CRUSOE JACK,

THE KING OF THE THOUSAND ISLANDS.

I0650730

BY

GEORGE EMMETT,

AUTHOR OF "THE PIRATES' ISLE," "MIDSHIPMAN TOM," "ALLS WELL,"
"WAR CRUISE OF THE MOSCA," &c., &c.

PROFUSELY ILLUSTRATED BY HARRY MAGUIRE.

OFFICE:
HOGARTH HOUSE, ST. BRIDE'S AVENUE, LONDON, E.C.

INDEX.

~~~~~

The Minute Gun at Sea 2
Twelve Years After 4
Hugh of the Red Hand 7
Tom Starboard 10
Crusoe Jack Begins his Wanderings ... 11
The Bell Bird 13
Crusoe Jack Captures One of his Subjects,
    and has a Hard Fight with Another ... 17
Crusoe Jack Alone in the Wild Beasts' Lair 21
The Fate of the Seagull 23
A Miraculous Escape from Death 30
A Phantom Ship—How Tom Starboard Lost
    his Ears 34
Catching a Shark 39
The Search for the Missing Heir 43
A Vision or a Reality—A Night in the
    Forest—A Novel Light—Hunting the
    Tapir 45
A Night in a Tree—The Fight with the
    Lions—Crusoe Jack's Rifle Does Good
    Service 51
The Fight with the Peccaries 55
Crusoe's Old Acquaintance Lured from his
    Lair—A Novel Attack 58
Adieu to the Island 62
Attacked by Sharks 66
The Coral Reef—The Castaways Pursued
    by Savages 70
Craft against Craft 74
Lela, the Indian Maiden 78
Our Hero Loses his Friend Tom Starboard... 81
How the Wrecker's Wife Plotted for the
    Wanderer's Birthright 83
Crusoe, like his Venerable Namesake, Finds
    Foot-prints in the Sand 86
Madge Collins and the Lawyer 89
A Dangerous Hiding-Place 92
An Indian Battle 95
The Antidote to the Wourali Poison ... 100
Alkay's Treachery 104
Mabel Meredith 106
A Strange Meeting 109
How Alkay Kept his Trust 115
Crusoe Rescues Lela from the Savages ... 118
Many Adventures and a Great Amount of
    Information 122
Crusoe Jack to the Rescue 129
A Dark Scene of Treachery... 131
Crusoe Captured by the Macoushi... ... 134
A Noble Action 136
On the Way to a Strange Adventure ... 139
An Unexpected Sight 147

Continuation of Tom Starboard's Adventure 15
A Singular Adventure 15
The Seagull at Last 15
Tom Starboard Meets an Old Acquaintance 16
The Thousand Islands — Jack Proclaims
    Himself King—Turtle Hunting 17
The Exploring Trip—Good Sport—The
    Captain's Hut — The Hammocks — A
    Strange Presentiment—The Mystery of
    the Strange Ship 17
Mabel is Still Persecuted—Then Rescued,
    and Encounters the Perils of the Deep ... 17
The Storm—The Shipwreck—The Raft—
    Exciting Scene—Providential Escape from
    Drowning—Jack and Tom Peril their
    Lives and do Good Service—Jack's Amaze-
    ment at Recognising Mabel 17
The Shipwrecked Party—Explanations—
    Mr. Meredith's Story—Jack is Told the
    Secret of his Birth—Mabel and Jack
    Make their Vows of Affection 17
A Generous Proposal—The Expedition to
    the Wreck—The Treasure—A Terrible
    Position—No Chance for Life—Saved at
    Last 17
Watching the Wreck—Terrible Suspense—
    Safe to the Shore—The Raising of the
    Seagull Accomplished—A Banquet at
    Jack's in Honour of the Event—Jack and
    Tom are Made the Heroes of the Day ... 18
The Launch of the Seagull—The Trial Trip
    —Jack and Mabel—Madge Collins's Letter
    —Tom Starboard's American Adventures
    —Buffalo Hunting—A Prairie on Fire ... 18
Tom's Prairie Adventures Continued—Jack
    and Mabel in Peril—A Terrific Struggle
    for Life—Is She Dead or Alive ?... ... 18
Jasper's Disappointment—The Pleasures of
    London Life—Jasper is Made a Dupe—
    His New Friend, the Captain 18
The Lawyer and his Visitor—A Startling
    Proposal—Who the Captain Really Was
    —His Remarkable History 18
The Indian Maiden's Adventures — The
    Sacrifice—The Invasion—A Wild Plan of
    Escape 18
An Unexpected Attack—A Fight on the
    Water—Timely Rescue 191
The Seagull—Jack's Reflections—He is At-
    tacked Treacherously—A Critical Position
    —A Desperate Fight, and a Final Victory 195
Jack's Escape—The Sea-Bird—The Seques-

tered Island—A Strange Discovery—A Secret, Mysterious, and Dangerous Adventure   197

Jack's Adventure Continued—His Remarkable Discovery—What Course Shall He Take?—The Danger Overpowers Him ... 199

The Alarm—the Search—Lela's Danger—Another Conflict with the Indians   ... 201

The Gaming House—The Course of Luck—The Two Schemers—Jasper Engages in a Rash Adventure—Mr. Meredith's Confidant 203

The Apparition—The Explanation of the Mystery—The Duel and Its Effects   ... 206

How the Pirates Treated Jack—The Cross-Examination — Disposal of Treasure — Another Encounter in Prospect 209

The Attack on the Seagull—A Terrible Encounter with the Pirates 212

The Chase for the Pirate—A Terrific Storm—Jack's Extraordinary Apparition on Board the Seagull 214

Our Hero's Unexpected Appearance on Board the Seagull—End of the Chase ... 218

Arrival at the Society Islands—Grand Reception—Instructive Account of the Customs of the Natives   220

The Festivities—The Sham-Fight—An Astounding Discovery by Captain Hastings 223

The Pardoned Mutineers—The Exciting History of the Escaped Convict 225

The Convict's History Continued and Concluded   228

The Story of the Second Convict   233

The Convict's Story Ended — Signs of Treachery 238

The Conference of the Conspirators   ... 242

The Flight of the Spies—Tom and Jack both meet with serious Disasters—A Treacherous Deception 245

The Invasion—Fearful Encounter—Tom Starboard proves himself a Hero 248

The Combat between the Chiefs—A Sanguinary and Universal Contest—The Victors and the Vanquished 252

The Prisoners—Tom Starboard Storms the Citadel of the Mutineers—Perils on Board the Seagull 256

The Attack on the Seagull—A Desperate Resistance—Fearful Peril of Mabel   ... 259

The Boarding of the Seagull—Desperate Struggle, and Fate of the Mutineers   ... 263

The Revenge of the Hopaws—The Second Invasion   267

The Landing of the Invaders—The Conflict and the Victory   269

The Seagull's Voyage—the Deserted Ship—Jack and Tom again at the Mercy of the

Ocean   274

Misgivings as to Jack's Fate—The Search—All Hopes Destroyed   278

The Pirates—The Abandoned Ship—The Desperate Position of Valdez—Hopes of Plunder   280

The Council of the Pirates—Conspiracy—A Cunning Scheme   283

The Pirates on the Raft—Their Danger and their Deliverance 287

Rescue of the Pirate Crew—The Capture of the American Vessel   289

Adrift on the Wide Ocean—The Perils of the American Crew—The Ship on Fire—Fate of Jack and Tom   290

The Seagull's Voyage—Tidings of the Lost Ones — Misgivings and Doubts — the Homeward Voyage—A Wide Separation 294

The Escape—The Storm—The Wreck on the Iceberg—Deadly Peril, and Strange Position of Jack   297

Further Perils on the Ice—A Frozen Sleeping-place—The Morning—Jack's Sufferings from Cold and Hunger—How he Obtained Food—He Builds a Hut and has a Terrific Combat with a Bear   ... 300

Fearful Position—Attacked by Wolves—The Icebergs Again—Fight with Polar Bears   306

A Further Chase of the Bear—The Esquimaux—The Reindeer and Sledge—Chased by Wolves — The Precipice — Narrow Escape—Death of the Indian Chief   ... 310

The Indian Feast—Zanoolah, the Indian Maiden—the Sudden Attack—A Fearful Conflict   317

Alone on Lion Island—Crusoe Jack's Hut on Flagstaff-hill   321

Crusoe Jack's Journal—The Mutiny of the Thunder   323

Quiet Days on Lion Island—The Mysterious Figure   326

The Skeleton 327

The Mysterious Arrow   328

Buoying the Wreck of the Thunder   ... 330

The Canoe—Another Mystery   332

On the Look-out   333

A Fruitless Errand 334

The Mysterious Scroll   335

The Princess of the Island 337

An Unknown Friend 338

Footmarks on the Sand!   340

The Nymph of the Lake   341

The Island Princess 343

Crusoe Lays in a Stock of Provisions   ... 345

Crusoe Fortifies his Hut   346

A Fleet of Thirty-five Canoes—Crusoe's Alarm   348

Crusoe goes out to meet the Savages ... 350
The Pursuit 352
The Island Princess a Prisoner 354
Crusoe Jack to the Rescue!—Attack on the
    Savages 355
The Fruits of the Victory—Crusoe Dis-
    covers his Mysterious Enemy and Un-
    known Friend 356
Crusoe Tends the Wounded Maiden ... 358
The Gigantic Tree—The Girl is Seized by
    the Savages 359
On the Trail of the Savages 361
Crusoe Again Rescues the Indian Maiden... 363
Crusoe Astonishes the Savages 364
Crusoe's Hospitality to the Indian Maiden... 365
Crusoe's Peace Again Disturbed by the
    Savages 367
Preparations for an Attack 368
Crusoe Makes Use of the Fire Balls — 369
The Savages Meet with a Warm Reception 370
Flight of the Savages 372
Left Alone 374
La-loo-hee-ah's Bower 375
The Field of Death 376
A Disagreeable Task... 377
The Island Maiden Finds an Apt Pupil in
    Crusoe 378
Crusoe Tries his Skill at Civilisation ... 380
La-loo-hee-ah's Narrative 380
The Island Maiden Gratifies Crusoe's Curio-
    sity About the Strange Metal 383
About the Wreck of the Thunder, and the
    Treasure Sunk Therewith 385
Honi Soit Qui Mal Y Pense... 387
Crusoe Jack and the Island Maiden Visit the
    Wreck of the Thunder 389
Explanatory 390
Alone! 391
A Rare Bird 392
More of the Feathered Mystery 394
A Pleasant Excursion 395
Crusoe Meets with a Still Greater Surprise 396
A Valuable Commodity 398
Crusoe's Resolve 400
Signs of the Enemy 401
The Savages in Possession of the Hut ... 402
In the Subterranean Store-room 403

Terrible Revenge 404
Crusoe Surveys the Wreck of the Hut ... 405
La-loo-hee-ah herself Again 406
Flagstaff Point Assumes a Brighter Aspect 407
Tutor and Pupil 408
Crusoe's Diary 410
Another Extract from Crusoe Jack's Diary
    —La-loo-hee-ah's Water Clock 411
Diary Continued—The Diving Dress and
    the Helmet 412
Preparing for the Fight 414
The Rival Fleets 415
Crusoe Surveys the Camp of the Savage
    Foe—A Terrible Means of Revenge Sug-
    gests Itself to him 416
Excitement in the Camp of the Huanitans... 417
The Safety of La-loo-hee-ah is Made Known
    to the King... 418
Crusoe in Command 419
Crusoe Witnesses an Extraordinary Scene 420
Moments of Horror 423
Crusoe's Deliverance... 424
Crusoe Becomes a Prince 425
The Coronation 426
Crusoe is Married 427
On the "War Path"... 429
Victory! 430
Crusoe Jack King of Huanita 431
The Savages Forward Crusoe's Work at the
    Wreck 432
Crusoe Visits the Wreck of the Thunder ... 435
Crusoe Again at the Wreck... 436
Crusoe's Prospects Brighten 437
Crusoe Estimates the Value of his Stock ... 439
The Huanitan's Become Alarmed 440
A Discovery 441
Crusoe's Encounter With a Monster of the
    Deep... 442
A Critical Position 443
Rejoicings on Lion Island 444
The Last Box of Gold 446
The King of Huanita Meets with a Sur-
    prise 448
A Sharp Engagement... 450
The First Shot 451
Explanatory 452

THE KING OF THE THOUSAND ISLANDS
OR THE ADVENTURES OF
CRUSOE JACK

CRUSOE JACK,

The King of the Thousand Islands.

By GEORGE EMMETT,

Author of " Midshipman Tom," " Frank Fearless," " Sheet-Anchor Jack," &c.

CHAPTER I.

THE MINUTE GUN AT SEA.

WHERE the ragged cliffs towered high above the troubled waters stood the lonely hut of Darrell Collins, the wrecker. Perched like a bird of evil omen upon the loftiest pinnacle of the mighty barrier that had withstood the storms of ages, the small structure seemed to defy the wrathful elements.

Half a century of storm and sunshine had passed since the lonely hut had been erected from the timbers of a stout vessel which had been driven upon the rocky beach beneath.

Bravely the thick planks had withstood the destructive hands of Time, and now, save a few places upon the roof, the wrecker's hut looked as though another generation might seek shelter beneath it.

Mighty trees had fallen, their gnarled trunks torn from the long fibrous roots by the force of the angry winds; palatial mansions had become dismantled, and left to decay; gallant ships had been riven asunder; and twice the small cluster of fishermen's dwellings which were scattered upon the face of the cliff had been levelled to the ground.

Yet, amid this desolation, the lone hut by the sea remained unharmed by the fierce storms.

To the simple-minded dwellers upon this portion of the rocky coast, especially those who had suffered from the destructive elements, this immunity from harm enjoyed by the dwellers in the solitary dwelling was ascribed to the aid given by a power that shall be nameless.

That Darrell Collins and his children had sold themselves to the Evil One was a settled truth; and none—not even the boldest of the hardy fishermen — would venture near the wrecker's dwelling after night had set in.

Peering through the only window of the hated dwelling, Darrell Collins' sour-visaged helpmate took a long searching look at the mighty waste of waters beneath.

The silvery moon had scarcely reached its zenith when Madge Collins first placed her wrinkled face against the glass.

"It is rising," muttered the crone. "There will be work to-night, in spite of the coast-guard and lifeboats."

As the slowly uttered words came from her lips, a low moaning noise arose from the slug-gish ocean, and the moon's bright disc became hidden by a long black bank of clouds.

The words of the wrecker's wife were prophetic. The storm was rising, and the ominous aspect of the night threatened danger to the homeward bound.

Darrell Collins was seated by the dying embers of a wood fire, which ever and anon shot forth a bright streak of flame that rendered the interior of the hut visible, and, falling across the morose, brutal face, and large, muscular chest, gave the wrecker an un-earthly appearance.

Upon a torn and dirty blanket at Darrell's feet was the form of an infant—a pale, sickly child. As the red gleam from the fire revealed the little slumberer, the face and hands twitched convulsively.

There was a savage look upon the wrecker's face as he sat moodily watching the child—an expression of such deep ferocity that had such a face been transferred to canvas it would have been cried down as a libel upon humanity.

From his moody reverie the wrecker was aroused by the harsh, grating voice of the wife.

"Heard you that, Darrell?" she said; "heard you that?"

He raised his head and listened, but made no reply.

The dull roar of the surge, and the howling of the wind as it swept round the hut, pro-claimed the storm had risen.

Broad flashes of light gleamed for a moment across the window—then became lost—then appeared again upon the bosom of the troubled ocean.

As the gale flew furiously on, the wrecker's eyes for a moment kindled brightly. The transient light passed away when his glance fell upon the slumbering child, and, dropping his head forward, he again became wrapped in gloomy thought.

With a sharp cry of anger falling from her lips, the woman turned towards her husband, and, in a high shrill voice, said—

"Are you deaf, Darrell Collins? Heard you not the voice of the storm?"

"Peace, woman! I have done with such work."

Madge came from the window, and standing before her husband, she folded her long shrivelled arms across her breast and said—

"Are you mad, Darrell? Know ye not that we have not even food to give that crying child

when he awakes. Out, man, and be doing!"
—she lowered her voice until it sounded like
the hiss of a serpent—"perhaps you may meet
the man who made that child fatherless."

The wrecker sprang to his feet, his face red
with passion, and, raising his clenched hand
on high, he said—

"Meet him! meet the slayer of my boy?
Could I but think that I—"

Boom!

The wrecker paused and ran to the window,
and to windward a sudden flash was seen to
glance upon the troubled waters.

"It is the lightning," he said. "Yet I could
have sworn— Ha! Madge, my axe! Fill the
brasier! It is the minute gun!"

Boom!

Above the howling of the pitiless storm came
the dread sound that told of a gallant ship in
distress. The sound that brought a brave
crew and a stout boat to the beach—men who
perilled life and limb to save those whom the
restless waters threatened to engulf.

Boom!

Three times had the report, muffled by the
roar of the surge, come across the dreary waste
of waters, and as the flash shone for a second
amid the darkness, the fierce eyes of the
wrecker blazed with a strange light.

He saw, by the flash of the minute gun, a
noble vessel driven before the gale. He saw
that there would be work for his fell hands,
should the plunging ship strike beneath the
towering cliffs upon which he stood.

Drawing his cap firmly over his eyes, and
gripping a long-handled axe, he issued from
the hut. A moment he stood as the fierce
wind hurled him backwards; then, rushing forward, he cried to his partner in sin—

"The next report, mind, show the light!"

He was gone; and the crone with bony
hands filled a brazier with coals, interspersed
with pieces of wood, fragments of tarred rope,
&c. When the loosely-packed mass of com-
bustibles touched the upper rim of the receptacle, she poured a quantity of oil, of an
inflammable nature, over the contents.

"The fiercest gale," she muttered, "will not
put this out. Ho, ho! So they thought when
they killed my poor Jasper, they had extinguished the death-light. A mother's curse be
upon the hand that killed him!" turning to the
infant which had awakened, "and made you
fatherless, my bairn! but I'll be revenged yet.
Woe! woe to the ship that drives before the
storm! Woe to those who pass the lone hut
when the moon is hidden! Jasper's blood shall
be washed out a hundredfold."

Swinging the brazier to and fro, and one
dark, shrivelled hand raised with forefinger
pointing to the warring elements outside, she
looked like those weird, witch-like women in
"Macbeth." As her harsh grating voice died
away, the minute gun at sea sounded upon her
ears.

* * * * * * *

About two hundred yards below the spot
where the massive cliff frowned above the roaring surf, a number of men were collected upon
the margin of the afflicted waters.

Here the long line of white-crested billows

broke upon the smooth sands. Either way
from this spot for miles, masses of sunken
rocks and jutting crags caused the surf to
break with a terrible roar—dire, portentous
sounds to those who madly cling to the storm-
driven ship.

Twice in the distant gloom had the bright
flash and dull roar of the minute gun excited
this knot of men to madness.

Twice had they launched the lifeboat; each
time had the surging billows hurled the boat
back to the beach.

Again sounded the signal of distress from
the ship; again the gallant fellows, nerved to
desperation, made an effort to succour the
helpless ship.

A loud huzza came from their lips as the
buoyant craft rose to the crest of a mighty
wave. A second cheer was given by the few
who stood upon the beach, and scarce had the
cry of hope found utterance, when a burst of
mingled grief and horror came from the lips
that had given back the cheer from the lifeboat.

The storm-spirit, as though incensed at the
puny efforts of men to save those who were fast
hurrying to destruction, hurled the lifeboat
back, and left it high above the reach of the
retiring waves.

Bruised, bleeding, and helpless, the crew
were assisted to their feet, and the little group
turned their eyes to the dim outlines of the
tempest-stricken vessel.

"There is a chance for her yet," said a
weather-beaten old coastguard, "and only
one."

"Which is that, shipmate?" asked a bruised
member of the lifeboat's crew.

"She must strike, it appears," said the old
sailor; this is the only place where a chance of
saving a few lives exists."

"Right, shipmate. Ha! there goes the gun
again. What are they doing now?"

Every man, with beating heart and over-
strained vision, leaned forward in their excitement to obtain a better view of the doomed
ship.

A blue light shot up from the vessel's deck
and rendered her dark hull and torn sails
plainly visible for a few seconds.

An exclamation of joy came from the old
sailor.

"See, see!" he said to those around. "Her
bows are as true as the needle to the pole for
this spot."

His hearers gave a deep sigh of relief; then
followed various excited comments.

"Beautiful! beautiful! Keep your wheel
down and you will be safe."

"She is falling off. Look! look! her bowsprit is straight for the wrecker's cliff."

"God forbid!" was the coastguard's first
ejaculation. No, my boys; the barky won't do
much harm if she—— Ha! what is that?"

The minute gun again boomed out, lighting
the weird scene like the lightning's vivid flash;
but it was not the blaze of the gun that caused
the startled ejaculation to fall from the old
seaman's lips.

High above them a bright sheet of flame
swung to and fro in the gale, shedding a red,

unearthly glare to all that came within its influence.

To the dismayed group who had been watching the doomed vessel with such keen interest the bright stream of fire which, meteor-like, shone on the summit of the wrecker's cliff, caused a burst of horror to fall from their lips, and from mouth to mouth the cry went, gathering strength as it proceeded, and higher, even than the howling winds and roaring waters came in startled, fearful accents, the words—

"The death-light on the cliff!"

There was no hope now for the vessel, and the group of brave-hearted men stood silent and appalled, watching the destruction they were powerless to avert.

Lured by the bright glow of the blazing brazier, the crew of the stricken vessel made a last and desperate effort to steer for this seeming beacon of hope.

Too well did they succeed.

Crash came the huge bowsprit against the massive rock; then the figure-head, as though riven by some unseen hand, dropped to leeward, and was tossed ashore; at the same moment the foremast swayed to and fro, then toppled over, and in a few seconds the stout vessel was broadside-to upon the sunken reefs. Now arose the shrieks that chilled back the life current of the hardy seamen who had thus heard the long, piercing cries of agony and supplications for help—heard them, oh, God! and yet could not relieve. Boats were cut away only to be dashed into fragments a second later. Again the cries for help could be heard above the shrieking of the blast; the vessel careened over—a mighty crash was heard—the hull gone to pieces—masts, rigging, spars, human beings, for a moment mingled in the whirl of waters—a moment later, vessel and crew had disappeared for ever.

The death-light had done its work too surely and too well.

CHAPTER II.

TWELVE YEARS AFTER.

Time had worked but little changes in the outward aspect of the lone hut by the sea.

Inside the solitary dwelling an air of greater comfort was perceptible than when we last beheld the wrecker sitting by the poor fire, gazing with moody bitterness at his grandchild.

The infant had now grown into a wayward, sickly, revengeful boy—one who, in spite of the great love that existed in the hearts of the wrecker and his wife for their son's child, often made them wish that he had never seen the light.

From the night when the minute gun called Darrell Collins forth upon his fell work of plunder, he had become a changed man.

Not a Spanish galleon loaded with golden doubloons, and fallen to pieces upon the rocks, would lure him from his dwelling.

That night was the last of his dire occupation; since that time he had lived at peace with the officers of the crown.

A great change had taken place in Darrell Collins since that night when the false beacon lured the tempest-tossed vessel to destruction —a change that robbed him of his former savage aspect, and made him appear like a man over whose head there hung a black cloud of hidden sorrow.

Whatever had so strangely changed her husband, even the termagant Madge failed to discover. That his moody silence and long fits of abstraction had something to do with the fearful storm which took place on the night this story opens, she felt assured, but its nature she was at a loss to imagine; and Darrell, when pressed by her artful interrogations, would cast a startled look around and order her to be silent. There was that in his eyes and disturbed countenance which told the woman it would be prudent to leave further questions for some future time.

But twelve long years rolled on, and the secret, whatever it was, remained locked in the wrecker's breast.

That his melancholy had some reference to that night's work there could be no doubt; for whenever his eyes rested upon the form of a dark-eyed, handsome boy—whom the wrecker had brought to his lonely hut after the good ship had fallen a victim to the treacherous light—his whole frame was strangely affected.

Much angry recrimination took place between Darrell Collins and his sour-visaged helpmate, when he returned with the infant, and the pitiless woman would have hurled the child into the raging sea had not Darrell snatched it from her arms, and, with a display of temper that was unusual with him, given the termagant to understand that any harm befalling the helpless child would be the precursor of a terrible punishment to the termagant Madge.

He gained his point, and the child, even with the scanty care that was bestowed upon him, as the years rolled round grew into a fine handsome boy.

His straight supple limbs and face glowing with health were such a marked contrast to the crooked form and sickly visage of Madge's grandson, Jasper, that it caused the crone's heart to fill with pitiless hate towards the poor little castaway.

The early years of his life had been passed wearily by the boy, and often when sinking under the undeserved cruelty of the vicious Madge, his eyes would wander to the boundless stretch of waters, and he would pray for the time to come when he would be old enough to seek his livlihood upon the treacherous element that cast him into the power of the cruel woman.

Jasper and the little waif were about the same age, and the little hunchback, whose temper was as crooked as his body, found a keen delight in causing his handsome companion to fall under the displeasure of his vindicative granddame.

No bond slave—no wretched negro, who toiled from morn till night for a capricious master, had a worse time than poor little Jack had with the malevolent young tyrant, whose drudge the harsh-tempered woman had made him.

Often did the hunchback, when backed by the presence of old Madge, strike the hapless boy with any weapon that his strength would permit him to grasp.

The latent fire in Jack's nature, when he recoiled from a spiteful blow by Jasper's hand, could be seen in his flashing eyes and quivering lips. Had they been alone it is possible that Jack would have taken the matter in his own hands, and inflicted such a chastisement upon the young tyrant that he would have been freed from a recurrence of his brutal malice.

In the presence of that awful woman he had to curb his rising passion, and, treasuring up the memory of his bitter wrongs, wait until the time should come when he could repay the blows with heavy interest.

Jasper hated the brave little fellow for that beauty which tended to make his body look yet more deformed than ever, and, with a strange longing to mar the handsome face and lithe limbs which filled his heart with envy and malice, he, serpent-like, waited and watched for an opportunity to carry out his wish.

Thus stood matters upon the stormy eve, exactly twelve years after Jack became an inmate in the lone hut by the sea.

By the light of a flickering candle Darrell Collins was mending a large fishing-net; opposite to him sat Madge, her head nodding to and fro as she yielded to the dreamy god of sleep.

Jasper was stretched at full length upon a sofa, which had once formed part of the cabin furniture of a ship; and little Jack, the hero of this story, was on his knees before the fire, deciphering with difficulty the pages of a book, which absorbed his interest to such an extent that he, for the time, forgot his wretched fate, and, mingling in the thrilling scenes of adventure so vividly depicted, imagined himself far, far away, and sharing in the wondrous exploits of the heroes of battle and shipwreck.

It was an old book of seafaring stories—glowing accounts of British seamen's daring, tales of wondrous adventure with terrible monsters of the mystic deep, and hand-to-hand encounters with skulking beasts of the forest.

But little time for learning had poor Jack, but what little he had gleaned from the many books which had found their way into the wrecker's possession was stored up, and afforded a solace for many a weary hour.

The boy's quick perception enabled him to master the stepping-stones to learning, unaided by the spectacled schoolmaster of the fishing village.

And, to Jasper's rage, he beheld his companion reading with ease books from which he could with difficulty spell out a dozen words.

This was another cause for Jasper's increased hate; not only was his companion's beauty the means of rendering his ugliness more distasteful, but, in spite of the care which the village schoolmaster had bestowed upon him, his dull intellect had not yet mastered the simplest words.

Jasper thought of this as he lay upon the sofa, his small ferret-like eyes darting angry glances at the absorbed reader by the fire, and,

prompted by the spirit of evil, he whined loud enough to awake the dozing Madge—

"I'm so cold—that Jack takes up all the fire."

Her darling's voice was enough for Madge. She was ready to pounce upon the excited boy, whose senses were enthralled by a terrible encounter between one of his heroes and a detested ground shark, and did not hear the pitiful whine from Jasper's lips, or the angry growl from Madge.

"Get your lazy carcase from the fire," screamed the latter, clutching Jack by the collar, and hurling him back; "do you think we clothe and feed you to do nothing but sit nose and chin together reading that rubbish?"

Poor Jack, thus rudely awakened from his ideal participation in the combat he had been reading, let the book fall from his hands, and cowered back from the uplifted hands of the shrill-voiced dame.

"Of course," she said, addressing her malignant pet, "my poor darling is to be left to suffer while you, beggar that you are, can hulk about the place doing nothing but eat, drink, sleep, and read a parcel of stuff that is not fit for grown men, much less children."

The wretched boy made no answer to the woman's words, but stood with his small hands clasped and his brain on fire at the rough treatment which had so suddenly broken his ideal worship.

How noble he looked as he stood silently regarding the virago!—the early elastic vigour of his well-knit limbs showing to advantage by the strange and half-defiant attitude he had assumed; his well-set head thrown back, and the glossy black hair falling in wild luxuriance over his neck and shoulders.

The crone saw not the graceful form and face, as the red glare from the fire helped to lend additional charm to the picture, but in harsh, grating tones her voice rang out shrilly—

"Don't stand there, fool, putting yourself in stage-player's attitudes, but pull the sofa near the fire!"

The little fellow's heart heaved with passion, and his dark eyes kindled angrily as he stepped across the room to obey.

How bitterly he contrasted his life with the hero of the book which Madge's violence hurled from his hands!

Better a thousand times, he thought, would it be to face the untamed denizens of the forest than to exist under the brutality of this revengeful woman and her tyrannical grandson.

With a heavy heart he tried to draw the cumbrous piece of furniture across the chamber, but the additional weight of Jasper prevented him from moving it.

Knowing by sad experience that the non-fulfilment of his task would be ascribed to anything but the right cause, he struggled with all the strength he possessed to move the couch.

It was too much for him, and his feet slipping, he fell forward, his head striking the chest of the grinning hunchback.

The blow was not heavy, but Jasper, who,

judging others by his own standard, believed that Jack had fallen upon him purposely, sprang up, and entwining his claw-like fingers in Jack's long curls, began to tug at them savagely.

It is the last feather that breaks the camel's back, and this indignity to our hero, when his mind was filled with the recollection of the heroic deeds performed by the gallant men about whom he had been so attentively reading, brought the hot blood to his cheeks, and clenching his hands he dealt his tormentor a rapid succession of blows about the head and face.

Jasper released the long jetty curls from his fingers, and began to yell for help.

Jack's sudden attack upon his tyrant so took old Madge by surprise that it was some moments before she could believe in the reality of the scene.

Her darling's yells, as he cowered before the enraged boy, caused her to spring from her chair, and, blinded by a sudden vortex of passion, she seized an axe that stood by the fire, and rushed towards Jack.

The ill-used little fellow knew that his punishment would be worse than ever for daring to resent Jasper's ill-treatment, and feeling that one blow would be as heavily punished as a thousand, he plied his clenched fists hard and quick upon his hated tyrant's face.

Too cowardly to resent a blow, Jasper filled the hut with his cries, and had not Darrell Collins, by suddenly extending his foot, tripped his partner up, she would, in her blind fury, have slain the little fellow.

With an ejaculation of anger, Darrell strode across the chamber, and kicking the axe aside as he passed, he took the panting form of the enraged boy in his arms, and bore him out of reach of the furious Madge.

"Attend to your cub," he said, angrily; "this is no more than I expected from the manner in which you have allowed that boy to tyrannise over one who is—"

Madge sprang forward, as though about to put her right to chastise Jack to the issue of a struggle with her powerful husband for his possession.

There was a gleam of anger in Darrell's eyes that warned her of coming danger to herself, should she push matters to an extremity.

"Keep back!" growled the wrecker, savagely; "this boy shall not be ill-used. I saw the whole scene, and Jasper deserved the thrashing."

Baffled in her design upon Jack, the virago vented her ill-humour in a torrent of abuse upon her husband.

When her breath failed her, she placed herself by her favourite's side, and muttering lowly fierce threats of vengeance against Jack, she wiped a thin line of blood from Jasper's face.

Darrell Collins, knowing sufficient of his wife's temper to feel that for some hours there would be no peace in his dwelling, threw his nets over his shoulder, and, bidding Jack follow him, left the hut.

"May the waters swallow the pair of ye!"

muttered Madge, as the door closed upon her husband. "Jasper, my darling, has he hurt you much?"

The swollen eyes and cut lip of her favourite proved how much he had suffered.

Blind to everything except the sense of her grandson's chastisement, the vindictive woman sat upon the couch and poured into the ears of Jasper—a mere child—such a hellish project of revenge that, bad as he was, he shuddered at her words.

That feeling soon passed away, and, drinking in the poison she so cunningly instilled in his mind, the child in years lent himself willingly to her subtle scheme.

They had barely concluded the fell project, when a loud, imperative summons at the door caused Madge to spring from her seat, and exclaim—

"Who's there?"

"Open the door, my good woman," said a voice outside; "we have had trouble enough to find this confounded nest without being kept outside."

Madge opened the door, and two gentlemen entered, one a dark-eyed, noble-looking fellow. His companion was old, ferret-eyed, and had a face which bore the impress of cunning and falsehood.

Madge eyed her visitors suspiciously, and waited for them to state the object of their visit.

She was not kept long in suspense. The younger of the two, throwing himself into a chair, said, with a light laugh—

"Hospitality does not seem a leading trait in the dwellers of this benighted place—eh, Mr. Twistem?"

"To judge from present appearance, Sir Harold, I should be much inclined to answer that—"

The lawyer's prolix reply was cut short by the gentleman whom he had called Sir Harold saying to Madge—

"Now, my good woman, I will state the object of my visit as briefly as possible."

Madge became more attentive.

"Do you remember," he continued, "a wreck taking place about twelve years since?"

Madge answered in the affirmative, and her red face paled.

The stranger's dark piercing eyes noticed the effect his words produced, and he resumed—

"You need not be under any apprehension; I am not a police officer, neither do I come to ask you for any little articles that may have been left on the shore when the vessel broke up."

Madge began to feel uncomfortable under the fixed look of the speaker's brilliant eyes. This feeling was not decreased when she fancied she saw a manly likeness of the ill-used Jack in the bold handsome face before her.

"I will first," said Sir Harold, "explain my connection with that ill-fated ship; it may tend to a better understanding between us. The Albacore was homeward bound from India, and among her numerous passengers was a brother of mine and his wife and child."

Madge almost suspended her breathing as these words came from the handsome stranger.

"A few months since," he went on, "I discovered by chance that a child was saved from the wreck, and, to be brief, I have travelled all this way with the intention of learning whether the infant is my brother's boy."

Madge did not answer at first, for, as the speaker explained the object of his visit, a bold scheme came to her cunning brain.

To gain a little time to mature her plan, she said—

"There is one question I should like answered before I enlighten you upon this matter."

"What is it, dame?"

"Should the child we saved from the wreck be the one you name, what are your intentions towards him? I ask you this, sir, because I have a mother's feelings towards the boy."

"No harm is intended," said Sir Harold; "should your surmise be correct, he will exchange this miserable dwelling for a—"

The lawyer placed his hand upon the speaker's arm, and said—

"That is—hem!—perhaps. You see, we shall be better able to tell you when we have seen the boy." He lowered his voice, and added in a whisper to his companion—"Your frankness will spoil all. Remember, should this brat be your brother's child, it will be better to pay these people to keep him here. You are not yet in a position to return the money you have wasted since the property came into your hands. Pray, my dear sir, let me conduct this affair."

The tempter changed the current of feeling in the young man's heart, and, loosing his hand, he answered—

"Be it so; do as you will."

Sufficient had been said to cause Madge's heart to leap with joy, and, to better prepare her plans, she invited the strangers to the second chamber in the hut.

"Step in here," she said. "I will bring the boy to you."

Closing the door carefully after them, she rushed to Jasper, who, hidden by the gloom, had escaped the stranger's observation.

He had cunning enough in his nature to understand the part Madge wished him to play, and, stimulated by her words of caution, the boy followed Madge into the presence of the strangers.

Sir Harold gave a start of undisguised repugnance at the crooked form and sallow face of the wrecker's grandson. Even the more practised nerves of the crafty lawyer sustained a shock.

One glance was all they bestowed upon the crooked form; then Sir Harold said—

"Impossible! that cannot be—"

Madge sent the boy into the next chamber, to spare him the pain of hearing the baronet's concluding words.

"I agree with you," the lawyer was saying when she re-entered the room; "such a thing seems impossible. Ugh! fancy that misshapen form having a coronet."

"Our errand is fruitless," said the baronet to Madge, "unless you can bring me a stronger proof of identity than that."

"There are the clothes," said Madge, "in which he was dressed at the time. Would you like to see them?"

"The very thing, my good woman," said the lawyer. "I suppose they are marked?"

"You shall see them."

* * * * * *

Standing at the open door of the lonely hut Madge Collins watched the strangers as they toiled down the steep declivity to the valley below.

A cunning smile was upon her wrinkled face as she chinked a heavy purse of gold which the younger stranger had given her as an earnest of his liberality.

"So," she muttered, "I am to burn all traces by which that proud man's relative can be discovered. Ho, ho! how he looked when he saw Jasper! Ho, ho! my generous lord, it will not be Madge's fault if the hunchback does not yet wrest your title and property from you. So I am to have gold as long as I keep the secret; more, should I send the boy away so that he may never be heard of more. Ho, ho! I will do all this. He shall be sent away—him—that brat who has raised his hand against my boy—he shall go—his shall be the fate you so well planned for my darling. It seems almost like a dream, yet it is true. Once rid of Jack—then, Jasper, you shall mingle with the best in the land, and strip the fellow of his riches, and repay the look of disgust with which he greeted you, my poor suffering lamb."

She closed the door, and, with a wild light dancing in her sunken eyes, sat by the flickering fire and indulged in roseate dreams of future wealth, when her darling should usurp another's birthright.

What trifles sometimes alter our lives! Had not Jack resented Jasper's cowardly attack in all probability he would have been taken from the wreckers by the young baronet, and placed in a position for which his birth and noble form so well fitted him.

Simple as the cause may seem, his absence with Darrell Collins at the time the strangers made their appearance at the hut was the forerunner of his becoming a lonely wanderer over an immense tract of unpeopled country.

Perhaps there is more truth in the old proverb that—"Fortune knocks once at every man's door," than most of us will admit.

Poor Jack's fortune came and was lost without him being there to give it a welcome.

CHAPTER III.

HUGH OF THE RED HAND.

No word of the strange visitors to the lonely hut by the sea reached the ears of Darrell Collins or Jack when they returned from their night's fishing.

Madge had the game in her own hands, and she determined not to lose it if possible.

The precious Jasper followed her instructions to the letter, and more willingly when he knew that by acting the part she had marked out for him he would be the means of injuring his young companion.

Jasper's hazy intellect was not strong enough to comprehend the great stake for which Madge was playing.

It was sufficient for him to know that by keeping a still tongue he was doing a spiteful act towards Jack.

Unknown to Darrell Collins, his wife, when absent, had several interviews with a somewhat mysterious personage, known by the name of Hugh of the Red Hand.

What passed between them, and why she gave a heavy sum in gold to her visitor, will soon be made apparent.

Since the night when Jack's lion heart prompted him to turn upon his tyrant, Madge had but few opportunities of venting her ill-temper upon him.

Darrell Collins, as though to make amends for some secret wrong done to the boy he had so strangely brought to his home, never allowed him to remain in the hut unless he was present.

This was gall and wormwood to Madge. She wanted to be rid of the handsome boy, yet, before he fell into her toils, she felt a strange desire to wreak a personal chastisement on him.

There were times when Darrell left the hut for the day; then Jack, to escape the indignity of being compelled to wait upon Jasper and endure Madge's ill-treatment, would spread the sail of his fishing-boat, and glide out upon the white-topped waves.

There was a freedom in this that well suited his daring heart. The small craft bounding from wave to wave, the dull roar of the surge as it broke upon the rocks, and the feeling of boundless freedom in thus skipping over the blue waters, brought a glow of happiness to his heart and a glad sparkle in his eyes, both of which he lost when the night came on, and he was compelled to turn the boat shoreward.

One lovely summer's eve, when the red sun flung its beams across the rippling waves, Jack escaped from the lone hut, his face red with passion, and his heart filled with wretchedness, launched his boat, hoisted the sail, and was soon dancing upon the waters.

Seated in the narrow stern of the frail craft, one hand grasping the tiller, the other the end of the small sail, he was soon carried out from the shore.

The boy's lips were compressed, and his brow set, and the silent working of his features told the agony that was at work within his breast.

"Why am I born to such a wretched fate?" he burst forth, as a large tear of agony rolled down his flushed and burning cheeks. "No dog could be treated worse than I am by that horrible woman, and her still more horrible boy. I wish this boat would take me out of sight of this hateful place. I would sooner die than suffer this continued ill-usage."

His hand, agitated by the workings of his mind, shifted the long narrow sail from side to side, and when he raised his drooped head from his breast he found that the fitful breeze had wafted him close in shore.

He was on the point of shifting his helm and letting the sheet go free to the wind, when a cry of terror smote upon his ears.

It was a young, girlish voice that broke upon the stillness of that calm eve, and Jack, turning his head, beheld the form of a young girl clinging with frantic energy to a tuft of vegetation that grew out of the rock.

The boy saw her peril, and with marvellous promptitude he shifted the helm of his boat, and tightening the sail, drove the boat upon the sands.

"Hold fast," he said, as he sprang upon the beach; "if you fall nothing can save you from being dashed to pieces."

As Jack sprang like a chamois from rock to rock he saw standing above the ledge beneath where the terrified girl was clinging the form of a boy, who, overcome by terror, in place of assisting the young maiden, stood wringing his hands and crying for help.

In the excitement of the moment Jack pushed the well-dressed young gentleman aside, and throwing himself face downward upon the cliff, stretched out his hand and grasped the girl's waist.

Jack's well-knit frame, developed already by the hard life he had led, was stronger than many a youth's of eighteen. With assuring words and comparative ease he drew the little maiden in safety to the ground, and stood at a respectful distance.

When the object of his care was safe, Jack recognised her as the daughter of an old admiral who dwelt near the shore, and in the person of the youth he had so unconsciously thrust aside, he beheld a proud, haughty young gentleman whose father had once ordered Jack to be whipped from his grounds.

Edgar Moreton, the boy who stood upon the edge of the cliff crying for help, was one of the foremost to lash poor Jack, and assist in his expulsion.

He had not forgotten this circumstance, and with something of a scornful look upon his face he turned to Edgar, and said—

"Perhaps you can take care of this young lady now she is quite safe?"

Edgar's face flushed angrily, and stepping between him and the little trembling maiden, he said loftily—

"This slight service makes you forget yourself, peasant."

An angry reply rose to Jack's lips, but its utterance was choked by the little maiden running forward with extended hands, saying—

"Thank you for the kind assistance you gave me. Come to my father's house, and let him reward you."

"I will do that, Mabel," said Edgar, throwing a shilling towards Jack. "Your father will not care about your bringing every fisher boy you may meet to the hall."

Jack turned fiercely, but Mabel Meredith's small white hands had grasped his rough palms, and in a voice of touching sweetness she said—

"Never mind my cousin—he is angry. Come with me, and papa will be glad to see you."

The kind voice and beaming eyes of the little pleader brought a mist before Jack's eyes. Poor boy, it was the first time such words had fallen upon his ears—the first time his hands had been grasped in such a tender, confiding manner.

As well as the varied emotions that filled his breast would permit, he answered—

"I require no reward, miss, for the little service I have rendered you. I would rather go back to my hut than return with you to the hall, where," he added, bitterly, "I was once beaten like a stray cur from the grounds, and I can—"

"You must forget that. Come, I will walk back with you."

Half yielding to the witchery of her voice, Jack was about to stammer out a half refusal when Mabel abruptly said—

"I have not asked you your name. Mine is Mabel Meredith—what is yours?"

"Jack," replied our hero, simply.

"Jack—Jack what? Anything else?"

"No. I have no other name; except old Madge sometimes calls me Lazy Jack, or Darrell Collins calls me Crusoe Jack."

"Crusoe Jack," repeated the young lady. "What a strange name! Why do they call you Crusoe Jack?"

"Because I read all about Robinson Crusoe, and wish I could be like him, away from everybody."

There was such a tone of sadness in the boy's voice that the little maiden felt insensibly drawn towards him. She was about to question him about the cause of his unhappiness, when an end was put to this conversation by Edgar Moreton striding angrily between them.

"Stand aside, beggar!" he said, in a tone that caused Mabel to start with terror, "or I will hurl you into the sea."

With one hand he drew Mabel's wrists away, and with the other he struck Jack full in the face.

The young aristocrat's pride was humiliated by Jack rescuing his young companion, and, giving way to the impetuosity of his nature, he had struck our hero before he well knew of the act.

Jack reeled violently back with the force of the blow; then, white with concentrated passion, he turned and faced his antagonist, and, with a skill and accuracy of aim which bespoke great physical skill, he dashed his clenched fist in the young noble's face.

Edgar recoiled backward; then, recovering himself, his eyes dancing with passion, he sprang upon his younger adversary, and sought to grasp him by the throat.

"Beggar!—low-born hind!" he cried, fiercely. "How dare you strike a gentleman?"

Jack calmly awaited the onset, and, seizing young Moreton by the collar, a sharp and desperate struggle ensued.

Maddened with rage, the young aristocrat tried to clutch Jack's throat, and in their many turns and struggles he succeeded in getting his fingers upon the latter's windpipe.

Jack felt the blood rushing to his head, and with a mighty effort he threw his adversary from him.

Horror! A piercing scream of agony came from Edgar's throat as he fell over the cliff into the surf beneath.

Jack and Mabel stood for a moment transfixed with terror, then the young girl, with shrill, piercing cries, ran towards the hall.

Amazed, dumbfounded by the suddenness of the terrible catastrophe, Jack stood and looked after the flying form; then, as the terrible knowledge of the punishment that would befall him if taken dawned upon him, he sprang down the cliff, and pushed his boat into the sea.

One spring brought him to his seat, and, loosing the sail, he shot out upon the deep.

"It wanted but this," thought the pale and terrified boy, "to fill the cup of misery. Yet why should I repine? Since the first hour I can remember I have been beaten and treated worse than a dog. What right had he to strike me? Was it because I am ragged and friendless that he had a right to kick and cuff me at his pleasure? He had not!" he added, vehemently. "Here upon the rocking wave will I make my home, and never behold the hateful land."

The poor boy sat for nearly an hour, his eyes fixed vacantly upon the rippling waves as his boat, wafted by a gentle breeze, sped from the shore.

"Boat ahoy! Starboard—starboard! Do you want to run into us, my young shaver?"

Mechanically he obeyed, and put his helm a-starboard. Then, looking up for the voice that had hailed him, he beheld the dark hull of a vessel, which contrasted strangely with the sails aloft, stretching from spar to spar their gleaming expanse of snowy white.

Without a word he drew aft the tack, and suffered the boat to run under the vessel's bows.

"What say you, my lad," asked the same voice that had at first hailed him, "will you ship?"

"Yes," answered Jack, joyfully. "I will."

Letting fall his single sail, he stood up in the boat, and, catching at a rope which hung over the vessel's bows, he clambered on board.

As his foot touched the deck, one of the men dropped a cold shot into the fishing-boat, and sent her to the bottom.

Before the first feeling of thankfulness had subsided for the happy change in his prospects he was taken below by one of the crew.

Upon the quarter-deck of the Seagull stood the captain, Hugh of the Red Hand; beside him, Dennis Campbell, his first mate.

"To think of that, Dennis," said Hugh; "I should as soon have thought of seeing the moon drop into the sea as that youngster coming aboard like that."

"It do seem strange, cap'n—'tarnal strange. But you ain't going to do as the old woman wants you with the boy?"

"No, Dennis. We must find another way of getting rid of him. It is not exactly in my line—that sort of thing."

"I thought not, cap'n. Shall we stand out to sea before any cussed revenue falls foul of us?"

"Yes, Dennis; we've got the cargo aboard. Go, pipe all hands to make sail."

The mate repeated his superior's orders, and the shrill whistle was heard in every part of the ship.

In a few minutes the Seagull, with her white canvas spread to woo the fitful wind, was gliding out into the deep blue waters.

Poor Jack!

He had fallen into the hands of those who had been hired to destroy him !

* * * * *

When the billows rolled towards the land our hero's boat, bottom upwards, drifted to the beach.

There was joy in the heart of old Madge and her misshapen son when the boat was found.

Crusoe Jack they believed—and rejoiced in the belief—was dead, and they were free to plot for his birthright.

The only one who mourned the gallant little fellow's untimely fate was Mabel, and while life existed she felt she could never forget the handsome boy.

There was one who stored up a deep hatred for Mabel's preserver—that one, the young patrician whom Jack had hurled from the cliff.

He alone discredited the story of the broken boat.

"It is but a lying subterfuge," he thought. "Though twenty years may pass, I will repay the churl."

He kept his word. And when the time came that brought Jack to England the young noble's malevolence caused him to seek among untamed beasts and desolate regions a resting-place for his weary spirit.

CHAPTER IV.

TOM STARBOARD.

THE captain of the Seagull marvelled much when he thought of the heavy bribe Madge Collins had given him to put Crusoe Jack out of the way.

Red-handed Hugh had seen much of the world. He had at different periods been connected with slavers, privateers, and once served on a pirate ship.

During the whole of his strange and adventurous career such a circumstance as the present had not come under his notice.

What motive could the wrecker's wife have in wishing to rid herself of the boy? was a question that occurred to his mind hourly since the boy had come aboard.

That she had one, and a very powerful one, he felt assured, as he remarked in a conversation with his first officer.

"The old hag would not have parted so freely with her money were it not a certainty that the boy's removal would amply repay her, but in what manner I cannot make out. In fact, the affair is a perfect mystery."

"It is," was the reply. "Can the boy throw no light upon the matter?"

The captain of the Seagull laughed.

"Hang it !" he said. "Why did I not think of this before? I will speak to him."

Jack was sent for, and, cap in hand, stood before his officer.

Red-handed Hugh could glean but little information from Jack.

He found, as he expected, that no relationship existed between Madge Collins and the friendless boy.

Jack, much puzzled by the captain's close questioning, returned to the forecastle.

"As wise as ever," remarked the captain of the Seagull. "Poor little devil, I suppose I must keep my word with old Madge, or she will repay me by putting my neck in a tie that will be too tight to be comfortable."

The first mate of the Seagull looked out upon the sunlit waters, and said—

"There?"

"No," replied the captain. "I am not quite so bad as that yet, though I told the old woman I would send him aloft in a gale, and put him in the way of breaking his neck or tumbling overboard. I have thought better of it since."

"What do you intend doing?"

"I will tell you when we pass the Straits of Magellan."

"What ! Put him ashore ?"

"Yes. He may stand a chance of being picked up by a ship."

"A poor one if you mean leaving him among those islands."

"I do. You must think I am an ass to leave him where he is likely to return."

When this conversation took place the vessel was upon the coast of Patagonia, and rapidly nearing the scattered group of islands whose existence in the midst of the mighty ocean has been attributed to the action of the volcanoes in the ocean bed.

Little imagining the fate in store for him Jack was standing upon the forecastle, listening, with a boy's delight, to the many wondrous stories of peril and adventure which the crew were wont to beguile the weary monotony of their life by detailing.

What wondrous things were revealed to him by the simple, unvarnished stories told by the rough seamen !

Tales of wild daring which caused his blood to run like liquid fire through his veins.

Even his favourite book was forgotten, as men told of their strange lives when cast ashore upon a barren island, or delivered by the waves into the power of savages, whose only garments were a string of beads or human teeth hung around their hips.

There was one man who had, from the hour our little hero had placed his foot upon the Seagull's deck, taken a strange interest in the friendless boy—Tom Starboard (so he was called), a man who had passed fifty years on the ocean.

The old seaman, though taciturn and morose with his shipmates, seemed to bestow the whole love which his rugged heart was capable of feeling upon the young lad ; and often, when the dull splash of the reckless seas and the sighing of the wind among the cordage somewhat damped poor little Jack's ardour for a seaman's life, old Tom Starboard would divert his mind from its melancholy by reciting strange scenes that he had passed through during the half century he had been buffeted about by the waves.

He told him of such wondrous sights by sea

and land that he forgot the dismal soughing of the wind and dull plash of the waves.

Forgot everything—even the cold, drizzling rain, which beat against his face as he kept on watch during the long dark nights upon his first voyage at sea. When they were relieved, and Jack lay in his hammock, he would keep awake the remaining part of the night thinking over all he had heard, and unconsciously laying in a stock of useful knowledge that was so soon to be called into use.

Upon the evening of the same day that the conversation took place between the captain of the Seagull and his first mate respecting Jack, the boy was leaning upon a gun, looking anxiously for land.

A few days previously old Tom Starboard had told him that they would soon pass the island of Juan Fernandez.

"I should like," Jack said to his companion, "to go ashore when we reach the island."

"You would! Why?"

"To see if there are any remains of Robinson Crusoe's hut."

Tom Starboard laughed as he answered—

"Alexander Selkirk you mean, Jack."

"No, I don't. I mean Robinson Crusoe."

"Impossible," said Tom. "Such a person never existed."

"Jack looked up at the grave, weatherbeaten face, and said somewhat reproachfully—

"You are joking, Tom."

"I am not," was the reply. "Shall I enlighten you upon the subject?"

Jack did not immediately reply; he felt half sorrowful to be thus robbed of his boyish faith in the existence of the lonely dweller upon Juan Fernandez, and kept repeating, in a low voice—

"So there is no Robinson Crusoe after all!" Then he added suddenly—"Yes, Tom, tell me all about it."

"I will," Tom said. "You remember me speaking of Captain Woodes Rogers?"

"Yes."

"He it was who discovered Alexander Selkirk, in the year 1709; that is seven years before the publication of 'Robinson Crusoe.'"

"Yes; but did this Selkirk live upon the island?"

"Yes, for many years, and when taken on board the ship he could not speak his own language."

"How was that?"

"From long disuse, I expect."

"Ah, I understand, but had he skins on?"

"Yes, he was clothed with the skins of goats, and it was some time before he would drink anything but water."

"But about the goats?"

"It is said that Selkirk killed upwards of five hundred, and marked a great number on the ear. Some of these were found thirty years afterwards by Commodore Anson's crew, still alive, and the marks yet visible upon their ears."

Jack asked no more questions that night. He turned into his hammock, and mentally wondered if Alexander Selkirk had led the same life as his favourite, Robinson Crusoe.

When the boy had gone below the old sailor took his place at the helm.

He had not been long at his post when Red-handed Hugh and his first officer came on deck to enjoy their cigars.

Walking to and fro within a few yards of the helmsman, they began to converse about the unfortunate boy.

"It's no use, Dennis," Tom Starboard heard the captain say. I shall put him ashore the first island we sight."

"Yes, and have him picked up before we return to England."

"Pshaw! you should know more about those isles. Why, man, there is no anchorage near them for the smallest vessel."

"Agreed; but a boat might touch there for water."

"Not very probable, as there is none, except a few drops that lodge among the rocks after rain."

Tom Starboard's fingers gripped the spokes of the wheel as though he would crush them in his agitation, and an involuntary cry of horror escaped his lips.

The captain turned at the cry, and muttered—

"Curse that fellow, he has overheard us, Dennis!"

"Sir?"

"Let Tom Starboard be placed in irons when he is relieved."

The chief officer looked up with astonishment depicted on his face.

"Tom Starboard in irons!" he repeated; "what has he done?"

"Nothing yet; but he will either desert with the youngster, or oppose his being left behind."

Dennis bit his lip.

"It is unfortunate," he said, "that old Tom should have overheard us. I know him well; he has taken a fancy to the boy, and might prove troublesome to us. He must be put out of the way for a time."

They soon after left the deck, and Tom Starboard, when he was relieved from the wheel, was ironed and placed where he could not interfere with the designs of the villainous pair.

So the night passed.

The only friend the poor boy had was placed, manacled like a felon, in the lower hold.

And Jack, buried in the sound repose which youthful innocence alone enjoys, knew not that the morrow would cast him forth helpless, friendless, and alone, upon a yet untrodden land.

CHAPTER V.

CRUSOE JACK BEGINS HIS WANDERINGS.

THE day, bright, clear, and glowing, dawned upon the Seagull, and the officer of the watch stood upon the weather gangway, gazing at the red dusky orb of light which was slowly rising above the waters.

The captain had left orders on the previous night to be called at sunrise. Little Jack who was in the middle watch, was sent below to rouse him.

The captain arose, and came upon deck.

"Is land yet in sight?" he asked, and his eyes were eagerly scanning the sunlit main.

"Not yet, sir," was the answer.

"Fetch me a glass."

The officer obeyed, and Red-handed Hugh mounted the fore-rigging, and from thence on to the fore-yard.

His scrutiny did not last long. By the aid of his powerful telescope he saw the haze of land, apparently about eight or ten miles away.

Satisfied that it was one of the lonely islands he sought, the captain of the Seagull returned to the deck, and ordered the steward to be sent to him.

"Place a few biscuits," he said, when that worthy appeared, "a piece of beef, and a bottle of water in a basket."

The steward replied—

"Yes, sir."

He then went below. Meanwhile, the captain kept his glass upon the low, dark object that every moment became more distinct.

His right hand, the unprincipled Dennis, was by his side, and peering through a glass at the island, which lay under the lee bow.

"Don't remember," he said, "having seen it before."

"Nor I," replied the captain; "there are so many of them that it would be impossible to say."

"The basket, sir," said the steward, coming forward; "all ready, sir."

"Very well. Pipe a boat away, Mr. Campbell, and send young Saunders to me."

While the whistle's shrill tones awoke the drowsy crew, the vessel was hove-to and the boat launched.

Edward Saunders, a youth of about eighteen, came upon deck as the boat was brought up alongside the ship.

"Take charge of that boat," said Red-handed Hugh, "and when you put that boy ashore return at once."

The midshipman looked into his captain's face, and saw by its stern expression that remonstrance would be useless.

With a sigh he turned away and descended to the boat, little Jack following him.

The bright morning sun was upon the deep waters when the boat left the vessel's side, and the poor boy, released for the first time from the confinement of the ship, gazed joyfully at the wild aspect of freedom around him.

The crew pulled merrily, snatches of songs enlivening their labour at the oars, and poor Crusoe Jack, unsuspicious of the sinister design meditated against him, joined his frank young voice in the chorus.

An hour's hard rowing brought them to the white sandy beach of a most beautiful island, about six miles in circumference.

Narrowing out from each end was a small tongue of land, over which the surf broke with a dull, heavy roar.

From what could be seen of the interior, it appeared to be covered with tall, graceful trees, and fluttering from branch to branch were birds of every colour and size.

The men rested upon their oars for a few seconds, gazing with envious eyes at the cool, shady groves so temptingly open before them. Fain would they have jumped ashore, had not the captain before starting given an order that none were to leave the boat without the officer's permission.

"Here, Jack," said young Saunders, "you are the lightest—jump ashore with this basket; and here, in case you should meet any wild beasts, take my sword."

He unfastened his belt as he spoke, and threw the weapon upon the sands.

Without a moment's hesitation, and glad of the opportunity to go within reach of the beautiful birds, Jack took the basket and went ashore.

When the poor boy had gone out of earshot, the midshipman said, in as firm tones as his agitation would permit—

"Shove the boat off."

Used to the strict discipline of the Seagull's captain, the men obeyed—possibly without thinking of the evil intended to the little fellow, who was running swiftly after a young bird which flew towards the trees.

The boat stopped when about three fathoms from the shore, and young Saunders called out—

"Here, Jack; come this way!"

The boy turned, and when he saw the boat so far from the beach, with her head towards the vessel, he stood still with amazement.

Yet no suspicion of the actual truth came to his mind until Saunders said—

"Good bye, Jack. It's the captain's orders that you are to be left here. Keep up your pluck—you can now be CRUSOE JACK in reality!"

A low murmur came from the rowers, and the bow-oarsman said, loud enough for the poor little castaway to hear—

"What is he to be left there for—a child like that? What say you, messmates? Shall we stay and keep him company?"

"You had better sit down," said the midshipman. "Come give way, men! If you have anything to argue about, the captain is the man. I am only obeying his orders."

The sailor reseated himself, and muttered, savagely—

"Yes, you are right, Mr. Saunders; and were all on board of my opinion, they would not suffer the vessel to leave without taking him on board."

The rowers, undecided how to act, still remained resting upon their oars. It wanted but a few words to cause them to run the boat aground, and either bring the boy away or remain with him.

Perhaps Red-handed Hugh knew what would take place when his cruel order was carried into effect, for the Seagull was seen to fill her maintop, and stand in towards them.

An exclamation from young Saunders caused them to turn their eyes towards the vessel.

That glance frustrated the carrying out of their wish; they saw two gun-ports open, and the grim muzzles of two carronades pointed at the boat.

"Give way, men," repeated the middy, "or he will fire into us!"

They knew sufficient of Red-handed Hugh not to neglect the significant meaning, and with sullen, determined faces, they pulled slowly back to the ship.

JACK'S ENCOUNTER WITH THE GORILLA.

When the dread truth came upon the boy's mind, he stood as though suddenly transformed to stone.

Fain would he have uttered a word of supplication to those who were so cruelly deserting him.

But his tongue clave to his mouth, and an involuntary throb of anguish caused him to clasp his forehead and reel back as though suddenly a bullet had passed through his heart.

For an instant the sunlit waters gleamed before his eyes—the tall, stately trees seemed to swing to and fro; then he fell to the yet untrodden shore, bereft of sense or motion, a wretched castaway upon a lonely isle in the great southern ocean.

The boat returned to the ship, and the grim, silent men, enraged at the treatment they had so recently witnessed, would have gone in a body and demanded the boy to be brought back.

In this they were frustrated. Red-handed Hugh had prepared for their return, and, presenting a gun loaded with grape, he ordered them below.

There was one upon whom the blow fell with crushing force—Tom Starboard. He had been released from his irons when the boat put off, and now with glaring eyes, and then with fear, listened to the atrocious act of Hugh of the Red Hand.

The conflict between rage, grief, and despair, for a time convulsed the old seaman's iron frame.

When these feelings passed away he made a deep but silent vow that he would seek out the little castaway, though he should have to sink the vessel to carry out his deep and settled vows.

No. 2.

CHAPTER VI.

THE BELL BIRD.

WHEN our hero's faculties, which had been so rudely stopped, returned, he arose from the beach, and as the full force of his lonely condition burst upon his mind, he felt as though his senses were about to desert him.

Disconsolately wrapped in his weary grief he stood upon the unknown shore, his eager eyes fixed upon the fast receding outlines of the vessel that had brought him over so many, many miles of ocean.

"Will she come back?" he said aloud; "or am I to die here, unaided, unmourned, and my body to lie until—— No, the thought is too horrible. It is but a trick of the captain's to try my courage."

He spoke thus as he paced wildly to and fro upon the silent strand; and, as the vessel gradually sank lower and lower in the far distant horizon, and at last became a mere speck, all hope died within him, and he felt he was alone.

Then, in a voice tinged with melancholy foreboding, he turned towards the unknown groves, and said—

"There is no hope here—I must die."

But as the words came from his lips his thoughts ran into a fresh channel, and, looking towards the glorious orb of day, which shed its bright effulgence upon the romantic spot, he mused—

"Why should I despair? Others have been placed as I am, and lived; please Heaven, so will I."

The bright boyish face shone with a glow of resolute courage, which gave promise of the fruit it would bring forth when manhood should strengthen his limbs and enable the brave heart to battle with his known fate.

The sudden change from wild grief to a heroic courage to combat the dangers and difficulties by which he was surrounded, imparted a vigour to his young frame, and without another murmur he went to the spot where he had left the small parcel of provisions.

It was small, indeed; and as he enumerated the articles and portioned them out day by day, he found his struggle for life must begin at once and in earnest.

Some half-dozen ordinary ship-biscuits, a bottle containing about three pints of water, and a square piece of salted beef.

"In three days at most," the brave boy said, as he gazed upon his scanty larder— "three days, and this will be eaten, and then—"

He paused as he caught sight of the sword and belt which the young midshipman had left upon the sands.

"Then," he repeated, fastening the weapon round his waist, "this must supply me with more."

The bright luminary of day, as though angered at the villainy that had been perpetrated, became suddenly overcast with dark clouds, and the winds arose sullenly, and came sweeping fiercely in from the troubled ocean.

The gay feathered denizens of the trees, terrified by the sudden change, flew away, filling the air with their shrill cries, and where the tall cane-balse reared its giant head, a rushing noise was heard as its occupants sought a place of refuge from the coming strife.

With his small stock of provisions in one hand, and the naked sword-blade in the other, Crusoe Jack stood for a few moments partially bewildered by the sudden change in the aspect of the scene around.

"The very birds," he thought, "warn me of my danger by staying here; I will follow their example, and seek a safer place."

Now as the brave boy advanced towards the grove of graceful drooping foliage, a chill feeling of awe came over him.

The first signal of the coming storm had passed away, and a dead silence ensued.

The birds of the air had gone to their roosts, the beasts to their hiding-places, and alone in that silent place, without a shelter from the coming storm, was the poor castaway.

Alone in the deep, solemn stillness of that strange region, every sound hushed, not even the rustling of a leaf breaking the mystic silence.

No wonder that the wanderer's cheeks turned pale, and his limbs trembled beneath him.

In this moment of chill desolation the sky became darker, and the haven which he sought became obscured from his view.

As his fears increased at this dread change he stood still, and lowering his head, awaited the coming of the tornado.

Then, as though the terrible silence had been but for the purpose of enabling the elements to gather their power, a sheet of vivid lightning swept across the blackened horizon, then a peal of thunder that caused the lovely island to vibrate; then following this dread sound came the roar of the surf, the dull noise of the rising waters, and the howling of the wind as it swept onward, tearing trees out by the roots and defacing the surface of the beautiful isle.

Struck by the branch of a wild tamarind tree, Crusoe Jack lay stunned beside the prostrate trunk, insensible alike to his fate and the fearful conflict of the elements.

The tornado flew around, shrieking aloud amid the devastation; following in its track the giant waves leapt madly upon the beach, and breaking with a sullen roar, as though in anger at being checked, swept every particle of vegetation away within their reach, changing a fair, smiling paradise into a scene of awful desolation.

The wind lulled as rapidly as it had risen; the waves lowered their giant heads and sank into the bosom of the deep blue waters; then, as the sun burst forth with redoubled effulgence, the dark clouds swept onward, and all became as fair as Eden when first trodden by the parents of mankind.

Crusoe Jack arose from the damp earth, his brain confused at the sudden blow he had received, and the swift, marvellous changes in the elements.

The luxurious vegetation, the stately elm and tamarind trees—save those uprooted by the tornado—glittered as though covered with a myriad of diamonds, as the rain-drops hung in small globules upon the edges of the drooping leaves and upon the tiny blades of grass.

Though somewhat appalled at first by the mighty voice of Nature, his courage returned as he looked upon the beauties of his island home.

Everything around was again fresh and beautiful; the birds again came forth and carolled joyously as the sun burst upon them; and from the centre of the rocky hills, the fresh sparkling water pursued its course, and fell with a musical sound into what appeared a chasm beneath.

Well aware, by brooding over the many books of travels he had read, and the strange stories of his old friend Tom Starboard, of the value of the limpid stream that flowed within fifty yards of where he stood, he ran nimbly forward to examine the spot where it emptied itself.

A cry of joy came from his lips at the wondrous reservoir which held the pellucid water, and sinking upon his knees, he prayed fervently to the Giver of all Good for the life-stream that lay beneath them.

Had the castaway been well versed in geology, he would have been able at a glance to account for the mirror-like pool.

The small hills which served as a conductor to the rain that fell upon the higher parts of the island had been upheaved by a volcanic eruption, as the many large pieces of rock and sandstone which were lying at their base testified.

Forming a tank of singular form was the chasm that held the falling waters, and around the edges were massive pieces of rock, covered with a creeping plant whose flowers hung in graceful festoons within an inch of the crystal pool.

Our little castaway stood for some moments in silent admiration. After he had uttered his prayer of thankfulness his lips unclosed, and he murmured—

"Wonderful, how these pieces of rock have been taken out to form a reservoir for the water!"

A sudden thought, not unmixed with awe, came to his mind, and he moved from the enchanting spot, muttering—

"Here, then, all the beasts are sure to come for water. I must not stay until I find out the animals that are upon the island."

Still holding his little stock of provisions in one hand, he walked towards the grove of trees.

"Poor old Tom!" he soliloquised; "I wonder if he knew, when he told me, should I ever be cast on a lonely island, to find out the enemies I should have to contend against, that I was to be put ashore? No, I don't believe he knew it, or he would have given me a gun to defend myself with."

Half thinking, half speaking, he reached the grove, and, lonely and deserted as he felt, he could not refrain from giving vent to an exclamation of admiration at the beauties by which he was surrounded.

"I shall have plenty of time," he thought, "to look at this beautiful place; now I must look for somewhere to sleep."

At the end of the grove (between two and three miles from where he stood) was a towering hill. Towards its verdure-clad summit the boy turned his eyes, as he strove to remember the course pursued by Tom Starboard when he was thrown upon one of the *Twelve Thousand Islands in the Indian Archipelago.*

"I must not," Crusoe Jack soliloquised, as he walked briskly forward, "sleep among the branches of the trees, for there Tom Starboard told me the most deadly snakes are sure to be found. Nor yet there"—he looked towards the thick cane-brake and almost impenetrable underwood as he spoke—"for the wild animals are sure to have taken refuge when the storm came on. In a hole or cave near the top of the highest hill is the best place; there I must go."

His spirits rose with the exhilarating effects of the cool fresh aspect of the place, and, with his sword firmly grasped, and keeping a wary look-out for wild animals or savages, he walked steadily onward.

When he reached the desired hill he found it much higher than he had anticipated; yet, despite the recent emotions caused by his heartless desertion and the blow he had received at the commencement of the tornado, he began the laborious ascent of its rugged sides.

The love of nature was strongly implanted in the young adventurer's heart, for, though footsore and tired when he reached the summit of the stately hill, he leant upon his sword, and, as his eyes wandered over the lovely view beneath, he exclaimed enthusiastically—

"Beautiful—beautiful! I could stand here for ever."

It was, indeed, beautiful; and well might a thrill pass over the castaway's frame when he thought that, of all God's creatures, he was the only one that had ever beheld the dazzling sight.

The glorious expanse of sunlit ocean, stretching out to that pale blue line where it became blended with the transparent canopy of heaven, looked like a gigantic mirror—the glittering surface without a speck to mar its sublime beauty.

Turning his enraptured gaze inland, the many hues of the mighty silent forest, the emerald tints of the grassy greensward, the purple and brown hues of the scattered masses of rock, formed a panorama of such rich beauty that it made his island-home seem too fair a spot for mortal to dwell upon.

Above this grand expanse the transparent sky, illumined by the orange tints of the afternoon sun, gave a finish to the beautiful reality that may be imagined but not described.

Upon the summit of the hill there stood a single tree, the glittering drops yet hanging upon the long pensile leaves. Beside the vigorous trunk, and within the protecting shade of the dense foliage, was the gnarled and barren remains of what had once been a giant representative of the mighty forest below.

Crusoe Jack, with a happy fearlessness in his countenance, and a bright hopeful look in his dark eyes, stood for a moment and contemplated the decayed tree and its leafy companion.

"This must be my resting-place," he thought. "From here I can keep a look-out upon the ocean, and watch for a ship to come within sight."

Placing his small basket of provisions upon the ground, he passed from beneath the shade of the long boughs, and said—

"This old trunk was once the only tree here. The younger one, which will serve as a protection against the sun's rays, I have no doubt has sprung either from a seed or a root of the useless old pine yet standing. Oh! now can I understand more about the wonders of nature that poor old Tom used to talk so much about."

Speaking in this careless, half-happy manner, he attentively examined the old trunk, and, carefully walking round it, he sought for a realisation of the hope that had sprung up within him.

Should the barren tree turn out to be hollow he would have a resting-place better than any hut he could have built now, had he the tools ready for its construction.

So sure had he felt that this would be the case that a cloud of disappointment came over his face when he found, upon every side, it was covered with thick impenetrable creeping plants, so closely interlaced that his sword was unable to cut through them.

One blow, harder than the rest, caused a cry of joy to escape him.

The tree was hollow.

Here, then, was all he desired; and, setting to work with a will, he again sought to find an entrance.

Still the same result.

Breathless with his exertions, he paused, and took another survey of the old tree.

The trunk at its base measured about fourteen feet in circumference, gradually narrowing towards the top to about five feet.

"In there," Jack thought, "there is a chamber fit for a king, and one where I should be safe from the elements and any prowling beast that might find his way up here. Ah! the top."

Quick as thought he sheathed his blade, and climbing by the aid of the clinging plants to the jagged summit, where the tree had broken, he paused, and, again drawing his sword, began to hack at the fibrous network of strong runners which grew across the aperture.

Joy! they yielded; and, looking through the opening, the young adventurer beheld the interior.

It was, as he surmised, perfectly hollow; and in one place, about three feet from the ground, the light struggled in through the network of the parasitical plant.

By the aid of one of the several runners he dropped lightly inside (about ten feet of the trunk was left), and stood motionless upon a heap of dried leaves.

Nothing stirred beneath his feet—no slimy creeping thing, no hissing serpent, no crouching animal—all was silent; and he could hear his heavy quick breathing as his breast rose and fell beneath the contrary emotions of hope and fear.

Not satisfied that he alone was the occupant of this strange dwelling, he turned over the thick layer of leaves with the point of his sword.

Satisfied at length, the boy began to examine his home.

He found the walls (so to speak) firm in every part, except the one before mentioned, over which the creeping plant grew.

It was a few minutes' debate whether he should remove the obstruction, and make the hole serve as a door, or keep only the opening as a means of ingress and egress.

"If I could," Jack thought, "cut away the lower part of this creeper, so that it would fall like a curtain, it would save me much labour in climbing up and down. I'll try."

He did.

Half an hour's sawing at the tough runners cut through nearly two feet.

He tried them with his hands, and found that, although so hard to saw with his sword, they were sufficiently pliable to yield to the pressure of his body, and allow him to pass through.

This completed, he brought his scanty larder to his chamber, and, drawing the fibrous plant as close as possible to his door, sat upon the heap of dried leaves, and, for the first time since he had left the Seagull, he partook of food and water.

With his biscuit and beef he was very careful. Water he knew there would be no lack of, and when his simple meal was concluded he remained for some time in deep thought, planning out a guide for his future mode of existence.

"I have," he thought, "a better hut than I could build, and a bed that is softer than I expected to find. These leaves must have blown in from the other tree; so as long as this trunk lasts I can keep the supply up. Water—ha! that I must bring up in this bottle every day. Food—that question, Jack you will be better able to answer when you have taken a survey of your kingdom, and seen which of your subjects are fit to eat; that is," he added, "if they will let me catch them."

Tired with the exertions he had already gone through, the castaway laid himself upon his bed of leaves, and, gazing up at the small patch of sky visible through the top of his strange home, his thoughts wandered to the Seagull.

The sun had sunk with a dusky glow, and night was coming on before he gave up the puzzling thought of his desertion.

He thought over every act since he had been on board—yet none would justify the captain in thus casting him upon the world.

Then he thought of the kindly old sailor whose spirit-stirring stories of dangers by land and sea had, in a measure, prepared him to encounter the sudden change in his young life. Thinking thus, his eyes closed, and he fell into a deep slumber.

A strange sight, had any eyes been there. A boy fast asleep in the hollow of a decayed tree, and alone upon an unknown island in the great South Pacific Ocean—alone amid a thousand dangers—but watched and protected by the Great Omnipotent, or he would, ere this, have fallen a victim to the hungry beasts whose fierce growls penetrated even his lofty resting-place as they wandered about in search of food.

It was early dawn when he awoke. The night birds and beasts of prey had retired to rest; the insect world were not yet warmed into busy life; the fresh dewy morn spread overhead its hues of grey and rose colour, which came through the opening above; and the roseate hues of morn lit up the glittering drops that hung upon the fragrant blossoms of the trailing plant he had broken on the evening before.

His senses steeped in a vision of the ship he was never more to see, he listened with closed eyes for the sound of a bell that had filled his ears during his long unbroken sleep, and, forgetful that he had been parted from the only friend he had ever known, he turned upon his side, and muttered—

"It is not yet ten bells, Tom !"

The words had barely left his lips when the clear ringing sound of a fine-toned bell smote upon his ears, and caused him to start from his leafy couch.

As he stood for a moment, as though about to hastily dress in obedience to the morning summons on board ship, the reality of his position flashed to his brain.

"It was a dream," he said mournfully; "yet I could have sworn bells struck just then. There it is again; the vessel has come to take me on board."

There could be no doubt of the reality of the sound—the clear ring of a bell, twice repeated, came wafted to his ears.

With the sudden hope of his release from his solitary existence strong within him, he crept through the leafy covering, and stood upon the hill, his eyes eagerly turned towards the sea, expectant to behold the hull and masts of the vessel that yesterday sank beneath the distant horizon.

His heart fell. There lay the noble expanse of sea, its surface undimmed, and, as though to make his agony complete, the bell yet rang out its clear ringing sound.

"She may be in some creek or inlet," he thought. "This time it is no delusion."

Again, the sound came wafted upward, and disregarding the birds which clustered upon the trees and poured forth their songs of praise to the new-born day, or the monkeys that frollicked from bough to bough, he started at a quick pace in the direction from which the sound proceeded.

Reaching the base of the hill, Crusoe Jack paused and listened anxiously for the well-known summons.

Again it rang out, and darting through the grove of trees, he rushed to the beach and looked anxiously for the ship.

Here his hopes were dashed away, and the certainty of being delivered from his lonely fate crumbled to pieces.

As he stood bitterly conscious that he had

been the victim of a fancied sound, the bell-like notes rang out close behind him.

Turning suddenly he ran back to the grove, his heart beating hopefully, and scarcely had he passed the opening, when he was brought to a sudden standstill by a ringing note sounding just above his head.

Transfixed with astonishment he looked up, and upon the highest branch of a tall tree, he beheld the cause of his anxiety.

It was the bell bird, whose clear ringing note sounds exactly like a fine-toned bell, that had caused the young adventurer to rush from his hollow tree, and search for the vessel he so fondly believed was waiting to take him aboard.

The companion, or bell bird, is about the size of a jay, but different in colour, the plumage being of the purest white. Upon the top of this singular bird's head is a black spire between two and three inches in height.

Jack's wandering gaze was fixed for some time upon the beautiful creature, who, regardless of the strange intruder, kept sending forth his clear notes.

"I shall be wiser in future," thought Jack; "and not so easily disturbed by the strange sounds I may hear."

He walked slowly, sorrowfully back to his lonely habitation, and set the contents of his meagre larder before him.

Breakfast over, the castaway, buckling on his sword and descending from his castle, went into the valley beneath to survey his domains.

CHAPTER VII.

CRUSOE JACK CAPTURES ONE OF HIS SUBJECTS, AND HAS A HARD FIGHT WITH ANOTHER.

THE lovely island seemed to have covered itself in its fairest garb to welcome the young monarch's survey.

Jack found everything as beautiful as on the previous day; his fair kingdom lacked but one essential to make it an earthly paradise—that was, a companion to share its beauties.

"Had I but a companion," he thought, "I do not know that I should have one regret at being compelled to end my days here."

Still walking and admiring the many strange but beautiful birds and animals that met him at every step, he sought to recall the first adventure that befell Defoe's hero in the celebrated romance of " Robinson Crusoe."

"Ah !" said Jack, sadly, "he was much better off than I am. When he awoke in the morning he found the ship so near that he could obtain everything he wanted, while I have nothing to help me in my loneliness."

He was passing close to the cane-brake at this moment, and for the first time beheld a specimen of its denizens.

It was a young puma (South American lion), not larger than a lady's spaniel, which came gambolling forth from the tangled brushwood.

The cub had never before beheld anything human, and with that curiosity so inherent in the feline tribe, it came towards Jack and rubbed its sleek sides against his legs.

Crusoe Jack knew no danger was to be apprehended from the infant lion, but the case was far different should either of the parents emerge from the cane-brake.

With a wary look Jack waited, sword in hand, for the appearance of either of these dreaded animals, but nothing appeared to excite his apprehension.

The young puma seemed to fancy Jack, for as he stooped and stroked its head, the animal made a low purring noise, not unlike a cat.

Crusoe Jack had often heard old Tom Starboard mention the South American lions, and he knew by the little animal's presence that beyond the cane-brake there must be a thick wood, for the pumas (originally natives of Peru and Chili) usually took up their abode among the close timber, or upon the highest mountains.

Remembering this gave Jack a disagreeable sensation, for should this class of animal be numerous upon the island, his castle (as he termed it) would be a dangerous resting-place.

Thinking thus he passed on to the beach, and, to his surprise, the young lion followed him.

Jack paused, and raising his sword, was about to plunge it into the little animal's body.

"No," he muttered, lowering the uplifted blade, " I will not kill the little creature; it can do me no harm; and if——" he paused—then resumed; " yes—why not? I may be able to tame it. Tom Starboard had one he brought up, and it used to follow him like a dog. So will I—at least, I can but make the attempt."

He patted the creature's head, which, as though pleased, rubbed itself against him, and when Jack moved forward trotted closely after his heels.

"I am not doomed to die of hunger," was Jack's exclamation when he reached the seashore. Near the margin of the waters, and evidently cast up by the storm of the previous day, was an assemblage of shell-fish.

Either way, as far as the eye could reach, the white sand was covered with every specimen of bivalves (having two valves), yet of such strange shape, that Jack was at first doubtful whether he should be safe in eating them.

Opening one of the larger kind with the point of his sword, he found the fish closely resembled an oyster, and stifling all compunctions, he swallowed the tempting morsel, with the remark—

"Here goes my first subject."

He found the flavour not unlike the luscious oyster, and, seating himself upon the sands, nearly a dozen of the species followed the first unfortunate brother.

"Were I Robinson Crusoe," thought Jack, I should have a shovel or a pickaxe to dig a hole beyond high water mark, let the sea into it, and fill it with these fish, then they would keep fresh for some time: but not having either I must do the best I can."

Afraid to risk the loss of his only weapon by using it as a pick, he began a search among the various pieces of rock, stones, shells, and other things which lay about in profusion on the beach.

Perseverance met its reward. He found a piece of stone about an inch and a half in thickness, and above a foot in length; and to make it more useful for the purpose in view, one end tapered off to a sharp, rugged point.

Jack's spirits rose with the success he had hitherto met. True he had not found two of the most essential things to keep life within him when the cold winds should whirl over the island, and the snow cover the emerald verdure that looked so fair beneath the summer sun. When this time should arrive fire and clothing must be obtained, or he would perish.

He thought not of this as he collected a goodly heap of shell-fish and carried them far above the reach of the water; but speaking lightly—nay, happily, to the young lion, which trotted after him with dog-like fidelity, he gathered upwards of two hundred specimens of the bivalvular tribe, and seated himself upon the heap to rest, for the work was one of time and much fatigue in walking backwards and forwards.

The cub threw itself at his feet, and resting its head upon his forepaws, looked up into our hero's face, evidently at a loss to understand what the two-legged animal could be about.

"Well," said Jack, looking at the little creature, "you seem quiet and tame enough now; but when your teeth and claws grow I am afraid my opinion will alter—unless I can tame you. Tom used to tell me it would be easy to make the most savage of your tribe as obedient as a well-trained dog. I will try; but look out—if ever you show signs of going the wrong way, it will be worse for you."

The boy's hand caressed the animal's head as he spoke.

"Now," Jack continued, "having made up my mind to keep you as a companion, the first thing to be done is to give you a name."

Jack thought over dozens of names, but rejected them as fast as they came to his mind. He looked at the young lion as it lay so tamely at his feet, the large eyes half closed in seeming enjoyment at the boy's caressing hand.

"Robinson Crusoe," Jack thought, "named the black man Friday. Let me see! This is Monday. Shall I call this little fellow Monday? Here, Monday?"

The young puma lazily opened his eyes as he received his name.

"Ah !" said Jack, half aloud, "that seems a funny name, eh? I have it. I'll name him after the poor dog that old Collins bred. Yes, Hector—that is a good name."

This difficult matter settled to his satisfaction, Jack took up the pointed piece of stone. Hector, closely following his companion's movements, watched Jack as he grasped his novel spade and threw the sand up with all the strength he could use.

Jack knew the value of time and worked with a will, yet the sun was in its meridian by the time he had made a hole sufficiently deep to hold his collection of fish.

The heat of the sun, too, began to tell upon him, and by the time the fish were thrown into the receptacle he was thoroughly exhausted.

Opening a couple more of the hard-coated

inhabitants of the sea, Jack, though weary, and his fingers cut and bleeding from the jagged edge of his spade, swallowed the fish, and then commenced to cut a channel from the hole he had made to the sea.

This task occupied at least two hours, but when he had finished he had the satisfaction of beholding the water enter slowly into the deep trench, and he knew that for some time he could rely upon a supply of good food.

When the hole became filled the young puma began to drink, but no sooner did he taste the salt water than he turned away, as though the brine was disagreeable to him.

"Poor fellow!" said Jack, stroking his head, "you are thirsty. Come along, we will leave these gentlemen in pickle, and go to that beautiful tank of cool water I saw yesterday."

Well satisfied with his work, and not dreaming of the many deadly perils in store for him, our young castaway, with Hector following at his heels, turned from the beach, and went towards the two small hills at whose base he knew the natural reservoir was situate.

Jack had no difficulty in finding the spot, and stooping over the crystal water he drank deeply, then laved his face and hands.

The young lion, much to Jack's astonishment, refused to drink, and stood a little way from the margin, his large eyes fixed upon an overhanging piece of rock which projected some feet over the pellucid pool.

Without looking for the cause of the animal's disinclination, Jack took off his little glazed hat and filled it with water.

This he held beneath Hector's mouth, and, much to his satisfaction, the animal drank the contents.

This operation was thrice repeated. Then Hector seemed satisfied; and giving a sidelong look towards the piece of rock before mentioned, drew back as though alarmed.

"There must be cause for this," thought Jack; "he does not dislike the water, evidently. What can it be?"

Where the piece of rock threw its deep shadow over the pool, Crusoe Jack felt assured that either an alligator or that most ferocious monster, the ground-shark, lurked.

Yes; it must be there, for in every other part he could see the stones that formed the bed of the pool, and distinguish the different plants that grew in wild beauty at the sides.

A moment's reflection caused Jack to smile at what he had regarded as a certainty, for, upon looking around, he could see no way by which either of the above dreaded monsters had reached the delightful clear pool.

"Yet," he mused, "there must be something to cause that little fellow's fear. Now, what can it be? Not a shark, because they could only be found among the pools which the tide can reach, and this is far away from the sea."

Suddenly picking up a good-sized stone from the ground he dropped it in the water, and as near as possible to the overhanging piece of rock.

Crusoe Jack, in spite of his brave heart, stepped back, with a cry of fear falling from his lips, and his limbs palpitating beneath him,

as he thought of the narrow escape from death he had when he immersed his face in the cooling treacherous water.

As the stone fell to the bottom of the water, an immense crocodile darted forth from his hiding-place, and, with his terrible jaws distended, caught the stone.

Jack heard the snap as the jagged teeth met. Then the jaw opened to eject the stone, and the monster, as though angered at being thus tormented, lashed the water with his strong flexible tail.

This portion of the crocodile is equally as dangerous as the terrible jaws. Being very flexible, for the purposes of propulsion, the animal is capable of moving it quickly from side to side, and being covered with a kind of plate armour, which forms upright ridges or crests in the centre, a blow would be certain death.

The crocodile, as though content to await a future time for his prey, swam slowly back to his lurking-place, and our hero, breathing freely when the monster disappeared, put his hand to his forehead, as though trying to remember some half-forgotten occurrence.

He was endeavouring to recall the description Tom Starboard had once given him of these dreadful creatures. This one, to which he had so nearly fallen a victim, he saw was upwards of seven feet in length—an adversary that would soon have made a meal of the young adventurer, had he, as he intended, stripped and jumped into the water to bathe.

"I might have expected it," Jack mused; "these horrible creatures infest the rivers and fresh waters of warm climates. Ugh! the monster! but if I live until to-morrow, I will destroy him, were he twice as big."

As Jack walked slowly from the lurking-place of the monster, he felt a cold thrill pass over him.

The more he thought of the horrible death he had escaped, the greater was the terror it inspired; for, be it known, that the crocodile tribe are incapable of swallowing under water; thus, when they seize their prey, they hold it beneath the water until suffocation ensues, then hiding the dead body in a hole in the bank until it becomes putrid, they eat it at their leisure.

No wonder, when he thought of this horrible fate, that the boy's face blanched.

As he neared the cane-brake where the young lion had met him in the morning Crusoe Jack began to reflect on the strange liking that the animal had taken to him.

Judging from its size, and the absence of either claws or fangs, Jack conjectured it could not be, at most, more than a few months old.

With these thoughts came others, not unmixed with dread, and the poor boy, grasping the only weapon he had, kept a good lookout as he neared the tangled brushwood.

"This cub," so ran his thoughts, "has strayed from its mother, and no doubt she is prowling about in search of him. If we are found together my chance of escape will be but small."

The wish to slay the young lion never entered Jack's thoughts; in fact, he felt that he owed his life to the animal's refusal to drink at the pool—had it not done so he would have plunged into the cool water and met his death, the very thought of which made him shudder.

Already he felt attached to the companion of his day's labour, and, fancying it would start away into the cane-brake, Jack kept stopping and patting the creature's head.

His only thought was to get the docile creature to his eyrie upon the mountain, without falling in with the enraged lioness—a task of difficulty he had yet to accomplish.

Keeping as far as possible from the dense underwood without departing from his path, he began to increase his pace; but, to his mortification, the animal, when passing a part of the cane-brake, which had either been trodden down by some heavy animal or broken by the tempest, put its nose to the ground, and, uttering a low whine, started off.

Fearful of losing the cub Jack forgot his caution respecting the mother, and ran after it, determined, if all other means should fail, that he would throw the young puma across his shoulder and carry it up the mountain.

The creature, to Jack's joy, made a dead stop when it reached the broken canes, and Jack jumped forward with the intention of seizing the animal before it could go any further.

His hand was on Hector's neck, when he caught sight of what he felt must be its mother, by the caressing manner in which the cub was purring about the full-grown lioness.

The boy drew back with a start, and stood upon the defensive, fully expecting the fierce beast to crouch ready for a spring.

But, to his surprise, it took no notice either of him or the endearments of the young animal.

As Jack's fears gradually left him he began more attentively to examine the recumbent beast, and from the position of the legs and body he soon found out the cause of Hector's attachment.

The lioness was evidently dead.

The position of the fierce brute, the marks of violence upon its body, and the pool of blood that lay near, had forced the conviction upon him, and without more ado he stepped forward to lead the young one away.

While stepping over the dead animal's form Jack thought of the use he could put the thick brown skin to.

"After I finish Mr. Crocodile," was his mental resolution, "I will skin this brute, and by the time my clothes are worn out it will be ready for use. Ha! What's that?"

Well might the poor boy spring backward with a loud cry, and bring the point of his weapon up to stay the onset of the terrible apparition that had burst upon his startled gaze.

Brushing down the cane-brake with as much ease as though the tough vegetation were rotten twigs, was a fearful-looking animal of the gorilla tribe. Its height, as it advanced upon its hind legs, was far above our hero's head, and the immense paws and large body covered with rough hair, gave the beast such a fearful aspect that Jack, though he knew every nerve would be wanted to aid him in getting rid of this unexpected monster, stood and trembled as though suddenly stricken with the ague.

"God help me!" said Jack, prayerfully; "for I have need of help now."

The young puma, when he caught sight of the huge monster, bounded from its mother's carcase, and took refuge among the trees behind Crusoe Jack.

The young creature saw in the horrible brute the slayer of its parent, and, with that sagacity which enables the lower animals to tell friend from foe, it flew with evident signs of terror at the huge ourang-outang's approach.

The beast, as it stood glaring upon the pale but determined boy, seemed to halt for a moment, as though astonished at Jack's appearance.

Our hero was the first of his species that the ourang had seen, and whether to take a better view of his little foe, or to gibber with rage at being disturbed in his lair by the presence of a daring mortal, the huge monster beat his shaggy breast with his paws, and gave vent to a series of discordant cries.

The sudden pause in his attack gave our hero time to better examine his enemy.

And as he stood there face to face with this denizen of the woods Jack's hand became steady and his nerves strung to the highest tension.

The ourang as he stood upright would have measured at the very least seven feet, with chest and limbs big, massive, and of wondrous strength in proportion to his great height.

It was an awful moment in our hero's life, that dread pause when he stood awaiting the attack of the fierce brute, whose long white teeth and sinewy limbs filled the boy's mind with uncontrollable fear.

The animal, as though satisfied with the scrutiny, advanced upon the young castaway with the evident purpose of crushing him, for the long anterior legs, or arms, were advanced ready to grasp Jack by the body.

The creature's hot breath fanned the boy's cheek, and nerving himself for a struggle which he knew would end in the death of one, he withdrew his hand, ready to plunge the long blade of his weapon into the brute's carcase.

It was evident that the ourang knew not the use of the glittering weapon which Jack held, for he advanced upon its point, one paw extended to grasp the young adventurer by the throat.

A partial blindness came over Jack as he lunged forward and buried one-half the sword-blade in the ourang's body.

The brute gave a scream of agony, and, pressing forward, sought to grapple with his sturdy young antagonist.

Nerved to desperation, Jack drew the weapon from its fleshy sheath, and as the animal's dark blood spouted in a jet, he stepped nimbly aside to escape the terrible embrace of the long hairy limbs.

Jack's agility saved his life, for the ourang,

maddened by the pain and the sight of his blood flowing, gnashed his teeth, and sweeping the air with his long paws, missed his aim as the boy stepped aside, and grasped the trunk of a young tree instead.

Howling with fury, the ourang tore the tree up by the roots, and in his rage crunched the branches off with his horrible-looking teeth.

While thus engaged, Jack came behind him, and taking good aim, drove his weapon into the centre of the ourang's back.

That blow brought the angry brute to the ground; the vertebræ were severed, and though not dead, it was unable to reach its young destroyer.

With flushed cheeks and his weapon red from hilt to point, Jack stood and beheld with awe the fearful efforts the ourang made to rise.

Biting and tearing the earth in his fury, and seeming more like a human being in agony than aught else, the monster tried to regain his feet.

Now one of the large paws was placed upon the wounded chest, as though seeking to stay the flow of the crimson tide; then with a convulsive effort, which only tended to accelerate hæmorrhage, it sought to drag itself towards Jack, who stood calmly, proudly, defiantly watching its maddened throes and futile rage.

The wounds were small, but Jack knew from the large circle of gore-stained earth that he had divided one or more of the large blood-vessels.

For upwards of half an hour the brute's terrible struggles continued.

During that time the excessive motion of the body as the animal tore up the earth with his teeth and nails, had so emptied the huge carcase of its life-stream, that it lay nearly still, a convulsive movement of the lower jaw and the closing and unclosing of the paws betraying that only an infinitesimal part of that tremendous muscular power yet remained.

Gradually these struggles were over. A sudden throe passed over the carcase, the limbs stiffened, and the ourang turned slowly over upon its back, dead; and the rays of the setting sun fell upon its dark shaggy breast and the flushed face of the brave young victor.

No mighty warrior at the close of a long and stubborn battle, heard the cries of victory from the lips of his men with a prouder glow of exultation than Crusoe Jack felt when he saw his huge foe lying prone, and the battle won only by his single arm.

No long-range rifle to shoot down a savage enemy from a safe retreat, but like a Roman warrior he had fought with his sword, and with that alone, aided by his stout heart, had vanquished a foe more terrible than the prowling jaguar or the venomous snake.

"Dead," said Jack, exultingly, "and I am alive. Ugh, you ugly brute! I should have had but little chance had one of those limbs reached me."

To make sure that every spark of vitality was extinct, Crusoe Jack passed his sword twice through the monster's neck.

Dead as he had appeared to be, a convulsive movement was perceptible in the wretch's limbs, and the horrible-looking mouth opened and closed as the keen blade passed through the jugular vein.

"Your race is run," said Jack, as he wiped the red sword blade with a handful of grass, "and that warm skin of thine shall make me a cloak. Rolled in that I need not fear the cold To-morrow will be a busy day. I have you to skin, and the dead lioness. Now, Jack, fortune smiles upon you. Now for home. Ah, where is Hector?"

A few yards from the dead carcase he found the young puma, its eyes distended with fear, and its limbs quivering.

Crusoe Jack caressed the frightened animal, and gently leading it away, said—

"Come on, Hector; you will know better soon than to be frightened at any animal that dwells in this island."

The beast followed him submissively, and by the time the red sun was sinking beneath the horizon Jack and his companion had reached the trunk of the blasted tree.

Here the pair sat upon the dead leaves, Jack sharing the remains of his biscuit with Hector, a proceeding that drew the little animal closer to his master, and when night came on the fearless boy placed his head upon the young puma's side, and slept as soundly as though he were in his berth in the Seagull's forecastle.

CHAPTER VIII.

CRUSOE JACK ALONE IN THE WILD BEASTS' LAIR.

THREE heavy months had passed since Crusoe Jack had been left upon the lonely isle—three months, and the autumn tints were beginning to merge into the dread winter.

It was now the middle of October, and the young castaway had not been able, in spite of every exertion, to procure the means of kindling a fire.

He had rubbed, according to the Indian method, two sticks together to create a spark, but in spite of every exertion his efforts had been unsuccessful.

During this time many changes had taken place in his dwelling. The skin of the ourang was spread over the leaves, and formed, under the circumstances, as good a bed as could be wished.

The hide from the dead lion had also proved useful, as it served him for a cloak during the cold damp days, and a coverlet at night.

Nor were these the only comforts he had obtained, for, with a courage and hardihood remarkable in one so young, he had traversed more than two-thirds of his kingdom.

He found upon the opposite side of the island a small river, the water as clear and as fresh as the lovely pool where his foe, the crocodile, still lurked.

Jack had devised several ways to rid himself of the wretch, but, for the want of a gun, he had been unable to pay off the promised score.

The river extended about two miles inland, and from the fact that no visible mode of emptying itself was apparent, our hero ca to the conclusion that the sparkling waters had their origin in a number of hidden springs.

He found an abundance of fish in the stream, but owing to his want of fire they were useless to him.

By dint of patient watching he had made himself acquainted with the different species of animals that dwelt in the thick woods.

This undertaking was fraught with danger, for Jack, to attain this knowledge, had to secrete himself among the pieces of rock that formed the margin to the (as he termed it) Crocodile's Pool.

To this place the animal creation were wont to come and drink, and our hero, much to his rage, had beheld the lurking scaly thing drag many an unfortunate victim beneath the surface.

The young lion Jack tried to teach to hunt for him; but Hector, now furnished with tolerable teeth and claws, invariably demolished what was caught, and by a low growl and lashing of the tail warned Jack that it would be dangerous to interfere with him.

An animal, closely resembling a rabbit, abounded in the woods, and Jack, followed by his docile companion, had often startled the timid creatures.

It was then the idea came to the young adventurer's mind to make his tame favourite useful in procuring food, for Hector, during the three months, had been Jack's constant companion, and knew the meaning of his master's words and gestures as well as dogs would.

To start him after one of the rabbits was the work of a moment, and the little agile animal soon had the trembling little creature in its fangs.

The taste of blood must have aroused the young lion's latent passion, for, as before mentioned, he would not leave his prey until it was gorged.

Then, as though aware he had offended his master, he would creep to Jack's side with downcast head, then lick the boy's hand, and look up in his face with an expression that seemed to plainly say—

"Do not be angry, master; it is my nature."

This was the interpretation Jack gave the half-frightened, faithful look, and stroking the animal's massive head, he said—

"It's my fault, Hector. Nature is stronger than your love for me, and it's plain if I let you taste more blood I may yet become a victim to your instincts."

But to return. More of Hector hereafter, and his devotion to his master.

In addition to the wild hogs, deer, and rabbits, Crusoe Jack found a kind of buffalo among his subjects.

The eatable portion may be thus enumerated:—Fish, deer, hares, rabbits, buffaloes, wild hogs, and turtles; but unfortunately our Crusoe had neither lines to catch his fish nor the fire to cook them. With respect to the other portion he had neither powder, shot, nor rifle; thus, in the midst of plenty he had to subsist upon the most Spartan diet.

Among the dangerous part of his subjects were jaguars (tigers), pumas (lions), alligators; the latter lined the banks of the river before mentioned, and were from four to seven feet long.

Scorpions, tarantulas (large venomous spiders), insects without number—some of them very dangerous and troublesome—serpents of great size, and mostly venomous.

Monkeys, parrots, snakes, and many birds of beautiful plumage, Jack saw in his travelling; and, though last, not least, the famous torpedo eel, a reptile which, if only touched with a stick, causes a numbing sensation to run through all the joints, not unlike the shock from an electrifying machine.

Such was the colony that Crusoe Jack reigned over, as he expressed it.

Some he wished to eat if he could catch them, and some wished to eat him if they had the chance.

Like all monarchs, Crusoe Jack had a deal of trouble with his subjects.

Sometimes he would attempt to run down a deer or rabbit; then the tables would be turned, and he would have to run from a prowling jaguar or lion.

This brief explanation will tend to better acquaint the reader with the class of wild brutes that the lonely boy had to contend with, and as Jack had only a sword to defend his life, the risk he underwent was triple as much as it would have been had he possessed any description of firearms.

Hitherto he had borne up against the meagre diet, which consisted of fruits, shell-fish, and milk.

"Milk!" the reader repeats, stopping short; "there must be some mistake." Nothing of the kind. We, the faithful chronicler of Crusoe Jack's adventures, again repeat—"Milk."

It had been our hero's custom to drop a stone in a hole close by his habitation every morning, to denote the number of days he had been cut off from the world.

Upon the thirty-ninth day of his loneliness he placed a stone as usual in the receptacle, and looked out seaward with the hope that he might behold the white sails of a vessel standing in towards the island.

Nothing met his vision save the sunlit bosom of the mighty ocean, and turning mournfully away he buckled his sword on, and, calling Hector, went to explore a barren rock about two miles from the base of the hill upon which he dwelt.

The one idea uppermost in Jack's mind was to discover some dried wood, that by rapid friction would act as a flint and steel.

For this purpose he had determined to visit the most barren part of his dominions—the dark naked-looking rock before mentioned.

Arrived upon its jagged summit, he beheld a dry ugly-looking tree, with large roots spreading out, fan-like, over the barren stony surface.

The trunk looked as though it had been dry since the first hour the beautiful isle was created from the ocean, and Jack, with the point of his sword, began to chip off pieces of the outside bark.

Several pieces lay at Jack's feet, and desistng from his work he picked up two of the most promising chips from the ground, and began the wearisome task of rubbing them together.

Until his wrists ached and his fingers were sore he continued the dispiriting labour, and worn out at last he threw them down, and exclaimed—

"Useless! I'll try no more."

The depression of spirits caused by this ever-recurring failure did not last long, for Jack's buoyant mind would not recognise the fact of any undertaking being fruitless.

So applying his sword-point to that portion of the trunk which was destitute of the bark, he began to pick out a piece which promised more success.

Scarcely had the sharp point pierced the trunk than Jack suddenly desisted, and an exclamation of astonishment fell from his lips.

From the hole he had made a thick, white, creamy juice began to flow out.

At a loss to account for what he conceived to be a strange phenomenon, he stood gazing at the white fluid. Then, prompted by curiosity, he suffered it to flow upon his finger; then, with the greatest caution, conveyed it to the tip of his tongue.

The taste he found cool and delicious, and, at the risk of being poisoned, he filled a shell which he invariably carried about with him for the purpose of dipping water from the Crocodile's Pool—the fear of the rapacious wretch preventing him from again trusting his lips to the treacherous water.

He had nearly conveyed it to his lips when a precautionary measure suggested itself.

He offered the shell to Hector.

The young lion Crusoe Jack had found of great assistance, for when about to partake of anything that seemed suspicious the animal's instincts proved a better guide than his own judgment.

Hector, in this instance, greedily partook of the white juice, and when Jack held the shell under the hole, the animal reared itself on its hind legs, as though anxious for a second draught.

For this he had to wait until Jack had refreshed himself.

When looking over another portion of the rock the young castaway found some trees of the same species, and resolving, by the aid of the only vessel he had (the water-bottle), to carry some of the delicious draught to his eyrie, he left the spot, and slowly retraced his way home.

During his walk he remembered for the first time that Tom Starboard had once mentioned a similar tree, which he called the "cow-tree."

The description closely resembled the appearance of the tree Jack had found, and our hero, in silent wonderment at the goodness of the Great Being who had provided so bountifully for him in his helplessness, uttered a mental prayer of heartfelt thanks for the discovery he had made.

It was a veritable tree of life for poor Jack, for he felt his limbs, which had begun to waste away from his meagre diet, soon grow plump under the generous nourishment from the delicious juice of the cow-tree.

There were but two regrets that Jack now felt. One was his inability to catch any of the animals that would have given him good wholesome food; the other was his failure at not being able to kindle a fire.

The latter began to seriously alarm him. The cold winter, he knew by the chilly mornings and damp evenings, was fast approaching; and he felt that, in spite of the warm skies, there was every possibility of being frozen to death before the warm weather would come again.

This was a matter which caused him many an hour's deep thought, and one day, while absorbed in melancholy reflection, the idea occurred to him to search the hill-side for a stone that would answer the purpose of a flint.

To think upon a subject likely to improve his condition was to act, and taking with him a lasso, made from thin strips of the huge monster's skin he had slain, he prepared, to use a homely phrase, to "kill two birds with one stone."

"Why," Jack thought, "can I not creep on top of one of those pieces of rock which surround Crocodile's Pool, and, when a wild hog or deer comes to drink, slip a noose over their heads, and secure what I stand so much in need of? I will try; but first to search for the stone—then for my plan."

He called his attendant, and, descending the hill, began a minute examination of the side.

His search was as unsuccessful as every attempt he had made respecting the fire.

Not discouraged, Jack went to a smaller hill, the base of which led to the thick wood where dwelt the wild beasts that had no good will to their young monarch.

Going direct to the summit of this barren hill, Jack, by descending in a circular manner, carefully examined every part of the surface.

He had nearly reached the bottom when he felt, or fancied that he felt, the earth move beneath his feet.

Somewhat surprised, he stamped heavily on the ground.

Horror! The earth gave way, and he felt himself sinking rapidly through a hole, and without the power to stop.

In a moment more a subdued growl came upon his ears, and, springing up from the heap of earth and stones which had tumbled through with him, Crusoe Jack cast a terrified look at a group of savage hungry-looking animals, and, mechanically grasping the hilt of his sword, gave himself up for lost.

HE WAS ALONE IN THE WILD BEASTS' LAIR!

CHAPTER IX.

THE FATE OF THE SEAGULL.

As long as the lonely island was in sight the captain of the Seagull kept his glass fixed upon the solitary figure of the young castaway.

Hugh of the Red Hand had passed through too many scenes of violence and bloodshed to feel any compunction for the villainy he had just perpetrated.

But there was one circumstance that caused

him at times to wish he had acted on Campbell's advice, and hurled the boy overboard
during a squall.

The secret would then have been safer; now
his mind misgave him respecting the fidelity
of his crew.

True, they had not openly expressed their
feelings upon the hated action, but he saw by
their sullen looks and the manner in which
they performed the necessary duties that a
fire was smouldering which only wanted a
spark to set it in a blaze.

Fully determined to make an example of the
first man who should dare dispute his authority, Hugh of the Red Hand paced the quarter-
deck, his fingers resting upon the butt of a
pistol which, primed and loaded, hung from
his belt.

Upon the forecastle stood Tom Starboard,
surrounded by a number of his shipmates.
The old seaman's heart was full of rage and
grief.

The heartless desertion of his young favourite
had aroused the old tar's latent fierceness, and
with a quivering lip and suspicious moisture
in his eyes, he addressed those around him in
his brief, homely language.

"Shipmates," he said, "man and boy I've
served on shipboard, but never in my life have
I seen such an inhuman act as this. Come!
What say you? We are forty to one! Shall
we go on our cruise and know that poor lad
is dying, or shall we compel the skipper to
put about and take him aboard again? I ask
you, shipmates, for a plain answer—yes or no!
If you say yes, he must obey; but if you say
no, I shall know what to do."

Many who, like himself, felt Red-handed
Hugh's act to be as cruel as it was uncalled
for, answered in the affirmative.

Possibly there would have been more on old
Tom's side, but the dread with which they
regarded their captain was sufficient to make
them fear a mutineer's death for asking that
justice might be done to the handsome boy
who had been such a general favourite among
them.

When old Tom saw the minority were of his
opinion his bronzed face reddened with shame.

"Very well, shipmates," he said, in low,
husky tones, "I see there are too many
against me to gain my point; but though I
die for it, I'll know why this vile act has been
committed."

He moved quietly from the forecastle, and
some of his companions were about to follow
him; but, waving them back, he said—

"Stand fast, shipmates; one is quite enough
to get into trouble."

They obeyed, and Tom walked boldly to the
quarter-deck.

There was more of grief than anger in Tom's
mind as, cap in hand, he stood before his
superior, and said—

"Cap'n, it's many a long day since old Tom
signed articles on board this craft—seven long
years, I think—and the whole of that time he
has never asked a favour."

"True, Tom; it is over seven years," said
Hugh, toying with the butt of his pistol.
"Now, what is the favour you wish granted?"

"Not much, cap'n; only that you will put-
about, and take that youngster aboard again."

The captain of the Seagull laughed as
though amused at old Tom's request; then said,

"I am very sorry I cannot oblige you, Tom.
Now go back to the forecastle, and, when
next you make a request, let it be one that I
can grant."

"You can grant this, cap'n."

"You are answered. Go to your duty."

"Very well, cap'n; since you won't take the
poor lad aboard again, tell me what reason
you had to leave him upon that spot?"

Hugh of the Red Hand turned upon his heel,
and, without deigning a word in reply to Tom,
said to Campbell—

"Turn this fellow off the quarter-deck. If
he refuses to leave, place him in irons."

Campbell moved forward, but at the second
step he halted. There was a menace in the
angry eyes and clenched hands which wanted
not old Tom's words to render intelligible.

"Keep back, sir!" said the old seaman. "I
don't want to do anything that will harm you,
but if you come near me until I have spoken to
that cowardly murderer, then the consequence
be upon your own head."

The old seaman's gigantic form, his well-
known muscular power, and his utter fearlessness, caused Dennis to cower back in dismay.

Not so with Red-handed Hugh. He turned
suddenly upon the daring speaker, and drawing
a pistol from his belt, levelled the tube at old
Tom's forehead.

"Leave the deck at once!" he said, "or by
the mother that bore me I will send a bullet
through your skull!"

Tom Starboard's steadfast gaze was fixed
upon the angry captain's face as he replied—

"I care not for your threat; you have done
all you dare do. I have been put in irons for
no fault; chained like a savage beast while
you perpetrated that act which would disgrace
a savage. No, cap'n, do what you like with
me; death I fear not—my old hull has been
too often among shot and shell to fear your
pistol."

There were among the Seagull's crew many
ruffians that Red-handed Hugh felt well
assured he could rely upon; singling those out
he stayed Tom Starboard's speech by calling
out—

"Here, Jacques—Lenery—Bill Johnson—up
and pinion this noisy lubber."

The men called by name ran quickly forward,
and with dexterous fingers soon secured old
Tom's wrists.

Tom Starboard, though quite a match for
the three fresh men, stood passive while his
hands were bound, then, as his face grew white
with rage, he said—

"Twice in twenty-four hours, cap'n, you
have done this to the best seaman on board
your vessel. I tell you this, 'twill be the last
time, for pull a rope or touch a spoke at
that wheel I never will." Then turning
his head to the silent group who were
watching his every movement on the quarter-
deck, said, "Listen to me, the fresh hands
who came aboard the night before we left
England, and hear for the first time

CRUSOE JACK AND HIS TAME ZEBRA.

that you are on board a slave ship, and there stands Cap'n Bernot, the man whose hands——"

"Silence! take him below; by —— I'll have the gratings rigged for you to-morrow!"

"No, cap'n, never will old Tom Starboard come beneath the cat; if man won't punish your cold-blooded act, *Heaven will.* Yes, that poor boy——"

He was hurried below before he could utter another word; then Red-handed Hugh confronted the seamen and said—

"There has been enough of this for one day; go to your duty, and remember, the first man who murmurs or refuses to obey an order dies, as sure as there is a sky above us."

The crew dispersed, cowed by the savage resolution of their captain's face and manner—dispersed to meet again in small groups and speculate upon the fate that awaited Tom Starboard.

The captain of the Seagull and his chief officer walked to and fro upon the quarter-deck; both, in spite of the bold front Red-handed Hugh had assumed, were evidently perplexed at the sudden change that had taken place in old Tom.

"I'll flog him," said the captain, in reply to a question from Dennis, "if I have to quell a mutiny for it."

Dennis did not reply; his gaze was riveted upon a mass of dark fleecy clouds that were at that moment crossing the sun's disc.

"Shorten sail," he said suddenly, "or we shall be blown to rags."

"What is it?"

"A tornado. Boats'n, pipe all hands——"

The sentence was never finished, for the swift storm that had swept over the lonely isle where Crusoe Jack lay stunned from a blow of the fallen tamarind tree

3

swept around, darkening the bright canopy of heaven, hurling the sea in dense masses before it ; and before a hand could touch a rope, or the spelled seamen seek safety in flight, a mighty volume of water swept over the Seagull's taffrail, and cleared her deck of two-thirds of the crew.

Among those who were thus suddenly swept into eternity was Dennis Campbell.

Then, as the full force of the storm burst upon the ship, and sudden darkness came over the face of the waters, Red-handed Hugh yelled out to those who yet hung to the shrouds, to lower the sails.

As the words left his lips the Seagull careened over on her side, and plunged madly forward, her yards under water.

Full seven fathoms of the raging billows were traversed by the vessel in this manner, and when a giant wave struck her and her masts arose, the wind blew every stitch of canvas into ribbons, and many of the lighter spars were snapped off and carried away.

Amid the tempest's roar and the howling wind there could be heard the screams and cries of the fear-stricken men as they were, one by one, swept into the sea.

On, on, rushed the ship ; the darkness of night above, the wrathful billows swelling over the decks. On, until a sudden shock caused the hull of the ship to shiver from stem to stern ; and the waves, as though exulting in their horrid work, leaped around the ship, and hove in surging masses over her sides.

The fearful truth came with terrible distinctness upon Red-handed Hugh and the few that had clung to the vessel.

She had struck upon a rock.

And at every attack of the fierce hurricane the stout timbers threatened to shiver to pieces, as though the vessel had been made of glass.

The captain of the Seagull and ten men were all that remained of the many who had one short hour before peopled her deck.

And these in such imminent peril that life was not worth one moment's purchase.

Dashing through the blinding spray, Red-handed Hugh, when the vessel became stationary, brought a lantern from below.

By its feeble light he discerned how terrible had been the work of the maddened tempest.

"This way," he shouted. "Quick, there must be land close by. Lower a boat—in five minutes she will go to pieces."

They had sufficient consciousness left to understand that certain death awaited them when the groaning timbers gave way before the storm spirit, and catching at their captain's words as a means of escaping this doom, the men rushed to the sides and cast loose one of the boats.

The waters were subsiding as they attempted to pull from the vessel's side. Then came a blast of wind from the sea, and the boat was thrown up. There was a crash, and a cry of hopeless despair as it shivered against the Seagull's dark side ; a compound mingling of fragments of wood, broken oars, and human forms—then all was over. The captain and crew of the slave ship had passed away for evermore.

Now were Tom Starboard's words prophetic, when

he said that Heaven would punish the evil-doer for that morning's heartless, cruel work.

*   *   *   *   *

As quickly as the change had taken place on the lonely island, so did the storm king pass onward. The waters became still, and the bright sun shone over the late scene of death.

The stricken ship rested peacefully upon the bosom of the rippling waves, and, save for the broken spars and tattered sails, no trace of the late fearful tornado was visible.

Though the storm-riven vessel was at rest, beneath the water-line two ridges of jagged rocks held her as though in a giant vice.

Full seven fathoms around the stately hull their white curling lines of frothy wavelets showed where the deadly reefs lurked.

Within ten fathoms of the broken bowsprit the barren shore of a volcanic island reared its rocky out-lines, and stretching inland could be seen a mass of dark tangled herbage.

Leaning against the shattered stump of the main-mast, was the solitary form of Tom Starboard, the only survivor of that dreadful gale which had burst upon the hapless vessel.

"Not a soul left," said the old seaman, in a low, melancholy voice. "Great Heaven, it seems as though thy wrath had risen to punish those who took part in the guilty work of the new-born day."

He became silent, and leaning his bronzed cheek upon his hand, thought long and deeply over the terrible events of that day.

In fancy he saw the wild waves closing over his fellow creatures, and upon his ears came their piteous cries for help ere they sank to their wide, wide tomb.

"It is Heaven's will," he said, as though answering a question, "that I alone should be saved. Yet why should I have been chosen among the many better and God-loving men whose cold forms lie beneath the treacherous wave?"

These reflections brought the rugged seaman's mind back to the time when his soul was far from sin, and kneeling upon the wave-washed deck, he uplifted his hands and uttered a thanksgiving which had the merit of being free from worldly motives.

Rising from his knees, he looked towards the rugged land, and thought of the poor solitary boy who had been left to die upon a strange shore.

"Yes," muttered Tom Starboard, "I can see a mightier hand than mortal's in this. The very fact of being sent below, which at the time excited every black passion in my heart, was for a wise purpose, that saved my life, in order that I might rescue that innocent boy from a long and painful death."

With this mission before him, the seaman's heart became filled with hope, and well knowing the value of time, he at once descended to the cabin, and sought, by reference to the log, to find the precise latitude of the islands where Crusoe Jack had been left.

To his disappointment there were no marks to indicate the precise spot ; but upon further search in the captain's cabin, he discovered the vessel's course since they left England pricked upon the chart.

Still no tangible clue to the lonely isle; not even upon the chart was its position denoted, and as old Tom's finger rested upon the black dots which marked the many isles in the South Pacific Ocean, he muttered—

"It is not one of these. No, it must be one of the ny that are not marked upon any map." Hurry-

to look over the log, and comparing it with marks the chart, he resumed, "It must be near the tropic of Capricorn, and, at most, not a day's sail from here."

Taking a small compass that stood upon the table, he went on deck.

The thought of exploring the island that lay so near did not enter his head.

Old Tom had heard from the men who placed Crusoe Jack ashore, that the isle was covered with verdure; this he knew would be incapable of yielding sustenance to a goat for many years.

"Waste of time to go ashore," thought Tom; "this island has not *risen out of the sea** many months."

After a careful examination of the longboat, Tom Starboard found it quite seaworthy, and before the evening had closed in he had placed a sail, a couple of rifles, a barrel of powder, a bag of bullets, and a week's provisions in the stern.

Thus equipped, the old seaman awaited until the morning's sunrise; then, alone, and in the full belief that he was working out his destiny, he started upon his lonely voyage to discover Crusoe Jack.

The sea was as calm as an inland river, and the boat, propelled by a light breeze, glided quickly through the mighty waste of water.

Twice before the night closed in did the intrepid old tar pull his light craft ashore upon two islands.

Each proved like the one he had left, barren and desolate, and still, with the hope of accomplishing the object of his voyage, he drew the boat ashore, and spreading the sail over the sides of the boat, prepared to pass the night.

The first beam of the young day found him once more upon the wide ocean.

Mile upon mile of waters was passed, still no sign of the verdure-clad isle where his young favourite, for aught he knew, might be dying from hunger.

The exertion consequent upon having the entire management of the boat had thoroughly worn out the brave old soldier's strength, and scarcely had he crept beneath the covering than he fell into a deep slumber.

So far was he lost to all that occurred around him, that the hardy, watchful seaman heard not the grating sound caused by a number of canoes striking sharply upon the beach.

Each canoe as it became stationary disgorged its freight of painted savages, and when all were disembarked they spread themselves around the low-lying coast, and protected only by the skins that hung from their shoulders, threw themselves upon the

ground, and, save for one whose duty it was to watch over his companions, were soon asleep.

It was a strong party of savages, who had come from an adjacent island to gather turtles' eggs.

Unsuspicious of the proximity of the host of dusky wretches, old Tom slept on until he was aroused by the canvas being rudely torn from above his head.

Opening his eyes, he beheld to his dismay a crowd of dark faces gathered round the boat, and from their gestures it was plain they were as much astonished at finding the lonely voyager as he was to behold them.

Luckily for our hero, old Tom had stowed away the rifles and ammunition beneath the loose boards which covered the bottom of the boat, or they would have shared the fate of the compass, which he saw was already in the hands of a savage.

With dire forebodings that his voyage was stayed, he arose to his feet, and before he could leave the boat a dozen hands were stretched out to grasp his clothes, and before two seconds had passed, cap, jacket, trousers, and shoes, were torn from him.

Resistance was useless, so the old seaman, calm and defiant, waited for the death he felt was near.

When every article of covering had been stripped from him, the savages collected in a group and held a long conversation respecting their prisoner.

Poor old Tom shuddered. A speedy death he feared not, but from the horribly significant actions of his captors, he knew that they were cannibals, and evidently canvassing the best mode of cooking and eating their prisoner.

This fearful fate blanched the bronze cheeks of the hardy seaman, whose heart had never quailed before the heaviest broadside or the fiercest storm.

One by one, as the discussion was carried on, a black skin would start from the group, and turning to th naked prisoner feel his flesh with his finger an thumb; then, as though their horrid instinct w excited by the touch of the white man's flesh, they uttered a short wolfish cry and darted back to the clamorous circle.

In spite of the dread feeling which these unmistakeable actions brought to the captive's mind, he could not repress a grim smile.

"After beating about all over the world," Tom thought, "to come to this. Well, if it is my fate I must die, but unless I am much mistaken they will find this old carcase tougher than they can digest."

Not satisfied with Tom's spare form and the hard wiry flesh, the savages, after a long discussion, came to the conclusion that it would be better to keep their prisoner and feed him until the flesh assumed a plumper appearance.

This arrangement having been assented to by even the hungriest of the gang, they dispersed, and began to collect the turtles' eggs which were found in abundance beneath the sands.

Urged forward by the muscular savages, Tom Starboard was compelled to assist in their labour.

A task that soon became arduous, for the sun, as it gained power, scorched his naked limbs and gave him the most excruciating agony.

From sunrise to nearly sunset the work continued; then the immense heap of eggs was placed in the

* In the year 1811, Captain Tillard watched the formation of one of these extraordinary islands, which, in four months increased a mile in circumference, and eighty yards high; and when the captain and crew climbed the lofty sides, the ground was too hot to walk upon.

CRUSOE JACK.

longboat, and Tom, by significant signs, was given to understand that he was to hoist the sail and join the canoes.

Tom Starboard's heart leaped with joy.

He knew the sailing powers of his boat, and as he prepared to leave the island a wild hope of escape came to his mind.

Hopes that were soon doomed to be dissipated, for a number of the dusky devils, armed with spears, the tops made with sharks' teeth, seated themselves in the longboat.

"While there is life there is hope," thought old Tom; "I am not to be eaten yet, it seems, and if they do not discover the rifles I may yet stand some chance of escape."

Several times during the passage from the island the longboat's sail, heavily freighted as she was, had to be taken in to allow the canoes to keep up with her.

This fact gave Tom infinite joy, once on board and the sail spread he should be able to escape from a fate, the bare thought of which caused a cold thrill to run through his veins.

About four hours from their departure from the island, the canoes grounded upon a rocky shore.

From the immense masses of stone and its dark colour, old Tom had no difficulty in discovering the latitude into which he had been so unwillingly brought.

The whole population, when the canoes grounded, ran to the shore, and to the captive's surprise, he saw that the whole of them were entirely naked.

The longboat was immediately surrounded by the women, who, without taking the slightest notice of the white-skinned captive, made a scramble at the cargo of eggs, and in an incredibly short space of time the boat was emptied.

Tom Starboard trembled with dread.

When the many eager hands were collecting the eggs that lay in the bottom of the boat, an accidental touch upon one of the boards that concealed his precious store, and all hopes of escape would be gone.

The harvest was at length gathered, and Tom Starboard was left with his grim guardians.

By this time the news was spread that a white man had been captured, and the savages gave vent to a long howl, expressive of their joy.

At a signal from one whose waist was garnished with a string of human teeth, the captive was taken ashore, and, followed by the yelling crowd of cannibals, they went to a cluster of huts, which evidently formed the town or village.

Here a short halt was made, and after a brief oration from the chief, Tom Starboard was taken further inland.

At every step the hope that had buoyed him became fainter, and when he passed inside a circular space, railed off by long stakes, he felt that death was silently stalking towards him.

A train of horrible thoughts, conjured up by the ghastly sight within the stockade, caused his blood to run cold; and, for the first time since his captivity, came the terrible reflection that his young favourite had been captured and eaten by the very tribe of inhuman monsters into whose hands he had

fallen. The anguish of this dread foreboding was more than the thought of coming death, and laying his hand upon his open brow, a deep groan of agony welled up from his heart.

Without a word, his guards placed their spears upon the ground, and while two held him firmly by the wrists, the remainder brought the long trunk of a young tree, destitute of its branches, and throwing old Tom Starboard upon his back, bound him with tough reeds to the pole.

Commencing at his ankles, coil after coil was passed round until they reached his armpits; then uttering a few sentences to the helpless seaman they left the stockade.

The tough reeds cut into his flesh, and at every attempt he made to rise, he was thrown back by the extremity of the pole, which exceeded his height by some feet.

Well did Tom Starboard understand this crafty mode of securing a prisoner. His escape seemed as impossible as though he had been in the deepest dungeon of the inquisition.

So beneath the quiet starlight he lay, his horrified gaze resting upon the pile of ghastly emblems of humanity that were within three feet of his body.

He needed no telling to inform him that he was in the temple consecrated to human sacrifices. The pyramid of skulls, and another of leg and arm bones, showed how many had suffered at the hands of the inhuman tribe.

Tom Starboard sought to shut out the fearful scene by closing his eyes.

But the horrible creations of his brain were more to endure than the sickening sight around.

While lying in this place of skulls, a fearful idea had taken possession of his brain. He could not divest himself of the conviction that among the bleached pyramid of eyeless sockets and grinning teeth, was all that remained of Crusoe Jack.

This mental torture, added to the bodily agony he was suffering, for a time maddened him; and in the whirlwind of fury that took possession of his faculties, he bit madly at the pole which held him so firmly.

And while his head swayed from side to side, a joyful cry came from his lips.

The ligature between his shoulders had been bitten through.

As though scarcely crediting this truth, Tom moved his body from side to side.

Joy!—here was a path to freedom.

One by one the galling bands were bitten through, and before morning Tom stood erect, his limbs unfettered, and a resolve in his heart either to die upon the weapons of his enemies or escape.

Unarmed and naked as he was, this task was full of danger.

The odds were fearful; one nude man against a tribe of fierce, bloodthirsty savages.

Creeping towards the entrance of the stockade, Tom was about to emerge and make an attempt to gain the beach.

The first step brought him face to face with an armed black, who had been left in charge of the temple

The long deadly spear was levelled at his breast, and the savage sought to drive him back to the interior.

Rendered desperate, and not caring whether his life was taken or not, Tom Starboard sprang aside, then, with a tiger-like bound, he closed with the cannibal.

There was a short struggle, then a sharp gurgling cry, and the black fell to the earth, his own spear transfixed through his heart.

Then Tom Starboard, with the blood-stained spear in his hand, stood over the prostrate form, and twice plunged the barbed point into the fallen man's body.

The Englishman's muscular power had soon crushed out the islander's strength; the weapon changed hands, and the deadly point drank its owner's life.

With a loud convulsive laugh, Tom Starboard stood over his foe until the last convulsive throe told that death had taken place.

Then, with set teeth and a murderous light in his eyes, the old seaman went towards the cluster of huts where lay the sleeping horde.

The dreadful fate which in a few hours would have befallen him had raised a savage feeling in the English seaman's breast, and he thirsted as eagerly for the blood of those who had captured him as ever the most fierce savage thirsted for the blood of a foe.

Carried away by this unnatural passion, old Tom crept into the first hut he reached.

The pale moonbeams dimly lighted the interior, and as he stood with the murderous spear ready to immolate the inmates, the low wail of a child came from the furthest corner of the wigwam.

The strong man's arm shook, and, creeping from the place as silent as he had entered, he muttered—

"Why should I make that babe fatherless? the poor wretches only obey the savage instincts of their nature. Shame on you, Tom Starboard, thus to become a midnight assassin in your old age! Shame on ye!"

The low wailing cry of the young child, as it clung to its dark-skinned parent, had changed the fierce inhuman passion which had crept like a species of madness to the sailor's heart.

He went forth from that dwelling fully resolved not to shed blood unless for his own defence. A great change for one who, but a few minutes previous, had determined to glut himself with the blood of the sleeping savages.

Abandoning the mud huts, Tom Starboard went swiftly towards the moonlit ocean.

The sharp-pointed stones cut and lacerated his feet at every step, and the cold night winds froze the blood in his veins.

Those feelings were unheeded. The tranquil ocean was before him, and the moon's silvery gleam seemed to guide and encourage him to regain his liberty.

It wanted but an hour to the dawn, and Tom, as he neared the spot where the canoes and his own boat were lashed, became sensible of some dusky forms moving about.

Creeping behind a massive piece of rock he watched their movements, and, after a few minutes' consideration, he muttered—

"They are keeping watch over the canoes."

The moon's rays gleamed upon their hatchets and the barbed points of their long lances; and as they paced slowly to and fro upon the rocky shore, Tom Starboard counted nine dark forms.

"Fearful odds, if I am seen," Tom Starboard thought; "but if I can once get to the boat in time their number would not stop me."

Between the piece of rock behind which Tom crouched and the next massive fragment that stood between him and the boat, was an open space of ground upon which the moon shone with wondrous brilliancy.

To pass this place was the most dangerous part of Tom's desperate venture; and baffled for a time, he stood silently calculating his chance of doing battle with the watchful guardians of the night.

"It will be daylight soon," he thought, "and unless I reach the boat nothing can prevent my discovery—death will follow that. What is best to be done? I can but die once; it is better to die fighting for my liberty than to be taken back to that horrible enclosure, and be slowly bled to death. I'll risk it; liberty or— Ha! what's that?"

A loud braying noise came from the direction of the huts, and the savages upon the beach turned suddenly round and ran swiftly past the very stone which hid Tom Starboard's naked form from their eyes.

Fully expecting to be discovered and immolated, the intrepid sailor waited with his spear lowered, to transfix the first who should come within reach of his arm.

Though two of their number passed so closely that he could have touched them, he was unseen; and, to his joy, the islanders ran nimbly to the peaks of the highest rocks, and appeared to be striving to make out the cause of the unusual sounds that had broken the death-like stillness around.

That signal was no mystery to Tom Starboard. He knew the sound was caused by a conch-shell, and it summoned his foes from their sleep to pursue their prisoner.

"Curse them!" was Tom's mental wish; "they have found the dead body of the fellow I killed, and discovered my escape."

He felt there was not a moment to lose. The distant flicker of torches and the angry hubbub of voices proclaimed the whole tribe upon his track.

Regardless of the savage forms above him, he darted boldly from his place of concealment and ran to the boat.

Exerting every muscle in his body, he pushed the heavy craft into the water, then scrambled inside.

Not a moment too soon did the boat begin to drift from the shore.

The islanders, startled by the keel grating upon the beach, sprang from the rocks, and with a wild yell rushed towards the fugitive.

There was no time to use either sail or oars, and Tom, with set teeth, stood in the bows, one trusty rifle in his iron grasp, the other leaning against the side of the boat.

Unaware of the danger that awaited them, the savages rushed into the water.

Not more than six feet intervened between them and the desperate, hunted fugitive.

One Herculean fellow soon came within reach of the boat—his hand touched the gunwale—a loud report echoed over the rocky, cavernous islands, and the savage fell back into the water, his skull shattered to pieces.

Tom Starboard had thrust the muzzle of his piece in his pursuer's face and fired, when the dusky wretch was about to snatch it from his hands.

As quick as thought the second rifle was taken up, and Tom waited but for a fresh victim.

Awed by the swift and terrible fate of their companion, the natives paused in their headlong career.

It was but for a moment; then, as though actuated by a sudden frenzy, they swam in a body towards the receding boat.

Brief as had been the check, Tom Starboard had set the single sail, and to his joy the boat swung round and began to glide swiftly through the water.

Not swift enough to escape the onslaught of the resolute natives, who, determined to slay or capture the white man, grappled the boat as it turned under the influence of the sail.

A wild laugh came from Tom Starboard's lips as the second rifle was fired point blank at the face of another foe, then clubbing his weapon he sprang upon the bow and sought to beat down those who had remained.

The loud report, and the warm blood of the slain man bespattering their naked forms, caused them to drop back into the water; then, as though urged forward by the wish to avenge the death of their companions, they again seized the boat and tried to scramble aboard.

Nerved to desperation, and fighting for life and liberty, Tom Starboard brought the butt of his rifle upon the head of the first who impeded the boat's progress.

The black's forehead was crushed in, and falling back with a yell of agony he sank beneath the wave.

Six yet remained.

Again the clubbed rifle performed its deadly work, and rid Tom of another foe.

Then, while battling with the fifth savage, the last one arrived beneath the boat and scrambled over the stern.

Tom had just despatched his fifth pertinacious foe, when the last of the gang, steadying himself in the boat, launched his spear at the sailor's body.

The rocking of the boat spoiled his aim, but the long weapon pierced the Englishman's thigh, and remained quivering in the wound.

More like two wild beasts of the forest than men, they closed, and clutching each other's throats, sought to decide the deadly fray.

In muscular power Tom Starboard was superior to his antagonist, but the recent fatigue he had undergone rendered him weak.

He felt the black's sinewy fingers tighten upon his windpipe, while upon the well-greased skin of his opponent he could barely retain his hold.

With the little strength left, and sensible that a film was coming over his sight, Tom Starboard closed his left hand and delivered such a "facer" that the black's nose was flattened upon his face.

The right hand quickly followed the left, and dealt such a succession of blows upon the astounded Indian's face that he loosened his grasp upon Tom's throat, and sought to ward off the tremendous club-like fists of the panting English tar.

No sooner was his throat free than Tom Starboard saw the victory would be his.

The black's spear yet quivered in Tom's thigh, thus they were both without weapons.

Calling to his aid all the skill he had acquired when a boy, he drove the savage step by step backward, until a well-aimed right-hander caught the savage between the eyes, and sent him like a rocket over the boat's stern into the sea.

Unfortunately for Tom, such was the impetus of the blow that he lost his balance and fell heavily into the water after his bruised and bleeding opponent.

Rising to the surface, he tried to clutch the boat.

Horror! a gust of wind caught the sail and sent it forward with a velocity that soon left Tom Starboard far behind.

His heart sank within him at this fresh misfortune, and as he struck out madly in the track of his boat the shore became illuminated by a hundred flaring torches.

The tribe had rushed to the beach.

A yell came from their lips when they beheld the white sail gleaming beneath the moonlight, and when Tom Starboard turned his head he beheld a dozen canoes being launched in pursuit.

At the same moment the black who had been so severely punished by Tom gave a loud shriek of agony; then came a fearful crunch that caused the cold drops of agony to ooze out of Tom's forehead.

The savage had been bitten in two by a shark!

There seemed no escape now from death; he was madly plunging after the boat, which increased her speed every moment.

A dozen canoes were skimming the waters, and would in ten minutes be close upon him.

To render death more certain, he knew one of those fearful sea monsters, the shark, would soon be upon his track.

In the midst of these dangers the pain of his wound was forgotten, until the limb began to stiffen and impede his progress through the water.

There was no hope—he must die; and closing his eyes, he gave himself up to the shark's triple teeth rather than face the death that awaited him ashore.

CHAPTER X.

A MIRACULOUS ESCAPE FROM DEATH.

APPALLED for the moment by the sight that met his eyes, our hero stood with his hand upon his sword, and his pale, handsome face turned towards the hungry, crouching beasts, who, disturbed by the sudden noise of the falling stones, uttered a low, savage growl.

It was a sight that would have blanched the cheek of the most lion-hearted.

Gathered around the cave were the fierce denizens of the adjacent forest—the terrible-looking puma, the sleek but deadly jaguar, were there in every size and age.

Crusoe Jack looked from one to the other as though waiting for the strife to begin, but beyond a repetition of the low growling noise the fierce animals seemed to take no notice of the intruder.

A noise above Jack's head caused him to look hastily upward, and to his surprise he beheld Hector with his fangs distended and his claws out, as though waiting to attack the first of his wild brethren who should advance upon his master.

His look was but brief; to his sorrow he bitterly regretted taking his eyes from a noble-looking brute, who, with his massive paws placed upon the body of a young deer, lay direct in his path.

The young castaway found that as long as he kept his gaze fixed upon the majestic animal, whose mien proclaimed him king of the wild beasts' lair, he was safe.

But no sooner had he looked upward than the beast arose, and sweeping the ground with his tail he gradually prepared for a spring upon the brave-hearted boy.

"Heaven help me," Jack said; "should I by a miracle sheath my sword in this fierce beast's heart, I shall be surrounded and torn to pieces by the remainder."

Through expecting never to escape from the dread place alive, the intrepid boy turned his weapon towards the crouching beast of prey.

He saw the fierce eyeballs glaring with a lurid light as the animal crouched lower and lower until his body became flat with the ground.

Then with a roar that caused the whole of the savage denizens to start angrily from their recumbent positions, the animal bounded upon our hero.

A prayer came from his firmly closed lips as he was borne to the earth by the animal's weight, and expecting every moment to feel the long white fangs tearing open his flesh, he closed his eyes, as he thought, for the last time in this world.

His sword had been wrenched from his grasp as the fierce brute sprang upon him, and now, when he felt a warm shower deluging his face and neck, life seemed to revive in his bosom and he unclosed his eyes.

The upper portion of his body was covered by the lion's form, and Jack, as he struggled to rise, uttered a short cry of joy.

It was then he discovered the cause of the long teeth not being fixed into his quivering body.

The kingly brute was in the last agony of death.

Crusoe Jack's weapon, up to the very hilt, was fixed in the lion's body, piercing the massive chest, and the point shining through his back.

The animal had been its own destroyer.

Crusoe Jack, when awaiting that spring which he felt would terminate his life, had held his sword directly in line with the lion's chest.

The ferocious beast, springing forward with a terrible impetus, had come upon the point of the weapon, tearing it from Jack's hand, then, as the huge form bore the gallant boy to the earth, the animal went forward, and the hilt of the sword coming in contact with a large stone, drove the blade completely through its carcase.

The warm stream that fell upon our hero was the life-blood of the fierce forest monarch.

As quick as thought Jack drew the blade from the quivering carcase, and with one foot planted upon the dead animal's side, he awaited the coming of the next terrible foe.

The scent of blood aroused their fierce natures, and with deep cries, which caused a third dread echo in the rocky lair, the deadly animals gathered round Jack and the fallen form of their late companion.

A young lioness, who had been the slain animal's mate, prepared for a spring, but ere she had time to carry her intention into effect, Hector, with a low savage growl, sprang through the opening, and seizing the lioness by the back of the neck, they both rolled into the centre of the den.

The events of the next few moments were like a dream to our hero.

He remembered the dread array of the fierce, fiery eyes gradually encountering his—he heard the roaring of the wild animals as they lashed themselves into a state of fury—then, as he staggered beneath the fierce attack of a jaguar, a *shot was fired* from the opening above.

He saw a form clothed in the skin of a wild animal bound to his side, then a second shot, then the jaguar's teeth, which had met in his shoulder, relaxed, and from excitement and loss of blood, he fainted.

When consciousness returned, it was like to awaking from a frightful dream.

Yet, to his amazement, when he beheld a man's form clothed from head to foot in skins, and his tame lion reclining by his side, he closed his eyes, as though he had passed from one strange phase of existence to another equally as strange.

"Are you better, Jack?"

These words caused him to start from his recumbent position and stare wildly at the speaker.

"Am I mad?" he thought. "Is this a vision of a diseased mind?"

Again the strange form bent over him, and asked—

"Are you better, my lad? Come; don't look so scared. Don't you remember me?"

The face seemed familiar to the boy's eyes; yet there was a strangeness about it that robbed the countenance of its identity.

Jack lay with wondering eyes. The speaker's strange attire was sufficient to arrest his attention, but our hero could not withdraw his glance from the upper part of his deliverer's face. There was *something wanting*.

At length Jack rose on his elbow, and said in a low, faint voice—

"Thanks to you, I am better and alive."

"Glad to hear it, my boy. You had a narrow touch for your life. Come; don't you remember me?"

Jack passed his hand across his forehead, and cried:—

"Your voice seems familiar, yet I can not—"

"What; forgotten old Tom—Tom Starboard?"

"Tom Starboard!" Jack echoed in astonishment, "and I not to know you; but you are much altered, Tom!"

"Ay, boy; I don't think the mother who bore me would know her son. Look here."

He turned his head round, and Jack was horrified to behold the place where his ears should have been, red and barely healed up from the frightful operation.

"Both gone," old Tom said, grimly, "and what's worse, they will not grow again."

"How, in heaven's name, did you lose them, Tom?"

Jack could not repress a shudder as he asked this question.

"It's a long story, my boy," old Tom replied. "I'll tell you another time. How is the wound?"

Jack raised his arm.

"Very painful," he said. "That brute's teeth must have met in my shoulder?"

"They won't meet again, Jack. I tumbled that jaguar over as neat as a ninepin, though I must say my hand shook a little when I saw how you were fixed."

"I had given myself up for dead," Jack said; "even now I can scarcely understand by what miracle I was saved."

"No miracle, boy. A good leaden ball—that was the miracle."

"How did you escape them, Tom?"

The old sailor indulged in a quaint laugh.

"I scarcely know," he said, "unless they took me for one of themselves. This is a queer rig, Jack, for Portsmouth."

Jack smiled faintly. The acute pain of his wounded shoulder was gradually numbing his faculties.

"But I think," old Tom continued, "it was the report of my rifle that scared the brutes, for when I came down to your assistance I fired right in among them, and they ran to their corners, regularly knocked over by the noise."

Jack looked anxiously towards his tame puma. A thought came into his head that filled him with alarm.

"He's all right," said Tom, interpreting the boy's anxious look. "I wouldn't have touched him for the world. Sky-scrapers and hammers! how that young beggar fought for you! He regularly clawed and bit a jaguar to death!"

"How did you know the animal was tame, Tom?"

"I know all about it. I'll tell you the yarn soon. Be—"

Jack's hand had fallen heavily to the ground, and his limbs became so rigid, that old Tom Starboard threw aside his rifle and uttered a cry of alarm.

His face soon brightened when he found his young companion had only swooned from pain and loss of blood.

Hector lay with his massive head resting upon his fore paws watching Tom Starboard's movements,

then, as though satisfied that all was right, he closed his eyes, and became motionless.

Old Tom's first care was to cut away the upper portion of our hero's jacket, and examine the wound. A troubled look came over his weather-beaten features when he saw the deep furrows where the fierce animal's teeth had entered the flesh.

"A bad wound," he muttered, "and unless I attend to it mortification will take place."

He laid the senseless form upon the ground, and rising, began to search anxiously among the mass of short vegetation that covered the earth.

Gathering the leaves of a shrubby, purple-coloured plant, he came back to the boy's side, then removing the covering from the lacerated shoulder, he began to slowly masticate the leaves, until they became a soft pulp.

With this strange remedy he covered the torn flesh, then tearing a portion of the boy's shirt-sleeve into narrow strips, he bound it tightly over the pulpy mass.

Crusoe Jack opened his eyes when the operation was over, and clutching Tom Starboard's hand, he pressed it gratefully.

"What have you done to my shoulder?" he asked. "When I fainted the wound burnt like a red-hot iron, now a delicious sense of coolness pervades the place."

"Not much, Jack; an old remedy for wounds I learnt from a South American Indian. Come; cheer up, my lad; you will be better soon. Can you walk?"

"I'll try, Tom."

By the assistance of Tom Starboard's arm Jack regained his feet.

"That's right!" said the old seaman, cheerily; "now lean upon me, and we will go to your den. Where is it?"

Jack pointed to the dark outline of the old tree.

"There!" said Tom; "it's a long way. Come; the sooner we are there the better."

As they slowly walked towards Crusoe Jack's eyrie the young castaway pointed out the peculiarities of his island home.

Suddenly he came to a standstill, and looking into old Tom's face, said—

"Tom, I can hardly believe the truth of you being here."

"True enough, lad, and from what has passed I did not come a moment before I was wanted. I have been a long time finding you."

"A long time?"

"Yes; over three months, as near as I can guess, and I have passed through more than I thought this old frame was capable of bearing."

Jack glanced up at the earless head, and sighed.

"That's not the worst, boy," said Tom; "but come, when you are better you shall hear it all. Never mind the past; here I am, Jack, and until King Death walks in and cuts my cable, I'll stand by you."

They resumed their walk, Jack's mind busy with a thousand perplexing thoughts.

He could see by the old seaman's strange attire that the ship had not come to the island. How, then, had his old friend found him?

Many were the questions he put to Tom, but the old fellow was obstinate. He would not clear up the mystery until he saw his young companion safely inside his dwelling-place.

It was a toilsome walk for Crusoe Jack to reach the summit of the hill, weakened as he was by the reaction of his overstrung nerves and the terrible loss of blood he had sustained.

When they reached the trunk of the old tree Tom Starboard shook his head, and muttered—

"A bad place, Jack; very bad."

The boy looked at his companion, surprise depicted upon his face, and asked—

"Why?"

"For several reasons," was the reply. "The first is, the insecurity of the tree itself."

"Insecure, Tom?"

"Ay, boy; the old trunk would not stand many of the fierce tornadoes such as we had when you were put ashore."

"It seems strong enough."

"To you it does, but ere we have finished our cruise about these islands, you will alter your opinion."

They had by this time passed inside the trunk, and both lying upon the couch of leaves, covered with the dark skin of the immense ourang.

Tom looked curiously at this, and suddenly said—

"Surely, you never killed this monster, Jack?"

"I did," was the modest reply, "more by luck than good management."

"Killed him in fair fight with your sword?"

"Yes, Tom."

"Then," said the old sailor, proudly, "you gained a victory that puts all our lion-hunters to shame."

Crusoe Jack did not think so much of the terrible encounter with this horrible wild man of the woods as he did of the terrible conflict in the wild beasts' lair, and without attaching much credit to his indomitable pluck, he told Tom Starboard of the encounter.

"Well done! well done!" exclaimed the old sailor. "Jack, you are a plucky fellow, and—but I must not make you vain."

Jack smiled, and said—

"Now, Tom, about this old tree; what other objection have you to it?"

"Other! why I've twenty."

"Tell me one more."

"I will, and in a few words. This place is too much exposed to the cold winds when the winter sets in."

"I had thought of that," said Crusoe Jack; "but as there was but little chance of obtaining a fire, I should not have wanted a place to live in long."

"No fire!" repeated Tom Starboard. "How have you existed? What have you eaten?"

Jack told him.

"Bad! very bad!" Tom repeated. "Upon such a diet you would not have been alive a week when the frost came on."

"I never," Jack said, "despaired, although I often thought of the long dreary time; but something seemed to whisper aid would come. I did not think of you coming to me, Tom—that would have

seemed a wild hope; indeed, my thoughts were that a ship might call at this island and I should be saved."

"A ship!" Tom Starboard said, gravely. "My boy, these islands are nearly a thousand miles out of the track of any vessel."

"I might have looked out until I perished," Jack said, "if this is the case."

"You might, lad. But now, what about a meal? A good bowl of broth would do you good."

Jack's eyes sparkled.

"Broth," he said; "that I fear is impossible to obtain. I have some berries, and a bottle of white juice from the cow-tree."

"You shall have something better, Jack."

Old Tom rose to his feet, and taking his rifle, was about to emerge from the hole in the tree. Turning, he said to his young companion—

"Lie perfectly still until I return, then Jack, my boy, for a feast that a king might envy."

Jack's spirits rose with the companionship of one he loved so well, and he said—

"And a king will enjoy. Am I not king of this island, and you my prime minister?"

Tom Starboard laughed, and began to descend the hill.

Jack listened for the report of his rifle, a sense of happiness stealing over his heart at the prospect of once more enjoying the sound of his fellow-mortal's voice.

Little did the boy imagine how soon his trusty friend was to be torn from him, and his bright hopes doomed to fade before the loneliness and desolation of the impending evil. Worse to bear from the short but congenial fellowship of his rugged but true hearted friend.

This is anticipation. To resume.

With a blissful feeling pervading his senses, Jack fell asleep, and when he awoke the evening shadows had fallen upon the island.

A confused recollection of the day's strange events crowded upon his brain, and for a time he thought the fight in the wild beasts' lair, and the coming of Tom Starboard, a dream.

No; joy! it was a blessed reality. There, outside the tree, was the staunch old seaman bending over a ruddy fire. Could it be true?—a savoury smell came through the opening as the night wind swept in fitful gusts over the hill-top.

Curiosity, and an appetite whetted by so long existing upon such meagre fare as had fallen to his lot, drew Jack to the opening in the hollow tree.

It was a strange sight that met his eyes.

A blazing pile of logs, evidently part of the ancient tree, threw a lurid glare upon Tom Starboard's weird figure.

His limbs clothed in the dark skins of several small animals, his tall form, long elf-like gray locks, and the bronzed face, gave him such an unearthly appearance that, had there been a stranger near, he would have taken the harmless old tar for a demon practising some kind of horrid rite.

From the uncouth figure Jack's eyes wandered to the dark object which caused the savoury incense to float beneath his nostrils.

What was it? It was not an iron pot, nor yet a kettle; yet, by its shape, it might have passed for either.

Jack looked long and earnestly at the strange object, but could make nothing of it; at last he thrust his head through the opening, and said—

"Tom, whatever is that you have on the fire?"

Tom Starboard desisted in his cooking operation, and looked up.

"You are awake, are you?" he said. "I found you asleep or I would have shown you how to make a mess fit for a king. Ha! ha! ha! Eh, Jack?"

"It smells good, Tom; what is it?"

"A stew."

"Where did you get the pot from?"

"Pot? Oh, the gentleman who came up with me lent us the saucepan."

"Gentleman! You are joking, Tom."

"No, quite serious. Can you come out and see it?"

Jack was through the opening in an instant, and old Tom, stirring the logs until they threw out a bright flame, revealed to Jack the mysterious article upon the fire.

The boy, though well versed in the ingenuity displayed by various unfortunate men who had been thrown by the waves upon a desolate shore, had never heard or read of such an astonishing contrivance as this.

"In the first place," said Tom, exhibiting the object of Jack's wonderment, "I knew you wanted something better than cow-tree juice and dried berries. And wanted it quickly; so without wasting time to shoot any of the animals, for the simple reason that I had nothing to cook them in, I went in search of an acquaintance, one I knew that would be a good meal, and answer the purpose of a good thick saucepan at the same time."

"Yes, but Tom——"

"Wait a moment, young impatient. This old friend, you see, is a turtle, and, by the way, I have turned another on his back for to-morrow. Now can you see the arrangement, Jack?"

"Yes; I wonder how you thought of it."

"Knew it years ago, when I was cast ashore in a worse place than this. Now bear this in mind, Jack, it will be useful some day."

"Like all your advice, Tom."

"Glad to hear it. Now, look here; first catch a turtle—see?"

"Yes."

"Then, having lit the fire, place the stones, one on each side, to rest the gentleman on."

"Yes, I understand."

"Then, turn him on his back, as I have done; but before you do this, cut off his head and feet. Then place him over the fire, and wait until it is ready."

"What is that on the shell, Tom?"

"Ah! I had forgotten; this is wet clay."

"What is it for?"

"To prevent the shell breaking before the soup is ready. Now, then, my hearty, stand clear while I bring the soup-dish inside."

The turtle, cooked within its own shell, and sending forth such a delicious steam that Jack's mouth began to water, was, much to Hector's disgust who

moved quickly away from the black, smoking object, brought inside the hollow tree, and each adventurer, armed with a shell of an oval shape, began to partake of the rich, invigorating stew.

There was a happy smile upon Jack's face as he sat down to partake of his strangely-cooked supper, and in spite of the recent dangers he had gone through, as the meal progressed, his light laughter pealed out at the quaint remarks of his companion.

CHAPTER XI.

A PHANTOM SHIP.—HOW TOM STARBOARD LOST HIS EARS.

"TOM, Tom, wake up; here's a ship close to the island!"

Such was the exclamation that aroused Tom Starboard soon after daylight upon the morning succeeding the supper of stewed turtle.

Our hero had awoke before his companion, and looking out from his eyrie, he beheld, to his astonishment and joy, a stately vessel within a mile of the island.

At first, scarcely realizing the truth, he stood gazing at the welcome sight; his eyes fixed upon the tall tapering spars, the delicate outlines of the cordage, and the dark hull, which seemed to loom out in the dull gray morn as though surrounded by a thin mist.

Waving his cap joyfully, he turned towards his sleeping companion, and gave vent to the above exclamation.

"A ship, boy?" said old Tom, rubbing his eyes. "Are you sure?"

"Yes, yes; a three-masted vessel—a man-of-war, I think. Tom, make haste and help me to signal, Hurra! We shall soon be away from this lonely— ha! Tom—it's gone!"

He had turned towards the vessel, and when the slowly-uttered words which had concluded his sentence came from his lips, he stared with mouth agape; his face alternately red, then pale, and his breast rising and falling, as though under the influence of some terrible feeling.

Tom Starboard had by this time reached the outside of the tree, and, seeing Jack's agitation, he said—

"What's the matter, lad? Where's the ship now? I thought so—you were dreaming."

The sound of his companion's voice broke the horrible spell that had fallen upon the boy's faculties, and as the colour came back to his lips and cheeks, he answered—

"No, Tom. I saw that vessel as plain as I see that white bird flying across yonder."

Tom Starboard shaded his face with his hand, and looked long and anxiously in the direction Jack had pointed out.

There was nothing visible save the tiny wavelets as they flowed towards their island home.

Afar in the east the sun, like a huge ball of fire, appeared to be rising from the bed of the sea.

There was no mist, no fog. Everything was bright and clear, and as the old sailor's eyes looked round alternately at the four quarters of the compass, he said—

"There is nothing, lad—not a speck; and the ship, had she been near enough to us for you to make out her rig, couldn't have gone below the horizon so soon."

"Tom," Jack said, solemnly, "as true as we stand re, *I saw a ship*—there--just below where those rge birds are flying."

Crusoe Jack's manner, his troubled look, and wondering, half-frightened gaze, carried truth with his words; and old Tom, in spite of his iron nerve, felt a chilling awe creep over him.

"I have heard," he thought, "of a phantom ship, but never saw one. I've heard, too, that it comes when anything bad is about to happen. The Lord have mercy on me, and keep the poor boy from harm."

"Tom," shrieked Jack, suddenly clutching his companion's arm in wild dismay, "look! look! There it is again."

Tom Starboard's heart sank within him, and he turned in obedience to the frightened boy's sudden cry of terror.

It was no chimera of the brain. There upon the sun-tipped waves a large vessel was plainly visible.

As he stood spell-bound at the strange sight, Crusoe Jack, with blanched cheek and distended eye, asked in a low whisper—

"What is it, Tom?"

There came no reply from the stout-hearted sailor; he heard not the question. Every sense was for the time deadened by a deep feeling of superstitious horror which harrowed his soul, and made the lion-hearted man's form shiver with dread.

True, his lips moved spasmodically, but no sound escaped them.

Fear that he had never felt when, with cutlass in hand, he sprang upon an enemy's deck, now, under the spell of this horrible vision, had stricken him dumb.

True there was a cause for the awful spell that had fallen upon our adventurers. There, precisely in the spot Jack had pointed out, stood *a phantom ship.*

That it was any other than an unreal vision, the mystic manner in which the semblance to a full-rigged vessel had burst upon their sight put aside all thought of it being anything more substantial than what it seemed.

Nor was the suddenness with which it appeared all. There was a misty, unsubstantial look about the vessel that made her look a thing of the spirit world.

The hull partook largely of the shadowy look of the spars and sails, and, to add to the horror of the spectacle, the *red dusky sun could be plainly seen through the vapoury outlines of her canvas.*

This left no room for a doubt of the dread visitant's spectral character, and as the startled pair became aware of the last addition to the strange and mystifying spectacle, their gaze became fascinated, and their deep, heavy respirations told how deeply their feelings were under superstitious control.

For nearly a quarter of an hour the phantom ship stood motionless on the waters, then the frail, mystic semblance quivered, and gradually melted away.

When the dread visitor had departed, Crusoe Jack's fingers relaxed their grasp upon his companion's arm, and he said, in a low, frighted voice—

"Tom, what can this dreadful sight be?"

Brought up from boyhood among men so prone to believe in superstitious legends as sailors are, Tom Starboard had not failed to imbibe strong feelings of horror at the story of the Flying Dutchman, and its never failing power of bringing evil upon those who witnessed it.

Fully believing at the time that the horrible vision was no other than the veritable sea spectre, doomed to be tossed about upon the waves until he should have expiated his sins, old Tom answered—

"The Lord have mercy on us, boy! That sight will surely bring some terrible calamity to us. I hope it will be upon my old hulk, not yours."

"Is it—is it," Jack asked, with terrified earnestness, "the—the Flying Dutchman?"

"Ay, boy; what else could it be? That it was not a real ship is certain, for we both saw it melt away before our eyes. The Lord help us, Jack! It's a warning, my boy, for one or both to prepare for the last voyage."

With such depressing sentiments weighing heavily upon their minds, the morning passed wearily away.

The many plans they had discussed on the preceding night were for the time unattended to, and with saddened hearts filled with that indefinable feeling of dread which cannot be explained, they sat upon their couch, and in silence ate a scanty meal.

The turtle formed the repast, and had it not been for that morning's fearful sight, old Tom had determined to again light a fire under the thick shell, and so partake of its luxurious contents until the inside was empty.

But under the depressing gloom that had fallen upon them, the appetite was forgotten while the mind remained so fully occupied by such chill feelings of dread.

But as the day wore on, Crusoe Jack reflected long and deeply upon their mystic visitor's appearance. The result of his ponderings chased the gloom partly from his handsome face, and going to old Tom, who was busy cleaning his rifle, he sat by his side, and began—

"Tom, I want to ask you something about that sight we saw this morning."

"Forget it, boy; forget it," said the old sailor. "It's a thing to be seen, and not talked about."

Jack was not so easily repulsed.

"Tom," he said, "everything you tell me I always know and find to be right, but I have been thinking and thinking about this phantom ship, until I feel that our judgments have misled us."

Old Tom stopped abruptly in the act of sponging out his rifle-barrel, and said—

"Misled us? Why the boy's gone mad!"

"No, Tom, no; answer me this. Did not the Flying Dutchman live, or was supposed to have lived, a very long time ago?"

Tom Starboard placed the butt of his rifle upon the ground, then putting his hands over the muzzle, he rested his chin upon the back of the uppermost hand, and looking down at Jack, he answered, slowly—

"Yes, a long time ago."

"A hundred years," asked Jack, "or more than a hundred ? "

"Quite a hundred, Jack, perhaps more ; but what on earth is the boy driving at ? "

"I tell you, Tom. If the Flying Dutchman lived so long ago as that, it was not him we saw this morning."

"Why not him ? "

"All that time ago," Jack said, "ships were not built the same as they are now."

"P'raps not."

"Not so long in the hull, and a very high poop, which gave them a stumpy appearance."

"Certain, boy ; certain."

"Well," Jack said, triumphantly, "the ship we saw this morning was not stumpy-looking. It was like the Seagull, only much larger."

Tom Starboard's gloomy face changed while Jack was speaking, then his lips puckered, and finally expanded as he gave vent to a hearty laugh.

Crusoe Jack was astounded.

More so when Tom Starboard threw his rifle upon the ground, and with a leap that a wild Indian alone could have successfully imitated, he sprang up and gave vent to a lusty cheer.

Jack felt certain his companion had suddenly become deranged, and with much concern in his voice, he asked—

"What ever is the matter, Tom ? "

"Matter, boy ? Hurra, hurra ! What an old fool I am ! Why, Jack, my boy, that wasn't the Dutchman after all."

"It was not."

"No, boy, no ; it was but the reflection of a ship, hat's all. Hurra ! "

"The reflection of a ship ? "

"Yes, boy, yes ; the shadow of a vessel in another sea."

"Of course, Tom," Jack exclaimed, jumping to his feet in delight. "How foolish we were to be so frightened ! I have often read of it, now I remember, but never thought it could be true."

"True enough, boy ; there are more wonderful things than this ship to be seen in the world."

"I think so, Tom. Such strange and terrible sights, that in a book we should think them mere invention."

"I don't know about your books, Jack,"—the old sailor extended his hand towards the sea—"there's my book, boy ; and I've read more wonderful things there than you will find in your books."

Jack could well believe the old seaman's assertion.

The gloom now dispelled from their minds, the partly-consumed turtle was dragged from the inside of the tree, and hoisted upon the supports.

Then Jack, collecting all the dry wood he could find, placed it beneath the shell, and old Tom, by using the lock of his rifle, soon had the stew in active progress.

As they sat by the fire, Jack with one hand buried in Hector's long mane, old Tom said—

"While this fellow is being warmed, suppose I finish the yarn I began last night ? "

"The very thing I was about to ask," Jack said, "for I am anxious to know how you escaped from those wretches."

"Where was I when you went to sleep ? "

"Where you had fallen out of the boat, and were swimming after it with a shark close behind you, and the natives in their canoes coming from the land."

Old Tom, though the fearful episode had long passed away, shuddered as he thought of the fearful moment when he was left in such dire peril upon the bosom of the mighty deep.

"That was a dreadful time, Jack," he began ; "I had given myself up to the shark, which I knew was close aboard of me, and had shut my eyes ; but even then it was hard to die, so I opened 'em again to have one more look at the sea.

"I looked towards the boat, and then I saw her with the sail flapping against the mast, and looking for all the world like as though she was waiting for me to come aboard.

"That sight gave me new hopes of life, and looking towards the black devils as was coming hand over hand upon the craft—for, d'ye see, they didn't know as I was in the water—I stretches out as hard as I was able to reach her.

"No good. A canoe full of them came up before I had gone ten fathoms, and while another canoe went and took the boat in tow, I was dragged aboard by the hair of the head.

"I didn't struggle. I felt it was all over with me, so sat down and waited for the thrust of the black devils' spears, but that didn't happen. They had something worse than a death so easy for me.

"Well, I was took ashore, and all the women— they is worse than the men, Jack—began a yelling and scraping round me. Look here."

The old tar opened his robe of tiger-skin, and showed Jack his breast all covered with scars.

"That," he resumed, "was done by the women. Some used their nails, and some their teeth, and I'd been torn to pieces by 'em hadn't a big black fellow drove them away. It was as much as he could do, and he had to knock a good many of 'em down with his club, afore they'd leave off biting and tearing my poor old body."

Jack's eyes flashed at this horrible recital, and he asked—

"Did you not resist them ? "

"Resist them, lad ? Did you ever see a pack of hungry dogs, when a piece of meat has been thrown in among them ? "

"Yes, once."

"Well, it was just like that. I was the piece of meat, and them horrible women the dogs, only they were worse than any dogs—they were devils.

"When the black fellow had driven 'em off, he drags me away to where all the men of the tribe were holding a palaver, and when they saw my chest all over blood, certain as you are there, Jack, if they didn't begin to lick their lips the same as a thirsty sailor would at grog time."

"Horrible ! "

"It was, Jack, it was ; and I took the old chief

AN AWKWARD ENEMY.

long time to palaver to 'em to let me be punished first, afore they ate me.

"So at last I was taken to a tree, and about a dozen of 'em held me tight, while some more *nailed my ears* to the trunk of that tree."

Jack's eyes filled with tears, and he said—

"Poor Tom!"

"It was dreadful pain at first, and I could have bellowed out; but I wouldn't let them hear or see I cared, so while the blood ran down my face I stood without flinching, and looked hard at a lot of the devils who were standing looking on.

"There I stopped until night; the blacks thinking I could not get away, went to their huts, leaving only one big fellow to keep watch over me.

"I don't know how it was, Jack, but I passed off all of a sudden, just as though I died. I can't call it anything else, for one minute I was looking at the big black fellow, the next, everything went round like, and I forgot my pain and where I was placed."

"You fainted from pain," Jack said, suggestively.

"Perhaps so; anyhow, pain brought me to life again. I don't know how long I was in that state, but when I came to, I found my body covered with blood, and a strange feeling each side of my head— *my ears was gone.*"

Crusoe Jack uttered an exclamation of horror.

"Yes, gone," old Tom continued. "At first I did not know what to make of it; but when I felt I was free, I thought more of escaping than of the loss of my ears.

"I could see nothing of the black who had been standing over me, and as the night was very dark, I determined to make an attempt to reach my boat.

"I knew where it lay, not more than two fath from the tree, and I knew the terror the natives of my rifles—they were both lying safely in the boat.

"My powder, shot, and swords, were safe in their hiding-place, and creeping forward as well as I was able to, I reached the beach.

"To the right of where I had been nailed to the tree, there was a small, cave-like place in the rock, and as I passed I saw a light inside.

"Creeping to it, afraid to disturb a stone, I peeped in, and saw—what do you think, Jack?"

"Your sentry, perhaps."

"What else?"

"I cannot guess."

"Yes; I saw the fellow who had been guarding me, Jack, and I saw him leaning over a fire roasting two pieces of flesh—yes, don't start—they were *my ears!*"

"Tom!"

"You can't believe it, lad? Look here."

Tom Starboard took from beneath the skin that hung over his breast two dark pieces of dried flesh, much resembling parchment, and bearing unmistakable signs of having been scorched by fire.

Jack turned his head away, and shivered at the sickening sight.

Old Tom replaced the horrible relics, and said—

"I've saved them both, however; I feel the day will come when I shall have a better vengeance upon the wretches than I have yet obtained."

"How did you get them?" Jack asked, shudderingly.

"I saw the cannibal," said Tom Starboard, "stooping over his horrible feast, and, weak as I had felt before, I became as strong as a giant with rage.

"Before he could turn and save himself, I had my fingers at his throat, and there, Jack, held them until the wretch's life had passed away.

"Then I took these emblems of my visit to that fearful island from the fire, and went to the boat. There was no one there to stop me, and I was soon out upon the sea; had I been followed, they never would have taken me."

"How was that, Tom?"

"The first thing I did," said Tom Starboard, "was to load this rifle, and as soon as the blacks had laid their hands on my boat I would have blown my brains out."

"A better death," Jack said, "then again falling into their hands."

"So I thought; but there was no pursuit, and before morning I was out of sight of the horrible place.

"For several days after this I must have been in a raging fever, for when I next remember anything, I found myself alone upon a beautiful island, the boat nearly full of water from the rain, and my body one mass of blisters from the sun."

Old Tom paused, and remained for some minutes in deep thought.

"I daresay," he said, "I was very ungrateful to the One above who had protected my life through all these dangers, but, Jack, I laid in the boat and prayed for death to come."

"Poor Tom! you must have b

"I was, Jack. Each side of my head was in a frightful state from the wounds not being attended to; my body was all blisters, and my legs, from being I don't know how long in the water that had got into the boat, were numbed and shrivelled up. I never thought one could be in such a state and live.

"But I thought of you, Jack, and made sure the island was the one where Captain Hugh had put you ashore; and, full of this hope, I dragged myself to the land and lay upon the cool grass.

"Creeping very slowly forward, I came to a tree, then fainted; for I was that weak that I could not raise my hand to my head.

"Then I should have died had it not been for the vampire bat."

"The vampire bat, Tom!"

"Yes; the little animal, by sucking a portion of blood from me, saved my life; otherwise I must have died from fever. Whether it was the bleeding or the drinking of cocoa-nut milk, I don't know, but in a few weeks I was able to take my gun and go in search of some animal; for I wanted a skin to protect me from the sun by day and the cold at night, for up to this time I was quite naked.

"My success gave me this warm covering, and by the time it was dry and made to cover my limbs, another week passed away; then I had to repair my boat, which I imagine from the state of the keel must have been driven ashore during a storm, for it was badly damaged.

"When I had refitted, I again started to find you —sometimes whole weeks without seeing land; at others, touching at an island every day. I began to fear you had either died or been eaten by cannibals or wild beasts, until yesterday, when I saw you and the young lion coming down the hill."

"Where did you see us from, Tom?"

"I had just run aground as you began to descend this hill, and being so surprised at the sight, I could not hail you loud enough for you to hear.

"I kept you in sight until suddenly you disappeared through the earth; then I ran forward, thinking you had tumbled into a chasm or a rift in the earth. You know the rest, Jack. Now, having cleared off the log, let me have your yarn."

Jack told him all that had transpired since he had been upon the island, and when he had concluded, old Tom said—

"You had a narrow escape, Jack, from that beastly thing in the pool; we must have him out from there."

"I have tried often," Jack said, "to have him out, but to no purpose."

"What would you have done had he come out?"

"Thrust my sword in his ugly carcase."

Tom Starboard laughed.

"You might as well have tried to make an impression upon a stone wall," said Tom, "as to have hoped to injure him with your sword."

"The lurking brute," Jack said, "I shall not be content until I get him out of there."

"All in good time, my boy; now what is our plan for the future?"

"That," said Jack, "I will leave to your better judgment."

This answer pleased the old seaman.

"Very well, boy," he said; "to begin, we must find a better spot than this for our dwelling-place; but first, let us fill our larder. Do you think you can use a rifle, Jack?"

"Yes; my shoulder does not pain me in the least."

"I knew it wouldn't. Nothing like the red-skin's remedy for a wound."

Rifle in hand, the adventurers began to descend the hill side.

Our hero, under the genial influence of companionship and the possession of a trusty weapon, felt none of that loneliness which had so weighed upon him before Tom Starboard's arrival.

At the base of the hill they came to a stand.

"Before we go in the house, Jack," Tom Starboard said, "let us pull the old boat well up among the trees, for we shall want her soon."

"Want the boat soon, Tom?"

"Yes, boy; there is the hull of our old craft not far away, and everything we want is inside."

"I had forgotten that. When shall we start in search of it?"

"As soon as we have laid in provision enough for a month's voyage."

"A month?"

"Ay, boy, a month; these islands are so plentiful that we may cruise longer than that before we find our way to it."

Our hero longed to be once more upon the boundless wave, and had it not been for the more prudent advice of his elder companion, he would have had the boat launched and trusted himself to the ocean, without either provision or clothing to guard against the many evils that awaited the voyagers upon their search for the dismasted hull of the once stately ship.

So with many a long, wistful look at the bright surface of the vast ocean, Crusoe Jack helped to place the boat under the protecting foliage of a huge tree.

Then, with their fingers upon the triggers of their rifles, and keeping a wary eye upon everything that resembled the fierce beasts which infested the island, they entered the forest.

CHAPTER XII.

CATCHING A SHARK.

THE glowing tints of the vertical sun shone over the beautiful island, as Crusoe Jack and his companion entered the thickly-wooded forest.

Passing beneath the cool shade of the mighty trees, the boy began to look eagerly around for one of the lesser animals which he knew abounded in plenty.

The society of his only friend, the late narrow escape from death, and the certainty that they could procure both food and raiment for the coming winter, drove the melancholy from our hero's face, and, with a light heart, he conversed gaily with his older and more staid companion.

"I've been thinking, Tom," he said, "about the turtles."

"The turtles, lad! What about them?"

"That it must take a great quantity to supply the different countries with their shell."

"Shell, eh? Oh, you mean to make combs, boxes, and that sort of thing."

"Yes; and, as you say they are not so very plentiful, it's a wonder the whole race is not exterminated."

Old Tom Starboard gave a quiet chuckle; the sailor never indulged in what may be termed a laugh, it was a sort of suppressed giggle, unaccompanied by any facial movement.

"So you think," he said, when he had indulged in this peculiar laugh, "that everything the landsmen call tortoiseshell is made from the shield of the turtle?"

"Yes. Why, is it not, Tom?"

"Bless the boy, no! Did they kill even turtles enough to supply the woman folks with things to stick in their hair, there wouldn't be a blessed turtle left in two years."

Crusoe Jack opened his eyes in astonishment.

"Well, Tom," he said, "all I know is, that the books I have read have been all lies, for they say that the shell of the turtle is used for the manufacture of many articles, and polishing brings out those beautiful streaks of red, yellow, and dark brown."

"No, lad, the books may be all right, not as I know much about 'em, but the turtle-catchers don't kill the fish to get the shell."

"I understand now, Tom; the turtles shed their coats and the men collect them."

"Wrong again, boy."

"Do tell me, Tom; I hate to be kept in suspense."

"I will, boy. I think it's right you should learn all these things. Well, when they catch the turtles, the men cover the poor devils' backs with pieces of sticks, grass, or anything that will burn, and set fire to it."

"While the turtle is alive?"

"Yes, boy; and when the heat causes the little square pieces to rise, they pass a knife underneath and take them off."

"Does not this kill them?"

"No, Jack, the fishers take good care of that; they do it very gradually, because, you see, too much heat would spoil the shell."

"The poor things must suffer fearfully."

"Yes, it do seem cruel; but the fishers often catch one some time after it has been shelled, and they find the outer coat has grown again."

Crusoe Jack was very thoughtful for a few minutes after this explanation of the cruel mode of shelling turtles.

Suddenly a look of intelligence passed over his face, and he said—

"I understand now, Tom; the thin outer covering is taken from the turtles' backs, not the hard, bony shell."

"That's it, boy; the scales only are taken away, but it must be, as you say, a most cruel operation."

"Yes, poor—ha! look there."

Within a dozen yards of the two adventurers a small wild hog was trotting away, evidently disturbed by the sound of their feet, as the dried twigs were snapped and broken by the first footfall in this untrodden part.

Our hero's gun was brought to his shoulder, and had not old Tom thrown up the muzzle, our hero would have fired.

"Not that," said Tom Starboard, kindly; "the report of your piece will bring out all the beasts of prey that lurk among these trees."

"I had not thought of that, Tom. What are we to do? We want game, and cannot have any unless we kill them."

"True—very true; that is just what has been troubling my old brain ever since we started. We want something as sure as our rifles, but without making a report."

"I'm afraid, Tom, we shall not obtain this useful article."

"We must try, Jack. Did you say there is a river on the other side of the mountain?"

"I did, Tom; at least, there is a stream of some width, but whether it is fresh water, or filled by the sea, I cannot say."

"The latter, I hope, Jack. Come, my boy, let us go in search of this place; we may, perhaps, find all we want."

Our hero had the most implicit faith in his companion. Although disappointed, boy-like, at not being permitted to fire upon the game, he quietly retraced his steps, and pointed out the direction of the water.

On their way, the adventurers passed the crocodile's pool, and Jack, with his finger upon the trigger, looked out for the scaly gentleman who had so nearly made a meal of his young form.

The monster was not visible, and old Tom, guessing the import of Jack's anxious gaze, said—

"Don't be in a hurry, my boy; we will have him yet."

"I hope we shall," said Jack, "for I never look at this pool without a shudder."

"Enough to make you, boy; had the scaly fellow once got you between his teeth, there would have been but short time to have said your prayers."

They passed on. The scenery at every step was bold and beautiful in the extreme, and several times our hero paused to gaze upon the glowing expanse of nature.

"This is very lovely, Tom," the boy said; "so beautiful that one can scarcely feel a regret at leaving the world."

"It is, boy, it is; but I have seen more beautiful sights than this, and yet have pined for home and friends."

"Home and friends!" repeated the castaway. "I have neither, Tom, therefore I suppose I feel less than others at our lonely condition."

"No friends, Jack?"

Our hero felt the gentle reproach these words conveyed, and answered—

"None besides yourself, Tom: and you are with me?"

Old Tom looked with admiration at the lithe form and handsome face, and shook his head, as he said—

"There is something I cannot make out, Jack, u."

"What is it, Tom?"

"Why the skipper who is now at the bottom of the sea should have been paid to leave you ashore?"

"Paid?"

"Ay, paid! for I heard enough to tell me that when I was at the wheel, listening to the cap'n and his first officer."

"There is but one," Jack said, "who would have done that; and she could not have given the captain money enough to recompense him for going so much out of his track to leave me ashore."

"There's a lot of wickedness afloat in the world, my boy; and we might flounder about a long time before we guessed anything near the mark. Come on, Jack; don't think any more about it. You'll be a great man yet, if you live long enough."

Our hero smiled at his companion's words, and, throwing the rifle into the hollow of his left arm, trudged manfully alongside.

"I don't think anything about it, Tom," he said. "The only thing that sometimes troubles me is the thought of the young squire I knocked over the cliff."

"Ah! you fear you have killed him—eh?"

"That's it, Tom."

"Hope for the best, lad. I don't think you have, as the water must have been pretty shallow thereabouts."

"You know the place, then."

"Well— Hallo! is that the spot?"

They had just turned a projection, and come suddenly upon a large extent of sand, still wet, and varied by small lines of rock and tangled seaweed.

"Yes; but the last time I was here this place was covered with water."

"It was high tide at the time, my lad. Bear ahead. It strikes me there is just the spot we want, over by those stones."

He pointed with the butt of his rifle towards a number of irregular pieces of rock, and as he looked to the priming of his piece, he continued—

"Those stones, Jack, have been upheaved by one of those volcanic eruptions that are common in these parts. See, here are some small pieces that have been carried away by the receding tide, and, unless I am at fault, at the foot of those high pieces of stone we shall find a nice nest of gentlemen, who will provide us with all we may want in the way of arms and tools."

By the time he had ceased speaking, they reached the objects of his remarks.

Between the bases of the pointed rocks they found a deep chasm, and old Tom, standing by the brink, said—

"Ten fathoms of water at least. Throw a stone in, Jack."

The boy obeyed, and watched with interest its swift descent.

The pebble had not sunk more than three yards, when a long, grayish-looking object darted out from beneath the shadow of the highest piece of rock.

Jack uttered a cry of alarm, and hastily brought his rifle to his shoulder.

"A shark!" said the old sailor, "I thought we should find one here, Jack."

Jack did not reply; he was too excitedly watching the dreaded monster as it rose within an inch or two of the surface, then, as though angry at being lured from its retreat, the dreaded creature caused the water to seethe and bubble by a few movements of powerful tail, then darted back to its lair.

When it had disappeared, the young castaway drew deep breath, and said slowly—

"Yes, Tom, it is a shark, and a large one. I cannot understand it scarcely; but every quiet-looking pool this island is the dwelling-place of some terrible monster."

"This is very easy to understand, Jack. This fellow has been left here by the receding tide, or else stays by choice."

"Choice, Tom?"

"Yes; it may be more profitable to his hungry stomach to stay here, than go out to sea and search for food."

"The wretch," Jack said; "I wonder if any poor sailor has ever fallen a victim to his jaws."

"Most likely, boy. I should think he is an old one by his length. It must be, at the least, eighteen feet from stem to stern. Throw in another stone, Jack; we will try what we can do for the gentleman."

Another stone was thrown in, and, as the voracious creature again darted out, the old sailor said—

"Fire at his head, Jack; don't miss him, boy, whatever you do."

Drawing a deep breath, Crusoe Jack drew the butt of the rifle firmly to his shoulder, and fired.

The ball sped true to its mark, and the water, which had been of a pale greenish tint, became encrimsoned with the fierce animal's blood.

"Bravo!" shouted old Tom, lustily; "well hit, lad! Load again—that's it. Always be ready, in case we might be attacked in rear."

Our hero, with flushed face, carefully reloaded his weapon.

"Come here, boy," said his companion, seating himself upon a stone near the brink, "and see the fun out."

Jack sat beside his old friend, and in silent satisfaction they watched the dreaded animal struggling with its slowly departing strength.

Our hero's bullet had entered the shark's forehead, and by the stream of dark-coloured blood that spouted upwards, it was evident a huge blood-vessel had been cut through.

For nearly an hour the wounded wretch lashed the water, and darted from side to side in the vain hope of escape.

Our hero suggested putting the animal out of its misery at once, but to this old Tom strongly objected.

"No, boy," he said, "never use two charges of powder when one will do; besides, you would not hit a better part, were you to fire a broadside at him."

The water by this time had been beaten into a foam by the shark's tail, and as this pretty dark-coloured froth began to subside, the shark was seen to float upon the surface of the little landlocked bay.

"He is dead!" our hero exclaimed, joyfully. "See, Tom, how quiet he lies!"

"Not yet, my lad. That won't happen till we see his ugly white belly uppermost."

The creature was so still that our hero thought for once his companion was mistaken, but, as he was about to give the thought utterance, he saw the large fins moving gently.

"You are right, Tom," he said; "the reptile is not yet destitute of life."

"No, my boy; old Tom has not been on the sea, man and boy, thirty-five long years without knowing a little about these varmints."

He then explained, in his homely way, to his companion that the muscular power which is necessary for a fish to have over the swimming bladder was just departing, thus it was that the huge carcase floated.

"You see, my lad," he said, in conclusion, "this varmint hasn't the power to compress the swimming bladder, so he can't go to the bottom. It's a wonderful thing, isn't it, Jack? Ha! there he goes."

They ran to the rocky edge of the pool as the lifeless brute rolled slowly over, and the red sun gleamed upon its white breast.

The next thing to be considered was how to bring the vanquished monster ashore.

An easy task had our adventurers been in possession of a goodly coil of strong rope, but as they had neither rope nor anything that would answer as a substitute, the victory they had achieved seem fruitless.

While old Tom stood gazing longingly at the shark, with a puzzled look upon his weather-beaten face, our hero solved the difficulty.

"We can do it, Tom," he said, joyfully. "Hurra! Come and help me."

He bounded swiftly towards a grove of tall trees, and before old Tom could well understand the cause of this sudden act, the boy was busily at work with his sword, hacking at one of the lower branches.

"Catch hold of the end, Tom, and bend it down."

Tom gave one of his peculiar laughs, and said—

"What on earth is the boy at?"

He held down the branch, and in a few minutes it snapped off close to the gnarled trunk.

Jack soon lopped off all the superfluous shoots, and when he had finished he held it before old Tom's face, and said—

"There, Tom. Won't that do?"

Old Tom rubbed his chin reflectively, and smilingly said—

"Well, Jack, you'll soon be ahead of me. Dash my old head! I should never have thought of that."

The object of his admiration was the shorn bough, which had at its smaller end a good-sized and tolerably strong crook.

Proud of his quaint companion's words of praise, Crusoe Jack led the way to the brink of the miniature bay.

Fixing the crook in the shark's gills, the castaways began to draw their prize towards the shore.

It was an easy matter while the dead shark was upon the water, but when they had succeeded in landing the huge ugly head and part of the shoulders, they were brought to a standstill.

The dead weight was too much for their united strength, also too much for the green bough which had done them such essential service, and the adventurers, much to their regret, were compelled to desist.

Old Tom looked wistfully at the huge carcase, and, as usual when in a dilemma, he began to stroke his chin.

"This won't do, Jack," he said. "We mustn't leave the beggar here, or the tide will carry him into the sea."

"What is to be done, Tom? It would take at least six strong men to drag him ashore. I have it," he added, suddenly. "Hurra! We shall manage it yet, Tom."

"Eh? Bless the boy! What has got into your head now?"

Jack whipped out his sword, and began to hack at the dead animal's body, as far as they had drawn it out of the water.

Old Tom was loud in his praises of his young partner's ingenious plan, and when the boy became tired, he took a spell, as he termed it, at the dissecting business.

"Right, Jack," he said; "we must bring him ashore in pieces. Good lad for thinking of that. We shan't be sorry for this victory."

When old Tom began to finish sawing the first portion of the carcase, our hero asked him what uses he could put the various parts of the shark to.

"Do with it!" was his exultant reply; "a hundred things, Jack. His jawbones will make saws. His skin, when dry, will be as tough as leather. The bones will make needles, arrow heads, spear heads, and all sorts of useful things, and from his flesh we can extract oil enough to keep a lamp going for—for a long time."

The pair worked with a determination not to be caught by the tide, and before sundown they had the felicity of beholding the huge monster upon the sands.

The carcase was severed in four pieces, and the mode by which they drew each piece ashore was by making a slit with the sword for the crook to fit in.

Old Tom measured the fierce ocean monster with the sword-blade, and said—

"Over five-and-twenty feet long, Jack. Come, we will go back to our peak, have some stew, and the first thing to-morrow morning return and finish this job."

On their way back to their lofty home, our hero had the good fortune to shoot a large rabbit.

This welcome addition to their scanty larder old Tom carried off in triumph.

Tired by the exertions they had that day undergone, and faint from want of food, our adventurers found a draught of milk from the cow tree, a refreshing luxury.

"Now, Jack," old Tom said, "stir the embers under the turtle while I make an oven to bake this rabbit."

A few dried sticks placed upon the red embers soon burst into a blaze, and while Jack was busy with the turtle, old Tom scraped a large hole in the ground near the base of the tree.

This he termed his oven.

Our hero watched with curious eyes his companion's movements, and when he saw old Tom diligently mixing a small mound of clay with the contents of the water-bottle, he could not help saying—

"What is that for, Tom?"

"This? Bless the boy! Why, this is our pie-crust."

"Pie-crust?"

"Yes," said old Tom, gravely; "and if you never have a worse mess than this will be when it is done, you will not fare badly."

Our hero shrugged his shoulders.

"It may be very good, Tom, but I think I shall stick to boiled turtle and milk. Fancy eating earth. Ugh!"

Old Tom desisted for a moment in making his paste, and said—

"Eating earth! Would you believe I have eaten earth before now, Jack, and been thankful for it?"

An incredulous smile played over our hero's lips as he said—

"I can believe anything you tell me, Tom, although some things are so strange and wonderful that I can scarcely realize their truth."

"Would you have credited that a tree could have given milk as freely as a cow?" *

"It seemed strange when you first told me about it."

"Yet you found it true?"

"I did."

"Well, Jack, perhaps before we have done our wanderings together I shall be able to show you the earth that is eaten not only by wretched castaways like ourselves, but by whole tribes of Indians, who eat the earth after slightly baking it over a fire."

"Is it similar to that which you are now kneading?"

"In colour only; the earth to which I allude is found upon a wide plain in South America after the river overflows the banks. When the water passes away it leaves the soil so rich that not even a single blade of grass will grow upon the ground."

"That is the reason, I suppose, the Indians eat the earth?"

"Right, boy; they must eat either that or starve."

"How does it taste, Tom?"

"Fatty, but not unpalatable. At least, I suppose I was too hungry at the time to particularly notice the flavour, for you may be sure I stood out as long as I could against the horrible stuff."

"Poor Tom, you must indeed have been in a sore strait."

"I was, but not worse than many thousands, for in Siberia, Africa, and Japan, this fat earth is frequently eaten by the half-starved natives."

"Poor wretches."

"Talking of strange food," old Tom continued, kneading the earth with both hands, "I do not know which of the two dishes I tasted in those parts was the worst."

"Worse than eating earth?"

"Yes; I was once near the great river called by the natives 'Oroonoco,' and by good fortune came upon a large hut just as night had set in. I was hungry and wanted food, and they gave me a piece of greasy, dark-looking paste, and just as I was

---

* Humboldt calls this singular tree Galactrodendrum.

about to convey it to my mouth, imagine my disgust to find the dark spots where large ants."

"Ugh! that would have been sufficient for me, Tom."

"It was for me until I found there was nothing else to be had, so I closed my eyes and eat my piece of ant pudding, and had I never seen the black spots, I should not have known the difference between it and rancid butter—the taste was exactly the same."

"If ever I travel in those parts, Tom, I hope I shall have my larder with me."

"I hope you will."

Old Tom gave a chuckle as he said this.

Jack, who knew the meaning of that sound, said—

"I suppose I should have to carry it a long way."

"You would, boy. Depend upon it, if there is anything to be obtained the red-skins will have it in place of dirt or ant puddings. Hullo!"

"What's the matter, Tom?"

Crusoe Jack received no reply, and to his astonishment he saw his companion spring suddenly to his feet and start off down the hill-side.

Jack caught up his rifle, not knowing for a moment what had caused this sudden movement, and was about to follow.

When he came to the brow of the hill he burst into a hearty fit of laughter, as he beheld Tom Starboard chasing Hector.

The young puma had quietly made off with the dead rabbit in his mouth, and when old Tom uttered the exclamation of surprise, Hector was in the act of creeping down the hill-side.

Jack called to his little favourite, and the animal, slipping past old Tom, ran to his master, and to Jack's delight dropped the rabbit.

He seemed to understand he had done wrong, for without waiting to receive a caressing stroke from his master's hand, he slunk away to the interior of the tree, and coiled himself upon the bed of leaves and turned his large eyes towards Tom Starboard.

"The young beggar!" Tom said, when he reached the brow of the hill, "he has taken all the breath out of my body."

Jack laughed and handed him the rabbit.

Old Tom covered the animal's skin with the soft clay he had been so carefully preparing; then filling the hole he had scraped in the earth with dry twigs, set fire to them.

"Two courses to-night, Jack," he said, as he placed the peculiar-looking object upon the blazing fire; "fish and game."

Whatever objections Jack had entertained towards the earthy pie-crust, vanished when the rabbit was taken out of the hard clay.

With this covering the hair and skin came away, and the flesh, owing to the gradual heat, was as white and as tender as that of a young fowl.

Old Tom watched his young companion partake of this food with pleasurable feelings in his rugged heart.

"It will do him good," he thought; "poor boy, he looks pale and thin."

Our adventurers' dinner table was not of the most elegant design, neither was there an abundance of glittering glass or silver plate to garnish the feast.

A square piece of stone served the double purpose of table and dishes. Plates were out of the question.

Their fingers were the only knives and forks they possessed, and for chairs they used the earth.

"Well," Jack said, gleefully, as he succeeded in disengaging one of the rabbit's hind legs, "this is a glorious supper, Tom; I never tasted anything so delicious before."

"Not bad, Jack, all things considered. Better than eating a dirt pudding, eh?"

"Better! There is not a nobleman's table graced with a dish so delicious as this."

"They want the appetite, Jack—he, he, he!"

"What are you laughing at, Tom?"

"I was just thinking, lad, that's all—thinking what a pair of cannibals we must look—no knives, no plates."

"Bother those things! Help me, Tom, to pull that leg off."

When the meal was over and the fragments put out of reach of Hector's pilfering claws, old Tom went in search of a herb which would supply him with a good substitute for tobacco.

Jack watched his companion examining the various shrubby plants that grew in profusion on the hillside, then with the help of the clinging plant that grew around the tree he climbed to the summit.

Seating himself upon this lofty peak, he took a survey of his island home.*

The sun was slowly disappearing like a ball of lurid fire when our hero looked towards the mighty ocean.

Glittering in the dusky rays, he beheld a flight of humming-birds flitting to and fro over the sweet-scented plants that grew beneath his lonely eyrie.

They seemed like winged gems as they rose and fell in their eager chase of the tiny insects† that rose from the bright petals of the beautiful blossoms.

When our Crusoe became tired of watching the tiny birds chase each other through the air, he turned his face again seaward, and suddenly straining his eyes, he exclaimed in astonishment—

"IS THIS A VISION OR A REALITY?"

Calling loudly to his companion, Crusoe Jack sat dazed, spellbound, and appalled.

CHAPTER XIII.

THE SEARCH FOR THE MISSING HEIR.

WHEN our gallant young Crusoe was being taken from the white cliffs of England to that far distant land where his strange and wondrous adventures took place, the beautiful fairy-like creature whom he had saved from a watery grave rushed wildly to her palatial home, and burst into the room where her father was seated.

The nobleman looked up with astonishment depicted upon his handsome face, and said, pleasantly—

"What now, my darling? You are excited. What is the matter?"

---

* See No. 1, front page.
† The supposition that humming-birds feed only on the honey from the flowers is not correct, for on opening the crop insects are always found.

She wrung her hands, and, in a voice choked at times with convulsive sobs, told him of the fight that had taked place upon the edge of the cliff, and the fate of her young companion.

She had just finished her recital when the young gentleman who had been so unceremoniously tumbled into the water made his appearance, his clothes wet, and his pale, handsome face white with passion.

"Here is the dead alive," Mabel's father said, smilingly. "Come, Harry, let us have your account of the terrible encounter with the young fisherman. Poor Mabel! she would have filled our minds with alarm upon your account."

The young aristocrat, with a malevolent look towards Mabel, said—

"It is soon explained, sir; one of Darrell Collins's boys saved Mabel from falling over the rocks, and became presumptuous, so I gave him a chastisement, that's all; though," he added, spitefully, "Mabel would have brought the fellow here."

A grave, noble-looking gentleman, who was seated with the baronet, repeated the wrecker's name, and said—

"That is the man; I had forgotten his name until this young gentleman mentioned it."

He looked surprised; then turning to his daughter, said—

"Now, young people, leave me with this gentleman; I will thank the fisher-boy for his gallant act to-morrow."

"Mabel has done so already," said Percy, contemptuously. "A pretty fellow, truly, for a young lady to speak with."

Mabel turned her large blue eyes towards the speaker, and said—

"He is brave and handsome, which you are not, Percy."

The young patrician's face became scarlet, and as he left the room, he muttered, severely—

"Curse him! the beggar's brat; I'll be revenged upon him for the blow he gave, if it is in twenty years' time."

He kept his word.

When the two gentlemen were alone again the stranger, who was an old friend of the baronet's, and a general in the Indian army, resumed a subject which had been interrupted by Mabel's entrance.

"This fellow," he said, "when I was washed ashore upon a spar—you remember that fearful storm, and how our vessel was lured to destruction by the wrecker's light?"

"Perfectly, Sir James."

"I had my boy clasped on one arm, and to the spar I clung wildly with the other, but I had scarcely touched the beach when this villain came and struck me a blow with a hatchet."

"Horrible!" said the baronet. "The merciless miscreant!"

"I remember nothing else until I was on board a pirate lugger; how I escaped drowning I know not, unless I became entangled in some portion of the wreck. The pirate seamen told me they had found me entangled in part of the rigging attached to a broken mast."

"And your boy?"

"I believed him dead until lately. There must have been a strange fatality that brought one of this fellow's companions to India. One night, by the watch-fire, I heard a number of men recounting their past lives. Among them was one who spoke of the manner in which vessels had been lured to destruction by a gang of wreckers to which he formerly belonged."

"It was, indeed, strange."

"You may be sure my attention became riveted when the fellow spoke of the very vessel which had brought me here; he also spoke of an officer being slain by this Collins, and a boy would have shared his father's fate had not the villain's heart been touched by its helplessness."

"You were the officer," the baronet said, "and the babe your son?"

"Yes."

"What became of the child?"

"The wrecker, I afterwards found, took the little fellow home and brought him up."

"The thing is clear; you have but to appear at the lonely hut and demand your son."

The officer shook his head sadly as he said—

"That plan, I fear, will not answer; the fellow may deny all knowledge of that night's work to screen himself from punishment."

"But you have the evidence of the man who told you the——"

"No; he was shot the next day, when we met the Sikhs at Gwalior."

The baronet reflected for some moments, then he said—

"Leave that to me; I will go at once to the hut, and, if possible, see the boy, and bring him here."

"Do, and my eternal gratitude shall be yours."

The distance was not far from the lordly mansion to the lone hut by the sea; and the baronet, concealing his person in a long cloak, soon reached the wrecker's door.

It was open; and, from the angry voices of old Madge and her husband, he soon became aware that something had happened to stir the black blood in Darrell Collins' heart.

The baronet's face went white when he heard Darrell tell Madge that through her he had slain a boy's father; and, had it not been for her harsh conduct, the boy would not have ventured upon the sea, in an open boat, and been drowned.

Madge's shrill voice was heard in reply; then a deep oath, followed by a blow; then a scream from Madge, as she fell backward, her mouth smashed in by her brutal husband's fist.

This passed so swiftly that the baronet was not aware that Darrell had left the hut, until he saw him striding down the cliff.

Mabel's father followed him, and, in a few moments, was by the wrecker's side.

A few minutes' conversation sufficed to fill the blanks in the angry dialogue he had overheard.

He learnt that a boy, for whom Darrell Collins would have given his life, had been drowned, and the boat, in which he had put out to sea, had been washed ashore, bottom upwards.

To the baronet's anxious inquiry, as to whether he could form any conjecture how the accident occurred, Darrell gave a surly answer, and turned sullenly away.

There was not much difficulty in identifying the poor boy who had been taken from the wreck of the homeward-bound East Indiaman as the general's son. Again, the brave lad had rescued his daughter from destruction. Then the baronet thought, fearful of the consequences of his quarrel with young Percy, he had spread the sail of his boat and come to an untimely end.

As he went slowly and sorrowfully back to his home, he thought of what might have been had his old friend's son lived.

He pictured the general's son and Mabel together; and, with a deep-drawn sigh of grief, he wished Sir John Moreland had arrived but a few days earlier from India.

Sir John saw, by his friend's sad face, that his hopes of finding his son were premature; and, with poignant anguish depicted upon his handsome face, he listened to the dreaded news.

The blow fell heavily, but the veteran only bowed his head in sorrowful resignation, and, when he could speak, he said—

"It seems hard to be borne, but I must endure it. One hour before you started from here my boy was with your daughter. Now,"—here the voice faltered, and a tear rolled down the bronzed cheek—"he is beneath the wave."

"It is a heavy blow, my friend; but the Lord's will be done."

"Amen! Now the only tie that brought me to England is gone, I will return to India, and upon the battle-field, perhaps, I may find a Lethe for my sorrow."

"But your estates here in England?"

"I shall not claim them. Had my boy lived, I should have done so. As it is, my brother can retain what he believes to be his inheritance."

"He believes you dead?"

"Yes; I have not contradicted the report that I perished in the wreck of the Fairy Queen. I should never have come to England again, had it not been in the hope of finding my boy."

To all his friend's entreaties, the sorrow-stricken man remained immovable. He wanted to leave at once the place fraught with so many saddened memories.

The baronet at last desisted, and Mabel was sent for, and, much to the young maiden's astonishment, she was questioned and cross-questioned respecting the appearance of the gallant boy who had saved her from death.

Her answers left no doubt respecting the identity of the supposed fisherman's son and the rightful heir of a brilliant fortune and an honourable name.

She heard the whole of the sad story from her father when Sir John Moreland had returned to India; and when Percy spoke of the beggar's brat, she told him her preserver was of nobler blood than himself.

The little maiden cherished the memory of Crusoe Jack in her heart; and, though she supposed him dead, as time went round his image grew more indelibly marked in her memory.

So while our hero was being conveyed to his lonely island, his father, whom he did not remember, had been in search of him.

And while he wandered among wild beasts and brutal savages, old Madge worked and plotted to place her crooked-back godson in Jack's stead, and sought to wrest the wanderer's inheritance from the general's brother to enrich the low-born Jasper—Crusoe Jack's bitterest foe.

CHAPTER XIV.

A VISION OR A REALITY—A NIGHT IN THE FOREST—A NOVEL LIGHT—HUNTING THE TAPIR.

TOM STARBOARD, when he heard his young companion's voice, ran quickly up the hill-side.

"What is it, lad?" he asked; "a ship in sight, or a shoal of whales."

"Neither, Tom. Look there!"

About two miles from the solitary island the old seaman beheld the water rolling and bubbling as though a mighty space of the otherwise tranquil sea was about to rise in dense volumes.

From the troubled waters a noise, like the rolling of innumerable wheels over a hard road, could be distinctly heard; then a mass of seething foam was hurled upward, and from the chasm there came a dense body of thick sulphurous smoke.

This strange spectacle held the young castaway spellbound, and he did not hear old Tom Starboard's exclamation, which explained this strange and wonderful freak of nature.

"A volcano!" old Tom said; "there will be an island there in a few hours."

The thick volume of smoke hung like a pall over the surging waters, and, from time to time, showers of stones could be seen shooting upward.

Crusoe Jack gazed upon this singular spectacle with thrilling heart; and, when the smoke rolled slowly away and a long dark line was visible several feet above the water, he said—

"Tom, this is a sight worth all the dangers and privations we may have to encounter. It is, indeed, wonderful. Please Heaven that I live to leave this island, I will travel every part of the world, if such wondrous spectacles are to be seen."

The boy spoke enthusiastically, yet the resolution was, as will be seen, fully carried out.

He saw more strange and wonderful things in his after wanderings than an island rising out of the sea.

"There are stranger things in nature than this," old Tom said; "as you say, boy, please Heaven, we will yet see them. This is not the first island it has been my good fortune to behold rising from the very depths of the ocean."

Crusoe Jack drew near his friend, and listened attentively to every word old Tom uttered.

"In 1810," the old sailor said, "I was at St. Michael's, and saw one of these strange and sublime spectacles. I passed the spot a month after, and beheld an island not less than a mile in circumference, and between seventy and ninety feet high—that is, the immense mass of volcanic matter was that height above the level of the sea."

"You saw this, Tom?"

"Ay, lad; not only saw it, but walked over it; and, what is stranger, six months after I was within pistol-shot of the place, and instead of an island, there was nothing but a small reef not ten yards in length."

"It had nearly disappeared."

"Yes; sank as strangely as it had come, and, save for the smoke that issued at times from the sea, it was almost impossible to make out the place where this wonderful phenomenon appeared."

"Marvellous!" ejaculated our hero—"most marvellous!"

"It is, boy. Such sights as these do not fall to the share of those who stay at home all their lives."

"I question," said our hero, "if one-half of those who have never been beyond England would believe such strange things."

"Perhaps not, lad, perhaps not; but those who see must believe. Come, the damp is falling; we will turn in, for we have much to do to-morrow."

The castaways sought their primitive couch, and, fatigued by the day's exertions, slept soundly for several hours.

Our young Crusoe, at all times a light sleeper, was aroused soon after midnight by a succession of unearthly cries, so much like a human being in distress, that he started up from his bed of leaves, every nerve thrilling with excitement.

"Tom," he said, anxiously, "awake! there is a terrible noise at the foot of the hill."

Old Tom raised himself upon his elbow and listened for a few seconds, then growled out—

"It's those cursed howling monkeys. I did not know we had any upon this island. All right, go it!" This was added when a yell louder than had come before reached their ears. "I'll settle a few of you to-morrow night."

In answer to our hero's interrogation, the old seaman told him that the howling monkeys were huge, and of a reddish colour, and had long beards. The difference between those midnight disturbers and their species was, the howlers never quitted a large tree they had chosen for a home; and, he added, that one tree alone would contain upwards of a hundred noisy creatures.

Jack determined, during his stay upon the island, to give those tenants immediate notice to quit; for old Tom, as he drew his portion of the skin coverlet over his head to shut out the horrible din, told him that he would have this serenade every night for at least nine months in the year.

Leaving our hero to this comfortable reflection, the old seaman went to sleep.

Not so our hero, whose mind had been excited by the commencement of the howling, and it was a long time before he could shake off the strange fancies that came to his brain.

At times the howls were subdued and sullen, and seemingly some distance from the brow of the hill.

Then, as our hero closed his eyes, the most unearthly discord would suddenly come upon his ears; so sharp and plain that he felt assured that his tormentors were grouped around the tree.

"I cannot endure this" he muttered, angrily. "I will send a charge of small shot among them; perhaps that will have the desired effect."

Swinging his gun, he went to the brow of the hill, and fired in the direction of the noise.

Never in the whole course of his life did our Crusoe so much regret anything as that.

The loud report of the rifle, so far from silencing the disturbers of his repose, caused an unwelcome addition to the concert.

The myriads of birds that were at roost among the trees, startled by the noise, began to flutter their wings and give utterance to the most dreadful cries.

Then came the deep, subdued growls of the jaguars and pumas, as they were prowling about in search of food.

Then the wild hogs—the tapirs—began to grunt and snort at the unusual sound, and Jack's friends, the howling monkeys, seemingly disgusted that others should join in their serenade, increased their yells threefold.

Our hero stood for a moment and listened to the horrible discord, then turned and rushed inside the tree.

He flung the gun from him and stopped both ears with his fingers, and in that position he went to sleep.

The faint blush of the new day found the adventurers busy preparing their morning meal.

Jack was busy stewing the turtle, and old Tom, after he had carefully cleaned their rifles, brought out the remains of the baked rabbit.

The larder was empty when they had finished their breakfast, and, as Hector lay quietly by crunching the bones, Jack said—

"Now, Tom, what is the day's work to be?"

"The shark first," was the reply, "then to the forest."

Jack had a lively recollection of the previous night's serenade, and, his mind filled with vengeance against his tormentors, he asked—

"Had we not better go and dislodge that howling crew first?"

Old Tom laughed.

"You won't mind them," he said, "in a few weeks' time, Jack; you'll get used to it by that time."

"Shall I? I don't intend trying, Tom."

"Very well, lad; but we had better dissect the shark first."

"Why so?"

"Well, lad, I don't want to use our powder and lead too much; one thing, it wastes it—and another, we can do our work better among the trees with a lance; you see, that is quieter, and not so likely to disturb the beggars."

"Be it so," Jack said, rather reluctantly; "you know best, Tom."

Shouldering their rifles, and Hector following at Jack's heels, the adventurers went to the place where they had left the severed portions of the shark.

Stripping the voracious monster occupied a goodly portion of that day; but when the bones were cleared of their covering, Jack gave a loud hurrah.

With an amount of skill which only stern necessity can call forth, old Tom made several useful articles of the monster's bones.

The jaws he fashioned into two very useful saws, and several of the smaller bones he set aside for needles, combs, and various small tools that would be useful to them in building a hut.

But the crowning triumph in Jack's estimation was the formidable teeth, the points as sharp as needles, yet of sufficient strength to penetrate the trunk of a tree.

Leaving the remainder of the bones to bleach, old Tom and his companion went towards the forest.

Though many hundred trees were examined, the old sailor shook his head, and when our hero offered to climb one, and lop off a couple of straight branches,

"Not that, boy—not that," he said; "we shall find it directly."

They did. In less than ten minutes after, old Tom uttered a triumphant cry, and pointing to a tree, said—

"There, lad, every twig is as supple as whalebone and as tough as iron."

The massive forest giant which had called forth these words from the old seaman differed but little from those they had passed—the bark, the foliage, and the long, spreading branches were alike.

But near the base of this particular tree a number of long shoots grew out; they were of different lengths, some not more than ten inches, others as many feet. Though this disparity in length existed, each was of a circular form, not much larger than an ordinary walking-stick.

There was not the slightest vegetation upon these singular shoots, and, as Jack expressed it—

"They grew long and thin, and looked as though the upper branches had robbed them of their foliage."

"May be so," old Tom said; "look here, lad, ugly as they are, do you think any of the handsome branches would stand this?"

He seized one of the shoots as he spoke, and drew the point down until it touched the trunk. A moment it was held in this position, then suddenly released, and to Jack's surprise the branch resumed its position, and became as straight as though old Tom's weight had not bent it double.

"It seems strong enough," our hero said, "and just the thing for our purpose."

"It is, my boy; the world could not provide us with such a lance-shaft as these will make."

Selecting two of the longest, old Tom held them down while our hero cut them off close to the trunk.

After considerable labour this was accomplished; then the old sailor's ingenuity was taxed to fasten the points upon the ready-grown handles.

The leathern strings from their shoes fastened the teeth in a slit made at the end, and when this was concluded, old Tom declared that they were in possession of a better weapon than all the muskets in the world.

Although our hero did not exactly agree with his companion's opinion respecting the relative value of the weapons, he allowed the old seaman to have his way.

"Now, my boy," old Tom said, "before we go in search of our dinner, let's have a little practice with the lance."

Selecting a small tree, the slender trunk, at its thickest part, not more than ten inches round, they began their first essay with the lance.

To our hero's amusement, old Tom's weapon went more than a yard away from the tree, and buried itself half-way in the ground.

"I could do it once upon a time," Tom Starboard said, "but I suppose my old arm has grown stiff."

Measuring the distance carefully, the young Crusoe poised the light weapon gracefully above his head, and with a precision that would have been creditable to an Indian, he sent it several inches in the tough wood.

Tom Starboard opened his eyes in amazement when he saw the light shaft quivering in the tree, and pulling his weapon from the earth, he said—

"Bravo! that was more than chance, Jack; where did you learn to handle a lance like a red-skin?"

"Since I have been left here, Tom."

"What! eh? you had no lance!"

"No; but during my walks about the island, I made it a practice to pick up any straight sticks I came across, and as I passed threw them at the trees or a bird."

"You did well. Come on; if you are as successful with a young deer, we shall have a dinner fit for the Lord High Admiral."

"I'll try, Tom."

When they entered the sombre depths of the mighty forest every sound was hushed, save the occasional screams from the throat of a noisy macaw.

The hideous noises that had so engrossed our young Crusoe's attention were stilled, and the night-prowling animals were hidden in their lairs.

In vain our hero looked for the bearded monkeys; they had disappeared, and, ghost-like, left no trace behind.

Beneath the spreading branches of a lordly palm-tree the adventurers saw a number of deer seeking shelter from the sun's burning rays.

With a quick movement of his hand, our Crusoe moved his companion back, and before the latter well knew what had occurred, he heard the whir of Jack's lance as it cleft the air.

Following the course of the weapon, he beheld one of the animals transfixed to the earth.

The lance had gone completely through the creature's side, and pinned it to the earth.

So quickly had death come upon the young deer, that its companions, beyond a wistful look at the quivering lance-handle, showed no signs of fear.

"There," old Tom whispered, as they passed through the thick tangled underwood, "is that not better than a noisy musket? You see, boy, we might, had we weapons enough, spear the whole of them."

"I can see the advantage now," Jack said; "shall we have another?"

"No, that would be waste."

The crackling of the dry leaves beneath the castaways' feet now startled the deer. Springing to their feet, they gave a timid look in the direction of the sound, then bounded away with the fleetness peculiar to their race.

A low growl came from Hector, as the drove entered into the thicket, and before Crusoe Jack could prevent him, the lion dashed in pursuit.

"Gone to forage on his own account," said old Tom, "but I question if he will overtake the herd."

"I wish," Jack said, "that I could cure him of that habit, but I fear it is impossible."

"Quite," was the reply. "You can't alter nature, Jack."

The heat was now intense, and the labour of skinning and cutting up the young deer caused the adventurers to feel thoroughly fatigued.

Crusoe Jack complained, too, of violent pains in his head, and old Tom, fearful that his favourite had been injured by the sun's rays, said—

"We must stay here, Jack, until the sun goes down; it will never do to venture out while you feel like this."

"The heat is stifling, Tom, and I feel thirsty."

The old seaman insisted upon Jack lying at the foot of the tree while he made him a cool shelter from the blazing heat.

The boy obeyed, and gladly, for he felt worse than he had really told his companion; not only was he suffering from the most acute pains about the head and face, but his limbs felt as though all power of motion was rapidly leaving.

In an incredibly short time the old sailor had erected a shelter for his companion.

A few branches from six to eight feet in length had been thrust into the ground, the tops meeting each other.

Over these a covering of palm-leaves was placed, and our hero found the shelter both cooling and pleasant.

His next care was to obtain water for the poor boy; this task to old Tom was not very difficult.

He had wandered many hundred miles over the vast regions of South and Central America, and knew the virtue of every tree and shrub indigenous to the mighty wilderness, and when he had constructed the palm-leaved shelter, he began to search among the trees.

Our hero watched him attentively for some time as he minutely examined the elegant parasitical plants that grew upon the trunks of the massive trees.

"What are you looking for, Tom?" he asked at length.

"Water, my boy."

Crusoe Jack was prepared to hear the most strange and wondrous explanations of Nature's works, but this reply surprised him.

"Water?" he said. "Water among these trees?"

"You find milk," old Tom said, "on the trunk of a dry, withered tree—why not water? Ha! here is one at last."

He sprang eagerly forward, and in the fork of a tree he detected a large leaf of peculiar form; it was rolled—to use a plain simile—as much like in form as the grocers roll paper to keep sugar in.

Each leaf of the rain plant when open is very broad, but as the rain or dew falls it rolls itself into the form just described, and keeps its contents, something over a pint, safe and cool from the sun.

Jack drank the contents of his natural goblet, still wondering at the strange works of Nature.

"Tom," he said, "every day brings forth some new and wonderful piece of Nature's work. Who would have thought these leaves contained such a refreshing draught of pure water?"

"It is wonderful, my boy; but there are yet more wonderful things for you to see."

With this Tom Starboard began to collect a heap of dried wood, and, as our hero's eyes closed, he heard the crackling of the pine over which old Tom was roasting the steaks from the young deer.

The cooking utensil was the iron ramrod of Tom's rifle.

When our hero awoke, all the disagreeable symptoms had passed away, and he jumped to his feet with a light laugh.

"Tom," he said, "your palm-leaf cottage has cured me."

"Glad to hear it, my lad. Come, here is a dinner for you."

Spread upon a palm-leaf were the steaks from the young deer, now, as Tom said, done to a turn.

Upon another primitive dish were a number of roots, not unlike the horseradish in appearance; these old Tom had dug up from a marshy kind of ground between the forest and the inlet where they had killed the shark.

"You'll find them good eating, Jack," the old seaman said, as our hero turned over the strange-looking roots; "they'll answer the purpose of bread and vegetables all in one."

Jack laughed, and commenced an attack on the viands, which proved the slight attack of fever had not injured his appetite.

Besides the deer-steaks and roots, there was a plentiful supply of water—a rain-plant grew near this grassy table—and they had but to extend their arms to obtain a delicious draught.

Minor accessories had not been forgotten by the kind-hearted old sailor. He thought the boy was not well, and under the burning sun's rays, he had walked to the sea-shore and collected a shellful of the white froth.

This he had dried in the sun, and it made an excellent substitute for salt.

A species of capsicum had also been gathered, to give a flavour to the steaks; and the feast concluded with a plentiful supply of wild berries about the size of a cherry, and exquisitely sweet to the taste.

This was the most luxurious meal our hero had partaken of since he had been cast away.

It was a strange picture of primitive life; the rich light of the fading sun tingeing the mighty forest with a crimson hue; the graceful foliage swinging pendulous in the evening breeze; the hum of insect life; the short, querulous notes of the gaudily-feathered macaws, and their not less brilliant companions, the noisy parrots.

Reclining upon the ground were our adventurers: old Tom gravely smoking dried leaves from a pipe—the bowl, a small shell; the stem, a piece of thin, hollow cane—Jack, in a half-recumbent position,

UNSEEN ENEMIES.

lazily watching the bright birds as they chattered, screamed, and quarrelled, upon the branches of the adjacent trees.

Neither for some time attempted to speak. The strange feeling of solitude produced by the soothing hum of the busy insect world caused even the castaways to feel a sense of happiness at being thus admitted within the grand arcanum of Nature, to view her unsullied beauties, unfettered by the restraints and conventionalities of civilized life.

"Tom," our hero said, suddenly, "there is a strange delight after all in being placed as we are—a sort of delicious charm out of which one expects every moment to awaken to the senseless ceremonies of the artificial world we have left."

"Ay, boy; old as I am I can feel the glorious sense of freedom in being thus untrammelled. No master to serve, but, instead, absolute monarch of as fair a spot as God has created."

The old sailor spoke enthusiastically; he loved the wild, adventurous life, and with our hero for a companion, he would have been better pleased to have wandered over the untrodden parts of the great continent than have become wealthy in his native land.

The boy's hot blood coursed through his veins as he caught old Tom's enthusiasm.

"It is indeed glorious," he said, "and to those who love adventure, there is more to be met with in our position than in the shock of opposing armies, or the close broadsides of fighting vessels."

From the spot where they were resting, the decayed tree upon the summit of the hill was plainly visible, and as Jack ceased speaking old Tom uttered an exclamation of surprise, then pointing to their eyrie with his extended finger, said—

"Jack, Jack, there is your favourite dragging something up the hill!"

Jack started up, and beheld Hector carrying what he supposed was a young deer to their mountain home.

"It is strange," Crusoe Jack said, "that he did not return to me!"

"Not at all strange, my lad."

"Not strange! The beast is much attached."

"May be; but the skin of the dead lioness is yonder, and who knows but the cub may be taking that carcase to its mother?"

"Perhaps so. Well, he is better there than with us, if we are to have a midnight hunt in the forest."

"That rests with yourself, Jack. If you feel equal to the danger and fatigue we will; for if not—"

"I would not miss the hunt for the world. I am better and stronger since the morning than I have been for some time."

"Very well, lad; we shall have some sport, and danger as well."

The sun's rays had nearly departed when the adventurers arose from their grassy couch.

During the time that Crusoe Jack slept beneath the shelter of palm leaves, his companion had been minutely examining the puma's footsteps upon the soft ground.

At one place, near a mass of thick underwood, he followed the trail of footprints, and by the broken vegetation he knew that one of the largest—in fact the largest—of the American animals had a lair near here.

"A tapir," muttered old Tom; "if the boy is well enough he shall have some sport to-night."

Within what he calculated would be the path of the huge beast the old seaman selected a large tree, and upon the thickest part of one of the lower branches the adventurous pair seated themselves.

The immense beast they were on the look-out for was peculiar for its habits and peculiar conformation, being able to exist either upon land or water.

In shape the tapir is not unlike a hog, the nose of the male species extending beyond the lower jaw and forming a slender trunk, which the animal uses as an elephant uses his proboscis; the legs are short, the eyes small, and the ears erect, and the hoof small, black, and hollow.

This remarkable animal sleeps during the day in the darkest and thickest woods adjacent to the water, and at night prowls out in search of food, which consists principally of grass, sugar-cane, and fruit. If disturbed in these midnight wanderings it takes to the water, and, like the hippopotamus, walks upon the bottom with as much ease as on the dry ground.

The silent pair waited long and anxiously for the sound of the animal's heavy footsteps, but the moon shone before any sign was heard.

Our hero began to tire of his uncomfortable position in the tree, and was about to suggest

a movement towards the howling monkeys who had just begun their horrible serenade, when an exclamation of astonishment came from his lips.

The ground beneath them had suddenly become illuminated with tiny bright stars.

By degrees the light grew stronger, and Jack was able to distinguish objects pretty clearly for some distance around.

"Fireflies," old Tom said, in answer to Jack's query; "pretty things, eh, Ja——. Ha! here he comes; ready with your lance, boy."

Crash! crash! breaking down every impediment that stood in his path, the immense animal could be heard approaching.

Our hero grasped his lance tightly, and rising upon his knees he held a small shoot of the tree firmly with his left hand, and concentrated all his energies for a swift and sure blow.

Crashing and plunging through the thick brushwood, the tapir came at a swift pace close beneath the tree.

By the gleam of the myriads of sparkling fireflies Jack made out the animal's crooked back, and with all his force he drove the lance into his thick hard skin.

Horror! The tender shoot snapped, and our hero fell within a yard of the heavy animal's feet.

Old Tom uttered a cry of alarm; he knew one tramp of those massive hoofs would crush out the gallant boy's life.

Regardless of his own danger he sprang in front of the angry tapir, and shortening his weapon drove it with all the strength of his muscular arm through the animal's neck.

The beast fell, then, with a whining noise, struggled to his feet, but before he had taken three paces forward our hero had shifted out of the way, and was now plunging his lance quickly into the animal's side.

There was a faint attempt upon the part of the tapir to turn upon his young antagonist, but in doing so he fell, pierced to the heart.

The contest had been brief but desperate, and though neither of the adventurers had received the slightest hurt, they both stood for some minutes contemplating the huge form.

The great danger they had incurred was forgotten in the excitement of the moment; but now, in the semi-darkness and solitude of that vast forest, the knowledge came back with redoubled force, that the merest trifle might have caused them to have found a grave where they now stood so bravely victorious.

There was not much time to stay in this spot, for the prowling beasts of prey possibly attracted by the smell of fresh blood, began to skulk through the forest, uttering as they came low fierce growls.

In an instant the gallant boy seized his rifle, and bringing the piece to his side was ready to contest the trophy he had so gallantly won.

"We must leave him," old Tom said. "Come, Jack, there will be a collection of skulking devils here directly that will pick our bones as clean as we did the rabbit this morning."

Jack, somewhat reluctantly, followed his companion from the dangerous place, and as they went towards the hill he came to a sudden halt, and said—

"Do you hear that, Tom?"

They had just passed one of the outlying trees when the howling monkeys set up such a succession of yells that it caused the young Crusoe's blood to tingle in his veins.

Before old Tom could stay him he threw his rifle to the ground, and holding the spear between his teeth, began to climb the tree where the melodious serenaders were congregated.

Old Tom, with a chuckle at the punishment he intended inflicting upon the disturbers, stood at the foot of the tree with his lance upheld ready to fall upon the monkeys as they descended.

Right and left among the branches Jack scrambled, and despite the many bites and scratches he received for thus intruding among the musical brutes, he laid about him with such good will that the howlers scrambled down the tree with wonderful speed.

Then, as they hopped to the ground and were about to make off, Tom Starboard's lance could be heard—thud, thud—as it fell across the noisy brutes' backs.

In the midst of the fun, and as Jack was descending the tree, his companion called out frantically—

"For God's sake, stay where you are."

The next moment he had scrambled upon one of the lower branches, only in time to escape the fangs of a powerful lion and lioness who came to the foot of the tree.

The adventurers could just discern the outlines of the deadly brutes' forms and the dusky glimmer of their green blazing eyes.

Here they were fixed until the hungry brutes were tired; unarmed in the tree, they were powerless, having left their rifles on the ground.

CHAPTER XV.

A NIGHT IN A TREE—THE FIGHT WITH THE LIONS—CRUSOE JACK'S RIFLE DOES GOOD SERVICE.

"JACK," old Tom said, "we have left our rifles below, and should these hungry brutes scramble up the tree our chance of escape will be but small."

"'What cannot be cured must be endured,' Tom."

With this sage axiom the young Crusoe scrambled upward, and sitting astride one of the topmost branches, looked calmly down upon the circle of admiring friends below.

It was not a pleasant position for our adventurers, and as they beheld the number of wild animals encircling them, there seemed a great probability that the siege would last some time.

The myriads of sparkling fireflies as they glided over the soft ground and up and down the lower limbs of the trees, gave a sufficient light to render the dark bodies of the prowling beasts distinctly visible.

There could be seen the sleek tigers walking with noiseless tread around the base of the tree, and ever and anon lifting their heads as they sniffed the dainty meal above.

A group of strong-limbed lions stood a few paces from the huge tree, their massive forms and blazing eyes looked strangely vivid by the dancing sparkles of light.

The night wore on, the adventurers rarely exchanging words; both silent, watchful, and not without a sense of dread, which the brave at all times feel when left to the calm reflections of a great and terrible danger.

Not a mailed knight of yore had a stouter heart or greater indifference to danger than our young hero. Had he been hemmed in by the skulking crew who stood beneath, he would have battled with them without one thought of the probable issue of the conflict.

The affair now wore quite a different aspect; the body and mind became chilled—one, by the cramped position they were in, the other by the certainty that unless the midnight prowlers returned to their lairs they would be starved out, or compelled to descend and become food for the forest children.

At times a subdued growl would escape old Tom Starboard's lips as he found his position becoming irksome.

The least movement in the tree was greeted by the watchful animals as a sign that their prey was about to descend, and in an instant every head would be upturned and a circle of blazing eyes looking doubly cruel in the dim light.

From the depths of the forest came the wild, startling cries of the peccaries and tapirs as they rushed through the dense tangled brushwood, pursued by their fierce and more voracious brethren.

From the banks came the noise of the crocodiles as they plunged into the water to stifle the prey they had seized.

Mingled with these sounds came short, angry growls from the wild beasts below, the plaintive cry of the water-fowl, and dull croaking of a colony of frogs filled the air with sounds that were neither pleasing to the ear nor soothing to the mind.

It was near daybreak, and a white vapoury mist began to arise from below.

Our hero, whose limbs were cramped, and whose eyes ached from their long vigil, uttered an exclamation of joy as he saw the white smoke curling up from the dark pools and marshes.

Old Tom, who had been sitting cross-legged in the fork of a large limb, looked up and asked—

"Are they going away?"

"No."

"Ugh! I thought they were, by the noise you made. What was it?"

"Look! do you not see that vapour rising?"

"Well?"

Old Tom's temper was evidently soured by his night's roosting.

"I thought," said our hero, "that we might possibly escape under cover of the mist, which seems to increase every moment."

"Did you think those fellows below were fool enough to let us escape, eh?"

"They will not see us. We can creep to the point of one of the lower branches and drop lightly to the ground."

"Can we?" growled the old tar. "No, boy; here we must stick until those devils are either too tired or too hungry to stay longer."

"I had hoped," Jack said, "that they would

have gone away when daylight came at the very latest."

"I'm afraid not, boy—afraid not.   We shall see."

There was a long pause, and as Jack's eyes wandered from point to point he beheld a faint streak of light in the east.

"The day is breaking, Tom," he said, joyfully. "Look, look!"

"Ay," the old fellow grumbled, "it won't make much difference to us, I expect."

Crusoe was silent; he knew by his companion's manner that conversation was irksome to him.

As he watched the speck in the distant horizon his mind reverted to the time when he was beneath the wrecker's roof.

He thought of old Madge, of her crooked-back, vicious son, and the morose yet not unkind Darrell.

From this unpleasant retrospection he beheld in fancy the fairy-like form of the beautiful Mabel, and for the first time since he had rescued her from an untimely death the lovely girl's image began to cause a stronger and hitherto unfelt sensation in his heart.

Every word, every look, came with vivid distinctness to the young castaway's mind, and as his cheeks reddened and his heart beat faster than its wont, the subtle, delicious dream of love broke upon the proud-souled boy.

So sweet was this vision of infantile beauty that Jack for a time forgot his peril and became lost in a delicious reverie.

"Had my lot in life been different," he thought, "I should possibly have served beneath the royal flag and in time become the commander of a vessel of war, then as a man I could have aspired to the beautiful——"

Jack's reverie was cut short by an angry growl from below; then old Tom's savage tones broke upon his ear.

"Growl away, you ugly, skulking devils," the old tar said; "had I my rifle here I would shoot two or three of you screamers."

The growls and old Tom's voice ceased, and Jack closed his eyes in the hope of bringing back his blissful waking dream.

The attempt was useless—the thread had been broken, and his mind wandered to other subjects.

The sun's resplendent rays had pierced the thick grey vapour until it seemed like a thin gauze veil hanging in festoons above the giant trees.

Little by little the graceful foliage of the surrounding trees became visible, then the green slopes and verdure-clad valleys, and like a curtain slowly rising to disclose a well-set scene, beneath the edge of the mist could be seen blue and sparkling streaks of the interminable sea.

The joyous chirp of the small birds as they fluttered from branch to branch, the heavy flopping of the gaudy parrots' wings and their sharp peculiar cry, the hum of the insect world as they awoke beneath the sun's genial warmth, gave life and additional beauty to Nature's wondrous panorama.

Forgetful of the crowd of hungry animals beneath, our hero drank in the beauty of the scene, and as his gaze wandered from one beautiful object to another still more beautiful, his thoughts were of the hour he scrambled over the bows of the slave ship in sight of England's white cliffs.

Uneasily he thought over every circumstance that had befallen him since that moment; and though but a few months had passed, what a wondrous change had taken place in the poor friendless, unknown boy.

He could scarcely realize that so short a time had passed; it seemed an age of excitement—new scenes and wild adventures had been compressed into a few weeks.

A new world had opened to him, and he marvelled when he thought how great would have been the change had he remained an ill-bred outcast beneath the wrecker's humble roof.

The low, fierce growls of the prowling beasts of prey broke upon his ear, and then he thought—how sadly came the terrible impression upon his mind!— that ere many hours passed he would probably fall a victim to the long white tusks of the greedy brutes, whose dogged, silent watchfulness had not for one moment ceased since they followed the scent of the adventurers to their place of refuge.

Little marvel the brave heart became heavy!   It was hard to be cut off at the outset of a life of wild adventure—a mode of existence so congenial to his temper and lion-like courage.

"I can't stand this any longer, Jack.   I'm —— if I can."

Old Tom was excited and angry, or he would not have used a word that would be bad in these pages.

Our Crusoe made a drive with his spear at a noisy macaw, who was screaming above his head, as he said—

"What can we do, Tom?   They are determined to stop."

The beasts had laid themselves flat upon the ground, their vicious faces upturned, and their hungry eyes watching the slightest movement of those they evidently looked upon as a legitimate meal.

"Do?" old Tom growled.   "Can't you assist me, lad?   Come, think of a plan to regain our rifles."

Perched twenty feet above the desired weapons, the young Crusoe had not an easy task assigned him.

"If we had a line, Tom," he said, "I think we might manage to recover one."

"With a line, of course—fish for them, eh?"

"Exactly."

Tom Starboard rubbed the spot where his left ear would have been, had not the dark-skinned cannibals taken a fancy to these useful ornaments, and said, with less asperity in his voice than he had before used—

"Yes, lad, that is the thing; but as we have not anything like a line——"

"Tom."

The old seaman looked up at the handsome, animated face and ejaculated—

"Well, boy?"

Crusoe pointed with his hand to a long, willow-like bough, as he said—

"How would this do, if we can manage to get it off?"

The old seaman scanned the long, supple branch

attentively; at length, satisfied with his scrutiny, he said—

"Ah! I see there is a small shoot at the end that would make a good crook. But is it strong enough, lad, that is the next thing?"

"We can but try it, Tom."

"True; how to break it off. I wish I had my old knife. The Lord help us, what is the boy doing? Hi, Jack, are you mad—there—oh, Heaven! I thought so. Hold on, my lad, for your life while I skewer that beggar!"

Whiz through the air Tom's long lance flew, and with a dull thud passed clean through the back of a large tiger, whose teeth were within a few inches of our hero's legs.

The beast writhed and growled savagely, and strove to scramble forward as the long, quivering weapon pinned him to the earth.

The cause of this terrible, and to the actors this momentous episode, was Jack's attempt to break the long branch from its parent stem.

The boy had scrambled above the doomed limb, and placing his spear between his teeth, then with both hands tightly grasping one of the uppermost branches, he placed his feet upon the supple limb he wished to detach.

For this purpose he jerked himself upward, his feet for a moment being suspended between the two branches; then falling with the whole weight of his body upon the lower branch, it snapped off close to the trunk.

Jack had expected more resistance, and to his and old Tom's horror, the supple branch which he grasped bent like a cane, and before he well knew what had befallen him, he felt that he was descending right into the jaws of the hungry fraternity who had so long and patiently awaited his coming.

Not a sound escaped his lips, though the brave boy could hear the sharp snap of a tiger's teeth only a few inches beneath.

When old Tom's lance cleft the air the tiger was in the act of crouching for a spring, and but for that timely and well-aimed blow there would have been an end to the gallant fellow's adventures and perils.

The tiger transfixed, old Tom, fearful that a second fierce brute would be more successful in dragging the boy from his perilous position, descended the tree with wondrous speed until he came within reach of our hero's head.

Then lying horizontally along the trunk, he seized Crusoe by the hair, and drew him upward.

The supple limb which had so nearly caused Jack's destruction, partly relieved of its burden, rose slowly, and as Crusoe clutched at a stouter branch flew upward and resumed its place.

Without commenting upon his hair-breadth escape from a deadly peril, Jack simply said—

"I think I detached that branch, Tom."

The old sailor, who had not recovered from the fright Jack had given him, blurted out—

"Detached it, eh? Why—why, do you know that skulking devil I have pinned nearly had you by the leg?"

"Yes, I know that—" this was said with all the sang froid imaginable —"lucky you picked me up in time, Tom."

The old tar was staggered by the boy's coolness, and as he gazed fondly at the flushed and beautiful face he said, proudly—

"Jack, had you served long on board ship you would have worn a pair of gold swabs (epaulettes) on your shoulder. Yes, you may laugh; it's true, and an admiral's cocked hat in the bargain."

Jack laughed heartily at his companion's earnest face, and said—

"Fancy, Tom, Admiral Crusoe Jack. Ha, ha, ha!"

"You young beggar! There you are laughing as though we were safely on the deck of a good ship. Have you forgotten the hungry, ugly, sneaking gang that is below?"

"No. Where's the long stick I broke off?"

Like a monkey he climbed from bough to bough until he reached the supple, rod-like branch, which hung to the tree by a small thread of bark.

To detach the branch was the work of a moment, and stripping off the leaves and every useless shoot, our hero began to descend the tree.

Arrived at the lowest branch, the boy thrust his spear into the trunk, then began to lower the long rod.

Stretched at full length along the massive limb, and gripping only with his legs, he tried to fix the crooked extremity of the long branch in the trigger-guard of the nearest rifle.

The circle of animals took but little notice of Jack's movements, and looked, if possible, more intently at the lithe figure stretched along the branch of the tree.

The task was not easy of accomplishment, and not until Crusoe had several times raised the rifle a few inches from the ground was the desired result attained.

Old Tom had eagerly watched every movement, and when he beheld the weapon slowly rising towards his companion he uttered a short cry of joy.

"Well done, lad, well done! Gently. Ha! it nearly capsized, then. So—that's it. Hurra! I have it."

During the time he had been speaking the precious weapon was in Jack's grasp, and the boy rising from the fearful position necessary to attain this desirable result, handed the rifle to old Tom.

"No, boy," he said; "no, you got the piece, keep it, and pepper away at those beggars."

Jack gave him the thin branch, and while Tom was busy fishing for the second rifle the boy settled himself firmly upon the stout stem, and carefully examined his weapon.

He drew the hammer back several times to assure himself that no injury had been sustained by the trampling of the brutes' heavy feet, then carefully loaded.

"Shall I begin," he asked, as his bright eyes glanced along the dark barrel, "or wait for you, Tom?"

"Blaze away," was the answer; "I can't get a grip upon my piece."

Crusoe could not resist smiling at the exertions his companion was undergoing.

One of the besieging force, a powerful, full grown lion, was watching intently the swinging to and fro of old Tom's body, as he tried to affix the crooked end of the stick in the trigger-guard of his rifle.

Crusoe covered the royal brute with the muzzle of his piece, then drawing a deep breath, he drew the butt close to his shoulder and pulled the trigger.

The animal uttered a wild cry, then sprang upward; a moment the fore feet clawed wildly at the empty air, then with a dull thud he fell to the earth lifeless.

The bullet had entered close beneath the shoulder and cleft the heart.

"Number one," said the young adventurer, as he began to reload. "Come, Tom; you will be too late for the sport."

"Ugh!" grunted the old fellow, "I can't get the plaguey thing up."

Jack rammed home the bullet, and asked—

"How's that, Tom?"

"Don't know, Jack. The rifle cants over when I begin to haul up."

Jack laughed at this woful speech, and again drew the rifle to his shoulder.

The fall of the lion had caused a movement among his companions, but whether of fear or rage it was hard to determine.

The whole of the brutes had risen to their feet, and as their white fangs glared horribly, and their tails swept the ground, a succession of low growls came from their massive throats.

Again the boy sped a bullet from the fatal piece.

This time a full-grown tiger was hit, but not mortally, for the animal, as the blood trickled from its neck, stood as though spellbound with rage at the sharp cutting pains, then suddenly raising itself upon its hind legs, made a grip at the weapon old Tom had at last raised from the ground.

One blow from the animal's paw sent the rifle flying far beyond the reach of the long branch, and as an expression, more remarkable for its force than politeness, came from the old seaman's lips at being thus treated after the trouble he had taken, the tiger turned suddenly upon one of its companions, and attacked it with terrible fury.

Such a fearful roar came from the assembled beasts, as the combatants bit and clawed each other, that the dense forest resounded with the terrible echoes.

"Give her another, Jack," old Tom sang out, as he dashed the pole he had been raising to the ground. "Aim well, lad; the coward brute has knocked my rifle beyond the tree."

The sharp crack of Crusoe's piece followed those words, and as the "ring" of the ball yet sounded in Tom Starboard's ears, the growling combatants rolled over and over for a few yards, then became motionless, save for a convulsive movement of their flanks.

"Pinned them both," shouted old Tom. "Well done, lad!—well done!"

Jack was getting excited with the slaughter he was executing among the enemy, and without noticing his companion's words, he loaded as quickly as possible.

The denizens of the forest that yet remained un-

hurt seemed suddenly to comprehend that something wrong had taken place among their fellows.

Round and round the carcases of the four dead brutes they walked; then, halting for a moment, sniffed at the yet warm blood; then, as Jack's rifle rang out for a fourth time, they gave a yell, and making towards the forest, soon decamped.

The last shot Jack saw had broken a puma's leg, for the animal limped after his companions, the off fore leg held up, and blood dropping from it at every stride.

Old Tom gave a loud huzza as the enemy turned tail, and without waiting to consider whether the four animals that lay so still were beyond the power of doing mischief, he rapidly descended the tree and clutched his rifle.

Our hero was on the ground a moment after his companion, and with flushed face and sparkling eyes he stood proudly regarding the fallen forms of the powerful forest kings.

"They'll remember the crack of a rifle," said old Tom, "eh, Jack? Four warm skins for our wigwam; we need not fear the cold."

Jack did not answer. The proud exultation he felt at having thus so effectually proved the power of man over the strongest brute, held him spellbound, and Tom was for the moment lost in a reverie from which they were both aroused in a manner as unexpected as mysterious.

Something came through the air with a sharp hiss, passing so near to our hero's ear, that he instinctively stepped back.

At the same time Tom laid his hand softly on Jack's shoulder.

"See," he whispered.

Crusoe Jack looked in the direction indicated. A feathered arrow still quivered in a tree immediately behind where they had stood an instant before.

"An unseen enemy," Tom continued. "We are not alone on the island; let us step aside out of danger, we shall have another messenger presently."

The expected whizz did not however come, and our two adventurers, cautiously approaching the tree examined the arrow.

"Of Indian make," Tom said. "It is possible, Jack, that whoever threw this dart is still in ignorance of our presence. Let us separate and explore cautiously."

With rifles steadily grasped, each went on the quest for their invisible enemy; but though they searched every thicket and climbed trees which enabled them to reconnoitre the surrounding landscape, no trace of the islanders could be discovered.

"We must trust to another chance of getting near our savage friend."

"I hope he won't make his presence known by planting one of his ornamented darts in our throats."

Tom laughed.

"We'll let the arrow remain where our friend planted it," he said; "to withdraw it would at once betray our presence here."

CHAPTER XVI.

THE FIGHT WITH THE PECCARIES.

PROMISING themselves the felicity of returning at the first opportunity to skin the defunct animals, our friends threw their loaded rifles in the hollow of their left arms, and, using their spears as a walking-stick, they went leisurely towards the place where they had left the huge tapir.

There was no difficulty in finding the spot, for long ere they began to sight the tall trees and the thick underwood, a flight of dark-coloured birds could be seen flying in a circle, and noisily uttering a sharp, peculiar cry.

"The beggars," said old Tom, when he saw the birds; "they are waiting for a feed."

Jack looked at the vultures, and said—

"Shall I bring down one or two?"

"No," was the abrupt answer; "waste of powder, boy. They are as tough as oakum; sooner gnaw a deal plank than one of those beggars."

"What is the cause of their peculiar manner of flying?"

"First soaring upwards, then coming down with a swoop—as though about to pick up something from the ground?"

"Yes. But look; directly they go below the lower branches of that tree, they scream in that peculiar manner and fly upwards again."

"Yes; the varmints," old Tom said. "You see, my lad, when they swoop down it is with the intention of digging their beaks in the tapir's tough hide, and, from the way in which they hurry upwards, there must be something more than the tapir's dead carcase to frighten them. Look to the priming of your weapon, lad; there is more sport for us before we have our breakfast."

The caution was not thrown away. Our hero stuck his spear in his belt, and with the muzzle of his rifle thrown forward and his finger upon the trigger, he advanced cautiously towards the low clump of bushes that concealed the tapir's huge carcase.

A low, fierce growl brought them to a sudden halt, and old Tom, peering through the thick tangled brushwood, uttered an exclamation of surprise.

Crusoe ran forward at the cry, and throwing up the muzzle of his piece, exclaimed—

"Hector!"

Lying with his fore paws across the tapir's neck was the young lion, and, from sundry suspicious marks, it was evident Jack's favourite had been trying to pierce the dead animal's skin with his teeth—an unsuccessful attempt, when the strength of the huge animal's hide is capable of resisting a musket-ball.

The young lion came to his master's side, and began to purr and rub against his legs, exhibiting much the same gestures as a cat would when in the presence of its mistress.

Crusoe caressed the massive brute, and then, leaning upon the muzzle of his rifle, he watched Tom Starboard decapitate the tapir.

The head and feet were soon secured, and the pair, carrying the spoil, began their retarded journey to their eyrie.

From his old companion Jack learnt that, with the exception of the head and feet, the flesh of the tapir was both tough and tasteless, and where better food could be obtained, there was no necessity to eat such unpalatable flesh.

When they reached their lofty home, old Tom placed the tapir's head in the hole where they had baked the hare on the previous day.

And while Jack cleaned the rifles with a care that showed how much the trusty weapons were valued, the fragrant odours from the primitive kitchen gave additional proof of the good things in store for the tired and hungry adventurers.

When the rifles were laid aside, Jack came and seated himself by his old friend.

Their conversation turned upon the perils of the previous night, and old Tom, in answer to a question from Crusoe, said—

"Yes, lad. Once before in my life I was in a similar fix."

"Where did it happen, Tom?"

"In Central America. I had climbed about half way up a mountain cabbage-tree, and—"

"Climbed a cabbage tree, Tom?"

"Ay, lad—cabbage. What do you think of having to climb a hundred and fifty yards to get one for your dinner."

Jack opened his eyes in astonishment as he said—

"That cabbage, Tom, must have had a pretty tall stalk."

Old Tom looked at his companion, a slight suspicion entering his mind that Crusoe was inclined to disbelieve his statement.

"Ay, boy," he said, "it had a long stalk; and when I tell you that the stem is no thicker than a man's leg you will be less inclined to believe my statement."[*]

"I never doubted it, Tom," Crusoe said. "I laughed at the comical idea of a cabbage growing such a tremendous height."

"It does not resemble a cabbage in shape," old Tom said. "The name 'mountain cabbage' I believe arises from a similarity of taste. Well, I had climbed more than half-way up the palm when I was nearly tumbled from my lofty perch by the long trunk swinging to and fro. As there was no wind at the time, I looked below, and there, to my horror, was a huge buffalo butting the tree with all its force."

"You may be sure," old Tom said, laughing at the adventure, "that I was not over pleased at the presence of this unexpected visitor."

"I should think not, Tom."

"Well, to make the yarn short, the beggar, when he found he could not shake me from my perch, very quietly laid down at the foot of the tree, and looked up, as much as to say, I shall have you yet, my fine fellow; but he was mistaken, although for six long hours he kept me clinging like an overgrown monkey to the stem of the palm. He would not have gone then, had not a party of mounted Indians sighted him and drove the fierce brute from his post."

---

[*] The tree referred to by Tom Starboard is called the mountain cabbage (*Arœa Obracea.*)

"What about the cabbage, Tom? I suppose you had no appetite for that."

"You are wrong, lad; it was early morn when I began the ascent of the tree, and not having had anything to eat since the previous day, in spite of the gentleman below I cut the tender vegetable and had a lofty breakfast, much, I dare say, to the edification of the gentleman in waiting below."

Crusoe laughed at his companion's adventure, and they proceeded to anatomize the baked tapir's head.

After breakfast the adventurers went to the creek, where the dismembered shark still lay, and old Tom cutting a portion of the flesh into thin flakes, they conveyed a large portion to their lofty habitation.

Here the small bones of the dead sea monster came into use to drive into the decayed trunk in lieu of nails.

Upon each bone a large flake of shark's flesh was suspended to dry, and soon the outside of the tree presented a curious appearance.

"Not a bad fishmonger's shop," old Tom said facetiously; "the only drawback is that we shall have to wait a long time for a customer."

"I expect so," Crusoe said, "therefore, we will devour our stock-in-trade when it is ready."

The castaways were now anxious to leave the island and go in search of the Seagull's hull.

This task was not the easiest of accomplishment, as they were without compass or chart, therefore it became necessary to lay in a good stock of provisions in the event of not being able to find the isle where the ill-fated vessel had struck.

The flakes of shark's flesh when dried would be of immense service to the voyagers, as they would keep fresh for a considerable time.

But as they could not live entirely upon this insipid food, a council was held, and they determined to levy a contribution upon the eatable portion of Crusoe Jack's subjects.

"First," Tom Starboard said, "we will relieve the lions of their skins. We shall find them useful when at sea."

This proposition met with Jack's approval, and old Tom having selected a flat, sharp-edged bone from the shark's anatomy as a substitute for a knife, they shouldered their pieces and descended the hill.

Hector was left at home, and long before his master was out of sight he scratched up the tapir's feet from the larder, and began to gnaw them.

The adventurers' larder, by the way, was nothing more than a square hole scraped out near the base of the tree, and the edibles being covered with palm-leaves were deposited there, the earth was replaced, and the castaways descended the hill in the belief that everything was safe.

It was so until Hector scented the provisions, and soon clawed the contents out.

The knife formed from the shark's bone answered admirably, and by the time the noonday sun blazed through the trees, the four skins were spread out to dry.

This task over, the adventurers refreshed themselves with a portion of the tapir's flesh and a draught of cow-tree milk.

Keeping a prudent distance from the beaten path which denoted the coverts of the prowling beasts of prey, the adventurers sought out the retreat of a drove of wild hogs.

Passing a clump of low trees, old Tom placed his hand suddenly upon our hero's arm, and whispered—

"Listen; the peccary."

Crusoe knew the meaning of these words, and, bending his head downward, he listened attentively to a peculiar sound; at first it seemed like the snapping of green twigs, but as our friends grew accustomed to the noise, they could distinguish the champ of teeth, and occasionally a short satisfied grunt.

Old Tom pressed his fingers upon his companion's shoulder, and whispered seriously—

"Peccaries feeding."

Crusoe nodded, and in the same still voice, asked—

"What are we to do?"

"Wait," was the whispered answer. "When I go down upon my hands and knees, cover me with loose leaves and dried wood; but be quiet as you do it."

A little surprised, our hero complied, and heaped a goodly stock of fallen foliage over his companion's back.

Thus accoutred, old Tom placed his rifle on the ground, and crawling forward, with his spear in his hand, passed slowly round the clump of trees.

Jack crept after him, keeping the stock of leaves between his body and the feeding drove of wild hogs.

This precaution was necessary, as the peccaries go in droves, and are very fierce when attacked. In size they resemble the wild boar, and like them have tusks of appalling length.

Creeping out into the open space, the adventurers beheld the busy droves—the bristling backs and white gleaming tusks were seen as far as the eye could reach; and Crusoe, as he peered through the cover of vegetation which he had heaped upon old Tom's back, saw the necessity of the stratagem.

As the myriads of porkers kept moving about in their search for food, a dim foreboding came to Crusoe's mind that an unlucky displacement of the tottering hide upon his companion's back would expose them to the fierce attack of the drove.

Had such an accident occurred our friends would have been either ripped up by the long tusks, or crushed by the multitude of horny feet.

There was not much time for speculation, for old Tom, in a sepulchral whisper, said—

"Be ready, Jack; there is one coming this way—he is sure to poke his nose among the leaves that conceal my carcase. By ready, lad, and when he moves round my head, drive your spear in sharp and silent. Mind, don't let your hand rise above my green coat. He, he, he—here he comes—the bait takes. We shall strike several if you are careful."

The wild boar alluded to by Tom came on at a swinging trot—a low grunt coming now and then giving evidence of the satisfaction he felt at being first to find the large heap of leaves and green twigs.

When the ugly-looking tusks were within a few yards of Tom Starboard's heap, the old fellow jerked out—

"Don't let him get his nose under the leaves, or I shall get a bite."

In spite of the danger, Crusoe could not refrain from a hearty but silent burst of merriment as the significance of Old Tom's words burst upon him.

In fancy he saw the porker making a rush at a tender twig, and taking a mouthful of old Tom's back instead.

When the porker reached the tempting heap he came to a standstill; then snuffing at the part which covered old Tom's head, he gave a dissatisfied grunt, as though suspicious that all was not right.

"The brute scents us," thought our hero, "and he will make a rush at old Tom directly."

As though determined to fully investigate matters, the wild boar began to walk slowly round the old tar.

The animal gave a squeal when he came face to face with Jack, and before he could either retreat or show fight Crusoe's lance was driven through his heart.

The animal fell on his side, and as Jack withdrew the fatal weapon a spout of blood came from the wound.

"Well done, Jack!" came in a sepulchral whisper from the mound of leaves. "Here's another."

An old boar, whose bristles were rapidly turning white, came grunting towards the adventurers.

He appeared to be the king of the immense drove, and evidently, from the cautious manner in which he approached and the malicious look in his bear-like eyes, the dying squeal of his companion had aroused his suspicions.

Crusoe held his breath and awaited, ready to drive his weapon through the patriarchal porker.

The old gentleman, without deigning the least notice of the heap of leaves and tender green shoots, trotted on to his companion.

No sooner did he behold the dead carcase than our hero raised his lance, but before he could strike, the old boar caught sight of Jack, and showing his long tusks, gave a squeal that was heard by the whole of the herd.

It seemed a signal of danger, for the peccaries left off grubbing among the grass, and turning sharply round, in a quick trot came towards the troublesome old gray-back.

The earth shook with the passage of the herd, and as far as the eye could reach the dark mass came pressing onward.

Every stone, every fallen leaf seemed to have changed into a peccary, and old Tom, who knew the danger that menaced him and his companion, sprang to his feet, scattering the leaves in a shower around.

This sudden movement caused our hero to pause in his thrust, and before he knew well what had happened, the old boar charged him as he was about to rise.

Jack's weapon was knocked from his hand as he fell beneath the animal's weight; he heard the fierce grunt of the savage brute—could feel his hot breath —and, oh, horror! the white fangs were within an inch of his handsome face.

Quick as thought Crusoe seized the animal's thick neck with both hands, and for a moment prevented the long white tusks from tearing his flesh.

So quickly had this taken place that old Tom was not aware of his companion's danger until he heard Jack's cry as the beast knocked him down.

The old seaman's face blanched, and for a moment his hand shook; the next, the trunk of the largest tree in that vast forest was not more steady than Tom Starboard's muscular arm.

He saw the fearful danger that was likely to occur through this misadventure—knew that unless the old boar was despatched and Jack upon his feet before the herd reached them, he would be torn to pieces:

Thud! The lance went clean through the brute's side, piercing his heart, and as the warm blood gushed out he fell upon the young castaway.

With a muscular power that seemed superhuman old Tom drew Jack from beneath the heavy carcase, and threw him over his shoulder.

He cleared the low clump of trees at a bound, then stooping to pick up his rifle, he kindly asked—

"Hurt, lad?"

Jack wiped the blood from his face, and said—

"No; another moment, and it would have been all over with me."

Tom thrust the rifle into Jack's hand, and said—

"Up, lad! here they come."

Imminent peril made them both active to an extent that seemed wonderful, and as the herd came sweeping round the clump of brushwood our adventurers sprang into the fork of a large tree.

The foremost of the pack snapped fiercely at their heels as they drew their legs sharply beyond the coming porkers' reach.

The place was alive with the excited brutes, and whether out of a desire to be revenged upon the slayer of their companions, or actuated by a horrible instinct to prey upon the flesh of the strange visitors to their home, the hogs seemed seized by a species of madness to reach the tree.

Many reared themselves on their hind legs, and bit savagely at the bark of the lower limbs.

Others from the rear walked upon their companions' backs, and tried hard to drag the castaways from their place of refuge.

Many, again, with a cunning that seemed impossible in such animals, rooted the ground up near the base of the tree, and all united in a succession of grunts intermingled with shrill squeals.

Upon every side the ground was covered with the fierce brutes; it really seemed as though they had sprung out of the ground.

The first feeling of dread over, our hero and his companion seated themselves firmly on their perch, and began to take the bearings of their situation.

Both rifles were loaded and at full cock, and held by hands that were able to use them.

Old Tom placed his rifle across his knee, and looking at the surging crowd, said—

"What do you think of this, Jack?"

"I am quite astonished," was the reply, "at the vast multitude of animals. I should scarcely have credited there could be so many in the world."

"Bless the boy! these little wretches multiply so fast that, were their numbers not thinned by the lion and other beasts of prey, they would soon overrun the vast continent of South America."

"So it appears. One thing, Tom, I don't think I shall ever like pork again."

"Why, lad?"

"Ugh! that brute's tusks just touched my face, when you put an end to our fight."

"You were in a sore strait, lad. Thank God you are safe."

"Amen. I have much to be thankful for."

"You have, lad. Ha!"

"What's the matter?"

Old Tom raised his gun and fired point blank at an old hog who was busy tearing up the ground with his snout.

"They cannot uproot the tree," Crusoe said; "this one in particular, I should think."

"Can't say, lad. You see there is a great number of them, and if all were to dig with their snouts, the tree would soon be level with the lower roots."

"Confound them!" Crusoe said. "What is to be done? It is no use firing at them, I suppose."

"Not the least. Look there—look at the varmints!"

Jack looked in the direction of his companion's finger, and beheld about sixty of their besiegers sitting calmly on their haunches.

"That's pretty plain," said Jack; "they don't appear to be in a hurry to leave."

"I expect we shall be kept here until night."

"Then——"

"They will make sail pretty quick, when the jaguars or pumas come from their lairs."

"That will not benefit us much."

"No, lad; I expect we shall have to roost here all night again."

"I hope not; one night is quite—— Hallo! Tom, what's the matter?"

The old seaman shaded his eyes and looked towards the path they had traversed when entering the forest.

That something unusual was taking place was very certain, for the peccaries were heard squealing at the highest pitch of their voices, and many darting hither and thither as though thrown into a sudden panic.

Whatever it was the drove soon seemed to understand it, for, when a prolonged squeal came from the direction of their startled companions, those beneath the tree gave a deep grunt, and, as though seized with terror, turned towards the forest and made off.

It was some time before the vast multitude passed beneath the tree, and, when it came near the last, there was such an outcry that Jack was compelled to put his fingers in his ears.

At length the cause of the uproar and sudden flight became apparent, and Jack, when he beheld their terror, became so excited that he shouted lustily—

"At them, boy—give it to them, Hector! Bravo! you turned that fellow over. Silence, boy."

And before old Tom could prevent him, the excited boy slipped down from his perch, and, clutching his rifle, he scampered after the flying herd.

Old Tom followed, and growled out—

"Never saw such a thoughtless fellow; he'll be hurt, safe as my name's Tom."

Jerking out the last word savagely, he dashed into the thicket and joined his companion.

We left Hector in the full and undisturbed possession of the castaways' larder, and the animal, after crushing the tapir's feet, also the remains of the baked head, licked his mouth, and running to the crest of the hill, looked after his master.

Satisfied that he was out of sight, the young lion slowly descended the hill, and gave hot chase to several nimble monkeys, who took the precaution, before dropping a stone upon the young lion, to place a discreet distance between themselves and the lordly brute.

Hector bore their impertinence with the utmost coolness, and following his master's trail, he reached the forest while Crusoe and old Tom were busy skinning the dead lions.

Hector had displayed much the same sagacity towards his master as would have been shown by a well-trained dog.

He heard our hero's voice as he neared the spot where the skinning process was going forward, and, making a détour to escape being seen, the intelligent animal found his way to the dead tapir.

His presence scared the hungry beasts of prey, and, after quietly partaking of the choicest morsels, he coiled himself beneath the shade of a huge tree and went to sleep.

From his *siesta* Hector was aroused by the squealing and grunting of the drove of wild hogs.

At the commencement of the noise he raised his head and listened. A lull took place in the horrible outcry, and Hector closed his eyes lazily and placed his muzzle upon his massive fore paws.

Scarcely had the noble animal closed his eyes when the squealing and grunting began with redoubled vigour.

Hector sprang to his feet, and lashing the ground with his tail, glanced around the thick underwood.

All trace of the docile exterior left the young lion's face as his latent instincts were aroused by the horrible noise.

Stalking majestically towards the drove of peccaries, he entered the glade. One glance at his master, and he seemed to comprehend the danger that menaced him.

As a well-bred terrier bounds towards a cluster of rats, so did the young lion fall upon the outskirts of the wild horde.

Tearing the peccaries aside with his terrible fangs and powerful claws—strewing the ground as he battled his way towards his master—Hector charged through the dense herd; and when they fled in wild confusion he ceased not the havoc, and when called by the well-known voice he loved so well, the little animal—so terrible in his anger—left a trail of bruised and bleeding carcases to mark his passage through the forest.

CHAPTER XVII.

CRUSOE'S OLD ACQUAINTANCE LURED FROM HIS LAIR.—A NOVEL ATTACK.

THE retreating host were followed to the depths of the vast forest, the route marked by scores of dark forms that had fallen by the adventurers' rifles or the teeth of their savage ally.

When the slaughter ended, and the peccaries had gone beyond the reach of pursuit, the castaways, exhausted by the hot chase, threw themselves beneath the shade of a tree.

Jack lay with one hand upon the young lion's |mane and the other grasping his trusty weapon.

Old Tom sat opposite, his bronzed faced covered with perspiration.

A few feet from them a large forked branch was thrust in the ground, and, suspended by a strip of lion-skin, was one of their foe's haunches, frizziing and smoking over a blazing log fire.

"I think," old Tom said, as he surveyed the scene of battle, "we have made a good morning's work, Jack."

"Yes," was the answer; "the result was not warranted by the beginning, and I question whether, had it not been for Hector, we should have ever left that tree."

"Not yet, boy, that is certain; however, we shall not have to run any more risks on this island."

"How is that, Tom?"

"Bless the boy! here is food enough to victual a three-decker."

"True. I was about to ask you what we shall do with these porkers."

"Use what we require; the rest the beasts of prey will consume."

The smoking joint was taken from the fire, and while the castaways were discussing the savoury meal, old Tom was busy maturing a plan to salt a sufficient quantity to victual them both.

Suddenly he paused in the act of slicing the joint and said—

"I have it! I'll make some salt, Jack; then we shall be prepared for contrary winds."

Our hero looked up in surprise, and repeated—

"Make some salt?"

"Ay, boy. Why not?"

"I did not think that salt could be procured except from a mine."

Old Tom gave one of his dry laughs, and said—

"Come; let us go to the sea-shore. I'll soon show you how it is done."

The young castaway knew the value of time too well to put off the operation, though every limb ached, and he could scarcely keep his eyes open, through the deprivation of sleep on the previous night and his great exertions since the morning.

Cheerfully shouldering his rifle, and the young lion following at his heels, he accompanied old Tom to the beach.

Here their arms were laid aside, and each with an impromptu spade, formed from two large shark bones, began to dig a large square hole in the sand.

This old Tom termed his tank, and when it was finished a trench was cut to the water side of sufficient depth to allow the sea to trickle into the tank.

When this tank was completed, a similar tank was made in rear of that, which was now slowly filling with water.

Crusoe worked until his hands were torn and blistered, without murmuring. Poor little fellow, he found that the life he loved so well was full of hardship as well as wild adventure.

From the back of the first tank to the second a trench was made, and the sand removed, except a small quantity at the junction with the first tank.

Old Tom, in answer to our hero's query respecting this, said—

"You see, lad, I want to filter the water from the first tank to the second, and very slowly, so that when the sun shines upon the water it will be gradually passing down the trench, and leaving the salt there."

He pointed to the first tank with his spade.

"But, my boy," the old tar said: "you look tired; suppose you turn in while I cut up a few hogs. We can leave this for a day or two."

"I would sooner assist you, Tom."

"Very well, lad; come on."

They went back to the forest, and by sunset both were staggering towards their eyrie under a load of the choicest parts of the peccaries.

Hector's theft was discovered when the adventurers went to the larder, but in consequence of the great service the animal had done he escaped punishment.

The next day was a busy one upon the island, the result of a long discussion being a determination to embark in search of the Seagull's hull in two or three days at farthest.

While they were busy carrying portions of the dead hogs to the pickling tank, old Tom, to be ready for any emergency, began to teach our hero the Indian language, such as is spoken by the various tribes of South and Central America.

He found his young companion an apt pupil, and before they had finished putting the joints in salt, Jack was able to answer several words in the Indian tongue.

Old Tom Starboard's mode of instruction might be followed with advantage by many spectacled pedagogues.

When he had given his pupil the Indian terms for every article they had in their possession, he made it a point of using the term until Jack, by taking the article denominated in his hand, could not fail to remember the words.

One example will suffice to explain the old tar's mode of instruction.

"Jack!" he would call out suddenly, "hand me the *obak*."

Crusoe picked up his gun.

"Good lad! Don't forget *obak* when you see your gun."

A moment after he would call out—

"Jack, where is the *kuma*?"

"There," was the ready reply, as Crusoe pointed to the forest, "and an *imuk* on that tree."

"Bravo—bravo! good; don't forget *kuma* means forest, *imuk* parrot. Good lad!"

So the lesson continued until the salting for that day ended, and as they turned to retrace their steps to the hill, old Tom pointed out many objects that grew in their path, and in his quaint manner so impressed the Indian terms upon his willing pupil's mind, that Jack seldom made a mistake when asked to point out a tree or a flower.

In this manner they had traversed nearly half the distance that intervened between the forest and the hill, and as they were emerging from the palm grove a loud crashing noise among the brushwood brought them to a standstill.

Ever on the alert, both rifles were brought to the full cock, and they turned about for the creature that made such havoc in the cane-brake.

The noise seemed to recede from them, and Jack, pushing aside the tall canes, followed the path which had been made by some huge and heavy body passing through.

Old Tom was close upon his heels, and as he looked narrowly at the trail, he exclaimed—

"The crocodile, as I'm a sinner!"

"The crocodile! are you sure?"

"Certain, boy, certain. Look at those marks. See where the brute has turned off and bowed down the tall canes."

"My old enemy," Jack said, gleefully. "However, we shall soon overtake him."

Easier said than done, Master Jack. Whether the brute has contrived to regain his watery home, or afraid of the smell of human beings, it is hard to say; but one thing was certain, when the castaways entered the cane-brake the crashing noise lessened considerably, and denoted the quickened pace of the scaly gentleman for whom our hero had such a cordial dislike.

In the excitement of the moment the pursuers forgot the cuts and bruises they received in their passage through the tangled vegetation.

At length the trail ended, and an open space lay before them, and to their disappointment they beheld the crocodile within three feet of the pool.

Quick as thought Jack's gun was brought to his shoulder, and, much to his surprise, when he fired, the bullet struck the brute's head and hopped off as though it had been an india-rubber ball; the next sight was the water splashing upward as the scaly monster regained his lair.

"Well," said Crusoe, as he reloaded, "that surprised me a little. Fancy, the ball hopped off without doing the least injury."

Old Tom laughed at his companion's astonishment, and said—

"You hit the hardest part, lad."

"Hang the brute! Has he a soft spot anywhere, Tom?"

The old sailor laughed at Crusoe's eagerness, and answered—

"That armour upon his back is the best place, Jack; fire at that next time."

"I will; but I'm afraid we shall not see the gentleman again for some time."

"Perhaps not. Suppose we entice him out."

Crusoe's eyes sparkled at the idea; he had not forgotten the manner in which the scaly monster had deprived his kingdom of many goodly animals, and he would have incurred any risk to have rid the pool of its voracious tenant.

The crocodile, of which so little is known in Europe, deserves more than a passing allusion; so with the reader's permission, we will explain the peculiarities and ferocity of this singular and terrible animal.

These animals are to be met with in many parts of India, Asia, and Africa; the river Nile, the Niger, and the Ganges abound with them, and in Upper Egypt they float along the surface of the water and seize whatever may come within the reach of their rapacious jaws.

When this mode of attack fails, they hide among the vegetation near the river side and wait in patient expectation of such creatures as may come to drink.

The bull, the dog, the tiger, or man himself, often falls a victim to their ferocity; the mode of destroying their prey has been related already in these pages.

Sometimes these amphibious monsters have been known to measure twenty feet in length. Perhaps the greatest peculiarity in this animal is the absence of a tongue; but in place of this useful part there is a sort of membrane attached to the two sides of the under jaw.

The nose is perfectly round and flat, not unlike a dog's, and of a soft spongy substance.

The skull is proof against a musket-ball; this part of the animal is rough and unequal in several places, and about the middle of the forehead there are two long crests about two inches high.

The fore legs have the same parts and conformation as the arm of a man, but they are somewhat shorter than the hind legs.

The hands have five fingers, the last of which have no nails.

The hind feet are provided with four toes, three of which are armed with long claws, but the fourth is without a nail.

Their toes are united and hollow, like a duck's foot, but much stronger and thicker.

The usual colour of these brutes is dark brown on the upper part, and whiter below, with large spots of both colours on the sides.

From the shoulders to the extremity of the tail is covered with large scales of a square form, this armour rendering them nearly invulnerable; and the powerful blows they are capable of striking with their tails render them dangerous foes, and, as a rule, to be avoided rather than attacked.

With this description of the monster who had so long dwelt in safety upon the lonely isle, the reader will be prepared to marvel at the daring hardihood of the castaways luring the terrible brute from his lair.

A portion of one of the peccaries was thrown by Tom Starboard into the pool, and, as a matter of course, was seized and carried away by the crocodile.

When he had thrust it in a hole in the banks he came to the surface in the hope of meeting another windfall.

Old Tom had by this time attached another piece of flesh to a thong of lion skin, and depositing it upon the surface of the water, he retreated the length of his line.

The bait took; the scaly thing came slowly towards the tempting morsel, but before he could snap it up, old Tom quickly drew it away.

To Tom's joy, the furious monster followed, until the whole length of his body was visible.

Here he stopped, and looking furtively at the adventurers, seemed to debate whether he should return or follow the tempting piece of pork.

His appetite gained the day, and he made a snatching grab at the bit, and before old Tom could jerk it away the scaly one had snapped it up, thong included.

This done, he fixed his small, vicious-looking eyes

CRUSOE JACK ASTONISHES THE NATIVES

upon Jack, and made a movement as though about to attack the boy.

Perhaps the greatest disadvantage the crocodile labours under is his inability to turn about.

This Jack knew, and when he saw the ugly brute making direct towards him, he bounded forward and took the enemy in rear.

The crocodile, as though fully aware that mischief was intended, began to paddle slowly round; his hind toes forming the point on which he turned.

"Give it him, Tom," said the young Crusoe, as he fired point blank at the crocodile's back; "shoot him in the eye."

The bullet from Jack's rifle either struck one of the thick heavy plates upon the brute's back, or merely buried itself in the skin, for the monster took no notice of it beyond swinging his flexible tail suddenly to and fro, as old Tom was in the act of lodging a bullet in his eye.

As ill luck would have it, the swing of the tail caught Tom Starboard's legs, and in a moment the old tar was struggling upon his back, and the ball he intended for the crocodile's eye went flying upward.

In spite of the serious aspect of affairs, our young Crusoe could not help laughing at old Tom's sudden downfall.

His laugh was brought to an abrupt termination by

6

the crocodile wheeling round and making at him open-mouthed.

Jack, at this moment, was in the act of ramming home a fresh charge, and in his hurry to get out of the brute's way he stumbled forward.

There was but two feet between him and his jaws; and old Tom, seeing the lad's imminent peril, clubbed his rifle and rushed in front of the fierce brute.

Active as a squirrel, the boy was upon his feet in an instant.

One look showed him the danger he was in; and to the surprise of old Tom, and no doubt, the crocodile as well, Jack turned a complete somersault, and alighted astride the enemy's back.

Tom Starboard's heart sank within him; not more than six feet distance was between the crocodile and the margin of the pool.

The blood curdled in his veins at the possibility of the monster making the fatal plunge with the beautiful, reckless boy upon his back.

Determined to sacrifice his own life to save the boy he so dearly loved, he gripped his rifle yet tighter by the muzzle, and rained a shower of blows upon the crocodile's soft snout.

This seemed to have no impression upon the brute, for he kept straight on towards the pool, as though determined to take his rider with him.

This arrangement, however satisfactory it could have been to the surly brute, was not agreeable to Crusoe.

The boy knew his danger; and when old Tom's white lips ejaculated—

"Jump off! jump off! or you will be carried under the water!"

He answered—

"Pitch into him, Tom—I'm all right."

Tom did pitch in. The rifle-butt rained such a shower of blows upon the only tender part of the unwieldy beast's body that he was compelled to pause for a moment, in consequence of the pain he underwent.

Jack had dropped his rifle while he performed the somersault, and after he had fixed himself firmly upon the scaly creature's back, a thought flashed to his brain, which was instantly put into execution.

From the position he was occupying he had a good opportunity of getting between the square plates which so well defended the fierce creature's back.

Out came Jack's sword like a flash of light, and with all the strength he could muster he began to dig at his charger's back.

Rendered savage by the attack in front and the sharp stabs above, the crocodile became terribly aroused, and, as though determined to rid himself of one, if not both, of his foes, he made a charge, open-mouthed, at Tom Starboard.

The old sailor stood his ground manfully. Though certain death would have been the consequence had the crocodile reached him, he made not the least effort to move out of the monster's way, but, if possible, increased the number and weight of the blows.

A loud shout from young Crusoe was followed by the sudden downfall of the scaly beast, and old Tom, pausing in his attack, looked towards his companion,

and beheld, to his joy, the boy's sword driven up to the hilt in the monster's back.

Jack paid no attention to the steed he bestrode stumbling forward, but drew his blade from its fleshy sheath, and plunged it again its whole length between the brute's shoulder and neck.

This was the *coup de grâce.*

A hissing noise came from the hot wound, as the air came from the animal's lungs.

The jaws opened and closed once or twice with a loud snap; then the carcase fell over, and as Jack sprang to the ground in safety, the crocodile's lower jaw fell and his eyes closed for ever.

The castaways gave a jubilant shout at their victory, and old Tom, to make sure, placed the muzzle of his rifle to the brute's eye, and sent a bullet inside the impregnable skull.

Thus, the beautiful pool which had so long been but a snare for the unsuspecting animals that dwelt in the forest, was deprived of its savage tenant by the indomitable spirit and reckless daring of our young hero, Crusoe Jack.

To those who are familiar with the terrible monsters, the great dangers our friends exposed themselves to in facing the unequal combat will be well known; to those who have not beheld a living specimen of the fierce creatures, let them study the previous description, and imagine how they should feel face to face with one.

CHAPTER XVIII.

ADIEU TO THE ISLAND.

Two days after their encounter with the crocodile the castaways prepared for their voyage of discovery.

The boat was launched, after being carefully examined by the old seaman, and the painter being made fast to a stout branch, the provisions and a pile of soft skins were placed in the stern.

The dried flakes of shark's flesh were stowed away, to be used only in the event of the store of salted peccary failing; but that seemed scarcely possible, as there was more than they would have consumed in a month, had not an unforeseen event occurred, which will be related in its proper place.

Their only difficulty had been in constructing vessels to hold water.

But this was overcome by making bags capable of holding from two to three gallons, from the skins of the wild beasts slain during that fearful night they sat in the tree.

A small shark bone formed the needle for this purpose—the thread was drawn from a piece of the boat's sail.

Four of these water-skins were placed in the boat with the provisions; then Hector, after much terror, was induced to enter the small craft.

Everything being ready, old Tom hoisted the sail and, wafted by a gentle breeze, the adventurers' boat glided slowly from the island.

Reclining at full length upon a soft pile of skins, Crusoe looked wistfully at the small black speck standing out so boldly against the azure sky—he looked and felt as though he was leaving his boyhood's home, for the humble trunk of that memorable tree had been to him the only happy resting-place his saddened heart had known.

He was going, Heaven only knew whither, leaving peace and tranquillity, for an unknown place, or, mayhap, to be engulphed in the treacherous ocean, which now like an island lake bore the boat forward.

Little wonder that he felt a strange yearning wish to return to the summit of that lonely hill, the eyrie, and the vast unpeopled tract of land wherein he had been a king.

Until the land became a mere hazy outline, he kept his gaze steadfastly fixed upon the place where he had passed both lonely and happy hours.

Then, as the dim streak became blended with the far distant horizon, he raised his hand, and said in tones of touching sadness—

"Tom, I never yet felt so desolate as I do now."

His old companion was standing upon one of the thwarts, one hand grasping the single mast, the other shading his eyes from the red sun.

He turned sharply as the boy's mournful voice came upon his ear, and gazing earnestly at the handsome young face, answered—

"Desolate, boy, desolate! Do you regret leaving the island? If so, we will—"

"No, no, Tom; I do not wish to return. It is not that feeling which oppresses me."

"Eh? Bless the boy! I would have not left the place had I known it would have made you so sad."

"You misunderstand me," Crusoe said. "I must repeat that I have no wish to return. I do not fear the dangers we may encounter during the voyage, neither do I wish to stay longer upon that island, lovely as it is; but, looking at it as we glided away from the shore, I felt as those must feel who leave home for the first time."

"Very natural—very natural, my boy; but we should feel thankful that we have the power to leave the place. There we might remain for years, and not behold the white sails of a ship; here, upon the blue waters, there is a chance of being picked up, or at least reaching the old leaky hull, and finding all we require to make our lonely condition endurable."

Crusoe was about to respond to this speech, when a peculiar appearance some twenty fathoms ahead of the boat caused him to exclaim—

"Look! What is that, Tom? Is it?—yes; it must be—a sail!"

Tom Starboard turned quickly, but before he could catch even a glimpse of the welcome canvas, our hero said huskily—

"It's gone; yet I could have sworn I saw—— Yes; look! There it is again!"

Tom Starboard's face flushed slightly at the object, which to the uninitiated had the appearance of spread canvas, but his practised eye soon saw the real nature of this, to him, unpleasant sight.

"Sail, lad," he said, in a tone that showed how heartily he wished the strange appearance anywhere but in the vicinity of their little craft—"no; it's a whale spouting."

As he spoke a second white object suddenly arose from the water, then a third.

Jack saw the look of gloom that passed over old

Tom's face augured danger from the presence of the spouting fizz of white vapour.

"What is it, Tom?" he asked eagerly. "Your face tells me that all is not right."

The old seaman shook his head, yet never for a second suffered his eyes to wander from the object of his dread.

"All wrong, lad," he said—"all wrong. If they come this way, one fluke of the tail and up we go. I hope," he mentally added, "the boy's feelings were not prophetic of what I feel almost sure will happen."

Several dark objects were plainly visible above the water, then the sea, which lay so placid all around, was seen to swell into white-topped waves, as though under the influence of a sudden squall.

Amazed, yet interested at the strange sight, Crusoe watched with suppressed breathing the swift approach of the horde.

"A large shoal," muttered old Tom, "and coming right upon us. Look out, lad!"

The warning was only in time, for Crusoe had been so intent with the movements of the whales that the possibility of them being cast overboard had quite escaped his mind.

He had but time to clutch the side of the boat, when the frail craft was turning to and fro in the swell caused by the passage of the whales through the water.

They escaped death by the merest trifle. Had the whales kept the same course they were pursuing when first sighted, nothing could have saved our adventurers' boat from being thrown on her beam ends by the fan-shaped tails or the huge back of one of those leviathans.

They had, much to the old sailor's joy, swerved a little as they came within a couple of fathoms of the boat, though the sea was agitated by their swift passage through the water to such an extent that the boat was at times lost in the trough of the sea, and at other times perched upon the crest of a white-topped frothy wave.

The exertions of both were required to keep the frail vessel from foundering, and though the timbers were untouched, neither felt safe until the waters began to subside and they were once more going free before the wind.

They had manned their little craft with hope when they left the island, and now, as old Tom watched the dark forms as they sped onward, ever and anon sending up a white misty column from their nostrils, he said—

"A lucky escape, lad; had one of those beggars fluked us, there would have been an end——"

Crusoe uttered an exclamation of surprise.

"What is it, lad?" the old tar asked; "has she sprung a leak or filling, eh?"

"Where is Hector?"

This query came with startling shortness from the young Crusoe's lips, and old Tom, looking aft, sought eagerly for the puma.

He was gone to all appearance. There lay the heap of skins upon which the young lion had been coiled—the place now vacant—a circular indentation showing the exact spot where he had lain on leaving the island.

"He's gone to a certainty," the old sailor said, regretfully; "now I remember, I have not seen him since the whales came close upon us."

Too much occupied with the danger that had menaced them, the adventurers had not noticed the young puma's terror when the boat began to rise and fall upon the undulating water.

The animal awakened among the pile of skins, and every fibre seemed to quiver with abject fear. The nostrils were dilated, and the eyes were distended to an unnatural size, and as the frail bark rolled from side to side, or rose almost perpendicular upon a mountain-like wave, the animal clung madly by its claws to the gorilla-skin, and gave vent to a low moaning whine of fear.

This lasted until the boat was suddenly dashed down between two waves, then the affrighted brute tore up the pile of skins and sought safety beneath them.

A pang of regret passed through Jack's heart when he thought of the noble animal's being engulphed by the seething water, and as old Tom let fall the sail, which had been hastily furled, he went slowly aft to resume his place at the helm.

Passing over the piles of skins, his feet came in contact with a soft object, and as a gleam of hope spread over his face he stooped, and to his joy found the object of his solicitude beneath.

The exclamation he gave caused old Tom to turn, and when he beheld Jack soothingly caress the trembling brute, he felt as pleased as though the young lion had been a human being.

"I'm glad you have found him, Jack," the old fellow said; "it wouldn't have been right at the beginning of our voyage to have lost our favourite."

The boy was too much engaged in his attempt to allay the lion's terror to answer Tom Starboard, nor did he look up until Hector crept from his hiding-place, and placed his great brown muzzle confidingly upon his master's knee.

The kindly tones of Crusoe's voice soon drove away all recollection of the recent strange fear that had pervaded the brave forest king, and, as though secure from further terror, he licked Crusoe's hand with his great rough tongue, and coiled himself at the boy's feet as docile and obedient as a spaniel.

Looking around at the boundless tract of water, Jack found that all traces of their late visitors had departed.

The boy had beheld, for the first time, a gathering of the ocean's strange and monstrous inhabitants, and with that thirst for knowledge which is inherent in every intelligent mind, he asked his companion to solve the mystery to him of that vast gathering.

Old Tom had, during his career, served on board a whaler, and with more intelligence than could have been expected from one to whom the very alphabet was as much a puzzle as a sheet of Egyptian hieroglyphics, answered every query both readily and intelligently.

The old man was a keen observer of Nature, and, as a boy, he had often been struck with the singularity of her works.

Deprived of the power of gleaning knowledge from books, he had studied the mighty volume which had opened to his eyes when he began his career as sailor-boy upon an east-indiaman.

Even then, although but a child in years, he had often puzzled gray-headed men by the shrewdness of his remarks, and the quick perceptive power he displayed of learning the habits of the strange denizens of the deep.

With them it was sufficient to know that, we'll say for example, a whale rose to the surface at certain periods; or that a shark was usually attended by a number of pilot-fish and suckers. He wanted to know why it was so—a question his shipmates, although they had served many years at sea, could not answer.

Crushed as it was in the outset of his desire to attain a knowledge of the ocean's strange denizens, the wish became stronger, and he patiently watched every trivial circumstance that took place among the finny tribe until he had acquired a better and more profound insight into the sea's natural history than many who are looked upon by the world as great and learned naturalists.

Such a man was a fitting companion for the brave, intelligent boy, and, as the sequel will show, the knowledge Crusoe thus obtained was a mighty power, and saved him more than once from the icy clutch of the grim Destroyer's hand.

"I never could have imagined," the young wanderer said, "that we should have been in such peril in consequence of these whales nearing us."

"Peril, lad!" the old sailor said. "Did you think those great brutes were as harmless as a shoal of mackerel?"

"No, Tom; I have heard that, when attacked, they often upset a boat, but never knew there was any danger to be apprehended when not interfered with."

"There is, boy, great danger; and I too well remember a circumstance that happened when I was a boy aboard a whaler. What think you of a stout ship being sunk by one of them?"

"How do you mean—lifted out of the water and upset?"

"No, lad; the biggest among 'em couldn't do that. But the one that I am speaking about was the cause of our vessel sinking, and sending forty poor fellows to Davy Jones's before their time. You look surprised, lad. Shall I tell you how it occurred?"

Jack's face brightened. It was not often of late that old Tom indulged him with a yarn, or, rather, truthful recital of perils that he had passed through, and strange hardships and sights, that would have been discredited by many who, forsooth, called themselves wise, and sent forth huge volumes of the wonders of Nature, without having seen one iota of the many strange things they professed to so well understand. There has been, and no doubt there are at the present moment, many rough, unlettered men before the mast who could enlighten the world with truthful and wondrous stories of Nature's mystic works, and, were they believed in preference to the many great naturalists, whose field of observation consisted in the limited extent of their own gardens, or a heap of musty books, the ignorant and untravelled would be nearer the truth than they can ever hope to be by poring over their calf-bound volumes.

"Every word of this, lad, is as true as we are in this boat," old Tom said, as he began his recital; "and this is how it occurred: The Mary, the whale-ship which I was aboard, was in the southern ocean, looking out for whales.

"One morning, as the captain or the mate—I forget which now—was in the *crow's nest*,* on the look-out, we all stood by the boats, ready to let fall the moment he gave the signal."

Old Tom paused, and drew his hand across his eyes, and Crusoe saw, by the working of his features, that the recital recalled unpleasant memories in the veteran seaman's mind.

"Don't tell it," the boy said, thoughtfully, wishing to spare his companion any painful feelings; "the recollection is too much for you."

The old fellow gathered the corner of their little sail tightly in his hand, and, making an effort to appear cheerful, said—

"Yes, lad; I've begun, and may as well go on. Now, Jack, I always see his pale face and blue lips when he said 'Good bye' to me."

Crusoe's interrogative look was answered by the narrator of the sad story.

"He was my brother, lad"—old Tom spoke as though making an effort to choke back the husky sensation that almost stayed his words—"the only one I ever had. Well—well, he went, I hope, to a better place than this world, for he was too good—much too good—to—to—"

Old Tom paused, and a tear trickled down each weather-beaten cheek.

Crusoe felt for the poor fellow; he could understand, although he had hitherto been alone and friendless, the strange yearning that clings to the heart of those who have lost for ever one that was dear to them. Again he expressed his wish for old Tom to abstain from recalling the details of that fatal day; the old man's answer was a quick gesture of the head, as though to imply silence.

"Where did I leave off?" His voice was firmer now, and the nervous twitching motion of the lips had passed away. "We were waiting for the look-out to give the signal. It came. Little did the gallant ship's company think the welcome words was their death warrant.

"It was," he resumed, after a slight pause, "although when the cry came from above, 'She spouts—she spouts!' we gave a cheer, and, like magic, down went the boats and the whole of the hands complete; six were soon pulling like mad towards the huge animal, who could be seen blowing about every half minute.

"We were not long getting alongside the whale; then, as he was about to sink, the captain called out, 'Peak your oars!' Up goes the shining blades, and, afore you could count one, I had sent the harpoon deep slap in the brute's carcase, for," old Tom added proudly, 'I was then harpooner, and, if what they record of me is true, as good as any man who ever drove a lance into a whale.

"After he was struck, the mate calls out, 'Stern all!' and we backed out of reach of the monster's tail, and, giving him plenty of line, down he went, sixty fathoms of good rope fastened to the harpoon.

"We followed the brute until he rose to the surface, and the headsman stood ready to give him the finishing stroke; but, quick as thought, his tail went up in the air, and as it descended our boat was struck, and the next minute we were splashing about in the water.

"That would not have mattered much, as the other boats were not far off, had it not been for a shoal of sharks which were swimming about near us—they always do when a whale is struck—in the hope, I expect, of getting the blood which runs from their wounds.

"Be that as it may, they were soon seen coming towards us, and before the boats—which came, you may be sure, as quickly as men could pull—arrived, three poor fellows were bitten in halves by the powerful teeth of the rapacious sea monsters.

"Poor fellows! they were saved from many long days of suffering by their dreadful fate, although none at the time knew the great danger that was creeping towards us.

"This accident," old Tom continued, "stayed the pursuit, and the whale, maddened with the pain of his wounds, appeared at times to spring out of the water, throwing up a mountain of white spray with the convulsive flappings of his fin-like tail.

"Never shall I forget it, lad; that dreadful moment when the men in the boat which was in advance of us called out, 'He's struck the ship!' Those who heard the cry could not at first believe the fearful truth. Alas! the matter was soon beyond dispute. We were not more than ten fathoms from the doomed vessel, when we saw a detached portion of the cutwater floating towards us. A minute after the whale rose to the surface, and, as true as I'm a living man, the powerful brute made a furious charge upon the Mary's larboard bow, and with his immense head crushed the planks; it seemed as easy as we would break an egg-shell.

"The ship filled, and before we could reach her she had lurched over on her side, and down she went with all on board.*

"There we were, lad, hundreds of miles from land; no food, no water, and our home engulphed by the treacherous water. There was nothing left for us but to die, and before we sighted a ship the whole of the Mary's crew, except myself and the second mate, had perished miserably in mid-ocean; among the first was my poor brother."

Then old Tom sat with his elbows on his knees, and, as he abruptly finished this sad story, he covered his face with his hands and wept.

Crusoe felt the unbidden tears rising in his eyes, and quitting his seat, he came beside the grief-stricken man, and placed his hands upon the poor old seaman's shoulder.

"Tom," he said, in gentle, soothing tones, "you have lost your brother; let me fill his place in your heart."

* A station at the mast-head.

* A similar accident befell a whale-ship in the South Pacific not many years since.

The veteran sailor upturned his gaze, and looking fondly in the boy's face, he took the small hand between his own rough palms and pressed it affectionately.

"You shall," he said—"you shall be my brother; next to him I have loved you more than aught else in this world."

"And I have loved you, Tom; you have been my only friend, now we will be as brothers."

The setting sun had thrown a dull red glare upon the ocean before old Tom Starboard recovered his wonted cheerfulness, and when the young wanderer had won him from the deep melancholy which so heavily weighed upon his heart, he asked a few questions about the leviathans of the deep.

"Do they always," he asked, "swim in such vast numbers as those we saw a short time since?"

"Not always, lad; that must have been a pod of young whales."

"A pod," Jack cried, with a marked stress upon the word; it seemed a strange one to use in reference to the great quantity.

"By a pod," old Tom said, "I mean a great number of young whales, which, under the guidance of some old ones, learn to swim and seek their food—at least, I expect this is the cause of the vast numbers of young I have seen, each horde attended by one or two old ones."

"Strange," Crusoe said, musingly, "these creatures have no power of speech, yet they are capable of being instructed."

"Nature, lad—nature," said old Tom. "Here comes the darkness. Help me to make an awning of the sail, then you can turn in while I keep watch."

The sail spread over the boat's stern formed a comfortable covering, and kept the night damps from falling on the castaways.

Crusoe, tired and unused to fatigue like his companion, was soon asleep, and old Tom, with an extra skin thrown over his shoulders, sat just within the sail keeping solitary vigil.

The hours glided slowly onward, still the old seaman sat with his head buried in his hands listening to the gentle ripple of the waves as they kissed the timber of the little craft.

The recollections connected with his brother's death, so long dormant, now recalled by the recital of the whaling adventure, saddened the hardy seaman's spirit, and he felt the honest love of his rugged heart more firmly fixed than ever upon the handsome boy who slept so near him.

So the long night passed, and morning's cheerful beams shone upon the gray-headed castaway, whose position had remained unchanged, but whose faculties were lulled to mute forgetfulness by the soft murmur of the rippling waves—the gentle murmur which had from childhood lulled him to sleep, and whose heaving breast had been his home both in sunshine and storm.

CHAPTER XIX.
ATTACKED BY SHARKS.

THE sun was shining upon the sea's glassy surface when our hero awoke from his slumbers, and starting up to a sitting position he glanced towards his companion.

A remorseful feeling came to his heart when he beheld old Tom still in the same position as when he had bade him good night. Rising softly, he crept forward and placed his hand upon the old seaman's shoulder.

"Tom," he said, "this is not right; you have kept watch the whole night. Why did you not rouse me?"

The veteran started at the boy's light touch, and instantly his senses, which had been buried in oblivious slumber, returned.

"I could not have slept, lad," he said; "besides, there was no need of keeping a good look-out. We are far from land, and a hundred miles away from the track of any vessel."

"Still, Tom," said the boy, "you ought to let me share the labour of the voyage with you."

"So you shall, lad—so you shall. Now begin, and help me to get breakfast."

He jumped to his feet while speaking, and with Crusoe's assistance the sail was hoisted and securely fastened, and as they went aft to partake of their frugal meal a light wind had carried them quickly forward upon the bosom of the trackless waste of waters.

The breeze fell about noon, and the sea became as smooth as the polished surface of a mirror.

The boy noted the anxious expression upon his companion's face when this sudden calm fell upon them, and following the old sailor's inquiring glance as he swept the horizon, he asked—

"What is the matter, Tom? You look anxious since the boat became motionless."

"There is nothing much yet, boy, but there may be something. Look there!"

Old Tom pointed to a bank of heavy, dark clouds that was at that moment gliding slowly over the sun's burning disc.

"I see them, Tom," he said. "What does it mean?"

Shading his eyes with his out-stretched hands, old Tom took a long and deeper scrutiny of the rapidly accumulating harbingers of a coming storm.

"That's what I can't answer yet," he said, in reply to Crusoe's query. "It may be only a gathering of rain-clouds—it may be the prelude to a heavy squall; if so, the Lord help us—this boat will never live it out!"

Crusoe knew his companion was not in the habit of magnifying any approaching peril—far otherwise. Knowing this caused a vague feeling of uneasiness to enter the gallant boy's heart; little wonder he should feel thus.

They were alone upon mid-ocean, and nothing to shelter them from the coming storm, their boat a frail structure that would not withstand the buffet of a large wave.

Checking the chill feeling that came creeping over his faculties, our hero stood beside his companion and in silence they stood watching the slowly-gathering storm-clouds."

Rolling upwards, as though they rose from the ocean, the dark masses drifted across the sun; then, as the wind came stealing gently across the water, the sail bellied out, and the boat, like a high-mettled racer when goaded by the spur, shot forward.

The white foam curled before her sharp prow in feathery streaks, and from time to time a shower of minute spray swept across the faces of the anxious castaways.

"To the helm, boy!" shrieked old Tom, when this change took place. "Keep her to it, and, please the Lord, we may yet escape."

Obeying this order with an alacrity that showed how deeply Crusoe shared his companion's excitement, the boy seized the tiller and kept the boat's head in the direction pointed out by a silent gesture from old Tom's hand.

Ten minutes passed in this manner—both silent; one grasping the sail ready to let fall should circumstances require, the other watching every movement of his companion's hands.

The wind which wafted the boat so swiftly through the water, also brought the storm clouds upon their track, and their only hope of salvation lay in being able to out-speed the mass of murky clouds.

"I think," old Tom said, as he suffered the single sail to go free, "we shall do it, lad. Ha! look, it has burst!"

Crusoe turned his head, and beheld the atmosphere about a mile to leeward now having a thick, misty appearance, and the water beneath appeared to bubble and froth upward.

Presently the minute spray increased in size, until the white-topped billows could be discerned rising and falling as the water was lashed by the sweeping gusts of wind.

Our hero knew by the misty appearance of the horizon that the rain-clouds had burst, and the water was falling upon the ocean in such force as to darken the air through which it passed.

He knew also that the white-crested foam and the undulating movement of the distant part of the sea was caused by the wind suddenly sweeping downwards.

Yet, strange to say, although these evidences of a terrible tempest were raging within a mile of their little boat, all around, save to leeward, was calm and beautiful.

The young castaway now understood the meaning of old Tom's exclamation, when he said their only hope of safety was the possibility of outstripping the gale.

"You don't think there is a possibility of the storm reaching us now, Tom?" Jack said, as the boat glided swiftly onward; "the clouds seem to me to be drifting this way."

Old Tom sustained himself by holding the mast, and took a long look at the seething water and deluge of rain that was falling.

"No, lad," he said; "I think not. The gale is nearly over now, and the clouds that you imagine are coming this way are gradually disappearing, the Lord be praised."

He concluded in such a faint murmur that Jack felt the danger, despite these assurances, was not yet over.

He asked his companion if such was not the case.

"You are right, lad," was the answer; "there is yet danger, but not one-twentieth part of what threatened us when the clouds began to gather."

The danger, from whatever quarter old Tom expected it, did not come; and soon after the sun shone out with a double brilliancy, the wind fell, and the seas again became calm.

"We must take a spell at the oar," said the old sailor. "I am suspicious of these seas; one minute a cat's-paw, the next a hurricane. Bend to it, lad; perhaps we may sight an island before dark: there are plenty hereabouts or I am much out of my reckoning."

The rudder was made fast, and Jack took the stroke oar.

"Are we far," he asked, "from the wreck?"

"Not far, lad; but there are so many islands hereabouts that we may touch at a dozen before we find the one we want."

They pulled for some time in silence, and Jack, who was watching the tiny wavelets, suddenly suspended his rowing and uttered an exclamation of surprise and admiration.

"What is it, lad?"

"A fish," was the reply. "Here, Tom, look! I never saw such a beautiful creature."

Resting for the time upon the oar, old Tom leant forward, and looked in the direction indicated by his companion's finger.

When the veteran seaman beheld the little creature, which swam close to the stern, so far from sharing Jack's admiration, a warning cry came from his lips.

That there could be anything to fear from the pretty little creature that glided so gracefully through the water was ridiculous to suppose. Yet Jack well knew there must be a cause for his companion's warning cry.

What was it?

Old Tom was by this time standing upon the thwart, his keen gray eyes directed first to one side of the boat then the other, and finally, as they turned to the stern of the boat, he exclaimed—

"I thought so—here he comes. To quarters, lad; hand me my rifle."

As quick as the words left the old fellow's lips, Jack was upon his feet and snatching up the rifles, which had been placed beneath the gorilla's skin.

He gave one to Tom, the other he held ready for use.

Following the direction of his companion's fixed gaze, he beheld a sight that for a moment sent an icy chill to his heart.

Making direct for the boat was one of those dreaded monsters of the deep, the white shark, the most furious and dreaded of the terrible species.

Every moment brought the monster nearer the boat, the huge black body was visible beneath the dorsal fin, which, like a sail, showed the speed at which the unwelcome visitor was approaching their frail bark.

Though startled by the sudden and unexpected appearance of the ocean monster, Jack's brain was busy trying to solve the connexion between the shark and the beautiful little fish that had been visible so close under their lee.

He noticed that the object of his admiration had suddenly disappeared, and well knowing the voracity of their grim visitor, his first thought was that the small azure-coloured fish had swum away terrified at the shark's approach.

His surprise was great when he beheld the small fish swimming a few yards ahead of the shark, and looking, to all appearance, as though it was guiding the monster to the boat.

He almost forgot the danger they were placed in, by his anxiety for the little thing. Nothing, he thought, could save it from the capacious jaws of the shark; but as he feverishly watched, he saw to his increasing surprise that the terrible animal took not the least notice of the tempting morsel so close to his jaws.

There was a mystery in this he could not fathom, and much as he wished to understand it, there was no time to ask any questions.

The boy well knew that had they been upon the deck of a stout vessel there would have been nothing to fear, even from this, the fiercest of the shark tribe; he also knew that, situated as they were, only a couple of feet above the water, there was every possibility of their terrible pursuer springing out of his element, and either seizing the boat or one of themselves. He had heard many such stories told on the Seagull's forecastle, and bravely as he had hitherto faced ordinary danger, his cheek now paled at the prospect of an encounter with this, the mariner's most inveterate foe.

There was not much time given him to prepare for the fight, for the shark, whipping the water violently with his forked tail, made a charge at the boat's stern.

The castaways thought their last hour had come when the huge creature struck the boat and sent it forward with the swiftness of an arrow.

Both were hurled bruised and bleeding between thwarts, and before they could regain their feet a crushing of wood was heard.

"Great heaven!" old Tom ejaculated, "he has torn the stern out. Jack, my boy, it is—"

His young companion was upon his feet in an instant, and as he arose he saw the terrible jaws above the gunwale; then, as the crash of breaking timber sounded upon old Tom's hearing, the boy called out—

"No, no! it is only the rudder."

The voracious brute had seized this useful appendage by his triple row of teeth, and torn it away from the fastenings.

The shock given to the small boat threatened to swamp it, and as the fierce brute rushed through the water with the piece of board between its teeth, the crew of the Hope had regained their feet, and stood ready to defend their lives.

The shark crushed the rudder between its formidable teeth and scattered the fragments, then with a sudden flap of the forked tail dashed for the second time towards the frail craft.

The hideous fin rose above the water, and the teeth seized a portion of the gorilla's skin which hung over the stern.

But before the skin could be whipped away old Tom's rifle rang out, and to the young castaway's joy the huge monster's jaws relaxed, the tail whipped the water into a white foam, then a convulsive throe traversed through the creature's body, and he rolled over dead, the sunshine gleaming upon the white breast.

A shout of joy came from Crusoe's lips at this sight, and he ran aft to assure himself that their deadly, dangerous foe was no more.

"Dead as a herring," old Tom said; "that shot hit the most vulnerable part of the monster's carcase."

Jack saw a thin, ensanguined streak rising to the surface from beneath the shark's head, and as he gazed with glad yet dread feelings upon the ocean terror, he said—

"The ball has entered his head, Tom."

"No, boy," was the reply, "the nose, fair in the middle, that is the place; though they are so strong, a blow with the butt end of a musket will kill any of them, if you hit the right spot."

"Heaven be praised you have done so, Tom, or the brute would have dragged our boat beneath the water."

"Very likely, lad, very likely. Now don't forget, when you want to kill one of these reptiles, hit between the nostrils, and it's all over with 'em."

Jack, whose eyes had been fixed upon the dead shark, suddenly cried out—

"Look, look, Tom! here is another coming."

Old Tom hastily but carefully reloaded his rifle, and looking to leeward he saw the dorsal fin of one of the species cleaving the sunlit waters.

Jack suggested taking to the oars, but his older and more experienced companion overruled this.

"It ain't a bit of use," he said, "trying to get away, we must let him come, and serve the varmint as this one has been served. You know the spot, Jack, 'tween the nostrils; let him have it; I'll reserve my fire, in case as you should miss."

As Crusoe, with compressed lips and flushed face, watched the second shark coming towards them, he saw, as in the former case, one of those beautiful little creatures, the pilot-fish, swimming a few yards in advance of the monster's snout.

There was a mystery in this that surprised the boy, and had there been time he would have asked his companion the meaning of this affinity between a creature so small and beautiful as the pilot-fish and the ugly-looking ferocious, white shark.

When the huge fish came within a few feet of the dead carcase, his fins became quiet, and the small evil-looking eyes were seen examining the lifeless form of his late companion.

The snout was within six inches of the surface, and Jack, taking careful aim, pulled the trigger.

Whether the wounded animal went to the bottom and died, or whether he shot away and rolled belly upwards out of reach of the rifles the castaways could not determine.

But after the shot from Jack's rifle the monster disappeared.

A red streak coming to the surface at right angles from that which came from the already slain animal, proved that the boy's shot had taken effect, though not so fatally quick as the old seaman's.

Too much elated at being thus rid of their enemies, the ocean wanderers did not trouble themselves respecting the terrible fate of the small shark, but taking to their oars, they began to move swiftly through the glassy-looking surface of the mystic deep.

The late exploit called forth no comment from the rowers. Deadly peril and hair-breadth escapes were too much a matter of daily occurrence to cause a second thought.

But Jack, as he laboured at the oar, could not dismiss the recollection of the shark and its beautiful little satellite from his mind.

When they paused to rest for a few minutes from their labour, the boy took the opportunity to clear up the matter.

"Tom," he said, "when you saw the small fish that came leeward before the shark, you seemed amazed. Had the little thing any reference to the other's appearance?"

"Ay, lad," was the reply, "it had. That was the pilot-fish; they always go in front of a shark."

"Does not the vicious brute ever eat them?"

"No, lad; the little things are too useful. Didn't you notice the pilot-fish, after looking at the boat, go away?"

"Yes—now I remember, I did."

"Then you saw it swimming in front of the shark, and guiding the brute to our boat?"

"Guiding the shark, Tom?"

"Ay, that's just it, lad—nothing else. It saw us, may be, and went back to its protector. I've heard—but that I can't say is true, 'cos of not seeing it; but those who saw it told me—that when the pilot-fish is in danger of being devoured by an enemy—for in the sea, my lad, the fish prey upon each other, the shark excepted—he sometimes gets killed by a thrust from a sword-fish—"

"Wonderful!" the boy said, deeply struck by Tom's words.

"Yes, it is wonderful, lad—very wonderful. Let's see—I was saying about the pilot-fish being in danger?"

"You were."

"When this happens, the shark opens his mouth and lets the little creatures stay inside until the danger is past. Then they come out again, and swim in front of their master's snout."

"It is strange, these things, Tom—very strange."

"Yes, lad, to those land-lubbers who know nothing of the wonders of the deep; but to the sailor, he so often sees them that they become matters of no interest."

"I think, to the reflective mind, Tom, the wonders of creation must be more interesting than morbid details of crimes."

"You are speaking of your book learning, my boy."

"I refer not to books of instruction, but to the mass of works that are to be found in which the interest lies in a secret murder, a ghost or a woman shut up in a dungeon—novels, I think they are called. I saw a large chest full of them in the wrecker's hut; he had collected them from different ships."

"Well, lad, well."

Old Tom was listening to his companion's words, but was not making much headway with their meaning.

"I can't explain my ideas, Tom," said the simple-hearted boy, "as clearly as I wish; but I'll try and——"

"Go on, my lad, I can understand you well enough, though a book would be as much use to me as a chart would to a marine."

"When I had time," Jack said, "I used to look over this store of books, although I did not know much about reading then. I used to take the books that were most worn."

"I see, lad, I see: you thought they would be the most interesting."

"Yes, but to me they were useless. I read one or two of them, and thick books some of them were, and found them filled with the finding of a dead body, or something of that sort, and the wrong person taken up for the murder, and so on, page after page."

"A long yarn spun out, eh, lad?"

"Yes, Tom. Well, I soon gave up reading those which were so well thumbed, and tried some which had to all appearance been scarcely opened. Those were the books, Tom—natural history, travels, voyages, and wonderful stories of men who had explored hitherto unknown parts of the world."

"You liked those, lad?"

"I did, and often have I hidden one under my jacket and sat in a fissure in the cliffs reading for hours."

"They did you good, lad."

"When I was left upon the island, I used to think over many things that had been done by the travellers over wild tracts of unpeopled country, and endeavour to do as they had done when exposed to starvation."

Old Tom nodded his head approvingly, and looked with pride at the bright, intelligent face which was now turned towards him.

"What I have often wondered at since," the boy said, in conclusion, "is the fact that the most useful, truthful, and interesting books, were scarcely read, while the others, which spin a long yarn about somebody being murdered, or a gipsy taking away a child, were half worn out."

Old Tom stroked his chin—a habit of his when puzzled—and turned the matter over in his mind.

"I don't know," he said, at length, "how it is, Jack, unless people like to read a lot of lies instead of the truth."

"But, Tom, the books of travel and adventure were more interesting than the others."

"Perhaps so—perhaps so." A long pause took place. Crusoe had driven his companion out of his depth. "I wish I had learning enough to answer you, Jack, but I—yes—I think I've got it. Was there any murders in the books of travel."

"Sometimes there would be a fight with savages or a man torn to pieces by a wild beast."

"Yes—yes, but the wrong man would not be taken up and put into prison, and a girl pipe enough tears from her eyes to sink a jolly-boat."

Crusoe became suddenly enlightened.

"No, Tom," he said, "no. In the book of adventures there would not be one of those girls that were always in a scrape. I see it now—I've got it, Tom!"

"Eh, eh! what is it, lad?"

"It was the girls that caused the books to be read Of course, everybody wanted to know whether she would be married to the man that had been put in prison. I know how I used to find that out," he added, laughing; " I couldn't go on reading a lot of things that didn't seem natural, so I looked at the last leaf, and every book ended alike—they all got married."

Old Tom settled himself upon the seat, and, seemingly glad the boy's cross-questioning was over, began to feather his oar.

Jack took the hint, and the light craft was soon gliding swiftly forward.

CHAPTER XX.

THE CORAL REEF—THE CASTAWAYS PURSUED BY SAVAGES

DURING the time consumed by the adventurers in the conversation related in the preceding chapter, the huge carcase of the white shark had drifted in a parallel line with the boat.

The monster was within a fathom of the frail structure his triple teeth had so nearly destroyed, and our hero, as he called old Tom's attention to the proximity of their late foe, exclaimed—

" As I live, Tom, there is a number of fishes growing out of the shark."

" Growing out of the shark, lad ? No ; they are suckers, and have nothing to do with the big varmint, except to make him useful."

The boy had ceased rowing until old Tom had turned the boat's head towards the floating carcase, then he bent to his task with a will that soon brought the boat alongside their late foe.

By the time this movement was accomplished, the shark had rolled partly over, and the suckers were under the water, but near enough to the surface to be visible.

The fish to which old Tom had given the peculiar name of "sucker" was about ten inches in length, and differed slightly in conformation from its fellows by a peculiar apparatus upon the top of its head ; it appeared not unlike a second mouth, for when old Tom bent over the edge of the boat, and forcibly detached it from the shark's sides, Crusoe beheld a row of small teeth in the strange conformation.

Old Tom struck the peculiar-looking fish a sharp blow upon the edge of the boat, and soon terminated its existence.

" You see, lad," he said, holding the curious-looking creature up by the tail, " this fish ain't got much of a pair of fins, so it can't swim very fast, but it ain't to be beat for all that."

Jack took the object in hand, and minutely examined the apparatus which nature had provided as a counterbalance to its feeble powers of progression through the water.

" That thing," old Tom said, " causes it to stick to the belly of a shark, a ship's bottom, or a floating plank. It ain't particular as long as it gets carried about."

Jack placed the fish in the bottom of the boat, and more than ever mystified with the singular inhabitants of the ocean, resumed his seat, and again plying the oar, thought over the many wonderful things he had become acquainted with since he had been cast away by the captain of the Seagull.

The dangers he had passed were all forgotten in the all-absorbing wish to penetrate yet further into the mysteries of animated nature—a wish that could not be eradicated by twice the peril—and seeking out the wonders of nature made him, as will be seen, a wanderer over the inhabited and uninhabited parts of the globe.

Old Tom, seeing the boy's abstraction, said—

" It's strange work, Jack, ain't it ? and it makes you think of curious things. Eh, lad ? "

" More than strange, Tom, more than strange."

He replied thus to his companion, and again relapsed into silence—a quietude only broken by the jerking of the oars in the rowlocks, and an angry, fretful whine from the young lion.

Nearly an hour they rowed thus silently, then the voice of old Tom awoke the boy from his trance.

" It's time to take a rest now, lad," he said, " so pass me over your oar, and come for'ard."

Crusoe resigned the oar to his companion, and stepping lightly over the thwarts, stood in the bow. The young lion, scared and subdued by the strange motion of the boat and sounding water, arose from the pile of skins, and crept after his master.

The ordinary nature of man and beast seemed changed. The young forest monarch now crept for protection to the feet of the youth whom he could have torn to pieces with as much ease as he could crush a fly.

Jack pitied his young favourite's terror, and with kind words and gentle caressing strokes sought to alleviate this unnatural feeling in the noble animal.

The act was understood and appreciated, for the large red tongue licked Crusoe's hand ; then the animal coiled itself within a few inches of Jack's feet, and from time to time uttered a low whine.

The golden sun threw its rays across the sea's vast expanse when our hero took up his position in the bows. Nothing was to be seen around save the azure-tinted sea in the wondrous yet monotonous aspect presented by its vast magnitude.

" Keep a good look-out, lad," said the old seaman ; " if the wind keeps down, we shall sight the island before night."

It needed not his companion's words to incite the boy to look for the promised land, and shading his eyes—for the slowly sinking sun shot its powerful rays directly in their path—he keenly scanned the horizon.

Nothing was to be seen but the gently rippling bosom of the great mass of the interminable water. Towards every point of the compass our hero strained his eyes, but nothing save the blue and distant horizon, which appeared to blend with the sea, rewarded his anxious vision.

There he stood until the orb of day sank like a lurid ball of fire below the horizon, and the dark shadow of approaching night descended with the swiftness peculiar to the tropics.

One short leap from sunshine to darkness—no twilight to give warning of the day's close.

With a sigh of regret the young adventurer went aft, and helped to spread the sail over their resting-place, and as they sat partaking of their frugal meal, both felt anxious for the morrow.

"I know these seas," the old sailor said; "we have had fine weather upon our voyage as yet, but before morning we might be tossing about, our only hope of safety a piece of the broken boat, or, may be, an oar."

Alone, and nothing but the frail boat between them and eternity, and that boat drifting at the mercy of the wind and tide! the sky overhead so dark as to render each other's face barely distinguishable—these words were not calculated to inspire the young adventurer with cheerful anticipations.

But so far from feeling any despondency at his companion's words, that indomitable spirit that had hitherto carried him safely through so many perils showed itself in the castaway's reply to this sombre speech.

"The night damps, Tom," he said, gaily, "are not favourable to your temperament. Pardon my rudeness, but your voice was for all the world like a raven's, croaking out all sorts of ill-luck. I know what it is that makes you so gloomy; you are out of your reckoning with the latitude of the island. Come, don't let that trouble you. I question if the greatest navigator in the world could do better in an open boat, and without either compass or chart."

"May be you are right, my lad; but it seems strange that we should have been all this time without sighting one island. When I found you I passed a dozen between sunrise and sunset, that's what it is troubles me, lad. I fear, and every moment the fear becomes stronger, that we have gone to leeward of these islands. If so, the Lord help us! we shall never leave this boat again."

"Why do you despair to-night more than last night, Tom?"

The old sailor bent over the side of the boat and placed his head as near the surface of the ocean as he could. He remained there for several seconds; then rising to a sitting posture he answered Jack's question.

"I'll tell you, my lad," he said. "If we are where —— Ah! there it is again."

Old Tom again leant over the side, and appeared as though listening for the repetition of the sound that had first caused him to assume this strange attitude.

Presently he arose, and as though speaking to himself, said—

"It's nothing; yet I could have sworn I heard the same noise before."

"What is the matter, Tom? You seem full of strange fancies to-night. What was the sound like, that caused you to listen so anxiously?"

Old Tom again turned his head to windward, as though not being satisfied with the result of his previous efforts to make out the cause of the strange sound that had hitherto baffled his efforts.

"As near as I could judge," he said, in reply to Jack's question, "it is like the roar of a heavy broadside, though at a long distance."

Jack attempted to peer through the gloom that surrounded them as he answered—

"If so, we shall see the flashes of the guns."

"That's what I've been thinking, lad; so perhaps, after all, it is but my fancy. Think no more of it, lad, but turn in; you have had a long spell at the oars to-day."

"No, Tom," was the reply. "If it is necessary to keep watch, I will do it. Last night you let me sleep undisturbed. Surely, if I am able to share your dangers, I am able to share your fatigues."

"Very well, my lad; I will turn in. I am not so strong, I find, as I was twenty years ago; then two or three nights without sleep wouldn't hurt me, but now—well, I suppose I don't get stronger as old Time puts his mark upon my head. Good night, Jack; arouse me if you hear that noise or if you feel sleepy."

"Good night, Tom, I hope to call you up with the cry of 'Land ahead.'"

"I hope so too, lad—good night."

The old seaman was thoroughly worn out, and no sooner had he drawn the coverlet of skins over his form than his long, regular respiration told how soundly he slept.

Jack kept within the shelter of the sail, to prevent the heavy mist which was falling from saturating his clothes and possibly laying the seeds of an insidious disease in his young frame.

Though thus sheltered, both eye and ear retained their keenest faculties, and were alive to the slightest sound.

"I cannot make old Tom out to-night," Jack mused; "it is not often he indulges in groundless alarm, nor is it often his practised hearing is at fault, yet he fully believed in that sound. I know from his manner that he did so. However, I do not— Ah!"

A rumbling noise—not unlike the sound of a distant cannonade—came upon the boy's ears, and caused him to run to the bow and endeavour to pierce the gloom that hung over the sea.

The bright flashes which he fully expected to follow this startling noise were not visible, and after listening anxiously for some time, he returned to his seat, and, feverish with excitement, noticed the recurrence of the sound.

An hour passed, and nothing was heard save the ripple of the waters and the sigh of the gentle wind.

"I wish the morning would come," our hero soliloquized, "this inky darkness gives one such peculiar sensations when anything occurs that seems out of the natural order of things."

The wind now began to freshen, and the boat, which had hitherto been nearly immovable, began to drift, as Jack conjectured, towards the distant sound.

"Anything is better than this suspense," muttered our hero, as he shipped the oars; "I will hail towards the noise, and set the matter clear."

Forced by the wind, and propelled by the skilful young oarsman, the boat skimmed swiftly onward.

Between each jerk of the oars the boy listened intently, but without hearing the mystifying sound repeated.

Suddenly pausing in his labour, he unshipped the oars.

"This," he thought, "will never do. I shall possibly get between the vessels that are engaged, and receive a shot that will send us to the bottom."

There was sufficient wisdom in this proceeding to emanate from an older head; and Jack, when he had arrived at this conclusion, resumed his seat beneath the awning, his mind fully occupied by the strangeness of the nocturnal disturbance.

He had fallen into a half-conscious state just before daybreak. The soothing ripple of the water had lulled him; in spite of every effort he closed his eyes, and, though the mind was in this semi-conscious state, the nervous faculties were alive to the slightest sound.

With an exclamation falling from his lips sufficiently loud to awaken old Tom, Crusoe sprang to his feet, and listened to a terrible roar which came from a point not, apparently, many fathoms from the boat.

The uninitiated might have supposed that the sound came from a contending fleet of vessels, but our hero and his companion knew too well the perils of the dangerous deep to be thus misled. Simultaneously the words came from their lips which explained the mystery—

"Breakers ahead!"

Neither were thrown off their guard by the proximity of this unlooked-for danger, but with one thought each seized an oar, and began to turn the bow of their little craft away from the frightful thunder of the heavy surf.

They felt that their escape from certain death had been miraculous, and as they bent to their oars and increased the distance between the boat and the terrible roar, a mute prayer of thankfulness came from their hearts to Him who had once more saved them from death.

"Didn't think he was so near us," old Tom said. "That's the first time, lad, I ever mistook breakers for guns."

"I was deceived the same way," Crusoe said; "but the roar of these is much louder than usual. Is it not so, Tom?"

"Well, yes, lad. When the sea breaks upon a flat shore there is not so great a noise."

"Where are these breakers?"

"A coral reef, lad, to a certainty; just such a sound as roared around us the night you were left ashore."

"You think this is the same island?"

"I think so; but these places are so much alike, that I wouldn't like to say for certain; however, when daylight comes we shall see."

Keeping within earshot of the heavy surf, the castaways anxiously looked for the first gray streak of dawn.

Should this turn out to be the isle where the Seagull's hull had found a resting-place, their wanderings would for a time come to a close.

They hoped that among the stores of the doomed vessel there would be found everything necessary to prepare for a long journey over the mighty wilderness of South and Central America.

It was possible with the stores thus found to make for a nearer post, where a vessel would take them to England; but neither Crusoe nor his companion had any ties to bind them to their native land.

Happy with each other, and both fond of the wild,

perilous existence, only to be found in the primitive forests of the New World, they had fully determined to gratify this passion to satiety.

This was the primary cause of setting off to seek the old vessel, and as far as they had yet advanced the venture seemed successful.

While keeping in good offings, and far enough from the rolling surge to ensure their safety, the mind of each was busy with the thoughts natural upon such an occasion.

Would they find the hull as old Tom had left it, high and dry upon the sunken reef, or had a terrible storm swept over the island and broken the stout hull into fragments?

These and other self-put questions were asked and pondered over again and again, but without either arriving at a satisfactory conclusion.

They hailed the first beam of morning with a glad shout, and as the murky vapour began to rise from the waters, the boat was again turned towards the roaring surf which had so nigh destroyed them on the previous night.

What a sight met their curious gaze when the hull became clearly visible under the light effulgence of the rising sun!

A sight, though it brought at first keen feelings of disappointment to their minds, each confessed was the most beautiful the eye could behold.

One glance told old Tom it was not the island he sought, and but for our hero's wish to explore the grand, yet tranquil spot, he would have put the boat about and ventured further in search of the object of his mission.

Within a quarter of a mile from the prow of their little craft, the sea was beaten into a long line of white, troubled foam.

As the eye became accustomed to the seething line of water, the adventurers beheld a white reef of coral, over which the dark blue waves sported, as though in mockery at the wish of those who gazed upon the sight to pass the beautiful but deadly barrier which stood between them and the island.

"No use that way, boy," old Tom said, shaking his head gravely; "a whaler wouldn't live two minutes in such a surge."

Crusoe's imagination was fired by the sight he beheld, and had the danger been ten times greater, he would have risked it to have explored the lovely isle.

"Let us pull round the other side," he said: "we shall, perhaps, find a channel wide enough to admit our craft."

Old Tom acquiesced, and the boat was soon skirting the dangerous coral reef, the voyagers calmly looking out for a break in the line of pearly foam.

It was worth the trouble and risk necessary to effect a landing, and to minds so constituted as our adventurers', the danger only added a zest to the enterprise.

Beyond the line of sparkling foam a sheet of clear water was visible, so little disturbed by the boiling surge that an inland lake alone could have vied with its glassy surface.

The sight of this was more than sufficient to call

GALLANT RESCUE OF THE ISLAND MAIDEN

forth the energy of so tried a seaman as old Tom Starboard.

"Look, lad," he said, suddenly; "we will have the little bark afloat in that quiet water, if we have to leap over those breakers."

They had rowed round the extent of the isle before noon, but still the same formidable white line stood between them and the tantalizing sheet of water which so peacefully bound the verdure-clad shore.

While thus engaged they had ample time to study the general outlines of this oasis in the desert of nature.

They saw the verdure-clad shore, and, rising in a gradual yet sharp pyramidal form, a tier of lordly hills, each crowned with vast numbers of the fairy-like fan palm, their graceful stems tapering upward in every fantastic yet beautiful form.

Resting for a moment upon their oars at another point which showed the opening between the vast hills, they saw a dense forest, with its giant vegetation rising hill above hill in a manner that added to its solemn aspect of impenetrable mystery and rugged grandeur.

The magnificence of the high mountain peaks, which seemed to blend with the heavy sky, added to this scene of beauty, and called forth an enthusiasm from the younger adventurer which peril or difficulty could not subdue.

Coasting upon another part of the romantic isle, and still looking eagerly for a break in the interminable line of foam, the sea breeze blowing from the opposite side brought with it such a fragrant odour of sweet-smelling flowers, that proved the desired spot was fraught with the gentle beauties of the flori-

7

cultural world as well as the wild and mighty trees of forest vegetation.

The sun reached its meridian, and the adventurers, baffled but not dispirited, were compelled from fatigue to give up the seemingly hopeless task.

"I'll tell you what it is, lad," the old seaman said; "there is but one chance of ever taking the little bark beyond those reefs."

"What is that, Tom?"

"We must wait, lad, and see if the tide goes down, and shows us a path big enough for the boat to pass through; but even then it will be dangerous, for the sea never gets calm upon such a reef as that."

"When do you think the tide will change, Tom?"

"Not afore sundown, lad; so we've plenty of time to try the passage. Let's pipe to dinner."

"Sundown," our hero repeated, and cast a regretful look towards the island; "that is a long time to wait."

"Not long, lad; and, in case there should be any red or black skins on the place, we will go on with the Injins' language."

Jack gave another look at the placid sheet of water between the surf and the shore, and hugging himself with the hope that the receding tide would enable them to reach land, went aft and assisted to prepare their meal.

Now that the excitement had partly died away, both felt the effects of not taking food since the preceding evening; so with appetites sharpened by the unceasing labour, they fell upon the dried shark's flesh with a vigour that looked like a fit of indigestion hereafter.

Having to wait as patiently as they could under the tantalizing circumstances, they passed the time by again taking a survey of the exterior of the lovely isle.

Old Tom put down its circumference at twenty miles at the very least; his companion, to whom the place seemed of vast size, guessed nearly twice that distance.

From this external examination they were suddenly aroused by an unexpected sight, and both, with one accord, grasped their ever ready rifles.

A number of pit-pans—boats hewn out of a solid piece of timber—were seen approaching the western side of the island.

They were six in number, and each held as near as could be seen about ten men.

One glance was sufficient to show that the travellers were savages, and as a matter of precaution the rifles were relinquished and the oars resorted to.

"We'll pull a little round to leeward, Jack," the old seaman said, "in case they've not seen us."

Barely had the blades dipped beneath the surface when a sudden shout from the savages, followed by a simultaneous movement of their paddles, showed that they were seen and pursued.

"Pull steady, lad," old Tom said; "if the worst comes, we can but make a stand, and if our rifles don't put some of them out of mess my name's not Tom Starboard, that's all."

CHAPTER XXI.
CRAFT AGAINST CRAFT.

THE adventurers soon found that in point of speed the pit-pans had much the advantage, and although both were well practised at the oar, they soon dis-covered that all attempts at distancing their pursuers were out of the question.

Seeing this, old Tom, like a careful general, looked towards the island to discover an opening between the ridge of white coral.

"Once through that, lad," he said, "we can draw our boat across the passage, and make leaden bullets stop the chase."

The idea was good, and under the circumstances, nothing better could be done.

The boat was turned towards the coral reef, and, to the adventurers' joy, they found the tide had considerably lowered, and in many places the hitherto invisible barrier was clearly visible above the white flakes of foam.

Old Tom stood up for a moment to take the bearings of the dangerous reefs, and to Jack's great relief, he said—

"There is an entrance, lad; it winds in and out very much, and at the widest point we shall have scarcely room enough to use our oars."

He was about to resume his seat, when a whizzing noise, followed by several splashes in the water, caused him to look towards his pursuers.

The leading pit-pan had considerably gained upon them—so close that the naked figures of three savages were plainly visible fitting arrows to their bows.

The noise that had attracted old Tom's attention was caused by their first attempt to pierce him as he stood upright in the boat.

"Give me your oar, Jack," he said, calmly. "You go aft, lad, and see what sort of a mark you can make of the leading pit-pan."

Taking both rifles, Crusoe stood in the stern, watching every movement on their pursuers' part.

The savages had reseated themselves when old Tom's body presented no further mark for their arrows, and were now busily plying their paddles.

Old Tom was straining every nerve to reach the dangerous opening in the reef, and the boat seemed to fly through the water.

It was of no avail. The light pit-pans came in a straggling line in their track, and as the old sailor turned his head and scanned the distance between his boat and the coral reef, he saw that, despite his efforts, they must be overtaken.

"Lookee, lad," he said, "we don't want to kill any of 'em, but if you don't stop the leading canoe, we shall have to make a stand-up fight afore we reach the reef."

The round blades of the Indians' paddles presented a glistening disc beneath the sun's rays, and to the young castaway's unerring aim a fair object for his skill.

"Yes," said old Tom, when he mentioned the paddles, "knock a score of them out, and we may, perhaps, get inside the reef afore the rest come hand-over-hand upon us."

Every nerve strung to its highest tension by the imminent peril that awaited them should the Indians overhaul their light craft, Jack brought the butt of his rifle to his shoulder.

The trees, the very rocks themselves, were no firmer than the boy's arms as he held his rifle and glanced along the barrel.

He chose a moment when the boat rose to the crest of a wave (for they were now in the surf), and fired.

The success of his shot was proclaimed by a yell from the Indians, and as the boy looked eagerly towards the pit-pans, he saw that two out of four paddles were gone.

Old Tom testified his delight by a deep-toned British hurrah, and despite the precious value of every moment that passed before the reef could be reached, he threw his oars up and said, gleefully—

"Try it again, lad—try it again. See—the varmints have stopped, and the others are gathering round."

The words were jerked out as Tom's body swayed to and fro with the exertion of rowing.

From what our hero could understand of their previous movements, it was evident the sudden loss of the paddles had for a time confounded the Indians.

He could see the pit-pans clustered together, and one form was plainly visible handing the paddle which had been shattered by Jack's bullet from one to the other.

"That's puzzled 'em, Jack," chuckled the old seaman, as he bent completely double. "Ha, ha, ha! they won't get over it for a—— By the Lord, here they come like so many vultures."

His self-congratulatory speech was cut short by seeing the pit-pans suddenly spread out and urged forward with all the speed strong arms could accomplish.

Not more than six times the length of the boat existed between the adventurers and the glassy sheet of water—their promised haven of rest and safety.

The pit-pans were a quarter of a mile away, so well had old Tom urged the boat onward while the savages were examining the mutilated paddles.

Although every moment decreased the distance between the pursuers and the pursued, the latter knew that unless their boat became fixed upon the coral reef, they could not be overtaken.

Already they were being tossed about by the seething foam which whirled and eddied around them, at times lifting the frail craft almost perpendicular, as the surge, forced forward by the mighty heave of the ocean, rushed tempestuously over the reefs.

Both knew the crisis was at hand—one more move and their boat would be shivered in a thousand pieces or floating in safety upon the calm sheet of water that intervened between the surf and the shore.

Our hero stood amidships, one hand grasping the mast to steady himself, and his eyes watching for the opening in the reef.

The surface of the water was one white mass of foam, and as the waves broke inward and the froth rushed over the blue bosom of the tranquil lake, it was at times difficult to detect the pathway between the sharp points of coral.

"Keep a sharp look out, lad," the old seaman said, as he caused the stout oaken shafts to give in his strong grasp, "and tell me when she goes wrong."

Once, when the breaking of a giant wave left the particles of the sunken rock perfectly visible, our hero caught sight of the narrow winding passage.

That momentary glance was sufficient, and keeping his keen gaze fixed upon the spot, he guided the old mariner with word and gesture.

He felt everything now depended upon his skill, and forgetting for the time the group of savages who were hurrying on to destroy them, he thought only of the task before him.

"So, so!" he said. "Gently, Tom, with your larboard oar—now pull! Quick; steady—again larboard; now give way—with a will. Huzza, huzza! We are safe!"

The roar of the boiling surf, the blinding showers of spray, the tossing of the boat—all passed away, as they shot through the opening and left the deadly entrance on their lee. It seemed scarcely possible that there could be such a vast difference in the time and space that had intervened.

The tranquil beauty of the scene was, if anything, enhanced by the roar of the breakers from which they had just emerged, and as the old seaman paused to recover from the long and arduous pull he had undergone, he looked towards the verdure-clad hills, and exclaimed—

"Beautiful, beautiful!"

They had little time to admire the surrounding loveliness. The angry yell rising even above the noise of the breaking waters told how near the foe had come.

"We will try the shore, lad," said old Tom. "There is a mangrove growing there; if we can once get under its shade, we can fight a hundred of those naked devils. Collect the ammunition, and be ready to spring ashore. There is nothing else left."

The pit-pans were now in the midst of the roaring surf, and the castaways, as they looked back at the white froth from which they had so recently escaped, beheld one of the boats turned upon the sharp-pointed coral.

There came a yell of despair from the dusky crew. The next moment there could be seen a compound medley of broken timber and human forms, as the angry wave bore them upward, then dashed them upon the sharp particles of the hard coral.

"One gone," said old Tom; "see, lad, it has beaten them back. No; one has passed. How far are we from the tree?"

"Three boats' lengths."

"God help us! if they—but they will. Fire, lad, fire! Disable one at least, and we are safe."

The sharp report of the rifle rang out, and was followed by a scream of pain from the Indian boat. One had fallen by the well-sped bullet. There was one paddle lost, but as the death-cry rang out a second pit-pan dashed through the surf, and came with the speed of light after the daring fugitives.

Old Tom answered their wild yell with a cheer of defiance, and as the cry left his lips the boat's keel struck the soft muddy bank.

"The mangrove!" he said; "this way, Jack."

They shared the ammunition between them, and, followed by the young lion, dashed beneath the shelter of the famous tree which old Tom had struggled so hard to reach.

Though our hero lived to become an actor in many a scene of peril, he never forgot the feelings that swept through his heart when he followed his companion through the thickly clustered trunks of the mangrove trees.

It was not fear, although his brave heart failed him

in that dreadful moment—it would but have been human. It was not akin to this feeling. Better had it been so; the suffering would have been less acute while it lasted.

The boy's blood ran like liquid fire through his veins, his temples throbbed, and a pale light shone in his fixed and unnatural-looking eyes, and with this strangely altered state of feeling there came over him a tigerish wish to behold human blood.

He wanted to revel in the life-stream from the bodies of his foes, and like an angry lion he would have turned and grappled with them had not his companion dragged him to a place of shelter.

The mental excitement he had undergone since the previous night had been sufficient to cause this strange state of feeling, and by the time they had sheltered their bodies behind the trunks of two large trees, the wild excitement passed away, and he became the cool, daring boy who had stood undismayed in the centre of a den of wild beasts.

By the time they had taken up their position the pit-pans had run aground, and the crews, like so many demons, sprang ashore, and with a swift pace came towards the fugitives.

Tom Starboard was too well versed in the crafty Indian mode of warfare to take the least notice of this demonstration.

He knew full well that it was but a feint to get them to expose their bodies, to become mere targets for the arrow and equally deadly javelin. With both these weapons they saw the Indians were armed.

There were not more than two yards between the adventurers, and they were able to converse freely without being overheard by the subtle foe.

Crusoe brought his rifle up when he beheld the Indians running towards the trees, and would have fired had not old Tom restrained him.

"Steady, lad," he whispered, "they will not come among the trees unless we move out and show ourselves. Down on one knee, lad, and be ready to let drive when I give the word."

The boy dropped on one knee, the barrel of his good rifle brought forward ready for instant use. Old Tom did the same, and both remained silent, invisible, and watchful, ready at any moment to cut short the lives of two of their foes.

The wisdom of this manœuvre was soon shown, for the Indians, when they had approached to the skirts of the forest, came to a sudden halt; then quickly raising their bows, sent a flight of arrows whizzing past the very trees where our friends crouched.

"I thought so, the varmints," muttered old Tom, as he ran his eye along the barrel of his rifle. "They want us to break cover."

Finding this did not dislodge the fugitives, the Indians spread themselves out and began to advance slowly and cautiously inside the thickly wooded forest.

The plan they had adopted promised to bring success, for while the right and left flanks advanced, the centre remained stationary until the extended line formed the third of a circle.

With the cunning of their race the warlike savages thought to drive the adventurers from their place of concealment, then by a quick movement the right and left flanks would join, and the fugitives would be hemmed in on all sides and entirely overcome.

Had this manœuvre taken place in the open ground, our friends would have had no difficulty in picking off the nearest of their foes as they advanced.

But in the thick forest, where the trees stood so closely together that in many parts there was scarcely room enough for even a warrior's naked form to pass, the matter wore a grave aspect.

To have fired would have been madness; they might have brought down two of their foes, but the smoke of their rifles would have betrayed them, and before they could have reloaded a score of swarthy savages would have pounced upon them.

Old Tom watched them with his keen gray eyes twinkling with an angry fire, and when he beheld the flanks begin to converge towards each other, he said in a still voice to his young companion—

"Lay yourself flat on your stomach, my lad, and creep to the next clump of trees—there, just beyond where those macaws are flying."

Without disturbing the thickly-grown underwood, the young wanderer crept with a serpent-like motion towards the spot indicated.

He kept the trunk of the tree he had just quitted between his body and the enemy, and in this manner reached a shelter some thirty yards farther away.

Old Tom closely followed, and the young lion, as though disdaining to crouch from a foe, walked boldly after his master.

The trio reached their new position without being observed, although at times the old seaman felt certain that Hector would betray them.

There is no doubt but that he was seen, but possibly the Indians felt more interest in hunting the pale faces than the young forest monarch, or they would have launched a javelin or two at him.

They had been but a few minutes in their retreat when the leading files of the foemen closed, and by this movement they passed through the very trees which had first sheltered the castaways.

Not a living thing could have escaped them in that circle, and old Tom chuckled when he beheld them look upward at the branches of the trees, as though expecting to find their prey among the stout limbs of the mangrove.

They were evidently at fault, and after a few words from one who seemed to be their chief, they spread themselves out, and began to repeat this manœuvre.

There could not be a better plan than this for searching the forest, for by continually repeating this movement they must pass through every part of the thickly wooded ground.

As they again advanced, the castaways again glided forward, and a second time the Indians closed without seeing their prey.

They were now upon the verge of the forest, and old Tom began to grow anxious as to the result of the next move.

There was a tall batch of high canes some thirty yards beyond the trees, and behind this a heap of fallen rock, but before they could possibly reach the cane-brake, there was an open space which must be passed.

Old Tom was not long in making up his mind.

The Indians were again standing in a circle, and he knew the next move would bring them clear of the trees.

"We must make a run for it, Jack," he said. "The varmints will close around this spot next time, and unless we are out of sight I would not give a purser's dip for our lives."

A sudden shout from their foes caused the adventurers to peer out, and they beheld their pursuers gathered round the trees which had last given them shelter.

The savages had found their trail. A few bushy-spreading plants had been pressed down by old Tom, and like so many bloodhounds they turned, and began to follow the tell-tale marks.

"It's all up, lad," said Old Tom; "they have found our trail, and will be ahead of us directly."

Crusoe shook the powder in the pan of his rifle and asked—

"What is to be done, Tom?"

"Nothing lad, but to make a running fight of it. We must fire as we go from tree to tree, and when we clear the forest make a dash for the rocks. Be careful, lad, never to fire until I am loaded, and I will do the same with you."

Crusoe understood the advantage of this, and at a single word from old Tom he sprang to his feet.

Two of the Indians who were in advance gave a shout, and like a pack of wolves the whole number dashed forward.

Showing no more of their bodies than was absolutely necessary to use their rifles, the brave boy fired at the advancing crowd.

The sharp crack of the piece resounded in a thousand echoes, and one of the red-skins sprang upwards and then fell flat upon his face; the bullet had gone through his heart.

The whole party came to a standstill when they reached the body of their fallen companion, and one, stooping over the prostrate form, turned it over, and sought for the weapon that had so swiftly sent the dusky spirit to the happy hunting grounds.

Taking advantage of this, the castaways dashed from the trees, passed the cane-brake, and with a glad cry scrambled over a huge piece of granite.

Never had Nature formed a better means of defence than this piece of stone; it was about ten feet high, with a jagged top, which had broken away from a towering mountain, half stone, half earth, and between the base of the mountains and the fallen fragment a distance of nearly two feet intervened.

The fugitives saw at a glance the advantages this place possessed, and standing behind this natural breastwork, they rested their deadly weapons upon the ready-made embrasures, and awaited the Indians, approach.

Though for a moment struck with dread at the strange death that had befallen their companion, the momentary feeling of fear passed away, and burning to avenge his fate, they gave a loud cry and bounded after the pale-faces.

A puff of smoke from old Tom's rifle, and a second Indian falling to the earth with a bullet in his thigh, somewhat checked the ardour of their advance. Though evidently unacquainted with the use of firearms

they seemed to know that a sudden onset would be the surest way of silencing the murderous weapons.

Drawn up two deep they stood before the piece of rock, and at a single word from their chief an arrow sped from each bow, and was buried in the base of the hill behind our adventurers' backs.

Crusoe, like his companion, had lowered his head when he beheld the Indians placing the shafts in their bows, and when he saw them quivering in the earth, he would have returned the discharge by a shot from his rifle.

"Hold your fire!" said Tom, energetically; "they will try and take us by boarding. Call the lion up, he can help. Be ready. Here they come!"

With long springing jumps rather than running, the Indians dashed towards the little fortress.

Six of the band dashed up the face of the rock, and would have sprung down upon the adventurers, had not the terrible crack from both rifles hurled two backwards, bleeding and senseless.

The remainder paused—it was but momentarily, for, urged on by the crowd below, they were compelled to advance.

Old Tom had by this time clubbed his rifle, and sweeping it round his head, he dislodged another pursuer.

Crusoe had placed his rifle on the ground and drawn his sword, and soon the bright blade was crimsoned by a red stain which proved that another of the enemy has been disabled.

Three of the attacking force were at the foot of the rock, and so swiftly had all this passed that those in rear were ignorant of what had happened until they came, breathless and panting, to the fallen rock.

Dismayed, but not conquered, the Indians would have hurled themselves upon the sturdy pair, and in the end must have triumphed.

But ere they could put this project into execution, the young lion, with a swift bound, sprang from beside Crusoe and dashed among the foe.

The mere weight of the animal's body bore two to the earth, and the remainder, though unappalled by the subtle power of the weapons used against them, were so terrified by this unexpected attack that they turned and fled towards the forest.

There they halted, and clustering again together, appeared to be holding a new council of war.

"Tom," exclaimed Crusoe Jack, as the young lion, with the docility of a Newfoundland rejoined them, "I think I have found out a new way of striking terror into the hearts of our foes—here are two of their largest javelins, I will make one of them a messenger of destruction. See!"

Drawing the slender, barbed weapons from the soft earth, he tried them one after the other in the muzzle of his rifle, and uttered an exclamation of delight when he saw that they fitted the opening.

"What are you projecting now?" asked Tom.

"This," Jack said, unravelling into threads a piece of his under garment, and binding this with the pith of a dry sapling round the javelin point.

Then he poured some powder into the pan of his rifle, and giving a glance at the still dismayed savages, he bade Tom hold the barbed point to the lock and pulled the trigger.

The dried pith and cotton immediately ignited, and Jack carefully rammed home a charge of powder, and again primed his rifle.

Then he carefully forced the stem of the javelin down the barrel, and blowing the burning head into a blaze, took steady aim and fired.

The blazing missile shot above the heads of the savages, and fell into the thickest of the wood behind them.

"We'll wait and see the effect of that," observed Crusoe Jack, "meanwhile, Tom, assist me to manufacture one or two more."

They had not long to wait. The ignited coil falling amongst the dry leaves and brushwood set the whole mass alight, and the savages uttered yells of terror as they beheld that part of the forest where they had taken refuge instantaneously on fire.

Tom clapped his hands in delight at the success of Jack's novel means of terrifying their assailants, and Crusoe Jack, who had again rammed home a javelin, took aim at the foremost of the distant Indians and fired.

The blazing weapon struck the savage full in the chest, and flinging his arms up in the air, he gave vent to a wild cry of agony, and fell backwards in the throes of death.

This second unexpected shot seemed to put a finishing stroke to the islanders' fears, and leaving their companion where he fell, they fled howling from the burning thicket.

The rifles were again carefully loaded, and leaving the fallen forms to be tended by their companions, the castaways left the spot and began to ascend the mountains.

CHAPTER XXII.

LELA, THE INDIAN MAIDEN.

FROM the pinnacle of the high mountain the castaways had a clear view of the island and the distant sea.

Our hero's eyes were fixed upon the yellow streak which divided the dark waters from the emerald tints of the luxuriant vegetation.

He saw the nude, dark forms of the angry Indians gathered round the boat which had brought them in safety through the perils of the deep, and as he clutched his companion's arm he gave vent to a few words which explained the painful feeling so visible upon his handsome face.

"They are destroying our boat, Tom!"

The boy's words were too true; the red-skins were breaking up the brave little craft and casting the scattered timbers far into the sea.

Old Tom Starboard saw the magnitude of this misfortune, and as he leant upon the muzzle of his trusty rifle, he gave expression to the gloomy forebodings that filled his mind.

"There is nothing," he said, "that could have befallen us equal in danger or more likely to shorten our days than the loss of this boat."

"It is a terrible misfortune," Jack said—"a terrible misfortune indeed."

"Ay, lad, it is. The red devils have not done this without a motive. If my suspicions are correct we have

a hard struggle before us; then," he added, sorrowfully, "when our ammunition is gone we shall be—— But there, boy, I will not tell you all my foolish old head wou'd suggest. They say the darkest hours come before daylight. I hope it may be so with us, for this is a dark hour indeed."

Crusoe made no reply; he was fully alive to the truth of old Tom's words, and though his heart fell at being thus cut off in the career of wild adventure he had marked out for himself, he felt that the same power which had protected him through so many deadly scenes of peril would not desert them in this hour of need.

"I should not have cared so much," old Tom said, breaking in upon our hero's thoughts, "had this taken place at the island where the old bark rides high and dry on the broken rocks; but here, without the means of ever reaching the place where everything we need is to be had in abundance, it seems like the beginning of a mis—— What is it, lad?"

He broke off suddenly, and with this interrogative turned to our hero."

The boy had brought his rifle to his hip, and as old Tom turned he drew the hammer back to full cock.

"There is some new movement about to take place," he said. "I have been watching the Indians ever since they destroyed our boat, and from time to time I have seen them turn their faces this way. Now, look! there is one of their number coming up the hill-side."

Old Tom followed the direction of his youthful companion's finger, and beheld one of the red-skins coming towards them. He saw the man was unarmed, and by the green bough which he held above his head, knew that his errand was of a peaceful nature.

"Ground arms, lad," he said; "yon green bough he carries means the same as our flag of truce."

By the brilliant head-dress worn by the stately Indian, old Tom knew that a chief of the tribe had brought the green offering of peace.

Long intercourse with the aborigines of South and Central America had made old Tom conversant with their habits, and a secret joy sprang up in his breast when he beheld the rank of the herald.

"They don't mean fighting again, boy," he remarked, as he stepped forward to meet the Indian prince; "if they did, one of the young men would have come, not a chief."

The Indian paused when the old sailor stepped out to the brow of the hill, and laying the green branch upon the ground, he bared his plumed head, and stood like a magnificent statue.

Old Tom had time to note the peculiar tattooing upon the chief's breast, and turning his head towards Crusoe, he said—

"He belongs to a tribe which were once kind to me, so be of good cheer, boy; I know their lingo, and will soon make them friendly to us both."

Jack inclined his head; he was at that moment lost in admiration at the faultless symmetry of the young Indian's splendid figure, and the matchless beauty of his grave features.

Old Tom placed his rifle upon the ground, and advancing to the green bough, touched it with his hands.

The Indian chief repeated this act, and extending his hand towards the adventurers, said, in the rich figurative language of his people—

"The aged white hunter and the young white brave have spoken with living fire to their red brethren. Is it right?"

"Why," old Tom said, in the same tongue, "do the children of the forest make war upon the solitary white men who sought this shore, not to slay, but to find safety from the great waters?"

The Indian chief's face wore a troubled look as he asked—

"Does my brother speak the truth? He is a mighty hunter by the skins he wears, and his hair is white with age. I cannot think he would lie."

"He does not lie," said old Tom, quickly; "he speaks the truth."

"Yet," the Indian said, "when we saw the white men's canoe, and followed it to greet our white brother as one hunter should greet another, there came the living lightning and killed one of our braves."

"Go back to your people," old Tom said, as he at once understood that the affray had begun through a mistake on both sides, "and say that the white hunter is sorry. Tell them we feared the red men, and used the mighty weapon which speaks like the distant thunder and slays like the lightning's shaft. Go, tell them that we would be at peace. Say to your chief, the great Aynoth, that the white man who slept in his wigwam in the forest of Cayane, would live on this island. Say this to him, and let him depart with his people."

The young chieftain's face betrayed the surprise and joy he felt at old Tom's words, and rushing forward, he took the old sailor by the hand.

"The son of Aynoth was saved from a puma's fangs by a solitary white hunter who came in a winged canoe. Say, how was the son of Aynoth saved?"

"The old chief," said Tom Starboard, "and his braves were upon the war-trail, and Red Plume, the son of Aynoth, was left with the women. He strayed to the forest, hand in hand with Lela, the White Rose, and met a puma prowling among the trees. The boy had left his spear in his father's hut, and would have died had not the white hunter slain the puma."

"I am Red Plume," said the young chief, joyfully. "The white hunter speaks the truth, and the boy is glad."

He wrung old Tom's hand with a fervour that told how deeply he rejoiced at thus strangely meeting the man who had saved his life.

Old Tom returned the pressure of the Indian's hand, and asked—

"What of Lela, the White Rose? Does she dwell in the wigwam of Red Plume?"

The young chief's eyes blazed with anger, and striking his breast, he answered—

"She does not. Red Plume slew her brother, and her heart was turned against him. Listen! she will be punished for this. Even now she is tied to a tree in the forest, that wild beasts may eat the heart that refused to love the son of Aynoth."

Old Tom had known the doomed maiden when she was but a timid, prattling child, and, fearful that his words would be realized, he pointed to the forest beneath, and asked—

"Does my son mean here?"

The youth bowed his head and cast his eyes upon the ground, as he answered—

"It was to place the White Rose in this peril that we sought this island, and when her cries came past upon the wind we left. It was then we met the white hunter and his brave companion."

Old Tom's blood curdled with horror, and as a plan to save the beautiful girl came to his brain, he said—

"When does my son leave this place?"

"I came," said the chief, "to ask the white men to let us bury our braves who have fallen before their weapons—to ask them not to kindle living fire as the braves are put beneath the earth; then we depart. What does our brother say?"

"Bury your braves in peace, and depart." The young chief broke the green bough in two—one piece he gave to old Tom, the other to Jack; then bowing with courteous-like grace, awaited the conclusion of the ceremony.

"Give him a piece of yon bough, lad," said old Tom; "let us get rid of them as soon as possible, or a horrid death will befall one that I knew when she was but a lisping child."

Crusoe looked the surprise he felt at those strange words; not having understood the conversation, he was ignorant of the terrible death that menaced a young and beautiful girl.

He gave the Indian a portion of the branch—a proceeding in which old Tom readily bore a share, and the Indian youth, as he received these tokens of peace, placed them in his belt; then, taking old Tom's hand between his own, he said—

"Red Plume does not forget that to the white hunter he owes a life; he is grateful, and will return when the hearts of his people have forgotten the work of to-day. Until then he will ask the Great Spirit to watch over you, and keep you from the teeth of the Masketees. Farewell!"

He turned as the last words came from his lips, and ran down the hill-side with the speed of an antelope, and old Tom, looking after the lithe, beautiful form, repeated slowly—

"The Masketees."

"What is the meaning of that, Tom?"

"Meaning, lad? Man-eaters, and we are among them."

"Here, on this island?"

"Ay, lad; they are but few, and live in the hollows of the rocks by the sea. I know them too well; but as long as we keep here on the high ground we are safe. Once go, Crusoe, within sight of their holes, and I would not give an inch of old rope yarn for our lives."

"What is that I heard you were saying about a horrid death befalling one whom you knew as a child?"

"Sit here, boy."

Crusoe seated himself beside his companion. The young lion, placing himself at their feet and resting his massive head upon his paws, watched with evident interest the movements of the Indians as they buried their fallen companions in the valley below.

Old Tom told the astonished boy the substance of the conversation between himself and the Indian, and when Jack heard that a young and lovely girl was in such imminent peril, he would have at once started to the forest.

"We must wait," old Tom said. "I am almost maddened by the knowledge of poor Lela's peril, but we must wait until they leave the island."

"But can we——"

"You know not their customs, lad; were they to suspect our enterprise, they would return and cut the poor girl in pieces."

"We can defend her," said Jack. "If we wait until they leave, the poor girl will in all likelihood be torn to pieces."

"We must hope for the best, Jack; thank Heaven the prowling brutes do not come out until after nightfall, and before that time I hope the red-skins will have gone."

"The cool manner of the old seaman somewhat checked the boy's impetuosity; but the task was difficult, and old Tom had need of all his reasoning powers to restrain his young companion from hurrying at once to the rescue of the Indian maiden.

The fiery, chivalrous nature he inherited from his brave but unknown father was perceptible in the restive spirit, which could ill brook old Tom's prudent council.

"The deed is inhuman!" the boy passionately exclaimed. "Is this the boasted chivalry of the redskins, to sacrifice a girl because she cannot return the affection of one who is hateful to her sight?"

"I don't know much about what you call *shivalry*," said old Tom, quietly; "but I know the red-men have some strange customs. Perhaps this is one."

"It is a disgrace to them."

"May be, lad; but all the palaver from a whole fleet of chaplains wouldn't make 'em believe so. But quiet, lad; we shall yet be in time to save her."

Jack set his teeth firmly, and looked towards the dark group that were filling in the burial-place of the fallen braves.

He could distinguish the noble features of the young chief who had visited them, by his brilliant headdress, and as he recalled the young Indian's features to his mind, he turned to old Tom and asked—

"Surely that handsome youth was not a party to this horrible sacrifice?"

"I think not," was the reply; "but you see, Jack, though he is a chief, and son of the ruler of that tribe, he dare not go against anything that his fellows wish. I knew the young fellow long ago, and I know, if he dared, he would take us to the village, and we should be treated as friends. But, you see, he must not do it; it would be against their laws, and perhaps cause his death."

"How cause his death?"

"This way, lad. The tribe would call a council, and bring it in that he had brought disgrace upon them by being friendly with the white men who had killed some of their tribe. What did he say to me as he left? Didn't he tell me that he would come when the hearts of his people were less angry with the white hunters? Doesn't that prove that he can't do anything unless the tribe give their consent?"

"It seems like it, Tom."

"Ay, boy; so don't put the young fellow down in your log as being chief mate in this business. Depend upon it, lad, he would like to save the girl, only he dare not."

"Dare not!" Jack repeated, fiercely. "Were it my love I would do so, even if I had to fight my way through the whole tribe."

"May be you would, Jack; but the young fellow is an Indian, and don't forget his bringing up; it's born in 'em, Jack. There they go—so you will soon be out of your misery, and poor little Lela out of hers, I hope."

The red gleam of the setting sun flashed upon the Indians' paddles, as they propelled their light skiff into the seething waters.

Our hero, despite his anger against the tribe, could not but admire the dexterous manner in which they navigated the breakers.

The pit-pans seemed in danger every moment of being smashed by the dangerous coral reef that girt the lone isle. At times they disappeared beneath the white spray, to appear a moment later upon the crest of a mighty billow.

The adventurers watched them until they had passed the coral reefs, and a long line of dark objects dotting the ocean's smooth surface told that all had passed safely, and were returning to their village to bring back the tidings of the deaths that had befallen the young braves.

Crusoe was thinking of the many huts that would be saddened by their return, and bitterly lamenting the stern necessity which caused them to raise their rifles against a fellow-creature, when old Tom's voice startled him from the painful reverie.

"To the forest, lad," he said; "it will be dark in another hour."

"I am ready," the boy said, grasping his gun. "Shall we go together?"

"I think not," old Tom said. "The poor girl is among those trees, and they cover more ground than we could walk over between this and midnight. So, lookee, lad; you and Hector enter by that clump of palms, I will go round by the brushwood, and we shall meet in the centre. Understand?"

"Perfectly."

"Well, in case we overhaul the girl—that is, whichever sees her first had better signal at once."

"In what manner?"

"That's what I am thinking about. It won't do to throw away a charge of powder; besides," old Tom gave Jack a sidelong glance, "the report of a rifle will not make the birds and beasts at all musical, eh?"

Jack smiled at this allusion to their adventure with the howling monkeys.

"Not at all," he said. "Suppose we imitate the macaw's scream."

"That will do, lad."

They had arrived at the base of the mountain by this time, and as they were parting, each to enter the forest by a different route, old Tom called out—

"Keep a good look-out, lad; there is sure to be plenty of prowlers among the trees, or the red-skins would not have chosen this place for the sacrifice."

" I will. If I am in danger I shall fire."

" Do, lad. Keep well behind a tree if you are attacked."

The last word was uttered as old Tom disappeared among the brushwood; then Jack, with the muzzle of his rifle held forward and the lion following at his heels, went towards the clump of waving palms.

There was a strange sense of loneliness at the young adventurer's heart as he entered the unpeopled spot, and for a moment he paused and listened to the buzzing of the insect world, the monotonous cries of the birds, and the zephyr breeze as it sighed gently among the branches of the tall trees.

He strained every faculty to try and hear the well-known footfall as his brave companion broke through the tangled brushwood. He stood thus for some time, and failing to hear the familiar sound again, went forward upon his mission.

Until the declining day deepened into night he sought the Indian maiden, and when the moon's silver rays streamed through the dense foliage, and he had not found the girl or heard the macaw's querulous note, a dim foreboding of evil stole over his senses.

He sought to shake off this feeling by talking to the docile creature who trotted quietly by his side.

The effort was futile. The presentiment grew stronger upon him that some dread evil was throwing its chilling foreshadowing upon his path.

What could it mean? Was it a harbinger of his death? Again, had harm befallen his companion? These mental queries gave him no clue to the strange sensations which had taken possession of his mind, and the moon's ghostly light added to rather than detracted from the spell.

As the time wore on, and he had wandered over two-thirds of the silent and thickly wooded ground, the boy stood with both hands clasped upon the muzzle of his rifle and gave a shrill cry.

The echoes gave back the macaw's note, but a sound to answer it there came not.

A horrible idea flashed through his brain, and his limbs shivered as though they were stricken with the ague.

" Tom Starboard," he thought, " has fallen a victim to the beasts of prey."

The thought was too horrible to entertain, and throwing his gun in the hollow of his arm he again moved onward.

He had not gone more than a dozen paces when the well-known hungry cry of the prowling tiger came to his ears.

So close was this sound that he turned his head as if expecting to behold the dreaded beast crouching for the deadly spring.

The cry was repeated, and Jack by this time having recovered from his surprise, knew that more than one of the dangerous animals were near.

Before him grew a dwarf palm, and beyond this the moon revealed a clear space walled in by the dense trunks of the mighty *ceiba*.*

---

* The trunk of the *ceiba*, or silk-cotton tree, has been known to measure fifty feet in circumference, and a hundred feet in height.

Our hero drew aside the screen formed by the dwarf palm, and when his eyes fell upon the scene illumined by the quivering moonlight, he reeled backward as though an arrow had passed through his heart.

Fastened to the trunk of a tree he beheld the Indian girl, and within a few feet of her were two full grown jaguars. As they glided nearer and nearer, the peculiar sharp cry and the angry sweep of the tail showed they were about to make the fatal spring, and rend the young and beautiful maiden limb from limb.

Our Crusoe saw that he had arrived too late to save the doomed girl, and as he smote his forehead with his open palm, he cried aloud in his heart-agony.

CHAPTER XXIII.

OUR HERO LOSES HIS FRIEND TOM STARBOARD.

THE young lion was startled by the cry of horror and agony which came from his master's lips, and following the direction of the jaguar's cries, the noble brute dashed through the palm branches.

This prompt act aroused the boy from the sudden spell which had fallen upon his faculties, and with a determination to save the girl he rushed forward, his trusty rifle levelled at the crouching brutes.

A glance of admiration suffused his handsome features when he beheld the Indian girl's half-clad form, and aiming at one of the hungry brutes, he pulled the trigger and shot it dead.

Without waiting to reload he dashed forward to the tree to which the maiden was bound, and regardless of the danger which menaced his life, began to unloosen her cords.

He had barely done this when the tiger, with a low growl, crouched ready to spring, and the boy, turning his head, beheld the brute's fierce eyes and bared tusks.

Quick as thought he clubbed his rifle, and prepared for the onset; but ere the tiger could make the fatal bound which would have terminated our hero's life, the lion sprang between them, and with a sullen growl seized the jaguar by the throat.

The tiger, though borne down by Hector's sudden onset, soon struggled to his feet. A moment after both animals were rolling upon the ground, fiercely contesting for victory.

Crusoe saw his favourite would, even if victorious, receive some injury from the tiger's fangs, and quickly reloading, placed the muzzle of his piece close to the brute's head, and shattered its skull.

The maiden, until the sharp report of Jack's weapon awoke the forest echoes, seemed to have been in a death-like trance. She had remained, although her bonds were severed, in the same position as when Jack first beheld her.

Her well-moulded arms hung lifeless from her shoulders, and her beautiful head drooped upon her breast.

From this posture she was aroused by our hero's rifle, and looking wildly in his face she passed her hand across her brow, and exclaimed wildly—

"Am I, then, in the happy hunting-grounds? I —but no—there lie the brutes that were about to tear me in pieces."

Jack's limited knowledge of the maiden's language kept him in ignorance of her words, but making a close guess at their import, by her startled gestures, he made an attempt to reply.

His words were but few, yet the girl understood he had saved her from a terrible death.

"Safe," Jack said. "Tiger's killed—come on—all safe."

Now, this speech was not worded as it would have been had he been master of the Indian tongue, or had the maiden understood English, but under the circumstances it sufficed, and Lela, her dark depthless eyes filled with grateful tears, took Crusoe's hand in her own, and looked heavenward, then laid her right hand upon his head, and invoked the blessing and good will of the Indian deity for her brave young preserver.

Crusoe responded to the maiden's kindly wishes by pointing to the dead animals, and then to his gun.

She understood his meaning, and in the sweet liquid accents of her native tongue said—

"My white brother is handsome, and poor Lela knows no fear. Come, let us leave the forest. Lela will be happy in the wigwam of the young brave."

Crusoe, thanks to old Tom Starboard, understood a portion of Lela's speech, and by disjointed words and expressive gestures told her that he had no wigwam, no shelter, no food.

The girl's eyes brightened, and as the forest began to echo with the cries of the midnight prowlers, she caught him by the arm.

"Lela," she said, "will cook the young hunter's food, and be his slave."

A dim consciousness came over our hero that the beautiful girl had made a proposal to become his helpmate, and as this flattering offer he felt had been made in grateful return for her preservation, he did not know how to refuse.

Crusoe was not of that class of soft-hearted youths who fall desperately in love with every pretty face and form they meet. To him the roar of the breakers, or the sullen growl of the forest denizens, had more music than the dulcet voices of the most beautiful maidens.

In the wild life he so fondly loved, he found more joy in the beautiful face of nature than he would in the features of the handsome Indian girl. Thus, when he began to calmly contemplate the probable result of his meeting with the White Rose, he was ungallant enough to wish she had not been so prompt in making her offer.

Other commonplace heroes would have gone in raptures at the good fortune thus unexpectedly thrust upon them. Crusoe did quite the reverse.

He had saved the girl because his nature was good and brave. He had given no thought of her ultimate disposal, even should her rescue be effected; but now, as they walked side by side, Crusoe began most ardently to wish for old Tom's appearance.

"The Indian wives," Jack thought, and the idea was not pleasant, "cook their food, chop wood, and attend to the drudgery of the fields, while their lords and masters bask in the sunshine or hunt in the forest. It may be very nice, but I don't want a wife; if I did, there is only one I should like, and that would be the pretty little girl I saved from falling into the sea. I wish old Tom would come; perhaps he wouldn't mind being this pretty Indian's husband."

Master Jack, in spite of his impregnability respecting the White Rose, had not forgotten the beautiful Mabel. Oft in the stillness of the night, when he had been alone on the summit of his eyrie, the lovely Mabel had been the subject of his thoughts. The remembrance formed the basis of the only wish he had to return to England, and though he knew it not, the seeds of a depthless love were implanted in his heart, and it needed but a loving companionship with the peerless English girl to develop the slumbering passion.

"I wish old Tom would come," he mentally repeated as they emerged from the forest; "he must have heard the report of my rifle when I shot the tigers."

The young pair came to a halt in a grove of beautiful palm trees, and Crusoe, as he listened to Lela's efforts to make herself understood, collected materials for a fire.

"This," he thought, as he applied a light to the heap, "will guide old Tom, and until he comes I will pass the time in making a shelter for this poor girl."

A dusky-skinned Indian could not have constructed a temporary hut with more speed than did our hero, and Lela, when she saw him collecting a number of long willow-like branches, began to gather a heap of dried leaves.

The thickest ends of the taper shoots were thrust firmly in the ground, and the tops, laced together with shreds of bark, formed the framework of the roof. Over this palm-leaves were so placed that even a tropical shower would roll off, and leave the interior quite dry.

He was proceeding to form the walls of the same leafy material, but Lela, who had by this time gathered sufficient leaves to cover the floor of the hut several inches in depth, approached with her arms full of long grass.

This she placed on the ground, and with a sweet smile took our hero's hand, and pointed from the little heap she had gathered to the framework of the hut.

"She wants me to use that for the walls," Jack thought, as his eyes followed her expressive gestures, "but I cannot see how that is to be done."

He shook his head, and laughed at her puzzled look when she found that he was ignorant of the mode by which the Indians plait the long grass into a covering of their huts—plait it so deftly that it is impervious to wind and rain.

"Lela," she said, "will teach her white brother. Come!"

She placed the ends of about a dozen blades of the long tough grass in his hand, then, with a rapidity which seemed to him marvellous, plaited them so firmly that he could not, when desired by her, pull them asunder.

Long before the moon had reached its orbit, the framework of the hut was covered by Lela's skilfully woven matting. A door was also formed by the same ingenious method, and to enable it to open and close Jack formed a pair of hinges from a strip of his tiger-skin jacket.

When the dried leaves had been spread, our hero led the lovely Indian girl to the entrance of the hut, and with a graceful courtesy handed her inside.

She looked up in astonishment when Jack closed the door and went towards the fire; then, reclining upon her primitive couch, she burst into tears.

Our hero heard her sobbing, and ran to the hut, and after some difficulty she made him understand the cause of this sudden grief.

"I am your slave," she said, "and when you turn from me the light of your countenance Lela's heart is sad—she thinks she has offended her lord."

Jack felt much tempted to kiss the tears away which trembled upon her long dark eyelashes, but repressing the inclination, he made her understand by disjointed words, half Indian, the other English, that he was not angry, but anxious to hear the footsteps of his friend.

There were visible signs of disappointment upon her sweet olive face when she heard that there was another white hunter upon the island, and when Jack had retired from the door, she threw back the mass of black shining tresses from her brow, and murmured—

"The heart of the handsome white hunter is turned from Lela; yet Lela would sooner die than love the son of Aynoth. She loves the pale-faced youth, and that love is spurned."

The large eyes blazed with anger, and the small hands clutched the leaves and ground them to powder.

Crusoe, who at that moment stood by the flickering pine logs, leaning upon the muzzle of his rifle, little thought that the gentle dove-like orbs of the beautiful maiden could glisten with such fury.

Master Jack had yet to learn that the blood of a hundred princes ran in the Indian maiden's veins, and though, until roused, the vengeful passions of her race were held in check by the natural sweetness of her womanly thought and feeling, yet there was but a frail barrier between all that was bad in the nature of that forest child.

He had yet to learn that it would be safer to rouse a sleeping tiger than repel the devoted love which had filled her heart when he stood by her side beneath the quivering moonbeams.

A touch from his hand, a kind word or look, and she would become his devoted slave, and at his command yield her very life. Coldness, neglect, and insensibility to the deep love in her guileless heart would change those feelings into those of implacable hate, and a keen thirst for his life.

Crusoe thought not of this as he stood painfully listening for the return of his friend, starting at every leaf that fell, and in the rustle of the branches and the sighing wind sought to distinguish the footfall of the friend whom he loved with a son's affection.

The night passed, and when Lela came forth from her hut she saw the handsome boy sitting upon the trunk of a fallen tree, his face covered with his hands, and the lithe, graceful form trembling with silent grief.

The lion lay at his feet, and unused to behold his master in so strange a mood, from time to time licked the clasped hands and brushed away the hot anguished tears that oozed through his fingers.

The girl stood silently regarding the wretched boy, and her eyes filled with sympathetic tears.

CHAPTER XXIV.

HOW THE WRECKER'S WIFE PLOTTED FOR THE WANDERER'S BIRTHRIGHT.

THERE had been many changes in the lives and fortunes of those with whom the reader had but a transient acquaintance in the first part of this work.

Sir James Morland, sick at heart and broken-spirited at the fate which he believed had befallen his son (Crusoe), went back to India, and, ever foremost in the terrible encounters during the Afghan war, sought a Lethe for his heart's sorrow in the wild charge of his dragoons against the mailed hordes of the famous Ackbar Khan.

He sought a hero's grave, but the god of battle brought him safely from every red field of slaughter, and he lived only to repine against his hard fate.

Sir Harold Morland, his younger brother, believed him dead, and since the interview with Madge Collins, related in the second chapter of this story, felt no apprehension of his brother's son ever coming forward to claim the princely estate which he enjoyed.

He had seen Jasper, and his soul revolted at the thought of kindred blood running in their veins. Thus, when he returned to London with the astute lawyer, he again plunged into riot and dissipation, a course of living which brought him to a premature grave.

He died two months after the boat in which our hero was supposed to have perished drifted ashore.

The Morland property thus became without a claimant—Sir James in India and under an assumed name, Sir Harold dead, and Crusoe supposed to have perished.

Madge Collins felt assured that the boy she so bitterly detested was no more, if he had not, as was generally supposed he had, died by the capsizing of the fishing boat. A ship came to England about three months after Crusoe had stepped over the slave ship's bows, and her captain made a statement which caused old Madge to fairly yell with joy.

He brought home a portion of the Seagull's pinnace, and from nothing being heard of the ill-fated vessel, it was apparent she had foundered in the fearful tornado that swept over the lone isle and vast ocean.

"He is dead, curse him!" old Madge would mutter exultantly, as she opened the box wherein the clothes Crusoe had worn when the wrecker brought him to the hut were kept. "Dead—ho! ho!—and the time will soon come when my darling shall be a gentleman."

The time did come, sooner than she expected, and

the only barrier to her plot was removed, as she thought, for ever.

George Meredith, the pretty Mabel's father, as the reader will learn, by referring to chapter xiii., was acquainted with the relationship between Sir James Morland and Crusoe; he knew also that the crook-backed Jasper was Darrel Collins, the wrecker's grandson.

Old Madge feared this gentleman. She felt that he would never permit the development of her well-laid plot; but hugging herself with the hope that he would die, or leave the vicinity of the lone hut by the sea, she applied the money Sir Harold had given her to destroy all traces of Crusoe's identity to the education of Jasper, in order to fit him for the position she determined he should fulfil.

For this purpose the crook-back was sent to a large school at the nearest town, and under the strict discipline of a spectacled pedagogue Jasper began his education.

He had not been long domiciled under the roof of Birchwood Academy, when strange rumours reached the old woman's ears respecting Mr. George Meredith. Rumours which, were soon verified by that gentleman selling his mansion and its contents, to satisfy the shareholders of a bubble company in which he had become a director.

Ruined, and destitute of even a shelter for his lovely child, the once rich man left Mabel to the care of a woman who had long been his housekeeper; then, with the hope of yet winning wealth for his beloved child, he took a passage in a sailing vessel bound to Chili.

In that far-off land he had a brother, reputed one of the wealthiest men in South America.

He left England penniless; all, even his last shilling, was given to the woman who promised to be a mother to the child until his return.

Madge heard of his departure on the same day that a notice appeared in the papers announcing the death of Sir Harold Morland.

The crone could not at first realize that so much good fortune could have befallen her, and after reading the editorial remarks respecting the virtues of the deceased baronet, and the lament that the fine old estate would pass into the hands of a distant branch of the family, she carefully cut out the welcome paragraph, and began to ponder over the first step to be taken in the great work.

Darrel Collins, since Crusoe's supposed death, had become a changed man. If he was moody and morose before, he was tenfold more so since the fishing boat, keel upwards, was found upon the beach.

He seemed at times as though his intellect had become deranged, and when this fit came over him he would, no matter the hour, wander in a dejected manner about the cliffs, muttering strange words, which told of dark deeds done by his hand when the death-light gleamed from the cliff. In one of these moods he went forth one stormy night, and from that hour Madge, to her secret joy, but outward lamentation, had never beheld him again.

He was supposed to have fallen from the precipice into the seething waters, and though the fishermen, forgetting their old animosity against the wrecker, searched every crevice in the rugged rocks, not the slightest trace of the mad "wrecker," as he was called, could be found.

Thus Madge and her precious boy were left unopposed in the execution of their plans, and Jasper, from the continual training he had received from his grandmother, was quite ready to devote the whole of his energies to the work before him.

He was brought from school when old Madge found the field clear, and after they had discussed every plan that seemed likely to prove successful, he threw himself back in his chair, and rubbing his hands gleefully, chuckled—

"There is nothing to stop me. Ho! ho! and to think that, after all, I shall have that hateful Jack's money."

"There is nothing to prevent you, Jasper. Old Meredith is out of the way, and the handsome gentleman dead that came here and gave me money to burn the clothes the young wretch was brought here in. No, there is nothing to prevent it."

"Old Meredith out of the way?" Jasper repeated. "What has become of his little girl? Has she gone?"

"No. Why do you ask?"

The youth showed his discoloured teeth savagely, as he answered—

"Because I should like, when I grow older, to have that girl for my wife."

"Why? Do you love her?"

"Love her? No; but if she were my wife I could beat her—kick her until she became black and blue; then cut off her long curls, and throw them into the fire."

Old Madge gave her hopeful grandson an approving look, as she asked——

"Why would you do this?"

"Why? I will tell you why. You remember when Jack was drowned?"

"I do."

"And the fuss old Meredith made about it. Don't you remember how he called him a noble fellow, and said he had saved his daughter's life?"

"Yes, yes; I know all that; but—"

"Don't be impatient, granny. I met this girl one day—soon after the boat was found. She was standing on the edge of the cliff, crying, and when I spoke to her she turned away, as though I had been a serpent. This is not all. Before I spoke I heard her sobbing, and calling out, 'Poor Jack—poor Crusoe Jack! You are not dead. Come back to Mabel; she loves you so much!' Nice to hear that, eh, granddam?"

The old woman's eyes twinkled, and she nodded her head for the young miscreant to proceed.

"When she turned away I went after her," he resumed. "I told her how glad I felt that Jack had been drowned. You should have seen her. Ho, ho! she turned on me like a little spitfire, and called me a low-born grovelling worm—ho, ho!—and while she was speaking, up came that cousin of hers, Percy Meredith, and no sooner did he see me than he called out—'Low-born hound! Dare you insult my cousin?' And with that he clutched me by the collar, and lashed me with his horsewhip. I feel my

JACK BUILDS HIS HUT.

back smarting now." He ground his teeth savagely. "It has smarted ever since, and will smart until I either have the girl in my hands, or push her cousin from the cliff."

Old Madge's face went white with passion as she listened to this recital, and her fingers twitched convulsively with her apron.

"What," she asked, "did the girl do while you were being beaten, Jasper?"

His face was fiendish in expression as he answered—

'She told him that I was a coward, and to beat me like a dog. He did, curse him!"

"You must," oid Madge said, "have much offended the girl."

"Perhaps I did. I mocked her words when she cried out for Jack to return, and told her how I hated him; and, when she called me names, I caught her wrist and twisted her arm round until she screamed out. It was the scream that brought her cousin Percy to her side."

"You were too spiteful, Jasper; but as she caused you to be beaten like a dog, *you shall marry her when you are old enough.*"

Jasper sprang from his chair, his little bead-like eyes glistening with joy, and his frame quivering with emotion. He knew that the strange old woman would not hold out a hope that could not be realized, and as he clutched the chair-back in his paroxysm of exultant feeling, he now hoarsely asked—

"How. granny?—how is this end to be attained?"

"I will do it," she said, "but my darling must not be impatient. It will take time—a long time—but she shall be yours, when you are the rich heir to the great Morland estate."

"Tell me how you will manage it," he said, eagerly; " it seems so wonderful that I can scarcely believe its truth."

"This is my plan," she said. " Old Meredith has gone abroad, and he has left his daughter with old Hannah Willis, and they live in one of Nicholas Harvey's cottages."

"Yes—yes."

" Old Meredith has paid the rent for six months, and promised to send Hannah some money at the end of this time. Well, he may not be able to do so, and as Nicholas wishes to sell the very cottage they are now in, I will buy it, and let them stay till they are in my debt."

" But suppose old Meredith sends the money, they can pay."

The old woman laughed. It was more like the hiss of a serpent than anything human.

"If he does," she said, "the letter must never reach them."

"I see; go on."

"I will lend them money to buy food when all they have is gone, and get them so in my power that the law will allow me to turn them adrift; and then, when they have neither bed to sleep on nor food to eat, you can make your offer. If she refuses the prison shall be her home—you understand ? "

"I do—I do. But can you do this ? "

"I will try, and I do not see much chance of failing."

"You are a dear old granny. Let me once have the girl, and I will make her wish her tongue was torn out before she—"

A summons at the door stayed his malicious speech, and when old Madge gave permission for the person outside to enter, the latch was lifted, and the ferret-like form of the lawyer who accompanied Sir Harold to the hut passed inside the door.

Old Madge's heart gave a throb when she beheld the visitor—instinct told the motive of his visit.

He entered the hut, and making a profound bow to the old woman, closed the door, and then looked uneasily at Jasper, who sat in the shadow of the room.

CHAPTER XXV.

CRUSOE, LIKE HIS VENERABLE NAMESAKE, FINDS FOOT-PRINTS IN THE SAND.

A LOUD sob from Lela caused the boy to raise his head, and when he beheld the maiden's sorrowful attitude, he arose and went to her side.

It was a long and wearisome task to make the maiden understand the cause of his grief, but when he had succeeded, she made a gesture with her hand to imply that he should search the forest.

A suggestion that Crusoe at once acted upon, and Hector accompanying him, he left the Indian girl.

Before he went upon this fruitless search, the young girl asked him for the long spear, barbed with a shark's tooth. He gave it to her, thinking at the time she required it to defend herself, should any of her foes you linger on the island.

It was a sad walk for our hero as he traversed the silent forest, and though he searched long and eagerly, he failed to discover the least trace of his old friend.

He came upon the old seaman's trail when turning a narrow opening among the great ceibas, and though he was faint and weary from his long search, he followed the foot-marks until he reached the smooth sands upon the farthest side of the island.

Here the trace became lost for some yards, and Crusoe was about to return, the horrible suspicion strong upon him that poor old Tom had been devoured by the beasts of prey.

But as he stood, his heart sick with grief, he saw the young lion, who had gone some distance ahead, suddenly place his nose near the ground and run forward towards the sea.

This peculiar conduct aroused the boy, and as a wild gleam of hope came to his breast, he sprang forward and passed the young lion.

Passing a broad tract of sand covered with seaweed, he came upon a smooth expanse, from which the receding waves had carried away the. *débris,* which had been so plentifully strewn about where it had been cast beyond the reach of the ebb tide.

Here he beheld the well-known footprints, and near them the marks of at least twenty naked feet.

The venerable hero of Fernando Po did not feel more amazed when, going towards his boat, he found a solitary foot-mark in the sand, than our hero did when he saw the impressions mingled with the marks of old Tom's mocassins.

There could be no doubt of the identity of Tom Starboard's trail, he had worn boots formed from two thicknesses of tiger-skin, and the impressions were double the size of the naked feet.

Bewildered by the sight, our hero saw that a struggle had taken place near the water, and pursuing his search further, he beheld the marks of three canoes.

Shading his eyes with his hand, he looked across the sea; but its surface was undimmed by a speck.

How bitterly the truth came to the young wanderer's heart! and for some time he prayed that he too had been taken to share his companion's captivity or death.

There was now no doubt respecting Tom Starboard's fate. Although the first horrible idea had passed away, there yet remained sufficient anxiety to fill Crusoe's breast with the most poignant inquiries.

Old Tom had been carried away by a party of Indians; but for what purpose?

It was this inexplicable mystery that kept the boy's mind on the rack.

Were his captors of the tribe that visited the island the day previous, there was a faint hope that the friendship of the young chief would be of service to his old friend.

The boy's mind was disturbed by the strange circumstance, and the more he pondered over the matter, the greater the mystery became, and the weight of sorrow was heavier at his breast.

He could not, no matter how he sought to solve the mystery, arrive at any solution that prom any safety for his friend. There was but one conclusion, and that was, he had lost his only friend, and for ever.

As this knowledge gained strength upon his mind, the young castaway bowed in anguish before the terrible calamity, and throwing himself upon the sand, covered his eyes that the glorious light of day should not add to the mental torture he endured.

This paroxysm of acute anguish passed away, and he arose outwardly calm, and turning his head from the spot rendered hateful by the loss he had sustained, he began to retrace his steps.

"Henceforth," he thought, "I shall be alone. That kindly voice which cheered our solitary life is gone, and perhaps silent for ever."

The thought convulsed his frame, yet he manfully struggled against the ever-recurring paroxysm of grief.

"Wailing," he thought, "will not return him to me. Though the blow is hard to bear, I must bring my mind to brook this affliction with more calmness. Yes; henceforth I must pass my days in solitude—solitude, the more irksome now that he is taken from me. But, with Heaven's help, I will yet track his cowardly captors, and though I fall in the attempt, he shall not die unavenged."

This resolution brought the fierce light to his eyes, and a settled determination was visible upon his features.

He knew not how the task was to be accomplished; he was without the means of conveyance from the island, but the heart that quailed not when he stood alone in the wild beasts' den was equal to the task he now assigned himself—to rescue Tom Starboard if living, to avenge him if dead.

His grief was somewhat allayed by this resolve, and as he wandered slowly through the forest, his mind again reviewed the circumstances that attended his friend's loss.

That he had not been carried off by the tribe they had fought yesterday he began to feel convinced, for they had watched the pit-pans break through the hissing foam that girt the isle.

Pondering thus, he saw a portion of a feather head-dress lying at the foot of a tree, and as he started forward to lift it from the ground a cry of amazement came from his lips.

Just visible among the brushwood was the butt of old Tom's rifle, and as the boy raised it from the ground he could scarcely repress a cry of horror.

Around the small of the stock and near the muzzle, the weapon bore the imprint of two blood-stained hands.

Crusoe gazed at these tell-tale marks, his very soul frozen with the dire mystery.

How came that rifle there? Were those marks the impressions of his friend's hands?

No, it could not be so, for the rifle was loaded, and he knew the old seaman too well to suppose that a foe would have taken him by surprise.

Placing his hands over the red stains, he found that the musket was clubbed when it received those marks.

His brain was in a whirl. Had old Tom been overpowered on the spot, the rifle would have been taken by the victors.

He rejected this hypothesis—rejected it because the weapon had been evidently hidden, and in such manner that he recognized the hand of his lost companion.

There was no trace to show that a struggle had taken place here, yet the broken head-dress showed that something unusual had occurred.

The more he thought, the greater the mystery became; greater still when he found the foot-prints of old Tom's mocassins—his alone. He turned, and followed them until he came to the verge of the forest. Here they ceased, and when they again became visible, it was among the marks of a dozen naked feet.

In the midst of his dire perplexity, the recollection of the Indian maiden's presence on the island came upon him. So great had been his grief that he had utterly forgotten the beautiful girl.

"Lela," he thought, "will tell me whether this head-dress belongs to her tribe."

His previous fatigue seemed to pass away under the impulse he received to learn more of the mystery which surrounded the disappearance of Tom Starboard.

When he returned to the hut, he found the young maiden busily engaged cooking the fore-quarters of a young deer.

She smiled sweetly when our hero returned, and ran forward to relieve him of the rifles he carried on his shoulder.

Crusoe, in the loneliness that had so suddenly come upon him, was touched by the girl's graceful act, and as she led him forward to the blazing fire, he felt the frozen barrier which he had placed around his heart gradually thaw.

He saw at once the consolation he would find in the companionship of the lovely girl he had saved from death, and for the first time since their meeting, he gave the Indian maiden a kindly smile.

She noted it, and her dark lustrous eyes beamed with joy, and when Jack held out the broken head-dress she took it from him, and placing it upon the grass, pointed to the smoking meal, and with expressive gestures signified that he must partake of the food before she answered his query.

The boy had not partaken of the slightest nourishment since he came on the island, and the savoury smell of the roast fawn added to an appetite already ravenous by long fasting.

He had expressed his surprise by words and gestures at the sight of the tempting meal, and the girl, after he had for some time been vainly trying to solve the mode in which she obtained the fleet animal, pointed to his spear, which lay upon the ground.

She made him understand that she had crouched behind a tree, and sent the barbed weapon into the young deer as he fled past her place of concealment.

She gave him also to understand that the island abounded with animals that were fit for food, and among the many vegetables that grew in profusion in the woods, there were to be found the prolific bread-tree and groves of cocoa-nuts.

This intelligence was pleasant to hear, and the boy thanked her as well as he was able in the language of her tribe.

Her eyes sparkled with delight at his words, and she told him that upon her would devolve the task of keeping their table supplied with fruit and vegetables, while his would be to hunt in the forest.

Crusoe, even in the short conversation they held over this meal, found a great respite from his sorrow; more so when she began to teach him the language of her people.

Jack was an apt scholar, and before a month passed away he could converse fluently in the Indian tongue, and Lela, who had taken a fancy to learn English, was equally quick at acquiring the language.

It was not until he had somewhat mastered the rudiments of the Indian tongue that he could understand Lela's words when she examined the broken head-dress.

He learnt that the circlet of feathers belonged to a tribe whose hunting-grounds were next to those of her people, and she accounted for their presence on the island at the same time as Red Plume's party, by telling Jack that the two nations were at war, and probably the braves who had carried away old Tom had started from the mainland with the intention of cutting off the party that brought her to the island.

Although she accompanied our hero to the place where the circlet had been found, and keenly examined the forest, she was as much at fault respecting the blood-stains upon old Tom's rifle as our hero.

One thing gave Jack's mind a reprieve from his poignant anguish—that was, he found that the tribe into whose power old Tom had fallen were not cannibals; far from it, they had upon more than one occasion befriended the white traders against the tribe to which she belonged; and the only reason she could assign for their capturing the old sailor was the wonderful weapon he possessed.

But when she found he had left the dreaded weapon among the underwood, she confessed herself at fault, and, like our hero, became quite mystified at the cause which led to the old seaman's disappearance.

As the days wore on and merged into weeks, Crusoe became more reconciled to his lot. The girl's gentle manner won upon him, and he began to find that life was quite endurable with the dusky but beautiful Indian; and but for the indelible impression Mabel Meredith had made upon his heart, he would have loved Lela with the same warmth that she loved him.

In this he had to play a hypocritical part; he had to profess a depth of feeling when the guileless child of nature spoke of the love she felt towards him.

He had not the heart to tell her that he loved her but as a brother would love a sister; it would have grieved her, and Jack could not endure the sight of her lustrous eyes filled with tears.

Lela was happy. She believed his profession of attachment; and when he built a hut from the parts of the boat and the lower branches of the ceiba tree, she cheered his labours with sweetly musical snatches of song.

The hut was soon finished, and the young pair passed a brief season of happiness therein—a dream-like existence that was doomed to be broken by events that both were unprepared for.

Our hero, though he had found the days glide happily past in the society of the gentle Indian girl, had not relinquished the resolve that he had formed to go in search of his old friend.

He had taught Lela to use the rifle, and the maiden had thus been able to bring down such of the timid animals as were necessary for their simple meals.

Thus, when the hut was built, he was able to devote the whole of his days to the project nearest his heart.

It was the labour of weeks to fell the giant tree, and prepare it for being hewn into a form that would make its exterior seaworthy, and the interior sufficiently large to hold himself, Lela, the young lion, and an abundant supply of food.

Slow as the work progressed, he never for one moment flagged in his exertions. It was a labour of love, and the thought of old Tom Starboard being in captivity gave his arm a giant's strength.

Thus the task, which at first seemed hopeless, progressed day by day, and Crusoe began to look forward to the time when he would once more float on the blue waters of the boundless sea.

Alas for the mutableness of men's projects! One brief hour brought the galling truth to our hero, that his long and arduous task had been without the least benefit to himself.

One morn, soon after the sunbeams had gladdened the earth, Lela and the young lion had gone in the forest; for, strange to say, Hector had transferred the greater part of his affection to the gentle maiden, and by her patient teaching had learnt to bring to her feet either bird or animal that fell before her rifle.

Crusoe watched the girl's handsome form until it became lost among the drooping foliage of the graceful fan-like palm.

"I should be thankful," he thought. "Here I have all that would make thousands, who are struggling from day to day for their bread, happy. A beautiful and devoted companion, a fertile and rich kingdom, yet I am not content. No; blissful as the days have been since I became a dweller upon this isle, there has been a drawback to my happiness. Poor Tom! it is your absence and uncertain fate that makes my life one of unceasing anxiety."

The tears came to the boy's eyes as he thought of the kindly friend he had so strangely lost, and, as he threw his axe upon his shoulder and went towards the unfinished boat, his face brightened and he resumed—

"I must not despair. My boat will be ready before another moon has waned, and with Lela for my guide, all my cruel uncertainty will be at rest."

Stripped to the waist, the boy began his labour, and save for the chattering of the birds, nothing was heard in the forest but the blows of his flint axe.

He had been at work nearly an hour, and the rough outline of the frame of his boat was becoming visible.

He stopped to regard the effect of his untiring energy, and to rest his body, which had become stiffened by the stooping posture he had been compelled to assume.

"It begins to look a little ship-shape," he said, in a pleased voice. "A little more off the cut-water, I think, will give her greater speed, besides lessening the labour of rowing."

In stepping backward his eyes involuntarily turned seaward, and in a moment he became as though turned to a statue.

His lips were parted, his breast rose and fell, and his eyes seemed as though they were about to burst from their sockets.

Looking beyond the fading line of the white breakers, he beheld a number of canoes, filled with men.

They were different in construction to any he had seen before, being much longer, broader, and each carrying a large square sail.

In number there could not have been less than thirty, and he calculated the crews at two hundred at the very least.

Crusoe knew enough from what Lela had told him of the bloodthirsty nature of the tribes which dwelt on the mainland, and as he gazed at the formidable flotilla he felt that their visit to the island boded him no good.

At first he hoped they were of the tribe to which Lela belonged, but a second glance at the canoes dissipated this hope.

Aynoth's braves, he remembered, came in pit-pans, while the flotilla which came so near the isle was composed of long, narrow pointed canoes.

"What could be the object of their visit?"

He asked this question over and over again, but his mind could not suggest any satisfactory reply.

Suddenly he snatched his jacket from the ground, then ran swiftly in the direction Lela had taken.

He found the lonely girl in the ceiba grove, gambolling with the young lion.

His abrupt appearance put an end to the gambol, and Lela, as she pushed her playmate aside, ran to her lover, her face expressive of the anxiety she felt.

"Lela," he said, hurriedly, "there are canoes near the island. Come and behold them."

"Canoes!" she repeated, her lips faltering. "The Great Spirit forbid that my people have come."

"It is not your people, Lela."

She clapped her hands joyfully, and said—

"I am happy again. We shall not be parted."

When they reached the rising ground the Indian girl stopped suddenly, and in a voice of terror said—

"Lost—lost! It is the Masketees."

"Masketees, Lela?"

She clutched his arm and looked up wildly into his face, and said—

"Lela speaks. It is the Masketees, and there is no hope."

Crusoe knew too well the significance of her words, and though he had at first felt a chill creep over his frame, the feeling passed away, and snatching the rifle from Lela, he said—

"Fear not, Lela; we can yet baffle them."

"No, no. They have the cunning of the serpent. We must hide away, or die."

"Neither," Jack said, resolutely. "Run for the other rifle. From this position we can sink every canoe that crosses the reef."

"No good," she said, mournfully. "The Masketees can swim faster than the beaver. Listen to Lela, who would die for you, and loves you more for

being thus brave. But what can one warrior, however mighty, do against a tribe?"

Jack lowered the muzzle of his rifle. He knew Lela's counsel promised the greatest safety, and with many a wistful look at the canoes, he took the young maiden's hand, and ran swiftly to the hut.

She would have prevailed on him to hide among the rocks, but our hero ended the matter by securely fastening the heavy door.

"No, Lela," he said. "These logs are proof against arrow or javelin, and as long as we have an ounce of powder we are safe."

The girl's eyes shone brightly, and taking the second rifle from the corner she came to her lover's side.

"We will die together," she said; "but before our spirits wing their flight to the happy hunting-grounds, there will be sorrow in the Masketees' wigwams."

Jack smiled sadly at the beautiful girl's words, as he placed the whole of their ammunition beneath the loop-holes he had luckily constructed when building the hut.

The prudent course he had adopted when he dived beneath the water for the barrel of powder and the bag of bullets, which had been thrown in the sea by the angry Indians, was a matter of self-gratulation in this moment of dire peril.

And he trembled at the knowledge that in his hands were the lives of the whole of the dusky horde that were at that moment yelling with joy as they crossed the reef.

CHAPTER XXVI.
MADGE COLLINS AND THE LAWYER.

BIRCHWOOD Academy had put an external polish on Jasper Collins, and a skilful tailor had done much to hide the deformity which had so disgusted the baronet when he visited the hut in company with his legal adviser.

Mr. Robert Twistem, when he saw the wrecker's grandson so much altered, gave a grunt of approval, and going towards the old dame extended his hand.

"I hope, madam," he said, "you have not forgotten me. You may remember I called upon you in company with my lamented client. Of course, you are aware that the baronet is no more."

"Quite," the woman said, scrutinizing the lawyer keenly. "I saw the account in the newspaper."

"Indeed! Hem—very sad, my dear madam, but young men, you know, particularly young men of fortune, are apt to forget the golden rules of life."

Madge evidently wondered what this prelude was for, and not knowing exactly what answer to make, she inclined her head. The old woman, though unlettered and reared from infancy among the rough fishermen, was not without a certain keenness of perception and natural cunning, that made her quite a match for Mr. Robert Twistem, the solicitor. She guessed his meaning, and determined, if possible, to play the leading card in the game.

"Such a fortune!" the man of law continued. "Very sad—very sad to think that the fine old estate must pass into a distant connexion of the family."

He was coming to the point, old Madge thought,

and she selected the card to play. She was premature, for the lawyer, as though suddenly recollecting Jasper's presence, rose from his seat, and said—

"A thousand pardons, my dear sir. I should not have known you were in the room had you not risen. You remember me, I presume?"

The loathing look with which the baronet had garded him had never been effaced from Jasper's mind, and knitting his brows savagely, he answered—

"I remember your companion better than I do you."

"Ah, indeed! Yes, poor gentleman. Alas! he has departed this life."

Jasper laughed bitterly, and the venom in his nature showed itself in his words.

"I am aware he is dead," he said, "and have wondered since that he could have remained in the same graveyard with his fellow-men."

"You are severe, sir, in your remarks. I have always heard my lamented client spoken of with the most profound respect."

"Very possible," was Jasper's reply. "Men that have eaten at his table, and fattened upon his bounty, may have cause to speak well of him; but I—do you know, sir, that I am human in feeling, and when your companion looked upon me as though I were a loathsome reptile I hated him, and have hated him even to his memory."

The lawyer was somewhat surprised at this speech, and giving old Madge a sidelong glance, he mentally exclaimed—

"She would have begun the siege. Hem! a cunning dame. She has prepared this boy for the field. I must be wary. Ah! she would possibly have contested the baronet's right to the estate had he lived, and with the proofs in her possesion it would have been a hard battle." He glanced furtively at Jasper. "Not a drop of the Morland blood in his veins; yet, as I said before, I must be wary."

The mental observation concluded, Mr. Robert Twistem smiled most affably, and answered Jasper—

"We have all our faults, Mr.—Mr. Col——"

"John Morland," broke in the sharp voice of old Madge, as she played the first card.

The lawyer was staggered a little, but not confused. He gave the dame a glance, which meant, as plain as man could speak—

"John Morland, if he can make it agreeable to my interest; otherwise, my dear madam, I will upset your schemes without the least compunction."

"I beg your pardon," Mr. Twistem resumed in his blandest tones. "I was not aware that you were really the son of the poor gentleman."

Old Madge leant over and whispered to Jasper, and the lawyer, in spite of his good breeding, left off speaking, and craned his neck forward to hear her lowly-spoken words.

In this he failed, but the import he guessed by Jasper rising and leaving. He had learnt to bow at Birchwood Academy; but it was the stiff, awkward bow of a peasant—a very different inclination of the head and body of the innate gentleman.

"I will retire," he said. "You have come upon business matters, I presume; therefore I will not intrude."

"No intru——"

Jasper was gone before the lawyer could finish the ready lie upon his tongue—gone to peer about the cottage of old Dame Willis, to gloat over the sweet child he longed to crush and humiliate.

When the door closed upon his misshapen form, Madge Collins and the lawyer remained for some minutes silently regarding each other. Both felt that the crisis was coming, and both sought to begin the battle of intrigue by taking up the strongest position. As they sat thus, their thoughts ran pretty nearly as follows :—

MADGE COLLINS—"This lawyer has come down here to either get the clothes that were worn by the boy Darrel saved from the wreck, or else to make an offer to put Jasper in possession of the property, if I will make suitable terms. He would not do this were it not for the means in my possession to bring Jasper forward as the true heir. So, under these circumstances, I have not much to thank him for."

MR. ROBERT TWISTEM—"Hem! a cunning old lady. Were it not a better paying affair to assist her in placing this ungainly brat in possession of the baronet's wealth, I would hand over the deeds to the claimant for the estate. He will, I have no doubt, contest this claim; but the proofs she has of the boy's identity will be too much for the jury. Ha! I knew, at the time Sir Harold gave her the money to destroy everything relative to the wreck, she would not do it; but I did not expect to find her so well prepared. Hang the woman! She must have commenced operations at least a few days after our visit. Here is the crook-back well dressed, and evidently schooled far beyond the requirements of his class."

When the worthy dame and her visitor had held this little self-communion, the lawyer commenced operations by remarking—

"I am glad, madam, that you have counselled the young person to leave us together for a short time."

He said "young person," until the time came to give him his proper name, or that of our unfortunate young hero.

"Indeed!" said Madge. There was a little asperity in the dame's voice that sounded as though the lawyer's words were not the most pleasant he could have uttered. "Indeed! Why, may I ask, are you so pleased?"

"I like to be frank, Mrs. Collins."

Old Madge smiled sneeringly at the lawyer's frankness.

"Because," he continued, affecting not to notice her peculiar smile, "it places us at once upon a perfect understanding with each other; it is by far the best way. Do you not think so, my dear madam?"

"Perhaps it is. Pray proceed."

"You may remember, when I had the honour of last visiting you, my lamented client totally repudiated the idea that any relationship existed between him and the youth who was so lately in this room."

"I am aware of that."

"To be brief, madam. When the estates were, so to speak, left in my hands, I at once thought it my duty to wait upon you, and learn whether my late lamented client's prejudice against the young person proceeded from his ungain—hem!—his wish to keep the property. Now that he is no more, I think, before the distant connexion of the family becomes possessor of the property, I am but doing my duty in endeavouring to find out whether there is really a nearer claimant."

"Your motives, of course, are purely disinterested?"

The lawyer shifted about in his seat and looked not unlike a baited bull. He sought to evade this pointblank question; but the old woman kept him to the point, and he began in his heart to wish he had stayed in his dingy office.

After a long pause, he looked straight at the cold gray eyes which were watching him with a cat-like expression, and answered—

"As the legal adviser of the family I think the question almost unnecessary."

"I am quite of a different opinion, Mr. Twistem."

"Indeed, Mrs. Collins. What cause——"

"Shall I be frank and tell you the cause?"

"I should be grateful."

Old Madge drew her chair close to the lawyer's, and fixing him, as it were, in his seat, she said—

"It is this, Mr. Twistem. You are well aware that the dead baronet would not—although, mind, he disclaimed all relationship with the boy—he would not, I say, have given me that heavy sum of money to keep the boy's existence a profound secret and destroy the clothes he had when picked up from the wreck, if he had not believed there was some truth in my statement."

"Hem! well, to a certain extent, he may have believed you could produce the *rightful heir;* but I can assure you, my dear madam, that he never would have acknowledged the boy you presented to us."

"The law," old Madge said sharply, "pays no respect to a claimant's form; he may be crooked and ungainly; but if he can prove his right beyond dispute, the delicate nerves of *your lamented client*," she imitated the lawyer's dolorous manner of pronouncing those words, "would not have kept him from his birthright."

"Perhaps not, madam, if he were the rightful heir."

A savage light gleamed in old Madge's eyes, and suddenly clutching the lawyer's arm with her long fingers, she screamed in his ear.

"Who dare dispute his title?"

Mr. Robert Twistem would as soon have been in the clutches of a wild cat; and the defiant words which rose to his lips were replaced by—

"No one; certainly, no one. But, my dear madam, you are digging your nails in my flesh."

She released his arm, and in the same high falsetto continued—

"Who dare dispute his right? Have I not the letters sent by the baronet? What does he say in them, sir?"

The lawyer had edged his chair further from the lady than when the conversation began.

"I really do not know," he said; "I was not present when he wrote—I was not really."

He spoke the truth. Had he been present he would not have suffered the careless baronet to place such a formidable weapon in the woman's hands

"Does he not say," she yelled, "that I am to keep his birth a secret? Has he not referred to him more than once as his brother's child? And was it not by his wish that I placed the boy at school, and with the sum of money he gave me to keep silent about the matter?"

When old Madge had thus electrified the lawyer, she threw herself back in the chair, and began to swing her body to and fro.

Mr. Robert Twistem began to perceive, unless he effected a skilful flank movement, he would be utterly defeated, and so far from taking a leading part in the transaction, he would play a second and very unproductive fiddle.

"It won't do," he thought, "to let the old hag bully me like this; I must try the same dodge, but," he added, "out of reach of her long nails."

"Madam," he said, rising, "whatever indiscretion the baronet may have been foolish enough to commit, I must beg to remind you, that as a man who has been for years mixed up with the most peculiar and complicated cases, I have a keener perception in this matter than my late—the baronet. Therefore I tell you, frankly, that I do not believe the youth you brought to us that day, or the youth I saw a few minutes since, has the slightest claim to the Morland estates."

He held the chair between himself and the old woman, by the time he had finished this speech, and, as a matter of precaution, took a careful survey of the means of exit from the hut.

Great was his surprise when he found that Madge, instead of giving vent to a violent outburst of passion, continued to rock herself to and fro, and in a voice of singular calmness, considering the late outburst, merely said—

"Have you done?"

"No," he said, her quietude making him bold, "I have not. I would remind you, if you wish to push matters to extremes, that I have, from the people who dwelt about here, made inquiries about this boy."

Madge gave a spiteful snarl, and uttered the single interrogative—

"Well?"

"These inquiries," he resumed, "have resulted in the elucidation of a few facts that I feel sure will place us, my dear madam, upon a better understanding with each other."

Old Madge made no reply. She now ceased rocking herself, and then sat bolt upright in her chair, glaring at the lawyer.

"These facts amount to this," he resumed. "At the time of my former visit there were two boys under this roof."

"That's a lie," old Madge said, bluntly. "But go on."

"If not under this roof at the time," he said, "they were residing here. Soon after one of the boys was lost through the upsetting of a boat, and from the description given of his appearance I have no hesitation in saying that he was nephew of my late client the baronet."

"But I say he was not."

The lawyer was out-flanking his antagonist, but she would not yield without a struggle.

"We will not press the matter any further," he said. "You know exactly how the case stands, and can tell whether a frank admission of the truth will serve our interest better than the way in which you have begun."

The victory was entirely on the lawyer's side, for Madge began to think that after all it would be the better plan to meet his advances half way, than to stand out and perhaps be worsted in the end.

"Our interest!" she said. "What inference am I to draw from those words?"

"What you like," was the cool reply. "Suppose we say that it will be more to my advantage to assist you in bringing this boy forward as a claimant to the property, what benefit am I to derive from it?"

"Benefit! What do you mean, present or prospective?"

"Present. But mind, if I undertake the matter, you or your grandson—he is your grandson, I believe?"

"You can believe whatever you think proper."

Met there, R. Twistem, Esq. Well met!

"I am convinced such is the relationship. Let that pass. I think I can safely assert, with the proofs in your possession, I can raise him from his lowly position, and by doing so, I shall expect a remuneration adequate to the service."

"You are not certain of its accomplishment. You spoke of a client who would contest Jas—Mr. Morland's right to the title."

"I did. But as he has already asked my advice upon the subject I think a mode may be found of causing him to change his mind. If so, there is nothing to prevent Jasper Collins or John Morland, from at once stepping into the dead baronet's shoes."

Old Madge was silent for some moments. She found she was, after all, to a certain extent in the lawyer's power, and despite the proofs she could bring forward, she knew there would be but little chance of success unless she acted as Mr. Robert Twistem wished.

"Would it be too much?" she asked at length, "to inquire the mode by which you would get rid of this claimant?"

"Not at all. I do not see anything to forbid me telling you. The facts are simply these. This distant connexion is a poor, needy wretch, and when I told him there was a heir to the property, he asked me whether it would be of any benefit to him to oppose the heir?"

"Well, your answer?"

"I bade him wait. He is not answered yet."

"I see," old Madge said. "If you cannot make your own terms with me you will at once espouse his cause?"

"Frankly, yes."

"What are your propositions?"

Mr. Twistem drew a sheet of paper from his breast, and glanced over its contents.

"Part of the estates," he said, "are mortgaged for two years. Thus, the net income from the remainder is considerably below the actual worth of the property. Now, what I propose is this. I am to have for my services the total annual income of the whole of the property for two years."

"But you say—"

"One moment, my dear madam. I know about the mortgage, but as I am in no hurry, I will take the money by instalments—say in a period of six years—that is, if I hold requisite security. Remember, out of this sum I shall have to buy off the needy claimant. So that, after all, my share will be but small."

Old Madge was not able to cope with her visitor in matters of finance, and so far as she could understand his offer seemed within a reasonable limit.

"What security," she asked, "do you wish to hold for the payment of this money?"

"Merely the young gentleman's signature to this paper."

He held out the paper to Madge; but she, after wading through a slough of unknown words, returned it to him, saying—

"You had better explain its nature."

"It is very simple," he said. "A mere matter of form, but quite necessary in business. It purports that I have advanced the young gentleman a sum of money which is to be repaid by instalments, and within a period of six years. If it is not paid I shall claim a small estate in Lincolnshire. This, of course, is merely a matter of form also; for out of the immense rent roll, the young gentleman can pay me in a third of the time if he thinks proper."

Old Madge, though she doubted the lawyer's honesty in the matter, did not know sufficient to put her on her guard, so after a few minutes' deliberation she said—

"Be it so. When do you wish that paper signed?"

"As soon as possible. You see, without this as a security, I shall not feel safe in paying off the needy claimant."

"Very well. Mr. Morland will soon be here. Ha! here he is."

The door opened, and Jasper entered the hut.

"I have seen her," he began; "seen and glo—"

He saw the lawyer and abruptly stopped.

"Come here," Madge said; "bring the pen and ink and sign your name to this paper." As he bent over the table she whispered—"John Arthur Morland."

The lawyer, in spite of his habitual self-command, could scarcely refrain from a cry of joy when he heard the scratch of the pen.

"Is this sufficient?" said Madge, when the signature was affixed.

"Quite," was the answer, as his willing fingers clutched the precious document; "now, madam, I must return to London and work in the good cause. With your permission, I will take the letters from Sir Harold and the infant's clothing."

An hour later he left the hut muttering joyfully—"I have outwitted them both."

CHAPTER XXVII.
A DANGEROUS HIDING-PLACE.

A DEEP silence reigned in the hut during the time the Indians were disembarking, and from time to time the young wanderer looked compassionately at the sad but beautiful face beside him.

He could not calmly contemplate the probable death of the devoted companion whose gentleness had won upon his heart. As he thought of that matchless form stricken low by the merciless hand of a dusky savage, a sob came from his lips, and the weapon he held was grasped with a firmer hand.

Lela heard the low cry and came to our hero's side, and placing her soft hand upon his shoulder, looked into the eyes she so well loved.

"My brother is sad," she said, and her low musical voice added to the grief that pierced the boy's heart. "Does he fear death? Surely not. One so brave and handsome will be given a place in the happy hunting-grounds."

"No, Lela," he answered; "I fear not death; too oft have I stood face to face with the cold, cruel tyrant to heed his approach. It was upon thy account my heart felt heavy."

Her eyes glistened, and she drew closer to him.

"Upon my account!" she murmured. "Does Lela's life hold any value in the heart of the brave young hunter?"

"More, Lela, than I knew until this dark hour; yet it is not strange. Have we not hunted the wild hog, the lobba, the maroudi, and the hannaquoi, together—have we not sat beneath the mighty mora, and listened to the whip-poor-will and the plaintive note of the houtou and the pi-pi-yo? and our hearts have grown together in those moments when the forest was filled with their cries, and the pale moon shed its halo over thy head. Can you ask me, Lela, if my heart would not be cold were you to die?"

She threw herself on his breast, and placing her soft cheek against his, murmured—

"Lela can now die, she is happy; her heart is more glad than the hannaquoi or the maroudi, when they behold the red sun peeping out from the dark clouds of morn."

Crusoe's lips touched the girl's forehead as she spoke, then raising his head he looked through the loop-hole towards the cluster of dark forms that stood out in bold relief against the glaring ocean.

"See, Lela," he said, "they disperse. Can you tell me what it is they seek?"

The girl no sooner beheld the Indians attentively seeking among the trees and long grass, than she clasped her hands, and exclaimed wildly—

"The eyes of Lela were blind when she first saw the red-men; they are not of the tribe she spoke. No, no; they are the Macoushi—the Macoushi."

Crusoe had a dim recollection of old Tom Starboard having once mentioned this tribe, but why they were to be feared more than others he could not divine, until the girl said in a low, frightened voice—

"THE WOURALI!"

This dread word caused even our hero's steel nerves to give way, and as he brought the butt of his piece to the ground, he said—

"They will gather the poison, Lela, and, perhaps, leave us in peace."

The girl shook her head sadly.

"No," she said; "it is worse that we are here. When they have gathered the poison it will be a test to try its strength upon our bodies."

"Heaven preserve us!" said Crusoe. "We have but little chance of outliving this fearful day. Quick, Lela!" he added; "see, they come this way! Ha! one points to the hut, and they fix the poisoned darts in the blow-pipes! Here, point your rifle, Lela, and bring down that chief with the head-dress of campan-e-ros feathers."

The hut was seen, and fifty nude savages, armed with the blow-pipes and poisoned darts, came swiftly towards them.

Keeping in view the object for which these pages were written—viz., to combine instruction with amusement, and to prove to those who cavil at the form in which this book is issued, that other and purer reading to that of elevating a common thief to a brilliant pinnacle of heroism—a false position, by the way, for though a highwayman may have lolled, decked out in scarlet and gold, and bestrode a sable, fiery steed, he or they were but wretched, hunted fugitives, and so far from mixing in the brilliant company found in the gilded fashionable saloon, they were wont to hide in the filthiest hovels while the sun gladdened the earth, then at night prowl forth like beasts of prey—as I before said, to show that better reading could be found in the usual low-price publications, I must pause for a short time and explain the cause of Crusoe's agitation when Lela uttered the single word—

"Wourali!"

To those who care not to learn the strange and terrible significance of this word, I say, Pass on to the next page, and stand beside the young wanderer as he bravely defends his hut against the power of a savage tribe. Those who have a thirst for knowledge will, I feel assured, thank the writer for this digression from the course of the story.

The wourali poison, which is used by most of the tribes of South America, is prepared to the greatest perfection by the Macoushi Indians; to them no toil or danger, is too great to collect the precious materials, and it was to this circumstance that Crusoe Jack's lonely island owed the sudden appearance of the nude savage forms which so alarmed the gentle Indian maiden and her lion-hearted companion.

In the silent depths of the mighty forests the ingredients which form this life-destroying essence grow in wild profusion.

A pine called wourali, from which the poison takes its name, is the first thing the Indian seeks. When he has gathered sufficient of this, he digs up a dark tuberous root. Tying these two together, the next thing to be found is a bulbous plant which contains a green and glutinous juice.

After gathering a small bundle of these stalks, the searcher looks under the brushwood for two species of ants, one large and black, and so poisonous that its sting produces a fever; the second is small and of a bright red, and stings like a nettle.

After obtaining these, a quantity of Indian pepper is gathered; then the deadly fangs from the labarri snake are extracted, and the whole of the ingredients are in the poison-seeker's possession.

The labour is not yet concluded, for the subtle poison has to be prepared, and the task is by no means easy of accomplishment or free from danger to those engaged in the manipulation.

With the above poisons in his possession, he proceeds thus to make an essence that will combine the power of each of the above, and reduced to such a form it can be easily carried about, either in the chase or on the war path.

First, the pine and bitter roots are scraped into thin shavings, and put into a sieve; this is held over an earthen bowl, and water poured on them; the bulbous stalks are then bruised, and the juice squeezed by the hand into the pot; and lastly, the venomous snake's fangs and the ants and pepper are added.

This pot is then placed over a slow fire, and as it boils, a little of the poisonous juice from the pine is from time to time added. This is continued until the whole of the ingredients become a thick syrup, and the operator, as he pours the subtle essence into a small earthenware jar, holds it at arm's length, in order that he may not inhale the powerful deadly vapour.

So great an undertaking is this esteemed, that the hut wherein it is made is considered polluted, and either burnt or levelled to the ground; and those engaged in the operation must fast during the whole time the work continues. The pot which is used for holding the syrup must never have been used before, or the virtue of the poison will be lost.

Though these and other precautions are taken, the Indians who attend the manufacture are ill several days after.

So much for the preparation of this terrible mode of death; a few words as to its use will be necessary.

The arrow is barely nine inches long, and is made from the leaf of a species of palm tree, called coucourite, hard and brittle, and as sharp as a needle. About an inch of the pointed end is dipped in the poison, and the other end is exposed to the action of fire, to render it hard, after which it is bound with wild cotton; this, again, it fastened with shreds of the silk grass.

Six to eight hundred of these deadly missiles are placed in a quiver made from the dried skin of the tapir.

The Indian, to guard against being pierced by his own weapons, fastens the arrows' points downwards to a long stick by strings of cotton. Thus, when he wants a fresh arrow, he draws the stick a little distance out of the quiver, and is enabled to handle the deadly weapon without danger to himself.

A thong enables the quiver to be slung over the shoulder, and with his blow-pipe in his hand, the savage warrior is better armed than the European soldier, with rifle, bayonet, and cartridge.

The blow-pipe is, perhaps, not the least singular part of the equipment. This extraordinary tube of death is found in the wilds of the unpeopled tracts of country near the Rio Negro. It is of a bright yellow colour, and grows to an extraordinary length. The Indians use pieces at the very least twelve feet long; both inside and out is as smooth as polished ivory, and of an equal diameter, and without the least sign of a knot or curve. This tubular reed, which Nature furnishes in abundance to her dusky children, is too delicate to stand the risk of coming in contact with the lower branches of the trees—accidents that would

happen either in the chase or in the heat of an engagement with a hostile tribe.

To obviate this, the Indians use a case formed from the straight lance-like shoots of a palma, called the samourah; first carefully extracting the pulp, then inserting the long delicate reed—polishing and pointing the end, which goes to the mouth, with silk grass, finishes the long weapon, and its possessor is ready to meet the largest brutes of the forest or the fiercest foe.

It was from the samourah that poor old Tom Starboard made the long shafts for himself and Crusoe when on the first island.

Inserting one of the poisoned arrows in this singular weapon, the Indian can send the missile with one puff the enormous distance of 300 yards, and so truly that the smallest bird can be brought down while on the wing.

The effect of the poison is instantaneous; the slightest scratch or prick with the envenomed arrow tip produces instant death. The victim does not expire as though suffering pain, but drops to the earth, every faculty numbed, and as the subtle essence becomes infused in the blood he droops and dies, but so gently that it seems more like falling into a gradual slumber.

The most reliable travellers assert that three minutes is the usual period which elapses between the time of receiving an arrow and the passing away of the earthly spirit.

There is but one antidote, and that will be mentioned in its proper place.

The reader may now see in imagination the exulting horde of fierce savages, as they drew up before Crusoe's hut, and each having his quiver full of poisoned arrows, he will confess that our little castaway had but little chance of escape.

The smallest opening in the logs would be sufficient for them to send a succession of deadly missiles to the interior, and Crusoe, for the want of tools, had unfortunately many chinks in the log walls of his island home.

When the young adventurer bade his companion bring down the Macoushi chief the tribe were running towards the hut, their blow-pipes carried in a similar position to that adopted by the soldier with his musket at the trail, but scarcely had the words left his lips when the Indians came to a sudden halt, and the chief, coming forward without his weapon, advanced to within twenty feet of the hut, and made signs that he wished to hold a parley.

Our hero would have fearlessly gone forth to meet the red man, had not his more cautious companion seized his arm, and said hurriedly—

"Stay! See you not a warrior behind the drooping palm?"

Crusoe peered through the small round hole from which he had withdrawn his rifle, and beheld an Indian crouching behind the palm-leaves, his long blow-pipe pointing towards the door of the hut.

The Indian chief became impatient, and, folding his arms, looked contemptuously at the log building, and exclaimed—

"Is my brother a squaw, that he fears to come and hear the words a chief would utter?"

Jack listened to this taunt with flashing eyes, and had not Lela gently held his hand he would have sent a bullet through the dusky warrior's brain.

"Be silent," whispered Lela; "the Macoushi knows not that the white hunter dwells within the hut. Be silent, and he may depart, and not know that any——"

She stopped abruptly and pointed to the Macoushi chief, who was cautiously advancing towards the hut.

"Down," cried the girl. "Let us burrow like the fox; he may not see us."

Crusoe comprehended her motive, and threw himself flat upon the ground, and so close to the side of the hut that detection by the Indian's prying eyes was impossible.

Lela crouched close by his side, her dark eyes eagerly watching the dusky form of the feathered chief.

He came with the panther's wary gait, and applying his eyes to one of the many crevices, looked long and carefully at the interior of the hut.

He saw not the recumbent forms of the young pair, and at last, as though satisfied that nothing living was within the log building, he walked boldly to the door, and tried to enter.

Three stout logs barred the door, and the Indian, after several ineffectual attempts to force an entry, uttered a grunt of dissatisfaction, then turning slowly away, he walked towards his companions.

"He is gone," said Lela; "and when the wourali is made, it will be beneath the roof of this hut."

Crusoe sprang to his feet, and looked wildly at the beautiful girl.

"Lela," he said, "no more shall we wander beneath the trees and listen to the whip-poor-will."

"No more," she cried, clasping her hands—"no more; and soon the owl will lament over our graves, but the——No," she added, suddenly, "he has forgotten. Let us burrow like the fox until the wourali is made, then we can come forth and look at the bright sun, and rejoice."

She pointed to the flooring of the hut as she spoke; and Crusoe, as he understood her meaning, gave a glad cry.

Beneath the pine logs which formed the flooring of their island home, the young wanderer had excavated a square hole to contain their provisions, and to sleep in when the cold winds should sweep through the imperfectly closed walls of their dwelling; he had made it deep and broad, and now, in the hour of their need, it served them as a sanctuary.

The portion of the flooring which covered this underground chamber was movable and easily raised.

Had Crusoe constructed it for a place of refuge from danger, he could not have made it to answer the purpose better with the limited means at his disposal.

To convey their weapons, food, and water to this place was the work of a moment. The greatest difficulty was to persuade the young lion to descend the few steps. Like an angry watch-dog, he kept gliding to and fro in front of the door, his long tail sweeping the ground, and every moment stopping to listen to the distant hubbub of the Indians' voices.

Soothed by Lela's caressive hand, Hector at length descended, and stretched himself at her feet. Then Crusoe followed, and closing the trap over his head, sat, rifle in hand, awaiting the coming of the Macoushi Indians.

It was a fearful time, and every moment seemed an age to the young pair as they sat in the murky light (a few rays struggled faintly through the narrow openings of the pine logs) listening to the sounds of the approaching foe.

When a heavy beam was applied to the door, Crusoe and Lela had the greatest difficulty in repressing the angry growls of their four-footed companion, and when the rude fastenings yielded, and the broken fragments gave way with a loud crash, the lion sprung to his feet, and gave a roar that caused Crusoe's blood to run cold.

Quick as thought he drew his sword, and held his hand back ready to kill the faithful brute, should he, in his anger, turn upon those he loved so well.

The growl had evidently not been heard by the invaders, for its utterance was blended with the crash of the falling doorway, and they came through the aperture and began eagerly searching the two small chambers of the hut.

The young pair heard their remarks as they found a hammock made from plaited grass in Lela's chamber, and their expressions of surprise at beholding in Jack's sleeping apartment a couch of dried skins.

They were puzzled by the strange sight, and held a long deliberation respecting the occupants of the two chambers.

To Crusoe's relief the supposition was that they had fled to the forest, and thither a number of the Indian youths sped, hoping to capture the fugitives.

Those who remained in the hut began preparations for distilling the subtle poison, and to Crusoe's horror, placed the large earthen vessel over their hiding-place.

He felt Lela's hand, cold and clammy, placed upon his wrist, and her words sounded like a death knell as she whispered—

"When the wourali is made, the hut will be given to the flames."

He pressed her hand, and would fain have uttered cheering words, but his heart became heavy as the utter hopelessness of their position came upon his mind.

There was no hope. He felt they must die beneath the blazing timbers of the hut, or dash through the trap-door and fall to the earth stricken to death by the Macoushi arrows.

As the cold, clammy drops of agitation stood out upon his forehead he bowed his head, and endeavoured to meet his fate with fortitude.

The task was hard and the struggle great for the fiery spirit to succumb to the grim destroyer without striking a blow for life, and as he heard the soft footfall of the naked feet above his head, a grim resolution came to his mind, and he determined to die with a weapon in his hand rather than perish beneath the blazing walls of his island home.

CHAPTER XXVIII.
AN INDIAN BATTLE.

BEFORE our hero could raise the trap and boldly confront the Macoushi Indians, the latter gave a yell, and seizing their blow-pipes, they rushed from the aut..

Crusoe emerged from his place of concealment, rifle in hand.

One glance through the open door showed the cause of this sudden movement on the invaders' part, and Crusoe, when he beheld the unexpected sight that met his gaze, called upon Lela to come forth.

She came, followed by the young lion.

"Tell me, Lela," he said, " are not these the pit-pans of your people ? "

She looked towards the smooth sheet of water inside the breakers, and clasping her hands, said—

" It is! They come! Red Plume and his tribe! May the Great Spirit be merciful to my people ! "

Crusoe looked at the excited girl, and asked—

"What dire misfortune is this my sister fears ? "

"See you not the Macoushi like a dark cloud hovering near the brink of the water ? "

" I do."

"See you not my people fitting arrows to their bows ? "

" I see that also."

" Can you, a white man, not tell the meaning of these things ? "

"By Heaven! yes. There will be a battle between the tribes."

"My brother has spoken true. There will be a battle."

"I knew not," Crusoe said, "that your people were at war with the Macoushi."

"When our chief, whose beard is white as the snow of winter, was a young brave, ay, as young as you are, there came to our wigwams one of the accursed Macoushi. He loved a maiden of our tribe, and would have taken her had not the chief—then not even a warrior—cleft his skull in twain with a tomahawk. From that day to this there has been war between them, and though so many moons have passed, and many heroes have fallen, they will fight until one tribe has gone to the happy hunting-grounds."

Crusoe knew the fierce passions of the warlike Indians were aroused against a hostile tribe. Neither would give in until one tribe would be so reduced in numbers that it would be impossible to take the field.

This result attained, the victorious tribe would compel the vanquished to become their slaves.

Lela's people were a brave, hardy tribe, more numerous than the Macoushi, of more robust form and constitution, before the long and fearful war broke out between them. The many sanguinary engagements had somewhat reduced their numbers, for although they at all times fought like heroes, the subtle weapon wielded by the Macoushi gave them an immense superiority over the arrows and tomahawks of their foes.

The meeting upon Crusoe's lonely isle was a surprise to both parties, but no sooner did they behold each other than both made preparations for the coming strife.

The Macoushi chief drew his men up in a semicircle upon the bank, and with their deadly blow-pipes held ready to send forth a flight of envenomed arrows, they crouched waiting for the signal to begin.

The warriors of Aynoth, except those who were using the paddle, stood up in the fore-part of their pit-pans, their bows bent, and their loud cries of defiance bidding the Macoushi fire.

In the foremost pit-pans Crusoe beheld the Apollo-like form of the young Red Plume.

His heart throbbed violently at the thought of the noble savage being slain by one of the envenomed barbs from the Macoushi pipes.

"Lela," he said, "is your heart turned from your people ? "

The dusky maiden's form shook for a moment, and her large eyes filled with tears as she answered—

"I could not love Red Plume, yet his was the only voice that spoke against the cruel order for me to be bound to a tree, and left for wild beasts to devour "

"I am glad to hear it," our hero said, "and you, Lela, in memory of this kindness, bring the rifle I have taught you to use, and we will aid the men of Aynoth in their fight against the Macoushi."

The girl's eyes sparkled; in spite of the cruelty of her people, her heart was yet warm towards those among whom her early days had been passed.

The warlike fierceness of her nature showed itself in the sudden clutch she made at the rifle, the trusty weapon that had once been in the possession of Tom Starboard.

" Come," she said, " Lela is ready; and when the living lightning goes forth from this tube of death, each time shall a chief of the Macoushi fall."

Our hero uttered an exclamation of delight.

"Lela," he said, "your woman's wit has suggested a plan by which we can aid the men Red Plume leads to battle. Yes, we will pick off the chiefs, and scatter dismay in their ranks. Ha! there is the signal for the battle to begin."

A shout from the tribe of Aynoth came upon their ears. At this moment a shout of mingled rage and despair as the poisoned barbs of the Macoushi dealt death among the little bands Red Plume commanded.

The young chief saw his warriors, stricken by the Macoushi's poison, fall forward as they madly urged their pit-pans through the water, their teeth firmly set, and their massive muscular chests heaving with excitement.

In spite of the showers of poisoned arrows they kept up their swift pace, and in obedience to their young chief's command, did not discharge a single arrow in return.

Red Plume, conspicuous by his circlet of white feathers, stood in the bows of the foremost pit-pan, his superb form was drawn erect, and as he bent his dark fiery eyes upon his hereditary foes, he gripped his glittering tomahawk, and said—

"Forward, men of Aynoth! the Macoushi is a dog—a coward—a squaw; he cannot fight but with poisoned shafts. Forward, and let your tomahawks drink their blood."

He was aroused by a yell louder and fiercer than any that had yet left their lips, and the light pit-pans sprang out of the water beneath the fearful arrows of the excited foemen

GOING FORTH IN QUEST OF ADVENTURE.

Red Plume had spoken the truth in one respect.

The Macoushi were not armed; but in warfare they relied solely upon their blow-pipes and spears.

A charge with the keen tomahawk was to them a matter to be avoided. They had no weapon to contend against a close combat, so they unwillingly retreated before the muscular tribe of Aynoth, taking refuge behind trees, and from thence sending forth their deadly missiles.

They saw the purpose for which Red Plume and his braves kept their bows unbent; saw the gleam of the terrible tomahawks in their hands, and they tried with might and main to keep the foe from effecting a landing.

Shower after shower of deadly barbs greeted the advancing braves; time after time the rowers were struck by the deadly poison and fell forward dead—the paddles held firmly even in their death grasp.

Not a word was spoken as the bodies of the fallen were thrown into the sea and their places taken by others, who, excited almost to madness by the fearful havoc the Macoushi's arrows were making among them, soon made up the distance lost by the change of rowers.

They were within a dozen feet of the beach. Red Plume, who had singled out the chief of the Macoushi, gave the war-cry of Aynoth, and waved his gleaming axe above his head.

The signal was understood.

As though by magic, a hundred dusky warriors sprang to their feet; the paddles were abandoned, and the braves, turning towards the Macoushi, sent a flight of arrows in the midst of the closely-packed

9

tribe. So sudden had this movement taken place that the Macoushi were, for a moment, taken by surprise.

Fifty of their number bit the dust as they were in the act of applying the blow-pipe to their lips.

Their yelling disturbed their companions' aim, and before they could reply to the arrows which had caused this change in the aspect of the fight, Red Plume gave a second whoop, and, at the head of his fierce warriors, dashed ashore.

The Macoushi feared those gleaming axes, and knowing the advantage they possessed by fighting with space enough to use their long weapons, they broke and fled to the cover afforded by a dense clump of trees.

Red Plume, though he panted to be avenged on his foes, gave the signal for his men to also take to cover.

The young chief knew that in crossing the open ground to engage the Macoushi he would run the risk of losing a number of his men before he could come hand to hand, and knowing that every wound, no matter how slight, produced death, he wisely, but reluctantly, gave the order for them to disperse.

The wand of a magician could hardly have produced a more startling effect than this order caused.

The band of warriors seemed to melt away, and none but the dead Aynoths and the dead and wounded Macoushi strewed the ground.

Crusoe had watched these movements between the hostile tribes with flushed cheek and blazing eyes.

He longed to place himself beside Red Plume when he saw that noble-looking savage spring to the shore and rush towards the foe.

He could scarcely restrain the hearty British hurrah which rose to his lips at the sight, and had it not been for Lela he would have rushed from the shelter of a clump of cane-brake and joined the Aynoth warriors.

"Stay," she said. "Does my brother wish to reach the hunting-grounds, his spirit taken from him by the tip of the Macoushi arrow?"

"I can pass round them, Lela."

"My brother is mistaken. He knows not the cunning of the Macoushi dogs."

"The trees," Jack said, "will hide me from their sight."

"The trees," Lela said, "will be used by the Macoushi when my people bear down upon them, as the jaguar springs upon the deer. The Macoushi are squaws. They will run behind the trunks to hide from the warriors of Aynoth. See, my brother, Lela speaks the truth."

As she spoke the Macoushi separated, and ran behind the protecting verge of the forest.

When she saw her people imitate this movement she said—

"See, the tribe of Aynoth behave with the wisdom of trained warriors. They hide their bodies from the Macoushi."

Crusoe could not help smiling at the girl's words.

When the foe ran behind the trees she likened them to cowards, but when her people imitated the movement, she likened it to their knowledge of the subtle tactics of Indian warfare.

The parties remained for some time under cover, the chiefs alone daringly exposing their bodies and hurling the bitterest taunts at each other to bring on the engagement.

"The Macoushi," said the young chief of Aynoth, "skulk like squaws. Let them come forth, that my young men may see the colour of their faces."

"Let the men of Aynoth seek the hiding-places of the Macoushi, not hide like women or old men. Faugh! ye are dogs."

Red Plume's eagle eye blazed with fury, but his handsome face, schooled to hide the workings of his mind, seemed immovable as he calmly answered—

"Many moons have come and gone since the Macoushi first met the men of Aynoth. Many scalps have been brought from the Macoushi, yet more shall be taken. Come from your hiding-places——"

The sudden report of a rifle stopped the young chief's speech, and to his surprise, one of the hated Macoushi fell from the branch of a tree.

Red Plume saw the Indian grasp madly at the air as he fell—saw a throe pass through his frame as he reached the ground, and the bronzed limbs became rigid.

The Indian had fallen within a few feet of the young chieftain of Aynoth, and as he bent his dark eyes upon the small circular wound, he muttered—

"The white hunter is abroad. He has saved Red Plume's life."

He knew that the skulking form, hidden by the thick foliage of the giant tree, had crept there but for one purpose—that purpose, to strike him with an envenomed dart.

In spite of the danger which the act incurred, the superb warrior sprang from the shelter of the tree, and with a loud shout of defiance, he stooped over the yet warm body, and quick as thought, cut off the reeking scalp; then waving the bloody trophy over his head, he darted back to his place of shelter just as the Macoushi sent a shower of poisoned arrows with unerring aim to the very spot he had just vacated.

The taking of the scalp caused a shout of joy from the chief's followers—a shout that was answered by a yell of savage anger by the Macoushi.

For some minutes after this not a glimpse could be seen of the lurking warriors.

Our hero, from his place of concealment, had seen the Macoushi Indian creep from his companions and ascend the tree.

He watched him until he reached one of the upper branches, and as he levelled his blow-pipe at the young chief the boy fired and brought him down.

The shot had somewhat astonished the Macoushi, and the sudden scalping of their companion had taken place while their attention was distracted looking for the daring hunter who had fired, as it were, from their very midst.

They saw Red Plume wave his trophy above his head, and when he darted back among his followers they had only recovered sufficiently to use their long deadly weapons.

A council was held, and the dusky braves, burning to avenge this insult, began to move from tree to tree to get nearer the foe.

They did this with such cunning that at times only the outline of their forms could be seen, shadow-like, among the small openings in the forest.

But cunning as they were, not a vestige of their bodies was distinguishable but the whizzing of an arrow told the men of Aynoth were on the watch.

A dozen of this party had been more or less hurt by the time they had glided to the verge of the forest, and when all were covered by the trunks of the trees and the thick foliage, they began to fire into the hiding-place of Red Plume's band.

Save for a smothered cry now and then escaping a falling warrior's lips, there was no perceptible sign that the peaceful place was tenanted by upwards of of two hundred savage men, each eagerly thirsting for the other's blood.

Closer and closer they crept to each other, until not more than a dozen yards of the clear greensward intervened between them.

Crusoe's heart beat wildly as he crept from bush to bush, following closely the steps of the Macoushi tribe.

He saw the crisis was at hand, and the dusky bands would soon be engaged in close and deadly conflict.

Oh, how ardently he longed to place himself beside the graceful form of the young chief of Aynoth! but the straggling band of the Macoushi tribe prevented this.

He knew that to pass them on either flank would be to expose himself to the deadly wourali poison, and thus for the time he had to wait and watch for an opportunity of obtaining his wish.

A mass of cane-brake and dwarf palm rising from a little hillock was reached by our hero, Lela, and the young lion, at the very moment Red Plume gave the loud signal for his band to rush upon the foe.

The dusky warriors, like hounds released from the leash, bounded from their place of concealment.

The gleaming tomahawks shone beneath the sun's bright rays, then came a sudden shout as the foremost rank of the Macoushi seized their spears and rushed to meet the bounding warriors of Aynoth.

There was a second rank yet of the Macoushi.

These kept among the trees, and as the foe advanced they sent forth shower after shower of poisoned darts.

Many of the Aynoth braves fell under the deadly fire, but the young chief, who was now fighting like a lion at bay, remained unscathed.

Crusoe and Lela held their rifles ready, awaiting for an opportunity to fire, when they could do so without injuring their friends.

At present their aid would have been as fatal to Red Plume's band as it would have been to the Macoushi, for the dark forms swaying to and fro under the fierce light were so mixed together that it became hard to distinguish friends from foes.

In spite of the superhuman exertions of the young chief and his heroes, they were compelled to retreat and seek refuge from the deadly fire which the foe kept up from among the trees.

The Macoushi gave a yell of triumph when the men of Aynoth fell back. Like so many demons they rushed from their cover to follow in pursuit.

Their joy was soon changed to despair.

When they reached the small open piece of ground which divided the tribes, the men of Aynoth suddenly turned and sent a flight of arrows among their foes.

The Indians' aim was true to the mark, and

twenty of the Macoushi fell, an arrow quivering in each of their hearts.

The thickly-wooded forests gave Crusoe's friends the advantage the Macoushi had hitherto enjoyed.

Red Plume formed his men in two ranks: the front rank down upon one knee, the second standing close behind.

In this manner they received their advancing foe.

First the front rank discharged a flight of arrows, and while they were preparing for the next discharge, the standing rank emptied their bows.

Thus checked in their onset, and too brave to retreat, the Macoushi stood their ground for some minutes, vainly endeavouring to use their blow-pipes against Red Plume's band.

Foaming at the mouth with passion, the chief of the Macoushi tried every inducement to urge his men forward. The attempt was futile.

The close, deadly discharge of the Aynoth arrows was too much for them, and with a yell of savage despair they broke and fled to cover.

Red Plume saw the confusion he had thrown them in, and calling aloud upon his warriors, he dashed in close pursuit.

He was too close upon them for the deadly blow-pipe to be used, and the Macoushi thus left with their spears, turned and met the tomahawks of the foe.

The fight was carried on with all the ardour of savageness inherent in the warlike tribes, and the Macoushi being nearly double the number of their foes, soon forced them back to the open space.

The ground was by this time strewed with the dead and dying of both parties, and it seemed that nothing short of a total extermination of one tribe would end the fight.

The long-cherished hate of over half a century was concentrated in the hearts of those remnants of the two tribes.

Both the chiefs were young braves, and felt that the honour of their nations rested in their hands.

The men under them were actuated by the same feelings, thus the battle was more desperate and bloody than it would have been had the whole of the tribes been engaged.

Had such been the case, there would have been men among them whose years might have been reckoned by the sinewy strokes in their bony bodies.

As it was, they were all young, and each felt how great would be the honour to return from the red field of strife and tell how they had exterminated the last of the hated foe.

Red Plume's tomahawk became reddened from the blade to the tip of the hilt.

Like a panther thirsting for blood, he destroyed all who came within reach of his valorous arm.

Blinded by the fierce passions that filled his breast he saw no danger, and once, when pursuing the foe, he was himself surrounded by a dozen of the Macoushi.

Twice his keen tomahawk struck off the handles of the foemen's spears.

Twice he struck down those who would have taken his life.

The third time he followed two stalwart warriors

who were retreating before his murderous weapon, and in aiming a downward blow at their heads he missed his mark, overreached himself, and stumbled forward.

His tomahawk fell from his grasp, and he was at the mercy of the remainder of the foe, who were following close upon his footsteps.

He turned like a tiger at bay. A short hunting-knife hung by a leather thong to his wampum belt, and seizing the weapon, he opposed it to the long spears his foes wielded.

With a glad shout they rushed upon him, and the brave warrior, whose name was a terror to the Macoushi, stepped back to evade the thrust made at his breast.

The step was nearly fatal.

His foot caught in a tuft of fibrous root, and he stumbled and fell upon one knee.

"Yield, dog," said the foremost of the foe, drawing back his hand to give the fatal stroke; "yield to the Macoushi, thou squaw."

The young chief hurled his hunting-knife far away from him, and baring his breast, replied—

"Never! Strike the son of Aynoth; he dies as a Maori should die."

The foe whirled his long-handled weapon high above his head, and lowering the point was about to slay the gallant youth.

Another moment, and the chief of Aynoth, the pride of the Indian country, would have been no more.

But before the barbed point could enter the brave heart, the terrible crack of the white man's rifle was heard, and the Indian, with a stifled cry, sprang upward, then fell upon his face dead.

Red Plume wrenched the spear from the stiffening grasp, and with the terrible fury of a wounded panther he sprang to his feet, and transfixing the foremost of his foes, cried out—

"The spirit of Red Plume shall never be sent to the happy hunting grounds by the hands of a dog."

He made the boast somewhat too soon, for in his fury he drove the spear so far through his opponent's body that he could not extricate it before the remainder were upon him.

Undismayed by this fresh misfortune, he seized one of his foes by the throat, and in spite of the captive's struggles held him up as a shield.

He had noticed the clump of cane-brake from which the puff of smoke came after the bullet struck his foe, and covering his body with the writhing form of the Macoushi, he retreated, step by step, to this new sanctuary. He judged, and judged rightly, that the friendly hand which had twice saved his life would use the terrible rifle upon his foes, should they follow him.

One by one he saw the pursuers fall, and from the rapidity of the firing he guessed that more than one rifle was at work.

By the time he reached the clump of thick brush-wood he was left with only the Indian he had seized and used as a shield.

The rifles of Crusoe and the beautiful girl Lela had rid him of all but this one of his bloodthirsty foes.

Hurling the half-strangled Indian from him, Red Plume was about to enter the cane-brake, when Crusoe issued forth, and pointing to the still savagely fighting tribe, said—

"Our place is there."

Red Plume made no reply, but seizing the boy's hand he pressed it warmly, and said—

"My brother has twice saved my life—Red Plume is grateful."

"When the men of Aynoth," said Crusoe, adopting the figurative language of the tribe, "have driven from the island the hated Macoushi, then we will talk, not teach."

"My brother is right; he is a brave, and though young, many scalps should hang at his belt."

With this word falling from his lips, the young chief stooped and picked up his tomahawk, and bounded towards the combatants.

The young lion followed close to his master, and when the former reached the scene of strife he at once placed himself by the side of the chief of Aynoth.

The battle began with but little advantage on either side, and though many fell both parties kept their ground.

The arrival of Crusoe and the fierce young animal upon the side of the tribe of Aynoth produced a change in the aspect of affairs.

Crusoe, handling his rifle with a dexterity that struck terror in the hearts of the Macoushi, caused them to fall back.

The young lion, watching every red-skin that approached his master, suddenly made a bound among the Macoushi, and seizing the chief in his terrible fangs, bore him to the ground.

Their chief fallen, and being torn limb from limb by the savage beast—the rifle of Crusoe sending death and dismay in their ranks—soon caused them to yield.

Fighting savagely to the last, they fell back towards their canoes; and as the setting sun glanced upon the waters they jumped aboard and pulled madly from the island.

Five out of the ten canoes which had arrived there filled with armed men were now empty, and the fragment of the band pulled as though a legion of fiends were upon their track.

Red Plume's followers plied their arrows upon the retreating tribe, and Jack's rifle did good service.

Once the beaten tribe paused in their retreat.

It was their last effort.

A shower of poisoned darts came from their long weapons; then they dashed towards the boiling surf, and disappeared beyond, to re-appear upon the blue waters.

This last discharge brought grief to the heart of Red Plume, for his young friend, the gallant Crusoe Jack, lay prone upon the earth, a barbed, poisoned arrow quivering in his shoulder.

CHAPTER XXIX.

THE ANTIDOTE TO THE WOURALI POISON.

WHEN struck by the fatal shaft, our hero sank upon the ground at the feet of the splendid chief of Aynoth.

The latter gave a mournful wail when he saw the brave boy fall, and the tribe gathering round at this cry from their chieftain gazed strangely at the plumed head bent so calmly over the stricken boy.

He saw their glance, and guessed the thoughts in the dusky warriors' brains, and placing one hand on the boy's clustering curls, he said, in a voice husky with grief—

"The warriors of Aynoth have a heavy sorrow upon their hearts. Behold, the brave white hunter who has twice saved Red Plume from the dogs of the Macoushi! Behold him dying! The poisoned fang of the arrow eating away his young life, and not all the great medicines of the tribe can save him."

The boy that had twice saved the life of their beloved chief had excited a debt of gratitude. And the dusky braves would have defended him to the last man; and when they found his life was slowly passing away they gave vent to their grief in a low mournful cry.

Red Plume held the boy's head upon his knee, and tried to induce him to speak.

"But one word," he said, "before your spirit wings its flight to the white hunters' paradise. But one word—it will be music to the soul of Red Plume, and balm for his bruised heart."

The rapidly glistening eyes were fixed upon the chief's handsome face, and the blue lips tried to give utterance to a few words.

It was in vain; the grim destroyer's fingers, cold and crushing out his young life, were closing around his heart; and those who knew the subtle form of the wourali poison knew that he had but a few minutes to live.

Crusoe, with the best effort of his failing strength, took the young chief's hand and held it firmly.

The warriors were touched by the spectacle, and many turned aside to shut out the affecting sight.

Like an infant falling into a deep slumber, the boy was succumbing to the grim destroyer, and those who were gathered around came yet closer to watch the dread separation of the spirit from the earthly clay.

The moment was not far off, and while they stood thus, hushed with quietude, a light figure sprang in among them, and, with a piercing cry, fell upon Crusoe's breast.

It was Lela.

And her appearance startled for a moment the proud-spirited Indian chief. His lips moved as though about to question whether an earthly shape stood before him or the form of the beautiful girl he had so vainly striven to woo and win for his bride.

For a moment this feeling lasted; then passed away as the truth came to his mind.

"She has," he thought, "been saved by the young brave, and loves him. Be it so. Red Plume loves the white youth, and could he but live I should be happy in seeing her in his wigwam."

Under other circumstances he would not have been thus calm.

The sight of the beautiful girl would have kindled a trait of jealous passion in his breast—a fierce flame that would not have been subdued unless his tomahawk had drunk his rival's blood.

But no; with his breast so filled with grief at the sight of the dying boy, the fierce passion of his nature was subdued, and he calmly beheld Lela's rounded arms entwining the gallant boy's neck.

"You have killed him," she cried, passionately; "killed all I love. May the Great Spirit blight your days, and refuse you admittance to the happy hunting-grounds when death comes upon you."

"Lela," said the chief of Aynoth, "there is not one of the tribe but feels towards the young brave as a brother. Say, would they kill one who has saved the son of Aynoth?"

She made no reply to the chief's words.

Her whole existence was blended in the great sorrow that had fallen upon her heart.

It was no evanescent affection the young Indian girl entertained for the gallant boy.

Time might pass—they might be separated until the snow of winter shed its silver threads in their locks—even then the love she felt would still live; and, though her spirit left its earthly form, it would be with the fond hope of joining him she had so well, so deeply, heartily loved on earth.

Aynoth's graceful chieftain pitied her, and his heart became yet heavier at the sight. A touching, melancholy sight it was.

The young and beautiful Indian maiden, lost to everything around, and clinging wildly to the breast of her dying lover.

There was another yet who mourned our hero. It was the young lion.

He lay with his massive head resting on his fore paws, the large eyes fixed upon his master's face with that strange wistful look which belied the words of those who tell us that the brute creation are incapable of feeling.

For several seconds a dead silence reigned among the sad group.

Even Lela's grief had subsided to an imperceptible moan, and it would have been hard to tell the poignant agony she suffered had it not been from the convulsive throe which ever and anon passed over her beautiful form.

Suddenly the silence was broken by the young chief saying, in the soft, rich tones so peculiar to the Alougual tongue—

"The bee draws the sunbeams from the petals of the flowers, and they suffer not. Say, White Rose, can the venomed sting of the hated Macoushi be drawn from the wound of the brave young hunter whom we all love?"

He had in his speech unwittingly hit upon the only antidote to the subtle poison.

Lela raised her head when he first began, and as her ears took in the sound of his voice her large eyes began to dilate with joy.

She understood his meaning, and the gentle, devoted girl, without one thought for her own safety, applied her lips to the wound and drew therefrom the venom.

The change that took place seemed miraculous.

The eyes that were fast closing in death, opened.

The fixed, glassy look left them, and as he beheld the lovely girl he gave her a glance that spoke more than words.

His limbs, too, which had seemed to lie listlessly and limp upon the ground, seemed now to begin to regain their wonted vigour.

He made an attempt to raise his right arm.

Joy! Once more the sinews were of use, and with a glad cry he placed it round Lela's waist, and drew her towards him.

He was saved.

Snatched from the very jaws of death, and the dusky braves rent the air with their shouts of joy.

But Lela, she who had saved her lover's life?

She had gradually sunk into a state of listless torpor, and our hero beheld with anguish this fatal sign.

He called to Red Plume, and in accents of the most thrilling nature, said—

"Will she die!—my beautiful forest bride! Will she die?"

Red Plume placed his small dusky hand upon the troubled boy's shoulder, and said—

"Unless the poison enters the blood through a wound there is no danger. Be of good heart, my brother; she will sleep, and wake to love and life."

Crusoe bowed his head in mute thankfulness, then bent over the lovely girl.

She was to appearance asleep. So placid, so gentle was the expression upon her features, that it seemed

as though she was under the influence of a sweet and soothing vision.

Crusoe placed her head upon his knee, and with a soft caressive touch smoothed back the long silken tresses from her brow.

A few words from the young chief caused the warriors of Aynoth to disperse, and taking their tomahawks they began to lop off the lower branches of the nearest trees.

In less than ten minutes a large screen was placed around Lela and her young lover, then the Indians left the spot and began to bury those who had fallen on both sides during the fray.

By the time this was finished the girl opened her eyes, and meeting those of her lover she gave a glad cry and flung her arms round his neck.

"The Great Spirit," she said, "has been good to us. We are safe, and the Macoushi dogs are beaten far beyond the breakers."

"Safe, Lela," he said; "safe, thanks to you, my gentle girl."

She looked in his face, and pointing towards the graceful form of Red Plume, who stood calmly watching his followers place their companions beneath the earth, said—

"Red Plume—has he come to take me from you?"

Our hero started, and a jealous pang shot through his heart.

He had not thought of the deep love the chief of Aynoth felt for the White Rose until the girl spoke.

"Stay, Lela," he said; "Red Plume spoke kindly of you. His men placed this cool retreat over us. Does this look as if his heart was turned against you?"

"It does not," she said; "but the law of our nation gives him a claim upon me now that I have escaped the wild beasts."

"I have twice saved his life," the boy said; "if he wishes to enforce his claim he is not worthy the name of a chief."

She crept down to him, and asked—

WOURALI POISON DARTS.

"Would you let him take me away?"

Crusoe's face flushed.

"By Heaven, no!" he said; "were he backed by ten thousand warriors he should not take you from me while my arm has strength to grasp a weapon!"

The girl's eyes filled with tears.

"My brother," she said, "shall not risk his life for me. See! Lela will stay with him or die."

She drew a short Indian knife from her girdle, and he saw, by the fierce glance in her eyes, that she would put the weapon to her heart sooner than yield to Red Plume.

He admired her fortitude, and imprinting a kiss upon her warm lips, said—

"Lela is not yet gone. I will seek Red Plume, and learn from him the cause of his errand here."

He drew aside the green boughs, and as he appeared before the Indians they suspended their operations, and gave a loud shout of welcome.

Red Plume looked up.

The young chief had been brooding over the past—thinking of the time when he had hoped to possess the lovely White Rose.

Dark thoughts swept across his mind when he pictured the late scene that had passed between Crusoe and Lela.

The kindly feelings towards the noble boy were for the time swept away by the jealous wound.

For a time he felt that he could have dashed the leafy screen aside, rushed upon the lovers, buried his tomahawk in their skulls, and felt happy.

Again the current of his feelings changed.

He saw the Macoushi warrior among the foliage of the tree—then heard the report of the boy's rifle when it brought the skulking assassin from his concealment.

"I am not much better than a squaw," he muttered, "to think thus. Do I not owe my life to the white hunter? Shall I requite the debt by robbing him of all he loves?"

His better feelings prevailed over the evil thought to destroy his successful rival, and when he beheld Crusoe emerge from the small bower he ran eagerly towards him with extended hands.

"My brother's face," he said, "tells me that the White Rose has returned to life. Is it so?"

"It is."

"My brother speaks, and a cloud of thought sits on his brow."

"Red Plume," our hero said, "the White Rose has a sad and heavy heart."

"How so?"

"She fears that Red Plume has come to claim her from the hut of the solitary white man."

The chief placed his hand upon Jack's shoulder.

"Tell her," he said, "that Red Plume is a brave. Tell her to be happy with the white hunter, and may they dwell in peace.

Crusoe's eyes brightened, and he shook the Indian warmly by the hand as he answered.

"Those words are spoken as a chief could only speak, and the heart of Lela will now be glad."

He ran swiftly back to the hut to impart the joyful news to the anxious girl, and then returned to his friend.

"What says the White Rose?" Red Plume asked. "Is she now happy?"

"She is, and prays that the Great Spirit may send you a maiden as beautiful as the stars, and worthy your love."

"She said this?"

"She did."

"Red Plume is happy," he said; "he has not turned the heart of the White Rose from him."

"You have not," Jack said. "She loves you as a sister, and loves her people in spite of the great wrong they would have done. It was her rifle, Red Plume, that aided you in the fight, but her heart was turned away from you and her people."

The young chief's eyes sparkled with delight.

"The time may come," he thought, "when she will love the chief of Aynoth. Until then I must be content."

Crusoe and the young chief were now walking beneath the very tree from which the Macoushi had been shot.

"Brother," said the Indian chief, breaking a small twig from the tree, then separating it in two he gave one part to Jack, "keep this; it will remind you of the debt the tribe of Aynoth owe to one who has done so much for them."

Crusoe took the small twig, and placed it in his belt.

"I will keep this," Red Plume said. "It will remind me how much I have to remember the visit of the young brave to this island; but"—he stopped abruptly—"where is the aged hunter whose form is as upright as the morra tree? He is not here."

Crusoe uttered an exclamation of grief.

"He is gone," he said, "and by the strange trail. My heart is heavy when I think of what may have befallen him."

"Gone," repeated Red Plume. "He went not with my people—he must be gone."

Crusoe drew his Indian friend towards the forest, and pointed out the strange marks that were yet left.

He told him of the red stain upon the musket, and how the imprints of many feet were visible upon the sods.

Red Plume paused for some moments over the strange story, and when he spoke his words caused our hero's heart to fill with grief.

"The trail," he said, "points to the Masketee. They alone have taken him from you."

"The Masketee."

Crusoe repeated the words, and his lips went white.

He knew that there was but little hope of ever beholding Tom Starboard again had he fallen into the power of this accursed tribe.

They were the most savage nation upon the coast, and loathed even by the red-men. They (the Masketee) ate human flesh, and their horrible rites filled the minds of those who beheld them with the deepest loathing.

"The aged hunter," Red Plume said, "shall be found, if alive."

Crusoe shook his head despondingly.

"Nay, my brother, the tribe of Aynoth are now upon the Masketee trail; the pipe of peace has been buried, and until the Aynoth tomahawks have drunk Masketee blood there will be no peace between them."

"On the Masketee trail; and how," Crusoe said,

"could my brother expect to find them upon this isle?"

"No," Red Plume answered, frankly: "we had to pass the island, and my heart yearning to learn the fate of the White Rose, and to once more behold the face of the aged hunter, this alone could have brought me here."

"Red Plume," Crusoe said, "I will accompany you upon the war trail; my rifle is at the service of the men of Aynoth."

"I would take my brother, but the great chiefs have had a vision that a white man will bring misfortune to our tribe. Thus my braves would not go upon the war path with you. Red Plume would be too happy, but he has but one voice; the chiefs have many, and all bow down when they speak."

Crusoe knew after this speech it would be impossible to alter the chief's determination, so, hiding as far as possible the disappointment he felt, he said calmly—

"My brother will come to the isle when he returns from the war path, and if the aged hunter lives, he will also come."

"He will; until then farewell. See, my people are waiting for me, and Red Plume must not be the last upon the trail of his foes."

He wrung our hero's hand, then bounded in the direction of the beach.

Crusoe watched the pit-pans leave the island and skim over the deep waters of the mystic ocean.

Then, as the last boat disappeared like a speck in the distant horizon, he turned from the sight and walked sadly towards the lovely Indian girl, who stood beneath a tree awaiting his return.

CHAPTER XXX.

ALKAY'S TREACHERY.

A MONTH passed wearily away before our hero heard from his friend, the princely chief of Aynoth. He came not in person to the island, but sent a lesser chief, named Alkay, with a message.

The red-skin came with twenty young men of the tribe.

These Red Plume had sent to remain with Crusoe upon the island to protect him and the White Rose in case a straggling party of the Macoushi or the Masketee came to avenge their late defeat, by destroying the young brave to whom the men of Aynoth owed so much.

When Alkay's pit-pan appeared off the island, our hero ran to the shore, his heart gladly beating with the hope of beholding his friend, the faithful old Tom Starboard.

In this he was disappointed, and his heart sank at the news Red Plume's messenger brought.

He told him that from intelligence gleaned from the prisoners they had taken, old Tom Starboard had been captured and sentenced to death for slaying two of the tribe when he reached the Masketee lodges.

But the night before he was to have been executed he strangled the sentinels placed over him, then escaped, and had not since been seen or heard of.

The news was somewhat comforting. It did away

with the dread uncertainty that hung over the faithful old fellow's fate.

So thought Crusoe, until Alkay told him that in the fastnesses of a thick forest, the Masketee had found a portion of their escaped prisoner's jacket, and as it was not far from a den of lions they abandoned the search, thinking he must have been torn to pieces.

"But," Alkay added, "the aged hunter was as cunning as a fox. He may have left his jacket among the trees to throw dust in the eyes of the Masketee, for they are but squaws."

There might be some truth in this, yet the chances were so much against an unarmed man escaping from the prowling beasts, that Jack felt as saddened as before, and looked upon his friend as for ever gone.

Jack felt pleased with Red Plume's friendly act.

The addition of twenty-one young and well-armed braves gave him a feeling of security, and he felt proud when Alkay placed a circlet of richly-coloured feathers upon his brow, and laid before him an exquisitely mounted tomahawk and shield.

He accepted these symbols of authority with a swelling heart, and then, placing a belt of wampum round his waist, he motioned for his little army to draw near.

They came, and Crusoe, drawing his princely form erect, said—

"Men of Aynoth, you have made me your chief. Until the dark wings of the spirit of death hover near me, may I be worthy of the trust."

Alkay answered for his followers.

"The young brave," he said, "whom the men of Aynoth love, and speak of as the Young Eagle, can command us to the death. He is a chief—a brave chief, and may his heart never be turned against us."

Crusoe's eyes sparkled with pride.

The title given him was one that none but the bravest warriors ever received.

"The Young Eagle," he said, "will forget he is white, and be a brother to his braves."

A shout of joy came from the Indians, and many rushed forward and prostrated themselves before the youthful chief.

"Go, my brothers," he said; "the White Rose will give you the flesh of the young deer. You are hungered and would eat."

His word was law with them, and led by Alkay they filed past their chief, their weapons lowered, and went towards the hut.

Crusoe watched their stalwart forms until they dispersed, then glancing at the symbols of Indian work, he soliloquized—

"Fortune plays strange freaks with us poor mortals. Here am I—not a year since, a miserable wretch, compelled to eat the bread of charity, endure the taunts and revilings of the vicious grandson, and the crone, old Madge Collins—now, what am I? A chieftain of a band of as brave men as ever trod the earth. Would that the pretty Mabel were here to see how different the poor friendless boy she so much pitied has become!"

It was indeed a great change, and well might the boy walk with a prouder step, and head erect, as his circlet of gorgeous feathers waved over his brow.

When he neared the hut he found his men seated upon the ground before the door, partaking of the food Lela had placed before them.

He passed among the dusky warriors—a smile upon his handsome face—as they arose, and paid him the same homage they would have paid to a chieftain of their colour.

Lela cried with delight when she beheld her lover arrayed in the showy symbols of an Aynoth chief, and twining her arms around his neck, she murmured—

"Men who have fought the Macoushi, men who have battled with the Masketee and the wild beasts of the lonely forest, speak of their chief, the Young Eagle, as a great and mighty warrior. Lela heard this, and her heart was glad within her breast."

"The braves of Aynoth," he said, "speak too well of me. I do not deserve it."

"My brother is wrong. Did he not save the bravest chief of a great tribe? Did he not help to drive the Macoushi from the isle, and made many a wigwam sorrowful by the wonderful tube which speaks with the lightning's flash and the roar of distant thunder? Why does not the Young Eagle wear the scalps of his foes? He is a warrior, and a chief."

"My people," Jack said, "are not cruel even to their foes; they do not scalp them, neither do they torture their prisoners."

"My brother forgets he is no longer one of the white braves, who cannot be better than the squaw, not to take the scalps of their enemies."

He tried to explain to the forest maiden the difference between the habits of his country and the savage tribe to which she belonged.

Lela listened with exemplary attention to all he had to say, and when he had finished, she shook her head and continued—

"The Young Eagle must forget that he belongs to a nation who know not what it is to fight; he must be a brave and wear the scalps of his foes.

Crusoe smiled as he muttered—

"I'll be hanged if I do, if I have to resign my new dignities for it."

The Indians soon built themselves a cluster of dwellings within sight of the young chieftain's hut.

And when the sun sank down, they would gather in the open space and amuse Crusoe with an exhibition of their warlike dances and the use of the tomahawk.

Many were the wondrous feats they performed with the deadly weapon, and soon was our hero called to join in their sports.

He found Alkay of great assistance to him in learning the various modes of the Indian warfare, and it became his chief delight to exercise them as though they were upon the war-path of a coming foe.

The time passed quickly now, and in the charm of this new phase in his wild life, Crusoe forgot all about the object of old Tom and himself leaving the beautiful isle upon which he was cast away.

Forgot, until a trifling circumstance revealed it to his memory, and caused him to at once conceive a plan whereby he could bring such articles as he stood most in need of.

The chief of them were powder and balls; for the late fight with the Macoushi had caused a woeful havoc in his little magazine.

He had the large pit-pan which brought Alkay and his followers to the island, and with this he determined to go in search of the Seagull's hull.

One morning, when he was about to start for the forest, he called his men together and made known the object in view.

"In the hull of the large canoe," he said, "I shall find enough of the lightning tubes to scatter far and wide the braves of the Macoushi or the Masketee; the journey is not far, and when my young men return, each with a tube of death in their hands, they will be glad."

Crusoe's weapon was venerated by his followers, for upon more than one occasion, when they were throwing the tomahawk and using bows, Crusoe had startled them by the fearful accuracy of his aim.

He had seen them set up a mark for their arrows—a thick log of wood—and though they were expert marksmen, not one shaft in six even struck the target.

It was then Crusoe brought his trusty rifle, and cutting a small notch in the trunk of a tree, returned about two hundred yards, then fired.

In spite of their stoicism, the red-skins could not help running forward to the mark, and when they beheld the notch split by the bullet, they gave vent to their surprise.

Crusoe knew enough of the Indian character to make him cautious in the use of his weapon.

Many of the braves manifested much curiosity in the construction of the rifle, and would fain have taken it from the boy's hand to try their skill.

Once, when it was not loaded, he gave it to Alkay.

The Indian, to Jack's surprise, drew the hammer back, brought the piece to his shoulder, and pulled the trigger, thus showing how narrowly he had watched the boy when using the rifle.

To the red-skin's surprise the hammer fell without having any report or smoke to issue from the muzzle.

Alkay stared with astonishment, and lowering the butt, peered down the bore, and then handing it to Crusoe—

"When the Young Eagle," he said, "points the wonderful weapon, fire comes forth, and unseen shafts strike the smallest mark. Will the Young Eagle tell his servant why these things are?"

Jack determined to inspire the minds of his followers with his powers, and after slyly dropping a charge of powder in the barrel, he brought the butt to his shoulder and fired.

The charge was rather a large one, and being dropped loosely in, the report was rather subdued, but a sheet of flame came from the muzzle.

At this sight Alkay stepped back with a cry of fear, and covered his face with his hands.

It was some time before he could approach the formidable weapon again; when he did so, our hero quietly assured him that to the white man alone was given the power of causing the lightning to pour from the dark tube of death.

From this time the Indians had become possessed with a desire to obtain a rifle each, and many-attempts had been made to fashion a similar weapon from pieces of hard wood.

With untiring perseverance, and great skill with the primitive tools used, they made some wooden rifles, but found that they were useless.

Thus, when Crusoe held out the hope of finding the wreck, and supplying them all with rifles, they were mad to go upon the search, and two ran to the beach to launch the pit-pans.

Crusoe called them back.

"Many moons may pass," he said, "before we find the remains of the great canoe; my people will be tired, and there are no hunting-grounds upon the surface of the great ocean, and they must eat. Let us hunt to-day in the forest, and kill plenty of game; to-morrow we will go in search of the big canoe."

The hunting party was soon formed, and until nightfall Crusoe's rifle and his followers' bows were at work.

They returned to the huts heavily laden with the day's spoil, and by the quiet moonlight birds were plucked, cleaned, and cooked. Two young fawns were also cut up and smoked, until the exterior of the flesh became sufficiently hard to resist the action of the sun's rays; thus prepared it would keep good for many weeks.

It was a tender scene, the parting between Lela and Crusoe Jack, and like a shadow of the dark trouble that was winging its flight towards them, Alkay's dusky form was visible for a few moments at the window as he watched the young pair.

Crusoe took but eighteen of his men with him.

Alkay and two braves were left to protect Lela until his return. The young lion also stayed with his mistress.

Crusoe little knew, when he left the devoted girl to Alkay's guardianship, that the Indian had conceived a violent passion for Lela, and when he peered through the window of the hut it was to gloat over the White Rose, whom he had vowed to possess when our hero's form no longer became visible from the island.

CHAPTER XXXI.

MABEL MEREDITH.

In a sweet little cottage, where the woodbine shed its fragrance through the open windows, dwelt Mabel.

It was indeed a great change for the young girl, who had been so long accustomed to the splendour of the great hall by the cliff, to become a dweller in the humble cot rented by their old servant, Hannah Miller.

The good old dame, though she kept her trouble to herself, was in hourly fear of being expelled from her dwelling.

The money Mabel's father had left was nearly gone, and she knew not when the promised remittance would arrive.

To make matters worse for the good dame, the cottage changed hands, Mrs. Collins having purchased the freehold.

The old dame little knew the motives that actuated the wrecker's wife in thus becoming the mistress of Woodbine Cottage; had the least suspicion entered the aged dame's head, she would have taken the child by the hand, and wandered from door to door to beg sufficient food to keep life within them.

Rent-day had passed nearly a month, and Mabel had day by day looked for the promised letter from her papa.

But it came not, and without as much as a loaf of bread in the cottage, the poor girl and her faithful old nurse sat by the open window, looking, and looking in vain, for the arrival of the village postman.

He came not, and Mabel, when all hope had fled, burst into a flood of tears, and threw herself upon the old dame's breast.

"Poor papa!" she said; "something must have happened to him. Another mail has come in, and no letter."

"Don't 'ee cry, my poppet," said Hannah, soothingly; "there will be another batch of letters coming in on Wednesday. It will only be two days to wait."

There was a little hope in this, and the child, drying her eyes, upturned her light, lovely face, and murmured—

"Perhaps one may come then, Hannah; but we have nothing to eat in the house."

"Don't 'ee trouble about that, because I dare say I can get a little credit at the shop. There, that's a good girl, don't 'ee cry."

It was not long to wait. Two days would soon pass away, and the letter would be doubly sweet in consequence of the long delay.

"I tell 'ee what," said old Hannah, suddenly, "if the letter don't come here it will be as well to write to thee Cousin Percy; he will give thee plenty of money if thee wants it."

Mabel's eyes dropped, and her face reddened as she said—

"Not for worlds, Hannah, would I apply to Percy."

"Would 'ee sooner starve, and be turned out of house and home?"

"Ten times sooner."

"Well! well!" and the old dame lifted her hands in astonishment; "and one's own relation, too. Why, lass, thou must be very foolish."

"No, Hannah; but I have many reasons for not applying to Percy."

"Reasons, lass?"

Old Hannah carefully adjusted her spectacles, as though their aid would enable her to understand the young girl's reasons for this—to her—strange behaviour.

"Yes, nurse; shall I tell you them?"

"Do, poppet, do."

"Percy," Mabel said, blushing, "used to tell me that I should be his wife some day, and I don't like him."

"Don't like him, lass? Deary, deary me!"

"No, nor shall I ever do so."

"Deary, deary me!" repeated Hannah, pulling the spectacles down to the bridge of her nose; "such a fine, handsome, spirited gentleman, too!"

"Yes, he may be all this, still I do not like him; neither should I like to tell him how badly we are placed. I know he would send me money. Then—then—"

"Then what, lassie? Tell me."

"He would have a claim upon me, and I should not like it."

"Thee knows best. Get my cloak, and I will go to the shop, for we maun have some supper."

Mabel passed to the inner chamber and brought old Hannah's cloak and hood, and while arranging them they were both startled by a smart knock at the door.

"Bless us!" the old dame muttered. "Who can this be, I wonder?"

She opened the door, and to her astonishment Mrs. Collins entered the hut.

The wrecker's wife was known to old Hannah, but not to Mabel.

Madge Collins was hard to recognize as the wrecker's wife. She had exchanged her old print cotton dress for rustling silk, and upon her head, where an old tattered bonnet was wont to reign, a costly fabric of lace and feathers was perched.

Her fine clothes did not become the gaunt form and coarse face. But Madge cared little for this. She had money, and those who were first to scoff and gibe at her when she was poor now bobbed and curtsied when she passed them in the village.

They saw the halo which gold sheds around its possessor, and forgot the hated woman whose fell hands had often held the death-light on the summit of the cliff, and lured many a proud vessel to destruction.

"Good evening, dame," she said, when old Hannah had stepped back from the doorway to let her pass. "Good evening, Miss Meredith."

Without waiting for any return to her salutation, she seated herself in the old Windsor arm chair, and in the most affable tone she could use, said—

"I suppose you are much surprised to see me here, Mrs. Willis?"

"Yes I am," the old lady replied. "But I ought not to be, though."

"How is that, Hannah?"

"Old Nicholas told me he thought you would buy the little cottage, and as he has not come for his money I expected that you had done so."

"Yes, dame," old Madge blandly said; "I have bought this and the two next cottages, so I thought I should come and tell my tenants that the property had changed hands."

"Yes, mum, but I hope you haven't come for the rent, because, you see, I—I—hadn't the money yet; but I dare say I shall be able to give it you on Wednesday night."

"Don't mention it, Hannah; any time will do for that—three months hence, if you like. I did not come to ask you for that, I assure you; merely a friendly visit, that is all."

"Yes, mum; thank you for calling, but I thought I might as well tell you about the rent, because there is no knowing when we may get a letter from abroad, and I thought you would think it strange if I did not pay."

"Not at all. I know the mails are very uncertain, therefore be quite easy; and should you not receive the letter you expect, pray make a friend of me. I should only be too happy in obliging you and that sweet young lady. I know," the treacherous woman added, "that we are compelled at times to suffer great inconvenience."

Old Hannah fell into the trap.

Although she had told Mabel she could procure what they required from the village, her success there was very uncertain, for the man (who was both old and disagreeable) that kept the shop made it a standing rule never to trust.

Madge's generous offer, old Hannah thought, would save her the pain of a refusal, and actuated by this motive, she said—

"Thank'ee, mum, for telling me that you would not mind being a friend to us, for, to tell 'ee the truth, we are put about sadly by Mr. Meredith's letter not arriving, and we have not any money left to get anything."

Old Madge's purse was displayed on the instant, and placing a sovereign upon the table, she said—

"I am so glad you have told me. Take this for the present, and should the letter not arrive, be sure and let me know."

Old Hannah would have accepted only one-fourth of the proffered amount, but Madge was firm, and insisted upon her using the sovereign.

Apparently to escape the delighted old dame's thanks, Madge rose and took her leave, and old Hannah soon after went to the general shop in a state of high glee.

Mabel had felt a chill pass over her frame when old Madge fixed her snake-like eyes upon the young girl's face.

She was glad when the wrecker's wife left the cottage, and would fain have dissuaded old Hannah from using the money.

"Hoity, toity," said the dame. "What now, lassie? What is the matter?"

"I do not like that woman," said the girl, "and I wish you had not borrowed that money from her. Don't use it, Hannah. We can do without until Wednesday; it is only two days, you know."

"Bless the child! she's full of fancies," said the dame; "first, she won't ask her cousin for money when we are so badly off; then, when we get some, she takes a dislike to the lender because she is not so handsome as herself. Go to sleep, lassie, for an hour, while I go out; it will do you good, and take the strange fancies from your head."

The young girl was silent. She liked not to vex her aged companion.

When partaking of the food old Madge's money had purchased, Mabel suddenly burst into tears, and exclaimed—

"I can't eat it; I really can't; it seems to choke me every mouthful I take."

"My darling lassie, what is the matter?"

"I don't know, nurse."

The old dame kissed the white smooth forehead, as she said—

"Your father's letter not coming has upset you, my child."

"Perhaps it is so, nurse, for I feel so sad and miserable that I know not what to do."

Old Hannah tried to comfort the poor girl, and after much persuasion tempted her to eat the food.

Mabel feared old Madge.

That instinct which caused this also filled her mind with a strange foreboding.

Poor child! Could she have but guessed the evil the old beldame had begun to work she would indeed have been miserable.

Soothed at length by her companion's caressive voice, she retired to her little cot, to dream of the noble-looking boy whom she believed buried beneath the waves.

To dream also of the evil, triumphant look which flashed from Madge Collins when old Hannah accepted the loan of that sum which was the forerunner of evil to them both.

It is lucky that we mortals cannot see into the future, or life would not be long endurable.

When Madge returned to the lone hut on the cliff, she found her hopeful grandson seated at the table busily perusing a pile of papers he had that day received from the conscientious Mr. Twistem.

He looked up when she entered, and asked—

"Well, have you seen her?"

"I have." She gave vent to a low chuckle of triumph as she spoke. "I began the work."

His eyes glistened at her words.

"They do not suspect," he asked, "that you have bribed the post-boy to secure the letter?"

"No," she said; "far from it; they look forward to Wednesday to bring them the remittance they require."

Jasper gave a diabolical grin.

"We have that safe," he said; "now what are we to do about the bank notes he sent?"

"Keep them," was the answer; "they'll help to pay the lawyer's account."

"True. Have you read this last letter from Twistem?"

"I have not. You can tell me the contents."

"Yes, in a few words. He has succeeded in paying off the claimant for the estate, and three days more I am to go to London."

"To London?"

"Yes; from thence to the old country seat, to take possession of that fellow's estate—at least, it would have been his had he lived."

"I am sorry he is dead."

"Why?"

"Because we lose half our triumph."

"I can't see that."

"I will explain," said Madge, spitefully. "Had he lived we could still have obtained possession of the estate, and while he remained here, performing the most menial services, you could have been in the enjoyment of his property, and in a position to have made him feel your hate."

Jasper's face would have done credit to a fiend's as he heard these words.

"True," he said. "All this could have been done. I wish he had lived."

"So do I. But it is no use doing that. Let us see about business."

"I am quite ready."

"When do you think you will return here?"

"After I go to London?"

"Yes."

"That will be vexatious. A few months, at the least.

"So much the better."

"Why?"

"For a very simple reason."

"What is that?"

"While you are away getting used to your new position I can keep a watch over the bird I have promised to snare for you."

"I had almost forgotten that. You will be compelled to remain behind. I had hoped you would accompany me."

"For what purpose?"

"To share in the good fortune to which you have raised me, to triumph over those who are ever ready to revile the wrecker's wife and her deformed grandson."

"Curse them!"

"Ay." Jasper showed his teeth as he spoke. "Ay, curse them!—three times curse them!—but they yet shall feel the cripple's sting. You know how I can hate, and it will go hard with me if I do not bring ruin and misery to all who have been ever ready to point the finger of scorn towards us!"

"You can do it, Jasper; you will have gold in abundance; spend it, boy, in the work of revenge. Ha, ha! how great is our triumph! the wrecker's grandson placed in the halls of an old family, and a coronet in perspective."

"It is, indeed, a triumph; you do your part, grandam, I will do mine."

"My part?"

"Yes; bring that proud, haughty girl, beggar as she now is, to my arms, and I will show you how I can repay her withering words and the lashing I received from her fine cousin.

"Do not trouble yourself about her; in less than six months she shall be yours."

"Enough; you have promised, and I never knew you yet to break your word."

"I shall not in this instance. Good night, Jasper; I shall not see you before you leave in the morning. Remember my parting words, *beware of that smooth-tongued lawyer*; he has overreached us I know, but how I cannot say."

"I shall remember your caution; keep a wary eye upon Mabel Meredith, for I would sooner lose the estate than lose her."

"She shall be yours by the time I have promised.

"I am content."

The next morning Jasper Collins went to London, and from there to Crusoe's inheritance. Thus he secured our hero's name, and began to look forward to the time when he should be made a baronet.

Madge, meanwhile, continued to plot against the peace of the gentle girl, and, by bribing the village postman, she obtained the letters sent by Mr. Meredith to his daughter.

A TIMELY SHOT.

The last letter she thus obtained told she had but little time to lose.

The father, in that epistle, spoke of the joy he should feel at once more beholding his child.

He told the gentle girl that he should return to England by the first vessel that left the port, and fetch her to the land of plenty.

Old Madge locked the letter up in a box, and, wiping her spectacles, muttered—

"I have no time to lose. Next week the blow must be struck that will give to Jasper's arms a beautiful girl; when he is tired of her charms, he can revenge himself for the haughty manner in which she has behaved to him, and the manner in which she spoke of that baby-faced ape, Crusoe Jack."

10

CHAPTER XXXII.
A STRANGE MEETING.

OUR hero and his men braved the dangers of the sea in their light boat.

From island to island they went, hoping at every new place to behold the remains of the great canoe.

The work lasted for upwards of a week, and still no signs of the Seagull. And one evening, when they had reached a leafy covering to protect them from the night dews, Crusoe was startled from his sleep by an exclamation from the look-out.

He sprang to his feet and ran to the water's edge, and for a moment he could scarcely believe in the truth of his eyes.

Seated across two logs, and drifting towards the island, was the well-known form of his friend Tom Starboard.

In less than an hour the boy was locked in the brave old tar's arms; and when the first greetings were over, old Tom told him that he had been carried away by the Masketee, and after making his escape as Alkay had described, he left his tiger-skin jacket in the forest to mislead his pursuers.

The *ruse* succeeded, but poor old Tom soon fell into further misfortunes; he made for the shore of the Masketee's country, but soon had the good fortune to meet with a ship's boat, that had come ashore for water.

The captain heard his strange story and took him aboard.

On board the Speedwell he received every attention, and fortunately met an old shipmate, named Ned Harley, who had sailed with him when upon that fatal whaling expedition when old Tom lost his only brother.

Lying side by side beneath the calm starlight, old Tom began to explain the mysterious marks which had so puzzled his youthful friend.

"Tell me that," the boy said, "when we have more time. I want to learn how you came upon those logs and floating about at the mercy of the waves."

"It is a long story, lad."

"So much the better —we have a long night before us."

"That's true, Jack—where shall I begin?"

"Where you like."

"Well, I will do so from the time I stood on the Speedwell's deck, and the vessel sailed from the island."

"That will do; you can tell me the other part when we return to the island."

"Very well, lad. You must know it was somewhere near Patagonia where I shipped on board the Speedwell boat.

"We did not go through the Straits of Magellan, as the passage was dangerous; but we passed them, and doubled Cape Horn. We went merrily on; now and then touching land, to take in water, fruits and live stock; now and then speaking a vessel bound for England; and now and then finding some new kind of fish or wonderful bird, until we neared the island of Juan Fernandez.

"There the weather changed, and such a storm came down upon us as I never experienced till then, or since.

"Before it reached its height, I remember poor Ned made me laugh; a gust blew my hat off, and he called out—

"'Tom, your hair will be blown off too, if you don't hold it on; my shoe-strings have been whisked out this half-hour!'

"The fury of the storm soon increased, so as to put all laughter and joking out of our thoughts. Night drooped around so rapidly that it seemed as if a mighty black shroud had fallen suddenly over us.

"You have witnessed a storm—a wreck—and have seen the wild waves, 'the wide, wide tomb,' closing over your fellow-creatures; so I will not dwell upon the dreadful sight that I was witness to, when the gallant vessel which had weathered so many storms struck on a sunken rock and went to pieces, as if she had been made of glass!

"I got entangled in some loosened rigging, which had been snapped and unravelled like twine; and this circumstance, which I expected would be the cause of my death, saved my life.

"Part of the topmast was attached to the ropes, which the furious blast twisted round me, as it swept off my shipmates in crowds into the fierce waters; and away I went also at the same moment, with my brave and true-hearted captain! I never afterwards saw a soul from that vessel, nor an atom of her stout planks.

"My past life seemed a dream, and that moving home a phantom—a fancy—when I recalled the circumstances of the sudden wreck to my remembrance.

"How long I floated in my net-work of ropes I cannot tell; sure I am that I did not lose my senses; for I well remember the wrath of the panting billows, as they were urged onwards by the furious hurricane; on they dashed over my defenceless head, swirling the shattered mist against my wounded limbs, and straining the cords till they cut into my flesh.

"I remember, too, that the storm seemed to subside as quickly as it had arisen, and that though the ship had struck during all the black horrors of night, I saw the gray dawn to the east, and the sullen masses of clouds rolling off as if they dared not stay to look upon the mischief of that awful night.

"Then a noise as of a vessel toiling through the waves, came over me, and a mixed feeling of fear and hope that it was the Speedwell, safe and close to me, passed through my confused brain. Then a shout, and a grappling with my coiling ropes. Then a sensation of the soft air, and of my mounting through it; and then a buzz of voices, as I lay in quietness on a solid floor.

"Alas! alas! how wretched I felt when I found that all the voices were strange, the language foreign, and the faces dark and unknown to me. A Portuguese merchant vessel, bound for the city and port of Guayaquil, had weathered the gale and picked me up.

"I cannot describe to you, Jack, the forlorn state of my feelings after this terrible wreck. The captain, with all his goodness and bravery, gone! my companions vanished! my beautiful ocean home, the gallant ship—the work of years—scattered on the waves!

"My own situation and the altered state of my mode of existence I did not consider, till I was compelled to feel it severely, by the coarse treatment I met with from those who had saved my life.

"I was made to work my way (that I expected, and could not complain of), but I felt sadly the difference in the manners of the captain and his crew, compared with those of the Speedwell.

"However, 'tis no use dwelling on that sad time, which dragged on so slowly, till I reached the port to which the vessel was bound, where we dropped anchor.

"I thanked the captain for saving my life, and told him I intended to leave the ship. To my surprise, he replied that I should not. I said that he had no control over me, that I was an Englishman, and would not be compelled to serve in a foreign vessel.

"'Then,' said the mean wretch, 'pay me for your passage from Juan Fernandez, and you may leave the ship.'

"This he knew it was impossible I could do, as I had nothing. I told him so, but he only laughed in my face, and said—

"'That's not my look-out. You shall pay me, or stay where you are;' and with an oath in which *Madre di Dios* (Mother of God) bore a large share, he turned on his heel, and left me to my own sad feelings; and they were sad enough, for I had not a friend within hundreds of miles of me, and I was in the power of a hard-hearted man.

"For a few minutes I gave way to despair, but my natural firmness soon returned. I reflected that I had, in fact, paid my passage, by working even more than my share in the vessel, and therefore I felt no scruple in quitting it, should an opportunity offer.

"I was resolved I would not remain with such a crew of dirty, superstitious fellows; but I was confident it would be no easy matter to leave them, for though I do not wish to appear boastful, I must say that I could not help knowing that I was a better sailor than any one in the ship, and I was confident that they all knew it, too; no wonder, then, that it was a desirable thing for them to keep me on board.

"I now found that I was closely watched; but I was much more kindly treated, in order, doubtless, to make me contented with my situation.

"We had dropped anchor as much as a league from the shore, partly, I suspected, to prevent me from attempting to escape by swimming such a distance; but they little knew what the resolution of an English tar could induce him to undertake in order to regain his liberty.

"I appeared to be quite satisfied with the captain's determination, and waited quietly for an opportunity to escape; the time, however, drew nigh for the vessel to put out to sea again, on a farther coasting voyage, and as yet no attempt had even been possible.

"On the very evening, however, before she was to sail, I had to take my turn in the night watch, with two others, who had orders to keep an eye on me.

"'This night, or never!' said I to myself, as I took my station.

"While I was walking the deck, one of my shipmates being at the masthead, and the other astern, the ship suddenly quivered, as if she were in an ague fit. Down slipped the fellow from on high, and fell flat on his face; the other rushed forward and knelt beside him, both crossing themselves and gabbling all the prayers to all the saints they could think of.

"I, you may be sure, lost no time; but immediately seizing a plank, I hastily lashed it at my back with a rope, which by great good chance lay near me; then slipping astern, I let myself quietly down, and dropped into the water. The noise of the splash, I feared, would betray me; but another shiver, accompanied by a shock, as if the vessel had struck ground (though she was at anchor and the weather calm), set the fellows off again at a fresh volley of prayers, and they did not hear me.

"I gave all up for lost, though, the next minute, when I heard the jabbering of the merciless captain and the rest of his crew, as they came tumbling up on deck; but I took courage when I found they were all praying; so I quietly struck off, though making but little way, owing to the board on my back.

"You may suppose that I made eagerly for shore, but it was a weary distance from me.

"The reason I encumbered myself with the board was that I might turn on my back and float, when I became fatigued with the exertion of swimming."

"But, Tom, what was the matter with the ship?" Jack asked.

"You will hear directly," he replied, "but you guessed, of course, that it was the effect of an earthquake, didn't you?"

"*I did*; so go on, Tom," said Jack, and Tom went on.

"As I continued my toilsome passage, sometimes floating with the tide, which was fortunately flowing—that is, setting in towards shore—and sometimes swimming, I heard a loud bellowing of the troubled earth, and felt the water jar me as if it had been a solid substance; suddenly a towering volcano, which I took to be Cotopaxi, for I had seen it on clear days at above a hundred miles distance, became illuminated, appearing like an immense lighthouse; the thundering increased, and shrieks and other frightful noises were borne to me over the water.

"At last, when I was nearly exhausted, I was thrown ashore, where I lay to recover breath and strength; but oh, the distress and confusion that then took place!

"Many of the inhabitants of the city came crowding down to the water's edge for safety. Houses had been destroyed; the earth was rocking and heaving like an angry ocean; streams of water had gushed out of the ground where no water had ever been before; suffocating fumes of sulphur burst up under the feet of the terrified and flying sufferers; and when morning dawned, the face of the country seemed changed.

"Still the town itself had sustained but little damage, and the inhabitants began to return to their dwellings and their business. They are so much accustomed to earthquakes all over the province of Peru, that it is not surprising they should so soon lose their terrors.

"In the general distress I met with but little compassion or succour, which I then thought wonderful; but I had yet to learn that affliction hardens the heart.

"No one relieved my hunger, so I ventured to steal a handful of chocolate nuts from a heap that had fallen out of a basket, which had been thrown down during the night. These I beat between two stones, and mixed with a little water; and this was my food for that day.

"As I wandered about among the shipping, looking in vain for a vessel, I recollected that the bay of Guayaquil is famous for a small shell-fish, about the size of a nut; it is called *turbine*, and produces a purple dye, reckoned the best in the world.

"So I boldly seized a small boat that was lying at anchor; and, pushing out into the bay, I caught a few of these little, valuable fish, and returned to shore again before the owner of the boat had missed it.

"I was now sure of a resource against starving, provided any one would buy my turbines.

"I was soon fortunate enough to find a purchaser; so I pursued this plan for several days; always taking the same boat, which no one appeared to claim.

"Perhaps the owner, poor fellow! had been destroyed during the earthquake.

"I slept every night in a hut close to the sea; and, on the fifth morning, I found a French vessel in the harbour, which was proceeding on her voyage to Buonaventura, and to Acapulca, in Mexico.

"I immediately went to the captain, and offered to work my way to the port of Buonaventura, if he would give me my passage; I told him my story, and he was kind enough to grant my request.

"In due time we reached the port; and, with gratitude for the captain's kindness, I left the vessel. I had formed the resolution of crossing over the continent of South America alone, and on foot! I longed to see you again, my lad.

"I must have seemed mad," said Tom, "and so the French captain thought, I believe; and was not sorry to get rid of me. He was a kind-hearted man, however, for he gave me thirty francs, a gun, and some gunpowder; saying, with a shrug of his shoulder, as he bade me farewell—'Eh bien, donc, vous êtes bien courageux! Mais souvenez-vous qu'il faut manger; et que ce fusil vous rendre de bon service.'*

"I was, you may be sure, grateful to the captain; and I hope he thought me so. But don't look so wonder-struck, Jack; you think me a mad-brained fellow: and yet if I had not done so we should never have met again.

"I provided myself with a wallet," continued Tom, "which was to contain shoes stockings, gloves, and a shirt; then inquiring the road to Zita, I set out before sunrise, towards the Andes.

"I was two months in crossing the desolate northern extremity of those giants of the earth. I bought—nay, I did not buy, I found—a mule, that was browsing on some prickly shrub—I forget its name—in a wild pass of the mountains. She was saddled and bridled, and had evidently lost her master. I looked in vain for some hours, but could find no trace of any traveller; so I felt justified in taking possession of her.

"It was well I did, for the sure-footed beast took me safely over dangerous passes that I never could have crossed without such assistance; many times, on the summit of a peak like a sugar-loaf, has that creature, with a sagacity that was quite astonishing, stood looking from side to side, then, slowly taking aim, has folded her legs under her and slid down with me on her back for many hundred feet!

"She played truant, however, one night, slipped her bridle, which I always had wound round my arm

while I slept, and wandered away, leaving me on the borders of a trackless forest.

"Once I crossed a mighty torrent that was boiling along at the depth of a hundred feet below me, through a narrow ravine; and what sort of a bridge do you think I ventured upon? Two large fragments of rock, one from either side, had fallen together during some earthquake, I suppose, and had formed a natural bridge, quite firm and safe, over which I crossed.

"Another time I had to pass a rift, or chasm of prodigious depth, near an ancient village, the ingenious inhabitants of which had constructed a bridge of rushes, in the following manner—two strong posts were fixed in the rock on each side, and to these were fastened ropes of rushes; the path upon them being made of the same material, plaited together. On each side was also a rope, for the passenger to steady himself by.

"These bridges, in fact, are the origin of our chain or suspension bridges; but the elastic and light nature of the rush makes the motion of the bridge very unpleasant; indeed, when I had gone about half-way across, my head seemed to swim, and I was obliged to sit down, to recover myself; I really thought I never should reach the opposite side of it! I sat there swinging in the high wind, in a most perilous, yet ridiculous situation.

"I wished much, while I was among the Andes, to see the interior of one of the mines; but they were all too distant from me; the quicksilver mine of Huancavelica is particularly curious, having a complete town, and its cathedral, 'deep in the bowels of the earth.'

"I shall not attempt to take you toiling on regularly, day by day, nor even week by week, my lad; nor shall I tell you of half the dangers, difficulties, and troubles I met with.

"I made the sun my guide by day, and the stars by night; I roosted in trees, like the birds; and ate fruit and herbs, like the beasts.

"I explored mountain torrents, which no human being, probably, had ever seen before, and found diamonds in their beds, which had been dried up.

"I collected gold, too, from the mud of the rivers, and curiosities out of number, which I was obliged to throw away for want of convenience to carry them.

"I became, however, in a few weeks so accustomed to my solitary life, that I learned how to avoid the dangers by which I was surrounded, in a surprising manner.

"I met with tribes of native Indians, who had never heard of the name of England, and had never seen an Englishman; and perhaps this ignorance surprised me more than anything that occurred to me; perhaps, too, it taught me the best lesson in humility that I ever met with.

"Ours is a great nation; and we are all so much accustomed to hear, and to believe this, that we are too apt to think that the world could not go on without our assistance.

"A sailor is particularly liable to feel too proud; for, go where he will, on every coast of every maritime nation (that is, nations bordering on the sea), he finds his fellow-countrymen and their ships.

* Well, you are very courageous! but, remember, you must eat; and this gun will be of much use to you.

"In the wilds of South America, however, as I tell you, I discovered that it was possible for our great and powerful England to be unknown; and that I was looked upon as a kind of savage, a something quite inferior to the uncouth and uneducated creatures among whom I wandered for months.

"I travelled about one thousand eight hundred miles, but I did not walk all the way; I frequently went with the Indians up their rivers; and for above five hundred miles I rode on mules, or wild horses, which I caught by stratagem.

"Once I had a narrow escape, I remember, from being devoured by a puma.

"One day, I had come unawares upon a herd of wild horses that were grazing quietly on the borders of a forest.

"I had been walking a long way, and felt tired; so I thought I might as well try to catch one of these horses, and vary my mode of journeying, by riding again.

"I had heard of the manner in which the Guachos (or South American peasants) catch them with a lasso, or long rope, which has a loop at the end of it; and this they expertly throw over the head of the animal that they single out; their dexterity is surprising.

"I feared, however, to attempt such an exploit, lest I should fail, and thus frighten them all away; besides, I had no rope that was long enough. So I set my wits to work, and thus I tried my scheme.

"I observed among the trees that skirted the plain a pool of water. To this pool I made my way, for, thought I, they will surely come there by-and-by to drink, so I climbed up into a cinchona, or bark tree.

"Having fastened one end of my rope tightly round one of the lower branches, I made the other into a slip-knot, or noose; and then I waited patiently for my expected prey.

"The cinchona, I should tell you, looks somewhat like a cherry-tree. I had leisure as I sat to observe the beautiful trees that grew around me, and to admire the exquisite loveliness of the flowers of the *parasitical* plants—that is, those which do not root in the earth, but which grow on other trees and shrubs (such as the *mistletoe*, that you have often seen on apple-trees)—which hung in wreaths and festoons from bough to bough, climbing to the very tops, and hanging out their rich clusters of various colours from among the dark leaves of the towering trees.

"Humming-birds, too, of the brightest plumage, were flitting about these flowers like winged gems; rubies, emeralds, topazes, sapphires, seemed chasing each other in the air.

"While I sat admiring these pretty creatures, evening drew on, and they quickly disappeared; I then noticed some rocks, in dark masses, that frowned out from amidst the foliage, clothed with fern-trees, among which I saw the bottle-shaped nests of the *orioles*, tropical birds, that were warbling harmoniously, but whose notes were almost overpowered by the hoarse cries of the flaring parrots and macaws, which were glancing and screaming about in all directions; their noise was so loud at times as to drown the roar of the silvery cascade, which I saw dashing its white spray through the foliage.

"At last, the whole herd of horses left their pasture in a body, and came neighing and gambolling towards the waters, with their tails sailing in the wind, and their long manes waving about with every graceful turn of their bodies.

"I assure you, it was rather an appalling sight to see myself close over the heads of so many powerful animals, that made the ground echo with their movements.

"I sat still, however, enjoying myself with a calabash shell full of milk, which I had drawn from a *cow-tree* that grew on the rock near me.

"I had just finished my bowl of vegetable milk, when a fine horse came under my cinchona-tree, and stooped to drink; so I crept to the end of the branch; and as he raised his head, I slipped the noose over his neck and drew it tight; the start he gave when he found himself confined, frightened his companions, and away they all scampered, leaving me and my prisoner alone.

"Instead of striving to break the rope and escape, which he might have done with ease, his courage seemed cowed by this new kind of restraint.

"I had some struggles, it is true; but I quickly conquered him by kindness and patience, and we were soon friends; but I resolved not to mount him in order to pursue my journey for some time.

"In the evening, then, having refreshed myself with some of the fruits that grew near me—for while I journeyed through the forests I never wanted food—I took a fancy to explore a cavern that I saw in the rock, near which the cascade tumbled. I resolved to be well prepared for any enemy, so I took my gun, and left my horse grazing at the foot of the bark-tree.

"As I drew near the lofty cavern, I was astonished at the noise—the deafening noise—of innumerable wings, and looking up in the uncertain twilight, I saw hundreds, I may say thousands of birds flying about, and preparing to leave their home in search of food; they were the *guacharos*, night-birds that somewhat resemble our fern owls; but instead of roosting on trees, these creatures build in caverns—their noise is prodigious.

"Indeed, the different sounds at night in those vast forests of South America, are not the least wonderful of the circumstances that attend travelling through them. The howling monkeys, the night-birds, the sharp calls of the jaguars, the roar of the pumas, the whistling of the alouetes monkeys, the flapping of wings, the rustling of ~~branches~~, and other noises are astonishing.

"How different from the lone solitude of our woods in England, where an owl hooting is the only sound that disturbs the silence of the night, except perhaps that a dog baying the moon in the distance, makes us aware that one other living thing is waking.

"Well, I stayed so long in the bird cavern, that it was dark when I got back to my horse, and I had not yet made up my nightly fire.

"So I had to collect leaves and sticks, almost in the dark. I was kneeling down, blowing away at the heap of fuel which I had just lighted, when my horse suddenly started, drew back to the full length of the cord, rolled his eyes, enlarged his nostrils, threw his ears forward, erected his mane and tail, and stood the very image of terror.

"I jumped up hastily, and looking into the gloom in the direction which his eyes took, there I saw a dark mass, moving softly along among the bushes. I was up the tree in an instant, and then I drew up my gun which I had rested against the trunk.

"All was quiet for a minute, then this gliding figure came nearer, but so quietly, that I should have thought myself deceived had not the horse shown such symptoms of alarm; I therefore levelled my piece, fired, and as I judged, wounded the animal, which bounded up and darted off into the thicket, at the moment that the fire burst into a bright blaze, and of course kept all the wild animals away.

"I rested, however, but indifferently this night, for want of my rope, which I had used to confine my horse. Hitherto, I had always looked for a tree with the branches going out in this way," said Tom, holding up his hand and showing his fingers, all rising from one centre, as the branches spread out sometimes from the trunk of trees; "and when I had found one I laced the rope in and out of two boughs, so as to form a kind of cradle; thus supported, I slept in peace, excepting that sometimes the vampire-bat would annoy me by sucking my blood.

"He did it though so quietly, that I suffered no pain; and perhaps it was serviceable to me to lose a little blood; it is not improbable that these flying surgeons kept me in health by their gentle bleedings. The vampire-bat does not subsist entirely by sucking the blood of living animals; it feeds also on insects and young fruits.

"One morning when I awoke and was coming down from my cradle, I found that a rattlesnake had coiled itself round the stem of the tree, and I thought it would be all over with me, but my presence of mind did not forsake me even in this case, for as the reptile reared his flat, wide, terrible head, I took such good aim, and was so near, that I blew it to atoms.

"Once I caught a poisonous snake called the *laburri* snake, that I might look for and examine the fangs which contain its venom. I saw it asleep, and creeping cautiously towards it I sprang at its neck, which I grasped tightly with my hands, its mouth was then forced open, then taking a small piece of stick I pressed it on the fang, the point of which communicated with the root where the bag of poison is, and I saw the venom ooze out; it was of a thick substance, and of a yellow colour.

"Well, I came at last to the dreary plain or steppe, and here my troubles were severe; all kinds of stinging insects, serpents, and horrible reptiles annoyed me. I suffered also from a scanty supply of food; sometimes I was lucky enough to find a plant called *tillandsia*, which resembles an aloe, and contains a quantity of pure water in its stem, but I rarely found it unless a few trees grew above it, for it loves a sheltered situation.

"When I had not this luxury I was obliged to drink the horrible water of the river, which swarmed with animalculæ to such a degree that I seemed to swallow as much solid as liquid; I wonder it did not kill me. I was obliged to destroy my poor horse, and leave him to be devoured by the condero, for he could find no food in these wide plains, where the rivers overflow every year.

"After travelling a long time, I came upon a wandering tribe of natives, consisting of three or four families, and entering one of their wretched huts, which were built with clay and leaves, I asked them for food in the few words I knew; but they did not understand me, so I had recourse to signs, and made them understand I was very hungry. They then gave me some food and turned away from me, lying down in their hammocks, which, with fourteen others, were slung from some beams above. I counted fifteen persons, all naked, lying indolently around me.

"I was so tired and wet—for it was now the rainy season—and so disgusted with my food, that I sought rest by following the example of the tribe.

"I stayed a few days with these Indians, not because I liked them, for they were the most apathetic and idle of human beings. They had no wants beyond eating and drinking, so that they had no employment. No clothes to make or mend, or domestic cares. I stayed because the rainy season was at its height, and the vast plain was now under water; but I quitted them as soon as I could, with no other feeling than thankfulness for their having given me food and for not having put me to death.

"But they would not have fed me, only it was less trouble than to refuse me, and they would have killed me only it was too much exertion; for I never saw such a set of indolent creatures in my life. I heard the word Oroonoco just before I left them, and found by signs that the larger of the next two streams I should come to, towards the south, was the river I was so anxious to reach. I did reach it, but had many hundred miles to travel before I should reach the island.

"Once I imprudently went into a pleasant, cool-looking piece of water, beautifully overshadowed by trees, that I might have a bath. I had scarcely struck out twice before I felt a shock as severe as ever I experienced from an electrifying machine."

"Was it a crab bit your foot?"

"No, Jack, the shock was given to me by an electrical eel; you remember me telling you of the torpedo?"

"Yes; if you even touch them with a long stick, you feel a great shock at all your joints."

"Yes," Tom continued, smiling. "The shock I felt was indeed great, as you may suppose. It took away all my strength, and my senses, too, and I should have died had not an Indian woman just then come down to the pool to dip water. She saw my situation, and guessing the cause, lost no time in dragging me out before the reptile could repeat his attack; this eel in its proportions somewhat resembles the torpedo.

"The rainy season was now over, and all nature became again fresh and beautiful. You can have no idea of the delicious feelings that I used to experience in the early morning; the comparro, perched on the top of a lofty mora-tree, used to awaken me by his clear ringing note.

"Just before sunrise, the night birds and prowling beasts of prey had retired to their rest; the insects were not yet warmed into their busy life, the cool dewy dawn spread overhead its lines of gray and yellow and rose colour, which shone through the boughs above and around me, the deep orange glow in the east came rich and warm through the glittering drops that hung upon the fragrant blossoms of the climbing shrubs above my leafy cradles; birds of every hue and form sang to me—monkeys frolicked from bough to bough with a happy fearlessness and agility that was astonishing.

"And the sloth, even that most harmless yet contemned of animals, would, at this sweet hour of prime, look in my face with less of woe in his own as I lay watching his singular movements with the most intense delight.

"I had now," continued Tom, "been a long time in this forest without meeting any of my fellow-creatures, and I began to want your companionship. True, I took a pleasure and pride in being independent, by making the wonderful productions of nature useful to me without the assistance of others, but my attempts were uncouth; for instance, having found a beautiful caoutchouc or india-rubber tree, from which the gum was flowing, I thought I might, perhaps, strengthen my shoes by letting the liquid flow on to them so as to form a new sole; this took some time, you may imagine, as it was necessary to allow each morning's running to set hard before another was added.

"I made hats by splitting some of the tough thick leaves of a species of olive, and so on.

"One night, on the verge of a forest, I had taken up my nightly quarters and was going to sleep in my cradle, when I saw a light glancing among the trees, and as I had been wishing to reach a village in order to procure a fresh rope, which the natives ingeniously form by twisting the long fibres of the leaves of the cocoa-nut tree,* I came down from my roosting-place and went towards the light. I was quickly at an open part of the forest, and as quickly up to my knees in quagmire, the treacherous beacon in the meantime changing its shape and position with every movement I made to extricate myself. Sometimes it was elongated and then it became contracted again; when in the former state it is called *draco volans*, or flying dragon; in the latter, *ignis fatuus*.

"Following this light, though it brought me into all sorts of scrapes at first, was the means in the end of meeting you."

"How was that, Tom?"

"Well, you see, after I scrambled out of the quagmire, I took especial care to keep away from those will-o'-the-wisps, and by skirting the forest I found myself upon the margin of a clear pool.

"Taking the direction of the water, I found it led to a small creek; this I knew by the course it was taking led in its turn to the sea."

"In a moment the idea of passing down the creek and trusting to a passing vessel to pick me up came

* Cocos Mescifera

to my mind, and without pausing to consider the rashness of the scheme, I spliced a couple of logs together and was soon aboard, or rather astride of them.

"When you saw me, Jack, floating about at the mercy of the waves, I had been twelve hours in one position. I dared not move for fear the craft would capsize, and send me to old Davy's locker.

"There, Jack," he said, in conclusion, "that's my yarn, and if I haven't had enough for the little time we have been parted, tell me."

CHAPTER XXXIII.

HOW ALKAY KEPT HIS TRUST.

"You have, indeed, had your share of adventure, Tom," our hero said, "since we parted."

"Ay, boy, I expect I was born to see strange sights, and pass through more than most men."

"I believe you have, Tom. "I have no doubt the strangest part of your story is yet to be told."

"No, lad, not the strangest, for my mind before I got a berth on the Speedwell was too much filled with plans of escape to note the wondrous works of Nature. I do not consider that the handiwork of man is at all strange; it is the sublime mysteries of this planet that always impress me as being grand, and beyond our comprehension."

"They are, Tom; still, the very fact of your escaping from that fierce tribe of Indians, and the strange marks you left, are wonders beyond the ordinary course of events."

"P'raps so, lad—p'raps so; I dare say you often wondered what it all meant."

"I did, and though many hours I spent in following your trail, the mystery only became deeper."

Old Tom laughed.

"No wonder, lad—no wonder," he said, "those marks that so puzzled you were made on purpose to puzzle more cunning woodmen, and had it not been for an unlucky slip, I believe I should have got away and been saved the trouble of my long, but interesting journey."

Crusoe opened his eyes wide with astonishment as he repeated—

"You made those marks, Tom?"

"Ay, lad; does it seem strange?"

"It does, indeed."

"Yet it is easy of explanation. Listen, lad; it will be a lesson for you when the red-skins are on your trail."

One of the Aynoth braves came towards our hero at this moment, and bowing low his plumed head, asked—

"Will the Young Eagle sleep beneath the shadows of the trees, or shall his men build him a cool retreat that the sun may not scorch his brow?"

"We shall leave the island," Crusoe said, "before the sun rides high in the heavens; until then, the Eagle would be alone with his aged friend. Let my young men go to the forest, they will find plenty of work for their bows."

A silent inclination of the head answered those words, and the dusky form glided softly away.

"Fine-limbed men those," old Tom said; "had you rifles enough to arm them, it would take a hostile tribe some time to drive you from the island."

"It would as it is," Jack answered; "these fellows fight like demons. Speaking of rifles, it was for that purpose I started in search of the Seagull's hull."

"You came the wrong way, lad; the old leaky hull lies a long distance to the north-east, or else I am much out of my reckoning."

"I have come in the opposite course, then."

"Sure to do that, lad; if there's two ways to do a thing, depend upon it we always go the wrong way first."

"I believe you are about right there, Tom. But come, let us have your explanation of those strange marks in the forest."

"Right, lad. Now tell me what you saw."

"On the sands," Jack said, "I found the marks of your moccasins; then there were the prints of about a dozen naked feet."

"Right, go on."

"A little farther off, I saw that three canoes had been grounded."

"Correct, boy; what else?"

"When I returned towards the hut, bewildered by your sudden disappearance, I saw the broken feather from a chief's head-dress lying at the foot of a tree."

"Yes, lad, correct again."

"Not far from this I found your rifle, hidden under the brushwood, and, on the small of the stock, and near the muzzle, the weapon bore the imprint of two blood-stained hands."

"Ha! ha!" laughed old Tom; "I suppose that scared you a bit, lad?"

"It did; I made sure you were slain."

"Not yet, boy, though I ran a pretty good chance of being eaten afterwards, as you shall hear; but first, I will explain the peculiar appearance my trail presented.

"This is how it happened," old Tom continued. "You remember when we parted to go in search of the Indian girl?"

"Yes."

"Well, when I reached the point I had marked out to enter the forest, I was a trifle scared by hearing a jabbering among the trees. Monkeys, I thought; but with the thought came the sounds in a louder key, and I knew that a party of Indians were not far off.

"A minute's listening told me they were not of the Aynoth tribe, and to my horror, when the moon suddenly burst forth, I knew by the yellow paint on the devils' breasts that I had walked into a nest of the Masketee Indians."

"A nest. How do you mean, Tom?"

"Thus," Tom Starboard said; "the party were concealed by a clump of dwarf trees, and I knew not of their presence until I found myself surrounded."

"Not a pleasant position."

"Far from it, Jack. Well, you may be sure I was more surprised than pleased."

"I can believe that."

"And," Tom continued, "did my best to get clear of the trap; but, bless you, they were upon me in an instant, and, though I knocked several of them down with the butt of my piece, I had to give in through an unlucky chop I received from a tomahawk; it was here."

Old Tom raised his cap and showed Crusoe a red seam, a little above the frontal bone.

"From this wound," he continued, "the blood trickled down into my eyes, and, as a matter of course, blinded me, and gave the devils a chance they would otherwise not have had. It was from occasionally cleansing this from my eyes that my hands became stained, and left the marks upon the rifle."

"But," Crusoe asked, "how came it under the brushwood?"

"You shall hear. When I found that fighting was no use, I made a sudden rush from them, and thrust the piece under the brushwood. They would have found it, had you not fired when they began to search."

"That," Crusoe said, "must have been the report of my rifle when I shot one of the tigers that were about to spring on Lela."

"I guessed as much, lad, and though I struggled hard to get away—for the signal you gave filled me with a giant's strength, and made me frantic to escape —it was no use, though I pretty well damaged some of their faces with my fist, they settled me with a blow from a tomahawk, then carried me from the forest."

"This accounts," said Jack, "for the absence of your footmarks between the forest and the shore."

"Exactly, lad; for I did not recover until we were close upon the canoes, then I had another set-to with them; but I might have saved myself the trouble, for they bound me with deer-skin thongs, and pitched my old carcase in the bottom of a canoe, then pulled like madmen from the island."

"Something must have startled them, Tom."

"Yes, boy; it was the second report of your piece. Well, the beggars were not long in reaching the mainland, and when they did so, I knew my doom was settled."

"Why?"

"Because, in place of taking me to their lodges I was taken to a stockade, and two fellows left to watch over me until the time came for me to be killed and eaten."

"A pleasant prospect!"

"Yes; but as it did not agree with my notions of a comfortable death, I knocked my sentinels on the head and escaped. You have heard how I put them off the trail by leaving my tiger-skin jacket in the forest?"

"I have. Ah! there is the first sign of the coming day, so we will have an hour's sleep before the sun comes upon us."

Old Tom was quite agreeable to this. He was weary and in pain when Crusoe first beheld him on the floating logs; but knowing how anxious his young favourite was to hear the story of his adventures since they parted, he bore up against his fatigue until the recital was finished.

*   *   *   *   *   *

Alkay, from the summit of one of the many hills

which stood like so many gigantic guardians over Crusoe's lone and rocky isle, saw the pit-pans cross the bar, and skim swiftly through the deep waters.

The passion he had conceived for Lela turned the innate goodness in the red man's nature to all that was bad. Had it not been for the girl our hero would have had a loyal and devoted follower in the exultant, passion-blinded man, who watched his departure from the island with such gestures of wild and exuberant joy.

"The Young Eagle," he soliloquized, "has gone upon the search for the big canoes and the tubes of death. May the Great Spirit keep him away until I have softened the heart of the White Rose, whose eyes are more tender than those of the fawn, and whose beauty is more to me than the young sun when it rises above the deep waters in the far east."

He turned slowly from the voice of the trackless ocean and descended the hill.

At its base he met the two young braves who had been left by Crusoe to guard his dusky mistress.

Unhappily for the girl and our hero, these two were discontented with the duty their chief (Red Plume) had placed them on, and when Alkay joined them they were looking wistfully across the sea, and speaking in low angry tones of their banishment from the beautiful land of Aynoth.

Alkay gliding behind a clump of brushwood overheard this conversation.

"The Great Spirit," he thought, "is kind to his servant. Now Alkay will find no opposition when he wishes to carry away the White Rose."

He watched his companions' dark forms as they left the hill side, and slowly followed. He was busy with the project at his heart.

The little village wore a strangely mournful look as Alkay passed the cluster of huts.

The level greensward which had so lately been trodden by the absent braves and their young leader was now deserted, save for the ludicrous pair of tame monkeys, who were walking about hand in hand and jabbering as though holding an argument.

The creatures had been taught by Lela and our hero, and with that aptitude for imitation which is so strongly inherent in this species, they were walking, or rather hopping to and fro, in uncouth imitation of the manner in which Crusoe and his beautiful companion were wont to enjoy the cool evening breeze.

A number of tame birds were perched upon the roof of Crusoe's dwelling, among them were two paroquets of the most brilliant plumage.

These birds our hero had taught to speak with tolerable distinctness, and whenever our hero appeared at the door of the hut, they would scream out his name, and hop to the ground to be picked up and placed either on the wrists of Crusoe or Lela.

When Alkay passed to his hut, these birds were silently watching the closed doorway, and evidently wondering at the unusual quietude which reigned around.

Alkay cast many a wistful look towards the closed door which hid Lela's form from his sight.

He watched the lovely girl bowed down by the grief caused by her separation from the fair handsome boy. The portraiture was not pleasing to the Indian's mind, and he ground his teeth angrily when he thought how fondly and devotedly she was attached to the gallant boy.

The two young Indians came towards the angry plotter, and seating themselves by his side, one said—

"My brother looks sad. Is his heart heavy when he thinks of the braves who are upon the great waters."

"Oroma," said the crafty Alkay, "has spoken. He has asked why I am sad. Does he never feel sad when he thinks of the beautiful maidens of Aynoth, and how they pine for the young braves who are far away from the land of the Macoushi?"

"My brother speaks true," Oroma said. "My heart is sad when I think of our happy hunting-grounds, and the dark-eyed maidens, whose eyes are like stars and whose voices sound like the music of falling waters."

"Good," said Alkay; "my brother knows the cause of my sadness."

Oroma looked towards the hut, and said in a low and hushed voice, "Many moons will pass before the Young Eagle and his braves will return. Why does not my brother visit the land of Aynoth?"

"The Young Eagle," Alkay replied, confided the White Rose to my keeping. Can I leave? No! but my brothers can. Alkay will watch until they return."

The crafty words had the intended effect upon his hearers, and looking into each other's face they gave a grunt of satisfaction.

"Alkay speaks as a brother," said Oroma. "We will go to the land of the Macoushi, and return before two moons have passed."

A gleam of joy shone in Alkay's eyes.

This was all he wanted. The Indians away, he would be alone upon the island with the peerless White Rose.

"When the Young Eagle," Alkay said, "returns to his hut he will find the White Rose. But my brothers are alone here, while the Aynoth maidens so loudly lament the absence of their braves."

"It is true," said Oroma.

"Go, then, my brothers," Alkay continued. "In the forest there is a pit-pan which the Young Eagle has fashioned from the mora tree; in it you can cross to the land of Aynoth. Return before the second moon has waned, and all will be well."

The Indians unsuspectingly fell into the snare the cunning Alkay spread for them.

Had they suspected the sinister motive which caused him to wish them away from the island they would not have gone.

They had sworn by the Great Spirit to protect the Young Eagle and the White Rose—sworn this before the great council of the tribe, and they would have died sooner than broken the oath which they believed, by so doing, would shut them out from the happy hunting-grounds, when their spirits appeared before the great Manitou.

The pit-pan which our hero had been at so much labour to construct was soon found by the young braves, and at sunrise next morning they dragged the heavy craft to the shore and tried its floating capabilities.

Alkay was with them. His heart filled with exultation when they took their seats and began to slowly paddle from the isle.

He watched them until they had crossed the foaming coral reef, then turned quickly away and went towards the hut.

Beneath the shadow of a drooping tree sat Lela. The young lion lay at her feet, its large eyes rolling restlessly about, as though in search of the much-loved form of his youthful master.

The poor girl sat with her hands crossed over her breast and her dark eyes fixed mournfully upon the broad expanse of water.

A large tear trickled slowly down her cheek, and showed how sad and lonely she felt at the absence of the boy she so well and fondly loved.

From this pensive attitude she was aroused by the hasty footsteps of Alkay, as he crossed the open space which divided the men's huts from their chieftain's.

She raised her sad face when Alkay approached, and said, mournfully—

"Does my brother bring news of the Young Eagle's return, that his steps are so quick?"

"He does not," Alkay answered, "but comes with a heavy heart to the White Rose."

She looked inquiringly at his not less handsome face, and asked—

"What is the sadness that weighs upon the heart of an Aynoth brave?"

"Much sadness," he said. "Heard you not the whip-poor-will's plaintive cry when the sun sank beneath the waters?"

Lela started. She had heard the bird's peculiar note as it sat among the branches of the very tree which now sheltered her from the sun's bright rays.

A chill crept over her frame at the significance of this warning note, and in a startled manner she looked across the sea, her breast sad and filled with gloomy foreboding.

The bird mentioned by Alkay is believed by the Indians to contain the departed souls of those who have lately passed away from earth.

Her mind filled with this strange superstition, and the fact of the bird having perched upon the tree which overshadowed the door of Crusoe's hut was sufficient to cause her the most poignant anguish.

Her lover had perished, and his spirit passing to the body of this strange, but beautiful bird, had made known his death by the low, plaintive cries, which are not unlike the moaning of a human being suffering the most exquisite pain.

Lela's head drooped upon her breast, and from her lips there came a sharp, long cry of woe, and swinging her body to and fro, she cried—

"Yes; it was the spirit of the Young Eagle that came to Lela. He came when the sun was hiding its bright face beneath the waters, for then was the hour that Young Eagle sat beneath the mora tree, speaking to Lela with the soft music of his voice."

"It was so," said Alkay, "and my young men, who saw the whip-poor-will, and heard his cry, have

gone to the land of the Macoushi to tell the chiefs that Young Eagle is no more."

Lela raised her eyes while he was speaking, and a faint cry of alarm escaped her lips.

She saw by the passionate, gloating expression upon his face that he was regarding her with feelings that awakened her woman's nature to a sense of danger.

"Alone!" she said; "are we alone upon the island, Alkay?"

"The White Rose has spoken," he said; "it is true. We are alone."

"May the Great Spirit protect me," she murmured, "from this man! There is evil in his glance and danger in his presence."

"But why," Alkay continued, "does my sister, look so strangely? Can she not dwell here as she has dwelt with the Young Eagle? Alkay is a brave, and will give the White Rose his wigwam."

She clenched her hands, and the fire of her race shone in her dark eyes at those words, yet no sound came from her lips.

"Alkay," he continued, "will be kind to his squaw. For her will he slay the beasts of the forest; for her shall the softest couch be spread. Alkay is a brave, and a man of Aynoth. Say, White Rose, will you become his squaw?"

She rose to her feet, and fixing her flashing eyes upon his face, said, scornfully—

"Is it thus a brave should speak to one whose heart is sad, and whose lord is far away? Go! Lela will not become thy squaw. She can die, but never live with Alkay."

The passion he had hitherto subdued while speaking to the lovely girl now burst forth, and with a mocking laugh of fell triumph, he answered—

"The White Rose speaks to the winds. Alkay has said she shall share his hut. We' alone, and she must do as he wishes."

She uttered a few words in the English tongue to the young lion, and, like an angry mastiff, the royal brute sprang to his feet, and placed himself between Alkay and the beautiful girl.

"Behold!" she said. "One word, and thy limbs will be rent asunder. Go; leave my eyes clear of your form, or, by the spirit of our race, I will have thee torn limb from limb."

Alkay gnashed his teeth with fury, and stepped back. He saw by the brute's crouching manner that one word from the girl would cause him to spring forward and tear him piecemeal.

CHAPTER XXXIV.

CRUSOE RESCUES LELA FROM THE SAVAGES.

She stood with one hand upon the lion's mane until the baffled Alkay sought safety by closing the door of his hut after he had passed inside.

Lela stood like a marble statue until his form was no longer visible. Then she raised her hand to her burning forehead, and, closing her eyes, tried to shut out the terrors of her position from her brain.

The first few moments were passed as though she had just awakened from a horrible dream; but soon she became calm, and prepared to meet the dangers that threatened her.

"Young Eagle," she murmured, "would not rest in his grave beneath the waters were he to know that I became the squaw of Alkay. No; Lela that has been beloved by Red Plume and turned her heart away from the music of his voice; Lela who has been loved by the white handsome hunter, can never open her ears to the words of this man."

She paced hurriedly to and fro, and thinking over many plans to escape from her persecutor.

"The whip-poor-will," she murmured, "may not speak the truth; Young Eagle may yet live. Lela will wait until the moon wanes before she dies. If he does not return, she will know he has gone to the happy hunting-grounds, and will join him there."

The Indian girl's firm belief in an after state of eternal happiness with the youth she so fondly loved made the prospect of dying by her own hand one of joy rather than of dread.

She had some days to live, for the moon was but young, and when her mind was resolved upon thus baffling her persecutor, she began to plan a scheme whereby she could live in safety until the time came for the knife she wore at her girdle to drink her young life.

A smile irradiated her lovely face when she at length hit upon a scheme to escape Alkay's persecutions, until all hope should have passed of Crusoe's return; and leaving the hut, she called her faithful guardian to accompany her, and took her way sadly and slowly to the yellow banks.

Seated upon a piece of rock, she gazed at the spot yet marked by the keel of the boat in which Crusoe and his braves had left the island.

She remained there until nightfall, then wearied with her grief, she began to retrace her steps to the hut.

In passing the clump of palms which marked the entrance to the little settlement, the young lion gave a low growl of anger.

The cry was succeeded by the crackling of dried twigs, and to Lela's horror she beheld the noble beast disappear, as it were, into the very bowels of the earth.

To one so well acquainted with the Indian manners, Hector's disappearance was no mystery, and as she peered down the large hole wherein her favourite was now hopelessly fixed, she clenched her hands, and muttered fiercely—

"Alkay is a dog; may the Evil Spirit tear him limb from limb for this cowardly deed!"

Her suspicions were correct; it was Alkay's head that had invented this mischief.

He had watched the girl as she sat by the rippling waters, and well knew that all chance of compelling her to become his wife was useless while the young lion was by her side, he therefore dug a large pit in the path she would pursue when returning to the hut, and covering it with broken branches, awaited the success of his plan.

It was a hard matter for the treacherous Indian to refrain from giving vent to a shout of joy when he saw the lion fall into the trap he had so skilfully laid.

The cry of exultation changed to one of surprise, not unmixed with terror, as he turned and gazed seaward.

Lela, guided by the sounds, looked out towards the boiling surf, and beheld six of the Macoushi's canoes cross the coral reef, and shoot forward into the clear space.

It needed no wizard to tell either Alkay or the forest maiden the meaning of this visit; both knew that the Macoushi had come to wreak their vengeance upon the young white hunter and his dark-skinned mistress, for the share they had borne in the late fight between Red Plume and the Macoushi.

Their common danger, for the time, made the Indian girl and her suitor friends.

Alkay came from his place of concealment, and began to cut a way for the young lion to ascend from the pitfall.

In the midst of his labour he was startled by the well-known war whoop, and before he could escape to the forest the foe were upon him.

One gleam of the tomahawk and Alkay rolled to the earth a corpse, then the exultant red-skins seized the trembling girl, and uttering loud shouts of joy, dashed onward to the centre of the forest.

The lion still in the pitfall escaped them, and in spite of the beast's endeavours to reach the surface, he fell back to the bottom of the accursed trap.

Haste, Crusoe and your gallant band, or you will find your huts a heap of smouldering ruins, and the beautiful girl slain, when you reach your island home.

*　　*　　*　　*　　*

According to old Tom's evidence of the spot where the Seagull's wreck lay, they would have to repass the island to reach her.

The pit-pan was soon got in readiness for the journey, and long before the mid-day sun shone on the waters the little band had embarked.

Crusoe and his trusty friend were seated in the stern, old Tom, as usual, passing the time by recounting portions of the strange scenes he had beheld in his adventurous life.

Stories that were keenly relished by the daring boy, as much for the adventure in them as the insight it gave him to the wonders of animated nature.

He little thought, when lying beside old Tom beneath the shelter of a canvas awning, the terrible danger that surrounded his dusky island queen.

When they were gliding slowly from the isle, Crusoe beheld a huge seal basking in the sun, and without a second thought, he called out to his men to pull towards it.

"Why do that?" old Tom asked. "The creature won't let you take him."

"I will try," Jack said, laughing; "so bear a hand, Tom, and steer the craft towards it."

When within a fathom of the amphibious animal, it raised its head, and shuffling off the line of rocks, plunged into the water and disappeared.

Old Tom laughed, and Crusoe gave vent to an expression of annoyance.

"Confound the brute," he said; "I should have thought that nothing could have been more easy than to have captured it."

"Wrong, lad," said the old tar; "appearances deceive you with that quiet-looking thing. Would you believe they are very troublesome, ay, even dangerous to catch?"

"I should not. Dangerous?—absurd!"

"You think so, lad; I did once, until I found out my mistake, when I was in the Polar regions."

"Ah, you promised to tell me, now I remember, about your exploits with the walruses and seals; suppose you do so now, it will pass the time away until we reach the island."

Old Tom was nothing loth to satisfy his favourite, so settling himself in the most comfortable position he could find, he began—

"Well then, you must know that I embarked on board a trading vessel, which had wintered in the Gulf of Obskoia. She was laden with valuable furs and seal skins.

"The farther we stood out towards the Polar regions, the more novel and beautiful the scenery became.

"Ice islands, in every possible form, floated around us; innumerable birds, fishes, and many amphibious animals, sported near us, as if they were aware of the shortness of their summer, and were resolved to enjoy it to the utmost.

"We soon ran through Waigatz Strait, which divides the continent of Russia from the sterile island of Nova Zembla; and in a short time we arrived at Archangel.

"Here I again took shipping; as I preferred coasting the whole of North Russia and Danish Lapland, rather than return home by land through Petersburg —the way I had before travelled.

"I had a great desire to visit Lapland. I resolved to double North Cape, coast the west of Norway, disembark at Heligoland, cross the country to Tornea, in Lapland, which is situated at the upper end of the Gulf of Bothnia, and so proceed to England through the Baltic.

"All this I did; but I must now go back to Archangel.

"I went on board there, and nothing occurred worth noting till we doubled those gigantic rocks, which form the extreme promontory of Lapland, called North Cape.

"Here we experienced a dense and dark fog, for several days, so that I lost a view of some part of that grand range of coast, the whole of which I was very desirous of seeing.

"Soon, however, the weather cleared again; and, the ship's crew resolving on a little sport among the walruses, we prepared our fire-arms, and other weapons, and lowering the boat, half a dozen of us got into it and pushed off towards an iceberg, on which we saw several of these creatures at their unwieldy gambols.

"As we approached they turned their heavy, unmeaning faces towards us, and ceased their play.

"Two or three of the Russian sailors now wished to fire at them; but a sturdy Dane, who was one of the crew, objected, saying—

"'That is merely killing for the sake of killing; there is no practice, no fun, no danger, no glory in shooting at them so far off.'

"He therefore proposed that we should row boldly up to a great fellow that was lying alone at a distance from the others, and attack him at once with a harpoon.

"The Russians, I suppose, did not wish to appear less courageous than their shipmate, so it was agreed that we should pull away towards the walrus that we had singled out.

"We now rested on our oars, and each of us stood armed.

"The Dane, rather too carelessly, took aim, threw his weapon, and struck the animal on one of his tusks.

"This jarred, without injuring him; he raised his awkward bulk, and sat like a sphinx.

"In another instant, a second harpoon flew from one of the Russians, and hit him in the shoulder; this roused him, and made him savage, so that he plunged into the water, and swam resolutely toward us.

"A third weapon was thrown, and with a truer aim, for the poor creature's side was struck.

"I had never before wantonly destroyed life, and a sudden feeling of disgust at the sport, as it was falsely called, made me withhold my harpoon, which was the last on board.

"The Dane, who had lost his own, saw me lower the weapon instead of flinging it, and called out to me to know why I did not strike it.

"I knew that I should only be laughed at, if I told my reason, and therefore did not reply.

"The furious animal had by this time gained upon us, so that, though two muskets had been fired, and one had hit the creature on the back, its fierce eyes and loud breathing were distinctly seen and heard.

"The Dane now began to fear for the safety of the boat, which the animal could with ease have capsized; and he hastily bade two of the men seize the oars; and darting suddenly at me, wrenched the harpoon out of my hand and sent it at the walrus.

"This unexpected jerk, with the motion of the boat, threw me off my balance; I fell forward, and pitched headlong into the water close to the huge paw of the animal.

"I had long been an expert swimmer, and had too often been obliged to exert my presence of mind, to let me now neglect my only chance of escape.

"I dived at random, and fortunately came up on the opposite side of the boat, which had lain-to the instant my disaster was known.

"Only two of the men were occupied in despatching the wounded walrus, the other three were busied in my affairs.

"They quickly helped me into the boat; and we rowed away towards the brig, laughing heartily at my accident.

"Another day, as we were becalmed, we resolved to land among the rocks, and explore their cavities; we wanted fresh water, too, and hoped to obtain it easily.

"We took weapons with us, of course; but I resolved not to attack any creature, excepting in self-defence.

"The view of the landscape, by a midnight sun, was very singular.

"I scrambled for a long time up one of the

ALKAY'S TREACHERY.

desolate peaks, and soon came to a lake of fresh water, nine hundred feet above the level of the sea.

"Crag rose above crag, white with the snow of ages; in little hollows of the mountains, sloping patches of lichens, and stunted Arctic plants, chequered the scene.

"White foxes and a solitary elk, were the only animals I saw.

"Towards the sea, the view was equally sublime; towering masses of ice were drifting in a stately and beautiful manner; the breakers were dashing their white heads against the bases of those stubborn rocks, that had withstood their vain fury for thousands of years in the same dreary solitude.

"Long shadows from the mountains stretched over the ocean, and added to the singularity, wildness, and grandeur of the scene.

"I turned to leave it, contrasting its sullen aspect and lonely desolation, its scanty life and niggard vegetation, with the richness of animal variety and the rapid growth of tropical climates.

"I reached the shore, where the boat was moored just in time to see a fierce attack made by a seal on one of the crew, who was unarmed.

"The foolish fellow had been teasing the creature, till it was so savage that it flounced itself into the water, from off the ledge of rock on which it had been basking; and when I came up it had swum to the spot so swiftly, and was making such a resolute assault on the sailor, that he was actually frightened, and was trying to scramble into the boat, looking back, in dismay, at its open mouth close to his heels.

"In his hurry the man's hands slipped, and he

11

fell sprawling on the beach, within a few feet of the seal.

"I could not help laughing at the position of the combatants; there was my shipmate kicking and struggling; there was the seal shuffling and flacking his tail, and trying to seize his prostrate enemy!

"The misfortune of it was, that I dared not fire at the animal, for fear of hitting the sailor; so, seeing there was no time to lose, I whipped out my cutlass, and attacked the seal pretty vigorously behind.

"This fresh enemy he was not prepared for; he turned on me at once, which gave the man time to rise.

"I threw him my gun; and then we soon despatched the creature.

"I resolved to have his skin; and, my shipmate offering to take the whole management of it on himself, I consented, and before I landed at Heligoland he had made it into a very tidy-looking cap, which he gave me, thanking me for having saved him from an awkward bite."

CHAPTER XXXV.

WHICH IS A CONTINUATION OF THE LAST CHAPTER, AND CONTAINS MANY ADVENTURES AND A GREAT AMOUNT OF INFORMATION.

"I SHOULD not," Crusoe said, "have thought that such a quiet-looking animal had so much fight in him."

"Neither did I," old Tom answered, "until this encounter took place."

There was a short pause, and the wanderers looked out upon the calm blue waters for the sign of the distant isle.

It was a beautiful scene. The arched canopy of heaven one mighty expanse of clear blue, the still waters, the absence of the smallest of God's winged creatures in the air, and no perceptible sign of the myriads of the sea's strange inhabitants.

It was a time to cause the reflective mind to become filled with wondrous thoughts—a soothing, dreamy state of feeling which the low chant of the Indians, as they plied their paddles, added to rather than detracted from.

Crusoe, when he found that the island was not yet in sight, and in blissful ignorance of the danger that menaced the beautiful Lela, upturned his face, and said—

"I never felt the strange influence of being, as it were, alone in the world until this moment."

Old Tom looked at the boy interrogatively.

"You don't quite understand me, Tom?"

"Not quite, lad."

"When you finished your story about the seals, I looked round at the great desert of waters, then upwards at the sky."

"A grand sight, boy, in a calm like this."

"It is; well, I thought what atoms we are upon the great planet. Here is a small boat far away from land, and so frail that one gust of wind would capsize us."

"I know what you mean, boy; I have felt so very many times when I have been far from the dwellings of man—a strange feeling, lad, and one that ought to make one feel thankful to the Great Ruler of the universe, for giving to us poor mortals the understanding to appreciate His gifts."

"We ought, indeed," said Crusoe; "but all are not like you, Tom."

"Nor you."

"No," Jack said, "they are not; but you, Tom, are one in a thousand."

"How is that, boy?"

"You have seen so much more than most men. Oh!" he added, "I only hope that I shall live to see as much as you have."

"Hope you will, boy. Just tell your men to pull and not go to sleep, or we shall not sight the island to-night."

Jack did as he was requested, then asked—

"How far do you think we are from the island?"

"Can't say to an hour, Jack, but should think about four, or may be five hours' pull."

Crusoe sighed.

"What's the matter?" old Tom asked.

"Nothing; felt a little dull, that's all."

"Dull! a young feller with the blood like fire running through his veins. Why, at your age I never knew the meaning of the word. Damme, lad, I was then poking about the untrodden wilds of South America."

"You there," Jack said, "at my age?"

"Ay, boy; and young as I was I shall never forget what I felt at first landing on those wonderful shores."

"I'm glad to hear it," Jack said, smiling, "for you will be enabled to tell me."

Old Tom laughed, and caressingly patted his young favourite's curly locks, as he said—

"Well, boy, perhaps I have not forgot all I saw and heard. Well, lad, it was the mighty trees, the magnificent plants, the beautiful birds, the astonishing reptiles, all so different from anything which I had ever seen, or even heard of.

"I might as well tell you," old Tom said, stopping abruptly in the story of his adventures, "that it was my first voyage, and being but a poor little shrimp of a fellow, I was more fit to attend upon the captain than do any part of a seaman's duty on board; so the captain thought, for he made me his cabin-boy much to the disgust of a lout called Swipes. How I repaid his kindness I will tell you if we have time."

"I hope we shall," Crusoe said; "your recollections, Tom, are the most amusing and instructive that I ever read or heard of, and I read a rare lot of books when I was at Madge Collins's."

"You will make me conceited, Jack," old Tom said, secretly pleased with the boy's words, "and it would not look well in an old hunks like me; but to the yarn, or we shall be in sight of the land before I am half way through."

Jack stretched himself at full length, and resting his chin upon his hand, upturned his face to listen.

Old Tom filled a rude pipe with a portion of tobacco, and lighting it, began—

"We intended to coast all along, from the great river Oroonoco, and as we were to remain some weeks at each principal town, on the eastern side of the continent, I had frequent opportunities of leaving the ship, through the captain's kindness. He had many friends to visit, and so great was his attachment to me that he always took me with him. The first time we quitted the vessel, to sail in a boat up the narrow part of the river Oroonoco, among the rapids, where no large vessel can enter, I remember I saw twelve alligators, all in sight at one time."

"How did you escape being swallowed up, Tom?"

"They do not attack boat-loads of persons, my boy," he replied; "but poor Glaucus, Captain Heartly's dog, was nearly killed by one.

"I was leaning over at the stern of the boat, to look at a large creature that was lying like a log in the water, when my hat fell off, and the dog darted over after it.

"In a moment the ugly monster swam towards Glaucus, who was not aware of his danger till the alligator was nearly upon him.

"Only think how keen the dog's instinct must have been! Like lightning he darted round, as if he had known that alligators cannot turn quickly in a rapid current.

"I hallooed to the captain, who caught up his gun and fired at the fierce reptile; but the ball, though it struck him, only frightened him. It could not hurt him.

"It gave Glaucus time to gain the side of the boat, and I was so anxious to help him in that I almost fell over myself.

"Poor fellow, how he trembled! But he had never let go of my hat!

"Alligators, as well as snakes, remain dormant during that part of the year which may be called summer, though the heat varies so little that the two seasons, in warm latitudes, instead of being named summer and winter, are divided into *the rainy* and *the dry seasons.*

"When the waters begin to subside these horrid creatures bury themselves deep in the soft mud of the rivers, and the sun hardens the earth above them, so that you may walk about with hundreds of them lying torpid under your feet, and hidden from your sight.

"A very curious circumstance once occurred to us, which I will relate to you:—

"We all agreed to sleep in a deserted hut on the banks of the river, and having looked to see if any jaguars were hidden, or snakes coiled up, within the cabin, we went in.

"The sailors spread their own and the captain's mats about the floor, and we all lay down to sleep. I put my mat on a kind of mud bench near the wall.

"Towards morning I felt my bed moving, and in another moment I was jerked into the midst of the sleepers, where I kicked and bawled till I frightened the whole party wide awake.

"'Look! look!' cried I, 'an earthquake! The bench running away; there! it has tumbled into the river.'

"It was, in fact, a young alligator on which I had spread my mat!

"It had, no doubt, entered the hut during the inundation of the water, which then flowed into it;

there the animal had settled itself for its summer's sleep, and the mud had caked upon him.

"I suppose that either the smell of the dog which slept by me, or a thump I had given him during my sleep, had roused my dreadful bedstead, and then the noise I made frightened him away!"

"Very terrible!" said Jack. "How large are the alligators, Tom?"

"They have been found to measure twenty-two, and even twenty-four feet in length.

"A young Indian girl, while she was bathing, was seized by one of these creatures, and as he dragged her under water she had presence of mind to force her fingers into its eyes with such violence that the pain obliged the animal to let her loose, after he had bitten off the lower part of her left arm.

"The poor girl swam to shore with the other hand; and she recovered from the wound, although she had lost so much blood.

"Accidents of this kind often happen to persons while bathing, or fetching water from the rivers.

"The next day we arrived at the house and plantations of the Spaniard, Don Caloa, whom the captain was going to visit.

"He was a merchant, and sold the oddest things, I then thought, in the world; monkeys, mackaws, turtles' eggs, &c. You have eaten turtle soup, Jack?"

"Yes."

"Well, you would wonder that any turtles could escape such a slaughter of the species, if you were to see the thousands and thousands that are destroyed by the Indians every year at the *Harvest of Eggs*, as it is called.

"I was there with the merchant, and saw the whole method of taking them.

"We all went in a boat early one morning to an island in the river, where the sand was smooth, and which the tide had left.

"A person then took a long pole, and walked about thrusting it into the sand in every direction: and wherever it went in very easily, the Indians knew there was a nest of turtle's eggs; so they dug away, and, when they found any, put them into baskets which they had brought for the purpose.

"Numbers of Indians were there from all the neighbouring shores, and immense numbers of eggs were collected.

"They make a kind of oil of the yolk, which is used in cooking, as well as for burning in their churches.

"It is supposed that not fewer than a million of turtles lay their eggs at the mouth of the great river Oroonoco.

"More than three millions of eggs were taken the year I was there.

"Each turtle lays, on an average, seventy eggs; but so many are broken, so many are hatched before they can be dug up, so many are hunted out and devoured by the jaghuars and other animals which feed upon them, that it is not surprising the number should be so reduced.

"I saw the whole shore of the Oroonoco swarming with little turtles just hatched, and scrambling towards the water to escape from the Indian children who were catching them.

"The turtles lay their eggs, during the night, in large holes which they scratch in the sand; they then cover them up, and leave them to be warmed into life by the sun.

"The eggs are larger than pigeons' eggs, and when well preserved, by slightly boiling or by drying in the sun, they are very pleasant food.

"We saw some large shells of turtles, which the jaguars had emptied as neatly as if the flesh has been cut away with a sharp knife.

"These animals hunt the poor creatures, catch them, turn them on their backs—for you know they cannot turn back again—and then devour them at their leisure.

"That same day, as we were sailing up the river, we saw the the largest jaguar that had ever been heard of on that coast. It had just killed a chiquire, or water hog; but it had not eaten its prey, on which it kept one of its paws.

"A large flock of vultures was hovering near, in order to devour the jaguar's repast, if he should chance to move. They came every now and then, within two feet of the beast; but the least movement he made drove them off again.

"The noise of our oars made the animal rise slowly and hide itself behind some bushes. The vultures now tried to take the hog, but the jaguar dashed into the midst of them, lashing his tail, and carried off his prey into the forest.

"Jaguars seldom attack boats by swimming to them, excepting when they are very much pressed by hunger."

"What fierce and terrible animals there are in the world!" said Jack.

"There are very disagreeable reptiles in South America, certainly," replied Tom; "but, I confess, that I think them more than compensated for by the variety of beautiful and curious animals which that country produces in greater number than any other part of the world.

"What think you of the Titi monkey, and the Widow monkey, for instance?"

"Titi and Widow monkeys?" said Jack; "I never heard of them!"

Tom continued: "The Titi is very small; its hair is of a beautiful golden colour; it is more like a child in its countenance than any other animal; it is very timid; and when anything alarms it, its large eyes fill with tears.

"It is very fond of insects to eat, particularly of spiders; and I have heard that its sagacity is so great, that when any engravings of insects have been shown to it, it would dart its little hand at a grasshopper or a wasp, in hopes of catching it; but that when pictures of insects on which it did not feed were placed before it, the little creature took no notice of them.

"The Titis are so fond of warmth, that if several of them be in a cage, and a sudden shower come on, they crowd together, twining their legs and tails around one another to keep themselves warm!

"One that was tamed used on such occasions to run after a person who wore large sleeves, that it might take refuge in them!

"The Indians say that they sometimes, in the forests, meet groups of ten or twelve of them, crying terribly, because those on the outside want to get in the middle, to be warmer!"

"I don't really doubt your word, you know, Tom," said Jack; "but really this seems unbelievable."

"I do not think it incredible, my boy; I have seen too many wonders to refuse my belief to a circumstance so well authenticated as is the natural history of these monkeys.

"Humboldt mentions the fact, and he was too respectable, sensible, and philosophical a man to assert improbabilities; those who devote their valuable lives, as he did, for the benefit of science are entitled to our respect and——"

"I beg your pardon, Tom. I might have been sure that you would tell me nothing that you did not believe to be quite true!" said Jack, rather abashed.

His friend patted his head, and said, "You need not fear to believe the assertions of modern travellers my boy; no man of credit would assert falsehoods, for fear of detection.

"Thanks to the blessing of printing, and to the spirit of adventure, people cannot now be gulled or deceived with such stuff as the earliest travellers and writers chose to relate.

"Suppose I were to tell you that, when I travelled in Africa, I saw a tribe of men walking about without heads, could you believe me?"

"No, Tom; to be sure I could not!" exclaimed Jack.

"And yet this has been asserted and believed," replied Tom.

"No, not believed, surely! Who asserted it?"

"St. Augustine, one of the Fathers of the Church, affirmed it. In his thirty-third sermon, he says, 'I was already Bishop of Hippo, when I went into Ethiopia, with some servants of Christ, there to preach the gospel.

"'In this country we saw many men and women without heads, who had two great eyes in their breasts. In countries still more southerly, we saw a people who had but one eye in their foreheads,' &c. Now what say ye?" added Tom.

"Ha! ha! ha!" shouted Jack. "Well that is famous!"

"When printing was unknown, think how imperfectly any kind of knowledge would be communicated! Reflect, too, that as the mind of man was not ennobled and strenghtened by the habit of reading, and by comparing the merits of authors, it was open to any assertions, any folly, any imposition, any superstition, that artful, clever, wicked men chose to invent.

"You say truly, Jack; you could never credit the story contained in that quotation from St. Augustine, and the reason is, that your mind has been kept free from the degrading power of superstition; because, too, you have never heard that modern travellers have corroborated the impossible circumstance; but, above all, because your good sense (though you may not have considered the matter exactly in this way), enables you to feel certain that if a man were but to cut his throat, he must die; and that, therefore, it would be impossible for him to live without a head!"

Tom had gone a little too deep for Jack's mind to

follow quite clearly; but he understood enough to make him feel pleased in having shown Tom that he was too sensible to believe impossibilites'; so he look-ed up in his face, and said—

"Now let me know about the Widow monkey."

"There is nothing that will please you in the account of the 'Widow in mourning' but the description of its body, which has caused it to have that name.

"Its hair is black, soft, and glossy; its face is of a whitish colour: the neck has a white band in front, about an inch broad; the hinder feet are black, and the hands are white.

"In these white marks on the black monkey, the inhabitants think they discover the veil, the neckerchief, and the gloves of a widow in mourning."

"Did you ever see an ourang outang?" Jack asked.

"No, my boy. I heard much of a monkey which the Indians called the 'Great Devil;' but none of them had ever seen one.

"We were just now speaking of the disagreeable animals and reptiles of South America; I'll tell you what I found much more terrible than serpents, jaguars, and crocodiles."

"What, Tom? What could be more dreadful than those creatures?"

"Mosquitoes, white flies, and ants," said Tom.

"You must be joking," said Jack; "why, you could knock the gnats or mosquitoes away with your hand, or handkerchief; you could have trodden on the ants; and as to the white flies, they are harmless. They did not trouble me much; and on our island, I do not remember that I saw one," Jack continued.

"That is because your cave was situated so high; if you had been situated on the low lands, or on the banks of a river, you would have wondered no longer at my expression just now.

"Why, my boy, we seemed to breathe mosquitoes instead of air; we were never free from them, excepting at midnight, and then other insects, huge bats, and jaguars, kept us ever in alarm.

"Sleeping rooms there are sometimes built on poles, or scaffolding, higher than these cruel insects ever fly, which is found to be about twelve feet from the level of the rivers; and in these apartments we were able to obtain a little breathing comfort.

"Vast regions of that grand country are rendered uninhabitable, by the different species of tormenting insects which infest it.

"When two persons meet in the morning, their first question is—

"'How did you find the zancudoes during the night? How are we to-day for the mosquitoes?'

"You never saw such a pair of legs in your life as mine were when we got back to the ship, owing to the wounds and swellings which the different insects had caused.

"In some parts the Indians bury themselves in the sand, with only their heads out, in order to sleep

"In other places they assemble all the cows in the village, and among them they pass the nights; for it is found that mosquitoes are not so troublesome in the neighbourhood of cattle.

"Sometimes the Indians build a kind of oven without doors or windows, having only a little hole, through which they creep on their hands and knees, then lighting a fire in it of wet brushwood, which makes a great smoke, the insects are driven away; and then, closing the opening of the oven, they go to sleep.

"I, however, could not bear the heat, smoke, and stagnant air of these holes. I preferred even the cloud of mosquitoes in the open air.

"The white flies are so very minute, that if you were even to use mosquito curtains, they must be wetted to prevent these tiny plagues from making their way through the cross threads of the curtains. Their sting, too, is very painful.

"There is a species of *termites* (a sort of ant) that eats paper, pasteboard, parchment, &c.; so that there are no ancient records of those countries in which these insects are found.

"There is another species of ant that devours green leaves, particularly of succulent (that is, juicy) greens, such as salads; so when the inhabitants wish for a few dishes of pleasant cooling herbs, they make a garden in the air."

"In the air, Tom? How?" asked Jack.

"They procure an old boat, or a frame of that description, raise it on dry poles, then fill it with earth, and sow their seeds. The destructive ants, which travel in close bands, thus pass the bare poles, or supporters, not knowing that anything is growing above.

"Really," said Tom, pausing, and speaking to himself—"really, the more I reflect on the vast mass of life in that wonderful country, the more I am astonished, and the greater is my admiration of the Deity who planned the mighty work.

"Animal life crowding the forests, the plains, the rivers, the air. Vegetable life loading the rich earth with its enormous growth. What would become of the vast mass if it had not a proper species to nourish?

"If alligators and jaguars did not devour the young turtles; and if ants and locusts in myriads did not clear the rampant vegetation from the surface of the ground, what would be the consequence? These things seem wonderful, do they not, Jack?"

"They do indeed," answered our hero, and raising himself, he looked ahead of the pit-pans to ascertain how far they were from the island.

Not unlike the dark fragment of a rain-cloud looked Crusoe's island home, and as the boy again stretched out his limbs, he mentally wondered whether Lela was upon one of those yet invisible hills, looking out for his return.

He little thought of the danger she was then confronting, or he would not have so quietly said—

"Thanks, Tom, for what you have told me, and as there is yet time for a little more, suppose you tell me how you requited the captain's kindness."

Old Tom shaded his eyes with his hand, and took a survey of the distant isle, then emitting two or three volumes of smoke from his lips, said—

"Let me see. Well, suppose I wind up with the mutiny, and my share in its suppression."

"A mutiny on board your ship?"

"Ay, lad; and had it not been for me, the captain and his mates would have gone to Davy Jones'."

Jack was all impatience to hear this, and fearful the pit-pans would reach the island before old Tom had finished, he said—

"Go on, Tom."

"No hurry, lad; it ain't much of a spin, so just wait till I fill my pipe."

Our hero had to wait—impatiently, it is true.

This process over, and the tobacco lighted to old Tom's satisfaction, he began—

"Well, when we returned to the ship, and got under weigh, Swipes, who believed that I did him out of a berth as the captain's attendant, began to show his hatred towards me, and to make matters worse I was in the habit of accompanying the captain on deck to begin my first lesson in steering the ship and learning the compass, and while thus engaged, Swipes was ordered to perform my work; this enraged him, and one day he had the folly to object to one of the captain's commands.

"I never shall forget the start, and angry flash of our usually kind commander's dark eyes, as, with a voice of thunder, he swore the fellow should suffer for his insolence.

"The poor wretch that very morning received fifty lashes, and was put in irons for two days.

"Discipline is so necessary on board ship, that commanders, however mild they may be, are obliged to show their power sometimes.

"Swipes' enmity to me now became deadly. He took an oath to be avenged on me for having been the cause, as he said, of his disgrace; and from that moment his whole soul seemed bent on contriving my ruin.

"There was also a young sailor, a Falmouth lad, on board, who early attached himself to me, in consequence of my once screening him from the captain's displeasure for a trifling fault; and I liked him, because he was good-tempered; and because he was so much like myself in manners, we became friends.

"Poor Ned! and he too went down.

"But I must not go on to that sad wreck.

"The day after our return to the vessel, I was sitting in the cabin as usual, when the door opened, and Ned's face looked in.

"Finding I was alone, he came towards me, very cautiously, and said, in a low, hurried voice—

"'Tom, there has been foul work aboard, while the captain and you have been ashore.'

"'What do you mean, Ned?' said I.

"'I mean that it's as much as my life's worth to tell you, if it should be known,' replied Ned.

"'Then why do you offer to tell?' asked I.

"'Because I deem it better to risk my existence, than to see two good fellows butchered for want of warning.'

"'Good fellows! Butchered! Warning! Ned?' I said, in alarm, starting up and running to the captain's closet, where he kept his firearms.

"'Nay, you're not killed yet, Tom,' said Ned, who could hardly keep from laughing at my boyish eagerness to be well armed.

"'Then pray make haste and tell me when I am to be killed, and who is to be my butcher; for I cannot understand you, Ned!' I replied.

"'In a word, then, Swipes has bred a mutiny in the ship.

"'His surly old uncle, the boatswain, has been so worked upon, and plagued about the rascal's flogging, not only by Swipes, but by three or four of the sailors (and he named them), that at last they've got him to promise he would head the mutineers.

"'The way I came to be among them was this.

"'I was asleep, three days ago, on one of the chests in the steward's room, which, you know, is dark; but happening to wake quietly, I heard Swipes and Dick Jink talking close by me; but they did not see me.

"'They were calling over the names of the mutiny band; and they agreed that six would be too few, so Dick said—

"'"Ned Luff's a sturdy little dog, let's have him."

"'"No," replied the other with an oath, "he's a sworn friend to that rascal Tom Starboard; he'd peach, I know?"

"'So there I lay, hearing all this, and wondering what the fellows were after; when Swipes went on, "Well, though there are but six of us, we're all stout-hearted, and, what's more, well prepared; while they'll all be taken unawares! They won't expect anything; besides, in the night, when they're asleep and stupid, how easy it will be to kill 'em! I'll do for Tom, and do you stick to the captain, Dick! Oh! never fear but we shall soon have the ship in our hands, and then, my boy, I shall be steward, and you shall have enough grog to swim in. My uncle will be captain, and you shall be mate, Dick."

"'Then with a laugh they moved off.

"'Amazed and terrified at what I had heard, I lay for full half an hour considering what was best to be done to mar their plot; but, as the captain and you were ashore, I could think of nothing better than to tell you of your danger as soon as you came aboard.

"'At first, indeed, I thought of letting Mr. Sterling, the mate, into the secret; but then, as I had not heard enough to enable me to answer all the questions I thought he might put to me, I resolved to let things go on, and keep a sharp look-out after the mutineers.

"'Once or twice, yesterday and the day before, I narrowly escaped their observation, as I was listening to their private conversation; and to-day I overheard Swipes saying to Dick—

"'"We must throw that fellow Ned overboard; he's always prying about, and I believe he suspects what we're after!"

"'"I don't believe a word of it," replied Dick, "for if he knew anything he would by this time have told his friend Tom, who would have told the captain. Besides, Ned is a hearty good dog, and parts with his grog as generously as if it were only water."

"'The fact is, every day since I overheard the conversation I have invited Dick to take a share of my grog, which he never refuses; and whilst he was drinking I was gradually drawing the secret from him. From his hints—for, you know, he don't half trust me—and from what I have overheard at different times, it seems that an attack will be made to-night at twelve; so mind and be prepared.

"'I shall probably be with them; for Dick told me not a hour ago, that he should want me to-night, and hoped I would stand by him like a man if any danger should befall him.

"'I promised to stand by him in all weathers; upon which he gave me his hand, and desired me to be with him soon after the watch is set, as it is his turn to mount guard to-night.'

"'To-night!' said I, looking at the priming of the pistols.

"'To-night, at twelve precisely, you may expect an assault upon the captain and you; so be prepared. Of my help you may be sure; and we must hope for the best. For the remainder—but hark!' said he.

"''Tis Swipes, Ned! In with you! into the closet—hush!' I said, pushing him in, and sitting down to my writing, though my hand shook so with the fright I had felt, that I could not form a single letter.

"The villain Swipes looked round the room quickly and went out again without speaking. Of course he suspected Ned Luff was with me, and had come to look for him.

"As soon as he was gone, I let Ned out of the closet.

"'Make haste,' said I, 'off with you! But don't let him see you come up the companion ladder. I'll talk with you again, if I can, before midnight.'

"'Well, but, Tom!' said he—

"'Go! go! that fellow will see you,' said I, pushing him out.

"I stood like one bewildered, after I heard his footsteps die away. I seemed to be in a dream; for I had never been in a situation so terrifying to a young and innocent mind.

"Murder was so shocking! and that our worthy captain should be the victim of these men quite upset me.

"Just then, his well-known quick step sounded on the stairs, and in he came.

"The moment I saw him, I begged him, hastily, to bolt the door, for I had something horrible to tell him: he looked at me, and was going to laugh, but seeing that I appeared distressed, he did bolt it, and then I told him all.

"He sat with an unchanging countenance while I was speaking.

"'Poor ignorant creatures!' he exclaimed; and then followed a volley of oaths, which I need not repeat to you.

"'Go and fetch Mr. Sterling to me,' said the captain; and I went.

"'Sterling,' said Captain Heartly, 'I've seen your courage well tried in an engagement, but I've never seen it in a mutiny; how will it stand that sort of work?'

"''Tis not likely to be tried, captain!'

"'Ah! isn't it though?' and then Sterling heard what I had just told the captain.

"'Dastardly villains! Murder in cold blood!' he exclaimed.

"'Hush! not so loud, my good fellow.'

"'Well, but as you know who the mutineers are, captain, you'll order them to be ironed—heavily ironed—and confined directly, won't you?' said the mate, whose hot temper was aroused.

"'No. Why, what a mad fellow you are! I have but Ned Luff's word for the truth of this business; and were I to have them punished upon so slight a testimony, I should breed a mutiny among the rest of the crew; for, of course the rascals would deny the charge, and how could I prove it?

"'No: we'll wait for them, and, if possible, disarm them without bloodshed; this will not only prove whether the remainder of the crew are true-hearted, but we shall then be perfectly justified in putting them in confinement till we reach the next port, where they can be tried by court-martial.'

"Don't look so anxious, Jack! I was not killed, you see; I have only this scar to show for my share of the fighting."

He bared his right arm as he spoke, and traced with his finger along a jagged-looking white seam across the flesh, below his elbow; he then went on:

"'Sterling,' said the captain, 'you, and Freeman (the steward), and Bilge, and Simpson, and Stowman—must be ready to assist us: I am sure of courage and fidelity in all of you.

"'Tell them what you know; contrive that the mutineers shall see you in your hammocks, as if you were really going to sleep for the night; then get up and come all of you, armed, into my cabin: be sure to come cautiously.

"'Tom had better go to his hammock, and stay there; we shall not want him. Time enough for your fighting, my lad, when you have weathered a few more gales!

"'Why, what ails the boy?' said he, seeing that I was ready to burst into tears.

"'Oh captain! sir,' I said, 'don't think me a coward, nor make me one! Pray let me be by you! I'll not flinch; I cannot go to my hammock and lie there like a useless hulk, while you are in danger!'

"'Let him be here, captain,' said Mr. Sterling, kindly; which made me seize his hand and thank him.

"'Nay, I don't want to make a chicken-hearted fellow of the boy, I'm sure! So pray join the brave band, Tom,' replied the captain, smiling.

"Well, I could not get near Ned all the rest of the day; the mutineers, I suppose, suspected him, and feared that he would tell me what they thought he knew of their plans, so they watched him closely.

"How long the hours seemed! How changed did everything appear about the ship! How my young heart beat as I passed the men whose names I had heard were among the cowardly set!

"Evening fell quickly around us; everything was beautiful and calm but the hearts of those blood-thirsty men!

"I sat at the side of the vessel playing with Glaucus, as if I were thinking of nothing but his tricks, though my feelings were anything but pleasant.

"I remembered my home! Thought that I might be killed! Fancied my mother's sorrow! Feared I might have to take the life of a fellow creature, of one of those with whom I had been for months in the daily habit of talking and of eating.

"All this was very sad.

"And I wondered how it was that the stars could come out sparkling, and twinkling, and brilliant, and joyous-looking; and that the moon should wear so placid a face when such a scene of bloodshed and wickedness was going to take place.

"Storms, and wild waves, and angry clouds, and a fiery sky, I thought, would suit that night better; and, I am sure, would have pleased me more.

"This calm quite fretted me, and added to the irritation of my feelings.

"The watch was at length set; and the rest of us retired to our hammocks.

"Now it so happened that I was not able to leave my bed, owing to the suspicious watchfulness of the conspirators; so that, to my inexpressible horror, I heard an unusual shuffling of feet on deck, while yet two of the band loitered near me.

"This was too much for me!

"I sprang up like a young panther, and with a cutlass in each hand, which I had concealed in bed, I dashed by the two astonished fellows, and was on deck in an instant!

At the top of the cabin stairs I saw Swipes standing with a pistol cocked, and unsheathed hanger, ready to shoot, or cut down the first that should come past him.

"I rushed at him before he was aware, knocked the pistol out of his hand, and seizing his collar, strove to throw him from me, that I might have room to run into the cabin.

"The strength of the ruffian was, however, greater than mine; he soon recovered his feet, threw himself against me, so as to make me stagger, then cut at me with his hanger with such force that my right arm was disabled, and my weapon fell clattering on the deck.

"Although I had another, I did not need it, for the villain sprang again at me, and tried to throw me down; when, at that moment, Glaucus flew out from his sleeping-place under one of the guns, and seized Swipes' leg.

"He roared and swore with the pain, while his passion and revenge only seemed to increase.

"We still struggled together, wounded as I was; but my strength was failing, and I reeled towards the side of the vessel; in another moment, Swipes' weight overbalanced me, and we both fell into the water!

"I remember nothing more, till I found myself in the ship's boat, and Ned Luff supporting me. The first words I heard were—

"'No, to be sure, that dog's too good a christian to save such a scoundrel as Swipes. You need not try to make him go after the worthless carcase any more, Bilge; the dog won't stir. Besides, I saw the fellow's white face, full in the moonlight, on the top of the wave. He's dead, I tell you!' said Ned.

"'I think poor Tom had but a narrow escape,' replied the good-natured Bilge, as he fixed the tackle that had been lowered over the ship's side for me to be hauled up.

"Though weak and faint, I could now thank them for their kindness; and then I begged to know if the captain was safe and the mutineers secured.

"'Yes! yes! Never fret about them; all's well! Let's get you into your hammock, and have your arm dressed, for I've found where all this blood comes from; and then I'll tell you about the mu-

tiny,' said Ned, as he fixed the ropes round me, and called to those above to haul away.

"As I swung off, I felt a weight drag my legs (as I thought) almost from my body, and a shout of mingled laughter and delight hailed my entrance to the ship; it was at poor Glaucus, who, having saved my life, would not quit me; but, seizing my trousers with his teeth, and clasping his fore-feet round my legs, was drawn up with me.

"The next day I was well enough to leave my bed; all were kind to me; and Ned told me, as we sat together, of the remainder of the last night's disturbance.

"'When you heard that noise of shuffling feet, Tom, which you told me of,' said he, 'your fears— no, not your fears, but your thoughts, must have deceived you; it was only Swipes, whose feet slipped and made him stumble.

"'The time had not arrived for beginning the attack, but Swipes had seen Sterling go downstairs, so he thought he might as well mount guard, and either keep him there, or give the alarm, if he should come up.

"'The two fellows, who you thought were staying to watch you, were Ben Ply and Jack Warely, who were talking the business over, and had agreed to keep out of the scrape; for Swipes had offended them just before, and they thought they should be fools to put their necks in jeopardy for him.

"'So, you see, the mutineers were reduced to four; Swipes, the boatswain, Dick Jink, and Bob Lanyard.

"'Dick is a drunken dog, who would kill his own father for a glass of three-quarter grog; and so, knowing how fond he is of it, and to keep him true, Swipes gave him his own allowance, and consented to receive me, at Dick's request, in lieu of the two who had fallen to leeward.

"'Well, this sudden fight of yours with that scoundrel Swipes, made such a noise, that the old boatswain, Jink, and Lanyard, were afraid the captain would come up to see what caused it; so they rushed down the cabin stairs, and I ran after them.

"'I had wetted the powder in their pistols, unknown to them; and as they were taken at unawares, they had not their cutlasses ready; so they were both disarmed by the captain and Sterling in an instant, for the noise above had warned them in time to be prepared.

"'As soon as I saw the three safe, I told the captain what had happened between you and Swipes, and we ran up to look for you (for I had not seen you fall overboard); there I found Ben Ply and Jack Warely lowering the boat; and I saw Glaucus struggling in the water and keeping your head up by holding your collar in his teeth.

"'As soon as you were taken into the boat they tried to make him go in again to save Swipes, but neither they, nor I, nor Bilge, nor the captain, even, could persuade him to stir from your side! and the body had now floated so far from the ship that no one would venture to swim to it.

"'Indeed, it was quite clear that Swipes was nearly strangled before he fell over; you had held his throat so tightly, Tom, that he had no breath to help to float him, I suppose.'

"It was long," continued Tom, "before I could get the wretched end of Swipes out of my mind. The three mutineers where landed at Buenos Ayres, where they took their trial, and being found guilty of mutiny, were hanged at the yard-arm.

"Thus ended the only crime of that sort that I have ever witnessed in the two-and forty years that I have been a wanderer."

As he ceased speaking Crusoe uttered an exclamation of surprise, and pointed towards the island.

CHAPTER XXXVI.

CRUSOE JACK TO THE RESCUE.

THE pit-pan was tossing about close to the coral reef when old Tom ceased his interesting narrative, and as the light craft shot through the spray into the deep blue waters, Crusoe suddenly exclaimed—

"Canoes on the beach! What can be the meaning of that, Tom?"

The old sailor took his rifle from the bottom of the boat, and quietly examining the priming, answered—

"That yellow streak round the bows of the strange crafts tells me they belong to the Macoushi tribe, and the meaning of them being there, lad, we shall soon find out."

A foreboding of the evil that had fallen upon the island maiden caused the blood to run cold through Crusoe's veins.

"The Macoushi!" He repeated this name with compressed lips and kindling eyes. "They have come here but for one purpose."

"A purpose," old Tom said, "which is soon guessed. They have not forgotten the share you took in the late fight, my lad."

Crusoe made no reply. His eyes were fixed with an eager, searching look upon a clump of dwarf palms.

He saw, by the waving of the leaves, that something was behind them to cause the foliage to be thus disturbed.

Standing erect in the bow of the pit-pan, his left hand grasping the barrel of his unerring rifle, his right shading his eyes from the blazing noon-day sun, our hero called upon the Aynoth braves to put forth their strength to run the pit-pan ashore.

The dusky warriors bowed their plumed heads to this command of their chief, and bringing every sinew into play, they fairly lifted the light craft out of the water.

"The Macoushi dogs," Crusoe said, adopting the mode of speech which his dark-skinned followers were wont to hear from the lips of the gallant Red Plume, "they have come when my young men were away looking for the winged canoe—come when but three of my braves were on the island, and by this the Macoushi tomahawk has drunk our brothers' blood, and the huts which my young men built are now level with the earth."

Incited by these words, the Indians' fiery passions were aroused, and compressing their lips, they pulled madly towards the isle.

Borne upon the wings of the soft westerly breeze came the joyful cries of the Macoushi.

The sound was like the blast of a trumpet to a mettlesome charger, and the Indians, with glaring eyes and dilated nostrils, bent lower to their task.

"Do my young men hear?" Crusoe resumed. "It is the cry of the foe. Hark! again it comes! They shout with joy at the thought of my brothers being away."

The Indians gave a low cry of anger, and turned their heads towards the shore.

"My brothers," Crusoe said, as he noticed the effect his words produced, "think with me that the Macoushi are dogs, and dare not wait to see the Aynoth tomahawk gleaming in the sun."

A growl of pleasure came from Crusoe's followers as he threw in this compliment.

"My brothers are pleased," the youthful white chief continued. "Yes, the Macoushi must fly before the heroes of Aynoth, and their canoes will bear them from the land. Say, shall it be so?"

The Indians turned their faces towards the speaker and looked confused. The expression upon their dusky faces told that his words were not fully understood.

Crusoe pointed to the canoes.

"My young men," he said, "are strong of limb. To them the canoes will be as reeds. Let their tomahawks splinter them, and throw the fragments to the sea. Then the Macoushi cannot escape our vengeance!"

They answered with a shout of approval, and the prow of the pit-pan was turned towards the canoes.

Old Tom Starboard had been a quiet, but interested listener to the words Crusoe had said to excite the young Indians' anger; and as Crusoe bent eagerly forward, vainly trying to make out the cause of the strange commotion among the clump of dwarf palms, he arose from his seat in the stern, and said—

"Brave lad! A red-skinned warrior could have done no better. Where did you learn this lesson?"

"From Red Plume."

"You are an apt scholar. Oh, curse the fellows, they nearly upset me."

The Indians, maddened by Crusoe's words, drove the pit-pan with such force upon the beach, that old Tom, had he not clutched one of the rowers by the hair of the head, would have been pitched overboard.

Like demons the Indians fell upon the Macoushi canoes, and with their sharp tomahawks split the thin timber into a thousand pieces.

Crusoe waited not until the enemy's flotilla was destroyed, but, with old Tom following close upon his heels, he started forward in the direction of the clump of dwarf palms.

Fully expecting to come upon a group of the foe holding high revel at their victory over the few braves he had left in charge of the island, Crusoe kept his eyes towards the upper branches of the trees (they were not more than six feet high).

Old Tom found it was as much as he could do to keep up with his young companion, and, as they ran side by side, he jerked out spasmodically—

"What's—the—mat—ter? They—are not among the dwarf palms."

"See," Crusoe said in reply, "how the leaves swing to and fro! There must be——"

Before he could finish the sentence, there was a crashing noise, as though he had trodden upon a heap of dry twigs, and, to his companion's surprise, Crusoe disappeared.

Tom Starboard halted in time to prevent himself falling into the trap the cunning Alkay had dug for the young lion.

Old Tom knew not for some moments what had occurred.

His companion's disappearance was so sudden that it seemed as though he had been swallowed by a huge chasm in the earth.

A half-smothered, sullen growl from the depths of the pit into which Crusoe had fallen caused old Tom to point the muzzle of his piece downward, and yell out—

"Stand clear, lad! I'm going to fire."

"Hold!" cried Crusoe, as he made an attempt to scramble up the side of the pitfall. "It is Hector they have trapped. The poor brute saved me from breaking my neck."

"How?"

Old Tom asked this question as he knelt at the edge of the pitfall, and held his rifle at arm's length, for Crusoe to clutch.

"I fell upon his back," was the reply, as the speaker's head became visible. "And, in place of being torn to pieces, as I fully expected, the poor brute licked my hand. But, Tom——"

He paused, and looked his companion in the face.

"I know, lad," said the old man, "what you would say. "Keep it in, lad, we shall know quite soon enough."

Crusoe bit his lips.

It was by exerting the most powerful self-control that he refrained from using the Indian girl's name.

"If she is safe," old Tom muttered, as he threw every branch and twig he could gather into the pit, so much the better when we find her. If not, we shall find it out quite soon enough."

Crusoe silently followed his companion's example, and in a few seconds they had thrown sufficient into the pit to raise the young lion within four feet of the level ground.

The intelligent brute, when within this distance, crouched low, and, gathering his haunches well beneath him, sprang from the pitfall.

The royal brute safe, our hero and old Tom dashed through the underwood, and went in the direction from which came a succession of joyful cries.

The sounds coming upon the lion's ears, caused him to pause for a moment; then, turning his head up, and sniffing the air, he gave a low, angry cry, and dashed forward.

Crusoe and Tom were soon distanced, but by the merry shouts of the triumphant foe changing to a yell of dismay they knew that the angry brute had dashed in among them.

A sudden turn in the tall cane-brake revealed a sight which for a moment caused the boy's heart to turn cold, and his older and less impassive companion to give vent to an oath.

Beneath the giant limbs of a mighty ceila tree were grouped together between thirty and forty of the Macoushi braves.

In their midst was the beautiful Indian girl, her arms and legs fastened by deer-hide thongs to an upright piece of wood, and scattered around her feet were several bundles of dry branches.

Crusoe saw the young lion crouched at the girl's feet, and two Indians lying prone upon the earth showed that Hector had made an effort to rescue the island maiden.

An effort which had nearly cost the noble brute's life; for, as he lay showing his gleaming fangs, and tearing up the earth with his claws, Crusoe saw the long shaft of a Macoushi spear protruding from his side.

The noble brute had only time to crush out the life of two of the exultant foe, before he was stricken by a dozen sharp spears.

Crusoe and old Tom took in these details at a glance; and the former, as a cry of mingled rage and horror came from his lips, brought the butt of his rifle to his shoulder, and fired at one of the Indians, who was in the act of applying a live torch to the mass of dry branches and tufts of sun-scorched grass.

The blazing brand fell from the Indian's grasp, and, springing upwards, he clutched madly at the empty space, then fell forward a corpse.

The Macoushi gave a yell, and, seizing their spears and poisoned arrows, turned in the direction of the report.

Crusoe, reckless of the consequences, threw his rifle from him, and drawing his sword, bounded forward, and stood beside Lela.

The Indians shrank back, as, meteor-like, he dashed into their midst, and with feelings of more than ordinary ferocity, they stood in a semi-circle around him, looking from the glittering blade he grasped, to his fearless face.

Old Tom Starboard had only time to utter a cry of alarm before the boy had sprung from his side, and stood thus calmly defiant—his graceful, well-knit form a mark for a score of poisoned weapons.

The old seaman lost no time in the attempt to overtake his young companion; but, dropping upon one knee, he brought his deadly rifle to his shoulder, and, motionless as a stone figure, he waited to slay the first of the Macoushi who should make a hostile movement towards the gallant youth.

He had not long to wait.

The Indians, though at first astounded at the report of Crusoe's rifle, and the swift death that had come upon their companion, soon recovered their wonted hardihood, and, uttering a fierce cry, they pressed closely upon him.

Two of the foremost spear-shafts were struck by the bright keen-edged sword, and one of the foe stooping to pick up the fallen blade, was seized by the neck by the wounded lion.

One of the fiercest of Crusoe's foes—a chief of the tribe and a colossus in form—sprang forward to grapple with the boy.

Crusoe turned his sword point to the savage's naked breast, but before he could drive the point through the painted skin, the Macoushi's fingers were entwined round his throat; and another of the tribe, standing behind, struck him senseless with one blow from his club.

Crusoe fell to the ground—the gigantic chief, at the same moment, toppled forward—a bullet from old Tom having entered the back of his skull.

Then came a shout of joy from the Macoushi, as they rushed forward to pin the galiant boy to the earth; and old Tom's blood seemed to freeze at the fearful doom which threatened the boy he loved so well.

CHAPTER XXXVII.

A DARK SCENE OF TREACHERY.

How long and dreary each hour appeared that brought the Wednesday nearer, the day that fair, beautiful girl had waited for with a yearning of hope and expectation for the letter from her father!

She sat at the window of the lone cot, and waited for the arrival of the village postman.

A sad foreboding oppressed her, a shadowing of danger seemed to surround her, and she felt that some evil would befall her before that glorious day that gave gladness to the little feathered songster, and drew a rich fragrance from the blushing roses around.

Her heart bounded with joy when she saw the postman cross the stiles in the distance, and wend his way through the verdant fields towards her humble homestead.

She did not, as was her custom, jump and run to the door, but waited for her guardian to bring her the letter.

The postman stopped at the gate, nodded to her, and, selecting a letter from the pack, he stood with it in his hand, as though hesitating; then, placing it at the bottom of the rest, he went on.

"No letter again for me," murmured the poor girl, in despair.

Dropping her head on a small table that stood before her, she wept bitterly with disappointment, and sobbed herself to sleep.

When she awoke the rose-tint had left her cheeks, and her eyes were red and swollen.

She looked vacantly around the apartment, as though she had forgotten where she was; and when she raised her eyes to the window, she was fearfully startled by the fiendish face of Madge Collins looking through the glass exultingly upon her.

Mabel was terrified by the apparition of the woman she so much dreaded. Giving vent to a piercing shriek, she rushed from the room.

Old Hannah, hearing the cry of alarm, hastened to see what had happened to her darling charge.

They met in the passage. Poor Mabel threw herself upon the good old lady's breast, and sought for comfort and protection beneath those arms that entwined her supple waist.

"What is it, my birdie, what is it?" inquired Mrs. Miller, kindly. "Tell me, Mabel, don't 'ee cry. Come, come, there's a darling child, you know how it upsets me when you take on in this way."

So saying, the old lady commenced to pout her lip, and, forgetting she had her spectacles on, took the corner of her apron to wipe her eye.

"God bless me!" she exclaimed; and, discovering her error, "how stupid! to be sure."

Mabel looked up and smiled through her tears at the comical expression of her guardian's visage, while she carefully examined her treasured glasses to see what injury she had done them with the corner of her coarse apron.

"Quite a mussy I hadn't knocked them off my nose, and broke 'em," said she, carefully adjusting them again just above the bridge of her nasal development.

"I prithee, my dear, tell to me what ails thee," said Mrs. Miller.

"Oh, nurse!" replied the poor girl, trembling with horror at the remembrance of the face she had seen at the window.

"Well, my poppet, what is it? Did you see anything to frighten you?"

"I did, nurse—something fearful!"

"Gracious me!" exclaimed old Hannah, glancing suspiciously over her shoulder, as though expecting to see some horrid monster preparing to devour them.

"Yes, nurse," continued Mabel Meredith, "I saw——"

"Yes, child! What?"

"The postman."

"Eh!—eh!—eh! There bean't nothing in him to frighten thee!"

"No; but he had no letter."

"Well—well! there was nothing to frighten thee in that. He may bring you one yet."

"I think not," said Mabel, sadly. "But, nurse, I saw something more fearful than the postman."

"Surely, child, did thee? And was it horful?"

"Horrible!"

"Ugh!" went Mrs. Miller, and a chill ran through her veins. "Come thee into the kitchen, my poppet, or you will catch cold."

"No, nurse, I shan't; but if you wish it, I will come."

"Yes, my dear, I do wish it—not because I am frightened—oh! no."

But she was, because the passage was rather dark. They retired to the kitchen.

Old Hannah fastened the door, and drew her pretty charge to her side, anxious to hear the strange story, yet half afraid to listen to it.

"There! there! Look! Hannah—look!" suddenly exclaimed Mabel.

"Eh!—ah!—what!—where, my dear?" stammered the old lady, jumping from her arm-chair in alarm, and running several times round the room.

Mabel caught her by the arm, and pointed to the kitchen window, where stood Madge, the wrecker's wife, with the same fiendish and unpleasant look upon her distorted visage.

"There!" said Mabel Meredith, in a strange, low voice, "that is what I saw before."

"Good gracious! how horrible the woman looks!" exclaimed Mrs. Miller, covering her face with her apron, to shut out the unpleasant glare of Madge Collins, that fixed upon them so gloatingly.

"Come away, Mabel, my pet, there is evil in that woman's eyes—she means danger."

Mabel did not hear the warning; she was too intent in trying to read the inscription upon an

epistle held in the claw-like hand of old Madge.
A startled cry of glad surprise left the fair girl's lips,
and before Hannah had time to remove the apron
from her face Mabel was gone.

The old servant stood bewildered.

The evil face of Madge had gone from the
window, and she had also gone from the garden—
gone, vanished like a shadow, nor could Mabel,
who had gone out to detain her, find a trace of the
treacherous woman.

She returned more downcast and sad than before.

"Nurse," she said, her voice breaking the silence
like a low, sweet strain of music.

"Well, my daisy?" returned the old woman,
kindly.

"That woman held a letter of mine."

"Nonsense, my child; your fancy."

"Nay, 'tis not fancy, for I read my name and
address upon it. I knew the writing to be that of
my dear father."

"What does thee think she could want of your
letters?"

"I know not; yet she may have some purpose.
I liked her not from the first time I saw her. I am
sorry, nurse, you ever accepted the money from her;
for since then there seems to be a dark cloud of
sorrow and unhappiness hovering over the house."

"Tut, tut! you must not fill your head with such
stupid fancies."

Well, we shall see," replied Mabel. "Give me
my hat and cloak, please."

"Where are you going?"

"For a little walk."

"Be careful of thyself, and don't go far, in case
that woman means thee harm."

"Very well, nurse. Good bye!"

A big tear trickled down the good woman's face,
as she kissed the pale, lily cheeks of her charge.

"Poor little darling!" she soliloquised, when
Mabel had gone. "It be a very hard life for her to
bear, after what she's been used to; but if she be
taken from me, I should break my heart, for I love
her, I does, as if she was my own—"

Breaking down, she indulged in a quiet flood of
tears undisturbed.

During that lapse of time she reflected upon
quite another train of thoughts, and, raising herself, quite refreshed, she commenced again—

"I don't know what the world be coming to now-
a-days," she began. "Girls are not like what they
was when I was young; they do seem giddy and
flighty, and if things don't go just as they like, they
mope and fly into their airs, and the world seems
upside down; but Mabel bean't like the rest. No!
She's been out a long time now, I fear something's
happened. I shall never forgive myself if there is."

Jumping up, she hastily adjusted a coal-scuttle-
shaped bonnet on her head, and throwing a huge
cloak over her shoulders, went out in search of her
fair charge.

The sad little beauty was wending her way to the
forest, where often she would go of a summer's
evening, to beguile away a part of her lonely hours.

She would sit beneath the shady trees, and pore
through the pages of a deeply interesting book of

dangerous travels, imagining the daring hero to be
her handsome lover, trusting and thinking how
happy should she be when he might return from
some far-off clime with the trophies of his adventures.

So strong was her imagination at times, she
would make herself believe that she was reading her
lover's life.

But, when she closed the book, she would awake
as though from a dream, to the sad remembrance
of his supposed fate, in going down with the ill-fated
ship.

On this evening, she had left her novel at home,
for she could not peruse incident after incident
without believing that such was the fate of her lover,
and it made her unhappy.

And such it was. But little did the poor, fond
girl dream of the happy truth.

The day was fast decreasing, the rich gleam of the
sun slowly sank far behind the horizon, and the
little feathered tribe were sending forth their evening hymns before they retired to their respective
perches to await the next awakening day, when
Mabel Meredith entered the forest.

She was startled by the appearance of two ill-
looking ruffians, who stood lounging against the
trunk of a large tree.

At a glance she saw they meant no good to her.

As soon as they caught sight of the fair girl they
shrank back out of sight, as though not wishing to
be seen by her.

That act portended an omen of evil. Mabel
judiciously retraced her steps.

A cautious tread of footsteps following close behind her warned her of danger.

She turned her head, and, to her terror, saw
both men not a dozen paces from her.

One had taken off his long cloak, and held it in a
position as though to throw it over her, and so
capture her in it.

The girl was quite sensible of the peril of her
position, and shrieked loudly for assistance.

Her cry of distress was answered by Hannah
Miller, who could be seen across the fields.

An oath from one of the ruffians terrified the poor
girl by its intensity.

Again and again she cried loudly for help.

"Now, then, Bill, clap a swab over her jawing-
tackle, or she'll bring half the village upon us," said
one of the seafaring fraternity, probably the wreckers
of the coast.

"Avast, there, yer lubber!" exclaimed the other.
"Why the —— don't you put yer grappling-irons
on her? You are the nearest."

Mabel sprang forward with the celerity of a
startled fawn, and ran fleetly in advance of the
caitiffs.

"Set sail, Bill," yelled the ruffian just addressed.
"Run her down! If we lose her, we shall lose the
prize-money. I'll be alongside yer afore her 'ave got
far."

Bill took to his heels—if that's what they called
setting sail—and gave chase to Miss Meredith.

Before many seconds had expired from the time
when Mabel had taken the lead, her vile pursuer

CRUSOE AND THE POLAR BEARS.

overtook her, and grasped her roughly by the arm.

"Release me instantly," demanded Mabel, with great composure.

"Certainly, my dear," coarsely replied the ruffian.

Ere the other worthy came up, puffing and blowing like a broken-winded horse, he took her other arm.

"What's the meaning of this?" she asked, coolly, though she felt a drowsy dizziness taking possession of her senses.

"Oh," replied Bill, "that you'll find out soon enough."

"Not a bad little craft, is she, Bill?" remarked the other.

"No!" Bill answered, "infernal sight too good for that cussed old Collins, an' if it warn't for the

prize-money we shall get for her we would share her 'tween us."

Imagine the poor girl's feelings of horror, held as she was between them, and compelled to hear their coarse, brutal remarks passed upon her.

"Come along, my lamb," said Bill.

Powerless in the clutches of these rude brutes, Mabel was borne up the rocks that overhung the sea, when old Hannah came upon the trio through another inlet that she had taken as a near route, and confronted the two wreckers like an enraged fiend.

She had provided herself with a thick cudgel, and with one blow on the head she stretched the ruffian Bill at her feet.

Then she set furiously upon the other—a scuffle took place between them, in which Mabel was released.

This gave her a good opportunity to escape, and she was not long in availing herself of the chance.

She was tearing down the perilous cliffs, with the intention of going to the village, and returning with the peasants to the rescue of her devoted guardian.

She had not got more than half way down the dangerous precipice, when old Madge, who stood upon a projecting crag, looking like Satan himself, caught Mabel, who was flying blindly down the rocks, in her gaunt arms, and, with a fiendish cry of triumph, carried her up again with the greatest ease.

Mabel had not seen the old wretch in her flight, and she was too bewildered to know where she was ; but the terrible truth soon made that evident to her when the wrecker's wife spoke.

" Mine ! " she exclaimed, gloatingly.

The poor girl knew there was no hope for her now, and, with a deep-drawn sigh, she gave herself up to her fate, terrible as it might prove.

Madge Collins now reached the summit of the cliffs.

The wreckers had overpowered their female antagonist, and dragged her to the most peaky point of the rocks overhanging the sea, for which they had received previous instructions from Madge.

The old wretch had taken Mabel into a cave.

" Look up," she said to the poor girl, who was almost fainting ; " look for the last time upon your kind guardian, before she is sent to eternity."

Mabel looked up bewildered, and shrieked when she saw the peril of Hannah Miller.

" Away with her to perdition ! " exclaimed Madge.

The men raised the helpless woman, who implored to be allowed once more to kiss her fair charge.

But she was sternly refused by the inhuman wretches who were about to cast her into the depthless sea.

They swung her two and fro three times, and then hurled her with fearful force from the rocky peak.

A piercing cry, coming from her heart's core as she rapidly descended through the air, rent the air, and struck, like a keen dagger, into Mabel's breast.

Madge then closed the rude door of the cave.

" You are in my power now, my fine lady," she said, tauntingly. " I am going to take care of you until Jasper, the cripple, whom you have despised and loathed, returns to make you his wife."

Mabel reeled round, a ghastly pallor came over her face, a low, gurgling cry escaped her lips, and she fell lifeless at the feet of her fiendish captor and tormentor, Madge Collins, the wrecker's wife.

CHAPTER XXXVIII.

CRUSOE CAPTURED BY THE MACOUSHI.

strong was the spell upon old Tom Starboard at he could not steady the rifle in his grasp.

Those iron sinews which had stood him in such good stead in all quarters of the globe, were for once relaxed, and though he beheld the Macoushi warrior poising the fatal spear to transfix the gallant boy to the earth, he was powerless to save him, and old Tom, closing his eyes to shut out the fearful sight, covered his face, and cried aloud in his agony.

There seemed no hope for the boy.

The angry Indians, with that thirst for blood so inherent in their race, drew closer, to behold the fatal stroke given.

The keen blade gleamed in the sombre light, and the frail shaft quivered in the Macoushi's strong grasp, as he drew back a second time, to take a surer and better aim.

This act saved Crusoe's life.

The island maiden, with a smothered cry, sprang towards a fallen brave, and with wondrous strength wrenched the weapon from the dead man's hand.

Like a lioness defending her young, the girl stood over her lover's body, and, as quick as the lightning's flash, her weapon found a sheath in the Macoushi's breast.

Buried in the dusky savage's flesh, far above the lover, was the long spear, and the shaft swayed to and fro with the force of the blow.

It was well aimed ; and the man fell without a cry, his heart cleft in twain.

The girl's eyes sparkled brightly as she beheld the Indian fall to the ground, and before a hand could be put forth to slay her, she snatched up Crusoe's bright sword, and turned quickly round to the dark cluster of men.

" Behold ! " she cried, " how an Aynoth maiden makes war with her foes ! Behold, ye Macoushi dogs ! how she can defend the white hunter, whose hand has sent many of your accursed race to the endless fields of eternity ! "

They levelled their weapons, and pressed closer ; and the girl, with a savage laugh, gazed at the bristling line, and said—

" Back ! There's a devil within me that will send your accursed spirits to the black guardian of your race. Back, I say ! "

The men, awed by her voice and manner, paused and looked into each others' faces.

Then the chief of the Macoushi spoke—

" Men of the land where the tiger hunts," he said, " make not war upon a woman."

The men gave an angry growl.

" We are braves," he continued, " and men of a great and mighty tribe. Keep your weapons for the Aynoth dogs ! This woman, who has slain a warrior, let her die with the white hunter—let the flames eat away their bodies, and the wind carry their dust upon its wings ! I have said. Are my brothers content ? "

They gave a glad shout, and, despite Lela's attempt to save herself and lover from their impending doom, she was disarmed, and again a prisoner.

They would have bound her to the form she loved so well, had not a mighty shout at that moment startled them.

It was the men of Aynoth, with old Tom at their head, who were now bounding forward to avenge their white chief's fall.

The chief of the Macoushi pointed with his spear towards the depths of the forest, and said—

"Take your prisoners hence, and, while our spears are being reddened with the blood of the Aynoth dogs, let the flames go upwards, as an offering to the god of battle."

They answered him with a yell, and four among those who stood near the captives seized them, and started at a swift pace towards the spot indicated by the chief.

The wounded lion, unobserved by the Indians, crawled after the doomed prisoners and their guard.

Scarcely had they disappeared among the trees, when old Tom and the men of Aynoth dashed through the cane-brake.

The Macoushi quickly formed under their leader, and, with levelled spears, prepared for the onset.

Crusoe's followers, furious at the loss of their leader and goaded to madness by old Tom's cries, bore down upon the bristling line.

There was a short and stubborn conflict for a few seconds, then the Macoushi line swayed to and fro, and then, beaten back by the heavy tomahawks wielded by the men of Aynoth, they broke and fell back upon the confines of the forest.

Old Tom, who was too well versed in the Indian mode of warfare, urged his men forward to cut off their retreat.

It was craft against craft—red-skin against red-skin—and the Aynoth men, though as swift in their movements as the eagle in its flight, were too late to intercept the foe.

Once among the trees the Macoushi disappeared as though by magic.

Old Tom glared savagely at the giant trees, and raising his clubbed musket above his head, he called out in the Indian tongue—

"Forward: men of Aynoth. Drive the skulking devils from their cave."

He led the advance bravely—and his heroes, taking a firmer grip of their reddened weapons, dashed after him.

From tree to tree the Macoushi were driven.

But not without laying low some of the Aynoth men.

The Macoushi, too, suffered severely in their retreat.

The slightest portion of their dusky forms, visible only for a moment, would be followed by the swift flight of a tomahawk through the air.

So true was the aim, that the weapon slew or maimed one or more of the foe.

Far into the sombre stillness of the mighty forest, pursuers and pursued kept up the fierce struggle.

The chief of the Macoushi knew they had either to conquer or die; for the young men of the opposing tribe with biting words, which the Indians knew so well how to use, taunted their foes with the intelligence that their canoes were now broken to fragments, and that they had no mode of escape unless they conquered those opposed to them.

The Macoushi hurled back taunts as bitter.

They told how they had landed, and slain Alkay; and how the island maiden and her pale-faced lover were at that moment being consumed by fire.

Old Tom Starboard, sheltered by the broken stump of a tree, plied his rifle with deadly skill.

But when the Macoushi told the fate to which they had given his young companion, the old man's eyes became dim, and his knees trembled with the throe of agony which passed through his frame.

The cunning Macoushi saw the old seaman's agony, and heard the yell which came from the men of Aynoth when this intelligence came.

They knew also that the foe would brave everything to rescue the young chief and the island maiden from the funeral pyre, and, with devilish subtlety, retreated in a direction contrary to that which had been taken by Crusoe's captors.

Old Tom looked eagerly around for the smoke which he knew would be visible should the fiendish work have begun.

He saw nothing to mark the spot.

The blue canopy of heaven was unclouded, and, as far as the eye could reach, the green, waving foliage met his gaze.

He had begun to think that the Indians' words had been used but to taunt him and his followers.

With the thought, his nerves became steady; and catching a glimpse of the man's face who had sent forth the dire words towards him, he pulled the trigger of his unerring rifle.

The Indian sprang upwards, then fell forward upon his face.

One convulsive contortion of the muscles, an effort to rise, and the red-skin's spirit fled to the mystic realms of eternity.

Old Tom quickly reloaded, and, in a voice that was heard by friend and foe, he said—

"The Macoushi is a liar, and with the lie upon his tongue, he has gone face to face with the great Manitou."

The chief of the hostile band stept boldly out from the shelter of a tree, and poising his long spear, he darted it at old Tom.

"Dog!" said the warrior; "the great Manitou never lies! His voice came to my ear, and bade me slay you. Thus do I obey!"

Tom Starboard had only time to throw himself flat upon the earth, when the spear came whirring through the air.

It struck the ground a few feet in advance of his prostrate form.

"Well aimed," muttered old Tom, as he turned over on his back, and fired at the retreating chief. "Take that in exchange!"

The ball sped onward, and struck the Macoushi chief in the leg.

In spite of his stoicism, and the stubborn spirit which actuates the aborigines to suffer the most excruciating agony in silence, he could not help a low cry of pain escaping his lips.

The Aynoth braves yelled derisively; and one, pointing towards the tree behind which the wounded chief had taken refuge, said—

"Listen to the cry of the squaw! Behold, men of the Aynoths, how your foes cry when they are wounded!"

A second yell followed these words. A yell that was again repeated; old Tom Starboard pointed with outstretched hand, to a thin, spiral column of light blue smoke which was slowly ascending among the trees

"To the rescue!" shouted the old seaman, clutching his rifle. "Behold, men of Aynoth, the work of the Macoushi!"

They understood the significance of his words and look, and, suddenly leaving the bush, they bounded after the old seaman.

The Macoushi were close enough to hear old Tom's words.

And the chief, following in the direction of his outstretched finger, saw that his men had begun their work of vengeance.

It was now impossible to keep Crusoe's friends in ignorance of the spot where the sacrifice was about to take place.

Knowing this, the Macoushi turned and fled before the resolute attack made by the foe, as they rushed towards the place of execution.

Keeping well in advance of their pursuers, the Macoushi reached the spot where the funeral pyre was beginning to blaze—a few yards only were between them and their pursuers.

But ere the men of Aynoth could pass over this small space, the fire had encircled the helpless victims, and one powerful ruffian sprang upon the pile of logs, and, flourishing his scalping knife above his head, pointed with his left hand towards Crusoe and Lela.

Old Tom saw the ruffian's purpose, and, regardless of all save the desire to be revenged upon the dusky devil, he broke through the phalanx that surrounded the pyre.

One bound brought him beside the Indian.

There was a short, but deadly struggle. Then the brave old Tom snatched the scalping knife from his foe.

Like a flash of lightning it descended up to the haft in the Indian's breast, and, as the man fell backward into the living flames, the Aynoth braves drove back their foes, and, with a glad shout, began to scatter the pine logs and dry brushwood on every side.

The scalping knife cut the captives' bonds, and Lela and her lover fell forward upon the charred wood, to all appearance dead.

CHAPTER XXXIX.

A NOBLE ACTION.

OLD TOM STARBOARD sprang like a tiger among the dusky forms that surrounded the captive pair.

Passion gave the old seaman the strength of a giant, and with his clubbed musket he dashed the Macoushi to the earth, as though the stout warriors were but reeds.

Right and left, the butt of his rifle fell with a dull thud upon plumed heads, and with every blow the men of Aynoth, and their white ally, numbered a foe less.

Crusoe's dusky warriors were close upon old Tom's heels, and their gleaming tomahawks did savage execution, until the Macoushi, awed by the prowess of the little band, broke from the position they had taken up, and fled wildly towards the forest.

The last of the Macoushi—a young brave, whose wampum belt was as yet unadorned with a human scalp, gave a longing glance at Crusoe's clustering curls, and before the boy's followers well knew what had taken place, the young savage sprang upon the heap of dried brushwood, and plunged his left hand among the cluster of dark curls which adorned our hero's head.

He gave a wild, exultant cry, as he drew his scalping-knife, and flourished it above his head—that cry was his last.

While its echoes were yet repeated among the mighty trees, old Tom seized him by the throat, and, with herculean power, hurled the exultant Indian many feet from his intended victim.

The Indian tried to rise and follow his retreating companions, but ere he could do so, one of the Aynoth braves cleft his skull in twain.

A wild cheer came from the conquerors' throats, and, with one impulse, they brandished their encrimsoned tomahawks, and dashed after their foes.

Old Tom released the captive pair, and as he wept tears of joy over his young favourite, he blubbered out—

"Don't mind an old man's weakness, Jack, I can't help it."

Crusoe pressed his friend's hand; then, drawing Lela from the smoking pile, he said—and a shiver ran through his frame as he spoke—

"Look, Tom. You were not much too soon.'

He pointed to the flames, which were rapidly ascending.

"Not much, lad. But hark!"

The trio listened to a distant shouting, and the Indian girl, clasping her hands, said joyfully—

"It is the Aynoth cry of victory! The men of my tribe are scalping the foe."

"This must not be," Crusoe said. "Come, Tom, let us save the poor wretches from being massacred!"

"Right, lad!" old Tom said. "Though the redskin devils would have roasted you, we must not, as Christian men, let 'em be butchered."

Lela placed her hand upon Crusoe's shoulder, and looking into his dark eyes, said, softly—

"My brother forgets he is a chief."

"How so, Lela?"

"He talks with the aged hunter," she said, "and Lela, who knows the white man's tongue, hears words that no chief of a great tribe would use."

Crusoe looked from the girl's face to old Tom's, and remarked—

"See how different are the feelings of this girl to the women of our nation."

"Nature, lad—nature!" the old sailor said. "It is born in 'em; and what's born in the flesh—you know the rest."

Crusoe smiled, then, pointing in the direction of the hut, said—

"Lela's place is beyond the mighty ceibas. Let her go. Young Eagle will behave as a warrior."

She bowed her head submissively, and was about to leave, when the cane-brake parted, and the young lion dragged his wounded body through the opening.

Lela turned, and a cry of grief came from her lips, and, dropping down on one knee beside her stricken favourite, she plucked the arrow from the animal's side.

Crusoe stooped to caress the noble brute, an act which was repaid with a low whine of pleasure, and the hot, feverish tongue licked the boy's caressive hand.

Old Tom gazed for a moment at the strange spectacle—the beautiful girl stanching the blood in the animal's side, and one of its huge paws placed fondly over her shoulder.

"That's a picture we don't see every day, lad," he remarked ; "and a pretty one too."

"It is," Crusoe said ; "and if eyes ever expressed words, the wounded lion speaks the gratitude he feels. But come on, we shall be too late."

They dashed among the trees, and, guided by the fierce shouts of the victorious Aynoths, soon reached the scene of slaughter.

Crusoe's fear had not misled him, the men of Aynoth were slaughtering the foe with that keenness for blood which belongs only to the red men of the forest and the fierce panther tribe.

Bravely had the Macoushi stood in a small open glade, in the vain hope of staying the pursuit.

There was a momentary struggle as weapon met weapon—a swaying to and fro of the dusky phalanxes—then the Macoushi broke, and fled towards the trees.

Their foes divined their intention, and, spreading themselves out like a fan, they intercepted the fugitives, who, being in small bodies, could make but a feeble stand.

Like flashes of light, the Aynoths' tomahawks gleamed in the air—then fell with crushing force upon the skulls of the foe.

Their pit-pans destroyed—pressed in the rear by the victorious Aynoths—no escape for them, save by plunging into the tranquil sea—the Macoushi threw down their arms, and sued for quarter.

The reply was a fierce yell, and the red weapons were plied more fiercely.

Another five minutes, and not one of the Macoushi braves would have been alive.

Bounding to the spot, and placing himself between the excited victors and their cowering foes, Crusoe, with flashing eyes, called upon them to stay the red work.

Their passions were too much excited to readily obey their young leader, and, save from one or two, the tomahawks continued to gleam in the sunlight, and each stroke sent a red-man's spirit to the mystic regions of eternity.

Crusoe snatched a tomahawk from the stiffening grasp of a dead Indian, and, placing himself before the Macoushi, he sternly waved his followers back.

"The men of Aynoth," he said, and his dark eyes blazed with passion, "are braves. They do not make war with a foe whose hands are empty, and whose weapons are thrown away. Such as do this are not braves ; and as surely as the red sun streams through the trees, will I slay the next that raises a weapon."

Two-thirds of the Aynoths shrank back from the raised weapon, and the clear, determined eyes that were fixed upon them.

But four of the band, disregarding the words of the young white chief, dashed towards a group of the beaten foe.

Crusoe saw the act, and, before their weapons could be raised, he was amongst them.

"Dog!" he said, "is it thus you obey your chief? Die!"

He struck one to the earth with his tomahawk, and the remainder, awed to submission by their companion's fall, immediately lowered their weapons.

Crusoe followed up the advantage he had gained over the fiery band by saying—

"You have sworn before the great council of your tribe—sworn by the Great Spirit, to serve and obey the Young Eagle. Is it thus you keep that oath? Go, men of Aynoth! seek your lodges, and when the tiger's thirst for blood leaves your hearts, come to the hut of Young Eagle, who loves his young men."

The Indian race, so quickly roused to demoniacal fury, are as easily subdued by a judicious appeal to the really honest depths of their nature.

I use the term honest, because the red-men, until they became *polluted* by the white traders, travellers, or the settlers, were honest, sober, brave, and chivalrous, yet quick at anger and as quickly appeased.

Mark how these traits, one by one, left them, as the mighty forests and endless savannas became peopled with the flow of emigration which pour out from the cities of the Old World.

The ring of the settler's axe in those vast regions awoke echoes that sounded strangely upon the ear the simple forest children.

They saw mighty trees cut down by the strangers' hands—saw the game, which was their only wealth, driven far away by the surging crowd of pale-faced strangers.

Tract after tract of land was taken from them—their hunting grounds given to the axe and flames ; and because the red-men resented this wholesale destruction of the land they and theirs had held from time immemorial, the needy adventurers laid aside their axes and took up the rifle against the naked and poorly-armed Indians.

What was the result? Wholesale massacre upon either side, and lying reports reached the old country respecting the red-man's ferocity and cunning—reports that originated with the very men who had robbed the Indians of their birthright, and driven them, with fire and sword, from their hunting-grounds.

With such chroniclers, there can be but little wonder that the simple forest children were classed among the most degraded of God's creatures.

The small band who served Crusoe were free from the evil traits so unjustly attributed to the Indian character.

Naturally brave, they loved the boy for his gallantry, and would have followed him to the death in any enterprise, no matter how rash or hopeless.

Young Eagle was to them a superior being, and they worshipped, admired, and loved him.

The disobedience they had shown when he ordered them to desist in the terrible slaughter was not through any disrespect or want of respect for their young leader.

It was simply obeying an uncontrollable impulse of their untutored nature, and the example he made of one of their number, in place of bringing angry feelings to their breasts, made them love the boy for his strict sense of justice.

A long digression, the reader will think, but necessary in a work that does not deal with fictitious scenes of excitement to render its pages interesting.

The readers of " Crusoe Jack " were promised both instruction and amusement, a promise that we have so far kept with them, and shall do so until the end.

To resume.

The men of Aynoth, with bowed heads, slowly left the field of slaughter, and went towards their lodges.

Then Crusoe, still holding the blood-stained tomahawk in his hand, turned towards the Macoushi.

" I have saved you," he said, " from death; for my young men were angry when they saw that the foe had come to the island during their absence and killed all that were left. Then, worse than the tiger, they took a poor helpless girl, and gave her to the flames. Say, is it right these things should be done by warriors of a great and powerful tribe ? "

The Indians were silent, and gazed from the youthful speaker to old Tom's statuesque form.

The old tar was leaning upon the muzzle of his fatal rifle, listening with pleased astonishment to his favourite's words.

" I have seen many a red-skin chief," he thought, " and heard them speak; but this boy is a wonder, considering the little he knows of forest life. It's nature, I suppose—nature; and, unless I'm far adrift, the lad is far out of the common."

Old Tom was not far adrift in his surmises, as the reader knows.

" Listen, men of the Macoushi," he continued, finding that none of the tribe answered; " the great forests, the mighty plains, and the troubled waters, are large enough for all to dwell upon."

An exclamation of approval came from one of the listeners.

" It is," Crusoe said. " Why, then, do the Macoushi seek to slay the men of Aynoth ? "

" Many a Macoushi scalp," said one of the tribe, " hangs in the Aynoth lodges."

" Is that a reason why you should thus war with each other ? "

" A Macoushi warrior," said the Indian, proudly, " is ever on the war path of his foes."

" Nature, Jack," old Tom said, in English; " you won't change it, lad."

" I'll try in this instance, Tom."

" Push ahead, lad."

Crusoe turned to the Indian who had spoken for his companions.

" Does the Macoushi warrior," he asked, " always return from the war path ? "

" Many," was the reply, " go to the happy hunting-grounds."

" But they would sooner live ? "

The Indian's reply was characteristic.

" They die as warriors should die."

" You can't get over that, lad," said old Tom, quietly; " better give in with the argument."

" So I think," Crusoe said, " for my dusky friend seems quite able to hold his own."

" Aye, lad, he'd do that ag'in a fleet of petticoats, and they love to show a good amount of jawing tackle."

Our hero laughed.

" But what, in the name of all that's good," said old Tom, " do you want these fellows to do, that you tack about from point to point ? "

" I should like," Crusoe said, " to put an end to this war between the tribes."

" Whew ! "

Tom's whistle of astonishment would have excited the envy of a bo'sun.

" What are you whistling for, Tom ? "

" Nothing, lad—nothing—exercise, that's all."

Crusoe looked straight at the old fellow, as he said—

" You are quizzing me, Tom; but never mind, I will try my hand at peace-making."

" Do, lad, do. It will save many a poor devil's scalp if you can get them to bury the war hatchet, and take to smoking pipes of peace."

Crusoe felt that old Tom was not very sanguine about a successful result of his meditation.

Hopeful of the issue, he again addressed the Macoushi.

" My brother tells me," he said, " that the braves of his tribe die as warriors should die."

The Indian bowed his plumed head, in token of acquiescence.

" Does my brother forget the empty lodge, the sorrowing woman he leaves when the spirit wings its way to the happy home beyond the sun ? "

" A Macoushi squaw," said the Indian, " lives to repeat the brave deeds of her husband."

" Go it, darkie," chuckled old Tom.

" Does she rejoice that he is dead ? " Crusoe asked.

The Indian was silent, he could not tell a lie.

" She does not," Crusoe said. " Neither do the young men of the tribe when they lose a brother."

" Young Eagle forgets," said the Indian, " that the Macoushi have many braves, and their young men can be counted by many hundreds."

" I do not," said Crusoe; " but the life of every brave is precious, and should not be wasted in this long war with the men of Aynoth. What say my brothers, will they bury the war hatchet, and be friends with those they have so long and nobly fought ? "

There was a few minutes' silence, and old Tom chuckled out—

" Why don't you try to wash their skins white, Jack ? It would be quite as profitable as the palaver you have wasted."

" Have patience, you tantalizing old sinner. I shall bring them round to my way of thinking, yet."

" Perhaps you will, lad—but not this side of twenty years."

Before Crusoe could reply, the Indian answered his suggestion.

" Young Eagle," he said, " is a mighty r ▃▃ for one whose years are but few."

" That's soft soap, Jack, and —— "

" Let him go on, Tom." ·

The old tar grinned as the Indian proceeded.

" When he speaks," said the Macoushi, " his voice is as soft as the fall of the dew upon the flowers."

" That's——"

" Do be quiet, Tom."

" When on the war path," continued the Indian, " his bound is like the panther's. We listen to the words of so great a warrior, and find them to be good. Thus do we bury the hatchet of war—thus do we become friends."

They hurled their weapons from them, and breaking a bough from one of the trees, each took a portion, and laid it at Crusoe's feet.

The boy, with a triumphant look, turned towards old Tom, and, raising his bugle—formed from a conch shell—blew three loud notes.

The sound was answered by the Aynoth braves suddenly appearing among the trees, and Crusoe, when all were present, told them of the termination of the long war between the tribes.

The men of Aynoth soon followed the example of the Macoushi, and the broken branches were exchanged.

At the conclusion of this ceremony, the rival tribes began to fraternise and embrace each other, as though they were brothers meeting after a long absence.

Crusoe and old Tom left them, and walked slowly towards the tent, the old sailor thoroughly astounded at the miraculous change the boy had effected in the hearts of the angry savages.

Old Tom hurried outside the hut to caress the wounded lion, whose wound had been dressed by Lela, and the grateful animal lay across the door—a grim, trusty, and watchful sentinel.

Crusoe stepped over the lion's body, and went inside ; and, soon after, old Tom was startled by hearing an angry cry from the boy's lips ; then followed the report of fire-arms, and Crusoe dashed through the doorway, a rifle in each hand.

" What on earth is the matter ? " old Tom began, when he saw the boy's face blackened and charred with gunpowder.

Crusoe grasped him by the shoulder, and, in wild, thrilling accents, said—

" Come, Tom. The island is no longer a home for us. Let us go."

" Why? Bless the lad ! What——"

" Ask no questions now," Crusoe said, " but come. Let us once more see the lovely waves beneath us ! "

" But—but—"

" For heaven's sake, Tom, do not seek any explanation now ! I will explain hereafter."

He turned towards the boat as he spoke, and ran as though pursued by a legion of furies.

Old Tom shook his head sagely, and putting one of the rifles Crusoe had dropped upon his shoulder, he closely followed.

When he reached the margin of the great ocean he found Crusoe wildly pushing the boat out from land.

Old Tom, still lost in wonderment, gave him a helping hand, and they were soon afloat.

As the boat glided from the shore, Crusoe threw himself upon the pile of skins, and remained for many hours silently watching the single mat sail as it flapped against the mast, or bellied out before the wind.

CHAPTER XL.

ON THE WAY TO A STRANGE ADVENTURE.

THE lonely isle had long sunk below the dim and misty horizon before Crusoe spoke to his wondering companion.

When he did so, old Tom was struck by the change in his voice, and the deep glitter in his dark eyes.

" Tom," he said, " come and sit beside me."

The old seaman went aft.

Crusoe said—

" I feel, old friend, as though my blood had changed to liquid fire. Come! can you not find something to turn my thoughts from the fearful scene I have—but there, you shall know all when I am calm enough to tell you."

" Something, lad ? What can I do to calm you ? "

" Recite some of the wonders you have beheld, anything is better than this mental torture I endure. Come, Tom, grant me this favour."

" I will, lad ; try and keep your mind from thinking upon the matter that has upset you. Though I fear you have exhausted my powers of amusement, still, I'll try, and if I am prosy, or fail to amuse you, tell me so."

" I shall not have to do that," Crusoe said, a faint smile flitting over his pale face.

" We shall see, lad ; put that skin round your shoulders, the evening is cold."

Crusoe did so, and old Tom went 'midships to fasten down the sail, one end of which had become loose.

When he returned to our hero's side, he drew a warm skin over his shoulders, and after a few moments' silence, and two or three long side looks at his companion, said—

" Would you like to hear a little about the Egyptian mummy pits ? "

" I should, very much."

" Very well, lad. Now fancy we have started from London or Plymouth, and reached the stormy waves of the unfathomable Bay of Biscay ; then, coasting the fertile shores of Portugal, we are round that vast headland, the impregnable fortress of Gibraltar, and enter the Mediterranean Sea.

" We touch at the island of Malta, where I am regaled with the finest oranges in the world.

" Then pass the southern part of Sicily, and see Ætna, its natural lighthouse.

" But I have beheld the mighty Cotopaxi, so that Ætna, and all European mountains, appear as mere molehills, after the giant heights of the Andes.

" In a short time we neared Nelson's Island, off the point of Aboukir, with the whole crew singing—

" 'The battle of the Nile
        Shall be foremost on the file ;
And Nelson, gallant Nelson's name, applauded it
        shall be !
Then huzza, boys! huzza!—huzza, huzza, huzza !
  Britannia still, Britannia rules the main ! '

"In the midst of this noise I observed a weather-beaten tar seated happily across a gun, and roaring away at the top of his lungs, very much to his own satisfaction.

"I drew near, and found he had altered the words of the old ditty to—

"'The battle of the Nile,
I was there all the while,
And Splicer's name, Ben Splicer's name, applauded it shall be!
Then huzza!' etc., etc.

"Poor old Ben! he looked quite as happy as if he had been the hero of the Nile!

"Aye, and much more happy than Nelson ever looked; for Ben was unwounded, and felt no care; while his noble commander had dragged on a painful existence for many years, owing to the agony of an unhealed wound; and his situation as admiral, having the lives of so many of his fellow-creatures under his control, and the honour of his country in his hands, might well weigh down his spirit with care and anxiety.

"Ben and I talked over the battle of the Nile together, and I gazed at the spots with interest, as he pointed them out to me, where so many human beings had lost their lives.

"Soon after, we landed at Rosetta, where I took leave of my shipmates, and hired a boat to Grand Cairo, at which place I stayed only a few days, to see the mosques, Jacob's Well, and other curiosities, for I was anxious to reach those wonderful pyramids of Dijza, which have astonished the world for so many hundred years.

"Never shall I forget the feelings of awe and amazement which took possession of me as I approached them, in their dreary solitude, with that mysterious colossal head of the Sphinx, which seems a thing of eternity—as if its mild face and upturned eye had borne the parching winds of the desert in everlasting patience. You have so often seen and heard accounts of those sublime works of man, my lad, that I must pass to other curiosities, for——"

"No, Tom!" exclaimed the boy, "for you cannot think how different it seems to me, now you tell me these things. I can hardly express myself; but you know what I mean. I am not so interested in those wonders that I meet with in books, but if I talk to any one who has seen these strange things, I feel that they are true. For instance, I have read accounts of eruptions of volcanoes. I never seemed to realise them till we saw that island rise from the sea."

His friend smiled, and, filling his pipe, resumed his narrative.

"You have heard that the largest pyramid is six hundred feet high.

"I went up to the top of the pyramid, on the outside, clambering up steps that were as high as my breast; and what a singular view I had from the summit!

"As far as my eye could reach, in almost all directions, I saw the sterile spots where now the Arabs' tents flap in the desert blast.

"Thoughts, feelings, musings, crowded into my mind, until I went down again, and entered the vast building. There is a well below the base of it, the depths of which has never been ascertained; and I had the pleasure of flinging stones into its dark mouth, that I might listen, in wonder, to their deep plunge into the water.

"I then hired an Arab guide, and proceeded about thirty miles farther, to visit the pyramids of Sacarah, under which are the mummy pits that extend for many leagues.

"The operation of descending into these dark abodes of the dead is very unpleasant.

"The guide and I slung ourselves down a deep hole for nearly thirty yards; and the loose stones from the sides came clattering about us in such numbers, that I expected we should have had a severe blow or two; but, fortunately, we escaped.

"When I got to the bottom, I found I had to creep through a long narrow passage, for twenty yards, so small and so dark that I would not venture; for, I thought, what will be the use of my going?—I shall see nothing. So I resolved to dismiss my guide as soon as we should return to open daylight, and then ramble about for a few days in this wonderful neighbourhood, and look for curiosities.

"This I did; and, having purchased eggs, dates, and coffee, I crossed the river again, and proceeded to the tombs that are excavated in the rocks.

"Here I was tormented with Arabs, all offering their services as guides; but I resolved to explore by myself; so refused all their offers, and entered the tombs alone.

"You will have some idea of the immense multitudes of human beings that have been buried there, when I tell you that I wandered the whole day by lamp-light, through numberless long lanes of coffins, or cases, piled in rows to the ceiling of the caverns, which have been hollowed out, with incredible labour, in order to receive the dead bodies. It was really a city of the dead!"

"I thought," Crusoe said, "Egypt was not a very populous country. Where could all these people have lived? for you say that the mummy pits under the pyramids of Sacarah extend for several leagues. In these wide deserts, how could they manage to collect such thousands and millions of mummies?"

"There *are* thousands and millions, Jack.

"The ancient and extensive city of Memphis is supposed to have been situated between Sacarah and Gizeh, or Dijza; and these plains, as the pits are called, were the burial-places of the city.

"There were, doubtless, many other towns and villages scattered over the desert, which were once crowded with inhabitants; and not the least wonderful circumstance of this country is, that the people themselves (in the state of mummies) are the only records we possess of their dwellings having formerly stood where the parched and ever-shifting sand now spreads, like a deep sea, over them. In other conquered countries, the inhabitants are gone from the surface of the earth, and their ruined buildings only remain.

"Evening drew on, then, and I seated myself at one of the openings of the rocky tombs, to catch the cool air which blows every night from the deserts.

"True, it comes loaded with light sand, which is drifted and eddied about in a very annoying manner, entering the houses of Cairo, and penetrating everywhere.

"But this evil is but a trifling drawback from the blessing of a cool breeze in that fierce climate where the ground reflects back upon the face gleams of heat, like those at the door of an oven.

"I had made myself a fire of some broken mummy cases—but I could not endure the thought of burning the bodies, as the Arabs do when they want fuel for their fires—and having boiled my coffee and lighted a lamp, I sat down to eat my dates, and enjoy an hour's meditation among the tombs.

"The long, winding course of 'old Nile' flowed away to the north.

"Grand Cairo stood in the misty west.

"The heights, in which the tombs are excavated, arose behind me to the south.

"And far to the east, stretched out beneath the brilliant stars, lay the dreary deserts.

"Two or three Arabs, in their picturesque dress, three or four camels, a Mameluke on a noble Arabian steed that seemed winging its way over the plain like a bird, were the only moving objects in sight.

"The short twilight was fading into night, and I was just thinking of my choice of a resting-place among the confused and dusky heaps of unburied bodies, when I was startled by a low moan from a broken pile of coffins near me.

"I sat quite still, with my date half eaten, listening eagerly.

"A slight noise, and a louder groan, now made my heart beat so that I could hear it.

"I raised the lamp, which flared in the breeze, while the smoke of it rolled towards the spot whence the noise proceeded; and, as I sat with my eyes straining in the same direction, I thought one of the mummy cases moved!

"The next moment a louder groan, and an uplifted arm from the same coffin, alarmed me.

"But my terror was at its height in another instant, for the whole crowd of cases came clattering to the ground about my ears, burying my coffee, and nearly smothering me with the cloud of dust which they raised.

"I had scrambled up as the coffins fell, which fortunately enabled me to save the lamp from being extinguished; but it shook so violently with my fright, as I stood trying to look through this suffocating dust, that I expected I should be left in the dark.

"The groans had ceased.

"But imagine my horror, when the breeze had wafted away the cloud of dust, on beholding a human being, alive, and covered with blood, raising itself on its elbow from the fallen mass, and gazing at me!"

"Horrible!" Crusoe said.

"'In heaven's name, who are you, and how came you in this place?' I said.

"'An Englishman, wounded by an Arab, and left here,' answered a faint voice.

"'Gracious heavens! what can I do to assist you? I have no refreshment—nothing to dress your wounds with!'

"Then, setting down the lamp in safety, and going towards the exhausted man, I found that the fall had caused his wounds to bleed afresh, and that he had fainted.

"I carefully raised him from the heap of broken cases, and brought him to the entrance of the tomb, hoping that the air might revive him; then recollecting that an old Arab lived about a hundred yards farther, in the same range of tombs (for it was he who had supplied me with my light), I hastily ran towards his dwelling: the noiseless sand yielded to my feet, and my own breathing was the only sound caused by my rapid flight.

"The aged man had not yet spread his date-leaf mat for repose, when I hurried into the dusky abode.

"I told him my errand, and requested him to return with me, and assist to recover the wounded traveller. I had found before that the Arab could speak and understand English, for he had been accustomed, during many years, to act as a guide to the numerous travellers who visit the ruins, so he easily comprehended me; and immediately going to an empty mummy case, he took out an earthen pitcher—so old, and of so singular a shape, that it looked as if it had come out of the ark:—it contained some date-milk and some boiled rice; from the same closet he then took a small pot of fragrant balsam, some fresh young date leaves, and a mummy bandage, for the traveller's wounds, and away he went.

"We found the poor fellow lying just as I had left him; so having quickly bound up his head and shoulder, which had been deeply cut, we supported him, and poured a little of the sweet, refreshing milk into his mouth. He soon opened his eyes, and in a weak voice thanked us for our care.

"I sat by him, as he lay on the ground, with my cloak rolled under his head for a pillow, and occasionally gave him water to drink, which old Barac had fetched for him.

"Towards morning, my poor wounded companion felt revived, and told me that he had left Cairo, where he had lodgings, on the preceding day, in order to visit the tombs; and having hired an Arab guide, they entered the recess.

"'I thoughtlessly,' continued the traveller 'drew out my purse with my pocket-book, and laid it by me, while I sat down hereabouts, to write a few memoranda.

"'The cowardly villain seeing my purse, resolved to have it, and, coming behind me, struck me a blow with his short sword that nearly stunned me, at the same time that it disabled my right arm; I jumped up, however, but before I could get my own weapon out, in order to defend myself, he had inflicted this other gash on my head, which brought me to the ground.

"'I suppose I fainted, or was stunned, for I remember nothing more till I tried to move, and fell with all those mummies to the floor; I suppose the wretch thought I was dead, and so procured some assistance to heave me up there.'

"I would not suffer the gentleman to talk any more, and begged he would keep from any exertion; 'But,' I said, 'you are not able to bear the motion of a removal to Cairo to-day, and I don't like to leave you, while I go—Perhaps the old Arab will go.'

"I went to the opening of the tomb as I spoke, to look for him; he had promised, when I dismissed him over night, to come back again in the morning. I could not see Barac, but I stood still to look around me; and I was as much delighted with the scene in the dawn of day, as I had been with it in the twilight.

"The glittering minarets of the numerous mosques in the city shooting up in the clear air—the distant groves of magnificent orange trees, towards Gizeh—the lofty sycamores, that render the island of Rhoda so pleasant—the waving tops of the plantation of date trees—and those mysterious pyramids, with their sharp, clear outlines, cutting against the morning sky—all the landscape too, bathed and refreshed with the cooling dews of night—formed a view so uncommon, and of its kind so beautiful, that I shall not easily forget it.

"Soon I saw old Barac's long white robe fluttering in the breeze; and, going to meet him, I gave him money, and dispatched him for a surgeon, desiring him to bring linen, refreshments, and, above all, a pair of pistols, a short sword, powder, and balls, all of which orders he faithfully attended to; and I had the satisfaction of hearing that the traveller's wounds were by no means dangerous, and that he might be moved with safety on the following day.

"As I sat by my companion of the tombs, he told me that his name was Austen—Harry Austen; that he was on his way, overland, to India; that he was desirous of seeing everything of note, and was not restricted as to time or expense.

"I was glad to hear this, as I liked the young man, and hoped to gain a travelling companion for a few months.

"So I told him my name, my story, and my plans, and asked him if he should object to our journeying together.

"He was delighted with my proposal, and our time was most agreeably spent in planning our future route.

"This was a matter of some difficulty, as I wished much to see the Lake of Asphaltites (or Dead Sea), which lay very far from our road across to India; it being situated near Palestine, and not very far from the eastern shores of the Mediterranean Sea."

Old Tom then resumed, "I, however, omitted going the Dead Sea, and complied with Austen's wish of turning our soles on the desert.'

So, the next morning, like two young mad fools, we were, we dressed ourselves like Arabs, mounted our camels, and hired a guide, who rode also on a camel, and led another, which was laden with provisions; and with merry hearts we set forward on our 'ships of the desert,' (as the camels are aptly styled by the Arabs), to traverse the trackless sands, instead of waiting for the next caravan going to Mecca.

"Harry's fine spirits were soon distressed under the fatigue of this dreary journey.

"He had been weakened, too, by his wounds; and he was, on all accounts, less able to endure toil and hardship than I was.

"The uneasy motion of the camels we soon became accustomed to; but the disappointment now and then at the wells, and misery of finding no water at spots where our guide had led us to hope for some, were trials that we all felt, but which nearly killed poor Harry.

"Towards the close of a day of great suffering, when our camels flagged and drooped beneath the fierce heat, they suddenly snuffed up the air, and all four set off to the left at a full gallop.

"Our guide told us that they scented water; so, fatiguing as their rapid pace was to us in our exhausted condition, we gladly hurried over the parched sand, although we saw no signs of the desired well.

"Soon we gained a rising ground, and, below us, saw a spot like enchantment.

"A verdant plot, green as an emerald, lay beneath us, watered by a stream which welled out of a rock, cool, pure, and clear.

"We eagerly rushed to it, and drank in such imprudent quantities, that I wonder it did not injure us.

"Having satisfied our raging thirst, we had leisure, before the red sun went down, to look round and admire this paradise.

"Date palms, tamarinds, acacias, and plane trees, the white-blossomed coffee, rice, grass, and flowering creepers, fringed the rocks, from which the silvery fountain bubbled: linnets, larks, bulbuls, bees, and chameleons, were singing and sparkling on all sides; and the scorching sunbeams, that had poured their fury on our heads as we crossed the desert, now glanced through the rich foliage of the trees with all the refreshing beauty of an English evening.

"Here we prepared our supper of coffee, honey, rice, and dates; and after having watched the stars as they came boldly out, twinkling with intense brilliancy, we laid ourselves down to repose for a few hours, covered with our cloaks, and resting our heads on the saddles.

"We were scarcely settled in our cool retreat before the quick ears of our guide distinguished the rapid approach of a large company of travellers, who were sweeping over the plain towards our delicious resting-place with the same velocity that we had used.

"He hastily roused us, warned us of our danger, raised our wearied beasts, and urged us all up a narrow passage between the rocks, that we might see whether our visitors were friends or foes, before we should trust ourselves among them.

"We were scarcely screened from view behind a cluster of shrubs, before a troop of Arabs, with their flowing white robes streaming in the night breeze, came thundering over the rocky ground to the fountain.

"They flung themselves from their impatient camels and horses, which crowded to the water; and their riders mingling among them, formed in one minute such a strange confused group, that I stood looking at it with astonishment, totally forgetting our own peril.

"A fire was now kindled, which quickly blazed up, and threw a glare over the wild party.

"At this moment I felt my shoulder touched; and turning quickly, I found, close to my face, the black eyes of our guide sparkling in the gleam from the fire light.

"He cautiously whispered, that he knew the tribe of Arabs, by the shiek, or rather, by the device on his scarf, which he desired me to look at, as the chief unwound it from his shoulders, and gave it to an attendant. I saw some stars and a crescent moon very distinctly upon it.

"The guide then told me that my friend was saddling the camels a little higher up the rugged pass, and that we must join him and pursue our journey immediately; assuring me that Kana, the shiek, or chief, was a very warlike man; and that he and his tribe never suffered any travellers to appear in sight without pillaging and capturing them.

"I was roused by this information, and cautiously followed the guide to the spot where Austen waited.

"We lost no time, but quickly mounted our wearied beasts, and, winding down the rocky path, which became rugged and barren as we approached the sands, we again struck into the desert, which we traversed by the light and guidance of the stars.

"Soon after sunrise we came to another eminence, and, having ascended it, we looked anxiously back in the direction of the well, to see if Kana and his warlike tribe were pursuing our route; and, to our terror, we beheld the horizon in that part peopled with men on horseback and on camels!

"Away we started again, and for a time lost sight of the objects of our alarm.

"By noon we were exhausted; a fearful sultriness increased the oppression of the usual heat: our pursuers gained rapidly upon us; the camels once more slackened their pace, and almost ceased to move, although we tried to rouse them by the usual mode of encouragement, by chanting or singing to them. Suddenly, our guide exclaimed, 'Alla! Alla!' and threw himself from his camel, desiring us to do the same; and pointing to the west, we beheld several enormous pillars of sand, twenty or thirty feet high, moving towards us with astonishing rapidity.

"We flung ourselves down, crouching under the camels, and expecting instant destruction.

"The stately columns were now so close to us that we actually felt some of the sand in our faces.

"But the wind just then shifted, and they moved off towards the tribe of Arabs who were in pursuit; and as we sat watching these terrible whirlwinds, one or two of them divided in the middle and dispersed. Whether they fell on the party and overwhelmed them or not we could not determine; but we never again saw the Arabs, who must either have perished or dashed off in a different direction, in order to avoid the dreadful death that awaited them.

"Our journey was a very fatiguing one; there were so many wonders to admire, and our repose at night was in general so delicious and refreshing

that we had always something pleasant to look forward to in our greatest periods of suffering. Many times we saw a large flock of ostriches in the distance, which at first we always mistook for a whole tribe of hostile Arabs. Sometimes we joined in a chase of them for amusement, and frequently obtained their eggs to eat, which formed a pleasant variety in our food.

"The hunters of some nations catch them by clothing themselves in the skins of dead birds. Passing their arms through the necks, they are able to deceive the flocks, and thus they are taken with less trouble than when hunted by the swift Arab horses.

"These birds are domesticated in some parts of Africa, and, though they are stupid to be taught any useful habits, they will submit to be mounted, and then they run as if they would never stop.

"We had been long enough in the deserts for us to wish to leave them, so we made the best of our way to the shores of the Red Sea, where we embarked on board an Indian vessel, and, passing through the Strait of Bab-el-mandeb, in due course we reached the city of Surat, on the western coast of Hindoostan; and there we remained some months, with an uncle of my friend Austen.

"I enjoyed myself exceedingly in this handsome city.

"One day, I remember, I was very much amazed to see a sheep that had been injured (and which I should have been inclined to kill, from motives of humanity) lifted carefully on the back of a Hindoo, and conveyed into a large building.

"I naturally inquired the reason of this, and was informed that, although there is no hospital for human beings, yet there is one for diseased and maimed animals, which are all brought here, and attended to by the humane Hindoos.

"I was now in the country where that noble animal, the elephant, is in constant use for the service of man.

"I never saw an elephant-hunt, but you may read entertaining accounts of it in several works.

"While I was up in the country, I once witnessed a singular instance of sagacity, or instinct, and, in my opinion, of reason, in two elephants.

"We were journeying on the western side of the Ghaut mountains, towards the town of Nassuck (about ninety miles S.E. of Surat), where another uncle of my friend Austen lived, and were crossing a wide, barren plain, having a powerful elephant in our train, when we came to a spacious well, at the same time that a smaller elephant, with his mohaut, or keeper, on his neck, came up also to drink.

"This man had provided his beast with a bucket to dip water with, and which was hung on his proboscis, or trunk.

"Our elephant was not provided with one; so what do you think the saucy animal did?

"He seized the bucket, and wrested it from his fellow servant, who was so much weaker and smaller than himself that he dared not openly resent the insult.

"But the cunning creature watched his opportunity, and while our great beast was standing with his side to the well, the weaker animal retired backward a few paces, and then rushing forward with all his might, drove his head against the side of the other, and fairly pushed him into the well.

"We laboured for fourteen hours before we could extricate him; for the surface of the water was twenty feet below the level ground, and there were many feet of water below him, so that he floated about very happily, and was in no haste to come out.

"We were obliged to procure fascines, or fagots, from a neighbouring encampment of the British army, which we lowered into the well; our mohaut then made the elephant comprehend that he was to pile them up under him, so as to raise him to the top; and he worked well for some hours.

"But when he found that he was gradually being raised out of his delicious bath, he refused to place any more fascines; and it was only by coaxing, and procuring him plenty of rack that he could be induced to continue his work; and the hope of this favourite beverage accomplished that which threats could not."

"How very wonderful the elephant's sagacity was, Tom! But what is rack, pray?" said Jack.

"Arrack, or rack, is a spirituous liquor, made from rice; it is frequently mixed with the other ingredients of which punch is made, which is then called rack punch.

"I have often drunk it, but do not like it. Austen told me of another curious anecdote of this most sensible of quadrupeds.

"A friend of his, in the army, had once occasion to cross the Jumna (which is a branch of the Ganges, you know) with a detachment of soldiers, and some young camels belonging to him, in a flat-bottomed boat.

"The camels were terrified at this novel way of journeying, and refused to get into the boat; upon which one of the mohauts called his elephant, and desired him to drive them in. The animal then put on a furious appearance, trumpeted with his proboscis, shook his ears, roared, struck the ground to the right and left, blew the dust in clouds towards them, and so entirely subdued one great fear in the terrified camels, by exciting a greater, that they bolted in the boat in the utmost hurry; then the elephant reassumed his composure, and quietly walked back to his post.

"We thought it would be a pity not to extend our excursion as far as the celebrated temples, or pagodas, of Elora, which are cut out of the rock, by a people who must have been well skilled in the arts; and yet these temples are so ancient, that the surrounding nations have no records of the work, but attribute the mighty buildings to the skill of their gods Brahma and Vishnu. Here, then, we wandered and admired for a few days; and then prepared to recross the Ghaut mountains; and down those precipitous passes, where the torrents in the rainy season rage and roar, we were borne, in two palanquins, on men's shoulders. In all my life, I never travelled in so delightful a manner! I had no drawback to my comfort, but from a sort of shame at the circumstance of being carried in ease and safety, by four of my fellow-creatures, who were thus converted into beasts of burden! I own that this fretted my spirit; I named it to Harry, who only laughed at my squeamishness, as he called it, adding, 'If the fellows like it, why need you object? If they don't carry you, they will carry some other person; if they felt this wonderful degradation that you talk of, I should, perhaps, be as unwilling as you to subject them to it; but really, I cannot see that they are worse off, or more to be pitied, in following their calling or trade, than our servants are, who wash their clothes, and wait upon us at our meals.' I was not convinced by his arguments, but I said no more.

"We agreed to go to Bombay, and there take shipping, and run down the whole of the Malabar coast, round Cape Cormorin, and across the sea of Manara to Columbo, the chief city of Ceylon.

"This we did, and went pleasantly on, scenting the perfumes of the spicy island for many leagues before we could distinguish its lofty shores, from the clouds that hung above them.

"Soon after we came to anchor in the open road—for there is no harbour—and were quickly in the extensive and populous city of Columbo."

Here a sullen cloud, that had long hung in the horizon, began to spread itself rapidly over the heavens; a heavy shower fell, and soon drenched the wanderers.

Old Tom paused, and covered his young companion with a piece of sail.

"Had enough, lad?" he asked, "or shall I go on?"

"Finish the yarn, Tom; it is most interesting."

Old Tom filled his pipe, and after a few thoughtful whiffs, resumed—

"Where did I leave off? At Columbo: aye, I remember, we had just landed.

"As Harry and I, the next day, sat eating a fresh-gathered, creamy cocoa-nut, and comparing its soft texture and delicious flavour with the hard, chucky stuff that we had eaten in England, Austen said—

"'Well, Tom, I little thought when I landed in Egypt that I should meet with a friend who would accompany me in my rambles. Are you tired of our roaming life, or shall we cross over this beautiful island together, and take shipping at Trincomalee or at Batacola?'

"'Why, Harry,' I said, if I found my long ramble across the widest part of America a pleasant stroll, I think I cannot fail to enjoy this walk exceedingly; I shall have your company, which, I confess, will delight me; the distance, too, is so trifling, compared with former travels—only a hundred and fifty miles—the country is so rich, so many productions are to be met with that are entirely new to us, so many birds inhabit the island which are never found elsewhere—besides, we have so long been confined on board ship, that I cannot hesitate for a moment. We will start as soon as you please; for I shall be glad to stretch my legs a little,' said I.

"It was thus settled; and in a day or two we started.

"We found the country wild and beautiful, beyond anything we had hitherto seen.

TOM STARBOARD ON THE LOOK-OUT.

"Immense cocoa-nut trees, the sacred banian, under whose extensive shade we frequently saw the simple native Hindoos worshipping at their bamboo altars.

"Groves of cinnamon trees, with their smooth, fragrant bark, were some of the productions of nature which we were never weary of admiring.

"I was surprised to find, from an old Indian, whom we saw stripping a cinnamon tree of its rind, that there are three distinct oils extracted from the different parts of it; that which is obtained from the leaves is called the oil of cloves; that from the fruit is extremely fragrant, of a thick consistence, and is made into candles for the sole use of the king of the island.

"The bark of the root not only affords an aromatic oil, called oil of camphor, but also a species of camphor, which is exceedingly white and pure.

"Mace and nutmeg-trees, too, were very abundant; and we were much interested by the manner in which the natives gathered and prepared this pleasant spice for exportation.

"The men ascend the trees, and gather the fruit, by pulling the branches to them with long hooks.

"Some are employed in opening them and taking off the first rind, or shells, which are laid together in heaps in the woods, where in time they putrefy.

"As soon as the putrefaction has taken place there spring up from the mass a kind of mushrooms, called *belati moschatyni*, much valued by the natives;

indeed, Harry and I ate them with the greatest relish."

"I thought, Tom, that mace was the shell of the nutmeg. Why then do they throw it away?" asked Jack.

"So it is, lad; that which is put aside, as I have just stated, is the outer shell, or husk; the mace, or inner shell, is carefully taken off with a knife, then dried in the sun, and squeezed very hard to extract all the moisture, lest it should decay; and after that it is fit for exportation; the nutmegs are dipped into a pickle, made of lime and salt water, to preserve them from mould and insects; and then they are sent abroad.

"It is very pleasant spice," said Tom; "but few persons are aware how dangerous it is, if taken in large quantities.

"The most beautiful tree we met with in our walk was the tallipot, which grows straight and tall, and as large as the mast of a ship; the leaves of it are of such a size, that one is sufficient shelter for fifteen men!

"When dried, they are round, and fold up like a fan; the natives wear a piece of a leaf of this tree on their head, to shade their faces from the sun; and the leaf is so tough, that it is not easily torn. Every soldier carries one with him, and it serves him for his tent. We did so too, and a most beautiful and pleasant green room it made.

"In the heat of the day we used to sit under the shade of one, if we happened to be distant from a forest, and near a village; and while we regaled ourselves with the delicate fruits of the island, we used to watch the Hindoo women getting in the rice harvest.

"After the corn was cut, they laid it in bundles at the bottom of a wide but shallow hole, about a foot deep and eight feet across (or in diameter), then they drove in half a dozen oxen among it, to trample it; and in this manner they would obtain forty or fifty bushels in a day.

"Sometimes we found the jungles or underwood of the forest quite impassable; and once, I remember, towards evening, we had advanced with great toil a considerable distance, when we found it utterly impossible to go a step farther in that direction, which was right as our compass proved.

"So we made our beds for the night, that is, we lashed our ropes into the form of cradles, in the same way that I used to manage mine in South America; agreeing to retrace our steps the next morning, and skirt the forest, instead of crossing through it; this would waste time, but we could not help it.

"Well, we were very quietly swinging in our nests, and watching the stars twinkling above us, when we heard a distant noise, that sounded like a heavy trampling, and a prodigious crashing of boughs, accompanied by yells and glancing lights.

"You may suppose we were astonished, and soon afterwards alarmed, when we found these furious sounds approaching our trees.

"In another minute, a herd of ponderous elephants came galloping under us, crushing the underwood with their weight, tearing away the lower boughs of some of the trees, and snapping the trunks of others, which stood in their way.

"The very earth trembled beneath the enraged animals as they tore along; and just as we hoped our hiding-place would be left in safety, a monstrous fellow, the last of the herd, came thundering on, whisking his proboscis in every direction.

"Unfortunately, the branch of the bread-fruit tree to which Austen had lashed his cradle was just within the creature's reach.

"He stopped an instant, caught it in his trunk, wrenched it from the stem, and lumbered on after his companions, just as another shout burst forth; and the approaching lights showed me poor Harry falling to the ground, with the broken branch cracking and splintering all about him!

"I hallooed to the people who were pursuing the animals, and begged them to stop, that I might have assistance for my friend, in case he should be hurt; then scrambling down, I went to him, and found that he was stunned by the fall, and lying with his legs bent under him.

"His face, too, was much scratched, and his clothes were torn by the boughs: fortunately, the thickest part of the branch had fallen against the bole, so that it did not touch him; if it had not been thus broken in its descent, he would have been crushed by its weight.

"I found the party to consist of hunters, employed by the king of Candy to drive the elephants into a part of the forest which had been already enclosed and prepared to receive them, that they might be ready when he should choose to order a hunt.

"You must know that tame elephants are always employed on these occasions; so, on the neck of one of these poor Harry was raised, and supported by the man that rode him, and I mounted another.

"In this way we travelled all night, having separated from the hunters; and in the morning I found that we were ascending the steep hill on which the city of Candy is built.

"Harry had recovered his senses during the night, and I was rejoiced to find that he was very little injured by his fall.

"One of his ankles, however, was sprained, which would oblige him to rest a few days; and we were therefore not sorry to pass our time in a city so singular as that of Candy.

"Our good-natured guide could speak a little English.

"He had been a soldier, during the time that the British troops entered Candy.

"He took us to his own house, which was situated in the principal street, very near to the king's palace, which is a square of immense extent, built of a kind of cement, perfectly white, with stone gateways.

"The large street, in which Yalee our guide lived, was very wide, and more than two miles in length.

"We stopped at his house; and, instead of dismounting from the necks of our gentle and tractable beasts, we stepped at once on to the stairs which ran up the outside wall; and, although the houses are but one storey high, we found the doors nearly up to the roof.

"This strange manner of building was adopted, Yalee told us, to prevent the mischief which the elephants would cause to the houses when they are hunted in the streets for the amusement of the king.

"We were astonished at the simple furniture, and the few wants of our hosts.

"Four or five earthen vessels, a copper basin or two, and two or three stools constituted the whole of the former.

"And rice, water, milk, fruits, and areka cakes, composed the latter."

"What are areka cakes, Tom?" asked Crusoe.

"They are made of a coarse kind of sago, my lad, which is manufactured from the stem of the bread-fruit tree; they saw it into small pieces, and after beating the pieces in a mortar, pour water on the mass, and leave it some hours to settle.

"It is then strained through a cloth, when the mealy substance runs off and the woody particles remain behind.

"The water is then poured away, and the meal when dried is made into cakes

"The same meal more finely pulverised, and made into round pieces, forms a substance resembling sago."*

"What is arrowroot, Tom?" asked Crusoe.

"The root of an American plant, called *maranta arundinacia;* but the flour of potato is so frequently used for the same purpose, that, very probably, you have never tasted the foreign production.

"Well, we stayed with Yalee, our simple Hindoo, for a week; during which time we had the honour of beholding the king, mounted on his favourite white elephant, and followed by his whole court.

"Harry's foot was in a few days sufficiently well for him to travel though not to walk upon.

"So, Yalee saying he had occasion to visit the sea-port of Batacola, we once more mounted his elephants, and, after passing through rich valleys, highly cultivated, we crossed the lofty range of mountains that divide the island, and terminate the effects of the monsoons, or winds which blow periodically in warm latitudes.

"Soon after we reached Batacola, where we found a vessel ready to sail for Calcutta, in which we embarked, having remunerated Yalee for his hospitality.

"As we approached the mouths of the Ganges, we encountered a violent storm; and, our vessel not being well manned, we were driven ashore on the eastern coast of India, within a few miles of Juggernaut.

"No lives were lost; and Harry and I soon congratulated ourselves on that which was a misfortune to others: for the festival of Juggernaut was being celebrated, and we should have been sorry to miss seeing so curious, though dreadful, a sight."

"I was wondering," said Crusoe, "if you could tell me anything about that shocking idol, Tom; for I remember, when I saw a picture of its great grinning head, over the top of a high tower drawn by elephants, I did not believe it was a real thing: so I am very glad to find that you have seen it."

"For more than fifty miles, before we reached this

horrid place, we found the roads strewn with human bones; they were those of the pilgrims who had died on their way to the temple of the idol: some of the groups of persons whom I saw told me they had been two months on their journey: many old people were coming hither to die.

"I saw one man, for a penance or self-punishment, lay himself down at every step he took, measuring the road by the length of his body.

"When we came in view of the temple, the multitude shouted, fell down, and worshipped; then, as we drew near the town of Juggernaut, we found the crowd so thick that we could not attempt to go on; the gates were kept shut until the pilgrims had all paid the tax.

"But such was their eagerness to get into the town, the gates were broken down, the guards overpowered, and the whole mass of people strove to enter at once.

"The temple is a very noble building; and numbers of priests and other attendants on the idols are handsomely paid for their services.

"The next day after our arrival, the enormous car, sixty feet in height, was made ready, and the frightful idol placed on the top of it; six ropes, each the size of a ship's cable, were attached to it, by which the people drew it along.

"Two other inferior idols, on two lower towers, each drawn by five elephants, followed the grand car.

"Flags, and bells, and crimson trappings, were profusely scattered, and the whole absurd cavalcade moved on.

"The shouts of the multitude were now quite deafening; and the self-murder of the poor ignorant creatures soon began.

"Persons of all ages threw themselves under the massive wheels of the car, and were crushed to death, and their bodies left to be devoured by dogs, jackals, and vultures.

"The horrible sight of half devoured carcases— the dreadful smell of those that were putrefying under a burning sun—the fierce and senseless shouts of the ignorant multitude were too disgusting to be long endured; so Harry and I speedily hired horses, and set off for the coast immediately, where we took shipping for Calcutta, at which place we arrived in safety.

"Here Harry found letters awaiting him from England, so we agreed to leave Calcutta in the same vessel.

"In a week we were once more on the ocean."

CHAPTER XLI.

AN UNEXPECTED SIGHT.

OUR hero, who had been listening with rapt attention to his companion's narrative, suddenly leaned forward, and pointing to a small dark object that was slowly floating towards the boat, exclaimed—

"What is that, Tom?"

"That, lad," said the old sailor, attentively watching the small black speck, "looks much like a piece of wood."

"Wood! and here?"

---

* The true sago is the production of a species of palm-tree— the *Cycas revoluta.*

"Ay, lad, and there ain't much to be surprised at in that, considering we are in the stream that runs direct from a cluster of more than a thousand small islands."

"A thousand islands!"

"Ay, lad! a thousand wonderful places, that have come up out of the sea's depths. Come up with huge bodies of smoke and flames, which the mighty waters could not extinguish."

"Volcanic islands, Tom?"

"Ay, lad, so they are termed."

"You said there was not much to be surprised at in seeing this log of wood here?"

"Nothing to be surprised at lad, when I tell you that hundreds of vessels strike upon the hidden pieces of coral islands, which are rapidly sinking again to the bed of the ocean."

Crusoe pondered for a few minutes.

"Tom," he asked, at length, "are none of these islands inhabited?"

"None, lad, except by goats and birds, and when a few men may escape from the whirling waters. You have passed them, lad, upon your voyage out from England; and—"

He paused, and as the piece of wood which attracted their attention rolled over, added—

"A piece of the Seagull, by heaven!"

It was a fragment of the jolly boat, and in white letters stood out the name SEAGULL.

Crusoe looked the astonishment he felt as he said—

"We are not far from the place where you were wrecked."

Old Tom shook his head.

"As for that, lad," he said, "we may not be a hundred fathoms, or we may be a hundred miles."

"The promised hope," Jack said, "for we have been long hoping to behold the remains of that beautiful vessel."

Old Tom was silent.

The well-practised gray eyes were watching the rippling waves, in the somewhat wild hope that a second piece of the ship would serve to guide them to the spot.

The boundless water, as far as the eye could stretch, was without a speck, save for the fragment of the Seagull's jolly boat, which by this time was slowly drifting past the boat.

At length Tom, startled, spoke—

"Look here, lad!" he said, "the stout craft has not gone to pieces, lad."

Crusoe loooked on interrogatively.

"I mean it," said old Tom; "and unless I am very far from the mark, the ship has been boarded since I left her."

"Boarded! by whom?"

"That," old Tom said, "remains to be seen. It may be a shipwrecked crew. Again, a party of Indians from the mainland may have come across the old hull; or what is as much to be feared, a gang of pirates, driven by stress of weather, may be using the spars for firewood."

"How do you know all this, Tom?"

"All what, boy?"

"That the vessel has been boarded since you left her."

"It's very simple, lad. The jolly boat, of which this is a piece, was half way down the hold when I left the Seagull, and was so fixed by the force with which the waves broke her from her fastenings, that it would have been necessary to cut away part of the hatches to have loosened her."

The explanation satisfied Crusoe.

"By the way," he asked, "what were you so intently gazing across the water for, just now?"

"To find out the way that piece of the jolly boat came."

"You are a strange fellow, Tom," said Crusoe. "Is finding a pathway across the ocean possible?"

"Ay, lad; when I know that the maelstrom is the point of attraction for the fragments of the wreck."

"The maelstrom, Tom?"

"Yes, lad; the place where two or three currents meet, and such is the attractive power of the vortex, that vessels have been drawn into it before now."

"Your opinion is," Crusoe said, "that this piece of the wreck is being drawn slowly towards the whirlpool?"

"Yes, lad; and, if I am right, we are going direct to the cluster of islands we have so long wished to find."

"I hope so, Tom."

"So do I, lad; for we shall be able to live more like Europeans, if we find the old vessel, than we have done lately."

"We have a few hours of daylight left," said Crusoe, "and with this wind we shall see the islands before dark."

"I hope so, lad; for I should not like to face a rough sea in this cockle shell."

"It would not be very safe, Tom."

"I think not, lad. Now, come, as I have told you enough to calm your mind, let me know the cause of the strange sounds inside the hut."

Crusoe's head drooped, as he said—

"Not now, Tom. When you have completed your narrative."

"Very well, boy. Let me see, where had I reached?"

"You had taken a passage home from India."

"True, lad; and a pretty roundabout journey I had to get to England. Would you believe it, I had to pass over the frozen regions of Siberia before I got to the old country again?"

"How was it that you were so far out of the way?"

"It was this, lad. I went with my young friend to Holland—there we parted, and I shipped on board a lugger, as third mate; but I did not wear my rank long, as you shall hear.

"I was an experienced seaman; and I found that we were likely to meet with such rough treatment from the weather, that a strong pair of hands, and I may add, a cool head and firm courage, might not be useless in the vessel.

"Before we were out of sight of the coast, the short wintry day was closing in; to the S. and S.E. the sky was of a dull slate colour, over which angry white clouds were scudding with surprising swiftness;

and it was the opinion of all on board that we should have a heavy night's work.

"It was a day or two after new moon, so that we were soon in utter darkness.

"The wind now suddenly swept over the troubled waters in one wild, tremendous gust, which nearly laid the lugger on her beam ends; but she righted again, just as the hurricane (for which we were now better prepared) burst over us, in all its head-long fury.

"For several hours we bore up under it; and by dawn of day we found ourselves in the Texel, beating up against the wind, which had chopped round to the N.W.; then we passed the Helder, and entered the Zuyder Zee, straining before the gale with bare poles, having lost anchor and cables.

"Towards evening we ran into a little harbour to the north of Amsterdam; for we found the helm so injured that we dared not risk it to the end of the voyage.

"I gladly left the strained and leaky vessel; and having secured a bed and supper at the little inn, I hoped to pass the night in comfort.

"About eight o'clock—an hour or two after I had left the lugger—I found that with the rising tide the gale had increased; and it shortly became so violent that the inhabitants began to assemble, and to talk with fear of the doorbraak,* taking every precaution in their power to prevent such a misfortune.

"The engineers who superintend the state of the dykes were on the alert; such parts of the dykes as were considered the weakest, were strictly watched; and the best means the Waterstatt† could suggest, were resorted to, in order to strengthen them.

"The whole village was soon in a state of commotion, and I felt too anxious at my novel situation to taste the supper I had ordered, or to take the repose I required; so I left the inn, and, proceeding to the dykes, was soon aware of the extreme danger of our situation.

"As I walked at the foot of the rampart, which the industry of that wonderful people, the Dutch, have raised to resist the fury of the sea, I heard the mighty waters above my head, dashing against the noble barrier!

"I was, in fact, with numbers of my fellow-creatures, actually below the raging ocean, which was now striving to force a passage through the bank, into the low and level country on the other side of it.

"I soon mounted on the top of the dyke, and beheld the fierce waves flinging themselves with merciless power against the terrace on which I stood.

"The new moon and the tremendous gale had united to raise the vast body of waters much above their usual height, which now threatened to destroy the labour of ages; for, if the rampart should prove too weak, we all knew that the whole flat country of West Friesland would soon be under water.

* Doorbraak is the Dutch term for breaking in of the dykes.
† Waterstatt is the name of the company or administration which is entrusted with the care of the dykes.

"This frightful state of alarm continued till midnight.

"The bells in the church were tolling widly, now clanging on our ears, as the blast rushed by us, now dying away amidst its distant fury.

"Lights were flaring in all directions, sometimes nearly obscured by the misty rain that mingled with the spray, and tore away inland, in sheets of foam; then, as the fuel was heaped upon the beacon fires, the flame gathered strength, and streamed wildly along amidst the dull red smoke, towards the devoted country.

"Terrific was the blue lightning!

"Deafening was the roar of the thunder!

"Higher and stronger came the breakers!

"Louder and fiercer were the gusts!

"When yells and shrieks of despair burst suddenly from a group of persons about fifty yards farther on the dyke, a double flash of lightning illuminated the scene, and showed us the savage billows overtopping the bank, the immense fabric yielding to their fury; and, by the light of another flash, we saw the whole mass washed on to the village and dashing among the houses!

"The consternation was now awful, the scene dreadful beyond my powers of description!

"The doorbraak became wider every instant; the sea poured through it like a cataract; huge stones, or rather blocks of granite, weighing many tons, were washed about like pebbles.

"The sides of houses were beaten in; trees were uptorn and carried forward by the flood, increasing the havoc!

"In short, dangerous as my station was on the trembling dyke, which was ready to give way with me every moment, I thought it safer to remain where I was, than to descend into the destruction of the village.

"I therefore waited in the total darkness that had followed the heavy thunderstorm; and soon had the comfort of feeling that the billows came less forcibly, that the gale was abating, and that the dyke was no longer breaking in.

"Many weary hours, however, wore away in terror and misery on the part of the wretched inhabitants, whose cries of distress broke mournfully on my ears, as the poor creatures were searching for their relatives in the dark desolation of the village.

"With the first faint streaks of dawn glimmering in the south-east the sky became clear; the stars shone out with an unusual tremulousness, as if they too had shared in the uproar and disasters of this cruel night, and had not yet recovered their placid twinkling.

"When the light grew stronger I descended to the village that I might render what assistance should be in my power to the afflicted inhabitants.

"Before I went I turned my eyes on the wide waste of waters that were stretched out on either side of me; the sea, which had now retired from the assault, like a savage victor but half satisfied with the proofs of his power, was lashing the patient shore in harmless rage; on the other hand, as far as my eye could trace, another sea was lying in sullen cruelty upon the rich lands of the patient Hollanders.

TOM STARBOARD AND THE BEAR.

"Fields just ploughed, and sown with corn; pastures of grass which had yesterday been crowded with well-fed cattle, were now covered with water.

"Hay and corn stacks, mangled bodies of men and animals, beams and timbers of houses, furniture, and wrecks of vessels were floating about in dreary quietness.

"I thanked Heaven that my dear friend was away from this sad scene, and then hastened down, just as a sparkling winter's sun rose over the ruffled surface of the Zuyder Zee, and showed me, to the south, the distant spires of Amsterdam, glittering like another Venice, above the waters of the inundation, which had the day before flowed in their proper channel, but which were now ruining the works of industrious man.

"The damage that had been done during the night was immense. Hundreds of human beings had perished; vast numbers of large cattle, besides sheep, were destroyed.

"Hundreds, nay, thousands of families, which had been in wealthy or comfortable circumstances, were reduced to poverty; in short, it was a calamity such as I never expected to behold, and which I could not have imagined to be so severe if I had not seen it."

"Tom, what are the dykes made of? Stone, or clay, or timber, or walls, or what?"

"Not any of these materials, my lad," replied Tom. "I have heard that, in the lowlands of England, a very simple and ingenious method employed to construct dykes is by driving stakes into the sand, near high-water mark, at spring tides; between which stakes the people weave osiers; the next gale then works up the sand, and weeds, and shingle, against this little barrier, which materials have time to settle and harden; and perhaps the seeds of the marine plants, as well as our strong-rooted couch grass, have vegetated, or grown before any more storms disturb them. Thus, fresh, solid work is added, from time to time, to man's ingenuity, until the barrier becomes strong enough to resist the fiercest hurricanes.

"Well, that barrier the ocean has thrown up without the ingenuity of man; that immense pile of shingle has been increased by the storms of many ages, until it has become a firm stoppage to the waves.

"It is not thus, however, with the coast of Holland; there, man has set his wits against the mighty winds and raging floods; and has so nearly conquered them, that scarcely more than once in a century does such a calamity occur, as that to which I was witness.

"I have been trying to recollect in what book I have met with the account of the manner in which those noble dykes are constructed, but I cannot succeed.

"I know, however, that sail cloth is said to constitute the groundwork, or rather wall, against which the mud and sand collect; but you will be surprised to hear that a little weed is the material on which the Dutch chiefly depend for their safety."

"A weed, Tom?"

"Yes, lad, a lowly plant, with lilac or pinkish flowers, called rest harrow, which you must have seen growing on barren spots, in England, possesses roots, so wonderfully strong, tough, matted, and spreading, that the Hollanders sow it on the tops of their dykes to strengthen them, and to enable those structures to resist the power of the sea."

CHAPTER XLII.

CONTINUATION OF TOM STARBOARD'S ADVENTURE

"You may be sure, lad," said old Tom, "that I did not stay longer than I could help in this country."

Crusoe was silent.

The boy's generous mind was dwelling painfully upon the vivid picture of desolation which old Tom drew.

In fancy he beheld the homeless families rushing frantically from the devouring waters, and it was not until old Tom again spoke, that he raised his eyes and said—

"It must have been a fearful sight, Tom."

"It was lad, and I was glad when I left the scene."

He stood up in the boat, and, looking in the direction the fragment of the Seagull's boat had come, resumed—

"I don't see any sign of the islands, yet, lad, so I will spin the remainder of the yarn, and tell you how I was taken in by a fellow to whom I behaved as though he had been my brother."

"Taken in," Jack said, a smile passing over his sad face. "I should have thought after what you had seen of the world, you would have been pretty well used to its rogueries."

"I thought so, too, lad. But I was mistaken. However, it will be sufficient to tell you that I was at that time in possession of a vast sum of money, more than two-thirds of which a cunning Dutchman —one Mynheer Vandergoldt—managed to swindle me out of."

Crusoe laughed at the savage manner in which Tom spoke.

"I was awfully enraged," old Tom continued ; "and I swore that I would follow him to the end of the earth to have revenge. I did go pretty near as far."

"Did you get your money ?"

"You shall hear. No sooner had he swindled me, than off he started for his home, in Amsterdam— never thinking, I expect, that the flat he had so well taken in would follow him.

"I did. But before doing so, I had to think how I could reach the place, for going by land was out of the question ; and as I did not wish Mynheer Vandergoldt to spend my hard-earned money before I renewed our acquaintance, I soon found out I must go by water."

"One moment, Tom."

"Ay, lad."

"How did the fellow swindle you ?"

Something very like a curse preceded old Tom's reply—

"It was this, lad. I had knocked about, as I thought, quite long enough, and, being pretty flush with money, tried to buy a small vessel, with the intention of trying my luck in the coasting trade.

"This fellow—this —— Vandergoldt, had just the craft I wanted for sale. A bargain was soon made. He got the money, I a roll of papers."

Old Tom looked savage as he added—

"But when I went to take possession of the craft, I found he had sold her to three parties besides myself."

"Strange work," Crusoe said.

"Rather !" old Tom answered ; "and as I was the fourth purchaser and an Englishman, I saw but little chance for me ; so, leaving the three Scotchmen to squabble and fight over the affair, I purchased a good thick stick, and went to pay my respects to my sharp-dealing friend ; and, as we shan't see the island for some time, lad, I'll spin the yarn in proper trim."

"Do," Crusoe said, his intelligent face lighting up, for, like all sensible boys, he loved to hear truthful descriptions of men and places, in preference to the cut-throat, imaginary stories of impossible boy (vagabond) heroes—heroes placed by certain writers at the head of gangs of ragged pirates or skulking footpads.

After these few words respecting the literature written for boys of the present day, we will allow old Tom to resume his interesting adventure.

"A fishing boat," Tom resumed, "fortunately had escaped the fury of the gale, and I took my short passage in it for the few miles I had still to sail.

"On my arrival, I was rejoiced to find that the capital, that rich and noble city, had escaped the havoc of the wind and waves, a few of the lower streets only being under water.

"Everything was at a standstill ; and you may suppose that the inhabitants were in a state of consternation.

"I inquired for the house of Mr. Vandergoldt, and, on going to it, was mortified at finding he had started the day before for St. Petersburg, which is the northern capital of Russia.

"Whether he had heard of my coming I could not discover ; but I resolved to follow him, and in three days I was off.

"The weather continued open and mild until I reached Riga, which is situated between the two countries of Russia and Poland.

"This city is very populous, and carries on an extensive trade. It stands on the river Dwina, which runs into Poland. Over this river there is a floating wooden bridge, 2,600 feet in length, which is removed as soon as the winter begins and is replaced in the spring.

"I crossed it the very evening before they began to take it down ; for the cold set in during the night, and on the following morning, so sudden was the change, the people were crossing the Dwina on skates.

"I waited a few days at Riga, for the weather to clear after the first heavy fall of snow, that I might enjoy my novel and curious journey ; so, under a clear frosty sky, wrapped up in furs, and skimming along over the smooth white surface of the ground, behold me now in a sledge, in company with twenty others ; some containing travelling merchants, and the remainder loaded with frozen provisions, for the supply of the markets of St. Petersburg."

"I don't think," Crusoe said, "that I should have gone so far after the money."

"It was not the money, lad, so much as the anger I felt at being made such a dupe."

"Go on, Tom," and Crusoe sank back on his couch of warm skins.

Old Tom rose and trimmed the mat sail, for the wind began to freshen a little, and the old seaman knew that a sudden gust would send their frail craft bottom upwards.

The gear fastened, a long look in the direction of the island, then old Tom resumed—

"I had ascertained the address of Vandergoldt, so I went on the very day of my arrival to the house; and I have every reason to believe that it was Vandergoldt himself who spoke to me; for, notwithstanding the circumstance of a large, bushy beard he wore, if he had not been a guilty person, who was afraid of being given up to justice, he need not have started, and looked so confused, when I inquired for Mr. Vandergoldt.

"The wily Dutchman, however, soon recovered himself; and seeing, I suppose, that I was only a poor, half-crazed, sailoring kind of creature, this ingenious person, addressing me in broken English, said—

"Ah, mine goot Got! vat a beedy vor you do gome al dees long vay vor noding! Mr. Vandergoldt ees my ver good vrend, and hees beesinees haves lead him do Dobolsk, do drade vor vurs mit de marjand, vrom Ghina; bod, os he ees not been gone more nor dwo howrs, you may oberdake heem."*

"I was delighted," continued Tom, "that the fellow was not above two hours ahead of me; so having procured some additional clothing to protect me from the severe cold I was going to experience, such as bearskin boots, with the fur turned inwards, and all that sort of thing, I hired another sledge, with a driver, to take me to a small town, the first hundred miles on the road to Yarensk.

"Before we reached this miserable village—I forget the name of it—I began to feel the effects of a Russian winter.

"A piercing wind, and driving sleet which froze as it fell, cut my eyes and cheek bones—the only parts of my body that were exposed, so that I was obliged to flap my fur cap quite on to my nose; how the driver managed, I cannot tell."

"He was used to it, as the woman said when she was skinning the eels, while they were alive!" said Crusoe.

"True, he was so," replied his friend.

"At this village we arrived towards the end of the third short wintry day; and, to your astonishment, you will hear, that as soon as the driver had taken a large measure of brandy at the miserable inn, he went off to the public vapour bath; whither I followed him, out of curiosity.

"It was a large wooden building in the midst of the hamlet, having seats ranged round the walls, raised one above the other, till the top seat reached within four feet of the ceiling.

"In the middle of the room were placed large stones, which had been made red-hot; and on these water was constantly poured, which sent up volumes of steam, that filled the building.

"According to the temperature which the people chose to be exposed to, they seated themselves on the higher or lower benches; for the coolest part of the room was at the bottom, and the hottest at the top.

"My sulky bear of a driver chose the warmest

berth; so, stripping off his clothes, he crawled up to the upper form.

"There were about two hundred other persons in this misty den when I looked in.

"In about a quarter of an hour, they came rushing out, looking more like raw beef than men, owing to the heat! then, naked as they were, away they ran, and tumbled over and over in the snow!"

"What a strange custom!" Crusoe said. "I love bathing as well as any one; but I never heard of such a peculiar bath as this."

"Each nation has its peculiar customs; and, of course, they are found to be agreeable, or they would not be followed," replied Tom; then continued—

"On the following morning, I hired another sledge, a driver, and six dogs.

"No, I did not make use of dogs to draw me, until I reached the confines of Siberia.

"Furnished with plenty of tobacco and brandy, I again set forward, stopping every night in some wretched hovel, dignified by the name of an inn, until I came within sight of the Ural mountains.

"At every village, I enquired if any travellers had passed the same road before me; and I generally found the boors were agreed in asserting that a sledge had gone forward on the previous day.

"I had now arrived at the last resting-place, before I could cross the mountains, and enter Asia, but still no Mr. Vandergolt appeared.

"My guide and I agreed very well together.

"He was a native of Siberia; and I found him, as indeed all his countrymen, much more hospitable and honest than the Russians.

"I am naturally quick at learning languages, and soon acquired sufficient knowledge of his native tongue to enable me to converse with Goskoi, the driver; and he told me that, as soon as we began to ascend the mountains, we should suffer much more from the cold than we had done hitherto, for wood was so scarce we should perhaps be obliged to sleep without a fire; that we must carry more food for ourselves, and take a supply for the dogs, as he intended to substitute those animals for our wretched horses, which had become so weak and bad as scarcely to be able to drag us along.

"He told me, too, that I should have no need of money, for his countrymen never take anything by way of payment from travellers. And all this I found to be correct.

"I had hitherto slept every night under a roof of some sort; for though the villages lie very wide from one another, there are post-houses at a day's journey apart, where the postmen, and other travellers, pass the long hours of darkness.

"On the following morning, then, we began our ascent among the barren chain of mountains that divide Europe from Asia; they are, however, barren only on the surface; inexhaustible riches lie beneath; gold, silver, iron, lead, copper, and coal mines exist throughout the range; but owing to the thin population, the barbarous ignorance of the natives, and the severity of the climate, the mines are not well worked.

"During the short, hot Siberian summers, which appear as if they burst out from amidst the snows

* Ah, my good God! what a pity for you to have come all this long way for nothing! Mr. Vandergoldt is my very good friend, and his business has led him to Tobolsk, to trade for furs with the merchants from China; but as he has not been gone above two hours, you may overtake him.

of winter, vegetation proceeds with great rapidity; and as we had passed vast forests of birch and pine trees we had had a fire whenever we wished to light one.

"Now we could no longer expect to find wood; we therefore eagerly seized any straggling bushes of the Daourian rose (the only fuel left us), which we tied up in bundles, and fastened to the back of the sledge.

"By noon, we were quite shut in among the passes of the hills; and, instead of a boundless tract of level snow, patched with leafless birchwoods, and the deep melancholy hue of pine forests, which had been my usual prospect for some weeks past, we were enclosed between dreary walls of ironstone, covered with drifted snow on every part that was not perpendicular.

"The silence of this savage wild, too, was unbroken, excepting now and then by the loud bark of a hungry wolf, and the screams of the little animal he might be destroying.

"Our progress was slow; the sledge was heavy; so Goskoi and I walked nearly the whole of the day; and as night approached we halted at a turn of the mountain, which projected like a shoulder, and would serve to screen us from the biting north-east wind.

"We fed our dogs with come of the frozen fish that we had brought for them; and, lighting our fire, we prepared to cook a white hare that I had shot about an hour before, but which in that short time had become frozen as hard and stiff as a stick.

"Having finished our repast, we wrapped ourselves up well in our furs, and laid down on the snow, with our feet to the cheerful blaze.

"Notwithstanding that I had smoked an extra pipe, and taken a large allowance of brandy, I suffered extremely in my new white bed.

"Fortunately, I could not sleep.

If I had dozed even, I really think I should never have waked again.

"As I lay thus, thinking of the contrast of my present situation, with what it had been during the many hot nights that I had passed in the torrid zone, and wondering that any of the French soldiers had escaped, who were exposed, during their retreat from Moscow, to the fierce rigours of a Northern winter, I thought I heard a low breathing near me.

"I listened.

"It was not Goskoi, for the noise sounded on my right hand.

"He was snoring on my left, and the six dogs lay curled round close to the fire, on the opposite side.

"I raised myself cautiously, and looking keenly through the midnight gloom, I saw a figure moving along on a ledge of rock within a few yards of me.

"By the flickering light of the fire I watched this white moving mass.

"As I was wondering what it could be, it disappeared, that is, it lost its footing, and slipped off the ledge of rock, carrying with it a quantity of frozen snow, which rattled and tinkled as it fell.

"This noise roused the dogs, who would have made their escape had they been at liberty; but being fastened all together for safety to a crag of our rugged walls, they could not run from the danger which threatened them, so they set up such a dismal howling that Goskoi awoke, and, in astonishment, asked me what was the matter.

"I told him that I had seen a figure moving, and he was on his feet in a moment, saying—

"'It was a bear! And if you do not wish to be hugged to death, defend yourself, Englishman!'

"I arose, but not quite so nimbly as Goskoi had done, and seizing the muskets, we prepared for our shaggy foe.

"He soon came round the shoulder of rock, with a sullen, determined look.

"It was evident that he was sorely pressed by hunger, or he would not have braved our party and our fire.

"I was in front, between him and the dogs, one of which he seemed resolved to carry off.

"'Fire! Englishman! My gun has flashed in the pan!' exclaimed Goskoi.

"I should not have waited for his directions, if I had been prepared, for I had been too long accustomed to nightly disturbances, to lose my presence of mind at this.

"But I had never before met with a midnight adventure in the frozen zone.

"My hands, in spite of fur gloves, were numbed with the cold, and I could not feel the trigger of my gun.

"In the meantime the white bear still made towards us.

"Goskoi yelled, and flung his arms about, to frighten him, while I, in vain, held my gun pointed towards the slow-moving savage.

"I could *not* pull the trigger!

"Goskoi now became half frantic.

"His fear of the animal gave way to his alarm for my safety.

"He rushed forward, wrenched the gun out of my hand, flinging his own weapon at the animal's head, and in a moment he fired, and hit the bear in the side of its neck.

"The blow turned the resolute creature but for an instant.

"I was roused by the danger of our situation, being in the power of a large and ravenous beast; so, seizing the burning brands from the fire, I flung them at him as fast as I could pick them up.

"This new mode of attack enraged and terrified him exceedingly.

"He turned half round, as if to make his escape, and at that moment Goskoi, who had reloaded the gun, quick as thought, fired a second time, and wounded the creature near the heart.

"My exercise among the warm embers had restored the use of my hands, and I ran to the spot where my companion had thrown his own weapon.

"I reprimed it; and by this time the bear had gone round the fire, and was just seizing one of the terrified dogs, whose noise was now deafening, mingled as it was with the yelping of the other five, the driver's shouts, and the growling of the bear.

"I ran up behind, and when quite close to him,

I fired at, and hit the back of his neck, just as the poor dog fell a victim to the creature's fury.

"As soon as I had fired, I laid hold of the muzzle of the gun, and began battering him on his hard skull.

"Goskoi now rushed up, and seeing my danger—for I had become the object of the animal's attack—the man took aim so well that his fourth charge brought the bear to the ground.

"We then despatched him with our long knives; and by the waning light of the fire, which was by this time nearly out, we skinned both the animals.

"The cold was intense, the fire all gone, and the wintry dawn had not yet appeared.

"Suddenly I recollected having heard of the dreadful method which the French soldiers employed to obtain a little warmth, when they lay perishing among the snows of Russia.

"I begged my Siberian friend to assist me to open the bear; and then, thrusting my hands and feet into the still warm carcase, and throwing the skin over my shoulders, I contrived to obtain, for a short time, a little extra heat."

"How horrible! You must, indeed, have suffered much, before you could have taken such a method of warming yourself!" said Crusoe.

"I assure you, my lad, it was frequently done by the French during their campaign in Russia: they killed their horses, and creeping into the empty carcases for warmth, were frozen to death in their strange abodes!

"Well, Goskoi being more accustomed to the severe winters of the north, bore the cold weather better than I did; so, as soon as he could see, he employed himself busily in preparing for our journey, and when I awoke from a wretched sleep, the five dogs were harnessed, and eating their breakfast, and their poor dead companion was dangling, without his skin, at the back of the sledge, with our other provender.

"We now started again, with a clear sky above us, and soon after came to a level space; our journey was very rapid. I own to you, my lad, that I often repented having undertaken this wild-goose chase; I had foolishly thought that what one* Englishman had done, I could do, forgetting that all constitutions are not prepared to endure so great a degree of cold, and that, indeed, I might probably feel the severity of this climate the more from my having passed so much of my life in the hottest parts of the world.

"As we drove along I began to thing very seriously of my foolish undertaking. What were we to do without a fire? No fuel of any kind now appeared, and I mentioned to Goskoi, my fear of our being frozen to death on the following night.

"The good-natured fellow told me, that while I slept he had found a store of the dried dung of animals, in a hollow of the mountain, near our resting-place, which the wild beasts of the district had frequented; and he added—

"'We always collect this stuff to burn—it is very useful; you will see to-night what a cheerful fire it will make.'

* Captain Cochrane.

"I found when evening came, that he was right; we had collected every morsel that we could find of this precious commodity during the day, and, by a little good management, the fuel lasted nearly the whole of the night.

"The next day we advanced still further into this truly savage region, and our situation became somewhat more alarming, for having depended upon obtaining plenty of game, such as hares, martens, etc., we had been too prodigal of our provisions, and we found ourselves and our dogs reduced to one small raw fish, and the poor frozen animal which the bear had killed, and which we now were too hungry to leave any longer.

"The dung, too, became so scarce, that during a weary sojourn of half the following day, we had not found sufficient of it to keep a fire alight for a quarter of an hour!

"My fears of being frozen to death the next night were again very great.

"I had walked the whole of the day. The cold became every instant more intense as we ascended the rugged mountains; the dogs flagged in their speed—their strength was failing, for they had not had, among them all, enough food for the meal of one dog.

"To add to my discomfort, the cheerful Goskoi, who had hitherto entertained me with the singularly wild airs and legends of his country—he who had kept up my courage (for I am not ashamed to confess that I never felt so little bravery in my life—it seemed pinched and frozen up within me!)—my good-natured driver was evidently as much out of spirits as I was.

"The evening drew on, and I asked him where he proposed to halt for the night.

"He turned his furrowed face full upon me, and said—

"'Englishman, I do not know! I have missed the road—we are in the heart of the mountains—I cannot tell what we are to do! I could, perhaps, pass the night in safety, but how will you bear the cold?'

"I was shocked, you may suppose, my lad; but my natural courage seemed to return with the need I found for it.

"I had, till this journey, in all my wanderings been either alone or the director of others, so that I had depended on no one for advice or assistance, and my firmness had never deserted me.

"Here, in Russia, I had not only been in an entirely new state of existence, but I had been directed instead of directing; I had depended on others, instead of my own exertions.

"Finding, therefore, that Goskoi had lost his courage, I roused my half-frozen faculties, and took upon myself to direct.

"I made my companion see and understand this change in me; showed that I was vexed that he had not sooner told me of our having missed the way; proposed that I should kill one of the dogs, while he should scramble up a craggy mass of rock on our right hand, and try if he could recognise any of the land-marks which had hitherto guided him; for, from his having several times crossed this barrier, he marked his road by several natural sign-posts; such as a round-headed piece of rock, a crag, shaped like a bear, a fallen mass of iron-stone, and so on.

"This plan he immediately prepared to execute, while I proceeded to the ungrateful task of killing the foremost of the faithful creatures that had dragged us thus far, so steadily and patiently."

CHAPTER XLIII.

A SINGULAR ADVENTURE.

"I HAD scarcely taken the poor animal's life, when I heard the voice of Goskoi on the rugged peak of a snow-covered rock near me.

"He called out cheerfully that he thought he saw our road on the other side of a deep ravine, or hollow.

"I looked round at him, as he stood in his wolf-skin dress, pointing from the summit.

"The dull gray of the eastern sky was at his back, while the crimson glory of the setting sun threw a warm glow over his weather-beaten features, as he explained our situation to me.

"Imagine my horror, my lad, when, at the moment I was answering his call, I heard him shriek, and, the next instant, saw him vanish from my sight!

"I instantly darted forward, scrambled up the icy sides of the rock, and reached the top, I know not how, such was my anxiety for the worthy fellow.

"I soon discovered his fate.

"He had lost his footing, had rolled over the projecting rock, and was doubtless dashed to death in the ravine, which lay dark and dreary in the coming shades of night!

"I stood for a few moments in despair, the calamity had been so sudden.

"I stooped down and listened, as near to the edge as I dared to venture, hoping, yet dreading to hear a groan.

"The silence was horrible.

"I would have given worlds, I thought, to hear the roar of the summer floods, whirling the melted snows along that frightful ravine.

"Any noise would, I thought, be preferable to this deep silence.

"But all around me was quiet as the grave, and I turned away from the dismal spot with a sickening shudder.

"Suddenly, it occurred to me, that it might be possible to discover some natural pathway, a water-track, or a cleft in the rock, by which I should descend into the hollow, and try to rescue poor Goskoi from a probably lingering death.

"He might be lying stunned and wounded in that terrible abyss, and so die from cold and neglect.

"This idea inspired me with strength and vigour.

"I thought not of cold—I felt none.

"I feared no danger from slippery paths nor midnight gloom, but I scrambled over crags and peaks; clung round shoulders of iron-stone; hung from icy ridges, and clambered among jagged points, till I must have traversed the edge of the gulf for more than a mile, and had just reached a flat surface of

the rock, when I felt myself sinking rapidly through a hole, without the power to stop myself!

"In a moment more the screams of women reached my ears, and I tumbled with a large mass of snow and soot, and boards, and bearskins, upon a large fire that was burning in the middle of a cavern!

"In my fall, I upset a pot of fish-broth, that was being cooked for supper; this, owing to my weight and the load of snow, put out the fire, and filled the place with steam.

"A lamp which had been burning in a niche of the wall, before the image of some patron saint, was knocked down by the terrified creature who was praying before it.

"Two or three children were running about crying and screaming with either pain or alarm, or both, for the poor little things had been splashed with the hot broth.

"A dog was growling savagely; and a man's voice praying and cursing, completed the confusion of this singular scene.

"I quickly rolled off from my hot berth among the hissing embers, you may be sure; waiting in silence and darkness, the end of my adventure.

"I was among human beings, but of what description I could not tell, excepting that I found by their language, they were natives: though whether they were persons who lived by plunder, or a harmless Siberian family, housed for the winter in this warm cave, I could not yet discover.

"Presently, a dead silence took place of all this clamour.

"There I sat in darkness, trying to catch a glimpse of the persons with whom I was in company; but not a ray shone from the dull red solitary brand that had escaped the water, and which, as it lay, looked as if it were flushing and panting beside me.

"This brand, with a star or two, twinkling in the deep blue sky—which peeped through the hole I had made in the roof—were the only objects I could discern.

"In a few minutes, the voice of a woman was heard, scarcely above a whisper, inquiring where the children were; and the little creatures, guided by the sound, and encouraged by the silence of the violent disturber of their home, crept quietly to her side, where I heard them whispering together.

"The man now gained courage, and asked where the slips of pinewood were, that he might light the lamp again; and having found them, he took one and came towards the expiring embers.

"I watched him, as he blew the fire with his breath; and I could not forbear smiling when I saw the hasty and terrified glance that he threw round, as the cheerful blaze shot up, and flickered, and streamed above his head, giving light and brilliancy to the whole place.

"It was impossible for me to remain long undiscovered.

"I arose, therefore, explained, and apologised; comforted the children in the best manner I could; and then entreated the peasant to go with me, that I might endeavour to find poor Goskoi.

"This he absolutely refused; adding, that it would be impossible to descend into that deep ravine without light to guide our steps. I was, therefore, reluctantly obliged to give up my plan till the morning.

"After a time, peace was restored; the fire again blazed cheerfully; the fish was put on once more to boil, and the man mounted to the roof, to replace the boards and skins, so as to leave only a small exit for the smoke, as the wide hole, through which I had fallen, would have admitted too much cold.

"I amused the family by attempting to relate some of my adventures, while our homely meal was being prepared.

"It was soon ready.

"Tables and chairs there were none; but there were large cushions, made of bear skins, stuffed with dried birch leaves, which the family used for beds.

"These made also very pleasant elastic seats, and on one of them I sat, eating my portion of fish.

"I tasted, too, some of the dried roots of the yellow sarine lily, which is a favourite article of food in Siberia; but I did not greatly admire the flavour.

"There was no brandy in the cave; but there was plenty of that coarse, ardent spirit, which is made from the dried stalks of the *sibiricum;* of this liquor the natives make use, when their favourite brandy cannot be obtained.

"This family consisted of the husband and wife, three children, and the wife's sister.

"They told me that they had wintered in this singular abode for two years, preferring it to the mud huts of the valley.

"It had been a silver mine; but the vein of the ore having failed in one direction, instead of seeking for another vein, the mine had been abandoned, and had remained neglected for many years.

"Zulof, the peasant, or boor, told me that he had enlarged the cave about a month before, and had found so much silver ore, that he intended to take the lumps of it in his sledge, on the following week, to Tobolsk, where the annual fair was to be held.

"The natives meet foreign merchants at this fair, to barter their valuable skins of sables, white hares, bears, red foxes, martens, &c., for tobacco, brandy, knives, &c.; and here Zulof hoped to exchange his pieces of precious metal.

"I was glad to find that my host was going so soon to Tobolsk, as I hoped to accompany him.

"I now reminded him of his promise to assist me on the following morning in my search for poor Goskoi and the dogs, then bade them all good night; and, notwithstanding my anxiety for the fate of the driver, I soon fell into a sound sleep, from which I did not wake till late the next morning.

"The savoury smell of cookery roused me.

"I could not, at first, recall to my recollection the strange adventures of the last evening; but lay still, trying to collect my thoughts.

"I suppose the——'

"Ay, I was just thinking, Tom," interrupted Crusoe, "that the strong spirit you mentioned had made you a little sleepy!"

"No, no!" replied Tom, smiling, "I do not recol-lect that my deep sleep was caused by anything more than the pleasant warmth of my apartment, with my previous fatigue and exposure to the severe cold.

"But I was going to say that the novelty of my situation, I suppose, tended to confuse me.

"When I opened my eyes, I found the three children close to me, listening to the ticking of my watch, which I immediately drew out and showed to them; it was a very fine musical watch.

"I then delighted them, as well as their parents and their aunt, by winding it up, and giving them a tune.

"I never shall forget the astonishment and awe, the admiration and uncouth rapture, which this wild melody excited among my uncivilised friends. Yet, why should I call them uncivilised? I have never met with half the kindness—disinterested kindness—in civilised society, that I have received from those uneducated savage nations, as they are called, who expect no reward for their hospitality; and who absolutely refuse to accept of any recom-pense.

"Well, the reindeer steaks were left to burn on the embers, while Escal (the wife) stood listening to my fairy music; Zulof left his fishing tackle, which he was mending, and came trembling and looking around, saying—

"'A Rusalki, a Rusalki! No one but a Rusalki could play such music! We shall soon see one of them, with her long green hair! Surely she will not come in anger with such music as that playing round her!'"

"Rusalki! What is that?" Crusoe asked.

"The Russians believe in a species of water and wood maids, called *Rusalki:* they are represented as of a beautiful form, with long green hair; they balance themselves on the branches of trees, bathe in the lakes and rivers, play on the surface of the waters, and wring their locks on the green meads, at the water edge.

"I hastened to explain my beautiful music to the delighted beings; then begged them to let me des-patch my breakfast quickly; and promised that on my return from my search for Goskoi, I would let them hear the *Rusalki music* for as long a time as they might wish.

"We soon finished our meal; and, Zulof having placed a ladder, we mounted to the chimney, carry-ing with us a long pole with a hook at the end of it, a rope, food for the man and dogs, in case they should have survived the night; and other things that might be useful.

"We wandered about the whole day, descended into the ravine, and found the exact spot where Goskoi had fallen, by the marks in the snow, which had been recently moved; but nowhere could we see any remains of the driver; the dogs, too, with the sledge, had all disappeared; and we followed the track of the vehicle, until it reached the right road to Tobolsk, so that my new companion cheered me with the hope that the driver had regained the sledge, and driven it on towards the city, to which he was going.

"We therefore returned to our cave; and you

CRUSOE JACK AT HOME.

may suppose that my heart was lightened of a load of care and anxiety.

"We had the good fortune to kill two white hares as we walked, which made capital meals for us on the following day.

"In a few days, his sledge being made ready, the provisions packed, and our two selves in good travelling condition, Zulof and I bade the women and children farewell, and away we started for Tobolsk.

"We arrived without accident; and, in less than half an hour after I had entered the crowded streets of the city, I recognised by old friend Goskoi, who was conversing with a Tartar merchant.

"The poor fellow seemed as much pleased to see me, as I really was to find that he had escaped the perils of the Oural* mountains. He insisted on my staying with him at his brother's house, so long as I should remain in Tobolsk, and then he turned to the merchant to finish his conversation.

"Finding that this person was well acquainted with the principal traders at the fair, I asked him if he had heard the name of Vandergoldt.

"He told me he knew the man, and had been informed, within a few days, that Vandergoldt did not intend to come to the city of Tobolsk this year, as he had hitherto done for many winters past, but that he had sent instructions to the different merchants, with whom he used to trade, to forward the goods which he ordered, to his warehouses at St. Petersburg.

* Sometimes spelled Ural.

"This intelligence, my lad," continued Tom, "was very vexatious to me, you may suppose. To find that I had only added to my stock of dangers, and that I had been of no service by bringing a rogue to justice, as I hoped I should, was very provoking. Besides, I began to be so ashamed of my exploit, it was so very absurd, so Quixotic, that I wisely kept it a secret, lest I should be laughed at for a fool."

"But you are making the worst of the business, are you not, Tom? You are rather more fond of improving your mind, of seeing countries, and of observing the different customs and manners of their inhabitants, than most people are," said Crusoe.

"Well, Jack, you are kind to make excuses for me," said Tom, goodnaturedly, as he continued—

"I enjoyed the novelty of the scene by which I was surrounded. Calmucks, Tartars, Russians, and Chinese, filled the streets, all engaged in the exchange of merchandise.

"I was now so inured to the severity of the climate, that I bore exposure to it nearly as well as the natives, and have had icicles dangling from my venerable beard, and even had my nose frost-bitten, without much alarm.

"In about a fortnight, Zulof, having bartered his silver ore and his skins, for tobacco, brandy, iron implements (or tools), and tackle for fishing, prepared to return to his snug home.

"So, as I wished to send the family something as a present—(a recompense I would not offer, as I knew I should offend him)—I obtained credit on a St. Petersburg merchant, and bought a common watch, which I desired he should let the children have as their own.

"He was much pleased with my kindness, as he called it, and I soon after took leave of him.

"I wandered back to St. Petersburg; but, as I expected, Mynheer had gone back to Holland."

Crusoe looked quizzingly up at his friend, and said—

"Of course you followed?"

"Did I?" said old Tom. "I had had quite enough of that business."

Crusoe indulged in a quiet laugh.

"After a time," old Tom said, "I left Russia, and shipped on board a merchant ship; but long before we came in sight of England, the Seagull overhauled her, and that devil in human form, Hugh of the Red Hand, sunk the ship, and sold all on board, save myself, for slaves."

Crusoe started; it was the first time he had heard the true character of the Seagull.

"I'm not sorry now," old Tom said, "that he let me live, for I have been the means of being of service to you."

"You have, Tom, I know! Now, what is that? Look among those old trees near the shore."

CHAPTER XLIV.

THE SEAGULL AT LAST.

OLD TOM sprang to the bow of the boat (they were now close upon the rocky shore of a large barren-looking isle) and his eyes followed the direction of Crusoe's finger.

He gave an exclamation of astonishment as his eyes fell upon the singular sight which had attracted Crusoe's attention.

Within the space of a dozen fathoms from the beach, lay the massive and gigantic form of a dead elephant.

Across the fallen leviathan's side, a large crocodile had taken up his position, and overhead a flock of hideous-looking vultures screamed and flapped their wings, evidently scared from their repast by the huge crocodile's presence.

To complete this picture, the form of a man could be seen, rifle in hand, crouching behind a piece of fallen rock.

"Well, lad," old Tom said, "this beats everything. What on earth can that fellow be crouching there for?"

Crusoe, during his sojourn amongst the haunts of the forest denizens and the savage tribes who came from time to time to his domain, had learnt the value of being prepared for any emergency.

So, during the time old Tom was gazing upon this strange scene, he loaded and primed both rifles.

He handed one to his companion, as he answered—

"Waiting to get a shot at the crocodile, I should think."

His words were barely uttered when the sharp crack of the stranger's piece rang out, and the crocodile fell backwards, clawing the ground, and lashing his tail with rage and pain.

"A good shot," muttered old Tom, as he handled his piece; "that bullet went in just above the scaly one's fore-leg."

The crocodile's death agony was by this time over, and he lay beside the huge carcase he had come to feast upon.

The stranger, when he beheld the scaly brute roll over, gave a joyful cry, and sprang to his feet, with the intention of examining the dead brute.

But as the cry escaped his lips the pit-pan grounded, and old Tom sang out—

"Ahoy! messmate, ahoy!"

The crocodile-slayer turned, then stood like a stone figure, and gazed wildly at the skin-clad forms of Crusoe and his companion.

He waited until they reached the shore; then, as though seized with sudden fear, uttered a wild cry, turned, and dashed madly from the spot.

"Well," old Tom said, "that's one way to give us a welcome. What ailed the fellow, Jack?"

"Perhaps," our hero said, "he has gone to give the alarm to his companions, if he has any."

"True, lad, such may be the case; so, before we go any further, suppose you go aloft and look out."

Crusoe selected one of the tallest trees for his post of observation, and, with an agility a squirrel could only have equalled, climbed from branch to branch.

Raising himself upon the summit, he had a clear view of the island; and after a long and searching look, became aware that, save the crocodile-slayer, the island was deserted.

He was about to descend, when a dark-looking object upon the opposite side attracted his attention.

At first, he thought it was a mammoth rock, which some mighty convulsion of nature had dislodged from the almost perpendicular cliff which surrounded the isle.

By degress the outlines of the dark form became clearer to the boy's eyes, and little by little, he made out the battered, but still distinguishable form, of a dismasted ship.

"The Seagull!" he exclaimed. "The Seagull at last."

Slinging himself off from the upper limb of the tree, he soon reached his companion's side.

"The Seagull, Tom!" he said. "The Seagull"

Old Tom looked upward among the branches of the trees, and said—

"Where, lad, where?"

"On the opposite side of the island."

"I'm glad to hear it, lad; but what about the fellow and his companions?"

"I cannot see a soul," said the boy. "The place seems as deserted as when it was first created."

"Well," the old seaman remarked, "if you did not see any one, it's my opinion that the fellow we saw took us for cannibals, and started to save his life."

"I am much of the same opinion, Tom, so let us go to the old vessel, and see whether there is anything yet on board likely to be of any use to us."

Crusoe made a forward movement, as though he would have started across the island.

"Come back, lad," was the old tar's caution. "We can sail round to the spot; it will be better than going across the island on foot, there may be more of the crocodile-killers about."

Crusoe saw at once the prudence of this counsel, and immediately turned towards the boat.

Crusoe's impatience could not brook the delay necessary to hoist the sail; but jumping in, he took the rudder, and asked old Tom to use the paddle.

The old seaman smiled at his companion's impatience, and as he paddled from the beach, said—

"By the way, Jack, you have not told me the cause of your sudden flight from the island."

"Nor you," Crusoe said evasively, "have not told me anything about Hugh of the Red Hand."

"All in good time, lad; but as I think I've spun you yarns enough to rig a three-decker, suppose you tell me the cause of that shot, and your hasty exit."

Crusoe was thoughtful for a few moments—the subject was evidently not pleasing to him, but feeling his old companion had a right to know the cause of his sudden departure from the beautiful isle, he said—

"Well, Tom, you shall know all things. When we started, I had made a resolution not to tell you."

"Would that be kind, lad?"

"Perhaps not, Tom, but when you know all, you will, perhaps, understand my feelings."

"I dare say I shall, lad; but I cannot believe that you should hide anything from me."

"You shall judge," said Crusoe, as the hot blood reddened his cheek at the revelation of the scene that took place in the hut.

At the conclusion of the strife between the hostile tribes, the Indian girl, who had been watching Crusoe as he acted the part of peace-maker, gave a savage cry, and went inside the hut.

Rage, contempt, and indignation filled the maiden's heart, and tearing off a circlet of gorgeous feathers which Crusoe had given her, she trampled them under her feet.

"Young Eagle," she cried, scornfully, "is a squaw, and Lela, a princess of the Aynoths, will close her heart against his."

Scattering the feathers of her circlet with her hands, she threw them out of the window.

Scarcely had she done this when our hero entered the hut.

He gazed with astonishment at the girl, and somewhat sternly asked—

"What is the meaning of this, Lela?"

She turned her angry face towards him, and answered—

"Young Eagle is a squaw, and the men of Aynoth are made squaws by his words."

Crusoe's eyes began to kindle with anger.

"When the Macoushi lay beneath the Aynoth's knife, and twenty scalps were ready to be taken, the pale-face dog told them to bury their knives, and be at peace."

"I did so, Lela, and they obeyed!"

"They were cowards, and afraid of the pale-face chief, whose blood is but water."

"Lela!"

"Aye. You can show anger to a woman. Go where the foe stands with their red spears, show it to them."

Crusoe bit his lips to prevent an angry reply.

The girl construed his silence into an admission of the cowardly feelings which she attributed as the cause of the peace which had just taken place between the warlike tribes.

"My brother," she said, scornfully, "feels that he is no longer a brave—feels that he should become a squaw, and stay in the hut to chop wood and cook the game which—"

Crusoe was stung beyond endurance at this. He knew the words used by the Indian girl were the most insulting that could be addressed to a warrior.

Justly indignant at this, he held up his hand to imply silence on her part.

An action which was misconstrued by Lela.

She imagined he was about to strike her, and, actuated by a sudden frenzy, she seized a rifle from the wall, and fired point blank at his head.

The bullet whistled so closely to his ear as to be felt, and the smoke and flame shot across his eyes.

Snatching the weapon from the island maiden, Crusoe reeled backwards.

"Lela!" he said, and his voice was tinged with bitterness, "we part at once, and for ever."

She would have spoken, but whether in tones of sorrow for her hasty act, or of farther defiance, it is hard to say; but ere one word left her lips, the door of the hut was dashed open, and Crusoe joined the astonished Tom Starboard.

"Well," old Tom said, when Crusoe had told him the particulars of this scene, "it's nature, Jack; the girl was savage because you deprived her country-men of the chance they had of obtaining a few scalps."

"Yes, but——"

"Wait a minute, lad; she knew nothing about what we term mercy. There ain't such a word in their language; so, perhaps, after all, you cannot blame her."

"Not blame her for firing point blank at my face?"

"Well, no," old Tom said, "perhaps not; but that act may, after all, have not been premeditated."

"It was within a hair's breadth of settling me!"

"Poor lad. Well, do you feel sorry at thus losing your dusky mistress?"

Crusoe was silent for some time.

"I'll speak the truth," he said, at last. "I am not sorry."

"Eh? Did you not care for the girl?"

"Not as she cared for me, Tom; and I have often felt that I was playing the hypocrite by encouraging her passion."

Old Tom rested on the paddle for a few seconds, and said—

"Well, lad, everything, they say, happens for the best; perhaps this has done so."

"Perhaps it has, Tom."

Crusoe knew not, when he gave utterance to these words, how soon his heart would be enraptured by the sight of one of his own country—a fair, beautiful girl, worthy to be the bride of Crusoe Jack—the King of the Thousand Islands."

———

BOOK THE SECOND.

CHAPTER I.

STANDING out boldly against the clear blue heavens was the massive hull of the stranded ship, and Crusoe, as they glided slowly under her bows, was struck by the melancholy grandeur of the sight.

Already had the keel begun to disappear with the effects of the many storms that had swept over the island since the vessel had become fixed upon her final resting-place.

"It is a sad sight," the boy said, "a very sad sight, Tom, this lovely vessel left thus to the mercy of the raging waters; sadder still is the remembrance that the gallant fellows who trod her deck are at the bottom of the sea."

"Some," the old sailor said, "deserved their fate; for though I served with them, I do not believe a more villanous gang ever sailed over the blue waters."

"Tom!"

"It is true, lad—too true; so you will say when I tell you some of the black deeds of that fiend in human form, Hugh of the Red Hand."

They had by this time made their boat fast to a gun's warp which hung over the side, and old Tom, breaking open one of the lower ports, scrambled through, closely followed by his youthful companion.

The port-hole led to the captain's cabin, and when old Tom had entered, he uttered an exclamation of surprise.

"What's the matter, Tom?"

"The ship has been ransacked, lad. Look here!"

He pointed to a locker. The lid, though strongly bound with iron, had been smashed open.

"Perhaps," Crusoe suggested, "the man we saw slay the crocodile has done this."

"Not likely, lad. There has been more than one hand in this business; and, unless I am much mistaken, the old barque has been visited by pirates."

"Why do you think so? A ship may have touched here, and a search may have been made for the papers."

"Honest sailors," old Tom said, holding a Malay crease towards his companion, "do not carry such things as this!"

Crusoe examined the deadly-looking weapon attentively.

It was the first time he had seen a blade fashioned in the serpent-like form of that murderous crease.

"A murderous implement," he said. "To what country does it belong?"

"To the Malays, lad."

Crusoe placed the weapon in his belt.

"I'll keep it, Tom," he said; "for close quarters it would be most useful."

Old Tom nodded, and proceeded to further investigate the ship.

Every locker and chest had been broken open, but nothing appeared to have been carried off.

A pile of arms stood in the rack just as old Tom had left them, when he started in quest of Crusoe.

Cutlasses and their pikes were still on the hooks they had occupied when the stout crew stood, full of life and strength, ready to seize their weapons.

Old Tom shook his head at the sight.

"I don't like it, lad," he said; "I wish they had taken the arms with them."

"Why?"

"I'll tell you why, lad; the pirates have been here and searched the old barque for money, which they have not found. You see the cargo and arms are safe. So, to my mind, this is how the matter stands: they have been disturbed by a sail appearing off the isles, and if that sail were a merchantman, they have captured her; if she were a man-of-war—which I hope—they have been taken. If this is not the case, mark my words, lad, they will come back, and, as sure as you stand there, we shall have a visit from them before long."

"You said, Tom, that they had not found the treasure on board; how do you know that?"

"Because, lad, our skipper was too wide awake to keep his ill-gotten pelf where a king's officer could find it. I know the spot," he said; "and if we live to see the old country again, we shall have more money than we can comfortably spend in an ordinary lifetime."

"There must be a vast amount, then."

"There is, lad. Come below and you shall see it."

They went below to the orlop deck, and at the end of a tier of water casks, old Tom paused.

"Give me a hand, lad," he said, "with this crow-bar."

Crusoe obeyed, and old Tom, after removing a square piece from what, at first sight, appeared to be a ponderous cross-beam, thrust his hand inside the small opening, and brought out a canvas bag from which came the musical chink of gold.

"There, lad," he said, "there's a sample of the hoard; and there's plenty more up here."

"Useless things to us, Tom."

"Aye, lad, just now, perhaps; but we shall not always be here, I hope."

Crusoe sighed.

He felt the romance of his ideal life wearing off day by day, and like old Tom, he secretly longed to behold the busy world again.

"What a strange hiding-place!" he remarked, as old Tom closed the aperture; "they would have sought long before looking here for gold."

"'Tis a strange place, lad, and the man who used it was a strange man."

"How did you find it, Tom? Surely he did not entrust this secret to the whole of the crew?"

"Not exactly, lad, trust Captain Hugh for that. No—I don't believe, with the exception of myself and the captain, that a soul knew of this goodly store."

"You were his confidant, then?"

"No, lad. I found it out quite by accident. It was this way. When we were off the Bay of Tunis, the Seagull overhauled a Spanish ship, and robbed her of a quantity of bullion."

"You were little better than pirates, Tom."

"Not a bit better, lad—pirate, slaver, buccaneer, and smuggler were parts in which Captain Hugh Dampier—for that was his proper name—played by turns."

"I expected as much; but about the discovery of the captain's hiding-place for his gold?"

"Well, we had scarcely cast off from the Spaniard, when a brig of war, with the Union Jack at her mizzen, came down upon us."

Crusoe's eyes lit up at the prospect of a sea fight being related by old Tom; but he was disappointed.

"There was no time for escape, and no chance of a successful issue, had we fought the gun brig. Well, I happened to be down here—just about this spot—when a gun was fired from the brig, and a boat sent to board us."

"There was no fighting after all?"

"No, lad, no. Well, I was busy about my work when I heard a noise just above my head.

"'Rats!' I muttered.

"But, no. The noise continued—thump—thump—thump. I hastily cut out this little square piece of wood from the beam, and, closely following it, came a bag of gold."

"A prize, Tom."

"Yes, lad, had I wanted it. Well, I took the bearings of the case, and soon found out the secret. What think you it was, lad?"

"I don't know, Tom."

"Well, just this: cunning Hugh had a small shaft leading from his cabin to this hollow beam, and when he had tied the gold in canvas bags, he dropped it out of sight. It was a good move, and by its means he was saved from the clutches of the brig. They made a stiff search for the money the Spaniard had lost, but the skipper's hollow beam was too much for them."

"So I should think. Now, Tom, we will go back to the cabin and turn in, for I am tired; and a comfortable bed is too much of a luxury to be despised."

"It is, lad; and as I know where to find plenty of preserved meat, and the captain's wine, it will be our own fault if we do not make ourselves comfortable for the night."

"It will," said Crusoe, "so let's steer for the cabin."

Old Tom soon found the preserved provisions, and, what was better, several bottles of good wine.

While he was thus engaged, Crusoe was looking over the contents of a portfolio.

An exclamation of astonishment caused old Tom to pause in his attempt to draw a stubborn cork, and ask—

"What's the matter, lad?"

"Listen," Crusoe answered; "here is a letter from old Madge Collins to Captain Hugh Dampier."

"Eh!—what, lad? Eh!—what is it about?"

"You shall hear; I will read it to you."

"Do, lad."

Crusoe moved closer to the open port, and read:—

"'You shall have the money I promised if you will take the boy; but mind, he must fall overboard during a gale. Remember, if you do not keep faith with me, I shall tell the commander of the man-of-war outside the harbour a few truths respecting the Seagull and her captain.—M. COLLINS.'"

They were silent for some minutes; then old Tom spoke.

"Look here, lad," he said, "keep that letter, it may be useful some day; for, if I am not far out of the bearings of this matter, that old woman had a very powerful motive in getting rid of you."

"She must have had," Crusoe said. "A mere feeling of dislike would not have caused her to go to all this trouble and expense."

"Never mind, lad; forget all about it until we see the old country again—that is, if we ever do; if not why it won't matter."

Crusoe placed the letter carefully away, and dismissing the matter from his mind, began to partake of the good things to which he had so long been a stranger.

"I wonder who that fellow can be," Crusoe said, "that took to his heels when you hailed him, Tom?"

"Don't wonder, lad, at it. We shall soon find out. Pitch in, it's not often we get such a feast as this."

Jack pitched in, and after supper old Tom slung a hammock in the cabin, and Crusoe took possession of the dead captain's luxurious couch.

They fastened the doors, not so much because they feared an intrusion, but the habit acquired of living in a state of continual danger had become a second nature.

Crusoe turned and tossed on the soft bed, and somewhat spitefully listened to old Tom's deep breathing.

"Hang it," he muttered, "I cannot sleep half so well as I did when I had only a bed of leaves."

He indulged in several impatient turns, first on one side, then the other—then began mentally counting until the total exceeded some thousands.

Growing tired of this, and finding that sleep still kept away from his aching eyes, he jumped out of bed and pulled the soft bed from the cot.

"That's it," Crusoe thought, "I shall sleep better upon the hard mattress."

He found himself but little benefited by the change. Do what he would, no sooner had his eyes closed than he awoke with a start.

The fact was, Crusoe's nerves were overstrung by the day's excitement, and, unlike his tried companion, he could not easily calm his mind.

At length he fell into a light slumber, and found himself surrounded by a legion of dark-skinned Malays.

He thought he stood in their midst, armed only with the deadly crease he had found on the Seagull's deck.

The weapon, he fancied in his dream, was knocked from his grasp, and in a second the Malays were upon him, and he felt their cold sharp blades enter his flesh.

With a shout of despair he sprang up in bed, and awoke.

The noise roused old Tom, who, in an instant, was upon his feet, his trusty rifle ready for action.

Finding everything quiet, the old tar said—

"What's the matter, lad? I thought we were attacked by a legion of Indians."

Crusoe told him his dream, and the old tar, clambering to his hammock, said—

"Glad it's no worse, lad; had it been those devils you never would have seen another day. Curse them! I once nearly lost my life by their treachery! but go to sleep, lad, perhaps I may tell you of it another time."

Crusoe tried to follow his companion's advice, but to no purpose; and old Tom, thoroughly aroused by Crusoe's sudden cry, found he could not again win the drowsy god to his pillow.

After listening to Crusoe, as the lad turned from side to side, he said—

"Can't you sleep, lad?"

"No, Tom; I can't get those fellows' faces from before my eyes. I wish I had not touched that crease. I believe it was thinking about that that caused my unpleasant dream."

"Most likely, lad; lie perfectly still, and think of something else, and you'll soon drop off again."

"Not to-night, Tom; so, if you are in the humour, you may as well tell me about your brush with the fellows who have so scared me to-night."

Old Tom filled his wooden pipe with dried leaves, and when he had succeeded in making them burn until his pipe bowl looked not unlike a small furnace, he said—

"You remember the mutiny I told you about?"

"Yes."

"Well, it was just after this affair that I met with an adventure that nearly cut my wandering life very short."

"If I remember, you were but a boy, Tom."

"Quite right, and on my first voyage. Let me see."

Old Tom paused for some minutes, then resumed—

"I'll take up the yarn from the point I left off at, after the meeting. Let's see—that was at Buenos Ayres, was it not?"

"It was. You had come to the time when the mutineers were hung at the yard-arm."

"True, lad. Well, we left Buenos Ayres, which, by the way, I found a very different place——"

"Hush!" Crusoe said, suddenly. "What is that?"

Old Tom listened, and as plainly as man's organs of speech could articulate, there came upon their ears a sad, mournful cry, followed by the words—

"Houtou, houtou!"

"It's only a bird," old Tom said, "don't be alarmed, lad."

"A bird, Tom, and able to utter words so distinctly."

"Ay, lad! and he takes his name from that mournful cry you have just heard."

"What a strange sound for a bird to make! I could have sworn the words came from a human being in distress."

Old Tom laughed.

"I should have thought, lad," he said, "that the campanero had cured you of that."

Crusoe could not help smiling at the recollection of the smart chase he had to discover the imaginary object.

"Is this bird," he asked, "anything like my old friend, the campanero."

"Quite different," said old Tom. "The one is of the purest white plumage, and the other of divers colours."

"How divers colours."

"The body is green, with a bluish cast in the wings and tail, and his crest, which he from time to time erects, is black in the centre, surrounded with the most brilliant blue, and most extraordinary, there is a black tuft on his breast, consisting of nine feathers, each of these tipped with blue."

"What a beautiful creature," said Crusoe. "I hope we shall be able to catch one."

"I dare say we can, lad, though he is awful shy."

"There, he is again calling out—but go on, Tom; I will not interrupt again, although I have gained much information by doing so."

"That's right, lad; learn all you can, it will do you no harm. I'll begin again. Where had I got to?"

"You found Buenos Ayres a different place from what you had expected."

"Right, lad. I may as well tell you it was so named by the Spaniards; and the meaning of the word is—good airs, or delightful climate."

"It so happened that the weather was very sultry, and during the short time we stayed, the court-martial was held, and the disgraceful death of three of the crew made the place ever afterwards hateful to me.

"I was glad when we were off again to other climates.

"We had on board passengers for the Cape of Good Hope, so we went by that passage to China, and were to return home by Cape Horn.

"Nothing material occurred during the voyage till we entered the Straits of Malacca, between the peninsula of that name and the island of Sumatra.

"An accident had happened to our casks of fresh water, so that that essential article began to run short, and the captain ordered four of us to go on shore to obtain a fresh supply.

"'Don't forget your cutlass, Tom,' he said, good-humouredly, 'for you may meet with rough usage.

"'I see no signs of inhabitants along the whole range of coast,' continued he, with his telescope to his eye, 'but some of those ferocious fellows, the Malays, may be lurking about. I would rather steer for Sumatra,' he said, turning to the mate, 'but the wind is foul for that tack, so keep together, my lads; and do you, Bilge, fire your musket, if any of the villanous Malays play you false.'

"Bilge, and Ned Luff, and Warely, and I, therefore," continued Tom, "armed ourselves, and put off towards shore.

"I was delighted to think that I was allowed to make one of the party, for my spirit of adventure was strong, and I longed to see fresh faces and fresh manners.

"We rowed away in high spirits, longing for the delicious fruits, which Bilge told us we should find in great plenty, for he had landed on this coast during a former voyage.

"We pushed into a pretty creek, jumped ashore, lashed the boat to the trunk of a cocoa-tree, slung our cutlasses, stuck our pistols in our belts, and away we sallied, Ned and I singing by snatches, as we pulled the fruit and ate them—

"'Ye gentlemen of England,
    Who live at home at ease,
    How little do ye think upon
    The dangers of the seas!'

"'I wish you'd think of the dangers of the land, you noisy fools,' said Jack Warely, who was peeping about, and fancying a Malay in every bush; but we were too thoughtless and too full of spirits to be warned by our companions, so we continued to sing, or rather roar—

"'Ye gentlemen of England,' &c.

"'Ye gentlemen of England, I'll make you both sing to another tune, you bawling fellows, I tell ye! Why can't you stop your blaring mouths with these?' said Warely, again, throwing two monstrous pine-apples at our heads.

"We only laughed the more at his anger; gnawed away at the pine-apples (in Malacca they are the finest in the world), and, between every mouthful, shouted—

"'How little do you think upon
    The dangers of the seas.'

"'Bilge!' exclaimed Warely, who was really angry, 'those dolt-headed fools of boys will cause some mis-chief. Here are we getting farther into this thick wood, and their noise will direct the rascally Malays where to find us! Do stop their singing, will ye? But look at Ned Luff! Why, what's the fellow at?'

"Bilge and I sprang forward, for Ned had dashed on a few paces; while I had stayed behind to laugh Warely out of his fears.

"Partly hidden by the trees, and among the brush-wood, there was Ned, cutting and slashing away with his cutlass at something which he could not see.

"But, in another moment, Bilge and I were in the thick of the fight between Ned and a floundering rhinoceros!

"The monstrous creature had been wallowing in the mud of a neighbouring river, and being awakened by our noise, had just raised up his cumbrous body as Ned got to the banks of the stream.

"The foolish boy began attacking the great hillock of flesh, instead of letting the animal remain quiet, which it would have done, for it is very inoffensive; but, being attacked, it never flinches from an enemy.

"Bilge knew the habits of the creature better than we did, and cried out—

"'God bless my life! but Ned will have the worst of it!'

"'Let's run down the bank, and attack it behind with our cutlasses,' exclaimed Warely, who was close after us.

"'You may just as well cut at the rock,' replied Bilge.

"'Let's all fire at it,' I shouted.

"'His tough hide will flatten your bullets for you; but we shan't hurt him,' returned Bilge.

"In the meantime, the creature had left the water, and was coming up the bank, preparing, with his head down, to strike his short, thick horn into poor Ned.

"I rushed up, whisked out my cutlass, and, while Ned stood on his defence, I aimed at the animal's eye, and struck my weapon into it.

"The pain made him pause for an instant.

"But, the next moment, he dashed up between us, while we slipped behind a tree.

"All escape seemed now over, for he instantly wheeled round, and ran with fury against the very tree which sheltered us.

"His weight and mighty strength jarred the stem, the leaves and blossoms quivered, and down it fell, snapping like a lath.

"Our danger was now frightful.

"The stamping of his ponderous feet was tremendous. His monstrous body (for he was twelve feet high) seemed waiting to crush us, as we crouched down among the fallen boughs; and his rage was quite awful, as he staggered with the pain of his wound.

"Terrified as I was, I would have rushed out upon him in the hope of injuring his other eye also with my cutlass; but the creature had come up the bank, and was now on a level ground, so that I could not reach him.

"At this moment I saw Bilge and Warely peep out from behind a mass of rock.

"The rhinoceros now fell from pain, with a weight that shook the ground.

"Bilge then fired at the only soft part of the animal—his belly.

"Warely darted forward at the same moment, with his cutlass raised on high, which glittered as he struck it deep into the same place.

"Ned and I flew out from behind.

"I aimed at the eye which was yet perfect, and blinded him, while Ned buried his weapon near the heart of our enormous foe.

His very agony now brought him on his feet again, but we were safe; for, as he could no longer see to pursue us, we stood on the rock (whither we had run for protection), watching the blind, headlong fury with which he kneaded the moist sod of the dingle with his feet, tearing down the surrounding trees, and trampling their branches into splinters.

"The next moment he staggered and rolled down the bank into the river, his huge bulk forming a stoppage to the water, which soon rose over his body, and dashed off in a sparkling cascade.

"All this, my lad, that has taken so long in telling, passed in less than three minutes.

"It was a frightful situation to be placed in; and I shall not easily forget our terror.

"When we had recovered ourselves, for I assure you, our cheeks told truth, whatever our lips might have said, we called a council of war, and agreed to go back to our boat, and bring her round the rocky headland, in order to fill our water vessels in the small river which we had discovered.

"So we tacked about again; and I give you my word," added Tom, laughing, "that we returned more quietly than we went.

"Like other heroes, we fought our battle o'er again; and, unlike some heroes, we gave each one a fair share of the glory!

"Well, we had steered round into the mouth of the rivers, and were still talking of our morning's work, when Bilge called out—

"'There goes an esculent martin!' pointing as he spoke, to a little bird that was flying over us, and which looked no bigger than a wren.

"'Is that,' I exclaimed, 'one of the birds that build the edible nests? Do, Warely, put the head of the boat round, and land me on this rock?'

"'The captain was telling me about the little esculent martins, last week; and he said, too, that he was very fond of their nests in soups.'

"'Put her head round, there's a good fellow; I won't be long clambering up the rock; and I dare say I shall soon find some nests, if there are any caverns.'

"'I'll come, too!' exclaimed Ned Luff, jumping up.

"'Yes, you idle fellow,' said Warely; 'you'll be off from the labour of filling the casks.

"'Bilge and I may do that, while you go a birds'-nesting, like a land-lubber, lads!'

"'No, no! I don't stand that fun; come, bear a hand; let's get the boat freighted, and then you may land and welcome; but you won't catch me among

you, though; I'll not put myself in the way for those wild wretches to run a muck* at me!'

"We laughed at Warely's caution," continued Tom, "but we lent a hand to fill the casks; for we felt he was right.

"'Ay,' muttered he, half aloud, 'I do hate those Malays. I wouldn't meet one—no, not if I might be made captain to-morrow.'

"'Why, Jack,' said Bilge, as he stood to rest himself, wiping the heat-drops from his sun-burnt face, 'why, Jack, if I had not seen you stand to a gun, with as good a heart as e'er a one of us, I should think you, and even call you, a coward!'

"'No, Jem Bilge—no! I am no coward! I never was one, but for two days, and that was when I would have lifted my hand against a fellow-creature—a countryman—my captain! And I do think, sometimes, that Swipes must have had a Malay in him, to tempt him to——'

"'Ay—ay! Well—well! that's all over long ago, Jack. Come, let's get this job done, for it's very hot, and we'll moor the boat under shadow of the rock, and cool ourselves, while those boys climb up it.'

"In a short time, we had finished our task, and Ned and I began our birds'-nesting.

"The face of the rock was nearly perpendicular, but bold crags jutted out here and there, over the water; bushes, dwarf trees, and beautiful flowering creepers fringed the rugged stone, and waved in the light breeze.

"We toiled up, catching and clinging to them for support, and, after a good breathing, we reached the top, about twenty feet above the water.

"We stood still to rest for a minute, and then turned round to look for those delicious nests.

"'Here's a prize,' I shouted, as I dashed into a small hollow, or cavern, near me, and brought away more than a dozen nests that I had taken from the sides of the rock, to which they had been ingeniously fastened, in the manner that the martins' nests in England are plastered to the eaves of cottages.

"I had just placed my nests safely on the edge of the rock, and had turned round to go and look for more, when I saw Ned creeping towards me, with his finger on his lip, as a sign that I was to be silent; he turned his head towards a thicket of coffee trees; and I, following the direction of his eyes, saw, to my terror, three or four tawny faces, with large black eyes and long glossy hair, watching us from among the lovely white blossoms of the coffee.

"Round I flew in a moment. 'The Malays, Ned! the Malays! Down the rock, my lad!' I shouted, as I kicked the little heap of nests over the edge, and scrambled after poor Luff.

"'Hallo, Ned!' bawled Warely.

"'What! Is the boy going to drown himself?' cried Bilge, as Luff, missing his footing, crushed through

---

* The Malays are deemed the most ferocious and treacherous people on the face of the globe, and when their natural disposition is increased by drinking spirits, they frequently seize a sword or other naked weapon, and, running through their villages like maniacs, cut at every one they meet. This is called "running a muck;" which is also a term of chivalry, and then means an action something similar, but without cruelty or bloodshed.

the bushes, and, sprawling like a frog, went splash into the water. 'Look at the nests, flying thick as hail! look at Tom Starboard! Bless my life! but they've seen a Malay! nothing else could have made such havoc!' exclaimed Warely, seizing the oars, and preparing to push off towards the ship.

"'Hoy! no sheering off and leaving our shipmates to go to the bottom, though, Warely!' said Bilge, as he pushed the boat towards Ned and me.

"We were soon in the little vessel; and were putting out to sea, when, looking up to the top of the rock, I said—

"'Well, we are most valiant heroes, it must be confessed! we ran from those men, as if they had been cannibals! why they do not think it worth while to follow us! So let me pick up some of the nests for the captain! I'm sure they cost too much (*fright*) to be wasted.'

"Warely was very unwilling to delay our departure for one moment; but Bilge said—'You see, Tom is right; there is no sign of a Malay!'

"The next minute, and before I had secured half-a dozen of my little floating treasures, a rustling among the bushes ahead of the boat caught our attention; and, immediately, we saw four ferocious-looking fellows fling themselves into the water in front of us, so that we must pass them to reach the ship.

"They had no fire-arms, of course, for they could not have used them in the water; but they swam towards us with one hand, and brandished a short sword in the other, similar to the one you have, Jack.

"We were well armed, and soon gave them a broadside, for we all fired at them together.

"But the active fellows had dived as we took aim; and to our terror, we found they had glided through the water like fish, and had risen close to our boat.

"We had no time to reload; so we pulled out our cutlasses, and succeeded in wounding one of them, which only made them more desperate.

"Warely got a cut across both legs.

"Ned had his weapon struck out of his hand with a violence that sent it spinning and glittering against the rock, which shivered it in pieces.

"Bilge and I would, in another minute, have become food for fishes, had not our jolly boat hove in sight.

"She came swirling round the headland in such style!

"How we cheered our messmates, when we found our deliverance certain.

"The tawny Malays no sooner saw them, than, with a wild sort of shriek, they dived once more, and remained concealed from our sight.

"We rowed about to look for them, that we might pepper their ribs; but they were too deep for us: we never saw them again; and, after this second adventure, we were not sorry to find ourselves at home again on the stout planks of our good ship.

"The captain had sent the other boat well manned in search of us; for he had heard Bilge's musket, when he fired at the rhinoceros; and the ship's crew feared we were fighting with the Malays.

"Captain Heartly seemed pleased with my atten-

tion in bringing him the edible nests; and laughed heartily when I told him of our adventure; though he added more seriously—

"'Poor lads! I should be sorry that those treacherous wretches, the Malays, should have had your lives.'

"He enjoyed his soup, which those nests made quite delicious—though I cannot describe in what way.

"In due time, then, we entered the river Si, on which stands the large and flourishing city of Canton, and there I——"

Old Tom paused, and listened to Crusoe's deep breathing, then added—

"What, asleep, lad?"

No answer came to his query.

"I thought so," muttered the old tar; "perhaps I've been spinning half that yarn to myself."

His supposition was not quite correct, for Crusoe did not fall asleep until he had finished the encounter with the Malays.

Old Tom carefully placed his pipe under his head, then drawing the blanket over his nose, he soon fell asleep, and, shall I add, snored in unison with his young companion.

Crusoe, remember, is not a tinsel hero—continually doing impossible deeds with equally impossible means at his command—he was mortal, and, being tired, lay on his back, and the usual consequence was the result: he breathed through his nostrils, and snored most unmusically, and seemed to enjoy it.

I wonder, courteous reader, if the thrilling heroes of modern romance were ever guilty of such a natural action; perhaps they have, and it has not been recorded.

CHAPTER II.

TOM STARBOARD MEETS AN OLD ACQUAINTANCE.

THE campanero, perched upon the summit of a mighty mora tree, welcomed the first blush of the new day with his clear, ringing notes.

The toucan, on a lower branch, from time to time awoke the echoes of the forest, by altering a peculiar series of notes, which sound in the distance like the yelping of a dog. The South Americans call this bird piapoco, from the peculiar noise he makes, which sounds at morn and eve as though he said Pi—a—po—co—eo.

Flying from tree to tree were numbers of gaudy-plumaged macaws.

When their noisy shrieks subsided for a moment, the sweet, plaintive song of the beautiful troupiele could be heard, like the sound of a flute, as it floated away upon the gentle eastern breeze.

These sounds, and the gently rippling water washing the Seagull's sides, greeted our hero and his companion when they awoke.

Old Tom rolled his eyes, and listened with much inward satisfaction to the well-known music; then, dropping from his hammock to the deck, called out—

"Are you awake, Jack?"

"I am," was the answer. "I was just listening to the strange sounds."

"That's more than you did to my yarn last night, lad."

"I must apologise for that, Tom, for I fell asleep in spite of all I could do to the contrary."

"It doesn't matter, lad; I'm glad you did so."

When they had dressed, old Tom suggested breakfast, and Crusoe agreed. They again partook of the good things Hugh of the Red Hand had taken on board for his own use.

The meal over, they took a fresh rifle each from the hooks of the cabin wall, and old Tom said—

"Now, lad, I think the first thing we had better do is to go in search of the man we saw yesterday."

"I think so, too, Tom."

The sun had reached its meridian when they came in sight of the object of their search, and the stranger, evidently regarding them as foes, stood on the defensive, his rifle at his shoulder, and his finger on the trigger.

"Stand where you are," he said, "or I fire!"

"Avast, shipmate!" said old Tom, "seeing there is but three of us here, and the three English, I don't see any cause for this."

The rifle was lowered, and the stranger, advancing with extended hand, exclaimed—

"Tom Starboard!"

"Yes," the old tar answered, rather taken aback. "who are you?"

"You soon forget, Tom."

The old sailor looked hard at the weather-beaten face for some few seconds, then exclaimed—

"Captain Hastings! as I live."

"Yes," was the answer. "We are both much altered since we last met; and no wonder, seeing you in that odd dress, I took you for a foe."

"I look much unlike an English sailor, captain," said old Tom. "But how, in the name of fortune, did you come here?"

"It's a long story," said Captain Hastings, as he seated himself upon the trunk of a fallen tree; "but, as I have but myself to blame for it, I must not grumble."

"Things do change in this world," said old Tom. "The last time I saw you the Seagull and your vessel were both at anchor in the River of Parrots."

"True, Tom; and there your captain wanted me to join him in a privateering cruise. Poor Dampier! I wish I had done so; it would have been better for us both. I need not ask his fate, I suppose, Tom."

"He is gone!" was the answer, "and all hands, save myself and this lad, went with him."

"Poor fellow! Well, he was a brave man, Tom, no matter what his other faults were."

"True, captain, but he was a tyrant, and a ——"

"Let the dead rest, Tom."

Old Tom was silent at this rebuke, and the captain, as though to pass over the somewhat harsh words, said—

"Come here, old friend, and sit by your companion."

Crusoe and old Tom took seats near the speaker, who resumed—

"Before I ask the cause that brought that stout vessel upon the rocks, I may as well tell you how I came here."

"Do," old Tom said; "I am anxious to learn."

"By the way," Captain Hastings said, "had we a dozen hands, Tom, we could get her afloat; and I could obtain such a revenge upon my cowardly, mutinous crew as would amply repay me for all I have suffered."

Old Tom opened his eyes with astonishment at these words.

"Is it possible," he asked, "that your men mutinied?"

"They did, and left me here; but, please heaven, we may yet get the Seagull afloat and manned—it's a wild hope, Tom, and you may well shake your head; but, wild as it is, I have cherished it from the hour I saw the scoundrels ransacking my old friend's ship."

"It was your late crew that broke open the lockers, then?"

"Yes. And, much to my joy, they did not find any gold on board."

Old Tom gave Crusoe a meaning look, and both smiled significantly.

"You remember the morning," the captain said, not noticing their bye play, "when your ship weighed anchor, and left me in the river?"

"I do well remember it, although I have made a voyage to England since that time."

"I think I have been further than that, Tom. But to my story. Well, after that I had the boats piped away to fetch water, before I left the river.

"About noon, as I was reading in my cabin, I heard the report of several pieces; upon which I ran out, and went myself to the mast-head, where I perceived my men, who were filling our casks at the river, surrounded by a multitude of Indians.

"I, upon the instant, let slip our cables, and having a strong sea-breeze, started full into the river's mouth at all hazards, ordering every man to his arms, and to load all our great guns with musket-ball.

"By good fortune the tide was almost at the highest, so that we came on broadside to the rivulet where the men were defending themselves.

"They had made a rampart with the empty casks, and had kept off the Indians with their pieces, but just as we came they had spent their ammunition, and resolved to submit.

"But as soon as they perceived us, they took to their heels, and ran towards the ship, and the Indians after them; but we soon stopped their career, by firing our double and round, which killed fifty men, and put the rest to flight.

"We took our men on board, and intended to fall out of the river, but found the tide turned; and before we could get out, our ship ran aground, so that we were obliged to wait till the next tide.

"In the meantime, not to be idle, I armed twenty men and ordered them to guard the rest while they filled our casks; which was done, and with the long boat, brought alongside the ship.

"I would not let them be hoisted aboard for fear of hurting the ship, now she lay a-ground, though it proved to be a clayey bottom.

"An hour before night we perceived an Indian

running very swiftly to us, who called to us in Portuguese to fetch him on board.

"As soon as he was in the ship, he told a man that understood Portuguese, that the Indians, to the number of a thousand, designed, in the middle of the night, to attack our ship, and that they would come down in canoes; for they well knew we could not get out till flood of tide.

"This man, whom we took for an Indian, was a Portuguese the Indians had taken prisoner a year before, and, understanding their language, learnt their resolution; and while they were calling their men together, he took the opportunity to make his escape.

"I immediately called the officers together to consult about the danger, and we agreed to send fifty men well armed.

"As soon as it was dark, we landed six of our guns, and raised a small battery without any noise or bustle.

"Two of our guns were loaded with double and round in the stern of the ship.

"The rest of our men were ordered in close coverts on each side of the river, with directions to let the Indian canoes pass them, and not fire till they were all gone by.

"Everything was concerted and settled, and every man ordered to his post, to repel the charge; and we had contrived it so well, that none of our fires could hurt one another.

"About one o'clock in the morning, we could hear their paddles in the water, and, soon after, perceived them silently sailing down the river, to the number of two hundred canoes.

"We let them come within fifty yards of our ship before we fired; but when we began, we made such a terrible slaughter among them, that I pitied them.

"When the morning dawned, we were amazed to see what havoc death had made. The very shores were stained with blood, and we had not lost one man.

"The Portuguese who gave us notice, I rewarded with a hundred pounds, and two suits of new clothes, both linen and woollen; and we made use of him for our interpreter.

"He told us we had one of their caciques among the prisoners, and a man of great power among the Indians.

"I ordered him to ask him the reason of his enmity to us, since we had never offended them.

"He told him that he took us for Spaniards or Portuguese, nations they hated from the barbarous usage they had met with from them; but he was sorry he had molested us, seeing we were Englishmen, and enemies to the Spaniards as well as themselves.

"But, however, he would pay sufficiently for his ransom, if we would spare his life; and accordingly we agreed for one hundred weight of gold-dust, and twenty in ingots, and he ordered one of his retinue to fetch it. In the meantime, we took advantage of the tide, and fell down to our old station.

"The next day, at noon, two canoes arrived, one with the gold, and several persons came to wait on their king; and the other laden with fruits and provisions, which I had parted between the ship's company.

"I took the ingots for my share, and the gold-dust was divided among the rest.

"We put the Indians on shore, and the next day weighed anchor again, and we steered our course with a fresh gale for the Straits of Magellan.

"I intended to pass through these straits into the South Sea, for I was of opinion it would shorten our voyage; and then my curiosity strengthened that opinion.

"But I was advised by my lieutenant to venture up to Buenos Ayres, a town belonging to the Spaniards, where he assured me we might drive a good trade under-hand with the merchants.

"I communicated the matter to the whole company, who unanimously agreed it was the best course we could steer.

"So we kept in with the shore, and steered for the Rio de la Plata, which we reached in twenty days without any accident.

"As we had war with France and Spain, I had hoisted French colours, that we might have the liberty to trade with more safety.

"When we were within two leagues of the port we came to an anchor in a little creek, in eight fathom water, with a sandy bottom.

"We did not care to go nearer the town, for fear the governor should have taken it into his head to have hindered our going out again.

"Though we were not in sight of it, yet we had canoes alongside of us in an hour after our anchoring; and some of the merchants came to be informed what we dealt in.

"One of them told me he believed it would be no difficult thing to dispose of my cargo, if I thought fit to make the governor a small present.

"Accordingly, I took his advice, and sent my steward, in my name, with a piece of holland, and half a dozen pieces of Italian silks, which he received as a very valuable present, and sent me word he would not in the least molest me, provided I did not deal too barefacedly.

"I understood him, and, therefore, was very cautious, selling but to one at a time, nor would I suffer another to enter the ship till the former was despatched.

"In two days I got rid of all the cargo I intended to part with, to a very great advantage; and then I allowed my men liberty to do what they thought fit with what they had, which gave them general satisfaction.

"The next day I invited the governor on board, with some of the principal merchants, and entertained them in my cabin; and in return I was to dine on shore at the castle.

"But I left a strict order with my lieutenant how to behave himself if I should be stopped, for I knew the Spaniards to be a very unfaithful people.

"The governor seemed to have less of the formality of the Spaniards than ever I met with in any of them.

"When I took my leave of him, he made me a present of two Indian slaves, and a bar of gold that weighed three pounds two ounces.

"When I came on board, I called a council, to know what course we should steer next, for, as to traffic, I had no pretence to go to the South Sea, seeing all my cargo was already disposed of.

"We debated for some time, and at last we agreed to go to the South Sea upon the score of privateering.

"We communicated our intentions to the company, and they all seemed much rejoiced at the resolution I had taken.

"Now I began to repent I had not joined with Captain Dampier, for I wanted men for any notable exploit.

"But I did not despair of meeting with him in the South Sea.

"We weighed anchor, and steered for the Straits of Magellan with a fair wind.

"One morning my servant roused me, and told me that a sail bore down upon us, and the lieutenant desired to know how to behave himself.

"I rose upon the instant, and, by the help of my perspective, I saw it was a vessel with English colours; but imagining they were put up only for show, I caused French colours to be hoisted, which was soon answered by the same in the ship that pursued us.

"I ordered everything to be prepared for an engagement, without any hurry; commanded my men not to appear upon deck, and kept on my course with crowded sail, that our pursuers might imagine I was willing to get from them; yet I ordered it so, by false steering, that they gained upon us.

"About three in the afternoon, they were within half a league of us, firing every quarter of an hour a gun to leeward, to let us know we were to take them for friends.

"I ordered my men to tack about, to hoist up English colours, and bear upon them.

"We soon perceived we had much surprised them, but notwithstanding they kept up their French colours, and seemed to prepare for the engagement, though they were much inferior to us.

"When we came alongside I hailed them, and (after owning they were French) commanded them to surrender, but was answered with a broadside, which we returned so fast that they soon struck and called for quarter.

"I ordered the captain to come on board, who informed me that his vessel was called the Felicity, belonging to Monsieur de Gennes, and had been separated from the fleet three days before.

"I used the captain very well. I gave him a small present, and dismissed him without taking anything from them.

"I found this action did not please some of my men; and, not wishing to make them uneasy, I summoned them upon the deck, and told them as this was a ship of war, there was not much to be expected from them; therefore I told them I would share five hundred pounds among them, to make them amends for their disappointment.

"But not one of them would accept a penny; and, in return, I told them I did not intend to make any more such compliments to the French, if ever they came into my power again.

"They were all very well pleased at my declaration, and some of them praised my generosity; for though most sailors are rough and blunt in speech, yet they can in their way admire a generous action as well as other men.

"Our officers were under some apprehensions of meeting with the squadron of Monsieur de Gennes, which, being a fleet of five sail, would certainly be too hard for us; and we were informed by the captain of the Felicity that they had sailed for the Straits of Magellan.

"I found their fears very reasonable, and it would be a fool hardy action to encounter a force so much superior.

"Humanity obliged me not to hazard the lives of so many.

"So I resolved to make for Le Maire's Straits, which in five days we discovered, known to the sailors by three rocks, called the Three Brothers, from their likeness to one another.

"We found a strong current setting northward, and an unusual tossing of the ship; but we got through the straits in two days with safety, and made for the South Sea.

"The next day we discovered the Magellan clouds, so well known to sailors, which convinced us that we were over against those straits which run into the South Sea.

"Those clouds are always seen in the same degree, and in the same orbicular form.

"We kept on our course, not intending to come within sight of the continent, for fear of a discovery; and the weather favoured us in continuing very hazy.

"About an hour after dusk we heard the sound of a trumpet, which we conjectured must be on board of some vessel, because we were well assured we were not near enough the land; upon which I immediately gave orders to put out all our lights, and steer our course the way we heard the sound, which sounding often gave us notice of their course.

"In half an hour, though pretty dark, we gained sight of them; but their mirth was soon changed when we got up with them, thrust out our guns, and hailed them.

"We understood they were Spanish, and I ordered them to be told, if they did not on the instant lie by, and send their commander on board, I would immediately fire upon them.

"They very readily complied with my orders, hoisted out their boat, and the captain came on board.

"He was employed by the Viceroy of Peru to carry condemned persons to Valdivia, which is the residence of most of the rogues of America.

"But we were also informed that they had the Real Situado on board, which is a sum of money so-called, that is sent from the Viceroy of Peru to pay and clothe the garrison, as well as to repair the fortifications of Valdivia.

"This sum usually amounted to four hundred thousand crowns, but we could find no more than two hundred and fifty thousand; but then, to make amends for the deficiency, we met with a great

THE ISLAND MAIDEN SWAM TOWARDS JACK'S BOAT.

many valuable East India goods, brought from thence by their Manilla ships; for the merchants always put their supply to Valdiva in the ship that carries the money to pay the garrison, that being the only time to dispose of their goods.

"This prize made my men mad with joy, and I feared it would make them think they would have enough, and consequently desire to return home.

"But I soon found it had the contrary effect, and they all expected from this earnest of good fortune, riches enough in the voyage we proposed to make them for ever happy.

"I treated the prisoners well.

"They numbered forty-six, including fifteen felons, who were well pleased to have changed their masters; expecting better usage from us than from the Spaniards of Valdivia, where they were designed.

"There was one Williams, an Englishman, among them.

"I entered him, two Frenchmen, four Spaniards, and the trumpeter, in my books, to reinforce my crew.

"I was convinced they were good sailors. But I

15

did not know how to dispose of the ship and the rest of the crew.

"If I should give them their liberty, they would of course alarm the country; and, if I kept them with me, provisions would fall short; for they were victualled but for a month's voyage.

"The Spanish captain, being informed of my fears; told me by an interpreter, that he had received such handsome usage from me, that he would, upon his honour, steer to what port I thought fit, and report, if I pleased, that I had sailed back again for the North Sea.

"I told him, though I could rely on his honour, I could not rely upon the whole of the ship's company; so, to make things safe, I gave him his ship, after first taking the guns, small arms, and ammunition away.

"This did not please my men, and the rascal Williams soon made himself the leader of those who were dissatisfied, and there was a sudden mutiny.

"All the officers were slain except myself.

"I, it seemed, was not to die.

"But the rascals, not liking to keep me on board, left me here almost two months since.

"There, Tom, what do you think of my adventures since we parted?"

"I think!" old Tom said. "Had I my will, I would soon be on their track, and find some means of revenging the villanous mutineers' allegations with interest."

"I may yet be able to do so.

"There may be a wreck. A ship may strike here upon these strange rocks; if so, I shall have some chance of getting the Seagull afloat."

The captain's words were prophetic, as it afterwards proved.

"Well," old Tom said, "we can join with you."

The captain was delighted at the offer.

The nucleus of a crew were thus formed, and with Tom and Crusoe for his first and second officers, he began to talk about putting the Seagull in fighting trim.

CHAPTER III.

THE THOUSAND ISLANDS—JACK PROCLAIMS HIMSELF KING—TURTLE HUNTING.

LEAVING the captain still sitting on the trunk of the tree, engaged in his own reflections, Jack ascended a neighbouring rock, and taking his seat upon its extreme point, gazed admiringly out upon the broad sea. He was shortly rejoined by Tom Starboard.

The island, our readers should be informed, was one of that sequestered archipelago called by Tom the Thousand Islands, all of which were of volcanic origin, and surrounded by those dangerous rock and coral reefs, which had been the doom of the Seagull's mutinous crew.

It was no exaggeration on Tom's part to call them the Thousand Islands.

Seated upon the high promontory that jutted out into the many-coloured ocean, Jack contemplated the boundless and beautiful prospect which his new territory revealed to him.

Island beyond island, peak on peak, and rock above rock, stretching in one magnificent panorama over the whole bosom of the sea as far as the distant horizon.

And now, bathed in all the glories of the rising sun, each point glistened with red or purple, or gold, and vied with the dancing waves in which it lay embedded.

Never had Jack, in all his wanderings, beheld a scene so lovely—so enchanting; and even Tom Starboard, with all his immense experience of the beautiful places of the world, expressed his admiration.

But Tom had seen the islands before, and consequently these beauties did not produce so great an effect upon him as on Jack.

The latter could not repress his admiration, but exclaimed—

"By Jove! but this is glorious. Oh, Tom! how glad I am that we have found these islands."

"I thought they would astonish you," the old tar answered. "Didn't I tell you there were a thousand wonderful places, and I'll warrant, a closer acquaintance with them will not lessen your admiration."

"No, Tom, no. I feel that I could live here for ever."

"Ah! my lad," replied Tom, chuckling. "What, so soon forgotten our last resting-place, with your glory and power as a chief, and the beautiful Indian girl into the bargain, eh?"

Jack looked rather embarrassed at these words.

"Do not talk about that, Tom," he answered; "you know the reason why I left the island—as for Lela, she will be far happier when away from me."

"Not by the signs I saw, she won't," returned Tom; "but you know best."

"At all events, I did well to get away," Jack replied. "I did not want to chain myself completely to Lela, and the happiness of both of us will be enhanced by the step I have taken."

"And your late subjects?" asked the old tar.

"Must look out for themselves. I have done all I could for them. And now, Tom, suppose we change the subject. Here we are, and here we must remain for some time at least. It will be long before we have thoroughly explored the Thousand Islands."

"Suppose we set about it at once?" suggested Tom.

"Stop a moment longer, this view is too beautiful for me to leave before I am compelled. It sets me thinking upon all sorts of things as I sit here. My past life, my present state, and a hundred vague longings and fancies come across my mind."

"In short, you've got a romantic fit come on, my boy," suggested Tom.

"That's it—a romantic fit—but not more romantic than my life has been. Just think of it; first, a wretched, ill-treated little castaway, flung on the English coast, after a voyage from—heaven knows where; then a sailor on board the Seagull, put ashore, goodness knows why, on an island where fate next made me a warrior chief; and now—"

"Well, what is your highness's present state and condition?" said Tom, smiling good-humouredly.

"THE KING OF THE THOUSAND ISLANDS!" cried Jack, suddenly starting up, his face flushed with enthusiasm and excitement. "That is what I am now, or, at least, what I will be. I've just thought of the title, Tom; isn't it a good one?"

"Capital; but, you see, titles ain't much good to anybody in your situation. Where your subjects are to come from, in the first place, I don't see. The captain and me won't make a very big nation."

"Are you quite sure that all the islands are totally uninhabited?" asked Jack.

"I should be as much surprised," answered his companion, "to see a man of any kind, as I should to see a mermaid in the water yonder, or a fine lady's kid glove lying on the beach."

"Well, at all events, there must be some birds, beasts, and fishes on the islands, which I will make my subjects. Adam and Eve, who ruled all the world, had no others. Or, even failing this, the islands are a kingdom in themselves."

"Yes, my lad; but a king without subjects is like a gun without powder. But stow this talk," the old salt continued; "I think we've been at it long enough. Let's turn to, and make ourselves generally useful. We shall want some breakfast; so get up, my lad, and help me to see about it."

Thus exhorted, Jack reluctantly quitted his post of observation, and accompanied Tom on a preliminary observation of the island, for the purpose of killing turtles and chopping wood for a fire.

After their breakfast, accompanied by the captain, the two friends set out on an exploring expedition through these wonderful islands.

So far from being barren, as it at first appeared, the island on which they had landed was a delightful region.

In extent, it was little more than three miles in circumference; but for fertility and beauty, it was a complete fairy land.

The whole of the ground was covered with a carpet of verdure, adorned by myriads of bright-coloured flowers; there were also gum trees and prickly pears, and almost every variety of tropical flowers and fruit trees, festooned with climbing plants, and forming complete bowers and arcades and groves of luxuriant sylvan beauty.

Cocoa-nuts, sago, the castor-oil plant, and a variety of seeds, all probably washed ashore in the first place from distant lands, and taken root in the island, abounded in all parts.

These, together with the turtles, the swarms of fish, the eatable lizards, and the birds and wild goats that inhabited the high rocks, gave ample evidence that our hero's new dominion was a land of plenty.

"No need to starve—eh Tom?" he cried, as he delightedly stood on the centre eminence and surveyed the rich prospect before him. "It seems to me a wonder why some of the South American Governments have not taken possession of these islands, and formed colonies on them."

"They would be little use for that, Jack," returned his companion. "They are too small to support large numbers of people, besides, and you forget," he added, "that, having been in the first

place cast up by volcanoes, they are liable at any time to go down suddenly in the same manner."

Jack started, and felt suddenly uncomfortable to think that all this glorious scene could possibly sink into the sea and be devoured! And, above all, the idea of sinking down with it—which would be certain death—was particularly unpleasant.

"No, Jack," remarked Tom, "the worthlessness of these islands are their only safety, and, though, they might support you and me, and perhaps two or three dozen more, they would be despised as a colony by any of the great neighbouring Governments. So, knowing they don't belong to any one else, you had every right to call yourself as you have done, "The King of the Thousand Islands."

The companions shot a great number of birds, mostly peculiar to the islands, and having short beaks like bullfinches, and Jack soon covered himself with feathered ornaments of all sorts of bright colours.

Then they destroyed a number of iguanas, great hideous creatures about three feet long, with great pouches under their mouths, and formidable claws. It was, as Jack remarked, "Quite a pleasure to get rid of them!"

CHAPTER IV.

THE EXPLORING TRIP—GOOD SPORT—THE CAPTAIN'S HUT—THE HAMMOCKS—A STRANGE PRESENTIMENT—THE MYSTERY OF THE STRANGE SHIP.

THE whole day was passed in exploring the island, and the neighbouring ones, all of which presented the same features and general characters.

Captain Hastings could, of course, tell all about the animals and productions of the territory, where he had so long reigned alone.

Jack and Tom used their pit-pan, and the captain one of the boats from the Seagull, which he had rescued and mended for his own use.

The captain had, during his solitary stay in the island, lived in a small hut he had built on the shore, not far from where lay the wreck of the Seagull.

In this hut he invited them in the middle of the day to partake of a repast, consisting principally of turtle, and many of the fruits and vegetables of the island.

It being a fine day, the companions had a glorious trip among and around the wonderful thousand islands, and the coral beds that encircled them.

They shot an immense quantity of game, and caught many turtles, both by jugging, netting, and shooting.

Jack had fine sport in one of the islands, where he shot a magnificent turtle through the neck, killing it instantly, just as it was scuttling into the water.

When night came, as it was fine weather, the party resolved to sling their hammocks upon the branches of a couple of strong spreading trees, not far from the captain's habitation.

This impromptu sleeping-place was constructed without much trouble.

By the aid of ropes, the adventurers securely

fastened their skin cloaks to the trees, in the position most comfortable for sleeping in, and spreading under and over their bodies their other garments, contrived, as Jack expressed it, "to make as good beds as you could get at a first-rate hotel."

When once comfortably settled, they found little difficulty in going to sleep.

They were weary with their day's adventures.

All around was calm and quiet as the grave.

The night was delightfully cool, and no troublesome flies or mosquitoes disturbed their repose.

Tom, Jack, and the captain were very quickly, therefore, as fast asleep as so many dormice, and there seemed no reason why they should not sleep undisturbed until morning.

But, somehow, Jack did not.

He awoke suddenly with a start, and a strange feeling of apprehension, just as the faint streaks began to tinge the sky above, and speak of the approaching day.

Jack's mind was confused.

He for a moment did not know where he was, and almost tumbled out of his hammock in his bewilderment.

What was the cause of that peculiar feeling of mental oppression that overcame him, and seemed to indicate some danger near, or impending?

Jack could not tell.

He only knew that he experienced it, and that a feeling of wakefulness had come over him on a sudden.

Hark!

Can that possibly be the sound of voices at this silent hour, and on this uninhabited island?

Jack started up, his brain throbbing, his heart beating quickly, and listened.

Yes, it was evidently voices engaged in rough, angry converse, and seeming to proceed from the opposite side of the island. These unexpected sounds were accompanied by a harsh grating noise, like that of dragging a boat along the beach, and Jack now fancied he could hear the plash of oars.

How near it sounded, too! What, and who could they be, that were about to depart from the island, and where had they concealed themselves on the previous evening?

A thousand vague conjectures chased each other through Jack's mind, but none were satisfactory. He was completely puzzled, and at a nonplus.

What should he do? Wake his companions, and acquaint them with what he had discovered, and accompany them to ascertain the cause of it?

Would it not, however, be best to remain quiet and concealed, for who knew whether the mysterious visitors to the island might not be deadly foes?

Jack, at length, determined not to wake his comrades, who were sleeping very soundly; but his curiosity was so strong, that he resolved, come what would, to see something of their mysterious neighbours.

So he silently glided out of his hammock, and, armed with his sword, stole cautiously in the direction of the sound.

Over hill, and mound, and valley, in that gray morning twilight, through thick underwood, and under tall trees, where birds were just waking into life he went. Wherever an open eminence occurred, an uninterrupted view of the sea, on every side, was to be obtained.

Jack at length reached the top of a rising ground, covered with thick clumps of trees, from which a grassy slope stretched gently down to the shore.

Here a most unexpected sight presented itself to his view.

A large bay, or natural harbour, evidently of deep water, and capable of sheltering craft of considerable size. Beyond that, the dull, gray, leaden ocean, clothed in the early morning's gloom.

But, above all, Jack could distinguish the outline of a large vessel, having the appearance of an English schooner, getting up sail, about a quarter of a mile from the shore, and slowly making her way from the island.

No other boat was to be seen, and it was evident that the one he had heard launched belonged to this ship.

Jack was very much puzzled and surprised. He stood watching the vessel, which, with a light breeze springing up in her favour, was making rapid headway, until she grew less and less, and faded away into the distance.

It was no deception, then. Some persons had visited the island during the night, but who they were it was difficult to conjecture. If they were the crew of any South American trading vessel, and had put in there for water, they had chosen a very peculiar time to do so, and one which argued a most intimate acquaintance with the island.

No strangers to the island would have landed under such circumstances, passing in safety the dangerous rocks that surrounded the archipelago.

It was evident, therefore, that the crew of this mysterious ship knew the island well, and were accustomed to put ashore on it either for water or some other purpose. Their choosing the night to do so looked suspicious, and rendered it all the more a mystery who and what they could be.

While he was pondering all this, the vessel gradually disappeared, and was lost quite out of sight. Jack felt it was no use pondering any longer, so, feeling suddenly weary, again he got back to his hammock, and joined the others, still sound asleep. He was very soon the same himself, and he slept until far into the morning.

When Tom awoke, the morning sun was shining in all its splendour over the wild scene of sylvan luxuriance in which he had passed the night, and far over the vast expanse of the golden ocean, gemmed with innumerable islands and islets of great beauty.

Jack sat up in his hammock, and gazed around him in a half-bewildered manner. Tom had risen some time before him, and was engaged a short distance off in chopping wood to make a fire. The captain was making breakfast in the hut.

"Come, my lad!" was the old tar's first exclamation to our hero. "This won't do, you know. to lie asleep of a morning like a land-lubber after a night's spree. Here I've been up ever so long, and been out hunting for our breakfast!"

"And what have you got for breakfast, Tom?" asked Jack, with considerable interest.

"Well, in the first place, I went and got some water from a stream out on the left yonder, using this skin-bottle. Then I began hunting for tortoises and turtles, which is no great difficulty, considering they abound in thousands in all the islands round about, and I felled this chap here, and I'm going to cook him in his own shell. I think we shall find enough in him to make a breakfast of, considering that he must weigh at least 200 lbs. I can tell you I had rather a job to carry him here with my jacket wrapped round him."

While Tom was thus employed with the tortoise at the fire, he had made Jack perform his ablutions at the neighbouring spring which Tom had spoken of. It was a fine stream, falling from a low cliff about thirty feet high, and thus forming a beautiful waterfall, encompassed by high rocks covered with luxuriant vegetation.

Jack gazed for some time in admiration at the beauties of this scene, and then, turning in the direction his appetite pointed—namely, where the breakfast was being prepared, he made his way along the beach, where he saw an immense number of turtles and iguanas, which scuttled out of his way as fast as they could. Jack made up his mind to have a good day's sport with these animals, and, when he looked out over the calm, bright sea, the thought of the mysterious ship of the night before came into his mind, and he determined, if possible, to solve that mystery.

When he got to the hut, he found the breakfast ready cooked, and the captain serving it out upon the shells of the turtle, which he used as plates.

They found this dish very agreeable, and with the water out of the skin bottle, mixed with some wine, they made a delightful meal.

In the process of cooking, Tom had also extracted a considerable quantity of oil, which he had preserved, as he knew it would be very useful to them for a variety of purposes.

While they were engaged on their repast, Jack thought it high time to acquaint his friends with the strange circumstance of the ship. Accordingly he said—

"Tom, you complained of me lying in bed a long while this morning, but I did not sleep quite so long as you. I was not only awake, but up, and walking about the island."

"And what was you doing then, my lad?" asked Tom.

Our hero answered with emphasis—

"Looking at a ship!"

Tom's looks expressed great surprise.

"Looking at a ship?" he exclaimed. "Nonsense! You must have been dreaming!"

"Not a bit of it; I was as wide awake as I am now, and I saw it as plain as anybody can see anything when it is half dark. It seemed like an English schooner, fully rigged, and had been at anchor.

"Some of the crew went ashore in a boat, and went away again.

"At last, I'm certain that I heard the sound of voices, and afterwards the boat putting out.

"When I saw the ship, she was just getting under way, and was bearing out for the west, with the wind in her favour."

Both Tom and the captain were beyond measure surprised at this recital, and put several questions to Jack in order to gain more particulars; but the latter had told them all he knew, and neither was able to fathom the mystery.

"I can't make out who they could have been," remarked the captain. "Such a thing has never occurred here before."

"They must have been intimately acquainted with the island to land safely at night on a coast so dangerous as this is for large ships."

"Then, again, what do they come for?"

"I don't believe it could have been a merchantman, English or otherwise, for no such vessels ever visit these islands under such circumstances. The only thing is that she must have been a pirate."

"Do you think so, sir?" asked Jack, eagerly.

"I do. Nobody but pirates and smugglers would act in that manner, and they would prefer making their secret harbours nearer to the mainland, where they could more easily dispose of their plunder. But if the vessel was really a rover, then we must keep a bright look out, for our stay here won't be a very safe one."

"They can't murder us for our riches, at all events," said Jack, laughing.

"No; but if they use the island as a hiding-place for their treasure," answered Captain Hastings, "it will fare hard with us if we are discovered here."

"We've got some adventures in store for us, I'll warrant," remarked Tom, "and precious ticklish ones, too, I shouldn't wonder!"

And subsequent events showed that the old tar was not mistaken.

CHAPTER V.

MABEL IS STILL PERSECUTED—THEN RESCUED, AND ENCOUNTERS THE PERILS OF THE DEEP.

OLD MADGE'S warning to her grandson to be aware of the smoothed-tongued lawyer was either forgotten or despised by Jasper.

Revelling in the command of Crusoe's fortune, name, and birthright, he had but little time to watch the lawyer's crafty doings.

It was a dangerous weapon the keen-sighted Robert Twistem had received from Jasper Collins.

The paper the latter had signed, though purporting to be merely a security for the payment of the sum the lawyer had demanded as a reward for placing the estate in Jasper's possession, was in reality a mortgage upon the whole of the Moreland estate.

Mr. Robert Twistem took his measures well. One by one he managed to introduce to Jasper men of desperate fortunes, and by degrees the banker's grandson was led, step by step, to become an inveterate gamester.

Robert Twistem, Esq., chuckled gleefully at the success of his plans, as he rubbed his spotless hands. He muttered triumphantly—

"The first step gained, the time will soon arrive

when the payment of the first portion of the money will be due. He will not be able to pay me; and, like Shylock, I will have my bond."

Pausing in his audibly expressed thoughts for a few minutes' reflection, a self-satisfied look passed over his face, as he resumed—

"Yes, there is but one way; he must make over to me a portion of the property, and piece by piece I shall have the whole of the rich lands, and that beggar's cub will go back to his hut on the cliff."

With this pleasing prospect before him, Mr. Robert Twistem went about his daily avocations.

Old Madge's letter, stating that she could not wait for the scheme she had first matured, but had forcibly taken possession of the girl, caused the crookback to start at once from London.

He found the poor girl a captive when he reached the lone hut by the sea, and, with the intention of at once taking her to London, he had the travelling carriage waiting beneath the cliffs until his return.

Entering the lone hut, Madge came forward, and, pointing to the inner room, said—

"Your bird is in that cage; and, now, what do you intend to do with her?"

"Carry out my original intention."

"Marry her?"

"Yes, and ill-treat her, until her life becomes a burden too heavy to bear."

Old Madge grinned spitefully.

"A grand revenge, Jasper," she said; "but rather tedious."

"I can wait."

"You can, Jasper. Would you like to see your captive?"

"Not now. It will be dark soon; then I will take her to London."

Base as he was, Jasper could not face the poor girl.

When night set in, Mabel was brought from the inner room, and Madge, with devilish glee, passed a gag across the girl's mouth.

Jasper gripped her by the hand as he led the way down the cliff, and the girl, stupified with terror, unresistingly followed her abductor.

The travelling carriage was at the base of the rocky pathway; and Jasper's hand was upon the door-handle, when Mabel, shaking off the terror that had hitherto oppressed her, broke from his grasp, and, tearing the gag from her mouth, uttered a shrill and agonising scream for help.

The sight of the gleaming lights from a ship that was moored within twenty fathoms of the shore, caused this sudden change in the young girl.

While the cavernous cliff yet sent back in loud echoes her piercing scream, a boat grounded on the beach, and several men sprang ashore.

"A woman's cry!" said a voice, which caused every nerve in the girl's frame to vibrate; "there must be something wrong."

"Perdition!" muttered Jasper, as he grasped her firmly, and attempted to drag her to the carriage.

She struggled desperately, and again her screams echoed upon the night air.

This time there was a response—an angry shout —then a man's form came swiftly to her side.

"Save me! save me!" cried Mabel; "save me from this man!"

In answer to her plaintive appeal, the stranger raised his clenched hand, and felled the crookback, stunned and bleeding to the earth.

Then, as the seamen arrived on the spot, the light from a boat house, revealed to Mabel's astonishment, her father's form.

She gave a cry, and threw herself upon his breast, and he, throwing his arms around her slender form, kissed the white forehead, and resumed—

"Mabel! my darling! What is the meaning of this?"

She told him in a few words, and the sailors, who were grouped around, listened to her story with breathless interest.

They gave a cry of rage, and before George Meredith could interfere, two of the number seized Jasper by the ankles and ducked him in the sea.

The driver of the travelling carriage made an attempt to escape, but the boat's crew dragged him from the box and hurled him into the water.

He scrambled out wet, and begged for mercy, and his worthless master, who had recovered under the rough treatment he had received, joined in the whining cry.

"To the boat, men," said Mabel's father. "We'll leave the punishment to a higher power."

The men obeyed, and as the boat glided swiftly towards the ship, Mr. Meredith told his child that he came to take her from England.

He heard with astonishment and anger that his letters had been stopped by the old harridan, Madge Collins, but the happiness he felt at being so providentially upon the spot to save his child, made him soon forget all the wrongs she had suffered.

*   *   *   *   *

The guard-ship driven by the furious gale, struck upon a sunken reef in the South Pacific Ocean, and all that were not washed away by the surging billows were landed upon a raft hastily put together soon after the ship struck.

The storm still raged, and the poor girl, when she heard there was no hope of life, gave one cry, and swooned in her father's arms.

High above the noise of the roaring waters, and just as the first raft began to split asunder, the castaways were startled by a loud noise apparently close upon them.

"We are saved!" came from the sailors' lips, and one hastily tying a shirt to a pole held it aloft as a guide to those who were coming to the rescue.

"There they are, lad," the strange voice said, "lay-to, Jack, pull captain, or we shall be too late."

A minute later, and a boat had dashed alongside the raft, and Mabel, who had revived when the hopeful cries struck upon her ears, opened her eyes, and beheld the strange-looking crew of the welcome boat.

Two, a man and a boy, were dressed in skins, the other in a torn officer's uniform.

Could she be dreaming? No; the voice, the bold, handsome face could but belong to one—that one her childhood's ideal—

CRUSOE JACK.

CHAPTER VI.

THE STORM—THE SHIPWRECK—THE RAFT— EXCITING SCENE—PROVIDENTIAL ESCAPE FROM DROWNING—JACK AND TOM PERIL THEIR LIVES AND DO GOOD SERVICE—JACK'S AMAZEMENT AT RECOGNISING MABEL.

CAPTAIN HASTINGS knew that without further assistance than that of Crusoe and Tom Starboard, it would be impossible to fulfil his cherished design of getting the Seagull afloat.

With a dozen trusty hands, as he had said, the hull could easily be raised, and in due time put into fighting order, but the island was totally uninhabited, save by that trio of castaway Englishmen.

If a ship should strike on any of the neighbouring rocks—not a very unlikely circumstance on the dangerous coral reefs—and they could contrive to rescue the crew, the captain felt certain that he would soon be at the head of a sufficient number of men to carry out his intentions.

With a gallant ship like the Seagull, well manned and in good fighting order, he could defy any enemies that were likely to menace him in that unknown region.

Above all, he could give chase to the mutineers, and punish them for their conduct towards him.

And then, how glorious would be the cruise upon that boundless ocean, dotted as it was with innumerable islands of immense fertility, where every means of profitable merchandise abounded!

Jack's eyes glistened with the delight of anticipation as he listened to the captain's project.

"How delightful, Tom!" he exclaimed to his companion, "to be again afloat, and cruising about among the beautiful islands of the Pacific."

"You're on a beautiful island now, my lad," returned the old salt, "and yet you're ready enough to leave, seemingly."

"Yes, it is very nice to be here for a time," replied Crusoe, "but not to be on an uninhabited desolate island without hope of escape, or any protection against the crews of pirates that may happen to come ashore. I like to be afloat on a ship like the Seagull, to be able to go ashore when and where we please, and to meet the pirates on equal terms on their own ground."

"Well, she's a neat craft certainly," replied Tom, looking admiringly at the stranded hull of the ship, "and she's got some fighting mettle in her yet, I'll warrant, if she could only get afloat again."

"She shall soon be got afloat, I'm determined," said Captain Hastings, "and after all, Tom," he added, flinging himself backward luxuriously on the soft grass bank on which he was sitting. "We're not so very badly off. We're on a desert island, it's true, but one abounding with all sorts of things on which all of us can live, and besides, some valuable property in the wrecked ship yonder, with nobody near to take it from us."

"It ain't much good to us now, though, captain; is it?"

"No, and that reminds me," said the captain, laughing, "of the old story about the man who was cast ashore on a desert island without a shilling in his pocket."

"That's just my case, captain," observed Tom.

"And mine, too; but that old joke is only to show the uselessness of wealth when we have no means of disposing of it; you see, if we had a million of money, we should be no better off as long as we are here."

"Not a bit," returned Tom. "Whereas if we can get the Seagull afloat, and begin trading on the South American coast, we might all make our fortunes, and go home to enjoy them."

This was certainly an agreeable prospect, and Jack thought so too, as he looked out over the vast many-coloured seas over which the clouds were lowering. Then his heart thrilled with pleasure and pride as he thought of Mabel, and the joy of coming home as a rich man to claim her hand; surely they could not refuse him then!

Where was she now?

Had she forgotten him?

Was he ever to see her, or hear from her again?

These thoughts chased each other rapidly over Jack's mind, as he gazed across the boundless ocean.

But the aspect of that sea was now changing from beautiful to terrible.

A dark heavy cloud was veiling the fine blue face of the sky, and turning the bright flower-covered glory of the coral isles into gloom and desolation.

A terrible tropical storm was coming on.

One of those fearful hurricanes which Jack knew well, and Tom Starboard knew still better.

Hurricanes which uprooted strong trees, destroyed houses and flooded towns on shore, and at sea proved the destruction of doomed ships.

Jack, Tom, and the captain looked at the sky; all remarked its ominously threatening aspect.

"We are in for a spell of foul weather, to a certainty," said Tom.

And they were not mistaken.

Bursting from the sky with fierce and overpowering violence, the storm cloud descended in heavy showers of rain, the thunder rumbled and boomed along the sky like the deadly artillery of a remorseless foe, and the lightning illumined the sky in lurid flashes of forked blinding magnificence.

The party on the beach returned without delay to the captain's hut, to avoid the violence of the storm, but still they could look out, and their hiding-place commanded a view of the sea.

The waves had arisen in obedience to the voice of the storm mountains high, frothing, dashing, tumbling—here in deep gulfs, there in surging gigantic waves. It revelled in its destructive and awful power.

Woe be to any unlucky ship that attempted to breast such a gale!

The trio thought of this as they gazed out from the window of the hut.

"Look! look!" cried Jack, pointing with trembling finger to a dark speck on the distant horizon.

"A ship! a ship!—English by the look of it—battling with the waves. Her masts are broken, her sails flap in the breeze, she will be wrecked!"

Both Tom and Captain Hastings strained their eyes to discern the vessel.

"Yes, yes," said the former. "I see her, she is doomed, sure as a gun; she can never live through this gale, and very likely will strike on one of the reefs."

His prophetic words were almost instantly realised, for the next moment the doomed vessel was observed to quiver in every beam and timber, and with a loud crash, only drowned by the raging voice of the storm, she was hurled upon the reef.

Her hull remained entire, but the masts and rigging fell from their several situations, and the other parts of the unlucky vessel were severed to fragments.

The horror-stricken observers could just discern the unavailing attempts of those on board to put out their boats. Each went to pieces ere it could be launched. The floating spars and fragments of the hull were evidently the only hopes of the shipwrecked men.

While their doom was thus threatening them, they managed to form a raft, on which all contrived to get, and to which they clung with the proverbial tenacity of the drowning.

The reader need scarcely be told that this ship was that which contained Mabel and her father.

How little did Crusoe Jack suspect this fact as he witnessed the terrific scene. Suddenly a natural impulse led him to exclaim—

"Oh! Tom, for heaven's sake let us try and help them. Cannot we put out our boat, and try to reach them?"

"Useless, my boy—quite useless," replied the old sailor. "We should be knocked to pieces long before we could reach them. No. See, they are manning this raft. It is their only chance."

"Heaven have mercy upon them!" exclaimed Captain Hastings, who was much impressed by the scene before him.

"Amen to that," added Tom. "I know what it is myself. I can feel for them, though I cannot help them. That raft is being terribly knocked about, but if it can only keep together till the storm gives in a little, they may be able to get ashore."

The captain thought of the Seagull, and wondered whether the crew on the raft were destined to help him to set her afloat. He had felt a hope that a wreck might occur in order that this end might be gained, but he secretly reproached himself for his cruelty, when he saw all the horrors of the wreck before him.

It was an exciting scene. The raft seemed to have but little chance of keeping afloat for any length of time. Every moment the heavy waves threatened to dash it to pieces. But though it was tossed like a light shell on the crest of the waters, it still remained intact. This fearful position continued for more than an hour. We have described the situation of those who clung to the creaking raft, and have only to add that the signal they raised was instantly perceived by those on shore.

"See! they are signalling for help," cried Crusoe Jack, much excited. "We must—we will try to save them."

"The gale appears to have decreased a little," remarked the captain, "and they are slowly drifting out to sea. I think we may venture to put out a boat now."

As soon as these words were spoken, Crusoe Jack and Tom Starboard hastened to where their canoe was moored, and by the time they had got it ready, the gale had so far abated that they had strong hopes of prosecuting their adventure in safety.

Tom, Crusoe, and Captain Hastings, all got into the boat, each with a couple of oars, and they commenced breasting the surging waves, and steering towards the raft.

And this proved a more difficult task than they anticipated. Not only were they proceeding in the teeth of a very strong wind, but each wave threatened to overthrow their frail vessel. It was only by the most skilful guidance, the most careful balancing, that they contrived to keep it afloat.

Still the gale was visibly decreasing, and by the time they arrived within hail of the storm-tossed raft, the water was much smoother.

No pen can describe the joy of those on the raft at this rescue, nor the amazement and delight of Jack when he recognized in the fair countenance of the shipwrecked English girl the features of his beloved Mabel.

How astonishing it was that Providence had destined them to meet again under such circumstances!

But Jack did not think of this, he only thought of the joy of meeting and saving her; and as he lifted her into the boat he clasped her to his heart in an outburst of pride and thankfulness.

Mabel, her father, and several more soon found room in the boats, which, after landing them, returned to take the remainder.

———

CHAPTER VII.

THE SHIPWRECKED PARTY. — EXPLANATIONS.—MR. MEREDITH'S STORY.—JACK IS TOLD THE SECRET OF HIS BIRTH.—MABEL AND JACK MAKE THEIR VOWS OF AFFECTION.

In half an hour the whole of the shipwrecked party were safely on shore, exhausted by the perils and anxieties they had undergone, but otherwise uninjured.

The rescued party consisted of Mr. George Meredith, who commanded the ship, his daughter, about six officers, and forty seamen—just the sort of crew that Captain Hastings required for the Seagull—and so he thought as he scrutinized their appearance.

The danger over, the party next proceeded to the work of raising two or three cabins to shelter them during the coming night.

A glass of spirits served out to all by Tom Starboard, out of the stores of the stranded Seagull, inspired the seamen with renewed strength for this work.

A thick clump of trees greatly assisted them in the erection of these structures, and in a very short space of time, with the assistance of tools, tarpaulin, and other articles from the stranded ship, they had succeeded in making a very efficient shelter—a kind of extension to the captain's hut.

Meanwhile Jack, Mabel, and George Meredith had found an opportunity of giving mutual explanations to each other.

Nothing could equal Mr. Meredith's surprise at recognizing Jack. It was not until the rescue was over that he had an opportunity of scrutinising him closely, and when he did so, he exclaimed—

"Is it possible that you are the gallant boy who has now twice rescued my daughter from a watery grave?"

"I am, sir," replied Jack; "and very glad I am to have been the means of doing her and you such service."

"But how did you get away—how came you here? We thought you were drowned off the Cornish coast. Do tell me all about it!" said the astonished Mr. Meredith.

Jack, as briefly as possible, related all the numerous perils and adventures he had met with since his being picked up by Hugh of the Red Hand.

Mr. Meredith and his daughter both listened with breathless interest and astonishment to the recital of Jack's adventures.

"And now, sir, it is my turn to ask you," said Jack, "about all that has happened to you, and how you came to be wrecked in this unfrequented region?"

"Of adventures," replied Mr. Meredith, "I have few to tell of any importance. I was ruined by a commercial speculation, and was obliged to leave England for Chili, leaving my daughter to the care of a Mrs. Miller; and Madge Collins, the wrecker's wife, since your disappearance has contrived—but now is not the time to speak of that. I will only allude to myself. I went to Chili, found my brother, as I expected, very prosperous, and, more than that, he received me with more kindness than, in fact, I ever expected—people change so when you are long separated from them.

"I told him my situation, and he was generous enough to offer me a share of his large coffee and sugar plantation, but this I refused, and merely desired to enter his service in a subordinate capacity. He made me the chief overseer on the estate, and even in this position my prospects were very hopeful. The trade continued prosperous, and the crops abundant. I lived frugally, saved as much as possible for the sake of my darling daughter, to whom I was enabled to send frequent instalments, which that odious woman, the wrecker's wife, fraudulently appropriated.

"I saved money, and speculated on my own account very successfully; in short, I amassed in a few years a comfortable independence.

"One cause of my anxiety was, that I left off receiving letters from Mabel—the cause being, as I now know, that they were intercepted.

"About three months ago I set sail for England to see Mabel, and bring her back with me to South America.

"I found her just about to fall a victim to the vilest machinations on the part of the grandson of the wrecker's wife; all these particulars Mabel will be able to tell you better than I; and, having no ties in England, I set sail immediately for Chili with my daughter, and, after a voyage hitherto prosperous, have been, as you see, wrecked on this island."

"And now you are again ruined," said Jack.

"Not quite," replied Mr. Meredith. "I have, it is true, lost this good ship the Silver Star, with a splendid cargo of English goods; but I am thankful to say that I have still a considerable part of my property safely entrusted to a London banker, and another portion left with my brother in Chili.

"How like you grow to your father," added Mr. Meredith, as he gazed admiringly on the handsome form and countenance of the youth. "By-the-bye, he is not returned from India, and I fear he is no longer living."

"My father!" faltered Crusoe, in extreme amazement.

"Yes, my boy, your real parent is no other than Sir James Moreland, of Moreland Hall. He is a naval officer, whose homeward-bound vessel was lured to destruction by Darrell Collins, the wrecker. All perished except you and your father, who was picked up by a pirate lugger. He believed you dead, until he heard evidence to the contrary in India, and returned home to claim you. By an unfortunate coincidence you ran away just at the time of the inquiries, and as you didn't appear again, it was for the second time supposed that you had perished."

"Can this really be true, sir?" asked Jack in great excitement.

"Perfectly true, I can assure you."

"Then my father is still alive, and I may yet be restored to him?" asked Jack, eagerly.

"He is in India, if anywhere," returned Mabel's father, "under an assumed name, though; believing you dead, he said he had nothing to live for, and has sought death on the battle-field."

"And Collins, Madge, and Jasper—what of them?" asked our hero.

"It is too long a story to tell you now. Ask Mabel when she has recovered from the exhaustion and excitement of this terrible day. She will tell you the sad tale of her wrongs."

Eager as our hero was to know all, he forbore, as desired, to question the agitated and delicate English girl, who had so recently undergone all the horrors of shipwreck. Still, he could not resist the temptation of again seeking a few words of conversation with the object of his love.

Accordingly, he took an opportunity, when they were unobserved, to say to her—

"Mabel, are you not glad to see me again, after this long separation?"

"Oh! how glad, and how thankful!" she replied, her beautiful face flushing with earnestness. "I have often thought of you, and lamented your death; and now to find you here alive, and to be thus rescued by you, it is like a dream."

"You are not in love with Percy, now?"

"Percy? Never. He is unworthy of all affection. Think how he slandered and insulted you, when your birth is even more noble than his own."

"I will prove myself worthy of it, if only for your sake," said Jack, proudly. "Mabel, I fervently hope and believe that better days are in store for us."

As he encircled the slender waist of the fair English girl with his arm, the arm that had twice saved her from a watery grave, he felt a degree of pride and happiness which neutralised all the perils he had undergone.

What would he **not** undergo for her sake?

CHAPTER VIII.

A GENEROUS PROPOSAL—THE EXPEDITION TO THE WRECK—THE TREASURE—A TERRIBLE POSITION—NO CHANCE FOR LIFE—SAVED AT LAST.

THE next morning rose fine and cloudless, no trace appeared of the terrific weather of the preceding day. The sea was unruffled, and smiling in placid beauty, and a delightful breeze stirred the fragrant leaves.

The first thing now to be done was to carry out Captain Hastings' grand project of raising the stranded Seagull, and getting her once more afloat and in fighting order. His scheme was heartily supported by Mr. Meredith, whose men readily undertook to engage in the work.

Captain Hastings and Mabel's father soon became great friends; both were true-hearted English gentlemen, and gallant sailors.

The captain proposed to share with Mr. Meredith the stranded ship and her cargo, but the latter declined this generous offer, saying he only wanted a passage to Chili for himself and his daughter.

Still, he thought regretfully of his own destroyed vessel, as he gazed over the broad surface of the waters, on which fragments of the Silver Star could be discerned floating about in many parts.

Then it was that an important idea first struck him.

"There are the remains of my poor ship," he said," and they seem to be drifting ashore with the incoming tide. "The hull is higher out of the water than I imagined she would be, perhaps there is still some of the cargo left in her. I tell you what, Jack, you had better take out your boat, and see if anything is to be rescued from the wreck, and I'll promise you that whatever you find, of whatever value, shall be yours exclusively."

Jack could not but be grateful for this generous offer. It had all the excitement of chance about it, too. Whatever he found on board the Silver Star should be his. He thanked Mr. Meredith, and proposed to set out at once.

"Tom, you must go with me," he said, "and you shall have a share of whatever we get. Who knows how rich we may become after all this!"

Tom consented, and in a short time they set out in their pit-pan, which had already done so much service.

It was large enough to contain a tolerable amount of treasure-trove; and, impelled by Jack and Tom, it flew over the smooth sea as swiftly as an arrow.

The mutilated remnants of the Silver Star lay firmly embedded on the coral reef, about half a mile from the shore.

The hull was still almost entire, but careened over in such a position that it seemed impossible either to get upon her deck, or get in at any of the portholes.

Her case was far more hopeless than that of the Seagull. Any attempt to move the hull would inevitably send it to pieces, and all that could be done was to try and make some sort of entrance into the part above water, and see if any of the cargo could be got at.

"Look, Tom! What a wonderful sight!" cried Crusoe Jack, as they glided over the calm, clear waters, and steered their way among the beds of coral. "All kinds of beautiful flowers, of all colours, growing beneath the sea. I never thought coral islands were so beautiful."

"Yes, my lad, they are one of the wonders of Nature, which everybody admires that sees them. They are what are called zoophytes—that is, half plants and half animals, half alive and half dead. The captain's steward, on my first voyage in this part of the Pacific, was what they call a naturalist; he knew all the names and properties of the plants; and used to tell us all about them. That rose-coloured one is a sea anemone; and those green ones, growing smoothly and thickly, are tubiporas astreas. Then there are meandrinas and cariophyllas, and a lot more names that I can't recollect. These high trees, growing out of the reef, are gorgonias and isis, and very beautiful they look, don't they?"

"Yes," replied Jack, "and see what a number of starfish and crabs, and sea creatures of all kinds, live among the plants, and many of the flowers seem to grow in the shapes of animals."

"There isn't a shape hardly that they don't grow into," replied Tom Starboard. "It's one of those wonders of creation that nobody can't exactly explain. But, see here, my lad, we're close on to the hull. Poor thing, she's been regularly knocked out of all shape. I'm afraid there ain't much to be got out of her."

It did, indeed, seem a hopeless prospect, for the ship's massive hull was not more than about twelve feet out of water in the highest part, and, to add to this, the tide was every moment making her deeper. The hull was so disposed, that her entire length was equally covered by the water, and consequently the upper row of portholes were all dry and visible. These portholes were all closed, but it was very doubtful whether those beneath the water had been able to resist its entrance, so far as to prevent the ship from being entirely filled. A network of broken rigging, spars, planks, and water-casks, floated around the wreck, and rendered it a matter of extreme difficulty to steer the canoe in safety to the hull.

Tom and Jack secured the boat to the main-chains of the vessel, just beneath the row of open portholes.

"Now, if I can climb up the hull, and break that

porthole window," said Jack, "we shall be able to see how far she is flooded, and then we shall know if it's likely there's anything to be got."

Jack found this a matter of no great difficulty. With the assistance of Tom, he climbed up and broke open the porthole, which was large enough to give them admittance. Cautiously looking around him, he found, to his surprise, the chief cabin entirely free from water; and, though all the interior furniture was knocked to pieces, a large chest of books, which stood in one corner, was quite uninjured.

Jack's eyes glistened as he gazed on this. If he could only reach that chest, he felt certain of a good reward for his trouble.

"All right, Tom!" he shouted, as he dropped carefully into the cabin. "She's wonderfully water-tight, considering what she's gone through. Here's a chest, and I will break it open, and hand you out the contents."

Full of eager anticipation, he made his way to the chest, and, placing his stout cutlass beneath the lid, had a wrench with all his strength.

For a long time the locks resisted all his efforts. At length, however, it opened, and his exertions were rewarded by a considerable quantity of all sorts of valuable property—money, jewels, plate, arms, rich wearing apparel, flashed before his eyes. He was rich at last. His eyes glistened with pleasure, and his hand trembled with excitement, as he proceeded to take possession of the wealth.

He almost completely emptied the locker of its contents, and placed them in a heap on the floor of the cabin.

Then he was about to hand them out to Tom, when he came across a beautiful miniature of Mabel.

His attention was arrested; he gazed long and intensely at the beloved face, forgot all around him, even the ominous sounds of the rising waves, thundering against the side of the wreck.

These sounds grew and increased. Jack knew what they portended. The tide was coming up, and the vessel would soon be flooded.

Unless he was quick in securing his prize, there would be the most pressing danger.

Still, impelled by some irresistible impulse, and imprudent as it was, Jack determined to seek the other cabins. He, accordingly, opened the door of the chief cabin, and proceeded with some difficulty up the hatchway, which was closed.

The vessel had begun to lurch and rock terribly. Jack could scarcely maintain his balance up the steep steps.

At length he opened the hatchway.

Just as he did so, a tremendous rush of water, pouring on to the deck, poured down the hatchway his very face. The ship seemed to give a terrific lurch, and sank more deeply into the waters.

Jack staggered back almost insensible from the shock of the waters. He knew he could not face the incoming sea, nor keep his balance on the almost perpendicular deck. So he half fell, half staggered back into the chief cabin, which was now flooded deep with unceasing and angry waves.

He tried in vain to shut the main hatch. He felt that his doom was imminent. If he stayed a moment longer, even to possess himself of the contents of the chest, he would be inevitably lost; even now, he doubted if there was any chance of escape.

How aggravating it was to have to relinquish his prize, when it was just within his grasp!

But a dreadful death stared him in the face. Rushing to the porthole, he mounted a broken stool, and attempted to climb through. One bound, and he would have been safe, but he suddenly lost his hold, and, falling backwards, struck his head against the heavy leg of the overturned table. He fell backwards on the floor, amid the rising and angry flood.

The fall had stunned Jack. He lay with his head bleeding, and his consciousness, for some moments at least, entirely left him.

Never did his death seem so near. Where was the hope of escape? Where the chance of rescue?

Tom Starboard saw Crusoe's accident, and his heart sank with a fearful presentiment. Was he to lose the gallant boy—whom the old sailor loved like a son? No, he would try to save him, even if he himself perished in the effort.

He sprang through the porthole. He saw Jack lying senseless, scarcely more than his head above the flood of water.

But there was no hope of rescuing the brave boy by bringing him through the porthole, especially as he was now insensible, and could not help himself. Tom felt quite unequal to the task, and knew that if he attempted it, both would inevitably perish.

The hatchway was the only chance, if he could once mount the sloping deck and force his way down the hatchway, he could carry Jack up the cabin stairs.

The resolution was taken in a moment. Collecting all his strength, Tom sprang over the bulwarks, and, with the utmost difficulty, got to the hatchway, through which the waves were now pouring with terrific force.

At the peril of his life, the brave old tar contrived to descend the cabin stairs; and, as he did so, the ship gave another shock and lurched yet more fearfully on the larboard side.

There was not a single moment to be lost.

Rushing with almost supernatural speed, Tom made his way to the chief cabin.

There lay Jack, still unconscious and bleeding, and in momentary peril of being drowned, without a chance of saving himself from a dreadful fate.

Tom seized the prostrate form of the gallant Crusoe in his still strong arms, and without even a look at the half-flooded and unattainable treasure chest, he fled with him up the steep stairs and again on to the sloping deck, battling all the way with terrific waves.

How he accomplished this difficult feat Tom could never afterwards satisfactorily explain; he supposed that his excitement gave him extra strength.

In a few moments he had dropped the now-reviving form of Jack into the boat, and was soon sitting beside him, supporting his bleeding head tenderly in his arms.

"Where am I? What is this? Am I safe?"

said Crusoe, opening his eyes and gazing at Tom bewilderingly.

"Yes; safe, lad, at last, God be thanked. But you had the nearest touch of death that I ever saw. Oh, good heavens! what an awful moment this has been!"

"In all my time I never passed such a fearful five minutes as this last has been!"

And the rough but kindly old sailor wiped the perspiration from his heated brow.

"Are you hurt, my lad?" he resumed, gazing anxiously at the pallid countenance of our hero.

"No—very little," Jack answered. "I was stunned for the time, and have cut the side of my head, and it is still very painful; but by binding this handkerchief round it, it will soon bring it all right again."

"How wet I am!"

"Why, dear Tom, you have saved me from a frightful death!"

"It was only my duty, my lad, and thank Providence that I was able to do it. I was an old fool to allow you to get upon the wreck at all, as I might have known that in that position there was no safety in her for a moment."

"We shall lose our prize, Tom."

"What signifies the treasure in comparison to your life?

"No; it is useless to try any more for that or any other portion of the ship's cargo. The hull is thoroughly flooded, and will certainly go to pieces in the next gale, or in a short time be covered and imbedded in the new coral beds which the insects are daily raising."

"What, can they raise the coral beds so quickly?" asked Jack.

"Yes, lad; in Brazil I have seen boats that have been moored ashore become so covered with the fungus in a few weeks as completely to disappear!"

"How wonderful!" cried Jack; "and what will be the effect if this happens to the remains of this vessel?"

"Only that we shall have some chance, at low tide, of digging out some of the remains of the cargo. There seems very little washed overboard."

There was indeed so little of value, apart from the hull, that beyond two or three water-casks, and a small keg of spirits, the two companions got little to repay them for the labour and peril they had undergone.

CHAPTER IX.

WATCHING THE WRECK—TERRIBLE SUSPENSE—SAFE TO THE SHORE—THE RAISING OF THE SEAGULL ACCOMPLISHED—A BANQUET AT JACK'S IN HONOUR OF THE EVENT—JACK AND TOM ARE MADE THE HEROES OF THE DAY.

ALL on shore watched the departure of the boat containing Tom and Crusoe with feelings of pleasure.

None grudged the gallant boy, who had been so instrumental in saving so many lives, whatever he could rescue from the wrecked ship.

On the contrary, all wished him the utmost success in his search.

But when, watching from the shore, they saw the peril of Crusoe when he disappeared in the hull, the hearts of all sank with fear, and all gazed horror-stricken at what they considered the inevitable doom of the gallant boy.

Poor Mabel clung trembling to her father's arm, turned as pale as death, and uttered a scream of terror.

Mr. Meredith bitterly reproached himself as the primary cause of the catastrophe.

"Fool that I was to send him on such a dangerous errand," he exclaimed, "and to have been the cause of his death. I shall never forgive myself for it."

"He is not quite lost, for Tom Starboard is rescuing him," cried Captain Hastings, who was gazing anxiously through his telescope.

"Yes—yes! the brave fellow will manage it. Look! up he comes through the hatchway, with the boy in his arms; and now he is in the boat again. How glad I am!"

The whole party of spectators gave a sigh of relief.

When Tom and Crusoe landed, they were overwhelmed with mingled questions, praises for their bravery, congratulations on their escape, and consolation for their disappointment.

"We've proved it's not much use, sir, in trying to get much out of the wreck of your ship," said Tom. "It ain't half so hopeful a scheme as raising the Seagull."

"You are right," replied Mr. Meredith; "and yet poor Jack may not quite despair of his fortune. As soon as we've got any boats fit for it, we'll have another try. In a few days the hull is sure to go to pieces, and then there will be more chance."

"As to the Seagull," added Captain Hastings, "I propose we all set to work at once. We've inspected the wreck, and come to the conclusion that there will be no difficulty about it; and this is as good a day as any for beginning the attempt."

So the greater part of the rescued crew got to work on the stranded vessel, according to the plan which Captain Hastings had arranged and was prepared to superintend.

It was a period of great excitement and pleasing anticipation.

All felt interested in the gallant vessel, which was their only prospective means of leaving the island.

No alteration had taken place in the position of the vessel. She still lay between the two jagged pieces of the rock, which at low tide were above the water line, and which still held her as firmly as a vice.

Added to this, a considerable mass of the coral formation had risen around her, and further imbedded her in this undesired resting-place.

To dig away and remove these incumbrances, and get the vessel high and dry on shore, so that she could be more easily repaired, was the chief object of the shipwrecked crew.

In order to do this, it was necessary to erect a kind of dock, or wooden support, to sustain her weight.

It occupied a whole day for the ship's company to saw down the trees and fix this construction in its place, and to dig away the rocky soil in which the body of the vessel was imbedded.

CRUSOE JACK STOOPED TOWARDS THE BODY OF OLD TOM STARBOARD.

When they had done so, however, they were well repaid for their trouble with complete success. The vessel was in a far better condition than they had expected.

By means of a framework of blocks, similar to those used in dockyards, laid beneath her keel, and ropes fastened to the sides of the deck, the Seagull was placed in such a position that she could be easily repaired.

A wooden breakwater, built along the beach before her, kept the vessel high and dry.

The carpenters, riggers, and other workmen, from the late Seagull, examined the vessel closely, and affirmed that it could soon be got ready for the sea.

She was emptied of all her cargo, including the late captain's treasure, the secret of which was entrusted by Tom only to Captain Hastings and Mr. Meredith. All these things were safely removed to the buildings the sailors had erected on the island.

The second day after the wreck of the Silver Star, when the Seagull had been thus rescued from the power of the waves, Captain Hastings presided at the general supper-table in the principal hut, and, indeed, it was a complete feast, in honour of the desirable event.

Every sailor received a double allowance of grog, and several bottles of wine were opened for the officers of the party.

Added to the preserved provisions from the wreck, a large amount of the game and wild fruits, with which the island abounded, had been obtained by Jack, Tom Starboard, and Captain Hastings, and were added to the general store.

Everybody was in high spirits, and our hero, sitting beside his beloved Mabel, with his arm slyly thrown around her waist, felt a thrill of pleasure in looking upon the brave and happy faces congregated around him.

Captain Hastings made a speech on the occasion, of which the following were some of the chief points—

"Now, my friends, I am glad to say that we have successfully accomplished our difficult task, and we have cause to be grateful to Providence, for we have a fine vessel, which will soon be ready for sea, a brave and efficient crew, and provisions to last us to the next port. Now, as I am thoroughly satisfied with the officers Mr. Meredith has brought with him, and as he has resigned all command over them to me, I must beg them not to be jealous if I give promotion to two persons fully worthy of it. I allude to Crusoe Jack and Tom Starboard, two of the staunchest and bravest sailors that ever went a voyage, and I design to give Jack the post of first lieutenant in my ship, and make Tom my steward. I only hope it may be their good fortune at some future time to rise still higher in the service. My friends, I hope you are satisfied with my decision?"

All expressed their approval in the heartiest terms.

"Well, then, suppose we all give a cheer, and drink a toast. I say—here's health to Tom Starboard and Crusoe Jack!"

All stood up, and responded to this toast with the most deafening applause.

Our two heroes were quite overwhelmed by the honours done them; and Mabel's eyes were lit up with a ray of pride and pleasure at Jack's good fortune.

Crusoe felt it incumbent upon him to return thanks, which he did in a capital speech, which gained fresh applause.

Old Tom next stood up, and spoke in his rough-and-ready sailor style, but in a manner they all appreciated and welcomed.

That night Jack's sleep was haunted by ambitious dreams, which this event had called up. He thought himself the commander of a splendid ship, with a brave crew under him, and Tom as his first lieutenant, cruising about among the rich islands of the Pacific, gathering cargoes of the most precious merchandise, and chasing and capturing no end of pirates and slavers.

Above all, his dream brought before him a beautiful face—that of Mabel—who, as his beloved bride and an ocean queen, accompanied him in his hour of triumph.

Blissful dreams! golden aspirations! would they ever be realised?

CHAPTER X.

THE LAUNCH OF THE SEAGULL—THE TRIAL TRIP—JACK AND MABEL—MADGE COLLINS'S LETTER—TOM STARBOARD'S AMERICAN ADVENTURE—BUFFALO HUNTING—A PRAIRIE ON FIRE.

IN about ten days the Seagull had been completely rigged, repaired, and re-decorated; and everybody confessed that she looked like a new ship.

It was a time of great rejoicing when she was launched from the temporary dock, and glided out into the calm blue sea, her white sails sparkling in the golden sunlight.

All the gallant sailors on the island—and none more loudly than Jack and Tom Starboard—raised a joyous shout as the flag of old England was once more fixed at her mast-head.

The Seagull took a sort of trial trip around the islands, and as great care had been taken to ascertain the position of all the rocks and shoals which abounded among them, she was steered safely into the deeper waters.

Captain Hastings, Jack, Mr. Meredith and his daughter, and several of the officers and men formerly belonging to the Silver Star, were on board the barque, and the trip proved entirely satisfactory.

The Seagull's sailing properties were ascertained to be of the first order.

Nobody felt more happy than our friend Jack, now first lieutenant, you must remember, under Captain Hastings, as, while the vessel sped swiftly along the smooth sea, studded with the "Thousand Islands," he stood looking over the bulwarks, with his own fair Mabel beside him.

The happiness of both was complete, and past sorrows were for the time forgotten.

"Mabel," said Jack, smiling, "these, as I've told you before, are the 'Thousand Islands.' I don't say I've counted them; but Tom Starboard calls them so. Now, my title, mind—perhaps I haven't told you—is 'King of the Thousand Islands,' and these are my dominions."

"Then I must do homage to your majesty," replied Mabel, as with a sweet smile she dropped a graceful curtsey to him. "Hail! King of the Thousand Islands!"

"But you know, Mabel, if I am king, you must be the queen, while we are here; but soon we shall have to leave our dominions, which I am getting rather tired of, I tell you, and start off on a long and glorious cruise.

"But now, Mabel, I declare that what with my being constantly employed on the Seagull, and one thing or another, we have not found time to relate the whole of each other's adventures.

"So I'll begin by telling you about how I came to be King of the Thousand Islands."

He related the whole of the adventures he had met with since his departure from England, how he was left purposely on the desert island, and how, like Mazeppa, he passed through many dangers, only to be raised to a throne.

He then spoke of Tom Starboard in the warmest terms, as he always did, and of all that had come to pass since he had been the chief of the Azmotas.

He felt some hesitation in speaking of the Indian maiden; but he could assure Mabel that his heart had been throughout constant to its earlier affection.

In return, Mabel related to him all that she had undergone by the cruelty of Madge Collins, and the malignant craftiness of Jasper.

When she came to describe how the wrecker's hump-backed grandson had endeavoured to carry her off, and her brutal treatment by him and the two hired ruffians, Jack involuntarily clasped his hand, and longed to have the dastard before him, that he might wreak summary vengeance.

The day previous to the trial voyage, Jack had confided to Mr. Meredith the secret of Madge Collins's letter, which Tom had found in the bottle on board the Seagull.

Mr. Meredith had pondered deeply over the matter; he could easily see the plots that were going on against our hero's inheritance; and he expressed his intention of communicating, as soon as he arrived in Chili, with a friend in England who would keep watch over Madge, the lawyer, and Jasper, and keep him informed of all that occurred.

He also said he would try and communicate with Jack's father in India, and inform him all about his son's circumstances.

While Mabel and Jack were thus conferring together, Tom Starboard came up to them, and Jack requested him to entertain them with one of the stories of his past adventures.

"Did I ever tell you," asked Tom, of any of the adventures I met with when I travelled across the North American prairies?"

"I don't think you did, Tom; and I'm sure I should like to hear them."

"Well, I had a nigh touch of being gored to death once by a buffalo in New Mexico, when me and a lot of other fellows, some English and Yankees, others half-breeds, and the rest Indians, were hunting them.

"Did you ever see a real live buffalo, Jack?"

"Never; but I guess they are rather awkward customers to deal with."

"You're right; the one I speak of was a particularly awkward customer. You know that the buffaloes, or American bisons, abound in vast herds in all the prairies in the west of the United States and in the north of Mexico. As many as 20,000 at a time have been known to congregate in one vast herd in the wild valley of the Mississippi. They are tremendous fellows, their fore-part covered with shaggy mane, like a lion's; with a large hump, and short horns, which can, however, do some damage, as you shall see from my story.

"We were crossing the large prairie between Fort Arbuckle and Walnut Creek, in a party of about twenty, seven of whom were my former shipmates (I was then in the common merchant service), about as many Yankees and half-caste hunters, and the remainder Indian guides. We had travelled three days without seeing any signs of buffaloes, until one of the Yankees, suddenly pointing out to a distant part of the prairie, exclaimed—

"'I'm darned if there ain't some buffaloes—a whole heap of 'em—coming down upon us. That dark streak that is growing larger every minute is a herd of buffaloes. What I propose is, that we ride on one side to get out of their way, and when they have passed, charge in amongst 'em from behind, and take 'em by surprise. When this is done, the critters are so skeered that they afford excellent sport.'

"We followed the Yankee's advice, retired to some distance, let the buffaloes pass us, and then we commenced our sport.

"All of us were eager for a buffalo adventure—every gun was well loaded and cocked, and everyone disputed for the honour of firing the first shot. The fact is, about a dozen of us fired at once; but, strange to say, we didn't kill a single buffalo.

"The herd was comparatively a small one, being a sort of advance-guard of the immense body that was to follow.

"They were evidently scared by the shots we had fired, and moved off with all the rapidity they were capable of.

"We prepared for a regular buffalo hunt in the Indian fashion, which is, properly, to kill them with arrows; but though only the Indians had these weapons, we thought we could do equal execution with our rifles.

"In this some of us, and myself especially, proved to be greatly mistaken.

"As soon as we came up to the herd, the Indians made a sudden rush into the midst of them, and with spears, in most cases, piercing the hides of their destined victims, and wounding them severely.

"This made them furious, and they rushed upon their attackers with such violence that it was only by the agility of their well-trained steeds that the Delawares escaped their vengeance.

"One poor fellow, named Arrowfoot, a young chief, was frightfully wounded in the encounter.

"It was a wild and stormy scene; the herd was completely dispersed, and rushed about madly in all directions.

"The Indians did great execution among them, and so did the rest of the party with their rifles; but where they missed—and you may judge that in such a scene of confusion it was impossible to take a good aim—or but slightly wounded the animals, they found themselves closely pursued by the infuriated beasts.

"That was just my case. I had shot—with first-rate aim, as I thought—a splendid buffalo. My bullet, I imagined, had gone straight to his heart.

"But I was mistaken. It had just grazed his skin enough to make him furious.

"He turned round, but I had by this time loaded again.

"Once more I fired, but the ball missed, and I had to port my helm and run, the buffalo after me with all his speed.

"A couple of dogs, belonging to one of the Delaware chiefs, had got in among the herd of buffaloes, and they gave chase to this particular one.

"This did not help me in the least; for, with the dogs after him, the buffalo went quicker than ever, and chased me till I was out of breath, and felt every moment that I must fall, and submit to my fate.

"At length I reached a tree that afforded good

foothold for climbing. I sprang up it like lightning, and seated on one of the branches, out of the buffalo's reach, I felt that I was out of danger.

"The animal waited some time for his vengeance, bellowed for me to come down; but I brought him down instead.

"As soon as I was able to load my rifle, this buffalo was my prize.

"I cut up the carcase and placed it on my horse, as soon as I could catch that animal, who had scudded away frightened when the encounter commenced.

"The rest of the party were, on the average, pretty fortunate, considering that some got wounded and others had been obliged to run for it, like I did.

"That was the first taste I had of buffalo hunting, one of the most dangerous sports in the world, I should say."

"I only hope I may have the chance of trying it," remarked Crusoe. "But I say, Tom, did you ever see a prairie on fire?

"What sort of a sight is it?"

"Sight! why a magnificent one, to be sure; better than all the fireworks that were ever let off put together.

"We saw a prairie on fire a short time after my buffalo adventure; in fact, we nearly fell a prey to it.

"I shall never forget that adventure.

"We had encamped for the night in a sort of hollow or valley, edged in with steep, barren rocks. The prairie above was covered with long, dry grass; but fortunately the valley was almost entirely bare of vegetation.

"We fixed our cattle in the corner, near the tents.

"None of us had thought of the dangers of fire, as there had been nothing that day to indicate it.

"Well, we went to sleep, and slept as soundly as only weary hunters can sleep.

"I had a beautiful dream about finding a stranded ship, with a heap of nuggets in her—enough to make me rich for life—when I awoke suddenly, and sat up in the tent.

"I looked around me drowsily; all was quiet, and everybody was asleep.

"Suddenly I began to become aware of a strong smell of smoke, and I heard the wind howling almost as loud as a hurricane.

"The thought of fire came into my head. I started up, looked out of the door of the tent, found our sentinel fallen asleep, and saw my suspicions verified.

"The prairie was evidently on fire, but the flames were a long way off, and, if we were careful, they need not alarm us.

"I ascertained that there was nothing that the fire could take hold of between the tops of the valley; and, as the faint gleams of the flames were just visible in the extreme distance, we might rest securely the remainder of the night. The wind, too, was luckily blowing against the flames, and I hoped it wouldn't change for some hours.

CHAPTER XI.

TOM'S PRAIRIE ADVENTURES CONTINUED—JACK AND MABEL IN PERIL—A TERRIFIC STRUGGLE FOR LIFE—IS SHE DEAD OR ALIVE?

"I WRAPPED myself in my Mexican cloak, re-lighted our fire, and began to keep watch without disturbing our sleeping sentinel. Excepting the loud wind, nothing was to be heard all through the solitary night. My sleepiness had left me, and so there I was, thinking of all the adventures I had been through in the course of my life.

"In about an hour the wind changed, and I could tell by the increased smoke that the flames were coming towards us. Then I began to hear in the distance the looming bellow of the buffaloes, and the prolonged howl of terrified wolves.

"These ominous sounds, occurring at that silent hour, had a most appalling effect upon me. I began to feel very uneasy, but still did not disturb my companions.

"The danger was still far off.

"Again the wind lulled, and all was quiet. I began to be sleepy again, and at last quite unconsciously dropped off.

"I was awakened in less than an hour, by a terrible confusion.

"There was a cry of 'Fire!' horrible at all times—and cattle tearing about, as if mad with fright.

"The fire was close upon us. It had been blown rapidly by the changing wind, and now there was no time to fly before the approaching danger.

"If we tried to escape by flight, the fire would overtake us, and our horses were so frightened that there was no depending on their being manageable.

"All we could do was to stay and take our chance.

"It wanted about two hours to daylight, and we calculated that before that the flames would have reached the valley.

"This proved to be the case.

"In less than an hour, the rush of the destroying element had brought it within a quarter of a mile.

"The smoke was unbearable.

"We bid fair to be suffocated.

"At last we could see the flames, the sheet of fire swallowing the high grass and trees on the head of the ravine, and sweeping around to the other side.

"The atmosphere was hot to suffocation. The smoke was almost enough to stifle any one.

"Showers of sparks were hurled into the valley, and could only be warded off by having all combustible articles covered with damp blankets or canvas.

"These fires, I must tell you, are very frequent on the prairie. Most of them are accidental, and when the grass is very dry the least thing sets it on fire; but sometimes the Indians set it on fire on purpose to burn down the old grass, that new and better may spring up.

"But how it was caused didn't matter to us then. There it was, and the question must be, should we escape it?

"We were certainly in an awful position, completely surrounded by a circle of flame, for the fire soon reached the other side of the valley.

"The crackling of the horrible flames, mingled with the cries of terror from numerous wild animals, all added to the horrors of the scene.

"Our horses plunged and neighed, and exhibited signs of terror, and as we lay beneath the wet tents, scarcely able to breathe, we felt that if this continued much longer we should die of suffocation.

"At one time we thought all was over with us.

"It was when a tongue of flame, creeping down a solitary tree at the other end of the valley, threatened to reach a clump of bushes.

"It would thus inevitably spread to some of our combustible articles.

"But we flew instantly to the tree, and continued for some time to throw water, obtained from the adjoining brook, upon it, which at last extinguished the flames.

"At length, after more than half an hour of fearful agony and suspense, the flames had passed us.

"All the vegetation around us had been totally destroyed, and, looking over the slope of the valley, we could see on one side an immense stretch of prairie, blackened and bare after the fiery ordeal, and on the other the triumphant flames pursuing their destructive course."

"Well, that was a position, Tom. It's a wonder to me you wasn't suffocated outright."

"To be burnt alive is what everybody considers the most horrible of all deaths. But dangers are very nice to talk about after you have escaped them."

* * * * * * *

A week after the trial trip was the time fixed for the starting of the Seagull on her voyage to Chili.

Captain Hastings intended on the way to visit the Sandwich Islands, and many ports on the coast of Central and South America.

This interval the party spent in a rather pleasant manner—shooting, fishing, boating, and making all kinds of expeditions, till they had thoroughly explored the wonders of the islands.

It was Crusoe's greatest delight to gather coral from the neighbouring reefs, while he fished in the clear waters, or with his gun took aim at the sea birds that skimmed the ocean's surface.

One beautifully brilliant day they were out upon an expedition of this kind.

Mabel in the bow of the boat—on which was fixed a small mast and sail—and Jack seated at the other end, waiting for a chance shot at some of the bright-coloured birds that flew tantalizingly around him.

Mabel had gathered a large heap of coral branches and beautiful marine flowers and plants, to which Jack had added a considerable quantity of game, so that the freight of their little craft was rather excessive.

They did not notice the circumstance until they were some distance from shore, when it became evident to Jack that, not only was the vessel weighed down very heavily by her freight, but she was slowly filling with water.

Jack started up, and ascertained the unpleasant fact at once.

She had sprung a leak.

How and where Jack could not ascertain.

Nor did it much signify.

The leak was there, and the question was, how to evade the impending danger?

"Over with the cargo!" cried Jack. "Mabel, I am sorry that you must sacrifice all your beautiful coral branches, and I must lose my spoil. The boat must be lightened, or we ——"

He did not finish the sentence, but continued hurling the cargo overboard, which much lightened and relieved the boat.

But the danger was imminent.

They were in deep water, a long distance from the shore of one of the most sequestered of the islands, far out of sight or hearing of any of their companions.

Notwithstanding all Jack's exertions in endeavouring to bale out the water, the boat was continually filling, and gradually sinking under them.

What was to be done?

Mabel turned pale, and could not repress her terror, even though Jack continued to exhort her to retain her courage and presence of mind.

She assisted him in baling out the water, but their joint efforts were of no avail.

Still, the water rose and the vessel sank.

Jack began to be seriously alarmed, not on his own account—for he could swim well—but on that of his companion, whose terror would, he felt assured, prevent her from using every effort to save herself.

It was very certain that the vessel could not hold out much longer.

The water had soon reached the seats, on one of which Mabel stood, clinging to the frail mast.

The incoming tide was agitating the sea, and every wave rose higher and higher over the sides of the doomed boat, which had soon become entirely submerged.

If they continued on it, they must sink with it.

Jack saw that a struggle for life had come.

He must try to swim ashore; and, what was still more difficult, save his companion.

Mabel, as he expected, had lost her presence of mind at this dreadful crisis.

She was completely overwhelmed by the perils of the terrible ocean.

She could only cling to him with the desperation of hopelessness, and implore him not to leave her to perish—a request that was needless.

Jack thought more of her danger even than his own.

Flinging off the upper part of his tiger-skin suit, so as to be more unimpeded, he instructed Mabel to support herself by clinging to his shoulder, and he would thus sustain her weight upon his back, which was the only means by which the rescue could be effected.

Thus loaded, he commenced to strike out into the deep water.

Jack felt that it would need all his strength, all his powers of endurance—strained, too, to the highest pitch—to support this double weight through the long stretch of water that intervened between him and the shore.

He prayed fervently for that strength.

He nerved himself for the task he had undertaken, and he was at first able easily to support the exertion.

Every stroke brought him nearer to shore, but how far off was that shore?

What a world of waters intervened between him and safety!

And how could he hope to struggle through it?

The water was comparatively smooth, and he could swim well, but the chance of ultimate escape was but faint.

Onward he struggled.

The shore seemed to recede as he advanced, and the weight he sustained seemed to increase every minute.

Mabel clung to him with all her strength, but the faintness of terror, the trembling of the arms that encircled his neck, made her doubt if she could long retain her position.

Would the shore never be nearer?

Jack could distinguish the beds of white coral, the gorgeous marine vegetation rising above it, and yet they seemed a terrible distance off.

His strength was beginning to fail him.

The terrific exertion was exhausting all his powers.

He drew his breath with great effort, and his arms seemed weighed down with heavy iron chains.

Still onward he pants and struggles.

Still, by mere force of will, he continues with giant strokes to cleave the waves that dash, and tumble, and foam around him, though luckily, by their weight and direction, they impelled him shorewards.

Once he thinks he must give up.

His strength is almost gone.

He seems to be carrying tons, and to be battling with monstrous waves.

But through the foam and spray he discerns, very near now, the welcome coral-bedded shore.

The sight gave him fresh exertion.

He urges himself onward.

Once more he collects all his failing strength, and again strikes out for the land.

In a few moments he has reached an outlying coral bed, and in a minute more he partly springs, is partly thrown by a gigantic incoming wave, on a bank of coral beyond.

Jack staggered forward inland, and then literally dropped from the sustained exertion.

The peril, the suspense, the anxiety were over, and they were safe.

He breathed a prayer of thankfulness; then knelt upon the ground beside the body of Mabel, who lay stretched out at full length beside him.

Heavens! how pale she was!

How cold were her hands!

How death-like the aspect of her closed eyes!

She seemed to have stopped breathing.

Her respiration was faintly discernible.

Could it be possible that she was dead?

The thought nerved Jack to fresh action.

He supported her beautiful head in his arms, and looked into her face.

A cold chill of horror came over him, and he gave vent to a loud cry of despair as he gazed upon her.

She had died, then, in his attempt to save her.

Terror, and the awful power of the waves, had proved her destruction.

And he was alone—bereft of the being he loved dearest of any on earth, and to whom all his visions of future happiness had pointed!

The thought was madness.

He pressed his hand despairingly to his heated brow, and looked around him with an expression of the utmost grief and anguish.

At this moment he was startled by a light footstep behind him.

He turned, and to his amazement beheld the form of Lela, the Indian Maiden.

CHAPTER XII.

JASPER'S DISAPPOINTMENT—THE PLEASURES OF LONDON LIFE—JASPER IS MADE A DUPE—HIS NEW FRIEND, THE CAPTAIN.

No pen can adequately describe the rage and mortification of Jasper Collins when, giddy and confused from the blow he had received, he rose to his feet, and staggered from the scene of the late conflict.

He looked out to sea. In the distance could be discerned the vessel that bore George Meredith's daughter far beyond the reach of his violence, and his base malignity.

He clenched his hand and ground his teeth in his baffled rage, as he saw that Mabel had escaped him.

He returned to the cottage of Madge Collins, bleeding and confused, and with fierce disappointment visible in his whole aspect.

"What! returned!" cried the wrecker's wife in surprise. "Jasper! What means this?"

"It means that she has escaped—that I am baffled, beaten, and insulted; it means that Mabel is far beyond my vengeance."

Old Madge looked disconcerted for a few moments, and then replied—

"But what matters it, after all? If her father has returned and taken her abroad, he will, this time, baulk you of your vengeance; but she will also be removed from any opportunity of injuring you."

"Curse her! she always hated and defied me!" cried Jasper through his set teeth.

"So did Crusoe Jack, and what followed? He was drowned, and you are in possession of his rich inheritance."

"I hope that Mabel and her father will meet with his fate," cried Jasper, in tones of devilish malignity.

"So do I, fervently," returned Madge. "They will thus be all removed from our path."

How little did this well-matched pair imagine that their vile wish would come true, but in a very different manner to what they desired.

But they did not suspect the truth, and when the news arrived that the Silver Star had gone down in the Pacific, they firmly believed that their fiendish hopes were realised.

*　　*　　*　　*　　*

The wrecker's grandson returned to the metropolis, and plunged wildly into its many dissipations.

Jasper Collins had now, as he imagined, reached the hour of his triumph.

The estates of Moreland were entirely in his possession. He lived in wealth and luxury, everyone around him rendered him the respect due to his exalted position.

His pride, his cowardice, his arrogant malevolence were all submitted to by those whose interest it was to truckle to him.

But in the midst of his wealth and splendour, his ceaseless round of vicious pleasures, the wrecker's crookback grandson was on the brink of a precipice.

The subtle lawyer had him in his power; had made Jasper sign away his whole future prospects, and was only waiting for an opportunity to ruin him, and for this purpose he had also employed efficient agents.

Various gamblers, swindlers, and scoundrels of every description shared Jasper's pleasures, and plundered him without remorse.

Jasper was every day sinking deeper into the slough of vicious courses, and hurrying on the road to ruin.

Among his boon companions was a certain Captain Crowther, a fine dashing young officer, and a thorough "man about town," who, as he himself expressed it, was "up to everything," and who seemed to take a special interest in Jasper.

He it was who first introduced the so-called Mr. Moreland to the gambling houses which he himself frequented, and to certain companions of his own stamp, who soon contrived to ensnare Jasper in their toils.

Jasper, cunning and malignant as he was, proved none the less capable of being imposed upon, being ignorant as he was of the manifold snares and pitfalls with which his circumstances surrounded him.

He thought Captain Crowther a true friend, believed all his stories about his adventures in India, etc., and bit by bit confided in him all his past life and present prospects.

The captain secretly exulted, he was not what he appeared, he had a double purpose in ruining Jasper.

The beginning of their acquaintance was as follows—

Jasper had formed a casual acquaintance with a very pleasant gentleman at the hotel where he was lodging.

This person, seeing that Jasper was new to London, determined to make a prey of him.

He accordingly contrived to introduce himself to Jasper, enter into conversation, and make himself so agreeable that he had no difficulty in persuading the wrecker's grandson to join him in a game of billiards.

They kept this up until Jasper found himself losing heavily, and then his companion proposed for him to retrieve his losses by a game at hazard.

So the dice and cards took the place of the balls and cues, and Jasper found himself winning.

Elated with success, he played deeply, and all the time his friend was plying him with champagne, and of course Jasper began to feel its effects.

Luck ran very high with the wrecker's grandson, until it suddenly changed, and he began to lose heavily.

Still he played on and on, and drank deeper and deeper, becoming mad with excitement.

He played deep into the night, until overcome with liquor and excitement, he lost all consciousness.

How he got to bed he could never remember.

The next day he of course felt the effects of his previous night's amusement in a splitting headache, and a feverish, wretched condition of mind and body.

He desired to leave the hotel.

Called for his bill, and wished to see his friend of the night before; but the latter had disappeared, leaving his account behind him for Jasper to pay.

He, however, found to his dismay that he had lost every farthing he possessed.

What should he do?

He had no means of procuring the amount, and he wished to proceed to his new estate without delay.

At this juncture, Captain Crowther, who also lodged at the inn, came forward, and offered to lend Jasper the money.

"I see how it is, sir," he said. "You have been swindled by that scoundrel I saw you with last night. It is a disgraceful thing that such rascals are allowed to go at large. I wonder, landlord, you are not more particular as to the guests you receive in your house."

"I am very much obliged to you, sir," remarked Jasper to the captain.

"Don't mention it. I am glad to be able to assist you. We ought to be friends. My name is Captain Edward Crowther, of the 17th Bombay Dragoons. I knew your father, the late Sir James Moreland, intimately in India."

Jasper winced and changed colour at this.

"Here is the money," pursued the captain, "and now, Mr. Moreland, I shall be happy to continue my acquaintance with you at any time you are in London, and shield you from any further attacks from swindlers."

Jasper repeated his thanks, and so their acquaintance began.

The more he knew of the captain, the more agreeable the latter proved, and Jasper was very much taken up with him.

At the railway station they parted, and Jasper invited the captain to come down and visit him Moreland Hall, at any time he liked.

"Ah, Jasper! if you had recognised that countenance, you would not have been so cordial!"

A look of gratified hate and malignant triumph up the captain's face as he left the station.

"So, my work is begun!" he murmured, "and it will be my own fault if I do not carry it out successfully."

CHAPTER XIII.

THE LAWYER AND HIS VISITOR—A STARTLING PRO-
POSAL—WHO THE CAPTAIN REALLY WAS—HIS
REMARKABLE HISTORY.

THE bland and agreeable Mr. Robert Twistem,
solicitor, was seated in his well-furnished parlour,
reposing himself after the labours of the day, when
who should call but Captain Crowther.

The captain sent in his card, writing on the
corner—"On urgent and private business."

The lawyer took the card in surprise, but at length
consented to receive the visitor.

The captain entered with a half-military salute,
and seated himself in a free-and-easy manner.

The lawyer scanned him intently. Where had he
seen that countenance before?

"Well, sir, what is your urgent business with
me?" asked Mr. Twistem.

"Entirely secret and confidential, Mr. Twistem.
In the first place, I know the whole affair of you
and Mrs. Collins and Jasper, from beginning to
end."

"The devil you do!" cried the lawyer, starting up
amazedly.

"And, moreover," proceeded the captain, "I know
what your own little game is now. What would you
say if I offered to assist you in it?"

"How assist me!" cried Mr. Twistem, in a bewildered tone.

"Well, look here. You want to ruin Jasper
Collins—known as Mr. Moreland. It's useless to
deny it. You want the estate, and you have it in
your power to get it eventually. Consequently, you
also want some skilful person to lead Jasper along
the road to ruin. Now, I'm a man of desperate fortunes; young as I am, I'm up to almost everything,
and I am an old and desperate foe to Jasper Collins.
My offer is this—I'll assist you, on certain terms, in
any way you desire."

Mr. Twistem pondered. The captain's assurance
astounded him. He didn't know whether to accept
the offer or not. The former course would be at
once acknowledging himself the scoundrel he was.
So he hesitated considerably.

"I can twist Jasper round my little finger," remarked the captain. "I'm ready to do anything
with him that will advance our scheme."

"Our scheme!"

The respectable lawyer did not like the term.
He was very much puzzled how to answer his
visitor.

"Sir," he said at length, "presuming that these
are really my views, how can you assist them? I
know what I'm about. I have the law on my side,
and as to Jasper, he'll quickly ruin himself, without
your kind offices."

"I'll help him in it, and I'll help you, and I'll
help myself, all at the same time," cried the captain.
"Mr. Twistem, it's no use trifling with me. I have
you a little in my power. I know your character,
I know your scheme, and I can betray you. We
had better be allies. I will be faithful to the
death, and help you to ruin Jasper, to outwit
Madge, and to gain the estates—for a consideration."

"And that is"—— faltered Mr. Twistem.

"One fourth of the estates—or its equivalent in
money," said the captain. "I will be your spy, your
agent, your jackal, in fact, and we'll share the
plunder. Strike the bargain, give me my instructions, and all will be well."

"I can't—I can't!" cried the lawyer, much
agitated. "What! a quarter of the Moreland estates—
an immense property! It won't do, sir. Who are
you that dare to make such a proposal?"

"Who I am does not matter; certainly as good a
man as yourself, Mr. Twistem. Will you accept my
offer?"

It took a long time and a great deal of persuasion
to agree to the proposal of this mysterious visitor;
but at length he was prevailed upon to do so, on the
latter agreeing to lower his terms.

At the demand of the captain, he promised to pay
to the latter, within the term of six years, a certain
large sum, under an agreement entered into between
them.

But, before he would sign this agreement, the
lawyer dashed down his pen, despairingly, and said—

"I am determined not to sign away all this property in the dark in this way. Who and what are
you? Tell me at once, and clear up this mystery."

The captain pondered. At length he said—

"You will swear not to betray my secret, as I will
not to betray yours?"

"Never!" cried the lawyer. "We'll both work
together, and be faithful to each other. What is
your real name?"

"Not quite unknown to you, Mr. Twistem. I am
Percy Meredith!"

"PERCY MEREDITH!"

The lawyer started from his chair in amazement.
He could scarcely believe his ears.

"What!" he cried, "Percy Meredith! It is not
possible. I cannot believe it!"

"It's perfectly true, though. Look in my face,
and, though I know it is somewhat altered, you will
be able to recognise it. Come, I'll prove it to you.
Let me relate my history."

A long private conversation occurred between the
lawyer and his new ally.

Secret negotiations were entered into.

The compact was ratified, and the "captain" departed, overjoyed at the success of his mission.

The reader may ask in surprise, "What can have
occurred to change the haughty young patrician,
Percy Meredith, into a swindler and a base adventurer?"

Alas! time and opportunity, coupled with depravity of heart, can work immense changes.

Let us review the history of the "captain," as he
called himself.

Henry Edgar Percy Meredith was the son of
George Meredith's younger brother, and through the
death of his parents had been left in the care of his
uncle, and brought up in the society of his lovely and
gentle cousin Mabel.

We know the disposition he early evinced, how
haughtily he behaved to Crusoe Jack, how incensed
he was at finding the despised fisher-boy was of
nobler birth than himself.

Percy was sent to a boarding-school soon after Jack's disappearance, and continued there until after his uncle's ruin and departure to Chili.

At this time he had grown up to be a fine, high-spirited youth, looking more than the three years difference between his age and that of Crusoe Jack, and far more embued than our hero with the wicked ways of the world.

Percy was distinguished at school for his haughty, tyrannical, and unruly disposition, and, as he advanced towards manhood, these characteristics increased.

Unknown either to his preceptor or his friends he fell into bad company and vicious courses, and found means of wasting his allowance in betting and gambling, and all kinds of intemperance.

Mabel had for a long time heard nothing of her cousin. She never loved him, and his affection for her seemed extinguished.

At length Percy was discovered in an attempt to appropriate some property belonging to his preceptor.

His evil courses were discovered, his depravity unmasked, and he was sentenced to be expelled the school.

The principal wrote to Mr. Meredith in Chili, acquainting him with Percy's delinquencies, and the just course he had taken, adding that he was willing to see to Percy's future welfare in any way Mr. Meredith might advise.

Long before any reply could be obtained, Percy saved his master the trouble of expelling him by escaping in the night, taking with him property to the amount of upwards of twenty pounds, belonging to the master and his family.

From that day Percy was not heard of, either by Mabel or her father.

Mr. Meredith soon afterwards returned to England, made all inquiries, but found them useless, and at length returned with his daughter on the memorable voyage we have described.

Entering the world at the early age of eighteen, already far advanced in depravity, Percy Meredith plunged into courses of the most reckless kind.

His money was soon gone, and unable to obtain any respectable situation, he was forced to enlist in the 18th —— foot, as a common soldier; but, after a few months, deserted.

From that time, under the name of Captain Crowther, and a host of other *aliases*, he subsisted by the most dishonest means.

He heard of his uncle's restoration to fortune, and his departure with Mabel; and too proud to make known his existence to them, he only nourished his envy in secret.

The supposed death of Crusoe Jack had given him great pleasure, and when the news reached him of the Silver Star's wreck, and his relatives' supposed death, he was still incapable of any deep regret.

Thus Percy continued his reckless courses, sometimes temporarily rich, sometimes in terrible straits, but always in fear of the law; wasting his years, his health, and his chances of reformation. He seemed entirely incorrigible.

At length, when he heard of Jasper's undeserved good fortune, he was filled with rage and envy, and resolved to injure the "wrecker's brat," and to obtain some of his wrongfully-gained inheritance.

He knew the character of Mr. Twistem, saw his aim, and began his designs by offering his assistance, as we have seen, to that gentleman.

Such was the curious position of these characters of our story. Snares and pitfalls surrounded the unlucky Jasper, the wrongful possessor of the estates, whose brave heir was battling with ocean perils in the far Pacific, while the unscrupulous lawyer and the once aristocratic Percy Meredith were plotting deeply to share the inheritance of CRUSOE JACK.

CHAPTER XIV.

THE INDIAN MAIDEN'S ADVENTURES—THE SACRIFICE —THE INVASION—A WILD PLAN OF ESCAPE.

YES, it was Lela, the Indian maiden, in all the splendour of her glorious tropical beauty, and with her lustrous eyes fixed earnestly on Crusoe and Mabel.

Jack started up, and in his surprise forgot for a moment his present position and his past perils.

"Lela!" he exclaimed, "is it indeed you? How came you here? For what purpose ——"

He paused, as with a warning gesture Lela advanced towards Mabel.

"Lela!" cried Jack, in tones of anguish. "See, my white sister whom I have saved from yon sinking boat is dead, and my grief is great for her loss."

The Indian maiden knelt down beside Mabel.

"The young Eagle is wrong, his sister is not dead," she murmured. "See, she breathes—is reviving."

As she spoke, Lela took from her girdle a skin bottle, containing some potent liquid, and placed it to the lips of the English girl.

Mabel gave a sigh, and started up.

Her eyes opened, and her cheek regained a portion of its wonted colour.

"Where am I? and who is this?" she murmured, faintly gazing around her.

"Safe, safe, at last, dear Mabel, and, thank heaven, not, as I thought, dead from your recent peril!" cried Jack, rushing towards her with an embrace of joy and thankfulness.

Lela started back, and a scarcely perceptible expression of jealousy arose upon her beautiful countenance.

"This is Lela, a maiden of the Aynoths," Jack said to Mabel, "who was very kind to me when I sojourned with that tribe."

"But who now asks forgiveness from the white chief," added Lela, "for the injury she sought to do him."

"Speak not of that, Lela," replied Jack, "but tell me how you came upon this island; and why have you left the united tribes of Aynoths and Macoushis, who must now be happy and powerful?"

"They are united and powerful, but not always happy," replied the Indian maiden. "They have fallen off from the state of brotherhood in which the Young Eagle strove to place them. Red Plume is gone, and now Oroma is chief of the tribe. Me he sought for his squaw, but I declined his attentions, for my heart is still with the Young Eagle.'

Jack looked much disconcerted, and Mabel much surprised at this announcement, but neither spoke.

"Oroma sought me," pursued Lela. "He continued persecuting me with his suit, but my heart is firm and faithful. Two days ago he visited me in my lonely wigwam. He strove to gain my consent to be his bride. I refused. He urged the greatness, the power I should gain by being allied to the chief of a powerful tribe. But I remained firm. His anger was roused at my obstinacy, and, in a sudden fit of passion, he called his men, and commanded them to seize me."

"'The daughter of the tribe,' he cried, 'has been bewitched by the white chief. She rejects my love, she despises the tribe who has reared her. She must die!'

"The priests of the tribe echoed his fierce determination.

"I was taken to the temple of the god of fire, in the middle of the island—the temple formed of ceiba trees, and beneath the mighty shades of the spreading banyan.

"To the post of sacrifice I was tied, and faggots of wood and dry leaves were placed beneath me.

"I felt that my fate would be horrible, but my resolution was still firm.

"Again Oroma charged me to change my resolve, and become his bride. Still I refused.

"'Fire the pile!' he cried fiercely to his men; 'and the great god of flame will accept the sacrifice!'

"A man approached with a burning brand, and inwardly I prayed for a speedy death.

"The pile was lit.

"The flame flashed forth, and the suffocating smoke arose.

"I had no hope, nor even desire for life; but death by burning is full of tortures.

"Still my heart remained firm.

"The flames rose, and crackled among the dry sticks.

"The smoke volumed forth in dense clouds.

"Just then, a loud and fearful cry resounded from the adjoining forest.

"The chief started up, and secured his spear and tomahawk.

"Every warrior grasped his weapon, and stood on the defensive.

"It was the war-cry of the terrible cannibals—the Masketees.

"They had invaded the island, resolved to conquer the Aynoths, and secure their possessions.

"Their number was immense—their ferocity unequalled.

"In a few moments, the Aynoth chief had called all his men to arms, and prepared to go forth and meet the foe.

"'Unbind the disobedient maiden,' he cried. 'The sacrifice must be delayed. She must not fall into the hands of the Masketees.'

"His orders were obeyed.

"I was unbound, and conveyed to the wigwam of the chief.

"Here I was guarded by the squaws of the tribe, while two of the warriors were stationed outside.

"A terrible conflict ensued between our tribe and the invaders.

"Each warrior fought for his country and his home, and valour strengthened every arm.

"From all parts of the island thronged the Aynoth braves, with spear, and bow, and tomahawk, to drive back the invaders.

"But the Masketees were fierce, and strong, and numerous, and were difficult to conquer.

"Many an Aynoth brave fell, never to rise again.

"Fierce was the fray, and uninterruptedly it raged until the sun had gone down and night shaded the heavens.

"But at this time another fearful catastrophe was discovered.

"The flames from the post of sacrifice had not been sufficiently extinguished.

"For a long time they had smouldered, until at length they had spread considerably, and broke out among the neighbouring trees.

"The temple of fire was soon a mass of flames.

"Driven by the wind, the fire spread until it enveloped the whole forest.

"It at length caught the wigwam where I was imprisoned.

"A terrible scene of confusion ensued.

"The sentinels fled, the squaws broke open the doors, and rushed out wildly.

"I followed, and beheld a fearful scene.

"A fiercely raging battle.

"Twenty thousand warriors engaged, hand to hand, in deadly conflict, and the whole forest a sheet of flame.

"Scarcely knowing what I did, I made my way safely through the wilderness and escaped to the seashore.

"Then I looked back, and the scene was grandly beautiful.

"A mass of red flames lit up the midnight sky.

"In the distance could be heard the yells, groans, and war-cries of the combatants as they continued their work of mutual destruction.

"Now and then the dusky forms of a party of warriors could be discerned engaged in fierce combat.

"All else around was still.

"Near me was the calm sea, and to the shore were moored many canoes.

"Almost mechanically I rushed down the beach, and getting into the nearest canoe, put out from the land.

"Before I did so, however, a well-known sound greeted my ears, and Hector, my tame lion, bounded joyfully from the thicket, and leaped into the boat.

"He licked my hands with joy, but soon crouched down at the corner of the boat, and became still.

"I urged on the canoe, resolved to leave the island, and trust myself to the mercy of the waves and the darkness, sooner than face the dangers which threatened me.

"I was reckless of life, and cared not for the future.

"Then my boat was partly propelled, and was

partly carried along by the out-going tide, and the island was soon left behind me.

"The water was smooth.

"The night calm and peaceful.

"I longed to get out of sight of the burning island.

"Whither was I going?

"I knew not nor cared not.

"Hours and hours I floated, half unconsciously, on the surface of the waters, until the sun arose in all its splendour, and recalled me to action.

"It was a glorious morning.

"I looked back; there were no signs of the island.

"I was many leagues away from it.

"But about two miles ahead of me, I discerned the outline of a coast which I knew was not the land of the Aynoths.

"I put forth all my strength, and steered towards it.

"Every stroke of the oar brought nearer to me a scene of beauty, far surpassing even that of my native soil.

"Here, at last, I hoped I could find safety and repose.

"No signs of human residence were visible, so I thought the island was uninhabited.

"At length I reached it, and found my suspicions correct.

"There was no one on the island.

"I landed, moored my boat by the shore, and rested beneath the spreading shades of the palm trees. Here I found fruit that would serve me as food, and a crystal stream of fresh water.

"For many hours—ever since that morning's dawn —I have been on this island, and have seen no human being until I heard your cries for help; and, hastening to the beach, I saw you struggling into shore with the white maiden."

Both Jack and Mabel were interested and astonished at this extraordinary narrative.

"And Hector?" Jack murmured.

At this moment the tame puma bounded forward from behind the trees, and recognising Jack, crouched down and licked his hand with much show of affection.

CHAPTER XV.

AN UNEXPECTED ATTACK—A FIGHT ON THE WATER —TIMELY RESCUE.

MABEL started back with a slight scream at the appearance of the animal.

But Jack told her not to be alarmed.

"And now, Lela," he cried, "what do you intend to do?—not go back to the Aynoths?"

"Never! never!" she cried, firmly. "It may be that I am believed to have perished in the flames; but if not, the fierce chief may seek me out, and I should fall by the arrows of his warriors. But I will never again return to the tribe."

"Will you stay with us, and attend on the white sisters of your former chief?"

"I will! I will!" cried Lela, joyfully, and then added in English, "if the sisters of the white chief will permit me."

"I shall be very glad of your company, my poor girl," said Mabel, tenderly. "Yes, you shall be my companion, and together we will roam the world in our gallant vessel, the Seagull. See, here comes my father."

She pointed out to sea where Mr. Meredith was seen guiding a raft with sails, on which were several articles, apparently taken from the wreck of the Silver Star.

Seeing the party on the island, he steered his raft towards them, and soon leapt upon shore.

He looked around, completely bewildered at the scene presented to his view.

"What means all this, Jack?" he cried.

"Oh, papa! such terrible perils! We have just escaped," cried his daughter, clinging to him. "See there!"

She pointed out to the wreck of their frail boat, now floating out to sea.

"The boat leaked, and sank, and once more has Jack been the preserver of my life."

"For which my gratitude is a thousand-fold increased," said Mr. Meredith.

Jack quickly explained all the rest, and the party assembled on Mr. Meredith's raft, which immediately put out from shore.

"You see these things?" remarked Mr. Meredith, pointing to two small chests and a barrel on the raft.

"They are from the wreck of my poor ship. They have floated to yonder island, where they have been cast ashore, and as I steered by on this raft, I secured them.

"They contain light English fabrics, fortunately uninjured.

"They are yours, Jack, according to my compact."

Jack was overcome by this generosity.

"But you found them, sir, not I," he protested.

"No matter. You have now once again saved my daughter's life, and these will but poorly express my gratitude. They must and shall be yours."

While Jack was expressing his thankfulness for his generosity, a wild, savage yell was heard on the island they had just left, and looking back they saw a party of Aynoths rushing down to the beach.

They were headed by the chief Oroma, whose rage at the escape of Lela was vividly depicted on his countenance.

The party of savages had landed on the opposite side of the island to which the Indian maiden had escaped, but had not reached the beach until the raft had put off.

"They will try to capture me!" cried Lela, in great terror, as she crouched down beneath the spreading sail of the raft, and beside the trembling form of Mabel.

"But they shall never succeed!" replied Jack, starting to his feet, and seizing his rifle.

Mr. Meredith did the same, and at that moment a shower of arrows struck the mast and the chests beside which they stood, but providentially neither of our friends were hit.

Mr. Meredith loaded, and Jack, kneeling down, and resting his gun on one of the water-casks, took a fair aim at the barbarian chief.

A report, a flash of fire, and though the ball merely grazed the crest of the haughty chief, one of his followers fell to the earth in the agonies of death.

Again a shower of arrows were aimed at the dauntless Englishmen.

Several times they were struck, but as chance would have it they escaped from any dangerous wounds.

Meanwhile, their guns did great execution among the savages.

At every report of the rifle, a warrior of the Aynoths measured his full length on the verdant ground.

At length a bullet from Jack's rifle struck the fierce chief Oroma in the shoulder.

He had received a dangerous, if not fatal wound, and with a wild cry of baffled rage, he rolled over on the earth, disabled from further action.

Several warriors bore the wounded chief from the ground.

With a terrific yell of fury at the defeat they had sustained, they discharged their last volley of arrows, and then proceeded to disperse.

But as they did so, a fierce roar was heard, and Hector, the puma, bounded forward and charged into the broken ranks of the disordered savages.

In the excitement of escape from the Indians, the puma had been forgotten.

Now, entirely stricken with terror, the Aynoths offered no resistance to the animal, but fled in a panic to their canoes on the opposite side of the island.

Then the noble animal returned to the shore, and plunging into the waters, struck out for the raft, which he speedily overtook.

With what joy was he welcomed by his mistress, and by all who had beheld his faithfulness and sagacity.

Lela overwhelmed him with caresses, and Mabel's fear was turned into admiration.

"We have conquered for the time," observed Mr. Meredith; "but we must still be wary, for probably some of the savages are still lurking among the rocks."

In this he proved to be correct.

Scarcely had the raft rounded the chief headland of the isle, when they were literally surrounded by canoes full of armed savages.

Their intentions were evidently to capture Lela, but when their eyes fell on the chests which they supposed contained treasure on the raft, the greed of gain was added to their other motives, and their hatred to the pale-faces was aroused in full force.

The party on the raft were in greater peril than ever.

Their course was obstructed by the canoes of their foes, everyone of whom stood up with tomahawk and spear in hand.

The odds were very great against Jack's party.

It was two men and two weak and trembling women against twenty fierce and well-armed savages.

But Lela showed herself worthy of her birth, her fear was gone. She started up, seized her bow, and stood with her beautifully-modelled form defiantly erect, waiting for the attack of her persecutors.

Placed as the party on the raft were, they felt it

would be prudent, in the first place, to attempt measures of conciliation.

Lela was the first to speak.

"Warriors of Aynoth!" she cried, "I have fled from persecution, and if I choose to abide with the pale-faces, why should you strive to prevent me?"

"Lela," replied the chief of the opposing party, "you have rebelled against our great chief Oroma, and the wise men of the tribe had doomed you to the sacrifice. You have fled, but you must not escape your just fate!"

"Warrior," replied the island maiden, "this pale-faced chief by my side is the Young Eagle, who was once the king of our tribe, nay, who can even now exercise his authority. Dare you to rebel against him?"

"The white chief is a squaw and a coward," replied the savage. "He has made the Aynoths and the Macoushis bury the hatchet of war, and become as women; and he has fled like a craven from his dominions to evade the consequences of his act."

These words fired Jack with indignation, and he arose with a flushed countenance and flashing eyes.

"Miscreant!" he cried, "dare to repeat those words, and I will show you whether the young Eagle is yet shorn of his plumes. Men of Aynoth, I am still your chief—your king, and I command you to lay down your arms and let me pass on in peace!"

"You have wounded our chief, Oroma, and slain many warriors," was the reply; "and you have besides bewitched the squaw of our chief. Shall we then let you escape unpunished? No! You are no longer our king. We despise, scorn, and disown you. Forward, my men, to attack the pale-faced curs, for they must die!"

Instantly the attack commenced. Urging their canoes to the side of the raft, the Aynoths plied their spears and tomahawks, and with their shields dexterously warded off the blows of the white men.

Leaping on the raft, they attempted to seize the form of Lela, but the Indian maiden held aloft the strong but slender hatchet that had hung at her belt, and defended herself vigorously.

Fierce was the hand to hand encounter between the Englishmen and the warriors of Aynoth, the former fighting valorously in the defence of their lives and their recently acquired property; the latter filled with the thirst for gain and the fire of hatred.

With the butt-end of his trusty rifle, Jack for some time effectually kept his foes at bay.

Hector, too, did good service. Disregarding the many wounds he received, he plunged into the midst of the dusky foes, and with teeth and claws wounded many a savage warrior.

But still the party on the raft were in imminent danger. The odds against them were fearful.

Rapidly were the savages getting the mastery, and not only was Lela overpowered, but the beautiful form of the fair English maiden was seized by her brutal assailants.

With all the energy of fierce desperation, Mr Meredith fought in defence of his daughter, but in vain.

The raft, the treasure, and the prisoners were si

JACK FIRED POINT BLANK AT THE FOREMOST WARRIOR.

about to fall into the hands of the victorious Ay-noths. At this moment, however, assistance arrived.

Unseen by the savages, a party of Englishmen, consisting of Captain Hastings, Tom Starboard, and two or three other officers of the Seagull, who were out in their boat shooting sea-fowl, saw the danger of their friends, and hastened to the rescue.

Slowly gliding behind the wall of canoes, they arrived, unobserved, within a short distance of the scene of conflict.

Standing up in the boat, Captain Hastings took a careful aim at the man who held in his arms the fainting form of Mabel.

The aim proved true. With a loud and unexpected report the rifle was discharged, and the ball entered the brain of the savage.

Without a sound he fell back into the sea, and Mabel was clasped to her father's breast.

At the same time Tom, perilous as he knew the act to be, discharged a bullet among the body of savages who were overmastering Jack.

This shot also had the desired effect, and another of their foes was slain.

Then the rescuers boarded the canoes, and by a short but vigorous onslaught, obtained a complete victory over the savages.

Many were slain, many sank struggling in the water, and the remainder, seized with terror, fled precipitately in their canoes.

Half an hour afterwards there was not a savage in sight of the islands.

The rescuing party were overwhelmed with thanks, and the whole of the gallant band of dauntless English hearts returned safely to the principal island

17

CHAPTER XVI.

THE SEARCH FOR THE TREASURE—ITS RESULT—
JACK'S DIVISION OF THE PROPERTY.

THAT night the party held another happy festival.

Their adventures were recounted, and the bravery of Jack and his reward of the treasure afforded subjects for general congratulation.

Mr. Meredith recounted his researches among the remains of the Silver Star, and his determination to continue them, accompanied by Jack and Tom Starboard.

Lela attracted especial attention. Her beauty aroused the admiration of all the gallant tars around, but her heart was indifferent to the impression she produced. She sat silent and reserved, her whole love and care being concentrated on Crusoe Jack and Mabel, her new mistress.

Perhaps she was filled with regret that Jack could never return her affection as she desired him.

The whole of the party, however, looked forward with pleasant anticipations to the sailing of the Seagull, and the fresh adventures they were about to encounter.

The next day, Jack, Mr. Meredith, and Tom Starboard again set forth on the raft, and visited the wreck of the Silver Star, with the hope of rescuing the remainder of the treasure she contained.

The appearance of the wreck was now very different to what it had been when Jack nearly lost his life in the stranded hull.

The vessel was now broken into fragments; the constant action of the waves, added to the power of one or two violent storms, had almost entirely demolished the semblance of her original form.

The hull was broken into several pieces, the cabins were utterly destroyed, and planks, and hatches, and furniture, and fragments of masts, floated about the surface of the ocean, driven by the tide far away from the scene of the disaster.

Several water and spirit casks and isolated articles of clothing had been washed on the shore of the principal island, all that was light enough to float had drifted on the waters and spread even so far as the shores of the neighbouring islands; while all the heavier things had sunk amid the ruins of the dismembered hull.

The contents of the principal locker, and the various arms and scientific instruments that filled the captain's cabin, were still embedded on the reef where the Silver Star had gone down.

On reaching the spot, the party found, as they expected, a great change in the aspect of the remains of the Silver Star.

The coral insects had commenced their work around the broken portions of the hull, the chests and all the heavy articles were half buried in the new edifice of coral-bed that had been raised around them.

Glistening white in the tropical sun, covered with marine plants and fairy flowers of unearthly loveliness, the coral reef was in itself beautiful, but to our worthy friends it only represented buried riches and the difficulty of rescuing them.

They had chosen a time when the tide was down, and they could easily land among the reefs, and examine closely the condition of the wreck.

They had brought with them all necessary implements for unearthing the treasure, and, without loss of time, they set to work.

Some of the larger chests, bales, etc., were still partly above the surface of the water, and these indicated the spot where they were to commence their labours.

Digging with a will all around the buried articles, destroying remorselessly the beautiful branches of coral and the many-hued flowers that grew beside them, they worked on steadily under Mr. Meredith's direction, until one of the smaller chests was raised to the level of the ground.

It was very heavy, and, when opened, proved to contain much jewellery and other valuable articles, all in an excellent state of preservation.

It was immediately placed on the raft, and the companions, exhilarated by their success, set to work afresh with renewed vigour.

Several small chests were unearthed in the same way, but none contained articles of such value as the first.

The captain's locker, as the reader must remember, was entirely emptied of its contents by Jack, in his previous disastrous attempt; it had been knocked to pieces, and its remains now lay buried among the fragments of the hull.

But its contents were all buried in the coral reef, and the resurrection of these proved the most difficult and arduous portion of their day's work.

One by one, however, they were brought to the surface—nautical instruments, arms, small parcels of jewellery, a cash-box full of money and notes, both English and foreign, ammunition, and wearing apparel (the latter entirely spoilt by immersion), together with other valuable property.

Jack also found what he considered by no means the least valuable of the treasures—namely, the small miniature of Mabel, which had dropped from him in the hurry of his former miraculous escape from the wreck.

It was enclosed in a strong case, tightly clasped, and was fortunately unimpaired by the waves.

All these articles were placed upon the raft, some in tin boxes, some in casks, and all strongly corded on for security.

The amount of property which had been either unearthed, or taken from among the ruins of the hull, or the surface of the waves, that day and the previous one, proved more than the most sanguine expectations of the shipwrecked party had ever conceived.

Many of the crew had their boats out, and assisted Mr. Meredith in conveying the goods ashore.

A great number of hammocks, sailors' clothes, and bales of cloth and linen goods, preserved eatables, etc., were also rescued, and though many of these articles were spoiled, a considerable quantity yet remained fit for use.

In the evening Jack assembled the whole of the ship's company, and made a formal division of the large amount of property which Mr. Meredith had made over to him in gratitude for his services to him and his daughter.

Jack commenced by restoring all wearing apparel, etc., to all the owners who were able to identify it, and giving a certain sum to each of the men and officers out of the cash-box, by way of recompense for their past perils. Tom Starboard, of course, was specially rewarded.

All the hammocks, sails, compasses, arms, mathematical instruments, and eatables, he considered as belonging to their new vessel, the Seagull, for the general use of all who sailed in her.

The jewellery, he said, was the most suitable for presents ; and therefore he selected the choicest and most valuable among it, and presented them in a casket to Mabel.

The latter would not at first accept them ; but at length Jack prevailed upon her to do so, and even overruled Mr. Meredith's objections.

Jack also presented some jewels of considerable value to Lela, who received them with great thankfulness.

As to the cargo, Jack accepted it as his own, on condition that he would be allowed to present twenty per cent. of the profit to Mabel's father as soon as it was disposed of ;—thus restoring, directly and indirectly, a large portion of the property to the rightful owner.

Mr. Meredith's approval of these arrangements was at length obtained, and thus all were equally satisfied.

Such was Jack's fair division of the spoil which Mr. Meredith's generosity and his own bravery had brought to him, and he proved himself not unworthy of his good fortune by the generous use he made of it.

All were delighted at the division, and cheered Crusoe with bursts of hearty applause.

By this last act he had gained the favour of every one on the island.

And still with the reflection that he had done his duty, Jack could recognise the agreeable fact that he had a large share of wealth yet remaining for himself.

CHAPTER XVII.

THE SEAGULL—JACK'S REFLECTIONS—HE IS ATTACKED TREACHEROUSLY—A CRITICAL POSITION—A DESPERATE FIGHT, AND A FINAL VICTORY.

IT wanted but two days to the time fixed for the sailing of the Seagull.

She lay at anchor in the commodious harbour on the western side of the principal island, a perfect model of a gallant English vessel.

All viewed her with admiration, and looked forward pleasurably to their approaching voyage.

Jack was impatient for action.

His life on the island had been very pleasant to him, but he had now wearied of it, and he longed to begin active service as first lieutenant of the Seagull.

With Mabel his constant companion, with her father his firm friend, and with wealth already his, and more in prospect, the dream of his life seemed in a fair way of being realised.

But many years were to pass ; many dangers and obstacles were to be overcome, before our hero could realise all the fervent hopes of his heart.

Who could calculate, even for a moment, on the events of the mysterious future !

These reflections passed through Jack's mind, as, leaving his companions, he strolled out in the calm, glorious evening to visit for the last time the now familiar scene of his island dominions.

Never had the landscape looked so beautiful, the birds sung so sweetly, nor the declining sun flooded the sky with more ineffable splendour.

Jack could not help a tinge of regret that he was about to leave this beautiful region.

He had read Byron's "Childe Harold," and the "Corsair," and he reflected how sadly the former had left his native land, and how the latter, after a life of wild adventure, had suddenly disappeared from his island home. He could not help comparing himself with those poetic heroes. Well might he have sung—

" Adieu, adieu, my native shore,"

or the stirring lines in the adventures of the Pirate Chief—

" O'er the glad waters of the dark blue sea."

Truly, the events of these poems had found some realization in his own adventures.

Indulging in these half melancholy reveries, Jack reached the rocky peak from which he had taken his first survey of the island.

Here he stayed for some time, to give full scope to his thoughtful mood.

In his cloak and plumed cap, that wild, half-Indian costume which he still retained, Jack stood upon the peak, and, leaning upon his rifle, looked out upon the prospect beneath him.

He little knew how gallant and handsome a figure he presented in this prominent situation and carelessly graceful attitude.

He only knew that the scene before him was beautiful, that the pale moon was just rising on one side of the heavens, while on the other the glorious sun bathed the whole landscape in a crimson glow.

Above all, his attention became rivetted on a solitary figure that guided a light canoe through the narrow and intricate channels that were interspersed among the verdant islets.

He recognised that graceful form, in whose every movement there was an inexpressible charm.

It was Lela, the Indian maiden.

She did not observe him, but he watched her intently, and his whole reflections and attention were instantly centred upon her.

She loved him still—her hopeless affection still saddened her heart ; and he, plighted to Mabel, could never return her love as she desired him.

Constantly in his presence, as an attendant upon the fair English girl, could she ever forget her hopeless attachment ?

Would she not rather continually feel the pangs of jealousy ?

Did she not already exhibit them ?

Would she not in her future travels come at length to pine for her island home—her former associates ?

Jack indulged in all these reflections as he stood watching Lela's light canoe, in fancied security.

He little knew what peril he was about to encounter; what treacherous danger lurked within a few yards of him.

A party of four fierce and cunning savages were concealed behind a neighbouring rock, glaring at him with a gaze of fiendish malignity.

They were evidently bent on some deadly purpose, and that purpose had not been relinquished since the memorable fight on the raft.

These savages had not, as it appeared, left the island. They had concealed themselves among the thick tropical vegetation of the farthest outlying islets, and waited for a chance of vengeance.

They could not forgive Jack for the defeat they had sustained at the hands of his party, and for their disappointment at not gaining the treasure carried on the raft.

Above all, Oroma, the fierce chief, regarded our hero with the deadliest hatred, for was not Jack his rival in the dignity of chieftain, and had he not wounded and defeated him, and bewitched the object of his love?

During several days Oroma had remained in a temporarily-erected hut on a sequestered island, chafing with mingled pain and disappointed rage.

Every day he had sent out parties of spies to watch the Englishman, and seek an opportunity of slaying Crusoe Jack.

Now they deemed this opportunity arrived.

It was with fiendish exultation that the savages proceeded to carry out the commands of their chief.

Gliding, snake-like, up the rocks, slowly, noiselessly, and with astonishing agility, they approached the unconscious form of our hero.

Their fiendish natures exulted in the prospect of overpowering him.

Never, in all his many adventures, had Jack been placed in a position of greater danger.

Slowly, but surely, the Indians made their way, crouching on all-fours.

At length they reached him; he was still unconscious of their presence, and still regardless of his critical position.

With a wild yell, the savages rushed upon him in a body, armed with their murderous tomahawks, and their deadly spears.

They were four to one, and he, too, was on the brink of a precipice, with no means whatever of escape.

This, however, was not the only peril.

In the glen below, immediately beneath the peaked rock, was a canoe in which could have been recognised the form of the vindictive young chief, Oroma.

He had partially recovered from his wound, and, restless with the desire for revenge, he had at length left his hiding-place with the hope of encountering Crusoe.

His desire was now fulfilled.

His scouts had been at last successful. Jack was at bay, and in a most critical position, and the young chief was not loth to take advantage of his enemy.

He determined that Jack should die by his hand alone.

With demoniacal exultation, the youthful chief fitted an arrow to his bow, rose up in his canoe, and took a deadly aim at the struggling figure of our hero.

Jack was thus encompassed by the most imminent dangers.

His heart sank; he gave himself up for lost; but it was only for a moment, and then the dauntless English bravery came to his aid.

Collecting all his strength, he raised his gun above him, and aimed a deadly blow at the head of the foremost of the advancing savages.

Just at that moment the arrow from the bow of Oroma whizzed past our hero's head, missing him by scarcely a quarter of an inch.

He gave a rapid glance in the direction of the water, and recognised the form of his dusky enemy.

Then he realised the full extent of his danger.

The foremost savage fell beneath the mighty blow from the butt-end of Crusoe's rifle, but his followers attacked our young hero in a body, and with great severity.

To keep off, for any length of time, the whole of the party, and, besides, escape the arrows of Oroma, was, as Jack knew, complete impossibility.

If he was once stricken down, the fall of his body from the high peak would surely complete the deadly effect.

On the other hand, to leap from the summit was the only chance of escape.

By a sudden spring he might reach the water, and if not rendered senseless by the shock, would yet succeed in evading his enemies.

His resolution was in a moment taken. With one wide sweep of his arm he swung his rifle around his head for the last time, cast it from him, and then plunged suddenly over the precipice.

A terrific fall of about thirty feet, a shock, a splash, and Jack, giddy, breathless, confused, all but senseless by the shock, rose to the surface of the water, which was here about ten feet in depth.

He had providentially escaped striking his head against a rock that rose above the surface, not more than three feet from the spot where he fell.

The whole scene, exciting and important as it had been, had taken place in merely a few minutes.

Jack's faculties, for the moment shaken, now returned to him in full force; he comprehended his situation, and the only course of escape from it.

Being an excellent swimmer, he struck out for the opposite island, which was not more than a hundred feet off.

To reach this would be, under ordinary circumstances, a feat of little difficulty.

On seeing his escape, the Indians gave a yell of disappointment.

They had missed their prey; but, nevertheless, they made sure he must be killed by the fall.

Oroma, on comprehending the position of affairs, hastened to prevent the ultimate escape of our hero.

Putting in motion his canoe, he glided with rapidity to the spot where our hero was struggling with the waves.

It was impossible for Jack to swim so quickly as the canoe would be propelled by the practised hand of Oroma.

Consequently, the remorseless Indian had soon overtaken his foe.

"Vile craven of a race of squaws," he cried, "now you will not escape me. You shall die at once, and thus recompense the Aynoth chief for the pangs you have made him suffer."

Crusoe, without reply, rose on the waters, and caught hold of the side of the canoe.

His aim was to board it, and attempt by force to take possession of the craft.

Oroma, however, perceived his intention, and hastened to prevent it.

Every time Jack placed his hands on the canoe, the Indian chief endeavoured by hitting his fingers with the paddles to make him relinquish his hold.

But with a sudden and vigorous spring, Jack accomplished his design of getting into the canoe.

He sprang at the throat of the chief, and a fierce and deadly struggle commenced between them, which several times threatened to overturn the frail canoe.

Both knew it was a struggle for life, and they continued it with the utmost energy.

But Oroma was weakened by his recent wound, and he was no match for the vigorous young Englishman.

He felt his strength leaving him, though he struggled with all his might.

At length Jack, by an almost superhuman effort of strength, succeeded in hurling his dusky foe into the water.

The young chief rose to the surface, and weak and confused, struggled unavailingly with the waves.

Jack saw his opportunity, and seizing the paddle, made off as swiftly as he could along the channel.

Meanwhile the party on the rock had watched the scene with surprise.

They were utterly incapable of rendering assistance to their chief.

They had no arrows, only tomahawks and spears. These they had several times hurled at the gallant boy, but without effect.

As Jack paddled his canoe swiftly away, a sudden thought struck him, which he had forgotten during the recent encounter—What had become of the Indian maiden?

CHAPTER XVIII.

JACK'S ESCAPE—THE SEA-BIRD—THE SEQUESTERED ISLAND—A STRANGE DISCOVERY—A SECRET, MYSTERIOUS, AND DANGEROUS ADVENTURE.

WITHOUT more than a passing fear on this subject—for he hoped that Lela had been placed in no jeopardy by her unconsciousness of the presence of the savages on the island, Jack propelled his canoe with all the speed his strength was capable of giving it.

He glanced behind him; no canoes were following him; his foes had not recovered from the confusion caused by the late conflict, and Oroma was still struggling in the water. Yet he knew not how many of his foes might be lurking treacherously behind the rocks and in the irregular channels.

Jack's object was to get to the open sea, and then steer round to the principal island, and rejoin his companions.

He was well aware that the Indians were not sufficient in numbers to do any harm to the large and powerful crew of the Seagull, but there was no knowing what injury their treachery might attempt.

So our hero determined to inform his captain of their presence on the island.

The sunset was still glowing in its full splendour as he left the narrow channel, interspersed with numerous islets that surrounded the chief islands of the group.

He at length reached a small isle among the most westerly of any in the whole archipelago—an island of the most delightful beauty and luxury.

Cocoa-nut trees, bread-fruit, and palm, seemed to abound here as in all parts of his dominions, and from the sea the view in that glorious tropical sunset was particularly magnificent.

It was just as Jack was resting a moment in his boat to gaze upon this scene of beauty, that a brilliant parokeet, one whose equal for splendour of plumage and elegance of form he had never seen in those islands, flew rapidly above his head, on its way to its island home.

An impulse of the moment determined Jack to secure this fine specimen of the winged inhabitants of his island dominion, and present it to Mabel, to keep in remembrance of this period of their eventful lives.

The bow and sheaf of arrows, formerly belonging to the chief Oroma, still lay at the bottom of the canoe.

Jack seized them, stood up in the boat, and took good aim at the bird, just as it was making its escape inland.

The arrow sped, and struck the bird, which uttered a loud shrill cry, and fluttered painfully among the thick foliage on the shore.

Crusoe moored his boat on the beach, leaped ashore, and hastened to secure his prize.

The island on which he now found himself was so thickly overgrown with tropical vegetation that it was with great difficulty he could make his way through it.

He did not remember whether he had ever explored this island before; it was a very sequestered one. Its position would have prevented it from attracting any special notice.

It was the haunt of innumerable birds, both aquatic and terrestrial, and insects of many brilliant species likewise abounded in it.

The bird Jack had shot had fluttered down among the leaves of a palm tree, on to some thickly growing grass.

Making his way with considerable difficulty, he at length reached the spot where it had fallen.

He thought it was dead, but as he approached it the creature tantalizingly collected its failing strength, and again hopped out of his reach.

He was determined to capture it, dead or alive, but the bird repeatedly foiled his efforts in the manner above described.

It at length flew into the midst of a thick clump of trees, and Jack was unable to note the exact spot.

Still, however, he determined to persevere in his search.

Jack now found himself in a thick grove of feathery palms, lit only by the oblique rays of the declining sunlight.

The scene would have been beautiful, but for the gloom and sombreness with which the stillness and increasing darkness had invested it.

On one side was a thick clump of tangled tropical grass and shrubs, and it was while observing this that a circumstance so remarkable as to fill his mind instantly with a host of new thoughts, arrested his attention.

All around the vegetation grew thickly and wildly, with all the luxuriance of Nature in regions where she is untouched by man.

But had this wild scene never been trod by human footsteps?

From the grove to the centre of the clumps of bushes, the grass grew high, but it had been trodden or beaten down, as if by the recent passage of human feet.

There existed no animals in the island large and heavy enough to produce the extraordinary effect the grass presented.

It seemed, in short, as if some person or persons had recently visited this sequestered spot.

Jack's attention was aroused.

Here was a mystery which gave good scope for conjecture.

Our hero felt a sudden, wild, irrepressible desire to unravel it.

Who knew what mighty and important discoveries it might lead to?

Retracing his steps, Jack surveyed minutely the whole of the stretch of ground from the shore where he had moored his boat, up the gently sloping incline, and along the grove to the clump of bushes.

Now he noticed it closely, the whole of this path presented the same indications.

The grass was trodden down, and in parts where the ground was damp and sandy, the prints of footsteps were to be plainly observed.

Another circumstance, still more conclusive, was that, near the shore, half embedded in the sand, lay a portion of a broken boat-hook.

A little distance off, was a strong hook fixed into the beach, and which had evidently been used for the purpose of mooring vessels to the shore. Indeed, Jack had unconsciously taken advantage of this in his own landing.

These indications plainly revealed the fact that, not only had the island been recently visited, but by persons who were accustomed to use it for some well defined purpose.

Crusoe's thoughts inadvertently turned to the night on which he had seen the mysterious ship—his first night on the largest island.

He could not help connecting the two circumstances, and feeling assured that the same persons, or the same description of persons, who had mysteriously visited that island had now visited this in the same manner.

For what purpose were these visits made?

He could only come to the conclusion that they were made either by pirates or smugglers for the purpose of landing and concealing property of value which they had become possessed of.

The larger island he had traversed hundreds of times, but had seen no indication like he saw here. If the pirates had used any place there for concealing their property, he had hitherto failed to discover it.

But here he felt both a hope and a conviction that he should do so.

Like every one else, when on the track of a mystery, Jack felt an uncontrollable desire to follow it up, and arrive at some important result.

No thought of danger, nor indeed of any other circumstance that surrounded him, occupied Jack at that moment—his mind was entirely filled by this new subject.

How completely he had forgotten the bird! It might escape for ever for what he cared.

Such is the power which curiosity has over the current of thought.

Jack again retraced his steps to the grove, and soon arrived at the clump of bushes.

He struggled through the mass of undergrowth which stretched beyond and around it, and at length reached a spot, and beheld a scene, which was not now entirely unexpected by him.

The bushes concealed the entrance of a kind of hollow of considerable depth, covered with trees of long, straight form, but destitute of underwood.

In the middle of this hollow was a pile of boughs, bushes, and leaves, evidently placed in their present position not by the hand of Nature, but that of man.

Jack's heart beat quickly as, bending down, he entered the hollow, and approached this strange-looking heap.

A half-suspicion of the truth filled his mind, and inspired him with a resolution to proceed in his strange adventure.

He turned over the heap with the point of his cutlass, and, in a few moments, scattered it all over the grass.

Then his suspicions were confirmed by what he saw.

A trap-door of wood, about three feet square, with a strong iron ring fixed in the centre of it.

The ring was not rusty, but bright, as if from the effects of recent use.

Nevertheless, the door and the surrounding earth were damp from the humid nature of the ground, and the leaves and boughs which covered it.

Jack took hold of the ring with both hands, and with all his strength strove to open the trap-door.

It resisted all his efforts.

He tried again and again, but all to no effect.

The reason speedily became obvious.

He at length noticed (which he could scarcely

do from the almost complete darkness) that the trap-door was securely fastened by a wooden frame let into the earth, to which there was a strong lock fastened.

With this lock, by means of a ponderous key, was the trap-door effectually secured.

The key was, of course, in the keeping of the owners of the cave, and, without it, any attempt to effect an opening was useless.

Jack felt for the moment bitterly disappointed.

Not to discover all, after he had discovered so much, was very aggravating, and yet there was no means of opening the trap-door.

No strength Jack could exert, no implements he possessed, no force he could use, would enable him to raise or break open the ponderous trap-door.

Consequently, he at length reluctantly determined to give up the search.

He was just turning away with this resolve, when and idea suddenly struck him.

What if he were to attempt to blast the opening with gunpowder? he had sufficient in the flask that hung from his belt for the purpose.

He had, moreover, some fusees that had been taken uninjured from the stores of the Seagull.

He instantly resolved to carry out this design, be the consequences what they might, and somehow he felt a vague foreboding that they would be disastrous.

Taking a handful of powder from his flask, he knelt down beside the trap-door, and scattered it along the interstices between the trap-door and its frame.

He also put a considerable quantity in the lock.

All round the edges of the secret entrance were at length completely filled with combustible matter—all connected together, so as to form a train that would fire at once.

Trembling with the excitement of this dangerous experiment, Jack struck a fusee, and fixed the unlighted end in the crack of the trap-door, near the lock.

He then started up, and retreated to some distance, anxiously waiting for the effect of his plan.

He had not long to wait.

The explosion followed almost immediately, but instead of being loud and instantaneous, it was uneven and disconnected—a succession of short, quick, sharp, half-smothered reports, consequent, as he believed, on the damp nature of the wood-work.

This had somewhat deadened, but not completely neutralised the effects of the powder.

It had not blown off the trap-door in one tremendous burst, but it had blackened and weakened the edges and the lock, and torn away, in many parts, pieces of the wood-work.

Jack saw that he could now, without much difficulty, force open the weakened door, and thus effect his entrance.

He placed his cutlass in a large crack made by the recent explosion, and gave a violent wrench. The door flew open immediately, but he found it still very difficult to lift it back on its hinges, for it was very heavy, being clamped with iron bars and nails.

At length, however, Jack had forced the ponderous weight back on its hinges, and the door was completely open.

A gulf-like depth below greeted his eyes, black as ink, and wafting upwards an atmosphere of damp earth.

He could just distinguish the top of a ladder reaching to the trap-door, the bottom was lost in the depths of shadow.

Indeed, the wood itself was now completely enveloped in darkness, which was, naturally, still further increased in the subterranean cave. Though the door was wide open, no light seemed to penetrate through it.

This alone made our hero despair of carrying out his design to its full extent.

Jack, however, determined to descend.

He did so cautiously, feeling the steps of the ladder with his feet, and finding his descent very steep.

He continued descending to a depth of twelve feet, as near as he could calculate.

Then he placed his foot on the bottom of the cave.

His first act was to strike one of his fusees, which shed around the faintest, most uncertain spark.

Jack could discern very little by this light. Nevertheless, when it burnt up a little brighter, he advanced further into the cave, and, to his joy, perceived a waxen torch fixed to a ring on the wall.

He applied the fusee to it, and it at length caught.

The light, however, was at first dim, and while it was burning up, Jack again ascended the ladder, and cast a rapid glance around outside.

All was still, and now perfectly dark; the stars were out, and nothing disturbed the serene silence.

CHAPTER XIX.

JACK'S ADVENTURE CONTINUED—HIS REMARKABLE DISCOVERY—WHAT COURSE SHALL HE TAKE?—THE DANGER OVERPOWERS HIM.

RETURNING to the middle of the cave, Jack found that the torch had now burnt up to a considerable degree of brightness, and by its light he took a minute survey of the subterranean chamber.

It was a cave of considerable extent—partly natural, partly enlarged by excavators.

The well at one side had been dammed up, and outside could be heard the dash of the murmuring sea.

This circumstance confirmed Jack in his opinion that this subterranean apartment was one of those natural marine caverns which abound among the Pacific Islands, and had been thus turned to account by the pirates for their own purposes.

A roughly-made table, and a couple of long benches formed the whole of the furniture in the cave, in one corner of which was a long pile of rifles, cutlasses, and weapons of all descriptions, in capital condition.

A kind of fire-place cut out of the solid rock still contained some embers and ashes, fragments of a plentiful repast, and the utensils in which it had been cooked.

Of ornaments, the cavern was entirely devoid, but all things that could be useful to a pirate crew on their hasty and secret landing were visible even by the most casual observation.

But what most attracted Jack's attention was an iron chest of considerable size in one corner; and though it was covered with clothes of sailors thrown carelessly over it, Jack's gaze was arrested by it at once, and he felt a conviction that it contained all that was most valuable of the pirates' ill-gotten possessions.

In fact he knew that he had reached a jealously-concealed, and therefore valuable mine of wealth.

But whether it was available was another matter, or whether he could satisfy his curiosity by opening the chest, was a question against which all probabilities contended.

The pirates were certain to have carefully locked it, and taken the key away with them.

Still, Jack could not resist the temptation of making a closer inspection.

He went to the chest, removed every article that covered it, and found it as he expected, firmly and immovably fastened.

It was secured, too, by such a complete lock, which together with its immensely strong and heavy construction, entirely precluded the faintest possibility of opening it.

Jack saw this at a glance, with a feeling of disappointment.

All his trouble, then, was to lead to no further results than he had already reached.

As he came to this conclusion, a secret spring connected with the lock flew open beneath his unconscious touch, and revealed a small cavity let into the thickness of the iron.

And in this hiding-place he found to his joy a ponderous key, which he conjectured was that of the chest.

He was not mistaken.

With considerable difficulty he fitted it in the lock, and turned it by no less than five revolutions before the ponderous lid showed signs of being opened.

At length, however, Jack's end was gained.

He proceeded, without loss of time, to carry out the principal and most exciting part of the evening's adventure.

In every human being there is that degree of fondness for gain that makes the finding of a treasure—and especially a concealed one—a pleasant occupation, and our hero was not without a feeling of triumph as he saw how his pains had been rewarded.

The locker which he had found in the cabin of the wrecked Silver Star, in the adventure that had nearly cost him his life, had contained a large amount of valuable property; but it was merely nothing compared to the mass of wealth which was now spread before him.

For at the top of the chest were various articles of wearing apparel of the most costly description, and of the fashion of almost every nation, inlaid with gold and silver and precious stones.

As he proceeded, he became more and more astonished at the value and splendour of the prize he had found.

He next came to jewellery and other articles of adornment, formed of gold, silver, pearls, diamonds, and every kind of valuable gem, in a profusion of splendour such as his wildest dreams had never depicted.

There were bracelets and brooches, diamond watches, and pearl ear-rings, chains of gold, and rings, and lockets of silver, in apparently endless heaps.

What was almost as striking as the quantity, was the variety of appearance and construction in the articles.

They were all of different fashions—each was evidently produced by a different nation to the others.

The spoils of the world seemed gathered together in that iron chest.

"My word!" exclaimed our hero, as one by one he removed these articles from their hiding-place, and inspected them separately by the light of the the torch, "if ever I saw anything like this in all my life! the rascals know how to enrich themselves, that's certain. I wonder how many bloodthirsty fights and shot and shell, hand-to-hand encounters they've had before they could gather all this together? Ah! after all, it must be glorious to be a pirate."

This last thought greatly impressed his mind.

He began to long for the life of a sea rover—the bold, wild, adventurous life, with that constant excitement, change of scene and hopes of plunder, that has led so many to become pirates.

This is how honesty is first undermined; and for a few moments, while he was gloating on the treasure before him, Jack's foundation of good principles was, I am afraid, rather shaken.

Who could wonder at it?

There was abundant excuse for such mental deviation from virtue.

But the feeling was but of short duration.

All the startling honesty of Jack's gallant English nature revolted against it.

He resolved to be all his life rather a foe than a friend to the fierce robbers.

Still, he regarded the taking possession of this treasure (if that feat could be effected) as a just retribution against them for the many atrocious deeds they were known to have committed in those seas.

"It is but despoiling the spoiler," he remarked, as he dived his head once more into the vast heap of treasures.

"This wealth might enrich many honest fellows who really deserve it. And yet, perhaps, it would be better for our peace and safety not to touch it; for they say there is a curse in ill-gotten gold."

He had now removed the greater part of the contents of the chest, and had arrived at the bottom, which was entirely covered with small tin boxes, closely fastened.

These were very heavy, and Jack speedily ascertained, by rattling them about, that they contained money.

"Here are their cash-boxes," he remarked; "full as they can hold of riches, once belonging to people who are now, perhaps, lying dead at the bottom of the vast ocean, or who have become food for hungry sharks."

The large heap of gold, silver, and notes that lined the lower part of the chest was, like the other articles, of almost every country.

There were English sovereigns, and other coins, American dollars, francs, pistoles, ducats, and Russian roubles, together with notes upon almost every bank in the world.

This circumstance showed the number and variety of the prizes the pirates had obtained, and the immense scale upon which they must have carried on their operations.

In his minute examination of the treasure—in his absorbing wonder at its vastness, Jack seemed to forget all other circumstances.

He let the time go by, without heed of its flight, and thought not of the danger which might accrue to him from this rash adventure.

When he had emptied the chest of its contents, he stood regarding the glistening heap he had thus made upon the floor of the cave, debating in his own mind whether he should take any of it with him to show the captain in evidence of the extraordinary tale he would have to tell; or place the interior of the cave as far as possible in the state it had presented when he entered it, and seek the advice of others before entering into so desperate a course.

While thus deliberating, his eyes fell upon the heap of clothes he had thrown carelessly on the floor, among which was a rich suit, such as are worn by Greek sea rovers.

"I wonder how I should look dressed as a pirate—a corsair, as I think they call them in the islands where that suit evidently came from. Supposing I go back and frighten the captain and all the lot of them, who will take me for one of the rovers?"

Thus soliloquising, half in jest, he attired himself in the rich suit.

The embroidered red velvet cap and tassel, the richly-worked jacket, the silk neckerchief and brilliant sash, with the two ornamental pistols stuck into it, and, over all, the wide cloak or capote of silk-lined snow-white sheepskin—formed, altogether, a costume which showed off the handsome figure of our hero to great advantage.

"This is something like," murmured Jack, as he admiringly surveyed himself. "I think I shall keep these clothes, after all, as a trophy and reminder of this adventure. What a pity there isn't a looking-glass here! I wonder whether I can find a sword suitable to the rest of the dress?"

He had just turned to inspect closely the pile of arms that stood in the corner, when an ominous sound greeted his ears.

Is was the murmur of voices.

Rough, fierce voices, growing nearer and more distinct each minute, and proceeding from the ground above, over the entrance of the cave.

The tramp of many feet could likewise be heard.

Then a light from the outside glimmered through the trap-door, and a general cry of surprise arose.

Above all, could be heard a fierce, deep voice exclaiming, in English—

"Hell and furies! What is this? The cave broken open! Some persons must be inside. By G——! if they have, whoever they are, they shall never depart alive!"

Next, there was the sound of the approaching party descending the steep steps, and then figures became dimly visible at the opening.

Our hero knew his danger, but he was overpowered by it.

He stood spell-bound—panic-stricken.

His figure rigid.

His eyes fixed upon the approaching foe.

From this peril, at least, there was no escape.

The entrance of the robbers, their discovery of him or his present position, was, he knew, certain death to him, and he could hope for no mercy.

Thus he stood despairing, resigned to the worst that could befal.

The party of pirates rushed in, and approached him with loud exclamations of surprise and fury.

He was instantly surrounded by about a dozen dark, savage ruffians, the whole of whose countenances expressed the incarnation of demoniacal ferocity.

Thus encompassed by deadly perils, stood gallant CRUSOE JACK IN THE PIRATES' CAVE!

CHAPTER XX.

THE ALARM — THE SEARCH — LELA'S DANGER— ANOTHER CONFLICT WITH THE INDIANS.

THE night had fallen, and the moon shone brightly, when the crew had, as usual, been mustered to the evening meal in the tents they had erected.

Every heart was filled with delight at the prospect of their approaching voyage in the Seagull.

"But where is Jack?" exclaimed Captain Hastings, suddenly missing our hero.

Jack was not wont so long to delay his return.

Tom Starboard replied that he had seen Jack just before sunset, standing on the highest peak on the island, but after that time did not remember seeing him.

"It is strange he has not returned before this," observed the captain. "Can anything have happened to him?"

"I trust not," said Tom. "I hope he hasn't fallen into the sea in the darkness."

At this suggestion everyone looked alarmed.

Mabel turned pale, and her heart beat quickly with forebodings of coming evil.

At this moment it occurred to her that her new attendant, Lela, had also been absent longer than usual.

She mentioned this to her father.

"Lela also absent?" exclaimed Mr. Meredith. "This is indeed strange."

They all joined in his surprise, and many conjectures were hazarded as to the cause of the disappearance of the pair.

"Perhaps they have run away together," said one of the men, with a laugh.

Mr. Meredith silenced the speaker with a look of stern reproof.

But these lightly-spoken words grated unpleasantly on Mabel's ear.

Could he have deceived her?

Had he, on the impulse of the moment, acted so as to prove that his heart was still really with the Indian girl?

But no.

He was incapable of such baseness.

He could never be false to his first love.

After waiting upwards of an hour, our hero's friends resolved to seek him and Lela.

They divided into small parties, each going in different parts of the island in search of the fugitives, with the exception of a few men who remained to take charge of the Seagull, to whom, of course, instructions were given to redouble their vigilance.

The party explored the whole of the principal island. But without effect.

Mr. Meredith, who, in addition to the other men, was accompanied by Tom Starboard, made a most active search.

But returning hopelessly from this expedition, he came face to face with Captain Hastings' party.

It is difficult to say which felt the most anxiety—Mabel's father or Captain Hastings.

"This is getting quite serious," exclaimed the latter, on seeing Mr. Meredith. "Your search has, I see, like mine, been useless."

"Utterly so," answered his friend, mournfully. "What is to be done?"

There was a deep silence.

None seemed able to answer this question.

It was a strange, wild scene, at that silent hour, with the bright moonlight playing upon the beautiful rippling waters and upon the anxious faces of the party on shore, and again dying away into the shadow and gloom of the thick foliage of the trees beyond.

Suddenly, in the distance, were seen a number of canoes filled with Indians.

"He may be among them," exclaimed Captain Hastings.

"The savages may have taken him prisoner. Let us lose no time in following them."

Accordingly, as quickly as possible, they manned their boats, and all being armed with the necessary weapons for combat with their foes, they followed in the wake of the Indians. They were of course soon observed by the Macoushi, and a most exciting chase ensued.

The Indians, who before had been paddling along rather leisurely, on finding themselves pursued, redoubled their speed.

Their example was instantly followed by the others, who soon had the satisfaction of finding they were gaining on the savages.

The chase continued.

The Indians saw that their foes intended to overtake them, but were apparently determined to prolong the chase, and by various manœuvres they continued to elude their pursuers.

At length, apparently finding their position becoming critical, the Macoushi stood up in their canoes, and discharged a fierce volley of arrows at the approaching foe.

Fortunately for Captain Hastings and his party, the moon was at that time partially obscured, and instead of the usually unerring aim of the Indians, their arrows fell harmless into the dark waters.

But the friends of our hero were not to be daunted by this hostile movement.

They immediately replied by a volley from their rifles.

These weapons were more deadly in their effect, and several of the Indians fell wounded and struggling in the waves.

Still our gallant Englishmen did not escape uninjured.

Several of their party were disabled, but the rest, still undaunted, continued the strife.

At this instant a piercing shriek was heard.

It proceeded from Lela!

She could now be seen crouching at the bottom of one of the canoes.

By her side stood the chief Oroma, who savagely repressed her frantic struggles to free herself from the cords which bound her arms.

"Daughter of the Aynoth!" fiercely exclaimed the chief, "in vain is thy resistance! Never shalt thou return to the pale-faces, whom Oroma will ever scorn and defy."

"Scoundrel!" cried Captain Hastings, whose boat was now within a short distance of the group of canoes, "dare you to act thus atrociously? Instantly deliver up the maiden whom you have stolen and the gallant English youth, or your life shall pay the forfeit!"

Oroma understood but little English, and that little he had learnt from Crusoe Jack.

He comprehended, however, the threat thus spoken, and the allusion to our hero called forth his deepest feelings of hate and revenge.

"The fate of the Young Eagle is unknown to Oroma," he cried furiously, in his own language. "He fell not by this arm. Would that I might find him, to wreak my vengeance on him!"

"What does the villain dare to say?" demanded the captain of Tom Starboard.

"He says," replied the brave old tar, "he says he don't know anything of poor Crusoe; that he is looking after him now to revenge himself on him. Depend upon it he is bent on mischief to the poor lad."

"I trust," said Mr. Meredith, "that we shall both find Jack and frustrate the designs of these savages. But, in the meantime, Lela must be rescued."

This, however, proved no easy task.

The Indians rallied round their chief, and a terrific hand-to-hand combat ensued.

The whole of the English party, and especially Captain Hastings and Mr. Meredith, were prepared to fight gallantly for the rescue of the Indian maiden from the power of her merciless persecutor.

Even in the short time she had been with them, she had awakened a feeling of interest and affection in all, and everyone was aware how she had dreaded to fall into the hands of her fellow-countrymen, and now that fate had overtaken her, and her implacable foe seemed about to triumph.

Oroma, on his part, had not the least intention of

relinquishing his meed of revenge at her slighting conduct towards him.

Still he assented, when, after a short conflict, the combatants paused, and Captain Hastings proposed parley.

That some understanding might be come to with Indians seemed a prospect which would be best endeavour to bring about.

Tom was chosen as interpreter, and standing up in the moonlight—all knew his sturdy form, and every Indian's gaze was fixed upon him—he thus commenced his negotiations :—

"Men of Aynoth and Macoushi! There's no occasion for us to fight if you'll listen to reason. You see, in the first place, the Young Eagle, as you used to call him, has disappeared mysteriously, and we can't help thinking that you know so nething of him. If you do, we require you to tell us.

"In the next place, you have taken away that Indian girl against her will and consent, and I tell you plainly, we're not going to allow it.

"She ran away from you because she wanted to, and I don't see why she shouldn't stop with us if she desires it. You've no right to keep her. So give her up; and if your chief will name any reward for agreeing to our terms, our captain says he shall have it. Now, what do you answer ?"

"This," returned Oroma, in a half-sneering tone of triumph. "We know nothing of the Young Eagle; but I hope fervently he has sunk beneath the waters where he left me struggling for my life. If he has, then I have no rival in the possession of my prize" —here he pointed to Lela, who, still crouching by his side, shrank from his gaze—"whom I refuse to relinquish to you, or any other man living.

"As to your gold, I scorn it. Keep it to bring you the valour whereof you need so much. The maiden is mine; and, moreover, she shall not disgrace the tribe by running away from it and joining the pale-faces. All I have said is as yonder rock, immovable, and I will die ere I retract."

With this insolent speech the chieftain seized his paddles, and, by a sudden movement, shot outward in the centre of the stream.

A piercing shriek of despair came from Lela, as she was thus carried away from any chance of rescue.

The whole of the tribe, as if in obedience to some signal, urged their canoes onward in the same manner, and at the same time as their chief.

The quick, unexpected movement took the Englishmen by surprise, and ere they could get in order to follow, the Indians were far ahead of them.

There was some deliberation as to whether they should continue the useless chase, but the same result would have ensued from either decision.

The Indians, who appeared to have hitherto been playing with their speed, and invited the pursuit in order that they might meet the pale-faces in a close encounter, now put on their utmost speed.

Their swift, light paddle canoes soon outstripped the heavier boats of the Englishmen, and they were soon speedily lost in the heavy darkness that clouded the horizon in the direction they took.

A vain chase, and the disconcerted crew of the Seagull returned to the island—returned to fresh adventures, but without having solved the question that had led to their expedition—what had become of Crusoe Jack ?

CHAPTER XXI.

THE GAMING-HOUSE—THE COURSE OF LUCK—THE TWO SCHEMERS—JASPER ENGAGES IN A RASH ADVENTURE—MR. MEREDITH'S CONFIDANT.

IT was night. The scene was in one of those gambling houses which are still numerous in the heart of our great metropolis.

The weather was sultry, but in this abode of dissipation the atmosphere was stifling and oppressively warm, for there was no ventilation, except through the trap-doors that communicated with the floor and the roof, while the gas, whose yellow, sickly glare shone from a dozen chandeliers, added to the intense heat.

Yet this room was filled to overflowing—filled with gamblers of all ages and ranks in the social scale. Young profligates, men grown old in vice, ruined men who strove thus to retrieve their fortunes, timid gamesters new to the dreadful trade, all were vieing with each other in the race for illegal gain.

Meanwhile, M. Beaulieu—the sinister-looking Frenchman who kept this house of ruin—hovered about the tables, exciting his guests to continue their game, and chuckling secretly as he saw the heaps of gold which continued to enrich him at their expense.

At the central table, where the dice rattled most incessantly and the wine flowed freest, and the most hardened gamblers were congregated, a conspicuous figure was Jasper Collins.

He was sitting deeply absorbed in a game in which a large party were engaged.

He had been losing heavily, and he was anxiously waiting for the scale of luck to turn in his favour.

He looked haggard.

Worn with dissipation, and flushed with excitement.

The cool and practised gamblers around him were far too hardened in their terrible work to exhibit either the depression or exultation they may have felt.

Captain Crowther sat by Jasper's side, apparently sharing in his ill-luck, but in reality profiting as much by his losses as the blacklegs with whom he was in league.

"Never mind, Moreland, my boy!" he whispered in the familiar tone he had now assumed. "Recollect that if luck flows in a stream against you, it's just as likely soon to flow like a river in your favour. Let's order another half-dozen bottles, and trust for better luck. You see I don't worry myself like you do, though, by Jove, I'm nearly cleared out!"

Jasper did not reply to this questionable consolation otherwise than with a shrug of the shoulders, but still kept his gaze firmly fixed on the throws of the dice which his unprincipled companion knew well were loaded.

The game proceeded.

Jasper took more wine to sustain his drooping spirits, but it only had the reverse effect.

Meanwhile the luck still continued for a considerable time to go against him; it at length turned more in his favour, and this beneficial change seemed entirely owing to Captain Crowther.

"Now I'll tell you what. I'm going to win, and no mistake," said the latter, as he took the dice-box in his hand, "and if you follow my lead you cannot help winning too. You see if my next move won't be advantageous to both of us."

And so it proved.

But Jasper, while he exulted and felt so grateful to his disinterested friend, would have been slightly uncomfortable had he seen the secret signal that passed between the captain and his accomplices.

"There, I told you how it would be," said the captain, as he swept a pile of gold towards him. We shall both get out of this place to-night, or rather this morning, as rich as Jews; then we can give three cheers for our good friend, M. Beaulieu. You see, in these affairs, I always make it a rule——"

He stopped suddenly, looked at a figure that had been for some time hovering near the table, watching the game and the players with intense interest.

Captain Crowther paused, and then a recognition or at least a suspicion of it, lit up his countenance.

But he strove to conceal it, went on with his game, finished the broken sentence, and in a short time retired unseen from the table, while Jasper was still deeply absorbed in his game.

The captain, who had kept the figure in sight, now sought to approach it, though the latter strove to avoid recognition.

The captain, however, touched his arm.

"I know you," he whispered; "your disguise does not deceive me. Let us retire into the ante-room yonder. I want to talk to you a little."

The other nodded, and they both, unnoticed, left the excited throng.

The stranger was no stranger to our readers, though he appeared so, seeing that he had a long white beard, green spectacles, a white hat, and shabby clothes.

But Captain Crowther knew him instantly.

It was Robert Twistem, the lawyer.

As they retired for their secret converse, the figure of a respectable elderly gentleman, who had been watching the game, though not engaging in it, very intently, proceeded to follow them cautiously.

He contrived so that they did not notice him, but he was able to catch now and then a few words of the following conversation—

"I never expected to see you here, Mr. Twistem."

"No; but I thought I'd just slip in and watch your little game personally; in fact, I've done so on many other occasions when you didn't notice me."

"The deuce you have!" exclaimed Percy. "Well, you can't say that I haven't kept to our agreement, that we're not getting on nicely with our friend yonder."

"He's on the road now, certainly," said the lawyer with a chuckle. "Deep in debt, all his ready money gone, and his estate mortgaged. I shall soon be master of the Moreland property."

"You! Don't be so fast; we, you mean. Recollect our agreement. Well, I'll tell you what, I have a capital scheme in my head, that cannot fail to do our work admirably and very quickly."

"And I have another," said the lawyer, "which I warrant is better still."

"What is it?" both cried at once, in an eager tone.

"No; we'll keep our own secrets," said the wily lawyer. "I'll tell you my scheme very shortly. But, first of all, tell me where our friend puts up to-night?"

"At the Northumberland Hotel, Brook Street," answered the captain.

"Well, somehow I don't think he'll sleep very well, remarked Mr. Twistem, mysteriously. "Circumstances will combine to prevent him. However, we had better go back to the room again, now. I'll communicate with you soon. In a short time we shall be able to work more together."

The two schemers separated.

The captain to return to the side of Jasper, and the lawyer to continue his secret espionage, previous to his equally secret departure.

The listener to their conversation moved away with an expression of deep and painful reflection.

Meanwhile, an exciting scene was taking place at the table where Jasper was seated.

The latter, whose luck was again unfavourable, had discovered evident signs of cheating in the movements of one of his less skilful adversaries.

Jasper started up.

His face was flushed.

His eyes were flashing with the fury that made his whole frame tremble.

The excitement, the disappointment, and the wine he had taken, had conquered Jasper's usually cowardly nature.

He stood now prepared for the most desperate course.

"You are a cheat and a scoundrel!" he thundered to one of his adversaries, who went by the name of Major Rawlings.

"Do you think I didn't see you making signals to your confederate?—and besides, those dice are loaded; and these cards have been tampered with. This is a den of thieves! I'm robbed! I've been mercilessly plundered all the evening."

"Gently! gently, monsieur!" cried the French host. "I am not accustomed in my house to have these disturbances."

"What do I care whether you are accustomed or not. I say that scoundrel—and goodness knows how many more of them—has been robbing me. Do you hear, sir—I call you a scoundrel!"

"And I reply, Mr. Moreland, that I will not be insulted with impunity," returned the unabashed gamester. "I am an officer—an officer and a gentleman; and I demand satisfaction—I'll have satisfaction!"

"So will I!" cried Jasper, in increased fury. "Confound you! do you think I fear such a rascal as you! I hereby challenge you to meet me at Finchley Common to-morrow morning at five. Let our weapons be pistols. I——"

"What's the matter here?" asked the captain, approaching at this time. "A duel? Good gracious!

CRUSOE JACK READS A STRANGE RECORD.

For heaven's sake, my dear Moreland, don't think of such a thing."

"But he shall—for I shall accept his challenge," interposed the furious Major Rawlings. "I will meet you, Mr. Moreland, without fail."

"And I will be your second," said Mr. Catchem, another of the blacklegs.

"Captain Crowther will be mine," Jasper retorted.

"He will take my part, and see that no further unfairness is attempted."

The major sneered sarcastically at these words.

There was something in his manner that betrayed a secret triumph.

Many of the inmates of the room, all of whom had gathered round to witness the contention, exchanged covert glances, of whose import Jasper was ignorant.

"I am sorry this should have occurred," remarked Captain Crowther. "Mr. Moreland, your have spoken in anger. Will you not recall your words?"

"Never!" cried Jasper, firmly.

"And you, major, will you not give some explanation?"

"No; I will fight him!" hissed the gambler, fiercely.

"Then I am afraid the affair must come off," said the captain. "Mr. Moreland, I will be your second. But now our harmony has turned to discord, I think we had better leave the place for to-night. A night's rest may bring us all to a better mind. Come, Moreland. Gentlemen, we bid you farewell until to-morrow."

And the captain and Jasper walked off arm-in-arm, leaving the inmates of the gaming-house to comment on the coming conflict.

Jasper and his friend jumped into a cab to be conveyed to the Northumberland Hotel.

A spectator could have noticed another cab following in pursuit of them.

Jasper threw himself back in his seat. His rage and excitement were still intense.

"I'm sorry you've quarrelled with that man, my dear friend," said the captain; "and especially that you are going to fight him. Do you know who the major is?"

"No."

"He is one of the most determined duellists in London—perhaps in England. Many a man of the noblest blood has fallen by his hand."

Jasper's face fell, his rage was abating, and his natural cowardice returning, at these words. Still he expostulated.

"He is a cheat and a swindler. He has endeavoured to ruin me with false cards and loaded dice."

"Nonsense, my dear fellow, you must have been mistaken. No friend of mine would resort to such base tricks, or I would shoot him myself."

"I tell you I am not mistaken. I must fight him now, and I hope I shall kill him."

"I hope he won't kill you, of which there is some probability," said the captain.

They became silent, and Jasper began to feel very uncomfortable.

In a few minutes they had reached the hotel.

Jasper returned to his own room, harassed by a variety of conflicting feelings. Still, the wine he had drank, and reaction after the excitement, soon combined to send him to sleep.

But in about three hours he woke suddenly with a chill of horror and a foreboding of imminent danger.

It was not without a cause.

Meanwhile, the middle-aged gentleman, of whom we have spoken, left the gaming-house, and returned to his own residence in one of the suburbs of London.

He was a respectable merchant, whose presence at the gaming-house, as our readers may judge, was certainly not in accordance with his own inclination, but for a special purpose, and in pursuance of what he considered a duty.

What this duty was our readers will speedily discover.

Retiring to his own apartment, without disturbing his family, Mr. Layland (as he was called) sat down and wrote a long letter to his old friend, Mr. George Meredith, of which the following is one of the principal points:—

"You have asked me to keep watch over certain persons in England who are inimical to your interests. I have done so. In my last I gave you a full account of the proceedings of Madge Collins, and have now to speak of her grandson, Jasper. He has the estate which is rightfully that of Sir James Moreland, but he is surrounded by disadvantages that are leading him to his ruin. Men of unprincipled character are by degrees absorbing his fortune. In particular is one young in years but old in crime, named Captain Crowther; but I cannot help thinking that he is other than what he appears. I will endeavour to ascertain more of him. Last night I followed him and Jasper to a gambling-house of the worst character, where I saw enough to convince me how the fortune of Jasper is being wasted. I also saw this Captain Crowther confer in secret with another man, who, from his appearance, I am inclined to think was disguised. He may have been the lawyer, Twistem. I tried to overhear their conversation, but without effect. I, however, gathered enough to know that some subtle schemes are going on against Jasper. There was also a dissension at the gambling-house. Jasper has discovered he is being made a dupe, penetrated the wiles of his blackleg comrades, and in his fury has challenged one of them to a duel. The man is known as a skilful duellist, and I think that Jasper stands but little chance with him. To-morrow they meet, and whatever the consequences may be, I know you will like to hear of them. I have a presentiment that to-morrow will be an eventful day. Meanwhile, adieu.

"Your affectionate friend,
"HENRY LAYLAND."

Mr. Layland did not seal or direct this letter. He waited to add a postscript the following morning, describing the result of the duel.

Meanwhile, he had a dim foreboding that events important to his absent friend were about to occur.

CHAPTER XXII.

THE APPARITION — THE EXPLANATION OF THE MYSTERY—THE DUEL AND ITS EFFECTS.

JASPER COLLINS had never experienced such a fearful waking as that when, sleep suddenly deserting him, he rose up in his bed in the chamber of the hotel, and looked around him.

It was still night, though the first streaks of morning were visible in the sky, and struggled faintly through the closed blind and curtains of the windows.

But the other side of the room was still enveloped in almost total darkness.

In an instant all the events of the preceding day returned to Jasper's mind, the thought of the gaming-house, the quarrel, and oh! worse than all! the duel he had to fight that morning.

His heart sank, and a chill perspiration suffused his frame as he thought of it.

Why had he quarrelled with Major Rawlings?

True, it was annoying to find that he was being thus pressed upon by sharpers, and that his fine inheritance was gradually slipping from him by his own folly and others' rascality.

But why place himself in such imminent danger as he now was?

He had brought on his own fate by a sudden fit of anger, which, for the time, had made him brave. Now all his natural cowardice returned, and bitterly he cursed the moment when he had given the challenge.

The idea of death to him was particularly terrible. But how could he secure himself against the probable fate that awaited him?

He fervently wished that he could find some means of withdrawing from the terrible engagement; but he knew that if he did, all his acquaintances would scout him as a paltroon, and begin to doubt his assumed noble birth.

Oh! how terrible it was to know that in an hour or two he must stand up probably to be shot in cold blood!

Jasper thought of running away, of doing anything that would remove him from his terrible position; but he was still undecided, and in his indecision and fear, tossed and re-tossed with feverish agitation.

In this situation he trembled at every sound.

A superstitious terror was added to his other horrors, and he thought he perceived in every half-distinguished object around him, some apparition sent to warn him of his approaching end.

Was this all mere delusion?

No, there was—there must be a figure moving on the side of the bed near the wall—a white, ghostly figure, apparently gliding from behind a screen, coming grimly upon him through the semi-darkness.

Jasper gave vent to a cry of terror, and strove to shut out the terrific object with his hands, but it fascinated his gaze like a basilisk, and still approached closer and closer to him.

He could not help returning its fearful gaze, and thus perceived it to be a tall form enveloped in white drapery, the features, half-discerned, were those of an old man, with a long beard of silver-gray, and an aspect, not venerable, but ferocious, and almost demoniac in its expression.

Jasper trembled with a mortal terror, which almost paralyzed him and rendered him incapable of motion, speech, or action.

"Jasper Collins, falsely called Moreland," said the spectre, in most sepulchral tones, "your life has been evil, but your last hour is now approaching."

"Oh, don't say that, for the sake of heaven!" shrieked the affrighted wretch, recoiling in his excess of terror.

"It is, and nothing can prolong it," replied the spectre. "No mortal hand can avert your danger. You have only one chance; and it is in me. I alone can save you."

"How?—how? Tell me quick," said Jasper, catching at these welcome words eagerly.

"You must sign this paper—a compact to remain faithful in all things to me."

"Who or what are you or have you been?" asked Jasper.

"An embodied spirit, whose existence some ignorant fools may doubt, but whose power over mankind is boundless. I was once Sir William Moreland, one of the ancestors from whom you unjustly claim to be descended. I was disinherited by my father, and shot myself through despair at my ruin, having sworn revenge against the whole race of Morelands. But my spirit has since wandered over the earth, ever invisibly watching over the destinies of the family. You I will befriend on the condition I have named, and I will in future ever aid you to carry on your deception and your usurpation of my ancestors' name."

"What if I agree not to your terms?"

"You die," responded the apparition, "by the hand of the practised duellist."

Jasper again shuddered with fear.

"Oh, no—no!" he cried. "I will do anything. I will agree to your terms."

The spectre drew out a paper from beneath his shadowy robe.

"Sign your name here—your real name, Jasper Collins," he said. "Here is a pen and an ink-horn, and I will guarantee that the duel of to-day shall be harmless to yourself."

Jasper clutched even at this extraordinary proposal.

He took the paper from the spectre's hand, and, grasping the pen, wrote his name as well as he could in the gloom in the place indicated.

"Rise up at the hour appointed," said the spectre, as he again took the paper, "and proceed to the ground cool and collected, and with at least the semblance of courage. All shall go well with you. And, mark my words, should you want me to aid you at any future time, I, who know even your inmost thoughts, will instantly appear before you. Farewell now, and forget not our compact."

The spectre was gone in a minute—how, Jasper could not discern.

He appeared to vanish instantly, and the wrongful possessor of Jack's inheritance was left alone to his reflections.

Unpleasant reflections they were.

Jasper was too agitated to reflect calmly on the extraordinary circumstance that had just occurred, or to suspect that there was any trick or deception in it.

He felt, too, for a moment, a little reassured by the spectre's promises to aid him and secure his safety in the forthcoming ordeal.

But this feeling did not last long.

When, after an hour or two's half doze in the growing sunlight, Jasper awoke to find the morning radiance shining brilliantly into the apartment, he began to think that the spectre's visit was a dream, and that no agency, either natural or supernatural, was at work on his behalf.

He looked at his watch—an elegant repeater, studded with diamonds—and found it wanted but three-quarters of an hour to the time appointed for the meeting.

He arose, made his toilet, and after a mournful gaze out on the sunlight, which he feared he should never see again after that day, he sat down and proceeded to write a letter to Madge Collins, explaining his position, and giving her directions should the duel be fatal to him.

A similar epistle was directed to Mr. Twistem.

Jasper had now lost all confidence in the spectre's assurances, all of which he held to be but parts of a vivid but feverish vision, and all his trembling fears returned as he wrote these epistles, which seemed like his death-warrant.

Just as he had concluded them, his friend, Captain Crowther, entered the room, as gay and smiling in demeanour as Jasper was the reverse.

"Well, and how do you feel now?" he said, after their first greeting. "The meeting must come off now, you know; there is no getting out of it. I have brought a case of pistols, and a medical man to be in attendance on the field. We will soon arrange all preliminaries. And, indeed, we have not much time to lose. If you get a good choice of ground, you have every probability of good luck."

Jasper shrugged his shoulders.

"Good luck to be shot," he said, gloomily.

"Now, what's the use of being despondent about it? Look at me. I've fought, I may say, hundreds of duels in my life, both in India, England, and in France, and I'm not dead yet. Luck is everything, and I've no doubt it will be on your side."

"I wish I could be equally sanguine," remarked Jasper; "but, of course, it isn't because I'm afraid."

"Oh, no, of course not."

"But no one knows what may happen."

"No, but I'd advise you to drink this glass of brandy and soda water, and a few biscuits to sustain your spirits. Now we must be off, for the cab is at the door, and all is ready."

Jasper, with ill-concealed reluctance, followed his friend to the vehicle, into which he jumped, and was soon speeding along on his way to the fatal ground, in company with Sergeant Bilke, a regimental surgeon, whose services he had secured in case of accidents.

Had Jasper not been overcome with fear, or had suspected the deception practised upon him, he would easily have penetrated the disguise of the spectre, and foiled its schemes.

And had he been able to watch the exit of the mysterious figure, he would have seen it glide cautiously behind the screen, and through the door, and then, noiselessly ascend to the chamber over, enter, and lock the door after it.

Then, he might have seen the apparition, casting aside the sheet in which it was enveloped, and the false beard that covered its countenance, stand triumphantly in the apartment, presenting to the view the bland countenance of Mr. Robert Twistem.

"Splendid! delightful!" he ejaculated. "Why, the fellow's completely a child, when his fears are appealed to. How capitally I kept up my bit of acting—as if I'd belonged to some theatre all my life. But at last I am successful. He is now entirely in my power, and I can wield this little document over his head, like the sword of Damocles. Robert Twistem, your fortune will soon be made. Let me read over this precious paper, which, in spite of the darkness, is signed so legibly with the so-called Mr. Moreland's real name."

The lawyer chuckled as he read over the paper, which we will in a future portion of our narrative detail to our readers.

Sufficient to say, for the present, that its purport, if made public, would instantly ruin Jasper Collins.

The lawyer smiled triumphantly as he again pocketed the paper, and then relapsed into pleasant reflections.

The sun shone brightly on the wide expanse of the common, when Jasper and his friends arrived at the place of meeting.

Major Rawlings, Mr. Catchem, and several others were already there.

There was an expression of triumph and determination on the countenance of the duellist, as he greeted his antagonist, which made Jasper's blood run cold.

The preliminaries were speedily settled.

The seconds loaded the pistols.

Then measured the ground.

Jasper obtained the choice of position, which was one favourable point gained.

While he stood in the shade, where he could obtain a good view of his antagonist, the latter had the sun full in his face.

But the practised duellist knew how to make the best of disadvantages.

He pulled his hat over his eyes, and took up his position in his usual calm and collected matter.

Jasper, though frequently reassured by his friend, the captain, still inwardly quailed and trembled, and felt such a degree of fear that he could scarcely stand his ground, and the pistol shook in his unwilling hand.

"Place your body in this position," whispered Jasper's second, "so as to present as little mark as possible to the enemy. I know you are firm and determined" ("very!" he added, in an undertone), "and that you can take a good aim. Now then!—one! two! three!"

Jasper took his aim, and closed his eyes in terror.

A loud double report.

Jasper opened his eyes, to find that neither shots had taken the least effect.

"Very harmless," remarked Captain Crowther.

"And not at all satisfactory," added Major Rawlings. "I demand another shot."

"Will you agree to this, Mr. Moreland?" asked the captain of Jasper. "Shall the duel continue?"

"Ye—es!" said Jasper, falteringly, still fearful of the imputation of the cowardice which he felt, "certainly."

"Then, gentlemen, we will again proceed to business," said the captain.

The seconds again loaded, and the duellists again took up their positions.

This time Jasper was more abjectly terrified, and his antagonist apparently more composed than before.

"Take a rather higher aim," suggested Captain Crowther, "even if you don't kill him, it will be the better plan."

Jasper assented, and took aim—as far as he could aim at all—at the shoulders of his antagonist.

Then he levelled his weapon, fully pursuaded by the terrible sinking in his heart that his last hour had come.

"Now, then, **again**. One, two, three!"

The opponent's **second** dropped his handkerchief as a signal.

Jasper once **more** closed his eyes and fired.

A loud report—as loud, it seemed to the wrecker's son, as the trump of doom—and then, with a wild cry, Jasper fell.

CHAPTER XXIII.

HOW THE PIRATES TREATED JACK—THE CROSS-EXAMINATION—DISPOSAL OF TREASURE—ANOTHER ENCOUNTER IN PROSPECT.

We have left our friend Jack in perhaps the most uncomfortable position he had ever experienced during the whole of his numerous and exciting adventures.

He stood in the centre of the pirates' cave, surrounded by the fierce band of desperadoes who had caught him, red-handed, in examining, and, as they thought, plundering their treasure.

Their astonishment had, for the first few moments, prevented them from doing more than gaze at our hero with an expression that led him to hope for little mercy at their hands.

The pirate chief was the first to speak.

Advancing close up to Jack, he seized his arm with an iron grasp, and exclaimed in a hoarse voice—

"*Carramba!* So this is the way our private property is endangered, and our secrets discovered! By San Jose! but you shall explain this. What have you to say for yourself?"

"Yes, what have you to say for yourself?" echoed all the rest, in one fierce chorus.

"Come, now, you had better speak," resumed the pirate chief, "so that we may see how much mercy you deserve, if you deserve any at all. Just tell us the truth, and the whole truth, or by all that's murderous, I'll put this creese in your thievish throat!"

Jack stood facing his enemies.

He knew that it would be both useless and dangerous to display the fear he could not help feeling in his terrible position.

Bold words and a fearless demeanour would alone save him from instant death.

He accordingly replied, in as confident a tone as he could assume—

"Captain, I can easily explain the truth. Appearances are against me; but this I can solemnly affirm, I didn't come here to steal your treasure."

"Ho! ho!" growled the chorus of ruffians. "You had better not try and make us believe that, my young powder-monkey. Not come here to steal our treasure! It looks like it, indeed! Why, what are you doing now?"

"Merely looking over it," said Crusoe, boldly. "I found this place by accident."

"What accident?" asked the pirate chief. "How did you find your way here? Tell me that. No prevaricating, mind."

Jack saw by the deadly gleam in the eyes of the incensed rover-chief that it would be dangerous to tell him anything but the truth.

He therefore gave him a detailed account of his discovery of the track from the shore of the island to the entrance of the cave, his following it up, and the means by which he effected his entrance.

The latter circumstance caused the pirates some surprise, not unmixed probably with a certain degree of admiration at his daring.

"Daggers and marling-spikes!" exclaimed the pirate chief. "But it's coming to something if all-weather rovers like us are to be overhauled by such insignificant craft as you! Blow up the trap-door, indeed! Perhaps you'd like to blow up the cave and all with it, and take our ship, the Black Eagle, into the bargain?"

And indeed Jack did not feel at the moment any disinclination to perform that feat.

"And how did you open our locker?" was the chief's next question.

"Eh? That's it, is it? Curses on the blind folly that made us use old Dietrich Hakluyt's money chest, as if it was fit for a pirate's locker, and especially to leave the key behind, and trust to the secret crevice, for its safety. Barnard, you must put a new double lock on that chest, and we'll ___ it somewhere before we again put out. ___ bodikins! but I did think it was safe here, at ____."

"Its safety's over, captain," remarked one of the rovers. "It seems to me that there's been all sorts of craft cruising about these islands latterly. You know we've sighted about four in the last two days near here, and my opinion is that this place will soon be too hot to hold us."

"I expect we've got a nest of hornets blown on us already," observed another pirate. "Who knows how many?"

"We hab cotched one lilly hornet, cap'n," said the negro cook of the pirate ship, with a savage and malignant grin, "and we can easy pull um wings off."

"We'll have the truth out of him, at all events," said the leader of the buccaneers, "and see how far we are in danger."

Accordingly the pirate chief put down his cutlass, seated himself on an empty barrel, and prepared for a regular cross-examination of Jack.

"Now, youngster," he said, in a milder but still determined voice, "listen to me. We've got you in our power, and it's no use trying on any tricks with us. I'm not a man to be trifled with. We want to know all about you, your history, your friends; how you came on these islands, what you're here for, and who you're with; what's the strength of your party, and how much they know or suspect about us. All these particulars we want to know—and we will know—and it depends entirely on your telling us all whether we shall deal mercifully with you or not. So begin at once."

Jack saw there was no way of evading this command.

So he commenced giving the pirate crew a

detailed account of his whole history, or, at least, all parts of it that had any connection with what they wanted to know.

The narrative, which necessarily included many of Jack's adventures, could not fail to impress the pirates with some admiration of Jack's spirit and bravery.

Anything in the shape of adventure appealed directly to their rugged natures, and they accordingly felt much interest in Crusoe's narrative.

"Well, my lad," said the captain, when he had concluded, "it isn't so bad as I thought; for your friends don't seem to have much suspicion that we're so near them. At all events, you seem a plucky one, and stick at nothing in the way of danger. You seem to have a little of the rover's spirit in you, or you would not have put on that dress and weapons. How say you to turning pirate yourself?"

Jack's countenance fell.

He was puzzled how to reply to this question.

It would have been, under some circumstances, a tempting offer; but when he looked at the fierce, swarthy, lawless band of ruffians who surrounded him, and contrasted them with the band of gallant Englishmen on board the Seagull, his heart revolted against the idea, and he shook his head in answer to the pirate's question.

"You won't! And why not, my young Columbus?" asked the pirate captain. "What can you say against a rover's life?"

"Well, there is a great deal to be said against it, captain. In the first place, it isn't honest—"

These words were received by the lawless band with a roar of derisive laughter.

"Honest! per Baccho!" cried the captain of the rovers, who seemed to make use of oaths derived from every language that existed. "By the beard of the Prophet! as they say among the Turks, that is a good one. No, my young philosopher, we are not exactly honest, as landsmen understand the word; but we have our own code of laws, and whoever transgresses them" (here the captain pointed significantly to his cutlass, his pistols, and a coil of rope beside him), "why, we make him own to the power of our justice. But, as to honesty, in your sense of the word—pooh!"

Here the pirate captain pulled out his pipe, and began filling and lighting it with great composure.

Jack saw that it was fruitless, if not dangerous, to go upon that tack any longer, so he turned his argument in another direction, and appealed to the pirates' interests.

"Without saying anything more about the honesty of it," resumed Jack, "look at the danger you pirates are continually living in. You are never safe two days together. You are tabooed at every port. You can only put into the more sequestered harbours, under cover of the darkness. The myrmidons of the law are ever on the watch, and you know not how soon you may encounter them. A price is set upon your heads, and hundreds are either swearing vengeance against you for despoiling them, else thirst for your capture, impelled by greed of gain. Now, if you were honest traders, you would be under the protection of every flag that was known and respected on the high seas. You could proceed on all voyages in safety, and your gains would be much more sure. And then there is the reflection that you need fear no man, that you are as good as any other, and no nation can withhold from you the protection of its laws while you continue to obey them."

"Bravo!" cried the pirates, who seemed rather astonished, if not much edified by this discourse. "Three cheers for honesty."

"Which we respect so much," remarked the captain's lieutenant, sarcastically.

"Especially at a distance," chimed in another sea-robber.

"Well, my lad," remarked the captain, who had listened to Jack's homily with much attention, "you seem to be able to 'talkee-talkee,' as the Chinese say, or have the 'gift of the gab,' as you Englishmen express it, but I'm afraid your arguments are thrown away here. You talk of the dangers of a pirate's life; well, that seems to me rather a cowardly line of argument, for the perils of our life form its greatest charm. It is the constant excitement, the wild exultant and continual hope of plunder, coupled with the perils we undergo to obtain it, that makes our life far superior to many others. You'd know what it was, if you had been a pirate as many years as I have. When I was your age, and I lived on my father's sugar plantation in Cuba, I should have rejected the idea of being a pirate, with the greatest scorn; but now circumstances have made me one, I feel I would not change my life for that of a king—nay, am I not as great as a monarch on land? I am a prince of my own making—the king of the seas."

Jack could not avoid being impressed by the proud tone in which the pirate chief spoke these last words, and the handsome, half-Spanish countenance, tall, commanding form, which made the pirate chief so superior in appearance to the crew he commanded.

"Besides," resumed the buccaneer, "where would be the safety of myself and my crew were we to turn honest now? I tell you it is too late. The name of Juan Hernando Valdez, known also as the Black Eagle, and still better as the Scourge of the Pacific, is too well known and universally execrated to allow its possessor any safety. Every government in South and Central America has set a heavy price upon my head, and if I could hope for mercy from one, the others would still be my remorseless foes. No, it is too late for honesty on my part, much as I may desire it secretly. Fate has made me a pirate, and pirate I must remain. But a truce to such talk as this. Hola, there, caballeros, let's get supper ready, and drown our cares in a deep carousal."

A cheer was the reply to these welcome words, and the tables, benches, and forms were speedily brought together, and all kinds of provisions were taken from the cupboards, and the ship's stores placed upon the festive board.

Jack, who had privately cast aside the portions of the rover's dress in which he had equipped himself, saw in the changed demeanour of the pirates some hope of his own ultimate escape, or at least the safety of his life.

Still he was kept strictly in surveillance, and any attempt at escape as yet would be madness; nevertheless, he was filled with anxiety as to his friends and Mabel, and the state of mind they would be in when they discovered his mysterious absence.

He, however, determined to follow up the favourable opinion he had gained from the pirates, and accordingly joined in their festivities with seeming enjoyment.

The feast, the mirth, and the wassail were carried on with that wild and reckless enjoyment natural to men whose lives are passed in an alternation of imminent dangers and temporary security.

Songs were sung.

Toasts of the most lawless nature given and responded to.

The scene was rapidly assuming the character of an orgie.

But though the captain apparently shared actively in the carousal, an acute spectator might have noticed that he carefully kept within the bounds of sobriety. At least, he seemed to retain to the full extent the clearness of his acute faculties, and he also used his authority to restrain, as far as possible in this particular, his lawless crew.

While the rest of his reckless company were deep in their carousal—too deep to pay any particular attention to the actions of their leader—Captain Valdez slipped aside from his position in the central table, and proceeded to converse with Benito, his lieutenant, in a low tone.

They continued thus for a long time, and it would have been palpable to a close observer—indeed it was to our friend Jack—that the subject of their private converse was one of considerable importance to them.

Among the crew of the pirate ship, however, not one heard a single word; but in our character of faithful chroniclers, we are privileged to place before our readers the main points of what passed between them.

The conversation was in Spanish, and ran nearly thus—

"Benito," said the captain, "an idea has just struck me about which I desire your advice. Yonder lad has let out in his narrative perhaps more than he desires about the ship Seagull. It seems she is lying in first-rate fighting and sailing trim, off the principal island, and I have a shrewd suspicion that she has much in her that would prove worth having. Now, what say you if we make a bold stroke and board her this very night?"

The lieutenant pondered deeply, his dark, fierce gaze fixed piercingly on his chief as he did so.

"Do you know what sized vessel she is?" he asked at length.

"Of course I do: you know we all know. Didn't we see her several times when we came here to hide our treasure, when her hull was embedded in the coral reef, and there didn't seem any possibility of getting her out?

"Didn't we try to clear her of all the cargo, without getting much worth having, as it proved? But it seems another wreck of a rich English vessel has occurred here since then, and her crew, who seem to be spirited fellows enough, have managed to save a great deal of the cargo, and stowed it on board the Seagull.

"How I wish we'd been here before, watched our chance, and made a thorough search of the second wreck! But the wealth may be still there, and I propose we proceed to secure it at once, for the Seagull sails to-morrow, and to-night is our last chance."

"They'll never go until they've searched through the islands to find the lad," said Benito; "and then perhaps they'll see our ship, and be upon us. Very likely they're on our track now."

"But their ship, like ours, will of course be at anchor all night. Whatever happens, there is nothing to prevent our sending a few of our fellows in one of the boats for the purpose of reconnoitring the enemy's position, and, if possible, making a raid on the ship."

"And suppose they happen to be all on board, and prepared for desperate resistance?"

"Sangre de Dios! Benito, but you are full of qualms to-night," cried the pirate captain, rather nettled.

"Well?"

"Suppose, as you say, they are all capable of showing fight, what then? They are but forty or so, and we are equally numerous. It is man for man, and when were we pirates afraid of a close encounter?

"All I know is this, that if we stay here all night, we shall not get off anyhow without a fight with the Seagull, and if on the other hand, we leave to-night, farewell to our chance of plundering her."

"Cannot we watch her course, and attack her on the high seas?" suggested Benito.

"Very bad policy, indeed. Recollect she's a vessel half as large again as my Black Eagle, and in the open sea we should stand no chance with her. While at anchor she is much more helpless."

Benito paused again, and reflected deeply.

"But about this boy?" he asked at length. "How can we prevent him betraying us? How do you intend to dispose of him?"

"Benito," replied the captain, determinedly, "whatever other circumstances occur, that boy must not be let out of our sight. We must take him with us. In fact, he must become one of our crew. While he knows the secret of our treasure, and of our retreat in these islands, it would not be safe to let him go. He could betray us at any time, and besides, he is a spirited lad, and I have taken a fancy to him. He would be a valuable addition to our crew, and I think that he would not want much persuasion to become a pirate in act and deed."

"What, then, are your present intentions?" asked the lieutenant.

"To stay here a few hours," returned the captain; "unload our vessel, stow the things away here, and make some of the fellows dig out a deeper and securer hiding-place for the chest which contains our principal booty. Crusoe Jack (as this young hero calls himself) must be taken on board and securely confined, and before morning I hope to have a fresh treasure from the Seagull."

"All this does not seem so clear to me," remarked Benito, doubtfully. "In the first place, I think these islands are no longer a secure landing-place for us, and that to leave that chest and our other cargo here after what has occurred would be sheer madness. What this young fellow can discover accidentally, may be discovered in the same way by others. Attack the Seagull by all means if you think there is a good chance of success. But have our own ship perfectly in readiness, and leave nothing here that you reckon of value—some more secure hiding-place can surely be found."

"I think your advice good," admitted the Black Eagle, after some deliberation. "To lose the fruits of all our most successful expeditions would be particularly maddening. The chest shall be conveyed on deck without loss of time, and our little fire-eater shall find himself condemned to the same fate."

Having arrived at this determination, the captain hastened to put his resolution into effect.

Having first ascertained that no signs of an enemy had as yet been discerned by those without, he directed them to load the boats with all the more valuable of the property in the cave.

Jack accordingly witnessed the removal of the treasure he had discovered by those who considered themselves its owners.

"Now, my men," said Captain Valdez, as he witnessed this operation, "we must remember that chest contains the united property of our whole band, and be careful accordingly. I will take an oar with you myself, and you, my young friend (touching Jack on the shoulder), will please to come with me, and then you will see what a pirate's ship is like."

Jack saw that it would be useless to resist, though he knew also that this order was tantamount to being taken away to a lengthened imprisonment.

His heart sank as he cast his eyes in the direction of the Seagull, which was, however, invisible in the darkness, and thought of the friends that missed him, and his slight chance of seeing them again.

But he had little opportunity to indulge in these reflections, for he was compelled to take his seat with four more in the largest boat, and take an oar in his hand and help to remove the treasure to the Black Eagle.

The formidable pirate schooner lay far out in the bay, and as her great black hull loomed dimly through the heavy darkness that had now overspread the whole face of the sky, Jack could yet perceive enough of her strength, speed, and probable fighting qualities to know that she would prove no despicable foe against the gallant Seagull.

There was not the faintest prospect of escape as they rowed to the ship.

The captain kept our hero too closely under his immediate surveillance, and watched his every motion with the acuteness of a hawk.

Jack and his companions soon arrived at the ship, and having clambered up her sides, and got aboard, the next great affair was the hauling up of the treasure-chest, which was a matter of some difficulty.

Captain Valdez took an active part in the operation, as well as in stowing it away securely in his own cabin.

The less valuable parts of their possessions were disposed of in the same place, and in the meantime the pirate chief had said to Jack—

"Now, my lad, I must trouble you to go down below, and stay there a few hours, when I will tell you what I have decided shall be your future destiny."

Jack, knowing that resistance was useless, suffered himself to be removed to the hold, and securely fastened therein.

Had he known that the pirates intended to attack his dear friends in the Seagull, he would perhaps not have been quite so quiet.

The captain having thus safely disposed of his prisoner, and superintended the removal of the rest of the property from the cave, set out with about thirty of the crew in three boats for their desperate expedition.

CHAPTER XXIV.

THE ATTACK ON THE SEAGULL—A TERRIBLE ENCOUNTER WITH THE PIRATES.

THE night was now far advanced, though it wanted some hours of daylight, when the party of the Seagull, after their unsuccessful search, returned to their ship.

Sleep was almost impossible to our hero's friends, and they spent several hours in fruitless conjectures as to the fate of Jack.

Captain Hastings was of opinion that our hero had been carried away by some other tribe of Indians, but still he advocated another expedition in the morning, and to thoroughly examine the island, in case the natives might yet be lurking in some part of the thick jungle.

"But," said Meredith, "if he has been carried away by Indians, they would not linger long on these islands, having obtained their object. Depend upon it, they are far away by this time. I am afraid we must give up all hopes of finding Jack: he could not be concealed long in so small an island as this."

"True," replied Captain Hastings, "but I am loth to abandon the search, while the faintest chance remains of finding Jack."

Mabel also earnestly implored them not to give up all hope.

"Who knows?" she said. "He may be lying wounded in some thicket, unable to move or call for assistance."

They resolved, therefore, to resume the search by daylight, by exploring the coast, which, if Jack were still alive and at liberty, he would be sure to make for.

With this resolution, they separated for their respective berths, to endeavour to gain a little sleep while yet darkness rendered it useless to commence the search.

Tom Starboard, however, was one of those who could not rest.

The uncertainty of Jack's fate filled him with grief, and he restlessly paced the main deck.

The anchor watch was being kept by three men, who stowed themselves away comfortably under the lee of the long boat, and other sheltered places, conceiving that that was keeping quite watch enough in a land-locked harbour.

In one of Tom's restless pacings, he fancied he heard a slight splash in the water, and leaning over the bulwark, he endeavoured to pierce the Cimmerian darkness which surrounded them.

In vain he strained his eyes, however.

He could see nothing.

Muttering to himself, "It was a shark, maybe—they are plentiful enough hereaway," he was about to resume his moody pacing to and fro, when the sound was repeated, and this time his experienced ears could not be deceived.

He knew it to be the sound of oars.

But who could it be?

Was it Jack, who had made his escape from the Indians, and, taking to a canoe, was endeavouring to reach the ship?

Possessed with this hope, the old tar was on the point of shouting, "Boat ahoy!" when it occurred to him it might be the Indians themselves, who had discovered the ship, and hoped to surprise the crew, and make themselves masters of her.

He resolved, therefore, to apprise the captain; and as no time was to be lost, he instantly proceeded to the captain's cabin.

He found Captain Hastings lying in his berth fully dressed, and wide awake, he having been unable to gain a moment's rest.

Tom, in a few words, acquainted the captain with what he had heard.

They both went at once to the deck, and endeavoured to ascertain the number of boats that were coming, or whether it was merely one.

Fortunately, a slight gleam of moonlight was for a moment visible, and after a minute or two, they were enabled to make out three boats filled with men pulling fast towards them.

In the uncertainty as to whether they were friends or foes, Captain Hastings thought best to assume the latter, and despatched Tom to rouse and arm the crew forward, while he went into the cabin to call Mr. Meredith.

No time was to be lost, and in a few minutes all the crew were armed with pistols and cutlasses.

The four-pounder guns which the ship carried were loaded with grape-shot and run out, and all ready to give a warm reception to boats if needed.

Mr. Meredith, revolver in hand, took his station near the cabin door, and Mabel, in a state of terror and anxiety, remained inside.

The mate was superintending the gun, and Captain Hastings stood at the head of twelve of his crew to repel any attack by boarding.

As the darkness would render it difficult to recognise friend or foe, lights were brought to the main deck, casting a lurid glare over the scene, and revealing the bronzed faces of the crew and their gleaming cutlasses.

Nor were these preparations made a minute too soon, for scarcely were they completed when the boats came alongside.

A ferocious yell proceeded from those in them, followed by a discharge of grape and canister from the ship, wounding several of the pirates slightly, but not doing much harm, the darkness rendering all uncertain.

The pirates were disappointed by not being able to surprise the Seagull, but hoping still to carry her by force, they clambered up the chains with the activity of tigers.

Several of them were knocked back into the water, but long experience in boarding had given them the advantage, and with fierce shouts, they leapt, inflamed with the hope of plunder, on to the deck of the Seagull, where they were instantly attacked by Captain Hastings and his brave men.

A fearful combat then ensued.

True it was that the crew of the Seagull outnumbered the pirates by about ten men; but the buccaneers were inured by long service to a desperate life, and fought with the ferocity of wild beasts.

The crew of the Seagull were brave but inexperienced.

For a time the pirates gained the advantage, and step by step the crew of the Seagull were driven back to the forecastle, on which they stood, having now the advantage of a platform.

Both parties now rested for a moment, wearied with their exertions, and stood regarding each other with looks of the fiercest enmity.

"At them again, my bullies!" shouted the pirate chief. "Carraja! but we will make mincemeat of the fat English traders."

"Stand firm, my brave lads!" cried Captain Hastings. "Let us drive these sea-wolves back to their lairs!"

"Easier said than done!" cried the pirate captain, firing his pistol full in the face of Hastings as he was encouraging his men.

The bullet fortunately only grazed the shoulder of the latter, inflicting a slight wound.

The crew of the Seagull were just on the point of leaping down on to the main deck, and making a rush at the enemy, when an event occurred which turned the scale in favour of the Seagull's crew.

Tom Starboard, who had been fighting desperately, laying about him like a Trojan, thought he perceived a way of putting an end to the combat.

Accordingly he whispered to a couple of his mates his design.

They crept over the bows of the ship, and making their way by the chains till they came abaft the mainmast, they clambered over the bulwarks on to the deck again; and silently slewing round one of the guns which had not been discharged, pointed it to the group of pirates in front of the topgallant forecastle, where the pirates held the ship's crew in a state of siege.

It was just then that the combat was about to be renewed.

Tom, seizing the critical moment before the crews were inextricably mingled together again, fired the gun directly among the pirates.

The effect was tremendous.

More than a dozen pirates fell dead or wounded, and the remainder, staggered by the unexpected blow, stood irresolute for one moment.

Then, seeing the hopelessness of any further attempt to carry the vessel, the pirate chief, who had escaped with scarcely a wound, gave the signal of retreat, and with the remnant of his crew, rushed to the boats, which still remained alongside where they had been fastened.

The crew of the Seagull, with loud cheers, rushed after them, to endeavour to cut off their retreat.

They succeeded, however, in cutting down but one or two of the pirates, who, with the activity of men flying for their lives, leaped into their boats, and cutting them adrift, seized their oars in a moment.

They were many yards away from the Seagull before the crew of the latter could get a gun to bear upon them.

The pirate chief, standing up in his boat, roared out, in an explosion of rage at his defeat—

"You have conquered me this time. But when next we meet the result will be different. I will hang your lieutenant to the main-yard, when I reach my ship, as an example of what you may all expect if ever any of you get in my power. Beware! for I tell you again, I will have my revenge on Crusoe Jack!"

Several muskets were discharged at random from the Seagull after the retreating pirates, but it was not expected much damage was done by them; and the boats were soon lost in the darkness.

CHAPTER XXV.

THE CHASE FOR THE PIRATE—A TERRIFIC STORM—JACK'S EXTRAORDINARY APPARITION ON BOARD THE SEAGULL.

THE wind was blowing rather strong from the south-east, as the Seagull stood under easy sail from the little harbour in which they had anchored during the night.

It need scarcely be said that the pirate was nowhere visible, but knowing that as the wind had held in this quarter for some days, he would not have made much way as his course was directly in the teeth of the wind, Captain Hastings was not inclined to carry much sail.

The party bade farewell to the islands where they had met with so many adventures, and which now lay covered with the gorgeous vegetation of the tropics as they had been when they had first entered them.

"We will hunt this rascally pirate to-day," exclaimed Captain Hastings to Meredith, who, glass in hand, was standing on the poop, sweeping the horizon with his telescope. "Once seen, he cannot escape us, for there are few vessels can hold their own with the swift-winged Seagull."

"I hope so," observed Meredith; "but a stern chase is proverbially a long chase, you know."

At this moment Mabel, who had not hitherto made her appearance on deck that morning, now came up the companion ladder, and asked her father anxiously whether the pirate had been seen.

"Not yet, my dear child," replied her father, "but we hope to sight him to-day, for we are as fully determined to rescue that brave boy from the power of those miscreants, as you will be glad to see him rescued."

"Alas!" said Mabel, "that I am but a girl, and can take no part in a glorious combat fought for so good a cause, else no arm should strike with more effect than mine."

"I do not doubt it, my dear Mabel," said her father.

At this moment his words were arrested by a cry that thrilled his soul with hope.

"Sail ho!" was shouted down by the look-out from the foretop-gallant-yard, and "Sail ho!" was repeated by one of the mates, who had stationed himself with a powerful telescope in the main-top.

"What do you make her out?" Captain Hastings called out through his speaking trumpet.

"I can't tell yet, sir," replied the look-out. "I can only just see the tops of her royals."

"What course is she steering?" was the next question.

"Due south, sir," replied the man.

"We have him at last, I hope," said the captain. "Set the top-gallants and royals. Get stunsails out alow and aloft; set the flying-jib and the fore and main top-gallant stay-sails."

This was done, and in a quarter of an hour the Seagull was dashing along at nine knots, with a fair wind, in pursuit of the vessel.

In less than an hour they could make her out distinctly to be a long, low schooner, painted black, carrying every stitch of canvas that would draw.

It was evident the schooner had observed the Seagull, for the strange vessel immediately altered her course, and stood to east by south, evidently determined to keep on a wind, close hauled, which is the best sailing point of a schooner.

This manœuvre compelled Captain Hastings to alter the course of his own vessel.

"Weather the main braces!" he sang out to the crew; "haul on the fore and mizzen braces! Look smart, my men. In three hours we will be alongside the schooner."

The Seagull being now close-hauled, the stunsails were useless, and were accordingly hauled down.

Captain Hastings had now leisure to converse with Mr. Meredith, and observed to him that, according to the description which had been given him, this must be the renowned pirate ship, Black Eagle, whose captain had taken Jack prisoner.

"I trust it may prove so, and that we may catch him," said Mr. Meredith; "but the rogue sails fast, and he has need to do so, for if we catch him on the open sea, he will fare very ill."

"But," said Meredith, "I hardly like the look of the sky to windward. It is banking up rather heavily."

"It is, indeed. We shall have a stiff gale before long, but not, I trust, till our vengeance is complete," replied Captain Hastings.

But in this, as will be seen, he was deceived.

If any difference in the position of the two ships was manifest, it was in favour of the Seagull, which had gained slightly on her antagonist.

In an hour they had considerably lessened the distance between them and the chase, the wind having freshened considerably—so much so that Captain Hastings had clewed up his royals and hauled down the top-gallant stay-sails and flying-jib.

The schooner, trusting to the strength of her spars, carried all sail, when suddenly the wind came down in frightful gusts, carrying away the top-gallant sails of the Seagull, and compelling them to double-reef the top-sails.

At the same time a drizzling mist came on, and they lost sight of the chase.

Indeed, they had little time to observe her movements, had she been visible, for the wind had now increased to a hurricane.

The vessel had to be reduced to close-reefed top-sails and storm-jib, and even with this reduced canvas, tore along at a tremendous rate, plunging her bows into the waves with a shock like a battering-ram, the water sweeping aft as far as the gangway, and Captain Hastings was reluctantly compelled to keep her dead before the wind to prevent the waves making a clean breach over her.

Mabel had long since quitted the deck and retired to her cabin, her mind agitated for the safety of the vessel and those on board whom she loved; nor less so for her lover, exposed in a similar vessel to this terrible gale.

"It is getting worse," said the captain to Meredith.

"We shall be compelled to heave to, if it continues," was the reply, "and then I fear we shall lose the pirate. There is no foreseeing what tack the schooner will go upon."

A noise like the roar of artillery stopped the conversation, and both rushed to the main deck to ascertain the cause. To their consternation they found that the top-sails were blown completely from the bolt-ropes, and had disappeared to leeward, like passing clouds.

They had now nothing but the stern-jib on the ship, and this was not sufficient canvas to steer her.

The storm stay-sail—a small, triangular sail set between the main and mizzen masts—was bent, and being a strong, new sail, they hoped it would stand.

For an hour they continued scudding with tremendous swiftness before the wind, when a voice from the forecastle sang out in tones which sufficiently proclaimed the imminence of the danger—

"Ship right ahead!"

Captain Hastings flew to the wheel to assist the helmsman.

The ship's head swung round, her jibboom grazing the main rigging of a vessel, that could just be discerned through the mist.

Meredith, who had hastened to the forecastle on the first cry of "Ship ahead!" immediately recognised the schooner, which had been compelled to heave-to from the violence of the gale.

Meanwhile, as he had rejected the pirate's proposal to enrol himself among the crew of his ship, Jack had been closely confined in the schooner's hold, thrust down among spare sails, old cables, and, worst of all, bilge water.

He was filled with anxiety for his fate.

What would the pirate do with him if he refused to join the crew?

Probably he would be thrown overboard, and no trace of his fate would ever be discovered.

And then, Mabel?

How would *she* ever survive his loss, uncertain of what his fate had been, to say nothing of his faithful friend, Tom?"

"But then," thought he, "if I turn pirate, Mabel will be lost to me for ever. She would refuse to be the bride of a buccaneer."

Agitated by these thoughts, he continued for upwards of an hour buried in deep reflection.

At length, recognising the uselessness of his attempting to resist the pirate captain, he resolved to assent to the condition which alone could give him that liberty for which he pined.

Pursuing this resolution, he told the man that brought his supply of food and water that he wished to see the captain.

The man then left, and returned in a short time, and conducted him to the presence of the pirate chief, whom he found standing in the midst of a group of his subordinates on the quarter-deck.

"Well, my lad," said the buccaneer, "so you have made up your mind to join us at last—eh?"

"Yes," replied Jack. "The captivity I have endured has soon determined me upon taking that course."

"Are you prepared to take the oath—that fearful oath—the slightest infraction of which is death?"

"I am," replied Jack.

"Deliver the usual oath, and make him sign our agreement," said the rover-chief.

So the oath which bound our hero to obey the commands of the chief, and never, even to save his life, to betray his comrades, was then administered to him, and Jack was then free to look about him a little.

The captain's majestic appearance we have already described.

It was shown to full advantage by a rich Spanish costume, he being, though half English, a native of a Spanish colony.

Close behind him stood his lieutenant and confederate in guilt, Benito, who was a short, but strongly-formed man, a native of Manilla, of Malayan parentage.

He carried in his belt a creese, which was said to be dipped in a poison so deadly that the slightest wound from it caused death.

The remainder of the crew consisted of a medley of desperate characters of almost every nation, but particularly from South America and the Spanish Main.

They were about forty in number, and as Jack scanned their ferocious faces he thought he had never in his life seen such a band of fierce and lawless desperadoes.

He had become by this time somewhat used to their rough manners and appearance.

But still Jack sighed as he reflected on the life he would have to undergo with such companions, and resolved, whatever happened, that he would never be an active sharer in their deeds of crime.

As he was walking forward with a heavy heart, he heard the cry of "Sail, ho!" on the weather bows.

and sprang up the rigging to catch a sight of the stranger, but she was too far off for him to distinguish her.

His heart beat violently, but he scarcely dared to hope it could be the Seagull.

"And yet," thought he, "they must have disvered my absence; and well I know they will use ry effort to rescue me if they know I am in the wer of so dreaded a pirate as Valdez."

While he was thus in suspense between hope and fear, he was ordered aloft, with others, to loose the fore-top sail and fore-royal.

The pirate then hesitated awhile as to whether he should pursue the stranger, or make all sail to get away from her.

At length he decided on the latter course, considering that as he had already a vast treasure abroad, it would be best to make for some point where he could dispose of his booty, than run the risk of falling into the hands of a Spanish man-of-war; for he well knew that his atrocities had at length roused the supine Spanish Government to action, and that a vessel had been dispatched in quest of him, a large reward being offered for him, dead or alive.

He knew he was not likely to fall in with any prize worth risking his neck for in such a part of the ocean as he was then sailing, so far from the ordinary track of passing vessels.

By the time all sail was set on the schooner, and everything done which could help her along, they were enabled to make out their pursuer to be a full-rigged ship, in which Jack, to his great delight, recognised the Seagull.

While he was still gazing with delight, the storm in which the Seagull was battling at length overtook the pirate, and Jack was again ordered aloft to reduce sail.

While so engaged he was speculating on the chances of escape.

But how was he to effect it?

To leap overboard, and endeavour to escape by swimming, was certain death.

He would sink beneath the waves, without possibility of help.

Jack resolved to trust to the chapter of accidents rather than throw away his life without hope.

Besides, he trusted to the speed of the Seagull.

At length the gale was so fierce that the pirate hove-to.

The schooner was under a close-reefed try-sail and storm stay-sail.

He trusted that the violence of the gale would effectually prevent the enemy (for he now recognized his pursuer, and knew the cause of his ship being pursued so closely) from overtaking him, and he hoped that in the darkness and the gale she would sail past him, without being able to see the Black Eagle in the midst of the violent storms which lashed the waves to fury.

They had now lost sight of their pursuer, and were hoping they had got quit of her, when one of the pirate crew, who was aloft gathering in the fragments of the fore-top-gallant sail which had been blown to ribbons, saw to his dismay a large ship

coming down full upon them, threatening to send the schooner and all on board her reeling to the bottom.

He endeavoured to shout out to those on deck, but the violence of the wind prevented his words reaching them.

There was no time now to descend and warn them.

All he could do was to hold on, and await the coming shock.

The ship was within a few yards of the schooner.

Another moment and she would be upon them, when her bows gracefully fell off to port, and, as before stated, just grazed the quarter-deck of the schooner.

Jack, who was standing by the mainmast coiling up a rope, happened to cast his eyes to windward, and thought he perceived a dark mass looming upon them.

Jumping into the main rigging to ascertain the cause, he saw the bowsprit of a vessel just crushing the rigging where he stood.

His mind was made up instantly.

With one powerful spring he jumped from the rigging and grasped at the guys of the flying jib-boom, which he reached.

His life now hung on the strength of his arms.

For a moment, all he could do was to cling for dear life.

One moment he was lifted high in the air as the ship rose on a wave.

The next he was plunged right under water, as her bows came surging down again, sending the white foam flying from her in cascades.

But still he held on, watching for one steady interval.

At length, just as he was on the point of leaving go, from inability to hold on longer, he managed to catch hold of the foot-rope, and lift himself up a little.

Then placing one foot on the guy, he seized the jibboom with both arms, and swung himself safely up across the bowsprit, from whence it was an easy matter to descend to the forecastle.

He had uttered no cry for assistance, as, in the first place, he was too much out of breath with the exertion he had made to hold on; and, in the next, the roar of the water from the ship's bows would have effectually prevented him from making himself heard by those on board the Seagull.

The night was so dark that Jack was unperceived by any on board, as he made his way from the bowsprit and reached the forecastle.

Passing the man who had the look-out, who had posted himself comfortably under the lee of the capstan, Crusoe descended the maindeck without being noticed by any one—if any saw him he was merely taken for one of the crew—and reaching the door of the after-cabin, which happened to be half-open, he peeped cautiously in.

Round the cabin table were seated Captain Hastings, Meredith, and Mabel.

They were discussing the manœuvres made during the escape of the pirate schooner from being ran down.

THE SOCIETY ISLANDS.—COMBAT WITH WOODEN CLUBS AND TOMAHAWKS.

19

"Another half-minute," said Meredith, "and she would have been cut in two by our bows."

"Yes," said Captain Hastings, "that would have been the worst thing that could happen, for Crusoe Jack would then have been lost to us for ever; besides the chances of danger to our own craft, we might have stove in our bows."

"Is there any hope," asked Mabel, "that the weather will moderate by morning so as to allow us to pursue the pirate?"

"I think," replied the captain, "we have had the worst of the gale, but whether the pirate will be visible is very doubtful."

"It is useless to try to bring a gun to bear on the pirate, I suppose?" said Meredith.

"Perfectly useless," replied Captain Hastings. "We have driven miles past him by this time, it is dangerous to lay-to in so dark a night as this, too close to the schooner, for of course he will show no lights. But, however, we will heave the Seagull to now."

Captain Hastings, on saying this, rose up, and walked to the door of the cabin with the intention of calling the mate of the watch, and giving him the necessary instructions to heave the vessel to, when he observed some one peering into the cabin.

This, as our reader knows, was no other than our hero, who was gazing on Mabel as she sat, with anxious countenance, listening to the conversation.

"What are you doing there, man?" asked Captain Hastings, sternly, and throwing wide open the cabin door.

The light from the swinging lamp fell full upon Jack's face, causing Captain Hastings to start back in amazement.

He thought it was his ghost, and Jack must certainly have presented a strange sight, appearing so suddenly, without his hat, his hair all hanging over his face, his clothes saturated with wet, and blood in streaks upon his face, caused by sundry scratches he had received in his scramble on to the Seagull.

Mabel and her father no sooner perceived him than they rose up, and rushed towards him with a cry of joy.

CHAPTER XXVI.

OUR HERO'S UNEXPECTED APPEARANCE ON BOARD THE SEAGULL—END OF THE CHASE.

"JACK, my dear boy, can it really be you?" simultaneously exclaimed Mr. Meredith and Captain Hastings, as their surprise at seeing our hero merged into delight at once more beholding him among them.

"Oh, I am so glad—so very glad you have returned!" cried Mabel, with her whole countenance brightening into a perfect sunshine of smiles as she greeted our hero even more cordially than the rest.

Old Tom Starboard, who from his station outside had caught some inkling of the scene that was going on in the cabin, appeared at the door at this moment, and joined in the chorus of joyful recognition.

"Crusoe Jack!" he exclaimed, regarding the resuscitated one, half doubtfully. "But no, it can't be. It's impossible; and yet—may I never cruise again if it ain't, too! Bless you, my boy! I'm almost mad with delight! I thought I should never behold you any more."

"My friends," said Crusoe, looking around him, "you may set your hearts at rest on that score. It is myself, and not my apparition, I assure you."

"Shiver me! if it ain't more like an apparition though, to come here unexpected in that manner. How in the world did you get away?" exclaimed old Tom. "Swim from the ship or put out in a boat in this stiff gale?"

"No, Tom," answered Jack, smiling. "Neither of those feats would be very practicable, I think."

"Well, but how did you manage it?" asked Captain Hastings. "I am sure your appearance took us all as much by surprise as if we had suddenly seen the Flying Dutchman. I can't conceive how you contrived to get away from the pirate ship."

"Well, then, I will tell you," said Jack. "But first of all, let me put myself to rights a little. You see I am drenched through with spray, and I'm bleeding where I got some ugly knocks in making my escape. Who will lend me a suit of dry clothes?"

"Who won't?" cried Tom Starboard, joyfully. "Why, my boy, you can have a dozen, as far as the willingness to lend you them goes. Come this way, and I'll help you to make yourself all taut in no time."

"I've got a first lieutenant's uniform that I will give you," said the captain; "one that I wore myself many years ago, and which, I think, will fit you. Remember, that is your mark of distinction for your present rank."

"I am afraid I shall have to give up the honour," answered Jack, "because, in the first place, I am a pirate."

Everybody looked at him in surprise.

"A pirate? How do you mean?" asked Mr. Meredith.

"Well, only that I've joined the pirates, and—but I'll tell you more of that presently. Wait a few minutes, and I will again rejoin you."

"And, Tom, you had better let us have some more grog here," said the captain.

"Ay, ay, sir. I reckon Crusoe Jack will want some, after all he's been through, and everybody will be glad to drink his health."

Tom and Jack quitted the cabin, and the first observation of the former, as he reached the main-deck, was—

"Hooray! the wind is veering round to the right quarter at last, and the gale is going down a bit. We've had it strong, lad, and no mistake; and I'm blest if there's much headway to be made, except down old Davy's way, when it blows as it has done this blessed night. As for the pirate ——"

Tom took a long and minute survey through his telescope, but in spite of the increasing lightness of the sky, could see nothing of the enemy.

"He's got clean away, and is driving before the

wind like mad," he continued. "Well, it's the best thing for him, for if he had engaged us in fine weather, I'm blessed if he wouldn't have had more pills in his inside than would do his constitution good."

"I have no doubt of that, Tom," replied our hero.

In a few minutes Jack rejoined the party in the cabin, and he felt much refreshed now that he had cleansed away the signs of his recent struggles, and experienced the luxury of dry clothes.

"Now, Jack," said the captain, "in the first place you must drink off this tumbler of grog, and in the next, you are bound to relate all that has happened to you since your mysterious disappearance that night. If we know as much as you can tell us about the pirates, we shall be able to see what track to go upon when we are once more in fair weather."

Jack complied with the first part of the stipulation—that of drinking the grog, without any opposition, and immediately commenced relating his encounter with the Indians, and his marvellous adventure in the pirates' cave.

After that, he came to his captivity by the buccaneers, and the oath he had taken, and which had bound him not to reveal anything relating to his late captors.

"I consider that solemn oath has placed me in a critical position," he remarked. "It has bound me to the pirates' gang as one of themselves. I am branded with the secret mark which distinguishes the band of the Black Eagle, and have signed my name to an agreement, ratifying my determination to devote my life to their cause. What dangers I may run in future from fear of their revenge and what a terrible thing it is to break an oath so solemnly made, are considerations which make me feel very uncomfortable when I think of them."

"They need not cause you a moment's uneasiness," remarked Captain Hastings. "An oath taken by a prisoner under compulsion can never be binding after the escape of that prisoner. It strikes me that I should not have any very tender scruples of conscience on such a matter; indeed, I never have, though I have been placed in a position rather similar to yours. But you have not yet unravelled the great mystery, how you got away from the pirate ship."

Jack related the desired adventure to his attentive auditors, who listened breathlessly, including our friend, Tom, at the door of the cabin.

"That's about the boldest stroke I ever heard of," remarked the latter, when Jack had concluded. "I never knew more than two instances of a fellow jumping from one ship to another in that way during a heavy gale. Both of 'em was in war time, and in the first case the poor fellow lost his hold on the jib-boom, and was driven under the keel and killed in no time; and in the last case a mate of mine, who tried the dodge, was shot by the enemy, just he was jumping on her deck."

"Thank heaven, I have got off safe of both dangers!" said Jack. "I hope I shall never have to risk them again."

It was with interest almost as great as that with which they had listened to him that Jack heard all that had occurred on the island since his departure.

"But now, about this pirate," said the captain; "I am very anxious to know what his strength is, how many guns he carries, how he's loaded, what his course is, and so on; and, of course, Jack, you are the only one that can tell us."

Jack's expression showed some doubt on the subject.

"I've sworn not to betray the pirates," he said. "I think the best thing we can do is to let them alone. I fancy they'll fight shy of us in future."

"But, my dear Jack, why are you so scrupulous with regard to the oath?" asked Captain Hastings. "I am sure there is nothing binding in it. They haven't treated you so well that you need consider them very much, and I am sure you never had any serious intention of turning pirate yourself."

Jack hesitated.

He certainly could not, with truth, have denied that he had lately felt a strong inclining to fall under this temptation.

"Besides," added the captain, "it strikes me that they very probably think you have tumbled overboard (as you say none of them observed you escaping), there would not have been the shadow of a chance for you if you had. Depend upon it, they fancy their prisoner at the bottom of the ocean, and little think he will ever be alive to oppose them again."

"Well, I can only tell you this, then," Jack at length began: "The pirate is, as you already know, the famous Black Eagle, Captain Valdez; he is far weaker in fighting powers and size also than our own ship, and as for his cargo, the only part I have seen of it is the treasure I told you of, but that is enough wealth for one ship."

"A great deal too much for those scoundrels," the captain replied. "Heavens! how I wish you had discovered the pirates' retreat before! We could have laid in wait, attacked them, and seized both themselves and their ill-gotten gains. The thanks of the whole of the South American States, and a substantial reward beside, would have been the beneficial results to us of such an achievement."

"It is little use talking about that now," said Mr. Meredith. "The pirate has evidently escaped us, and if he is wise will never venture again within the reach of our guns. I think that now Jack has been rescued, or rather rescued himself, we had better not pursue the chase, but make for the Sandwich Islands, previous to our departure for Chili."

"But the pirate may be always following on our track, with the hope to take us unawares," said the captain.

"No. Depend upon it, he has other enterprises and other dangers to encounter," Jack returned. "He runs some danger in these seas, now there are so many vessels on the look-out for him; and he knows now the islands are no longer safe as hiding-places for his treasure. I shouldn't wonder if he changes his field of operations."

"Let us hope he'll give the Atlantic a turn," suggested Mr. Meredith. "Only let him venture in the track of English vessels of war, and his doom is sealed to a certainty."

Captain Hastings and Mr. Meredith, soon afterwards left the cabin to take an observation of how matters stood on deck; and, in the meanwhile, Jack was left alone with Mabel, a consummation that was by no means unwelcome to him.

"Dear Jack," cried Mr. Meredith's daughter, as she gazed into his face with the expression of affection that so completely enhanced the loveliness of her own, "you cannot think how anxious I have been on your account, nor how delighted I am to see you once more safe."

"I can fully comprehend your feelings by judging from my own, my dear Mabel," replied Jack, tenderly.

"Your joy cannot be greater than mine, and, indeed, I thought I should never see you again."

"And I had given up all hopes of your life," she returned, "when I heard the ruffianly pirate express his intention of killing you in revenge for his unsuccessful attack on our ship."

"It was what he never seriously intended to do," replied Jack; "for he was too anxious for me to join his crew, and give my assistance."

"But there is another thing, Mabel, which I am very much concerned about, and that is the fate of Lela. I am indeed sorry she is again captured by that fierce savage, Oroma, for I dread the fate she will probably have to undergo at the hands of a people so naturally ferocious as the Macoushi. Her only chance is to return, or pretend to return, the affection of the implacable savage, and to forget entirely her attachment to " ——

"You?" suggested Mabel, half slyly, seeing that Jack hesitated.

"Yes, Mabel, we will say, if you like, to me," Jack answered, boldly, "for it's unfortunately the truth. Still, as you know, the love is entirely on her side; but I had hoped in constant companionship with you, and in fresh scenes of civilised life, she would forget all her old passions and attachments, and become happy in a new state of existence."

"From my short experience, I am afraid she is too wild and wayward ever to become happy by such means," said Mabel, doubtfully: "she would have pined for her native woods and the wild excitement of the chase. Perhaps now she has returned to it she may, in time, become happy."

"Let us, at least, hope so," returned Jack. "I trust at some future time to ascertain more of her; but at present her fate is not in our hands. The perils that strew our own path to happiness are not yet over."

* * * * * * *

The next next day the wind had changed, the gale had considerably abated, but a strong breeze was blowing from exactly the quarter favourable for the new course the captain intended to take.

Relinquishing the fruitless chase of the pirate, who now seemed to have made his escape altogether, Captain Hastings designed to visit the Sandwich Islands, and many other portions of the great Pacific Archipelago, to dispose of the cargo of the Seagull, in exchange for the natural productions of that fruitful region.

CHAPTER XXVII.

ARRIVAL AT THE SOCIETY ISLANDS—GRAND RECEPTION—INSTRUCTIVE ACCOUNT OF THE CUSTOMS OF THE NATIVES.

THE breeze continued favourable, and on the third day after their encounter with the pirates, the crew of the Seagull came in sight of a small, but beautiful and fertile island, which they ascertained to be an outlying portion of the group of Society Islands.

From the sea, this spot presented a scene of great beauty; the undulating sweep of verdurous hill and dale rising from the sea in gentle acclivities, covered with gorgeous tropical vegetation, the whole surrounded by a beautiful coral reef; the birds rising from their sylvan homes, and skimming over the surface of the smooth sea, all combined to perfect a picture which no powers of description could adequately pourtray.

To our friends of the Seagull, the scene had the charm of novelty; but still it so far resembled the islands they had just left, that it did not impress them so forcibly as it would have done a spectator who beheld, for the first time, a specimen of the beauties of nature abounding in the wide bosom of the Pacific.

As it was Captain Hastings' intention to visit all the points of importance on their journey, and as, moreover, the ship was in need of supplies of food and water, he determined to put in at this island, should there be sufficient harbourage, and, above all, if the natives proved pacific and friendly.

On the latter point, our party of cruisers had soon an opportunity of satisfying themselves.

No sooner had they arrived close enough to the island to attract the attention of the natives, than the latter exhibited all signs of commotion and excitement.

The advent of an English ship, with the white men, bringing the welcome allowances of fire-arms and spirits (two things which all savages most covet) was at that time so rare an occurrence that it is no wonder the natives regarded it as an important event.

A universal shout, echoing from point to point, greeted the appearance of the Seagull, and an innumerable fleet of canoes of all kinds put out from the shore, and surrounded the vessel even before she had anchored.

As soon as a safe harbour was found, the Seagull lay at rest in it.

The natives essayed to get on board, or at least to open communication with the white men.

The natives were a tall, handsome race of people, warlike, but not particularly ferocious in appearance.

They were mostly tattooed, and carried clubs, wooden-headed hatchets, and spears, their dress was in general formed of a rough kind of cloth manufactured by themselves.

Their hair was worn long, and generally ornamented with feathers, the chiefs being especially distinguished by the towering height of their plumes.

They managed their canoes by means of spoon-shaped paddles with exquisite skill, and even the women, whose appearance was in general very at tractive, guided their light and slender craft with much grace and effect.

It was fortunate that among the crew of the Seagull were several sailors who were well acquainted with the language spoken in these islands; so that there was no difficulty in communicating with the natives.

The oft-repeated salutation of "*Kao va kooe?*" or "How do you do?" was instantly answered by "*Nue nue moe. tackey,*" and thus commenced a conversation in the native tongue, which was duly interpreted to the captain and other officers.

The number of canoes that flocked around the ship, and the clamorous greetings of the hundreds of natives who had turned out to receive their visitors, led the party of Englishmen to keep up a bright look-out, in case any disagreement should occur, or the intentions of the islanders be less pacific than they appeared.

The captain, standing on the maindeck, held communication, by means of his interpreter, with the natives; but he would permit none to enter the ship before he had made his arrangements with the principal men of the island.

He therefore demanded to see their chief, or king, whom he said he had come to visit, on a friendly errand, from the grand white chief beyond the sea.

This intimation produced a great commotion among the natives, who instantly proceeded to summon their king to visit the great chief of the floating island, as they called Captain Hastings and his big ship.

Very shortly a large canoe, gaudily coloured and ornamented, and propelled by twenty men, put out from the shore.

This was the king's canoe, and it was followed by the canoes of all his principal chiefs.

The king and queen of the island were soon brought on board in great state, and, indeed, their appearance was sufficiently imposing to command respect.

The king was over six feet high, with a martial countenance, and a figure of great muscular strength.

He was dressed in a *teboota*, or cloth robe, beautifully ornamented, and hanging down low, both in front and behind.

His well-formed limbs were adorned with various ornaments formed of shells and whales' teeth.

Upon his head he wore a kind of hat made of the palm tree, and crowned by a towering crest of feathers.

His majesty was armed with a club, a long spear, and a tomahawk in his belt, which, together with the profuse manner in which he was tattooed, gave him a very formidable appearance.

The queen was a woman of great beauty and majestic appearance.

She was attired in tasteful drapery, formed of the cloth of the island, and on her head she wore a kind of bonnet made of the leaves of the cocoa tree, and adorned with various beautiful flowers.

The train of chiefs and other great personages who accompanied the king were attired in a very similar manner, though somewhat less magnificently.

"Hail to my white brother, who comes in his floating island from the great nation across the seas!" was the king's first greeting to Captain Hastings, not, however, in the native language of his country, but in a kind of broken English that surprised the party of the Seagull greatly.

"Hail to the great king!" replied the captain, "who I am much astonished to find can speak to me in my own language."

"I have learned some of it from the white men I have in my dominions," the king explained.

"Have you, then, Englishmen in your country?" asked the captain in surprise. "Have they become as *Canaccas* (the name given to the South Sea islanders in general)?"

"Some have been wrecked here," replied the king; "and others have escaped from captivity, and fled to my dominions. You shall speedily see them, but now I desire that the king of the ship shall become my *tayo* (brother), according to the custom in these islands."

The captain readily agreed to undergo that ceremony, which was as follows:—

He and the king were to exchange names, in token of becoming *tayos*, or brothers.

This privilege entitled the captain to protection and hospitality from the king and all his subjects, and raised him at once to a rank equal to that of the king himself.

So the latter placed his own hat on the head of the gallant captain, and they exchanged names—the king calling himself Captain Hastings, and the latter assuming the monarch's appellation of Nookeevah.

This ceremony also took place between the other officers of the Seagull and the chiefs under the king.

Jack and Mr. Meredith, and all the mates and lieutenants, and Tom Starboard, all became chiefs and *tayos* of the dark-skinned warriors.

A present of a musket each, and some powder and spirits, were given to the king and the principal chiefs; but the captain knew from experience that it was necessary to be careful in this particular, for while fire-arms are the things that savages in all countries most covet from the white man, they are also the most dangerous gifts that can be made them.

The captain accordingly refused a great many natives who were clamouring for fire-arms, giving them instead some wearing-apparel of English manufacture, and other articles of less value.

In exchange the captain received a large quantity of cocoa-nuts, yams, bananas, guava, and the preserved flesh of wild hogs, which abound in these islands in immense numbers.

The followers of the king, and indeed the whole of the party who came on board, inspected every part of the ship with great interest, and, of course, asked for almost everything they saw. It required a strict guard to be kept on all articles of value, lest their love of plunder might break out.

As the captain had determined to stay a day or two on the island, the ship was safely anchored in the principal bay, of which we have spoken, and the whole of the officers of the Seagull were invited on shore to dine with the king at his own palace.

Had the gallant captain even faintly suspected the perils and disasters that were to spring from accepting the invitation, he certainly would have refused it.

They, however, went on shore, rowed in canoes by the king's own men, while hundreds were collected on the shore to receive them with great cordiality.

The chief town in the island proved to be of considerable extent, situated close to the shore, and embosomed picturesquely in groves of cocoa-nuts and bread-fruit trees.

Most of the houses, or huts, were of bamboo, the entrances covered with woven leaves of the cocoa-nut tree, arranged with great effect.

The king's palace was of greater extent than any other house on the island.

It was formed also of bamboo and other woods, profusely ornamented both outside and within.

The principal room, into which our friends of the Seagull were led, was adorned all round the walls by mattings, on which a variety of designs were painted in gay colours; while groups of spears, tomahawks, and other arms, and various costumes, adorned with whales' teeth, completed the ornamentation of the apartment.

A long table was opened in the centre, and on this all the choicest luxuries of the island were placed.

To this scene of festivity Jack and his companions were conducted—all carried on the backs of natives, as a sign of their rank, the king and queen going first in a superb litter.

Throughout the whole procession a concert of music, consisting principally of horns and tom-toms, kept up a continual discord, which our hero could readily have dispensed with.

"My precious eyes!" exclaimed our old friend, Tom Starboard, who was carried on the backs of four men, on the supposition that he was a chief of great rank, "if ever I was treated with such honour as this—as if I was the Lord Mayor of London, or the Lieutenant of Ireland, or some such great person.

"What a fuss to make of a few English tars, who would have to knuckle under at home—eh, Jack?"

"You are right, Tom," replied our hero; "but recollect it's always the best way to respect the customs of the country, and if they take us for great persons, why should we undeceive them?"

"These natives seem the right sort," observed Tom. "I hope they won't turn out bad, after all."

"I think we can protect ourselves, if anything should occur," returned Jack. "But what makes you suspect treachery?"

"I don't suspect anything," Tom replied; "but I've had a little experience among savage nations, and I know they ain't to be trusted much further than you can see them. Luckily, we have left a good watch on the ship. Howsomdever, we don't seem so bad off at present. My word! to think of old Tom Starboard ever dining with a king!"

As Tom made this reflection, they arrived at the king's palace, where an efficient body of natives were keeping guard, armed with spears at least ten feet in length.

These were lowered as the grand procession entered, and the natives bowed almost to the ground to the king and his guests.

On entering the banqueting-room, the king and queen took up their position at the head of the table, under a canopy of state, Captain Hastings, Mabel, Jack, and Mr. Meredith being placed nearest to the royal personages as a mark of great distinction and favour.

The dinner was certainly plentiful and satisfactory, consisting of roasted bread-fruit, fish, cocoa-nuts, ahee nuts, yams, poultry, and pork, which is roasted, or rather baked, by covering it over with leaves, and burning it on hot stones.

Besides this, they had pancakes, and a variety of fruits, the whole of the viands being well prepared, and served up in calabashes or cocoa-nut shells, the knives and forks, all formed of bamboo, being as handy for use as English ones.

The principal liquor was cava, or the fermented juice of certain leaves, mixed with cocoa-nut milk.

This was very intoxicating, and the English party took the precaution of mixing theirs largely with water, and advised the king to do the same.

All the natives, however, partook of the liquor in all its strength, and its effect was speedily apparent in their manner and conversation.

During the dinner the captain put several questions to the king relative to the state of affairs on the island, which were proved to be anything but satisfactory.

King Nookeevah, and his queen, Waheene, though the rightful sovereigns of the island, were placed in great difficulty by the rivals with which they were encompassed.

"I have a cousin," thus ran the king's explanation, "named Pakayo, a mighty chief, and one who can lead to the field many thousand warriors. He is king of the neighbouring island of Typee, but he desires to conquer me, and become chief of the nation of Hopaws. My father, the heir to this throne, was killed by his father in a fit of jealousy.

"The old chief, my uncle, came with many warriors, and would have seized the kingdom, but I, though young, was not a coward, and I defended the island from his warriors. Fierce was the battle, and continued throughout the long day. Many gallant warriors fell, but the enemy were at length driven away, with great loss, and the old chief, Tiara, was slain by the arrow of one of my braves. Now, the double fierceness of ambition and revenge animates his son, Pakayo, against me, and we have been all our lives enemies.

"Many times has he come in his war canoes, with his fierce warriors, armed with deadly club and poisoned arrow, but the Great Spirit has assisted me, and given me strength, and mine has ever been the victory.

"The war has raged for years, and never, as long as we both live, will Pakayo cease his fierce contention; but never, I swear on the altar of the Great Etooa, shall he become chief of the Hopaws."

"What kind of men are the natives of Typee?" asked the captain; "are they more fierce than yourselves?"

"They are warriors and brave," replied King Nookeevah; "but they are without mercy, eaters of men, and scoffers at the Great Spirit, Etooa.

"Frequently they have nearly conquered us, but my warriors, and even their wives, would fight until they had spilt the last drop of blood, ere the honour of their nation should thus be clouded.

"Soon, a great expedition will be prepared, with mighty canoes and fire-weapons, and poisoned spears, and thousands of brave warriors, and we will go against the fierce Typees, and destroy their homes, their warriors, and subjugate the island into the power of the Hopaws."

CHAPTER XXVIII.

THE FESTIVITIES—THE SHAM-FIGHT—AN ASTOUNDING DISCOVERY BY CAPTAIN HASTINGS.

AFTER the feast was over, the king gave orders for a grand dance to be performed in honour of the English guests. The performers were the male and female attendants of the king and queen, all fancifully and gaily attired; and the dance was superintended by a native master of the ceremonies. Each of the male performers wore the teboota, and curious hats of cocoa-nut fibre, with plumes; but the female dancers were attired still more fantastically, in hooped petticoats, similar to those distended by the modern crinoline, and adorned with feathers and a variety of other ornaments, while their head-dress consisted of a kind of turban beautifully embellished with brilliant and sweet-scented flowers.

The beauty of those damsels, both in form and countenance, was of the highest order, and many of them were almost as fair as Southern Europeans.

The dance took place on a large platform, fastened to two large bamboo trees, in the gardens of the king's palace, which were a complete paradise of tropical vegetation, in all the wild luxuriance of nature.

The native musicians performed on drums, like those used by the Hindoos, beaten with the hands, and composed of hollow bamboo, or other wood, covered with shark-skin. Flutes were also used, and a kind of harp or lyre in its primitive form of the turtle shell, with fibres or sinews stretched across it.

The dance was very lively and quick, and must have been a great exertion to the performers, especially the female dancers, who indulged in various contortions and extraordinary movements, which displayed the elegance and suppleness of their statuesque forms.

The wild and rapid turnings, and twistings, and variation of figures contained in the dance were almost bewildering to the English spectators, who had never before beheld anything like it.

"This is not much like the dancing at the balls and parties in England, I should think?" Jack remarked, smilingly to Mabel, who was sitting between him and the queen, regarding the performance with much interest.

"No," she replied; "this scene resembles nothing I have ever seen before, except, perhaps, those curious performances in the pantomimes that I have witnessed in England. While I sit here, surrounded by this gorgeous tropical landscape, and these fantastically-attired savages dancing before me, I cannot help fancying myself at the theatre, witnessing some extravagant burlesque, where all is singular, fantastic, and unlike real life."

Mabel had received her share of consideration as a distinguished guest. Her beauty, so contrasting to that of the dark daughters of that tropical clime— so unearthly in its fair English loveliness, to eyes accustomed only to the glowing beauties of the south, added to the knowledge that she was the daughter of one of the principal white men in the ship, and perhaps a princess in her own country, had caused her to receive special attention, and to have already become a great favourite with Queen Waheene. The savages she now found herself among were so superior to those whom she had recently had so much cause to dread, that Mabel could not do otherwise than fully appreciate their kindness.

When the dance was over, and the performance had been rewarded by the distribution of various ornaments by their native chiefs, and of English money by the party of the Seagull, there were some fresh spectacles, consisting of feats of wrestling, slinging stones, and hurling javelins, all of which were performed with great skill and dexterity.

In the slinging of stones especially the natives showed great address, and their skill at hitting small birds at a very great distance struck their English visitors as perfectly astonishing.

Another curious amusement among them was for two or three men to get into a wooden tub, formed like a dish, and which, when placed on the water, would sink down till only an inch remained above the surface.

In this position the natives would whirl it round and round with great rapidity, by means of paddles, until it generally ended by the whole party upsetting their fragile craft, and falling headlong into the water. Not in the least disconcerted, however, they would speedily rise to the surface, and commence the sport afresh.

"This sort of thing might do for these fellows here," was old Tom's remark on this strange amusement; "but I must say I should not much like it out at sea, with sharks on our lee quarter, or even out in Old Father Thames, where one would stand a precious chance of an ugly ducking in the foulest water. Besides, I don't know any Englishmen who could do all these feats with the same dexterity as these brown-skinned rascals, who seem to be made of India-rubber, and to have no more bones than an eel!

"But see, they are going to have some new sport, that threatens to be serious."

And serious indeed it seemed. An elderly chief of powerful build, armed with an immense club and a wooden tomahawk, took his stand in front of . number of active young warriors, who were likewise supplied with wooden tomahaws, knives, and clubs, with which they made a terrific onslaught upon their single foe, who however by the skilful way in which he manœuvred his club, not only kept his yelling assailants at bay, but had successively floored several of them with a well-delivered blow upon the skull, when the king ordered the fray to cease, giving to him the palm of victory.

The last grand spectacle to which the king of the Hopaws treated his guests was a review or sham fight between different regiments of his warriors. About a thousand of these dusky soldiers marched forth in double file to an extensive plain near the king's palace, his majesty being carried as before, on a litter, and all the English guests conveyed to the scene of action in the same manner.

To prevent accidents no deadly weapons were used, the warriors being armed only with sticks for clubs, bamboo canes for spears, and bread-fruit instead of stones for the slings.

Each army was composed of two lines—the principal warriors, with clubs, standing in front, a row of spearmen behind, and the slingers drawn up on the flanks.

The commencement of the engagement was a combat between several chiefs, and afterwards the signal came for the general onslaught.

With a terrific and hideous yell the two parties rushed together.

The slingers hurled their projectiles with great fury, but were obliged to retire in the face of the approaching spearmen.

At length, the whole of the combatants rushed together in a grand closing encounter, with great confusion.

By the shouts, yells, sounds of blows, and general fierceness of the fight and the combatants, every spectator might have imagined the combat to be in earnest.

Clubs, spears, and slings, wielded in the hands of mighty and ferocious chiefs, seemed to do great execution, and to be used with deadly effect.

Both parties seemed to have entered as fully into the spirit of the scene as if they had been opposing their most deadly enemies.

At length, by the signal of the blowing of a conch-shell, the parties separated, both gradually forming in a line, and proceeding in opposite directions, the slingers passing behind each phalanx to secure their retreat.

Both continued throwing their mock-stones until they were out of sight of each other, and thus ended the sham engagement—a most interesting sight to all who beheld it.

"Thus, my English brothers, fight the warriors of the Hopaw," said the king, triumphantly; "and it is thus the vile man-eaters of the Typee tribe are kept from conquering my dominions. None can say that we are unworthy of the liberty for which we would lay down our lives."

"I greatly admire the skill and bravery of your warriors," remarked Captain Hastings.

"And now, having shown you some of the manners and customs of my own people," said the king, "it is time I should introduce you to some of your own countrymen, of whom I have a complete colony on the island. They are mostly men of great skill in the art of making things useful to the white men, and in this they have proved of great service to my people."

"How did they first come over here?" asked Captain Hastings.

"Many of them are English sailors, who have deserted from their ships at different times. But they are mostly composed of the crew of a ship which was wrecked here two months ago. Others are prisoners escaped from the islands where the king of the white men sends those who have committed crimes against him."

"Botany Bay and Norfolk Island," whispered Tom in Crusoe Jack's ear. "Bad fellows, depend upon it!"

"But see, here they come to welcome their brothers from beyond sea," said King Nookeevah, and as he spoke a large body of men were seen approaching from the other side of the plain. The party of the Seagull observed them with great interest.

They soon came fully into view, a party of not less than fifty men, the majority being English, but a few Spaniards and Frenchmen. In dress and appearance they were half Britons and half Canaccas.

Their countenances were all deeply embrowned with long residence in the island, their hair and beards were long and wild, their attire was somewhat similar to that of English sailors, but many of them wore the tapa, the teboota, or other Indian articles of dress, and each one had a cocoa-nut hat, adorned with parrot's feathers.

But what struck the party of the Seagull, and old Tom Starboard in particular, was the half-savage, forbidding aspect of their countenances, and the quick, restless motion of their eyes at everything around them.

"Just as I said, convicts and deserters, and bad characters, all of them," remarked Tom Starboard, loud enough to be heard by Captain Hastings. "My advice is, to keep a good eye upon them."

These words produced a profound impression on the mind of Captain Hastings, though he said nothing at the time.

As the party advanced, the king spoke to those among them who appeared to be their leaders, and introduced them to Captain Hastings as his Tayos.

This event was the cause of an astonishing and totally unexpected scene to all.

As soon as the leader, a tall man of forbidding aspect, saw Captain Hastings, he started back with exclamation of surprise.

Captain Hastings did the same.

"Williams, as I'm alive!" cried the latter, unable to suppress his astonishment and anger, "and the other scoundrels, too. Ha! so our chase has not been in vain!"

He paused for a moment, regarding fixedly the body of recreant Englishmen before him, all of whom gazed at him with a degree of dread that had almost deprived them of utterance.

The next moment, however, the captain again came forward, and, in a firm voice, he thus addressed the expectant and astonished crowd around him:

"King Nookeevah and chiefs of Hopaw, and you also, officers and men of the Seagull, I hereby declare that this body of men I now see before me, who have made this island their home, are the same band of villanous mutineers who left me to perish on a desert island, killed all my officers, and seized my ship. I hereby charge this man, their leader, John Williams, with mutiny and piracy on the high seas, and demand that he and his accomplices small be instantly seized and brought to account for their crimes. This I demand, in the name of the British Government, at the hands of the king of this island."

There was a deep and terrible pause after this declaration—the hush of amazement kept dumb every man among the thousands assembled.

Captain Hastings' party at once understood the importance of the discovery he had made, while the majority of the native chiefs sufficiently comprehended English to know the purport of this extraordinary declaration.

The mutineers themselves seemed overcome with terror.

There stood their former commander—the man whom they had so deeply wronged, returned to them like an avenging spirit—thousands of miles away from the scene of their crime, but fully prepared to ensure their punishment.

There was his trusty crew of gallant Englishmen, ready to obey the first command of their leader, and, worse than all, they were encompassed by a mighty army of fierce native warriors, against whom any opposition on their part would prove utterly fruitless.

They were completely in a trap—not the faintest chance of escape existed.

The king was the first to break silence.

"Am I, then, truly to understand," he asked, "that my white brother declares these men, whom I have trusted and held in favour so long, are but thieves and murderers, who are deserving of death for many deeds of blood?"

"I declare it!" replied Captain Hastings.

"Then," said the king, "they shall be brought to account for their crimes; for the cause of revenge is sacred, and he who rebels against his appointed chief is worthy of death. My soldiers, bring forward the miscreants to be examined as to their guilt, and let the heralds sound the signal for the whole of my chiefs to assemble in a great council of judgment."

Readily did the warriors of the Hopaw proceed to execute these commands.

The mutineers had been so struck with bewilderment and dismay at the sudden change from safety to the most imminent peril which had befallen them, that they were at first incapable of action.

They all looked dismayed and hopeless, but the leader, Williams, was a man who never entirely lost his presence of mind.

He looked around him and measured his chances of escape or resistance, and found them small indeed, and after a hurried and whispered conversation with his comrades, he came to the conclusion as to what course he should pursue.

He therefore set the example of non-resistance, by surrendering peacefully to the guards of the king.

And the whole of his men followed that example.

Before, however, the council of judgment could be formed, he advanced towards Captain Hastings, and with humble obeisance to him and the king, and an expression of deep humility, he said:

"I desire, in the name of the whole of my party, to be heard in the defence of myself and my comrades. Let me make one declaration before you pronounce judgment."

Captain Hastings hesitated, but at length gave the required consent, in which the king also joined.

"I declare, then, this," said Williams, "that I, in conjunction with all the mutineers here assembled, are truly, sincerely, and deeply repentant for the crimes of which we have been guilty, that we shall be ready instantly to deliver up to the captain the ship we took from him, but that the vessel, as many here assembled know, was wrecked on the shore of these islands and utterly destroyed on the day—three months ago—that we first came here, providentially rescued from the waves. We have always regarded the wreck as a judgment of Heaven against us, and I call the king and all the inhabitants of this island to witness, that we have, during our sojourn on this island, lived honestly, peacefully, and loyally, and not in any way returned to our former lawless course. We therefore surrender ourselves up to Captain Hastings, trusting he will extend to us his mercy and clemency, and will take into consideration our determination to live honestly all the rest of our lives."

What could be said, by one of such a generous heart as the gallant captain, against such an appeal as this?

The men were, at least apparently, truly repentant of former atrocities, in which they had all shared so equally, that the captain could not bring one to punishment without compromising all.

The only clear course, therefore, was one of mercy and forgiveness.

Deep as was his resentment, he could not well come to any other decision under present circumstances, and this view was confirmed by the king, who assured them of his power to make the mutineers keep to their promises in future.

In place, therefore, of a council of judgment, followed by condign punishment, the captain granted a free pardon, on condition that the mutineers should never attempt to leave the island, but continue to live peacefully with all men, both natives and visitors.

Was this leniency ill-timed and injudicious?

After events will enable our readers to judge for themselves on this point.

CHAPTER XXIX.

THE PARDONED MUTINEERS—THE EXCITING HISTORY OF THE ESCAPED CONVICT.

THE decision of Captain Hastings, with regard to the mutineers, was received by them with great, apparent thankfulness, and though Mr. Meredith and the principal officers of the Seagull somewhat doubted the effect of such clemency, they could not prove their suspicions to be sufficiently valid to oppose the course adopted by their commander.

Captain Hastings argued that, be the mutineers ever so inclined for treachery, they did not outnumber his own gallant crew, who had, moreover, the whole of the powerful island warriors on their side.

The mutineers did, indeed, run far more danger by any hostile measures than they would by submission.

So the band of island-Englishmen were allowed to join the festivities, provided in honour of the crew of the Seagull; and, indeed, they speedily ingratiated themselves so far into the favour of the latter by their good-fellowship, that the two parties became excellent friends.

Just before the sun went down, a supper, on a scale of magnificence equal to what the first banquet had been, was served up in the king's palace to the now largely augmented number of his guests.

Not only the Seagull's crew, but the party of island-Englishmen, and the whole of the principal natives, took part in this entertainment.

This assembling together gave the officers and crew of the Seagull a good opportunity of becoming acquainted with the recent adventures of the mutineers and their allies.

The party of mutineers have been described as Englishmen, but it will be remembered that there were among them several Spaniards and two Frenchmen—the prisoners of war, who had first incited Captain Hastings' crew to mutiny in his last South American expedition. The party was further increased by some runaway sailors from other ships, and about a dozen convicts, who, as the king had said, had escaped from Norfolk Island and Botany Bay.

The latter, however, proved by no means the worst members of the band, and, indeed, Captain Hastings and his crew were more willing to trust them, and believe in their assertions, than the gang who had supplicated mercy, and whose natural characters he knew only too well.

It was from one of the convicts named James Greenley, and who seemed the most straightforward of the motley band, that Crusoe Jack and Tom Starboard learned some curious particulars, both of the events on the island, and the wild, adventurous life of escaped convicts in New South Wales.

"How did you manage to escape here?" asked Tom of the fugitives.

"Well, sir, in order to tell you that, I must relate the whole story of my life, which has been a desperate one, I can promise you," said Greenley. "I was the son of poor but respectable parents, in London, where, when I was fourteen years of age, I obtained employment as a clerk in a large wholesale grocery establishment. I had been brought up in principles of honesty, and I have no doubt I should have retained them, but bad example has been the rock which has been my destruction, as well as that of thousands more in this world. Well, to speak briefly, I was led by degrees into a course of betting and gambling which soon swallowed up all my limited allowance, and brought me deeper and deeper into debt, unknown either to my parents or employers. At last, my affairs were so frightfully complicated, that I was tempted in despair to falsify accounts, and appropriate money belonging to my employers. No doubt you will suppose that my ruin came from being discovered, but it was not in this way. I carried on my delinquencies for a considerable time, and evaded discovery, or even suspicion; but at length I was so far sunk in the gulf of ruin, that nothing but a bold stroke would save me. So, after having for some time laid my plans and watched my opportunity, I ran away from my employers one Saturday night, taking with me the whole of the day's returns of the establishment, amounting to upwards of thirty pounds; besides this, I had forged a cheque of my master's that day successfully at two bankers, to the amount of fifty pounds, so that I considered I had a very good haul.

"For some time I subsisted in reckless profusion, sinking deeper every day in vicious courses, until, the whole of my money being gone, I was easily tempted by an unprincipled companion to join him in a gigantic system of forgery, by which immense sums could be obtained.

"The scheme was a very brilliant one, but unfortunately it failed just at the eventful moment.

"We were both discovered, tried, and as my former master came forward with the old charge against me, my guilt in both cases was clear, and I was convicted and sentenced to transportation for life, to the unconquerable grief and affliction of my parents and friends.

"My companion had so managed affairs that he got off much easier; seven years was the term of his sentence, and even that he managed, by carneying the parson and shamming religion, to evade, after three years' transportation; and though he was many degrees worse than me, he got a ticket-of-leave, and went back to England a free man, while I still pined in captivity.

"If ever I meet him again, I sha'n't forget that I owe that man a grudge."

"So, I suppose, you made up your mind not to go through the whole of your sentence?" asked Tom.

"Yes, that I did, and more than that, I swore a solemn oath not to go through half, nor a quarter, nor a sixteenth part of it!" cried the convict, smiling grimly and savagely—"but resolved to make a clear escape on the very first opportunity.

"So, in the fifth year of my transportation, when I had gained a little confidence of the governor and other officers, I petitioned to form one of the body of convicts whom the government were sending out to settle in Norfolk Island.

"Somehow or other, I had an idea that from an island there would be more chance of escape than from the mainland.

"In this I proved to be wrong, for, on my arrival, I found the island to be strictly guarded with at least a hundred soldiers, and a large number of police, and that the gangs were always strictly watched.

"I began to wish I had stayed in New South Wales, but, eventually, my settling on the island proved the means of my ultimate escape.

"We were employed in boiling salt, and a variety of other employments.

"Many of the convict settlers had their wives and children with them, others were single, and they were of all characters—from the most atrocious to the comparatively innocent.

" I saw there was no chance of instigating them to rebellion, for, indeed, it would have been madness to attempt it, so vigilantly as we were guarded.

" I saw I must keep my plans to myself if I ever intended to escape.

" To get away from the island appeared impracticable, for there were no ships or boats of any kind to seize, nor opportunity to seize them.

" No craft ever came near the island but the government ships that called at regular intervals.

" At length, driven desperate, I came to the conclusion that, if I could not leave the island, I would at least have some liberty while on it.

" The island was deeply wooded, and large enough to conceal a man who could make his escape into the interior.

" I resolved that I would be that man.

" Accordingly, one day, at the time when I was sent into the town to draw my weekly allowance of provisions, I carried out this intention successfully, pocketed my allowance, and took the first opportunity, while the gang were being mustered, to escape into the woods.

" It was evening. The mighty forest was dark and gloomy; every step brought me deeper into the wild and magnificent scenery, whose thick luxuriance would afford me excellent cover.

" I made my way with difficulty through the thick undergrowth for several miles, and until I reached an open space, far away from the remotest sign of human habitation.

" I sat down to rest—a wild exultation filled my heart.

" I was free for the time at least; no one knew where I was, and it was probable that my escape would not be discovered before morning.

" I had a week's allowance of food and a blanket, which I had used every artifice to conceal, and which would serve me to sleep in.

" There were abundance of streams of fresh water, and the mighty pine-trees, that towered above me on all sides, afforded wood enough for all my necessities.

" Above all, I should no longer have to work—to labour through a long day, under the eye of a stern overseer.

" I resolved to be like the wild birds—to roam through the woods, free as the wind, with no man to compel my will.

" This intention I carried out in a very effectual manner.

" My first care the next morning, after a refreshing night's sleep on the grass, was to provide some habitation that should be at once comfortable and secret.

" Now I knew that, if I built a hut, the base that would be made after me would soon end in the discovery of my retreat, and my subsequent capture.

" Nevertheless, I must have some protection from the cold, wind, and rain.

" Accordingly, I hit upon a novel idea. I determined to build no hut, but to rest like the birds—on the branches of the grand pine trees.

" I must tell you that I had secreted with me a large knife, a hatchet with the back part like a hammer, and a number of large nails; with these I proceeded to carry out my intention.

" I looked out for one of the smallest pine-trees. This I cut down with my hatchet, and fashioned with my knife into a number of boards, of which I could construct a sort of box, large enough to contain me comfortably.

" I also twisted some flax fibres I had picked up on the way into a rope of considerable length.

" I sought out the highest pine-trees in the most sequestered part of the island, and finding a thickly-leaved group that would just do for the purpose, I ascended one by means of the rope, and commenced constructing my habitation.

" Between the strongest boughs on the top of the pine tree, I nailed the boards in the shape of a kind of platform, which would easily support my weight.

" This successfully accomplished, I built the sides of it by means of other boards placed upright; and, in short, formed a sort of box, which would serve me as hammock and as resting-place either by night or day.

" Over this I fixed a broad roof, sloping up the sides, so as to allow the rain to run off.

" My edifice was thus completed.

" It was on the top of the pine tree, at least a hundred feet from the ground, and effectually concealed by the thick leaves from the sight of any one below.

" From the entrance or door I could see, even when lying down, all that occurred at the foot of the tree; and I should thus be easily able to perceive my pursuers, even while I was completely invisible to them.

" My means of ascent and descent were partly the long rope, which I had fixed to the higher branches of the tree, and partly a series of wooden pegs, too small to be seen by a casual observer, fixed into the sides of the trunk.

" By these means I could enter or quit my retreat at a moment's notice.

" Having placed all my provision stores in this strange hiding-place, I rested from my labours on the tree, and pondered over my situation with much satisfaction.

" 'The police will have sharp eyes, indeed, to find me here,' I thought.

" So effectual did my hiding-place prove that though, as I afterwards learnt, every possible inquiry was made after me, and many searches instituted, they all proved ineffectual; indeed, no pursuers came anywhere near my retreat.

" I thus passed a week in comparative safety, living on my provisions, drinking from the brooks, and resting in my little nest on the top of the pine tree.

" The rain descended, the thunder roared, the sun blazed fiercely, and the cold wind at times pierced through the forest, but I was safe, and sheltered from all these afflictions.

" I felt like another Robinson Crusoe, a true solitary; and, if not monarch of all I surveyed, I was no man's slave, and giving neither allegiance nor homage to any of my fellow-creatures.

"But this bright feeling of liberty came to a speedy end.

"At the conclusion of the ensuing week I had finished all my provisions, and now, as there was nothing in the forest on which I could subsist, I must make frequent hazardous depredations on the other parts of the island, or starve.

"This, I knew, was more likely to ensure my capture than anything else; but still, necessity compelled me, though I was well aware that it was only at night that I could hope to commit these depredations in safety.

"So, on the following night, I issued forth from my retreat, and when I had got to the end of the thick wood, and entered the open plains, where there were huts, and other signs of human habitations, a faint, sickening sensation of mortal fear came over me.

"If I were captured now, what mercy could I hope for?

"But I knew that a bold stroke and consummate dexterity could alone be my salvation, so I grasped my hatchet, the only available weapon I possessed, and went on with bolder steps.

"The village, or congregation of huts, was situated in the centre of an open plain. It was mostly inhabited by convicts who had wives and children, and who were employed in rearing sheep and other cattle.

"The only military guard consisted of a small body of police, who were stationed in the centre of the village, which they ever and anon patrolled to see that all was safe.

"I was well acquainted both with the locality and habits of the people, and knew in which houses I should have the best chance of successfully accomplishing my designs.

"So I first directed my steps to the back of the cottage occupied by Bill Stammers, a careless fellow, who was every bit as likely to have left the back door open as not.

"My expectations proved correct.

"The back door opened easily, and admitted me into the kitchen of the little cottage.

"All was dark as pitch, and as still as the grave.

"I entered noiselessly, felt for a match, and, to my joy, found a whole box, which I immediately pocketed, after having first lit a piece of candle.

"It did not occupy me long to take possession of all I required.

"I had brought my blanket with me to hold the plunder, and, I can tell you, I completely filled it.

"Half a week's rations of salt-beef and pork were in the cupboard.

"I bagged them.

"A pound of butter and the same of tea were the next articles; a couple of half-quartern loaves followed next, then a lot of potatoes, pumpkins, and melons, and, in short, a variety of eatables of all kinds.

"A bottle of spirits I likewise seized, as I knew it would prove particularly useful, and likewise a few useful tools out of a basket lying in the corner.

"Add to these a few useful articles of wearing apparel, and my swag was so bulky that prudence told me I had taken as much as I could carry without great inconvenience.

"So I put out the light, and proceeded to leave the cottage as silently as I had entered it; but at that moment the police were filing past, and, with a beating heart and a cold perspiration all over me, I waited breathlessly until they had departed.

"At length their footsteps died away, and I cautiously emerged from the cottage, found that all was clear, and made my way to the forest, staggering under the weight of my plunder.

"Just at that moment, a dog in a neighbouring yard began a fearful barking, and, fearing that this would give the alarm, I accelerated my pace until I nearly dropped from exhaustion.

"I contrived, however, with many rests, to reach my retreat, though I had such great difficulty in doing so, that I feared I should have to relinquish the attempt.

"However, when I had regained my nest, I slept soundly till morning, and then woke up with the blissful consciousness that my perils were over for a time, at least.

"I had enough provisions to last me nearly a week and several things to make me more comfortable than before.

"The next day, as I afterwards heard, was an eventful one at the settlement.

"Bill Stammers, of course, had discovered the robbery, and accused several of his mates of it.

"The governor questioned them, and made all sorts of inquiries, but could not find the culprit.

"At length I was suspected, the fact of my being in hiding told against me, and a grand search was instituted that very day.

"The pursuers were hot on the scent; a large reward was offered for me, and you may judge my feelings when, after having finished a comfortable dinner, in my nest, I heard the sound of a large number of men approaching my retreat."

CHAPTER XXX.

THE CONVICT'S HISTORY CONTINUED AND CONCLUDED.

"No words can describe the sensation I experienced as these ominous sounds struck my ear. I knew I was to some extent safe, but having been so long secretly sheltered from even the approach of those who desired my capture, their penetration into my retreat now seemed like a certain forerunner of my return to slavery.

"I shrank back in my little box at the top of the pine-tree, and, as I heard the crackling of the under wood that heralded their approach, I dared not even look out to ascertain the extent of danger.

"I at length, however, found courage enough to do so. I perceived that the party of pursuers consisted of six persons, all of whom I knew to be vigilant officers belonging to the military of the settlement.

"That they had every desire to capture me I easily perceived from their actions and faces, and that they brought a considerable amount of acuteness and experience to bear upon me I

THE TYPEEAN SAVAGES ATTACK THE SOLITARY BOAT.

was well aware; and knowing this, I felt that my position was precarious to a degree, and that it was but the turn of a hair whether they would discover me or not.

"Luckily, I had taken the precaution to light my fire (whenever I required to do so) at some distance from my concealed habitation, and there was no indication whatever in the spot immediately surrounding the tree to betray me.

"The officers perceived this, as they looked round the thickly-grown wilderness; and it was a great relief for me to find, from their conversation, how far they were off from suspecting my close proximity to them.

"'Confound the fellow!' was the first distinct exclamation I heard, proceeding from the mouth of Sergeant Steele, the chief of the police, 'where can he have got to? I could have sworn, from the indications we have just seen, that he had constructed his retreat somewhere here; but now here we are, and not a sign of a hut, or a tent, or a fire, or anything in the world to show where he has settled.'

"'My opinion is,' remarked another officer, 'that he don't stop at any particular spot, but shifts about from day to day, for fear of being caught. He'll particularly keep out of the way, you know, on account of that swag he carried off last night.'

"'Of course he'll keep out of the way—but where? that's the question,' cried Sergeant Steele.

"'Here we've been searching the whole island round, as if we had been hunting for the proverbial needle in the bottle of hay, and with about as much success.'

"'If I only catch him—'

"And the sergeant's eyes wandered around him savagely, and even fixed on the group of trees wherein I lay concealed, but so thick was the foliage that I was entirely invisible to him.

"How glad I was that I had coiled up my rope, and removed the pegs from the trunk of the tree, so as to leave no indication that might arouse the slightest suspicion!

"I began to breathe freely as I saw the vindictive officer's eyes wander around the very spot where I had hidden, and fail to discover the faintest indication of my presence.

"'Well, it is no use staying here!' remarked the sergeant. 'He must be further on, that's certain, if he's anywhere at all—if he hasn't vanished and become invisible, like a ghost.'

"'Perhap he's found a cave, or something of that kind,' suggested one of the party, 'and burrowed himself up, like a fox, beneath the earth, where he can laugh at all pursuers.'

"'If he does, he shan't laugh long, unless it is on the other side of the mouth,' said the sergeant.

"'But come, we must make a fresh start.'

"'We shall very likely come across Joe Dalton's party somewhere in this scrub, and then we can see if they've had any more success than we have.'

"Accordingly, the party again moved on, and had soon disappeared among the thick underwood through which they made their way with an amount of difficulty that made some of them swear not a little.

"You may imagine what a deep sigh of relief I gave when I knew they had departed. I felt myself, in a manner, more secure than before the search; for, not only was suspicion allayed, but entirely diverted from the direction of my hiding-place.

"The remainder of the search would, undoubtedly, be carried on in other parts of the island.

"But still I judged it a matter of necessity that I should not stir from my hiding-place, even for a minute, all the next of that day; but, like the wild denizens of the forest, whose habits I was now imitating, I should make the solemn hours of the night my only time for activity.

"So I lay for several hours, listening for any sound that might indicate a further prosecution of the search in any direction; but nothing was audible, and so I gradually dropped off to sleep—about the only thing I could do under such circumstances.

"When I awoke it was night—the search had probably concluded, and I could descend in perfect safety.

"I accordingly did so, and, feeling very hungry, I lit a fire and cooked some of the provisions I had purloined from Tom Stammers, which made a capital meal.

"I continued this wild, solitary life, hiding in the day, and every now and then stealing forth from my retreat at night, in order to purloin food and other necessaries, for several weeks.

"One or two more searches were made after me, but as they were unsuccessful, the authorities came to the resolve of leaving me unmolested; and I accordingly remained the undiscoverable and mysterious person which circumstances had made me.

"And after all, what was my crime?

"I stole nothing but the common necessaries of life, which the authorities would have been compelled to provide for me.

"I had never run away at all.

"My great offence was that of evading the laborious occupations which my comrades had to perform; and even these I came in time to long for, or, at least, regard them as but slight hardships compared to the disadvantages of my solitary position.

"The authorities, as I afterwards learned, considered the subject almost in the same light; for it was obvious to them that I suffered quite as much by my wild, solitary, and precarious existence as I should have done by any amount of hard labour.

"It was this feeling that made the governor abandon any future search, and resolved, even if I was captured, to deal with me leniently.

"This, however, I did not know at the time; for I thought, on the contrary, that if I was once caught, I should be punished in the severest manner.

"There was one grand project that occupied the whole of my time, labour, and attention, and that was, the manufacture of a boat.

"I had made, during my secret explorations, a minute survey of the coast, which was not above three or four miles from the spot where I had fixed my habitation.

"I had ascertained that it would be practicable, in calm weather, to launch my boat at one point on the shore; indeed, the mere act of doing so would have been in itself a matter of small difficulty, if I could only contrive to avoid the coast-guard that were employed to watch every part of the coast which might be made available for purposes of escape.

"At night, when the whole of the gang had retired to rest, and the usual supervision was kept up in the villages (of course, the guard on the coast was, to a great extent, relaxed), this, I knew, would be the only time I could hope for a chance of getting away.

"But the first thing I had to think of was the construction of the boat, or rather canoe, for it would necessarily be a vessel of rude construction; and sufficiently light to enable me to carry it to the shore.

"Such a vessel I knew well how to construct, and luckily I had sufficient tools for the purpose, so that a few days sufficed to accomplish this part of my project.

"There was a vast number of trees in the forest of a sufficient lightness, and yet durable, for the purpose, and from these I equipped myself with the vessel in question—a long, light canoe, capable of cleaving the water swiftly, and of bearing the weight of myself and all the necessaries I could take with me on my adventurous enterprise.

"A couple of paddles, such as I had seen used effectively by the natives of New South Wales, I also constructed, and these would, I knew, form excellent adjuncts to the boat.

"I tried my canoe in sailing it on one of the small streams in the forest, and found my first essay in boat-building so excellent that I had no doubt of its proving capable of performing the work for which I designed it.

"I concealed my boat in a certain hollow, covered with a thick growth of vegetation—a hiding-place which the strictest search would probably have failed to discover.

"I got together as many necessaries as I could conveniently carry with me, and then paused in my work, and lay down to rest that day, with the delightful reflection that but a short time intervened between me and liberty.

"When I say I got together all things necessary for me on my adventurous voyage, I must not omit to relate an adventure I met with in this, my last expedition, into the settled portion of the island.

"I had started off, late on the previous night, on my usual plundering expedition, and had met with my usual success, when, returning from one of the cottages, I most imprudently crossed one of the principal roads of the island, in order to get to my forest lodging by a short cut.

"Now, it happened just then (being daybreak) that a gang of convicts were about to proceed to their labour, and, on seeing me flit across their path, naturally guessed who I was, and raised the alarm accordingly.

"'Hooray!' they shouted. 'A chase! and if he gets away from us this time, he must run quicker than a kangaroo!'

"I did escape them, however, for all that.

"I saw my danger, and it inspired me with mortal terror, and yet the instinct of self-preservation urged me on.

"I darted into the forest at a speed almost inconceivable, considering the way in which I was loaded, and knowing so completely, as I now did, every turn any track in its multitudinous sylvan windings, I was soon enabled to leave my pursuers far behind, and reach my nest in safety.

"The gang, however, still kept up the chase, but without effect, and, though another grand hunt for me was that day instituted, I succeeded in baffling the efforts of my pursuers, who did not, indeed, even closely approach my effective hiding-place.

"Neither did they discover my canoe, on which point I was all day in a state of great alarm.

"The next night was the one I had appointed for my grand achievement—my final escape from the convict island.

"It was a calm, clear night, the moon shone with magnificent brilliancy—a circumstance which, unlike many persons bent on secret designs, I had no cause to fear.

"It is impossible for any one who has not witnessed it to describe the beauty and sublimity of moonlight in those grand primeval forests—an effulgence only seen beneath tropical skies, and which renders every object around as distinct and clear as day.

"I accordingly should have the less difficulty in pursuing my bold enterprise, for which I now felt every nerve strung and my whole energies concentrated.

"The whole of the articles I wished to take with me in the boat I tied up in one bundle in my blanket. This I tied firmly round my neck, while the canoe, which, though light, was still a considerable weight for one man to carry, was supported on my back.

"Thus the weight was, as far as possible, evenly balanced; and, as I set out, I felt a degree of unwonted strength animating me, which made the toil seem absolutely as nothing.

"This feeling, however, gave way to fatigue, long ere I had reached the end of the four miles that had intervened between me and the coast.

"The place that I had fixed upon to embark was a small bay in one of the wildest and most rugged parts of the island, tenanted only by hosts of various kinds of sea-birds.

"There was no coast-guard station within miles of it, so that on this point I felt perfectly safe.

"I was terribly tired by the time I had reached this spot, notwithstanding that I had rested sometimes on the way.

"The small, winding stream, on which I had tried the powers of my boat, ran from the heart of the forest into the sea very close to the bay; and it would, of course, have been an immense benefit to me could I but have traversed it in my boat.

"But, though in some parts deep and navigable, it was so obstructed in other parts with snags and weeds, and other obstacles, that I knew such a course would have been impracticable.

"However, here I was at the coast, the beautiful moon-lit sea stretching out before me, in a vast sheet of blue and silver.

"The tide was going out, and a gentle, agreeable breeze springing up in the south-east quarter.

"I dragged my canoe down the beach, after having

rested a little while, and launched it in the billows, more fervent in my hopes of its success, you may be sure, than any fine lady who christens a splendid frigate in the London Docks, by breaking a bottle of port wine over her bows.

"My little skiff, loaded as she was, glided into the water like a swan, and even when I had jumped in and she had sunk down in consequence, she was still high out of water, and evidently capable of doing her work well.

"I used the paddles as a man only can who works for liberty, and I glided out of the bay with considerable swiftness.

"'Farewell, old sea-girt prison!' I cried, looking back to the island, with a wildly exultant heart. 'Whatever happens to me in this perilous voyage, even if I am capsized and drowned, I shall still have the consolation of knowing that I have left *you* behind, and that I die a free man.'

"But whither was I steering? What course did I pursue?

"That, my friends, I left entirely to chance; for beyond the fact that there were some islands about sixty miles to the north-west, I was perfectly ignorant of the adjoining coasts.

"My sole care had been to get away from the island; and that once accomplished, I regarded the worst of my perils as over, though, in reality, they were no more than begun.

"However, I had a firm trust that Providence would watch over my safety, and I was not mistaken.

"Taking the north-west course, for which, fortunately, the wind was in my favour, I paddled my frail craft for hours and hours, till the brilliant morning had dawned over the gleaming ocean, and exhaustion had greatly relaxed my strength.

"I took some refreshments, rested, and then feeling slightly refreshed, again pursued my way, until about an hour after mid-day, my efforts were rewarded by my coming in sight of a small group of tiny islands, covered with beautiful verdure, right in my path.

"'Here,' I thought, 'is my destination, or, at least, the first stage of my journey.

"'I will land and rest here, and though I shall find the island in all probability uninhabited, I have no doubt Nature, at least, will be hospitable to me.'

"In this I was certainly not deceived, for a more fertile island for its size than the principal one of that isolated group I have never beheld.

"Cocoa-nuts, bananas, bread-fruit, and a whole host of other natural luxuries, including that greatest blessing to the way-worn voyager—a spring of fresh water, gladdened my delighted gaze on all sides.

"But the island was evidently uninhabited—I had come to that conclusion the first moment I set foot on it.

"So, reflecting how fortune had again made me a Crusoe—on a regular island this time—I sat down and enjoyed the luxury of some fresh-gathered fruit, and the draught of some delightfully clear water out of a hollow cocoa-nut.

"I was thus blissfully employed when all of a sudden a terrific sound, that made me tremble, greeted my ears, and sent me into the cold perspiration of mortal terror.

"It sounded like a terrific roar, as of some wild beast, apparently close to me in the adjoining bushes.

"I grasped my pistol (a weapon I had fortunately managed to purloin from one of the huts), and, turning round, resolved that I would not very easily be deprived of life.

"To my surprise, however, the sound proceeded from a very different source to that which I had at first ascribed it to.

"It was no lion, nor tiger, nor indeed a wild beast of any kind, but a being bearing some resemblance to a man, though so disguised that it was at first difficult to distinguish its human lineaments.

"The matter was however set at rest by the voice again repeating, in a rough, loud, guttural tone, that I am bound to say was scarcely human—

"'In the name of the demons! what man is that who dares to trespass on my private grounds?'

"I looked at the questioner in amazement.

"He was tall—almost Herculean in height, though fearfully lean and emaciated, and ghastly in hue.

"His beard covered his whole countenance, and hung down far below his chest, mingling in the upper part with a shock of unkempt shaggy hair, which added greatly to the wildness of his appearance.

"Take, in addition to this, a hat of palm-leaves and a costume, once that of an English sailor but now fallen into rags, eked out by all sorts of savage and fantastic adornments, and a formidable club, and a musket, and you will be able to form some idea of the apparition I had before me on that desert island.

"I gazed at this extraordinary figure in amazement that rooted me to the spot.

"I knew I had become very wild and uncouth in my own appearance; but I was conscious I was not so bad as this.

"'How dare you trespass on my domain?' he repeated, coming closer to me, and stamping his club on the ground, with a menacing gesture. "Know you not that I am the king of the ocean—the presiding spirit of all the demons who haunt this secluded spot, and torture the souls of the drowned men, whom they lure to their doom?'

"I was somewhat taken aback by these strange words, accompanied as they were by grinding teeth and flashing eyes, and a general demeanour and appearance that made me think this being was indeed some demon in human form, rather than a man. But I found courage to answer—

"'I am not trespassing. I am a poor voyager, just escaped from bondage, who seeks a resting-place on this shore.'

"'These islands,' remarked the strange being, looking around him, and flinging his arms about wildly, 'are no resting-place for mortal men. Demons, spirits of wrong, and evil water-spirits are its only legitimate tenants, and over them I, Alboracio, their dread monarch, preside with a rule of iron, and I forbid, I scorn, all human companionship.'

"The fact was now completely apparent to my comprehension. The man was undoubtedly mad. Solitude, and perhaps the constant presence of haunting and guilty thoughts, had unsettled his intellect, and gave him up as a prey to the powers of superstition.

"The knowledge of this fact was no pleasant one to me. I felt it should be, however, my first care to conciliate him by humouring his delusions. I accordingly bowed down before him in the humblest manner, and said deferentially—

"'Most mighty king, whose power all feel and tremble at, deign to receive, as your guest, a poor man who has fled from persecution, and who now throws himself on your gracious clemency. Let me entreat you to receive me kindly, and I will for ever bow down to your mighty power.'

"He seemed somewhat soothed by this speech, the wild frenzy that seemed coming upon him vanished, and in a kindlier tone, he said—

"'Will you swear allegiance to the king of the elements, and become his faithful and unswerving slave?'

"'I will,' I replied, in a humble tone.

"'Then you shall be spared; otherwise, death—the fate of tortures only worthy of the vile race of mankind—would have been your portion. Come with me, and such hospitality as I can afford shall be yours.'

"I followed him to the centre of the island, where stood his habitation, a hut built of cocoa-nut trees, and thatched with leaves and branches; it was strangely decorated with feathers and skins, most fantastically arranged.

"Here were, however, many such conveniences of domestic life as my host had been able to procure.

"He lived principally on fish, land-crabs, cocoa-nuts, and other plants, and the flesh of the wild hog, all of which were abundant.

"He proved himself hospitable, and willing to share with me all his supplies.

"In conversation, however, we could not meet on equal terms, for his mad delusion of seeing and ruling over the demons of the sea precluded all other subjects.

"At times, he was very violent, almost delirious, and if contradicted was so extremely dangerous, that I was compelled to act very cautiously for my own safety.

"As, however, I had made up my mind to stay for a time at least on the island, I gradually managed to reason him out of these fancies and to bring him back to a sense of his position.

"It was then I learned that his name was Joshua Dyson, and that he had been a convict like myself. He related to me his history, and I told mine, and from that time we became fast friends.

"We lived a wild life alone together on the island for several months, until a crew of Canaccas visited the island on a fishing expedition, and we agreed to return with them to their native country.

"We did so.

"We were hospitably received by the king, and have been here ever since."

"But you have not told us how your companion came to be alone on the island?" said Tom, when the convict had ended his strange history.

"That is a long story," replied the convict, "but if you wish to hear it, there is the man himself—that tall fellow on the other side of the tent—he will no doubt tell it you."

CHAPTER XXXI.
THE STORY OF THE SECOND CONVICT.

JACK and Tom Starboard both turned their eyes with great intentness towards the man whom the convict had pointed out.

He was tall and thin, and though still somewhat rather wild and eccentric in appearance and demeanour, he had evidently greatly changed from the fierce maniacal aspect that had characterised him when Greenley had discovered him on the island.

While the rest of the large party assembled in the large room were more or less occupied in the general conversation and festivity that prevailed, Tom and Jack were, for the time, so engrossed by the strange adventures of the convict, that they could give their minds to no other subject, and greatly desired to hear the singular narrative completed by the second convict's relation of his adventures.

Accordingly, James Greenley summoned his companion in adventure by the following words:—

"Josh, I know you are quite as good a hand at telling a tale as myself, and so as I've been spinning to these gentlemen the yarn of my escape from the old prison, over in Norfolk Island, perhaps you'll cap it by going through all your adventures to them, which, I know, will interest them as much as my own."

The second convict seemed at first to exhibit some disinclination thus to reveal the strange and painful details of his past life, but, on his companion persuading him, he commenced. His narrative is in the following terms:—

"I was born in a little fishing village, on the coast of Somersetshire.

"My father was a poor fisherman, whose utmost exertions could scarcely obtain us more than the bare necessaries of life.

"I was an only son, and accustomed from my youth to accompany my father in all his expeditions.

"My life passed uneventfully and calmly, until I had reached my twenty-second year, when an event occurred which completely changed the course of my hitherto peaceful life.

"My most intimate friends were an old fisherman, named William Maynard, and his nephew, a young man a year or two older than myself, and who was my constant companion.

"No two persons could be more firm friends than Robert Alwyn and myself.

"One beautiful evening, I called at Maynard's cottage, with the intention of asking Robert Alwyn to go out with me in my boat, the weather being very favourable.

"Both Maynard and Alwyn were out; but to my surprise, the door was opened by a lovely girl, who was a perfect stranger to me.

"The deep blush that suffused her countenance on seeing me, made her appear more beautiful still, as she told me her father and cousin were out.

"Her father!

"I then remembered having heard Maynard speak of his daughter, who was living with an aunt in London. She was to have returned, and this fair and refined-looking girl was the daughter of a fisherman.

"She looked, I thought, more suited to be the inmate of a palace.

"I went away with a strange and new sensation which I had never experienced before.

"My first sight of Alice Maynard seemed to have changed my whole nature. I had only gone a short distance when I met Robert Alwyn. He greeted me with his usual boisterous welcome.

"'And what did you think of my pretty cousin?' he asked, on hearing that I had been to the cottage to inquire for him. 'Alice came home last night and is going to live with us. Are you going out to-night? I hope we shall be more fortunate than we have been lately.'

"I answered his question concerning his cousin with apparent carelessness, and to his inquiry as to whether I intended going on a fishing excursion that night, I replied in the negative, feeling that I must for a time be alone to think over my meeting, for the first time, with the daughter of my old friend.

"To no other subject could my mind give its attention in the mood I was then in. For a few days I saw nothing of Alwyn, he having gone to a large town at some distance to procure some necessary articles for his occupation, which could not be purchased in our own village, as well as to transact some important affairs for his uncle.

"Anxious as I felt to see Maynard's pretty daughter again, I did not care to call at the cottage without some reasonable pretence; but as soon as Alwyn returned, I hastened to renew my visits.

"Alice received me with great kindness, as a friend of her father and cousin; and, short as had been my acquaintance with her, I felt that she must influence my future life, either for good or ill.

"How completely subsequent events realized this belief!

"For some months things went on as usual, and although I carefully watched the conduct of Alice and Alwyn towards each other, I thought I saw nothing to show more on either side than cousinly regard, and as Alice always appeared to treat me with the same attention as she bestowed on Alwyn, I fervently hoped that I might stand an equal chance of gaining her affections, and determined that nothing should be wanting on my part to convey to her the feeling with which I regarded her.

"At length I felt that I must learn my fate and fortune. So I sought a pardonable opportunity of declaring my love.

"Meeting Alice one evening, as she returned from a visit to a neighbour, I poured into her ear the tale of my love and hopes.

"She appeared both surprised and agitated by this declaration.

"She listened, with downcast eyes, and after a few minutes' silence, with deep blushes she told me that her love was bestowed on another, and that she could feel for me only the regard of a sister.

"'And that other,' I exclaimed, with bitter feeling, 'is your cousin, Robert Alwyn! Am I not right?'

"She answered not, but her embarrassment increased, and, with faltering steps, left my side, while I, tortured with a newly-aroused feeling of the deepest jealousy and disappointment, walked hastily away, caring little whither my footsteps led me.

"It so chanced that I presently met Robert Alwyn, my intimate friend, but whom, at that moment, I regarded as my most bitter enemy. He greeted me with his usual warmth, without appearing to notice my disturbed appearance, and I, glad to escape unquestioned, in some degree recovered my composure, and answered his greeting in much my usual manner.

"We arranged for our usual fishing expedition on the following evening, and parted with apparent friendship on both sides.

"By degrees my feelings calmed down somewhat, and, before I slept, I felt more kindly towards my rival than in my first passion I had thought possible, for I then felt that I hated him for ever.

"But was I not unjust in entertaining jealousy at all?

"Deep as was the blow I had received, I justly considered that Robert had done nothing to alienate my affections from him, although he had been the cause of my life's disappointment.

"The following day I saw nothing of Alwyn until the time appointed for our expedition, and when I reached the beach, Alwyn was there before me, with all things prepared.

"There was a degree of constraint in his manner, which told me that he knew of our unconscious rivalry.

"Little, heaven knows, did I anticipate the terrible end of that night's journey.

"We put off with a very favourable wind, and, for a time, were both occupied arranging the ropes and nets.

"When this was done, and we were gliding smoothly along, Alwyn, as I expected, alluded to the subject that was present to both our minds, and I think now I see his handsome, manly face as, with general sympathy, he held out his hand to grasp mine, saying, with frank heartiness—

"'Josh, old friend, I am so sorry that you feel any disappointment with regard to this matter, but I hope you will soon find another Alice.'

"I answered with as much composure as I could muster, and, by degrees, we turned our attention entirely to the sport on which we were engaged.

"We presently began to find the wind rising considerably, and Alwyn, whose spirits always seemed to rise with the storm, began to laugh and joke, and, seeing me look gloomy, as indeed I felt, asked me, laughingly, how I ever came to think such a girl as Alice could like such a grim old curmudgeon like myself better than a devil-may-care sort of fellow he was.

"Now Alwyn had a habit of thus bantering, by making a jest of observations of this sort.

"I was not then in a mood to appreciate them.

"I made no reply, though I felt my anger rising.

"Why should he, my successful rival, be thus happy, while I, who surely deserved happiness as much as he did, experienced all the misery of jealousy and disappointment?

"The words of Alwyn, though so lightly spoken, seemed to me full of triumph, and again I felt towards him that bitter enmity which I had thought conquered; his foolish words had roused the feeling again in my heart.

"I would have borne angry words, or even coldness, but to be laughed at in my misery!

"The increasing violence of the wind roused us both from our individual thoughts to a knowledge of the great danger that threatened us.

"The sea, which had hitherto been but slightly agitated, now worked up to a terrific pitch of fury. The waves dashed madly over the deck of the little vessel, which was tossed wildly to and fro, and our sails seemed in danger of being torn from the masts.

"Our utmost efforts were of scarcely any avail against the violence of the storm. We were both engaged in trying to shorten the sail, when a tremendous wave broke over us, and, so soon as I was recovered from the shock, I turned to speak to Alwyn.

"To my horror I saw him struggling in the raging waters. He had been washed overboard.

"I have said my first feeling was that of horror; and so it was. Indeed, the wildness of the storm seemed to have communicated itself to me.

"I was confused, maddened. My brain seemed phrenzied.

"Mingled with my horror was a feeling of delight that he, my triumphant rival, was in such peril.

"Overcome by this sudden madness, I stood mute. I made no effort to save him, and, after vainly struggling and appealing to me to save him, a terrific breaker dashed him backwards, and he sank for ever beneath the foaming waves.

"Great heavens! that I should live to say it! he, my childhood's playmate, the loved companion of my youth, perished before my gaze. I might have saved him, and I would not. I am his murderer, and his blood is on my head. I felt it then, and I feel it more now whenever I allude to that awful moment."

The unhappy narrator here gave way to the emotion which agitated him. When he had in some degree recovered his composure, he continued his story.

"Who can imagine my agony when the violence of the storm abated? I stood the one living creature in that boat, on the lonely sea.

"Alone in the darkness and depth of gloom, alone in my bitter remorse and unavailing grief.

"Even now the remembrance of that awful scene rises before my eyes with vivid distinctness.

"I know not how I reached the land.

"I only remember that the night had fallen when I reached Maynard's cottage with the terrible intelligence.

"Can you imagine what an errand this was for me to perform?

"As soon as I entered, they rushed towards me.

"'Is he drowned? Is he dead?' they asked, and I stared and repeated their words like a maniac.

"I cannot dwell on the painful scene that followed.

"I had only sufficient presence of mind to keep the terrific secret of my own guilt, and only relate—heaven knows in what words—the fact of Alwyn's death.

"The intense grief of Alice, I could only trust, would be assuaged by time, while, for myself, I knew that bitter remorse and despair would haunt me for evermore.

"I strove to appear as before, and carried on my occupation of fishing for some months, hoping that I might, in time, venture once more to ask Alice to become my wife.

"When I thought a sufficient time had elapsed, I again addressed Alice as a suitor, but it was only to endure a more decided rejection even than before.

"She told me that her heart was buried with her first love, and that she could never love again.

"She assured me of her friendship, but begged me never again to renew the subject.

"My cup of wretchedness was now filled to the brim.

"I had lost the hope of even such happiness with Alice as I dared think might be mine.

"My native village had become hateful to me.

"My father was now dead, and I was alone in the world.

"I determined at once to leave for ever the scene of my past life, and seek in other countries, if possible, a relief from the misery I endured in the this.

"I left the village early one morning without one farewell, leaving my departure a matter of conjecture to all.

I proceeded to a large seaport town, some miles distant, where I hoped to meet with some means of carrying out my plans.

"I was fortunate, as I thought, in meeting with the very thing I wished for.

"I was sitting in the parlour of a public-house the day after my arrival at the seaport, when there entered a man of commanding figure, who, although he was dressed as a landsman, I conjectured to be a naval officer of some authority, and, by his bronzed complexion, I concluded he had seen some service.

"I soon found my conjecture to be true, as he quickly entered into conversation, telling me he was captain of a merchant vessel just about to start to the West Indies and that he was short of hands.

"Here was the very thing for me.

"I immediately offered myself, and, to my great joy, was accepted with very little question.

"I was to be prepared by the next evening, as the captain explained that his vessel must necessarily leave the port at a certain hour at night, but that I need not come on board until the time for sailing.

"I gladly presented myself at the time appointed, and found the ship in that state of confusion which usually prevails when a vessel is leaving port.

"There seemed a great amount of caution and anxiety among the officers and crew; but this, of course, may have been only natural, the real cause of this secrecy I was to discover afterwards.

"The breeze was in our favour, and ere the middle of next day we were far out on the bosom of the vast Atlantic.

"When we had got out to sea, I began to have some doubts as to the real character of my companions, and suspicions that they were other than they appeared.

"It the first place, there did not seem to be the strictness and discipline on board that I was accustomed to believe prevailed in the merchant service.

"Then their sailing at night, and under circumstances of great secrecy, struck me as exhibiting a fear to meet honestly the gaze of the world.

"Then the wild, lawless appearance and character of most of the sailors, and the rough speech and manner of the captain.

"All went to confirm the belief I had begun to entertain.

"In short, I could not help thinking that the vessel was engaged in some nefarious and unlawful trade—not smuggling, for of that, though I had never taken any part in, I entertained no very strong abhorrence—but of the greater crime of piracy.

"It was easy enough for a captain to call his ship a trading vessel, bound for the West Indies, with English goods, and sailing under the protection of British colours; but it was equally easy to be all the time a pirate in disguise, and when we had got out to sea I found all my suspicions on this head were correct.

"I found that I had fled from the consequences of one crime to engage in another; that I had sworn to continue honest all my life, and strive by every means to repair the evil I had committed, only to become a pirate.

"I did not like the idea, and I said so boldly to the captain, in the face of all the officers.

"I told him that if he was on the look out for an unprincipled man, who was willing to turn pirate, he should have told me so at first, and not deceive me with an idea that I was joining the crew of an honest merchantman.

"The whole of the officers, however, received this intimation with contempt, not unmixed with ridicule.

"'Now, look here,' cried the captain to me, in an emphatical and rather fierce tone. 'I've engaged you on board my ship as an able seaman. You are here to obey orders, and not to dare to tell me what you are, and what you don't like. I may be sailing under private orders, or on my own responsibility. I may be a merchant, or a privateer, or a buccaneer, or whatever I please, but in any case I have the command of this ship, and I am not called upon to give any account of my actions to any one under me at least. I intend to be obeyed, or know the season why. Curse your impertinence! if you don't like to join our expedition, you can be pitched into the sea, or hung upon the yard-arm, whichever you like. But, if you suppose I am going to put back to let you go on shore, and set you free to blow upon us, you were never more mistaken in your life. So don't dare to say another word to me on this subject, or, by George, it will be considerably the worse for you!'

"I saw it was useless to make any further resistance, so I passively resigned myself to my fate, sadly reflecting how one crime committed ever draws the culprit slowly but surely on the path of guilt and misery.

"I had forfeited the happiness of my life. I had fled, conscious-stricken, from my native land, to seek consolation in change of scene, and I found I had become but one among a crew of men whose lives were devoted to deeds of guilt.

"But I determined that, come what would, I would never take an active part in their lawless deeds."

"And you kept to that resolution?" asked Jack, who was struck by the resemblance of this incident to his own recent position.

"I kept to it," returned the convict, "until circumstances overpowered me, and it became a matter of life or death whether I should obey the captain or not.

"We were about half way between the Azores and the West Indies, when we overhauled an Italian felucca, bound from the West Indies to Genoa.

"The captain had no sooner spoken this ship, and ascertained her strength to be far inferior to his own, than he resolved to engage her, and showed himself for the first time in his true colours, as a fierce, remorseless, and unmistakable pirate.

"'Now, my boys, for an engagement!' he cried, in fierce excitement; 'a prize is at hand, the first we have taken, and one that will make us much richer than we are now, if I am not greatly out of my reckoning. No shirking, no cowardice among any of you, or, by Jove, I'll shoot any man with my own hand, if he but dare to hesitate in obeying my orders!'

"What could I do? All my companions were both compelled and inclined to obey the will of their fierce commander; and I, if ever so far from willingly, knew that I must do the same, or resist under pain of certain death.

"So, when the action came, I took part in it; and, so potent is the result of example, I fought with as fierce a desperation as any pirate among them.

"Moreover, I felt like a man inspired by the strong passion of excitement, coupled with gain.

"I was poor. There was plunder in store for me, if I would but take part with the rest.

"I soon, therefore, found myself in the thick of the fight, hot, excited, my every nerve strung up to its highest pitch of fierce energy, and did my part so well that I was honoured by special notice, and began to be respected for my bravery.

"The felucca proved a splendid prize.

"She was laden with the richest merchandise that fertile region can produce, besides considerable private property belonging to the passengers.

"All this fell into the hands of our captain and crew.

"A short, sharp, hand-to-hand engagement, and it was ours.

"And it was only when the prizes were given out to each man according to his services that I felt some degree of remorse mingling with the wild exultation of successful plunder.

"The struggle ended in the final triumph of the more evil part of my nature, and I became a pirate at heart, as well as in deed.

"The splendid vessel after having been plundered of everything of value, was set afloat on the wide Atlantic without boats, compasses, or supplies of sail.

"The passengers were all chained together in the hold, the captain, with incredible barbarity, even refusing the necessary supplies of food to support their already gravely-imperilled existence.

"This deed of piracy proved the first of a series of successful engagements, by which we made a considerable amount of plunder.

"There were several ports about the West Indies and the coasts of North America, where we had many confederates stationed to assist us in disposing of our plunder.

"The more he engaged in actions and encounters that proved him to be a fierce pirate, the more our captain assimilated his private conduct to that character.

"He became harsh, brutal, and overbearing with every prize.

"He was subject to frightful rages, and severe to every man who offended him—a manner that surpassed everything I had ever heard of in the way of swearing, though I have listened to many a strong oath in my time.

"He flogged unmercifully every man who had in the slightest degree incurred the charge of disobedience.

"More than all was his brutal and inhuman conduct towards one of the ship's boys—a little fellow who was much liked by all on the vessel.

"This boy was sent aloft once to set the fore-royals—a dangerous duty, and one to which a youngster on his first voyage should not on any account be put.

"Well, he was afraid to go aloft, and prayed not to be sent on so dangerous a venture, at least, until he had become more accustomed to the duties on board ship.

"But the captain got in a tremendous rage, and swore that if he didn't instantly obey the orders given him he should be half flogged to death.

"Still, however, the boy refused, and the captain, worked up to a fearful pitch of rage, seized the iron sounding-rod, and, with a violent blow, felled the boy to the deck of the ship.

"The youngster fell with only a slight groan, but he never spoke nor moved afterwards.

"That one blow had been the death of him, and the brutal captain had the deadly guilt of murder on his soul.

"But though this deed struck even that lawless crew with horror, the captain treated it with great indifference, saying—

"'Well, it was his own fault : he wouldn't obey orders. I only intended to give him a thrashing, and the death-blow was entirely accidental,' and so on, ordering the body to be immediately lowered into the waves.

"This sad ceremony, always fraught with melancholy, was on this occasion invested with peculiar horror.

"While I am sure not a man on the ship, however hardened, regarded it with complete indifference, on me its effect was most powerful, and I loathed the sight of the captain ever afterwards.

"Many more instances I could relate of the ferocious cruelty and barbarity that characterized Captain Blackheart, as he was called, though whether it was his own name or not, I didn't know.

"He certainly deserved it.

"But at last his career came to a stoppage, if not a conclusion.

"In one of his piratical expeditions he imprudently engaged a large English ship, secretly engaged on the preventive service.

"The enemy proved too much for him.

"As he was known to have attacked many English vessels, we were all taken prisoners, and expected no mercy.

"Our vessel was captured, and we were conveyed to England, where our trial took place, and created intense interest.

"Strongly suspected as our captain was of having committed many worse crimes than mere piracy, there was no evidence to substantiate such charges.

"Many of the crew seemed desirous to bear witness against him.

"I alone came forward with evidence as to the charge of the murder of young William Stevens, to the great surprise of the court and consternation of the captain.

"I related, circumstantially, all I knew, and the rest of the crew, on being closely cross-examined, in a great degree confirmed my evidence.

"I said that I had considered it my duty to bring this charge, as I abhorred such brutality, adding that I had not, in the first place, been willingly a pirate, but had been entrapped into the service under false pretences, and now heartily repented all the deeds of piracy I had been engaged in, though originally under compulsion.

"This had so great an effect on the jury, that while the captain and officers were condemned to transportation and hard labour for life, and each of the crew for twenty years, my sentence only amounted to that of ten years' transportation.

"I need not say how the rage and revengeful feelings of the captain were raised against me for what he considered my treachery against him, and I know that he swore, and would, if ever he should be able, carry out the most deadly revenge.

"Previous to my second departure for England, I had ascertained that Alice Maynard had died of grief for the loss of Robert.

"Her father had, a short time afterwards, likewise sunk into the grave.

"Thus all my dearest friends were removed from me, and I, the prime cause of their deaths, a felon burdened with the double weight of known and secret guilt, was about to pay the penalty of my evil deeds.

"I wept at this reflection, for I was not quite hardened.

"But now repentance and remorse were too late, and I knew I must submit to the worst that might befall me.

"The whole of us were sent out to New South Wales in the same convict ship, thus traversing as condemned prisoners, the same sea on which we had long roved as dauntless pirates.

"I could not help reflecting how inscrutable was the great principle by which guilt is ever followed by punishment—punishment in the same proportion, and of the same kind as the guilt itself.

It must have made the fierce captain almost mad to pass splendid prizes, which, a few months before, he could have engaged and plundered, and brought the crew to his feet for mercy, knowing that he was now but a condemned prisoner, bereft of all his splendid treasures of ill-gotten wealth, and powerless to retaliate.

"This alone, added to the bitter remorse he must naturally have felt, must have been sufficient punishment; but added to that was the reflection of a future life of grinding slavery.

"Heaven knows what extent of fierce revenge raged in the captain's breast with regard to myself!

"I did not feel my position so acutely as I might have done, filled as I was with remorse and melancholy.

"I regarded the worst as over, and was prepared for anything that might happen to me.

"Little, however, did I imagine the horrors I was about to undergo, and the unexpected change which events would work in the manner of my punishment.

"I never went to New South Wales.

"I never served out even a portion of my punishment as a convict.

"Another and even more wretched fate was reserved for me."

CHAPTER XXXII.
THE CONVICT'S STORY ENDED—SIGNS OF TREACHERY.

"ONE day, as we lay in a dead calm off the island of St. Paul, in the Indian Ocean, the captain thought it a favourable opportunity for getting in a supply of water, of which we had lately been on a rather short allowance.

"Accordingly, a gang of eight convicts, under a strong guard, were sent ashore to fill the water-casks.

"A party of us, about forty in number, were permitted to stroll up and down the deck, as well as we could for our irons.

"The crew, armed with cutlasses, were engaged in their ordinary occupation.

"The marines were on the quarter-deck, and as the captain was below, enjoying his usual siesta, they were by no means very vigilant in watching us.

"Indeed, they had nothing to apprehend, as the crew and marines more than outnumbered us, even if we were free and had arms.

"I could not help wishing we could suddenly break our chains, and, seizing the capstan-bars or belaying-pins, or any weapons that came to hand, overpower our masters, set free our comrades below, and so take the ship; but my wishes, unfortunately,

were unavailing, though I little thought how soon they would be fulfilled.

"As I was musing on our chances, to my astonishment I heard the cry of 'Sail ho!' and, turning my eyes to the entrance of the little bay in which we were anchored, saw a large ship coming round the point of the bay.

"On she came, her white sails glistening in the bright morning sun, and we could see that she carried several guns.

"The English colours were at this moment run up on the stranger, and our captain, who thought she might be an homeward bound Indiaman putting in for the same purpose as himself, ordered the ensign to be hoisted, and getting his speaking-trumpet ready to hail her, she came down fast with the sea-breeze, and ranged up within fifty yards of us.

"The captain was just upon the point of hailing her, when suddenly she shot up into the wind, presenting her broadside to us, then a wide sheet of flame flashed from her sides, and, with a rustling noise, a torrent of grape-shot tore into our ship, carrying death on all sides.

"So sudden and unexpected was the discharge, that those of who where left behind, stood dumb with surprise.

"I cast my eyes round for a moment, and saw that out of about forty of us convicts, more than a dozen of them had been killed.

"But the officers and crew had suffered still more severely, and the mariners had lost many of their number.

"A regular panic now ensued.

"As for myself, I fell flat on my face, and the rest of the convicts followed my example.

"The crew, recovering themselves a little, began to rush to their guns, the captain, who was uninjured, giving his commands in a stern, sharp voice, and the officers encouraged their men to stand to their guns.

They thought the stranger must be a French privateer on the look for English merchant ships, which had perceived the Centurion lying at anchor in the bay.

"I thought to myself—let it be how it would, we convicts could scarcely be worse off than we were.

"I rose up to take a look at the stranger, and saw that she had hoisted, in place of the English colours, a black flag: she was therefore, evidently a pirate.

"Our men had barely time to bring a few guns to bear upon the stranger, when she came alongside of us, her bowsprit projecting over her bulwarks, and fifty grim freebooters came pouring on to our decks, armed with boarding-axes and cutlasses. They were headed by a gigantic individual, of a most ferocious appearance.

"Captain Jones, our commander, at the head of his crew, rushed to repel them, and a desperate conflict ensued, but it did not last long.

"The crew of our ship were too much taken by surprise to make a very long resistance.

"They were soon overpowered, many of them were killed, and the remainder threw down their arms and fled to any place which seemed to offer a momentary chance of concealment.

"The pirate, seeing that we were in irons, and could offer no resistance whatever, had not molested us in any way yet.

"Captain Jones, who was infuriated at the loss of vessel in such a manner, rushed at the pirate tain, determined to be avenged before he died.

"Aiming a terrific blow with his sword, he broke wn the pirate chief's guard, and inflicted so severe a ound on the temple, that he sank lifeless to the deck.

"But Captain Jones did not long enjoy his triumph, for one of the pirates instantly sent a bullet through his brain, and he fell prostrate upon the body of the fallen pirate chief, never to rise again.

"The pirates were now undisputed masters of the Centurion, and began rummaging the ship for booty.

"Several of them asked why we were in irons, and, on our telling them the reason, they said we were just the men they wanted, as they were short of hands, having lost two boats' crews in an attack of the natives of the Ladrone islands, with whom they had had some dispute.

"The pirates made no doubt of our joining them, and we informed them that there were many more of us below.

"They began to take the hatches off, to set free the rest, who were below in a state of great terror, not knowing what on earth had happened.

"The first of them that issued forth was Captain Blackheart.

"He was immediately greeted with a shout of recognition by several of the pirates.

"'What! Blackheart, our old commander? Why, we thought you had danced on nothing long ago.'

"'Well met, old bully. We will make you captain of a better ship than the one you lost.'

"'Faith, lads,' replied Blackheart, 'I've managed to elude both the yard-arm and Davy Jones, as yet. But it was touch-and-go with me. But take off these cursed irons.'

"This was soon done, and the rest of the convicts set at liberty.

The pirates then called a council, at which those pirates who had known Captain Blackheart proposed that he should be elected captain in the place of the commander they had lost.

"There were but few objections raised.

"Most of the pirates had at least heard of the renowned Captain Blackheart, and were quite willing to sail under a commander who, though fierce and tyrannical, was certain to fill their ship with plunder, if there was anything at all to be got by any means whatever.

"Accordingly, Blackheart was formally made captain of the Black Eagle.

"The convicts joined to a man, and most of the crew who remained did so.

"A few of them, together with the officers, refused to do so.

"They were savagely shot, and thrown overboard.

"I, who had been standing unobserved by the foremast, was then noticed by Blackheart.

"He instantly ordered me to be brought before him.

"My heart sank at this command.

"I knew I could expect no mercy.

"'Well, Dyson, are you going to join us?' asked the fierce captain.

"'No, I replied. 'I will die first! I have had quite enough of your dreadful trade, and I am determined I will not any longer be a pirate.'

"'You won't, eh?' said he. 'No matter. I owe you a grudge, and by heaven I will pay it! Away with him below, lads! I will, at my leisure, concoct a scheme which shall fully revenge me upon the traitor who dared to betray me in open court.'

"I was then thrust below in the lower hold, and left to my meditations, which were anything but of an agreeable nature.

"I should have mentioned that the boat—which had been sent ashore for water—had returned.

"The men, alarmed by the report of the guns, had been seized instantly, and those who refused to join the pirates, had shared the fate of those unfortunates who had been thrown overboard.

"To make a long story short, the vessel sailed for about a fortnight, during which time I was confined below.

"One morning I was brought on deck, and found we were anchored off a small, barren-looking island.

"'There,' said Blackheart, 'you can enjoy the rest of your life on yonder pleasant spot.'

"And I was hurried into a boat, and, without provisions or water, left ashore on that desolate island, from which, in about an hour, I saw the pirate ship, under full sail, fade quickly into the horizon.

"Luckily, I found the island by no means so barren as I at first supposed.

"I contrived to live here, in fact, very comfortably; but for the loneliness which preyed upon my mind, and caused visions and delusions that, at last, made me almost like a maniac.

"I was in this state when a companion arrived—an escaped convict like myself—one who had passed through almost as many dangers.

"We stayed together on the island for several months, during which time, as it was so far out of the track of vessels, we found no prospect of escape.

"At length, however, a whaling vessel, filled with Canaccas, arrived on the island, and rescued us, as you have heard.

"As to the pirate, Blackheart, I subsequently heard that he became the terror of the ocean by his lawless and frequent deeds of piracy.

"He was never captured, but, at length, fell in action.

"His successor was far more brave and desperate, and yet a more humane commander—Juan Fernando Valdez—the renowned Black Eagle."

"Yours is about the most exciting and adventurous history," remarked Tom Starboard, when the second convict had thus concluded his narrative, "that ever I listened to, though I've heard some remarkable yarns in my time, and told them too, for I've seen some life myself. And do you and your mates feel thoroughly contented and willing to stay on this island?"

The convict here looked round with a glance of terror, as if afraid that the last question of Tom had been heard by his companions.

But finding that they were all apparently engaged in the other conversation that was going on in the hall of festivity, he turned once more to Tom, and said—

"Hush! Don't ask that question. It's a dangerous one, and one I dare not exactly answer. I can, however, speak for myself. I am contented with my present life, and willing to live peacefully and honestly in the island, and so is Greenley, but as for the rest——"

He paused, and Tom filled up that pause in his own way.

"They long for their old life of piracy, I suppose?"

The convict did not reply, but gave another fearful glance around him.

"To-night," he said in a mysterious whisper, apparently in half-musing soliloquy—"heavens! to think of the horrible change a few hours will bring forth!"

"What change, messmate?" asked old Tom, sharply.

"Good heavens! Did you hear me say anything about to-night?" said Dyson, turning pale with terror. "No, no! you are mistaken! I meant nothing! I mustn't betray secrets, or——"

Again he paused in his frightened hesitation.

Tom comprehended that the man was half inclined to divulge the fearful secret that was troubling him, but was afraid to do so.

"Depend upon it, lad," said Tom in a whisper to Crusoe, "there's something in the wind to-night among these mutineer fellows. Some mischief's brewing, I'm certain. This fellow's stammering shows it is so. We must keep a bright look-out, and perhaps we may find out more."

At this moment Jack, on happening to look round, saw the eyes of Williams, the mutineer leader, fixed upon the group with an expression so dark and fierce, that it was perfectly demoniacal.

Did he suspect that Dyson was betraying his secrets?

*   *   *   *   *   *   *

In a short time the festivities came to an end, the guests dispersed, and the king, bidding adieu to the captain and all the party from the Seagull, proceeded with his queen to their private palace.

The native chiefs also sought their own abodes, each separately departing with his train of warriors and retainers.

The party of the Seagull put out in boats for their ship, and though they had passed a very pleasant day, and met with a friendly reception, the captain resolved, all things considered, on keeping an extra watch on the ship all through the night.

He had seen enough to comprehend that it were as well to be prepared for danger.

This feeling was confirmed by Tom Starboard's relating what he had heard to increase his suspicions, as well as the following incident, that almost turned them into certainties.

As the guests were leaving the king's palace, Tom observed Williams standing beneath the shade of a cocoa-nut tree in the grounds, conversing secretly with one of the native chiefs.

They did not observe him, but separated just as he approached, and he could distinguish the following words from the lips of Williams :—

"Never mind, we'll let them come to our council to-night, and then seize them, the traitors! So, farewell, till we meet at Banana Valley."

That these words were very important as evidences that some underhand proceedings were contemplated Tom felt certain, and so did the captain, when Tom mentioned it to him on board the Seagull.

"There's something wrong; but what do you think it is, Tom?" asked Captain Hastings.

"Well, I tell you what, your honour, I think it's this," replied the old tar. "A meeting, or something of that kind—perhaps to hatch a conspiracy or to carry out one already hatched—is to take place to-night, at a place called Banana Valley—wherever that may be—between Williams and that chief, and, perhaps, a lot more. Probably Williams thinks, because those two convicts talk to us, that they have betrayed his secrets, and intends to seize them when they arrive at the place of meeting. What their intentions are—perhaps to seize our ship, perhaps to work some foul play against King Nookeevah—that's the mystery."

"We must solve the mystery, though," said the captain; "and that can be only done by keeping a secret watch on their movements. The question is, how is that to be done? and who will undertake so dangerous an enterprise?"

"I will," said Jack and Tom Starboard simultaneously. "Let us go on shore in an hour or two, and act as spies on the mutineers."

"Think of the danger," said Mr. Meredith, and Mabel echoed this warning.

"It's no man's duty to shrink from danger, captain," said Tom; "and if Jack's like me, he'll be precious ready to foil these scoundrels. Oh, captain, what a pity it is that you let them go safe from punishment!"

"You don't even know what time they will assemble, do you?" asked Mr. Meredith.

"No," replied Tom; "but that makes no difference. We'll go on shore, say in an hour—they can't well assemble before—fully primed, and make our way secretly through the woods to the Banana Valley—which Bill Orton says he can give me directions to find. After that, let me alone for carrying out the rest of the enterprise safely."

The captain at length agreed to this arrangement, and in an hour Crusoe and his staunch friend prepared to set out for their desperate adventure.

Just at this time the captain, on taking an observation through his night-glass, exclaimed suddenly—

"By Jupiter! There is a bright light, like a beacon, or a watch-fire, suddenly appeared on the very part where that place of rendezvous must be."

"Then, depend upon it, the conspirators are assembling!" cried Tom, in great excitement. "Hurrah! we shall manage capitally; for, with that light to guide us, we can easily find the place,

CRUSOE JACK SAVES THE LIFE OF THE DOG.

and be there in a quarter of an hour. So, as we're all ready, we'll put out a boat at once."

"Let Opton and Peters go with you," said the captain, "and hold the boat on shore, in readiness for you, when you escape. Whatever you do, be very careful, for it will be all up with you if you are discovered."

"Ay, ay, sir! but we'll take care of our precious lives, depend upon it."

"Good-bye!" said Jack to Mabel, who was greatly concerned for her lover's safety. "You will see what important services I shall perform to-night. Be not concerned for my safety, for you know that Providence watches over all."

*   *   *   *   *   *

In little more than ten minutes, our adventurers had reached the shore of the island, and plunged into its woody recesses, on their way to the scene of their desperate enterprise.

"Hark, what is that?" enquired Jack of his companion, catching him by the arm. "Is it not the baying of a dog, think you? Stay here, and I will creep back and reconnoitre."

"Not alone," said Tom; "I'll go with you."

Crusoe Jack motioned him to be silent, and, with the stealth and activity of a tiger, he crept back through the underwood, and found himself on the sandy beach.

Here the cause of their alarm was quickly discovered. A huge Newfoundland dog was struggling with two Indians, who, armed with heavy clubs, were endeavouring to beat out its brains.

The poor animal was severely wounded already, and the sight of two other savages suddenly appearing in the distance, made Jack's very blood boil with indignation.

"Back, villains!" he shouted to the dusky fiends; but they answered him only with a hideous yell, and one of them turned his attack upon our hero.

Thus relieved, the dog soon made short work of his adversary; with one deep growl he hurled him to the ground, and tore the windpipe from his throat.

Cutlass in hand, Jack met the blows of the Indian's iron-wood club, and with a well-aimed thrust, wounded him in the arm. One swift blow sent his head rolling on the sands, and Jack stood ready to meet the attack of the advancing foes.

The new comers, who quickly reached the spot, were more powerful, and if anything more hideous, than their predecessors; with a wild whoop, that seemed to string the poor boy's nerves, they rushed upon the gallant youth.

"Avast, take that."

Jack recognised the voice immediately.

It was Tom Starboard's.

He soon made his powerful arm tell against the enemy. His presence, too, gave Jack additional courage.

The supple steel, if not very deftly handled, would have been but a frail weapon to have come in contact with the heavy iron-wood clubs.

The Indians did not fail to take every advantage in their power, with sheer brute force they were determined to conquer, their hideous howls had already brought some others of their tribe to their assistance,

and Jack saw that it was time to put some stop to their proceedings or they would do more damage to their enterprise than they could easily repair.

Jack gave Tom to understand this, and he as quickly comprehended their danger, so without more ado they plucked up all their strength and stretched their adversaries bleeding on the sands.

The approaching Indians, on seeing their comrades fall, yelled more furiously than ever, and tore like very fiends themselves over the burning sands to intercept the pair as they made for the thick underwood.

———

CHAPTER XXXIII.

THE CONFERENCE OF THE CONSPIRATORS.

TOM STARBOARD and Jack made their way, secure from observation, and without meeting anyone, into the deep recesses of the wooded island.

Night had fallen—the beautiful night of the tropics, when a glorious moon, and stars of diamond brightness pour down their flood of radiance upon such scenes of luxurious natural beauty, entranced by serene repose, as no imagination can adequately picture.

Not a sound was audible but the splash of the glittering waves upon the silver beach; not a living object disturbed the peacefulness of the tropic landscape.

Every wild bird had stilled its lay, and reposed peacefully in its nest among the perfumed groves; the hum of the multitude who had taken part in the festivities of that day was hushed in the primitive streets of the town; never, to an unsuspecting eye, did a place appear so peaceful as the realm of King Nookeevah looked on that calm tropic night. But our friends, Jack and Tom Starboard, knew that danger lurked under this mask of peace; knew that rebellion and deadly treachery were at work beneath the cover of night.

From the very first, ever since Captain Hastings' startling discovery, the cute old sailor had *suspected* the designs of the former mutineers, doubted their sincerity, and disbelieved in their seeming repentance.

And now he felt certain that mischief was brewing, and fervently hoped he would be able to check it by his present expedition.

"It must be a mighty fine thing for these *Canaccas*," remarked the old tar, looking around him as they passed through the streets of the principal village, "a mighty fine thing indeed to live in a place where everything to eat and drink and wear grows spontaneous-like, and nobody need work hardly, much more steal, and there ain't any call for police to walk about in the night to see that all's safe, even though everybody leaves their doors open, and thinks nothing of it."

"Yes, that's all very well," said Jack; "but it don't, seemingly prevent treachery and conspiracy, which is about ten times worse than all the robbery in the world."

"See there," he said, "how bright the light is shining through the trees!"

"It's those fellows, sure enough," returned Tom, "just assembling round their council fire. Now we must be very careful, and remember that a dangerous enterprise it is we've come upon. So you follow me cautiously, while I go forward, and make a survey, to see what's going on."

Followed by our hero, Tom plunged into the thick grove of trees in the direction of the light, which was not more than fifty yards off, treading cautiously, so as to make his way through the underwood without noise.

As they proceeded, their caution increased, and when they at length found themselves sufficiently close to the assemblage for their purpose, their footsteps slackened considerably, and they stopped at length in a spot that secured them well from observation.

This was a tangled growth of shrubs, beneath the thickly-leaved branches of a group of bananas, crouching down beside the trunk of the large tree, their forms concealed behind it, and with their faces on a level with a small opening in the thicket, they could effectually become unobserved witnesses of the scene before them.

And a strange, mystic, weird, and romantic scene it was.

Around a fire of dried branches and leaves, evidently lit more for purpose of light than of heat, a large assembly was congregated.

It could not have consisted of less than seventy persons, including not only the whole of the convicts and mutineers, but a considerable number of natives and half castes.

They were all armed to the teeth with guns, cutlasses, spears, tomahawks, and in short, every weapon, both native and English, and their attire was of an equally motley description.

The English islanders were attired as we have previously described them, in a costume resembling that of English sailors, but with cocoa-nut hats and plumes, and, now in addition, many of them had the *tapa*, or native cloak, over the rest of their dress.

The half-castes and the natives, among whom were many chiefs of the high rank, were attired in their full war costume, with their towering plumes, tattoo, spears, and murderous hatchets.

Fierce was every countenance set, and with an expression of stern determination, and the red fire-light glaring upwards on their dark savage features, and glittering weapons, gave, in conjunction with the tropic sylvan landscape around, a wild terrible aspect to the scene.

Crusoe and old Tom settled themselves as comfortable as they could in their post of observation, in which they felt tolerably safe, for they had no suspicion of the presence of observers.

The first words they heard spoken was a sufficient testimony—

"So the coast is all clear, eh?" said one of the men, who was standing up, and whom the two spies now recognised as Williams, the leader of the mutineers, to a couple of half-castes, who approached the group from the opposite side.

"Not the ghost of any suspicion," returned the scouts. "The Seagull is still out at anchor on the bay, with all her crew on board; and as to the old king, he's shut up in his palace with all his warriors round him, evidently thinking himself as safe as a fish in the water."

"Well, but you've still left some fellows on the look-out at the points I told you of?" said Williams.

"Yes, Stephen and Pari Hela are there, and they'll give us warning if there's any sign of danger."

"Well, you had better start off now on the north side, down by the rock of Kaheena, and station yourselves where you can have a good view. Come back in half-an-hour, and I'll give you further instructions."

The two scouts disappeared in obedience to the order of their leader.

The latter looked round him, and said—

"Well, are we all here now? Is the number complete?"

"Everyone, captain," returned one of the mutineers.

"Even Dyson and Greenley?" asked the chief of the conspirators.

"Yes, we are here," replied the two convicts, who had that day related their adventures to Tom Starboard.

The latter had noticed them sitting near the leader, and of course came to the conclusion that they were after all as bad as the rest, thus to take part in what he knew was a conspiracy of a deadly character.

But how he had wronged them, and how the very next moment undeceived him!

"Oh! you are there, are you?" said the treacherous mutineer, in a sneering yet firm tone. "Then I'll tell you what, my friends—I know your game. You've come to our meeting because you know very well you were compelled, or at least, if missed, would have aroused suspicion. But I know you are here as spies. I noticed you were precious friendly to-day with those fellows from the Seagull, and if you haven't betrayed our scouts, you intend to. Here, you fellows, just tie these two up to one of the trees, then gag their mouths, and let's see whether they can do any harm there."

Great was the evident discomfiture of the two convicts, who, to tell the truth, really intended to betray the conspirators, and thus save much fierce contention and bloodshed.

They had joined the conspirators through compulsion.

They knew to refuse would be at the risk of their lives, and now they found their intentions discovered, and their lives still in jeopardy.

A party of three stalwart half-castes approached near to the convicts, and, securing them in a manner that would have effectually overpowered resistance, had any been attempted, proceeded to carry out the commands of their fierce leaders.

Greenley and Dyson, however, did not struggle, but they remonstrated strongly thus—

"Captain, I don't call this fair at all. How do you know we were going to betray you? What do you think we came here for, but to join in the conspiracy? and besides, how could we turn traitors, even if we wanted?"

"It's no use jawing—not a bit," replied Williams, "your game is to be spies on us; and, as I won't have anybody around me who is not bound hard and fast, heart and soul, in this night's enterprise, you must be rendered harmless. Now then, you fellows! look alive; tie them up, and, if they struggle, you know how to quiet them."

So the half-castes proceeded to tie the two convicts to the very tree behind which our friends, Tom and Jack were concealed, waiting impatiently for the conference to commence; when, however, they saw this unexpected event, they were rather embarrassed, and retreated abruptly from their hiding-place into the thicket.

In a few minutes, however, the convicts were securely fastened to the trunk of the largest banana, and the gags, tied not only round their mouths but their ears, prevented them being even listeners to the discussion that was about to take place.

The spies, therefore, resumed their post of concealment.

"Now," said Williams, "as all is safe, and the time's getting on, we must come to some conclusion as to what must be done. So my mates, chums, and Tayos, I should like to hear what you've got to propose. From the first minute I saw that ship—little thinking who was commanding her—I determined that, by fair means or foul, she should be ours; and we will have her—as sure as my name's what it is. To find out that Hastings had come back to us—curse him! I wish he had been at the bottom of the sea long ago—regularly knocked me over, I must confess, and though he was spooney enough to believe us when we shammed penitence, still his crew suspect us, and have made the king do the same. Now, what will be the consequence to all of us? If we remain here we shall be closely watched, always under suspicion, and perhaps have some bother with the natives, and come badly off. We want to seize the Seagull, and to take all her crew prisoners. Well, but if we do that to-night—which, unluckily, happens to be the time fixed for our other great enterprise—the invasion of Prince Pakayo—they will interfere with each other. I ask you, therefore, which shall we do? Secure the Seagull now—the most dangerous and difficult of the two enterprises—and, making off with her set up as pirates, and sweep the seas, or give all our help to Prince Pakayo; and, when we've conquered the island, and killed that old fool, Nookeevah, in his own palace, and live here comfortably on the plunder we get? Which shall it be?"

"Neither, if I can help it, you scoundrels!" said old Tom Starboard to himself.

A tall, fierce-looking warrior now rose, and thus answered his English comrades in treachery—

"Tayo, there is no need to deliberate on this matter. There must indeed be no hesitation. I stand here as a messenger from Prince Pakayo, to whom you have bound yourself to betray this kingdom, and to give him all the help you can in his invasion. From this promise you cannot now retract without breaking your compact with my great chief,

which will be at your own peril. Therefore, you must give up at once all thoughts of seizing yonder Pritance (British war ship), until you have done your duty to Prince Pakayo. In two hours, as you know, the appointed time will arrive when the great chief, with ten thousand warriors, will make his invasion on this doomed nation. His victory is sure, but if you break faith with him——"

And the Typee made signs indicative of the most terrible punishment.

The chief of the conspirators paused.

His mind was evidently wavering between fear and desire, and he half muttered to himself—

"Still, I should like to seize the ship, and become a bold pirate, with such a splendid crew as we could muster. I'm thoroughly sick of this island, and long for the sea again. Don't you, mates?"

Many of the conspirators echoed this opinion with great emphasis, and it was evident that the pirate's life was the one most agreeable and congenial to these lawless characters.

Again there was a pause of deliberation.

"Time is flying," said the Typee warrior, impatiently. "We must not deliberate longer. I propose that you give up all thought of seizing this ship, which can only complicate matters, and give all your attention to the exciting and important events that will occur to-night."

"Curse the Seagull!" said Williams, still hesitating. "I wish I had never seen either her or her captain. If I tried to seize the vessel now, independent of the crew to contend with, we should have the alarm given, King Nookeevah and his warriors would instantly rise in arms and help the captain, and thus not only prevent my scheme, but perhaps be the death of all of us, and frustrate the invasion besides. Whereas, on the other hand, if we don't attack her to-night on the very first sign of the coming conflict between the Typees and the Hopaws, she'll be off, and I shall lose her for ever."

"But remember, captain," observed one of the mutineers, "as my old messmate used to say, there are as good ships on the sea as ever went under it, and you may, perhaps, soon be able to seize another every bit as fine as the old Seagull."

"Perhaps," suggested another conspirator, "she'll stay, and as soon as the battle comes on, help the king, who has treated the crew so kindly."

"Not if the captain's in his right senses, she won't," replied Williams. "Why, now, you know as well as I do, what the Typees can do when they once get fairly in a country. They'll smash up all King Nookevah's army, even if they had two men-o'-war crews to help them."

"How is it, then, the Typees have never been successful in their invasions?" said the other; "they've tried it often enough?"

"Tororo!" cried the Typee warrior, fiercely. "Say one word against the valour of the Typees, and I'll silence your tongue for ever. They will fight this time but to win. I say again that we must think no more of this ship, but devote all the strength of our minds and arms to the service of Prince Pakayo."

"Your chief, then, is certain to come at the appointed time?" said Williams.

"As certain," replied the Typee warrior, "as that the sun will rise on to-morrow's dawn—rise on a scene of slaughter and a conquered nation—rise to see Pakayo king of the Hopaws!"

There was another pause of a few moments, during which the wild assembly appeared all lost in deep reflection.

At length Williams suddenly exclaimed, in a burst of fierce and reckless determination—

"By the fiends! I don't see why, after all, I should worry myself about this matter. Why can't we do both—help Prince Pakayo and fight the Seagull. Once get the Prince's legions here, and they will readily help us in this, as it will be but part of their conquest. Besides, look how useful the cannons of the Seagull would be to us."

"My Tayo, thou speakest truth!" replied the Typee chief. "If we could only get into our own hands the great fire-tubes of the white men, we might fire upon the Hopaws from the sea, and thus attack them both by land and water."

"But how to seize the vessel?—that is, after all, the question," said the English leader. "It would take quite all the men we have here to do it, and that the attempt would, as I have said before, be certain to arouse the whole island."

"A great deal might be done in a couple of hours," remarked another conspirator.

"Yes, a great deal of harm as well as good, Harry," returned Williams, half sneeringly.

"But, though we had better not make any attempt to board the ship, in that time, still we might be able to secure her."

"How?"

"Why, by cutting the cable, and letting her drift on shore. The sea-breeze is now blowing, and she'll go on the coral rocks like a cockle-shell. If this is done just at the time of our allies' arrival, it will give the crew enough to do to take care of their own safety to interfere, and we can thus have them in our power, and they will be an easy prey."

"This seems a desperate scheme, O chief of the white warriors!" replied the Typee; "but it will be a magnificent one if carried out, for it will at once rid us of all our enemies."

"What do you think, Harry?" asked Williams of one of his principal associates. "Shall we carry out this scheme?"

"Well, captain, my opinion is, that you had better not. Don't you see how dangerous and desperate it is, and how unlikely to succeed? No—my idea in all such matters as these—cunning is better than force. Wouldn't it be better to overreach the English crew by some dodge?"

"What dodge do you think would do the business?" asked Williams.

"Well, suppose, as soon as the invaders have got securely on shore, we send a message by one of our natives to Captain Hastings, purporting to be from King Nookeevah, informing him of the arrival of the dreaded Typees, and entreating him earnestly to despatch a party of his men to his palace to assist him in this emergency, and, if possible, send him

some weapons and ammunition; and, by this means, the vessel would be weakened both of men and fighting material; and while the party on shore would be cut to pieces on their landing, a large body of our gang, kept in waiting ashore, should jump into the boats, and instantly attack the ship. If this is done with proper spirit, the Seagull won't fail to fall into our hands."

This subtle, treacherous, and cowardly scheme so far met the approbation of the unprincipled crew assembled, that they all agreed to it unanimously.

Williams himself was especially delighted with the ingenuity of his subordinate.

"By Jove! Harry Martin, but you beat us all at this kind of scheming," said the leader of the mutineers. "I don't know that any better idea could possibly be brought forward. It will suit us to a T; but will, of course, need great skill in its execution."

"If there were more Hopaws on the island favourable to our party," remarked the Typee chief, "it would be all the better, both for the invasion and the seizing of the ship, for our side would be unconquerably strong. But, as it is, it will, as you say, require great caution. At present, all our thoughts should be concentrated on the coming struggle that is to decide the fate of this nation."

One of the conspirators pulled out an old silver chronometer, and remarked, "It is now half-past one."

"And in less than an hour the canoes of Pakayo will arrive," said the Typee chief. "I doubt not that the fierce warriors, impatient with the thirst for blood, plunder, and revenge, have already left their native land."

"The wind is favourable to them," remarked Williams. "Thirst for plunder and revenge, do they? Not more than I do, I can tell you. How I long to serve out Captain Hastings and that old fool, Nookeevah, who has kept us screwed up here so long, working for our bread like humdrum mechanics! I'm sick of this life, and am resolved to go on the old desperate course. How we've stood it all so long I can't think. However, it's all settled now; so let us proceed to dispose our forces."

The whole party now arose, and the scene became one of disorder.

This was, therefore, a perilous moment for Tom Starboard and Jack, whose place of concealment was now more likely to be discovered.

Our two friends, however, had acted with their accustomed bravery and determination, and succeeded in evading the dangers that encompassed them

---

CHAPTER XXXIV.

THE FLIGHT OF THE SPIES—TOM AND JACK BOTH MEET WITH SERIOUS DISASTERS—A TREACHEROUS DECEPTION.

JUST as the assembly of conspirators was dispersing and amid the disorder resulting from the movement, an irresistible though imprudent impulse seized our friend Jack, and led him to act in a manner highly imprudent for one in his perilous situation.

During the latter part of the conference, the two

unlucky prisoners, who were tied in a half-stifled condition to the banana tree, appeared to be quite forgotten.

The watch-fire, too, had gradually sunk lower and lower, until nothing remained of it but a few scattered embers, giving forth a flickering and unequal red light.

The valley in which the conspirators' conference had taken place was of no great depth, but surrounded on three sides by thick groves of banana and other tropical trees.

The shade thus cast greatly defended it, and when the watch-fire was at its height, its lurid glow, so contrasting with the back-ground of black foliage, had shone with such great relief and effect, that it had been clearly visible, as we have seen, even from the deck of the Seagull.

But now the fire was almost extinguished.

The shade was very deep, and the spot where the two prisoners were tied, and in which our two friends, Jack and Tom, were concealed, was but very dimly discernible to those of the insurgent assembly who stood at any distance from it.

Greenley and Dyson had submitted to their punishment in the only way they could—without resistance or attempt at escape.

They stood gazing earnestly at the savage faces of their persecutors, unable to speak or hear, and waiting as patiently as the circumstances would admit for the moment of relief.

It was nearer than they thought.

They were not entirely surrounded by enemies.

Friends also were at hand.

Within two feet of them crouched Jack and Tom, both of whom observed their situation, and desired to free them from it.

But to do so would place them also in jeopardy.

Notwithstanding, the heart of our hero began to entertain compassion for the only two among the conspirators who seemed at all inclined to befriend them.

Jack had a long Spanish knife in his belt among his other weapons.

Just at the time when the most confusion prevailed among the assembly, and when the most flickering and uncertain light played upon the spot from the expiring fire, he edged closer up to Greenley, and in a minute cut his bonds in several places.

Tom observed the action, and seemingly impelled by the same motives, severed in the same way the cords of Dyson, who was nearest to him.

Then, touching the two men lightly, our two friends whispered to them, in a low voice—

"You are free. Quick! Get behind the tree, and escape with us."

The convicts looked round with a startled expression, and could scarcely repress a cry of wonder at the sudden appearance of their deliverers.

They, however, recognised Jack and Tom Starboard, and hastened to obey their orders.

In far less time than it would take to describe it, the two men slid behind the tree, tore off their gags, and, following Jack and Tom, plunged into the thicket with all their speed.

They hurried on, without saying a word, for a considerable distance, until at length they reached an open space in the most sequestered part of the wood.

Here they stopped to exchange a few words of hurried explanation.

"Now, then," said old Tom Starboard to the convicts, "of course you're ready to join our side?"

"Yes, yes," returned both, without the least hesitation. "We will help you anyhow we can."

"Very well, then. That is as I expected. We will help you, too. Here are some weapons. We must foil these scoundrels, if possible, in both their enterprises. We must give the alarm without a moment's delay; therefore you, Dyson, come with me to the palace of King Nookeevah to inform him all about the conspiracy that is being carried on against him, and urge him to order out his forces instantly. As for you, Jack, go with Greenley down to the Seagull, and tell Captain Hastings how matters stand, so that he may know how to act. If any of us meet the scouts of the conspirators, we must kill them instantly, or our efforts will be of no avail."

So our friends thus parted, each party taking a different direction, each on a similar errand, and destined, as will be seen, to end in equally disastrous results.

The appearance of the island was as yet undisturbed.

The greater part of the inhabitants still slumbered peacefully, unconscious of the crisis of the peril and ruin to which they had arrived.

Tom Starboard and Josh Dyson—who, in his gratitude to his preserver, expressed his willingness to aid the crew of the Seagull with his very life—made their way through the most frequented paths, where they supposed they would be least likely to meet with the scouts of the insurgent party.

In this supposition, however, they were deceived.

Cautiously they proceeded, and had arrived in safety within sight of the palace of King Nookeevah; but before they could enter into the garden adjoining, a body of four gigantic and fully armed warriors rushed upon them from a neighbouring thicket, where they had evidently been lying in wait.

Our two friends were now indeed in a dangerous situation, but the stout heart of Tom Starboard, and the desperate courage and great strength of Dyson promised to make the contest more equal than it at first appeared.

They accordingly prepared for a gallant resistance.

Springing back, they drew their pistols and cutlasses, and stood boldly on the defensive.

"Spies! spies!" cried the chief of the scouts, who was a native warrior of herculean stature, "foes to our cause, and that pale-faced hound Dyson, too. Craven dog! you at least shall not be allowed to harm us!" and raising aloft his mighty tomahawk, would have inflicted on the head of the renegade such a wound as would have been instantly fatal.

But Dyson evaded the blow, and returned it by a discharge of his pistol full in the face of his fierce assailant.

The shot was not fatal, but it took terrible effect.

The ball grazed the cheek of the Canacca, taking

off much of the skin, wounding the ear, and lacerating his whole features.

With a yell of pain the dark warrior staggered forward, but weak from the shot and the blood that was streaming from his torn countenance, he was easily stricken to the earth by the next blow from the cutlass of Dyson, and lay bleeding and powerless.

There were now but three assailants to two, but the odds were still sufficiently great to render the position of the Englishmen exceedingly dangerous.

Incensed at the loss of their companion, the three Canaccas set upon Dyson and Tom Starboard with redoubled fury.

The latter, however, defended themselves with lion-hearted valour, and though wounded, gave no signs of surrendering.

"Treacherous scoundrels! come on," cried the gallant old tar, presenting a couple of pistols to the heads of his foes, while Dyson followed his example, "I will die for the honour of England and your rightful monarch, King Nookeevah, before I give way to such vile conspirators."

Incensed by these words of defiance, the natives proved how deep was their enmity by the fierceness of their attack; but, as Tom afterwards remarked, in describing the contest—

"They got as good as they gave."

The combat raged long and fiercely; wounds were given and inflicted, but at length our gallant friends of the Seagull were obliged to succumb to the power of their foes.

Dyson fell, wounded, beneath the tomahawk of one of the warriors, and Tom, seeing how dangerous his position had become, endeavoured, for about the fourth time, to make off in the direction of the palace.

In this he was successful; for, though covered with wounds, and faint with loss of blood, he continued to tear himself from the group of Hopaw warriors, and half ran, half staggered down the path closely followed by his inveterate foes.

"Let not the dog of a white man escape!" hissed the native warrior, through his clenched teeth. "If he once reaches the palace our secret is discovered, and all our designs frustrated. He must die. This spear-throw shall be his death stroke!"

Planting their gigantic forms firmly on the pathway, the two remaining warriors threw themselves back to give full force to their spears, which both threw at once.

Tom had, by exerting all his nearly-exhausted strength, proceeded up the path with considerable speed, and was at length within a few yards of the king's residence.

He saw a couple of native sentinels stationed at the rude primitive gate that formed the boundary of the grounds.

Could his strength but hold out sufficiently long to reach them, he might explain all to them, and thus have the intelligence conveyed to the king, even if he should fail to convey it himself.

Onward, panting and exhausted, he urged his fainting form, and had at length approached and attracted the attention of the sentinels, when one of the spears, sent with terrific force, struck him on the shoulder, and, with a wild cry, he ——— earth.

He still, however, retained his senses long enough to cry to the sentinel, in broken sentences—

"A conspiracy against the king—go instantly, and tell him to assemble his warriors—quickly, for the sake of heaven!" and Tom fell senseless at the feet of the native.

Meanwhile, Jack and Greenley made their way to the beach, where an exciting scene presented itself.

The three men who had been left in the boat were defending themselves desperately against half-a-dozen of the natives.

There was no time for hesitation, and Jack and Greenley threw themselves eagerly into the fray, but not in time to rescue their comrades, two of whom fell pierced by the spears of the natives.

Firing his pistol at one, Jack, with a single blow of his cutlass, cleft the skull of another, while Greenley, less fortunate, aimed a blow at a very active savage, missed him, and was himself knocked down by the tomahawk of the infuriated warrior, who, instantly drawing a knife from his girdle, stooped over the prostrate form of his enemy to complete his work.

Just then Jack perceived the danger of his comrade, rushed to his assistance, and with a blow from the butt-end of his pistol levelled the miscreant to the earth.

He then turned round and made towards the boat, to assist the only remaining man in it, but at that instant a war-club from one of the Canaccas, thrown with great violence, struck him full on the side of the head, and he fell senseless on the beach.

The man in the boat was also wounded by the natives, who quickly tied the hands of Jack and Greenley, making them close prisoners.

Meanwhile, Captain Hastings, who had seen from the deck of the ship that something was wrong on shore, ordered a boat to be lowered, and with a dozen men in it, well armed, made all haste to the beach, where he arrived just as the natives were making off with Jack and Greenley.

Captain Hastings was on the point of ordering a volley to be fired at the departing savages, when a chief of great rank, accompanied by five or six dusky warriors, came out of one of the leafy avenues of cocoa-nut trees, which led down to the beach,

"Hold thy hand, great chief of the pale-faces," cried he. "I have a message from the King Nookeevah. Terrible are the events of this night. Thousands of Typee warriors, under their fierce chief, Pakayo, have landed on the north of the island, and are advancing to the king's palace. These miscreants, who have attacked, slain, and secured your men, must be some of the invading savages. The king desires thee, O great chief of the pale faces, to go with your principal officers to his palace, and confer with him on this terrible crisis. Unless all the Hopaw warriors and their white brethren of the Seagull sally forth and meet the advancing foe, they will conquer the island."

"And the king sent you with this message?" asked the captain.

"He did," replied the chief. "Witness his signet." And he displayed a glittering string of beads set with gold, known to be a private talisman of the king's.

"And moreover, he desires his white Tayos to lend him the aid of the great fire-weapons of the white men. Two cannons mounted on yonder hill would do more execution among the foe than even the tomahawks of a thousand Hopaw braves."

"It would be difficult, if not impossible, to convey them on shore at present," replied Captain Hastings, "and would, besides, place my own ship in danger. But I will go to the king, and see in what way, consistent with the safety of my own vessel and crew, I can assist him in this emergency."

"And the blessings of the whole Hopaw nation will reward you," returned the chief, fervently. "Come with your chiefs, and I and my warriors will attend you as an escort to the palace."

"I must first give some instructions to those left in charge of the ship," replied the captain. And here, turning to one of his men, he said, "Wilkins, go on board, and inform Mr. Meredith how matters stand. Tell him I entrust him with the command of the ship during my absence. And," he added this in a lower tone, "tell him to make all ready for sailing at a moment's notice, for it strikes me we may have to beat a hasty retreat. Say I will return as speedily as possible, but not till I have rescued Crusoe Jack and Tom Starboard. Tell Mr. Meredith, also, to send a few more men, for I must send off separate parties in different directions, in search of our brave scouts."

The execution of these orders occupied nearly a quarter of an hour, during which Captain Hastings remained on the beach, attending to the disposal of the poor fellows from his own ship who had fell by the hands of the remorseless savages.

The Hopaw chief showed great impatience, for every moment, he said, was precious in the fearful crisis.

Captain Hastings put several questions to him with regard to the mutineers, whom the chief seemed to hold in great abhorrence, as he said they would probably assist Prince Pakayo in his invasion.

The boat having returned with about six more men, and considerable ammunition, the captain's party, thus augmented, joined the followers of the Hopaw chief, and left the shore for the interior.

A couple of boats were left on the beach to serve the returning party after their expedition had concluded.

As the party proceeded up the verdant slopes, the commotion that was beginning to rage in the devoted island was plainly visible in the scene that presented itself.

Natives of every grade were rushing about, armed, in every direction.

Small parties of warriors were being hastily formed, and hundreds were wending their way in the direction of the king's residence.

In the distance could be heard the fearful tramp and the yet more fearful war-cry of the approaching invaders, who having succeeded by the aid of the conspirators in landing on the other side of the island, were now marching towards the scene of intended contest with all the insolent triumph of conquering usurpers.

Captain Hastings' heart sank as he looked around him and perceived the dangers by which he was surrounded. He almost wished he had stayed behind, and not endangered his own life and imperilled the safety of his crew by so fool-hardy a venture.

But then, when he thought of the uncertainty that enveloped the fate of Jack and Tom Starboard, which filled him with great anxiety, he resolved to brave any danger rather than not do all he could to assist them.

Before they reached the palace they met with very large numbers of warriors, among which, to his astonishment, the captain recognised the greater part of the body of mutineers.

Beginning to suspect foul play, the captain was about to turn for explanation to the warrior chief who accompanied him, when, in obedience to a signal from the latter, a number of the mutineers and native warriors rushed upon the captain's small party, taking them entirely by surprise.

The treacherous warrior-chief, who, as our readers may have suspected, was in league with the invaders, and had practised the ruse we have described, to get possession of the captain and principal officers of the Seagull, gave vent to a wild peal of malicious laughter.

"Ha! ha! noble pale-face!" he exclaimed, "you are conquered. Did'st thou think I really intended to lead thee to King Nookeevah? No, that monarch will soon be powerless, and your aid cannot assist him. Your own fate is also sealed. Tororo! what a cunning scheme was that of mine! Bind them, my warriors, every man, and convey them to my house as prisoners, under a strong guard."

"Villanous traitor," cried the incensed captain. "I demand to see King Nookeevah!"

"It's no use. You must give in, captain," cried Williams, the leader of the insurgents, approaching, with fierce triumph in his demeanour. "You're caught now, so are those infernal spies of yours! So you must pry into our affairs, must you? By G——! if your messengers are not dead yet, they very soon shall be! and as for yourself——"

"You ungrateful scoundrel! Remember how I pardoned you only yesterday!"

"All's one for that. You are in my power now, and we're masters of the island, or very soon shall be, and of your ship too. What do you think of that? But away with them, my men, we can't stop jawing here. We'll have quite enough to do to-night without that."

So, despite their resistance, the captain and his followers were hurried away to their undeserved imprisonment.

CHAPTER XXXV.

THE INVASION—FEARFUL ENCOUNTER—TOM STARBOARD PROVES HIMSELF A HERO.

THE treacherous Hopaw warriors—traitors both to their country and its brave allies the Seagull—dispersed like lightning into the shades of the forest with fiendish exultation at what they considered their victory over the gallant old tar who had striven to frustrate their machinations.

In vain the native sentinel at the gate of King Nookeevah's palace hurled after them his deadly war-spear.

They succeeded in escaping his just vengeance.

Meanwhile, old Tom Starboard lay stretched senseless on the grass, having, as we have described, just retained sufficient sense and strength to explain in broken sentences the object of his mission.

The Hopaw warrior—as gallant and trusty a warrior as ever trod the earth—bent over the fallen man, raised him in his sinewy arms, and summoning a companion, conveyed him to the palace of the king.

The monarch was seated in the largest room of his primitive palace, holding a council of war with his principal chiefs—for it seems that some rumours of the coming invasion of Pakayo had already reached his ears.

They were debating as to the best method to be pursued.

On the entrance of the two warriors, with the body of Tom Starboard, and shortly afterwards, the arrival of the body of Greenley, who in the same manner had been found lying on the ground, the king was struck with consternation at his recognition of them.

On being questioned, the sentinel explained, as far as he had seen, the event that had led to this mishap, but was of course unable to do more than repeat the words Tom had spoken to him ere he fell.

These, however, were of sufficient weight, when coupled with other circumstances, to impress the king with the full extent of the dangers that surrounded him.

He saw the coming invasion was the result of a conspiracy.

That he had not only enemies without, but traitors within his citadel.

A source of danger which has been the ruin of many a mighty nation.

Accordingly, while Tom and his companion were being taken to an inner room of the palace, and attended by the private physician of the king—a half-caste, and formerly surgeon in an English ship—the brave chief of the Hopaw nation proceeded without delay to call the whole of his warriors to arms.

The palace speedily became a scene of the greatest excitement and confusion.

Every chief who kept faithful to his allegiance to the king came forward, with his band of dusky warriors, fired with patriotism, and burning for the strife.

From every side, through the gloom of advanced night, poured crowds of Hopaw braves, armed with clubs, spears, tomahawks, and slings.

An immense blue banner, bearing upon it the representation of a golden star, was planted on the roof of the king's palace, and round this central emblem of their national unity and national existence the brave warriors flocked in thousands.

Spies, scouts, and messengers were secretly despatched in all directions.

Some did not return, which filled their comrades with grave misgivings as to their fate, and others brought back such accounts of the state of affairs, as showed the greatness of the perils by which the whole nation was suddenly environed.

Prince Pakayo had landed.

He was marching on to the capital, followed by thousands of Typee warriors, whose ferocity was only equalled by their skill and determination.

None opposed him.

For no band strong enough to do so had been as yet organised.

While, on the other hand, vast bodies of men in league with the treacherous mutineers, were assisting the progress of the invaders, Captain Hastings, Crusoe Jack, and several other officers of the Seagull, had been taken prisoners by the basest treachery, and were now incarcerated under a strong guard in the residence of one of the traitor chiefs.

The Seagull was still at anchor.

On the shore a number of insurgent scouts were stationed to prevent any communication with the land.

The whole of the inhabitants of the island were in a terrible state of consternation—each true man of the Hopaw tribe, seizing his trusty spear, and resolving to die in defence of his country, while hundreds of women and children were endeavouring to escape from the power of the fierce invaders, and wandered through the woods in a state of distraction.

Such was the perilous and critical condition in which the brave monarch of the Hopaws now found himself and his people.

Spite of all his precautions in his large and efficient army, his scouts and guards stationed on every point of the coasts, in spite of his grand boast that the Typees never had and never should effect their conquest over the Hopaws, those fierce foes were now in the heart of his territory.

And how was this?

Not from any mistakes on the part of him or his chiefs.

Not from want of bravery or weak hesitation, but from the machinations of vile conspirators.

Treachery, treachery, had done it all!

This was confirmed by the testimony of Greenley and Tom Starboard, who, by the efforts of the king's physician, were speedily brought back to consciousness, and were able to inform the king of all they had seen and heard at the conspirators' meeting.

How the king deplored the blind faith that had led him to place reliance in the words of men so deeply hardened in crime, and the mistaken leniency on the part of Captain Hastings, which had prevented their just banishment!

But it was too late now to regret past indiscretions.

The present only was the time for action, and on that depended the liberties—the very lives—of a whole nation.

So the king disposed his forces around his palace and throughout the capital, and made every preparation for the coming struggle that was to decide the fate of his people.

Tom Starboard, weakened as he was with the

numerous wounds, and despite the advice of the physician, insisted upon rising, arming himself, and joining the king against his enemies.

The fate of his beloved captain, and his gallant young companion, Crusoe Jack, filled him with anxiety, and he resolved to ascertain their danger, and, if possible, rescue them from it.

So, with one arm in a sling, and a bandage round his wounded head, faint with loss of blood, and trembling with mingled weakness and anxiety, the dauntless and lion-hearted old sailor prepared to do his part in the approaching fray.

Greenley would have followed his example, but his wounds were even more numerous and dangerous than those of his companion, and precluded all possibility of his joining in the encounter.

So he remained prostrate in the king's residence while the wave of battle rolled around his resting-place.

Hundreds of women and children, carrying with them such property as they could rescue from their deserted homes, had fled to the king's palace and the adjoining houses for safety, and for the defence and protection of their helpless ones.

Every Hopaw warrior exerted himself to the utmost.

Thus, all being prepared, the Hopaw nation stood ready for the coming struggle.

* * * * * *

The faint glimmer of approaching dawn lit up the sky, when first the long, loud, hideous, war-yell of the Typees greeted the ears of their gallant foes.

Then followed the tramp of thousands of feet, making the very earth tremble, and the fierce cries of contention, or death and despair, that marked the progress of the invaders against every small band that attempted to oppose them.

They had spread themselves in every direction; not a part of the island that did not contain some outlying picket, either of their own party or of the traitors who had leagued with them.

The ocean on the north side of the island was dotted with war-canoes, and in these many warriors proceeded to encompass the island, and thus attack it both by sea and land.

What, however, formed the principal source of the danger, and the most formidable object of attack and resistance, was the great central army of Typee warriors, headed by the fierce Pakayo himself, which proceeded in a compact mass towards the chief point of attack—the principal town of the island and the king's palace.

Fearful, indeed, was the appearance of that formidable body of inveterate warriors pursuing their path of blood in the gray, weird light of early dawn.

Gigantic in stature, terrible in aspect, and tattooed in such devices as could but strike terror into the souls of their victims.

Decked with the sports of the chase, and armed with ponderous war-clubs and death-dealing stone-tomahawks, yelling war-cries as appalling as the howls of wild beasts, and flourishing around their plumed heads the scalps of bygone enemies.

Alas! that such monsters in human form should be allowed to pollute the fair earth, and too often make their path of slaughter a high-road to victory over the brave and humane.

But so it has frequently been, so, indeed, it threatened to be on the present occasion.

But the Hopaws were not daunted by the terrific appearance of their foes, their souls were not cast down by their fearful situation.

A spark of dauntless national pride animated every breast, and there was not a warrior but who felt a heaven-given increase of strength vibrate through every nerve and sinew in his frame.

Leaving a numerous guard in defence of his palace, and sending several smaller bodies in various directions to take up such positions as would enable them to surprise and harass the enemy, King Nookeevah issued forth at the head of five hundred picked men, among whom were Tom Starboard and the sentinel who had befriended him.

"Men of Hopaw!" was the brave monarch's watchword to his trusty adherents, "we fight this day for all we hold dear—our lives, our liberties, our dear native isle, which has never yet fallen under the chains of the invader. There stand your enemies, your deadly, remorseless foes—scorners of the Great Spirit, and eaters of men. They are powerful; but strike! strike! with strong arms and hearts of iron, and they shall fall, and we shall conquer!"

Though a deafening shout rent the air, in answer to this appeal, no such encouragement was required by the gallant braves of the Hopaw nation. Already in their souls burned the glow of victory, and before them stood the foe whom they had resolved to conquer, or perish in the attempt.

Accordingly, the long line of warriors that had followed the king raised their usual war-cry, flourished their mighty weapons aloft, and rushed forward on their foes in a dense, heavy mass like a thunder-cloud.

The forces were disposed in exactly the same manner as at the sham-fight that had been the day before exhibited to the English visitors. That is, the principal warriors, with clubs, standing in the front line, the spearmen behind, and the slingers on the flanks.

It was the foremost row of this body that first advanced, headed by the king, on the front rank of their foes.

The latter, led on by their chief, Pakayo, had arranged themselves in a similar fashion, the most powerful warriors, armed with clubs and hatchets, occupying the most prominent position.

The two armies rushed together simultaneously, yelling their fierce war-cries.

The shock was terrific.

The very earth seemed to quiver with the violence of that hostile meeting.

Not even the deadly artillery of civilized warfare could have added to the fierceness of the opening contest.

The king seemed inspired with the strength of a giant—the bravery of a lion.

With one strong hand grasping the richly-ornamented handle of his ponderous tomahawk, which had descended to him from a long line of noble chiefs, and the other the shield on which the royal emblem was embossed, he charged into the very thick of the fray.

Nor were his principal chiefs backward in following his example.

Each man fought as though upon his valour alone depended the issue of the conflict.

Tom Starboard, notwithstanding his wounded condition, used his cutlass and pistols with such effect as proved highly injurious to all who opposed him.

The conflict was fierce on both sides.

All knew it must end in the triumph of one and the total annihilation of the other.

It was a fight to the death.

No mercy, no courtesy of warfare were to be thought of.

The invaders and the invaded regarded each other with a fierce and long-standing hatred, which could only be quenched by the blood of the opposite party.

The flower of both armies, the bravest warriors of each nation, were contained in the two contending ranks.

Should one conquer, the victory would be decided, for all the smaller bands were but adjuncts to the two great ones.

They assisted their efforts, but did not influence the main tide of victory.

Foremost among the opposing ranks, girt with his fiercest chiefs, stood Prince Pakayo, a warrior of the most ferocious aspect, wielding his dreadful war-club, so that at each blow a man was levelled to the earth, and a life was sacrificed.

The black eyes of Pakayo gleamed with a demoniacal light as he recognized his principal and hated foe, King Nookeevah.

"Vile leader of a race of cravens!" he thundered, in a tone that rose even above the roar of conflict. " The blood of my father, Tiaro, shall be this day avenged! Thou shalt not escape!—thou shalt fall into my hands, which alone must work thy punishment."

"Accursed cannibal and blasphemer!" shouted the brave king of the Hopaws, goaded to fury by these mocking words, "never till every human being perishes from off this island shall it become your prey! The great Etooa will aid those who obey him, and work his vengeance, by my hand, upon his vile enemies—thus!"

And bounding like a tiger upon his prey, into the dense body of Typee warriors who fought around their chief, the lion-hearted Nookeevah made towards his hereditary foe.

Prince Pakayo stood ready for the onset.

He rejoiced fiercely at the turn of events that had brought him and Nookeevah face to face. Not that he wished at once to slay him—no; his fiendish nature exulted in refined torture, and he desired only to take the king prisoner, load him with chains, and in this position of disgrace let him witness the final downfall of his country.

He had goaded the king to the attack, but prepared himself to stand only on the defensive, and in a short time gain his chief end.

Rash, indeed, was the action of King Nookeevah

in thus casting himself in the thick of danger, for he was immediately surrounded by Typee warriors, who aided the chief in this momentous conflict.

But King Nookeevah, swinging aloft his tomahawk, cleft the ranks that attempted to oppose him, and forced his way successfully to Pakayo's side.

He attempted to seize him by the throat, but the giant arm of the Typee chief warded off his arm.

Blow after blow was hurled with ever-increasing fury at Pakayo by his incensed rival, but one and all were warded off by the shield of the former, who, resolute to his intention of acting only on the defensive, returned not the attack, which he thus rendered harmless.

It seemed as though he desired to continue this course until Nookeevah was exhausted, and would fall an easy prey.

But as yet no sign of failing strength or spirit exhibited itself on the king's part.

While the two leaders were thus occupied, their followers carried on the contention in a manner well worthy of such an example.

The dawn, which was now spreading its new-born glory over the skies, fully revealed such a scene of universal contention as that lovely island had never hitherto beheld.

Far as the eye could reach, in every wood, around every cluster of huts, upon every spot that could be used as a vantage-ground for hand-to-hand warfare, contention reigned supreme.

Thousands of warriors of the two nations were fighting desperately, frantically, unsparingly cleaving skulls, wounding limbs, and stretching tall and stalwart forms unconscious on the ground.

The pathway of all was heaped with slain, and the wounded and dying groaned as they lay weltering in their blood.

All order seemed now destroyed.

The ranks of each army were broken, and the orders of leaders were scarce obeyed in the fierce passions that had taken possession of every breast.

The air was thickened by the constant shower of stones hurled from every direction by the slingers of the opposing parties.

The crested plumes of many a victorious chieftain were broken.

The gay attire of many a proud warrior was disarranged and soiled with blood.

But not alone were the Hopaws and Typees engaged in this fierce contention.

Their treacherous allies, the mutineers, aided them with every means in their power, acting as outlying and harassing parties, and rushing into the thickest of the fight whenever the tide of victory waxed sluggish.

In this old Tom rejoiced.

He longed, above all things, to be brought face to face in fair fight with the traitor Williams, and repay his villany with a well-deserved bullet, or fatal blow with the cutlass. And he had his wish.

Sending on the troop of warriors and half-castes, which the king has entrusted to his command, he had performed prodigies of valour, and made his presence an encouragement to his men, and a terror to his enemies.

The tide of combat, now so tempestuous, frequently separated Tom's party from that of the king; and on one of these occasions he found himself hand to hand with a party of mutineers led by Williams, and armed with muskets and cutlasses.

They recognised each other.

Fierce was the hatred that inflamed the hearts of both.

"Vile traitor!" cried the gallant old Tom, "is this the way you repay the captain's generosity? Such wretches as you deserve the yard-arm, and you shall yet swing on it. Forward, my men, and cut this band of wolves to pieces!"

"That's easier said than done, old tarpauling," returned Williams, levelling his piece at the head of old Tom.

But the ball missed, through a rapid movement on the part of the latter, which saved his life.

The muskets of the mutineers proved far less effective than they thought against the slings and clubs of Tom's followers.

They were too heavy weapons for a close encounter, when there was no time to load.

The only way of turning them to account was by using the butt-ends.

In this way they were about equal in utility to the war-clubs of the opposing legion.

Williams especially desired to kill, wound, or seize Tom Starboard.

He knew him to be his enemy.

He had ascertained how Tom, in company with Jack, had that night played the part of spy.

Already the villanous mutineer had accomplished the imprisonment of our hero and the gallant Captain Hastings.

Now he only required Tom to render his triumph complete.

"He's a lame cock, my boys, and can't fight," the mutineer shouted to his men. "See, his arm is in a sling. He hasn't recovered from the peppering he lately received from our scouts. Shame on you if you let such a foe escape!"

"Shame on me to be taken, villain, or give in to such as you!" said Tom, aiming a terrific blow at him with his cutlass. "Scoundrel! what have you done with Captain Hastings and his party?"

"Safe in a prison, where you'll soon be, too," returned Williams, warding off the blow with his own weapon; "and not only that, but the Seagull will soon be ours."

"It shan't!—it shan't!—I'll die first!" old Tom replied, his rage redoubled at this taunt, while his heart was filled with anxiety for the fate of his beloved ship. "You villanous scoundrel! are there no bounds to your infamy?"

The mutineer only replied by another blow, directed at the head of his enemy, but which was providentially warded off.

The combat between the party of Tom Starboard and that of Williams had now become as fierce, close, and deadly as that of the rival chiefs.

Tom's party was the smaller of the two.

But they were well armed, and the fierceness of desperation inspired them with increased strength.

A cry having arisen among Tom's party that Captain Hastings and his companions were imprisoned in a particular house, with which many of them were acquainted, old Tom resolved to break his way through all the intermediate obstacles, and set them at liberty.

The undertaking was a desperate one.

Williams, discovering his intention, redoubled his efforts to frustrate it.

Forcing their way onward, however, with dauntless determination, Tom and his followers gradually made Williams's party lose ground.

Each little piece of success was a spur to further exertions.

At length, by stratagem mixed with force, they contrived to break through the ranks of the enemy, and put them to the rout.

Williams, despite his disappointment, saw that he was compelled to retreat.

With a curse of baffled fury he proceeded to follow his disorganized and decreased party into the woods.

With a shout of triumph Tom and his followers pressed forward towards the place of Captain Hastings's incarceration.

"We will rescue them," said the brave old tar, "or ourselves fall victims to the rash attempt. Oh, how I long to have all my mates of the Seagull around that I may fight, and, if it is to be so, die by their side."

As he uttered this heroic wish, Tom came in sight of the prison which contained his gallant comrades.

It was a long, low, rudely-constructed edifice, closely barricaded without, but of itself containing little strength.

It was, however, effectually defended by a large body of Typee warriors and mutineers, armed with spears, clubs, and muskets, encompassing it on all sides.

Every prisoner that could be taken was brought to this place.

On seeing the desperate chances that existed of effecting the rescue, Tom prepared to dispose his forces for a sudden and vigorous onslaught.

They made it gallantly.

But a shower of spears, slings, and musket-balls was instantly directed towards them, and drove them back.

They did not, however, depart, but proceeded to recommence the attack.

———

CHAPTER XXXVI.

THE COMBAT BETWEEN THE CHIEFS—A SANGUINARY AND UNIVERSAL CONTEST—THE VICTORS AND THE VANQUISHED.

STILL fiercely and bravely did King Nookeevah attack the Typee chief.

Still wielding his tomahawk with the strength of a giant and the skill of a practised warrior, he sought to gratify the feelings of patriotic revenge that animated him.

But Pakayo continued to defend himself with taunting and desperate resistance.

THE INVADING INDIANS FOUND THEIR PLANS FRUSTRATED.

He seemed to take delight in baffling his foe, and yet contemptuously declining to return his attack on equal terms.

He appeared determined to let the king spend his strength in vain efforts to slay him.

Wherever the mighty blows of the king's tomahawk fell the shield of Pakayo was ready to receive them.

Wherever the terrific war-club was aimed it descended harmlessly on the impregnable defences of the Typee chief.

The contest had continued long.

The chief and followers on each side, at the express desire of their leaders, had refrained from interference in it, but renewed their attacks on foes of their own rank.

Nevertheless, there was many a chief who, on perceiving any imminent danger menace his leader, was ready to spring forward to his side, and give him the aid of his powerful arm.

The necessity for this devotion was soon apparent, for though Pakayo stood so resolutely on the defensive, he was evidently ready to take advantage of any rash movement on the king's part that would give him an opportunity of inflicting a wound.

Thus it was that when Nookeevah, almost frenzied at his ill-success, sought by a feint to break the guard of his enemy, the very action gave Pakayo an opportunity of gratifying his hate ; and he, taking advantage of it, aimed a deadly blow at the head of the king.

But at this moment a chief, distinguished throughout the whole Hopaw nation for his bravery and devotion to the king, bounded like lightning before Nookeevah, and caught the blow on his shield.

Had he been a quarter of a second later the brave chief of the Hopaws would have been a mutilated corpse.

He had saved the king's life, and so disconcerted his foe, that the latter drew back, paused, and regarded him with rage mingled with surprise.

"Vile chief of a race of demons!" cried the brave Hopaw warrior, flourishing his war-club, and preparing to take up the combat on the part of the king. "Back! back! or by the great Etooa, your hours are numbered!"

"What! dog of a craven tribe! darst thou speak thus to me?" cried the prince, almost livid with rage. "By the gods of my fathers! those words shall be blotted out in your blood!"

"But thine shall flow first!" cried the Hopaw chief, springing, with renewed energy, on the enemy of his country.

It is impossible for any words to describe the rapid action, the heat and confusion of the conflict after this new attack.

King Nookeevah had been driven back—but only momentarily.

He again rose, and plunged into the thick of the fight with fresh vigour.

Many a chief flocked to his side and aided him, while those of the opposing party arranged themselves around their leader.

The fight again became general, again raged with the fierce volume and velocity of a torrent.

The Hopaws, hitherto gradually succumbing to the superior numbers of the enemy, now seemed inspired with a fresh access of strength and spirit.

The fierceness of desperation drove them to redouble all their efforts and skill.

Their loss had been fearful, though their enemies had also suffered.

And now the desire to revenge their slaughtered relatives was added like fuel to the flame of their wrath.

They paused, therefore, for a moment.

They gathered themselves together in a compact body, and, collecting all their strength, rushed in a sudden and overwhelming mass upon their foes.

The Typees, in their insolence of approaching victory, had relaxed the energy of their efforts, and were therefore unprepared for such an attack.

They had, besides, become scattered and separated into detachments.

When, therefore, the Hopaws rushed upon them, as fiercely and mercilessly as a pack of wolves to the slaughter, the effects of the attack became speedily apparent.

The Typees began to give way.

The impetuosity of the torrent overcame them.

Their foes were equal in skill, strength, and bravery—in all but numbers—to themselves, and desperate vigour had removed even this inequality.

The Typees went down like reaped corn before the mighty onslaught of the Hopaw braves.

Hundreds of warriors fell dead and disabled.

All order was destroyed.

All skill became ineffectual.

The invaders had lost ground, and with it confidence.

That gone, the tide of victory necessarily began to flow against them.

Little did they imagine how desperate would be the resistance of the Hopaws.

They supposed they would prove an easy prey, and paralysed by the presence of the enemy in the very heart of their territory, would be struck with a panic, or at least offer little resistance.

But now they saw and felt, to their cost, what a foe they had to deal with.

They began to estimate truly the strength of the Hopaws.

With a wild war-cry, echoing from man to man in fiercely triumphant tones, the Hopaws, encouraged by the advantage they had gained, pressed onward with superhuman vigour.

Every man flocked around the great central vortex of battle, and gave his aid in increasing its destructive force.

Not only the men, but many of the women of the tribe, rushed from their places of safety with a furious valour that would not be resisted, and wielded the weapons of war with all the heroism and effect of ancient Amazons.

The Typees could not stand against so universal an onslaught.

Even the assistance of the mutineers, skilled as they were in the use of European arms, failed to give their efforts an increase of weight.

The tide of victory—a complete torrent, a cataract—flowed back upon them with redoubled force.

They saw the mighty banner of the Golden Star, the emblem of victory—like the black raven of the Saxons—hovering above their triumphant foes, and every moment verging nearer to them.

It was the sign of their approaching destruction, and it struck terror into their hearts.

To vanquish or to die!

The invaders had come for the former.

But if they failed, they knew how surely the latter fate would engulph them.

They saw the dreaded retribution overtaking them, when, their ranks utterly broken, they dispersed, as if panic stricken, and fled before their enemies into the forest.

In vain Prince Pakayo strove to rally his shattered forces.

In vain his frenzied efforts essayed to stem the current that was overwhelming him.

With the bitterness of heart such as a condemned angel must have felt on his defeat and disgrace, he saw his hated and despised foe, King Nookevah, pursuing him to the death.

But it was no use to resist.

He must go with the stream.

His life and liberty hung on the merest thread, and even that would now be inevitably snapped by further resistance.

So he fled, wildly, desperately, to the sea-shore.

Through tangled thickets and balmy groves, down deep tropical valleys, through primitive villages, and around rocky defiles, his scattered legions fled.

His victorious foes pursued.

From every point sprung up bands and parties of Hopaws to intercept their progress and thin the ranks of the vanquished.

Many fell, but few resisted.

The rapidly decreasing numbers were too disheartened to strive for aught but escape.

But even that was surrounded by difficulties.

Their canoes were scattered around the coast, but few remained where they had left them, and even these were intercepted by bands of Hopaws.

The bay to which Prince Pakayo led his men was, however, apparently clear from foes.

But this security was not real.

As the disordered army of warriors reached the shore, and were hurrying down to the canoes, a report, as of thunder, shook the air, and a volley of shot further decimated their ranks.

Prince Pakayo looked up, and saw, half concealed among the rocks, a body of Hopaws, armed, not with their native weapons, but with the more deadly fire-tube of the white men.

They had lain in wait, and well, indeed, had they carried out their stratagem.

Without, however, stopping to heed these dangerous foes, Prince Pakayo hurried down into the canoes that were waiting for him off the beach, and essayed, together with his principal chiefs, to avail himself of this last hope of safety.

But King Nookevah, following in hot pursuit, saw his design.

He determined to frustrate it.

He was furious at the idea that his foe, thus conquered, should ultimately escape him.

"Tororo!" he cried. "He shall never escape—he must be conquered. Haste! haste! and secure his boat ere it can be put off. Hurl your lances, and discharge your slings at him! Slay him at once, rather than let him thus evade us before our very eyes!"

He had scarcely any necessity to give this order, for a hundred spears were raised even before he had spoken it, and a hundred slings sent forth their stony projectiles at the form of the vanquished prince.

But, as chance would have it, they all fell harmless, as far as the leader of the invaders was concerned, though many of his companions were stricken down by them.

Pakayo was uninjured, and succeeded in leaping into the canoe before his pursuing foes could frustrate his intention.

But the band of scouts who were ensconced among the rocks resolved to act their part, and being nearest the shore, were best able to prevent the escape.

Hastening, like lightning, in a body, down to the beach, they charged in among the disordered ranks of the fugitives, and tried to force their way onward to the chief's canoe.

But a crowd of desperate Typees, while using every effort to escape, prevented their intention, and, though themselves cut down and slaughtered remorselessly by the pursuing foe, stood faithful to their unworthy leader.

The main body of Hopaw warriors, led by King Nookeevah, had now reached the beach and joined their allies.

The fearful conflict continued between them and the remains of the invading army.

The latter suffered severely, but they fought with more deperation. But quite unavailingly.

A great many contrived to make their escape to the canoes.

Hundreds leaped, in wild desperation, into the sea, and struck out for the nearest boats.

In this way a fearful number perished.

Death—with the slenderest possible chance of escape from it—encompassed them on all sides, and the mission of the Hopaws as avengers was indeed dreadfully fulfilled.

No one was ever more thoroughly incensed or filled with bitterer disappointment than King Nookeevah, when he beheld the escape of his hated enemy.

He strove all he could to effect his capture.

But the prince had taken the fullest advantage of the universal confusion that prevailed, and, urging his canoe with almost superhuman swiftness over the calm bosom of the ocean, was already far away from the land.

With incredible baseness he had left thousands of his trusty followers to perish on the beach, without even bestowing a thought on their danger.

He was accompanied only by his principal chiefs, and such others of his followers as could manage to enter the canoes.

This craven act showed that the bravery of this fiendish savage was but the bravery of the wolf, which holds on its course remorselessly when impelled by the thirst for blood and rapine, but when brought face to face with imminent danger, flies, panic-stricken, with cowardly and selfish fear.

"Craven fiend!" cried the noble King Nookeevah, regarding the escape of his rival with the fiercest rage, "to fly thus from the danger that he has left his poor tools of followers to face. Why, even I can be more generous to my foes than this miscreant is to his friends! Therefore, my trusty men, stay now this slaughter—it is useless."

"What shall be done with all these prisoners?" asked one of the Hopaw chiefs.

"They must be taken into safe custody, but I charge you to treat them well; for it shall never be said that the Hopaws acted with barbarity towards those whom they have conquered."

"Pakayo shall not escape thus!" cried the king, with a sudden outburst of renewed anger. "Bring hither my war canoe, and I will follow and seize him."

"Great chief," replied one of the king's most trusty adherents, "it would not be wise to do so, for your presence is now requisite to restore order among your distracted people. But I, who burn for conquest over yon craven chief, will hasten after him with my followers, and will not return until I can bring him back, either dead or a prisoner, to your hands."

"Your zeal and bravery are great, my trusty Powaca," cried the king, in admiration. "Go, then, take an efficient force, and strive to overtake this miscreant before he reaches the shore of his own land. I am resolved that my victory over him shall be complete. Hark! what is that terrific sound?"

A booming, like a peal of thunder rolling across the island, greeted the ears of all, as the king spoke.

"It is a report from the guns of the Seagull," said one of the chiefs. "She is being attacked by a number of the mutineers, and the captain and his companions have not yet gone to her rescue. Her position is indeed perilous."

"I will accompany a body of men to the ship," said the king, "and my tayo, Captain Hastings, shall be liberated. Shame it were on us if we aided not our brave allies."

And the king instantly set off on this expedition, rejoicing in the victory he had obtained, and resolving that, if human efforts could effect the design, it should be followed up to the utmost, and culminate in the downfall and punishment of the treacherous mutineers.

CHAPTER XXXVII.

THE PRISONERS—TOM STARBOARD STORMS THE CITADEL OF THE MUTINEERS — PERILS ON BOARD THE SEAGULL.

WE must now go backwards a little in the date of history, to record the adventures of Tom Starboard and his brave little band, in their attempt to rescue Captain Hastings and his companions from their undeserved captivity.

We have related how, on their first attempt to effect this desirable result, Tom's party were repulsed by the strong guard that encircled the place of captivity.

But the trusty old tar was not to be daunted even by this formidable opposition.

His party had no intention of abandoning their enterprise.

They retired for a few seconds. Then reloaded, and recommenced the attack with the vigour of desperation.

A somewhat exciting scene was presented by the interior of the house in which the captain and his companions were confined.

It was like all houses in Hopaw, built of rough logs and thatched with the twisted fibres of the cocoa-nut tree.

Its size, judging by an English standard, was but small, and its form was an oblong.

It consisted chiefly of one long, low room, with a fire-place, chairs and tables, glass windows, and other European luxuries, obtained from English ships, or made by the English workmen who dwelt on the island.

Every door was closely locked.

Every window was firmly barred.

But the combined strength of the crowd inside would have been sufficient to break through these obstacles, if, unharmed as they were, they had not to cope with the powerful guard outside.

Their position was, indeed, the aggravation of hopelessness.

With a large band of trusty companions, willing and eager to fight to the death to ensure their escape, Captain Hastings was perfectly powerless to carry out any such design, for the simple reason that not only every weapon, but everything that could serve as such, had been taken away from the prisoners as they were thrust in.

To break from their captivity would, therefore, be an act of madness, as it would certainly expose them to the fire of their well-armed foes, and result in their own inevitable destruction.

Rescue could only come from without, and knowing as they did the condition of the island, they had but little hope of its arrival.

The number of prisoners in this place was scarcely less than forty, among which were Captain Hastings and his party, Dyson, and all such Hopaws and half-breeds as had been captured when fighting against the mutineers.

Our hero, Crusoe Jack, lay on some matting in one corner of the room, with many other wounded persons beside him.

His injuries, it is true, were not dangerous; he had been stunned, but had now recovered; but, like Tom, he was weakened by the loss of blood, ensuing from the blow he had received.

Nevertheless, he felt able, or at least extremely willing, to start up at the first sign of rescue, and, grasping his cutlass, take his part in the fight for liberty.

Captain Hastings paced the room in extreme agitation, and ever and anon took an observation, through the barred windows, at the battle raging fiercely at a short distance from the hut.

None of the prisoners were manacled—they had been thrust in too hastily for that—so that their movements were unimpeded; and they waited in dismal groups whatever fate should await them.

"Heavens!" cried the captain, regarding the conflict through his telescope, "the Typees are winning. The devil take them for a crew of remorseless savages! What our fate will be when they've conquered the island, I dread to think."

"I fear there is little chance either for us or King Nookeevah," remarked Lieutenant Elton, an officer of the Seagull and an especial friend of our hero, Jack.

"Nookeeva? No; and I am sorry for it; that man's the most gentlemanly savage I ever came across, and that is no slight thing to say; for we see from these Typees what the natives of the South Sea islands usually are."

"I wonder what has become of Tom Starboard?" said Jack.

"And Greenley, too," added Dyson.

"I am very anxious on both their accounts," remarked the captain; "but especially on Tom's, whom I wouldn't lose for any amount of riches you could name."

"He never ought to have gone on such a desperate mission as spy on the mutineers," observed another of the Seagull's officers.

"He never did go with my willing sanction," returned Captain Hastings; "but he would go, so would Jack; and now look at the consequence of it. Confound it! I wish we had stayed in the Seagull, and let the Csnaccas fight their own battles, for a pretty position this interference has brought us all into!"

"We have done little good, sir, certainly," remarked Jack.

"Good! No. But a great deal of harm. The worst day's work I ever did in my life was pardoning those mutineers. If ever I get hold of them they shall all be hanged on the yard-arm as the only punishment fit for such wretches. They may beg and pray, and sham repentance, as much as they please, but they shall swing, to a man!"

"I only hope that we may get the chance of punishing them as they deserve," murmured Jack, turning to his nearest companion. "But at present we ourselves seem to stand the most chance of swinging."

"Poor Mabel!" thought our hero, as he placed his hand on the bandaged wound on his head, which at times gave him great pain. "She says I am always getting into danger, and she is quite right, for, somehow or another, I am continually in hot water. It's my fate, and I'm powerless to resist it. If I ever return to England—"

And here he relapsed into a bright vision of future prosperity and peace in his native land, with Mabel, the guiding star of his life, the sharer of all the joys earned by the many perils he had undergone!

One train of thought ever suggests another, and Jack's reflections reverted to Lela, her truth and love, her burning, passionate devotion to his every

wish, and above all the mournful uncertainty of her fate.

What had become of her?

Had she died from grief, slain herself in despair, or fallen a victim to the sanguinary customs of her country?

Perhaps, indeed, she had accepted her fate with resignation, allied herself to Oroma, or better still, to Red Plume, and now ruled as queen over a wild nation.

Who could say, and what availed such surmises?

The present was sufficiently critical to absorb all consideration, and, under existing circumstances, the fate of Mabel was of far greater importance to Jack than that of his dusky Indian admirer.

"Our ship will certainly be attacked by these mutineers and savages, according to their base design," remarked the captain, "and a great prize she will prove to them if they manage to take her. But I hope Meredith will give them such a broadside of bullets and powder, and shot, as will sink their miserable shells to the bottom of the ocean."

"Our companions, however, stand a better chance than we," said Jack: "for they have the power of getting away, and they will doubtless frustrate the mutineers' plan of cutting the cable. At last the wind is favourable for an escape."

"Which they will never make while we are in this peril," said the captain; "but they can, of course defend themselves against all the powers of the invaders, who luckily have very few guns, and regard cannon like the thunder from heaven, as something dreadfully destructive that cannot be resisted."

At this instant a booming sound met their ears.

The captain, and, indeed, the whole of the party, started as they heard it, for they knew instantly what it portended.

"It is a report from the ship!" cried several simultaneously. "She is probably attacked by the mutineers."

"I hope Williams is among them," said the captain, "and all his ruffianly gang have sunk in the bay, their boats riddled by the shot of our gallant men."

"Luckily there are enough on board to take care of her," said Jack.

"And I hope they'll do so, and not let any efforts to rescue us interfere with our safety," answered the captain. "I'm afraid, as far as we're concerned, that there is little chance of escape. Mr. Meredith had better leave us to our fate, and get the ship under way as soon as possible."

"A very unselfish way of looking at it, eh, Jack?" said Lieutenant Elton to our hero, in a low tone.

But the captain considerably altered his tone a few minutes after, when, after watching the confused scene that was going on without, he suddenly exclaimed in great excitement—

"By Jove, those rascally Typees are giving way. The Hopaws will win after all. We may escape yet! for if King Nookeevah once more regains his power, we shall win the day. Then, suppose we take advantage of the confusion, make a sudden rush, and burst open the door!"

All appeared ready and willing to carry out this proposition, and only waited their leader's orders to commence it.

But the captain stood gazing through his telescope, on the momentous struggle on which their fate depended.

"If we could once break through the confounded guard, we might meet with friends," he muttered; "but, desperate as I feel, I don't like the chance of our being shot down like dogs, without any means of defence."

"Look, look! how that large body of Typees and mutineers are being cut up by those brave fellows," cried Lieutenant Elton, with joyous animation. "See, they are disappearing fast into the woods. What a number of wounded and slain! Perhaps the Hopaws may attempt to rescue us."

"Here is one party coming this way," said the captain; "natives, half-castes, and ——, by all that's glorious, if there isn't old Tom Starboard at the head of them, cutting and slashing away for dear life!"

"Tom Starboard!" echoed every voice in the room, in joyful accents, and Jack started from his couch, and fairly sprang to his feet at the sound of that welcome name.

"Yes, there he is, wounded and bandaged, but still alive, and fighting like a lion. I know he'll rescue us if he can!"

"If there were only more fellows with him, the guard would stand no chance against them," cried Jack.

"They don't as it is!" cried the captain, joyously. "See how the brave fellows are slashing away. They cut their way through the band of miscreants with the valour of Trojans. Tom sees us, for he is making a signal of recognition."

With a shout of defiance, the party of gallant warriors, led by Tom Starboard, rushed upon the opposing guard of their foes.

The skirmish threatened to be as desperate and fierce a one as ever occurred between two such small parties of combatants.

Though the mutineers outnumbered Tom's party, and were better armed, yet the desperate courage and fierce determination to conquer, which characterised the latter, greatly counterbalanced those advantages.

Tom Starboard and his followers felt all that increased strength which is imparted by the consciousness that the tide of victory flows favourably.

The Hopaws were rapidly gaining the day, and the Typees, with the same rapidity, giving way before the lion-hearted attacks of their foes.

The consciousness of victory, therefore, produced two opposite effects upon the contending parties, and those who took their respective sides in the contest.

A hand-to-hand combat, even on a small scale, is always more exciting than a fight between two large contending parties, whose evolutions are conducted with the cautiousness of military evolutions.

The brave followers of Tom, with their cutlasses and tomahawks, and the mutineers with their guns, now useless for the ordinary purpose, grasped by the barrel and used in the same manner as war-clubs, formed a scene sufficiently exciting to rivet every faculty of the heart and brain, more particularly when witnessed by those in the position of Captain Hastings' party, whose liberties depended on the issue of the contest.

The clash of cutlasses, the blows of contending war-clubs, tomahawks, and the butt-ends of muskets, mingled with the cries and execrations of the combatants, and the more distant roar of the general battle, continued for some time without either party seeming to be any nearer victory.

Many a stalwart warrior of both parties fell wounded on the grass.

Many a blow was given and received, ere Tom Starboard's little band of trusty followers had achieved the victory which they were so resolved to accomplish.

The mutineers, frequently made to give way, as frequently rallied and formed themselves again and again into an impenetrable barrier against their enemies.

They had determined that nothing short of their entire defeat should make them deliver up their prisoners.

Rather than this should happen, they would themselves kill the unarmed men whom they had so treacherously immured.

To prevent the rescuing party's entrance, the whole strength and skill and energy of the mutineer's were directed; and, when they found themselves losing ground, they drew yet closer around the place of captivity, and arranged themselves so that they could as readily attack those within as the now formidable party before them.

They had lost several more men than Tom Starboard, and their numbers were so thinned that equality in this respect had almost been obtained.

The whole of the combatants knew now that the struggle had reached its closest and most critical point, and but a few moments would decide the question of supremacy.

But in their calculation of resistance the mutineers seemed to have almost forgotten those inside, or at least underrated their power of assisting their rescuers.

They knew the prisoners were securely imprisoned; and that even if they could break through their fastenings, it would be easy to cut them down as they emerged from the openings.

But it was far less easy to do this when a powerful body of friends of the prisoners were attacking them in front.

In short, the mutineers were encompassed by a double danger.

Captain Hastings, seeing the position of affairs, was now certain of their rescue, and prepared in the best manner possible to assist Tom Starboard's heroic efforts.

The whole of the prisoners were gathered in a conjoint mass behind the larger door of the prison, around which, outside, the principal body of the mutineers were assembled.

At a signal from the captain, the final rush was made.

The whole of the captives pressed themselves against the door with all their strength and weight, and, though at first this united effort proved a failure, the fastenings outside were not strong enough to bear the strain, but at length gave way, and, with a grand crash, the door fell.

That was the supreme moment of excitement.

With a wild shout of triumph, the whole of the prisoners bounded out over the prostrate and broken door, rushed in a body among the mutineers, wrested arms from the grasp of many, and assisted the attack of their gallant friends, and with such force and bravery that, in the space of a few moments, their victory was complete.

The mutineers, dispersed and conquered by overwhelming opposition, gave way, and sought that safety which flight alone could give them.

They fled in all directions as if stricken by a sudden panic; and, as they were now completely defeated, their victorious foes sought not even to pursue their triumphs further, but turned their attention only to those whom they had so gallantly rescued.

"Tom, my dear fellow, we owe you our liberty, if not our lives," cried the captain, enthusiastically.

"How glad I am, Tom, to find you have got safely over your perils," said Crusoe Jack, as he grasped the hand of his victorious friend.

"Well, as to safety, lad, I don't know," returned the old sailor, bluntly. "I'm pretty well knocked about by the events of this blessed night; but, thank God, I'm not killed, but have been able to rescue you."

"Oh, captain, if we ain't been through plenty of danger during this last few hours, I don't know who has."

"You're right, Tom; we have had a terrible time of it, and it strikes me I have been in a great degree the cause of it through my mistaken clemency to a parcel of scoundrels who ought to have been hanged right off. But, though the Hopaws are getting the victory, our perils are not yet over."

"No, they ain't, sir. But this is no time for talking. Hark! there is another signal from the Seagull. We must all start off to the rescue of those gallant fellows we have left aboard her, for I expect the scoundrels have by this time harassed them considerably. We may do something, however, if we attack them from the shore."

"Yes, yes," cried the captain, assuming a voice of command. "Arm yourselves, my men, and quickly as possible let some of you look to the wounded, and take them into the house, where a guard of you must remain while we go on our expedition."

These orders being obeyed, the now greatly-increased body of gallant men started off upon their perilous enterprise.

CHAPTER XXXVIII.

THE ATTACK ON THE SEAGULL — A DESPERATE RESISTANCE—FEARFUL PERIL OF MABEL.

THE party who, under the command of Mr. Meredith, were left in charge of the Seagull, were of sufficient strength to protect their vessel from every description of danger which they imagined could menace her.

The vessel was well armed, and certainly there seemed little cause to fear any foes they might meet in those uncivilised regions.

As far as their knowledge went, there was not a single ship within hundreds of leagues, of sufficient strength to cope with theirs.

What did they care for canoes, be they ever so large or numerous?

What harm could accrue from the attack of foes to whom the use of fire-arms was almost unknown?

The Seagull stood alone in her proud consciousness of superiority on the broad bosom of the midnight ocean—her vast hull looming dark and grim amid the clouds that ever and anon obscured the bright moonlight.

Captain Hastings, and indeed all on board, felt the most implicit confidence in the gallant vessel which had already undergone the perils of shipwreck, and had braved the dangers of the battle and the breeze in many adventurous cruises.

When Crusoe Jack and Tom Starboard started on their desperate expedition, it was for their safety alone that Captain Hastings and Mr. Meredith felt any degree of anxiety.

They had little fear of danger on their own account.

They judged that the mutineers, be they ever so treacherous, would scarce attempt to attack the vessel, knowing how little chance they had of success in boarding her.

The fears and warnings of Tom Starboard concerning the treacherous followers of Williams, were not fully shared in by the captain.

He did not regard them as enemies to be much dreaded.

A strict watch set on the ship, the crew well armed, and prepared at any time for an encounter, were surely sufficient safe-guards, and, at the worst, the Seagull could weigh anchor on the shortest notice, and depart in the favourable breeze from the island.

Accordingly, it was not thought necessary to do more, when Tom and Crusoe were conveyed ashore, than to let the boat, with two or three men, be in readiness on the beach to convey them back in the same manner.

Whatever treachery the mutineers contemplated, it was only necessary for Tom and Jack to return with the tidings of it, and the whole of the Englishmen could get off immediately from the scene of coming danger.

Little indeed did anyone on board the Seagull anticipate the deadly peril, the disasters, the universal conflict which that eventful night was destined to bring forth.

The first intimation of danger was seeing Jack return to the beech, not with Tom, but accompanied by Greenley.

Then the unexpected appearance of the party of scouts, their attack upon Jack and his companions, and the fatal struggle that ensued on the shore.

Long before those on the Seagull could put out a boat to hasten to the rescue of their comrades, the latter had been slain and wounded by their treacherous enemies, Jack himself was stricken down, and as to Tom Starboard, who knew what catastrophe might not have befallen him?

The captain went ashore too late, as we have described, to rescue our hero, and just in time to be summoned, as he thought, to the palace of King Nookeevah, but in reality to be treacherously captured.

From that time the danger was perceived, though its extent was not even suspected, but the party on board the Seagull were all filled with the deepest anxiety.

"How I wish Jack and Tom Starboard had never started on this ill-advised expedition," remarked Mr. Meredith, who was restlessly pacing the deck with Mabel. "We have lost some of our poor fellows already by it, and I'm afraid Jack, too, is slain."

"Oh! don't say that, dear father!" cried Mabel, in inexpressible anguish. "Anything but that!"

"My dear," said her father, in a tone which combined tenderness with some degree of reproof, "I was merely expressing a surmise, which I fervently hope will not be realised. But at the same time remember that in the eyes of that great Providence that watches over us all, lives are of equal value, and that of Crusoe Jack, impelled by his own rashness, is no more to be lamented than the lives of the poor fellows who fell victims to his imprudence."

"And can you talk like this?" said Mabel, bursting into tears, such as showed how those words cut her to the heart. "You who loved him so much. Oh, father, remember that *my* life is bound up in his, and, if he falls, then I must soon follow him."

"My dear child," said her father, more tenderly; "you distress yourself without a cause. At least, so far as I am concerned, I meant not to speak harshly, nor did I do so; I only deplored the rashness of Crusoe Jack and old Tom Starboard, which has at least caused the loss of several valuable lives. It was, however, merely through an excess of zeal and bravery; and, both for your sake and his own, I fervently hope that Jack has escaped death. But, at least, his position is very perilous."

"It is—it is," cried Mabel, "so perilous that I cannot rest this night through anxiety on his account. Oh! how I hope that he and his brave companions will escape the perils that surround them."

"No one can hope that, my dear Mabel, more fervently than myself. But you, at least, need take no part in these perils which you dread so much. Retire, my dear child, to your cabin, and, ere you wake to-morrow morning, the whole of the dangers that surround us may be overcome."

"I cannot," returned Mabel, firmly; "I have said just now that I cannot rest, nor can I until Jack and his companions return safely from their expedition. The blood that has been already shed fills me with horror, and who knows how much may flow ere to-morrow. No, I will stay here with you, and, if there be danger and death, let me at least share them!"

Seeing that his daughter was determined on this point, Meredith offered no opposition, but continued watching the shore with his telescope, in order to perceive any signs that might inform him of the position of affairs.

The captain had departed with the treacherous chief.

The mutineers had evidently dispersed from their meeting in the valley, for the light no longer gleamed across the wide waves.

In short, all was for the moment peaceful, but it was but the deceptive calm before the raging and deadly storm.

Scarcely for a moment did Mr. Meredith relax his personal vigilance.

Though he had been much fatigued during the day, he continued to keep watch.

Neither his inclination nor the anxiety that filled his mind would have allowed him to sleep.

Nevertheless, on seeing no present indication of danger, he returned to the cabin with Mabel, and endeavoured, as he could not rest, to sustain nature with the stimulus of a glass of wine, and to prevail on his daughter to do the same.

They were sitting thus together in the chief cabin of the ship, when suddenly a considerable emotion was heard on deck.

It was a combined cry of surprise from several of the crew, evidently purporting that something unexpected had occurred.

At the same time a slight vibration quivered through the vessel.

Mabel turned pale and clung to her father; but Mr. Meredith, starting up, seized his cutlass and pistols, and, with a hurried word of encouragement, rushed up the cabin steps.

"What's the matter here?" he cried, anxiously.

A dozen voices immediately answered—

"Please, sir, the cable's cut; and the ship's afloat."

Mr. Meredith's heart sank, but it was only for a moment.

"The cable cut!" he cried. "Great heaven! is it possible? Who can have done it?"

"A party of those rascally mutineers, sir, must have put out under cover of the darkness," replied the boatswain. "They evidently mean to send us ashore."

"And you've not heard nor seen any indication of them?"

"No, sir. Depend upon it that's what the devils have been at during this last quarter of an hour, when all seemed so quiet. The next thing they'll do will be to attack the vessel."

"They shall meet with a warm reception," cried Mr. Meredith, excitedly, as he hurriedly peered through his telescope at the shore; but, in consequence of the dense clouds that just then obscured the face of the moon, could distinguish nothing.

"Yes, they've certainly cut our cables, the scoundrels," cried Mr. Meredith. "They are lying quite slack. Now, my men, we must bestir ourselves; and get to hauling at once, and we'll see what can be done."

The order was obeyed as soon as given, but, as everybody expected, it only confirmed the reality of the danger thus menaced.

The first pull brought the ends of the cables on board.

The ship was clean cut away from her anchor, and had commenced drifting, though at a slow rate, on to the coral-bedded shore.

Mo. cover, the vessel was in less than eight fathoms of water.

The peril that these facts portended was indeed grave.

The destruction of the ship and the doom of her gallant crew was imminent.

"Out with another anchor, or she'll go to pieces!" cried Mr. Meredith. "The breeze is beginning to freshen, and unless she can be stopped, we shall not keep clear ten minutes longer!"

Another anchor was immediately got out, and thirty fathoms of cable having been attached to it, the longboat was lowered, and the anchor carried out.

The ship was with great difficulty hauled seven fathoms out from the reef, and the anchor was safely in eighteen fathoms of water.

It was while this was being done, that the moment of peril arrived, and a sudden daring attack on the Seagull was made.

A number of boats, filled with armed men, both English and Canacces, suddenly appeared under the stern of the vessel.

It was too dark to distinguish otherwise than imperfectly their movements, or recognise the countenances of those who guided them, but the crew of the Seagull knew too well what it portended.

The party in the longboat were evidently the first point of attack.

Starting up suddenly in their path a canoe filled with Typees and mutineers barred the progress of the boat, which had just returned from fixing the anchor.

To cut off communication with the ship, or at all events, hold that power of communication in their own hands, was evidently the object of the attacking party, and for this purpose they bore down on the crew of the longboat.

Guiding his canoe so closely up against the longboat that they struck, and a fearful shock was communicated to each, a warrior of gigantic aspect sprung up, tomahawk in hand, and followed by his men, tried to force his way into the boat.

But the gallant tars of the Seagull were prepared.

They grasped their cutlasses, collected their energy, and commenced returning the attack with as much spirit as it was made.

They found, however, that their position was an extremely desperate one, for they had to contend with a body of men greatly outnumbering their own, and composed, moreover, not entirely of unskilful savages, but of desperate characters, armed with European weapons, and well accustomed to use them in sea skirmishes.

"White-faced dogs!" cried the Typee chief, as he forced his way into the boat, "give way before the mighty invaders of the Typee, who will soon be masters of this island, and all your war canoes, and ill-gotten wealth."

"And don't think we've turned into land-lubbers because we've been so long ashore," cried one of the mutineers. "We can fight, by G——! and if you don't give way, we will show you pretty plain!"

"Scoundrels!" cried the leader of the life-boat's crew, "we're ready for all you can do!" and presenting a pistol, with skilful aim he shot the savage through the heart.

The fight was a desperate one.

The object of the Seagull's party was to force their way back to their ship, that of the mutineers to prevent them, and gain possession of the longboat.

In this the latter stood every chance of succeeding; for, besides the attacking party in the boat, the water seemed suddenly alive with canoes of armed men, all making their way towards the Seagull, and endeavouring to compass her round.

It would take all the bravery and skill of the Seagull's crew, to prevent them boarding her.

Mr. Meredith, standing on the quarter-deck of the vessel, had watched through his night-glass the efforts of the crew in the longboat.

When they had successfully grounded the anchor, his heart began to beat more freely, for he thought that the greater part of their peril was over.

But the next eventful moment the whole of these hopes were dashed to the ground.

Never did so great a change, so momentous and universal an indication of approaching peril, present itself in the space of a few seconds.

A fearful shout—the war-cry of thousands of fierce invaders—suddenly broke the stillness, and resounding from the opposite side of the island, was echoed from peak to peak along the shore.

The sound alone was enough to appal every heart, however brave.

For what did it denote?

The advent of an army of fierce, relentless, and bloodthirsty foes, bent on the destruction of the gallant Hopaws.

Those on the Seagull knew not this yet, but they surmised it when the roar of battle rose in their ears, and their anxiety respecting Captain Hastings, Crusoe Jack, and Tom Starboard increased greatly.

Then, at the same moment, the moon, bursting from her cloudy prison, shone over the surface of the ocean, and showed Mr. Meredith his own gallant crew engaged in a fierce hand-to-hand unequal contest with a large body of enemies.

Morever, these enemies were formidable in numbers and appearances, and were encompassing the vessel on all sides.

"To your guns, my men, instantly!" cried Mr. Meredith. "We are surrounded, and must make resistance. Put out a boat to the rescue of those gallant fellows whom these scoundrels are attacking."

But before these orders could be obeyed, a strong party of the mutineers, unobserved, began climbing the chains.

In a few moments the miscreant Williams—armed to the teeth and followed by a number of his fellow-ruffians—leaped on the deck of the ship, and commenced a bold attack on the crew.

The confusion gave them the advantage.

But the crew of brave and faithful Englishmen soon recovered from the surprise of the sudden attack.

They made a desperate resistance.

Every man was speedily armed.

Mr. Meredith, at the head of his crew, found himself again in the same position as when the pirates had boarded the Seagull.

He trusted that the result would be the same—victory on his side—but of this there seemed at present but the most uncertain chance.

"Surrender at once," cried Williams, presenting his revolver at the head of the captain. "There's not a shadow of a chance for you. The ship's surrounded, many of the crew absent, and as for the captain—"

"Villain! what have you done with the captain?" cried Mr. Meredith.

"He's a safe prisoner ashore, if you must know," returned the desperado; "and, curse me! if either he or anybody takes the side of these cowardly Hopaws shall escape this night. Now, then, do you intend to surrender the ship, or not?"

"Surrender?—never!" replied Mr. Meredith, fiercely and determinedly; "not for you, nor twice your number."

"Then die!" thundered the leader of the mutineers, firing his revolver at his intended victim with an accuracy which would inevitably have been fatal, but that a blow from one of the crew jerked the weapon on one side and diverted its aim.

The mutineers, having once effected an entrance, poured into the devoted vessel in numbers that overpowered the gallant efforts of their foes to repel them.

Their attack had been so sudden, their determination was so great, that to dislodge them from their position was a matter of no small difficulty.

In vain their number was thinned by the loss of many a ruffian, who fell back wounded into the sea.

Their determination was too great to be overcome by anything short of total annihilation.

They fought with the ferocity of tigers.

Williams urged his men on by recounting the plunder that was to be obtained by the victory, and, above all, the future joys of their pirate life.

"Now, for the cabin!" roared the miscreant, as he flourished his weapon around him, and forced his way through the dense mass of his opponents. "To the cabin! Quick! Arms, and gold, and everything of value will be found there, and we will make them our own. "Besides," he added, still more vauntingly, "the captain has a beautiful daughter, and she must be mine!"

No words could have spoken so calculated to arouse the fury of Mr. Meredith.

He sprang at the ruffian, planted himself in his path, and opposed all the strength of his stalwart frame against his further progress.

"Back, scoundrel!" he cried, fiercely. "One step more towards the cabin, and you shall be shot like a dog!"

"Will you try and prevent me?—then take that!" and, quick as lightning, the mutineer chief aimed such a fearful blow at the head of Mabel's father as, taking effect, sufficed to stretch him senseless on the deck.

The leader of the Seagull's crew was, if not slain, thus rendered powerless, and the mutineers felt certain of victory.

This certainty seemed to inspire them with almost superhuman power.

With a triumphant shout at his last feat, Williams again urged his men on.

While they collected the whole of their strength in their renewed and desperate attack, their opponents, struck with consternation at the loss of their captain, showed signs of confusion and disorganization.

"Hurrah!" cried Williams, "there's our chief obstacle gone, and now I'm captain of this ship, and I'll blow out the brains of the first man who disputes my title!"

"I will dispute it, scoundrel!" cried the first lieutenant. "I will take the place of Mr. Meredith."

"And share his fate!" said Williams, aiming his revolver at the head of the last speaker.

Unluckily, it took effect—not fatally, but so as to render the gallant young officer as powerless as his superior in command.

Amid the confusion that now prevailed among his opponents—amid the yells of rage—the clash and fire of weapons—the groans of the wounded, and the irregular, though heroically-desperate resistance of the Seagull's crew, Williams succeeded, inch by inch, in gaining ground, and at length forced his way to the cabin, burst open the main hatch, and sprung down the steps with a wild yell of triumph, followed by his lawless followers.

"And what," the reader may ask, "has become of Mabel all this time?"

She had remained in the cabin, from which, indeed, there was no escape.

Her position was, indeed, indescribably painful and perilous.

As soon as the action commenced, and the mutineers had boarded the ship, she saw that her only chance of safety lay in keeping below, according to her father's wishes.

Accordingly, barricading the door of the cabin as strongly as she could, she cowered down in a corner, fearfully agitated, no less with the anxiety for the fate of those she held dear, than for fear on her own account.

That there was a terrific conflict going on above she knew only too well.

That it was the mutineers she surmised.

But she could not venture to ascertain these facts; and she consequently felt all the tortures of suspension and doubt.

Every shout of the rough, brutal besiegers, every man that fell wounded, every volley of fire-arms, filled her with dread.

For how knew she not that her dear father had not fallen a victim to the power of his foes?

She had many times almost been tempted to rush upstairs at any cost, and end her doubts, even with her life.

With this view she had seized some arms from the pile always kept standing in the captain's cabin.

But could her frail hands wield such deadly instruments with success?

She knew not.

But it was at least a wise precaution to arm herself with them.

And this she did.

She afterwards had cause to be glad that she had taken this precaution.

When her father fell, she was ignorant of the distressing fact; but she knew how probable it was that, being foremost in the fray, he should fall an early victim to its rage.

Not till the struggle took place near the cabin did she imagine the full extent of her danger.

When she heard the mutineers bursting open the hatch, her heart sank, so that it was with difficulty she could keep from fainting.

Nerving herself, however, by a powerful effort, she grasped a loaded revolver in each hand, and placed a cutlass within her reach.

She then stood up, prepared for the worst.

It was with a prayer to heaven for strength—breathed inwardly, yet how fervently!—that this fair, gentle girl, whose loving nature had been so often tried by a constant succession of frightful and appalling dangers, then prepared to act such a part of heroism as even many a strong man fails to accomplish successfully.

Every moment increased the danger, lengthened the agony of suspense.

She heard the powerful efforts of the ruffian crew to burst the hatch.

She heard it crack.

She saw it finally give way, and a number of men, ruffianly in aspect, and flushed with the excitement of bloodshed, enter the cabin with a wild and appalling yell.

Mabel shrank back at their approach.

But her heart, nerved by desperation into a strength and courage that overpowered its natural terror, sustained her in that trying moment.

"Hurrah!" burst in a chorus from the savage crew. "Three cheers for the captain's daughter, the prettiest prize we've taken for a long time!"

Williams approached Mabel.

She recognized him with an abhorrence and dread that she could not conceal.

"Ah! my dear young lady," he cried, with a sardonic mock politeness, more abhorrent than any degree of fierceness. "My dearest Mabel (you see I know your name), behold in me the new captain of the ship. Say, will you be a pirate's bride?"

"Back!" she cried, presenting the revolver direct in his face, while her beautiful eyes flashed with indignation and desperate courage. "Back, ruffian, or I fire!"

Williams was evidently rather taken aback by this unexpected exhibition of courage.

"Stay!" he cried; "put down your weapon. Who wants to harm you, do you think? I merely wished to ask you to become a pirate's bride and the Queen of the Ocean. Put down the weapon, I say."

But still Mabel stood defiantly, with the deadly weapon in her scarcely-quivering hand.

"Come, come," said the ruffian, "put down that murderous pistol, and show a little complaisance. You'll find it not only useless, but dangerous to resist me. Why not accept me as your protector, now that your father is dead, and "——

A wild shriek, an involuntary look of inexpressible horror and grief proceeded from Mabel, as these fearful words reached her ears.

Her strength seemed gone.

She dropped her extended arm and the weapon she held.

"Dead!—my father dead?" she cried.

"Yes. And if he is, my pretty sea-queen, it served him right. Why did he resist me then? He tried all he knew to kill me, and got peppered himself instead—that's the only difference."

"Monster!" cried Mabel, gathering fresh strength from desperation, and again presenting her weapon. "Back! I say, once more! Come not nearer, or, by the Providence above us, it will be at the risk of your death or my own. You have already done evil enough to—to "——

A burst of tears—tears of bitter sorrow and despair at her father's death—choked Mabel's utterance.

The patience of the ruffian seemed exhausted by this.

His mock civility changed to his naturally fierce and brutal tone.

"Curse this whimpering!" he cried. "I'll bring you to your senses presently. Now, my men, let's set to and take possession of everything of value here. Come, overhaul, overhaul—quick!"

The men hastened eagerly to obey this welcome order.

Suddenly the thunder of a cannon-report was heard above, and the ship trembled with the shock.

"Halloa!" cried Williams. "What's that? Go on deck, some of you, and see how matters stand. Perhaps they are making more resistance."

CHAPTER XXXIX.

THE BOARDING OF THE SEAGULL—DESPERATE STRUGGLE, AND FATE OF THE MUTINEERS.

RUSHING with great haste to the deck, the chief of the mutineers found that he was not likely to retain peaceful possession of the ship.

Some distance off he perceived several boats making for the Seagull with all speed possible.

The space the vessel lay from the land was about half-a-mile, and the boats were not yet half-way, so he could without difficulty recognise Captain Hastings, Jack, and Tom Starboard, and all the crew ashore.

Suspecting that their friends were being rapidly overpowered, they were urging their way with all their strength.

It was at them the gun, which had alarmed Williams, had been discharged by some of the mutineers who had not been entirely absorbed in the pleasant task of plundering the Seagull.

Cursing the men for not calling him before, the mutineer began to consider his means of defence.

The vessel contained six 8-pounders.

These were at once loaded and run out—three on each side.

A small swivel gun, carrying a 3-pounder ball, was loaded on the forecastle, ready to be slewed round in any direction required.

The Canaccas, armed with tomahawks and spears, were placed to repel any attempt by boarding, the mutineers working the great guns and small arms.

The boats were by this time nearly alongside, and Captain Hastings saw with grief that the Seagull was in possession of the mutineers and Typee braves.

Ordering his men to lay on their oars for a few moments, he deliberated on the best course to be pursued.

He knew he would be helped by King Nookeevah and his warriors, but it was necessary for himself and crew to board the vessel first, as the Indians, although they would be of the greatest service in creating a diversion in his favour, were not to be trusted to board a ship in the face of the guns of which they had the greatest dread.

Casting a glance around, he was glad to see upwards of thirty canoes, well-filled with Indians, putting off from the shore.

His mind was made up, and, addressing his men, said—

"Now, my lads, you see our position; either we take the ship, which you yourselves know will be a tough job, or we must be content to live on the island, as followers of the native king, and have the prospect of passing the rest of our lives in this out-of-the way part of the world. What say you, my men—shall we attempt it? We shall have the help of the warriors in yonder canoes."

The men, one and all, agreed to stand by him, and gave a ringing cheer.

"Give way, lads," said Captain Hastings, and, with a few strokes of the oar, they dashed alongside.

The mutineers had not yet fired upon them.

They hoped that Captain Hastings would be intimidated at the sight of the reception that awaited him, and they did not wish to commence hostilities till it was impossible to avoid it.

Seeing, however, that the attack was determined on, they fired their starboard guns at the boats just as they came alongside, and with fearful effect, for one of the boats was sunk, and nearly all in her killed or wounded.

The few that remained, clinging to the wreck, were picked up by Captain Hastings's boat; but this incident filled him with grief for the loss of so many of his brave but limited band.

Crusoe Jack was the first to spring on to the deck of the Seagull.

Parrying with his cutlass the blows that were showered upon him, he was closely followed by Tom Starboard and Captain Hastings and his men, who all fought with desperation.

Nor were the mutineers slow to follow their example.

Williams, backed by all his stout forecastle men, fought like a hero; and had he been engaged in a good cause, it would have been impossible not to have admired his bravery.

He seemed to bear a charmed life.

Wherever the strife was thickest, there was to be seen the flashing of his cutlass, which dripped with blood.

In fact, he presented a terrible spectacle.

With his shirt sleeves rolled up, displaying his browned and brawny arms, the knotted veins of which were like ropes—with his eyes flashing fire, and curses falling thick from his lips—he never needed to repeat a blow.

Before his sinewy arm the strongest enemy seemed to fall like corn from a sickle.

As the fight had now become so desperate, the whole of the mutineers had rushed up from the cabin, leaving the main hatch open, and Mabel, almost distracted, followed them.

Judge her consternation at beholding the scene that presented itself; and, above all, on perceiving her father stretched upon the deck, to all appearance dead.

She flung herself down beside him in an agony of grief.

Crusoe Jack had been engaged with a light, active mutineer, who seemed like a cat, so difficult was it to take his life.

At length he rid himself of his foe; and seeing that the terrible pirate chief was driving everything before him, determined that he should fall, or he would himself lose his life.

Accordingly he rushed into the thickest of the fight, and, clearing the way with his cutlass, confronted the pirate.

"Turn, ungrateful villain," said the brave boy, and meet the fate which you have deserved a hundred times!"

"Well crowed, my young David!" cried the pirate chief, as with one sweep of his cutlass he felled a couple of men who barred his path. "Brave words for such a stripling. Take that for your trouble."

He aimed a blow which, had it reached its mark, assuredly our hero's career would have come to a summary end.

But Crusoe Jack was too quick of eye to be so easily disposed of.

Springing lightly aside, the mutineer's cutlass but swept the air, and, descending, struck against a belaying-pin on the mainmast, and was shivered to atoms.

Jack, seeing his chance, was on the point of rushing on his foe and passing his sword through him, when, to his vexation, the tide of the combat, which had hitherto raged more fiercely on the other side of the vessel, now swept his way, and in the hurry and scuffling he was separated from the chief, who, having lost his sword, he could discern wielding a huge capstan-bar as if it had been a straw.

His tall body towered among the throng, and his weapon rose and fell like a thresher's flail.

The Typee braves had hitherto held aloof.

Such close and terrific fighting was not to their taste.

They contented themselves with throwing an occasional spear or two, as opportunities offered.

Seeing now that the battle was going in favour of their allies, they descended from the poop, where they had mustered, and mixed in the melee.

The fray now baffled all description.

The ringing cheers of the brave, but now sadly-diminished English sailors, the oaths and curses of

THE SAVAGE WAITS FOR CRUSOE JACK.

the mutineers, and the thrilling war-cry of the Typee braves, together with the shivering of swords, the occasional report of pistols, and the dull thud of the deadly tomahawk, followed by a groan of anguish from the sufferer, made up a scene which resembled a pandemonium upon earth.

And now, the wind having died away, the combatants were enveloped in a sulphurous canopy of smoke, which rendered it difficult to distinguish friend from foe.

Captain Hastings, who, with Jack and Tom, and the remnant of his men, were now clustered together near the mainmast, perceived, with great regret, how few of his followers remained.

The mutineers had also lost a great many of their men.

But this was counterbalanced by the help of their Indian allies.

"What was keeping Nookeevah and his men?" thought the captain. "Could it be that the king had broken faith with him, and left him to his fate?"

But no. He wronged the brave and noble warrior—he would be true; and this belief was soon verified, for, with a loud Hopaw war-cry, hundreds of dusky warriors leaped suddenly upon the deck of the Seagull, and speedily changed the aspect of affairs.

Encouraged by this help, Captain Hastings and his men threw themselves with renewed ardour upon their foes.

"Revenge our comrades?" cried Starboard, who, followed by Jack, rushed into the thickest of the combat; and well did his brave mates respond to his call.

The Typee natives, unable to withstand the fierce onset of the Hopaws, and seeing that the hope of capturing the vessel was vain, leaped into the sea.

To men like them, swimmers from their earliest infancy, the distance to the shore was but a trifle, and they preferred taking their chance on shore to remaining to meet certain death from the revengeful Hopaws.

Williams and his men, though greatly disheartened by this defection, fought with the courage and desperation of men who knew they had no mercy to expect from their foes if taken alive.

But they were gradually driven step by step to the fore part of the ship, where they made a final rally.

"Dog of a mutineer!" said Hastings to Williams, " at last we have you; and in half an hour, you and your miscreants of followers shall swing from the main yard-arm. In vain you may plead for mercy. Vengeance for your manifold crimes and, above all, your atrocious treachery, has at length overtaken you."

"Ha! ha!" laughed the pirate, scornfully. "Talk of that when you have me in your power. But a short hour ago, and, but for the help of your infernal black thieves, every one of you should have had a long and silent swim to the sharks. But, like all cowards, you can threaten when out of danger. As for me, I scorn you and your threats, and reply to them thus"——

So saying, and calling on his men to back him, he made a tremendous onset on to the English allies; and with such desperation did the pirates fight that for a short time it seemed as if they would have cut their way through all opposition.

But Captain Hastings and his brave comrades closed round them, and the majority of the mutineers were cut to pieces, the Hopaws bravely seconding their friends.

Williams, however, managed by his great strength to break through them, and determined to rush over the bulwarks and endeavour to escape to shore in one of the canoes which was made fast to the ship's side.

This resolve he was putting into execution.

He was springing over the side when he saw Mabel, who was bending over what she supposed to be the dead body of her father.

Here was a grand opportunity of revenge, could he but carry her off and escape with her into the forest.

With a ferocious laugh, it was but the work of a moment for him to snatch her up in his strong arm and spring lightly with her into one of the canoes; then, seizing the paddles, he plied them rapidly, chuckling at his escape, and congratulating himself on the fact of getting off unperceived.

But in this, as we shall see, he was mistaken.

Crusoe Jack, who was determined not to let Williams escape, had marked his desperate attempt to cut through them, and had, as quickly as he could, extricated himself the melée—in which he had received but a few slight wounds—followed him with the intention of frustrating his project.

Great was Jack's consternation, therefore, at seeing him escaping with Mabel, and he determined to rescue her from the miscreant or perish in the attempt.

He was too late to seize the mutineer as he leaped into the canoe.

So, drawing a pistol from his belt, he waited for a favourable opportunity to shoot without injuring Mabel.

For a time he was unable to effect this, and called loudly to some of the Hopaws to go in pursuit of the fugitive.

But Williams hearing this, drew his knife from his belt, and threatened to stab Mabel if he despatched any one to rescue her.

Jack, in an agony of grief, countermanded the order, and for a moment was irresolute what to do, when chance in a moment altered the current of events and gave him the opportunity of revenge he longed for.

Williams had hitherto held Mabel before him as a shield, knowing that his foes would not fire upon him while there was the slightest chance of her being hit.

Inadvertently, but as he could not use the paddles and hold her too, he was compelled to relax a little his grasp of her.

The brave girl instantly made an effort to free herself from his clutches, and fortunately with success.

Finding herself free, she rushed to the opposite end of the canoe, determined, if no other mode of escape presented itself, to leap overboard.

But she was spared this alternative, for Jack was enabled to fire at Williams, which he did, taking a most careful aim.

Scarcely had the report of the pistol died away, when Williams stood upright for a moment, stretched one arm out towards Jack in a threatening manner, and then fell headlong into the water, shot through the brain.

Such was the terrible end of this fierce and desperate mutineer.

It is needless to say that not a moment was lost in getting Mabel on board the ship, and she was soon clasped to the loving breast of our hero—no one can describe with what gratitude and what deep, fervent thankfulness to her brave preserver.

The fearful death of Williams was practically the end of the conflict.

On seeing their leader fall, and themselves entirely surrounded by their foes, those of the mutineers who were still resisting gave up all opposition, and surrendered themselves to the victorious party of Captain Hastings, thus once more put into possession of their own vessel.

Comparative order was soon restored.

The attack on the ship, like the invasion, was now quelled.

The mutineers and their native allies were below, heavily ironed, and all attention was then turned to the wounded.

Mr. Meredith was found to be severely injured, but not killed, as Mabel had supposed, and this circumstance filled her with fervent thankfulness, and at once removed a heavy weight from her mind.

Many had been slain, but he still lived; nor had Jack nor Captain Hastings fallen victims to the fury of the fray.

All dangers for a time were over.

Great were the mutual congratulations and expressions of gratitude that passed between Captain Hastings and the brave King of the Hopaws.

The latter spoke proudly of his victory over the Typees, which, he said, had now been thoroughly accomplished; and, next to his gratitude on this head, was his joy at being able to render so great a service to his tayo, Captain Hastings.

Mr. Meredith was conveyed on shore, and both he and Mabel were accommodated with apartments in the palace of the king, and every attention was bestowed upon the sufferer by the king's special physician.

The wounded on both sides amounted to a great number; and both the captain and King Nookeevah showed great humanity in the way in which, without distinction, they caused them to be taken every care of.

The Queen Waheene and the wives of the chiefs also exhibited such fondness and consideration as few barbarous nations are supposed to possess; and their care of the wounded, added to their skill in the healing art, were productive of the best results.

As to the mutineers, and the Typees, and treacherous Hopaws who had assisted them—that is, such as remained after the fearful carnage that had so thinned their ranks—they were tried with great fairness and impartiality by a court-martial, composed of native chiefs and the officers of the Seagull.

Some were sentenced to death, and shot forthwith; others to terms of imprisonment, according to their degrees of guilt.

At least, the king and Captain Hastings had now once more regained their respective authority.

CHAPTER XL.

THE REVENGE OF THE HOPAWS—THE SECOND INVASION.

SUCH were the great changes that a few short hours had wrought upon the state of the island.

First, tranquillity, without any suspicion of the dangers that were so imminent, and which threatened to overwhelm the entire nation; then, the sudden convulsion, the fierce and momentous struggle, and lastly, victory, all the more glorious from the fearful contention that had preceded it.

Both Captain Hastings and the king of the Hopaws had the greatest cause to be thankful to the kind Providence who had thus secured them victory against what had seemed overwhelming odds.

And now they were all assembled together among the ruins of the by-gone struggle, the corpses of the slain, the dismantled habitations, the wrecked canoes, and the wounded and captive warriors of the great army of the conspiracy and invasion.

The victory had been complete, decided, overwhelming, but much yet remained to be done before its effects could be entirely remedied.

The Seagull had been so injured by the past struggles that some repairs were already necessary. This alone necessitated the ship's remaining for some days longer at the island.

Then there was the care of the wounded, whose recovery was necessary for the full-manning of the ships, and the more mournful ceremony of the disposal of the dead.

All these matters, were of course, at once attended to, and on the same day as that of the great double victory, the king, in honour of it, gave a grand festival, in which a general festivity and rejoicing prevailed throughout the island.

But these peaceful scenes were not destined entirely to supersede the red horrors of war.

Another and final struggle was imminent.

The chief, who had been sent by King Nookeevah in pursuit of the Typee chief, Pakayo, had returned with the intelligence that he had failed to overtake him until he had reached his own land, and then he found it impracticable, with his small body of followers, to attempt an invasion of the Typees' territory.

The latter were, however, so completely crushed by their defeat—so great was the disorder prevailing throughout their island that it would be an easy matter for the legions of King Nookeevah, especially if assisted by the Seagull, to effect the entire subjugation of the island.

The king, therefore, determined to lose no time for putting this grand project into execution.

"It is now my turn!" he said, in a voice of stern resolution, "and I will carry out my vengeance to the uttermost. It is but just retribution, and will conduce to the ultimate peace and security of these islands. Two days shall find me monarch of both nations!"

"Pakayo may show a desperate resistance," said Powaca, the brave chief who had pursued the retreating enemy.

"He will, doubtless; but let him shed every drop of his blood in defence of his kingdom, it must and shall be mine. Something whispers to me that I am to become conqueror; that the fate of two nations, so lately trembling in the balance, shall be decided by my efforts. My white brother," he said, turning to Captain Hastings, "will surely not now refuse to give me his powerful aid?"

"After the great services you have done me," returned the captain, "I will not shrink from danger to aid you, but my ship must be put in good fighting condition again ere I venture on such an enterprise. The Seagull shall accompany your fleet of negroes, and under cover of her guns, your brave troops may easily land and invade the fierce enemy."

"That will secure our victory!" cried the king, joyfully. "My tayo, I thank thee. Rest assured that the spoils of the conquest shall be shared with you and your brave crew. The fertile lands of the vile Typees once ours, no greater pleasure shall I ever experience, than paying the debt of gratitude by giving you part of them as your rightful dominion."

"I do not want that," replied the brave captain, smiling at the king's eagerness. "Neither I nor any of my crew have any desire to remain longer upon these islands, far less to obtain dominions upon them. We cannot as peaceful traders, and it is chance that has made us share the perils and disasters of a vast national conflict. Now we are desirous of departing, and will say farewell when we have assisted you in your brave, and, we hope, effectual attempt to repay these invaders."

"In a few days," said the king, "if all can be got ready, we will start on our grand expedition. My whole soul is bent on conquest, and that I will accomplish, with the aid of the great Etooa, whose providence has already assisted me."

The next few days were spent in preparations for this great enterprise.

Canoes were constructed, weapons made, and the crew of the Seagull were set to repairing the injuries of their vessel.

Many of the wounded had by that time sufficiently recovered to take part in the expedition.

Mr. Meredith was recovering but slowly, and Mabel had great hopes of his life.

Dyson, Greenley, and those of the English islanders who had not taken part with the mutineers, joined the Seagull's crew, whose vessel, in capital trim, weighed anchor on the day appointed, and sailed forth, surrounded by the canoes of King Nookeevah, carrying the formidable army of invasion he had collected together.

It was a glorious day even for the tropics, where nature luxuriates in an almost eternal summer, when the fleet started forth on its expedition.

Beautiful, indeed, was the spectacle presented by the gallant array of canoes filled with the bravest warriors of the Hopaw nation, all well armed and burning for revenge and conquest.

Thousands thronged the beach, the rocks, and every point from which a good view of the departing expedition could be obtained, eagerly and proudly gazing upon a sight which epitomised the whole glory of the nation.

There was not a man, woman, or child among these brave people who doubted for a moment that their king would lead on his gallant legion to certain revenge and victory.

Proudly towering above all the other craft that thronged the bay came the stately form of the Seagull, with all sails set, and every rope, and spar, and beam shining and sparkling in the golden effulgence of the morning sun.

Who could gaze upon this proud array of fighting power without regarding victory and triumph as certain?

Could the barbarous and disorganised Typees stand against the death-dealing guns of the gallant English vessel there, combined with the whole strength of the Hopaw nation?

Assuredly not.

The right would prevail.

It was in this conviction that the spectators of the noble scene rent the air with loud and continual acclamation.

There was a calm, four-knot breeze that sufficed to carry along the Seagull in a smooth, gliding, unbroken course—calm as some giant conscious of his innate strength; and the canoes, guided by the experienced hands of the king and warrior, kept up well with the vessels through the voyage.

The party on the Seagull could not look without considerable satisfaction on the formidable expedition and their own proud position in it.

Captain Hastings agreed with his allies in their sanguine expectation of victory.

The Typees, formidable as they had proved themselves, were now far less to be feared.

Their strength was broken, and little indeed were they fitted to cope with any brave crew of Englishmen prepared to vindicate Britannia's dominion over the waves.

"Once more for action, Mabel," said Jack, as they sat together on the taffrail, gazing out into the sea, and enjoying the double pleasure of beholding the warlike spectacle, and listening to each other's conversation. "Once again have we surmounted dangers that seem overwhelming, and at last obtained our reward by victory and glory."

"No glory or advantage, dear Jack," returned Mabel, "can compensate for the fearful perils we have all undergone. For my part it seems now almost incredible that I did not die of terror on seeing that scene of carnage on the deck; my dear father apparently dead, and every chance of my becoming a perpetual prisoner of one whom I could not regard without the deepest possible abhorrence."

"Thank Heaven we were in time to save you!" said Jack, "and deal out such punishment among the miscreants as they deserved. As for Williams he has met a just doom. He was a villain of the most atrocious description, and no fate he could have met could have exceeded his deserts. Falling as he did saved him from a more disgraceful fate. But it is idle to talk of that now; retribution has overtaken him."

"It is fearful to think of him!" said Mabel, shuddering and turning pale at the mere thought of the the dangers and indignities she had undergone. "Let us talk of something else. I am tired of all these dreadful perils and continual threats to our life and liberty, and long for quiet and safety. I never could understand what charm men can find in continual peril and excitement."

"The charm of glory, Mabel, and of overcoming the wrong, by the sheer strength of the right," returned Jack. "To me a life of danger and excitement is as my very breath. I could not endure to live without it. I could never settle down to a peaceful, humdrum life, even if I had all the riches man could desire. Give me adventure, excitement—something to fight for, and the consciousness of strength and right on my side. Then only am I happy."

"But everyone, even the greatest of warriors, has loved to enjoy peace sometimes," said Mabel.

"True, Mabel, and I am no exception to them in that respect, however far I may be from deserving the name of hero. My idea of happiness, if carried out fully, would be, first, a voyage round the world, a visit to every point of interest in the vast regions of Europe, Asia, Africa, and America—aye, to Australia, too, for that matter—gathering glory, meeting adventures, and achieving victory over wild beasts and men who act too much like them, making my name known, becoming a hero, in fact an independent man, who would owe all his riches to his own strong arm and energetic will, instead of the benevolence of others. After every voyage I should like a pleasant, beautiful home to come to, where I might enjoy rest after my perils, and in that home, Mabel, whom do you think I should like to find?"

Mabel turned her head slightly downwards and away from him.

Was it to conceal embarrassment, the expression, the deepening of hue, that these words called up on those beautiful features?

Jack scarcely knew, for Mabel did not reply.

"Well, Mabel," he continued, "in the first place, I should like to find Mr. Meredith occupying the position of honour and respect to which he is entitled. With health, repose, and happiness, all his. Then"——

"Who else?" said Mabel, who seemed to have regained some of her composure.

"Next, Tom Starboard—dear old Tom Starboard and Captain Hastings—stop, though, both of them, it strikes me, would be always with me on my voyages. Nothing could keep them on land long, I'll be bound. However, if not, they should always be welcome guests at my house."

"Well, who else?" asked Mable, her voice slightly faltering.

"Let me see, I won' say Lela, for it is very unlikely she would be there, though she would make an excellent companion for"——

He looked at Mabel.

It was not possible that she could fail to comprehend his meaning.

But she spoke not, nor did she return his ardent gaze.

Her eyes still avoided his, so he continued—

"Mabel, you know whom I mean. There can be but one person who could make my home supremely happy. With you, dear Mabel, such happiness, as I have described would be complete. Say, shall it not be realized?"

"That depends not upon ourselves," returned Mabel, yielding to his embrace. "Dear Jack, your happiness is mine also; and therefore, I need not say how ardently, supposing your dreams are realized, I shall try to ensure it. But if you thus roamed the world, how long and frequently you would be absent!'

"Necessity would compel me to be so," returned our hero. "But with a gallant vessel and crew under my command, I should be in some way consoled for your absence; and the perils past would only make our meeting more welcome."

"But suppose that, conquering my aversion to dangers and adventure," Mabel said, "I were to consent to accompany you in all those voyages and scenes of excitement to which you seem to be attached—I might do this."

"Then, Mabel, my happiness would be complete," returned Crusoe, enraptured by a proposal that showed so fully the affectionate devotion of her heart. "So shall it be, Mabel. I will be a king of the sea—not as a pirate, but as an enemy to pirates and a friend to the oppressed—and you shall be my queen."

"It strikes me, however," said Mabel, somewhat archly, "that we are looking a long way into the future, and calculating upon it hastily. It is scarcely time yet to lay our plans so minutely. My hopes are now centred in the conclusion of this voyage. How glad I shall be when we arrive at Chili. I have heard my father say it is a beautiful country. Have you ever been there?"

"No, but Tom Starboard has; and many a wild adventure has he met there. I hope I may be able to follow his example in that respect. All our dangers are, however, over for the time."

"What! all our dangers are over, and just entering into another engagement?" said Mabel.

"You surely cannot think lightly of the perils of this invasion?"

"It will be nothing to what we have undergone."

"Ah! then I hope you do not intend to take an active personal part in it?" said Mabel, anxiously.

"It will surely be enough to assist the natives from the sea, without joining the battle on shore?"

"No, Mabel. That would not be fighting at all. If we offer to assist these brave savages, we must do so fully. Whenever there is fighting going on I like to do all I can to aid those whom I believe to be in the right. So does Tom Starboard; so does Elton; and, indeed, of all of us."

"But this will be your last battle, I hope, for a long time,' said Mabel.

"As far as present appearances go, it will," returned Jack. "Once away from these islands, we shall be out of the way of conflicts and skirmishes, unless we meet with that confounded pirate, who will scarcely dare to make the first attack."

CHAPTER XLI.

THE LANDING OF THE INVADERS.—THE CONFLICT AND THE VICTORY.

THE island of Typee lay at not more than half a day's sail from the country of their deadly foes; and, long before the sun went down, the cutter came in sight of the line of beautiful green verdure just rising above the surface of the ocean, and denoting their proximity to the scene of forthcoming contention.

King Nookeevah's eagle eyes glistened, his proud form dilated, as, standing up in his canoe, he pointed with his spear towards the island.

"There stand our future dominions," he said: "Warriors of Hopaw! no resistance, no danger, must discourage us in our path of conquest. This is an eventful day, for it must witness a memorable struggle—a final victory. This day must the long enmity and constant hostilities that have subsisted between the Hopaws and the Typees be quenched in the blood of the latter. After that, peace, progress, and adoption of the arts—the power and greatness of the white men! Out of evil comes good. Thus spake the great Etooa, and thus must it be."

A chorus of acclamations answered this address. From every canoe rose the cheers of many warriors, each grasping his weapon to prove how eager he was to fulfil the commands of his king.

The Typees proved to be not quite so disorganised and unprepared for resistance as the Hopaws expected to find them.

Anticipating the fearful retaliation of their powerful foes, they had used the time in active preparations for a desperate struggle.

Every available warrior on their island had been made to join the legion of defence.

Arms of every kind had been manufactured with all possible despatch.

Fortifications of the strongest description that they were capable of constructing had been reared by the energetic natives in all points that offered, and were available either for defence or over for attack.

With a few guns the Typees might have defied their foes, even assisted by the Seagull; but as they had no fire-arms, substitutes were found in the slings and bows and arrows which were used for fighting enemies at a distance.

All round the coast, bands of well-armed warriors were stationed, both in canoes and skilfully concealed among the rocky defiles that abounded on all parts near the shore.

Every town and village was well defended, and the palace of Prince Pakayo was thronged with dusky warriors.

Bitter revenge, and firm, remorseless hatred had almost driven the Typee chief to madness.

His defeat was so unexpected to him.

He had so fully calculated upon a victory that would enable him to glut his hate and thirst for conquest to the utmost, that the whole of the long-cherished plans and hopes of his life had been shipwrecked by that one blow.

Many an invasion had he attempted; but none so gigantic in dimensions as the last.

In that he had put forth his whole strength—the entire fighting power of the nation had been collected together.

His fortunes were cast on that one enterprise, and it had failed.

The nation could never recover the blow it had received sufficiently to make another invasion.

Fearfully reduced in numbers and powers as it was, such an attempt would be madness.

But if the Typees could not attack, they could resist, and Pakayo resolved to do this to the death.

He was, in spite of appearance, no coward.

He had fled on beholding his utter defeat, knowing that in his own life was bound up the existence of the nation; but for that nation, now the grand final struggle had come, he was prepared to shed the last drop of his blood.

Fierce and gloomy had been the mood of Prince Pakayo on the first day of his defeat; but on the next, his resolution and activity returned, and a universal effort was organised for the purpose of ensuring defence.

Spies and scouts had yet remained faithful to the Typee chief, and enabled him to gain all necessary information with respect to the movements of his enemies.

Great was his dismay on hearing that even the attack on the Seagull had passed in exactly the same manner as his invasion, namely, in victory almost secured, and then ending in a miserable defeat.

By the death of Williams he had lost a powerful ally, and many of his most trusty chieftains had also fallen or been taken in the fray.

Fortune was clearly against Pakayo, and of this he seemed to be conscious.

"The Etooa of those detested dogs," he remarked to one of his chiefs on the day after the fight, "if he had been, as they believed, a powerful and great spirit, would have aided me and not them. Had I not my father to avenge? Right was on my side more than on that of the Hopaws. The gods we worshipped smiled favourably upon our enterprise, and it would have succeeded. Victory was nearly secured when suddenly all was changed. The strength fled from each warrior's arm, the force from each warrior's weapon. What caused this? It must have been the witchcraft of the detested Hopaws!"

"More likely, great chief, the services of the pale-faced magicians who assisted them," responded the warriors, "whose powers are so boundless, and whose fire-tubes are so deadly. If they assist our foes, our dangers are great."

"Silence!" cried Pakayo, sternly, his dark eyes flashing fire. "Thy words are that of a coward! Speak not to me of the possibility of further defeat. No danger that may menace us now can be too great to encounter. We must not shrink nor flinch, not if the whole nation of white men aid the hated Hopaws to invade us!"

Stern in this fierce courage, inspired as it was by the desperation of his position, the Typee chief collected all the strength of his scattered army, and strained every nerve to form an efficient defence against the coming invasion. On the day appointed, every means of resistance that could by any possibility be made available, had been brought into use, and the hope of triumph, faint as the chance really was, rose once more in every breast.

Victory or utter annihilation was now the only alternative, and the knowledge of this nerved every Typee with superhuman strength.

The fleet sailed slowly for a short distance along the coast, in order if possible to find a good landing place, but everywhere the Hopaws found the same preparations made to resist their landing. So, choosing out a spot where the soft sandy beach presented the best chance, they at once commenced operations.

The Seagull was ranged as close to the shore as she could get, and anchored with her broadside ready to sweep the beach clear of the hostile natives, and facilitate the landing of the Hopaws.

King Nookeevah himself, in his great war canoe, led his warriors to the assault. They were promptly met by the Typee braves, who dexterously interposing their own canoes between the shore and those of their enemies, thus rendered themselves safe from the guns of the ship, for a time at least.

The bitter hatred of the two tribes now had full opportunity to display itself, and the fight was deadly. Spears flew in showers, and many of the canoes, in their eagerness to close with each other, were capsized, and in the hurry of the combat none thought of picking up the survivors.

The tall form of King Nookevah was ever conspicuous.

His canoe contained upwards of sixty of his bravest warriors; and the animated words that fell from his lips instilled fresh ardour into breasts already inflamed with deadly hatred to their foes and a determination to subdue their country.

"Onward, my braves!" cried the King. "The loathsome vultures of Typee shall fall before the noble eagles of Hopaw. Vile miscreants! their hour has come! This day shall the rivers of Typee run blood, and their maze-fields be stained with the gore of the treacherous tribe!"

The combat between the canoes continues.

It is now at its height.

The sea is white with the foam of their paddles.

Neither side seems to have the advantage.

Victory hangs trembling in the balance.

THE LANDING OF THE INVADERS.

At last the impetuosity of the Hopaw warriors prevails.

The Typees begin to give way; their spears slacken fast; they ply their paddles swiftly; their canoes' heads are turned towards the shore; and amid the exultant cheers of the Hopaws and their English friends, the Typees fly for their lives towards the shore.

So far a great advantage was gained; but a much harder task was yet to be done, before the conquest of the island was achieved.

Pakayo had not yet taken part in the fight, but stationed in a thicket close to the beach he awaited the coming of his foes.

At the head of hundreds of warriors he was confident of victory, and though for a moment discouraged at the defeat of his canoes, he was burning with impatience to meet the hated King Nookevah in fair fight.

At a signal from the ship, the Hopaw canoes were brought close to the side of the vessel which was towards the sea, and Captain Hastings now gave orders for his men to fire upon the retreating Typees, by which great numbers of them were killed and their canoes sunk—those of the natives that escaped to shore immediately flying to the shelter of the forest.

Broadside after broadside was poured from the ship, and Prince Pakayo was compelled to lead his warriors farther into the woods, out of the reach of her fire.

This gave a favourable chance to the Hopaws to land, and their canoes were soon grating against the beach.

King Nookeevah thus stood upon the long-coveted soil of Typee.

The Hopaw chief divided his men into two bands—one under his own command, the other under that of Tom Starboard and our hero, who, in spite of the advice of Captain Hastings and the wishes of Mabel, could not be restrained from joining in the attack.

They began their march at once, and cautiously entered the dense forest—King Nookeevah on the right, while Jack and Tom entered from the left.

For about a hundred yards or so, Jack and his band encountered no opposition; and Tom Starboard was just remarking that the ship's guns seemed to have frightened the enemy to the other side of the island, when a spear which came whizzing close to his ear, undeceived him.

At the same moment the war-cry of the Typees rang through the forest, and hundreds of warriors who seemed to start from the ground, so suddenly did they make their appearance, stood ready to bar their passage.

These were a band which Pakayo (who had, though unseen, closely watched every movement of the enemy) had detached to meet them.

They thought as those only do who fight for the very existence of their country, and but for the powerful aid of our two heroes it is doubtful if they would not have gained the victory.

Jack was in his element—heedless of the spears and arrows which fell around.

He and Tom Starboard loaded and fired as fast as they could, knocking over many of the natives.

The Typees, finding that they were rather at a disadvantage by this open warfare, resorted to their old tactics of concealing themselves as much as possible.

In a few moments not one was to be seen. They were sheltered behind every tree or bush that would afford a hiding-place, and kept up such a shower of arrows and spears that our hero's party were fain to follow their example.

By remaining exposed, they were mere targets for their enemies, without the least possibility of returning their fire with success.

Jack and Tom were behind contiguous trees. "This way of fighting," said the latter, "reminds me of some of the skirmishes I have been in down Nebraska way, when we were lying in ambush for a tribe of the Blackfeet Indians."

Jack was so busy taking aim at the head of a Typee, which the owner had incautiously exposed, to reply to this speech.

The report of his rifle was heard.

At the same moment a Typee, who had been behind a bush some distance off, sprang to his feet and then fell dead to the ground.

"Bravo, Jack!" cried Tom. "You potted him in fine style. I wish one of the beggars would give me a chance."

A triumphant yell from the Hopaws followed this successful shot.

This so irritated the Typees that once more they sprang from their ambush, and, tomahawk in hand, resolved to put an end to the fight by coming again to close quarters.

A great many of them were shot down as they emerged from their hiding-place.

But the rest came on with such impetuosity that the Hopaws had great difficulty in maintaining their ground.

Still, they fought desperately against their more numerous enemies.

At last success seemed about to reward their endeavours.

Tom and our hero were about to lead on their men to a final charge, when they were attacked from their rear by an overwhelming number of Typee braves, who, from the other side of the island (where they had been stationed in case of the invaders landing), had made a quick march to meet the Typees, a message from Pakayo having summoned them in all haste.

This at once turned the tide of victory in favour of the Typees, who attacked their foes with great fierceness.

Step by step the Hopaws were compelled to retrace their path.

As they were unable to notice which way they were retreating, they unfortunately entered one of the beds of the many torrents, which in the rainy season came down to the sea like cataracts.

It was, however, now dry.

The Typees observed this with great joy, and made renewed efforts to drive their enemies still further into the rocky defile.

Then, closing round the top of the ravine, they threw down large masses of stone upon the Hopaws, and, by stationing numbers of men before the land entrance of the gorge, effectually prevented all egress from that way.

The mouth of the valley where it entered the sea was so narrow, and blocked up with boulders of stone and tangled masses of vegetation, that the fugitives found great difficulty in making their way over it.

Crusoe Jack now sought some shelter for his men.

He found one, it was a deep chasm made by a fissure in the barren rocks.

Seizing a piece of rope that had been left inadvertently by one of his followers, he made one end fast, and began a descent to ascertain what it might afford.

It was dark and gloomy enough.

He could hear the roar of water as it rushed through some subterranean passage far beneath him.

Then his eyes became accustomed to the gloom, he looked about him, but, horror! what did he see in the dim, uncertain light?

A dusky form, crouching behind a projecting rock, and a poisoned spear that was levelled almost in a line with his heart.

Quick as lightning he mastered the qualm that for a moment crept over him, and the next instant his nerved hand sent a bullet through the brain of his dusky, lurking foe.

"Treachery!" he muttered, and with the agility of a cat he reascended the rope and breathed the fresh air again.

Tom looked at his companion strangely, but asked no questions, the brave boy's features betrayed, not in the least, the terrible ordeal he had undergone.

It was no time for thinking or questioning.

Tom and Jack endeavoured to rally their men —but, for some time, in vain.

But the Hopaws, perceiving that all hope of flight was vain, turned, like the stag at bay, and faced their triumphant enemies.

Again the conflict raged.

But the Typees so outnumbered their foes that our two heroes saw with dismay that their men were fast falling around them.

In vain they exerted themselves manfully.

What were the efforts of two men, though armed with rifles, against such fearful odds?

"I am afraid this is our last adventure," said Jack. "What folly urged us to take part in this war? I wish we had taken the captain's advice. Mabel this night will be plunged into grief for my loss; and, as for you, my brave friend——"

"Never despair!" observed Tom. "I feel sure we shall get out of this scrape, as we have out of so many others. See that thick clump of bananas, growing in front of that huge rock? Let us place our men behind it. Once there, we can hold for hours, and by that time perhaps King Nookeevah will be able to come to our assistance."

"I hope he will," said Jack. "But perhaps he is himself in need of help. These Typees fight like the Romans of old."

The remainder of the Hopaw braves were led, as quickly as they could be, to the shelter of the bananas, which for some time screened them somewhat from their enemies, many of whom fell dead or wounded in their desperate efforts to storm the stronghold of the Hopaws.

Still our hero's band were continually thinned.

Though their deadly rifles lessened the number of their foes, the latter still pressed onward with undaunted hearts.

At length they succeeded in placing several large stones against the rock, by the aid of which they mounted into the very midst of the little band of Hopaws.

The brave followers of Crusoe Jack defended themselves resolutely; but, cramped into so small a space, were overpowered at last, as, with exultant cries, the Typees cut them down on all sides.

Jack and Tom defended themselves with the butt ends of their rifles.

Again was our hero brought face to face with death and defeat.

. . . .

Meanwhile, King Nookeevah and his warriors were, on there part, more successful.

After a short march the king encountered Prince Pakayo at the head of his stoutest braves.

The prince, on beholding his hated foe, was inflamed with rage.

The opportunity he had so long sought had now arrived.

He prepared for a long and deadly combat.

"Vile Hopaw!" he cried, "at last thou art mine! Thou shald die in pain and disgrace— die a conquered king—the last of the Hopaws. Upon them, my chiefs! Drive the invaders of our land into the ocean! Let the sharks feast on their carcases!"

Proud and defiant as were these words, King Nonkeevah laughed scornfully.

"This night, bloodthirsty miscreant," he cried, "I shall reign in the palace of Pakayo, whose head shall decorate my spear in his own lodge. Braves of Hopaw, to the fight!"

The combatants now closed with each other, fighting with the utmost ferocity.

King Nookeevah's men made repeated assaults upon the Typee, who fought around their king with equal valour, repaying the taunts of their foes with others equally bitter.

The combat raged with the greatest fury.

Pakayo, animated both with a desire for vengeance and the preservation of the liberty of his people, found scarcely an equal.

His dreadful war-club made terrible havoc among the Hopaws, while King Nookeevah, equally fired with wrath, made many unsuccessful efforts to reach him.

But though both were equally desirous of a personal conflict, the press around them was too great.

The efforts of the Hopaws at length prevailed.

The ranks of the Typee warriors were broken through.

Prince Pakayo and his men were compelled to retreat a little further into the forest.

Here, on the banks of a small river, they made their final stand.

On the opposite shore were the Hopaws, flushed with victory, and confident that in a short time Typee would be theirs.

"Yield!" thundered Nookeevah, "yield to your superior, and become slaves to the brave Hopaws!"

"Never!" roared Pakayo, in defiant tones. "Never shall a prince of the Typees yield to the Hopaw dogs. Rather shall the river redden the sea with our blood!"

So saying, he whirled his mighty club two or three times round his head, and then launched it with all his force at the head of King Nookeevah.

A sudden movement of the latter prevented the club from striking him.

It, however, caught one of his bravest chiefs full in the forehead, and crushed in his skull.

"Revenge! revenge for the brave Tynea!" shouted the Hopaws.

Some of them endeavoured, by swimming across the river, to reach the Typees, who, rushing to the water's side, speared the greater part of them.

King Nookeevah, perceiving this, ordered some of his men to go a little further down the stream to see if it was fordable.

A place was soon found which permitted of crossing.

King Nookeevah, with most of his men, was soon on the same side of the river as his foes.

Those whom he had left on the other side sent flights of arrows among the Typees; while he himself immediately proceeded to assault Pakayo and his warriors in person.

Thus attacked on both sides, the Typees fell fast.

Soon scarcely a dozen remained round Pakayo.

A great many of his men, on seeing the Hopaws were successful in crossing the stream, had fled into the depths of the forest.

There they could defy pursuit, though they could offer no successful resistance to the Hopaws.

Pakayo and his few braves disdained to fly.

Though they knew how hopeless it was to resist, they refused to surrender when summoned to do so by King Nookeevah.

At length, Pakayo alone remained.

Springing out upon a fallen tree which hung over the river, he for a time defied all efforts of the Hopaws to reach him.

The tree was so narrow that but one could get upon it at a time.

Several Hopaws who attempted it fell beneath the war-club of Pakayo.

King Nookeevah himself was for a moment stunned by a blow which he received while endeavouring to spear the great Typee chief.

At length, an arrow from one of the Hopaws struck Pakayo in the shoulder, wounding him severely.

The end had come.

The brave but erring chief of the Typees stood on the brink of eternity.

"Nookeevah," said the Typee chieftain, "you have conquered, but never shall the body of Pakayo fall into the hands of one who has been his deadly foe through life, and whom in death he defies!"

Then he died, still unconquered, before the eyes of his foes.

The strong current soon carried his body out of sight.

His last words were true.

The Hopaws never possessed the body of their great foe. It was hurried by the stream into the great sea.

So finished the last chieftain of the Typee race.

The conquest was, however, not yet complete.

King Nookeevah was still in ignorance of the fate of the band led by Jack and Tom.

If they had been unsuccessful, but half his work was finished.

Orders were therefore given by him to his warriors to proceed immediately to that port of the island to which the expedition had gone.

Meanwhile, we had left our two heroes in a position of the greatest danger.

Their allies were being rapidly killed by the Typees, and they themselves were worn out with the exertions they had made.

To save their lives they could not have held out many moments longer.

At length, to their great joy, their assailants suddenly recoiled from off the rock, and, with every sign of dismay, began a hasty retreat.

"I said so," cried Tom Starboard, after a quick glance round to ascertain the cause of their flight.

"I knew we should be rescued. Here is King Nookeevah and his brave warriors. Heaven be praised! for we shall soon be out of danger."

It was in truth the king.

They had heard from a distance the reports of the rifles, and had made all haste to the rescue.

The Typees made one effort to rally, but it was in vain.

The Hopaws fell upon them like a torrent, scattered them to flight, pursuing them with relentless fury.

A better acquaintance with the intricacies of the forest, enabled many of the Typees to save themselves.

All resistance was now at an end.

The land of the Typees was in full possession of the mighty Nookeevah.

The king, from long intercourse with the whites, had so far subdued his savage nature as to order that the wounded on both sides should be looked to, and then advancing to where Tom and Jack were standing, shook them by the hand, and thanked them for the gallant defence they had made in his behalf.

The Hopaws then took possession of Prince Pokayo's palace.

Strong detachments of warriors were placed in positions to overcome any attempt of the scattered bands of Typees to regain possession of the island; of which, however, there was but little fear.

The king, accompanied by Jack and Tom, then went on board the Seagull, where they found Captain Hastings in a state of anxiety for the fate of our heroes.

Great was his joy at beholding them unharmed, while Mabel, and indeed everyone on board the Seagull, declared they had had no peace since the fight began, and were almost upon the point of landing, at all risks, to ascertain the fate of Jack and Tom.

Captain Hastings then congratulated King Nookeevah upon his victory, and asked him what he intended to do with the island.

"I shall," replied King Nookeevah, "appoint Pakeeno, my brother, to be governor; leave half my men here for security, and then sail back to my own country, to which I am anxious to return."

Captain Hastings then intimated his intention sailing at daybreak next morning back to Hopaw, to take on board the men he had left there, and Mr. Meredith, and bid farewell to that part of the Pacific.

A grand feast was then held that night, to celebrate their victory.

Jack and Tom went on shore to join in the festivities, Captain Hastings refusing to leave his ship, and Mabel preferred to remain on board.

Next morning the canoes of the king were got ready for sailing.

King Nookeevah had placed his kinsman as chief of the island, giving him all necessary instructions; and at about midday the ship and canoes left the shores of Typee for the Island of Hopaw.

On arriving there the ship was once more anchored in the bay; after a few hours, spent in taking on board wood and water, and in feasting with the king, our adventurers bade a long farewell to their friends, the Hopaws.

The king accompanied them some distance with his canoes.

As they set sail from the island, our heroes, from the deck of the Seagull, watched the fast-fading form of the island in which they had experienced so many exciting and daring adventures, until it melted away into the horizon; and, with all sail set, and with a fair wind, the good ship, Seagull, ploughed her swift course to the Sandwich Islands.

CHAPTER XLII.

THE SEAGULL'S VOYAGE—THE DESERTED SHIP—JACK AND TOM AGAIN AT THE MERCY OF THE OCEAN.

A FAVOURING breeze bore our adventurers to within a hundred and ninety miles of Honolulu, the capital of the Sandwich Islands.

It was yet early morning on the eighth day after leaving the Hopaw Island, when Crusoe Jack came on board to inspect a sail which had been reported in the distance.

He found Captain Hastings himself taking a look at the stranger through his telescope.

"She is a good way off, Jack," said he; "and I can't tell what she is. The breeze is so light, it will be many hours ere we get near her."

Tom Starboard also, in the intervals of his duty, occasionally took an observation of the strange vessel.

But, like Captain Hastings, he could make nothing of her.

As, however, it was of not much importance to them what she was, after an hour or two she was almost forgotten, and a breeze having sprung up, all hands were busily employed in trimming sail to catch every breath of the favouring wind.

Captain Hastings expected to arrive at Honolulu by the evening of the next day.

But the wind, as yet, only came in faint puffs, and they made but little way.

A little before sundown they found themselves within two or three miles of the stranger; and, on inspecting her closely, they were surprised at the strange appearance she presented.

As her sails were hanging in disorder from her yards, and she seemed not to have even steerage way upon her (as she yawed to port or starboard), our friend, old Tom, after gazing a long while in silence, gave it as his opinion that she had been abandoned by her crew.

"In this case," said Jack, "I vote for boarding her. There may be somebody left on her yet."

He applied to the captain for leave to undertake the enterprise.

"Well," said Captain Hastings, "you can go if you like. But don't be away long; it will soon be dark, and I think we shall have a rough night of it, by the look of the sky. You know our old proverb—

'A mackerel sky and mare's tails
Make lofty ships carry low sails.'

And there is no mistaking the warning written up yonder."

"I suppose Tom will go with me," said Jack. "We two and another hand will be sufficient for the enterprise. We shall be back in an hour or two."

The quarter-boat being lowered, our heroes quickly stowed themselves away in her, and Jack waved an adieu to Mabel, who had in vain endeavoured to persuade him to relinquish a project of so much danger.

The boat soon shot out into the wide ocean.

"I say, Tom," observed Jack, "have you got any grog? It will be as well to take some, in case there are any persons on board starving."

"Devil a bit," replied Tom, "except just a taste of rum and a couple of biscuits, in case of having a long pull back to the ship. I don't think there's anybody about, myself. But give way there, lad. The night is coming on fast, and we shall barely have time to get back before it is quite dark."

A row of about half-an-hour brought them to within a hundred yards of the stranger.

The sight she presented was so singular that they involuntarily rested on their oars to gaze upon it.

Not a soul could be discerned upon her decks.

Her sides were all covered with barnacles.

Her ironwork was quite rusted away.

Huge strips of seaweed hung down her weather-beaten ribs.

She rose and fell upon the sluggish waves—now rolling to port till her copper-sheathing, or what little could be discerned of it for the barnacles, was exposed almost to her keel; then, rising again, she came over on the opposite side, till all her deck was plainly visible.

A mournful creaking noise accompanied her movements, caused by the pintle of her rudder being loose.

Her masts were tottering at every movement, and threatened each moment to come down with a run.

They could also hear the wash of water inboard, plainly telling that she was filling with water, and that however long she might have been abandoned, her end was near.

The winds and waves, together with the absence of man's fostering care, had done their worst.

Her doom was sealed.

On pulling round to the stern, to see if they could make out her name, they found the letters almost obliterated.

They could discern the letters M—Y NE—, L—DON, which they supposed to be "Mary Anne," or "Mary Jane, of London."

She appeared to be a brig of about two hundred tons.

All these particulars they made out in far less time than it takes us to transcribe them.

Having satisfied themselves as to the outward appearance of the craft, they came close alongside, and clambering up her worm-eaten timbers, they soon stood upon her deck.

There was but little on deck to notice.

Her bulwarks, galley, &c., were all gone.

Indeed, she presented nothing but the bare deck.

The hatchways were carried away.

At every wave which came over her the water would pour over the combings.

This appeared to be the cause of the water in her, as much as from leakage.

"There's nothing to pick up here." said Tom. "She appears to have drifted about for a twelve-month."

"Not quite so long as that," said Jack. "But let us try to get below."

This was a matter of some difficulty, as she was more than half-full of water.

But, after some time, they succeeded in exploring the after cabin, which was highest out of water, as the vessel was a good deal down by the head.

Nothing met their view capable of affording any clue as to the fate of the crew.

The cabin was devoid of all furniture, except the berths, which were still there, and some few articles of bedding, which floated over the cabin floor.

Not an article of any value was left, and it was evident either that the vessel had been visited before, or the crew had had time to carry away all portable articles of value.

Emerging from the after cabin, they passed on to the fore-hatchway.

Jack boldly jumped down to explore that part of the ship, if possible.

But he found it too dark to see much; and being up to his knees in water, it was very little good stopping there.

He turned round, with the intention of once more returning to the deck to rejoin Tom.

Suddenly he stumbled over something on the floor, and fell flat on his face, half drowned by the water which was in the cabin.

On regaining, after a short struggle, his upright position, he found he could not move.

His left foot, had somehow got jammed in some obstacle or other, and after fruitlessly exerting himself for some time to get free, he was obliged to call to Tom for help.

The latter put his head down the hatchway, and asked Jack what was the matter.

"Nothing much," said Jack; but I am not able to move, and the water is confoundedly cold. I think I have jammed my foot in a bight of an old cable. See if you can give a hand out."

Tom immediately proceeded to his assistance; but the depth of water made it a very difficult matter to extricate his comrade.

"I am caught like a rat in a trap, Tom. I can't think what holds me so fast, and it is quite dark, too. We shall have Captain Hastings sending a boat to look after us."

At last Tom, by dint of groping with his hands, found out the cause of Jack's detention.

A chest lashing had got coiled round his foot, and the more Jack pulled, the tighter it became.

Tom Starboard's knife soon settled that matter and the two adventurers made their way, as quick as they could, on deck.

The delay in releasing Jack had occupied full half-an-hour, and it was now quite dark.

Ominous clouds could be discerned flying swift overhead.

A long, heavy sea was gradually rising.

The tops of the waves were tipped with a whitish gray, while the occasional heavy puffs of wind, all presaged the coming storm.

The vessel was now rolling very heavily, having no masts to steady her.

"I can't see the Seagull," said Tom, after a minute's vain search with his eyes in the direction he supposed the vessel to be. "But let us get into the boat."

But where was the boat?

They had left her alongside, with their companion in her, but now she was nowhere visible.

They shouted till they were hoarse, but could elicit no response.

"Confound that fellow!" said Jack. "What is he up to? He can't have gone back to the ship."

Tom shook his head.

"I am afraid he went to sleep," said he, "and either the painter carried it away, or the rolling of the vessel unhitched it."

What was to be done?

Captain Hastings would be anxiously watching for their return.

They listened intently for the sound of guns, which they knew he would fire, as a signal of return, and also to tell them his position, so that they would know in which direction to steer.

But the wind was now loud and boisterous.

Dark waves toppled over on to the deck of the hulk; and, with nothing to cling to, our heroes had great difficulty in keeping their position, while, to add to their discomfort, they became aware that the vessel was gradually settling down.

A very few hours would decide their fate.

At length, finding it impossible to keep their footing, Tom Starboard made another descent into the fore-hold, and emerged in a few minutes with a coil of small rope, which he had found, and an axe all covered with rust.

With all the rope they lashed themselves to the stumps of the masts, and awaited in silence what seemed their inevitable fate.

"This is our last cruise, Tom," said Jack. "What unlucky chance made us stop so long on board? But why does not Captain Hastings come to our help? He must know that something is the matter."

"I am afraid," replied the old tar, "he has enough to do to take care of his own ship. Think how dark it is, too, and how easy it would be to run into this old hulk, which I wish had gone to Davy Jones a month ago," he added, bitterly, as he thought of the distressing scene there would be on the Seagull when morning broke, and revealed no sign of the missing men.

At times Tom and Jack fancied they could hear the report of a gun, but they had no means of ascertaining the truth of their surmise.

Meanwhile, the weather was growing worse and worse.

It was evident the brig would not swim much longer.

"We shall have one chance for our lives," said Tom, unlashing himself.

"What are you going to do?" asked Jack, beginning to free himself also, to help him in whatever plan Tom intended to carry out.

But Tom told him he had better keep fast, a

he could render him no assistance, and would only endanger his own life.

Jack watched Tom with great curiosity, as well as he could for the darkness.

He could hear the sound of chopping, which continued for upwards of an hour; at the end which time, Tom returned to his old post, and detailed to Jack what he had done.

"I have cut away part of the deck," said he. We can, perhaps, manage to get on that when she sinks. At any rate, it is our only chance.

"And a very poor one, too, Tom," replied Jack; "but let's hope for the best. I am getting uncommonly hungry; but it won't do to eat up all our provisions at once, which we could easily do, little as it is."

"We can take a sup of rum, though," said Tom.

This they did, and it, in some measure, deadened the feeling of hunger and thirst which they were now beginning to experience.

At length a peculiar vibration of the hulk, and the steady down-rush of water over her hatchway, admonished them that the crisis of their fate was at hand.

"Look sharp, Jack, and place yourself just here," said Tom, indicating the place where Jack was to station himself.

Then Tom severed the rope with which he had fastened the planks he had cut out to the deck, placed himself alongside Tom, and both, grasping the rope that the old sailor had left to hold on by, awaited the coming event.

"It is an even chance, Jack, whether we are drawn down by the hulk or not," observed Tom; "but now we shall very soon know, for—hold fast, Jack—she is sinking. Yes," he added, speaking very fast, "she is certainly sinking."

And indeed the vessel's deck was now level with the water's edge.

The hulk gave a few consulsive groans, reeled slightly from side to side; reared her stern high out of the water, and then slid, head foremost, into the depths of the ocean.

For some time the fate of our adventurers was doubtful.

At one time, the frail raft was almost perpendicular; then it shot downwards at a terrific rate, as if to follow the ship, of which it had so long formed a part.

Then it was whirled round and round like a feather, and finally remained quite steady on the spot where the unknown vessel had disappeared.

"Safe, so far," cried Jack, with a sigh of relief. "But our position is far from desirable We shall be washed off if the gale continues."

"I am in hopes it is breaking," answered Tom; and his words were soon verified, for, after an hour's tossing about at the pleasure of the waves, the wind subsided, and the sea soon went down, while overhead the moon shone out brightly.

It was one of those changes which are to be seen only in the tropics.

But a short hour ago they were tossing over mountainous waves in pitchy darkness.

Now they were gently heaving up and down on the constantly decreasing billows, while not a cloud obscured the glorious tropical sky.

Not a sign, however, was to be seen of the ship or the boat.

"I'll tell you what I will do," said Jack. "It is very probable that we may not not be picked up, and no one know our fate. You have the bottle that we brought the rum in. I'll write a few words on a piece of paper, cork it tight down, and throw it into the sea. Perhaps it may be found; and so our end will be remembered. I only hope we may escape, but I see little chance."

Accordingly, Jack took a leaf out of his pocket-book, and wrote with his pencil the following words:—

"We are drifting on a raft from the wreck of the deserted ship. But slight hopes of being saved.—

(Signed)   "CRUSOE JACK.
                                "TOM STARBOARD.

"The finder of this is requested to deliver it to Captain Hastings, of the ship Seagull."

"I expect that will drift to one of the Sandwich Islands," said Tom. "The currents set that way from here."

"At all events," observed Jack, "it may give some information of our probable fate."

The wind still continued to moderate, and the sea to go down; but our heroes could not help reflecting on the smallness of the chances of their escape—with only a few morsels of biscuit, no water, and without means of guiding or propelling their frail craft.

Their sole hope lay in being picked up by some passing craft; but vessels were not very plentiful in that part of the world.

At length morning broke on the ocean wanderers, and eagerly their eyes roved around the horizon, but nothing was in sight.

After a slight breakfast, consisting of one mouthful each of biscuit, they began to examine into their means of progression, and see whether it was possible to rig a mast of any sort.

At length, Tom Starboard with his axe managed to hew a long splinter off one end of the raft.

This they fastened, as well as they were able, to their raft, and Jack took off his shirt to serve as a sail.

They found, however, that it was of little more use than a signal of distress.

It did not urge the raft along more than half a mile an hour.

Thus the weary hours of this day passed over slowly, and the horrors of thirst began to assail them.

Night, however, threw her friendly shade over them; and they managed to forget their sorrows in sleep.

Next morning the sun arose in its usual brilliancy, and the pangs of thirst became difficult to bear.

"I must drink the sea water," said Jack, despairingly. "My tongue is parched in my throat."

Tom, however, earnestly dissuaded him from this; telling him instances of people in a similar position to themselves, who, having drunk sea water, had become raving mad, and thrown themselves overboard.

"It will be better," said he, "to bathe ourselves; this you will find is some antidote to the pangs of thirst."

They did so, and it afforded them some relief.

All that day the raft continued in this position, exposed to the full glare of the tropical sun

JACK SPRANG TO HIS FEET ON THE RAFT.

The only relief they could get was by throwing water over themselves occasionally.

The sky was vainly watched in hopes of some indication of rain.

Thus the second day passed slowly, and once more night reigned on the lonely wanderers of the Pacific.

Sleep, however, they could not; and it was evident that, unless help came next day, they would both be beyond the reach of assistance.

But few words were exchanged between them, though each was busy with his own thoughts.

The lassitude of weakness had overcome both.

Daybreak came at last, and once more were their glances directed in quest of any passing sail.

None was visible; and, in despair, Crusoe Jack, after wringing Tom's hand, stretched himself at full length on the raft to await his coming death.

Tom, leaning his face on his knees, also waited in silence his approaching end.

Some hours had passed away in silence, when Starboard Tom was awakened from a half-delirious dream by a loud shout.

Half mechanically he raised his head and looked around.

A large ship was hove to close to them, and it was from some of her people that the shout proceeded.

As his position gradually dawned on him, Tom, in a transport of joy, which inspired him with sudden strength, called to Jack, who, hearing a noise, languidly raised his head.

The deep hoarse bay of a dog roused him from his stupor, and as the noble animal leapt from the taffrail into the sea, Crusoe Jack leapt to his feet.

A sea at that moment broke over the raft and thoroughly roused Tom to a sense of his position; he arose on all fours and glared at the strange ship that had thus providentially come to their aid.

In the meantime a boat was lowered, and the oars plied by willing hands, then a few words of greeting, and our friends found a home on board the welcome stranger, where they received every necessary attention.

Thus once more had they been saved from the imminent perils which abound in a life passed upon the mighty ocean.

CHAPTER XLIII.

MISGIVINGS AS TO JACK'S FATE—THE SEARCH— ALL HOPES DESTROYED.

THE party on the Seagull had regarded the expedition of Jack and Tom Starboard with but little anxiety.

That a certain degree of danger attended it they were well aware; but that danger would not be great if the weather continued favourable.

But when the gale arose—when darkness began to close around the angry waters, shutting out from their view the ruined hulk and the gallant adventurers who had boarded her—then did Captain Hastings' party begin to fear that some harm had occurred to them.

"I told them to return before it became dark," remarked the captain to Mr. Meredith. "But it will soon be night, and the gale is rising fearfully. I'm afraid something has happened to them."

"It is impossible to distinguish anything at such a time as this," remarked Mr. Meredith, holding his telescope in his trembling hands, and vainly endeavouring to catch a glimpse of the wreck. "It is becoming so dark, and the hulk is so far off. How sorry I am you let them go!"

"So am I," returned the captain. "But Jack and Tom are both alike in that respect. They are so fond of adventure that they want to go on any desperate expedition that offers, and they are such favourites of mine that I do not like to refuse them."

Mabel had regarded Jack's departure on the expedition with great misgivings and anxiety.

They were doubled as the gale increased.

The night came on.

No signs were discovered of the adventurers.

That he had passed through so many dangers and escaped so frequently with his life, was to her a subject of great thankfulness, but no sign that Providence would always extend to him the same clemency.

She could not help thinking, too, that he frequently rushed into danger unnecessarily.

But then her admiration at his bravery outweighed any deprecation of his rashness.

How often had he perilled his life to save her own?

And, above all, was he not allied to her by the closest and strongest of human ties—the tie of love?

And Tom—gallant old Tom Starboard—so worthy a companion to our hero, she would lament him also.

She would lament and pray for both—for all engaged on that desperate enterprise.

"Oh, papa! do you think there is so much danger?" she asked, in eager anxiety.

"My child," he replied, "it is useless for those who, like us, are continually encountering the dangers of the deep, to speculate on the consequences of those dangers. We can only hope for the best."

"Why—why did they go?" she asked, in increased anguish. "Why have they gone so frequently in scenes of perils, filling us with anxiety, and tempting death in all its most frightful forms?"

"My dear Mabel," returned her father, "I own they were rash, and the captain was imprudent to let them go on that journey; but you must remember that if they perilled their lives, it was with the intention of saving others. There may have been many a poor creature struggling on yonder hulk to whom a rescue would have been been as a gift of life."

"True, true," returned Mabel; "and I only hope Jack has been able to perform another act of humanity."

"A true hero, Mabel, is one who faces death and danger for the benefit of his fellow-creatures rather than a fierce warrior who slaughters thousands for mere hollow fame and victory."

"Yes, papa; I think as you do, and I hope Jack may be numbered among the true heroes. He has been delivered from many dangers. May he escape from this, and may it prove his last."

"I can fervently echo that prayer, Mabel," returned Mr. Meredith. "If human aid can effect his rescue it shall be accomplished. But we are also ourselves in some danger and in great difficulties. To bear up against this gale, and to reach the wreck in this adverse wind, will need all the captain's seamanship."

This opinion was strengthened by the indications Mr. Meredith observed on regaining the deck.

The gale had increased to the height of intensity.

The blackness of the sky had something in it more terrible than the ordinary hue of night.

Black storm-clouds rolled over the once clear heavens.

Every moment the waves became more disturbed.

The sky blacker.

The rising gale grew more violent.

For the Seagull herself little fear was entertained, for the captain had good confidence in his trusty vessel.

But much anxiety was felt with regard to the fate of our adventurers.

"They do not return," remarked the captain, "and I fear they'll never be able to do it in this gale. A sinking hulk, and nothing but a quarter boat to take to, are desperate odds in a storm."

"If we could bear up to the hulk ourselves?" suggested Mr. Meredith.

"I fear it's too late now," returned the captain. "The wind's dead against us. I wish I had done it before, though."

"However, any chance, any risk to save their lives," said Mr. Meredith, eagerly.

"You are right. We ought to do anything to save fellows in their position. I'm not the man to desert them; but, as to reaching the hulk, I am afraid it's a clear impossibility. However, we will try. Mr. Hayward!" said he to the mate, "all hands 'bout ship; then double reef the topsails."

These orders were executed.

The yards were braced sharp up.

They endeavoured, by constant tacking, to get as near to the supposed position of the hulk as they could.

Great caution was required.

A good look-out had to be kept to prevent the Seagull from running down the hulk in the darkness.

After tacking several times, Captain Hastings judged himself to be somewhere near where the hulk should be.

But nothing could be discerned of her.

The Seagull was then hove-to for an hour.

Guns were fired and port-fires lighted at intervals.

They illuminated the ocean around them with a lurid hue.

Anxiously they listened for a response to these signals, but heard nothing, save the howling of the wind, the dashing of the spray as a wave came thundering occasionally upon the deck, and the hoarse cry of the sea birds.

Thus the night passed away.

Still no news of the wanderers.

As may be imagined, great distress was exhibited in the cabin of the Seagull.

Mr. Meredith and the captain kept the watches on the deck.

They were unable to sleep from anxiety.

Mabel, who also passed a sleepless night, became a prey to the most fearful terror and suspense as the weary hours went by.

Daybreak!

Though it brought with it a promise of a glorious day, in strong contrast to the storm of the previous night, yet it brought no alleviation of the distress of those on board the Seagull.

Men were stationed in the tops.

A reward of £20 was promised to the one who first reported any traces of the lost ones.

This, as may be supposed, was a great stimulus, and many were the pair of eyes eagerly scanning the ocean.

Several times something in sight was reported in various directions.

But all these proved, on closer inspection, to be the tops of the waves, or else some sea bird quietly resting on the liquid element.

At length the look-out man stationed in the foretop called out that he saw some object floating that looked like a boat, but at a great distance.

Sail was accordingly made in that direction.

In about two hours they came near enough to the supposed boat to make out distinctly its true character.

It was a boat.

It was floating bottom upwards, and as it came drifting towards them, its stern being lifted up a little, they read, to their great grief, the words—

"Seagull, of Plymouth."

"Heavens!" said Meredith. "My worst fears are confirmed. The fate of our loved comrades is now too plain."

"Yes," said Captain Hastings; "in endeavouring to regain the ship, the boat must have capsized. They have perished beyond all doubt."

Mabel spoke not.

She uttered no scream of terror.

But she turned pale at these fearful words.

She clasped her hands in anguish.

She trembled fearfully.

"No, no!" she cried, in a voice terrible in its intensity of emotion, "it cannot be. Oh, do not say that they have perished!"

Her father, himself terribly agitated, supported her trembling frame in his arms.

"My dear child," he said, "bear up against it. I fear there is no hope, and to know the worst is better than continued suspense."

It was easy to speak words of consolation.

But it was difficult at such a terrible moment to derive support and relief from them.

Mabel's tears flowed freely.

They were tears of genuine, unmixed grief, unbrightened by the faintest ray of hope.

Crusoe Jack had perished!

The hope, the joy of her whole life, was blotted out.

She cared no longer for existence.

It was a burden too great to bear.

Could she live on and on through coming years, without the hope of ever again beholding the object of her first, her only love?

Was there anything in the wide world that could afford her consolation?

She knew not.

But in the cabin of the Seagull, after she had heard the fate of her lover, she experienced the bitterest, intensest anguish of despair.

Notwithstanding the uselessness of further search, Captain Hastings and Meredith were loth to leave the spot where our gallant heroes must have gone down.

All that day they cruised slowly about, not that they had the faintest hopes, but still there was a melancholy satisfaction in reflecting that they had used every effort to rescue their comrades.

At length, it being evident all further efforts were thoroughly useless, Captain Hastings reluctantly gave orders to keep the ship on her course.

With every sail set that would draw, the Seagull speeded on towards her destination.

The wind kept favourable all that day, and at sunrise next morning, the Sandwich Islands were in sight; not the principal of the group, but some outlying islands not far from the main one.

The two islands before them were very small, and a narrow channel separated them.

Beautiful indeed they looked in the bright morning sun, their shores fringed with the dark cocoa-nut trees.

It had been Captain Hastings' intention to have doubled the southernmost of these islands, but on getting within a few miles of the cape that terminates that island, the wind hauled round, and blew directly in their teeth.

As the cape stretched a good distance into the ocean, and moreover ended in a number of jagged coral-reefs, Captain Hastings decided on trying the passage between the islands.

It was practicable he knew from the charts he possessed, though it was a rather a difficult passage.

It would, however, save a considerable distance.

The vessel's bow was then pointed towards the entrance of the channel, and the Seagull had entered between the two islands.

The current was rapid, and running adverse to the course of the ship, which, but for the favourable wind, would have found it more difficult to make her way.

As it was, their progress was slow, and the most skilful seamanship was requisite to guide the vessel safely.

The circuitous form of the channel, which was besides scarcely a mile across, and the abundance of high rocks that bounded it in every direction, intercepted the breeze, which, in an open sea, would have sufficed to send the vessel along at more than double her present speed.

As they proceeded, these difficulties increased.

"This is an awkward place," remarked Mr. Meredith, as he looked anxiously over the chart with Captain Hastings. "Goodness knows how long we may be getting to Honolulu at this rate. If we could only have kept out in the open sea, how much better it would have been."

"The chart seems clear enough, however," returned the captain. "I don't think we are in much danger, though this course will undoubtedly add to the length of our journey. I am sorry we entered this channel, with such a breeze as this, too, when we might be making nine knots an hour."

By dint of continued tacking about, the vessel made good way, but at length the wind lulled gradually, and the ship made a corresponding slackening in her pace.

This greatly added to the difficulties with which the party had to contend, and it promised to make their escape from so tedious a course a matter of uncertainty.

"If we keep on in this way we shall have to anchor," said the captain, who was examining the shore through his telescope.

"When the wind goes to sleep in a place like this, it's almost impossible to get along. Get out the long line," he added to the chief mate, "and let us see if all's clear for sounding."

The order was therefore given to heave the lead, for which purpose a number of sailors took their stations on the spritsail-yard, the cat-head, the fore-chains, the waist, and the main-chains, each holding a part of the line coiled up in his hands.

The captain and Mr. Meredith watched this operation with great anxiety.

"By the mark four!" was shouted by the leadsman.

"This will do if it gets no shallower," said Meredith; "we only draw eleven feet."

The next heave of the lead less than three fathoms, showed them how suddenly the depth decreased.

This was due to the rapid formation of coral reefs, which render the charts almost useless in a few years.

The Seagull was then put about at once, and only just in time.

Another five minutes would have seen them fast upon a coral rock, the top of which they could just discern.

By dint of keeping the lead constantly going, they managed to avoid the numerous shallows; but now the wind having almost died away, they made but little way in endeavouring to stem the tide.

CHAPTER XLIV.

THE PIRATES—THE ABANDONED SHIP—THE DESPERATE POSITION OF VALDEZ — HOPES OF PLUNDER.

THE crew of the Seagull thus battling with the difficulties of their position, little suspected that they were forming an object of considerable interest to a party of men on shore.

Amid the undulations, rocks, and declivities, at some parts barren, and at others covered with all the teeming vegetation of the tropics, were many nooks, capable of affording concealment to such persons as required it.

And concealment, with an excellent cause, was certainly the object of the unseen spectators of the Seagull.

The party consisted of about twelve men, not, however, Canaccas or Sandwich Islanders, but apparently natives of every clime but that in which they were now located

They were principally Europeans, but by no means favourable specimens of the inhabitants of that pre-eminently civilised quarter of the globe.

Ragged, haggard, unshorn, sunburnt, and bearing marks of hardship and privation, which greatly increased their natural expression of ferocity, there was not a man among them but would have sufficed to inspire the mind of a spectator with terror and abhorrence.

They were evidently desperadoes of the worst class—men to whom habitual crime was not only an occupation, but a means of subsistence.

It must have failed them now, however, or they would never have been brought to such a situation as the present.

Why were they lingering and hiding on that wild region, far from the haunts either of savage or civilised men?

What chance or design led them thus to be cut off from the society of their fellow-men?

Above all, what could they be, who neither resembled the natives of the island, nor the visitors who frequented the shores of the prosperous little kingdom of Hawaii?

One word of explanation will be sufficient, or at least throw some light upon this subject.

They were Captain Valdez, the pirate, and the remains of his crew.

Standing or seated on the ground in a huddled group among the thick cocoa-nut trees, their appearance was that of a band of neglected social outcasts, presenting a great contrast to the once fierce and desperate, but dashing and triumphant crew of the pirate's vessel; and that haggard, fierce, moody-looking man, who stood apart from the rest, with his eyes fixed steadfastly on the ocean, could that be the gallant Captain Valdez?

It was, and his lieutenant, Benito, sat at some distance from him, outvying his commander in the gloom and despondency of his attitude.

What had brought this brave and reckless crew to such a deplorable condition?

Let us proceed to explain to our readers, for the narrative is one of interest.

Wind, weather, and darkness had combined to prevent the pirate chief from overtaking and boarding the Seagull.

This he had every intention of doing, for he knew he could hope to come out safely from the attack.

Seldom had defeat been his portion, and his desperate courage scorned the supposition of it.

But when in the storm that was raging his vessel had been carried so far beyond the object of attack, the opportunity was lost, and other circumstances soon combined to divert his attention from the Seagull.

As for Jack, the pirate and all on board his ship had no doubt of his fate. That he had perished in the gale was the pirate's full conviction, though his disappearance was certainly rather mysterious.

It looked almost like suicide, but surely Jack's desperation was hardly so great as to drive him to that course.

"He must have fallen overboard in the gale," was the buccaneer's comment on the event. "He was but a young sailor, poor fellow, and didn't know how to keep his position on the yards in darkness and storm. I was sorry to lose him, Benito, very sorry indeed. He was a lad of spirit, and would have been very useful to us. What a capital pirate he would have made! He had all the energy and determination and daredevil bravery that is necessary to make a first-rate sea-rover Well, he's gone, and it's no use lamenting now, though there's many a fellow among the crew I could have seen overboard with greater pleasure."

With this reflection did the rover-king dismiss from his mind a circumstance which, to one accustomed as he was to scenes of death and danger, was, after all, but a circumstance of comparatively trivial character and frequent occurrence.

His amazement would have been greater had he learned the real fate of our hero—his gallant and almost miraculous escape in the raging storm.

Other circumstances, as we have remarked, soon, in a great degree, obliterated all thoughts of Jack from the pirate's mind.

Chief among these was the chase and capture of what he considered a splendid prize.

This was no less than an English trader, bound on a cruising expedition among the Pacific Islands and along the Western Coast of America.

She had a miscellaneous cargo of European goods, consisting of articles of great variety, and some of considerable value.

Though as large as the Black Eagle, she was not so well armed—in fact, she carried only a couple of guns, and her crew was not sufficiently numerous to cope with the large and desperate crew of the gallant sea-robber.

"A chase! a chase!"—that welcome sound that thrills the heart of every pirate, and inspires him with the awakened thirst for plunder and longing for the strife—resounded through the vessel, which, with every sail set, and the wind in her favour, was soon speeding in the wake of the doomed craft.

In vain the crew of the latter became conscious of their danger.

In vain every effort was made to escape.

That was useless; and resistance, which alone remained, proved equally so.

After an exciting chase of five hours, during which the powers of both vessels were strained to the utmost, the pirate at length succeeded in overtaking his prey.

The heavily-laden trader proved herself to be, unfortunately, no match in speed for the light, swift, active vessel, which fully deserved her appellation, the Black Eagle.

Desperate was the stand made by the trader's crew, even when overtaken.

But the short struggle which ensued showed how unavailing was all the bravery they could display.

The vessel, with all its wealth, was seized by the pirates.

The crew were confined in chains, and the greater part of the cargo removed from the ship to that of the pirates.

With a degree of prudence and foresight that distinguished him from many others of his desperate trade, Valdez also took possession of a considerable amount of spare masts, sails, and rigging which was carried by the English vessel.

Never had he taken a better haul, and with more marked and complete success.

Such articles of value as were most easily portable, and occupied the smallest space, were, of course, preferred.

Of these the pirate had soon as much as his vessel could conveniently hold.

A considerable quantity of less valuable goods, however, he left untouched, as he found they might incommode his subsequent flight.

Then the renowned pirate-chief performed a ceremony which was habitual to him in taking his prizes, and which showed the vaunting desperation of his character.

This was marking the ship with some memento of his victory.

For this purpose, he placed one of his own blood-red flags on the mast-head, with the well-known Black Eagle represented on it, and under that the dreaded name, Valdez.

As the crew were all in chains below, they would be for some time unable to displace the signal of defeat, which could not fail to be observed by any vessel which might overtake them.

With this he also put up a signal of distress.

"There! that's what I call showing the world what I can do," remarked the daring adventurer, as he prepared to leave the ship. "What's the use of achieving a victory and not getting any fame for it? I don't see why a sea-fight, fairly won, is not as great an affair as a battle on land. Whatever vessel overtakes this one will fancy that they have caught the renowned Valdez, and that he is making signals of distress; but, on coming nearer—ha! ha!—how much they will be undeceived at finding the true state of the case!"

Thus exulting in his victory, the pirate left his prize on the open ocean, the crew helpless, and the vessel plundered of all her valuable treasures, and much damaged by the recent encounter.

"Now, Benito," said the pirate chief, "I mean to turn honest for a little while."

"Turn honest?" said the lieutenant, in some amazement.

"Yes, Benito. Honesty is the best policy after all. To get rid of goods such as we've got aboard now, I mean to transform myself into an honest trader for the nonce. I mean to become Captain John Smith, of London, and trade among the Sandwichers and along the American coast with all these honest goods."

"A rather difficult job though, captain, on the well-known and dreaded Black Eagle."

"Ah! but I'm such a magician that I can change anything—the ship included—at a moment's notice. So, with a little paint, and rigging her up like a brig, I'll turn the dreaded Black Eagle, of Anywhere, to the peaceful trader, Mary Jane, of London!"

Acting on this ingenious suggestion, the crew so soon transformed the vessel that she stood little chance of being recognised by her enemies.

Under the guise of Captain Smith, of the Mary Jane, Valdez made a long cruise—first among the South Pacific Islands, and latterly to the Sandwich group, and the more northern part of the great ocean achipelago.

He disposed of his cargo to great advantage among savages, to whom European goods were great luxuries, and who were willing to purchase them at a high price.

The inhabitants of the Sandwich Islands especially (who are far more advanced in civilisation than any other of the South Sea Islanders) made good customers to the supposed English ship, and paid for their purchases in good American dollars, instead of articles of barter.

The captain had good cause to plume himself on his address and ingenuity which had enabled him unsuspected to make such good use of his plunder.

He at first contemplated a lengthened stay at the Sandwich Islands, but he could find no place where he could with safety conceal the immense treasure he had on board with safety; and besides, among the many English and American vessels that thronged the port of Honolulu, he might at last be recognised by some of his foes, or, at all events, fall under suspicion.

"I'll make for the West Indies after this cruise," he said. "I have friends there, and I shall be able safely to dispose of our wealth."

But how little did the rover chief calculate on the chance of events!

How little did he imagine how soon retribution would overtake him, and turn his triumph into despair!

With a considerable quantity of the cargo still on board, as well as the secret treasure, he set sail from Honolulu under favourable auspices.

His intention was to make the best of his way to Central America, and dispose of the rest of his cargo in his new character.

For a time the weather was extremely favourable.

The first day the captain had cause to congratulate himself on the swiftness of his gallant vessel.

Towards evening the aspect of the sky became extremely threatening.

The wind veered round to the eastward.

It blew strongly from that quarter, compelling the pirate to reduce his canvas.

The wind continued to increase.

Towards night it blew a perfect hurricane.

The gale continued without abatement all that night.

Next morning it had, if anything, become worse.

Valdez cursed the obstinacy of the wind, in blowing from the very direction he wanted to go.

He earnestly scanned the heavens, in hopes of seeing some probability of a change.

Towards noon he was gratified by the wind first falling to a dead calm, then a few puffs came from the westward.

All sail was then set to catch the breeze.

The brig was once more set on her course.

This favourable change did not last long.

The wind soon veered round to the eastward again, and began to blow very strong.

Captain Valdez was loth to take in sail till it was unavoidable, but finding that he must either ease the ship or lose his masts, he reluctantly gave orders to reduce canvas.

Before the sailors could start tack or sheet, a strong blast made the brig reel over till her yards dipped.

At the same time the cargo shifted over to leeward, bringing her still further on her side.

"Bring axes!" shouted Valdez, "Be smart, men, for your lives! Cut away the weather lanyards of the mainmast!"

Extended to their utmost power of endurance by the vast weight they upheld, the lanyards parted one after another at the first blow of the axe.

Then came a loud, crashing noise.

The mainmast fell over the side.

"Does she come up at all?" shouted Valdez, to the man at the wheel.

"No, sir—not an inch," was the reply.

"Then cut away the foremast!" cried Valdez.

A few strokes from the keen axe, and the foremast also yielded, and tumbled into the sea.

To their dismay, however, the vessel refused, even after this, to right herself.

It was evident that all the ballast must have shifted, and that in a very short time she would go down.

All discipline was now lost on board the ill-fated craft.

In vain Valdez exerted himself to maintain order.

For a time his efforts were unheeded.

The weather quarter boat was filled with about fifteen of the pirates, and they endeavoured to lower her, but she was smashed to pieces alongside the vessel.

In spite of their comrades' efforts to save them, but two escaped.

A mighty wave now struck the unfortunate craft, and swept half-a-dozen more of the pirates into the deep, beyond all hope of rescue.

Captain Valdez then called to the remnant of his crew, consisting of about a dozen, to help him launch the longboat, which perhaps might live in that rough sea.

After long and difficult labour, this was done; and hastily conveying all the provisions they could get at, they left the wreck.

They were compelled to leave behind them all the wealth they had accumulated—even the treasure chest.

It was impossible to get at it; besides, they expected the vessel to go down every moment, and they did not like to lose time even for their precious gold.

They managed to get safe from the wreck.

Spreading what little sail they dared, they contrived to keep their little vessel before the wind, back in the direction of Honolulu.

They continued on this course all night and next day.

On the third day from leaving the wreck, they landed safely on one of the outlying Sandwich Islands.

Their lives had been mercifully saved, but their situation was anything but enviable.

Every farthing of the vast treasures that had rewarded their many successful plundering expeditions was lost beyond any hope of recovery.

The vast ocean, on whose bosom they had obtained so much ill-gotten wealth, had engulphed it in a fit of grim retribution.

In the hour of Captain Valdez's triumph, he found himself suddenly ruined.

An immense fortune for himself, and a competency for every member of the crew—an amount of wealth on which each and all could have turned honest, and have done some good to atone for their many evil deeds—lay useless in the vast abyss of the ocean.

Never was the pirate chief so filled with consternation, rage, and despair.

His triumph was turned into wretchedness.

With the remnant of a powerful and gallant crew—but how wretched and reduced a remnant!—he might have done something to retrieve his fortunes, if his vessel had been spared him, but even that was utterly destroyed.

Without money, without friends—but rather hundreds of deadly enemies, ready to deliver him up to justice, if they discovered his identity—what could Captain Valdez do?

He at first contrived to take what advantage he could of circumstances, by carrying out his disguise of an honest English trader.

He pretended still to be Captain John Smith, of London, who had been thus disastrously shipwrecked, and who solicited the assistance of the benevolent on behalf of his gallant and unfortunate crew.

He said he only wished for sufficient money to take them home to England.

The appeal was not unheeded.

The brave Hawaiians, and the foreign residents, were ready to help Captain Smith, and liberal in their manner of doing so.

He was for some time the lion of the nation.

His bravery was extolled, his misfortunes deplored, and both he and his crew treated with great benevolence.

But many experienced English and American captains had their suspicions.

They began to believe that Captain Smith and his crew were impostors, to make awkward inquiries as to their ship, and what port in England they sailed from.

They even began to suspect that he had been engaged in piracy, or at least some contraband trade.

The so-called Captain Smith soon found the island too hot to hold him, and when at length he was recognised by a former victim, and the whole affair disclosed, he saw that the crisis of danger had arrived.

He would have left the island, but he had no ship, and he knew how dangerous it would be to attempt to get a passage on any vessel.

Everybody was anxious to capture him, and claim the reward set upon his head.

There was no way of leaving the island.

Even his boat had been knocked to pieces on his escape.

So Captain Valdez and his crew took the only course open to them.

They fled into the woods, and subsisted, like savages, on the wild productions of that fruitful country.

Amid the thick tropical vegetation, the varieties of hill and dale, the abundance of rocks and defiles, admirably suited for concealment, they might have contrived to evade pursuit, and live agreeably on the natural productions of the country, but that they were surrounded by enemies, who pressed them very sorely.

All through the islands continual chases were made.

The reward stimulated everybody to exertion, and that the renowned pirate was not caught was owing only to his own dexterity and valour.

But it was a wretched existence.

Perpetual concealment, without clothes, ammunition, or the necessaries of civilised life.

No wonder the pirate and his men were despondent.

No wonder they were ragged, haggard, and presented the appearance of hunted wild beasts.

Adversity had overtaken them, and their former crimes were being fearfully atoned for.

The small island to which they had at length contrived to escape presented great facilities for concealment.

Here they found themselves more safe than at any other part.

The place was very sequestered, thinly inhabited, and considered the wildest portion of the Hawaiian king's territory.

The appearance of an English vessel, therefore, in so unfrequented a spot was of course a matter of curiosity and interest.

The concealed outcasts, on seeing her heaving in sight, started up with eagerness.

It seemed to them an epoch in their lives—the turning point of their fate.

How much their surprise increased when Valdez, looking at the vessel attentively, suddenly exclaimed—

"Per Baccho! It's the Seagull!"

CHAPTER XLV.
THE COUNCIL OF THE PIRATES—CONSPIRACY—A CUNNING SCHEME.

"It's the Seagull!"

At these words every member of the outcast pirate band started up, as if electrified.

The exclamation had on them almost the effect of a magic spell.

It was not that they had anything in particular to hope or to fear from the appearance of the gallant vessel.

It was not the hope of seizing her, nor the dread that Captain Hastings might wreak upon them some terrible vengeance, nor was it entirely amazement at so unexpected an apparition, but a mixture of all three impressions.

All the rovers thronged around their chief.

Every eye was strained in the direction of the interesting spectacle, and each pirate speedily satisfied himself by the evidence of his own senses of the truth of the captain's exclamation.

Concealed among the wild, wooded undulations of the shore, they had ample opportunity to observe the vessel's movements, themselves unseen by those on board.

"*Carrajo!* But I was never more surprised in my life!" and Valdez, gazing as if fascinated on the form of the ship. "It is our old friend, or rather enemy, as sure as fate! There is not anything I so little expected to see!—such a large vessel and more especially this one. I wonder what brought her here?"

"And I wonder where she is bound for, now she is here?" added Benito.

"To Honolulu, probably; but she'll never make it in this gale. Her coming through such a dangerous place as this shows her crew's ignorance of the coast."

"They'll be ready to repent it when she strikes on one of the reefs yonder."

How she tacks about!" exclaimed Valdez, "and in first-rate style, too. Depend upon it those on board her know how to manage a ship. It was a bold stroke, trying to get through this channel; but if it's to be done, they'll do it."

"What a capital prize she'd make!" suddenly exclaimed one of the pirates.

These words had a most powerful effect upon his companions.

They looked at each other with an expression which showed how completely they acquiesced in this sentiment.

The thirst for plunder and wild excitement was awakened in every breast.

The captain was not exempt from the same feelings, but he knew how useless it would be to entertain them.

"A prize?" he cried. "Yes, she would, indeed. No one knows that better than we do, and no one knows more thoroughly how difficult a prize to obtain. We tried to board her when we had every advantage, a powerful crew and a trusty ship, and even then we failed. What chance, then, should we have, situated as we are now?"

Everybody was silent, for the truth of these words were too self-evident not to be immediately felt.

Still, the pirate's eyes glistened in a wild, passionate longing, as he gazed at the ship.

"Diavolo!" he cried, stamping with impatient fury. "How vilely fate has used me! To see a fine ship like that, with no chance of taking her, drives me almost to madness. Here's a splendid chance of bettering ourselves, and here we stand, outcast, starving, reduced in numbers, and without arms and ammunition. With a few canoes, and a dozen and a half of muskets or so, we might do something even now; but as it is, any attempt to attack them would be worse than useless—it would be dangerous."

"We are not in a position, though, to stick at danger, I think, captain," remarked one of the pirates, who was apparently more desperate and venturesome than his commander.

"No, Carlo, not if it is likely to lead to success; but as it is—there, it is useless to talk about it. And yet," he added, still watching the ship with longing eyes, "the sight of such a chance to get away from this accursed island, and, what's more, commence our old cruising life again, is almost enough to make a man dare anything."

A short pause, during which each member of the pirate band seemed occupied with his own reflections.

"She'll not need any attack to be destroyed, I am thinking, as appearances go now," remarked the captain, at length. "This tacking about's dangerous work in such a channel as this, and there are plenty of rocks remarkably handy. Well, here's my wish to you, my friend, Seagull—may you and your whole crew go to the bottom!"

It was with fierce envious asperity that the desperado uttered this malignant wish, which, indeed, stood some chance of being verified.

The gallant Seagull, which had passed so victoriously through so many dangers, was now experiencing far from the least of them.

Never was there a more tedious and difficult passage than that of the channel she was now in.

Mr. Meredith, Captain Hastings, and Hayward, the mate, all acknowledged that they had made a mistake in entering it, and that it would have been better had they tried to double the headland.

But now it was too late to rectify their error, and, indeed, under the pressing force of the weather, it was doubtful if it would have been practicable to do so.

The chief aim of the vessel was, of course, to keep out in the open part of the channel, and avoid the shore as much as possible.

This also enabled her to catch the wind, and take advantage, as far as possible, of its various movements; but these were so capricious and perpetual in their changes that the progress of the vessel continued to be extremely circuitous, slow, and uncertain.

The pirates on shore watched these movements with as much interest as if their own fates were bound up in that of the vessel.

The Seagull seemed to have a fascination to them.

"If there were any way," mused Valdez, "of getting some good out of this precious vessel, then I'd retract my wish and hope she *wouldn't* go down. We're terribly in need of supplies—biscuits, and rum, and tobacco, and that—for I'm sick of existing on these wild bananas and cocoa-nuts. If we could only, by any chance, get something good out of the vessel yonder, I should not so much care."

"It would be indeed a fine thing to get what we all so much long for," returned Benito, "which includes arms and ammunition. But that, of course, is out of the question. It would scarcely be very sensible to go to our mortal enemies for weapons to use against them—something like asking a lion for the loan of his claws."

"Is there no scheme by which we could ascertain the present strength of the crew on board?" asked Valdez. "Come, Benito, set your wits to work, and think of some stratagem that will serve us. It's nothing short of a complete sin to let the vessel go by without getting *some* advantage out of her. Force is impossible; but cunning may do something."

Benito pondered.

Valdez looked at him anxiously, as did all the rest of the pirates.

"We're so precious sure to be recognised, captain," remarked one of the rovers. "I think we've seen and felt enough of what the Seagull crew can do; and if they came across us again "—and here he paused, as if fearful of thinking what might be the consequences

"I'm not quite so sure of that," returned the rover chief. "We are very much changed since our last attack. That wreck and the hardships we've been through have turned us all into such scarecrows as we would have scorned a short month ago. Donnerwetter! if I could see myself in a mirror now, I'll warrant I should not believe I was Captain Valdez."

"This very circumstance may be turned to account," said Benito. "The mere fact of our being so changed gives us some little hope of success. We ought to try and make ourselves as unlike ourselves as possible."

"Well, and what then?" asked the captain.

"Couldn't one of us make signals to be taken aboard, and offer to pilot the ship."

Valdez shook his head.

"That would not be much use," he said. "We don't look like pilots. We look like just what we are—outcasts and wanderers. Besides, supposing one of us as a pilot, and a couple more as assistants, were to be accepted on board, what then?"

"Just this. The vessel is now in some difficulties. She'll never get through this channel—or, at least, not without great time and difficulty. Now, a pilot who could steer her safely out of this difficulty would be very welcome to the crew."

"But if the whole of us were taken on board and steered safely into Honolulu, you will admit we shall have done no wise trick—only run our heads into the lion's mouth!"

"You don't fully understand my scheme. It is this. One of us goes on board, offers himself as pilot, says, if asked, that he is an American who has lived for some time in the Sandwich Islands, and knows every rock about this coast. He can declare that, on seeing the ship struggling up the channel, he determined to offer his services to take her into the nearest port. Once accepted, he can say that the ship wants more men to man her."

"Well?" said the captain.

"Acting on his pretence, he may bring the rest of his companions aboard, who will take their place with the other sailors. Then, the first thing he'll do is to turn the ship's head back, and make for the entrance of the channel again, under pretence that it is full of rocks and shoals ahead, that it would be highly dangerous to attempt to navigate it."

"But, would they believe all this, Benito?"

"That is the chance. If they do, there is some hope of ultimate success. Once on board, and forming part of the crew, we may by stratagem make ourselves masters of the vessel. The pilot can keep her beating about at least until night comes, and then we can easily manage so that our party shall keep one of the night watches. The captain and the crew once below are easily secured, a rush must be made to the cabin to get the weapons, and then it will be our own fault if we don't turn the Seagull into a pirate vessel."

Loud and boisterous expressions of approval came from the outcasts.

"Well, Benito," said the buccaneer chief, with some satisfaction, "there's certainly something in what you propose. But you have forgotten one great point—the crew of the Seagull are far superior to us in numbers."

"But the stratagem I have suggested," returned Benito, "will enable our small party—provided they unite in one sudden and vigorous action—to be more than a match for all of them."

Valdez fully appreciated the ingenuity and, at the same time, the danger of this scheme.

One important drawback, however, especially presented itself to him.

"The difficulty will be in the first part of our conspiracy," he said. "When you or I present ourselves on board, we very likely shall not be recognised as old enemies. But our ragged appearance—and I don't see the least means of altering it—will still tell against us, and suspicion will be aroused when we talk about bringing our fellows on board."

"But 'any port in a storm,' you know," said Benito; "and, I may add, 'any pilot on an unknown coast.'"

"That proverb won't always hold good, Benito. The Seagull is manned by able sailors; and, depend upon it, they'd sooner trust to their chart and their own skill than take any suspicious character on board."

"Then my suggestion," Benito said, in a dejected voice, "falls to the ground."

"Not entirely," was the captain's response. "I admit it to be admirable so far as the method of seizing the ship goes, but the first part's not so clear. We are all right when once on board; but the thing is to get there, and that will take a deeper scheme than yours to accomplish."

"What, then, do you propose?" asked Benito.

"Why, I've just thought of a plan! Carrambo! a splendid one, if well accomplished—that cannot fail to get us berths on board the ship without suspicion."

"What is your grand scheme, then?"

"A brilliant one, and one not thought of before. Suppose we have a sham wreck?"

"A what?" cried Benito, in amazement, which was audibly shared by his companions.

The idea of a sham wreck seemed to them very extraordinary.

Real wrecks were bad enough, as they knew to their cost.

"Yes," proceeded Valdez, much excited. "Suppose we make a raft—it will not be difficult to do that in these parts—and, unseen by the crew of the Seagull, put out on the other side of the island, and steer round to the open sea just where we can intercept her course. Then, when she has passed the channel—which she may do safely to-morrow, if the wind changes—the first thing she'll see on the open sea will be a raft drifting about in the open sea, with a lot of shipwrecked seamen on it, making signals of distress."

"Splendid, captain! splendid!" cried several pirates, in admiration.

"Don't you see how our appearance favours the deception?" continued Valdez. "We look like shipwrecked seamen—indeed, what else are we?—and the generous Captain Hastings cannot refuse to take us up. When questioned, we can declare that we belonged to a Spanish or American ship which foundered out in the open sea during the gale, and that we are the only men saved out of forty or four hundred—anything you like. I'll leave that to you, Benito—you are such a genius for fictions of that sort. Then I think we can manage to disarm suspicion."

"There is only one drawback to this admirable scheme," remarked the cautious Benito. "And that is, that we are so closely watched, as you know, by the vessels of the Sandwich Islands, who are all on the alert to catch us. It would be dangerous to attempt to leave the island on a raft. They'd give chase directly, and then where should we be?"

"Safe, I hope," replied the pirate chief. "It won't do, Benito, to be too cautious, I know. I'm desperate, and ready to dare even capture sooner than continue such a life as this. There is another advantage in our scheme. That if the Seagull don't pick us up, some other vessel will, and we shall have our choice of benefactors, whom we can repay with our peculiar mode of gratitude."

"But suppose our rescuers recognise us?" said Benito.

"Little fear of that. We have lived so long wild in the woods here that we look far more like savages than ever the islanders did even in the days of Captain Cook. It will be as difficult to many people to recognise Captain Smith as Captain Valdez."

"We must, however, try this scheme," said Benito. "But night is the only time when we can hope to do it successfully. There is little chance but what the Seagull will be beating about this channel all night."

"None at all," acquiesced Valdez, turning again to the ship. "She won't make much way before the morning, and will have a hard time of it unless she anchors."

"Ah, if she anchors!" was echoed from mouth to mouth.

That would indeed have offered a better chance of success to the conspirators than even the subtle scheme the captain had propounded.

If the Seagull anchored near the land, and any of her crew came ashore, the pirates might attack them, cut them off from their party, and seize their boats.

Such a chance would open a prospect of fulfilling, by one bold vigorous stroke, the dearly cherished hope of the pirate crew.

But then, again, the Seagull might anchor far out in the channel, and hold no communication with the land.

Then the pirates would be powerless to carry out their design.

It was curious that the identical thought entertained by the pirate chief was at the same time passing through the mind of Captain Hastings.

"We shall have to anchor if the weather continues like this," he remarked to Mr. Meredith. "It will be tedious to remain here all night, but we could scarcely be making less way than we are now. I have a presentiment that we shall have better weather to-morrow, and then we can make up for lost time."

Notwithstanding this assertion, the captain was very reluctant to pursue this course, and continued deferring the orders necessary for its accomplishment.

The pirates fully resolved on carrying out their intention of making a raft.

They only wondered that the ingenious device of a mock shipwreck had never struck them before.

It was, however, they knew, one difficult of accomplishment—not so much in its ultimate part as the preliminary step of leaving the island.

Ever since they had, in imminent peril, fled to this place of refuge, their capture, as we have stated, had been continually attempted, and only warded off by their own skill in taking advantage of the thick forests and defiles with which the island abounded.

It was seldom they ventured near the shore.

They knew there were always many speedy vessels in sight of the island, which formed a perpetual menace.

They precluded the hope of escape.

Night was the only time when any chance offered itself.

They had no boat.

They had no tools to make one.

Whither could they have gone if they had?

They could only hope to drift out on the surface of the ocean with but the faintest chance of final escape.

The novel idea of the mock shipwreck, however, opened up a path out of all these difficulties.

A raft was not difficult to make.

They had only to get together some of the logs and fallen trunks that abounded in the forest, and secure them together by means of the long grass and vegetable fibres that grew in luxuriance around.

Whe wood was admirably adapted for the purpose.

The largest and longest log was to be placed in the centre.

The others were to be fastened to it.

A couple of squares, or large planks, set up vertically at the stem and stern, would serve, by moving them in accordance with the direction of the wind, to regulate the movements of the raft.

This mode of constructing vessels had been learnt by Captain Valdez in South America, where the natives employ rafts thus made, (called balsas) for all purposes of navigation.

Valdez suggested that if, when out at sea, they should be picked up by the Seagull, or any other vessel, they would declare that they had formed the raft of the drift-wood that was frequently met with floating about the island, and that they had providentially contrived to cling to it just at the time when the vessel went down.

They had no doubt that this pretext would be sufficient to disarm the suspicion of those whom they treacherously intended to make their victims.

So, as soon as night fell, they launched it from one of the creeks of the channel, at some distance from the Seagull.

The result fully realised their expectations.

The raft was completely watertight, of convenient size, and presenting just the appearance that would correspond with their concerted false account of its construction.

The pirates embarked on their extemporaneous vessel, with such necessaries as their situation enabled them to procure.

Previous to their departure they made a thorough examination of the adjoining coast and seas, to satisfy themselves that they were not perceived by any of the native vessels.

The intricacies of the channel would easily enable them to avoid the observation of the Seagull's crew, who, besides, were not likely to be keeping a very strict watch; for the wind had now considerably abated, and the sea had become so calm that a ship could scarcely have made more progress than in the late veering gales.

The Seagull lay so still that the pirates believed she had anchored.

The moon was shining brightly in the heavens, but ever and anon obscured by dense masses of clouds.

As the pirates' party put out from the shore the silver queen of night, suddenly emerged from her cloudy surroundings, lighting up the waves, and shining full on the path of the adventurers.

CHAPTER XLVI.

THE PIRATES ON THE RAFT—THEIR DANGER AND THEIR DELIVERANCE.

THE pirates had now embarked upon about the wildest and most venturesome enterprise they had ever taken part in.

As things looked now, however, it promised a successful result, at least, so far that they would leave the island behind them.

They were literally casting themselves upon the mercy of the ocean, which had been the scene of so many crimes, so many dangers, so many triumphs.

Men of their stamp, accustomed to continual dangers, and rapid alternatives of good and ill-luck, are ever full of confidence, which no reverses can completely quench.

They looked upon the present scheme—wild and preposterous as it really was—as one certain to lead to some ultimate advantage.

They followed their dauntless captain with good will and confidence.

"If we go out of one danger into another," remarked Captain Valdez, as he ordered his men to put out the raft from shore, "which we may be doing by this expedition, I must say that I'd sooner go through the worst that's likely to happen to us at sea, than stand any more of such a life as we've had on this accursed island, where we've been mewed up almost like rabbits in a burrow."

"It will certainly be most agreeable," returned Benito, "to escape from such a position; but let us take care that we don't find ourselves trapped like fish in a net by some of our American or Hawaiian enemies."

"By San José! Benito!" cried the captain, impatiently; "you are the nearest approach to a raven—to be a seaman and a brave man—that ever I met with. You are always croaking out danger, whether there is any or not."

"That's very likely, captain; but it's always best to be on the safe side, and be prepared for the worst that may happen. If everybody did this, many dangers might be safely evaded."

As the Malay gave vent to this delightful bit of moralising, the raft shot out into the channel, and the pirates were able to take a good observation of the position of the Seagull.

She lay, scarcely moving, at a quarter of a mile distant from them, her head pointing the opposite way to that in which, to escape observation, the pirates were steering.

Their intention was to gain the open seas, and, keeping as far out as possible, work gradually round the headland, so as to meet the Seagull

afterwards, and, if possible, put their pre-arranged scheme into execution.

"She's as fast asleep as a dormouse!" exclaimed the pirate, gazing eagerly at the vessel. "Every width of canvas set, and not moving an inch. How I wish the crew were all fast asleep too, and, likely to remain so while we boarded her. She's just the cut I admire," he added, critically; "long in the hull, sharp in the bows, and yet strong enough to carry such an armoury as would overawe every enemy we have. With the Seagull in our possession we might do anything. And we'll have her yet, as sure as my name's Valdez! But, pshaw! what am I talking about? What chance have we against such a crew, and such a vessel?"

"Not much, captain," returned Benito; "and I think the best thing we can do is to leave off wishing, and make the best of our present chances."

"You are right, Benito. Your advice is always good, after all," returned the captain. "By Jupiter! they'll see us if we don't look out! Steady, my boys; put her back a bit. We must make for the entrance of the channel. Once meet a bit of breeze in the open sea, and I know how to make our *balsa* go along like a revenue cutter."

But after events proved how vain was the captain's boast—how mistaken the confidence with which he endeavoured to inspire his men.

They steered safe out of the channel, and soon left the Seagull far behind.

They met no vessels, nor any indications that their escape was discovered.

By these means, they got safely out into the open sea, and as a light breeze began to spring up, the captain was able to guide his primitive craft with considerable skill and effect.

But a great deal of veering and tacking about was required.

The raft made but slight progress in the direction he desired to reach.

All that day the pirates were on the open sea.

The winds had again begun to be so adverse that they relinquished their intention of intercepting the Seagull, and kept out before the wind in hopes of finding some vessel that would pick them up.

None, however, appeared.

They began to realize the full extent of the dangers into which they had voluntarily rushed.

The wind increased as the day advanced.

They soon found they had no control over their frail vessel.

At length a violent squall arose, and they were completely at its mercy.

Its violence continued to increase; and all the mighty powers of the waves, the lightning and thunder, were aroused.

Bitterly did the pirates lament their rash and ill-judged expedition.

Their danger was now imminent.

They had intended to feign shipwreck, as a means of rescue, and now its real horrors had come upon them.

Far out on the bosom of the angry ocean, without sufficient food or water to last them more than a day, exposed to all the perils they knew so well and dreaded so much, they had indeed good reason to curse the infatuated folly that had brought them to such a pass.

The raft was tossed upon the crest of the enormous billows with a violence which threatened every moment to dash it to pieces.

Frail and light as it was, it formed but a poor defence against the giant fury of the engulphing waves.

It was with the utmost difficulty the half-drowned wretches could cling on to this last shred of safety.

All their necessaries were soon washed overboard, and this they had no power to prevent.

Their anxiety was, perforce, centred in the preservation of their own lives.

Hope seemed almost madness yet, still they clung to it with the proverbial tenacity of men in their terrible situation.

The darkness that overspread the sky, deepening the ordinary hue of night by the darker powers of the tempest, would have rendered it a matter of impossibility to have seen any ship, even if any had appeared that might rescue them.

Thus passed the night.

The day, while it exhibited some abatement of the storm's violence, brought but little alleviation to their sufferings.

They were alive; it is true, but in such a plight as rendered life scarcely endurable.

The pangs of hunger had begun to take hold of them.

That maddening thirst, which the water around mocks like a fiend exulting in a deadly temptation, began to oppress them.

Bodily weakness was added to mental desperation.

They had not yet arrived at that fearful climax of despair when the most horrible of all necessities—the necessity of cannibalism—should fill their minds; but they knew that, unless succour arrived, it would come at last.

To heighten the horror of the situation, if any thing were needed for that purpose, one of the pirates had the reputation of having lived on human flesh.

The circumstances were as follows:—

Once, when in the Dutch merchant service, the ship in which he served foundered, and he with seven others were the only ones saved.

They had succeeded in hurling officers, crew, and passengers, amongst the latter several women, on one side, while they with a mad rush lowered the only available boat, and jumping off pushed her rapidly away from the ship's side.

They had shame enough left to feel that they had acted like brutes. They soon found that, like brutes, they had acted without thought or reason.

They had forgotten that food was a necessity for existence.

Their mistake was soon discovered.

When the pangs of hunger had gnawed their vitals for many a weary hour, two or three of them began to look with frightful meaning at one another, as one of the weakest seemed about to sink under his terrible position.

Without any words one of the mutineers, for such they were, came to a tacit understanding that the weakest should die—or be killed, it mattered little which—and then, horrible thought, eaten!

By this time one of the boat's crew was dead, and the four would-be flesh-eaters, now in a majority, boldly seized the body, and commenced hacking the flesh away with their knives, and ravenously stuffing it into their mouths.

The other three refused to participate in the ghoulish banquet, and, in turn, met the same fate.

At last, when the cannibals were looking with longing eyes at one another, a sail appeared.

They were all four saved, and, having coined a story to suit the occasion, were put on the books of the vessel which saved them.

The horrible truth leaked out, however, and the cannibals had to leave the ship to save their lives from their messmates' fury.

How the one in question became a pirate is not in our province to narrate.

But, even among the scourings of the seas, with whom he now messed, he was looked upon with horror and disgust, as the rumour spread that he was a cannibal.

What, then, must have been the feelings of those with whom he was now cast away?

His presence must have brought the horrid fact vividly before their minds, that, unless a miracle occurred, some of them would probably share the fate of his former messmates.

Now was surely the time, if ever, to repent of past crimes—to feel their sufferings as a deserved punishment.

Now was the time to make sincere resolutions of amendment, if their lives were ultimately spared.

Did that lawless crew experience any of these feelings?

We cannot think but what they did.

Men of their class are at least proverbially superstitious, though hardened.

They could not but believe that their afflictions were the work of some avenging power.

It is certain that Valdez, being a man of better education and originally of better character than most of his companions, reflected more deeply, and began to entertain some feelings of remorse for the ill deeds that had produced so fearful a retribution.

Pale, emaciated, and with a wild, haggard countenance and demeanour, the pirate chieftain sat in the centre of the raft by the stump of the temporary mast which the wind had broken.

He gazed, with hopeless fixedness, over the stormy surface of the ocean.

The raft was still tossing about from side to side, though far less violently than before; but it made no progress; it was still at the mercy of the waves.

The breeze had considerably abated, but was still violent, capricious, and changing.

The sky was less black, but still shrouded by heavy masses of clouds, while on the horizon it was clear; indeed, too clear, for how welcome would have been the merest speck to indicate an approaching sail!

But no such sign was visible.

There was no hope of such an event.

Nothing but the most merciful chance could direct a vessel to their path, for the pirates were now thoroughly beyond all calculation of their position.

They might be but a few miles, or a hundred, from the land; they knew not, but the danger was great in either case.

To attempt to guide the raft would have been a task as hopeless as impracticable.

THE CASTAWAYS' VIEW THE BURNING SHIP.

CHAPTER XLVII.

RESCUE OF THE PIRATE CREW—THE CAPTURE OF
THE AMERICAN VESSEL.

WITH sullen terror the pirates had now abandoned themselves to their fate, when, with an unearthly shriek, Benito sprang to his feet and shouted—

"A sail! A sail!"

In an instant all the crew of the raft seemed galvanised into life, as they started up, and gazed piercingly in the direction indicated by Benito.

There, sure enough, was a white speck in the distance, which none but those accustomed to a "look-out," could have told from a sea-bird.

Gradually she drew nearer to the raft.

Would she see them, or would she pass them by, and leave them to their terrible fate?

Doubt was soon removed; she was rapidly bearing down on them.

She was now near enough for Valdez and Benito to make out that she was an American trader.

Untaught by the terrible lesson they had not yet recovered from, the pirate and his lieutenant began scheming how their accident might be turned to their advantage.

Valdez was the first to speak.

"I have it," he said, "we will carry out our original intention; once let us get on board, and the Yankee will soon be ours."

"How so?" asked Benito.

"Why, when we are taken on board, we will feign extreme exhaustion, and, without narrating our adventures, ask to be allowed to pitch ourselves down anywhere. We must so arrange our positions that the whole deck shall be under our command. Then when only the watch are left on deck, we can soon master them, and as the half-sleeping crew come tumbling up from below, we can soon secure them. and by having the boat ready lowered. we can throw them one by one into her, until we are sole masters of the ship."

"A noble scheme." cried Benito.

In a few words the pirate crew were informed of the scheme, and one and all expressing approval, they awaited the arrival of the American.

At last she hailed them, but they, as arranged, pretended to be too exhausted to answer, and when taken on board by the ship's boat, they threw themselves down on deck, and asked for food and water, which were soon brought.

The captain of the Yankee singled out Valdez as being chief man among the party, and began questioning him as to his position.

Valdez begged that he and his crew might be allowed to rest where they were, promising that in the morning they would give the story of their wreck.

Gradually the shadows of night drew over the ship, and as everything soon became quiet. save the tramp of the men on watch. the pirates began to brace themselves up for the struggle which was about to take place.

Exhausted as they had really become by their long exposure and fasting, the excitement of their position lent them almost fabulous strength.

At last Valdez gave a low whistle, and in an instant the pirates sprang to their feet, and. each seizing the man who was nearest to him, pinioned him with the loose ropes that were lying on deck ; while the remainder of the pirates stood at the hatchways to seize the crew as, roused by the noise, they came from below.

The American captain was the first to appear, and seeing his men bound and prostrate he shouted—"Treachery ! treachery ! "

In an instant he was gagged, and thrown heavily on his back, but his shout had warned those below. and they did not come tumbling into the trap set for them.

An alteration of their plans was inevitable.

Valdez now ordered his men to bind all of the crew who were on deck together, and then directed them to go below and seize the crew one by one and bring them on deck, while he and Benito lowered the boat.

With a wild shout of triumph his men hastened to obey this order, which was speedily accomplished.

The boat was soon lowered, and a general rush was made to the cabins by parties of armed pirates, against whom twice the number of their now helpless foes could make no resistance.

In a few minutes, amid an uproar and commotion that had now spread throughout the vessel on the former crew finding how they had been treacherously entrapped, all the principal officers were bound securely, and hurried on to the deck, and slipped over the side into the boat.

The American captain, who had by this time contrived to get his mouth out of the gag, gave vent to an explosion of rage and maledictions on his victors at finding himself disposed of.

"You darned sneaking everlasting villains !" he cried, "after my saving your lives, and treating you as honest men ! Darn me thoroughly, if ever I come across a crew on a raft again, if I don't leave 'em to die like dogs !"

"That's well resolved, captain !" cried Valdez, in sarcastic triumph ; "but we're not so completely ungrateful as you think. We will give you provisions and water, and some of your money. You'll be picked up safely, soon, probably. It's only turn and turn about. Now, my men, up with the other prisoners !"

Benito had meantime gone below. informed the conquered men that his party had got possession of the ship, and told them how they intended to set adrift all who refused to join the pirates.

A few of the most desperate volunteered to take the latter course.

Several others of the most experienced of the seamen were selected to become pirates without their own consent.

This, while it would augment the rover's crew to the number of twenty, would yet leave the original party so far in the majority over the new members that they could easily crush any attempt at insubordination on their part.

All the rest, who saw it was of no use to offer resistance, were secured, bound, and set afloat with the captain and others in the boat.

Then Valdez lowered them some provisions, water, and clothes, as well as a few cutlasses, and a chest containing some of the captain's property.

"Adieu, my friends !" said Valdez, with mock cordiality. "I hope you'll soon be rescued by some passing vessel. Don't forget how kindly you have been treated by the rover, Valdez !"

The last word startled the conquered party like a thunderbolt.

"Valdez !" cried the Yankee captain. "What, the all-fired cuss of a pirate ! Ah ! I see how it is now ! We've been regularly done—swindled like 'coons ! Damnation ! To think that I could have got a thousand dollars for delivering him up, if I'd only have known it ! and now here we are chawed up, and whittled away to the small end of nothing !" And with this he relapsed into moody cogitation, scarcely looking back at his stolen vessel, which, with the pirates on board and with the rightful occupants thus left in peril on the wide sea, bore off and soon increased the distance between them.

Loud, prolonged shouts of triumph from the pirates echoed across the wide ocean as the vessel gradually disappeared from the sight of its former crew.

"And now, my lads, for a splendid cruise !" cried Valdez. "Once more we are rovers, and ready to brave the perils and share the triumphs of a pirate's life ! I mean to give the eastern seas a turn now ; there's splendid prizes to be taken among the rich islands of the Malays. So, hurrah for the Vulture !—that will be a fine name to give our new vessel—and may she soon pounce upon some prey.

CHAPTER XLVIII.

ADRIFT ON THE WIDE OCEAN—THE PERILS OF THE AMERICAN CREW—THE SHIP ON FIRE—FATE OF JACK AND TOM.

THE American captain and his crew having thus, against their will, changed places with the treacherous pirates, found themselves in a position little better than that in which they had found Valdez and his companions.

They were on the open sea, in a small and frail boat, without compass or any means of ascertaining their position.

It is true they had sufficient provisions to last them some time.

They had also a small mast and a sail, by which means they had some control over their frail craft; and, above all, the weather was clear, the sea smooth, and no signs of approaching gales were visible.

These were advantages; but how long they would continue was a matter of great uncertainty.

In the event of such a storm as that which had nearly destroyed the pirate and his crew, the Americans knew how perilous their situation would become.

"What, in the name of thunder we're to do," cried the American captain—whose name, we must inform our readers, was Whittle—"beats me—and that's a fact! I'm regular downright flabbergasted. To be set upon by a lot of tarnation rascals, and give way to a mere handful like that, is what I never thought I should come to. As to escaping, now, I goldarned if I care whether I do or not! for I should be e'en a'most ashamed to show my face to the shipowners of Boston again, after being chawed up in such a manner."

"It wasn't your fault, not by long chalks, captain," said Tim the Whaler. "We're all in the same boat (I don't mean that as a joke though); and we're all to blame for not keeping a smarter look-out among such all-fired cusses. If we'd only found out their game sooner"—

"Every one of them should have been strung up in half no time, I can tell you," said the captain, through his clenched teeth. "I'd have punished the whole lot by regular Lynch Law— the tarnal rowdies, I would! Wal, I hope they'll split upon the first rock they come to, or be found out and taken by the first honest vessel they come across."

"That Valdez is the most desperate villain that ever cruised," remarked the first mate. "There's no taking him, for all our Government, and the Chilians, and Spaniards have tried. He's such a one to find out dodges to enable him to slip through people's fingers, that it's like catching an eel."

"He'll have to try some powerful smart dodge to get away from me, if ever I come athwart his hawse again," cried Captain Whittle. "I'll tell you what I mean to do, my men. If we get out of this confounded position, and can get to California by hook or by crook, I'll instantly communicate with the Government, tell them all I know about Valdez, and get them to organise such an expedition as will crush this varmint like a whip-snake. It will be all up with his career for ever if we only catch sight of his sail."

"A nearer way to go to work will be," suggested the mate, "to engage with the first vessel that we come across—if she looks strong enough —to accompany us on a cruise to catch this pirate. We can promise them a good reward, in addition to the heavy one offered for his head."

"You're right," returned the captain. "Snakes and sawdust! I'll give them every farthing I'm possessed of for the mere satisfaction of trapping the skunk. If I can only get a chance, I'll follow him to the end of creation before I'll give up the chase!"

Firmly determined as the American was on this extreme course, he little knew how circumstances would cause him to relinquish it. Revenge and retribution are as futile as all other human aims to oppose the irresistible course of events, which a higher power than man has pre-arranged to thwart his designs. The American adventurers were destined to many ocean-perils before any hope of such retribution would present itself.

The weather all next day continued fair, and the wind so still that the boat made but small progress. Captain Whittle's intention was to steer in a north-easterly direction; for, as near as he could calculate, they were about 2,000 miles from the North American coast. There was still some chance of achieving this distance if the wind continued in the quarter favourable to it, but otherwise nothing could be done. At present what little wind there was blew from directly the opposite quarter to the one desired. The day passed, and the night followed, bringing no change in the position of the adventurers. No ship hove in sight, although it is needless to say how strict a watch was kept by all in the boat. Then hopes began to sink as the desperation of their situation became more apparent to them. Their provisions were rapidly decreasing, but it had not become so far reduced as to cause them any great anxiety. But they were little calculated to stand out a voyage of weeks, exposed to all the dangers of time and weather which such an extended period would inevitably bring upon them. The Americans, we must add, did not possess quite so much desperate bravery and reckless hardihood as the pirates who had conquered, and they had been so little prepared for their present desperate situation that they felt it in its full bitterness.

However, there was nothing to do but keep a bright look-out, and hope for the best. The third day the wind increased and veered to the east; the clouds gathered, and the sea began to be more turbulent. A gale arose, not a very powerful or dangerous one for large ships, but to the small masted boat it proved rather troublesome. The small sail was clewed up directly, but they could not prevent the frail mast snapping through the violence of the gale.

No other piece of timber was there on board, except a couple of oars, and the mere stump of a mast that was left was almost useless to influence their progress.

The boat pitched, and rolled, and tossed, on the increasing crests of the waves, and it was only by great exertions that the crew managed to keep her afloat.

Their provisions, however, had been so well secured that they remained in safety, though not entirely uninjured by the sea.

After thus tossing about for some hours, the crew of the boat saw with some satisfaction that the wind was abating, and it was at length considerably lulled.

But though they had weathered this gale, it had been enough to give them a foretaste of what their peril would have been had it continued, or greatly increased in strength.

They were now drifting hopelessly on the wide sea, before a wind still powerful enough to render nugatory all their efforts to guide the boat.

Miles and miles, hours and hours, they continued this slow, uncertain progress.

Still no vessel was to be seen.

No distant white speck gladdened their vision.

Another day passed with the same results, the same uncertainty, and weary monotony.

They were now beyond all possibility of ascertaining their position or course.

It was entirely a matter of conjecture.

Even if they had known in what direction they were proceeding, it would have been useless to attempt to change the course for another.

At length, however, on the fourth day after being set afloat, at evening, just as the sunset blazed in splendour over the boundless ocean, a sail became visible.

She was very distant, and could only be discerned by Whittle by means of his telescope, which the pirates had allowed him to retain.

However, there she was : the difficulty would be how to communicate with or reach her.

It is needless to describe the joy with which this event inspired the wanderers.

Though they were in a far less desperate situation than that of the pirates when they had sighted a vessel in the same manner, their hopes and fears were nearly as strong.

"Sail ho!" resounded in a chorus from the small crew of that frail boat in as loud and boisterous a tone as if they had still been on their own vessel.

The sail was again hoisted as a signal.

Every effort was made to attract the attention of the vessel, towards which their involuntary course was taking them.

"She is steering nor'-east, I do believe," cried Whittle, with much excitement, as he gazed at her through his telescope. "By Jupiter! the very direction we want to go! She is spanking along splendidly; bound for the States, I guess, or, perhaps, Central America. If we can only catch her up we're saved!"

But, alas! their hopes were as futile as those of the pirate had been.

The vessel was too far off to discern the small boat, whose means of making signals of distress were so limited.

Gradually the swift course of the ship took her farther and farther away.

She grew more and more faint until she was at length hidden in the mists of approaching night.

Who shall paint the bitter disappointment, the utter revulsion of delusive hope that the benighted ocean warriors felt at this event?

Like King Richard III., they had "Set their lives upon a cast," and the "hazard of the die" had proved against them.

But their case was not so very desperate.

They were still drifting in the direction of the vessel, making way in her course, and might eventually hope to come within signalling distance of her.

The night fell once more.

It was clear and cloudless; but the wind still kept in the same direction.

Under her very limited canvas, the little vessel continued to drift on towards some unknown goal.

"I somehow have a sort of presentiment that we shall fall in with some craft or other soon," said the Yankee captain, "though we've got no means of signalling in the dark. It won't do, however, to lose any chance, so I mean to keep a look-out myself to-night. You can keep me company if you choose, Mr. Fleming; but, as for the others, they can sleep if they feel like it."

"Precious glad to be woke up, though, captain, with the cry of 'Sail ho!'" remarked old Tim the Whaler; "and I hope it will be a real sail this time, and not a regular Flying Dutchman like the last."

"We may be nearer to her than you think," returned the captain; "and, as to being a Flying Dutchman, we should find her real enough if we only got the chance."

So, while the others tried for a few hours to forget their troubles in sleep, the captain and mate kept their voluntary watch over the surface of the ocean, in hope of discovering some light that would guide them to safety and rescue.

An hour, however, passed without any such agreeable result.

Neither of the watchers spoke much to each other.

Anxiety and their own thoughts appeared sufficient to keep them awake, and to occupy both.

On no other occasion had such night watches been rewarded by any success; and it was only the captain's presentiment that made him hope this would prove any more efficacious than the rest.

At length, however, Captain Whittle and Fleming, the mate, started up simultaneously with a wild cry, not of joy, but of surprise and alarm.

A red, vivid light, immense in its extent, made itself visible to their astonished eyes at about three miles' distance—lighting up the wide expanse of the ocean with a flood of fiery illumination, that cast a deeper relieving shade over the surface of the sky, every moment increasing in intensity and strength, growing in flaming power and destructive might.

They could not for a moment fail to comprehend the cause of this portentous and fearful spectacle.

It was a ship on fire!

There is not, in the whole range of the wondrous sights to be seen on the mighty deep, a spectacle so beautiful, but, at the same time, so terrible, as a vessel in flames.

It is a scene of fairy-like beauty, but of demon-like horror.

The engulphing flames, circling around every beam and spar; the forked tongues of fire, darting like snakes from every window and outlet; the volumes of half red, half black, smoke that are belched forth and roll aloft o'er the darkening sky; the outline of the tall masts, begirt by the blackening shreds of half consumed sails; and, above all, the fearful knowledge that this scene is a double peril of destruction and death, which shuts men up between two destroying elements, both ready to engulph them, and both cutting off the chance of escape.

All this renders a ship on fire a sight of more than earthly horror.

Such was the spectacle presented by the ship which the crew of the boat had now drifted within an easy distance of observing.

The flames could not have broken out long, but had already made great way, and performed terrific destruction.

Already were the masts half consumed, the flames rushing forth from the hold, the deck one mass of ruddy flame and smoke.

The peril of those on board was indeed terrible.

The quarter-deck had been almost consumed, and they were all crowded on the taffrail, half paralysed with terror, and nearly choked by the intense heat and the thick masses of smoke that poured from the deserted vessel.

Among these unfortunate persons were two in whom our readers are particularly interested, and whose perils and escapes had been already numerous.

They were Crusoe Jack and Tom Starboard.

Our readers are, perhaps, anxious to learn what had brought them to this terrific position.

We will hasten, in as few words as possible, to allay their curiosity.

The vessel by which our friends had been rescued from death on the raft was an American trader, which, after a successful cruise among the islands of the Pacific, was now returning with many native productions, and a considerable quantity of money realised by merchandise.

Her last port had been Honolulu, from which she had sailed about the time when Captain Hastings was approaching it under such unfavourable circumstances.

Her course was therefore north-east, but for nearly three weeks she was impeded by adverse and changing winds, and it was during this time that they sighted a small object at a considerable distance.

"A raft, and making signals of distress!" was the report from the mast-head.

The captain knew at once that this assistance was required.

Few commanders of vessels are too wanting in humanity not to rescue persons thus situated, even by going out of their course, but in the present case there was no such necessity, for the raft was directly in the course of the trader.

There was little difficulty, therefore, in putting out a boat of half-a-dozen stout seamen.

Rowing as if for their lives, they were soon alongside of the frail craft that contained our heroes.

They perceived at once how matters stood.

They were only just in time to rescue them from death.

This, however, they did manfully.

The starving and exhausted wanderers were taken on board, where all means of restoring their strength was immediately put into requisition.

Their story powerfully interested their rescuers, for whose kindness and humanity they had every cause to be grateful.

But in answer to Jack's earnest appeal to be sent back to the Sandwich Islands, in the hopes of finding and relieving the minds of his friends, he was shown the difficulty and delay such a course would occasion to the whole crew, though the captain, sympathising with his distress, promised to send him and Tom back by the first vessel they might come across, bound for Honolulu.

As luck would have it, however, no such vessel appeared.

Days passed, and the American trader spoke to no craft of any kind.

Meanwhile Jack and Tom took part in the working of the ship, and being both able in their duties, and zealous to perform them well, in gratitude to their preservers, they soon gained the favour of all on board.

Jack was especially a favourite.

His adventures had been of no common kind.

His manner and appearance showed him to be superior to many other lads in his position.

A few light gales, but no dangerous storms, winds sometimes adverse, but on the whole favourable, marked their course, and there was nothing in this to cause anyone on board anything but satisfactory feelings.

Unconsciously the American vessel passed at different times two parties very singularly situated and under similar circumstances.

The first was the case of the pirate, Valdez, and his companions, who had made signals, as we have previously described, to Jack's vessel, near whose course they had drifted.

Their signals, however, had passed unheeded, and thus Jack was spared from an unexpected meeting with his old captor.

In the same manner, a week or two after Captain Whittle and his companions were set afloat by the pirate they made signals to the sloop, but were also unperceived.

It seems singular, that two such similar events, connected, too, so closely with each other, should occur under such similar circumstances.

Now, however, the pirates' victims had overtaken the ship.

But how little was she capable of affording them assistance in the situation she was herself placed in!

The cause of the fire was a mystery, as fires frequently are at sea.

It had originated, and it was believed accidentally, in the hold, but whether from accidental ignition among the stores, or the carelessness of any of the sailors, who had incautiously approached with a light some combustible materials, could not be ascertained.

But, however it had been originally caused, the fire had burst out, and extended, in an extraordinary short space of time, and was soon past all efforts to subdue it.

The pumps, the hose, playing upon the deck and rigging, with all the energy that could be combined, failed to do more than slightly smother the flames.

They speedily burst out again with renewed fury.

It was no time to make inquiries as to the culprits who had caused it, accidentally or otherwise, or to punish them for the act.

All was confusion.

The whole of the sailors seemed struck with a complete panic.

The authority of the captain was disregarded.

Attempts were made to put out the boats, but some had already caught fire, and from the insufferable heat and smoke upon the decks, the others could not be launched.

There was no means of making a raft.

There was, in short, no escape.

Nothing could be done but cling in despair to the only unconsumed part of the ship, till that should catch fire, and all hopes be entirely cut off.

It is one of the horrors of a ship on fire that that there are so few means of escape, and even these are frequently rendered useless by the general confusion that prevails. Many of the crew. driven to desperation, leapt overboard, but they found this was an escape from one death to another, for there was nothing to cling to, and all either sank from exhaustion, got struck on the head by falling timbers, or fell victims to the sharks. Every one luckily had contrived to escape from the cabin, which was so far fortunate as their deaths in such a situation would have been inevitable and instantaneous. No one, however, saw a shadow of a chance of escape ; all resigned themselves as well as they could do to death; but the majority were prepared to jump overboard at the last minute.

The taffrail, was as yet untouched, but every moment it was threatened by the all-devouring flames. Luckily, the wind was blowing the flames and smoke in the opposite direction, or the close proximity of them would undoubtedly have suffocated the doomed crew.

Jack and Tom, and indeed the whole party (which consisted of nearly 30 persons), frequently turned their glasses despairingly out to sea, in the vain hope of distinguishing some vessel that would rescue them, although they knew that this would be such a perilous duty on the part of a ship that few captains would undertake it.

" We're doomed now, my lad," old Tom Starboard said to our hero, in despairing accents. " There isn't a grain of chance for any of us; after all we've been through. too ! But there, the Lord's will be done. We'll die together, and I'm resigned as much as any of 'em."

" Yes, our time's come at last, Tom," replied Jack. " Often as we've escaped dangers before, there's no hope now. I'm prepared to die, too, but not by fire. I shall make one effort in a few moments, and jump into into the sea ; drowning is better than the torture of burning. But see ! see !"—he cried with an animation and excitement which greatly contrasted with his previous mournful aspect—" See ! there is a boat—a small boat with a sail. She has men in her—she is approaching ; we may be saved, after all !"

Every one rushed to the side at these words, and many were driven overboard, by the eagerness of all to distinguish the chance of rescue, to take advantage of the finest thread on which to hang a life.

" She is approaching ; but she can never take us," cried Tom, whose voice could scarcely be heard among the wild and frantic shouts of the others. " She is full already ; they won't try and save us at the risk of their own lives, it ain't likely ; for if she comes much nearer she'll catch fire herself."

But Captain Whittle had a humane heart, and he wished to do everything to save the struggling wretches on the doomed ship, though he knew how little he could hope to accomplish. His boat might, though with inconvenience, yet hold three or four more persons, and even this number of lives was worth saving.

So, guiding the boat with his oars, he ran her as close as he could with safety under the ship's counter, and shouted, " Hold on there ! We'll try to save some of you, if you have got any ropes or stern ladders ; quick, for God's sake."

A fearful rush was instantly made to secure this last chance of safety ; the ropes and ladders were speedily fixed, and a struggle for life was made to descend to the boat.

It was a fearful scene. The natural feeling of self-preservation prompted all to attempt to escape, to the exclusion of others. No one cared for anything but saving his own life. The struggle to reach the ladders, to get an inch of hold on the rope was terrible to witness in its grim despairing eagerness.

The strongest succeeded, the weakest failed, or perished, for many were driven into the water, or were left to be consumed in the flames, and suffocated by the fast-increasing smoke.

Jack and Tom had not waited for these doubtful aids to escape. Amid the fierce struggle that was like a battle, they had both, almost simultaneously, and actuated by some irresistible impulse, leapt into the sea close by the boat, and struck out for it. Tom reached it in safety. Jack was not quite so fortunate. As he struggled to the side of the boat, a portion of a burning spar, red-hot and hissing, fell into the boat, narrowly missing his head, hitting and burning his hand, causing him to relinquish his hold. It was thrown into the water immediately, and Jack was pulled in, and, though terribly suffering from the burn, he tried to be very thankful he had escaped with his life at all.

By this time many of the others had followed his example, leapt into the water, and attempted to reach the boat ; but their efforts were in vain, for Whittle's party, seeing that the boat was now in considerable peril, pulled back with all their might, after having saved Jack, Tom, and three more sailors, who had escaped down the rope. The rest, calling in vain for assistance, clung to the wreck, dropped into the sea, and continued their frantic efforts to reach the boat ; but she was now full, and to try and save more would be to lose all.

So the party in the boat pulled off as fast as possible from the scene of disaster, leaving those who were less fortunate struggling with inevitable death !

It was a ghastly scene—a terrible spectacle of despair and destruction ; and never till the end of his life did Jack forget that united wail, the fearful shriek of despair that came from the dying wretches who were left behind in the doomed ship.

CHAPTER XLIX.

THE SEAGULL'S VOYAGE—TIDINGS OF THE LOST ONES—MISGIVINGS AND DOUBTS—THE HOMEWARD VOYAGE—A WIDE SEPARATION.

WHILE the above exciting events were taking place, the Seagull had happily escaped the dangers by which she was surrounded, and arrived safely at the port of Honolulu.

By the utmost skill and care, and the expenditure of time, the ship had at length passed through the dangerous channel ; and once on the open sea the remainder of the passage was comparatively easy.

The Sandwich Islands, the most interesting and remarkable group in all the great Pacific Archipelago, afforded a marked contrast to the other islands which the Seagull had previously visited.

Here were no painted savages, decked in barbaric plumes, and wielding the tomahawk in incessant war! No rival tribes, engaged in perpetual contention for power and dominion; but a civilised nation, presenting but little contrast to the people of Europe.

The progress of this gallant people in the arts of civilised life is one of the most remarkable events of the present century.

Less than a hundred years have passed since Captain Cook discovered the Hawaiians, a savage and implacable race, and, as all our readers know, fell a victim to their fury.

Now they form a compact and powerful kingdom, with an extensive trade, newspapers, and other literature, manufactures, and agriculture, and an army and navy that render them far more powerful than any of their neighbours.

This immense change was mainly due to the exertions of one individual — the powerful monarch, Kamehameha I., whose descendants still rule over those island realms.

For many years has the Hawaiian nation been enrolled among the civilised nations of the world; and thus Captain Hastings and his party found it when they arrived at the port of Honolulu.

A town, well built and of good size, with shipping of every nation thronging the harbour, billiard-rooms, public-houses, evidences everywhere of commerce, wealth, and prosperity, met their eyes.

Yet still were the islands beautiful, fertile, picturesque, and the feathery palm and the cocoa-nut-tree waved in their forests and groves; and still, in the noble forms of the men and the bewitching and graceful dignity of the women of that island nation could be traced the lineaments of the proud, fierce warrior, and the wild but lovely Amazon of an earlier age.

Mr. Meredith, Mabel, and Captain Hastings were all delighted with the island.

They resolved on a stay of several weeks.

It was something, after all the dangers they had passed, to arrive at a place where peace prevailed, and where the turbulence and continual bloodshed prevailing among such people as the Hopaws and Typees did not exist.

The captain met with considerable success in trading, and disposed of all the goods left from the remains of the cargo of the two ships to great advantage in exchange for sandal-wood and Spanish and American dollars.

Mr. Meredith saw in this successful venture such an increase in his fortune as to remove all anxiety as to his own and his daughter's future prosperity.

Their only trouble now was the loss of Jack and Tom Starboard, as well as the sailor who had accompanied them on their ill-judged expedition.

Of the fate of all three they had little doubt.

The evidence of the overturned boat and the sunken hull was too strong to leave any hope that they had escaped.

There was not a person on board but who felt the loss he had sustained.

In Tom Starboard they had lost such an experienced, brave, and trusty seaman, as could not be easily replaced.

In Jack they were deprived of a companion who was the favourite of all who knew him, who had in him the genuine lion-heartedness of which the heroes of the world are made.

Captain Hastings sincerely lamented our hero.

Mr. Meredith mourned him as a son, and whose fate he had destined should at some future time be allied with that of his daughter.

And as to Mabel, what shall we say of her affliction?

It was bitter, intense, overwhelming—with no chance of relief, no hope of ultimately proving groundless.

Jack had perished—of that she felt assured; and notwithstanding the many dangers he had escaped, it now seemed madness to hope he had again met with such good fortune.

And so Mabel mourned him as one in whom the whole happiness of her heart was bound up, and by whose loss all that happiness had fled.

On the fourth morning of their stay in Honolulu, an event occurred which afforded them still a gleam of hope.

When Captain Hastings was on his ship, superintending the disposal of the cargo, and Mabel and her father were on shore examining the city of the Hawaiians, a boat put out from the shore, and rowed towards the Seagull.

One of the inmates, a man bearing the aspect of a Yankee fisherman, came on board, saying that he had a message for Captain Hastings.

On being confronted with the latter, the man pulled out a piece of paper, on which, as our readers may guess, was written, in Crusoe Jack's hand, the declaration of their desperate state on board the raft.

"I picked this up in a bottle, sir, that came ashore with the tide this morning, just as I was getting my smack under way out in the bay yonder. The surf dashed the bottle against the rocks with such force, as to smash it; but I secured it, and found this piece of paper, which I brought to you as soon as I could."

Captain Hastings took the paper, and read it with much surprise.

He did not know whether to hope or despair at the intelligence it conveyed him.

"Thank heaven!" he exclaimed, "some intelligence of them at last! but is it good or bad? That's the question. Drifting away on a raft from the ship! There is some chance of their safety."

"And I hope, your honour, it's good news?" said the messenger, regarding the captain as he read the intelligence."

"I don't know what to make of it, my good fellow. Here are three people who go out on the open sea, to overhaul a deserted hulk on a rough night, and never return the next morning. We find the hulk sunk and the boat overturned, and no sign of them, and we give them up as lost; and now by this we find they managed to make a raft, and got drifted out to sea."

"Whereabouts did that happen, sir, if I might be so bold?" asked the fisherman.

"About two-and-a-half degrees on the southeast from here, a deserted hulk of a brig, apparently, lay there, and these poor fellows went aboard her."

"Ah, then, your honour, I know. It must have been the pirates' vessel, the Black Eagle."

"The Black Eagle?" cried the captain, in astonishment.

"Yes, your honour. She was wrecked near that latitude, and probably drifted up to where you found her. That atrocious pirate, Valdez, had been cruising about here under the disguise of an English trader. Then he tried to get off, but was caught in a gale, and the ship was lost. Me and a mate of mine went out one day in our smack to overhaul the hulk, when we heard of the affair. But devil-a-bit, if anything did we find in her, except water."

"And Valdez and his men perished, I suppose?" asked the captain.

"Some of 'em did, your honour; but the rest got ashore on the islands, and still making believe to be English traders, they properly victimised the people here, who gave them money, food, and lodging, and I don't know what-all, until they were found out, and escaped into the woods in the island of Attowaie, where they hid themselves safely for a long time. They ain't been seen lately, so it is supposed that they must have got out to sea somehow, and got drowned in the late gales."

"They deserved such a fate, whether they met with it or not," returned Captain Hastings; "but I don't know what to say about those friends of mine."

"Depend upon it they are safe, if they took to a raft," returned the fisherman. "If there is any hope of your life out in a gale, that's the best chance of securing it."

"Well, my good man, I hope it is. At least you've brought us some good news that will relieve our minds a little. I won't keep you any longer. Take this."

The captain slipped a sovereign into the hand of the man, who touched his hat respectfully and departed, apparently much satisfied with the result of his expedition.

When Mabel and her father returned to the ship they noticed that the captain's manner was that of one whose mind was agitated by some unusual event.

Mr. Meredith took the first opportunity of trying to solve the mystery.

"You look as if you had received some unexpected intelligence?" he said.

"I have," returned Captain Hastings; "but I don't know whether to be glad or sorry."

"Is it about Jack and Tom?" asked Mabel and her father in a breath.

"It is; and not only about them but from them. See here." And the captain showed them the paper.

Mabel and Mr. Meredith scanned it eagerly.

Both, however, it seemed to inspire with a confirmation of their worst misgivings.

"Great Heavens! then there's no hope!" cried Mr. Meredith. "They've certainly perished!"

"We need not be too sure of that," said the captain.

"What have they written here,—'Drifting on a raft from the wreck, with slight hopes of being saved.'"

"Yes, there may have been no hope at the time; but there is always a chance when drifting on a raft of being picked up by some passing vessel."

"Very—very little, I think, in the present case," returned Mr. Meredith, not much reassured, while Mabel in an agony of surprise looked from one to the other for a ray of encouragement to her hopes.

Presently, Mr. Meredith asked the captain—

"What can we do? Is there any means of ascertaining their fate?"

"None that I see. We can make inquiries of every vessel here, and all that come in during our stay on the island; but we can do no more."

"Unfortunately we should not have any idea in what direction to look for them," said Mr. Meredith.

"Not in the least. They may have been driven hundreds or thousands of miles away from here, and they may have been picked up in a vessel bound for China, Australia, or any other distant latitude."

"But in any case they would endeavour to be sent back to the Sandwich Islands?" suggested Mabel's father.

"No vessel would go so far out of her course to put them ashore, though. It is scarcely likely, at least."

"In short, then, we have no chance of deciding as to what has become of them?" said Mr. Meredith, despairingly.

"We can only await the course of events. There, I do not entirely despair on their account, they may still be alive; but poor Bill Casey, I'm afraid, went over in the boat, you see—he is not mentioned here."

"I fear so."

"It was a rash and foolish expedition altogether," said the captain; "and I shall never forgive myself for yielding to them, and giving them consent to undertake it."

Such were the unavailing regrets and vague anxious surmises that the friends of our heroes indulged in with regard to their fate.

The Seagull stayed more than three weeks at the islands, but gained no tidings whatever, calculated to throw any light on the fate of Jack and Tom. It became evident that no vessel bound to Honolulu had picked them up, and it was therefore more probable that they had been rescued by some ship bound on the opposite course.

In this we know how far they conjectured rightly. At length seeing it was useless to delay further, the Seagull set out on her voyage to Chili.

That voyage was marked by no incidents worthy of special description. All the perils of their extended cruise were apparently over, and they could have afforded to look back to them without regret, but for the loss of the companions they so much valued.

With the wind in her favour almost all the way, the Seagull made a very quick passage to the port of Conception, the capital of Chili, where she was laid up for some time for repairing and unloading.

The party so long united in many adventures and ocean perils now separated. Mr. Meredith and his daughter took leave of Captain Hastings, with whom their acquaintance, so strangely commenced, had now developed into a firm friendship.

The captain, however, accepted Mr. Meredith's invitation to visit him at the residence of his brother, for whose estate, some eighty miles up the country, he was now bound.

Dyson and Greenley, at their own desire, accompanied the party, having been offered situations on the plantation, which they were prepared to fill with such zeal and honesty as would evince their gratitude for the kindness that had been shown them.

Mr. Oswald Meredith, Mabel's uncle, received his relatives warmly, deplored the vicissitudes they had met with, and offered them such a home as would place them in comfort, and with all the enjoyments that could enhance the value of life.

And certainly Mabel could not but feel happy, or at least consoled, in that beautiful region of fertility, where all was bright and serene, where nature revelled in all the exuberance of tropical wealth, a land of flowers and forests, and plantations and lovely savannahs, and gardens of indescribable magnificence.

Living as she was now to live, in luxury and affluence, protected from the chance of all such dangers as she had undergone, Mabel required the presence of her heart's only love to complete her happiness.

Captain Hastings, having stayed with the Merediths until the Seagull was completely ready for another voyage, and having shared with Mabel's father the proceeds of their merchandise, took his departure, though he parted with them with considerable regret. His design was now to sail for England, to see his own family and settle some important affairs he had in hand there.

About this period Mr. Meredith received the letter in which his friend in London, Mr. Layland, had detailed the proceedings of Jasper Collins. It greatly interested both him and Mabel, though their interest in the Moreland estates was considerably modified by the uncertainty of Jack's fate.

Mr. Meredith, however, wrote back to Mr. Layland to continue keeping him informed on these subjects.

He also wrote letters to all the shipowners he knew in the ports of North and South America, and prosecuted inquiries at a considerable expense in all quarters where there was any chance of obtaining information; but no tidings could he learn of our hero or his friend, Tom Starboard.

Mr. Meredith and his daughter were soon settled down in their new home.

Mr. Meredith purchased a handsome country house, adjoining his brother's estate, and here Mabel became the queen of his household.

Thus, by a strange fatality, were Mabel and her lover separated by the mighty length of two great continents. While one, in happy circumstances, had found a home in the south of South America, the other, as we shall speedily see, was destined to undergo a long period of adventurous peril and hardship on the opposite end of the American continent, more than 6,000 miles distant!

CHAPTER L.

THE ESCAPE—THE STORM—THE WRECK ON THE ICEBERG—DEADLY PERIL, AND STRANGE POSITION OF JACK.

IN the terrible period of excitement and hurried struggling for the chance of life, it was no time for our heroes and their preservers to exchange explanations of their relative situations.

The only object of all now was to get away from the burning hulk, and out of sight of the terrible spectacle presented by the dying struggles of those they were powerless to save.

The boat had now upwards of twenty men in her, the utmost she was able to contain, and, indeed, with their provisions and other cargo, the little craft was loaded almost down to the water's edge.

The event of a gale, to a number of persons in so inadequate a vessel, would certainly involve the most serious danger.

Add to this, the provisions would naturally be scanty in proportion to the increased number of the party, and the allowance, however sparingly doled out, would not last any great length of time.

The weather was still calm, but land was very far distant; and its direction, and the prospect of reaching it, were very difficult to ascertain.

The party thought of all this as soon as they had become sufficiently calm to reflect on their position, when they had rowed more than a mile from the burning hulk.

When its fiery outline had become more indistinct and remote, when the shrieks of agonising despair of the drowning or suffering wretches died away, fainter and fainter in the distance, the party could then turn their attention to the position in which they were themselves placed.

"You've had the nearest squeak for your lives, my lads," said Captain Whittle to the rescued men, "that you have ever had in all your born days, I'll venture to bet. I don't care what adventures you've been through."

"A good many I've seen in my time," answered old Tom Starboard, "and so has this lad here, but I'll own you're right. By the Lord, it was awful!"

"Still more awful for the poor creatures left behind, though," said the captain, looking back at the fiery glow that still lit up the sea for miles.

"The Lord have mercy on 'em!" cried the old tar, fervently. "Jack, my boy, we owe an extra prayer to heaven in thankfulness for our escape, and I'm sure I can give it from my heart. Poor creatures! indeed, I can judge their feelings in my own. The best thing we can wish them is a speedy death out of their misery."

"It's a calamity, I'm glad to say," resumed the Yankee captain, "that I've never had happen to me in all my voyages. I've struck on a rock, foundered at sea, got stuck among icebergs, overhauled by pirates, and tossed by whales, but was never in a burning ship."

"Once is as often as people do go in one, generally," observed Tom.

"There's frequently so much carelessness on board," said the captain, "and that causes fires nine times out of ten. I've always looked precious sharp after my fellows, and, please Providence, if ever I get my ship again, always will!"

"You've been wrecked, too?" asked Crusoe Jack of his new companion, who was next to him.

"Wrecked? No!" returned the other; "cast adrift by pirates; and this'll be a desperate voyage for all of us, let me tell you."

"Pirates?" asked Jack and Tom together, much excited. "How did that happen?"

The American sailor in a few words explained the events that had brought their party to their present pass.

When he mentioned the name of Valdez, Jack and Tom started with surprise.

"What! Valdez, the renowned buccaneer?"

"Yes, worse luck! But we little knew whom we were taking up, you may be sure, or our captain would have rescued them with a pair of handcuffs a-piece."

"That man's a complete wizard," observed Jack, "he can do anything! Nothing comes amiss to Valdez! And so he got off with your ship? I wonder how he came to lose his own?"

"Devil a bit do we know or care!" answered the American. "We heard something in Honolulu of his ship having struck somewhere out off the coast, and they said he was hiding in the islands."

"My lads," observed the captain at this juncture, "I can tell you one thing, our provisions have run very low already, and you'll all have to make up your minds to go on very short allowance."

Such a declaration was not inspiring, but after the near escape from death, through which they considered it a boon to be alive at all, our heroes did not feel the misfortune as acutely as the others.

"Nevertheless," resumed Captain Whittle, "I can afford a taste of something now to you fellows who have just been through so many dangers. Here, Johnson, deal out to the five new men a sup of brandy and a biscuit a-piece."

The offer was far from unacceptable, for Jack and his companions were exhausted by the exertion they had so recently undergone.

They accepted, therefore, gratefully, the captain's humane offer, and felt much refreshed by the stimulant.

As it fortunately happened that a small bottle of vinegar was among the provisions on board, Jack had some given him to apply to his burnt hand, which was still very painful.

Wrapping a piece of rag thus moistened around his wrist served in some degree as a relief from the pain.

"I wonder," suggested Captain Whittle, looking back again to the now almost invisible fire as he spoke, "whether there is the slightest chance of any stores, provisions, or anything that will be useful to us, being left in the hulk of that ship when the fire goes out?"

But the rescued men hastened to dispel any such fallacious hope.

"None, whatever," said Tom. "I doubt if there'll be anything left of her in a few hours but a heap of cinders. Everything that is of any use is past praying for already, I'll wager."

Having ascertained from the rescued men the position of the ship at the time she caught fire, Captain Whittle put his vessel, as near as he could calculate, on the course he wished to take.

There was scarcely wind enough to make their progress very rapid, and as their oars were useless to propel a craft so heavily laden, they managed to split up the remaining stump of the the mast into two more, with which four men, being relieved in their turn by four others, contrived to send the boat on at a considerably increased speed.

Thus the night passed.

A bright look-out was, of course, kept, but with no satisfactory result.

As the morning broke, the captain was confirmed in the correctness of the course he was taking by the position of the sun, as that luminary burst out in unclouded splendour over the watery horizon.

The fineness of the weather and the progress they had already made, inspired the adventurers with increased hope that they would in time be able either successfully to reach land, or come across some vessel that would pick them up.

In this, however, the lingering experience of the next two weary days proved that they were doomed to disappointment.

No vessel picked them up, nor, indeed, did any indication of a sail present itself.

Meanwhile, the weather, which at sea is a thing of a more capricious nature than on the wildest spot on land, began to be again unfavourable.

A violent gale arose, the waves became turbulent, and the frail craft was threatened with destruction.

Heavily laden as she was, her peril was very great.

The danger of being overturned, so serious to a small boat in such a position, was perpetually imminent.

Happily, however, though small, she was strong; and her crew managed to weather the gale, which in a few hours abated.

The weather cleared up, and hope again arose in the hearts of the adventurers, only to be followed, however, with renewed anxiety.

The next day a strong gale arose in the south.

The weather again became thick, and the peril as great as before.

As it was impossible to conjecture how long this terrific position would continue, and the provisions were now much decreased, it became necessary to put the whole party upon shorter allowance.

It is needless to say how far this increased their sufferings, and the pangs of half-satisfied hunger had every prospect of being followed by those of utter famine.

Thus days and days did the little vessel drift upon the wild waste of waters.

The mercy that had sustained them from destruction in the frequent gales was not extended to further aid or rescue.

No sight of a sail rewarded the long and anxious watchings of the imperilled crew, except on two of those occasions when the wind, the waves, and the distance prevented their communicating with them.

Whenever the abatement of the gales would allow them, they reared the two oars, fastened together with ropes to the stump of the broken mast, and these, with the only remaining and much tattered piece of canvas on board, formed an apology for a mast and sail.

But they were hopelessly beyond all calculations of their latitude; and what was still more serious, after a few days more, the wind set in to blow strongly and constantly from the south, thus carrying them northward with irresistible force.

Signs of greater impending danger became apparent.

The weather became bitterly cold, storms of snow and sleet were frequent, thick fogs frequently covered the face of the sea, and ominous darkness settled over the whole expanse of the sky.

From these indications, it became evident to the more experienced among the sufferers that they were approaching the Arctic regions, or at least the desolate shores adjoining them.

This prospect was even more terrible than not reaching land at all, for there was the continued danger of their vessel being dashed to pieces on some iceberg, or immoveably fixed between the great blocks of ice in some frozen waste where they would perish for want of food.

But they were powerless to avert the danger.

The wind, like an evil spirit bent on their destruction, perpetually urged them in the same direction; and every day the increasing violence of the storms of snow, and the winterly bitterness of the cold, added to their sufferings.

Their gloomy forebodings were almost confirmed when, after a few days of these terrible hardships, their provisions were at the lowest ebb, and all nearly perishing with cold—great blocks of ice loomed grimly in sight through the Cimmerian gloom.

When the mist cleared away, they were enabled to perceive, to their dismay, the region into which they had drifted.

They were almost completely surrounded by masses of ice!

Now, indeed, their position was truly appalling; exposed to the biting winds, encompassed by darkness, almost frozen with the bitter cold, drenched with the blinding snow, and expecting each moment to be dashed to pieces on the enormous masses of ice that surrounded them, there seemed nothing that could add to the horrors of their situation.

"Ah, cap'n, and messmates all," was old Tim the Whaler's comment on their position, "we'd better give ourselves up for lost. Nothing can save us now. I know these regions well; for, if I ain't very much mistaken, we are in the very latitude where the Sylphide of Boston—she was a whaler, she was, and I was out in her at the time—came across a vessel floating about, under bare poles, with the whole crew aboard frozen to death."

"Frozen!" said the captain, with a thrill of horror that communicated itself to all his companions.

"Clean dead and stiff as they sat in the cabin, and many on deck as well. We made signals to the vessel, for we were in a ticklish strait ourselves; but there was no reply, and we followed and boarded her, and such a sight as we saw I shall never forget in all my born days. We thought the crew had gone to sleep at first, and so they had for ever, for there was no waking them; and when we examined them close, we found every man as cold as a stone. They must have been dead for days."

Such a story was not cheering to men in the position of Jack and his companions; they knew it was only too probable to doubt, and too mournfully serious to be received in that half-amused spirit in which they had frequently listened to Tim the Whaler's yarns.

Hour by hour and day by day, the world of ice expanded its grim and rigid proportions before their eyes.

It was impossible even to ascertain the extent of their danger.

The white icy mountains that were perpetually in view, and the fixed, inflexible blocks of jagged and pointed ice that adjoined them, were not the only sources of danger.

Frequently, huge bodies of ice, not waiting till the force of the waves hurled vessels to destruction against them, float themselves on the ocean's surface, and, impelled by the currents, dash against frail vessels and shatter them to pieces instantaneously.

It is awful to drift thus on the wide waste of waters, not only exposed to any hardship but with the constant prospect of this fearful death in view.

Thus, however, it was with our hero and his companions.

No bravery, no strength, could avail them at this dread crisis.

Another storm—another fearful battle with the darkness, and snow, and sleet, and piercing winds.

Without a mast—for even their last extempore one had been destroyed—without a rudder, and with every seam strained open by the violence of continual shocks—the wretched little craft seemed near her death struggle.

Dark rolling clouds, and still darker fixed gloom and fog, obscured all around, and was only pierced by the thick falling snow.

Thunder crashed, and boomed, and rattled through the firmament; winds howled, whistled, bellowed through the frozen atmosphere.

Billows roared, and tossed, and hurled their frothy foam aloft in ungovernable rage.

The whole of the heavens and the sea seemed engaged in a terrible, uncertain warfare.

Above all, there loomed through this horrible gloom the treacherous, deadly-white bulk of the rocks of ice, like constant warnings of an impending doom.

Death to man— destruction to the frail craft on which he trusts his frailer life—will they not soon achieve their triumph?

Hark! the wind lulls; its fury has died away suddenly. Can it be that the tempest is breaking; that the darkness will soon close, and the waves sink to repose?

Blissful thought! there is hope yet!

But no! Treacherous, doubly treacherous are such signs of safety! The danger is nearer—more imminent than ever!

Captain Whittle started up; and, half-concealed as he was by the darkness, he was seen to point to a white object close to them—was heard to give vent to the terrible words—

"Good God! We are lost! We are on the ice-islands!"

"The ice-islands!" every tongue repeated in horror, for they knew that the words meant doom and death.

"No, no! it cannot be!"

"It is, it is! See!" said the captain, in a hoarse voice. And as he spoke a flash of lightning, terrible in its vivid intensity, overspread the heavens, and cast its light on the fearful scene. The sea and sky for one awful moment were flooded with a blaze of light. This revealed their doom, confirmed their worst fears. Close to them—not more than a few yards off—were mighty masses of ice, rolling, and tossing, and rocking on the heaving waters; and towering above all this was an immense rock of solid ice, a vast, looming, mountainous bulk, carrying destruction in its very lineaments. One moment

始

sufficed to exhibit this danger, which then again became enveloped in gloom. And now, to add to the roar of the winds and waves, was to be heard the grinding and crashing together of these vast, adamantine masses of the congealed and destructive element.

"We are under its lee—it is upon us!" echoed from one mouth to another among the doomed crew.

"See!—it is coming closer!"

Another flash, momentary as the first, again revealed the increasing horrors. The mountain of ice was terribly near now; in fearful distinctness could they perceive its thousand sharp points, reflecting the effulgent radiance of the electric light.

All stood up with one accord in the boat; for now, indeed, the death struggle had come: anguish, intense, indescribable, filled every breast.

However brave men may be, however ready and prepared to die, such tortures, such struggles, such gloom and darkness, and confusion add horrors to death which the stoutest hearts must quail under.

Jack and Tom grasped each other as in a last embrace. They would die together. They had suffered many dangers together before now, let them then suffer thus, for it will be the last.

Crash! like an earthquake, like the jarring of two opposing armies—with a jerk that makes every man lose his balance and clutch, stunned and breathless, at the object nearest to him—the boat sinks beneath their feet, sinks to destruction, shattered to fragments.

A wild, fearful, united cry of horror and despair rends the air like a death-knell.

Jack loses his hold of Tom, and both are hurled forward, they know not where, for they are struggling in the midst of a mass of human beings, all fighting for their lives with furious breakers and jagged blocks of heaving ice.

Jack falls forward with a violent shock, his head strikes, or at least grazes an immense block of ice, and for a moment he is stunned. Then he rises, bleeding and pained, with a throbbing brow, and every nerve strung to its highest pitch of intensity.

Above, around, below him, are tremendous masses of ice, all seemingly bent on involving him in, or sucking him beneath them.

All this has occurred, as it seems, instantaneously.

Darkness, confusion, a whirl of conflicting sensations, renders every man insensible to all sights and sounds and knowledge—but that he is engaged in a battle for the faintest chance of preserving his existence.

Jack struggled and struggled with all the strength of limb and of heart which desperation gives.

He was separated from Tom; he saw not his companions—could distinguish nothing—the darkness was over all, and the waves tossed him to and fro like a powerless and insensible thing. Never in all his subsequent life did he forget the violence of that struggle for existence.

At length he had managed to mount a floating block of ice, and sat clinging to it above the level of the waves. but their strength still impelled him onward. In a moment comes another crash, that seems to rend his limbs apart.

It is the piece of ice shattered beneath him, driven against a larger rock. Jack is again hurled forward with a terrible shock, and finds himself clinging, half stunned, to the icy ruins.

CHAPTER LI.

FURTHER PERILS ON THE ICE—A FROZEN SLEEPING-PLACE—THE MORNING—JACK'S SUFFERINGS FROM COLD AND HUNGER—HOW HE OBTAINED FOOD—HE BUILDS A HUT AND HAS A TERRIFIC COMBAT WITH A BEAR.

IT was some time before our hero could collect his scattered faculties sufficiently to have a distinct perception of the terrible situation into which he was cast.

Still in the storm and darkness; still surrounded by the conflicting elements; still stunned by the roaring of the wind, the dashing of the waves, and the constant creaking and grating of the ice.

As far as he could calculate, he had been thrown upon a floating island, or dense mass of ice, high, rocky, and mountainous, full of hollows, caverns, and fissures of the most grotesque and fantastic shapes, and rising up on two sides in sheer steep walls that shut out the view of all beyond. Yet even this vast mass, he could feel, was agitated and rocked by the violent force of the waves; and through its various interstices the wind roared, and howled, and whistled, as it does through caverns, and ruins, and forests on land.

Yet the ice-island, if such it was, was evidently drifting, and that rapidly, in one direction. It tossed and rolled about like a vessel; but it was far more strong than any ship ever built by man's hands, and the greatest force of the tempest could not crack or separate it.

Jack struggled to his feet, and endeavoured to look around him; but it was with the utmost difficulty he could keep his standing position for a single moment—the ice underfoot was so slippery and uneven, and kept up such a continual rocking motion.

Clinging to the icy walls on each side of him, our hero looked over the angry sea.

Very little could he distinguish. The darkness was too intense for the strongest sight to penetrate. Still he could both see and feel the immense flakes of snow that poured from the sky, and the breakers that dashed over the icy rock.

Where were his companions? It was impossible to say. No sign of the shattered boat, no human form in the waste of ice was visible, no cry mingled with the roaring of the tempest

Had they all perished? Jack could not hope otherwise; it seemed impossible they could have escaped such appalling dangers.

Yet even if so, he was little better off than they; for in his position he saw no chance of ultimately preserving his life.

Must he not perish with cold and hunger on the ice-island.

Jack began to despair. He lamented his friends as dead; himself he regarded as doomed to a speedy fate.

"They, are gone!" he mentally ejaculated.

"There was no chance for those who were not, like myself, thrown upon the rocks. Poor Tom! I had hoped we should have escaped or died

HE SPRANG FROM THE SLIPPERY LEDGE INTO THE ICY PRECIPICE.

together : but you are gone first. Well, I shall not be long in following you, for I've no more chance of escape than——"

He paused with a sharp cry of pain, for something large and flapping hovered about him, striking his head and breast with repeated sharp blows. Jack was half-stunned. He fell back on his knees on the ice. He could not distinguish what it was that attacked him. But he conjectured that was an albatross, or sea-eagle, or some other bird of the stormy deep, which had passed him on its flight. In a moment it was gone; it had passed him like a phantom; but a wild, shrill cry, as it darted away, showed the correctness of his conjecture.

"Heavens! what am I to do?" cried our hero in anguish; "liable to be thus attacked by fierce birds of prey, and utterly helpless, without any weapon to defend myself from the attacks of my enemies!"

He put his hand on his head ; it was bleeding, stunned, and confused ; his brain throbbed, and in every limb he felt stiff, and sore.

Besides that, the cold was still intense, though the high walls of ice, in a great extent, served to shelter him from the wind.

Jack had no other clothes warmer than the jacket, and shirt, and trousers, in which he had been saved from the burning wreck.

Alas! though they had felt hot enough in the excitement of that moment, how inadequate they were to protect him against the present inclement atmosphere !

What a complete contrast was afforded by the two situations!

Jack could not help thinking of this, and how he had been through the utmost extremes of heat and cold, and had been menaced with destruction by the two opposite elements—fire and water.

It was a grim comparison, and yet, situated as he was, he could reflect upon it with deep cogitation, as if it were some abstruse problem.

Such are the inexplicable vagaries in which the human mind, even in positions of danger, will sometimes indulge.

The ice-island still drifted rapidly, the tempest that drove against it still continued fierce and violent.

It was impossible to try to escape from this unpleasant resting-place ; such an attempt would have ended in inevitable death.

Jack knew he must pass the night, however long it might continue, on this block of ice. He therefore proceeded to find out that part of it that would afford him the best shelter.

Groping his way along on his hands and knees with immense difficulty, he endeavoured thus far to explore the island.

We have said how rugged it was, how full of caverns and intricacies.

Among these Jack groped anxiously, and with the constant dread and expectation of falling through some of the crevices into the sea beneath.

He crept along between the high walls of ice, and feeling his way like a man deprived of sight ; and, indeed, the darkness rendered his sight of no avail.

As he proceeded, the wind seemed to lull, or become more distant and powerless, but it could be that the tempest had subsided suddenly

No! He felt that it was in consequence of the more sheltered situation of that part of the island which he was now approaching.

He crept at length into a kind of cavern or grotto, not much larger than could contain him, its rugged walls and roof hung with icicles as hard and sharp as a knife.

The floor, if such it could be called, of this frozen apartment, was very thin, for he could hear the rushing of the waves beneath.

This constituted his present danger ; if it cracked beneath him, and he fell through, no power could save him from instant death.

Beneath such an immense block of ice he would be powerless, even to struggle for life.

Still this cave was the most eligible portion of his singular resting-place.

It was something to be sheltered from the winds, the falling snow, and beyond hearing, except faintly, the roaring of the storm.

If Jack had possessed a blanket, a cloak, or even a thick great-coat, he might have rested in something like comparative comfort.

But he had nothing on him but the insufficient clothes we have described, and he felt the cold intensely.

It was not, however, so bitter and so deadly as that experienced on land amid the snows of an Arctic winter.

The cold was caused more by that of the wind than the atmospheric temperature, and there was some degree of warmth to be obtained even from this cavern of ice.

Jack endeavoured to take advantage of it, as far as he could. Coiling himself up in the smallest possible compass, so as to counteract the heat of the body, and so disposing his clothing around him as to obtain the greatest amount of warmth therefrom, he endeavoured to find some repose after his sufferings.

But he feared to sleep.

He knew, or at least he had heard, that those who suffered themselves to sleep in the snow during the wintry cold of the Arctic region, never woke again.

Would it be the same in a cavern of ice ?

Jack feared so, and, of all things, he dreaded to die in a manner so awful and uncertain.

"I will not go to sleep," he murmured ; "it may be my death if I do. It surely cannot be difficult, in such a position as this, to keep awake."

But, alas! he felt that it was very difficult. By degrees he felt the power of sleep begin to overcome his resolution.

He strove to shake it off, to use every means to ward off a repose so likely to turn to a fatal one, but in vain.

He must go to sleep.

A drowsiness which nothing could combat, an insensibility even to the cold and discomfort of his hiding-place, gradually overwhelmed him.

He began to experience difficulty in fixing his thoughts on any subject—a sure sign of coming sleep—everything in his mind became confused, melted to unconsciousness, and at length into the sleep that he had dreaded.

He slumbered soundly ; his woes were forgotten, and, as far as his mind and his body could distinguish the difference, he might have been in the safest, most luxurious place of repose on land.

Suddenly Jack awoke, so bewildered that he thought he was still in a dream—for he *had* been dreaming—and his mind could not, at present, realise his situation.

He was so benumbed and cramped by being so long in one position, that he feared that he had lost the use of his limbs.

Then he began to feel the bitter intensity of the cold.

But yet it was some degrees less freezing than it had been before he slept.

With immense difficulty, Jack staggered to his feet, over which he seemed to have no control ; and it was only by long chafing and brisk rubbing, to bring back the long-suspended circulation, that his limbs began again to feel as if they were his own.

" Thank God that I'm alive at all ! for I never expected it," he cried fervently. " I dreaded sleep, lest it should be an unwaking one ; but it came upon me, and now I feel much refreshed by it."

He groped out of the cave, and came upon the block of ice.

All had now undergone an immense transformation.

For it was now day.

The sun had arisen, and shone brightly over the glistening ice.

The winds were stilled.

The waves had abated their tempestuous force.

Jack felt hope again revive in his breast.

For, under this changed aspect, there seemed much more chance of escape or of sustaining life in this icy rock than there had been the night before.

In order the better to examine his position, Jack climbed up, by means of the various jagged peaks and masses of ice that were piled around him, to the highest point of the rocky wall that had sheltered him, and standing there, surveyed a scene that for the moment rivetted his thoughts to the expulsion of all other subjects.

Before him stretched, as far as his eyes could reach, a succession of immense fields of ice, piled in ragged, stony lumps, rising to peaks and mountains, and spreading out in boundless glaciers of a smooth frozen surface.

On all these the now brilliant sun produced an effect almost like that of magic.

Refracting his rays, every peak and icicle glistened like diamonds and crystals and precious stones in every conceivable colour and variety of form.

The smooth sea looked like a sea of silver, the valleys might have been sown with diamonds, like that famous spot mentioned by Sinbad the Sailor, while the icy peaks and rocks rose in the forms of towers and spires and ramparts, like a city of ice, such as anyone might imagine to be the abode of the monarch of the Arctic regions.

Jack remarked all this with admiration.

And, indeed, how could he do otherwise ?

For the scene was one of surprising beauty ; and such a panorama as he then beheld, wrought by a skilful painter, and produced in the fairy region of pantomime, would have caused a sensation.

But Jack was not in a position that would enable him to enjoy it fully.

He was in the midst of hardships and privations, and his thoughts, of course, reverted to the consideration of the manifold difficulties he had to encounter.

The sky above was now blue and cloudless, save a thin haze that made the sun seem red and fiery.

The ice-island on which Jack had been cast was motionless.

Indeed, it appeared to have joined the range of icebergs beside him, and the unfrozen sea could only be discovered on one side at a great distance.

From all these signs it became obvious to Jack that he had floated many miles during the night on this ice-island, which, tossed and driven by the waves, had at length drifted so far among the masses of ice that its progress was stopped, and it lay completely locked and enclosed by them.

In short, Jack was now in a region of immense glaciers, stretching he knew not whither—a region that was neither sea nor land, but situated between both.

It was probable that he was near some shore—that is, in a few miles he might hope to reach solid ground ; but how to traverse this region was the difficulty.

It would consume an immense amount of time and toil, which, exhausted as he was by want of food, was doubly difficult to encounter.

As to his companions, Jack had no hope of seeing them again.

He had drifted so far away from where the boat had struck, and he had not the slightest idea in what direction to look for them.

Accordingly, as further anxiety on this matter was useless, he proceeded to do the only thing he could—that is, look out for himself.

"I am terribly hungry," he soliloquised ; " and I see not the slightest chance of getting anything to eat. It will be a fearful thing, after going through so many dangers, to perish at last of starvation !"

At this moment a harsh, discordant cry struck his ear.

It proceeded from an albatross, which, with spreading wings like those of an eagle—which bird indeed it resembled from its immense size and the rapidity of its flight—was cleaving the air seaward with the evident intention of darting down upon its finny prey.

Jack followed it with his eyes, for the sight interested him.

It was the first sign of life he had seen since the wreck.

The bird was followed by others of the same species, which took their flight from the same direction, and were soon far out at sea, engaged in their skilful fishing.

And not only these, but other aquatic birds such as swarm in all inclement and stormy regions, rose in the view of our hero.

Gulls, pelicans, sea-swallows, petrels, and other winged denizens of the frozen water, with every harsh and discordant cry, were on all sides.

Some had evidently made their homes around the towering rocks not very far distant, and others appeared to have taken a longer journey ; but all, in the first place, arose in the same direction.

Our hero noticed this, and the fact inspired him with hope.

"I must watch the flight of these birds," he said; "they all seem to make for the sea, and most of them cross those glaciers yonder. I will try and get across them, too, for whatever direction they come from there is most likely to be land."

Following this idea, our hero commenced the difficult task of climbing over the masses of ice and reaching the glaciers.

Hungry has he was, it was useless to attempt to kill or capture any of the sea birds, for he had no weapon, and, even had he possessed one he had no means of making a fire to cook his quarry.

His only chance was to cross the glacier, and reach, as he fervently hoped, the dry land.

This, however, was a matter of considerable difficulty.

The ice was so smooth and slippery, and uneven on its surface, that every step promised our hero a downfall.

It needed the tenacity of a cat to grasp hold of such uncertain supports as the jagged peaks of ice by which he made his descent.

He contrived, however, to reach the lowest part of the island, and from that to leap on to the adjoining block; in doing so, however, our hero slipped and fell, falling on his hands with a degree of force, which, had his fall been a backward one, would have probably been productive of serious results.

"This won't do," our hero remarked, as he picked himself up, still preserving his equilibrium with almost as much difficulty as a drunken man.

"One wants a pair of skates to get over such a place as this in the proper manner."

"Stop! I know what I'll do."

He took out his pocket handkerchief, tore it into exact halves, and tied each securely round his boots.

By these means his footing was made more secure on the slippery surface, on which, with ordinary leather soles and iron nails, it was impossible otherwise to walk.

"Now, if I only had a stick or a pole, like the alpenstocks, I think they call them, used in crossing the glaciers and mountains in Switzerland, I should be all right; but, as it is, I must do without."

He had now reached the level open fields of ice, which, according to his calculation, must be crossed to arrive at the land. Over this he was soon able to make better progress than he had imagined at first, for it was tolerably flat and even, consisting, for the most part, of small jagged lumps of ice, which had the appearance of having been ground from larger ones, and laid out evenly over this immense surface, in the same manner as the stones are on macadamized roads.

Stepping from one to another of these pieces was, after Jack's struggle across the larger rocks of this icy region, a matter of comparative ease.

Thus Jack went on and on, until on resting and looking back, he was surprised at the distance he had accomplished.

He was going further from the sea, too, and evidently approaching the firm land; for, as he proceeded, more signs of life presented themselves.

The birds became very numerous.

The albatross winged its flight above his head, and frequently passed so near him that, remembering his unpleasant rencontre of the previous night, he placed himself in a position of defence.

The stormy petrels screamed as they flocked in vast numbers on the piles and peaks of ice, or took their way in immense flocks out to sea.

Soon, too, Jack began to come in sight of creatures of a different kind—a great, ponderous elephant—an animal with formidable tusks shining out in contrast to their black skins.

These he knew to be walruses, and knowing their fierce disposition, he did all he could to keep out of their way.

Still more did he fear the moving white, shaggy masses, which he could distinguish perched on some of the rocks of ice; for he knew he was now in the home of that most dangerous devourer of the Arctic region—the Polar bear.

"If any of them should attack me, I shall stand but little chance," Jack murmured. "If I only had a gun, now, or even a whaling-lance, I should not fear so much."

But, fortunately for our hero, the bears were some distance from the track he pursued, and were too much engaged in hunting seals and walruses to notice the unusual phenomenon of a human being in their haunts.

The Polar bear, too, seldom attacks man; though, when he does so, he is a formidable enemy, as Jack soon afterwards was destined to discover.

In the course of a couple of hours Jack had made considerable progress on his Arctic journey, and he had the satisfaction of perceiving that his trouble had not been in vain.

He was approaching land—barren, bleak, desolate land, perhaps; but still something that held out some prospect of ultimately reaching human habitations, and at least escaping from the eternal region of ice.

He had at length entirely passed the glaciers, and entered upon the rocky shore, which was his first promise of deliverance.

The place, to any other eye but that of a man just escaped from Arctic perils, was desolate in the extreme. It consisted of level plains of bare, half-frozen earth, every now and then interrupted by masses of ice, which seemed either congealed ponds or channels communicating with the adjoining sea.

The rocks around were bare and bleak, and only in the distance could be seen mountains of every height, the tops of which were covered with eternal snow.

Jack cast himself on a large projecting lump of rock; he felt in need of rest, for he was already weary of his exertions.

"So far so good!" he said. "I have reached land, and that's more than ever I expected. But I fear it will be my fate to starve in this place, and I am almost dying of hunger now!"

It was rather aggravating to see so many birds around, such as a hunter, had he but fire-arms, could so easily bring down, and which, by the aid of a fire, might make a very good meal.

But Jack was without both these necessaries.

So, after a while he again set forth on his desolate journey. He crossed the wild, bleak expanse of country before him, and found himself again among a ridge of high rugged rocks, over which he had to climb.

On reaching the top of this elevated ground, he observed with some satisfaction that it was covered with short stubbly grass—the first sign of vegetation he had as yet come across.

But what gratified him more than this was that he could perceive that the higher mountains he was now approaching were thickly grown with dark, majestic fir-trees.

"I am approaching a wooded country," cried Jack, with delight; "and wherever wood is, there is, at least, shelter, and probably food and fresh water."

His whole aim was now to reach the desired country.

He toiled on manfully, though he was by this time very much exhausted; but the sight of the opening prospect of a more agreeable region cheered him onward.

His efforts were soon rewarded by his reaching one of the lower hills, and entering a wide expanse of hilly country, thickly grown with fir-trees.

If the air was no warmer, the appearance of the place was far more genial, and our hero's spirits rose in consequence.

"This is about my idea of what Norway must be," he soliloquised. "Well, that's better than the seas of ice I've just left, which are a great deal more like Greenland."

As he spoke he gazed over the more level ground before him, which sloped gradually down to a half-frozen channel, and was covered by a thick growth of short bushes.

In the centre of this region, a flock of wild geese were congregated together.

Fine, splendid birds they were, too.

And Jack felt all the instinct of a sportsman rise in his soul as he beheld them.

"If I only had a good rifle now," he cried, "couldn't I make some havoc among them?"

But, as he approached them, the birds flew away with deafening screams.

He hurled some stones after them, but they missed their aim.

An agreeable surprise was, however, in store for him.

As he was making his way along, he discovered, carefully concealed among the bushes, a number of nests belonging to the geese he had frightened away.

Many of these contained young birds, but these Jack was too humane to injure.

"I won't kill you, you unlucky little creatures," he said to these infant geese; "but I mean to have a feast here nevertheless. The very thing! One can eat eggs raw, even if they cannot eat flesh or fowl without its being cooked."

So he collected as many eggs as he could conveniently carry.

Many of them being of a very large size, he promised himself a very good meal.

He tied them up as well as he could in his handkerchief, which now he had no further necessity to wrap round his feet, and proceeded down the bank of the stream.

He soon reached a very snug little spot, where a mass of bushes grew thickly down to the water's edge, and the roots of the trees intertwined with one another in every variety of form.

He found a natural seat among these roots, and the foliage growing over his head gave him a shelter in the form of a sort of bower.

"Now I can rest in something like comfort," said our hero, with much satisfaction. "So I'll taste and see whether my breakfast is good."

It proved very good, indeed.

The eggs were of excellent flavour, and Jack making a hole in each end with the smallest blade of his pocket-knife, sucked them with great gusto.

Then, when he wanted to drink, he had only to dip the cups formed by the egg-shells into the unfrozen part of the stream before him, and take a draught, which but for its coldness would have been delicious, for it was of purest fresh water.

While Jack was disposing of this meal, which immensely refreshed and strengthened him, he could not help feeling gratitude to that Providence which had thus singled him out to be saved from destruction, and sent him, in the midst of such hardships, the means of supporting life.

But even this thought was greatly saddened by the reflection that he had lost his companions.

Poor old Tom Starboard was no more.

Tim the Whaler had spun his last yarn, and Captain Whittle, who so kindly rescued them from the burning ship, had now lost his own life.

Then, too, what an immeasurable distance he was separated from Mabel, and Captain Hastings, and Mr. Meredith!

They probably believed him dead, and, at least, would never see him more.

His destiny was now to traverse mighty deserts and prairies; undergo terrible hardships; meet with fearful adventures and escapes; and communicate only with such untutored savages as inhabited those desolate wilds.

After his meal was concluded, Jack rested himself for a considerable time, until he at length rose, now greatly refreshed, and prepared for further exertion.

Fixing his course by the sun, which still shone brightly, he saw that the westward was the direction to take, and he was confirmed in this by the increasing amount of vegetation that he discovered as he went.

"I wonder when I shall reach human habitation," pondered Jack. "Whoever lives here, whether Esquimaux or Red Indians, would surely give me shelter and food,"

But he was not destined that day, at least, to meet with any of his fellow-creatures.

Miles of wandering brought him not the slightest signs of human residence—all was as desolate and uninhabited as the home of the famous solitary hero whose name Jack bore.

"I am Crusoe by name and by nature," was our hero's soliloquy; "and it seems as if I am destined always to be cast ashore where there is no human aid or companionship."

The short Arctic day was now drawing to an end, the sun was getting low, and the prospect of a night in such a region without a shelter was getting unpleasantly imminent.

"I must try and build some sort of hut for the night," murmured Jack; "but how, with only a penknife to do it with? That is the question."

He looked around him.

The place was densely covered with trees of all sizes interspersed with brushwood.

Much of the latter was so thin as to be easily cut with the knife, and Jack thus formed a number of poles of a few feet in length.

Then having chosen his position, he cleared a small space of ground beneath some fir-trees and commenced his work.

He drove the stakes firmly into the earth in an upright position with the forks upwards for the purpose of supporting the cross-beams.

The latter were also partly supported by the trunks of the larger trees beneath which they were fixed.

Jack thus made himself four walls and a roof, very fragile certainly, but he hoped efficient for the purpose.

These he covered with "boughs" of small pine branches and leaves, so soft that they are frequently used by the Indians for carpets and mattresses, and some of these Jack placed carefully under his little tent.

For the purpose of a door he could only close the entrance up in the same way after he had crept into it.

He had thus a snug little nest, far more comfortable, he hoped, than his icy lodgings of the night before.

While he was busily employed in the construction of this shelter, Jack had another adventure which was sharp and dangerous while it lasted.

He was cutting down some of the stakes, when he thought he heard footsteps behind him. Turning round immediately, he perceived a large dark object creeping towards him in the gloom, from among the trees.

Jack grasped his knife, and the pole, his only weapon, for he could see the intruder was no man, but probably some wild animal.

He was not long in doubt, for in a few moments, an enormous black bear rushed upon him.

Jack started back; he was ill-prepared for defence against such a formidable assailant, but he determined to do his best.

Just as, with a savage growl, the monster leaped up close to him, our hero, grasping his cudgel firmly, brought its whole weight down with a well-directed aim on the bear's head.

This, however, served only to infuriate the animal; for, with a roar of pain that seemed to shake the forest like thunder, he rose on his hind legs, and with his formidable fore-paws strove to bear Jack to the earth.

The latter, despite his desperate resistance, was soon in the grasp of his shaggy antagonist —a position of great peril.

But Jack's presence of mind did not forsake him.

Though torn and bleeding with one stroke of the bear's paw, and half enclosed in its embrace, one arm was free, and with that he fought for his life.

The largest blade of his knife was open; it was long and sharp, and quite as efficient a weapon as a dagger.

Jack collected all his strength, and brought it down upon the bear's skull.

He knew that could he but touch a vital part, the little weapon would be as fatal as a gun shot.

His bravery was rewarded with success.

The blade entered the eye, and from that penetrated to the brain.

The bear's death was instantaneous.

With a wild dying roar of rage and pain, he reeled back, unclasped his powerless limbs from around his destined prey, and fell sideways upon the earth, which trembled beneath his immense weight and the violence of his fall.

Jack had triumphed. The struggle had been a short, sharp, and perilous one to him; but he had met with success, and pride was mingled with gratitude as he ascertained this fact.

With inadequate weapons, his courage alone had enabled him to gain a victory that seemed almost hopeless.

On assuring himself that the bear was dead, he resolved to turn his victory to some account.

With great difficulty and labour he cut open the immense carcase of the bear with his knife, and tore off the yet reeking skin.

It was terrible work, one that covered him with blood, and made him feel almost like a person committing some cannibalistic deed; but at last it was accomplished.

The greater part of the skin was severed from the body, and it was so large and thick, that Jack knew it would be of immense value to him.

He dragged the carcase as far as he could from his resting place for the night, and having cleansed the skin as well as he was able, wrapped himself up in it and crept into his hut, which he closed after him.

By this time it was dark, and he soon slept soundly.

CHAPTER LII.

FEARFUL POSITION — ATTACKED BY WOLVES— THE ICEBERGS AGAIN — FIGHT WITH POLAR BEARS.

JACK was awakened suddenly, after an uninterrupted sleep of a few hours, by a sound which filled him with the utmost horror and dismay.

It was a wild, terrible, unearthly sound to hear in that dead stillness and darkness—a sound which no one, even in a more secure position than Jack, could listen to without trembling.

A loud, prolonged howl, not from one throat alone, but from hundreds, all joining and blending in one dreadful chorus.

Our hero started up; he was wide awake in a moment—wide awake and alive to his danger, for he knew what this ominous sign portended.

He was surrounded by wolves!

Picture to yourself, if you can, any position more fearful and perilous than that in which our gallant hero now found himself.

Alone in the frozen forest, in the darkness of an Arctic night, without weapons, without any security from attack, and menaced by the presence of such bloodthirsty foes!

He got up and listened breathlessly. The wolves were very near him, and believed from the sound that the pack of these savages of the northern forest probably amounted to some hundreds.

At length Jack ventured to peep cautiously out of his fragile tent.

All his worst fears were more than confirmed by the spectacle he beheld. In the night-gloom, now melting into the coming light of morning, he could distinguish the dark forms of his enemies, relieved by the whiteness of the frozen and snow-covered ground.

An immense, apparently innumerable, pack of wolves were assembled round the body of the bear he had killed, which they were devouring eagerly.

It was a revolting and appalling sight; hundreds of these horrid beasts of prey were leaping and tumbling over each other in their frantic endeavours to get a portion of the prey. Growling and snapping as ferociously as so many demons. One would be successful in reaching a portion of the bear, and try to drag it away, when he would be instantly surrounded by dozens of others, who would soon tear it from him piece-meal.

The carcase did not last them many minutes; its bones were soon picked clean, and almost before our hero could fully ascertain the peril of his position, nothing remained of the bear but a few scattered bones.

Jack saw that he was now in the greatest danger; armed only with a knife, it was useless to contend against such a horde of howling monsters.

His only chance of escape lay in reaching a tree, and he lost no time in selecting one high enough to afford him shelter.

Already the famishing creatures were scenting him out.

One huge gaunt monster, whose eyes seemed balls of fire, was standing not ten yards from the tent, and it was evident he regarded Jack as his destined prey.

The horrid monster licked his sanguinary jaws as he regarded our hero, with horrible expectancy.

Dozens of others soon joined him.

Jack was now compelled to act quickly to secure the chance of saving his life.

One wolf had leaped upon the poles of the tent, and was endeavouring with teeth and claws to tear down the frail structure.

Thrusting his knife through the interstices of the hut, Jack reached the heart of the wolf, who, with a loud, quick howl, fell dead instantly.

This was as a signal to the main body of wolves, who, smelling the blood, came at full speed to the hut.

The dead body of their comrade was eaten in a few moments, and Jack, profiting by the trifling delay it afforded, dashed down the poles at the back of the tent, and ran with the desperation of fear towards a huge pine, whose long drooping boughs promised a comparatively easy ascent.

Nor was he an instant too soon in his flight.

Before he had got a dozen yards his tent was utterly destroyed by the trampling of the wolves, who the instant they saw him gave chase.

Jack sprang up with a superhuman effort, and caught and clutched with the desperation of extreme peril at the nearest branch within reach.

With what tenacity he clung to it, with what terrified muscular force he leaped higher, until his whole frame was securely clinging to the bough, it is scarcely necessary to record.

Extreme danger gives extra strength; and men, under the pressure of imminent peril, have been known to achieve feats which at other times they would have found impossible.

Step by step our hero reached an altitude where he might consider himself safe; and, resting on the strong bough of the pine, looked down at his enemies.

The first rays of dawn were lighting up the sky, and he could now distinguish the forms of his enemies, rendered all the more horrible by the still uncertain and hazy character of the light which revealed them to him.

No sound that ever Jack had heard more appalled him than the ferocious and combined yell of baffled rage which came from their throats as they perceived him.

They saw that he had escaped them, for a time at least; and that nothing but watching till he was exhausted would give them any chance of making him their prey.

They leaped up repeatedly in frantic efforts to reach him, their eyes glistening like red-hot coals, their cruel slavering jaws and blood-red tongues evincing their sanguinary hunger and eagerness for destruction.

Add to this their rage at being baulked of the prey they expected, which goaded them almost to fury.

Jack felt that he was comparatively safe, and yet there was a cold, sickening sensation at his heart which he could not resist.

Though beyond their reach, there is a degree of terrible anxiety in being thus so near to such bloodthirsty foes.

One moment's loss of strength, and he might fall from his resting-place in the midst of them.

And what fate can be imagined more awful than that of being devoured alive by ravenous wolves?

How tightly our hero clung to the tree!

He was not of so bold a character as to be able, as some might do, to taunt his foes on their inability to reach him.

He knew his danger was still great, for there was the prospect of being thus besieged for hours without chance of deliverance.

For the wolves seemed determined not to leave him.

They are patient, and, like cats, can wait for their prey, if they see no more immediate chance of satisfying their hunger.

On this course they seemed disposed to act in the present instance.

Clamouring and surrounding the tree on all sides, they spent their strength in vain endeavours to bring their prey within their reach.

After a time, however, they saw the fruitlessness of such efforts, and they became more calm.

Still they did not move—not a single member of that vast herd.

Seated on their haunches, they looked up at Jack with eyes as fierce as they were fixed.

Not for an instant was their gaze turned from him.

This alone afforded a good reason for mortal terror.

There is something so powerfully affecting in the basilisk glance of a pair of ferocious eyes, whose presence denotes deadly peril.

How much, then, is it increased by the numbers of such orbs being counted by hundreds?

As the daylight grew, Jack was able more distinctly to perceive them, and they had a kind of ferocious glitter which gave them almost the aspect of demons waiting for their prey.

Thus, benumbed with cold, his heart filled

with irrepressible terror, did our gallant young hero cling to the branches of the tree, surveying the terrible prospect of menaced death beneath him.

Would the wolves never go away?

They sat watching him with a constant, deadly, and patient intentness that was in itself terrible.

Hour after hour passed away in this manner, the wolves evincing no signs of being wearied of their vigilant watch.

Jack was terribly cramped, and very hungry, while the cold was so intense that he could scarcely maintain his position in the tree.

There seemed no chance of escape; his only hope lay in his being able to tire out the ravenous brutes.

It was now mid-day, and still no relief.

Jack revolved in his mind project after project, but could hit upon no plan likely to succeed.

One thing was certain: he could not maintain his hold much longer, he must soon drop from exhaustion; and then what a fate was in store for him!

Casting for the hundredth time a glance upon his expectant enemies, he saw that he was no longer the sole object of their attention.

On looking around to ascertain the cause of their relaxing their vigilance, he perceived a troup of about twenty reindeer at a great distance.

They evidently scented danger.

One enormous creature, perhaps the leader of the herd, was standing some ten yards in advance of the others.

The wolves, from being on rather lower ground, were at first unperceived by him; but at length, catching sight of them, he gave a stamp with his fore-feet, and the whole herd instantly started off at full speed, followed, to our hero's great delight, by his besiegers.

They had now a prospect of other prey.

Thus, once more, was Jack rescued from what at one time he regarded as inevitable death.

He waited till the chase was out of sight; and then, descending from his perch, he endeavoured by exercise to restore warmth to his benumbed frame.

His next purpose was to form a hut, which he determined to make of snow, the material most abundant around him.

The Esquimaux, near whose country he now supposed himself to be, were in the habit of building, as Jack well knew, very snug and commodious residences.

There were piles and mountains of snow in every direction, and Jack would have no difficulty in collecting sufficient of it for the purpose.

Having a flat, heavy piece of wood as a kind of trowel and also as a spade to carry the lumps of snow upon, he fixed for the site of his new habitation an open space of ground, well protected by the neighbouring fir trees.

Here he set to work with considerable industry, removing loads of snow and piling them one upon another in the form of a wall, beating them together flat and hard with his wooden spade.

In this manner the four walls of his residence were soon raised, a small opening left to serve as a door, and a smaller one placed much higher up to give admission to the light.

All was soon finished except the roof, and this was not difficult to make.

A few branches and pieces of brushwood placed across each other, seemed to support the snow which Jack heaped upon them.

This was also beaten flat and hard, and our hero had the satisfaction of seeing his dwelling complete.

He lined the interior with soft brushwood, as he had done that of his smaller hut, and found he could easily, after he had crept into his resting-place, secure the door behind him by placing the remains of the bear-skin over the opening.

"This will keep out the wolves, or bears, or anything, if I am not much mistaken," said Jack, looking with satisfaction at his work. "They will hardly try to besiege such a hut as this, with the walls a solid foot and a-half thick. If it freezes before the morning it will be as strong as a castle."

Feeling now very hungry, Jack proceeded to set out in search of something that would afford him a breakfast.

He had no weapon but a long, stout pole, or staff, which would serve him both to make his way over the uneven ground, and, he hoped, knock down some wild bird or small animal he might come across in the frozen forest.

Ascending with this purpose a neighbouring rising ground, which rose to a height that embraced an extensive view, he paused and surveyed the surrounding country.

It was now mid-day, and the sun gilding the spotless waste of snow and ice, stretching out on one side to the ice-berg covered sea, and on the other to deserts unknown, turned the otherwise desolate landscape into a scene of beauty.

But Jack had not contemplated it many seconds before a distant object arrested his attention, and made his heart bound with exultant hope.

It was a ship, far out at sea.

He could distinguish it well in the clear light, its white sails and its black hull.

It was apparently some European brig or trading vessel, becalmed, or at least proceeding at a very slow pace.

Could he communicate with it?

Here was a chance of rescue from the hardships he was now suffering.

Jack waved his pole over his head and shouted loudly until he remembered the uselessness of such efforts.

It was impossible for those on the vessel to hear him at that distance.

No, he must try and traverse the frozen waste, of ice and snow, get nearer the sea, and on one of the icebergs sufficiently high up to render his form observable.

Hesitating not an instant, Jack set off on a long and difficult clamber over endless masses of snow and ice and jagged glaciers, keeping in the direction of the ship.

At last he reached the side of the unfrozen water, on which were numberless pieces of ice floating about.

Standing on one of these, a few feet in length, but large enough to bear his weight, he again looked out to sea, and saw he had approached much more closely to the welcome vessel. But it was still a long distance off, and he did not see how he could communicate with it.

He at length formed the extraordinary design of chasing the ship on a lump of ice.

He could use it as a boat, guiding it with his pole until it had got some distance from shore, and the current was setting on the sea strongly.

But how was it possible that he could thus traverse the large distance from the vessel?

He could scarcely hope to accomplish this, but he might be enabled to come sufficiently near it to make signals.

At all events it did not require much exertion of strength to push this strange craft from shore, which Jack readily did.

For some time he went on swimmingly, but he had not proceeded far before the real difficulties of his journey commenced.

He could not steer the small iceberg, safely through the large masses of ice that studded the channel on all sides.

It seemed to have a tendency to run against, and remain fixed to, one of these masses.

Meanwhile he kept his eyes anxiously riveted on the ship.

She had apparently not moved.

"It is my only hope of rescue," he murmured. "1 hope it will not fail me."

Suddenly a terrific and continued growl, fearful and startling, echoed and reverberated from among the ice islands near him.

He started, turned his head, and perceived upon an adjoining block of ice a group of Polar bears.

They were not less than three in number, and the largest and fiercest of their species.

Their ferocious eyes were fixed upon him.

Jack's heart gave a great leap, "to his mouth," as the saying is.

It was impossible he could regard this danger without fear.

Armed only with the pole, how far he was fitted to cope with such formidable enemies can be imagined.

Alone, too, and on the ice, from which there was no escape.

To make his position worse, the small iceberg on which he had imprudently trusted himself, was now jammed fast against a large one.

To move it was beyond all that his most strenuous exertions could accomplish.

Jack stood face to face with his enemies. Their eyes were fixed upon him with that deadly glittering intensity with which beasts of prey regard their intended victims.

If ever Jack's stout heart almost completely failed him; if ever he needed most presence of mind, but stood most chance of losing it, it was now.

The suspense was short, for the bears all at the same moment sprang towards him.

One mighty bound, and they had alighted on the iceberg on which he stood. But they could not at first succeed in securing their footing.

Their weight gave such a shock to the fragile piece of ice, that it rocked and plunged, while one end sank for a moment deep into the waters.

This caused the bears to slip with a loud splash into the waves; but they had loosened the piece of ice from its fixed position, and propelled it again on its course.

Jack saw an opportunity, and gave it a tremendous push out from the shore.

His three assailants had completely lost their hold, but only for a moment were they disconcerted; they were soon cleaving the waves, and swimming rapidly after him.

As long as he could, Jack propelled the iceboat, using his pole as an oar, at some speed, but far from sufficient to distance such foes in their native element.

They had soon reached the iceberg, and began trying to climb up its sides; Jack stood up and endeavoured to ward them off with his pole.

Such a contest could not be sustained any length of time; in fact, the odds were too fearful to leave Jack any chance.

Luckily the iceberg had again struck against a larger one.

Could he possibly climb up the latter, and perch himself securely out of the reach of his enemies?

But he knew that even here the bears could follow him.

Still the experiment was worth trying.

Clutching hold of a projecting crag of ice above his head, our hero collected all his strength in one mighty bound, and then drew himself up a few feet above his late dangerous situation.

In doing this, necessarily, he had to drop his pole—his only weapon.

But he did it to save his life

He was only just in time, for one of the bears had already reached the top of the smaller iceberg, and was pursuing the chase.

The fall of Jack's pole attracted the attention of the animal, who stopped to observe it.

Meanwhile, Jack was climbing and struggling up the peaks of ice.

He cut his hands and bruised himself fearfully in this operation, and even then he could scarcely accomplish it, and expected every moment to slip off into the water.

Above all, he found it impossible to keep his footing for a moment in such a position with his boots; accordingly, the first time he could manage to steady himself, he tore them off.

There was no help for it, he must abandon these useful articles of clothing, although from being so torn about by his recent travels, they had become but of slight utility to him

Climbing as fast as he could, Jack at length reached the extreme top of the iceberg, which was of enormous size.

Climbing to one of its peaks, he looked over to observe his enemies.

They were rapidly climbing up after him, and in a few moments a hand-to-hand struggle with them would be inevitable.

How could he release himself from his fate?

Near him lay, in a confused heap, some jagged irregular lumps of ice.

They must have weighed two or three hundred-weight each, and some of them were too heavy for Jack to move.

He determined, however, to avail himself of these means of defence.

Seizing, therefore, one of these ponderous masses, our hero hurled it with all his strength, and with considerable accuracy of aim, down upon the head of the foremost bear.

It descended with a tremendous shock, and the animal, unprepared for so desperate a method of retaliation, fell backwards with a loud growl.

He was stunned by the weight of the missile, and, for a moment at least, was rendered harmless.

His companions, scared by his accident, started backward, and seemed disposed to give up the chase.

Jack now clambered with all his might and speed over the masses of ice before him, until he reached a more level expanse of broken blocks of ice mingled with drifted snow, along which he could make his way with comparative ease and celerity.

CHAPTER LIII.

A FURTHER CHASE OF THE BEAR—THE ESQUIMAUX THE REIN-DEER AND SLEDGE—CHASED BY WOLVES —THE PRECIPICE—NARROW ESCAPE—DEATH OF THE INDIAN CHIEF.

THE excitement of his contest with these formidable Arctic foes had made Jack almost forget the vessel.

Now, however, he remembered how all his hopes were centred on it, and looked eagerly out to sea for the welcome sail.

But, alas! it made some way during the skirmish with the bears, and in any case it was useless to hope for communication with it.

Jack could do nothing but gaze sorrowfully at its vanishing form.

" All my hopes cut off!" he exclaimed. " What shall I do?"

There was nothing to be done but retrace his steps inland, and make up his mind to traverse vast barren deserts.

More immediate dangers, however, were not over yet.

A scrambling sound behind him showed that one of the bears was still on his track ; in fact, pursuing him with the most savage fury.

" I must run," thought our hero ; "that is, as quick as I can, on such a surface as this. How lucky it is that I am coming to snow instead of ice, on which I should stand a chance of slipping every moment."

But he found that snow was, at all events, very different to solid land, and that it was hopeless to expect that he could distance the bear, which every moment gained upon him.

Still he pursued his way with all the energy he could exert.

If he could only reach his hut, without being overtaken, he might consider himself safe.

His enemy, however, was approaching him with fearful speed.

His flight seemed almost hopeless.

His resistance would be certain death.

Suddenly he remembered a stratagem that he had heard attributed to one of the messmates of old Tom Starboard, during the latter's Arctic voyages.

Taking out the two torn halves of his pocket handkerchief, he threw one down behind him, right in the path of the bear, when the latter was within a few yards him.

The bear, according to the habit of his species, stopped to examine this strange object, snuffing and smelling at it with considerable curiosity.

While he was doing this, of course, Jack made off with all the speed he was master of.

The delay on the beast's part was thus very advantageous to Jack.

But his enemy was not long in perceiving that the half of the handkerchief was of little use to him, and that he was losing his prey through it.

He therefore recommenced the chase with great vigour.

He had soon made up for the lost time, and Jack was again in the most imminent peril.

What would succeed once, however, was, in this case, likely to be efficacious the second time ; and Jack, as soon as the bear had again come within a few yards' distance, threw down the other part of his handkerchief.

The bear stopped again, and sniffed at this as he had done the other half ; but he seemed moved to wrath on perceiving what it was, and, with a fierce growl, shook and tore it between his teeth.

Jack had by this time made more progress than before ; but the bear followed him with proportionate speed.

The next time Jack threw down the battered cap, which he had still preserved all through his late adventures, and the bear stopped again to examine it.

In this way Jack proceeded till he came in sight of his hut, but, finding he could not reach it before being overtaken, he lost no time in springing up and ascending the first tree he came to, and, seated upon its branches, baulked his enemy in the same manner as he had done the wolves.

The animal was naturally disappointed and aggravated—it was lucky that he did not belong to the American brown or black species, which climb trees with great agility ; but, as this bear could not do this, though he made several ineffectual attempts, he seemed determined to wait till Jack came down.

The latter was not disposed to do so in a hurry ; but he contemplated with dismay the prospect of another such siege as he had with the wolves.

One enemy, however, was better than a hundred ; neither did the bear show so much patience as the wolves ; for, after a time, he saw that his chase had been useless, and came to the determination of abandoning it.

A loud growl of disappointed rage, and then the animal turned tail and started off in pursuit of seals or walrus.

Jack's immediate danger was now over ; but how many more perils hovered closely around him it was impossible to say.

He could only trust to Providence, which had so frequently and mercifully befriended him.

The hut would shelter him if necessary for a day or two ; but, without weapons of any kind, he would be unable either to kill game for food or to defend himself against such enemies as had recently attacked him.

What weapon could he make that would be of any service to him?

A bow and arrow would be the most useful, as well as practicable to make, and Jack, therefore, reflected in what way he could manufacture these.

There were many stunted trees growing near the place where had constructed his hut, and some of these were fitted admirably for the purpose.

Some were supple and pliant, as a bow should

he; others long and straight, and promised to make good arrows.

Jack immediately set to work to turn these materials to account.

"There is one thing in this sort of life," he soliloquised; "it makes a fellow learn to shift for himself. Not that I want to learn that now, for I have had plenty of it in my time."

He had soon cut and notched with his knife the piece of wood for the body of his bow, as well as several of the slender, reed-like pieces of underwood, which he cut into the ordinary length of arrows.

"But, about the string of my bow!" the thought suddenly struck our hero. "Where and how shall I procure that?"

He remembered that the Indians were in the habit of cutting strips of bear-hide for this purpose, of the required length and thickness, and that they formed admirable substitutes for more artificial materials.

The carcase of the bear he had slain on the preceding night had been so thoroughly devoured by the wolves that it would be idle to expect to find the least portion of it, but some fragments of the hide might still remain among the ruins of his temporary hut which the wolves had destroyed.

Acting on this supposition, Jack searched the spot, which presented many signs of the ravages that had been committed.

The ground was torn up, the grass trampled, the mangled and mutilated skeleton of the bear lay half imbedded in heaped fragments, and only a scattered pile of brushwood and piles marked the site of his recent hut.

Among the latter, he had the satisfaction of discovering a portion of the torn and mangled hide of the bear, and out of this he hoped to cut a strip long enough to answer his purpose. His knife, that useful implement, without which he could have done nothing, soon severed the required portion, and pruned it into the necessary shape. Overjoyed at his success, Jack strung the bow tightly, and, though a rude one in appearance, it promised to be a good and useful weapon.

Jack tipped his arrows with some small splinters of bone, severed with great difficulty, from the skeleton of the bear, and scraped sharp at the point. He had as yet no feathers to steady the aim of his arrows; but he hoped that the first trial of his new weapons would enable him to do so.

The bear-skin—even what remained of it—was yet large enough to furnish other useful articles.

"Why shouldn't I form myself a whole dress of skins, like my namesake, Robinson Crusoe?" he asked. "My present clothes are not much protection, and these would keep me warm."

He set to work, cutting strips and pieces of various shapes from the skin.

First, he formed himself a sort of coat, or tunic, of one piece. The sleeves, being fastened only by the strips of hide, cut as thin as was practicable in the same way, a hat, covering the entire head, and protecting the sides of the face, like a hood, was made; then a pair of shoes, fastened by thongs of bear leather, run through small holes; and, lastly, a broad bandage of leather, tied round the legs, served in lieu of boots or gaiters.

Jack also made a pair of mufflers, not quite so well fitting as ordinary gloves; but serving, in some degree, to protect the hand from the biting cold.

In all these impromptu articles of dress, the fur was turned inwards, the best way of securing the utmost degree of warmth.

The manufacture of all these things involved a considerable amount of time and labour; but Jack did not care for that, the result was so satisfactory.

"There!" he exclaimed, "that is the way to make the best of opportunities. Necessity teaches one to do things which we are apt to consider so difficult as to be almost impossible. I don't look much unlike Robinson Crusoe, now."

And he certainly did not, although he had no skin umbrella, which was less requisite in those barren regions than the fertile sunny isle on which our old favourite was cast.

Jack's last performance was to carve a heavy wooden club out of a bough of pine-wood, and make a broad, strong hide girdle, which would serve both to fasten the skin round his waist and hold his weapons.

Thus equipped, Jack set off in pursuit of game. It was rather late to do so, for the adventures had worn away the day, and the night was fast approaching.

Jack had tolerable sport, for he killed in a short time several wild birds, and then, the gloom of an Arctic night coming on, and the roar of wild animals being heard in the distance, he returned to his hut, faint and hungry, with a fast that had now lasted twenty-four hours.

With the steel blade of his knife and a piece of sharp flint he at length made a fire of dry brushwood, on which he piled branches of trees.

It flared up bravely, and thrusting a skewer through one of the birds he had shot, he broiled it over the embers.

The heat soon cooked it, and almost by the time the feathers had been quite singed off the interior was fit for eating.

Hunger is the best sauce; and Jack enjoyed this rude meal as much as he had ever enjoyed anything in his life.

Then he turned into his hut, closed the opening with the piece of skin, and wrapping himself in his warm clothes, slept undisturbed till morning.

Early the next day he was up again, cooking breakfast similar to his meal of the night before.

After that he wandered forth again in hopes of perceiving another ship; but none appeared that day.

Jack had resolved the next day to start off inland, for which purpose he cooked several of the wild birds, and cut the flesh into slices, and packed it into a skin pouch he made of the small animals he shot.

This would give him provisions on the long and uncertain journey.

His bow and arrows and club had proved trusty weapons, inferior only to a gun and pistol, while they were far less heavy to carry.

While disposing of his dinner that day Jack thought he perceived some figures moving along the snow at some distance.

He started up eagerly, and could plainly distinguish the forms of reindeer sledges and men.

Overjoyed at the sight, Jack rushed towards them, shouting wildly, and soon found himself in the centre of a group of astonished Esquimaux.

They were about ten in number, with four reindeer and as many sledges, and were crossing the country to the northward.

Their wild, dark countenances, stunted forms, and dresses of furs, ornamented with the feathers and down of birds, gave them altogether an appearance different to that of any persons Jack had ever beheld.

Of course he could not comprehend their language, and could only communicate with them by signs.

Jack pointed out to sea, made signs of distress, and tried to make them comprehend that he had been wrecked in a vessel out there ; then pointed to the snow hut he had built, and, lastly, made signs entreatingly, as if he required their assistance.

They understood it better than he at first supposed.

And then ensued a long confabulation between them in their strange language.

It ended in one, who seemed to be the chief of the party, motioning Jack to jump into one of the sledges ; and when he had done so, gave him some pemmican, whale's blubber, and other provisions.

Jack, however, made them understand that, though he was grateful, he had other food with him more congenial with his taste—namely, the flesh of the wild birds in his pouch.

His new friends made him understand that he could not accompany them, for they were going out northward for hunting, but that he was more likely to reach human habitations by proceeding in the opposite direction.

Jack, overjoyed with delight, obeyed these signs with every expression of gratitude, and leaving these generous friends, to whom he could offer no remuneration, sallied forth with a light heart in the southern direction.

His reindeer took him along in beautiful style, clearing the waste of snow at a brisk trot, and seeming to skim the surface rather than to run over it.

As he proceeded, the country became more open.

The snow lay thick, and the trees gave more signs of leaf and verdure.

Jack thought, too, the atmosphere was getting rather less intense.

In short, he had strong hopes that he should, in time, reach more genial latitudes.

For many hours he journeyed without misadventure.

But at length he heard a prolonged growl behind him.

He turned in terror, and perceived that an immense herd of wolves were giving chase to the sledge.

He immediately urged the reindeer to the utmost speed.

Not that it required any application of the rein or the stick he carried.

The animal, on hearing the wolves evinced the greatest terror, and flew along the frozen surface with all his speed.

For a time he gained on his pursuers, and he had strong hopes of distancing them altogether.

But these unwearying creatures, accustomed to chasing deer, still kept up the pursuit.

They always gain their prey, tiring it out by incessant exertions, and giving it no respite in its wild career over the snowy ground.

The chase kept on.

But Jack, to his dismay, could see that his brave animal was getting fatigued.

Large drops of foam fell from his mouth.

His eyes were wild, and he became almost unmanageable.

Still the wolves continued in hot pursuit.

At length the foremost wolf was not more than ten yards from the sledge.

Jack, drawing an arrow from the sheath, shot at him, and with fatal aim, for the wolf immediately rolled over in the snow.

This proved a slight check.

The main body of the wolves stopped, and commenced devouring their companion.

This was soon done.

Again the race for life was recommenced.

Jack kept on shooting at the foremost.

In most cases he was successful in his aim, but at length his arrows were exhausted.

The wolves were now closing round him.

One leapt right upon the back of the sledge.

His head was quite close to Jack.

His eyes were glaring at our hero, and his mouth distended, showing his gleaming teeth.

His hot breath was felt by Jack, who, raising his club, struck him several heavy blows, and at length tumbled him over on to the snow, where he shared the fate of so many of his comrades.

At the moment, too, the reindeer, who had struggled so bravely, began to swing from side to side, reeled, and then fell headlong to the ground.

The shock precipitated our hero out of the sledge. He fell, and expected nothing less than to be devoured immediately ; but, to his surprise, he found himself slipping along the ground at a rapidly accelerating pace.

The reindeer had fallen on the very verge of a precipice, the top of which was covered with overhanging snow, and the weight of Jack was sufficient to precipitate him into the abyss.

In vain he endeavoured to grasp at some object to retard his fall, the smooth surface of the snow baffled all his efforts, and half blinded by the white masses, he was compelled to resign himself to his fate.

The precipice was about fifty feet in height, and almost perpendicular ; fortunately for our hero, there was about five feet of snow at the bottom, where he found himself at length up to his neck, but otherwise uninjured. Though somewhat confused by his unexpected fall, he had, however, escaped from his enemies. The wolves would be totally unable to descend the precipice, which extended for miles.

Our hero sighed as he thought of the fate of the brave animal which had borne him so swiftly from impending death. But it was necessary now to think of his own position, again sufficiently perilous ; alone, without a sledge, in the desolate, north without any weapons but his knife in his belt, for he had lost the others in his fall, and no means of procuring food. Shaking himself from the snow, Jack glanced around to see the most probable direction to meet any tribe of Indians or friendly Esquimaux.

A HERD OF WILD BEASTS SCOURED THE PLAIN.

At length he determined to continue the same southerly direction as the most likely way to obtain success.

After walking in the forest for two hours he had the satisfaction of reaching a dense thicket, where, at all events, he could obtain firewood.

Setting himself down on a fallen log, he was thinking over the best course to pursue, when he was startled by hearing loud growls from a direction in the forest where he was unable to see much, on account of the dense brushwood.

Knowing that he was in no condition to cope, single-handed, with a bear, he walked quietly away from the spot, when he was arrested by the sound of a human voice, seemingly in great agony.

This was enough for our hero.

All thoughts of danger to himself were lost, and, drawing his knife from its sheath, he rushed quickly to the spot, and a sight presented itself, which caused him to start back with involuntary terror.

An enormous bear stood over the prostrate form of an Indian, who seemed at the last gasp.

An angry growl from the bear, as he turned his shaggy head, and perceived the approach of our hero, caused the unfortunate man to look in his direction.

His eyes met Jack's with an expression of imploring entreaty, and at the same time of suddenly aroused hope.

Determined to make an effort to save the man's life, Jack darted forward, and, grasping his knife, approached the bear, and struck him on the head with all his force.

The blow was effectual, and the fierce animal fell senseless to the ground.

This gave Jack an opportunity of despatching the bear without further trouble.

He then turned his attention to the unfortunate victim, who was still sensible, though frightfully lacerated.

He lifted him up, and perceived that he was bleeding from several frightful wounds.

At this moment, a quick, light footstep close behind Jack, caused him to turn.

He found himself confronted by another Indian, many years younger than the first.

They gazed at each other in surprise for some moments.

Jack had leisure to admire the finely-formed figure and handsome features of the other.

But the gaze of the red man was fixed in dismay on the prostrate form of the Indian, and he gave an exclamation of passionate grief.

He darted towards him.

He knelt down beside Jack, and supported the form of the elder warrior.

"My white brother has used his weapons well," he said, in good English, gazing on the prostrate form of the bear. "But, O Great Spirit of the pale faces! he was not in time to save the venerable Walinquan, the beloved chief of my tribe. Oh, my father! art thou indeed wounded—killed by the talons of the savage foes, against which your arm was unerring?"

"He is not dead," said Jack, "though I fear seriously hurt."

The bear was of the largest and fiercest kind, and the old chief was close in his embrace.

"And my brave white brother killed the savage enemy?" said the young Indian, in grateful tones. "Monalqua thanks him for trying to save his father's life. If he will come to the tents of our people, they will all do honour to the brave white chief; but I entreat thee assist Monalqua to remove the body of his beloved father."

Together they lifted the form of the now insensible Indian. The young chief led the way with hasty steps, and Jack followed. They proceeded some distance in silence, while the shades of night closed more deeply around them, and the forest became more dense.

The Indian led his companion through numberless intricate paths, and at length brought him out suddenly in an open space, where several tents stood almost completely hidden by the neighbouring trees.

The young Indian penetrated the largest and most important-looking tent, followed by Jack, who now found himself in the midst of a dusky array of Indians, all armed with spears, clubs, and tomahawks, and bedizened in savage grandeur.

They regarded him with astonishment for some moments, but their attention was speedily centred on the prostrate form of their chief.

They crowded around it, and turned to Jack's conductor for an explanation.

The young Indian spoke rapidly and excitedly in the language of his tribe, which was unknown to Jack, who, however, understood the appropriate gestures of the young man, which betokened the grief he felt and communicated to the rest.

The instant he had done speaking, the whole tribe rose from the ground, as with one consent, and surrounded Jack with tokens of approbation. Gratitude at his gallant conduct in striving to save the life of their chief at once made them his friends.

But his efforts had been in vain, for the old Indian was so fearfully wounded that his last hour had come.

Jack who was, meanwhile, in another tent, had surveyed intently the strange group which surrounded him.

One of the chiefs moved his hand towards a heap of skins, inviting Jack to be seated.

He gladly availed himself of the offer.

A profound silence succeeded the former excitement for nearly an hour, which seemed ages to Jack, when it was suddenly broken by an unusual wail of grief, which caused him to start to his feet.

The chiefs also rose, followed by their bewildered guest.

The cause soon became apparent.

Standing round a litter, a number of Indians were exhibiting signs of the utmost grief, while the shrill cries of the women announced that the Indian chief had died from the effects of his encounter with the bear.

Jack turned away from this scene so fraught with horror, and again seated himself in the tent.

The whole of that day, although they extended hospitality towards their guest, the entire soul and attention of the Indians seemed absorbed in grief for the bereavement they had met with.

In the night Jack retired to the tent of one of the warriors, where, exhausted with his many exertions, he slept soundly.

Not so the others, who nearly all kept up a

vigil throughout the weary night around the body of their chief.

On the following day the funeral obsequies of the Indian were to be performed; and these as our readers may have heard, are conducted with great ceremony among all the North American tribes.

The scene presented a singular spectacle in the eyes of a white man.

Arrayed, seated as in life with the most valuable ornaments the tribe possessed, the corpse of the aged chieftain seemed as if he was still in life, save that the glazed eyes and stiffened limbs showed that the last spark had fled.

Grouped around the dead were the forms of his son and all the chiefs of his tribe.

The young Indian warrior concealed his anguish with stoical firmness.

He alone seemed to possess the power of repressing all outward evidences of emotion.

He sat gazing at the lifeless form of his parent, as one whose thoughts were far away, or too rivetted and concentrated on one subject to be influenced by any other.

Meanwhile the women of the tribe were engaged in carrying on the pathetic ceremony which is used among the North American tribes.

Gathered in a circle around the body of the aged chief, they scattered wreaths of flowers, gathered from the adjoining forest, on his bier, all the time giving vent to a wild and plaintive chant, a kind of funeral coronach, which, begun by one singly, was gradually taken up by all the rest, and swelled into a soft harmony.

It is impossible for language to describe the effect of such a sound, echoing through the depths of the vast primeval forest; but it was completely in keeping with the wild and warlike figures of the Indians, and their attitudes of grief.

They understood the full force of the words they heard, which to Jack were meaningless; but from the expressive gestures that accompanied them he well knew that the maidens of the tribe were bewailing the dead, were extolling his virtues, his bravery, his wondrous skill as a hunter, his mighty valour in the deadly field of battle.

Sometimes this chant would sink to the softest and most pathetic tones; at others a sudden burst of grief or of warlike excitement would thrill through the soul of the audience.

Nothing at all resembling this had Jack ever before seen or heard; and, though he comprehended not the wild language, the scene was sufficiently intelligible to affect him powerfully.

Not a word did he speak.

No means did he take to gratify the curiosity he felt; for he judged it best to respect the customs of the tribe who had treated him so kindly, and not to interrupt a ceremony so solemn.

He found enough to do in watching the mourners—the appearance of all was attractive and striking.

Among the women, albeit they were bowed with grief, and many concealed alike their countenances and their emotions, were forms of matchless beauty, features of classic regularity and loveliness.

Pre-eminent among all stood the only daughter of the chief, to whom Jack's attention was involuntarily directed.

It was not that she was attired more sumptuously than the rest; it was not that her intense grief made her more conspicuous; but there was a majesty, a queenliness, an almost preternatural beauty in her whole demeanour which attracted his fixed and absorbed attention.

There was something in her beauty, too, different from that of any other woman Jack had ever seen—a peculiar distinctive quality which separated it from all others.

Zanoolah, for such, he was destined to learn, was the name of the chieftain's daughter, was a full-blooded Indian of the Arikara tribe; and yet it was strange that she was so different and so superior to the others around.

The contrast seemed to bear out the tradition that had prevailed among the tribe—that she was no mortal being, but half supernatural, endowed by the Great Spirit with magic power over the souls of others.

There was a legend attached to her birth which we cannot at present detail to the reader.

She did not observe how steadfastly Jack's gaze was fixed upon her.

She seemed conscious of nothing but the mournful ceremony in which she took the most prominent part.

The funeral songs, the kneeling and wailing ceremonies, lasted until the sun began to decline to the deepening shades of twilight.

The great Wanilquan was to be buried in a deep glen, thickly grown with firs, which had been for ages the sepulchre of his race.

There was something deeply affecting in the manner in which the brave tribe conveyed the warrior chief to his rest.

Every man in the tribe, fully armed with all his weapons of battle and chase, took his position in the long line, which was prepared to follow, in single file, the ornamented wooden coffin which contained the chief's remains.

This was borne by six of the principal chiefs. Then followed as many more bearing Wanilquan's weapons, accoutrements, and sowed deerskin canoe.

The rest followed in regular order, the most distinguished chiefs taking precedence, and the others succeeding according to their rank.

The women seemed as if their active part in the obsequies was over; for they did not follow the coffin to its last resting-place, but remained among the tents, kneeling reverentially as it was carried before them.

Jack did not know what part he was destined to fulfil in this strange scene until Monalqua motioned him to follow the procession.

Thus the long file of warriors slowly and solemnly wound along the narrow rocks, ledges, and downward-sloping paths that led to the place of interment.

They were not long in reaching it; and then all mustered around a spot in the centre, where the grave was already dug.

An aged and venerable man, the chief priest of the tribe, performed the latter part of the funeral ceremony, by delivering prayer and incantation as the body was lowered into the grave.

The renowned Wanilquan was buried with all his weapons of war, his implements of the chase, his robes of distinction, and his splendidly-ornamented canoe.

Nothing that was mortal of him survived, except his memory, and that the mournful and grief-stricken countenances of his warriors showed would long survive.

When the grave was filled up, the whole of the warriors again formed in single file and marched from the burying-place, headed by Monalqua.

The next ceremony was the formal election of Monalqua as chief of the tribe of Arikaras.

This was done according to the peculiar notion of the tribe, which was not unlike that in vogue among the early German kings.

Four of the principal warriors lifted the chief-elect upon his shield, and carried him into the centre of the tents, where, with spear in hand, he swore to protect, lead, and justly govern the tribe, and received the acclamations and congratulations of his new subjects.

A kind of diadem, formed of a corale of silver, profusely ornamented with gems, beads, and plumes, was placed upon his head, and a splendidly-adorned robe of buffalo-skin fastened on his shoulders.

Nothing could exceed the cordiality with which the gallant Indians welcomed their new chief.

Monalqua, the brave, the young, the gallant, a warrior before whose deadly rifle the stoutest foes quailed; a hunter whose unerring arrow wrought instant death among the wild game of the forest.

Monalqua was the pride of his tribe, and now, by the sudden and melancholy death of his father, he was unexpectedly called upon to occupy the position of leader.

Not a dissentient voice was heard.

But the young Indian, at this time of pride and triumph, did not forget the gratitude he owed to the white stranger.

As soon as he was thus formally invested with the symbols of power, when he had thanked his followers, and their acclamations somewhat abated, he motioned our hero to stand beside him, and introducing him to the others, made a speech which may be thus translated.

"Arikaras, here stands my white brother, the brave warrior of the pale faces, who strove, at the risk of his own death, to save the life of my father. That he did not succeed is owing to the supreme will of the Great Spirit, but not the less is gratitude due to the stranger. Arikaras, I receive him as my brother, I request that he may be made a chief, and received into our tribe; let him be invested with the crested plumes of the kingly eagle, the embroidered blanket, the deer-skin robes and mocassins of our tribe; let him become as one of the Arikaras, and may he prove as a warrior and a huntsman, that he is no longer an alien to our tribe."

This proposal was heartily accepted by the rest, although Jack, the principal party concerned, did not comprehend the terms in which it was couched.

He was soon, however, by gestures made to understand the part he was to play, and deemed it best to show every sign of assent.

"I may as well turn Indian in name," he reflected, "since I must necessarily live as one, and to adopt the customs of this brave tribe will ensure me friendship and protection."

So he unresistingly prepared to go through any ordeal the customs of the tribe might impose upon him.

These, however, were neither numerous nor tedious.

They consisted in obeying the chief's commands, by clothing Jack in the complete costume of the tribe, except the weapons of war and the plumed head-dress, which it seems were to be adopted last, and with some degree of ceremony.

The most important part of the investiture had now arrived, though Jack scarcely expected the part he was to undergo.

"Stay," cried the chief, in an authoritative voice, "let us first assure ourselves that the skill of this white man is worthy of the honours destined for him. Place up that target at the distance of one hundred paces, let the stranger string his bow and try his power of aim."

The command was instantly obeyed.

A large round target, on which was painted an immense hideous face, the centre of which, the mouth, was the object of aim, was fixed at the required distance, carefully measured from where our hero was to stand.

A magnificent Indian bow and arrows, far superior to the rude weapons Jack had recently made himself, were placed in his hand, and he was directed to make trial of his skill.

The Indians retired in a ring around him, leaving him a large clear place to stand in.

Our hero stepped forward, and took up his position.

He felt that the moment was an important one.

He saw that he would need all his skill to satisfy the spectators.

Who could tell what punishment, notwithstanding their apparent friendliness, they might bestow on the unskilful archer?

To be deemed unworthy of the honour about to be conferred upon him was, perhaps, the least evil consequence of such a failure.

Accordingly, Jack prepared to do his utmost to retain the good favour of the Indians.

He felt rather nervous, nevertheless, as he placed his arrow in the bow, knowing that hundreds of sharp critical eyes were fixed upon him, and that men, who were themselves astonishing archers, were to be the judges of his skill.

How distant the target was, too! It seemed an immense distance to shoot.

The target, however, was as plainly observable as if it had been day, for at the door of each of the tents that intervened in a long line before Jack's eyes, a pine torched was fixed, blazing brightly.

Jack raised his bow.

He was fearful at first that his nervousness would mar his efforts, but the strength of will soon returned in full force, and Jack felt that he was equal to the task before him.

One, two, three!

The final signal was given, and our hero, who had taken a long and careful aim, discharged the projectile from the bow.

The arrow whizzed through the air, and, to the satisfaction no less of the marksman than the spectators, hit the exact centre of the target.

A continued shout of approval rewarded Jack's efforts, and the young chief gave vent to the pleasure he felt in terms that were no less gratifying for not being understood.

"How bravely does the white man shoot!" he exclaimed. "He deserves, indeed, to be made a chief. No pale-face that I have hitherto seen has been able to perform such a feat. But he has another trial to undergo. Let him try his skill with the spear."

The Indians lost no time in obeying this order. A splendid spear of hard lance-wood, tipped with a sharp steel point, was handed to him, a young moose-deer, which the Indians had recently trapped, was set free at a certain distance, and Jack was directed to aim at it running.

He hurled the spear with all his force.

It shot through the air and struck the animal in the neck with such force that it brought him to the ground and killed him instantaneously.

Another outburst of acclamation, more enthusiastic than the last, evinced the delight of the Indians at Jack's skill, and Monalqua declared himself not only satisfied, but astonished, at the unusual dexterity of his white-skinned brother.

"He deserves to be made a chief of the first rank; for if now he is so good a huntsman, how great will be his fame in the battle of the forest, when he has been years in our tribe, and become a stalwart warrior. My white brother," he added, taking Jack by the hand, with great cordiality, "from this time you are next only to myself; let your name in future be Kewagie, the Arrow-speeder; receive, according to custom, the brand of our tribe, and the plumes that mark you out as a chief of the first rank."

There was not an Indian that showed anything but cordial approval of this agreement, and Jack had accordingly to undergo the most important part of his ordeal.

He was taken by the medicine-man of the tribe to the centre of the tents, where two attendants, baring his breast, punctured it with a sharp steel instrument, forming in the incisions a mystic emblem, something resembling the head of an eagle, which was the peculiar symbol with which every member of the tribe was marked.

This they rubbed over with a dark blue powder, which at once stopped the bleeding and rendered the effect complete.

The operation was somewhat painful at first, but the pain soon subsided.

This was the only tattoo that Jack was called upon to undergo, for it was not the custom of that tribe to adorn themselves further in this way.

Accordingly, when Jack was fully invested with the dress, the arms, and the crest of a chief, his English countenance and youthful form alone marked him out from the native children of the tribe.

Another cordial and universal expression of admiration burst from the Indians as their chief, grasping our hero by the hand and leading him to his own tent, exclaimed triumphantly, "Kewagie, you are now a chief of the Arikaras."

CHAPTER LIV.

THE INDIAN FEAST — ZANOOLAH, THE INDIAN MAIDEN — THE SUDDEN ATTACK — A FEARFUL CONFLICT.

IN the large tent, to which our hero was led after his admission into the tribe, considerable preparations had been made for festivity.

A large table, covered with a snowy cloth—unusual articles of luxury in Indian dwellings—with wooden stools and benches ranged around it, held a considerable quantity of viands; or, as the expression goes, "groaned under the weight of good cheer."

All kinds of wild birds, as well as the flesh of the bison ox, the moose-deer, and many other wild denizens of the forest, smoked upon the board, in company with bread, new Indian corn cakes, and such wild and hardy fruit as grew in the adjoining woods.

A number of attendants, or Indians of inferior rank, mostly taken as prisoners from the adjoining tribes, hovered around the tents, prepared to officiate during the repast.

To these had been entrusted the preparations of the banquet; and it is but just to say that they performed their part well.

It was the custom of this tribe that feasts of this kind should take place at the election of a new chief, however great may have been the lamentations for his predecessor.

By this we must not suppose the mourning of the Indians to be very brief or very limited; for, in many countries, funerals as well as weddings are ushered in by the outward signs of festivity.

Over this banquet, in which Jack took a prominent place, Zanoolah, the chieftain's sister, presided; but her grave demeanour ill accorded with the scene.

Jack took her notice, and though he understood not the language in which the introduction was spoken, it was a source of considerable pleasure to him, for she was supremely beautiful, as we have before had occasion to observe, and the expression of her dark eyes, as they fixed upon him, was something to thrill his heart like a magic spell.

Zanoolah, he felt at once, was a being to adore, to worship.

It would seem almost like presumption to love her, with that unearthly dignity that seemed to interpose between her and other beings.

But stay! What had he to do with love?

Was not Mabel Meredith's image his only guiding star?

True; but the heart of man is weak, and Jack was not entirely proof against other fascinations.

The banquet, at which all the principal chiefs were assembled, lasted long, and time flew by rapidly as the festivities increased.

Truth compels us to admit that the "fire-water" of the white man, or, in other words, the brandy and rum, which the Indians drank unmixed, began to have considerable effect upon them, and increased both their hilarity and their excitement.

They pledged each other from the leathern flasks in a thoroughly English fashion, and vied in their enthusiastic praises of the white man who was their guest.

Some related deeds of daring; others sang songs of war and the chase; and, in short, the hilarity increased to an extent which formed a complete contrast to the previous day of mourning.

Suddenly, in the midst of this hilarity, a sound was heard which all, under the circumstances, dreaded—a loud, prolonged, terrible, unearthly sound, which made them start up with blanched faces, and every sign of terrible consternation.

It was the war-whoop of the Osaga Indians.

In the dead of night such a sound to those who knew what it portended was horrible.

Swelling to a chorus of fierce yells, resembling the howling of a pack of wolves thirsting for the blood of their prey, it burst upon the ears of the revelling Arikaras.

It was so near, and so loud and echoing, that they knew at once that the fierce tribe, their deadly enemies, were surrounding their camp in vast numbers,

How to escape, or at least avert the danger, was the question.

It would have been different in broad day, when they could see their foes, and fight on equal terms; but now it was dark night, and the besiegers had all the advantage.

Scared and confused as in a panic, a number of scouts rushed into the tent, crying out in terrible alarm—

"The Osagas!—the Osagas!"

The whole of the chiefs started up, grasped their weapons, and prepared to resist.

"We must drive them back or perish," cried Monalqua. "Fools that we were to be thus unprepared, to give our time to unseemly revelry slighting the memory of the great Wanilquan, who shunned the fire-water of the white men; we are rightly served. But we must resist our fate."

Monalqua grasped Jack's arm.

"Now is the time," he cried, "to prove you are really an Arikara. Strike with all your power and strength, for the Osagas are deadly foes, and show no mercy."

Jack understood not the words, but the gesture was sufficient, and he followed Monalqua's warriors out of the tent, with a full determination to do his part in the affray.

The whole of the encampment was now in terrific confusion. The scouts and warders who had been scared from their posts by the advent of an overwhelming number of foes, could do nothing but give the alarm.

The Osagas finding their advantage, had already broken their way through the outer line of tents, and were rushing with terrific yells towards the centre of the Arikara encampment.

The latter lost no time in preparing themselves for the attack.

With lightning speed they armed themselves with rifles and pistols, used only for war, as the bow and spear for hunting, and began to form into ranks as regularly as the confusion would permit.

When thoroughly aroused, and especially if heated with spirituous liquors, the Arikara tribe were notorious for their desperate bravery, but their foes were fierce, treacherous, and implacable.

They soon came in sight, clothed in buffalo robes, tattooed in a manner that made them appear hideous and appalling, and armed to the teeth with gun, pistol, and tomahawk.

They stormed the outer tents, and soon reduced them to heaps of ruins, seizing all the cattle of the Arikaras, and pressing onward for further depredations.

Their opponents had not time to make a barri-

cade that would effectually oppose their entrance, and though they hurriedly piled up every available article that would serve the purpose, still the Osagas advanced.

Such an obstacle was nothing in their victorious path, and they soon destroyed it.

They were subtle, too, in their movements, and attacked the camp on every side.

Jack, Monalqua, and his companions, who judged the place of honour to be that of danger, were in the foremost rank, ready to receive the besiegers, and the critical moment soon arrived.

In a few moments a party of Osagas, bursting through the line of tents, Jack was brought face to face with the dreaded Black Plume, chief of these foes.

Formidable, indeed, was the fierce leader of the Osagas.

He was of immense stature, tattooed in a most hideous manner, and accoutred with a tremendous number of death-dealing weapons.

Waving aloft his mighty tomahawk, he mounted, leading his braves, on the top of the ruined barricade, and pointing to his foes, shouted—

"Death to the hounds of the Arikara! Let not a single warrior escape, nor a single scalp remain upon the heads of their chiefs. Let each stroke be a death-blow."

"They shall never conquer!" cried Monalqua, in his turn. "We, too can raise a war-cry. Onward, my men, and meet them ere they cross the barrier!"

He gave the signal for the attack, and the pealing war-cry of both tribes intermingled; a more terrible sound or a more fearful and exciting scene than the conflict that followed it, cannot be imagined.

The two tribes closed in terrific combat.

The Arikaras made a fierce and headlong charge at the enemy, who, not expecting the attack, recoiled, and were, for a moment, forced to waver.

But they soon renewed their attack with redoubled fury.

It was a battle to the death.

Neither thought of showing quarter.

Jack, keeping close to his new friend, Monalqua, strove eagerly to distinguish himself as a chief of the Arikaras.

The Osaga leader soon singled him out, spite of his Indian costume, and sought to seize him as a particular prize.

"A dog of a white man," he shouted, "among the ranks of these Arikaras. They are doubly craven to seek such allies. He must be mine! Long have I sought the scalps of the pale-faced dogs, but here is one who dares assume the garb and weapons of an Indian. He must die, and with every torture!"

But this fierce vaunt was not so easily carried out.

Jack was no novice in the art of fighting, as our readers well know, and he could do his part in an engagement with iron English nerve and steadfast valour.

He knew how to defend himself in a close encounter, but as yet the battle was more open, though by no means less deadly.

No sooner did the Osagas appear than they were received by a volley of rifle shots from the

Arikaras, but almost instantaneously met this salute by another equally fierce.

The consequences were fearful.

Dozens fell dead on either side.

It was a miracle that Jack and his companion chief were not among the first victims.

Both parties fell back to recover breath after this first encounter, and reload for a fresh attack.

Altogether, the Osagas had found they had met with an unexpected vigorous repulse.

Their chief, rendered furious by such resistance where he had expected an easy victory, urged his men on to a desperate and overwhelming attack.

"What! shall we be baulked by such foes?" he cried, "who are half women at heart, and herd with the white-faced dogs, more craven than themselves. No! we fight for plunder, for scalps, and for the triumph of victory; and neither shall we relinquish."

The attack was renewed, another double volley of rifles did double destruction, and fearfully thinned the ranks of each party.

Meanwhile another body of Osagas had striven to force their way in at the other side of the encampment, and take the Arikaras by surprise, but the latter were fully prepared for and averted the danger with great bravery.

The Osagas pressed onward, but the Arikaras still maintained their position.

All the women and children had retired into the innermost tents, where they lay trembling with apprehension of the fate which the issue of the day might bring forth.

Many, however, could not be restrained from rushing out and rending the air with shrieks and lamentations for their warriors slain or wounded in the deadly encounter. Among them all Zanoolah alone was calm, sustaining, consoling, and supporting the rest, and regarding the contest from the principal tent with a flashing eye, and a heart that beat with more than female heroism. To her the raging battle brought no fears; it was defeat alone that was ever a source of terror and shame. The combat had now become too close to render firearms available. The combatants had recourse to tomahawks, clubs, and the butt-ends of their guns and pistols. They closed in a fierce encounter, which could alone decide the issue of the day, and the fate of one or other of the tribes.

Both parties had lost fearfully, but the Osagas had not as yet taken any prisoners.

Their horrible thirst for blood, and longing for scalps, as well as their natural hatred of the Arikaras, urged them on to the wildest and most desperate attacks.

They wielded their tomahawks like demons in human form.

At each stroke a skull was cloven or a blow of fearful effect inflicted.

The scalps of many of his foes adorned the belt of the Osaga chief before his foes could prevent the horrible desecration.

The Arikaras on their part, resisted to the very death.

They threw themselves into the fight with the reckless daring of desperation, and their efforts were not entirely fruitless.

Fearfully decreased in numbers as they were, they were still a match for their enemies.

Like lions at bay, they seemed inspired with more strength and firmness the more their danger increased.

But they did not forget warlike stratagems.

Monalqua sent a band of scouts to insinuate their way through the encampment by an outlet unmenaced by the enemy, and open a fire upon them from behind.

The attempt succeeded, in so far that the Osagas, dismayed at the unexpected attack, were for a moment confused and wavering in their ranks.

Now was the time for their opponents to act with advantage.

"Warriors of Arikara!" he shouted, "there stand your deadly enemies—men whom it were a deed of virtue to sacrifice to the Great Spirit. Shall they die or conquer?"

A wild defiant shout answered his address, as his followers renewed their onslaught.

They rushed on to the scattered ranks of the Osagas, and by a sudden attack drove them backward to seek shelter in the wood.

But even in their retreat they fought desperately, cutting down their pursuers as they fled across a path strewn with the dead and dying of both tribes.

"The fiend's curse on these Arikaras," cried the fierce Black Plume through his clenched teeth, "are we to be foiled thus? It must be that demon of a white man, whose spells have bewitched and defeated us. Die, pale-faced hound."

He discharged his piece full in the face of our hero, but that young warrior was well versed in the manner of averting such perils, and diving on one side with incredible speed, he escaped the shot by the breath of scarce a quarter of an inch.

"You, at least, shall die," roared Black Plume, now as furious as a tiger at bay, and he discharged his remaining pistol at Monalqua.

The latter had as near an escape for his life as his gallant comrade, for striking against the spear he held in his hand, the course of the bullet was averted from a fatal part.

The Arikaras, with wild shouts of triumph, pursued their advantage to the utmost.

They gave chase to their foes in a compact body, cutting down as they fled all small isolated parties, and adding to the already fearful heaps of slain and wounded.

"We will have back our stolen goods," cried the young Indian chief, triumphantly, "the Great Spirit has turned in our favour, and his strength inspires us. Vultures of rapine and plunder, you shall no longer retain your prey."

A wild yell of disappointed rage and baffled hate burst from the lips of Black Plume and his followers as they saw how good a chance Monalqua had of carrying out his threat.

The Osagas had now become so scattered and disorganised, that, notwithstanding their superior numbers, all the advantages they had gained seemed about to slip from them.

They knew their only chance was to regain the cover of the wood, and there reorganise again and concentrate their strength for another attack.

This they succeeded in doing.

The darkness of the night aided their escape.

"We have conquered!" cried Monalqua, as,

flushed with the victorious excitement of chasing his enemies, he returned to his encampment to reassure the women of his tribe that the danger was over.

"My white brother has fought well!" he added, gazing at Jack with admiration.

"His plumes are torn, and he bears marks of the fray; but he has upheld the honour of the Arikaras as if he had been born in the tribe."

Jack made an acknowledgement, as far as he was able to do from gestures, to a compliment which he understood in the same manner, for he could not doubt that Monalqua was sounding his praises to Zanoolah when her large dark eyes were fixed with such a tender gaze upon him.

She came afterwards, pressed his hand, and looked upon his face with an expression far more eloquent than words.

Jack, however, was not quite so confident on another subject, and that was the victory of the Arikaras.

He dreaded the treachery of their foes, and feared they would find some means of renewing the attack with more deadly effect.

The young chief had, in truth, decided hastily. Once secure in their cover beneath the trees the treacherous Osagas plotted a more fierce and effective onslaught.

After some consultation, the chiefs determined to work their way gradually towards the tents of their foes, like snakes, under cover of the woods, picking off their foes as they came across them.

Strong bands of Arikaras were dispersed to the open spaces around the tents, and these were carefully on the watch for the least sign of a renewed attack.

Crusoe Jack, at his own request, headed one of these parties, and in his experience of the subtle tricks of Indian warfare, he judged, because he saw no signs of the enemy, that they had retreated in final defeat.

But his more experienced comrades knew better than this.

They knew that danger was never so imminent as when unseen, and looked about them with sharp and eager glances of distrust, into the dark and treacherous wood that sheltered their foes. Their suspicions were not unfounded; for when, all seeming quiet, they at length ventured to leave their shelter, a volley from a dozen rifles showed that the Ossagas were still on the watch.

This brought several of the Arikaras to the ground.

The Osagas were a mighty and merciless tribe.

Like their leader, they were only happy when revelling in blood.

Exasperated at the Arikaras not coming forth, they gave a wild whoop, and rushed upon their foes.

Crusoe Jack found himself suddenly opposed to a dozen of the red-skinned wretches.

Placing his back against a bush, he prepared to defend himself.

The Indians were astonished to find a white man among them.

Their astonishment increased to superstition when the bush opened and Crusoe disappeared.

Jack found himself precipitated some thirty feet down a gully, but, fearful of discovery, he lay till morning, when, climbing to the brink, he had the pleasure of beholding the sea at no great distance.

Turning his eyes from the sea he beheld a herd of wild beasts scouring the plain, followed by an incongruous host who were chasing them.

In a moment, as it were, they were past and with a sinking heart Crusoe Jack saw them disappear.

He was once more alone, but the brave youth was still undaunted, "that destiny which has carried me through so many dangers," he murmured, half aloud, "will not desert me now."

"No," he added, mechanically raising his voice, "I will never despair, for, weak and faint as I am, I feel that within me which is capable of battling against a thousand deaths. Ah! what is that, surely my eyes deceive me?"

"No," he ejaculated, "no," it is a sail, a vessel bearing down upon the island." With a cry of joy he bounded to his feet, and climbing the summit of a steep crag near him, he fixed his gaze on the nearing ship.

One hour later our hero was on board of her, she had taken in wood and water, and now she steered away again from the land.

The incidents of the last few hours had passed so rapidly, that Jack had exchanged situations without hardly comprehending the truth of his position.

He had not even inquired in what trade the vessel was engaged.

It astounded him when he discovered she was a sort of half pirate, half slaver, and the unsavoury, hideous-looking wretches that formed the rest of her crew made him feel somewhat uneasy.

The captain, like the mate, was not so bad to talk to, but his hard-set features showed he was not one given to persuasion.

Our hero was asked to join them, and as he did not readily comply he was informed, in no ceremonious manner, that he could either walk the plank or be put in irons in the lower hold.

One glance down the dark, stifling hold, and the sickly smell it gave forth, soon decided the question, and so for the nonce Crusoe Jack became a pirate or a slaver, he knew not which.

One year passed in this floating scourge of the seas, chasing the unguarded merchantman, and being in turn chased by British cruisers. At length, in one of her kidnapping voyages, among the South Sea Islands, she struck on a sunken reef and went down, giving Crusoe Jack barely time to seize a hen-coop and jump overboard.

Next morning he was picked up by a small craft laden with cedar wood, bound from the Fijis to Australia. There he soon gained the friendship of a wealthy merchant, who was about to embark his all, his fortune, in a vessel named the Thunder, bound for England.

This wealthy merchant, who had speculated largely and profitably in the purchase of, and bartering for, gold, had amassed over half a million, and so great was his confidence in our hero Crusoe Jack, that he persuaded him to ship on board, so that there might be some one to keep a watchful eye over the immense treasure. And so Crusoe Jack became second mate of the Thunder, and now we bring our story to the end of

BOOK THE FIRST.

BOOK THE SECOND.

~~~~~~

CHAPTER I.

ALONE ON LION ISLAND—CRUSOE JACK'S HUT ON FLAGSTAFF-HILL.

FROM the top of a mountain peak, the highest accessible point, a solitary man—alone on an uninhabited island—surveys the sea.

An island, sparkling like a bright emerald on the bosom of the vast Pacific, with other emerald specks to be seen, dotting the placid surface of the deep blue sea.

This lonely man stands on this high peak, and with admiration, mingled with awe and wonder, gazes on the grand and glorious panorama spread beneath him.

A vast expanse of blue ocean, quilted and rippled by little wavelets, stretching in every direction as far as the eye can reach, canopied by a sky of lighter azure.

To the east, to the south, to the north—one broad expanse—a glorious blue plain, sprinkled with little flashes of light and foam on the tops of the rippling waves.

To the west a little archipelago of islands, islets, rocks, and coral reefs, the nearest about half-a-mile from the island on the summit of which the cast-away stands.

Other islands and islets lie in a group further to the westward—verdure-clad, dark green patches, and spots and tiny dots, scarce perceptible with the naked eye—bright gems in the sea.

A soft westerly breeze is blowing, just sufficient to make the waves break is lines of sparkling white foam on the reefs, the shores of the islands and the black rocks, which here and there rear their crests above the surface of the water.

A group of islands spreads out in a fanlike shape, and this one, on the highest eminence of which the solitary observer is posted, is the most western, and forms the apex of an irregular triangle—the handle of the fan as it were.

The hill, on the top of which he stands, rises about the centre of the island, and all for a long way below the summit is very rugged and precipitous.

Then, after a descent of about a quarter of a mile, the ground grows smoother, and the descent is more gradual.

From the top there runs down, eastward, a narrow spur—at first abrupt, then, as has been said, sloping more gradually.

Then the spur of the hill still going on, but with very little fall, except on either side, where the descent is much more precipitous, there comes after a time a rise for a bit, until the top of a wooded hillock is reached.

And here there is an open space, and a keen eye might discern the evidence of a man's residence in the clearing of the timber and brush, and, above all, in a straight pole on the highest point, like a flagstaff.

And now to give the reader an idea of this island. We will ask him to imagine a lion *couchant*, his fore paws spread before him, and looking to the west.

On the highest point, that is to say, the head, stands our solitary adventurer.

From the head there is a rapid descent eastward to the shoulders.

We will suppose a man to be walking down from the lion's head eastward. He advances along the spine, which is elevated like that of a camel, or what is called a razor-backed horse.

Presently, at the haunches, there is a slight rise again, and, right between the two hips, he stands on the highest part of the lion, the head excepted, on the top of which our solitary observer is.

Here there is a clearing, and abundant evidences of man's handiwork to be spoken of hereafter.

From this second vantage-ground there is a clear prospect of the sea and shore to the eastward.

The ground again slopes rapidly over the tail of the lion down to the shore of as lovely a little bay as ever eye beheld.

The shore is of pure white sand, and on this tiny waves come rippling in the gentlest manner.

Even when there is a strong wind and rough sea farther out this heavenly haven is always calm and smooth.

For at distances of about a third of a mile from the shore there is nearly all around the island a coral reef, the top of which is above the surface of the water, and never more than a foot or so beneath.

And so in all weathers the lagoon, as we may call it, was tolerably calm, and, in fine weather, as placid as a lake.

It was swarming with fish and shellfish.

Along the shore was a strip of sand about a hundred yards wide.

Thence the ground began to rise in a gentle slope, and a little higher up was covered with verdure, low scrub, bushes and green turf.

Then there came trees, in groves and patches at first, afterwards a continuous wood, until the clearing, where was the flagstaff on the rump of the lion, was reached.

The ground was clear and rugged all along the spur, which represents the backbone of the lion.

It sloped sharply—almost precipitously—on either side to a dense forest of trees—fir, wild fig, cocoa, palm, bread-fruit, and others.

So rugged was the ground, so steep the path, that to ascend to the lion's head otherwise than along the spur or peak was almost an impossibility for a human being.

To ascend even to the clearing and flagstaff, except from the direction of the bay, would be a work of great difficulty.

And to approach either the flagstaff or the

lion's head, where our observer was posted, without being seen from that vantage ground, would be absolutely impossible.

Hence it will be seen at once that any man, or body of men, occupying either of these two places or both, would be in a position of great strength to resist a hostile attack.

Indeed, a determined man, standing on the highest point of all, might keep scores at bay by simply hurling down some of the huge fragments of rock and boulders, which were plentifully scattered about.

We have not yet spoken of the aspect of the land on the westward side—that is, over the lion's head.

The descent here was made even more rugged; in fact, in places a sheer precipice, and utterly impregnable to ascend.

At the foot of the deep declivity there was, as on the other side, a thick wood, then brush, shrubs, and verdure of various sorts, and then a strip of sandy beach, and then the sea.

On either of the lion's flanks, and facing the ribs, when the descent was over, there was a level land for about half a mile on either side.

So, then, to understand the nature and position of this place, let the reader imagine an island about two miles and a half long, a mile and a half broad—the length running from east to west.

Then, in the centre of this island, let him conceive a hill or mountain in the shape of a lion, the tail to the east, the head to the west.

It was, in fact, as though a gigantic lion were crouching along the centre of a level island in a smooth plain, looking to the west.

And now, having, we trust, made this plain, let us return to the solitary figure on the highest eminence.

He is attired sailor-fashion, in duck trowsers, blue shirt, and wears on his head a straw hat. Over his left shoulder he has slung a musket. He carries in his belt a revolver, pistol, and a small hatchet, called a tomahawk in Australia; and in his hand he has a telescope with which he frequently sweeps the field of view.

He is in the prime of early manhood, apparently about twenty-six or twenty-seven years of age.

A clear, keen eye, brown hair, and a handsome sunburnt face had this solitary inhabitant of what we will call Lion Hill Island. In body he is vigorous and well formed.

It is evening. The sun dips below the western horizon, painting the sky and sea with gold, purple, and scarlet.

Slowly the orb of day sinks beneath the horizon.

The young sailor closes his telescope with a bang; and then, extending his right arm towards the fan-like group of islands to the west, he speaks aloud—

"My kingdom! I, Crusoe Jack, must subdue all these islands and their inhabitants to me. Their inhabitants! Have they any? They have, I feel sure; and must own me as king, emperor, the supreme ruler!"

Then he turned to the east, and, looking out over the lion's tail to a spot beyond the coral reef, he again extended his hand, holding the telescope as might a field-marshal his *bâton*.

"My treasures! Yes, there beneath the waves, lies the gold which I will reclaim!—there, amidst the ribs and timbers of the wreck of the Thunder!"

Notwithstanding the utter solitude in which he found himself—sole inhabitant of an island, where hitherto no white man certainly, probably no human being, had ever set foot—our hero was by no means gloomy and cast down.

And, indeed, though he was alone, nothing but the boundless ocean, sprinkled with about a score of islands, such as this one on which he stood, in sight, there was much to cheer and exhilarate.

The balmy evening breeze, the glorious sunset, the placid sea, the luxuriant vegetation everywhere abounding, the conviction that he could neither want for food nor water—all this was sufficient to keep up the spirits of any man of ordinary energy.

But Crusoe Jack, sole denizen of "Lion Island," had much more to uphold him and steel his heart to bear up bravely under his desolate position.

He had a fixed purpose, an object in view, which he meant sternly to strive for and attain.

He, and he alone of all men on this globe, knew the exact spot, on the edge of a certain coral reef, where lay buried a vast treasure in gold.

And this treasure it was his stedfast resolve to reclaim—to wrest from the bosom of old ocean.

It lay there somewhere amidst the wreck of the one-time good ship Thunder, now sunk beneath the waves of the Pacific.

Before he descended from the little tableau, or flat patch of ground on the top of the lion's head, he once more swept the sea with his eye.

To the west, the group of islands and the sea beyond; to the east, only the ocean and the coral reef, on the sea face of which lay the wreck of the Thunder and the sunken treasure.

Again he murmured as he had done before, as though the thought haunted him—

"My kingdom—my treasure. Both shall own me lord and master."

His bronzed cheek flushed as he gazed around on the lovely scene, and there was in his eye the light of enthusiasm; on his face an expression of stern resolve.

"I shall win—I will win! It was not to make a feeble effort ending in failure that I, of my own free will, chose to be left alone on this island. As I did in the mutiny of the Thunder, in protecting the gold and defeating the mutineers, so will I now. I stuck by the Thunder while she was afloat, did my duty, and fought for the treasure. Now that she is sunk, and with her the boxes of gold, I will stand by the wreck until I recover every ounce."

After indulging in this soliloquy, the truthful expression of his thoughts, he proceeded to descend from the lion's head.

Down over the neck of the lion he slowly went, until, reaching the shoulders of the imaginary beast, the ground became clearer, and he was able to walk along the spur representing the backbone at a more rapid pace.

And presently—just as the twilight merged into night, and the stars began to peep forth—he reached the clear space where stood the flagstaff on the lion's rump.

Under the shade of a grove of palm and cocoa-nut trees, about fifty yards from the flagstaff, almost entirely concealed, there was a large hut covered with stout tarpaulin, firmly planted and supported. A few yards in front of this lay the trunk of an "iron bark" tree which had been felled.

And against this, as a back log, there was a quantity of dry brush and smaller wood. To this he applied a light, and the fire catching, there was soon a ruddy glare, illumining the small clear space, and sending the blazing beams far out over the placid sea.

But though the glare of the flames was bright enough to be seen for a score of miles, no human eye but his knew of it.

Every night for a week the beacon flame had shone out on to the ocean and the slopes of the island ; but save the wild birds in the trees hard by, and perchance the fishes in the lagoon, there was no living thing but himself to see the light of his bonfire.

Every night since he had been sole inhabitant of Lion Island he had lighted a similar fire—not with the expectation or even hope of its being seen, but for his own comfort and convenience.

By the fire he placed a quart pot to boil, and then, entering the tent, lit an oil lamp, which hung from the cross-pole overhead.

It was by this time dark, the transition from day to night being much more rapid in the tropics than in higher latitudes. The light of the lamp fell on as strange-looking an abode as ever man rigged up for himself and dwelt in.

From the outside it appeared to be merely a tarpaulin tent tolerably stout and well secured, but still only a tent.

Inside, however, it was quite different.

It was more like a log hut, with something of the rough slab, Australian shanty. The tent was but the outer covering at the sides, though it formed the only roof.

It was nearly square in shape, and along the three sides were planted close together stout logs.

They were set upright in the ground, and but that trees never did and never could grow so closely, they might have been taken for stumps. They were nearly as high as a man's shoulder ; on top of them were placed other logs horizontally, so that the whole rose to nearly six feet, forming a barricade and shelter.

The small interstices were filled up with branches, forming a sort of wicker-work, and behind this a layer of stones and stiff clay.

So that the hut was, in fact, a stronghold—arrow proof—that was the idea of the constructor —and even bullet proof.

The roof was, however, of tarpaulin only.

As for the floor, that was smooth and hard as a macadamised road.

Crusoe had made it thus :

He put down a layer of stiff clay mixed with small stones and gravel, wetted it thoroughly, then stamped and hammered it down tight with as big a log as he could lift ; and then, when he had got it all solid and smooth, he strewed hot ashes over the whole, and kept renewing these for twenty-four hours.

The result was a floor as hard as a stone pavement.

In the centre of this hut or tent was a small table, formed of two upright logs and a couple of rough slabs laid across.

A log on end served as a seat.

All around, and especially at the back, were small barrels, casks, wooden cases, bags, sails, canvas, tools, chairs, loose iron, two or three buckets, a sack of flour, a barrel of biscuits, and scores of other things, which at this place need not be enumerated.

Obviously, the solitary inhabitant was not in danger of starving, and was not wanting in appliances to make himself tolerably comfortable in his island kingdom.

After lighting the lamp, Crusoe unhooked it from the chain by which it hung, and proceeded to the back of the tent.

Here, close to the logs, was a square hole, like the forecastle hatchway on board ship.

It was covered over first with matting, and beneath that was a rude hatch.

Crusoe at once went down, taking the lamp with him.

This was his armoury.

With great labour he had dug this hole, and excavated a short tunnel with a subterranean chamber beneath.

The tunnel ran in the direction of the lion's head for about ten yards, and of course when he stood in the chamber at the end he would be quite clear of the tent.

So that if he should choose to burrow upwards he would reach the surface some distance at the back of it, and in the midst of a clump of wild fig trees, with thick brush all about their trunks.

In this strange subterranean chamber there was very little to attract attention.

A flannel bag, carefully wrapped in canvas, contained about 15lbs. of gunpowder.

Then there was a bag of biscuit and a quantity of loose iron, and a few old-fashioned muskets and cutlasses.

Besides these things, there was a small tin box, such as is used by lawyers to keep deeds and documents in.

This he proceeded to open, and taking therefrom a book, like a sea log, and a folded piece of parchment, he made his way once more by the tunnel into the interior of his strange abode, half log hut, half tent.

Then, hanging up the lamp and trimming it, he laid the book on the table, and opening it took pen and ink and prepared to write.

Before doing so, however, he turned to the first leaf, and proceeded to read over what was there written in his own hand.

CHAPTER II.

CRUSOE JACK'S JOURNAL—THE MUTINY OF THE THUNDER.

" SEPTEMBER 4th, 18——

" I am alone—the vessel sailed away last night, and this morning at sunrise there was not a spec to be seen on the horizon—nothing but the boundless ocean and the archipelago of islands lying to the westward. In case that I should perish by disease or misadventure, I here leave on record what are my aims and intentions in thus voluntarily taking up my abode on a desolate island, probably never before visited by white man, in the midst of the vast Pacific. Also, a brief account of the terrible events which resulted in the loss of the ship Thunder, and the death of all on board, save myself.

"The Thunder sailed from Sydney harbour two months before this date, having on board for cargo, wool, tallow, and other colonial produce. There was, moreover, gold in boxes, to the value of about half a million sterling. She carried also thirty cabin passengers — men, women, and children, and a sufficient crew. Among the latter were some of the most desperate ruffians who ever trod a ship's deck. I believe that many of them, notably the ringleader, Richard Smith, known as Death's Head Dick, shipped on board the Thunder solely with the view of seizing the treasure and murdering all but their own gang.

"I was second mate of the vessel, and soon became cognisant of the fact that there was a mutiny being hatched.

"It burst forth unexpectedly, and then there commenced a terrible struggle between the mutineers, who had barricaded themselves in the deckhouse, and the other party, who had fortified themselves in the cabin.

"This party consisted of the captain and officers, passengers, some petty officers, and a few good men and true of the crew, who had made their escape from the mutineers, and joined us.

"Shortly after the struggle commenced, the captain went mad, and leaped overboard; the mutineers made many furious attacks, but were uniformly beaten off, but with loss in killed and wounded on both sides.

"They were the more numerous, and could afford to lose man for man better than the small party of defenders in the cabin.

"One by one our men fell beneath the bullets of these murderous scoundrels; then there arose a terrible storm, and there was danger of the ship foundering with all hands.

"A suspension of this cruel warfare was agreed upon by both sides, in order that the sails might be reefed, and the ship made snug.

"Our men were aloft on the mizzen topsail-yard, when, with infernal cunning and cruelty, the mutineers contrived to throw the ship aback, at the same time cutting the stays; the mizzen topmast went, and all on the yard perished in the sea.

"Notwithstanding this disaster, I and a few survivors did not surrender. I was determined to defend the gold till the last.

"Having got a small cannon in the cabin, I pointed it down the lazarette hatch, fully determined, should they make a rush at the cabin, to fire it, and blow a big hole in the ship's side, and thus cause the foundering of the vessel in a very short space; for I knew we had no mercy to expect from these wretches, and that if we surrendered, we should nevertheless be murdered; and so I resolved that when our last moments came, they too should lose their lives, and be baulked of their booty.

"This threat, which they knew I should carry into effect, deterred them from making a rush on the cabin, and they proposed terms.

"These were, that they should be allowed to leave in the boats with half the gold.

"We, in the cabin, were wounded, weary, utterly worn out with many days of desperate danger and watching. I was urged by the few survivors, who still stood by me, to accept these terms and save our lives.

"I did so.

"Taking with them half the gold, the villains left the ship in two boats, doubtless thinking to make some port on the South American coast.

"But even in this last transaction there were treachery and murder intended, for before leaving they scuttled the ship.

"Fortunately, however, we were able to get at the auger holes, and, after desperate exertion, plugged them.

"And then there came another and crowning disaster.

"Another gale arose, and a huge green sea, breaking on board over the bows, burst through the cuddy, and out of the stern windows, sweeping overboard every living soul save myself.

"Ere many days the just retribution of heaven was made manifest, for, drifting about amid the equatorial calms, I one day beheld two boats. They were those in which the mutineers had left the ship with the gold, and now were laden with the treasure and the corpses of those villains, who had perished miserably from hunger, thirst, and exposure, having failed to reach the land.

"I lowered one of the ship's boats and rowed towards the others, and having committed the dead bodies to the sea, I again possessed myself of the treasure which was in the boats.

"But now came a fresh misfortune.

"A breeze sprang up. Through an accident the ship passed off before the wind, and I found myself, without food or water, in an open boat on the bosom of the vast Pacific.

"Once more kind Providence befriended me; and after days and nights of agony and hardship I regained the ship.

"One night, as the ship sailed along whither the wind might waft her, she struck on a coral reef of this island.

"She remained fast wedged in among the coral rocks, and there seemed but little danger of her sinking.

"But another storm arose, the hull of the Thunder was broken up, and now her precious cargo lies buried only a few fathoms from the shore.

"I took to one of the boats, and, after a short time, an American whaler hove in sight and eventually picked me up.

"But I would not remain on board, I had conceived a fixed resolve to stay on the island, a solitary adventurer, and endeavour to recover the gold which lies in the sea, amidst the timbers of the Thunder.

"It might seem a mad resolve, but I had made up my mind, and faithfully I carried out my purpose.

"I had money in a belt which I constantly carried round my waist, and so was able to purchase, from the captain of the whaler, provisions, tools, arms, ammunition—nearly everything I could require.

"The crew helped to build this hut, or tent, and then going on board the ship, she spread her sails to the wind, and I was left alone.

"And here I close this record, which, should I perish, and it ever falls into the hands of civilised man, will account for the presence and death, on this island, of the solitary adventurer, Crusoe Jack, one time second mate of the Thunder."

CRUSOE JACK PREPARES A MEAL.

CHAPTER III.

QUIET DAYS ON LION ISLAND—THE MYSTERIOUS
FIGURE.

FOLLOWING this brief record of the events which
caused the narrator, Crusoe Jack, to be alone on
this island in the South Seas, were some other
notes in the form of a journal from day to day;
these we will give, and having brought the
reader up to the present date, will then proceed
with the story in the third person.

"Sept. 5th, Evening.—My second day alone
here. I have been busy all day exploring, and
have named it Lion Island, because in shape it
bears a singular resemblance to a gigantic couchant lion.

"The result of my explorations hitherto have
been to confirm me in the belief that there is no
human being but myself, no animal life whatever, except a few lizards and bright-plumaged
birds. These lizards are from a foot to eighteen inches in length, of a bright yellow hue,
glistening like gold in the sunshine as they dart
among the crevices of the rocks and in the thick
green brush.

"I have ascended the highest point of the
island—the lion's head; the view from thence is
magnificent.

"Valleys and gorges clothed with a dark green
verdure, running down in all directions from the
high land to within a few yards of the sandy
beach. Here and there little silvery streams
are observed trickling down these gorges, at
times leaping from rock to rock like tiny cataracts.

"Some of the valleys running down from the
heights are extremely beautiful—sweeping, in
wavy undulations, to the white sands and blue
rippling waters beyond.

"These valleys, or gorges, are hemmed in on
either side by steep and green heights, the
rocks mostly covered with a sort of lichen or
moss; but the great peculiarity and beauty of
the prospect is the universal and abundant
verdure.

"Everywhere, from the extreme height where
I stood, the lion's crown, as I call it, the surface
of the island, the gorgeous hills, the sloping
vales, present one mass of dark green foliage;
the trees standing so closely and in such rich
profusion as to make it almost impossible to distinguish one from the other.

"And beyond, the calm blue ocean, the slow,
solemn Pacific swell rolling steadily onwards,
the surface of the sea broken by little tiny waves
sparkling like diamonds in the sunshine; here
and there a shoal of flying-fish rising in the air,
their fins and scales glittering like silver, and
after a brief flight sinking again into their native
element.

"Above, around, the sky, cloudless, and of a
delicate pale blue, save near the horizon, where
thin, mist-like clouds may be observed.

"The few sea-birds circling and wheeling
over the lagoons, and near the sandy shore,
hunting for their prey—fish; these were the only
living things my eye could discern.

"Away to the coast, like emeralds dotting the
blue ocean, is an archipelago of islands, yet to be
explored by me.

"I stood and gazed, seeming never to get tired
of the glorious panorama! but the shades of

evening closing over the scene warned me that
it was time to return to my tent on Flagstaff
Point.

"There, in front of a blazing fire, I sat and
pondered over the eventful past, and speculated
as to the future—what would be the result of
this my daring adventure. And then I turned
in and dreamed of the sunken treasure, and thus
ended my second day on Lion Island.

"Sept. 6th.—I have been at work all day in
my hut, carrying out a project on which I have
set my mind. It was a strange idea, and,
though I could scarcely account for it, it seemed
urged on me by some indefinable influence.

"This was to excavate a tunnel from the floor
of the hut to some distance in the rear, where I
could construct a secret chamber, or store-room,
and also by which I might, if advisable, find
another mode of egress.

"I am weary, weary, weary with hard toil,
and now, sitting by the fire, will close my journal
and shall seek Nature's sweet restorer—balmy
sleep.

"Sept. 8th.—I have been to work all yesterday and to-day at this precious tunnel of mine. I
have excavated a passage nearly ten yards long
towards the rear. The earth is soft, and I make
good progress.

"This evening, just before sundown, tired as
I was, I climbed to the lion's crown to reconnoitre. The same glorious prospect—the green
vales and hills of Lion Island, beneath and
around me—beyond, the blue, boundless ocean,
above, the pale azure sky. The wild birds have
gone to roost, and the lizards have sought their
nests in the rocks, and I stand alone amid the
vast solitude.

"I descended from the lion's crown with a
strong mixture of emotions—loneliness, sadness,
mingled with sweet calm, caused by the quiet
loveliness of the scene.

"I dreamed last night that, after great hardships and exertions, I had recovered all the gold,
conveyed it safely to England, and been awarded
£250,000—quarter of a milion sterling—for salvage. May my dream come true!

"Sept. 9th.—At work all day at my tunnel
and subterranean chamber.

"Sept. 10th.—Finished my mining operations
early in the afternoon, also constructed a small
wooden hatch to fit over the opening, above
which I can, when I think it advisable, spread a
thin layer of earth and clay. Then, after wet-
ting this, and trampling it down, it will look like
the other part of the floor and there will be no
trace apparent of what there is beneath.

"This evening, before sunset, I started sounding the shores of the bay, and began making a
sort of little dock for my boat. Saw a number
of fish, about a foot and a half long—silver, with
bright pink stripes across their backs—very
beautiful. I will try and catch some to-morrow
and see how they eat.

"I have not yet shot a bird, although I could
easily do so, for they are marvellously tame, allowing me to come within a few feet of them,
and then fluttering off in a lazy unconcerned
manner. I cannot find the heart to shoot them
merely for wanton sport and curiosity.

"Sept. 14th.—Three days have passed since I
made the last entry in my journal. I have been
at work strengthening my hut, digging drains

around it to carry off the water from the heavy tropical showers which occasionally prevail; I have cleared all the timber and brush away for yards around my hut, so as to have an open space. I think I have made it tolerably secure; solid logs all round, shoulder high, surmounted by horizontal logs. The space I have left at the entrance is so small that I can immediately barricade it if necessary. I think that, provided as I am with firearms, I could successfully resist and beat off any attack, unless taken unawares.

"But why do I speak or rather write of an attack? Am I not, in all probability, the only human being who has ever trodden these verdant slopes or bathed in the pellucid waters of the lagoon?

"Yes, it is true. But what of those other islands dotting the sea to the westward?

"Are they too, as desolate as this, with birds and lizards the sole denizens of their woods?

"I think not.

"I fancy that some of these islands are inhabited, perhaps by fierce and savage cannibals, whom it may be my task to subdue and bend to my will.

"Already I have thought I could discern signs of life—of motion. It was but yesterday eve that I thought I could make out dark specks moving along the sea around the shores of one—perhaps a fleet of canoes.

"To-morrow or the next day I will launch my boat, set sail, and have a cruise round this island, perhaps venturing to explore the archipelago I see to the west; but I must be cautious.

"The enterprise I have undertaken is one of difficulty, of danger, must necessarily occupy a long time, and before taking any steps I must well weigh the consequences.

"Sept. 17, Evening.—I have sailed all round the island without discovering anything fresh. Everywhere the same belt of white sandy beach, with valleys, groves of trees, and scrub and verdure of every description sloping down thereto. I have discovered several little inlets and gulfs, but none to compare to this long bay upon which I look down from Flagstaff-hill.

"The view from the west, looking over what I may call the lion's face and breast, is magnificent.

"Here there is only a very narrow strip of sand, and in place of verdure-clad sloping vales, huge towering rocks rising precipitously thousands of feet.

"When the wind blows from the west the long rolling Pacific waves come thundering up against these rocky cliffs, sending their sparkling spray high up in the air.

"Sept. 18, Morning.—Last night I had a scare. Either it was the offspring of a distempered imagination or I saw a human form.

"I was sitting in front of the hut smoking a pipe in deep meditation, and gazing dreamily into the fire, when suddenly through the smoke and flame, I beheld a human figure—a human face.

"It appeared to stare motionless for a moment, as if gazing in surprise. I was so utterly astonished and taken aback for some time that I sat staring in stupid wonder; then I started to my feet and ran round to the other side of the fire; the figure vanished among the trees by the clearing.

"I was unable to make out anything but that it was a human figure, for I was looking at it through the partial obscurity of smoke and vapour.

"I do not think it safe to venture out into the darkness, and, perchance, fall into an ambush of the savages, but to-morrow, well armed and on my guard, I must make careful search and fathom the mystery.

"Was it indeed a human form, or a phantasm of my imagination?"

CHAPTER IV.

THE SKELETON.

NARRATION in the form of a journal or diary is convenient, and sometimes very effective, but is apt to become tedious. There are other disadvantages. For instance, if the hero writing down his own adventures in diary form should fall ill, die, or be killed, of course there is an end of the story.

One of these things may happen to Crusoe Jack in the course of this story, for it is one thing to undertake a perilous adventure, another to succeed in carrying it through; one thing to risk life, quite another to do so successfully—to escape that fate that was risked. So, for these and other reasons, we will, for the present at least, continue the story in a narrative form.

. . . .

The last of the few brief extracts we have given from Crusoe Jack's journal was dated September 18. Now, when we resume this story, he has been for a fortnight the sole human inhabitant of Lion Island—at least, so far as he knows.

The last entry in the journal related how he saw through the fire a shadowy form, which, immediately on his rising and going round, vanished.

If it were a delusion, it was a very strong one, for the memory haunted him all through the night, and he got but little sleep.

In the morning, after a hearty breakfast, he armed himself with a revolver, rifle, and cutlass, and sallied forth to explore and see if he could discover any evidence of human presence beyond his own on the island.

First he carefully inspected the neighbourhood of the spot where he had seen the shadowy figure, thinking that perhaps he might observe footsteps.

But in this he failed entirely.

From an hour after sunrise, till the glare and heat of the noonday sun warned him to seek shelter and repose, he roamed vainly about, watchful, nervous, looking to the right, to the left continually, half-hoping, half-fearing to set his doubts at rest, by actual sight or by some visible signs indicating the presence of man.

Through the fervid heat of the day he slept under the shade of his tent, thus making up for a bad night's rest, and about four hours after noon again sallied forth in search of what he might discover.

For, strange to say, notwithstanding his utter failure to find anything corroborative whatever, he felt more and more certain that it was indeed a man or woman he had seen.

On this occasion he resolved to explore certain parts of the island, into which, by reason of the dense brush, he had not hitherto penetrated.

This was on the southern side, which was covered with the thickest possible scrub—so thick, indeed, as to be quite impenetrable, without freely using the sharp cutlass he carried to clear a path before him.

We have explained that the island mainly consisted of rising ground, which had a fantastic resemblance to a crouching lion ; but although the general character was hilly, there were many flat plateaux and valleys where there was a considerable expanse of perfectly level ground.

Presently, after cutting his way through many yards of dense brush, he came suddenly upon a clear space or glade.

It was about two hundred yards in circumference, and it showed Crusoe instantly that this clearing had been effected by human agency.

Nearly in the centre was a grove of palm trees, and, on making his way to them, an extraordinary sight met his eyes.

Here was undoubtedly the work of man's hands—a monument of stone of a pyramidal form.

As he approached this, wonder and awe possessed him.

This monument, or whatever it was, was evidently of vast antiquity. As the trees, in the centre of a grove of which it stood, were in regular order, and at exactly equal distances, it appeared that they must have been thus planted by human hands.

They were now great woody columns, with tops covered with verdant foliage, sixty or seventy feet in height.

As Crusoe gazed around, this thought forced itself on his mind: These are now great trees. When they were planted, they could have been but saplings. How many generations—how many centuries ago was that?

He proceeded to examine the pyramid.

It was four-sided, and rose, step by step, to a height of about sixty feet ; each step formed a terrace about four yards wide and ten in length, and was formed of enormous blocks of solid stone.

The height of each step was about three feet and a half, and the whole was thickly covered with moss, ivy, and wild vine, presenting the appearance, at a little distance, of a pyramid of bright green rising from the earth.

Cutting and scraping away the moss and vines which everywhere clung around, Crusoe discovered that the huge stones, of which the pyramid was composed, were laid one upon another, without any cement or mortar, with considerable interstices between.

He now proceeded to clamber to the top, which was comparatively easy, on account of the vines and ivy.

And here an extraordinary sight awaited him.

The topmost stone of all was a huge block about twelve feet square ; in the centre of it was hewn out an oval basin about seven feet long by three broad, and there lay, without any covering whatever, bleached white by the sun, a human skeleton.

On the one hand lay what were evidently weapons of war and the chase—a club, arrows, and the bow, from which the string had long since rotted.

On the other, a small axe, some spears, or javelins of wood, tipped with some metal.

The skull rested on a sort of shield, and, a few inches off, lay a circlet, of crown-like shape, which was evidently made of some metal.

After gazing on this strange spectacle from the brink of the basin for some time, Crusoe Jack determined to descend and make a closer examination.

He lifted up the circular object, which was extremely heavy.

"Gold !" he cried, "as I live."

He then proceeded to scrape off with his knife some of the incrustation with which it was covered ; but to his surprise instead of the yellow glitter of gold, he perceived that it was some metal of silvery brilliancy.

"It is very heavy for silver, but I suppose it must be," he said to himself.

Laying this down he soon proceeded to examine the weapons.

The arrows and javelin were tipped with metal which he thought at first was iron ; but using the scraping test again, he discovered to his surprise, that this also was a white, bright metal.

It was too hard for silver—that was quite certain.

What, then, could it be ?

He was unable to reply.

A mystery.

A metal, the like of which he had never seen or heard of before. Hard, white, and brilliant, apparently heavier than silver—heavy enough for gold.

After some thought, and careful examination of the skeleton and its surroundings, he resolved to leave everything as he found it—to respect what was probably the last resting place of some savage chief or king.

He now proceeded to make his way down the pyramid, and walked thoughtfully among the grove of palm trees, pondering and wondering as to the meaning of what he had seen.

By the state of the bones, it was evident it must have lain there for many a year, watered by the rains, and bleached by the tropical sun.

The more he thought the less able was he to account for such a monument, composed of such enormous stones, and built in such a place.

The size of the blocks of stone was such he felt certain that it would be no acceptable task for an English engineer, with all modern appliances at command, to have built it.

He remained here till sundown—lost, bewildered ; and then slowly made his way back to Flagstaff-hill, following the same path through the brush he had hewn out for himself with his cutlass, and arrived at what he called "home."

Another astounding surprise awaited him.

CHAPTER V.

THE MYSTERIOUS ARROW.

WHEN Crusoe arrived back at Flagstaff-hill, wearied out by bodily exertion and mental excitement he found the smouldering embers of the fire he had left in the morning.

After throwing on a handful of dry brush and a couple of small logs, he went into the tent, and throwing himself down on his couch, lay still until the fire should burn up.

He was by no means a teetotaller, but he fully appreciated the virtues of the leaf "which cheers but not inebriates." He put a quart pot on the fire, and made preparations for a cup of tea.

The fire was now blazing up fiercely, the logs which he had put on coming from a resinous tree, which he had very soon discovered.

When he went out from the tent, with the water in his hand, to put it on the fire, he did not look about him, but stooping down, placed it on the embers, where he knew it would quickly boil.

When he rose to a standing posture again, he did not start or cry out, but stood gazing in stupid amazement at that which met his eyes; for there, close by his left hand, in front of the fire, stuck up in the ground, was a long, thin wand, as it appeared to him, with a little bit of white stuff floating, pennon-like, from the top.

"How the deuce did that come there?" was his very English exclamation.

He looked at it and moved further back, as though bewildered—almost frightened.

He seemed afraid to touch it.

Daylight was gone, but the glare of the fire was sufficient to show him every minute point about this wand.

At last, as though waking from a sort of dream, he took hold of it and pulled it out of the ground.

A javelin, dart, or spear—he scarcely knew what to call it, but such it was—of white bone or ivory, and tipped with glistening metal, more brilliant than silver.

And again there broke from his lips another exclamation of surprise.

Crusoe Jack was never more flabbergasted in his life.

When, during the mutiny of the Thunder, the bullets of the villainous crew were whistling about his ears—weak, weary, and wounded though he was—he had never lost his presence of mind.

But now, a child with a wooden sword could have attacked him with advantage.

He took the javelin, for so we may call it, slowly into the tent, and laid it on the table carefully, tenderly, as though it were glass; then lit the oil lamp hanging overhead, and, seating himself on his log chair, stared at it like a stupid oaf.

This state of mind on his part was caused by the sudden shock of the discovery after great exertion and consequent weakness.

"I'll have a cup of tea," he said to himself, "and think about it."

Thereupon he brewed himself a pot hot and strong, with no milk, but a dash of rum in it in place thereof, and walked slowly up and down between the fire and the tent, pondering and wondering what was the meaning of all this.

"Last night I saw a human form through the fire and smoke," he said to himself; "this morning I vainly wasted in searching for anything which could point to the presence of man on this island, and in the afternoon I discover the stupendous monument, doubtless the sarcophagus of a king, the bleached bones of a tall man, with weapons of war, crown, and insignia of rank, and now this javelin, planted, as though in defiance, in front of my tent."

Then he re-entered the tent, and, seating himself, proceeded to make a closer examination.

The javelin seemed to be of ivory—perfectly white and hard; but, said Crusoe to himself—"There are no elephants here, and, besides, they have not tusks six feet long."

Then he bethought himself of the scraping test; but on feeling for his knife, found the sheath empty.

"I must have left my knife at the pyramid," he said to himself. "I don't suppose it will be of any use to old grizzly bones, so I'll go back to-morrow and fetch it."

Light words accompanied by a light laugh, perhaps a little forced. But great consequences sometimes arise from little events. However, he was possessed of another sheath knife, and scraping a little off the surface, it seemed to him that it was the best and purest ivory; after a close search he convinced himself there was no join, and that this six-foot wand was all in one piece.

"H'm!" he said to himself, making a sort of grave joke. "It seems to me elephants run rather large in these parts."

"Six straight feet of ivory! such a thing was never heard of!"

The wand or javelin was carefully scrolled and carved, evidently with infinite labour; and presently, after examining it all along its length, he came to the point where was attached the little white flag.

He looked at it, felt it with his finger, and said, aloud—

"Silk! and such silk! I once bought a girl a dress, and gave a guinea a yard for it; but this is worth a guinea an inch!"

And, indeed, it was a most extraordinary fabric.

Glistening as satin, thick as the best silk, and softer than eider-down, of so fine a texture that he could discover none at all.

It was of the purest white, pennon shape, about a foot across at the broadest part, and eighteen inches long.

Crusoe was a man who could make little jokes to himself under difficulties, and said aloud, quietly, for he was not afraid of listeners—

"Ah! I'll have my shirts made of this stuff when I get the half million!"

Then he came to the spear point, which was of the brightest white metal, sharp as a needle.

Again he used his knife; but the metal was too hard for him to scrape anything off.

"Too white for steel," he said to himself; "too hard for silver. What on earth can it be?"

"A new metal?"

"I must give it a name—what shall I call it?"

"I found it on Lion Island—I will call it Leontine!"

But though he tried to think lightly of this extraordinary incident, it was not possible for him to dismiss it from his thoughts.

Those who have read the "Mutiny of the Thunder" knew that Crusoe Jack was no coward; but again, that night, haunted by vague and undefinable terrors, he slept not till grey dawn began to peep out.

And at sunrise, waking suddenly with a start,

his eyes fell on the cause of his unquiet night; and again, as he started to his feet, there broke from him another very English exclamation—

"Confound that javelin!"

He made up the fire, boiled his pot of tea for breakfast in the old way he knew so well; but for once in his life could not eat.

He brought the javelin out with him; as he sat with his pot of tea before him, it lay by his side, and looking down on it he said—

"Confound you, you spoil my appetite. I feel as if you had gone right through my stomach!"

And all the day he prowled moodily about, fearful, watchful, starting at the rustling of every branch, rendered utterly unnerved.

It was the impalpable nature of his enemy—it was the mystery, the terrible suspense, which so prostrated him.

There were few braver men than Crusoe Jack; and could he have but seen a living foe he would have taken his chance of death or victory, but the consciousness of being seen by those he could not see—subject at any moment to an arrow or spear through the body, coming he knew not whence, appalled him.

And it was now that he began to realise the magnitude and danger of his undertaking.

His presence on the island was known.

That was a certainty.

The javelin and silk pennon were evidence enough of that.

True, he could stand a siege in his fortified hut; but how could he provide against phantoms—the invisible?

A hundred howling savages could not have stricken so much terror to his heart as did the shadowy forms he saw through the fire, and the ivory javelin which lay at his feet.

The day passed on without any sign of human being or vestige of human presence.

Night came; and Crusoe, now tired out, began to look upon things in the light of a fatalist.

"If it be so, let it be so!" he said, in the words of the poet Tennyson. "If I am to die by the hands of an invisible enemy, I must. I cannot fight shadows."

And just at that moment some rustling or crackling in the trees attracted his attention.

Snatching up his cutlass, in a fit of sudden frenzy, he rushed out, and waving his sword and shrieking his defiance in a most melodramatic manner, cried—

"Come on, you naked vagabonds—half a hundred of you!"

But to this bold challenge there came no answer.

No sound could be heard, save the sighing of the wind and the far-off murmur of the sea on the shore.

He seated himself before the fire on the ground, leaning his back against one of the logs which formed the hut; and, looking dreamily into the glowing embers, got into a half-dozy state, and feeling something brush his ear like a wasp or large fly, he put up his hand, and felt that which caused him to look round.

And there, driven hard into the log by the side of his head, was a feathered arrow!

It was this which had brushed his hair and touched his ear.

CHAPTER VI.

BUOYING THE WRECK OF THE THUNDER.

THIS incident of the arrow, equally mysterious with the planting of the ivory spear in front of his abode, was far more alarming; for, as regards the former, he might hope that it was a token of friendship, or, perhaps, meant nothing in particular. But there could be no mistake about the significance of a sharp-pointed arrow whizzing past his head and actually brushing his hair.

Having drawn forth the arrow, and carefully examined it, he sat in moody silence, pondering over the mysterious events of the last day or two.

Said he to himself, with forced resignation—

"I must abide by what fate has in store for me. I cannot fight an invisible foe, nor can I guard against an impalpable, unknown danger."

And, in good truth, it seemed he was utterly powerless.

What could he do?

Rush forth among the trees in the darkness, cutlass and pistol in hand, in search of his invisible foe?

That would be folly—more than folly—courting danger.

For if an enemy were concealed among the trees, by approaching closer he would only give opportunity for a sure aim with a second arrow.

After a bit he bethought himself, however, that he might secure present safety by withdrawing into the hut and barricading the entrance.

He did so. Having extinguished the oil lamp he knew that he could not be seen.

He was now on equal terms with the invisible foe—in fact, so long as he remained thus he had rather the best of it; for there was a young moon, and it was, of course, much more light without than within the tent.

So, taking a light double-barrelled rifle, he carefully loaded it, and seating himself on his rude table with this in his hand, so as to command a clearer view of the ground in front of the tent and of the trees beyond, he waited and watched, determined to fire at any moving object he might observe, without stopping to inquire who or what it might be.

A sudden rustle and motion among the brush caused him to start to his feet and level his rifle over the logs; but the next moment a small grey owl, breaking cover, flew across, and he knew the cause of this alarm.

Minutes, hours passed, and Crusoe Jack still kept his vigil. Silent, gloomy, with a look of savage determination on his features, eager to send a bullet whistling through the breast of the unknown enemy that had shot at him.

Probably he had never before been in so bloodthirsty and relentless a humour.

For, be it observed, it is when men are thoroughly alarmed, as well as angry, that the most cruel passions and instincts are called into full play.

During the whole terrible time of the desperate struggle on board the Thunder he was animated chiefly by a desire to put down the mutiny; and though he would, and did, whe-

opportunity offered, shoot down the mutineers like wild beasts, he had not much personal animosity.

Now, however, as he thought of the keen arrow just brushing past his ear, he ground his teeth, and swore that, if ever the chance came, the savage should pay with his life for his treacherous attempt.

But it seems that his amiable intentions were not to be gratified, for midnight came and passed, the sky began to cloud over, and the moon sank to the horizon.

Shortly it would be quite dark, and further watching would be useless.

Crusoe Jack was on the point of concluding his vain vigil, and had even risen from his seat and was about to hang up the rifle, when, taking one last look, something struck his eye in a grove of trees in front and a little to the left of the clear space.

The moon shone on this part, and he distinctly saw a white flashing gleam—a sort of metallic glitter.

He watched intently, and presently distinctly made out something in motion.

It seemed to him like the sheen of some bright object on which the moon's rays fell.

His mind was made up in an instant.

Getting a rest for his rifle on the breast-high logs, he carefully levelled it at the spot, and watched until again the gleam should appear.

He had not long to wait.

He could not discern in the slightest the nature of the object he saw moving slowly among the trees from his right to his left.

However, covering it with the greatest care, he fired.

The report of the rifle and the whistle of the bullet was followed instantly by a faint, sharp cry of pain or alarm, as it seemed to him.

Then there was a sudden rustling in the brushwood.

Jack bounded forth and ran in the direction he had fired, hoping to find a dying or, at all events, wounded savage.

But in this he was disappointed.

When he reached the spot there was nothing whatever to be seen, and the most profound silence reigned.

The moon was now overshadowed by clouds, and to attempt to prosecute a search in the dark would be not only highly dangerous but foolish and utterly useless.

So he returned to the hut, gloomy, disappointed, and very ill-satisfied with the result of the adventure.

It seemed that his life was at the mercy of an invisible enemy, who might return at any moment and, concealed among the trees, despatch another arrow with truer aim.

Although he lay on his couch again, he passed a sleepless night, snatching only a few winks an hour before sunrise.

The day broke bright and glorious; but though, now that it was daylight, he had not so much to fear from an ambuscade, he felt low-spirited and almost despondent.

Mystery succeeded mystery, each more impenetrable than the other.

First, there was the shadowy form he had seen through the fire; then the enormous monument or funeral pile, which he had discovered and climbed; then this ivory javelin, with white silk flag, planted, as it were, defiantly in front of his abode; next the white ivory arrow whistling past his ear, and burying itself in a log behind him, and, lastly, this mysterious gleaming object, which he had seen in motion, and at which he had fired, apparently without effect.

It seemed like a will-o'-the-wisp dancing among the trees.

Altogether he felt himself surrounded by mystery, and was intensely uncomfortable and worried in mind.

That day he did not venture far from the tent; but, keeping always a vigilant look-out, busied himself about many home or domestic matters which required attention.

The day and the night passed without further incident or adventure, and his alarm gradually subsided; and as day after day went on, and there were no further tokens of the presence of his mysterious enemy, his confidence returned.

"Perhaps some prowling savage," he said, "landing here by accident in his canoe, discovered me, and half in wonder, half in terror, shot an arrow; and doubtless the report of my rifle, and the whistle of the bullet, has effectually scared him away."

And so, though not altogether at his ease, he endeavoured to dismiss the subject from his mind, and turn his attention to such measures as were necessary for the prosecution of his object.

Taking a number of small light logs and some half-inch pieces of rope, a hand-lead, and other articles, he carried them down to the little dock he had formed, where lay his boat.

Having placed them in it, he embarked, shoved off, and hoisting the sail was soon gliding over the placid waters of the bay.

The wind was fair; and sailing easily through the opening in the reef, he brought the little craft up to the wind, and in a short time floated directly over the wreck of the Thunder, which he had previously marked by a buoy.

He now proceeded to take careful soundings, so as to ascertain exactly where the hull lay.

He managed this by a simple expedient.

Dropping a light grapnel, attached to a rope, he let it drag until it caught some part of the sunken vessel; then he sounded with his lead close by, and having fixed upon a place near to where the grapnel held when he had got a sandy bottom, he lowered a piece of iron with a line and buoy attached.

He repeated this operation some yards distant, his intention being to mark out thus by a series of buoys the exact outline of the wreck.

By evening he had fifteen of these buoys, and calculated it would take forty or fifty to complete the work.

When this was done, the form of the sunken vessel would be clearly marked out by these floating pieces of wood, and of course he could tell where was her head, her stern, her midships, or any part; and knowing this, he would know very nearly the position of the treasure, which, of course, would greatly facilitate any future operations he might determine upon.

An hour before sunset he ceased work, and hoisting the sail, steered the boat for the opening in the reef.

He was leaning lazily back in the stern-sheets,

moving the tiller to larboard or starboard as was
needed, when a sight met his eyes which caused
him to start to his feet, and made his heart bound
in his breast.

CHAPTER VII.

THE CANOE—ANOTHER MYSTERY.

SUCH was his astonishment that he let go the
tiller, and holding on by the halliards of the sail,
which were belayed to a cleat close by him, he
stood gazing towards the shore.

Thus left to himself, actually at the very entrance into the lagoon, the boat was as nearly as
possible drifting against the sharp coral reef,
which, at the least, would have cut a hole in
her planks, sunk her, and given him cause to
swim ashore.

But this danger he had just escaped.

And what was it he saw?

What wondrous sight seemed to strike him
daft with astonishment, even dismay?

A very simple thing, some might think.

The lovely bay he had pitched upon for his
harbour and the mooring-place for his boat, swept
round in a gentle curve, nearly the semi-circum-
ference of a circle, perhaps three miles along the
shore, from point to point.

There were numerous little inlets and creeks,
some of which, after penetrating the white sand
for a few yards, were completely lost and hidden
by the dense overhanging foliage.

About half a mile further south, at a somewhat
wider inlet, which he had selected for his boat's
dock and place of shelter, he could perceive a cleft
in the sandy shore, like a tiny stream running up
inland; after a few yards it was lost to the eye,
smothered by the dark green bush and gloriously
abundant herbage.

But from just within this leafy shelter there
arose aloft a thin column of white smoke.

His reasoning faculties came to his aid something in this way.

Although it may seem absurd that a strong,
well-educated man should have to arrive, step
by step, at such a simple matter just like a
child.

"That is smoke!

"Smoke comes from fire!

"I didn't light a fire there!

"Something must have done so!

"Birds and beasts don't light fires; so it must
have been a man or a woman—perhaps my
enemy—he who shot that sharp arrow at me
with such deadly intent."

He now proceeded to trim the sail, and again
seated himself at the tiller.

At first he turned the boat's prow towards the
little column of smoke, which wound slowly upward like a silver-grey ribbon from the dark
green foliage; but after sailing a hundred yards
or so in that direction, he altered his plans, and,
bringing her head two or three points more
to the northward, steered for the creek, where
he docked her.

Having run her safely in, he slung the carbine rifle over his shoulders, and, with a revolver
pistol in his belt and cutlass in hand, leaped on
shore and proceeded to make his way towards the
mysterious smoke.

"Be the consequences what they may," he said
to himself, "death or capture by savages, I must

and will do my very utmost to penetrate this mystery—to find out what manner of man or men it
is, of whom I have certain trace on this, which I
thought an uninhabited island."

He thought it best to avoid the sea-shore, for
any object moving along the white sandy beach
could be seen from all the slopes and valleys
which commanded a view of the bay.

Accordingly, he struck up among the groves
of cocoa-nut and palm trees, keeping well under
their shade, but avoiding, as much as possible,
the thick and almost impenetrable brush which
prevailed higher up.

Making his way cautiously thus, he presently
came to the head of the inlet or creek, near which
he had observed the smoke.

He could now no longer see it, for the trees
were thick, and their leafy summits, spreading
wide out, almost excluded the light of day,
giving, in place thereof, a soft, subdued twilight,
even when the sun was shining.

This little creek was in many places not six
feet wide, and a luxuriant growth of shrubs and
creepers in many places met together, and formed
a complete leafy canopy over the water.

And now, looking carefully to the right, to the
left, stepping with the utmost caution, and endeavouring not to make the slightest noise, he
advanced slowly towards the shore, keeping as
near to the bank as the exuberant verdure all
along its edge would allow him.

Presently the smell of burning wood was
wafted to his nostrils—an aromatic, spicy smell
it seemed to him; and pushing his way slowly
forward through the tall dank grass and
creepers, and other vegetation which impeded
his steps, he came suddenly upon a small open
space.

In the centre thereof he perceived the cause
of his alarm as he was returning from the wreck
of the Thunder.

A small fire, carefully built of small pieces of
wood in a pyramidal form. It had been lighted
at the top, and such was the nature of the fuel
that it kept burning down slowly and regularly,
with but little flame.

A light puff of wind wafted the smoke over
to him, and he could now perceive that it was
highly scented—in fact, the smoke resembled
incense.

Proceeding to examine the materials of which
this strange fire was made, he found there were
two sorts of wood, each cut into little slabs or
slates about six inches long by four wide; these
were next carefully and artificially built up into
a hollow pyramid about four feet at the base,
and shoulder high.

One wood was of a pale, rich yellow; this he
knew to be sandalwood—a most valuable commodity in the Chinese market; and this surprised him a good deal, for hitherto he had not
seen the trace of a sandalwood tree on the whole
island. Had he have come across one he would
instantly have recognised it, for he had been on
a trading voyage, as it is called, to a group of
islands about a thousand miles to the eastward
of Sydney; and, having succeeded, by barter
and purchase, in procuring a cargo of the precious
wood, had safely carried it to China, where a
large profit rewarded the speculation.

But the other wood of which the fire was
composed was to him a mystery.

Black as ebony, but unlike ebony, soft, almost pliable—indeed, it was highly odoriferous, even when not burning, and s one like polished tortoise-shell.

Using his knife, he found that it scraped like nutmeg, at the same time emitting a most fragrant odour.

"This is a most extraordinary material," he said to himself. "I think a cargo introduced into European markets would prove of enormous value.

"Is this an enchanted island? Wonder upon wonder, mystery upon mystery, burst on my astonished senses.

"First, I discover a new ivory—probably ivory wood; then a new material—a new silk, I may say, although that little pennon at the top of the javelin was never spun from the worm. A new metal, too, is presented to my bewildered observation; and now behold a new wood! Wonder upon wonder—mystery upon mystery!

"Fortune seems to be having rare sport with me. Perhaps the wayward jade is but trifling with me at first, before she bestows on me the full sunshine of her favour."

CHAPTER VIII.
ON THE LOOK-OUT.

LOOKING around the open space where smouldered the fire of aromatic wood, Crusoe Jack beheld a little opening, where the brush had been cleared away or pushed on one side, and examining this more closely, he plainly perceived that it was a pathway, which had been several times traversed, and leading to the creek at a little distance; following it, he suddenly came to a small canoe moored to the bank, almost entirely concealed by the overhanging foliage.

He was struck with astonishment at the wonderful little vessel he beheld.

Cutting down some of the brush and bushes, vines, and creepers, which hung in bunches all around, he soon got a clear view.

It was certainly not more than six feet long, about a foot or a foot and a quarter in depth from gunwale to keel, and was altogether the most charming bijou little object he ever beheld.

It seemed only fit for a museum and a glass case.

Each end rose in a curling manner, and curled over inwards like a ram's horn. It was lined with fine soft skins and feathers; the skins appeared to him to be those of some kind of antelope; but it was the hull itself of the little vessel which most astonished him. It was all mosaic work of white and black, or rather yellow and dark brown, in diagonal squares like those of a chess board.

Stooping down, he examined it closely, and perceived that it was composed of two sorts of wood, the very same scented ones which slowly burned in the fire.

It was inlaid and ornamented with ivory of the same sort as the mysterious javelin planted before his hut.

Inside, lying along the bottom of the canoe, was an ivory paddle and a quiver of arrows, with the feathers of some gaudy bird, such as those of a pheasant or peacock.

Drawing one of these from the quiver, he perceived that it was of the same description as that which had so narrowly missed his head, and at the prow of the canoe there lay a little circlet or plain tiara of the same glistening white metal, which he had discovered at the monumental pyramid.

Having ascertained all this, he slowly withdrew, pondering what course of action he ought to follow.

Still pondering, he went and seated himself under the shade of a grand old palm tree, and tried to put his thoughts into shape.

Resting his shoulders against the huge trunk, rising sixty clear feet from the ground before there was a branch, the fibrous substance which wraps round the base, and of which the South Sea Islanders make a sort of cloth, forming an admirably soft cushion and pillow, our lonely adventurer had, for the present, every advantage of calm repose in which to ponder on the past and lay plans for the future.

The sun was just dipping into the sea to the west, and the red glowing hues of sunset were beautifully tempered by the groves of trees and everywhere abounding verdure.

A little further up this green canopied creek a mountain brook rippled down into it, and, seated where he was, he could just hear the gentle murmur of the water.

A pleasant breeze rustled the broad leaves of the huge palm and cocoa trees, and all nature seemed about to sigh herself to repose.

Crusoe Jack had taken up a position, so as to command a view of both the fire and the canoe, a part of which he could just discern through the bushes.

"It is certain that the owner of this canoe—the person who made that extraordinary fire—will return here. It is also certain, from the exact similarity of this arrow I have taken, that it belonged to the same savage who shot at me. He must return, and I will wait here and watch until he does; and then—ah! then"—

He set his teeth hard, and, carefully examining the caps of his carbine rifle, laid it across his knees.

"A bullet through the chest for you, my treacherous savage," he muttered, "in return for the arrow aimed at me. We shall see whose aim will prove to be the truest."

Crusoe Jack was sternly determined on the course he laid down for himself; and it is quite certain that if any living thing in the shape of a savage head appeared at that instant, he would have raised his piece, aimed, and driven a bullet through it.

For Crusoe Jack was an excellent shot, and very unlikely to miss at anything like close quarters.

But now there came this rather unpleasant thought to his mind.

"Supposing that this fellow, to whom the canoe belongs, should have made his way up to Flagstaff Point, that would be the very deuce. While I was sitting watching here for his return, he might be turning everything over—plundering, destroying, burning.

"No, I don't think he would make a blaze. I fancy he would be too astonished at what he saw; the tools, arms, &c., would seem to him too strange and wonderful to be wantonly destroyed."

So he argued and reasoned to himself. And indeed there seemed much sense in the view he took of affairs.

For it seemed certain that the savage must return to his canoe, and also that if he stole anything from Flagstaff Point he would bring his plunder down with him.

"I only hope I may catch sight of the vagabond!" said Crusoe to himself, "humping any of my property on his back, and thinking perhaps to embark it in his canoe. If I don't drive a hole right through his dusky body, my name's not Crusoe Jack!"

And so he sat and watched, full of fixed and deadly purpose.

Woe be to any man of savage aspect who should be unlucky enough to come within sight of our hero, and within range of the carbine rifle lying across his knees.

This latter was a most handy and convenient weapon, one which he had especially selected from the arms of the Thunder, and put in the boat before the ship was entirely destroyed.

It was an American patent, one barrel rifled, the other smooth-bore, adapted either to carry small shot, slugs, or a bullet.

There were two hammers and nipples, but only one trigger.

The first pull at this trigger fired one barrel, and another pull without having to move the finger discharged the other.

On the present occasion, both barrels were loaded with ball.

Daylight waned, and the shadow of night closed over the scene.

It was clear overhead, however; and the firelight threw a bright ruddy glow around, so that he could still clearly make out the smallest object at the extremest point on the opposite side of the little clearing.

The time passed on at first without uneasiness on the part of the watcher; but, after a bit, he began to grow impatient.

"I wish this fellow would show, and let me settle his business for him, and have done with it," he muttered amicably. "However, if it is all night, I don't stir from here until he comes back. I'll wait and watch, and my chance must come."

The fire burned lower and lower—the moon sank slowly down towards the sea as the night waned.

Crusoe waited and watched, till, by degrees, in spite of himself, there stole over his senses a sort of listless dreaminess.

He did not sleep—was not near falling right off asleep even—but sat in a sort of half reverie, certainly not very vigilant.

He was aroused from this pleasant state in a sudden and extraordinary manner—far from pleasant, undoubtedly, especially after what had previously occurred.

He heard a whistling rustle, like the wings of a swift bird, followed by a sharp little thud.

Starting to his feet, he beheld, sticking in the tree against which he had been leaning, and barely an inch above his head, another arrow, the very counterpart of the one which had been before shot at him, and that which he had taken from the canoe.

His heart beat wildly for a few moments, and then nearly stood still

CHAPTER IX.

A FRUITLESS ERRAND.

CRUSOE JACK stood glaring around him like some wild beast disturbed in his lair.

Rage, terror, bewilderment—all were expressed in his face.

Suddenly he thought he saw in the shadow of the trees, on the other side of the clearing, an object moving.

It was but as a momentary gleam of something white, and then gone.

With a cry, almost a howl, of fury, he rushed across, and plunged into the umbrageous wood and brush on the other side.

Cutting savagely right and left with his cutlass, as though every bush, cane, and stalk of rank grass which fell before his keen blade was a live enemy, he rushed about like a madman, almost foaming at the mouth.

Presently he stopped from sheer exhaustion. In his mad career he had cut his way into the centre of a brake of cane and tall rank grass.

He now sat down, wearied out, panting for breath, utterly discomfited.

His thoughts and feelings were none of the pleasantest.

He was just considering what should be his course, now that his former plan had been so completely frustrated by the superior keenness of the savage or savages.

For a while he flattered himself that he was lying in wait for him or them, and to make deadly use of his fire-arms; he discovered that it was he himself who was watched—it was he who was at the mercy of these his invisible foes.

He had just got breath, and was listening, thinking, perhaps, to catch some sound, some rustling in the bushes, some crackling branch, which might denote to him the whereabouts of his enemy.

"For now, at least," he said, "in the midst of this brake of cane and rank grass, I am concealed."

Then suddenly there arose on the still night air a strange, clarion-like, sweet sound.

A human voice beyond all doubt.

"La-loo-hee-ah!"

It rose softly from the first syllable, swelling to a rather high pitch in the centre, and again falling with the most exquisite musical cadence in the last.

Anything more beautiful and melodious he had never heard.

The notes of a silver bugle floating over the placid waters of a lake have often been instanced for their soft melody; but this articulate sound—whatever it might mean—thus intoned by a human voice, transcended anything that had ever fallen on his ears.

He rose and stood listening intently, hoping for a repetition of the sound.

The sound seemed to be borne on the night air from behind him—that is to say, from the direction from which he had come.

After a bit he roused himself to the necessity for action.

"That's the chap who shot at me," he said. "Confound his pretty voice! I'll spoil his whistle if I get within a sight of him at fifty yards."

Whereupon he commenced to retrace his steps; not with the same furious recklessness as heretofore, but steadily and with a certain stubborn determination.

Emerging out of the clear space, in the centre of which he had discovered the pyramidal fire made of scented wood, he paused and looked around him.

The moon had not yet set, and the clouds, passing slowly, cleared off from the sky. There was sufficient light for him to discern all objects dimly.

The fire had nearly burnt down to its base, and all was one red glow.

Silence and solitude reigned around.

No sound came to his ear, save the distant bubbling of a little brook which trickled into the creek—no sight of any living thing; nothing but the trunks of the grand old trees, standing out like huge columns towering to heaven in the gloom.

He bethought himself of the canoe, and instantly turned his steps in that direction.

Just as he reached the little path in the bush, which he had first discovered leading to the creek, there again broke out on the still night air the strange, melodious sound he had before heard—

"La-loo-hee-ah !"

This time it seemed to be much closer than when he had heard it before—apparently coming from a little grove of trees on the other side of the clearing.

Crusoe did not hesitate a moment ; drawing his revolver with his left hand, his cutlass in his right, he ran straight towards the spot from whence the voice proceeded.

Distinctly he heard the rustling of brushwood and the crackling of decayed branches—such as might be caused by rapidly retreating footsteps, and he even thought he caught a glimpse of a figure flitting swiftly through the trees.

Be that as it might, however, he could get hold of nothing tangible, either for sight or hearing, and ran on amidst the cocoa and palm groves, until brought up by a dense tangle of cane, jungle, and tall grass, such as that into which he had before cut his way.

Once more he came to a halt—once more baffled and wearied. Scarcely had he rested a few seconds, when again was wafted to his ears the strange refrain—

"La-loo-hee-ah !"

This time it seemed to come further from the right, and again he started in pursuit of the phantom voice.

Though tired, he was undaunted, and more determined than ever to solve this mystery, though it should cost him his life.

After ten minutes' half running, half pushing through the vines, creepers, and dank grass, he was forced to come to a standstill.

"La-loo-hee-ah !"

Again rang out in the same silvery tones, this time from a totally different direction.

Notwithstanding his previous disappointment and inward weariness, he again made for the place whence he supposed the sound came.

This led him to the edge of an open space, and skirting this he plunged into the thicket, walking as fast and as silently as possible, ardently hoping to come unawares upon the mysterious being who had caused him so much terror and uneasiness.

He climbed a slope which led to the top of a low mound.

Arrived here, he halted to rest for a few moments, and reconnoitre as well as he could amidst the prevailing gloom.

And then, to his annoyance and bewilderment, again rang out, clear and flute-like, on the night air—

"La-loo-hee-ah !"

That syren cry by which he was to be haunted, and which, perhaps, would ere long be the signal for his death.

This time it again came from behind him—that is to say, from the direction whence he had come.

Once again he stood in the open space, and suddenly noticed that the embers and remaining fuel of the pyramid fire of scented wood were scattered in all directions.

That this was the work of human hands there could not be the slightest doubt whatever.

And were any other proof wanted there was a crowning one—a most tantalising and annoying proof to Crusoe Jack.

He had left the white ivory javelin, which had been so defiantly planted outside his tent on Flagstaff-hill at home, not wanting it, and, of course, thinking it was perfectly safe.

And now here it stood before his eyes, planted in the very middle of the place where the fire had been built !

Dawn was beginning to break now, and by its dim light he discovered something else which did not improve his temper.

A strip of bunting had been torn from one of his flags, and fixed beneath the white silk pennon which the javelin originally bore.

Whoever it was that planted that white metal-pointed wand where it now stood had been to his abode on Flagstaff-hill, overhauled it, perhaps pillaged it, and fastened to the slender spear a piece of his own bunting.

As he thus mused, he again heard the cry—

"La-loo-hee-ah !"

This time he thought in mocking accents.

It seemed to come from the direction of the creek.

He suddenly remembered the canoe, and made a rush for the little path in the brushwood leading to the place where it had been moored.

The canoe was gone.

And far away down in the lagoon he again heard the sweet syren mocking cry—

"La-loo-hee-ah !"

CHAPTER X.
THE MYSTERIOUS SCROLL.

The canoe was gone. The withes by which she had been fastened to the shore had not been unbound, but cut, for part of them still remained ; and once in the light craft, the owner, with a few paddle strokes, had doubtless sent her down the creek into the lagoon.

Crusoe followed the course of the narrow inlet, ran down the sea-shore, and seeing nothing on the side on which he was, the northern and eastern, he did not hesitate a moment, but plunged in and waded across.

About half a mile ahead of him was a point of sand and coral rock, covered with young cocoa-trees and scrub. The canoe might have had time, urged by a skilful rower, to have rounded this point, and so got out of sight; but he thought if he hastened to take up a position there he could not fail to discover the fleeing savage.

For this point commanded a complete view of the sea and the bay beyond it for miles, and he was certain he could run along the hard smooth sward much more quickly than any canoe could be impelled by any human agency.

He was a swift runner, and had excellent wind, and tore along the shore at a tremendous pace.

In his mad course he passed many creeks and inlets—"bayous" as the Americans of the Southern States would call them.

Some of them he leaped over; others he ran through as if they were puddles.

And so he tore along, and probably in a shorter time than he had ever done before, covered the half-mile, and stood on the point, and then what met his gaze?

The sea, the sky, the island, the coral reef.

He sank to the ground, overcome, not altogether by fatigue, but by mental exhaustion—bitter disappointment—almost despair.

It seemed as though he was marked out for the sport of spiteful fairies—shot at by arrows that grazed but did not hit him; tormented and defied by flag-bearing javelins planted right in front of his tent; tantalised by finding an elaborately carved canoe, whose owner eluded all his efforts to discover him; mocked and insulted by the sweet syren voice beguiling him on, yet ever receding.

It is enough to break down the nerve and crush the spirits of a brave and stout-hearted man such as Crusoe Jack undoubtedly was.

A week back, had anyone told Crusoe he would be thus harassed and terrified, his life made a misery and burden to him by an invisible foe, an airy nothing—vox et præterea nihil, as Ovid says—he would have laughed the thought to scorn.

In good sooth, all that he knew to a certainty as to the presence of a human being on the island was a voice. Beyond all possibility of doubt, those sweet-sounding syllables—"La-loo-hee-ah!" were uttered by a human voice, and one of singular melody.

But where was the body belonging to that voice?

The more he thought the more staggered and more aghast he grew at the aspect of affairs.

The canoe, which he had watched nearly all night, had been cunningly stolen away.

Whoever it was that had thus eluded his vigilance in this instance, could not possibly have got ten minutes' start of him.

He had run like a racehorse, and quickly gained a position, from which he could command the prospect for miles, and yet no black speck, denoting the presence of a canoe, dotted the surface of the sea.

Humanly speaking, it was impossible she could have put out from that little creek, and gone out of sight in so short a time, and yet there was nothing to be seen.

He lay there on the sand, and presently fell off into a deep heavy sleep.

The sun rose in a cloudless sky, and shining down on the weary dispirited adventurer, absolutely burned and blistered one side of his face and neck, and yet for hours he did not awake, and when he did so, he felt stupid and staggered like a drunken man.

His clothes, wetted by swimming through the water, had dried on him, and his wet shoes shrinking, caused him intense pain.

Taking them off, his feet swelled so prodigiously in a few minutes, that it was hopeless to think of putting them on again, so, slinging them round his neck, using the cutlass as a stick, Crusoe painfully commenced to retrace his return to his abode on Flagstaff-hill

But what a sight! Scarcely when he had been at his worst during the mutiny of the Thunder had he presented such a spectacle as he now did.

Step by step, and yard by yard, he toiled along the point of the shore, keeping entirely to the sand, on account of his bare feet.

He almost shuddered as he thought of the terrible task before him, in making his way thus shoeless over the rugged slopes covered with thorns and brambles, which he must traverse ere he could reach his hut.

However, when it was necessary to leave the belt of smooth sand by the shore, and strike inland through the groves of trees and thickets, he bethought himself of a mode by which he might avoid lacerating his swollen feet.

Taking off his shirt he tore it up and bound it round his feet, and then was able to make his way over the rough ground without much pain.

Several heavy showers of rain broke over the island as he toiled up the valleys and slopes, and by the time he reached his hut he was drenched through and shivering with cold.

There was some dry wood inside; so, throwing some on the cold embers, he set light to it, and piling on logs there was soon a cheerful blaze.

He brewed himself a pot of tea, of which having partaken, he entered his tent, utterly wearied and broken down, intending to sleep.

Hitherto he had not made any close examination.

He saw that, in a general way, the hut and its contents were almost as he had left them; and though he knew from the fact of the piece of red bunting on the javelin he had found stuck amidst the embers of the scented wood fire, that a visit had been paid by a savage or savages to Flagstaff Point, he felt far too listless, weary, and unnerved, to make close search.

All at once, however, he observed something on his rude table.

A piece of white paper he at first thought it.

But on taking it in his hands, he found it quite soft and pliable, and discovered it was the little banner on the ivory javelin.

Looking closely at it, he saw it was covered with figures and characters.

These however were to him incomprehensible.

They seemed to resemble ancient Egyptian inscriptions more than writing, properly so called.

He fancied he could make out certain outlines and devices intended to represent the human form, trees, &c., but so rudely and irregularly was it all done, and surrounded by flourish and ornament, that it was impossible for him to decide even whether it was meant for writing, or merely a sort of ornament scroll.

THE ISLAND PRINCESS.

However, there it was, and more evidence of human presence on the island.

Folding it up, he placed it in the breast-pocket of his coat; and then, dragging out a rug of opossum skins to the front of the tent, and selecting a place shaded from the burning rays of the sun, he threw himself down.

"Perhaps I shall fathom all these mysteries some day," he said. "Now I must sleep. My head aches desperately; it feels as though it would burst asunder."

CHAPTER XI.
THE PRINCESS OF THE ISLAND.

He slept as he had before done, on the sandy point, a deep, heavy sleep, but not one of those quiet slumbers which bring repose to the wearied frame.

When he awoke it was near sundown.

He felt dizzy, heavy-headed, and very thirsty. His skin was hot and dry, and his temples throbbed most painfully.

The fire was out, but he felt as though he had not energy enough to re-light it; and it was only by a great effort of will that he could nerve himself to the task of piling on some more brush and logs, and setting it alight.

He had soon reason to be thankful he had done so; for, after the burning heat in which he awoke, there succeeded great cold, especially of the hands and feet, and a shivering fit which lasted fully half an hour.

He was surgeon enough to know what all this

portended, and, with a heavy heart and sinking spirits, made the best preparations he could to meet and combat the fell spectre, fever—intermittent fever, which had now, he knew too well, got its cruel hand on his throat.

He got out the medicine chest, and mixed himself at once fully twenty doses of medicines, principally quinine and saline draughts.

He took a strong dose of quinine at once—that magic drug. the only one which can touch ague or tropical fevers.

Then he got water handy to his couch, a biscuit, and everything he thought he would require, should he be utterly prostrated by the fever, which he felt rapidly gaining on him.

Then he bathed his head and face, and piled a great quantity of logs on the fire, sufficient, he thought, to keep it burning for at least twenty-four hours.

And then he laid himself down, aching in every joint, every limb; his head throbbing, his skin again hot and dry after the cold fit.

"And now," he muttered, "I am in the hands of fate."

"If the savages, my enemies, come, I shall fall an easy prey to their rage. So be it. I almost wish it were over."

And then, ill and suffering in body, broken in spirit, and tortured in mind by rapid, indefinable terrors, he laid himself down on his rude couch.

No sweet refreshing sleep visited his weary eyes and aching brain.

He tossed and tumbled all the night through.

Occasionally he would drop off into a sort of doze, but haunted by strange fancies and phantoms he would quickly awake with a start; and this occurred many times, until shortly before daybreak the fever had so gained in its intensity that he was quite delirious and light-headed.

He knew where he was, and that was all.

The tent and all around it he peopled with creatures of his imagination. Old shipmates, and friends, and chief among them a female figure.

He thought this figure walked to and fro round his rude couch, wringing her hands and looking extremely wretched. Occasionally she would stop, sometimes at the head, sometimes at the foot, of his bed, and gaze down into his face with a glance full of unutterable pity and sorrow.

And then crowds of other phantoms would arise and drive away the vision. The mutineers, with Death's Head Dick at their head, blood-smeared and ghastly, shook their clenched fists at him, and threatened him, scowling horribly the while, whilst Death's Head Dick looked more horrible than when in the flesh.

Then there appeared another figure on the scene—a stern old man, with iron-gray hair, and wearing a long brown coat.

This latter, whirling some weapon round his head, quickly cleared the tent of its other phantom occupants, blaspheming and cursing at them right and left.

Until Crusoe Jack saw him standing at the foot of the bed silently regarding him.

It was Noah Plunkett some time captain of the Thunder, who, in his madness, had leaped overboard.

The fever-stricken man saw him, as he thought, in his delirium, produce the deadly revolver carbine from under his coat—that murderous weapon which he, with grim humour, used to call his telescope.

He levelled it.

Crusoe, with a shriek, rose to a sitting posture, and strove to struggle out of bed.

Just at that moment another phantom appeared on the scene—Schraeder, the unhappy Finn, whom Noah Plunkett had murdered.

With a scream of rage, the Finn flew at the throat of the late captain of the Thunder, and then there commenced a desperate struggle.

Over and over they rolled, the Finn holding his antagonist tight by the throat.

Crusoe, to whom all this appeared reality, watched the struggle with intense interest; his face flushed, his eyes bloodshot with the fierce fever which consumed him.

And presently he thought the Finn was choking Plunkett.

In their desperate struggles, rolling over and over on the floor of the hut, they approached the head of the bed. Noah, he thought, by a desperate effort, struggled to his feet, the Finn keeping his deadly grasp on the throat.

He thought he could see these two phantoms, glaring at each other with their ghostly eyes, their ghastly faces within a few inches of each other. They were close to the couch where he lay, hanging over it, and he thought that in their desperate struggle both would fall on him.

With a shriek of terror he bounded up, leaped from the bed, and made a rush to the entrance, to escape from the arena of this terribly ghostly conflict.

Weak, tottering, and giddy, and almost blind with delirium and horror, he managed to gain the outside of the tent, and then, staggering, fell heavily with his forehead against one of the logs forming the buttresses of his abode.

Then for Crusoe Jack all was darkness, oblivion.

The moon sank, and in due course the sun rose, red and glorious, in the east. He lay there till near high noon, his head in a pool of blood, with which his hair was matted.

This was, perhaps, fortunate, for thereby the pressure on the brain was relieved; and when he slowly woke to consciousness, though still light-headed and wandering, there was none of the furious delirium of the previous night.

He felt consumed by thirst, and endeavoured to rise, but was unable to do so.

His limbs had no longer the strength to obey the mandates of his will.

But he contrived to raise himself to a sitting posture, and presently saw, dimly, a few feet from where he was, outside the tent, a bucket of water with a pannikin. With great effort and difficulty he managed to crawl to this, and after drinking a full measure, he poured another over his burning head and face.

Then, with the end of a log for a pillow, he sank down, and went off into a state half trance, half sleep, muttering continually to himself.

And presently there came visions, if visions they were, of a more pleasant nature than the terrible scene which had driven him screaming from the hut.

Again he saw a female form and sweet lovely face flitting about him.

He could see this female form as through a mist, surrounded by a rainbow-like halo.

Jewels sparkled on her wrists, her hands, her neck, her brow, her eyes themselves the brightest gems of all.

Gently and noiselessly this new and strange phantom glided about him.

He could see but dimly, as through a cloud, and watched her with pleased curiosity, like that of a child, wondering whence came this fairy, nymph, angel—whatever she might be.

And presently he had a dim knowledge of a bowl being presented to his lips, and drinking deeply of a cool beverage—a sourish sweet, with a slight bitter taste clinging to it.

For a little time longer he thought this jewelled phantom with the gleaming eyes hovered about him; then soft strains of music seemed to arise on his ears; the mist grew thicker, and the fairy form was altogether hidden by the rainbow halo.

Then he closed his eyes, and slept—this time a calm, deep sleep—visionless, dreamless.

CHAPTER XII.

AN UNKNOWN FRIEND.

WHEN Crusoe again awoke it was daylight. The sun was just rising.

He had slept all through the night a calm deep sleep without once awaking or being disturbed by any dream or vision whatever.

He was very weak, but the delirium had entirely left him, and the fever also seemed to have burned itself out.

Looking around, he saw first that the fire still burned, and, observing more closely, he saw that a great number of logs must have been piled on over night, for there were the halves of some unburned, while others were scarcely touched at all by the fire.

"I did not put all those logs on the fire, I am sure," he murmured to himself, faintly. "I could not have done it. I remember now I was too weak. I have been very ill, in a raging fever. I have had visions, dreams; all sorts of wild fancies have haunted me."

"I thought I saw Noah Plunkett and that unhappy Finn locked in a deadly struggle. And then I have a dim memory of a female phantom, an island nymph, a siren, a fairy, a lovely lady, with jewels on her wrists, arms, neck, brow; gorgeously attired and surrounded by a rainbow halo."

" And yet this last vision seemed to me more palpable, more constant, than the other. "Ah! I remember! my head, I hurt it, it was bleeding."

He put up his hand mechanically, and a faint cry escaped him.

Wonder of wonders!

It was neatly and carefully bound up with a band of some soft fabric, and he felt that it was cool and moist as though it had not long since been wetted.

This was a discovery indeed, and could lead but to one most obvious conclusion.

During his insensibility some one had discovered him, bound up his wounded head, and otherwise done the part of the good Samaritan.

It could not have been an enemy.

An enemy, finding him under such circumstances, would simply have murdered him and taken possession of all his goods, as is the fashion with savage people, and too often with civilised people also.

A friend!

It could only have been a friend who had done this thing.

But who, then, could be this mysterious friend?

He had found that he had an unknown enemy on the island.

It would seem now that he had also an unknown friend.

The thought was cheering.

But was it warranted by the facts?

Was it not possible that he himself might, in his delirium, have bound up his head and forgotten all about it?

But this he soon dismissed from his mind as absolutely impossible.

And then there came to his senses all at once other evidence, utterly incontrovertible—making assurance doubly sure.

Near where his head lay, and within reach of his right hand, was a small bowl or gourd, halffull of some liquid.

He had not placed it there—had, indeed, never seen anything in the least like it.

He had strength enough to raise it to his lips, and then recognised the flavour of the liquid as the same sweet-sour bitter which he had tasted in what he thought was his vision.

It was, then, no vision.

Some human being had taken compassion on his wretched, forlorn condition—ill and helpless, all alone—and had come to his aid and succour.

Probably the beverage contained the juice of some medicinal herb, and by killing the fever and producing sound sleep had saved his life.

He took a deep draught, then lay back and lapsed into thought—thoughts of a more pleasing nature than he had enjoyed since the first mystery broke on his mind.

And presently, as the sun rose and it grew warm, he dozed off again into a sweet, gentle sleep.

The beverage, amongst its medicinal properties, seemed to possess that of a narcotic, and in a powerful degree, for it was sundown when he again awoke.

He felt greatly refreshed, clear-headed, and entirely free from fever.

He was, however, extremely weak, which might well be accounted for by want of food and loss of blood, to say nothing of the fever.

He was slightly thirsty too, and remembering how cool and grateful the acid-sweet beverage was before to his palate, he reached forth his hand to the bowl, in some doubt as to whether there remained any.

It was quite full!

During his sleep it had been replenished, and put back in the same place.

He was still, then, watched over and cared for.

A delightful feeling of grateful joy and satisfaction stole over his senses as he realised this fact.

It is only those who have found themselves in the like desolate and wretched condition of Crusoe Jack who can realise his feeling of sweet delight at the sure knowledge that there was some one in the world who cared for him, or, at all events, took compassion on his forlorn and helpless state.

By degrees, other proofs of tender care for his health and comfort were made apparent.

He discovered that his head rested on a pillow of matwork, apparently stuffed with feathers.

And by his side lay a roll of most strange material.

It was like the finest silk, quilted over eider down, at once soft, delicate, warm, and light.

And then he perceived close to the bowl of drink another vessel, with a wooden or cocoanut spoon.

He found it contained a thick, viscous mass, like very strong gruel.

This he judged at once was intended for him to take as food; and having already experienced such great benefit from the cooling acid drink, he did not hesitate to partake of this fresh offering from his unknown and mysterious friend.

It was far from disagreeable though he had never before tasted anything in the least resembling it.

It was thick and viscous as paste, and hung in strings to the spoon.

Like the drink, it was slightly acid, but had also a sort of nutty flavour, with just a tinge of saltness.

He got quite to like it after he had taken a few spoonfuls, and did not fail to finish the whole contents of the little calabash.

Then another drink from the bowl, and he began to feel sleepy from fatigue, weakness, and the narcotic virtues of the beverage combined.

Before composing himself to rest, however, he unrolled and drew around him the soft rug or coverlet of strange material, which he found so considerately placed by the side of where he lay.

And before yielding to the embraces of the god of sleep, he thought over the events of the last few days, especially the latest discoveries he had made of so much more pleasing a nature.

Who could be the person—man or woman, civilised or savage—who had thus taken compassion on him, tended him, cared for him, and probably snatched him from the jaws of death?

There came a sort of vague vision-like memory of a lovely female, richly bedizened with jewels, and, though in savage style, gorgeously arrayed.

But this seemed only like a dream, and he put it down to his delirium when the fever raged.

The fire, well provided with fuel, burned with steady glare and glow. The sun set, the moon rose; the gentle night breeze swept over the cabin scene, and Crusoe Jack, his head just under shelter of the tent, slept the sleep of the weary.

CHAPTER XIII.
FOOTMARKS ON THE SAND!

IN that tropical latitude there was no such thing as weather in our acceptation of the word—no variations of fine, wet, cold, hot, thick, muggy, and so forth.

Except for occasional heavy, tropical showers, during which tons of water came down in torrents, deluging the surface of the islands, and actually making a thin layer of fresh water on the surface of the sea, there was one continual round of fine weather.

Morning after morning the sun rose in a cloudless sky, climbing the blue vault of heaven to the meridian, deluging the sea and coral islands in a bath of golden sunshine, sinking down to the west, smiling over the calm Pacific, rippled by little waves, and the verdure-clad slopes and vales of the islands of the sea, till, leaving the horizon, the long shadows of the evening breeze proclaimed the approach of night.

A night, calm, beautiful, the gentle ripple of the swell on the reefs, of the little waves on the sandy shore, were the only sounds breaking the solemn silence of this island solitude.

And so, day by day, night by night, lovely, entrancing, but monotonous, was the calm of the weather and climate.

To one in Crusoe Jack's condition, just recovering from a severe attack of fever, nothing could be more favourable than such quiet pleasant times.

When he awoke in the evening, after the discovery of the roll of soft fabric with which he had covered himself, though very weak, he felt better in spirits, and with more energy.

He was no longer tormented by the terrible anxiety as to his mysterious enemy, for he knew now that he had also an unknown friend.

He was able to rise, wash himself, comb his hair, and make himself look less like a seaman and more like a civilised being.

Looking into a small circular mirror he had brought with him, he was horrified at the ghastly appearance he presented.

Could it be possible that three days' illness, even of a tropical fever, should produce such a terrible change in his appearance?

The skin of his face was like yellow parchment, the bones round the orbits of his eyes, his cheek bones and chin seemed to start out; his lips were of a livid blue colour, and his hair, which curled slightly, hung in straight dark masses.

It is not too much to say that it would have been hard even for an intimate acquaintance to recognise in the skeleton-like inhabitant of Flagstaff Island, the handsome, stalwart second mate of the Thunder.

He found the bucket replenished with beautifully cool spring water, and it had not been taken from any of the casks he had in the hut he was certain; from its appearance and temperature it must have been procured from some of the mountain springs, and carried to his hut by his unknown friend.

After a wash and a clean shirt, he felt refreshed, although tired even by that slight exertion.

The fire was burning brightly, also evidently the work of the unknown, and having made himself a pot of tea, he seated himself, with his back to the logs, and proceeded to seek solace in a pipe of tobacco.

The day passed without incident.

He was too weak to move away from the hut; but as he was now able to eat, he felt he was gathering strength slowly but surely.

At eventide, he made up the fire himself, took a light supper of tea and biscuit, turned in and slept soundly, nor woke till the warm rays of the morning sun fell on his face.

He had been visited during the night by his unknown friend, for the bowl was full of the acid beverage, the calabash of that strange food of paste-like consistency.

As he felt that his recovery was mainly due to the medicinal proportions of this drink and food, he took nothing else for his breakfast.

The effect was that he shortly felt drowsy, and, dozing off, slept for full two hours, basking in the warm sunshine.

After a wash, on looking in the glass to comb his hair, he was astounded at the appearance his face presented.

The yellow dry skin was all coming off in flakes and scales, and it really seemed as though he were going to moult, or cast his skin altogether; but he felt wonderfully better in every way, and rendered strong enough to walk some distance without fatigue.

He employed himself on light, easy work, making a number of buoys of rope, with weights attached, ready to finish buoying the wreck of the Thunder.

In doing this, writing up his journal, and drawing as accurately as he could a chart of the island, its creeks, and coral reefs, he occupied the time till evening.

And then, in quiet, delightful monotony, passed two or three days; no incident, no worry, no anxiety retarding the sick man's rapid recovery.

By the end of that time he was quite reinstated in health. Of course in so short a time he had not entirely recovered the strength and flesh he had lost; but his skin was clear, his eye bright, his appetite good, and, better than all, he was in excellent spirits.

Now it happened that on this, the fourth day after the fever had left him, he felt exceedingly well in health and spirits, and yet disinclined to do any work, in fact what is called a lazy fit; and after having taken breakfast, sat for fully an hour outside his hut, dreamingly smoking a pipe, puffing out the smoke at long intervals, thinking of things in general, and nothing in particular.

"I think I'll just take a stroll about the island," he said to himself. "I don't feel inclined for work, and a walk will do me good."

Accordingly, slinging the light carbine rifle over his back, sticking a revolver in his belt, and with a cutlass in his right hand, he started on a reconnoitring expedition.

The cutlass he found extremely useful.

He employed it as an axe in clearing away weeds, and cutting down brush, and as a stick on which to lean, to support his steps—not yet quite firm and steady.

He had no definite object in view, and was indifferent which way he bent his steps, so he found himself shortly at the head of the valley sloping from the mountain which led to the open space where he had found the pyramidal fire of scented wood.

Arrived here, he stopped at the tree, at the foot of which he was seated, when the white shafted arrow whistled into the wood within an inch of his head.

He examined the incision, probed it with his knife, and found it had gone into the solid wood full an inch and a half.

"D——n his eyes!" he muttered; "if he had aimed two inches lower, it would have gone clean through my skull."

He now walked to the remains of the fire. There were the burnt ashes, half-charred pieces of the two scented woods, the yellow and black, and besides these there were also many pieces entirely untouched by the fire.

It struck him it might be worth while saving them for curiosity's sake, even if they did not prove valuable.

So he set to work and quickly collected all that were not touched by the fire.

He ranged them in two little piles—the ebony wood in one, the sandal wood in another.

Looking round the clear space, his eye fell on the opening in the bushes which had first drawn his attention to the nook in the creek when he had discovered the cause.

Almost without thought—certainly without any definite object in view—he strolled thither, and made his way slowly through the brush to the creek, and, arrived there, a sight met his eyes which caused an exclamation of astonishment and wonder to break from his lips.

There was the canoe—the very same canoe—moored in the very same manner, and in the very same place.

He stood for a few moments gazing in speechless astonishment; but, after a bit, recovering himself, proceeded to make a closer examination.

Everything was exactly the same as on the previous occasion, except that the light diadem of the bright white metal was no longer there.

The water was lower in the creek, by reason of the state of the tide, than on the previous occasion, and she was now resting on a narrow slip of sand on the edge.

There was enough of this for him to get a footing, dryshod, and, standing, he made an examination of the canoe and her contents.

He tried her weight, and found that, weak as he was, he could, with ease, lift the light craft easily.

"I've a great mind to go for a row on the lagoon with her," he said; "but I'm afraid she would upset with me."

So he relinquished this idea, and replaced her exactly as he found her.

As he did so, his eyes happened to fall on the smooth white sand, still damp from the water, which had not long retreated, and there he beheld that which made his heart beat fast in his breast.

Footmarks!

The plain imprint of human feet, small, delicately-shaped, naked feet, leading in a direct line along the narrow strip of sand up the creek.

CHAPTER XIV.

THE NYMPH OF THE LAKE.

As soon as he had recovered from the first astonishment at the footmarks on the sand, he resolved to follow and see whither they led.

"I see a great discovery before me," he said to himself. "By following these footprints I shall probably be led direct to the place where is my mysterious unknown enemy, for I believe the maker of these footmarks is the owner of the canoe, and the owner of the canoe, with damnable malice, shot an arrow at me as I sat under the tree."

So, keeping his eye fixed on the narrow strip of sand, he advanced slowly up the creek, now walking on dry ground, at other times wading more than ankle deep in the water.

The sand was in places completely covered, where he, of course, lost sight of the footprints. These, however, always reappeared as soon as there came another dry strip, showing that, whoever it was, they had done as he was doing—partly waded in the water, partly walked on the sand.

The creek grew narrower and narrower as he advanced, and was so overhung by bushes, brush, and creepers, that at times he had to wade almost in the centre.

The dry sand soon disappeared altogether, and of course he lost sight of the foot track.

However, he continued his way, feeling confident that whoever it was had gone straight up the creek. Ere long he came to the end of it.

It finished abruptly, with a sloping wall of wet moss-grown rocks, over and among which tumbled a little rivulet of fresh water, whose gurgling and rippling could be heard far down the creek.

After some little delay for deliberation he commenced climbing the rocks, determined to penetrate to the place whence the little stream came.

The only difficulty he had in climbing up was from the slipperiness of the rocks, the ascent, otherwise, being tolerably easy.

After winding upwards in a zigzag fashion for about forty yards, he reached the top, and found himself suddenly on level ground.

Before him was a pond of fresh water, bordered by damp green turf and mountain moss.

He still pressed on, keeping a vigilant lookout, casting keen glances to the right and to the left, and, on reaching the end of the pool, he saw through the bushes a larger sheet of water before him, and, hewing himself a path with his cutlass, he found himself, in a few minutes, standing by the side of a lovely little lake.

It was almost circular in figure, and about five hundred yards across it seemed to him.

Its beauty was indescribable. All around its placid shores were luxuriant masses of tropical verdure, while, a little further back, there rose out of this green sea of foliage the tall slender stems of the cocoa palm and bread-fruit tree, with their tufts of dark green branches waving like gigantic plumes high in the air.

This charming little lake, which, in all his rambles he had never discovered before, was surrounded on all sides by mountain slopes, everywhere covered with trees, and a luxuriant undergrowth; at some places steep, with huge mossy rocks sticking out, at others with a more gentle incline; but everywhere the same glorious green.

The surface of the water was smooth as a mirror; not a wavelet rippled on the shore, and as he gazed he thought he had never beheld such a scene of calm loveliness.

Strolling slowly on, drinking in with his senses the placid beauties of nature before him, his eye fell on a white object near the centre of the lake.

Watching it for a moment or so, he perceived it was in motion. He had not his telescope with him; so, shading his eyes with his hands, he strained his vision to find out what it was.

It seemed like the white sail of a boat or canoe; but though he gazed his keenest, there was no craft of any sort or kind carrying this sail.

It was approaching him in a diagonal direction—that is to say, it was not coming direct to the place where he stood, but towards a point on the shore further up the lake.

Seeing this, he walked on quickly, thinking thus to get a better view, and all at once he came to a dead stop, and gazed around in utter astonishment.

He was walking a distance of about five feet from the shore, and two or three feet from a line of bushes and shrubs that ran parallel thereto.

In a little semi-circular nook in these bushes, where the overhanging branches formed a sort of natural harbour, he beheld a variety of objects, obviously for human use and ornament.

There was a pile of soft white material, with a gloss like satin; there was white glistening metal for what he took to be bracelets, studded with coloured stones, which were doubtless jewels; other strange ornaments—rings, and a chain, all of the same glistening white metal, lay in a heap together, and close by them a light diadem of singularly chaste and elegant workmanship.

Then there were a bow of black wood, white-hafted arrows, such as had been shot at him, and several white javelins with fluttering white pennons, exactly like that which had been stuck up before his hut.

There were other things, but he did not stay to observe more, for he perceived that the white object on the lake was rapidly approaching, and, looking again, he saw beneath it a human face, apparently floating on the surface of the lake.

He now bethought himself to be cautious, and and see what he could without himself being seen; so he walked quickly on about forty yards, and then ensconced himself in the bushes, so that he could command a view of the lake and shore without himself being seen. The object he had first observed was now sufficiently near for him to make out exactly its nature.

It was a human body floating, holding in each hand a light rod or pole, to which was attached the white fabric forming the sail.

This, extended by the two light rods, caught the slight breeze which sighed over the bosom of the lake, and the human form beneath glided smoothly and swiftly along, only the face and hands above the surface.

This was certainly the most picturesque mode of navigation which had ever fallen under his notice, and he gazed at the novel scene with mingled wonder and admiration.

As the floating, gliding figure came nearer and nearer, he saw that long hair was floating on the waves, and could distinguish the elegantly-turned limbs through the water, and in a few minutes' more this human bark reached the shore, the sail suddenly collapsed, the figure stood erect, about knee-deep in the water.

Crusoe Jack gazed with entranced delight on a lovely female form, almost veiled, and concealed by the luxurious masses of hair which fell over her neck, shoulders, and bosom.

After furling the sail by a few quick turns of the wrist, she let the light bamboo rods rest on her shoulder, and with an easy grace, advanced towards the little arbour, utterly unconscious of being observed by a man's eye.

He remained spell-bound, gazing on the beautiful vision, until she disappeared behind the sheltering bushes.

"My enemy!" he muttered. "A woman—an Amazon!—a beautiful tigress!"

CHAPTER XV.

THE ISLAND PRINCESS.

CRUSOE JACK remained in his hiding-place for some short time, pondering on what he had seen.

"Who can this woman be?" he said to himself, "and what means her presence here, apparently alone. Certainly she is no ordinary savage woman; probably the wife or daughter of some chief.

"And why should she seek my life, as undoubtedly she has done; for it was her hand and bow which sped the arrows which so nearly cost me my life.

"What must I do?

"What course shall I adopt?

"My life is not safe whilst this savage beauty roams the island at large, amusing herself every now and then by letting fly an arrow at me.

"Twice she has missed me only by an inch or so. The next time her aim may be more deadly.

"I must see to it. Self-preservation is the first law of nature.

"Despite her sex and romantic beauty, I must kill or make her prisoner."

And having formed this resolve, Crusoe Jack proceeded to act.

And a very foolish course it was indeed that he took.

Strange it is sometimes that the keenest and most quickwitted and prudent men will make the most egregious blunders.

Such was the case with Crusoe Jack.

At a little distance, armed as he was with rifle, carbine, and revolver, a savage man or woman, with bow, arrows, and spears, would be utterly at his mercy; but face to face, within a few yards, they would be on an equality—nay, the advantage would probably be on the side of the savage weapons.

Of this, however, he thought not, but advanced cautiously, keeping close to the bushes, towards the leafy bower where, doubtless, this island nymph was attiring herself.

He walked as noiselessly as possible, thinking to come upon her unawares.

But the quick ears and eyes of this child of Nature defeated his plan.

Probably she heard him approaching, and then, peering through the branches, caught sight of him.

Certain it is that, when within about ten or or twelve yards of the arbour, she bounded forth like a she-panther from her lair, and, with a short, sharp exclamation of anger, stood, statue-like, with javelin poised ready to hurl it at him.

Mechanically he sought his revolver.

She bounded forth another space, and again gave vent to a sharp exclamation.

He did not understand the language, but by her gesture he knew right well what she meant:

which was, that if he attempted to draw a weapon on her, she would drive her sharp spear through his body.

They were not more than seven or eight yards apart, this white man and this savage woman. She knew that his life was at her mercy.

Notwithstanding his critical position, he could not help gazing in rapt admiration at this island beauty.

Her figure was the very perfection of female grace, and would have driven a sculptor mad in vain endeavours to emulate.

She had put on her armlets, her bracelets, her ankle chain, suspending a purple stone, and the elegant little tiara or diadem; her long luxuriant dark hair she had twisted up in a classic coil at the back of her graceful head.

Reaching from her waist to her knee was a tunic of spotless white material, fastened by a crimson girdle.

Her back and shoulders were entirely bare, as were her feet and legs; indeed, the only covering she wore was this tunic and girdle.

The colour of her skin was a bright olive, fairer than that of many a Spanish or Italian lady.

A faint pink flush of excitement could be discerned on her lovely cheeks as she stood regarding the white man.

Her face was a perfect oval, nose thin and straight, mouth small, lips rich and full; a dimpled chin, whose slight prominence bespoke a firm and undaunted nature.

These lips, half parted, disclosed teeth of dazzling whiteness.

Her hair was not black, but of a deep rich brown; her eyes, too, were neither black, blue, nor brown, but of a deep violet hue most lovely to look upon.

Her hands and feet were soft, small, and delicate, and were as beautifully shaped as those of the most celebrated European belle.

Such was the lovely living statue which for some time stood motionless with poised javelin in front of Crusoe Jack.

He was a brave man, as the reader of "The Mutiny of the Thunder" knows; but he felt absolutely abashed, and quailed before this beauteous Amazon.

She said a few sharp words, waving her left hand with an imperious gesture.

He understood not the words, but knew right well what she meant.

She wished to retire and leave him, and somehow his will succumbed to hers, and he felt bound to obey.

So, still keeping his face to her, he walked slowly backwards.

Shortly he might have considered himself almost out of spear shot; but, strange to say, the thought of using his revolver or carbine never entered his head now.

He felt as though utterly defeated, and, for the time, incapable of acting on the offensive.

He was, as it were, under a sort of spell, and, having fallen back as far as the place where he had first concealed himself, he re-entered the bushes, and disappeared from her sight.

There was a tumult of wild thoughts and emotions in his breast.

At last he had discovered this mysterious being who shot arrows to terrify, and planted javelins with fluttering white flags to bewilder him.

He had seen his unknown enemy face to face, had looked in the eyes, and heard the voice of the agile siren, whose musical cry had some nights before led him such a wild-goose chase.

He had sworn that he would slay his unknown enemy ruthlessly, the first instant they met, and behold, woman though it was, he shrank from the encounter like a timid, frightened child.

Crusoe remained amidst the bushes for some four or five minutes, and then recovering his presence of mind, and collecting his faculties, he again issued forth.

This time he advanced prepared, holding his cocked revolver. In his right hand he held, on the point of his cutlass, a white handkerchief, as a token of peace, for on consideration, he felt loth to slay a woman, and such a choice specimen of nature's handiwork as this.

Advancing to within twenty yards of the arbour to which she had retired, he called out—

" Hallo, there !"

No answer.

He advanced a little further cautiously, and again called out.

Still with the same result.

And then a suspicion began to dawn upon him that she had taken advantage of his submissiveness to her orders to get out of the way.

This filled him with anger, and he walked rapidly on to the arbour. He now feared nothing; soon he was at the arbour whither she had retreated.

He now feared nothing; for, having his revolver in his hand he knew he could level and fire at least as quickly as she could throw her spear, or discharge an arrow.

His suspicions were well founded; for, on arriving at the shady retreat where he had first discovered the javelin, spear, bow, arrows, and white fabric, everything had vanished with the fair owner.

And just at that moment there came, borne on the calm air, as if in mockery of him, the melodious cry—

" La-loo-hee-ah !"

It came from the direction of the creek, and the sea from whence he had come, and he judged, not without reason, that this intrepid and lovely Amazon was bent on effecting her escape.

This he resolved, if possible, to prevent.

" For," said he to himself, " so long as she is at liberty and on the island, I am never safe. Urged by mere savage cruelty and wantonness, she may at any time, from a secure ambush, drive an arrow into me, and thus I shall perish ignominiously by the hand of a woman, unwept, unhonoured, and unsung."

Accordingly he started in pursuit, but though he was active, his descent of the rocky hill-slope, up which he had climbed, was a much more slow matter than that of the agile island nymph.

It was like a bullock chasing a chamois among its native hills. She, bounding from rock to rock, with graceful agility, accomplished the descent in a fourth of the time it took him, and ere he reached the bottom again, he heard the mocking, musical cry—

" La-loo-hee-ah !" coming from far down the creek.

Arrived on the level ground, at the foot of the slope, he made the best of the opportunity, and ran on down the creek full speed.

But when he had reached the place where he had left the canoe, it was gone, and away down on the open waters of the lagoon again he heard the melodious refrain—

" La-loo-hee-ah !"

He ran on till he came to the sea-shore, and from thence he saw, just shooting through a narrow opening in the reef, the canoe with spread sail, the lovely Amazon seated in the stern, steering with a paddle.

Her bright diamond diadem and jewelled ornaments gleamed in the noon-day sun for a moment or two; and then, as she went out to the open sea and rounded to, the canoe and its lovely burden were hidden from his sight, only the sail being visible.

He watched it gliding on for some half hour, growing smaller and smaller, till he could discover nothing but a white speck; and then, slowly and moodily, he made his way back to his hut on Flagstaff-hill.

This adventure, although it had partly unfolded to him the mystery of the arrows and spears, was by no means satisfactory.

He feared, nay he scarcely doubted, that emboldened by impunity, she would return, and even, if she did not cruelly assassinate him, keep him in a perpetual state of terror and anxiety.

To do him justice, he did not regret his not having slain her, but he wished he had made her a prisoner, or at any rate come to some arrangement, either of friendship, or, at all events, neutrality.

There was just a chance that she might have received such a scare as would keep her away altogether, but of this he had no sanguine hope.

So he resolved to bear up with a brave heart, and put his trust in Providence and his own courage and watchfulness.

" Fortune has willed," he said, " that I should discover the nature and sex of the mysterious enemy who has of late made my life wretched— a very burden. Perchance, ere long, I shall discover my unknown friend, and the one may prove an antidote to the other."

It was now the hottest part of the day, and the sun blazed down from a cloudless sky upon the island and surrounding sea.

Fatigued and languid from the intense heat, he sought the shelter of his tent, and reclining on his rude couch, slept till evening.

He awoke refreshed and invigorated, and having partaken of a pot of tea, he resolved to visit the highest part of the island—the Lion's Crown.

It wanted an hour of sundown, so he would have ample time to make the ascent, reconnoitre, and return before dark.

His strength had returned with marvellous rapidity, and he believed he was now as vigorous as he was before the attack of fever.

Slinging his telescope over his shoulder, in place of his carbine, he started, and, without misadventure, reached the high point.

He had reason to congratulate himself on his expedition; for, looking out towards the archipelago of islands to the west he saw that which greatly excited his curiosity.

He could discern, even without the aid of the glass, a number of black specks, between and amongst some of the nearest islands; and using the telescope, he discovered that these black spots were in motion—were, in fact, a fleet of canoes.

They seemed to be moving from south-west to north-east, and were, in fact, moving in the direction of Lion Island.

He could make out that the great majority had sails set, whilst those that were not so provided, he knew, though it was too far to see, were propelled by oars.

What was their object?

What their destination?

Had the savage maiden, who had escaped, carried the news of the presence of a white man on this island, and were they coming now to attack him, perhaps by a night enterprise?

A question easy to ask, but impossible for him to answer satisfactorily.

He lingered and watched this fleet of canoes till the sun sank beneath the horizon and the shades of evening began to close over the scene, without being able to come to any determination in his mind when they were coming or what their object.

In a few minutes it would be too dark to see; so he made his way back to his hut, and at once took measures to put it in a complete state of defence, resolved to keep vigilantly on his guard and be prepared for an attack at any moment.

CHAPTER XVI.

CRUSOE LAYS IN A STOCK OF PROVISIONS.

The night passed without incident or alarm of any description.

Crusoe slept well and soundly; nor were his slumbers disturbed by dreams of the lovely savage maiden whom he had discovered under such extraordinary circumstances.

He was awake and up shortly after dawn, and by sunrise had climbed to the highest peak of the island—the Lion's Crown—which commanded a view of all the broad expanse of ocean and the archipelago of islands to the west.

He was in considerable anxiety with respect to the great assemblage of canoes he had seen on the previous evening, anticipating, not without some alarm and misgiving, a visit from the savages.

He thought it most probable that the wild island beauty whom he had surprised bathing in the lake would carry the news to her people of there being a white man on this island—an intruder on their domain.

And what more likely than that they should then set out on an expedition to kill or capture him?

Thus reasoned Crusoe Jack, and he resolved to use the utmost vigilance to obviate this very undesirable consummation.

The keenest research, however, both with the naked eye and through the telescope, revealed nothing but the expanse of ocean and the group of islands.

Nowhere could he discover the faintest sign of a canoe, or, indeed, of human life at all.

Satisfied on this point, he returned to Flagstaff Point to breakfast, for he had now quite recovered his appetite, and, as if Nature were determined to make amends for the time when he could not eat at all, he was now at meal times as hungry as a hunter.

This excellent appetite of his brought round his thoughts to the important subject of a supply of food.

He had a tolerable supply of biscuit and salt meat and fish, besides a small stock of preserved provisions—a few dozen tins only.

Now, he was well aware that even if the beef and biscuit would last for ever, a diet composed exclusively of such food would be very unwholesome, and, sooner or later, would bring on that curse of mariners, the fell disease, scurvy.

So he came to the conclusion to lay in a good stock of fresh provisions before proceeding further with the preliminary operation even of buoying the wreck.

The principal vegetable productions of the island fit for food were bread-fruit, cocoa-nuts, and a species of small wild yam he had discovered, and a very succulent and nourishing description of seaweed.

By far the most important production of the South Sea Islands, exceeding even the cocoa-nut in value, is the bread-fruit.

Crusoe, in previous cruises among more southern and better known islands, had become familiar with this wonderful production, and was acquainted with the native mode of preserving the fruit for food.

The bread-fruit tree, when full grown, in its prime presents a splendid appearance.

It is not unlike a grand old elm tree in the spread of its branches, and great height and size.

The leaves of the bread-fruit tree are very large, and the edges are serrated in a fantastic manner.

As they grow to maturity, and decay they go through many changes of colour—from the rich green of their prime to a golden yellow—auburn—and various shades of rich brown.

The fruit is not unlike a small lemon or large citron.

It has a green rind, covered with little conical protuberances or knobs.

This rind is about an eighth of an inch in thickness, and when this is peeled off, the fruit, consisting of a beautiful, snowy-white pulp, is revealed.

The whole of the inside, with the exception of a very small core, easily removed, is eatable.

It is, however, never eaten in its raw state, nor, indeed, is it either wholesome or palatable until cooked.

The quickest and simplest method of cooking it is by placing the newly-plucked fruit among the embers of a fire, and roasting or baking it just as one might a potatoe or yam.

In a short time the green rind turns brown, and, cracking, shows the white pulp beneath.

It is then taken from the fire, and, when cool, the rind is easily detached, and there is the baked white fruit in the utmost purity and perfection.

At this period the bread fruit was at its highest perfection.

It must be borne in mind that it is not ripe and ready for use all the year round, like the cocoa-nut, but must be plucked at certain seasons.

Now was the time; so Crusoe Jack made his preparations to lay in a good stock.

It has been already remarked that it grew on the top branches of very large and lofty trees, and, consequently, was not easy to get at.

Crusoe cast about him for an easier method of obtaining the fruit than climbing the trees, and presently hit upon a plan.

First, he cut a straight bough of supple, elastic wood, about an inch in diameter, and six feet in length.

This he formed into a rude bow, and fitted thereto a string.

Next, he cut an arrow of the heaviest wood he could find, tipping it with iron.

To the shaft of this he affixed a long, thin line, scarcely stouter than string.

This done, he tried a shot, and found that he could propel an arrow higher than the loftiest tree.

His plan was a very simple one, and proved entirely successful.

Selecting a tree bearing plenty of fruit, he fired the arrow, with line attached, over the top.

He then fastened one end of the line round the stem of another tree, and going to where the arrow had fallen on the other side, hauled the line taut and proceeded to walk with it in a circular direction.

This had the effect of sweeping the branches with which the line came in contact, of their burden, and the result was, that, in a few minutes, scores of fine ripe bread-fruits lay around the trunk and beneath the branches of the great tree.

This operation he repeated again and again, until, by evening, he had nearly stript a score and a half of the finest trees.

He now laid a floor of large stones, and early the next morning built thereon a huge fire, which he allowed to burn for several hours, until he thought the stones were thoroughly hot.

Then, clearing away the fire, he piled the bread-fruit on the hot stones, covered the whole over with leaves and branches, and over all a layer of hot ashes.

By evening his mound of bread-fruit was thoroughly cooked.

All the next day he occupied himself in wrapping each particular fruit in a large leaf, and, when the whole had been thus treated, he piled them up in a pyramidal form some thirty yards at the back of the hut, covered them with a plentiful layer of leaves and over all a foot or two of loose earth.

Thus cooked and wrapped up and covered he calculated that the bread-fruit would keep good for many months, until again another crop should have arrived at maturity.

His favourite way of eating the bread-fruit was as follows, and, in his opinion, formed a dish fit for a king.

He first proceeded to grind up and powder the cooked fruit in a mortar, with the milk of a young cocoa-nut, in the place of water; then, taking a ripe cocoa-nut he would proceed to scrape the luscious, juicy meat into the pulp of bread-fruit.

The milk, cocoa-nut, and juicy pulp form, with the bread-fruit, a semi-fluid mass of most refreshing and delicate flavour.

Taken with a little salt only, he preferred this to any other dish it was possible for him to concoct with his limited resources.

Having then laid in a goodly stock of bread-fruit, he proceeded to gather a store of cocoa-nuts, wild yams, and sea-weed.

As regarded fresh meat, of that there was no hope; but he resolved, as soon as he had collected a good supply of the vegetable productions of the island, to turn his attention to catching some of the fish with which the waters of the lagoon abounded.

CHAPTER XVII.
CRUSOE FORTIFIES HIS HUT.

BUT though as an article of vegetable food, the bread-fruit stands pre-eminent, and is the mainstay of the natives of the Pacific Islands, the cocoa palm, for general utility, for the multiplicity of uses to which it can be put, is superior.

The appearance of this tree is grand and imposing in the extreme—rearing its tall crest with crowns of gigantic leaves, far above the other tropical trees which abound.

The natives of these fortunate islands, where nature does all, and man's toil is not needed to bring forth the fruits of the earth, repose year after year amidst the shady groves of cocoa-palms.

The nut it bears furnishes them with both food and drink.

With its boughs and leaves the native covers his hut.

He makes a fan of the young leaves, and also uses them to form small baskets.

He makes a species of cloth of the fibrous-like material, which wraps the trunks of all the large trees.

The cocoa-nuts, denuded of the husks and polished, form excellent and elegant drinking bowls, goblets, and cups.

With the husks he lights his fire, and uses the smaller nuts as tobacco-pipe bowls.

Of the fibrous husk he makes cords, lines, and ropes, also nets to catch fish.

He extracts an oil from the meat, with which he lubricates his body, and uses for many other purposes.

The wood, too, is of great value. It is very hard and durable.

Of it he builds his boat, and makes his war clubs and spears.

With the charcoal he obtains by burning it, he cooks his food, and impels his canoe by a paddle made of its wood.

This remarkable tree, once planted in suitable soil, needs no further attention or care.

The process of planting is a very simple one.

A fully ripe nut is placed in a hole in the ground in a moist place, and covered with earth.

In a few days a shoot pierces the shell and husk; and, burrowing up to the air and light, puts forth a few pale green leaves.

At the same time, two roots force their way through the holes to be observed at one extremity of every cocoa-nut, and commence burrowing down into the earth.

In a short time the nut bursts of its own accord.

The young plant now thrives and grows

rapidly, and, at the end of the year, is a stout sapling.

It needs neither culture, care, pruning, or manure, but steadily gaining size and strength, bears fruit in about four years, and continues to increase in grandeur for a full century, when it has probably attained its full growth.

Its fecundity is marvellous.

So long as it flourishes it bears fruit, and that all the year round.

The strange spectacle may be seen of nuts in all stages of development, from the full-grown ripe one ready to drop off the tree to the white blossoms which will take a whole year to form the perfect fruit.

It flourishes best near the sea-shore, seeming to have an affinity for the salt air, and somewhat sandy soil.

Crusoe Jack now proceeded to gather a considerable supply of cocoa-nuts, and piled them up in another heap near the mound of baked bread-fruit.

There was no necessity for accumulating such a quantity of the nuts as of bread-fruit, for, unlike the latter, the cocoa-nuts were in season, and ripe all the year round.

It was more for convenience sake, to have a store always handy, than from any necessity, that he collected a supply of some eight or ten score—about half young green ones, for the sake of the delicious beverage their milk made.

This done, he next set to work collecting sea-weed, of which there were several sorts fit for eating.

These were all a description of kelp, and when soaked with vinegar and a little rock salt, of which he had a plenty, made a delicious pickle.

He filled a small keg with this, and next bethought himself of collecting some wild yams. With these latter he was by no means satisfied. They were small, stringy, and slightly bitter.

Said he to himself—

" I may be on this island for years—aye, perhaps, it may be my fortune to spend my life. What a fate—what a mockery of success, should I succeed in reclaiming the gold, and yet be able to find no means of making my way to the realms of civilisation! However, be that as it may, I must make the best of my situation. These yams must be cultivated. I must have a garden."

And forthwith he set to work, and dug up about half an acre of ground, which he surrounded with a light fence—not, indeed, that there was any great necessity for this latter, there being no cattle or beasts of any kind to trespass, so far as he was aware.

Crusoe Jack, however, had a great idea of the picturesque and comfortable, and it appeared to him that an unfenced garden would look very desolate and ugly.

So he went to the extra labour of running a thin fence of bamboo and branches of trees round his garden, and also brought this fence in front of the hut on either side.

His abode now began to look quite homely. He had made the hut itself as secure and comfortable as possible, having covered over the tarpaulin roof with sheets of bark, which he stripped from a tree, very much resembling the " iron bark " tree of Australia.

And over this again he put a layer of boughs, so that his hut was not only sheltered from the sun and rain, but capable of resisting anything in the shape of savage missiles.

These various operations, the collecting, roasting, and storing bread-fruit, getting together a pile of cocoa-nuts, sea-weed pickle as he called it, and yams, and digging up and fencing his garden, occupied more than a week.

During that time no event whatever had occurred to break the monotony of his solitary life.

Day by day the sun rose in a cloudless sky, climbed to the zenith, then sank to the sea in the west.

Day after day he went up at sunrise to the Lion's Crown, as he called the highest point of the island, returned, breakfasted, and then worked on at whatever there was in hand until within an hour of noon.

Then, yielding to the intense tropical heat, he would take a siesta of clear three hours, and, as the sun sank towards the horizon, would finish his day's work—once more went his way to the high point in order to reconnoitre, and then would seek his hut and couch.

He had everything he could reasonably want. He enjoyed good health, a glorious climate, while the fruits of the earth were ready to his hand, and only required plucking.

Since the escape and disappearance of the savage maiden whom he had surprised, he had been troubled with no further alarms.

So far as he knew, the island would never again be visited by either this mysterious and lovely female, who had so terrified and tortured him, or by any other savages.

And yet he was far from happy—indeed, grew day by day more discontented and restless.

The utter solitude, the monotony of the life, which in time amounted to dreariness, in spite of the lovely scenery, climate, and surroundings, told upon his spirits.

And then he bethought himself of his object in thus voluntarily " marooning " himself on an uninhabited island.

The treasure!—the gold!

It was his object and intention to reclaim that; but the more he thought on it the more hopeless did the task of doing so single-handed appear.

He had cherished some sort of idea at the outset either of making a friendship, a sort of alliance, with some of the savage tribes which doubtless inhabited the other islands, if not this one, and bending them to his purpose.

He had visions of conquest, and dominion, of being a white king or chief over myriads of these children of the Islands of the Sea.

But things had by no means turned out according to his wishes or expectations.

At the first he was annoyed and terrified by an invisible foe, who seemed to hold his life at command ; and now, when this cause of alarm had ceased, he found himself utterly alone, a solitary denizen of this his kingdom—Lion Island—always excepting the wild birds and the golden lizards.

And so it came to pass that Crusoe Jack, who fretted and famed himself into a fever when arrows were being shot at him by a mysterious foe, now fretted and fumed at his utter solitude, and even said to himself that the excitement of danger, even unknown danger, was better than this sense of dreary solitude.

And one day there came a change—desolation, solitude, monotony, changed as if by enchantment to scenes of wild excitement and tumult.

But this we will leave to another chapter.

CHAPTER XVIII.

A FLEET OF THIRTY-FIVE CANOES—CRUSOE'S ALARM.

CRUSOE had finished all his arrangements about the hut, the garden, and surroundings, and had made his abode really most neat and charming.

Flagstaff Point presented the appearance of a model farm; the hut, garden, &c., in a clearing surrounded by groves of wood palms, gigantic bread-fruit, and wild fig-trees.

He had now been six weeks on the island, and had kept account of every day, both in his diary and by notches on the flag-staff.

This latter was really quite unnecessary, and, to tell the truth, he only did it from a sort of romantic feeling.

It looked so picturesque and dramatic—the use of notches, with a long one for Sunday, day by day lengthening out.

Well, on the forty-second day on which he had dwelt on Lion Island, he went up as usual, shortly after sunrise, to the Lion's Crown, in order to reconnoitre.

Contrary to his usual habit he had taken his breakfast before starting, and arrived at the summit of the rocky eminence; he felt not exactly tired, but languid and lazy.

So, after a brief look round through his telescope, by which he discovered nothing, he selected a comfortable seat, with his back to a huge stone, commanding a view of the sea and islands to the west, and, lighting his pipe, proceeded to make himself very comfortable.

He was in good spirits that morning, and proceeded, as he often did, to build castles in the air, planning out for himself a grand and successful career in the future.

The time slipped on, and, as the sun rose higher in the heavens, the genial warmth and the soothing influence of the tobacco, had upon him a soporific effect, so that he actually dozed off to sleep from lassitude and laziness.

This enervating effect of the delightfully mild climate of the islands of the Pacific is well known to voyagers, and in many cases the most vigorous and energetic men become quite indolent and apathetic.

And so it was with Crusoe.

The quiet, monotonous, uneventful life he had led of late—unbroken by incident or adventure—had had a numbing effect, as it were, upon his energies, and he now sat calmly with his back to a great rock, and, lazily puffing at his pipe smoked himself to sleep.

When he began to arouse himself from this half sleep, half-reverie, it was within an hour of noon, and lazily taking up his telescope he took a look over the sea.

And scarcely had he done so, than he started to his feet and proceeded to focus the glass more accurately.

About half way between the nearest of the islands to the west, and this one on an eminence of which he stood, he could plainly discern a little black speck on the surface of the calm sea.

A small canoe!

He was able to decide that for certain; but though he strained his eyes to the utmost, he could not make out whether it held one person—two—or none at all.

And, most provokingly, just at this time a light sea mist or vapour swept over the sea, which, though it did not entirely conceal the canoe, rendered it impossible to discern anything with certainty.

This mist seemed densest about the shores of Lion Island, around which it clung.

And as the canoe was obviously moving in this direction, it grew more and more dim, until, after a time, he could scarcely see it at all.

But if this solitary canoe thus slowly faded from his sight he soon had other things to attract his attention.

For, just rounding the southern point of the nearest island, he presently perceived several black specks in motion.

At first he counted six; but scarcely had he done so than others appeared, until he was able to reckon thirty-five canoes.

These were all much larger than the solitary little one he had first discovered, and their sails and numerous oars made them much more conspicuous objects, although at a greater distance.

He very soon discovered that they were pushing boldly out from land, and steering direct for Lion Island.

There was a brisk and favourable wind for them, and, urged also by many oars, they came on at a rapid rate.

The rapid approach of a whole fleet of canoes, apparently bound for his island—certainly steering straight for it—was a serious matter, and one which might well cause him considerable concern.

He had enormous advantages on his side, it was true, should their purpose prove to be hostile, in his fire-arms, and superior knowledge.

But then they, too, had the great advantage of numbers, and also, strange as it might seem, ignorance.

For, until they had tasted the deadly effects of powder and bullet, they would not be daunted; and though he might, if attacked, kill or maim perhaps a score, still one well-aimed spear or arrow might, nevertheless, put an end to all his plans and dreams of ambition, and his life at the same time.

He waited a short time longer, until there could be no possible doubt that the whole fleet of thirty-five canoes were making straight for Lion Island, and that at a very speedy rate, too.

As to the small canoe, a mere speck on the sea, which he had first descried, that had disappeared from his view altogether, hidden either by a promontory of land, or by the mist which hung about the shores of the island.

Crusoe Jack now hastened back to Flagstaff Point, impressed with the necessity of putting the hut in a thorough state of defence.

With spade and pickaxe, he at once set to work, and threw up a breastwork in front of the hut.

POINTING AT SOME DISTANT OBJECT THE ISLAND PRINCESS SUDDENLY BOUNDED AWAY.

What he had seen sufficed to dispel all that listless, lazy indifference which he had before felt, and he now toiled until his arms ached, and he was drenched with sweat.

Having thrown up a light parapet, he next proceeded to loophole the hut both in sides and rear.

Next he got up all the firearms he had, and having carefully loaded every piece, placed each one at a convenient place with several charges close at hand.

He neglected no precaution he could possibly think of, and, before sun-down, had put his dwelling, on Flagstaff Point, in such a state of defence, that it must prove a task of danger and difficulty, even for a small body of white men properly armed to carry it by assault.

He was now greatly divided in his mind, and felt keenly the disadvantage of being alone.

He was extremely anxious to reconnoitre and ascertain whether the savages had effected a landing, and, if so, where?

But then he fully realised the terrible risk of leaving his stronghold, containing his stores, arms, ammunition, everything which could be useful and necessary to him, unguarded.

And from Flagstaff Point he could see nothing. The whole fleet of canoes might have put into some convenient harbour, not visible from the Point, and he be in utter ignorance of it.

Again and again he felt tempted to make his way boldly down to the beach; and, skirting the southern shore of the island, ascertain for a certainty whether the savages had indeed landed.

But prudence prevailed, and he decided not to run the risk that such a terrible catastrophe as the capture of the hut with all his stores and ammunition by the enemy must prove.

And so he resolved to keep within his fort that night and wait and see what the morning would bring forth.

That evening no cheerful fire blazed on Flagstaff Point.

Our solitary adventurer, after a brief look round just before dark, retired to the hut, barricaded himself in as securely as possible, and with no light, save that of a very small fat lamp, kept his lonely vigil.

The hours passed slowly enough, he not venturing to sleep, but sitting awake, vigilant and watchful.

The night waned, the grey light of day dawned, and the sky in the east began to glare with red, purple, and golden hues.

And just as the upper part of the blazing orb of day appeared above the horizon, there arose on the morning air a strange sound—a sort of musical wail or chant, mournful but melodious.

Crusoe listened in rapt attention. "Human voices—a number of human voices afar off. It seems as though they thus greeted the rising of the sun. Can they be sun-worshippers, these savages?"

CHAPTER XIX.

CRUSOE GOES OUT TO MEET THE SAVAGES.

THAT the sound which fell upon our hero's ears came from human throats there could be no doubt whatever.

He stood and listened intently, trying to catch the words of the song or chant.

But this he was unable to do.

It began first in a low key, then rose and grew louder and louder, till a high, shrill pitch was obtained, and then again sank, and died away in a mournful, wailing sort of sound.

Altogether it was not unmusical, and, under other circumstances, this distant chorus of human voices greeting the rising sun would have had a pleasing effect.

As it was, however, it gave rise to other and more serious thoughts than the harmony and accord of the song.

Although it was at a considerable distance, he felt sure that the volume of sound which came rolling to him on the morning air was produced by a great number of human voices.

He thought of the fleet of canoes he had discovered steering straight for the island, and remembered that he had counted no less than thirty-five.

He now made a brief and rough calculation, founded on his own former experiences, and what he had heard concerning the manners and customs of the Pacific Islanders, especially with regard to their canoes and war parties.

He reckoned that the larger war canoes would carry nearly twenty men each, while the smallest would not have less than five or six.

So he resolved to fix upon ten men as the average number in each canoe.

With thirty-five canoes, this would give three hundred and fifty.

"A pleasant prospect, truly!" he said to himself. "This peaceful island of mine invaded by three hundred and fifty howling savages, all of them most likely eager for my blood! However, I must arrange to give them a warm reception. I'll bet a dollar that a score or so of them bite the dust before I go down!"

Now that he was in face of a certain and known danger, his spirits rose to the occasion, and he felt willing and able to make a good fight of it.

He did not hurry himself, but, keeping all the while a vigilant look-out, proceeded to light the fire and cook his breakfast.

"I've heard it said that Englishmen don't fight well on an empty stomach; and, as it's quite likely there may be hot work before the day's over, I'll just lay in a good foundation."

The distant sound of shouting and singing continued for fully an hour, and this had the effect of putting him at his ease for the time, for he felt pretty sure that until they had finished their rites, or ceremonies, or whatever they were then engaged in, they would not molest him or indeed commence anything serious of any kind.

Having partaken of what was really a sumptuous breakfast, he proceeded to accoutre himself, as he jocularly said, for the "war-path."

And certainly, if a most formidable array of weapons could make a warrior he was a most redoubtable and terrible one.

In the first place, he buckled on a belt, with a sharp cutlass or sword in a leathern scabbard.

In this belt he stuck a tomahawk, or small hatchet.

Also, three revolver pistols, and a large double-barrelled gun, of old-fashioned make, but carrying a heavy bullet.

Also he carried a broad-bladed, doubled-edged knife in a sheath.

Nor were these all his armament. It might be conceded that he was sufficiently formidable.

But this was by no means the case.

He carried in his hand a double-barrelled rifle, and had slung over his back a short-barrelled blunderbuss-sort of looking piece—in fact, almost a small cannon.

This redoubtable firearm was bell-mouthed, and as wide as a tea-cup, and he had loaded it with fully a quarter of a pint of slugs and small bullets.

Fired amongst a crowd, the havoc it would make must necessarily be terrible.

A telescope, also slung over his shoulder, a powder-horn, cartridges, and bullets, completed his outfit, and thus equipped, he sallied forth on his expedition—on the war-path, as he said to himself.

And certainly, if a number of weapons could give a man a ferocious appearance, Crusoe Jack might fairly calculate on striking terror to the hearts of the savages and conquering them almost without a battle.

So far he had not been able to form any definite plan, his first object being to reconnoitre and ascertain the exact whereabouts of the savages, and what they were doing, or might seem likely to be about to do it.

It has already been said that this lion-shaped island lay east and west, the head of the beast facing the setting sun.

The sound of human voices so plainly borne on the quiet morning air obviously came from some point on the southern shore, so in that direction Crusoe Jack directed his investigations.

He was well aware of the advantage of perceiving them and watching their movements before they could discover him, and consequently resolved to exercise the utmost vigilance and caution.

First, then, he advanced along the spur of high land representing the lion's back, and climbed to the high peak—the crown—thinking that from this elevation he would be able to discover the whereabouts of the savages.

But in this he was disappointed.

It is true he could see the whole seashore, the coral reefs, and the lagoons. These latter enclosed from him their stand-point, but he could see no sign of life—nothing to denote the presence of human beings.

This, however, he was able to account for.

The shore was pierced with numerous creeks and inlets, such as that one where he had discovered the canoe of the wild island maiden.

Some of these were of considerable size, and could easily accommodate a fleet of thirty or forty canoes.

Once under the cover of the dense brushwood and the luxuriant vegetation with which their banks were smothered, it would be extremely difficult to discover anything which might lie there concealed.

He had then no doubt in his mind that the savages had selected one of these creeks or inlets, and taken their canoes out of sight.

His object now was to find out where they had moored their canoes and pitched their camps.

He came to the conclusion that it was absolutely necessary for him at all hazards, no matter what the risk and danger, to approach close enough to the savages to ascertain what he could of their intentions by means of his ears.

For he had, as has been before remarked, had some experience of the islanders of the Pacific, though in regions far away from where he was now.

Nevertheless, he was aware that there was a strong resemblance running through all the dialects and languages of the almost innumerable islands of the Pacific.

So much so that the natives of islands hundreds of leagues apart could, when brought together, understand much of what each said.

Crusoe Jack had picked up a good deal of the language of the islands which he had visited, being quick at that sort of thing, and hoped that it would now stand him in good stead.

And, moreover, the captain of the American whaler, which had sailed away, had made him a most valuable present.

This was neither more nor less than a rough-and-ready vocabulary of the various dialects of the Pacific Islanders, compiled by a missionary, resident in one of the group called Society Islands.

It would be strange, indeed, if none of these bore any sort of resemblance to the language spoken by the savages of this, as he believed, hitherto undiscovered group.

After some deliberation, Crusoe Jack descended from the Lion's Crown, and advanced boldly down one of the numerous valleys sloping from the highland towards the spot where he judged by the sounds that the savages were assembled.

The valley, or path down which he went, was about half way between the lion's head and tail, and it ran as nearly as possible due south.

Arrived at the end of it he came to an abrupt wall of high rocks, which threatened to bar his further passage.

But walking along the edge of this he presently came across a narrow, winding, zigzag defile, and through this he proceeded as fast as the rugged nature of the ground would permit him.

The passage grew narrower and narrower, till his shoulders almost brushed the damp rocks on either side, which were so lofty and overhanging, as to make it quite dark and gloomy.

All at once, and quite unexpectedly, he came to the end of this defile or passage, through the rocks, and found himself in the midst of a clump of thick brushwood.

Pushing through this, and also using his cutlass to cut down some of the more obstinate bushes, he came out into open ground; and behold! spread before him, in all its calm, placid beauty, was the lovely lake—sailing along on the surface of which, in such novel fashion, he had discovered and surprised the beautiful savage maiden—heroine of the arrows aimed at himself, and the javelin with white silk pennon.

This was indeed a surprise; for he had thought that the only access to this lake was by way of the sea-shore the creek and the rocks, down which the little rivulet trickled.

CHAPTER XX.

CRUSOE MEETS WITH THE ISLAND PRINCESS.

THE waters of the lake rippled up on to a slip of land of beautiful green turf and moss, and along this, skirting the shore, Crusoe Jack advanced, unable to resist a feeling of delightful langour which stole over him as his senses drank in all the calm loveliness of the scene.

No costly carpet was ever softer or more sound-deadening than the green grass and moss on which he walked, and assuredly no landscape by a painter—no splendid panorama could compare with the actual reality before him.

He advanced slowly—dreamily, in a languid manner, as though the beautiful surroundings had so affected his mind and soul as to make him unwilling for action. From the other end of this lake valley, the end by which he had before gained admission, there presently burst on his ears a wild, discordant yell, obviously from many voices.

It was very different in its nature from the musical sort of chorus or song he had heard at sunrise, and seemed to him more in the nature of a war-cry.

The high rocks all around the lake concentrated the sound, and the savage howl was echoed and re-echoed many times.

This seemed to have the effect of thoroughly arousing him. He walked on much more briskly.

The noise died away.

He had arrived within about thirty yards of the arbour or shady nook in the bushes to which the savage maiden had retreated when he had disturbed her, when again a wilder, shriller, and more discordant yell broke on his ears.

And the next instant, like a startled fawn from her lair, out bounded the same lovely and mysterious damsel.

At first she did not see him, facing, as she did towards the southern end of the lake, the creek and the shore.

She stood in a singularly picturesque attitude, her head and shoulders bent forward listening intently.

She was attired in the same manner as when he first saw her—scantily, it is true, but not too much so for such a form of exquisite grace.

On the light diadem of bright white metal she now wore a sort of wreath of feathers.

Around her neck there hung a beautiful necklet of white flowers, strung together, and in her delicate, shell-like ears there were also two flowers of the same description.

Over her left shoulder she wore, scarf-wise, a strip of white material, the ends floating gracefully down her back.

All this Crusoe noticed, and last, not least, that she was unarmed.

She carried neither javelin, bow, nor arrows.

Probably she had left them in her leafy retreat, not dreaming she would be disturbed, or at all events, relying on being able to get them at a moment's notice.

Crusoe bethought himself of this, and saw his advantage.

He was more prudent and cautious now than on the previous occasion, and walking as noiselessly as possible, stole along so as to get between her and her arbour, where he suspected she had left her javelins, bows, and arrows.

Fortune seemed to favour him, for she now commenced to move farther away from the bushes, advancing slowly along the shore of the lake towards the outlet at the southern end.

He now observed that she walked quite limpingly, and that there was a slight bandage around her left foot.

He saw, too, that it was marked by crimson spots and splashes, and judged that she had accidentally cut or in some way injured her foot.

This was all in his favour; and when he had succeeded in placing himself right between the retreat in the bushes and herself, he judged that her capture by him was a certainty.

And to Crusoe this seemed a most fortunate thing, for he doubted not that it was she who had told of his presence on the island, and had brought all these howling savages to kill or capture him.

It was not without a feeling of triumph he thought how the tables were turned, she being now, in his opinion, completely in his power.

"I will not kill her," he said, "on any account. She is a woman, and it would be unmanly and cruel; besides, would do me little good. But I will make her a prisoner, and hold her has a hostage for my own safety; for I doubt not from her appearance but that she is a savage princess, or, at least, the daughter of some powerful chief."

Thus thinking, he immediately proceeded to act.

Advancing rapidly and stealthily towards her, he had arrived within about twelve yards, and was just going to make a rush to seize her, when she heard him.

Suddenly turning round, she uttered a few hasty words in her own language, totally unknown to him, and pointing with her left hand at some object he could not see, she turned her gaze from him.

A start, a scream of dismay and terror, and away she bounded like a frightened deer.

CHAPTER XXI.

THE PURSUIT.

FOR the first fifteen or twenty yards the maiden flew over the ground like the wind, impelled by her terror at suddenly discovering Crusoe so close to her.

Then, however, she suddenly halted, and stooping, placed her hand to her foot.

When next she proceeded, it was more slowly, limpingly, and with obvious pain.

Still, however, she made good progress, and having gained a good start of the white man, it seemed certain she would gain the bushes, concealed behind which was the outlet from this lake valley.

A thought—a cruel thought—flashed across Crusoe's mind.

He fell on one knee, and taking a steady aim, deliberately covered the fleeing girl.

His finger was on the trigger—the deadly tube was levelled at a spot between her shoulders.

He could rely both on his marksmanship and

the rifle, the accuracy of which he had often tested.

She was not more than fifty yards distant. To miss would have been nearly impossible.

One slight pressure of the finger, and the little leaden pellet, reposing now so quietly at the bottom of the barrel, would be sent hissing through the air—a messenger of death.

He hesitated.

His better nature prevailed over the cruel, bloodthirsty instinct, which urged him to stop her flight at any cost.

"No!" he cried, "I will not—I cannot fire on a woman, unless absolutely in defence of my own life; and now she is fleeing in terror. I will capture if I can, but not kill a woman."

He then started off in pursuit at his best speed.

He was a very fast runner, and being now in first-rate health and condition, got over the ground at a rapid pace, despite the heavy load he carried.

As she plunged into the bushes he was scarcely twenty yards behind her, and gained at every step.

Here, however, she had the advantage. Slight in figure, and agile, despite her wounded foot, she made much better progress through the dense brush than he was able to do, encumbered with such an arsenal of arms as he carried.

In emerging upon the open ground at the top of the rocks, over which trickled the little rivulet from the lake, she was about forty yards ahead, and had accomplished nearly half the descent.

Here, however, her injured foot proved a serious drawback, and she continued to clamber down, with obvious difficulty, and every now and then a sharp cry of pain breaking from her lips.

Crusoe now observed that the rocks over which she passed were spotted and splashed with blood.

A feeling of deep pity took possession of him.

Crusoe Jack was by no means a cruel man, and now that he saw this poor girl fleeing before him, wounded, in pain and terror, all his anger vanished.

For a moment he thought of giving up the pursuit; but then there came to his mind the thought of the hundreds of howling savages, and he said to himself—

"I will not harm her. Under no circumstances will I fire at or endeavour to wound her; but I must make her prisoner, if possible. My very life may depend upon it."

And so he started on again with renewed energy, and leaping in almost a reckless manner from rock to rock soon reached the bottom.

His delay, however, short as it was, had given her a further advantage, and she was again fully fifty yards ahead, and running swiftly over the smooth sand which bordered the creek when he got on level ground.

This was much more advantageous to her, with her wounded foot, than the rough, slippery rocks, and though he strained every nerve, he gained but slowly upon her.

She ran straight down the creek; now splashing knee-deep in the water, now speeding along on the sand.

He remembered now that a little further down was the place where she had moored the canoe on the two occasions he had discovered it.

It now occurred to him that she was hastening there in order to embark.

This, however, appeared to him a hopeless idea on her part, so far as escape from his pursuit was concerned.

It was, he thought, utterly impossible for her to cast off the ropes, or rather withes which fastened it to the shore, embark, and ply the paddle quickly enough to elude him.

However, he ran on at his best speed, and felt sure he was gaining on her, although he was only able to catch occasional glimpses of her figure, so dense and luxuriant was the growth of brush, bush, creepers, and vines all along the edge of the creek

Presently the rifle he carried caught in a branch, and very nearly caused him to fall.

The lock of the rifle got entangled, and giving it a hasty snatch, in order to loose it, the hammer fell, and one barrel went off.

This was annoying, and altogether he was delayed more than half a minute.

Scarcely had he again started on in pursuit of the fugitive maiden, whom he had determined to make captive, when the splash of water fell on his ears—the quick sound of a paddle, vigorously plied. Then he knew that she had gained her canoe, had cast off, and now sought to escape by way of the lagoon.

And just at that moment there came a reminder to him that he might, in pursuing her, rush into the hands of his enemies.

A wild, unearthly yell from hundreds of throats fell on his ears most unwelcomely.

He bethought himself. "She is paddling down the creek full speed, and the moment she comes out into the open lagoon she will be in sight of her friends—close to them—and can at once seek protection with them. Doubtless it was the report of my rifle which thus astonished them, and caused them to howl in this unearthly manner. It would be neither prudent nor even safe for me to show myself in the open in pursuit of her. I must give up the chase."

In coming to this determination, Crusoe Jack felt certain that he was acting wisely.

And so, perhaps, he was, although he was not aware of all the facts of the real state of the case.

Knowing that there was a horde of savages on the island, and close at hand, he had reason to think that she would at once seek shelter and protection with these, of course, her own people.

However, he kept on his course down the creek, using great caution, and not rushing on at headlong speed.

What, then, was his surprise, when he observed that the girl fleeing before him also slackened, and as she approached the mouth of the creek, where it opened into the lagoon, ceased paddling altogether, and bending forwards in an attitude of earnest, intense attention, seemed to be listening and endeavouring to pierce the leafy screen between her and the lagoon with her eyes.

His footsteps, as he marched steadily on, seemed to rouse her, and to cause her to act promptly.

With a glance over her shoulder, followed by a sharp cry of alarm, she dashed the double-bladed paddle into the water right and left, with remarkable skill and effect.

The light canoe shot ahead like an arrow, and, in half a moment, emerged from the shade of the bush into the open water of the lagoon.

Crusoe Jack followed more slowly, being careful not to expose himself to view.

And peering through the bushes, he got sight for the first time of the savages whose howls and yells he had heard.

In a sort of inlet or bay—not a creek running far up inland like this—he discovered the fleet of war canoes moored.

The savages were spread about over the sand, lying down in huts of boughs they had roughly thrown up.

They seemed to be just awakening, as might a hive of bees when disturbed; and, aroused by the howls of the others, those who were asleep joined in the general clamour.

He had no doubt whatever but that it was the report of his rifle, accidentally discharged, which caused this commotion.

From these people he turned his attention to the canoe of the maiden he had given chase to.

To his astonishment, she did not steer towards them; but, on the contrary, seemed bent on putting right out to sea, for the prow of her little craft was directed straight for an opening in the reef.

The savages did not seem to observe her for some time.

All at once, however, it was obvious they did so, for a most terrific and discordant yell rent the air.

Then there was a wild commotion, and a rush for the canoes, a dozen of which were quickly launched and manned by a crew of naked savages.

And now, to his utter astonishment, he perceived that their object was to chase and capture the girl in the canoe, who was using most frantic endeavours to urge on her little craft and escape.

While some of the canoes steered straight for her, others made for the opening in the reef, so as to intercept her if possible.

Crusoe was utterly mystified.

"What on earth is the meaning of this?" he asked to himself, but could not answer the question.

CHAPTER XXII.

THE ISLAND PRINCESS A PRISONER.

CRUSOE was now fairly bewildered, and knew not what to make of the extraordinary behaviour of these savages, and the girl, who, having escaped from him, now seemed to be chased by them.

Perhaps this is only some freak or sport—a trial of strength and skill.

This idea, however, was very quickly dissipated, for just then a flight of arrows came from the canoes, and many of them passed quite close to the girl.

Crouching low down in her little craft, so as to get as much shelter as possible, she redoubled her efforts, and the light canoe almost flew over the water.

In speed she greatly outstripped the fleetest of the pursuing canoes; but they had the ad-

vantage of being able to cut off a corner, and so intercept.

Still, however, so swiftly did the canoe shoot through the sea that it seemed almost certain that she would reach the opening in the reef for which she was making, before the foremost canoe even could interpose.

Once through this she would be out in the open sea, and with a start—being obviously swifter than her pursuers—her escape seemed certain.

But an unfortunate and unforeseen event dashed her hopes.

Crusoe, watching the whole affair keenly from his place of concealment, saw a tall savage stand up in the prow of one of the largest canoes, and, fitting an arrow to his bow, take slow and deliberate aim.

By a gesture of the hand he caused the paddlers to cease, so that the canoe might be as still as possible, and his aim not be deranged.

Crusoe saw the winged dart speed through the air, describing a graceful curve, and the next moment was aware it had been despatched with true aim.

For the girl, suddenly dropping her paddle, started upright; and, using his telescope, he was able to see the arrow sticking in her arm, between the elbow and the wrist.

The sight was not a pleasant one, and he forgot, in his pity at beholding a woman—a young and lovely girl—cruelly wounded, his former anger against her for having shot at himself, and caused him such uneasiness, and even terror.

He could see that she was trying to extract the dart, which was fixed in her flesh, and through his telescope, which was an excellent one, he could clearly discern the expression of her features—pain from the wound, mingled with terror of her pursuers.

Her efforts to extract the dart were vain, and as during the brief delay the nearest canoes had come quite close, she seemed to come to a sudden and heroic resolution.

With the arrow still sticking in her arm, she hastily seated herself, and again plied the paddle, as best she could.

The agony must have been terrible; and even at that distance he could see that her features were twitched and distorted by pain.

Her heroism and fortitude were all in vain, for in the space of a couple of minutes, and while yet at least a hundred yards from the opening in the creek, the foremost canoe shot ahead, and crossed the bow of hers.

She attempted to elude this one, but another instantly darted forward on the other side, and in a few more seconds she was surrounded and overpowered.

Resistance was obviously useless—probably worse than useless, and she attempted none, but appeared to resign herself to her fate, whatever it might prove to be.

Crusoe Jack, who had watched this singular scene from beginning to end with the most lively interest, was as much mystified and bewildered as it was possible for a man to be.

His first thought that this wild rush of the savages in pursuit of the maiden was not in hostility, but perhaps a part of some sport or ceremony, was utterly confuted by the fact of her having been cruelly wounded by an arrow.

He could still make out the tall figure of the savage who had shot the arrow.

Levelling his rifle, he took steady aim at him, and hesitated for some time whether or no to fire.

But on consideration he resolved to remain quiet—for the present at least.

In the first place, the man at whom he aimed was distant evidently over a quarter of a mile, and though his rifle would kill at more than twice the distance easily, it must be a matter of uncertainty for even the best of shots to hit a mark at that range.

Moreover, even if he succeeded and hit the savage, the smoke of his rifle must be seen and the report heard, which would alarm the savages, put them on their guard, and reveal to them his whereabouts.

So he quietly proceeded to load the barrel of his rifle, which had been accidentally discharged, and then crouched behind a convenient bush, and kept vigilant watch.

The prisoner—for such the girl obviously was —was dragged from her own little craft, and forced into the largest of the war canoes, where she was at once securely bound.

Then, with loud cries as of triumph, he supposed, and horrible yells, the canoes made for the shore.

So soon as the canoes grounded on the beach, the unfortunate prisoner—for as such he might fairly consider her—was dragged ashore, and, with blows, showers of stones, and every description of contumely, was rudely hurried along towards the encampment.

Here there seemed to be a sort of council held. A number of savages, with plumes of feathers on their heads, seated themselves in a semi-circle, the others falling back with some respect, though they still kept up a most infernal din.

He now took advantage of the opportunity to observe them closely, and take note of their shape, colour, features, and attire, such as it was.

They appeared to be all strongly-built, athletic men, though with a certain clumsiness of gait and heaviness of the shoulders which gave them a rather awkward appearance.

A huge bush of hair, either artificially plaited or clubbing out thus naturally, caused their heads to appear too large for their bodies.

They were all tall, nearly six feet in height he reckoned, while some were of almost gigantic stature.

Even from where he was he could not but be struck by the dazzling whiteness of their teeth.

Their skin was of a light copper hue, by no means an unpleasant colour, and their movements were free, agile, and graceful. As for clothing it was of the very scantiest.

A small cloth of white tappa, attached to a belt going round the waist, passing between the legs, and fastened before and behind, was every rag of which they could boast.

They made up for the want of clothing by the most elaborate tattooing on their bodies, arms, and legs.

This he at first actually mistook for some close-fitting garment, and it was only when he brought his telescope into play that he discovered his error.

After a while the tumult subsided, and there was some sort of order.

The prisoner girl was brought into the centre of the semi-circle, and, it seemed to him, was undergoing an examination, or being tried before the assembled chiefs.

The whole affair, whatever it might be, did not occupy long; for a tall warrior, in the very centre of the arena, arose about five minutes, and Crusoe knew by his gestures that he was delivering an excited harangue.

When he ceased there arose a tremendous yell.

The crowd of savages, who had been seated, patiently listening, leaped up, and dancing shouting, and howling, gave way to the wildest excitement.

Then there was a rush made for the prisoner, who stood calmly awaiting her fate, as it seemed, and with many blows and rough treatment, they commenced to drag her along the sand.

Crusoe's blood boiled.

A woman—weak, wounded, alone, and unprotected, and thus cruelly ill-used.

"My British blood won't stand this. It must be—CRUSOE JACK *to the rescue!*"

CHAPTER XXIII

CRUSOE JACK TO THE RESCUE!—ATTACK ON THE SAVAGES.

THESE wild islanders continued to drag and drive their prisoner on in a direction approaching the place where Crusoe was crouched concealed in the brush.

When within about forty yards only, he who seemed to be the principal chief gave some orders, and the crowd of savages came to a halt.

Then some ran off back to the camp, others sought the wooded ground, whilst a third party made their way to the sea beach, and commenced collecting large pebbles and rocks, which they proceeded to convey to the place where the prisoner was surrounded by several score of her captors.

The stones they laid on the ground until they had piled up a square heap about a foot and a half high.

Some others now brought a pole, a young cocoa sapling with the leafy top and branches lopped off.

This was about eight feet long, and they at once proceeded to erect it in the centre of the sort of platform of stones and rocks.

The watcher in the bushes was for some time at a loss to understand what it was they were about to do.

By-and-bye a number of them came up, carrying wood logs, sticks, and dry brush and leaves.

These latter were placed first on the stone platform, and the sticks and logs on top all around the staff or pole, which stuck up right in the centre.

Next they proceeded to bind the unhappy girl to this pole.

And then all at once the meaning of their proceedings burst upon him.

They were going to set light to the wood, and burn her alive!

Horrible idea! and one which filled him with pity for her, and indignation and rage at these cruel wretches.

"Probably they are cannibals, and after making her suffer all the agonies of death by fire, they will proceed to eat her. But if I don't spoil their banquet and give some of them a pill or two they little expect, my name is not Crusoe Jack."

He now carefully examined all his firearms, cocked and loosened the pistols in his belt, and got the blunderbuss he carried slung across his shoulder in readiness.

He laid down the telescope, and also took from his belt the powder, bullets, and cartridges, in order to be as free and unincumbered as possible in the dangerous enterprise he was about to undertake.

This was no other than to attack single-handed and endeavour to put to flight a horde of some hundreds of savages who, though they had no firearms, were yet well supplied with spears, bows and arrows, and war clubs.

He remembered that the report of his rifle when it went off accidentally, though it had startled and surprised them, did not seem to have caused any great alarm.

It was quite possible that they might prove to be unusually brave and warlike, and show fight vigorously.

In case, when he discharged all his firearms, doing as much havoc among them as possible, they were not cowed, but stood their ground, he would be in a position of extreme peril.

For of course he could not expect time or opportunity to reload, unless, as he hoped, they should be completely terrified and panic-stricken by the suddenness and desperation of his attack, and at once take to flight.

However, although he looked ahead and fully realised all the danger of what he was about to do, he did not for a moment waver in his purpose.

He saw the unhappy prisoner—a young and lovely woman—bound to the stake, and about to suffer an agonising death.

His manhood revolted at the thought; his soul rose in arms at the contemplated atrocity, and, having made all his preparations, he went to work—as he always did—calmly and deliberately.

He could plainly see the wretched prisoner, and observe the look of wild terror on her features at the impending and dreadful death staring her in the face.

He could see the agonised glances she cast around, looking vainly for pity or mercy in the ferocious countenances of her enemies, who danced and capered about, yelling and shouting like a lot of demons.

On either side of the prisoner was a tall savage, each employed in binding her arms to the stake.

These men, he felt sure, from their air of authority, the plume of feathers they wore, and other signs, were chiefs. One of them was the tall fellow, who, standing up in the prow of his canoe, had shot the arrow which, wounding the fugitive in the arm, had disabled her, and caused her to fall an easy prey into their hands.

At this man, then, Crusoe took steady and deliberate aim, getting a rest for his double-barrelled rifle on a small branch.

Waiting until no other body intervened, and taking advantage of a moment when the savage was facing towards him, he fired.

The crack of the rifle and whistle of the bullet was followed by a sharp cry.

Then the savage gave a leap in the air, and fell forward on his face, dead!

The bullet had struck him full between the eyes, of course killing him.

There was instantly the wildest confusion and running to and fro.

At first they did not discover whence came the report and the invisible missile which had slain their chief.

Crusoe Jack did not waste time in looking on at the effect of this his first shot, but quickly taking aim, fired the other barrel.

This shot was also a fortunate one, for it struck the savage on the other side of the prisoner full in the chest.

It did not kill him instantly, as the other, but he fell writhing and howling in the agonies of death.

Throwing down his rifle, our hero unslung the blunderbuss from his shoulders, and, with a loud shout, rushed from out of cover into the open, and running towards the savages, got within twenty yards of them almost before they were aware of it.

And when they perceived him, the greater number were so astonished and aghast as to be absolutely unable to fly.

Our friend was not one to do things by halves, and bearing in mind the atrocious and cruel deed they were bent on, he had not the slightest remorse in slaying them as he would wild beasts,

Aiming at a group of them clustered together, he fired the huge, heavily-loaded blunderbuss.

Terrible was the effect of this discharge; the slugs and bullets it carried scattered far and wide, inflicting desperate wounds on the naked bodies of the savages.

At least twenty were killed or wounded by this one discharge.

A most dreadful howling and yelling now arose from the wounded and dying; and, following up his advantage, Crusoe Jack dashed in among them, a revolver in either hand, firing right and left with great rapidity and deadly effect.

Having fired all the barrels of his revolvers, he drew the double-barrelled pistol, and having discharged this, sword in hand he followed up the attack, and, cutting, slashing, and thrusting, completed the work so well begun, and inflicted on the howling wretches, a most bloody defeat, without himself receiving a scratch.

In five minutes after his first fire he was in possession of the field, surrounded by the dead, dying, and wounded savages.

All the others had taken to flight, and were now hastily launching and embarking in their canoes, having, he hoped, received a lesson which they would not forget.

CHAPTER XXIV.

THE FRUITS OF THE VICTORY—CRUSOE DISCOVERS HIS MYSTERIOUS ENEMY AND UNKNOWN FRIEND.

No victory could have been more complete and decisive, and, standing panting from exertion, Crusoe Jack looked around on the scene.

The savage girl, whom he had rescued from a dreadful death, remained still bound to the stake.

She gazed around with an expression of horror and fear impossible to describe, and when he approached her, for the purpose of cutting the thongs which bound her, she cried aloud.

It seemed that she was as much terrified of him as of the savages he had put to rout—her would-be murderers.

By gestures and soothing words (she could not understand the language, of course, but she could the tone and manner) he made her understand that he would not harm her—was her friend, and not her enemy.

He then proceeded to cut the bonds, which fastened her to the stake by the arms.

While he was doing this, she watched the keen sheath knife which he used in a suspicious manner, as though doubtful whether or not he intended to plunge it into her breast.

When, however, he had cut the last withe, and, stepping back a pace, motioned to her that she was free, she seemed filled with astonishment.

Bound as she had been with her back to the mob of savages, amongst whom Crusoe's fire-arms had done such havoc, she was not aware till this moment of the slaughter which had taken place.

On either side, a little to the rear of the stake, lay the two chiefs—the one who had wounded her with the arrow stone dead, shot through the skull, the other in the last gasp of agony.

All around, and back for a distance of fully twenty yards, the ground was strewn with wounded savages, writhing and crying in pain, and dead bodies.

Crusoe, though by no means a hard or cruel man, who had seen a great deal of death by violence, had no compunction for what he had done, feeling sure that he was perfectly justified.

He was able to survey the scene calmly, and look forward to and lay his plans for the future.

When first scattered and driven away in panic and terror by his sudden and desperate attack, they had fled to the shore, and then to their canoes.

But having pushed off some few fathoms, they ceased paddling, and all the canoes gathered round one large one, in the prow of which there stood an old grey-bearded chief, evidently haranguing them.

His gestures and attitude semed to denote that he was endeavouring to inspire them with courage; and as he often pointed towards the girl and Crusoe, the latter judged that he was urging them to pluck up heart, and, attacking in their turn, avenge their disastrous defeat.

Every now and again cries of approval broke out, and when the old warrior concluded, the whole of them leaped up in the canoes, to the imminent danger, Crusoe thought, of upsetting them all, and gave vent to a loud and discordant yell of fury and defiance.

Our friend now came to the conclusion that it would be prudent for him, as the Yankees say, to make tracks, and pointing first to the fleet of canoes and then to the brush and forest, signified to the girl he had rescued that it would be advisable for them to beat a retreat.

At first she seemed doubtful, and appeared half inclined to start off and take to flight.

But Crusoe noticed with pity that the arrow was still sticking in her arm, down which a thin stream of blood trickled; also that her wounded foot was bleeding.

He called her attention to this—for in view of the horror of her late situation the greater terror of certain death, she seemed comparatively careless and insensible of her wounds.

But Crusoe, taking her arm, proceeded quickly, skilfully, and with as much gentleness as possible, to extract the arrow.

Of course, it was impossible to avoid giving considerable pain. When, however, the girl understood that what he was doing was meant in kindness, she submitted without a murmur, not a cry or a whimper escaping her.

He was successful in drawing out the arrow, and this done, proceeded to bind up the wound.

He carried a small flask of fresh water, in case he should find himself where there was no spring or stream.

With this he proceeded to wet a strip of white calico he had wound round his hat to keep off the heat of the sun, and then bound it round the wound.

She expressed her acknowledgment for this service by a grateful look, and also raised her two hands to her forehead and bowed her head according to some savage custom, as he supposed.

He next pointed to her wounded foot, and by signs asked whether she was able to walk, for he thought it useless to bind up this until she was in a position to rest it, and he determined in his own mind to take her up with him to his hut on Flagstaff Hill, and there treating her with respect and kindness, win her over to be his friend and ally.

He thought it likely he might get very valuable information from her if he could make her understand his questions, and if he in turn could gather the meaning of her answers.

She was now utterly submissive, and when he pointed to the brush where he had left his rifle and ammunition, she at once motioned him to lead on, signifying that she would follow.

After a glance back at the fleet of canoes which he perceived still lay-to at some little distance from the shore, the savages evidently watching his movements, he made haste to gain the cover of scrub and brush.

So soon as they perceived he was beating a retreat they let fly a shower of arrows, the greater part of which, however, fell short.

Some, however, whistled overhead, and stuck in the ground in front of him, but neither he nor the girl received any hurt whatever, the only effect the discharge had being to hasten their movements somewhat.

It showed, moreover, that, despite the severe and terrible lesson they had received, these people were not effectually cowed, and he judged it possible, and even likely, that they would pluck up heart and attack him in overwhelming numbers, or perhaps endeavour to fall upon him unawares before he could bring his fire-arms into play.

He resolved then to make the best of his way to the hut, and make preparations to give them a hot reception, to inflict on them such a bloody repulse as should effectually prevent them from ever making another attempt.

From their appearance, manner, and the hardihood with which they stopped in their flight, after having suffered so heavily in killed and wounded, he judged that this tribe must be most warlike and ferocious.

As he wended his way up a sloping valley he pondered over his present position and future prospects, and, despite the signal victory he had achieved, did not feel by any means satisfied.

He could not but see that difficulties and dangers thickened around him, and that, though this was the second month of his sojourn on the island, he was really scarcely any nearer his object—the treasure sunk on the outside of the reef in the hull of the Thunder.

All that he had been able to accomplish hitherto had been to partly buoy the wreck.

Still he remembered that he had not been idle, and congratulated himself on his forethought in having so fortified his hut as to be almost secure against assault.

And as he thought over what he had done and what remained to do, his spirits rose with a sudden elastic bound, and he half fancied he heard a voice whispering in his ear—

"Courage, Crusoe Jack! Keep up a bold heart, persevere, and success awaits you."

Arrived at his hut, the girl meekly accompanying him, it struck him that he would accuse her of having attempted to murder him, and reproach her therewith, if he could make himself understood.

So he got out the arrow which had been fired at him, showed it to her, made her understand that it was hers; and then also pointing out the place in the log where it had stuck, close to his head as he sat when it was shot at him. He laid his hand on his breast, signifying thereby that she had intended it for his heart, but had missed her aim.

This, however, by her gestures and exclamations, she seemed vehemently to deny, and tried to convey something to him, which he, through ignorance of the language, was unable to understand. Her eye presently falling on the calabash, which had been so mysteriously placed within his reach, filled with a cooling drink, when he lay ill of the fever, she seized it and pointed to herself.

"By Jove! Then this girl, in whom I thought I had discovered my mysterious enemy and would-be murderer, was, in fact, my unknown friend!"

CHAPTER XXV

CRUSOE TENDS THE WOUNDED MAIDEN.

It is scarcely too much to say that had she unfolded a pair of wings and flown away, Crusoe Jack would not have been much more surprised.

Although, now that he knew the truth, there seemed nothing so marvellous in it, not the faintest shadow of suspicion had hitherto crossed his mind that the same person who had shot arrows within an inch or so of his head, and had caused him such terror and anguish of mind, had acted the part of a friend—a good Samaritan; and when he lay in a burning fever, with a bad cut on the head, had bound up his wound, and given him a cooling and medicinal drink which he believed had been the main cause of his rapid recovery.

Now, however, it all burst on him at once,

and he wondered how he could have been so stupid as not to have guessed it before.

Nevertheless, he felt some difficulty in accounting for the arrows, so skilfully planted close to his head, and could scarcely see how that fact could be made out as a demonstration of friendship.

The ivory wand and the strip of silk-like stuff with strange inscriptions left on his table were puzzling and mysterious; but in these there was no danger to life or limb.

He determined to ascertain from his rescued captive the meaning of her conduct.

In the meantime he observed that she was suffering from her hurt foot, which was greatly swollen and inflamed, and seemed to give her more pain than the arrow wound in the arm.

Wishing to give her every aid and comfort in his power, he got out a flat tin dish, filled it with water, and also gave her a piece of calico with which to bandage her foot.

She understood, and thanked him with as sweet and graceful a smile as could any fine lady in Christendom.

But she shook her head at the calico, and pointed out into the trees, at the same time picking up a leaf from the ground.

The leaf was of the wild fig tree, and understanding her meaning, as he thought, he went and got a handful.

But she shook her head; then, with great quickness and dexterity, picked out pieces all round the edge of the leaf, so as to give it a serrated or saw-like appearance.

Then she gave it to him, and again pointed to the woods.

From this he gathered that she wished him to go and get her leaves in shape like this of the wild fig, as she had altered it.

So he started, leaving her at the hut.

For some time he saw no tree with a leaf at all like what he wanted, and in the course of his wanderings came across a gigantic cocoa-palm, standing on a rising piece of ground.

This was certainly the loftiest and most tremendous tree he had yet seen.

As he gazed up at the wide-spreading arms of this forest giant, towering scores of feet above all the other trees, it struck him that from the top of this tree there must be a magnificent look-out, and that from thence he could command a view of creeks and inlets on the southern side of the island, which were not visible even from the lion's crown.

So he resolved to return here, and, carefully noting down the direction in which this monster tree stood relatively with Flagstaff Hill, he proceeded on his search for the leaves.

At last he came across a little stunted shrub like a gooseberry bush, and at once saw that it bore leaves such as he wanted.

So, gathering a large handful, he made the best of his way back to the hut, where he had left the maiden he had rescued.

He found her seated outside the hut sprinkling water over her bad foot.

She had now taken off all bandages, and he beheld a nasty gaping wound on the ankle, laying bare a part of the bone.

On so tender a place a wound of such a nature must be, he knew, intensely painful, even if he had not observed the occasional twitchings of the girl's features as she suffered a spasm of pain.

When she beheld him coming with the leaves her eyes brightened, and, with an eager expression on her face, she held forth her hands.

He gave them to her, and, without a moment's delay, she proceeded to wet them one by one, and lay them on and around the wound.

So soon as she had thus covered the ankle completely with these leaves, she bound over all a piece of the original bandage, which had become loosened and disarranged in her flight from him, and before she was so unlucky as to fall fall into the hands of the savages.

Crusoe Jack doubted not but that she had taken the best possible means for a rapid and complete cure; but, at present the inflammation was at its highest, and she was evidently suffering intensely.

Amongst some of the many articles he had purchased from the captain of the whaler before that vessel sailed away was an assortment of drugs, and a few surgical instruments.

He now proceeded to mix a strong composing draught of morphia and chloric ether, which he brought out in a small cup, and made signs to her to drink.

She hesitated; so, by closing his eyes and feigning sleep, he gave her to understand what would be its effect.

She looked in wonderment; but hesitated no more, and drank it off, making a wry face, however, at its bitter taste.

Determined to perform the hospitable duties of a considerate host to his wounded guest, he got out the rug of opossum skin, and spreading it on the ground just shaded from the sun by the shadow of the overhanging boughs he had purposely placed on the top of the hut, he motioned to her to lie down, giving her to understand that he was going away up into the woods.

She bowed her head, and, with a roll of calico for a pillow, reclined at length.

He waited about a short time, and soon had the satisfaction of observing that the opiate was beginning to take effect.

A heavy look came over her eyes, and gradually the lids closed, and the long eyelashes rested on her cheeks.

She slept.

As she lay thus calmly slumbering, he looked with curiosity and admiration on this lovely child of Nature.

The short tunic she wore descended scarcely to her knees, and the fine white fabric, which, when he saw her standing by the lake, she wore loosely, scarf-fashion, just thrown over one shoulder, was now torn, and, moreover, stained with blood.

Nevertheless, though from the waist upwards, as nearly as possible, nude, she was much more modestly covered than such of the South Sea Island damsels as it had been his lot to see hitherto.

In her ears were small ornaments of white metal, and even in her sleep she wore the light sort of diadem, which seemed in no way to incommode her.

On one arm, the uninjured one, she had an armlet of the same metal, which looked like silver, but was, he thought, purer and brighter.

Her limbs were modelled in nature's loveliest mould, and as she lay thus calmly sleeping, in a most easy and graceful attitude, he thought to himself what a study for an artist for a sleeping Venus.

He remembered the light quilted sort of coverlet of the strange and fine material which he had found by his side when he lay ill of the fever.

This he got and quietly spread over her, for, to his English ideas, the slumbering beauty displayed too much of her elegant form.

Then, not forgetting to reload his pistols, and slinging his American carbine rifle over his shoulders, he started for the big tree he had discovered, determined to climb it, if possible, and get a view from the top.

CHAPTER XXVI.

THE GIGANTIC TREE—THE GIRL IS SEIZED BY THE SAVAGES.

HAVING carefully taken the bearings of the big tree, Crusoe Jack had little trouble in finding it.

But when he stood by its gigantic trunk, overshadowed by the huge umbrella of leaves its crown formed, the question was—How to get up there?

For the first twelve feet or so the trunk of this tree was covered with a fibrous sort of growth, something between rough bark and a creeping plant.

This it was easy to climb; but after that came the hard, smooth stem of the tree, without branch or protuberance of any kind.

This was a bit of a puzzler, and it gave him a great deal of trouble and anxious thought to devise a plan by which he could get to the top.

That which he had hit upon and decided to put in practice was slow, but he thought sure.

Having with him both knife and tomahawk, he soon cut from the branches of small trees a score or so of sharp-pointed pegs, about nine inches long.

At the back of the tomahawk was a sharp-pointed sort of spike, of sugar-loaf shape.

With this slung about his neck, and a number of pegs loose in the breast of his shirt, he climbed the trunk of the tree as far as the fibrous sort of stuff went.

A couple of feet higher up, and a little to the right, he struck another one with the tomahawk again with a like result.

And now he proceeded to fix the pegs he had cut in these holes, driving them in by plentiful hammering with the tomahawk.

Ascertaining that the pegs were sufficiently well fixed to bear his weight, he got a footing on the first, and drove in another, two feet above the second.

Then shifting up on the next peg, he drove in a fourth two feet above the third.

And so he went on, getting a rise of two feet each time.

In a little time over an hour he was able to grasp some of the branches of the wide-spread-crown of the tree, and haul himself up.

And presently climbing to the very top, he got his head through the canopy of great leaves, and looked around and beneath him.

It was a splendid panorama which lay spread out in all its beautiful tints of green verdure, blue sea, black rocks, white rippling waves, and smooth, white, sandy shore.

As a look-out point, commanding a general view of the island, and especially of its south coast, his perch on the top of the cocoa palm was all that could be wished, greatly superior to the lion's crown in many respects, though that point was really higher.

His eye swept the coast from the east all along the southern shore to the extreme west.

But though he carefully scrutinised every little inlet or creek, he could see nothing of the fleet of canoes or of the savages who had come in them.

He then turned his gaze seawards towards the islands to be seen on the west, and whence he knew these people must have come.

But he could discover no trace of canoes—not a speck dotting the surface of the sea.

"Strange," he thought; "they could scarcely have had time to have put to sea and get clean out of sight in so short a time. I must be on my guard; they may be concealed somewhere, waiting an opportunity to attack me unarmed."

Presently his eye fell on a small object by the sea-shore.

At first he thought it was the log of a small tree; but, using his telescope, he discovered, to his surprise, that it was nothing else than the little canoe of the maiden he had saved from torture and death.

He thought it strange that the savages should have left this on the sands openly in view, and it struck him that it was thus left as a bait, in the expectation that either he or she would endeavour to get possession of it.

So far as he knew, they had not yet discovered the existence of his own boat, which lay securely moored in dock; and such being the case, they would know the importance of a canoe, and, doubtless, imagine that the girl would run a great risk to regain possession of her little craft—the only means by which she could possibly get back to her own people, and her own island, wherever that might be.

And as he thought on that subject Crusoe Jack began to ponder and wonder as to what was the reason of the presence of this strange, mysterious, and lovely savage far away from her friends, and, but for these people he had given such a stern lesson to, and who evidently were enemies not expected by her here and himself, alone on this island.

What brought her here unattended, armed only with a little bow and arrows, and light spear?

What was the meaning of her extraordinary conduct towards himself—capricious, changeable, unaccountable?

Why did she first seek to terrify and annoy him, even granting that when she shot her arrows so close to his head she meant no harm?

And why did she afterwards take compassion on him, bind up his wounded head, and tend him carefully whilst smitten with the fever?

And lastly, what was the meaning of her being pursued, captured, ill-used, and doomed to death so soon as she was perceived by the wild men who came in the fleet of canoes?

He could answer none of these questions satisfactorily, except the last.

The savages who had given chase and captured her he felt sure must belong to a hostile tribe.

Also he had little doubt that she was the daughter of some prince, chief, or important personage of her own people, and so, with the wild cruelty of these savages, they resolved to take vengeance by ruthlessly torturing and murdering a poor unoffending girl, a daughter of a chief of their foes.

So far so good. That seemed plain enough, but all else was dark, bewildering, mysterious, and he resolved to lose no time in becoming sufficiently familiar with her language to be able to ask questions and understand the answers.

In this he did not anticipate any great difficulty, relying on a certain generic resemblance which pervades all the tongues and dialects of the Pacific islands.

He knew a little of the language of some Southern groups, and, having the valuable dictionary left to him by the captain of the whaler, did not doubt that ere long he would be able to learn all he wanted, and perhaps make some astounding discoveries.

He had no doubt whatever that he had quite won the girl over, and that she had no longer any fear of him.

Presently he bethought himself of looking for the place where he had inflicted such slaughter on the savages, and did not doubt he should easily distinguish it by reason of the dead bodies lying about.

But in this he was greatly disappointed.

For, although he discovered the scene of the intended murder of the girl by burning alive, the pile of stones and stake being plainly visible through his telescope, he perceived that both dead and wounded had been removed.

It was obvious, then, that the savages had landed again almost immediately after his own and the girl's departure.

This was not a pleasant thought, for it convinced him that these were bold, warlike, and determined fellows, and he thought it likely they would make an attempt to avenge their first defeat by killing or capturing him.

He was thinking over this and other things it led to, ever and anon sweeping the south shores of the island with his glass, when all at once there fell a strange sound on his ears.

It was from a distance, and he could not make certain as to its nature.

After a second it was repeated—a shrill cry in a human voice he thought.

"Perhaps it was only some wild bird," he said to himself, striving to quiet the uneasiness which possessed him.

But he remembered that he had never before heard any cry of a bird like this which now fell on his ear, although he had been on the island nearly two months.

He remembered that he had left the girl asleep in front of the hut under the influence of an opiate.

His heart smote him for having left her unprotected, and he hastily proceeded to descend the tree. This was a longer and more difficult job than ascending, as is always the case.

Just as he reached the ground the strange cry in the distance fell on his ears.

"I wonder what new peril awaits me? Dangers and mysteries seem to multiply every day," he said to himself.

CRUSOE JACK STRIKES TERROR INTO THE INDIANS.

He came upon the hut from the back, and running round he at once perceived that his fears had been realised, and that something had befallen the girl he had left calmly sleeping.

She was gone!

The rug and covering were all in disorder, and there were splashes and spots of blood on the ground.

And presently his eye fell on her little ivory javelin, lying a few feet off.

The metal tip was stained with blood!

CHAPTER XXVII.

ON THE TRAIL OF THE SAVAGES.

THE ground in front of the tent gave evidence of there having been a struggle.

There were footmarks and a piece of white stuff, which he judged had been torn from the girl's tunic, and presently his eyes fell on a long lock of hair—woman's hair.

He was not long in interpreting all this.

Some of the savages had followed them at a

afe distance—had watched the girl dress her wounds, and lie down to sleep—had seen him, who had proved so formidable, go off into the woods, and had then taken advantage of her being alone and helpless, to pounce upon her and get her again in their power.

That she had not suffered herself to be made prisoner and carried off without resistance was sufficiently obvious.

Witness the marks of the struggle on the ground—the torn piece of white stuff—the lock of hair, and the little javelin, its point stained with blood.

He quickly made up his mind, and resolved to start in pursuit, and, if possible, rescue the girl a second time from her cruel and determined foes.

For of a surety this second seizure of her, after she had been saved from them once with such slaughter, showed that they were not to be easily intimidated or driven away.

He had not great difficulty in finding the way they had gone; for the ground being rather soft, he could make out their foot-prints, and judged that there were four of them.

And after going a very little distance, he became aware of spots of blood in a regular track.

Some one of the party was wounded.

Was it the captive girl or her enemies?

That remained to be proved; but he was inclined to think from the spear tinged with blood that she had been able to use it to some effect before she was overpowered.

This track of blood rendered his pursuit easy, and carrying the little spear in one hand (he had picked it up mechanically, and now carried it he scarcely knew why), and a cocked revolver, he passed on, at times running.

Pursuing a southerly course towards the shore, he became aware, after going about three quarters of a mile, that he was close on the heels of the girl and her abductors.

He could hear the crackling of branches as they made their way through the brush, and even their voices speaking together.

Also he could make out, he thought, every now and again, a low wailing cry of pain and grief, and doubted not it came from the girl.

This urged him to increased speed in the pursuit, until he suddenly came in sight of four dusky forms, about fifty or sixty yards ahead of him, carrying a fifth.

These he knew to be the savages, who had again got possession of their victim, and it now behoved him to hit upon the best plan to attack them with success and rescue her again.

There was less than a quarter of a mile now of forest and scrub before the open ground by the sea-shore, towards which they were making, would be reached.

It occurred to him that the best way to discomfit and terrify them utterly was to get ahead of them—to lie in ambush in their path, suddenly fire at them when quite close, and then, springing out, finish the work with his cutlass.

There were only four of them.

This fact he ascertained to his great satisfaction.

He could make out that they were all tall, powerful men, armed with clubs, spears, and bows and arrows.

He now started off at full speed, describing the arc of a large semicircle, so that it should bring him about a hundred yards ahead of them, and right in their path.

At the foot of a wild fig tree there was a clump of bushes as high as a man, and amidst these he hastily concealed himself, and panting from the exertion of running, waited for their approach.

He could make out that the girl was bound hand and foot, and was being carried on a sort of rude litter made of a few boughs.

As they drew near he could hear a sort of monotonous song or chant, with which they enlivened their progress.

And mingled with this were occasionally low plaintive moans and wails of pain from the unhappy prisoner.

He now perceived that one of the four savages walked lame, and was wounded in the leg, for blood was trickling down it.

Ever and anon he would stop, and, with ejaculations of intense pain, put his hand on the wound.

But the others, in angry tones, appeared to urge him on, and, with many a groan and complaint, he would proceed.

It was now evening, and the slanting rays of the setting sun shone through the trees, and lighted up the group of four savages and their prisoner, so that Crusoe could observe the smallest particular.

He had a better opportunity than he had hitherto enjoyed of observing these savages at his leisure, as they advanced straight towards the place where he was concealed.

The upper parts of their bodies were entirely naked, but tattooed all over in a most elaborate and surprising manner.

Their features, naturally by no means bad, were also disfigured, and made to look quite hideous by the same process.

All had rings through their ears, and the two foremost had also rings hanging from their noses, the cartilage dividing the nostrils being pierced.

Each had around his throat a necklace of coral and shells.

Their hair seemed to be artificially arranged into a sort of mop-like clump, which made their heads look disproportionately large, and presented a most hideous appearance.

In this mop of hair were stuck feathers and other ornaments, the nature of which he could not make out.

Altogether, our adventurer watching them from his concealment as they approached, completely unconscious of their danger, thought them as truculent and brutal-looking savages as it was possible to conceive.

If he had been inclined to mercy and forbearance, the sight of the unhappy captive, bound hand and foot, the sound of her low moans of agony and terror, and the thought of the dreadful death they doubtless had in store for her, steeled his heart.

Nearer and nearer they came.

He could see their white teeth and fierce rolling eyes.

He held his breath, and when they got absolutely abreast of him, at a distance of about five yards, he fired all the barrels of the revolver pistol he had in his hand, and then, drawing the second one, rushed out.

CHAPTER XXVIII.

CRUSOE AGAIN RESCUES THE INDIAN MAIDEN.

THREE of the savages fell, including the wounded one, but the fourth escaped unhurt.

Of course the captive girl was let fall, and the unhurt man bounding off in terror and surprise, Crusoe instantly proceeded to cut her bonds and liberate her.

Save that she had been roughly handled, she had received no hurt, and at once sprang to her feet.

He still carried the javelin in his hand, not from any particular reason or intention of using it, but merely from the accidental circumstance of having picked it up outside the hut.

The girl snatched it eagerly from him, while he levelled and pulled the trigger of the other pistol.

The first barrel missed fire, and so did the next, and the next, and he then discovered that he had been so careless as to forget to put caps on the nipples.

The unwounded savage, who was evidently a most determined fellow, had, by this time, made a stand, and a spear whizzing by within a foot of Crusoe apprised him that he could not reckon upon an easy victory without danger to himself on every occasion he might come in conflict with these people.

The savage was preparing to hurl another spear, whilst the white man was hastily placing caps on the nipples of his revolver, when the girl interfered with good effect.

With sure aim and considerable force, she sent the light javelin flying through the air.

It struck the savage in the shoulder, going completely through it.

With a howl of rage and pain, he endeavoured to draw forth the sharp-pointed little weapon, and then, evidently discomfited, he turned and took to flight.

The Englishman, having capped his revolver, sent a couple of bullets after him, but was unable to say whether or no they took effect.

And so ended, again triumphantly for him, his second encounter with the savages.

A second time he had been successful in rescuing this island beauty from her foes.

Her gratitude was great, and she proceeded to evince it in characteristic fashion.

Falling on her knees at his feet, she bowed her face to the very ground, and then sought to place his foot on her head.

This, however, he would not suffer, and made her rise.

He now turned his attention to the three savages who had fallen beneath his pistol.

Two were already insensible—dying—having been shot through the head.

The third had received a bullet through the body, and Crusoe knew, by the bright crimson stream, which came in quick jets, that an artery was wounded, and that he must die in a very few minutes from loss of blood.

They were now close to the edge of the wooded ground, and within a hundred yards of the sea-shore.

And looking through openings among the trees, Crusoe observed that they were opposite the spot where lay the girl's little canoe, which he could now see hauled up on the shore.

It was an audacious idea, and one fraught with danger in the carrying out, but a sudden impulse possessed him, and he determined to possess himself of the little craft.

Hastily loading all the barrels of his revolver-pistols, he made signs to his companion to remain where she was.

But she let him understand, in the same way, that she was terrified, and afraid to stay there with two corpses and a dying man.

So he conducted her to another clump of bushes about fifty yards distant. Here she ensconced herself, and he started on his dangerous mission, greatly to her wonderment, for she had no idea at all of his intentions.

Once in the open ground, he crossed the strip of sand between the wood and the sea at a run, and was quickly alongside the canoe.

It was a light, delicate little thing, and, hoisting it on his shoulders, he started back. It was not destined, however, that he should gain the shelter of the bush and trees without being observed and molested.

From out of a grove of trees, about three hundred yards further to the westward, there suddenly appeared a body of ten or a dozen savages.

With loud yells they instantly gave chase to our hero, who, laden with the canoe—light as it was—could not, of course, make such good progress.

He soon became aware that before he would be able to reach cover the savages would be within arrow range, at all events.

Suddenly he stopped in his course.

This was greeted by a chorus of hoots and yells, and they came on rapidly, brandishing their spears and getting ready their bows and arrows.

Crusoe had a reason for thus stopping. He bethought himself of using the canoe as a protection from the arrows and spears.

It was not much more than six feet long ; so, placing it on his back, the keel outwards, it formed a complete shield for him from head to foot.

A tremendous howl greeted this manœuvre on his part, and a minute later he had reason to congratulate himself on his forethought.

As he ran he heard and felt several arrows or spears—he could not tell which—strike and stick into the bottom of the canoe.

He ran on vigorously, and though the savages gained on him every moment, he reached the shelter of the brush and trees at least fifty yards ahead of the foremost.

Then selecting a large cocoa-palm, he took shelter behind it, and stood at bay.

The savages came on in the most determined manner, and he proceeded to get his cutlass ready.

For he really saw a chance of a hand-to-hand encounter, feeling by no means so certain as he could wish that his revolver would be sufficient to keep them at bay.

He resolved to keep his fire till the nearest were within twenty yards, so as to make sure of hitting one fellow each time he fired.

On they came, yelling, shouting, capering,

dancing like madmen, probably to strike terror into the heart of the white man.

In this, however, they were not successful.

Three fellows were in advance of the rest, and, as if by common consent, made a rush altogether—two approaching to the right and left of the tree, behind which he had taken shelter, the third coming straight on.

Crack, crack, went Crusoe's revolver in rapid succession; and the two on either side fell, each shot through the body.

The third, or centre, still came on, and when he got within ten yards Crusoe pulled the trigger.

His pistol missed fire, and with a yell the savage bounded towards him, first hurling a spear, then raising his heavy war-club.

CHAPTER XXIX.

CRUSOE ASTONISHES THE SAVAGES.

It had now come to a hand-to-hand encounter, and all depended upon Crusoe Jack's skill, strength, courage, and agility.

The white man and the naked savage were now pretty well upon an equality.

The former had his cutlass and sheath knife, while the islander had spears, a small hatchet, and a formidable war-club, studded with large spikes.

As he sprang forward, the club, whirling round his head, described two circles in the air, and then, with a rushing swoop, was brought down, and aimed at Crusoe's head.

Had the blow taken effect, the combat would have been ended then and there; for if it had not crushed the skull like an egg-shell, it must have brought him to the ground stunned and bleeding. To parry such a weapon successfully with only a cutlass was an obvious impossibility; the blade would most likely be shivered, and the force of the blow scarcely broken.

Crusoe adopted a different course.

He had an eye like a hawk, and his motions were quick to follow.

Instead of trying to avoid the blow, by springing aside or backward, he made a rapid bound forward, so as to bring him a foot or two nearer to his opponent.

At the same moment he raised his left arm, to shield his head as much as possible from the force of the blow.

The result of this was that, though he did not escape it altogether, the heavy spiked end of the club—which, of course, descended with the greatest force—went over and beyond him, and the part nearer the handle struck his uplifted arm and left shoulder.

It staggered him, and brought him on one knee.

He was on his feet again, however, instantly, and managed to spring back—his left shoulder very sore.

The savage again raised his heavy war-club with the intention of repeating his blow, which had almost been completely successful.

A terrible yell of triumph showed his confidence in victory.

Crusoe had time to have got out of reach, and sought safety in flight.

But such a course would be only a very temporary relief from danger; for, seeing him flee, the other savages would be vastly encouraged, and would, of course, press on in pursuit, and he would lose all the advantage which the fact of his having hitherto defeated them with terrible slaughter gave him.

Instead, then, of ignominiously fleeing, he made a vigorous leap forward, and, despite the pain it gave him, by reason of the blow on his shoulder, seized the savage's wrist with his left hand.

The latter was utterly taken aback by this vigorous and unexpected action on our hero's part, and, yelling loudly, sought to disengage his wrist; while, at the same time he attempted to get the small hatchet from his girdle with his left hand.

But he was too late now.

Crusoe, muscular, vigorous, and active as a wild cat, had him at his mercy.

Drawing back his sword hand, he got the point of the cutlass to the breast of the savage, just in the centre, and below the ribs, where there was nothing but flesh and skin.

Then, with one fierce thrust, he drove it right through the unhappy wretch's body.

The cold steel went hissing through the flesh, the point coming out behind, and the cross of the hilt striking against the chest.

As the weapon was driven in, the savage only gave a sort of gasping moan; but when Crusoe suddenly drew it forth, the most terrible, unearthly, piercing shriek pealed out on the evening air.

Never before had the vales and groves of that quiet lonely island echoed with a sound like the death-cry of that savage.

It was, in tone, a shriek of the shrillest pitch, prolonged and dismal like the howl of a wolf or jackall, only infinitely more shrill and painful to the ear.

He did not fall at once, but staggered about, waving his arms, blood pouring from the wounds in front, where the sword went in, and at the back, where it came out.

There was fully half a minute of this terrible shrieking—his features distorted with agony—eyes rolling—teeth glistening—and Crusoe Jack shuddered at the sight, and turned away his eyes in horror, though he could in no respect blame himself for what he had done.

The unfortunate wretch looked in his agony like some demon undergoing the tortures to which he was doomed.

Suddenly, with another fearful shriek, the savage fell forward on his face, and commenced tearing up the ground with his hands, even biting the roots and grass with his teeth in his last agonies.

This was a most useful and important victory for Crusoe Jack, though a dreadful one in its attendant circumstances.

The other savages now ceased to advance, evidently deeply moved by the fate of their other companions, who had advanced so boldly and confidently on the solitary white man.

They had witnessed this same solitary white man slay the chiefs who approached to the right and the left, while yet they were yards distant.

But it was this latter victory which impressed them most.

The white man had engaged, in single combat, with the most redoubtable warrior of their tribe, and, after a brief encounter, had slain him too.

This might well cause them to pause in their bold and rash advance, for it seemed that their single foe had the power of killing them afar off with invisible weapons, or in a hand-to-hand encounter.

It is to be remarked that, hitherto, they had not seen any of the pistol bullets under which they fell; for these had, in every case, lodged in the body of the victim, or gone right through and out again, and so were lost.

Crusoe now got behind shelter of the tree, and keeping a sharp look-out, proceeded to reload all the chambers of his revolvers, being especially careful that every nipple was properly capped.

He kept a bright look-out all the while, and presently observed a group of them collected about one of the wounded.

This fellow was standing up; and, using his spyglass, Crusoe saw him holding up some small object between his thumb and finger, which he was showing to the rest, who were eagerly examining it.

This Crusoe at once decided was a pistol bullet, which the wounded man had himself extracted from his body or arm.

So the discovery of the missile, which had laid several of them low, did not seem to inspire them more with wonder and astonishment than alarm. Indeed, he fancied they seemed to gather courage a little after this discovery.

However, let that be as it might, they did not beat a hasty retreat, as he had hoped they would, but stood consulting, it seemed, and looking all the while earnestly towards him.

Having reloaded his revolver, he now again shouldered the canoe, and proceeded to make his way slowly and cautiously, pausing at every tree, to observe whether or no he were followed, towards the place he had left the girl.

He soon saw, notwithstanding the stern lesson they had received, the savages were yet unsatisfied, and not willing to give up the contest.

Probably it was from the fact of his being one man only which made them determined and persistent. They even began to follow him, and he resolved to put a stop to this.

So, halting behind a big tree, he unslung his carbine-rifle from his back, and waiting till one fellow rashly exposed himself within easy range, took most careful aim, and fired.

Purposely he aimed low, not caring so much about killing the man, as hitting him somewhere.

In a second after he had pulled the trigger he knew the effect of his shot.

The savage fell instantly, gave a howl of pain, and clapped his hand to his left leg.

This was by far the greatest distance at which he had hit any of them, and it produced a great effect.

They ceased to follow him, and he safely arrived at the place where he had left the girl, near the three dead bodies of the men he had first slain.

Great was her wonder and admiration at his prowess and safe return, and, above all, was she delighted with the recovery of her canoe.

CHAPTER XXX.

CRUSOE'S HOSPITALITY TO THE INDIAN MAIDEN.

THIS had, indeed, been a day brimful of excitement, startling adventures, danger, and bloodshed, ending with complete victory and triumph for himself up to this time.

As he, with his young companion, the Island Princess—for so, in his mind, he had christened her—slowly made his way towards the hut on Flagstaff Hill, just as night threw her mantle over the scene, he reviewed in his mind all the stirring events and perils he had successfully passed through since the sun rose that morning on his island kingdom.

First, there was the discovery of another way of access to the Valley of the Lake, as he called it—in itself an important thing.

Then there was his surprise of the savage maiden; her swift flight, despite her wounded foot, his pursuit, and her escape from him by means of her canoe.

And then the astounding incident of all the savages giving chase to the unfortunate girl, wounding her, making her a prisoner, and preparing to torture and kill her with the greatest cruelty.

Then followed his furious attack on the savage horde, his slaughter of them, and complete victory, followed by his retreat in triumph with the maiden, the Island Princess, as he had named her, whom he had rescued from their cruel hands.

And next followed his discovery, till then unsuspected, of this same girl being both the mysterious foe who shot arrows at him and otherwise annoyed him, and also the unknown friend whose care and attention probably saved him from succumbing to the terrible fever under which he suffered.

Then he thought of his folly or carelessness in leaving the girl asleep under the influence of an opiate while he went to climb the giant tree, he knowing all the time that the savages were either still on the island or somewhere close about.

And after his discovery that she had been seized and carried off, followed his pursuit of her abductors—his coming up with them, and the short, but decisive conflict, in which he slew three out of the four, while the brave girl wounded the fourth with her javelin.

And, lastly, his perilous, even rash enterprise, to recover the canoe, which by good fortune, skill, strength, and sheer pluck on his part, also turned out a glorious triumph, to the utter discomfiture of the vindictive and evidently determined savages.

This had been, indeed, a day overflowing with adventures and perilous escapes all ending fortunately and triumphantly for him; and as he arrived inside the enclosure of the hut, and stretched his weary limbs on the rug and matting, in fact he said to himself in perfect sincerity that he never wished to go through such another.

It was over now, however, and it behoved him to make arrangements for the future.

After a few minutes' repose, which he much needed, he rose, went out to the front of the stockade or bear-trap he had constructed, and carefully reconnoitred, keenly peering amongst the trees and shrubs for any trace of a foe.

It was now night, but not dark, for the sky was cloudless, and myriads of stars cast a subdued, silvery light on the calm scene.

Although he could discover no trace of an enemy, our adventurer here decided that it would not be safe to light a fire outside the hut; for it was extremely possible that some of the savages, though keeping carefully out of sight, were prowling about.

And, indeed, on consideration, he did not think it advisable or safe to remain outside.

For it was possible for an enemy to creep up to the stockade, and, looking over, shoot an arrow or hurl a spear with, perhaps fatal effect; for, as has been remarked, the stars gave plenty of light.

Accordingly he withdrew within the hut, and, signifying to the girl to do likewise, he dragged in the rugs and mattings, and proceeded to barricade the door by placing big logs, he had prepared for the purpose, across the entrance, forming a solid shoulder-high barrier.

So long, then, as they kept their heads on a lower level than this they were safe from the darts and spears of their enemies, should there be any hovering about,

He was so secure on this point that he did not scruple to light the oil lamp, trimming it, however, so that the flame should be very small.

He hung it up at the back of the hut, so that its feeble glimmer, while sufficient to enable him to see about the hut, did not dazzle their eyes, or prevent a clear view of the outside.

The stockade or breastwork he had thrown up only went round about four-fifths of the hut, at a distance of some ten yards, leaving an opening in front of about twenty-five feet.

Through this outlet he could see the trees and bushes on the slope of the hill leading down over the lion's tail to the shore.

So small was the flame of the lamp that within the hut it was comparatively dark, while he could clearly discern every object outside, and felt certain he would be able to see at once anything moving near the edge of the wood and scrub.

It happened that among the many articles left by the Yankee whaler was a small American stove, such as are used in the cabins and forecastles of ships in intensely cold weather.

This was little more than a cylinder of iron, about nine inches in diameter, fixed on three legs, with a lid and hole near the bottom, opening and shutting with a slide.

There were plenty of dry chips and pieces of wood; so, while his companion was again binding up her wounds, he proceeded to light a small fire at the back of the hut in the stove.

Crusoe Jack had a great fondness for two things—a pipe of tobacco and a pot of tea, and it was to have the latter that he had lighted the fire.

The girl, having finished dressing her wounds, which she accomplished with great skill, crouched in a corner of the hut, regarding his proceedings with evident astonishment.

There was no chimney to the stove, so he had to do as many savage tribes did—let the smoke escape through a small hole he cut in the roof.

Having made his arrangement for a pot of tea, he turned his attention to his companion, and perceived that she was still in considerable pain.

So, from his stock of medicines he mixed her an anodyne.

She shut her eyes to signify sleep, and then shook her head to convey to him that she did not wish to slumber again.

He gave her to understand that this would not have the effect, and she drank it off, thanking him with a grateful look.

He now proceeded to explain to her as well as he could by words, aided by signs, that it was needful for one of them to keep constantly on the watch.

She quickly caught his meaning, and made signs for him to lie down, and that she would keep watch.

But though fatigued, he was not sleepy, and smilingly declining her offer, brewed the tea, lit his pipe, and seating himself on his log stool, proceeded to enjoy the double luxury.

Tea is often considered as the especial beverage for weak women, querulous, gossiping, scandal-loving old maids, but in the Australian colonies great brawny fellows six feet and upwards set as much store on their pot of tea as ever did an imaginary jolly sailor for his grog.

No one ever starts on a journey without having as part of his equipment a quart pot and pannikin slung over his shoulder for the purpose of brewing the much-loved beverage.

But to return to our story after this digression.

In the position in which our hero sat he could just see over the logs which barricaded the entrance to the hut.

The girl arranged the soft fabric she had brought him when he lay ill with the fever, so as to form a sort of couch, and then seated herself at his feet.

Presently she began to chant a low monotonous refrain, which, nevertheless, was full of sweetness and melody.

He could not understand what it was she was singing, but ever and anon he clearly distinguished the syllables La-loo-hee-ah! the same mocking sound which had so tormented him on the evening when he vainly gave her chase.

He wondered much what was the meaning of this strange word, and resolved to endeavour to ascertain from her at a fitting opportunity.

Presently the sound of her voice grew fainter and fainter, until the song was only soft murmuring music—scarcely articulate.

And then weariness began to overcome this poor savage maiden—Crusoe's island princess.

Her head sank on his knee—the low, melodious voice died away, the eyes closed, and she slept.

Crusoe Jack gazed down on her beautiful face and form as she thus trustingly reclined on him and slumbered, one shapely arm thrown across her head in most graceful attitude—the other, the wounded one, supported in a sort of sling she had arranged—her long hair floating over her naked shoulders and down her back.

As he looked, he thought he had never seen a more lovely and graceful figure, even in the masterpieces of the ancient Greek sculptors.

"Sweet child of Nature," he said to himself,

"innocent, beautiful, and brave! And I was about to shoot at you. Ah! thank heaven, my better nature prevailed!"

CHAPTER XXXI.

CRUSOE'S PEACE AGAIN DISTURBED BY THE SAVAGES.

IT was a strange, an extraordinary, and most romantic and picturesque scene the interior of the hut presented.

The lamp shone with a flickering yellow flame, giving just sufficient light for the contents and general arrangement of the place to be dimly seen.

The huge upright logs which formed the walls and the tarpaulin covering formed the framework and background of the picture.

On one side, near the back of the hut, was spread a sheet of bark, raised about a foot from the ground by being placed across logs laid horizontally.

Blankets and a great rug of opossum skins on this formed Crusoe's couch.

Over the head of this rude couch two muskets, several cutlasses, and a broad axe hung in beckets attached to the logs and the tarpaulin roof.

At the back, and around the other side, was a strange conglomeration of articles—stores, and so forth.

There were barrels, bags, and wooden cases, all piled up together, and amongst them coils of rope, pieces of chain iron bolts, canvas, calico, lead in bars, and a keg of bullets, ready cast, tools, nails, odds and ends of all descriptions, a small cask of whale oil, a box of blue lights and ship's rockets, half a bale of raw hides, a grindstone, a coil of copper wire, loose copper, brass, zinc, iron hoops, hooks, tackle, whips, and scores of other things of all descriptions, which might or might not be useful.

And there, in the centre of this picture, with such a strange background and accessories, the two human figures—the white man in shirt, trousers, straw hat, and shoes of untanned leather, seated on a log stool at a rude table, on which lay before him his double-barrelled carbine, rifle, cutlass, belt, and pistols, and the savage maiden, with her bare shoulders and beautiful hair flowing down her back in wild luxuriance, reclining in an attitude of negligent grace, her head resting on his knee fast asleep.

A scene as wild, strange, and picturesque as ever a painter conceived and painted on canvas.

Crusoe smoked on in silent thought for nearly an hour, keeping, however, a vigilant look-out on the forest over the barricade at the entrance.

He refrained from moving for a long time, not wishing to disturb the girl who slept so calmly and peacefully.

But by-and-bye he began to feel inconvenienced from remaining so long in the same attitude, and sought a change.

Reaching forth his left hand, he drew towards him the opossum-skin rug, and, folding it up gently, raised the sleeping maiden's head, and placed it so as to form a pillow.

Then he quietly rose and left her still sleeping, her head now resting on the opossum rug and log stool.

Hours passed on, midnight came and went, and still she slept.

Crusoe kept vigilant watch, for more than once he thought he had heard sounds amidst the trees.

And as he knew there were no animals to cause them, and the birds did not fly by night, he was suspicious and watchful.

However, though he strained his eyes to the utmost, he could not discern anything—not even the shadow of a human form.

At about two hours after midnight the girl awoke, stretched herself, and murmuring some words he could not understand, arose.

He was leaning over the breast-high barricade at the entrance to the hut, looking out among the trees through the opening in the stockade.

Coming noiselessly up to him, she placed her hand on his shoulder, and then closing her eyes, put her head on one side.

By this she signified that he should sleep, and she went on in the same pantomimic manner to make him understand that she would keep watch.

After a little consideration, he gladly accepted her offer; for, in truth, he was both weary and sleepy.

Stretching himself on his bark couch, he lay for a short time thinking ere sleep stole over him.

The girl took her post near the barricaded entrance, moving slowly to and fro, but all the while keeping a vigilant look-out.

He watched her handsome, half-nude statuesque form and graceful movements for a few minutes, and then Somnus, the drowsy god, laid hold of his faculties, and he slept.

Shortly there came also Morpheus, and his brain teemed with strange fancies; he dreamed.

In his dream he again went through, though in a condensed form, all the scenes of the terrible mutiny of the Thunder; and events marching with rapid strides, his dream brought him down to the present time.

In fancy he went through all the events of the day from his first discovery of the girl to his second rescue of her.

And then he thought that the hut was surrounded by myriads of savages, who swarmed amongst the trees, and, yelling, leaping, and dancing, prepared to attack and storm his fortress.

And just as his dream reached this point, he was conscious of a hand being laid on his shoulder, and heard these words, whose meaning he did not at the time know, "Batumero putih marananna il hanko."

Awakened from his sleep, he raised himself on one elbow, and saw the girl standing by his side.

Directly she found he was awake, she pointed with her finger to the forest in front of the hut, and repeated her last words—

"Il hanko."

Now he had not the least idea what "il hanko" meant; but, judging from her manner, that it was something important, he at once rose and looked out over the barrier.

The girl stood by his side; and, pointing again, said—

"Borango!"

This, he judged rightly, meant "see," or "look there."

And, straining his eyes to penetrate the gloom, which the overshadowing trees cast, he could dimly make out forms—human forms it seemed to him—flitting to and fro.

From his post inside the hut, he could only command a view of the space opposite the gap in the stockade or fence, the latter more than shoulder high, being sufficient to hide a man or any number of men from his sight.

"Borango, borango!" the girl cried again, clutching his arm, and pointing this time to the branches of the trees.

And there he could make out also moving objects, but whether the forms of men or monkeys or of what, he was quite unable to say.

Crusoe Jack at once grasped the situation, and knew, by a sort of intuitive perception, that there was mischief afloat—danger to be encountered.

He thought it advisable to get a better view, and piling two cases one on the other mounted on them, and with his knife quickly cut a hole in the tarpaulin roof.

Then he tore on one side the branches of trees and other outer covering, and soon had an open space, through which he could get his head and shoulders.

When he did so, and looked around, he saw that which warned him he had yet to make a hard fight of it to escape the fury and determined malice of his savage foes.

CHAPTER XXXII.

PREPARATIONS FOR AN ATTACK.

IT was still dark, but the cloudless sky of the tropics allowed the starlight free play, and now that his head was outside of the hut, and he escaped the glare of the lamp, slight as it was, he could see much better.

His first glances were directed to the edge of the wood and brush, where he had already discerned moving figures.

He could now discern them much more distinctly, and could tell for a certainty that they were human forms.

Not only in front of the hut where he had first seen them, but on either side and behind the woods seemed alive with them.

He had now reason to rejoice that he had adopted the precaution of making a clearing all around his log-hut fortress, and was disposed to regret he had not further enlarged it.

As it was, the clear space extended fully sixty yards in all directions, and this was a great advantage, for the hut was quite out of the reach of spears, and though not beyond arrow-shot, yet was a sufficient distance to make accurate aim uncertain.

He judged that it was about three hours after midnight, and day would not begin to dawn for more than two hours yet.

His position was now extremely critical, as he had little doubt but that the savages meant to attack him under cover of the darkness, hoping to take him by surprise.

This obstinate pertinacity on their part, after the severe lessons they had received at his hands surprised him much, and caused him no little alarm.

"For," he said to himself, "despite my fire-arms and superior skill and knowledge, if they persist in keeping up these attacks, heedless as it seems they are of the slaughter and wounding of many of them, they must in time succeed by the mere force of numbers."

After a very brief look around, during which he satisfied himself that the woods were swarming with human beings—his savage foes, no doubt—he hastily came down, and proceeded to make arrangements for defence.

First he commenced loading the fire-arms, and having done this to his pistols and rifle, carbine, and blunderbuss, he next bethought himself of the rusty ships' muskets he had got from the American whaler.

These were all old-fashioned and out of date, most of them having flint locks.

However, he knew that at a short distance they would kill as surely as the most precise and accurately bored rifle.

Some of them he loaded with a brace of bullets, others with about a dozen slugs each.

While he was thus employed, keeping a sharp look-out all the while, the girl, who was intently watching his movements, touched him on the arm, and made signs to him that she would help.

This was very fortunate, and he wondered how he could have been so stupid as not to have thought of it before.

She seemed quick and intelligent, and was obviously anxious to aid him, as, indeed, she had proved by the skilful manner in which she had hurled her spear, and wounded the fourth savage in the encounter on the previous day.

He now carefully instructed her how to load one of the muskets, showing her how much powder to put in, and impressed on her the necessity of placing wadding between the powder and the slugs, with which he decided that she should load.

For it would be easier for her to drop in four or five leaden pellets than to ram down a tight-fitting bullet, and she could do it in much less time.

This done, he gave her an empty musket and the powder-horn, and showed her the barrel in which he kept the big swan shot and slugs.

The priming of the flint-lock muskets and the capping of those which were fired by percussion he reserved to himself, and for that purpose slung another powder-horn round his neck, and provided himself with a bag of caps.

She proved herself more apt than he had ever hoped, and in the space of a few minutes he had all his firearms loaded, and reckoned rightly that he could at any moment open a pretty considerable fusillade. With his two revolvers he could fire twelve shots, and with the double-barrelled pistol two.

These he meant to keep to the last until it came to close quarters, if ever the conflict should reach that stage.

Then he had the double-barrelled rifle carbine, which had already done him such good service, the blunderbuss, and an English army rifle.

Besides these modern weapons, on which he could count for eighteen discharges in all, there were eleven muskets. So that he could fire twenty-nine barrels in rapid succession.

He now set about loopholing the roof, so as to be able to fire upon the savages from a vantage-ground.

One after the other he cut four holes in the tarpaulin, which formed the cover of the tent, and partially pulled on one side the branches, &c., which he had laid over, so that he could see and protrude the barrel of rifle or musket.

One of these loopholes he made on each side of the tent, so that he could from them command not only the ground to the right and left, but also that in front.

And, foreseeing the possibility of an attack at the rear, he made two loopholes at the back of the hut.

Under each of these he placed cases, or something else, on which to stand, so as to bring his head and shoulders far above the level of the breast-high logs.

Having made all these arrangements, in which his companion aided him, showing unexpected intelligence and quickness at learning what was wanted, he cast about him as to what he should do next.

That the savages meant to attack him he had no doubt whatever, and he had good reason to anticipate that they would make a sudden and simultaneous rush upon the hut.

Now, in spite of his fire-arms, he looked forward to this prospect with anything but satisfaction, as, though he would probably be able to shoot down several of them, they might overwhelm him, as a pack of furious hounds might a hare or fox.

He had already experienced the advantage of acting on the offensive—fighting first—and felt strongly desirous of doing so now.

But there was a serious difficulty in the way, and one which seemed almost insurmountable.

So long as the savages kept in the shelter and shadow of the trees it would not be much use firing at them; indeed, little better than a waste of ammunition.

For though from his look-out holes in the roof of the hut he could at times dimly perceive forms flitting to and fro, they were in no case distinct enough to give him a fair chance for a shot.

Presently, however, a bright idea flashed across his mind, and he instantly proceeded to put it in practice.

The captain of the whaler had left him as a present a box of blue lights, some port-fires, half a dozen Chinese fire-balls, and a dozen signal rockets.

Without losing a moment, Crusoe Jack took two blue lights, and arranged the fuse of each so that it should flare up in about half a minute.

Then he took an arrow from the girl, affixed to the point a fire-ball, and laid it down on the table with the little box belonging to it.

The Island Princess, as he had named her, watched his every motion with great interest and curiosity, but said never a word, appearing to have the utmost confidence in his skill and power, as, indeed, she had reason to do, after what she had seen of his prowess.

This done, he took down the little oil lamp and placed it in a half-empty barrel, so as to make the interior of the tent nearly dark. Then he proceeded to clamber over the barricade at the entrance, with a blue light in each hand, his cutlass girt on, and revolver-pistols in his belt. He got outside the tent, and, crouching down, made his way rapidly and noiselessly to the fence and stockade.

Here he went on his hands and knees, and keeping close to the fence, crawled along until he came to the opening or gap.

Then, silently and swiftly, he stuck up the two blue lights, side by side, on top of the barrier.

Next he put fire, taking all the care he could to prevent the light being seen.

The fuses would burn about half a minute, and before that time he had safely gained the shelter of the tent.

With beating heart he took the bow and arrow, the latter loaded with a fire-ball, and prepared to mount to one of his loop-holes the instant the blue lights should blaze up.

He had in his hand a piece of touchwood, with which he set light to the fire-ball when the proper time came.

The few seconds which followed seemed minutes.

At last, with a fizzing and sputtering, the blue lights caught fire, and flared forth their brilliant ghastly blaze.

Instantly there arose a tremendous yell of astonishment or terror (perhaps both), which made the night air hideous.

CHAPTER XXXIII.

CRUSOE MAKES USE OF THE FIRE-BALLS.

CRUSOE JACK got his head through one of the loopholes he had cut in the tarpaulin roof just as the blue lights burst into full blaze, revealing to his gaze an extraordinary and unexpected sight.

He was aware that there were men amongst the trees and brush beyond the clearing, because he had seen their shadowy forms moving to and fro.

But he had no calculation of their number, and thought roughly that there might be thirty or forty, or perhaps a few more of them.

The loud, shrill, and prolonged yell which broke out when the blue lights burned up seemed to convince him that there must be a very large number of them, for the discordant howl seemed to proceed from all directions, front, sides, and rear.

It seemed from this that the hut was entirely encompassed by them.

And this notion of his was thoroughly confirmed when he looked out through the loop-hole.

First he directed his eyes to the front, and there saw a great number of the savages dancing and capering about in great excitement.

All were armed with spears, clubs, and bows and arrows.

He observed that, though they were evidently greatly astonished at the sudden blazing forth of the blue lights, they did not take to flight, or, indeed, seem very greatly alarmed.

Altogether, their conduct, under the circumstances, gave him the impression that they meant fighting, and though momentarily surprised and taken aback, would certainly attack the hut before long.

And the more he looked, the more serious did such a prospect appear to him.

For, turning his eyes to the right and left he saw that the trees and brushwood were swarming with them, and, even in the direct rear, he could make them out flitting to and fro.

All the while an unceasing din was kept up of jabber, shouting, and screaming.

And soon the unpleasant conviction was forced upon him that the savages who had originally landed on the island had received a very considerable reinforcement, for he was quite certain that there were now three times as many as even the large number that he had first seen.

How and when they had come he could form no idea whatever; but there was the disagreeable fact. And making a rough estimate, he reckoned that the hut was surrounded, beleaguered by six or seven hundred of these howling, dancing, naked devils of savages—all eager to kill him, and perhaps eat him afterwards, for he was by no means sure they were not cannibals.

Presently some motion amongst the branches of the trees attracted his attention, and he then saw, to his astonishment, that the tops, or leafy crowns of the trees were swarming with savages.

This was a most serious discovery; for, from such a vantage point they would have an excellent opportunity of shooting their arrows, and it would be unsafe for him to expose himself in the slightest degree, even so much as he was doing at present, when they perceived him.

And scarcely had this thought gone through his mind than an arrow came whistling through the air, grazed his head, and actually cut his ear.

It passed through the loop-hole, and stuck, quivering, in an empty wooden case.

"Ha!" cried Crusoe, "you've opened the ball, have you, you confounded vagabonds? All right! I'll find you some music to dance by, or I'm a Dutchman!"

The blue lights had by this time nearly burned out, and of course it would be unsafe for him to venture out to replace them with fresh ones.

He had, however, another plan all ready for execution, one which he thought would serve his purpose much better than even the blue lights, useful as they had proved in lighting up the forest, and revealing to him the number, nature, and disposition of the forces about to attack him.

This plan was in connection with the Chinese fire-balls, which the Yankee captain had so kindly given to him.

They would burn for a much longer time than the lights, and although the flame would not be so brilliant, it would be white, and show all objects in their natural colours.

He had already fitted one to the point of one of the girl's arrows; and now, after fitting the dart to the bow, he set light to the fire-ball, and, drawing back a little, shot it through the loop-hole in the direction of the trees in front

Hastening to watch the effect of this shot, he quickly put his head through the hole, and was in time to see the arrow, with its flaming point, describe an arc—attaining a height equal to that of the highest trees, and fall at a spot about a hundred and fifty yards distant from the hut.

Directly it fell it burst into full blaze; and all around that spot, for many yards, it was perfectly light, and he could see every motion of his enemies.

Satisfied with the result, he hastened to re-peat the manœuvre, and fired in quick succession three other arrows similarly loaded.

One to the left, another to the right, and the last one to the rear of the hut.

All were successful shots; and the effect was that the forest on all sides was lighted up with the white glare of these fire-balls, which are so made as to burn for fully ten minutes, and are not to be extinguished by water or any other known means of quenching fire.

So he had now this great advantage, that while the hut remained dark the forest retreat of the savages was lighted up.

He now observed that a sort of council was called; and then one, who was evidently a great chief, by the ornaments and the huge plume of feathers he wore, addressed the others in a short but vehement harangue.

Crusoe now thought it time to assume the offensive, and, if possible, prevent the anticipated attack by inflicting such damages and slaughter as to strike terror into them, notwithstanding their stubborn nature and fierce and savage dispositions.

So he called to the girl, and pointed to the blunderbuss, which was loaded with a heavy charge of powder, and nearly a tea-cup full of slugs and swan shot.

The instant the chief concluded his harangue he raised aloft his spear, and with a loud shout of encouragement led his followers to the attack.

As he advanced into the open the glare of the fire-ball clearly revealed his tall handsome form to the white man, who, himself unseen, could from his loop-hole see all that passed.

"That fellow must die!" said Crusoe, aloud; and then, turning to the girl, he added, "hand me up the rifle."

She could not understand his words; but, with quick perception, she followed the direction of his eyes, and handed him the deadly-accurate weapon.

He laid the blunderbuss on the case on which he stood, cocked the rifle, and looked out.

The chief, followed by some threescore naked savages, in no sort of order—nothing more nor less than a mob—came steadily on—perhaps unconscious of danger.

When he was within about a hundred yards Crusoe deliberately covered him with his rifle, aiming at the pit of the stomach, to allow for its throwing high.

Crack!

Away sped the leaden messenger of death on its errand.

CHAPTER XXXIV.

THE SAVAGES MEET WITH A WARM RECEPTION.

AT such a short range, and with a weapon of precision, it was scarcely possible for a good shot to miss.

Crusoe had taken accurate aim, and the bullet whistled through the air and struck the savage chief with deadly effect.

It hit him full in the centre of the chest, going right through the body and out at the back, fracturing the spine at the same time.

The unfortunate man gave vent to a death-yell, and then fell forward on his face.

Crusoe hastened to fire the other barrel of the

piece, and again succeeded in hitting one of the enemy.

A number of them now clustered around the chief, who, though grievously wounded—dying, in fact—was not yet dead.

They seemed not to be aware how fatal such tactics must prove to them; or perhaps they were determined, at all hazards, to bear off the wounded man.

There were, at least, a score of them, all in a crowd together, and offering a mark impossible to miss.

"The blunderbuss—give me the blunderbuss!" cried Crusoe, forgetting, for the moment, that the girl did not understand English.

He remembered himself in a second, however, and was about leaving his post to get it himself, when, to his surprise, she placed it in his hands.

She had heard him name the word blunderbuss before—had seen by his actions to what it referred, and had kept the fact in her memory.

This was a source of both surprise and gratification to him, and he rewarded her with a smile, and said—

"Good girl! You are, indeed, a valuable ally."

The words she could not understand, but their purport she gathered from his tone, and immediately after giving him the blunderbuss she took the discharged rifle from his hands, and commenced loading it.

Although he had determined to load the rifles and pistols always himself, he did not interfere with her, thinking that doing so might discourage her; and, besides, he was anxious to know whether, indeed, she was intelligent and skilful enough to load properly a rifle—at all times rather a delicate operation.

All this, which has taken some time to describe, occupied only a few seconds.

When Crusoe again looked through the loop-hole in the roof, the cluster of savages was still as thick as ever about their fallen chief.

They now appeared to have raised him and to be bearing him off. If, however, he had expected that the fall of two of their number—one a man of mark and rank—would deter them from prosecuting the attack, he saw quite enough to undeceive him.

They were dancing, leaping, yelling, and shouting in all directions, apparently working themselves up to the necessary pitch of excitement and fury.

"All right, my fine fellows!" muttered Crusoe between his teeth. "I'll give you something to jump and dance about presently!"

Then he levelled the blunderbuss, and fired.

It was heavily loaded, and the recoil knocked him backwards into the tent, to the dismay of his companion, who feared that he was wounded.

However, he was quickly on his feet again, and mounted to the loop-hole to see the effect of the discharge of slugs from the blunderbuss.

"Quick! quick! give me muskets!" he cried, as, with a rapid glance, he took in the situation.

The discharge of the huge piece—quite a little cannon, with its heavy charge of slugs and swan shot—had produced tremendous effect.

Of all the savages clustered around the dying or dead chief there was scarcely one who escaped without a wound.

The slugs and shot scattered and spread just enough, and a second after the discharge howls and yells from a score of throats told of its deadly effect.

Many of the savages lay on the ground moaning with pain and terror, while others made themselves scarce, limping off as best they could.

The girl now handed him a musket, and, levelling this at two or three together, he fired.

This he repeated again and again, now firing on one side, now on the other, now in the rear, but always keeping a bright look-out ahead at the gap in the stockade.

The effect of this rapid fusillade, under which at least half-a-dozen savages fell, was to disconcert them greatly, and prevent them from making an assault upon the hut.

The fire, however, had another result, and that not by any means a pleasant one.

It drew on the hut a flight of arrows, which stuck into the logs and roof, some coming in unpleasant neighbourhood to his head in all directions.

The flashes of the firearms revealed his head and shoulders to the enemy, and, with a determination and persistence which did them credit, they did not fail to take advantage of the opportunity.

The arrows could not penetrate through the strong tarpaulin roof, and instantly after firing he immediately got under shelter, so that the danger he ran was comparatively slight.

But, to his great surprise and annoyance, there came other missiles besides arrows—long, sharp-pointed spears, with hafts of heavy wood.

These, by their weight and the force with which they were hurled, came clean through the tarpaulin into the interior of the hut, and one went within a foot of the girl, while several came dangerously close to himself.

He was at first at a loss to account for these missiles, for he thought he was quite out of spear-shot.

Soon, however, he perceived the meaning of it.

The spears came from the tops of two huge cocoa palms, where were perched a number of the savages.

From their high position they were enabled to hurl their weapons with sufficient force to reach the hut, and their weight alone falling from such an elevation was sufficient to cause them to penetrate.

The fire-balls had now almost burnt out, and Crusoe Jack, crouching behind the logs of the hut, proceeded to affix some more to arrows in the same way.

All at once it struck him it would be a good thing to send one or two into the tops of the trees where the savages who were hurling their spears had their perch.

They were comparatively in the dark, and sheltered also by the huge leaves, he could not see them distinctly enough to get a good shot.

No sooner thought of than done.

In quick succession, he shot two arrows, laden with fire-balls, into the topmost branches of the trees.

Most prodigious was the effect.

The two great trees, amongst the thick branches of which a number of savages had established themselves, were the nearest to the fence and hut, and nearly right in front.

One of these trees died for some reason or other. Crusoe often thought it must have been struck by lightning.

The effect was this.

All the branches and leaves were withered, and the scorching tropical sun had dried them till they were like tinder.

The two trees stood closer together than is usual with large specimens of the cocoa palm, and, indeed, the branches touched and even interlaced at places.

Both the arrows, with the lighted fire-balls attached, fell amidst the withered leaves and branches, forming the tuft and crown of the withered tree.

Almost instantly the dry parched leaves and dead wood caught light, and began blazing furiously.

And this was not all.

Both trees had no branches, not even the smallest sprig, until the top or crown was reached.

But, clinging to the otherwise bare columns, was a quantity of moss mixed with creeping plants, a great part of which was thoroughly dry.

This instantly caught fire, and Crusoe Jack witnessed the strange spectacle of two huge trees on fire; the top a blaze of flame, and the flames slowly unfolding and creeping down the trunks.

And now there commenced a terrible scene; and as Crusoe Jack stood and looked on with pity and horror, he could not help remembering the death those cruel savages had intended for the poor girl whom he had saved, and thinking that this, which, on his part, was pure accident, was a just retribution and judgment on the savages for their meditated atrocity.

The firing up of the tops of the trees (for the second one, though not dead and so inflammable as the first, was dry enough to catch light) soon caused hideous yells and screams from the savages, who had climbed up and now found themselves caught in a fiery trap.

The flames gained ground with great rapidity, and shortly after the arrows and fire-balls had lodged among the branches the crowns of both trees were one blaze of fire.

The unhappy wretches, thus imprisoned by an unexpected foe, endeavoured to descend by the trunks; but these, too, were all on fire for at least a fourth of the way down.

The glare now lit up the surrounding scene, and everything, was plainly visible as daylight.

The savages beneath gazed with terror and astonishment on the extraordinary sight, and shouted and yelled.

And from the tops of the trees there came in answer the most dreadful screams and yells of agony.

And presently, to escape the raging flames, and preferring mutilation or death from the fall to being roasted alive, the unhappy wretches commenced falling from the trees.

Before each one dropped he gave utterance to a wild unearthly yell, then there was the rush of a dark body through the air, followed by a dull, heavy fall, and a lifeless mass, a bruised pulp, all that remained of what was, a few minutes previously, a strong, athletic man, lay at the foot of the tree.

CHAPTER XXXV.

FLIGHT OF THE SAVAGES.

THIS terrible scene lasted for some five minutes, and the white man, watching the destruction of his foes from his secure stronghold, counted thirty-three who fell from the trees, and all of whom must have been killed, for, from such a height, escape with life was as nearly impossible as anything can be in this world.

The scene—sight and sounds combined—was terrible, awful in its grandeur, and was one not ever to be forgotten by any one who witnessed it.

The savages had now ceased shooting their arrows and hurling their spears, apparently aghast at the terrible fate of their comrades, who kept falling, with awful yells, from the blazing tree tops.

For a quarter of a mile the whole expanse around the blazing trees was illuminated. The hut was plainly visible to the savages, and they, in turn, could be seen distinctly by Crusoe.

He could, had he chosen, have shot many of them, so excellent was the light, and so moderate the range.

It was a singular fact about these fierce but ignorant savages, and one that he now noticed for the first time, that they seemed to have no idea of getting out of danger from his firearms by retiring to a greater distance.

They seemed to have no idea of range, and it struck him that very probably they thought his weapons would kill as surely at a long distance as at a short one.

After a time the burning branches of the trees broke off, and fell, red hot and blazing, to the ground.

All the unhappy wretches who had sought the lofty perch in the crown of the cocoa-palm trees had now fallen and perished, and the frightful howlings and screams of agony ceased.

The tops of the trees, in particular the dead one, still burned fiercely, and there was abundance of light. Still it was obvious that, before long, the blazing trees must burn themselves out.

Strange to say, the savages, though evidently scared and disheartened, for they had ceased hostilities altogether, did not beat a hasty retreat from the scene of their discomfiture.

This obstinacy on their part, their seeming insensibility to the very severest and most terrible lessons, gave Crusoe much trouble.

"Shortly they will gather heart once more," said he to himself. "Some fanatic chief will harangue them and lead them on again. Again shall I have to do my utmost to repel them with slaughter, and I am weary of bloodshed."

And presently he bethought himself of the signal rockets the captain of the Yankee whaler had left him.

The blue lights and fire balls had already done good service, and he decided to finish up with these, and see what effect they would have.

He had by no means great confidence in the result, but resolved at all events to see what would come of it, trusting that fortune, which had in many respects been so kind, would bestow on him further favours.

Having loaded all the muskets, in which

CRUSOE JACK'S NOVEL MODE OF DEFENCE.

girl proved of the greatest assistance to him, he got out three rockets and carefully laid them horizontally on the top of the barricade, so that when ignited, they should shoot along parallel with the surface of the ground.

He had no rocket tube for directing them, and was obliged to lay them at hap-hazard.

All being in readiness, he fired them one after the other.

Every one who has witnessed a rocket let off knows the whizzing and hissing noise it makes.

The result exceeded his expectations.

The first one flew straight ahead, but far above the crowd of savages in front of the gap in the fence at which he aimed at.

Nevertheless, as it went roaring and sputtering through the trees some thirty feet over their head, breathing forth fire and sparks, they were seized with a sudden panic and were scattered in all directions with loud cries of alarm.

It was evident from this that visible weapons, such as these rockets, had far greater terrors for them than the more deadly bullets which sped on their fatal errand unseen.

The second rocket had even greater effect. It struck the ground about twenty yards from the fence, then ricochetted, and plunged, hissing, blazing, and scattering sparks in all directions, right amongst a group of ten or a dozen.

The rocket then made several erratic bounds of twenty or thirty yards—now to the right, now to the left, now backwards, all the while roaring like an engine blowing off steam.

There is little doubt but that the savages looked upon this fiery monster as an animated being, able to leap hither and thither where it pleased.

The third rocket completed their discomfiture, and sent them all flying, screaming, and yelling with fear.

Its effects were terrible.

It struck a savage full in the body, completely impaling him, and then exploded with a loud bang, mutilating and scorching the poor wretch fearfully.

Of course death was almost instantaneous, and he could not have suffered much pain.

But terror and horror at the sight finished the work Crusoe's bullets, the fire-balls, and the other rockets had commenced ; and as the fire at the tops of the cocoa-palms burned low, the whole horde of savages who had come on to the attack, confident in their powers and numbers, had sought safety in flight, and only the dead were left on the field, for, despite their panic, they managed to carry off their wounded.

So far as Crusoe was concerned, this was a complete and bloodless victory; but as dawn slowly broke and revealed the scene of conflict —strewn as it was with corpses—it was with a feeling of shuddering horror he regarded it.

At sunrise, having washed off the powder-smoke, which grimed his hands and face, he went forth to reconnoitre and survey the scene.

CHAPTER XXXVI.

LEFT ALONE.

ALTHOUGH once again the victory over the savages fell to the gallant mate of the Thunder and his companion, La-loo-hee-ah, the Island Princess, his heart was sad and heavy as he surveyed the battle-field.

Under no circumstances is this a pleasant sight after an engagement, but the scene he now gazed upon had peculiar elements of horror.

A great number of the savages were badly scorched and burned, while all who fell from the trees were, of course, sadly mutilated and crushed by the fall.

Then there were many slain by the bullets, and, lastly, those who had been struck by the rockets presented a shocking spectacle.

The sun rose bright and beautiful over the island, lying so calm and placidly, surrounded by coral reefs, on the bosom of the grand Pacific.

All nature seemed to speak of peace and happiness and beauty.

But what a scene was that on which Phœbus rose this glorious morning—a scene of havoc and death which might well appal the heart of a man

as brave and more cruel by nature than Crusoe.

Leaning his back against a tree our hero moodily surveyed his work.

And the thought arose to his mind—

" Am I justified in thus slaughtering the savages ?"

The answer came in the form of another question put to himself—

" How can I avoid it ? They will not leave me in peace. They seek my life with persistent fury. If to avoid them I fly, it will not avail me, for they can follow. Even if I took to the broad ocean in my boat, in the hope of being picked up by some vessel, or making land—an act of madness, almost—they could, if they chose, overtake me in their swift canoes. How can I secure my own safety against their attacks, save by defending myself to the utmost of my power, and in inflicting the greatest possible damage on them ?"

Presently there arose in his mind, in a vague sort of way at first, gradually shaping itself into form, this thought—

" It is the fact of having rescued the girl they had captured and doomed to death which caused them to attack me. It is because she is still with me that they are so determined in their attack. If she were away they would no further trouble me."

Not for a moment did he think of delivering up the Island Princess into their cruel hands, feeling tolerably certain as to what would be her fate should he do so. Such an unworthy thought never crossed his mind.

But he did seriously consider whether it would not be possible to arrange for the girl's escape.

He had, it will be remembered, not only rescued her from her enemies, but had also recovered the canoe from their hands ; and he argued with reason.

As she came here from her own country in this little vessel, why should she not—choosing a good opportunity—make her escape back to her own people?

Thus pondering in his mind, he turned his back on the scene of death and walked slowly towards the hut.

The girl, La-loo-hee-ah, was standing outside, her arms folded across her breast, gazing in a sorrowful, dreamy manner out to sea.

She looked, as well she might, very different from the time when he first saw her by the shores of the lake, in all the glory of her savage beauty—her luxuriant hair flying loosely in the wind, her bright eyes sparkling, her figure the ideal of female grace.

Now she was powder-grimed, wounded in the arm and foot—her fair body stained with blood —marked with scratches and bruises from the rough treatment she had received at the hands of her captors.

Her form still retained its elegance of outline, but it was like a drooping flower, and the handsome delicate features were haggard ; and there was a strange staring, frightened look in the eyes—an expression seeming to betoken despair and utter weariness of spirit on the face.

As Crusoe approached her, she turned her gaze on him ; and saluting him in her fashion, holding one hand on her forehead, the other on her breast, she waited for him to speak.

Pity for the exhausted and wounded maiden

caused him to turn his attention to her, and, touching her arm, he inquired, as well as he could, whether it pained her, and she repli..... bowing her head quietly, but at the same t.. by a sad smile and peculiar gesture, endeavouring to make him understand that it did not hurt very much.

Pointing to her foot, however, she made a face expressive of great pain. Regarding it, he could see that the whole foot and ancle were greatly swollen. The exertion and excitement of the strife having caused burning inflammation to set in.

He at once saw that the poor girl must have rest after such a night of fatigues and horrors, and did not think it worth while to broach his idea that she had better make her escape from the island at that time.

And he, too, was badly in want of repose; in fact, he felt that, at all risks, he must have rest, and as there was no sign of the savages he thought it would be tolerably safe for them to barricade themselves within the hut, and seek the rest they so much needed.

For it was not altogether weariness of body which he felt, but exhaustion of energy. The vital force required time, rest, and repose of mind to recover former vigour, and this could best be attained by sleep.

And so he resolved to risk it, and having first, with true chivalry, procured cold spring water and assisted to bathe his companion's foot for some time to ease the pain and reduce the inflammation, he proceeded to signify to her his idea that they had better both barricade themselves within the hut.

At first she did not appear to understand him, and presently she quite misapprehended it.

For she bowed her head gently in token of assent, and signified to him that she would remain and watch while he slept.

When he made her understand by signs and words, that it was not safe for her to sleep outside, and that she must rest, she absolutely refused to enter the hut, and shook her head vehemently in token thereof.

CHAPTER XXXVII.

LA-LOO-HEE-AH'S BOWER.

CRUSOE was, it may well be believed, considerably astonished and puzzled at this girl—her unwillingness to enter the hut and seek that repose so necessary to her.

Presently she explained her own plans and intention, and to his still greater astonishment, he found that she wished to build a sort of bower of branches, a leafy tent, and there take up her abode.

To this Crusoe could have had no possible objection, except on the ground that it would be dangerous.

For whereas, when barricaded within the hut, he could not easily be taken by surprise, it was a very different thing in the case of anyone sleeping, sheltered only by a hut of tree branches and leaves.

He had tact enough to perceive that her unwillingness proceeded from a sense of maiden modesty, and much he marvelled at this trait in the character of the island maiden.

Turkish women go with bare feet and legs, but consider it the height of immodesty to allow a glimpse of their faces to be seen, which, besides the veil, are nearly covered with a linen cloth called *yasmack*, so that nothing but the eyes can by any possibility be seen.

This savage girl, who from the waist upwards, was scarcely clothed at all, and felt no shame thereat, yet scrupled to share the hut (the safest possible stronghold under the circumstances) with the white man, who had rescued her twice from her enemies and saved her life.

Gently—almost pleadingly—she made him understand that she would make for herself a bower of branches and leaves, and there take her rest.

When Crusoe thoroughly understood her, he at once consented, and did his best to assist her.

Taking a tomahawk, or small hatchet, he went out to where there were some small trees and cut a number of branches, which he brought to the back of the hut.

We have before related how, a few days after, being left alone on the island, he had dug a pit within the hut, and thence driven a tunnel for a considerable distance to the rear.

At the end of this tunnel was a subterranean chamber, where he had stored gunpowder, arms, and other things.

By a strange chance, La-loo-hee-ah selected a spot for the erection of her fragile abode immediately above this underground storeroom.

Crusoe had ascertained the exact direction in which the tunnel ran by means of the compass, and he got the distance by measuring with a log line; so he was able to mark by a small peg the exact spot beneath which lay the subterranean chamber.

At the time he treated this as a curious coincidence, and of no importance, and thought how he could astonish her if he chose by making his appearance from below into her bough hut when she had finished it.

This he could easily do, for there was at one place of the arched roof of the chamber, less than a foot of soft earth, through which he could, in a few minutes, drive a hole with a small pickaxe.

However, thinking it of no importance, he did not acquaint her of the fact, but set to work to help her, and in a short time they had, between them, erected a charming little bower—an excellent shelter from the sun; the broad palm leaves, with which it was covered, also serving as a protection against rain.

It was the most fragile and airy-like structure possible to conceive.

For, about a dozen branches fixed on each side, and two at the back with their stems stuck in the ground, their tops meeting in the centre, formed the framework, so to speak, of the affair.

Then, cross-wise, were woven in between a few smaller branches, and the whole was covered over with large plantain and cocoa-palm trees.

This completed La-loo-hee-ah's bower.

It was situated in the midst of a clump of bushes which our hero had purposely left at that spot, and was thus almost entirely concealed.

At least, being itself built of branches and leaves, what could be seen of it appeared like a part of the surrounding foliage.

The palm-leaf covering excluded the glare of

the sun, but in the interior of this little abode there was a soft, subdued, green-tinted light, quite high enough, like that which comes through stained glass when the sun is shining.

La-loo-hee-ah's bower being finished, Crusoe brought up some matting and soft fabric she had brought for him when he lay fever-stricken. This, with a number of leaves, proved an excellent couch, and Crusoe could not but envy the lady, so far as comfort was concerned.

It was, in fact, a charming little bower, cool and airy, the very thing for the climate, and its very lightness and fragility made it appear all the more beautiful.

Here, sheltered from the sun by a leafy canopy, and fanned by gentle zephyrs, this weary and wounded child of Nature could take her rest, whilst the white man would be in very different quarters—cooped up in a dark and close hut, into which little light and less air could penetrate.

However, Crusoe consoled himself by the thought that, barricaded within the hut, he would be all but safe from surprise.

Nor was he by any means unmindful of the safety of the girl whom Providence had cast, helpless, upon him for help and protection.

He made her understand that she was in a dangerous situation, and that it was necessary for her to be as watchful as possible.

She let him know, in a pretty and ingenious way, that she slept very lightly.

She took his hand in one of hers, and then, resting her fair head on her other hand, she closed her eyes and said the word Narhoo—sleep.

Then she caused his hand to touch her shoulder very lightly; instantly she opened her eyes with a start.

This pretty bit of pantomime concluded, Crusoe Jack proceeded to put in practice a device he had hit upon for her security.

He procured a ball of twine from the hut, gave her the end of it, and then took the other end back to the hut, and put it through a crevice at the back.

Thus there was a communication established between La-loo-hee-ah's bower and the stronghold.

She was quick and intelligent, and he had no difficulty in making her understand that, in case of any alarm, she was to pull the string, the other end of which being fastened to his arm would at once awaken him and bring him to her aid.

This done, these two weary people—the white man and the island maiden—retired to their respective couches, and slept the sleep of the weary.

CHAPTER XXXVIII.
THE FIELD OF DEATH.

THE sun had climbed to the zenith, and was again declining, when Crusoe awoke.

Nothing whatever had occurred during this time to alarm or disturb the two sleepers—the island maiden and the white man.

The latter, after a preliminary reconnoitre, removed the logs which barricaded the door, and went out.

All was still quiet

Save the distant murmur of the ocean and the rustling of the gentle breeze among the trees, no sound broke the universal silence which reigned.

It was pretty evident that, for the present, at least, the hostile savages had gone away, perhaps satisfied with the terrible lessons they had received, to return no more, but, perhaps, also, to devise another plan of attack, and come back with hordes of fresh savages.

However, the coast was now clear, and our hero proceeded to have a good wash, and, having performed his toilette, went out to the front of the fence.

And there, as a foil to the lovely scene on which the glorious sun shone down, was the ghastly field of death.

Already thousands of flies had begun to congregate. a strange species of bird was seen—a sort of carrion crow—doubtless attracted, with the keen sense of smell all the vulture tribe possess, by the scent of blood.

Crusoe turned away in horror and disgust, and again he communed with himself as he walked slowly up to the leafy bower where the island princess still reposed.

"And this was all my work! It has been my unfortunate fate to transform this lovely scene—this island paradise—into a place of death and horror. I could not help it, unless I chose to throw away my own life, or deliver up the unhappy girl under my protection to certain death. The first, by all the laws of God and man, I could not be expected to do; and the other alternative—giving up the girl to her enemies—honour and manhood alike forbade. No. What I have done was forced upon me; and though I may deeply regret, I cannot reproach myself, and, under the same circumstances, should so act again."

One thing, however, was at once apparent to him. It was absolutely necessary to remove the dead bodies, and that without an hour's delay.

So he proceeded to the shady retreat of the girl, in order to awaken her.

He walked softly up to the entrance, and noiselessly removed the bough which, standing upright, served as a door.

She still slept, and, despite the rough treatment, terror, and anguish both of mind and body, looked very beautiful in the green-tinted light which came through the plaintain leaves, having a softening effect, and partly hiding the marks of wounds, bruises, and scratches, stains of blood, and powder-smoke on the fair body of La-loo-hee-ah.

He called her by her name, and in a second she was awake and on her feet.

She seemed much refreshed by the sleep she had enjoyed, and he was glad to see that the inflammation of the wounded ankle was nearly all gone.

In fact, she was now able to walk almost without limping, so beneficial had been the effect of the bathing with cold spring water in the early morning.

Crusoe went and fetched her plenty of fresh spring water, and then, with the true instincts of a gentleman, left her to perform the task, which, in good truth, was a very easy and simple one.

Meanwhile he passed the time in striking out a plan for the removal and burial of the dead bodies.

The sandy beach would, of course, be the best place to bury these slain savages, as it would be so much easier to dig a big grave there than up on the higher ground, where there were rocks, stones, and boulders to be encountered.

But that was half a mile distant, and how were the corpses to be conveyed there?

He knew that, as a matter of physical strength, he could carry them down to the sea-shore one by one; but he revolted, shudderingly, from such a thought.

Who, indeed, would like to undertake such a horrible task?

At last he hit on the plan of constructing a rough sort of truck or waggon, on which he could place a number at once, and without trouble drag it down the incline to the sea beach.

He saw that the construction of this vehicle, however roughly it were done, would occupy him the whole of the day, even if he could accomplish it before dark at all.

However, after partaking of a simple though late breakfast, he at once went to work to make this, his first wheeled vehicle of any kind—a hearse it might be called.

For axles he took two long crowbars which had been left him by the captain of the Yankee whaler, and on these he proceeded to construct his waggon, La-loo-hee-ah watching him all the while with wondering curiosity, and doubtless puzzling her savage brain as to what strange machine the white man was now employed in constructing.

All the while she eagerly watched every opportunity of assisting him, and to her quickness in handing tools, nails, and such things, really rendered the job both easier and shorter.

Of course, he could not make regular wheels, but four "slices," as it were, of a large tree cut across, and about half a foot wide, would serve the purpose very well.

A few planks secured together, with another plank edge-up to form the sides, completed this primitive vehicle; and he found to his satisfaction that he could drag it along with tolerable ease on level ground, without a load. And as the land from where the bodies lay, sloped all the way down to the sea, he doubted not that he should easily be able to do so when laden to the utmost of its capacity.

He had finished the work just about sundown, and then he and his companion repaired to the hut to take some supper; after which, Crusoe determined to set to work again and complete his task that very night—convey all the bodies to the shore, dig a large pit, and bury them.

And this, after a hard day's work, and the fatigues, excitement, and dangers of the previous night!

He did not consider it safe to light a fire outside the hut, for though they had neither seen nor heard anything of their savage foemen, they might at any time return, and, lurking about in the darkness, seize a favourable opportunity of driving an arrow into his body. And what better chance could they wish for than see him sitting outside the hut in the full glare of the firelight?

So he made himself a pot of tea—this, with a little salt-fish and bread-fruit, formed his simple repast.

As for La-loo-hee-ah she would touch nothing but bread-fruit and biscuit, to which, strange to say, she seemed to take a fancy.

It is probably the simple healthy vegetable diet of the South Sea Islanders, which renders their skins so clear and smooth, their teeth so marvellously white, their health so good, and and last, not least, amongst savage tribes always quarrelling amongst each other, wounds on their bodies, even the most dreadful gashes, (when no vital part has been injured or artery cut), so easy to heal.

Cold water and certain leaves, which they believe to have wonderful healing powers, are the sole means in use amongst the South Sea Islanders.

The meal finished, Crusoe went forth to commence his dismal and dreadful night's work.

With a large shovel over his shoulder, his double-barrelled carbine slung over his back, and revolver in belt, he made his way to the field, where lay the dead bodies of the victims of last night's fight.

CHAPTER XXXIX.
A DISAGREEABLE TASK.

CRUSOE JACK took no lantern or lamp of any kind, and the pale, uncertain light of the moon, struggling through a cloudy sky, was all he had to guide him.

It was a horrible task, and again and again his very soul revolted at it; but still he stuck to it manfully, and soon had placed ten corpses on the rude conveyance.

Then he commenced his first journey down the hill with what might fairly be called the "waggon of death."

Arrived on the sandy beach, he at once commenced to dig a pit a considerable distance beyond high-water mark.

This was a task requiring some time, but by no means difficult, for the sand was soft and easily shovelled out.

It occupied him about two hours, and then having deposited one by one the ghastly burden of his death-cart, he had to think of dragging i up again.

This was task which, as he feared, was slightly beyond his strength, and although he strained his very hardest, he was compelled to fire off his pistol, a pre-arranged signal, on hearing which La-loo-hee-ah was to make her way towards him.

To his great surprise and delight, he had very little difficulty in making her understand this; his slight knowledge of the general dialect of the South Sea Islanders being of great assistance to him with this intelligent girl, who was as eager as she was clever in making out his meaning.

He had not long to wait when he heard the musical cry, "La-loo-hee-ah," as she drew nearer, and, replying to it, she was soon by his side.

With natural aversion she shuddered and turned away from the dreadful pit, but willingly joined him at the rope to drag the waggon up the hill again.

Her aid, weak woman as she was, proved sufficient to turn the scale in his favour, and, after half-an-hour's hard work, they were once again at the clearing on Flagstaff Hill.

Two more such dismal journeys our hero performed alone. The girl came to his aid to drag the empty waggon up the hill the first time, and then he dismissed her, bidding her by words and signs to go and barricade herself in the hut, and sleep, or at least rest, until he returned.

For of course, having taken down his last ghastly load, he need not trouble himself to drag the "death-waggon" up again.

The grey light of dawn had already appeared in the east when he had finished his dreadful task, and filled in the sand over the bodies of his slain foes.

None but a young and vigorous man of strong constitution, iron nerve, and great courage and determination could have got through a night's work at once so horrible and so laborious, and it was with feelings of intense relief that Crusoe plunged into the sea, clothes and all, to wash himself free from the loathsome contamination he could not help receiving in handling and pulling about the bodies of men slain in such a manner as were these unfortunates, whose funeral mound of sand now marked their last resting-place.

When he emerged from the sea, all wet and dripping as he was, Crusoe Jack kneeled, and by the side of the great grave where lay his slain foes he returned thanks to the Supreme Being for the mercy hitherto vouchsafed to him, and prayed fervently for further help and guidance.

For our hero, though he had nothing of the Pharisee or the canting, uncharitable Puritan—though not perhaps even a good man, in the strict religious sense of the word—was not either cruel or wicked, and felt deeply the terrible necessity which had compelled him on two occasions—now on this island, and before, during the terrible mutiny of the Thunder—to take the lives of his fellow-men.

When he got back to the hut, weary and utterly worn-out with his terrible day and night's work, it was broad daylight.

La-loo-hee-ah was half sitting, half reclining outside, and as he approached, he could tell there was something the matter. Her face was turned on one side, her head leaning against the logs at the front of the hut, and, with one hand, she partly covered her face.

A sort of twitching of the features, and occasionally little starts, accompanied by sharp cries which she vainly endeavoured to stifle, proved that she was suffering acute pain.

He asked her where she suffered pain, and she pointed to her foot which was covered over with the sheet of white fabric, or tapa, which, by its softness and delicacy, had so surprised Crusoe.

He gently removed the covering, and then perceived that the injured ankle was terribly swollen.

The skin was red and shining, and, placing his hand on it, he found it was quite hot.

He at once mixed an opiate, and gave it to the girl, who drank it readily and thankfully. Also he placed rags, wetted with water and laudanum, on the foot and ankle, and then went off to procure a bucket of cold spring water, which, heretofore, had proved such an excellent remedy.

"Poor child!" he said to himself, as he made his way to the spring. "She strained the wounded ankle again in helping me to drag the waggon up-hill. I was loth to call for her assistance; but it was absolutely necessary—impossible to do without her aid. She must have suffered intensely; but brave girl that she is, she did not utter a cry or a moan."

Assiduous bathing with cold water, and the soothing effect of the opiate combined, soon reduced the inflammation and eased her pain; but still she was quite unable to use the wounded ankle—indeed, to put it to the ground even.

CHAPTER XL.

THE ISLAND MAIDEN FINDS AN APT PUPIL IN CRUSOE.

CRUSOE knew that the sun's rays would soon stream down with scorching heat; and, thinking it best for her to rest under his immediate eye, he explained this to her, and carrying her inside the hut, laid her down on the sheet of bark which formed the couch.

Having given her food and water—she could drink nothing else—he left her to rest, which, with plenty of cold water and time, he knew would be the best cure for her wounds.

Then he slung his telescope over his back, took his carbine in hand, and started for the highest point of the island, the lion's crown.

On his road there he mounted the gigantic palm, which in some respects was better as a look-out place than the other.

Neither from here nor from the highest peak of all could he discover any signs of the savages, or, indeed, of life of any sort, and it was with a sigh of relief he said to himself, as he turned his footsteps back towards the hut—

"Thank Heaven they are gone for good! It has been a terrible time; but by the good fortune and hard fighting, I have succeeded in beating off the savage horde. They have taken their departure, to return no more; and now—now I can turn my attention to the wreck of the Thunder and the sunken treasure.

*   *   *   *   *

"After a storm there comes a calm" is an old saying which now, in the case of Crusoe on Lion Island, was verified.

We will not dwell very much on the quiet time which succeeded the days of desperate excitement since the landing of the savages, but briefly chronicle how affairs progressed, and the steps he took for carrying out his great design—the recovery of the sunken treasure.

As time passed on, the tremendous difficulty of the task he had set himself grew more and more apparent every day. Obstacle after obstacle appeared to him, if not actually present, yet hovering in the future.

In the course of a week he had completely marked out by a series of buoys the exact position of the wreck, and had taken and marked them down on a chart of the reef and surrounding sea.

This done, there remained now the most difficult part of the work before him.

He knew where the wreck lay, and the exact position of every part of her. He even knew very nearly exactly the spot where were the boxes of gold.

But to get at them—that was the question.

They lay fathoms deep beneath the surface, probably smothered up with broken timber planks, cargo, rocks, sands, and all the *débris* of the wreck of a large ship.

There lay the gold somewhere in the after part of the wreck of the Thunder.

When the sea was smooth, he could actually see the outline of the vessel, although fathoms deep, and could plainly make out the stump of the mizzenmast, the cabin sky-light, and the after hatch.

Yes, there lay the gold!

But how to get at it; that was the question, a most momentous one and requiring long and careful consideration, and patient thought—as well as unflagging energy and resolute hard work.

After having buoyed the wreck, Crusoe desisted for a time from further efforts in that direction, until he had devised and matured some plan, even to the minutest details.

But he had the good sense to see that the most brilliant idea might prove an utter failure through neglecting some little precaution or act.

Just as the most valuable chronometer is rendered utterly useless if only one of the smallest and most insignificant wheels is removed or injured.

Though his thoughts were principally occupied in devising a plan of operations, he found time to pick up a great deal of the language spoken by La-loo-hee-ah, and in the course of a week could converse with her with tolerable ease.

The wound on her arm quickly healed, whilst the ankle, which was really the more serious of the two, was also nearly quite well, and she could walk about without showing any lameness.

Crusoe had now given up entirely his idea of proposing to her to make her escape from the island in her canoe.

Indeed, she was so extremely useful, so quick, willing and intelligent, that he would have missed her very much.

In fact, he had grown not only accustomed to her, but actually attached to her; not in the romantic love sense of the word, he said to himself, but as he might to a beautiful and faithful animal, such as a gazelle or fawn.

The thought of being again left alone in utter solitude on this island, beautiful and fertile as it was, was extremely repugnant to him.

Once he asked her if ever she intended returning to her own people, and she replied in a significant manner.

Pointing to the sun, she waved her hand from the east, where he rose, to the west, where he sank in the sea. Then she held up her two hands three times, and he understood that she would not return to her people until after the sun had risen and set thirty times.

He did not clearly understand whether she meant thirty days from the present time, or from when she landed on the island.

As has been said, he was able to converse with her with tolerable ease, and every day—every hour, added to his knowledge of the language.

His previous experiences on a trading voyage amongst the southern groups of islands proved a great help: for, always quick at picking up foreign words and idioms, he had acquired a rude outline of the language common, more or less, to all the Pacific islands.

It is true that there were great differences in dialect, so much so that the people of one group could not understand those of another; but, nevertheless, there was a sort of general similarity, and many of the principal words were the same, only differently pronounced, or with some little variation.

The vocabulary left him by the Yankee captain of words in common use, which he had learned in his many scores of visits to the islands during his seafaring life of more than thirty years, was also extremely useful to him.

The girl was exceedingly quick and intelligent; and, having learnt a great number of the principal verbs and adjectives, it was an easy matter to increase his knowledge of substantives. Even if it were not something, he could point to such as a tree, a stone, a cocoa-nut, and so forth; he was able generally to make her understand, she, on her part being most anxious to gather his meaning.

For instance, he wanted to know the word in her language which answers to our "enemy," He first said the word in English, and she repeated it after him. Then, taking her javelin, he threw himself into an attitude, and, looking as fierce as possible, seemed about to hurl the spear at her.

After looking grave for a moment, her face suddenly brightened up as she caught his meaning, and she gave the required word "Vetango," repeating it again and again with great glee.

And then by easy steps he became proficient; the soft melodious tongue, redundant with vowels spoken by the Island Princess, as he called her at first in fun, though he soon discovered that such in fact she really was, being the daughter of a king or great chief, who ruled over a large island and a group of smaller ones away towards the western horizon.

He did not press her much for her history, and the reasons which brought her to this island to play such extraordinary pranks with him, first terrifying him by shooting arrows at him, and then doing all she could to aid him when he was taken with the fever, for she seemed averse to speak on the subject; and on one occasion, pointing to the sun, let her hand fall gracefully towards the west three times.

"Ah," he said, "she will not speak upon the subject until after three days."

After she had signified this to him, he observed that she took from her girdle a small article, it seemed to be of the same white ivory material as that of which her javelin was made.

Also she produced a little bright shining object, and with this she commenced carefully marking the little white stick.

He watched her with great anxiety and presently said—

"What is that you have there?"

She looked up, and, with a smile, handed it to him.

He saw that it was a plain piece of ivory, about four inches long and half an inch broad, the ends rounded, and a hole bored in each.

It was not unlike a very small paper knife,

and the blades on each side were about as sharp.

On one were a considerable number of notches, from fifteen to twenty, he guessed, for he did not trouble to count, and on the other, one only.

When he asked her for an explanation, she laid her finger on the side with the notches, and said the word Soremo (the sun); and then, doing the same on the other side, she said, Matalona (the moon).

Crusoe Jack now understood.

This was her calendar, her diary, by which means she kept account of the days and lunar months.

And looking at the number of notches on the one side of the stick, he judged it represented the number of days either since she left her own island home, or since she landed on this island of his.

He now felt anxious for the expiration of the three days, after which time he intended again to press her for some account of herself.

And, meanwhile, he occupied himself in picking up more and more of the language; for the more he thought of it, the more difficult, almost hopeless, seemed the task of recovering the treasure alone and unaided.

And who could say that, knowing their tongue, and backed by La-loo-hee-ah (on whom he felt sure he could depend), he might not gain such influence over her people as to induce them to come and work for him at the recovery of the wreck?

It was a grand idea; and the more he thought of it, the more it impressed him, until he was inclined to cry, like Archimedes of old, " Eureka !"

CHAPTER XLI.
CRUSOE TRIES HIS SKILL AT CIVILISATION.

NOTWITHSTANDING the faultlessly graceful form of this island beauty, and the artless innocence with which she moved about, with scarce any covering above the waist—thinking no harm, and therefore knowing no shame—our hero felt a good deal embarrassed sometimes.

He had prevailed on her to wear as a cloak some fine white calico, two breadths of which he himself stitched together for her; but when he tried to persuade her to put it on, and wear one of his shirts, he found the task utterly impossible.

At his urgent request she put it on, and he helped her to tuck it inside her girdle.

Then she looked down at herself, and, bursting into an immoderate fit of laughter, she tore it after a few moments.

She knew that it did not become her, that the stiff clumsy folds of the calico were not nearly so graceful as the elegant flowing lines of her own matchless person.

But though she could not consent to make herself look hideous by such an incongruous mixture of sailor's shirt above the slight and rather scanty, but still very pretty, tunic, a skirt she wore attached to her girdle, and which did not come near her knees, she gave way to his wishes so far as to wear a sort of shawl or scarf of calico over her shoulders.

As he designed it, this peculiar garment would have completely enveloped her like a cloak; but to this Miss La-loo-hee-ah would not agree.

She cut it down, altered its shape, turned and twisted it about, and finally it came out of her hands a sort of scarf, which she wore in a graceful fashion enough across one shoulder, much in the same manner as an officer wears his silk sash over his uniform.

The young lady, however, who was by this time on excellent terms with Crusoe Jack, having lost all fear and shyness, did not half like it, she pouted and made faces, and pretended, by dumb show, that she would tear it to pieces; but after a great deal of persuasion she consented to wear it; even this scanty covering seeming an intolerable nuisance to this child of nature, who had seldom worn anything over her shoulders, except sometimes a sort of cloak of the soft white material before spoken of, and this only to shield her from the sun.

She had, too, an awkward habit, of which he could not cure her.

Did this calico scarf get in her way in the least bit?

If she wanted to hasten anywhere, off it came instantly, without the slightest hesitation.

Crusoe at one time thought of making her a regular dress, but soon relinquished the idea as utterly hopeless.

Quick, gentle, and intelligent, this wild, untutored, beautiful savage maiden would, he felt convinced, never submit to the trammels of civilisation as regarded dress, or anything of that kind.

He felt certain that he could teach her almost anything which an English girl could learn, so willing was she. and, moreover, clever —her answers to questions (when she understood what he meant thoroughly) being often so shrewd as quite to astonish him.

The more he saw of her, the better he became acquainted with her, the more he felt attracted towards this wayward and beautiful savage maiden.

Agile as a chamois, graceful and tender as a gazelle, with a face the features of which were he thought absolutely perfect in their regular beauty, and, withal, full of expression; eyes which laughed and sparkled, or flashed and gleamed with each changing emotion—he compared this wild island beauty with city belles he had seen, and could not but own that La-loo-hee-ah had infinitely the best of it.

CHAPTER XLII.
LA-LOO-HEE-AH'S NARRATIVE.

LA-LOO-HEE-AH wanted no persuasion to tell all she knew of herself and people. Of course, having only a very cursory knowledge of the language, Crusoe Jack was often compelled to interrupt her, and get her to explain her meaning.

But these little pauses in the narrative were advantageous rather than otherwise, serving as breaks, lightening up and relieving the monotony of one person's speaking continuously.

Crusoe had constructed outside the hut a sort of rustic arbour or portico.

This, consisting of the tender branches of young trees interwoven together, and covered at the top and sides with the leaves of the cocoa palm, and the bread-fruit tree, formed an agreeable shelter from the scorching rays of the sun, and, adding greatly to the appearance of the hut fortress, by no means detracted from the strength of the position.

The day had been intensely hot—so much so that our hero, who, even while revolving in his mind plans for the future, liked to be doing something, was forced to desist from even playing at work in the little garden he had fenced in.

Strolling down to the beach, he stripped and plunged into the waters of the lagoon, which were placid and smooth as a river, the reef effectually keeping off the swell of the sea.

After this grateful bath he retired to the shelter of the thicket which bordered the sandy beach, and took a mid-day siesta—in other words, went to sleep for a couple of hours.

This occurring day after day, and no work at the wreck going on, might seem to indicate laziness and flagging zeal on the part of the one-time second mate of the Thunder.

But such was not the case. Crusoe was well aware that it was useless to go blundering on like a bull at a gate, and that, above all things, system and a definite plan were necessary to success.

So, while as far as actual work was concerned, he was only pottering about in his own garden, making little improvements in the hut, reconnoitring, exploring the island, or catching fish in the bay, he was working out in his brain a scheme he had for recovering the gold from the wreck of the Thunder.

He proposed to gain his end by means of diving.

At first he thought of a diving bell, but afterwards came to the conclusion that such alone would be of little use, for it was not as though he had a smooth bottom to deal with. Of course there would be all sorts of irregularities about the wreck; and even if he could lower the diving bell on to a level part of the wreck, how could he get down the hold?

The answer to this came after a time.

By means of a diver's helmet, with tubes attached, and communicating with the diving bell, he hoped to be able to walk about freely among the crumbling timbers of the Thunder, and penetrate into the hold, so as to be able to get at the treasure.

Although he had not yet commenced the diving-bell, he had made plans and calculations, and decided what materials were necessary, ascertained that everything he might want could be obtained, thought about the piping for the tubes, and, indeed, in his mind provided for every possible contingency—at least, he thought so.

But, failing this plan, he had hatched another idea in his busy brain.

And a most extraordinary chicken it was—an audacious idea, if ever there was one.

It was no less than this—to construct a wall all round the wreck, a solid wall of rocks, coral, and earth, and clay, brought from the island—not sand, for that would very quickly be washed away.

He thought it possible to surround the wreck with a sea-wall—in fact, to build her into a dock, from which he could pump or bale the water.

This he well knew, even if practicable, would be a work of enormous labour, requiring hundreds of human toilers to carry it out.

He persuaded himself, however, that it was quite possible, and all he wanted was—a few hundred workmen!

Only a few hundred!

A modest requirement on his part, certainly —a solitary white man, on an island in the midst of the vast Pacific, and, were it not for the accidental presence of the girl, absolutely alone on Lion Island:

Surely the man must be mad!

How could he ever hope to procure the necessary labour?

And yet there was method in his madness.

Daily he saw, or thought he saw, a prospect of getting as many labourers as he required.

And this prospect, this hope which unfolded itself to him, was connected with the girl La-loo-hee-ah.

He thought it possible, probable even, that with her good will he might procure the aid of her people to carry out his great work—that which might almost be called the object of his life—the recovery of the treasure sunk to the bottom of the sea, and now lying amongst the broken and mouldering timbers, beams, and planks of the Thunder.

And, moreover, it occurred to him that if friendly savages, from their natural indolence, could not be prevailed upon to undertake the task, hostile savages might be subdued and compelled to toil at his bidding, as did the Israelites of old under the yoke of their hard taskmasters, the Egyptians.

Hence the reason why he was so anxious to hear the history of La-loo-hee-ah.

He wished to know the nature, disposition, and numbers of her people, whether they were brave and warlike, as undoubtedly the savages he had just succeeded in beating off were, or indolent and effeminate, as he knew to be the case amongst many of the groups of Polynesian Islands.

He was of opinion, from words she let drop, that her people were brave and warlike, and had a sort of standing enmity or feud against another tribe, to which he guessed the savages he had so signally defeated belonged.

It was, therefore, with great satisfaction that he seated himself by the side of the island maiden, under the shelter of the rustic portico he had built outside the hut, and prepared to listen to her story.

After pondering for a few moments, with cast-down eyes, she commenced all at once.

"I am the daughter of a king, the sister of a great chief. The kingdom of my father, the home of my people, is away yonder, under the setting sun."

These opening words she spoke with an air of noble pride fitly becoming a king's daughter.

At the words "setting sun" she arose, and standing in a most picturesque attitude, pointed with outstretched arm to the westward.

Crusoe was a practical man, and had a definite object in view, so though he could not but admire the lovely living statue standing before him in such a grand attitude, graceful, natural, and unstudied, he asked—

"How far towards the setting sun is the kingdom of your father?"

"Talanaki sango fah lah"—literally : Canoe sun—from rising to setting.

This he at once understood to mean that it was a canoe's voyage from the rising to the setting of the sun—that is to say, about twelve hours.

And allowing from five to six miles an hour for the speed of the canoe, which was quite sufficient, he calculated that the island of which she spoke was about sixty miles to the westward.

He had not yet been able to get over the difficulty of enumeration with her. Up to ten or twenty she was clear enough, but he strongly suspected that in her language there really was no word to express a number beyond twenty.

"How many people are there in your father's kingdom?" he asked.

She lifted up her hand and cried—

"Oh! nuee! nuee! nuee!" which meant, in English, plenty—a great number; and this was all the information our hero was able to obtain on the point; and he then discovered that there was no word to express any number beyond twenty, and that if forty had to be signified, it could only be done by saying the word which represented twenty twice over.

"Are there as many people in your kingdom as in that of the savages who made you prisoner, and would have killed you?"

"Ah, nargo! (no), those bad fellows plenty—plenty—plenty—plenty, many times more plenty."

She said this in her own language, of course, but the rough and literal translation given best expresses the manner of her speech.

"But our fellows—rabah, nuee rabah omani (fine, brave warriors)—soon make them fly back to their own place on the edge of the world."

It was some time before Crusoe could make head or tail of this. At last, however, he succeeded, and elicited from her that the islands occupied by the other tribes were situated right at the edge of the world, which, as all savage nations believe, is a flat expanse of water and sea.

Indeed, Crusoe was informed, to his no little amusement, that this edge was crumbling away, and that already some of his enemies' islands farthest to the west had been destroyed.

Hence she explained their inveterate hostility, and continued desperate assaults on her people.

"So long since I little, little child, once every three, four moon Talanaki omani (Talanaki warriors) come plenty, plenty Talanaki warriors."

Talanaki was, he ascertained, the name of the principal island, where dwelt the ruler of Talanaki and the neighbouring islands—a bloodthirsty, cruel, and warlike tyrant, known as King Junga.

Her father, who ruled the rich and fertile group of which the large island of Huanita was the principal, was called Akah Malatieta (King Malatieta), and her brother—a great chief and warrior, she explained, with just pride—was called Malatieta Nina (Prince Malatieta).

"And you—what is your royal title?" asked Crusoe, smiling.

"Faler-a La-loo-hee-ah," she replied, the words gliding off her tongue in the most charmingly soft and melodious manner.

"And what caused you to leave your own country, where you had your father and brother and troops of friends around you, to venture alone in a light canoe on a voyage to this place?"

She thought some time before she replied, puzzled, probably, how to make him thoroughly understand her meaning.

"Many, many suns ago—more suns than there are shells on the shore or fish in the sea—there was a great chief of our people. He was amani akah and kadodo."

The first two words signified warrior and king; but the third it is more difficult to translate—sacred man or holy man is perhaps the nearest to it in English.

Crusoe having understood this, she went on—

"He was killed in battle with the enemy; but before he died he laid his last commands on his son, who would be king after him, and promising, if these his dying wishes were complied with, to be present always and fight for our people in all their battles. For though his body was dead, his spirit would be alive for ever and ever to strike terror into the hearts of the foe."

"And what were the commands of the dying king?" asked Crusoe.

"He ordered that he should be buried in the island nearest to the rising sun."

"That is this one," said Crusoe, "on which we now are?"

She bowed her head in token of assent, and went on—

"He gave instructions that a monument of great stone should be built, and at the top of this his body should be laid in an open tomb, his royal crown at his head, his weapons of war by his side. The monument was to be square at the bottom, tapering to the top—like this."

And to illustrate her meaning, she placed the tips of her fingers together, keeping the palms of her hands asunder, so as to form the two sides of a pyramid.

Crusoe, however, did not require this to understand what she meant, for he recognised by her description the strange monument, with the skeleton in the sarcophagus at the top, which he had himself discovered and explored.

He was about to say so, but checked himself, and was afterwards glad he did so.

"The monument was built of enormous stones, and the body of the great king laid thereon, according to his wishes. It was also his command that either the King of Huanita, or whoever might be reigning at the time, or his son, or daughter should spend one moon in every twelve on this island where is the monument, and should three times ascend to the top, and place flowers of the cactus, a sacred plant, at the head of the remains of the dead kadodo and king—once on the day of landing, once before the noon should have passed, and once on the day of leaving.

"On those conditions the great king promised ever to be present when our people went forth to battle, and, though unseen, to discomfit and defeat the enemy."

She paused for a moment, and then said, silently—

"He has kept his word. Always have we beaten off the enemy, though they had ten warriors to our one. On many occasions our people have seen the spirit of the great king and kadodo seated on a cloud above the strife, and hurling spears and javelins into the enemies' ranks, who invariably fled when this took place."

"But will it no do," asked Crusoe, "for any one else but one of your royal family to spend a month on this island, and visit the tomb of your royal ancestor?"

"No, no, no!" she cried, shaking her head, vehemently. "I had forgotten to mention another, the last solemn charge he laid upon his son before he died—that no person whatever, save one of his descendants of royal blood— king, prince, or princess—should ever visit his monument. He caused his son to swear, on behalf of himself and his warriors for ever, that any person, be he who he might (save a member of the royal family) who should dare to intrude on the solemn privacy of his last sleep, should be punished with death, and that the penalty should be inflicted as early as possible within view of the monument."

Thought Crusoe to himself—"It seems, then, that I have incurred this death penalty."

He thought first of telling her that he had broken through this solemn charge of the dead king; but, on consideration, held his tongue on the subject, observing with what solemnity and awe she spoke on the subject.

"And where is this monument situated?" he asked—well knowing all the time.

"Do not seek to know," she replied, gravely. "It is best you should not. You might be tempted by curiosity, and you know the penalty is death; for even if my people did not discover you, the spirit of the great king would himself slay you in vengeance of the insult."

"The deuce he will!" said Crusoe to himself, with a half smile. "I reckon I'd better give the ancient monument a wide berth for the future, or I shall have old grisly bones jumping up and hitting me on the head with his royal war club."

He resolved to leave the completion of La-loo-hee-ah's story for the morrow, as what she had already told him furnished him with ample material for thought.

CHAPTER XLIII.

THE ISLAND MAIDEN GRATIFIES CRUSOE'S CURIOSITY ABOUT THE STRANGE METAL.

THE following day passed much as usual. At early dawn Crusoe ascended to the Lion's Crown, and thence, scanning the sea with his telescope, ascertained that there was nothing in sight.

This he did three and sometimes four times, the girl, however, who thoroughly understood his motives, sometimes making the ascent in his place.

His reason was a very simple and satisfactory one. If, when he looked out first, shortly after sunrise, there was nothing in sight, it was quite certain that a fleet of canoes coming from the direction of the islands to the west could not reach Lion Island under about six hours, and as before that time had elapsed he could again take a look-out. it was impossible for him to be taken by surprise.

The last thing in the evening, too, whilst La-loo-hee-ah was preparing supper (she had quite fallen into his ways, and, although she herself would partake of nothing but the vegetable diet to which she was accustomed, she cooked admirably for him), he would again make the ascent, and assure himself that there was nothing in sight.

Such being the case, he knew he was safe till the morning, for he had learned from La-loo-hee-ah that both the hostile savages and her own people had the greatest horror of trusting themselves on the water by night—in fact, nothing could induce them to make a night voyage.

After he had despatched his simple supper of biscuit and fresh fish (La-loo-hee-ah had caught some in the lagoon on that day, with a little net of her own manufacture), he seated himself by her side, and she went on to give him further insight into her history and the habits and manners of her people.

Especially he felt great curiosity as to the glistening, heavy white metal, the strange white metal of which her javelin was made, and which looked and felt like the finest ivory, and the soft fabric of silky nature, a sort of scarf which she had over her shoulders when he first saw her.

The bright diadem of this metal which she wore had been lost or seized by the savages when they captured her. But there still remained the javelin, which was tipped with the same extraordinary substance.

And, although the fine, silk-like fabric had been torn to ribbons, there yet remained many scraps and pieces.

As regarded the latter, she had no difficulty in making him understand that it was the product of a plant growing much in the same way as the cotton tree.

About the mode of manufacture he did not stay even to inquire.

He could see that it was not woven, in the usual sense of the word, but seemed rather to consist of a very fine description of knitting—so fine, indeed, that it was almost impossible to distinguish the separate stitches.

And as for the ivory, he learned, as he expected, that it was of vegetable origin—being obtained from the topmost branches of a tree bearing as fruit a small nut of the pistachio species.

It was only the smaller branches on which were the nuts that had this ivory appearance and hardness.

The largest of these branches were about the thickness of her arm, she explained, and were sometimes ten or twelve feet in length.

These large specimens, however, were the exceptions, the ordinary size of the ivory branches being about an inch and a quarter in diameter, and four or five feet long.

Both this tree and the plant which bore the silk-like material were only to be found on one particular island, which was under the sway of the king, her father, Akah Mulatieta, and she was unable to explain to him its exact whereabouts.

Up to this point he was able clearly to gather her meaning; but when he proceeded to question her about the metal he had named Leonine, he could not, for a long time, even guess at her meaning.

She drew his attention to the fire, which

smouldered in front of the hut, and then proceeded to throw on some green branches.

This caused a dense smoke to arise, which appeared to be her intention, for she pointed to it, and said, again and again, the words—Sarkah ramo—the meaning of which he could not discover.

But, after considerable thought and uncertainty, he at last grasped what it was she wished to convey to him by the fire and smoke—a burning mountain—a volcano!

Soon he felt certain that he had arrived at her meaning, which he interpreted thus—

The white glistening metal was only found on a certain small island, where there was a burning mountain.

He gathered from her that it was found at the foot of this mountain in large lumps, and smaller pieces mixed with sand, and stones, and dirt.

The rough ore was first washed and then submitted to the action of fire, in the same way as iron ore is melted, only with, however, an important difference. To melt iron ore, costly furnaces provided with all the latest inventions to preserve intense heat, as the hot-air blast, &c., have to be erected.

But as he understood her, nature in the case of these savages provided the furnace, so that but little labour was required on their part to purify the ore in the first place, and afterwards to soften it and render it malleable, so that it could be applied to the various uses for which it was fitted.

The implements with which it was worked were of stone, both hammer and anvil.

The volcanic island where it was found was one of the group which her father, Akah Malatieta, ruled; but the hostile savages of Talanaki frequently made predatory incursions there, in order to provide themselves with this precious metal, with which they tipped their spears and arrows, and applied to many other uses for which no other substance was so applicable.

On the occasion of these incursions there was always fighting, and the enemy were usually beaten off after a hard struggle, notwithstanding their great numbers and ferocity.

But still it too often happened that they obtained a quantity of sapuloh, as this metal was called, which they took away with them, and so contrived to keep up a supply for weapons.

La-loo-hee-ah ascribed the victories of her people, and their success in holding Sapuloh Island against desperate and oft-repeated attacks, to the aid of the great king, who died ages ago, but whose spirit was still present, and fought for his people of Huanita.

Though by no means believing this, Crusoe did not think it worth while to cast any doubt on the subject, but accepting her theory sought to acquire all possible information he could.

As regarded the future, La-loo-hee-ah professed to have little or no fear.

The enemy had managed to elude the vigilance of her people, probably passing the island with their fleet of canoes in the night, notwithstanding the great aversion of all the islanders to venture to sea after dark.

But in returning she felt certain that they would be seen, attacked, and destroyed by the brave warriors of Huanita.

Crusoe asked how it was, such being the case, that her father's people did not come to see after her safety, and she replied that probably they were unaware that the enemy had visited Lion Island, and made her prisoner. And it would be only a matter of absolute necessity which would induce them to set foot on this sacred island, as, by doing so, they would break the solemn injunctions of the great kadodo, by which it was required that one of the royal family of Huanita should remain alone on the island for the stipulated time, and should alone visit the tomb.

If, as she believed, the enemy had been attacked and defeated, they would take to flight, and escape to their own islands if possible.

The dead could tell no tales, and as for any prisoners who might have fallen into the hands of the Huanitas, it was not to be supposed that they would incur certain death at the hands of their captors by avowing that they had seized and illtreated the king's daughter.

La-loo-hee-ah seemed to feel thoroughly satisfied that the enemy would return no more, but Crusoe was by no means so confident.

He thought from the persistent determination with which, in spite of defeat and disaster, they attacked him again and again, that possibly he had not seen the last of them yet, but that they would return in great numbers, and with a settled plan of attack, the result of their experience of his weapons and mode of warfare.

As a consequence of this misgiving on his part, Crusoe kept a vigilant look-out, never failing to ascend to the Lion's Crown, morning and evening, and carefully scanning the sea to the westward.

Day by day passed without any incident worthy of note, and with scarce anything to break the quiet monotony of life on Lion Island.

At sunrise, our hero was wont to start away for the high peak he called the Lion's Crown to reconnoitre.

On his return, La-loo-hee-ah would have breakfast ready, having quite fallen into his habits and cooking admirably.

And then, embarking in the boat which lay moored in the dock he constructed, he would, with his companion, go out to the wreck of the Thunder, where he would remain till near noon.

Then, during the heat of the day, he would return to the hut, and whilst La-loo-hee-ah indulged in a *siesta*, sheltered from the sun in her leafy bower, he would sit and work at what he had in hand.

This was the construction of a quantity of canvas hosing of about the diameter of two fingers. This was in connection with his plan for making a diving helmet and dress, for he knew that he must have tubes or piping of some sort in order to get fresh air for breathing, and also to discharge the foul air.

Then, in the afternoon, he would again go out to the wreck, and get on with the work.

After this, and while La-loo-hee-ah was boiling water for a pot of tea, he was wont to ascend to the high peak, and ere the sun sank beneath the horizon take a careful survey around.

And then back to supper, a pipe, a chat with La-loo-hee-ah—for now he could converse with tolerable ease in her language—and then to bed,

IN THE HOLD OF THE WRECK.

and then to rest—himself barricaded in the hut, choosing to sacrifice comfort to safety, while the girl sought her bower of branches and leaves at the back of the hut.

And so passed day after day in the same quiet, even monotonous manner—a veritable calm after the storm.

But though for the time leading a comparatively easy life, Crusoe made steady but sure progress towards the object in view.

He was never idle, mentally and physically, and when not actually at work with his hands his busy brain was ever planning and scheming.

CHAPTER XLIV.

ABOUT THE WRECK OF THE THUNDER, AND THE TREASURE SUNK THEREWITH.

IT is now time we quit, for a space, such stirring scenes and war's alarms, as those in the previous chapters, and see how fares the attempt of the bold adventurer, Crusoe, to recover the gold, and what are his chances of success.

The sunken vessel lay on the outside of the coral reef, which ran parallel with the shore at a distance of about a quarter of a mile, enclosing a space of calm water.

The coral reef, at low tide, just showed above the surface; but at high water it could only be made out by the white water, or foam, where the waves broke over it.

Now, Crusoe had carefully reconnoitred all round the wreck, and had marked out the exact portion of the hull by a series of buoys.

The water was very clear, and when the sea was smooth he was able even to see the wreck, though it lay fathoms deep.

It was not possible to get anything like a clear view; still, he was able to make out that sand, stones, and broken coral were gradually accumulating over and about the wreck; and it seemed but too probable that, by the slow and ceaseless heaving of the waves and flow of tide and currents, the hull of the sunken vessel, gold and all, would be completely covered with sand, rocks, stones, and coral.

This was a serious matter, as he well knew; for when once sand began to accumulate it was a most difficult task to stop the encroachment.

It has been said that the reef, in which lay the wreck of the Thunder, only showed above the surface at low tide, and even then every wave swept over it.

At other times it would be covered by water, and any one standing thereon would be often waist deep.

Now Crusoe saw the necessity of having a firm "standpoint" at all times, where he could land implements, tools, &c., and prosecute any operations he might have in hand.

Accordingly, for several days, he had been occupied in bringing out to the reef boatloads of rocks, of sufficient size to resist the wash of the waves by their own weight.

These he placed on the roof, carefully wedging in as many as he could between the inequalities of coral.

He thus made a rough wall around the edge, enclosing a space on the top of the reef about ten feet in width and twenty in length.

This done, he set to work and filled up the enclosed top of the reef with heavy rocks and stones, until he had constructed a sort of raised platform, which was a foot or so above water, even at high tide.

The reef was almost precipitous; and looking over the edge of this on the seaward face, he could, on a calm day, when there was little swell, plainly see the hull of the Thunder as she lay over on her beam, half covered with sand and sea drift.

Having completed this platform of rocks and stones, and so secured a firm and dry footing overlooking the wreck, he next bethought him of the best means to prevent the hull being further covered with sand.

The novel idea occurred to him of constructing all round the wreck a submarine wall, of sufficient strength and height to resist the wash of the waves, and keep back the encroaching sand, which threatened to engulph wreck and treasure.

Accordingly, he set to work on this at once, and very soon perceived that he had undertaken a long and most laborious task.

The first day he commenced on it, he took out to the wreck two boatloads of rocks and stones, and hove them into the sea close outside the wreck.

Again and again he repeated this, aided most efficiently by La-loo-hee-ah, who though but a slender girl, was for her sex and size strong and active as a panther.

She would assist him in loading the boat, and having done so, would accompany him in her own little canoe, which she managed with marvellous grace and skill.

Swifter and lighter than the heavily-laden boat, she would hover about him in her little craft, now darting ahead, now falling astern—now shooting up alongside, and keeping up an incessant fire of merry talk and laughter, which had the effect of cheering up his spirits and lightening the work.

Did he want anything from the shore?

Away would dart La-loo-hee-ah in her fleet little craft, and return with it in less time than he could accomplish half the distance in the heavy boat.

In the course of a day, he would take out and throw into the sea four boatloads of rocks and large stones, being careful always to select the heaviest sort, so that they should, by their weight, remain at the spot where they sank.

Two of these boatloads he would heave over at exactly the same spot. This would create a mound or heap of large stones at the bottom, plainly visible when the sea was calm.

Then a few feet distant, and on the line marked out by the buoys, he would throw over two more boatloads; and so on, again and again, until there was a line of six or seven heaps of stone, with small intervals between them.

Next he proceeded to fill up the gaps or openings by throwing over more boatloads of rocks, and gradually there was thus formed, at the bottom, a submarine wall about four feet high.

But it was very—very slow work.

After about ten days' hard work at this, during which he had thrown over about forty boatloads, quite eighty tons, of rock and stone, he found that the wall only extended to about twenty-five feet.

It was only about four feet in height, and his intention was to keep carrying rocks and heaving them over until the wall reached the surface, and extended all round the wreck, joining the reef at the head and stern.

The hull of the Thunder, when this was completed, would lie enclosed in an artificial dock, in shape like the letter D, the reef forming the straight part, and the half hoop consisting of the wall of rock and stone.

Of course he did not suppose that such a rough contrivance could be made water-tight without an amount of labour and appliances which it was impossible for him to furnish.

He knew that the water could penetrate through the crevices in the rough blocks of stone and rock as freely as though there were no wall there at all.

Thus the wreck could not be enclosed in a dry dock, but in a wet one.

The advantages, however, he expected to reap from this laborious and tedious work, were these:—

In the first place, he reckoned with reason that, though this wall would not keep out water, it would sand and sea-drift, so that the danger of the hull of the sunken vessel being overwhelmed and buried in the sand would be obviated.

And furthermore he knew that the wall, when complete, would ensure almost completely calm water in the space it enclosed.

This would be an inestimable advantage, for with the water smooth at the surface, it was possible to see the wreck, and as, moreover, the sheltering wall would also act as a break-water to the rolling swell of the Pacific, there would also be smooth water at the bottom.

For diving purposes this was an enormous advantage. Indeed, he felt sure that no diving operations could be successfully carried on unless there was almost a perfect calm, not only at the surface, but beneath.

The task before him was prodigious, but he did not shrink from it, nor feel in the least disheartened.

Ten days' hard labour had only completed from twenty-five to thirty feet of this subterranean wall, and that only about four feet high.

To enclose the wreck completely would require more than three hundred feet, probably about three hundred and fifty.

And that only to a height of about four feet.

Consequently, even at that low height he had accomplished less than a twelfth of the first part of his task. And as he had worked hard for ten days to do this much, it followed that even under the most favourable circumstances, supposing him not to be interrupted in any way, it would occupy him one hundred and twenty days, or four months, to construct a submarine stone and rock wall, four feet high, around the wreck.

And after that there loomed in the future the still more tremendous task of enlarging the wall, and bringing it up to and above the surface, from a depth of from three to four fathoms.

Such a prospect might well appal a stout heart, and would be no easy task to an engineer with a staff of workmen under him. Crusoe, however, was not in the least staggered or disheartened at the work which lay before him, but worked steadily on, day by day, increasing the wall.

He also occupied himself in sounding, practising diving, and exploring generally.

One morning an extraordinary incident occurred, breaking through the quiet monotony of his life, and giving rise to a tumult of strange thoughts and old memories.

CHAPTER XLV.

HONI SOIT QUI MAL Y PENSE.

CRUSOE found his time pretty well occupied with his reconnoitring excursions to the Lion's Crown twice a day, and loading and throwing overboard at the proper place several boatloads of rock and stone between sunset and sunrise.

And this was not all.

He was continually exploring the wreck, sounding with the hand lead, and so ascertaining the exact depth of every portion.

He was a good swimmer and soon became tolerably expert in diving, being able to remain under water for fully three quarters of a minute, sometimes nearly a minute at a stretch.

But in this respect he could not approach La-loo-hee-ah, who, like all the Pacific islanders,

seemed as much at home in the water as on dry land—in fact, almost a fish.

He himself, though he could remain under water for nearly a minute at a stretch, was not able to do much effective work. The pressure of the water and the painful effort of holding the breath rendered any prolonged exertion impossible.

The buoyancy of the water, too, was another difficulty; but this he overcame in an ingenious way.

He took an old pair of sea boots, and loaded them all over the feet and lower part of the legs with lead—about twenty pounds on each boot.

Before he descended he used to put these boots on, and then taking in hand the heavy deep-sea lead, leaving the line attached thereto in the care of La-loo-hee-ah, would leap overboard feet first.

The weight of the deep-sea lead and the loaded boots would quickly bring him to the bottom, and the lead about his feet would also serve to keep his body in an erect position.

Without this or some such contrivance it would have been almost impossible to keep steady at the bottom for even a few seconds, and quite impossible to walk at all.

It is only those who have had experience at a considerable depth who can form any idea of the strength and buoyant power of water, especially sea water.

The weights on the boots kept his feet down pretty well, but when it became necessary to use the hands, he had the greatest difficulty in stooping in order to do so.

After repeated excursions to the bottom and on to the wreck itself, remaining below each time about three quarters of a minute, he had arrived at a thorough knowledge of the position of the hull and the nature of the bottom all about. On the wreck itself there was a considerable amount of débris—stones, rocks, and broken spars, timber, &c.—partly covered with sand.

The hatchways were off, and stumbling along, awkwardly enough, he on one occasion found himself on the edge of the afterhatch, and looking down into the great dark cavity, he fancied he could distinguish certain portions of the cargo, behind and beneath which the boxes of gold were stored.

He felt almost tempted to venture himself within the dark cavern-like hold; but he had already been below nearly a minute, and holding his breath was becoming painful.

Besides, it would have been worse than imprudent, almost madness, to have done such a thing, inexperienced as he was, and with no means of getting a breath of fresh air.

So, after another eager, lingering, longing look into the dark profound, where lay the treasure he had made his mind up to reclaim, he slipped off the loaded boots—they were attached by a thin cord to the lead line, and he had so arranged as to be able to free himself from them instantly—and shot to the surface, coming up close to the canoe of La-loo-hee-ah, which lay moored a few feet from his boat.

She had been paddling about in great anxiety about him, frightened at the length of time he remained below—much longer than he had ever done before.

To his great surprise he found, on looking at his watch, when he regained the boat—for he always accurately noted the time before taking a plunge—that he had been under water for nearly two minutes.

Now this, for anyone but an experienced and hardy diver, was a tremendous feat.

Even the Ceylon pearl-divers seldom exceeded two minutes, although some, with extraordinary powers of endurance, had been known to remain under for five minutes.

Still, this he knew was quite out of the common way, and the man capable of doing it was regarded as a prodigy.

A pearl-diver who remains below a clear two minutes, and in that time fills his bag with oysters, was looked upon by his fellows as at the top of his profession.

This fact, of his having remained so long below without serious inconvenience, was very pleasing to Crusoe.

It satisfied him that he was improving rapidly by practice, and might hope to be, ere long, an accomplished diver.

Nevertheless, he did not fall into the error of self-deception.

At the very commencement of his diving experiences he had come to the conclusion that he could not hope to do anything effective without an apparatus of some kind, by which he might be supplied with air—either a diver's helmet, with tubes for inhaling fresh and expelling foul air, or a helmet and dress complete.

And, to reap the best advantage from this, it would be also necessary to have a diving bell, from which, lowered near the bottom, he could make prolonged excursions, returning, when necessary, for air, for tools, or any other purpose.

His present diving attempts he could only regard as advantageous, as serving the purpose of exploring and familiarising him with the wreck and its surroundings at the bottom of the sea.

This, and nothing more.

Before he could hope to recover the gold, he had many months of hard labour before him.

First, there was the heavy task of completing the sea wall around the wreck.

He dared not attempt to calculate the time this must occupy him—labouring alone, or at least aided only by his Island Princess.

And thinking on the latter point, what she had said concerning her stay on the island being only limited occurred to his mind, and he proceeded to question her on the subject.

Her reply was not at all satisfactory.

It seemed to him as though she had kept back something—was prevaricating, in fact.

She appeared grieved at the idea of leaving Lion Island, but would not make any promise, or, indeed, give him any idea of the time she would remain.

She seemed distressed and uneasy when he mentioned the subject, and endeavoured to draw his attention off.

On the particular occasion of the long dive she escaped from further questioning in a very peculiar way. This is what happened—

On coming to the surface, he swam to his boat and clambered in. Being a great deal exhausted—for let it be know that the work of the diver is terribly hard—he reclined in the stern sheets on the boat's sail, basking in the glorious sunshine which rapidly warmed his body, chilled by the cold water at the bottom, and also quickly dried his canvas trousers, the only thing in way of covering he wore when he made his submarine excursions.

La-loo-hee-ah paddled her little canoe up alongside his larger and clumsier boat, and, leaning over the gunwale, proceeded to fan his face, and brush away flies with a plantain leaf she carried.

All the while she kept murmuring words of admiration and praise at his skill in diving, sometimes breaking into a melodious chaunt, and ever and anon stopping, laughing, and clapping her hands in great glee. Indeed, it was a sort of song of triumph, which, with variations, suited for different occasions, she often favoured him with.

It was something in this style, though it is impossible to give it word for word—

"Great is the white king who came from the distant clouds. He slays his enemies, afar off with thunders and lightnings, brought from Heaven, his home. He is strong as a thousand men, and more beautiful than the handsome Sah-noo, the young chief of Tidoro. His heart knows not fear, and he is swift of foot as the wild antelope. He bravely rescues the daughter of the great king of Huanita—Falor-a-La-loo-hee-ah is her name, and she gratefully sings the praise of the white king. La-loo-hee-ah is his slave, and he shall be king of all the islands," &c.

He was now sufficiently versed in the language to understand most of what she said; and could not help smiling at her extravagant praise.

Nevertheless, he felt also gratified, for he knew that it was in all innocence, and came from her heart.

Well, to proceed.

After she had finished this laudatory hymn, or, perhaps we should say, rather when she considered she had favoured him with enough of it, he rose from his recumbent position, rested and refreshed.

It was about noon, and the sun was intensely hot; so he gave up all thought of serious work, for the next few hours, at all events.

So he proceeded to spread an awning he had fitted to the boat, and then proceeded, in a leisurely manner, to haul on the deep-sea lead line, wishing to pull up the lead and his loaded boots which were also attached to the line.

Now, it happened that when he let go the lead, when he arrived at the bottom, it sank down the open hatchway, near which he stood, into the hold; and there, by some means or other, had become jammed.

This did not trouble him greatly, and he continued jerking at the line, occasionally in a languid, indifferent sort of way.

However, La-loo-hee-ah, whose quick glance little escaped, noticed it.

Still lazily playing with the line, thinking that the jammed lead would shortly get clear, he proceeded to talk to La-loo-hee-ah on the subject of her stay on the island.

"La-loo-hee-ah—do you remember when last I asked you if you purposed to go back to your own people, and leave me here in solitude, you could not reply. If it must be so, I must submit; but I shall deeply feel the loss of my Island Princess."

La-loo-hee-ah looked to the right, to the left, down into the sea, and up into the blue sky: and was obviously grieved and embarrassed how to answer.

Tears stood in her gentle eyes, and presently she replied—

"Yes—yes. La-loo-hee-ah must go to her people; but she will return with many warriors, who will call the white king their chief. And they will bring prisoners they have taken from King Junga and his men; and they shall be the slaves of the white man, and he shall order them to work and build his wall under the sea. And the brother of La-loo-hee-ah, the young prince Malatieta Nina, shall be his brother, and the daughter of the great King Akah Malatieta, who is called Faler-a-La-loo-hee-ah, shall be his sister. And he shall be great and powerful amongst the islands, and all the people shall bow their heads when they see him. Yes, it shall be so; and the white king shall live for ever on the islands of the sea."

Now this, though a very liberal and generous programme, would hardly have suited Crusoe Jack, could it even have been carried out literally, and the gift of immortality bestowed on him the power of living for ever in this delightful climate, and amongst those lovely verdure-clad islands.

Such a prospect of long life and charming indolence might suit some people, but certainly not Crusoe Jack. So he proceeded to question her closer.

"But when do you propose to go to your people, La-loo-hee-ah?—and how?"

She made some reply, the meaning of which he was unable to gather, and he went on.

"And if you go, when shall you return?"

No answer to this.

"Ah! I see. You do not intend ever to return. When you go to your people, you will leave me for ever."

At this she seemed much distressed.

"Is it not so, La-loo-hee-ah?" he pursued.

"No! no! no!" she cried emphatically again and again; and, rising to her feet, leaned over and took in her hand the lead line.

This was obviously to divert his attention, and prevent him from questioning her further.

"Ah! you want the great weight gone to the bottom of the sea. La-loo-hee-ah will bring it."

Then, without any more words or hesitation, she proceeded to divest herself of the sort of scarf she wore, thrown over her shoulders, and not of this only, but also of the short skirt fastened around her waist.

Then, standing for a few moments in a state of perfect nature, her faultless form in nowise covered, save by the long luxuriant hair which fell over her shoulders, back and bosom, she raised her two hands aloft, and plunged into the sea.

Crusoe Jack was a little bit confused at this sudden proceeding on the part of the Island Princess.

Vainly had he tried to instil into her mind some of the ideas of civilisation as to the impropriety of divesting the body of clothing, at all events in his presence.

But all these lessons seemed to be in vain.

She would listen respectfully, and even with interest, and, apparently, would quite agree with all he said.

And indeed it would seem that she really intended to profit by his advice, and be more circumspect and modest, according to civilised notions.

But when it came to practice—when the effect of his lecture had to be put to the test—ah! then it was a different thing.

As in the present case, her savage nature and instincts seemed to overpower everything else.

To take to the water with any clothing on, seemed to the island maiden a most absurd proceeding, and so, innocent of all evil, she followed the custom of her people with regard to her water toilet.

Honi soit qui mal y pense!

CHAPTER XLVI.

CRUSOE JACK AND THE ISLAND MAIDEN VISIT THE WRECK OF THE THUNDER.

CRUSOE JACK seated himself on a thwart of the boat under the shade of the awning, and looked lazily out on the placid water.

It was a dead calm, and the sea was as smooth as possible—that is to say, there was nothing but the gentle and solemnly slow Pacific swell to disturb the level.

A half minute passed, and he began to look out for her re-appearance.

A minute.

This, however, did not disquiet him in any way, for he was well aware of her excellent qualities as a swimmer and diver.

But when a minute and a half passed and she did not re-appear, he began to grow a little uneasy, and his lazy, careless gaze, gave place to one of interest and expectation.

Two minutes!

He held the watch in his hand now, and looked at it anxiously every few seconds.

Two minutes and a quarter!

Not a ripple disturbed the calm surface of the sea.

Two minutes and a half!

He now pulled and jerked at the lead line in a state of great excitement.

The lead still remained fixed, and there was no giving—no yielding—to indicate that she had hold of the line.

"Great heavens!" he cried aloud, "some accident has befallen her. Perhaps she has struck against a portion of the wreck, or, maybe, the ground sharks have come over the barrier. I cannot let her perish thus, without an effort to save her."

He had now no loaded boots—no lead even to assist his descent—both were at the bottom of sea attached to the line.

However, this did not daunt him, or even delay him beyond a couple of seconds.

Seizing a "pig" of iron which lay at the bottom of the boat, to serve as ballast when there was no cargo in her, he jumped headforemost into the sea.

The weight of the iron dragged him down faster than was pleasant, but, nevertheless, he did not let go.

As fortune would have it, the boat, being moored loosely, had shifted slightly from her former position, and now lay right over the after-hatchway.

As a consequence, when he leaped into the sea holding the heavy iron pig in his hands, it dragged him down through the hatchway into the hold of the vessel before he knew where he was.

As he was swept down through the water by the weight of the iron he held in his hands, he was conscious of some object darting past him in an upward direction.

The rush of water and the darkness prevented him from forming a certain opinion as to the nature of the object; but he had a sort of vague idea that it was a huge fish.

Perhaps a shark!

The thought was by no means a pleasant one, and the instant his descent ceased, by reason of his being brought up by a quantity of sand and sea drifts, which had accumulated in the hull of the wreck, he let go the iron, and holding on to a piece of chain-cable his hand came in contact with, he glared around him, vainly endeavouring to penetrate the gloom.

The only light there was came through the hatchway, and this, dimmed by between twenty and thirty feet of water above, was very faint.

His rapid descent had been both painful and exhausting, and now the pressure of the water and inability to breathe were distressing in the extreme.

But, notwithstanding physical pain and danger, he would not attempt to make for the surface without endeavouring to ascertain the fate of La-loo-hee-ah.

Clenching his teeth firmly and compressing his lips, he checked the impulse that seized him to call upon La-loo-hee-ah, and which attempt would have been fatal to him.

This effort, added to the excitement, sent the blood flying to his brain, and it seemed as though his head was about to burst. In that moment his imagination conjured up all sorts of horrible visions. It seemed to him that he was not the only occupant of the dark hold of the wreck.

Hideous monsters flitted about him. In imagination a dark swarthy figure was there in search of the buried treasure, and a demoniacal, armless, hideous-looking object was driving him away.

Crusoe Jack could contain himself no longer, the suffocating sensation was too overpowering, he let go, and allowed himself to rise up through the hatchway, which was, fortunately, right above his head.

Here he held on for a short time, and looked around as well as he could.

But, though there was a better light, he was not able to discover any sight of the girl, and, finally, utterly unable to hold out any longer, he struck out for the surface, aiding his ascent by using his arms and legs.

Fortunately, he came up quite close to the boat, for he was utterly exhausted, and it was with the utmost difficulty he succeeded in getting on board.

This achieved, he lay down on the sail in the stern sheets, and was, for a short time, almost unconscious from the effects of fatigue, excitement, the want of air, and the great pressure of the water.

Blood flowed from his nose, mouth, and even ears; and when he recovered, he leant over the side to wash the crimson stains from his face.

It was not until some time afterwards that he could collect his faculties so as to remember exactly what had occurred; but when he did so, he gazed wildly around on the surface of the sea in the hope of discovering her.

He had only lain in a half-fainting state for a few seconds, and she had only plunged beneath the sea some few minutes previously, and yet it seemed to him hours.

Seeing nothing of her, he sank back with a groan of despairing grief.

"Lost! lost!" he murmured. "The cruel sharks have seized her, and torn her fair body to pieces!"

Just at that moment, however, as he lay back, conscious of his own inability to do anything further, his left hand touched something wet and cold lying on part of the sail spread over the stern sheets of the boat.

Looking, he saw, to his utter bewilderment, a small heap, about a couple of handfuls, of sand and small stones—but not sand and small stones only.

What were those bright shining particles of a rich yellow metallic hue?

He grasped some, and with frantic eagerness proceed to examine them.

"Gold! gold! gold!" he cried aloud, starting to his feet, and for the moment forgetting everything else—the probable death of La-loo-hee-ah, and scarce even thinking at first as to how the gold could have come there.

"Gold! gold! gold!" he again cried, in a sort of feverish ecstacy. "Yes! part of the treasure sunk in the Thunder!"

"This is the first instalment, only the first. I shall have it all yet—every ounce of it."

For the moment he was, in good truth, almost delirious. The excitement of the sudden discovery had really been too much for him after his previous exertion and suffering in diving.

But after a bit his sober common-sense came back to him, and he asked himself the obvious question—

"How did this come here?" A question to which he could find no answer.

There it was.

Gold!—several ounces of it. Of that there could be no doubt.

Another mystery!

A mystery connected with a terrible disaster —the death, by drowning or sharks, of his Island Princess, La-loo-hee-ah!

CHAPTER XLVII.

EXPLANATORY.

THE events just narrated occurred in a very brief space of time.

Probably less than three minutes had elapsed from the moment he took his plunge from the boat to his discovery of the gold and wet sand and gravel on the sail in the boat.

He was just beginning to collect his scattered thoughts, when another surprise burst upon him.

Nothing less than the girl, La-loo-hee-ah, herself.

Like a mermaid, her head and shoulders suddenly appeared above the surface, at some few yards from the boat.

Darting through the water like a fish or mermaid, she was quickly alongside the boat, apparently not in the least exhausted after her dive.

Shaking the hair from her face, and laughing merrily, she reached forth over the gunwale of the boat, and deposited on the sail, close to where lay what he had just discovered, another handful of sand, gravel, and small stones, mingled with bits of gold.

Then she swam off to her own canoe, and skilfully embarking in the frail craft, without upsetting it, donned her tunic and scarf, and then proceeded to paddle up alongside Crusoe.

What had occurred was briefly as follows :—

The girl, half seriously, half as a freak, had plunged down into the depths to release the lead, which had become fixed in some way.

Having some little difficulty, she remained beneath an inordinately long time.

Crusoe, after a while, became alarmed, and fearing some mishap had befallen her, dived to render her assistance, or, at all events, to ascertain, if possible, what had happened to her.

But as luck would have it, as he was plunging downward, dragged by the heavy piece of iron he held in his hands, she was shooting to the surface.

It was the swift rush of her ascending body as she swept past him, which he had mistaken for a huge fish—perhaps a shark.

When she reached the surface, she saw that he was not in the boat, nor anywhere in sight, and with quick perception knew that he had dived.

When she first dived, she went right down into the hold where the lead had sunk, and swimming about with perfect ease amongst the *débris* of the wreck, presently descried some sparkling yellow objects amongst the sand, which partly covered everything to the depth of half a foot or so.

Grasping a double handful, she rose to the surface, and deposited her prize in the boat, much wondering what these shining yellow particles could be.

Having thus placed them, she again dived—the idea occurring to her that it would be capital sport to puzzle him on his coming up by the fact of her not being to be seen.

In the meantime he came to the surface, and not finding her, was terribly dismayed, his worst fears being now confirmed.

It was just at this time, when he had resigned himself to despair of ever seeing the lovely companion of his solitude again, that he discovered the bits of gold on the sail.

When he had, in a measure, recovered from his surprise, he was able to account for this, and in a satisfactory way.

The real state of the case broke on his mind suddenly, and he knew now that during her dive she had fished up these particles of gold, and having come up to the surface while he was still below, she had placed her prize in the boat and again dived.

This was all plain enough, and the sight, and touch of the gold had an inspiriting and cheering effect upon him. He felt now as does the exhausted and storm-beaten mariner when the wished-for harbour is in sight.

He had actually seen part of the gold which went to the bottom in the Thunder.

In fact he might say that he had actually commenced his task, and had on that day recovered a portion of the treasure—at least Laloo-hee-ah had for him, and that was all the same.

Having done so much, it seemed to him that there was no reason at all why he should not carry out his purpose fully, and recover the whole of the treasure—less, perhaps, a small quantity which, like this, had been scattered from broken boxes.

There was a brilliant prospect before him, and he felt more hopeful than he had ever done before.

But he was destined once more to be sadly discouraged.

CHAPTER XLVIII.

ALONE !

On the morning after diving for the gold Laloo-hee-ah did not join him in the front of the hut, as was her wont; but, on leaving her own leafy abode, started off down the sloping ground to the sea beach.

At first Crusoe took no notice of this, but ere long he observed that the fire was not lighted, and he missed her graceful form flitting about preparing the morning meal, chattering and laughing pleasantly all the while.

He now felt the misery of utter solitude, and the thought occurred to him—

" She is offended at my taking so little notice of her. Her canoe is by the shore, perhaps she has embarked and sailed away."

This had the effect of fully awakening him to the knowledge of how useful—almost necessary, indeed—she had made herself to him, and how deeply he would feel her loss.

Indeed, now that it was presented to him, the prospect of being left to prosecute his task in utter solitude seemed to him terrible in the extreme.

Perhaps, had he never fallen across this wayward, bright-eyed, lovely savage, he would by this time have become accustomed to his solitary life.

She had come across his path like a gleam of sunshine, and like that also seemed to have warmed his heart, to have exhilarated his spirits, and made the great work before him appear pleasant and easy.

And now that he had for a time basked in the pleasant sunshine, it appeared to him it was to be withdrawn and succeeded by dark, heavy clouds—a great gloom.

As these thoughts passed through his mind, he rose and proceeded to the bower at the rear.

He did not expect to find her there, as he had seen her descend the slope; but a chill struck to his heart when he noticed that she had taken with her her bow and arrows, and her little javelin, and several other objects.

This seemed to indicate that she had not gone down to the beach merely to bathe, as he at first thought, or rather hoped, but had certainly started on some expedition or other.

He immediately turned his footsteps towards the landing-place, where, on the previous day, they had left both his boat and her canoe safely moored.

It was as he feared, and again he felt a bitter pang when he found that the canoe had disappeared.

He quickly embarked in the boat, and, setting the sail, steered out into the bay, thinking to see La-loo-hee-ah. But neither she nor the canoe was in sight, and that which was before but a vague surmise became now almost positive conviction.

"Yes, she is gone, he muttered, bitterly, "and I am again alone. Ill fortune bears on me with a heavy hand. Scarcely had I secured the companionship, the willing assistance, even as I thought the attachment, of this savage girl, than she takes to flight and leaves me."

Considering with what complete immunity and success he had passed through the most desperate perils, it was very unreasonable on his part to complain of fortune.

Rather should he have considered himself lucky in having been favoured by the cheerful company and active, intelligent assistance of the island maiden, to say nothing of the valuable information he had derived as to the group of islands to the west, also of the language.

Such, however, is too common a trait in human nature. Men at the least disappointment or check are apt to forget all past favours, and complain bitterly of their ill fortune.

Though Crusoe was not free from this weakness, he was not the man to give way to vain repining and inaction. Trimming the sail to the wind, he passed through the gap in the coral reef, and made a reach out to sea of a couple of miles, so as to command a long view of the coast. No sign, however, could he discover of the girl, and with a deep sigh he slacked off the sheet, and turned the boat's prow again towards the shore.

"Once more alone, again do I find myself left to prosecute my tremendous enterprise, without human aid, companionship, or sympathy."

Not without reason he was downcast and gloomy, but by no means gave way to despair.

Remembering that he had neglected this morning to ascend to the Lion's Crown for the purpose of a good look out on the sea and islands to the west, he slung his carbine across his shoulder, and started off.

The morning was an unusually lovely one even for that balmy climate, and he stood gazing long out on the splendid natural panorama spread before him.

The calm beauty of the scene had a soothing effect on his mind, and when he made his way back along the ridge to Flagstaff Point his previous depression and low spirits had subsided into a sort of gentle melancholy.

As he walked, not taking any particular heed of anything, his eye was several times attracted by the flash of glittering yellow amongst the foliage at the tops of the tall trees.

At first he was puzzled what to make of this, but presently looking more keenly, he discovered that these were birds of most bright and beautiful plumage.

They were only to be seen in the thickly timbered ground far down the slopes of the hill, and, though he watched the bright flashing yellow of their plumage as they darted from tree to tree with a sort of quiet pleasure, he was altogether disinclined to make a nearer approach so as to ascertain what description of bird it was.

"A new species of bird," he said to himself, "for certainly I have never seen any with such gorgeously coloured plumage hitherto."

However, he did not trouble himself on this point, but made his way slowly back to Flagstaff Point in a state of lazy indifference very unusual to him.

His feelings—mind and spirits—had received a severe shock, and he could not recover from the consequent depression all at once.

When he arrived at the tent a surprise of a singular nature awaited him.

He saw, as he approached, that the ground at the rear of the tent, and in front of La-loo-hee-ah's bower, was covered with bright yellow patches and spots glistening bright in the sunlight.

"Gold, by all that's holy!" he exclaimed.

But the action of this bright yellow appearance on the ground being caused by gold in any shape —nuggets or gold dust—was very quickly and entirely dissipated; for a gentle puff of wind sweeping over the point, sent scores of yellow particles whirling and flying in the air.

Crusoe advanced full of wonder, and quite unable to account for so extraordinary a phenomenon.

And as he walked on, one of these glistening yellow particles was wafted by the wind within reach, and catching it in his hand, he found it was not gold nor anything like it, but a feather from some gorgeously plumaged tropical bird.

Soon he saw where these stray feathers proceeded from—nowhere else than the umbrageous retreat where La-loo-hee-ha had taken up her abode.

He stood still in doubt and bewilderment when within a few yards of the clump of brush, which was sufficiently thick to prevent his gaze penetrating. But he he heard a rustling—the sound of some object moving.

"Ah!" he thought, his heart beating faster. "La-loo-hee-ah—she has returned."

Then he quickly advanced, and called her name.

"La-loo-hee-ah, are you there?"

Instantly he heard her voice reply in her own tongue—

"Nargo! maika. Nargo! gilola!"

(Do not come—go away.)

CHAPTER XLIX.

A RARE BIRD.

So Crusoe, much wondering, though greatly relieved in mind, walked slowly to the front of the hut, and seating himself under the shady porch he had built, lit his pipe.

"Well, she's come back; that is so far good," he said to himself, with a sigh of relief, "I wonder where she has been, and what is the meaning of these feathers fluttering about?"

Then he bethought him of the glimpses he had caught of bright plumaged birds fluttering to and fro amongst the trees.

"Ah, I see! thought Crusoe, she went off on an excursion to shoot some of those birds," the arrival of which she doubtless was aware of long before himself. She is but a wild savage girl, but yet I cannot disguise from myself that any human companionship is preferable to absolute solitude, which must, under any circumstances, be dismal and disheartening. It is more so after having tasted of the bitter cup of utter loneliness, and then been relieved by the society—not of a fellow-Christian, or one of any civilised country, but of a fellow-being. The prospect of prosecuting, unaided and alone, the hard task I have undertaken appears to me now in all its horrors."

Whilst Crusoe was still speculating on the disadvantages of utter solitude, La-loo-hee-ah suddenly appeared before him, bursting on his gaze like some dazzling vision of beauty from Fairyland.

Wondrous was the change wrought in her appearance!

His countenance expressed his delight, his rapture at again beholding her.

A bright smile, like a burst of summer sunshine, broke forth on her features.

She took his hand, and, after the fashion of her people, placed it to her forehead.

Quiet, freedom from care, and, we may fairly assume, contentment with her lot, had removed all traces of suffering and ill-treatment from the form of the island maiden.

No bruises were visible and the soft skin, of rich olive hue, scarcely showed the scar of the now healed arrow wound on her arm.

The magnificent climate, a mode of life as simple as it is possible to conceive, a pure, vegetable diet, and a good constitution, with all the vital energies unimpaired either by bad air, bad food, or hereditary weakness—bodily or mental—all conduced to this desirable result in the case of La-loo-hee-ah.

It is probable that a civilised lady—a city belle—though, certainly, no lovelier than this savage maiden, would have been months recovering from the effects of such injuries and ill-treatment, and would, probably, have never regained entirely either health or appearance.

La-loo-hee-ah now appeared in the zenith of her beauty—a lovely child of Nature, not to be imitated or approached by the choicest work of art.

All this Crusoe's admiring eyes drank in, and more.

It is said that "beauty when unadorned is adorned the most."

This certainly requires some qualification.

The rarest—the most beautiful gem, is improved by a tasteful setting; a fine picture is all the better for an appropriate frame; and, as regards "the human form divine," though an excess of finery or profusion of ornaments does more harm than good, yet an elegant shape and a handsome face may be displayed to better advantage by means of taste and judgment.

La-loo-hee-ah, as she stood before Crusoe, was absolutely dazzling in her beauty—a nymph set in a halo of bright colours.

Crusoe Jack had sufficient excuse for the sudden fit of enthusiastic admiration which possessed him as he saw her unexpectedly appear before him.

And what was it over and above her beauty—which long ere this he had observed and acknowledged—which so especially attracted his attention?

It was that her natural charms were embellished by accessories, and of such a sort as no white man but himself had ever before seen.

The tiara, or diadem she wore when he first saw her on the shore of the lake had been lost during the conflict with the savages.

But it was gloriously replaced.

In its stead, carefully arranged so as to form a semi-circle from brow to brow, was a plume of feathers of a rich, dark orange tint.

Amidst these orange feathers were smaller ones of a deep brown, or chocolate colour, which served the purpose of a foil—as a diamond is placed on black velvet to display to best advantage its glittering splendour.

The scarf she wore over her shoulder was also spangled, as it were, with these same rich, brown feathers, which again contrasted well with the white material.

All these feathers had a sheen like that of polished metals, and the effect was very beautiful.

But the crowning splendour was the skirt which she wore round her waist.

It was so skilfully and tastefully made as to appear a work of Nature.

A stranger might almost imagine that the long bright feathers of which it was composed grew on the body of the wearer.

The largest of these feathers were over a foot in length.

At the base, or quill end, these were of a rich dark orange, gradually fading into a golden yellow, then to a straw tint, and finally, about two inches of the top or feather end was of a pure cream white.

Mingled with these hues of orange and gold, amber and white, gleamed the colours of other feathers—dark emerald green.

These were smaller in size, but the brilliant metallic lustre which they possessed caused them to gleam like flashes of light.

The effect, altogether, was magnificent in the extreme, and this brief attempt at description is scant and bald, and can scarcely give an idea of the glorious reality — La-loo-hee-ah herself.

As she stood before him, attired in plumage borrowed of the birds of heaven, she seemed rather a fairy, or visitant from some higher sphere, than a simple child of the Pacific Islands.

It was not for some time that our hero could discover the cause and meaning of this extraordinary change in the appearance of La-loo-hee-ah.

For, with the exuberant vivacity of her savage nature, she gave vent to her delight at his wondering and admiring looks by peal after peal of musical laughter.

And proceeding to question her, he for a time got no better answer, until at last, having laughed to her heart's content, she proceeded to explain it all to him.

He knew, vaguely, that these were birds' feathers, with which she had so tastefully decorated herself.

But as to what description of bird, or how she obtained them in such profusion, he had not the least idea.

So, having compassion on his ignorance and curiosity, she took him by the hand and led him up the slope to her bower among the bushes at the back of the hut.

The open ground, as they approached, was strewn with feathers, the same which, blown about by the wind, had first attracted his attention

But when they entered the patch of brush-wood, and arrived outside her leafy abode, the earth was literally strewn with feathers.

And looking around he perceived many dead birds, stripped of their gorgeous plumage, lying about.

Several of these he examined, and was much puzzled by their strange appearance. These, however, were mutilated and imperfect specimens. And seeing his anxiety, La-loo-hee-ah suddenly darted into her bower, and, returning quickly, placed a bird in his hands.

A bird!

Could it be called a bird?

It had feathers, and was shaped like a bird, and had a beak like a bird.

But it had neither legs nor wings, and these had evidently not been removed, but the creature was in its natural state.

A *rara avis*, indeed.

CHAPTER L.

MORE OF THE FEATHERED MYSTERY.

FOOTLESS and wingless, such was Crusoe's first impression. This, however, was not the case, for presently he discovered rudimentary wings, and, quite concealed by the luxuriant soft down on the lower part of the body, feet, having four claws on each.

The wings, however, were so small and undeveloped as to be quite useless for flying purposes. They resembled those of a young duck a week or so out of the shell. The feet, too, were proportionately not larger. To all intents and purposes the creature was really wingless, and as to the feet, it seemed impossible they could be of any service to stand upon.

And yet, on the other hand, it seemed equally impossible that the bird could be always on the wing.

Such small feeble appendages, no bigger than large mussel-shells, could not be called, with any reason, wings, and must be utterly inadequate for flying purposes, or to support for a moment the body in the air.

For the size of the bird was about that of a small goose or large duck.

Not having wings, then, whence its power of floating and motion in the air?

This was the thought which occurred to Crusoe Jack as he took it in his hands.

Scarcely had he done so than he experienced a most extraordinary sensation. It seemed as though by some mystic means it had the power of locomotion within itself, for it almost slipped from his hands, and at the very same moment it appeared to become suddenly lighter; in fact, to lose so much weight as to be almost imponderable—able to float in the air.

He held it fast, however; and this without difficulty, as the beautiful creature made no struggles, merely turning its head from side to side.

He proceeded to make a closer inspection of this most wonderful bird, if, indeed, bird it were, which he really felt almost inclined to doubt, such an extraordinary anomaly did it appear to him.

Although provided with such absurd little rudiments of wings, there was an abundance of plumage of the most gorgeous kind.

The body and tail (for though so deficient in wings it possessed a most magnificent tail) were of a rich, deep coffee brown, and on the breast a darker brown, variegated with green feathers.

The head and neck were of a very pale yellow or straw colour, the feathers being so fine, small, and closely set as to resemble the finest plush or velvet.

A band of dark green stretched across the forehead as far as the eye, which was dark crimson.

On the body, springing from what should have been just under the wings on either side, were long tufts of long and most delicate feathers—in fact, luxuriant plumes, which met over the body, and, spreading behind and on either side, almost enveloped the body.

At first our hero thought these magnificent tufts or plumes were wings, but he soon discovered that they possessed no wing bones, and also beneath, and smothered up in this feathery glory, those small appendages which should have been wings.

The beak was a pale blue, with a crimson tip.

These magnificent plumes, absolutely forming a bright robe of feathers completely enveloping the bird, were of a most intense golden orange colour, and very glossy, with a splendid metallic lustre.

Towards the tips they shaded off into a deep brown.

Our hero discovered that, though these gorgeous plumes were not attached to any wing or other bones, the creatures had the power of motion over them, and could at pleasure erect or spread them out fan-wise.

Not only was this the most magnificent bird in plumage he had ever beheld, but it had yet greater claims on his wonder.

A question he asked himself, but was unable to find a reply thereto.

Then he turned to La-loo-hee-ah, who all the while stood regarding him with quiet amusement.

His wonder, admiration, and bewilderment, were in no ways shared by her. Doubtless, she was aware that the plumage of this bird was very beautiful, or she would not thus have used it to attire herself in the magnificent style she had when she appeared to him.

But the bird itself was obviously not strange to her, and she appeared quite conversant with its habits and powers.

"Can it fly?" asked Crusoe, at the same time pointing up to the heavens.

"Yes," she replied. "Apoda Wanga (the birds of heaven) move in the air like fish in the sea."

This was very nearly true, though for the moment he did not fully comprehend it.

She took the bird from his hands, and then, holding it at arm's length, let it fall.

Instantly the splendid plumes were spread out like an immense fan, and to Crusoe's utter amazement it glided slowly and gracefully away, out into the open ground.

He followed, full of wonder and quite unable to account for the phenomenon, for he could perceive no motion of the plumes at all. Indeed, as the feathers were not attached to bones, and worked by muscles, as was the case with other birds, it would have been strange, indeed, could the bird have used these plumes as wings.

Instead, however, of mounting into the air as he expected, the bird slowly descended in a slanting direction, and gently alighted on its breast and belly about thirty yards from its starting point.

La-loo-hee-ah, laughing gaily, ran and caught it again, the bird seeming unable or unwilling to make an endeavour to escape.

Having it again in her hands she now called Crusoe's attention, and suddenly threw it aloft as high as she could.

To the astonishment and dismay of our hero it slowly glided away, and this time not alighting as before, rose higher and higher, and disappeared amongst the trees.

But it accomplished the ascent in a most extraordinary manner.

Of this in the next chapter.

CHAPTER LI.

A PLEASANT EXCURSION.

It has been remarked that the bird glided along in a slanting manner, gradually sinking lower and lower until it rested on the earth.

But on the second occasion, when La-loo-hee-ah threw the bird high aloft, it did not descend quite to the earth, though it once very nearly touched the ground.

Darting forward with great rapidity, it described a curve, rising again when at the lowest to a point higher than that from which it started.

Then it made another swoop downwards and forward, this time rising higher still.

And so it continued, until it had risen to a sufficient height, when it disappeared amongst the trees.

Crusoe felt a good deal disappointed at the escape of this extraordinary bird, and said as much to the girl.

"No matter," she replied, showing him her little bow, "La-loo-hee-ah soon get plenty more."

He was anxious to start at once, and getting out a fowling-piece, asked her to accompany him in search of other specimens.

But at this she shook her head, and gave him to understand that it was too late in the day now, and that the birds had all gone off.

On the morrow she would go and get him some more.

It was now late in the afternoon—too late, he thought, to do anything at the wreck.

And, besides, he was not inclined—a lazy fit, for a wonder, having possession of him,

This had been hitherto an entirely idle day—the first and only one with which he had to reproach himself so far.

Not feeling quite satisfied to allow the day to be an absolute blank, he bethought him that he would set to work and clean and oil some of the firearms.

He soon discovered that this was an operation much wanted, as some of the pieces were very rusty, and all needed cleaning.

At the same time he resolved also to get out the cutlasses and polish and sharpen them up a bit; and, in fact, got out in front of the tent his whole armoury of weapons.

There was no possibility of completing the task that night, so he contented himself with scraping and hammering the rust off the muskets, and oiling the locks.

At sundown he gathered them all into a heap, and covering a tarpaulin over, left them for the night, intending to finish on the following morning.

At the time he had forgotten that the next day was Sunday, which, hitherto, he had strictly observed as a day of rest.

However, on this occasion, he resolved to break through the rule, and finish cleaning and oiling all the pieces.

So, setting to work after breakfast, he got through his task about noon, and proceeded to stack them all together in the sun, intending to put them all away in their proper places in the evening.

Shortly after noon he perceived, some distance off in the forest, a number of bright yellow objects flitting about in the trees, which he knew now to be the same mysterious and gorgeously-plumaged birds of the day before.

He proposed to La-loo-hee-ah that they should go on an excursion and shoot some, to which she willingly assented.

To his surprise, however, she objected to his taking a fowling-piece or fire-arm of any description, pointing to her own little bow and arrows, and giving him to understand that a gun or pistol would cause too much noise, and scare the birds away.

So, yielding to her wishes, he did not take even a revolver-pistol with him, and started on the expedition, armed only with a cutlass and tomahawk.

A short walk along the high ridge of land brought them in close vicinity to where these extraordinary creatures had assembled.

They were to be seen in great numbers, flitting about amongst the leafy branches at the tree tops like flashes of golden light, their motion being so rapid as to render it quite impossible to distinguish any more.

La-loo-hee-ah, when within about fifty yards of the trees, about the tops of which they disported, signified to him to halt and conceal himself in a clump of bushes.

Having seen that he was well hidden from view, though he himself could see, she proceeded herself to get under cover at a little distance.

Crusoe watched her actions with all the eagerness of a schoolboy in attendance on an expert bird-catcher, anxious to learn how himself to catch, shoot, or snare the feathered denizens of the air.

La-loo-hee-ah ensconced herself at some few yards' distance from him, and was particularly careful to get well under cover.

There was here a circular fringe of bushes skirting a broad belt or patch of lofty trees, which the birds seemed to prefer to all others, for it was only where these trees stood thick together that they were to be seen.

The bushes were low, with overshadowing umbrella-like branches, which effectually concealed from view all beneath them, while any one crouching there could see through the breaks in the foliage with tolerable distinctness.

La-loo-hee-ah took up a position on her back, her head resting against the stem of one of the bushes, her body slightly on the right side, so as to give free play to the left arm.

Having thus disposed herself, and ascertained that he, too, was effectually concealed, La-loo-hee-ah commenced operations.

Crusoe could but dimly discern the outline of her form through the leaves and branches; but very soon there fell on his ears a strange sound.

A sort of low cooing, like that of a pigeon, but more distinct, and divided into two syllables, the second rising sharply to a high pitch.

The effect of this sound, which he knew was caused by her, was most singular.

Instantly there commenced a great commotion amongst the bright-plumaged birds.

They flew to and fro with increased velocity, seemingly greatly disturbed by the strange sound.

And, presently, they seemed to discover from what direction the sound came; for, in their strange erratic moving flights, they approached nearer and nearer to the fringe of bushes where he and La-loo-hee-ah lay concealed.

Adopting always the same mode of flight as the bird La-loo-hee-ah had tossed up into the air, these creatures moved down again and again, but always rising to as great, or greater a height, without absolutely touching the earth.

The strange cooing sound continued, which seemed to increase the excitement, and to attract myriads of other birds to the neighbourhood.

Minute by minute they increased in number until the air seemed absolutely alive with them.

Darting hither and thither in wild confusion, swooping down close to the earth, to rise again in a manner both grand and graceful, and all the while giving utterance to soft plaintive cries, the scene was absolutely bewildering in its gorgeous splendour.

Gleams and flashes of golden-coloured light filled the air, and darted noiselessly to and fro.

Save the low plaintive call with which these magnificent creatures replied to the decoy note of La-loo-hee-ah, there was no sound.

Their motion was, as nearly as it is possible to conceive, noiseless.

Only when several of them swooped down together, and passed very near to our hero, could he hear any noise of their passage, and then it was only a low rushing sound, like the sighing of the wind.

Always he observed they made their flights in the same manner. First, there was a swift swoop downwards, followed by a slower rise in a graceful curve, until an equal or higher elevation was reached.

Crusoe noticed that just at the place where the bird reached the lowest point of the curve, there was an obvious slowness of motion, almost a pause, indeed, before the ascent again began. And it was during this brief interval that he had the best opportunity of observing the bird alive in all its glory.

CHAPTER LII.

CRUSOE MEETS WITH A STILL GREATER SURPRISE.

LA-LOO-HEE-AH seemed to take great pleasure in exhibiting to him her skill in decoying these birds of magnificent plumage all around her.

In numbers, in beauty of feathers, and even in size, they continually increased, for larger and more splendid specimens of this unknown and gorgeous bird of the Pacific Islands constantly flocked on the scene, in answer to her continually low murmured decoy call.

"The cry was—'Still they come!'" Until the whole air and forest around was thronged and surrounded by these bright-feathered, wingless birds.

Crusoe looked on in pure wonder and delight for a time. But ere long, as he gazed on the gorgeous scene, there intruded on his mind one thought—born of civilisation and culture, almost an instinct of the civilised man—

"What wealth is here displayed before me! Those gorgeous plumes are worth—to adorn the brows of beauty—ten times their weight in gold."

La-loo-hee-ah seemed intent on affording Crusoe as brilliant a display as possible before shooting her arrows in order to bring down any of the birds.

She had with her a lump of stiff blue clay, and previously to fitting an arrow to her bow placed a small piece of this on the tip of the arrow, so as to make it terminate in a round knob in place of a point.

At the proper moment, with the slightest possible movement—so slight that Crusoe did not perceive it—she let fly an arrow.

It struck a large and magnificently plumed bird full on the body, and instantly it fell to the earth, and there lay at a distance only of a few feet from Crusoe.

His first impulse was to rush out from his concealment, and seize the wounded bird, so that it might not escape.

But La-loo-hee-ah stopped him with a few warning words, in a low tone of voice—

"Move not—the burra wanga not fly away."

He soon perceived that she was right in this, for the creature remained motionless, save its head, which it turned restlessly from side to side.

It seemed to sit on the ground as composedly as might a swan on the lake, resting on its belly and breast.

And now it was that the cause of its resting thus quietly struck our hero.

Having once touched the earth, it was unable to rise again, from the almost total absence of wings or feet, and though not hurt, was forced to remain thus calmly awaiting its fate.

La-loo-hee-ah now commenced discharging her arrows in rapid succession, and so timing each shot that after striking the object aimed at, it should fall back within her reach.

The scene was now a most extraordinary one. She kept up a constant flight of arrows at the rate of about twenty a minute, and aimed with such skill and precision that she never missed her mark.

As each bird was struck it fell instantly, always alighting on its breast and belly, in which position it would remain motionless, all save the head and ever restless eye.

Still keeping up her low, musical decoy-call, the birds continually swooped down close to where the lovely toxophilite lay concealed.

They did not seem to be diminished in numbers, or in any way alarmed by the constant

LA-LOO-HEE-AH WARNS CRUSOE JACK OF DANGER.

falling of their companions—victims to the too fatal bow and darts of La-loo-hee-ah.

The ground all about now presented an extraordinary spectacle, which each moment rendered more wonderful and gorgeous.

It was as though a flock numbering several score of swans—only of the most gorgeous plumage, instead of plain white—were floating placidly on a lake of dark green.

Their perfect immobility, the grand and graceful attitude in which they sat, the resplendent plumage of their breasts and bellies, all increased their resemblance to the most graceful of water birds.

Even the splendid plumes rising from each shoulder were folded back, and very much resembled in shape the wings of swans sitting at rest on the water.

Crusoe had ample opportunity to observe them in motion now.

He was utterly puzzled to understand how they contrived, without the aid of wings, to rise, after swooping down to the earth.

He could discover no motion whatever. The splendid plumes, which spread out fan-shape, seemed to serve the purpose of wings.

But he did observe on several occasions a slight fluttering motion between these false wings so to call them.

And after a bit he came to the conclusion that the real wings, or rather the rudiments of wings, had a motion of their own. And presently, availing himself of a favourable opportunity, and watching very closely, he perceived that these little wings had a very rapid revolving motion, like that of the wheel of a piece of steam mechanism.

It was not an up and down motion, nor a flapping motion, nor any motion at all resembling flying or swimming, but a purely circular motion, similar to that of the fan of a screw propeller or the paddles of a side-wheel steamboat.

It was, indeed, a wonderful discovery, but even this did not suffice to satisfy him as to the manner in which this extraordinary bird darted so rapidly through, and ascended in the air.

It did not seem to him feasible that such small objects as these rudimentary wings could alone give so great a propelling and ascending force to so large a bird.

He thought it likely that these swiftly revolving little wings might render some assistance, especially for steering purposes.

Meanwhile, La-loo-hee-ah kept up her flight of arrows, despatching them with untiring skill, and never failing to bring down a bird at each shot.

It seemed to Crusoe that the slightest tap was sufficient to bring them to the ground, and that there was no necessity whatever to inflict even a slight wound in order to bring their flight to a sudden termination.

Only a few minutes had elapsed since La-loo-hee-ah commenced the battue, and the ground was now covered with these extraordinary and magnificently plumed creatures—all sitting in the same posture, and motionless, save their heads and eyes.

A strange, almost comical resemblance struck him. It seemed as though they had been floating, swan-like, on a lake of water, which had suddenly congealed and frozen them all fast.

Crusoe could not restrain a burst of laughter at the conceit.

This instantly alarmed all those birds which were still flashing about in the air and sky above.

The tiny arrows of La-loo-hee-ah seemed to cause them no alarm; perhaps even they did not observe them.

Nor did they appear to take any notice of the fall of their companions, scores of which now rested on the earth, unable to rise.

But the sound of Crusoe's sudden and uncontrollable burst of laughter produced an instant effect.

There arose, first, a single loud call of alarm, which was instantly taken up by others—

" Wauk—wauk—wauk-k-k-k !"

It was a shrill and discordant noise, and simultaneously these extraordinary birds commenced to ascend, always in the same way, swooping down towards the earth to mount higher each time, until, after repeating the manoeuvre two or three times, they no longer descended lower than the tree tops.

Their captive companions—for, though neither caged nor bound, they were fast prisoners, unable from their nature to rise—replied to these cries of alarm by other calls, in a low note, which seemed to Crusoe to have something sad, plaintive, and mournful in their tones.

Poor creatures! though entirely uninjured, the swift arrows of La-loo-hee-ah had brought them to earth, from which they were doomed never to rise again save with the consent and assistance of the appointed master of all dumb creation—man.

Now that the birds had taken flight, La-loo-hee-ah and Crusoe, rising, emerged from their concealment.

The girl was in great glee, laughing and clapping her hands gaily at his undisguised wonder and admiration.

It was, indeed, a most marvellous and magnificent scene, and looked like a picture from Fairyland.

CHAPTER LIII.

A VALUABLE COMMODITY.

Now that the battue was over by reason of the flight of the game, Crusoe asked himself, as he looked around him on the spoils of the chase—

" Cui bono?—to what advantage or use can I turn these captured birds ?"

Though knowing little of millinery and the arts of adornment employed by the fair sex of his own and other civilised nations, he yet could not but be aware that such splendid plumes as he now beheld must be of great value.

Nothing approaching thereto in magnificence of colour, gloss, fineness of feather, and size had ever before been seen.

Of that he was quite certain, and felt well assured that the plumes of each bird must be worth at least ten guineas. Nor, indeed, did he confine himself to this amount, feeling pretty well assured that the value must prove much greater.

And so he rapidly made the following calculation.

La-loo-hee-ah's battue had lasted less than ten minutes.

He now from where he stood counted a hundred and forty-five birds, victims of her skill. Putting the value of the plumes of each at the lowest estimate (ten pounds), that would represent a sum of one thousand four hundred and fifty pounds.

It had only taken ten minutes to secure the birds.

It might take a day to kill them and remove the gaudy plumes.

Now, allowing for loss and damage, and supposing it possible to obtain a constant supply (which, from what he learned from La-loo-hee-ah, he had no reason to doubt), that would give him at least a thousand a day profit.

Always supposing that he should succeed in transporting his merchandise to a civilised country, or, at any rate, some trading port.

As to the value of the feathers he had no doubt. He had seen Bird of Paradise plumes, not nearly so magnificent, offered for sale at fifteen and twenty pounds.

So he felt confident of being on the safe side in estimating these at only ten pounds. And La-loo-hee-ah assured him that for half the year these birds abounded in like proportion, and that she could always secure as many as on this occasion.

A thousand pounds a day, at the very lowest estimate!

Probably at least double that sum in value to be realised in an easy and pleasant manner.

Perhaps much more.

It was a brilliant and dazzling prospect, and might well make him pause and think.

In one half-year, reckoning only a hundred and fifty days, he would thus amass property worth, at the lowest estimate, a hundred and fifty thousand pounds.

And this, to all appearance, was a certainty—at least, so far as obtaining the necessary supply of these magnificent plumes was concerned.

But then arose two other questions.

Question No. 1:

Would he ever have the opportunity of transporting himself, to say nothing of his merchandise, to a civilised country?

Question No. 2:

What about the treasure—the gold sunk in the wreck of the Thunder?

The possibility of recovering that was, to say the least of it, doubtful; and even should he succeed, after many months of labour, in bringing it up from the depths of the sea, it was more than probable that it would prove utterly worthless to him—that, having in his possession gold to the value of half a million, he might be fated to end his days on this island.

It was but too probable.

But, then, on the other hand, his chance was the same should he determine to procure and prepare a great store of feathers.

He might never be able to convey them and himself over the ocean to a civilised land.

But then, again, on deliberate consideration, it occurred to him that, in either case, the chance of reaping the fruit of his successful labour would be the same.

But it appeared to him that the question of obtaining a large quantity of feathers was much more nearly a certainty than recovering the treasure.

And so, for the first time, Crusoe wavered in his mind.

It would be hardly fair to say that his heart faltered in view of the task he had set himself; but he could not disguise from himself the enormous difficulties before him as regarded the recovery of the gold.

While, on the other hand, it was tolerably obvious that he would experience little, if any, difficulty in securing a large supply of these magnificent feathers.

On either hand the chances of his being able to turn the results of his labours to good account were equal.

But, on the one hand, was an apparently simple task — merely a question of time and labour.

On the other, an undertaking of enormous magnitude and difficulty.

Not only arduous, but essentially dangerous and painful, for diving operations of all kinds may fairly be so considered.

And then on the top of these reasons was yet another one, which, with most men, would have been of overwhelming weight.

Should he recover the gold, or only a part thereof, it would not become his property, but he would have to accept such salvage as the Admiralty Court might award him.

While, on the other hand, all that he obtained of valuable merchandise, other than the gold, would be his own, absolutely and without drawback.

A splendid scheme unfolded itself before him.

He might, he thought, accumulate on this island a great store of valuable merchandise—not only of these magnificent plumes of feathers, but other products of these extraordinary regions.

There was the vegetable ivory, of which the haft of La-loo-hee-ah's spear was made.

The extraordinary silk-like fabric, also of vegetable origin.

And then the heavy, glistening white metal—bright as silver, and, as he believed, more valuable.

All these things were to be obtained by enterprise and energy.

True, they were not here on this same island, but they were to be obtained amongst this same group.

And it was his business, he said to himself, to conquer and subdue the savage inhabitants to his will.

And when he had collected a vast stock of merchandise—ivory, leonine (as he called the new metal), vegetable silk, these splendid plumes of feathers, strange scented woods, and extraordinary productions—what a proud position he would stand in—the possessor of vast wealth!

Not only the recoverer, as he would be should he succeed in bringing up the sunken gold from the wreck of the Thunder, but the absolute owner of vast wealth.

Of course, there would still remain the task of transporting his property to a civilised land.

But that he did not consider, by any means, a hard task.

He calculated that he could equip and rig his boat so that she could perform the voyage to some port on the South American coast.

He reckoned that with ordinary weather he could reach Valparaiso in a month and a half at the longest.

Of course, supposing that he was not baffled by continuous head winds or tempests.

He thought that he could take with him in the boat a sufficiency of valuable commodities to charter and equip a vessel—a brig, or bark, of about three hundred tons—navigate her to Lion Island, and embark on board her all merchandise, to the value, perhaps, of millions sterling!

A splendid prospect!

A magnificent dream!

CHAPTER LIV.

CRUSOE'S RESOLVE.

AND now there arose this question in his mind:

Was he bound to sacrifice his own interests, lavish his labour, and risk his life, recovering a vast treasure, principally for the benefit of others, when there was a fair opportunity of obtaining valuable merchandise sufficient to make his fortune?—and this, too, without any very great difficulty, so far as he could see.

At all events, the task of collecting the plumes of these marvellous birds and other merchandise must be both less arduous, more pleasant, and safer than his projected diving operations.

Crusoe was sorely troubled in his mind how to act under the circumstances.

He felt greatly tempted in his mind to throw up his original plan altogether, and go ahead on this new tack.

But nevertheless there was a feeling of stubborn disinclination to give up that which he had undertaken, and by so doing to acknowledge himself defeated.

There was inherent in his nature and disposition a great reluctance to give up any enterprise once undertaken until crowned by success.

It seemed to him to be a smack of cowardice, and to be unworthy of a sterling man.

But yet, on the other hand, the advantages were so obvious and overwhelming, that worldly considerations bade him hesitate how he threw away such a magnificent opportunity of wealth.

Crusoe Jack was by no means a hankerer after riches; but every man must naturally be desirous of making his way in the world, and of course he was not free from this wish—natural to all mankind.

The more he thought on the subject the more sure he felt that he could succeed in reaching the mainland of South America in his open boat, properly strengthened, half-decked, and with her bulwarks raised a few feet.

Everything seemed in his favour.

The delightful weather which prevailed in these latitudes, the calm surface of the vast and justly named Pacific Ocean, usually only rippled by a pleasant breeze.

His knowledge of the latitude and longitude, possession of compass, chart, and quadrant, and lastly the by no means immoderate distance he would have to sail before striking the west coast of America.

All seemed to point to the calculation that he would have an excellent chance of reaching the mainland, even in an open boat.

There were but two dangers he had to dread—of exactly opposite natures.

The first was of tempest—of one of those furious and sudden tornadoes which occasionally break over tropical seas, carrying wreck, ruin, and havoc in their track.

The other danger was a dead and prolonged calm.

He well knew that, should there be such a state of affairs, he could scarcely hope to reach land in a heavy boat by means of the oars only. And, of course, the quantity of water and provisions he could embark must necessarily be limited.

For, beside these, it would be needful for him to take some valuable merchandise, in order to raise sufficient money to charter and equip a vessel—a brig or schooner—in which to return to Lion Island, and ship the rest of his treasure.

He had very rapidly sketched out his plan of operations; but, of course, could not absolutely depend on everything turning out exactly as he wished and hoped.

Nevertheless his scheme seemed to him feasible, and likely to succeed.

Of course there was always the chance that Dame Fortune might play him a shabby trick, and foil all his dear calculations and plans; but that was only a chance.

He reckoned that he could accumulate in a store or depot, well protected from the weather, sufficient valuable merchandise — plumes of feathers, new metal, vegetable ivory, and valuable scented wood — to make him one of the wealthiest men in the world in the course of a year.

Whereas he foresaw that his unaided efforts to reclaim the gold must involve a vast amount of labour, and—what was worse—it might be labour in vain.

And lastly there was that unpleasant fact that, even should he recover the treasure, it would not be his property, the only claim he could have on it being in the nature of salvage.

And so, as a matter of prudence and worldly advantage, it seemed there could be no hesitation on his part.

And yet, strange to say, he did hesitate — feeling all the while he debated the subject with himself a strange, unaccountable disinclination to adopt the course which seemed the easiest, the pleasantest, and the most favourable for himself.

It is doubtful which course he might have ultimately adopted had not another consideration influenced him—the birds themselves, the plumes of which were to make his fortune.

As he looked at them, seated so helplessly on the ground, incapable of any motion beyond that of their heads and eyes, and a slight rustling of the magnificent feathers, his heart revolted from the thought of killing them in cold blood.

And such must be his course if he decided to turn their gorgeous plumes to profit.

For it would be even greater cruelty to strip them of their feathers, and leave them to perish.

For he saw enough of their nature and formation to be certain that these glorious creatures were dependent for flying—if, indeed, that was the proper expression for their mode of locomotion through the air—on these very plumes of which he must rob them to carry out his plan.

It would be quite a different thing were the victims to be slain in the ardour of the chase.

He saw that it was necessary to adopt the plan of La-loo-hee-ah—of shooting them with blunted arrows—to avoid damaging their plumage.

And that involved killing them in cold blood.

Now this simple fact was sufficient to turn the wavering scale in Crusoe's mind.

It was so utterly repugnant to his feelings to commit such wholesale butchery that he finally decided against it, and spoke his decision aloud.

"I will not do it. At least I, the solitary white man privileged to see all these wonders and beauties, will not inaugurate a reign of cruelty and bloodshed. I will recover the treasure if possible, and will also enrich myself by any inanimate treasures I may discover. But wholesale murder—no! Humanity forbids it; my conscience, my feelings as a man forbid it. It shall not be. I will shed the blood of neither men nor dumb creatures, save from dire necessity!"

No sooner did Crusoe Jack come to this determination than, as was his wont, he proceeded to act upon it.

He had before seen La-loo-hee-ah toss one of these birds high in the air, and witnessed it take its flight away in the remarkable manner already described.

He now at once proceeded to imitate her example, and was greatly gratified at the result.

The birds evinced not the slightest fear at his handling them, but, on the contrary, seemed conscious that his intentions were friendly.

La-loo-hee-ah, so soon as she perceived his intentions, readily lent her assistance, and in a very brief space of time the air was again filled with flashing gleams of yellow light, for so swift were the movements of these richly-plumed birds when making their ascent as to make them almost undistinguishable.

But before he had given them all their liberty he discovered the secret of their mode of flight—penetrated the mystery which had at first so utterly mystified him.

It was an extraordinary discovery he made, and one which well repaid him for his trouble.

Briefly, then, he ascertained beyond all doubt that these birds had the power of rendering themselves heavier or lighter at pleasure.

A little consideration of the effect of this peculiar power will reveal to our reader the mode of their ascent.

The exact mode in which this was accomplished he was unable to discover with any certainty, but had good reason to believe that the increase of weight was gained by condensing air within the body.

And when the creature wished to render itself lighter, this condensed, heavy air was suddenly got rid of, and of course the body became instantly considerably lighter.

Probably every one knows that a pendulum allowed to swing freely, will rise nearly as high on one side as the point from which it started.

Were it not for friction, and the attraction of gravitation, it would oscillate backwards and forwards for ever, rising each time to exactly the same height as from that which it started.

CHAPTER LV.
SIGNS OF THE ENEMY.

Now, let us suppose that the weight of the pendulum was five pounds at starting.

It would descend to the lowest point, and then would rise on the other side to very nearly an equal height.

But not quite, because its own weight of five pounds would have a slightly more retarding effect than the impulse or force of the descent.

But let us suppose that the instant the pendulum reached the lowest point it was suddenly lightened, say to the extent of two pounds, so that it should now weigh three pounds instead of five.

Well, then, it would only be dragged back or retarded by its own weight or specific gravity of three pounds, while it would have received a descending impulse of five pounds.

Consequently, it would rise to a higher point than that from which it started.

Now, arrived at this higher point, we will further suppose that the last two pounds of weight were suddenly put on again—the pendulum would sweep down from its higher point with an impulse of five pounds.

Again, arrived at the lowest, we will suppose the two pounds of weight again removed—the pendulum, thus relieved, would sweep upwards to a still higher point.

Again, at its highest point, weight is put on, again to be removed at the lowest, and so on, alternately—the pendulum rising higher and higher each time.

Now this is exactly what took place with these wonderful and mysterious creatures.

Being animate creatures, and endowed with intelligence and certain physical powers, they were able to lighten their bodies at pleasure.

And instinct, or whatever it might be called, taught them to lighten their bodies at the proper time, and to increase their weight when gathering impetus for the downward swoop.

And so, by this strange power, these wingless birds were able to mount high in the air, always supposing them to have the advantage of a slight elevation to start from.

And the more he considered the matter, the more he felt that he had divined the secret of their mysterious flight.

He knew that certain fish had the power of rendering their bodies heavier or lighter by means of air bladders, which they could empty at pleasure.

It did not seem to him by any means impossible, or even improbable, that these birds should be gifted with the same power; and finally, he came to the conclusion that, in fact, it was so.

And so, having solved this apparent mystery, and made up his mind definitely not to abandon his attempt to recover the gold, Crusoe turned his attention to matters immediately in hand.

* * * * *

This day was Sunday, and it was the first which he had failed to keep as a day of rest—although not strictly as a day of religious observance.

Somehow, he felt vexed with himself for having broken through this excellent rule without some better cause than the pursuit, capture, and subsequent release of the beautiful and richly-plumed birds.

He did not exactly reproach himself, though he felt an inward dissatisfaction for which he could not account.

There was yet another thing which gave him some little uneasiness.

This day he had neglected to ascend to the Lion's Crown to make his wonted reconnaissance out to sea.

He resolved that such carelessness should not be repeated, and, forthwith, started to mount the high peak.

La-loo-hee-ah accompanied him; and, having satisfied himself that there was nothing in sight, they made their way slowly along the high ridge of land towards Flagstaff Point.

As they advanced, he observed that La-loo-hee-ah grew restless and uneasy; pausing every now and then, and listening intently.

He was unable either to see or hear anything; but it seemed her keener senses could detect something to cause her uneasiness.

Presently she came to a dead stop, grasped his arm with one hand, and with the other made a gesture for him to stand still and listen.

He fancied he could make out a faint, uncertain, distant sound away in the direction of the hut, but could not be certain.

La-loo-hee-ah, however, evidently heard or saw something, for she was in a great state of excitement; and, holding Crusoe by the hand, led him on at a rapid pace.

Muttered words broke from her lips as she almost ran forward, and our hero now began to understand that there was something serious the matter—something in the nature of a calamity.

After rapidly traversing some two or three hundred yards she again came abruptly to a halt.

Trembling with excitement, she again listened —bidding him do likewise.

And now he could just make out an unmistakeable sound — that of human voices. It seemed like that of the murmuring of a great crowd at a considerable distance.

La-loo-hee-ah had heard it long before he had, and had, moreover, put a most unfavourable construction on it.

Her face wore a startled, scared expression as, pointing towards Flagstaff Point, distant now about half a mile, she cried—

"Ketango! Ketango! Talanaki ketango—nuee nuee Talanaki ketango!"

(The enemy! The enemy of Talanaki—plenty, plenty of the enemy.)

This was terrible news; and Crusoe, remembering, suddenly, that he had no firearms, was instantly awake to the desperate nature of the peril.

All the firearms were piled in the open space in front of the hut, where he had left them before finishing cleaning them.

It appeared that the savages had effected a landing unknown to him. It would also seem that they were in the neighbourhood of the hut —his stronghold and arsenal on Flagstaff Point.

What if they should have taken possession of, or destroyed the hut?

Or what if they had possessed themselves of all the arms and ammunition?

The thought was a terrible one.

CHAPTER LVI.

THE SAVAGES IN POSSESSION OF THE HUT.

THERE was no time to be lost. Whatever was to be done must be done at once.

Crusoe hurried on, reviewing the situation, and thinking what was best to be done as he ran.

As to the situation, it was but too palpable.

The enemy had effected a landing, and were now on Flagstaff Point.

All his stores, arms, and ammunition were at their mercy.

This was enough to cause him desperate alarm.

The question now was, what course to adopt.

Under any circumstances, to gain possession of the hut—his only stronghold and store-room. That was an undoubted necessity.

Also to get possession of the firearms, which he had so imprudently left about in front of the hut.

This must be done.

But how?

They were but two; La-loo-hee-ah, armed only with her little bow and arrows, he having no weapon save a ship's cutlass.

Bitterly he regretted, now that it was too late, his folly in neglecting to make his usual excursion to the high peak he called the Lion's Crown.

Great was his self-reproach when he thought of his weakness and rank stupidity in failing to take the most necessary precautions, for the sake of seeing La-loo-hee-ah make prisoners of some scores of bright-plumaged birds.

All regrets, however, were now useless. It only remained to repair the mischief done as well as possible, if indeed it were possible at all.

As they advanced quickly towards the hut, keeping under cover of the trees, and avoiding the open as far as possible, the sound of voices became plainer, and he gathered but too well the unpleasant fact that there was a great crowd of them.

Presently they came in sight of the hut and Crusoe realised the full extent of the disaster which had befallen him.

In front of the hut was a crowd of, certainly, a couple of hundred savages.

Well he recognised them by the style of their tattooing, feathers, arms, and adornments, as his old and desperate determined enemies of Talanaki.

Crouching and concealing himself as well as he possibly could, he formed his opinion on the state of affairs.

The state of affairs was very easily understood, at once simple and disastrous.

The savages had entire possession of the hut, and he could see them passing backwards and forwards, in and out, examining the, to them, wonderful contents, each appropriating any article he fancied.

The hut was rapidly being gutted of its contents; the scene in front, were it not of such terrible danger for him, would have been amusing in its grotesqueness.

They had sufficient sense to be aware that it was principally by means of the firearms, which were piled carelessly in front of the hut, that the white man had been able to inflict such disastrous defeats upon them, and these they had at once taken possession of.

They were, however, as may well be conceived, perfectly useless to them, for they had not the least idea of how to load them, nor indeed were they aware that any such process was necessary.

Were it not a matter of such serious import, Crusoe would have laughed at the barbarous antics of the savages with the firearms.

They had observed him raise the piece to his shoulder, and noticed that immediately after this there came a flash of fire—smoke, and a loud report, followed in most cases by the fall of one of their number.

Great, then, was their disappointment when, on imitating his movements exactly, there followed no fire, smoke, and thunder.

However, they did not fling the strange weapons away in disgust, as might have been expected, but retained them, and set their great man of mystery, the Kadodo, whom they had brought with them, to exercise his magic power, and compel the familiar spirits of the white man to do their bidding, and supply them with fire, smoke, and death-dealing missiles to order.

This worthy declared without hesitation that he could do so, and our hero listened to a long and loudly-shouted incantation—the meaning of which La-loo-hee-ah, in low whispered words, explained to him.

The great Kadodo, a tall old man, with a long white beard reaching to his waist, was evidently regarded with respect—even awe.

His appearance was more than grotesque, it was frightful.

He was tattooed all over in the most elaborate manner, and with hideous designs in dark blue and red.

Across his face were three horizontal bars of tattooing, the centre one indigo blue, the others vermilion.

The upper lip, either by design, in battle, or by accident, had been entirely cut away, and a row of fang-like teeth, gleaming from out of his tattooed face, gave it a hideous expression.

As if to make his appearance the more horrible, he wore over his forehead, as a sort of head-dress or raiment, the skull of some very ugly fish of the shark species, the mouth half-open, and the double row of teeth seeming to grin at the observer.

A considerable crowd was gathered about this personage, for the purpose of having the strange weapons charmed, and made do the same service to themselves as they had done to their terrible enemy, the white man.

These listened with great respect, all the while turning over and examining the muskets with mingled fear and curiosity, as though expecting to see the mysterious spirit at work.

Others, by far the greater number, were moving to and fro, keeping up a continual chattering, above which the loud clanging voice of the Kadodo, as he yelled forth his incantation, could be plainly heard.

They were occupied dragging about and wrangling over the contents of the hut, which had, by this time, been pretty well pillaged.

All were armed with spears, clubs, and bows and arrows.

Some, who appeared to be chiefs, stood aloof from the noisy crowd assembled in front of the hut, looking on at the tumultuous proceedings with silent haughty contempt.

Crusoe had now satisfied himself that they had no intention of taking their departure—that this was not merely a sudden raid, and that they would not beat a retreat.

Nor, indeed, would it have suited him for them to do so, for he felt perfectly sure that, in any case, they would carry off the arms and other plunder.

But what was to be done?

He felt inclined to rush in amongst them, single-handed, in the hope of scaring them off, in sudden panic at his unexpected appearance.

He had done so once before, successfully.

Yes, but then he was possessed of fire-arms, and before he rushed into their midst some of their best and bravest had fallen before his deadly weapons.

Now it was a very different matter, and should he make the rash attempt, he would, probably, be quickly struck down by a club or transfixed by a spear.

Something, however, must be done, and that at once.

And, as if by happy inspiration, Crusoe hit upon a plan.

Nor did he lose a moment in putting it into execution.

CHAPTER LVII.
IN THE SUBTERRANEAN STORE-ROOM.

In order to carry out this plan it was necessary for Crusoe to gain the patch of brushwood and clump of small trees (amidst which La-loo-hee-ah had erected her bower of leaves), unobserved by the enemy.

This was a task requiring great caution and fraught with danger, but absolutely necessary for Crusoe's purpose.

"Follow me," he said, in a low tone to La-loo-hee-ah; "it is necessary that we should reach yonder clump at the back of the hut where your arbour is, and that unseen by the foe."

There was all over the ground a rank growth of tropical grass.

This would afford some concealment; but, unfortunately, it only attained a height of above a foot and a half, and in some places was quite scanty.

But, on the other hand, in several patches of two or three yards in diameter, it attained a growth of fully three feet.

There were also shrubs and creepers dotted about between the place where they were and the spot they wished to reach.

On his hands and knees, Crusoe commenced crawling along in the proper direction, so varying his course, however, to the right and left, as to keep as much as possible covered by those patches of taller grass and stray bushes.

It was, however, a most dangerous and ticklish operation, for there were several open spaces which must be crossed, and on which there was not sufficient grass for concealment, or any object intervening.

It is true the savages were not keeping any look-out, being wholly occupied with the spoils of the plundered hut; but by chance, at any moment, one of them might cast his eyes in their direction while crossing one of these open spaces.

Then, of course, there would be a discovery, an alarm, and he could expect nothing better than a desperate struggle and a violent death.

Without the aid of fire-arms, he could not hope to make a successful defence against such overwhelming odds.

However, by extreme care, and favoured once more by kind fortune, Crusoe and La-loo-hee-ah gained the welcome shelter of the clump.

There was not a moment to be lost, for there was imminent danger that one of the savages, wandering about, might come in this direction, and discover them.

Accordingly, he set to work at once on the execution of his project.

It will be remembered that, when he first built the hut, he dug a shallow pit at the back part of it, and thence excavated a subterranean passage, at the end of which, many yards to the rear of the hut, he hollowed out an underground store-room, or cavern.

The height of this chamber was only four or five feet, and there was but a foot or so of earth between the roof of it and the surface.

He ascertained, by accurate measurement, the exact spot, beneath which lay this subterranean chamber, which he used as a sort of store-room for powder, spare-arms, and other things which he would not immediately require.

This place he marked, and, to make sure that he was correct, drove his cutlass through the intervening soil from the surface to the cabin below.

Singularly enough, this spot happened to be in the very centre of the clump, and La-loo-hee-ah, without knowing it, constructed her light and airy abode exactly above the gloomy excavation Crusoe had made below. It was purely a matter of chance, and he had not hitherto even informed her of the fact. Great, then, was her surprise when he commenced vigorously, but quietly, to dig up the earth with the cutlass he carried.

In a very brief space he made an opening sufficiently large to admit his body, and immediately descended, just bidding La-loo-hee-ah keep a vigilant look-out.

In the subterranean store-room was, amongst other things, a small bull's-eye lantern. This he at once lighted, then proceeded with his plan.

Besides a keg of powder and a quantity of ready-made cartridges, which were in the hut, there was a barrel in the underground store-room.

This he had placed there from a vague idea of greater security, in order that, should anything happen to what he had in the hut, he might still have a reserve.

This latter barrel, which was full of powder, he rolled along the tunnel until it was right under the trap-door leading to the hut. This he had covered with earth, and placed matting over all, so that the savages who had now possession of his abode, had no idea of its existence, or that their enemy, the white man, who had before inflicted such slaughter upon them, was beneath them, with a barrel of gunpowder.

Crusoe could plainly hear them talking, yelling, and tramping about overhead, and judged that the hut was full of them; and, wasting no precious time, at once proceeded to broach the powder-keg.

This done, he wedged it carefully right under the trap-door, and, retracing his steps, laid a train along the tunnel to the cavern at the end, where he scattered a quantity of loose powder about the ground.

This done, he ascended, taking the bull's-eye lantern with him.

He had some tinder in a box he carried for striking a light with flint and steel; and lighting a bit of this, all was in readiness for the blow-up.

He waited a short time, however, watching for an opportunity when there should be a great number of the savages in and about the hut.

While so doing, he turned over in his mind the probable effect of what he was about to do.

A great explosion, of course, which would partly destroy the hut, kill, scorch and maim many of the enemy, and by its suddenness strike them with panic and terror.

He doubted not that those who were uninjured would immediately take to flight.

Then he would have an opportunity of regaining possession of the fire-arms.

But what of the powder and the loose cartridges?

The latter he thought would be fired by the explosion, but believed that the keg in the hut, which was strongly bound with iron, would resist the fiery blast.

And now the time had come.

Warning La-loo-hee-ah to stand back, he leaned over the hole with the burning tinder in his hand.

The next instant he let it fall on the gunpowder scattered below.

CHAPTER LVIII.
TERRIBLE REVENGE.

CRUSOE was perfectly aware that the explosion of so considerable a quantity of gunpowder must have a most violent effect; and the instant he had dropped the lighted touch-paper on to the train, he started back from the hole in the ground.

But he was scarcely prepared for what took place.

First, there was a low, hissing sound, as the powder burned along the train, then a sharp report, and a flash of fire ran along the tunnel, and shot up into La-loo-hee-ah's bower, which it utterly destroyed, and burned up in a second, scorching everything within many feet around with its fiery breath.

Crusoe and La-loo-hee-ah did not escape.

The gay attire of the girl, the gorgeous plumes so tastefully arranged, which had excited our hero's admiration, were instantly torn and burnt from her body.

Crusoe, whose garb was of a more solid description, was also severely scorched, and the shirt and the canvas trousers he wore were burnt in holes, and torn in many places by the violence of the explosion.

The tunnel acted, in effect, like the barrel of a gun, the barrel of gunpowder at the other end representing the charge.

A vivid column of flame shot through the opening in the ground and high into the air, and it is fortunate that neither he nor La-loo-hee-ah was close to the hole, or both would have been blown to pieces.

Although the effect at this end of the tunnel, where the flame and gases engendered by the explosion had free vent, was more immediate, that at the other end, beneath the hut itself, was far more terrible in its consequences, though slower to develope to its full extent.

First, there came a heaving and rocking of the ground like the waves of the sea. This lasted for a second or so, and then jets of flame broke out, till, all at once, the hut and the ground around seemed to be split asunder, and cast on either side—a great column of lurid flame shooting up into the air, followed instantly by dense volumes of smoke and the loud rumbling roar of the explosion, quite different from the first sharp report.

La-loo-hee-ah was thrown down by the shock; but Crusoe, though scorched and a good deal shaken, only fell on his hands and knees, and was able to witness the effect of the ground blown up.

In a second or so all around was enveloped in a dense, sulphurous smoke, and as the echoes of the explosion died away, there arose other sounds, amply testifying to the success of his venture, so far as destruction amongst the savages was concerned.

He had a glimpse—a sort of vision of human forms, whirling in the air, amidst fire and smoke, and pieces of timber, and logs, and sank back, stunned into insensibility by the shock.

He had not calculated on its being so violent; but he had, perhaps, neglected to take into consideration the gunpowder within the hut and a keg of rifle cartridges, all of which exploded instantly after the barrel beneath.

He did not long remain senseless; indeed, he never altogether lost consciousness, but was only momentarily " knocked out of time," as the prize-fighters say, by the great concussion of the air.

Crusoe Jack's first act was to inquire if his companion was hurt.

" No, I am only a little scorched," replied the Indian maiden.

They were both in a terrible state, La-loo-hee-ah especially presenting a most dismal appearance—blackened by smoke, scorched by the fierce powder blast, all the picturesque and beautiful adornments she had bestowed so much taste and trouble on burned and torn from her body, her hair even singed, and more than one scorch and blister on her soft skin—now hot and dry, grimed with smoke, she looked, as indeed she was, in a pitiable plight.

Crusoe forgot his own smarts and pains, which were considerable, as he looked on the island maiden.

She seemed perfectly bewildered and scared, to be in a state of mental collapse, though bodily he was glad to see no bones were broken.

The contents of the hut were blown in the air and scattered in all directions, and close to the ruins of La-loo-hee-ah's bower there fell a scorched, blackened roll of calico.

Very quickly, however, he unrolled the outer folds, and soon found some which were uninjured.

Tearing off some yards he wrapped them around the girl, who was beginning slowly to recover, and then, perceiving at some little distance a bucket which had been blown from the hut, he got it, and made all haste to the spring, where he literally splashed himself to cool his burning skin. Hurrying back he did the same with La-loo-hee-ah, and in a few minutes the pain of the burns, which most fortunately were slight, abating, he was able to turn his attention to other matters, and realise all that had occurred —the extent of the havoc and destruction wrought amongst the savages, and also the damage he had himself sustained—not in person, which was trifling, but in property, stores, and ammunition.

He almost feared to investigate the extent of the catastrophe.

It was, indeed, a scene of wreck, desolation, and horror which now met Crusoe's eyes, as, walking slowly towards the immediate neighbourhood of the explosion, he looked around him.

The hut, his carefully-constructed stronghold, was utterly destroyed, blown to pieces, in fact— only a few blackened logs standing upright in the ground, marking the place where it had been.

On the spot where it had stood there was now a pit or hollow in the ground, caused by the explosion, and this was strewn with smouldering fragments, stones, *débris* of all descriptions, and last, and most shocking of all, limbs and portions of human bodies.

It was a ghastly sight, and, what rendered it more horrible, was the faint, sickly scent of blood and burning flesh.

All around, for some twenty or thirty yards, in every direction, the ground was covered with the ruins of the hut and its contents, and it was with feelings of sorrow and bitterness that Crusoe Jack gazed on this wreck, which seemed to him so, not only in a physical sense, but also the wreck of all his hopes.

CHAPTER LIX.
CRUSOE SURVEYS THE WRECK OF THE HUT.

WHERE now was his strong fortress he had carefully built?

Where now his stores, his ammunition, arms, and all the accumulated treasures of hut?

Gone — scattered — burned — smashed — destroyed!

Moodily he surveyed the scene, gazing, with folded arms, on the dismal prospect.

Then his glance swept out seaward, and rested on the buoys marking the situation of the wreck of the Thunder.

The smoke still hung about, and the smell of this and burning wood, and the grass and leaves singed by the powder blast, and the whole aspect of the scene was a striking and most unpleasant contrast to the state of affairs a short time previously, when all was peaceful and calm, and the air redolent of the perfume of wild flowers, herbs, and the aromatic trees with which the island abounded.

With a sad heart and gloomy face, on which might be read horror and disgust at the task before him, he set about clearing away the wreck, and collecting the scattered remnants of the hut's contents.

In the first place, it was necessary he should remove the bodies and parts of bodies of the blown-up savages, for already the air was quite pestiferous.

He had hoped, when he had before carted away the corpses of his dead foes by means of the rude waggon he had constructed, that he would never again have such direful and dreadful work.

And now, behold, he had to go through it all again, and this time under much more dismal circumstances.

For now, the hut, at once his home, his fortress, his store-room, and armoury, was a wreck, a ruin, and all its contents, arms, provisions, stores, scattered and destroyed.

It so happened, however, by one of those strange freaks of fortune, for which there is no accounting, that a small keg of brandy, though blown to some distance, was not burst open, and Crusoe proceeded to revive his spirits and nerve himself to his dismal task by a good stiff drink of the eau-de-vie.

On this occasion it really proved to him the "water of life," for it not only gave him fresh energy and vigour, causing a reaction after the shock of the explosion, but also it served to fortify his senses against the sights and smells which surrounded him.

Once more, then, the dreadful dead cart was put into operation, and again did he dig a pit in the sand, and therein deposit the charred remains of his dead enemies.

As to those who were still alive—the savages who had escaped the explosion—there were no signs of them, and he had every reason to believe that, after such a terrible and overwhelming disaster, such convincing proof of his power to kill and destroy them wholesale, they had taken to flight in their canoes, and finally given up all thoughts of attack.

It was long past sunset ere he had buried the bodies and fragments, and partly cleared the ground.

Tired out in mind and body by the exertions and excitement of the day, he hastily rigged a hut of tarpaulin and such remnants of canvas and old sails as he could find, and with the bare ground for a couch slept the sleep of the weary.

La-loo-hee-ah disposed herself at his feet, and thus, amidst the ruins of their one-time home, these two companions in danger and misfortune sought rest and fresh energy in Nature's sweet restorer—balmy sleep.

The sun rose in the morning bright and glorious, flooding the island and sea around with his golden rays.

And notwithstanding the scene of wreck and desolation immediately around him, which seemed to betoken also the ruin of his hopes and prospects, Crusoe's spirits rose, and he felt animated with fresh vigour, fresh resolve.

"Courage!" he said to himself, as he gazed over the scene, amidst which, despite all that had occurred, he was still "monarch of all he surveyed." "While there is life there is hope. Nil desperandum!—the future lies open before me. I will persevere. Again will I try conclusions with fickle Fortune, and perchance tire her out by my persistence. I must—I will succeed, and ere I leave this island I will have achieved my object—recovered the gold, and made a successful dive for half-a-million!"

CHAPTER LX.
LA-LOO-HEE-AH HERSELF AGAIN.

FIRST and foremost—before again turning his attention to the Thunder, Crusoe proceeded to make as much salvage as he could from the wreck the explosion had wrought.

Of course all the light and fragile articles were either totally destroyed or badly damaged—some so as to be entirely useless.

This was the case with the nautical instruments —compass, sextant, and so forth.

All books and papers were burned and torn, and the charts completely ruined.

The lighter sort of fabrics, too, such as cotton, calico, of which he had a tolerable supply, were also scorched and torn, so that it was no easy matter to get even a few yards of tolerably sound material.

His signal flags were all torn and defaced, but he hoped he might patch them up for use.

Then, as to provisions, the barrel of flour had been riven open, and the contents scattered about—the same with the biscuit; and as for the small stock of preserved meats, all was total destruction.

The tools, from their being principally made of iron, fared better, and he recovered nearly all unharmed, save a few smaller ones, such as gimlets and so forth.

As for the canvas, that fared better, from its stouter nature, so did tarpaulins.

But his soft and warm opossum rug, and everything of that kind, was totally destroyed.

As regarded fire-arms, these were comparatively uninjured, as they were mostly outside the hut ; and, of course, such as the savages as escaped death from the explosion threw down their prizes, and skedaddled.

But of what use were they to him now—either clumsy musket or elaborately-finished American repeating rifle? Alas! none.

Not so long ago he had said to himself that though the savages had possessed themselves of his firearms, they were utterly useless to them as weapons either of offence or defence, for they had not the remotest idea how to load them.

And now he, though possessed of ample knowledge, was in the same position, for he had no ammunition, save enough powder for a few rounds.

The remainder of the rockets, blue lights, &c., of course were ignited and lost to him ; and so, too, was his only can of oil.

It was rather mechanically than as a result of thought that he collected the firearms, and piled them all together.

La-loo-hee-ah, who for some time had looked on in a doleful, half-frightened manner at the scene of ruin and desolation, seemed to pluck up heart now, and seeing how cheerful and energetic he appeared, pleasant smiles irradiated her truly charming face, which by great good fortune was scarcely scorched, though the long drooping eyelashes had been singed off by the fiery blast, and the ends of her beautiful hair slightly burned.

Finding amidst the wreck her own little needle of fish bone and some portions of the beautiful silk-like material she had brought with her, she pointed to the seashore, and said in her own tongue—

"I go to bathe—my skin is hot and parched. I will return soon."

"Be careful of the enemy," said Crusoe. "They may still be prowling about, and I might find it impossible to rescue you from their hands a third time."

La-loo-hee-ah made a gesture of disdain, replying—

"Ah! they are children. They will never again dare to provoke the wrath of the great white king, who can destroy them utterly by his thunder and fire, and death-dealing weapons."

Crusoe smiled sadly, but did not undeceive her.

Too well he knew that the virtue had departed from the death-dealing weapons, and that they were now of no use beyond that of the iron of the barrels and the wood of the stocks.

La-loo-hee-ah was by no means cognisant of the full extent of the disaster to Crusoe. She saw that the enemy had received a tremendous blow—had been slain wholesale, and scattered in all directions, and imagined that her white companion had foreseen all this, and was perfectly satisfied with the result.

Such, however, as the reader knows, was not the case, for Crusoe had never anticipated an explosion of such terrific violence, nor had he calculated on the total loss of his gunpowder.

La-loo-hee-ah, then, who had now recovered from the shock and fright, hastened away to the shore, and plunging into the calm, warm water, disported herself as might a mermaid or other inhabitant of the sea, and, after thus amusing herself for the space of an hour, returned to land, and taking a position on the margin of the sand, under the shade of a cactus tree, proceeded nimbly and skilfully to shape and piece together something in the way of covering.

This she very speedily accomplished, and presently surprised Crusoe by appearing before him radiant with smiles, and as tastefully, albeit scantily, attired, as when he had first seen her.

On her way back she had gathered some wild flowers, something like lilies in appearance, and of these she had made a chaplet encircling her brow.

In her ears, with fish bones in place of wires, she wore two small pink shells—far prettier than any jewelled ear-ring to be purchased of a fashionable jeweller.

Her hair, which had been slightly singed at the ends, she had bound around her handsome head in quite a charming style, as though she had seen and taken pattern by a Grecian statue.

Looking at the handsome island maiden, elegant in shape, graceful and agile in movement as a gazelle, it was hard to believe that she had been the heroine of such stirring and perilous adventures, and subjected to such injuries and hardships.

Her large dark eyes were lustrous as ever, though the loss of her eye-lashes singed off by the fire robbed them of one beauty.

Her olive skin, softer and more delicate than the finest satin, had received scarce any visible injury from the powder blast, and, more than that, she was refreshed and invigorated by her morning's bath.

She was as active, as full of graceful energy as ever.

Crusoe, after a few pleasant words, congratulating her on her appearance, proceeded with his work, and she, perceiving that he regarded it as a matter of importance, insisted on rendering him assistance, though he wished her to rest, merely keeping a look-out for the enemy.

But La-loo-hee-ah declared this was totally unnecessary, as they would not return, and, as usual in small matters, having her own way, proceeded to aid him in collecting and arranging the scattered remnants of his stores.

By noon the ground had been pretty well cleared, and everything collected and arranged.

Crusoe now knocked off work as the heat was almost insupportable, and, following the example of La-loo-hee-ah, made his way to the sea shore, and there indulged in the luxury of a sea bath—a luxury which he was fully able to appreciate, hot, parched, and dusty as he was.

In the afternoon, when the heat had somewhat subsided, he proposed to make a reconnaisance, in order to make sure of the final departure of the savages; and after that, to set about rebuilding the destroyed hut.

CHAPTER XLI.

FLAGSTAFF POINT ASSUMES A BRIGHTER ASPECT.

A WEEK passed on, at the expiration of which time, a great change had been wrought in the appearance of things at Flagstaff Point.

The ground had been cleared of the *débris*, and again there was to be seen a hut of timber and bark, built close to the same spot, and in a great measure composed of the wreck of the other one.

It was by no means so strongly or carefully built as the former one, for Crusoe did not feel inclined to devote more time than was absolutely necessary to it, as he was anxious to get to work again at the wreck of the Thunder as soon as possible.

When he had collected and stowed away such of his stores and so forth which were not utterly destroyed, he found that he was much better off than he had imagined possible on first viewing the scene immediately after the explosion, for many things he thought utterly ruined he found but slightly injured.

The powder-blast which had shattered the hut had been quite capricious in its effects.

Many articles of considerable strength had been broken, burned, and destroyed, while, on the other hand, many very fragile things had escaped destruction, and, in some cases, even had suffered no injury.

A remarkable instance of this was a box of teak wood which he used as a medicine chest. In this were sundry bottles, jars, and phials, containing drugs and chemicals; also, there were surgical instruments, some chemical apparatus, a retort and alembic, a small still, a Leyden jar and small galvanic apparatus, and many other things—some of the most fragile description.

Seeing this box overturned at some little distance from the actual scene of the explosion, he thought that, of course, its contents—most brittle—would be broken, and all his medicines and chemicals lost to him.

This was a heavy blow to him, for he set great store by the drugs, chemicals, and apparatus, having ulterior designs, especially with regard to the latter.

Great, then, was his astonishment when, on righting the box and opening it, he found only two or three bottles broken, and these not containing anything of consequence.

Even the Leyden jar of thin glass, and the ~~retort~~—even more fragile—had escaped breaking.

This was a source of great satisfaction, and caused his spirits to rise considerably.

As regarded tools, he recovered nearly all; axe, saw, auger, chisels, adze, wedges—everything.

His stock of nails, screws, iron bolts, and rivets, and iron-hoop wire and so forth, he recovered; for these could not well be destroyed but were only blown about, and scattered in all directions.

A good deal of his rope and stores of that kind was damaged; but there remained still a considerable quantity fit for service.

The same was the case with the canvas and tarpaulins.

His spare clothing, however, and all light fabrics were badly injured, and it was but very little he could pick out likely to be of any use.

Only a very small quantity of his stock of flour could be recovered, as the barrel had been burst asunder, and its contents dispersed in all directions.

This, however, was not a matter of great importance, by reason of the wonderful fertility of the island—in bread-fruit, corn, and nuts, and such indigenous productions.

Of his stock of ship's biscuits he collected about a third. His stock of preserved meat and that sort of thing, hermetically sealed tins and bottles, were, however, all destroyed.

He had eight or ten pounds of tea in a quarter chest, and this was utterly lost.

But, on the other hand, by a great good fortune, he saved nearly all his bag of coffee, over which a tarpaulin had been blown by the explosion.

He picked up, too, nearly all the cakes of ship tobacco given him by the captain of the whaler; and this was a great source of joy to him, for Crusoe Jack, like most seafaring men, would, for a choice, have gone without dinner rather than his pipe.

He was able, too, to recover a considerable portion of his bag of salt, which was an important matter, as to manufacturing this most necessary article by evaporating the water of the sea would have been a most tedious business.

It has before been stated that a small keg of brandy had escaped destruction. Not so, however, with respect to a large jar of oil—that had been broken, of course, and the contents lost.

A half-barrel of pitch had been melted and caused to run over the ground in a liquid state by the great heat of the explosion; but it had solidified again, and he was able to collect the whole of it.

He was able to scrape up and save nearly a bucketful of a small barrel of tar which had been burnt open.

These two last were of great importance to him, and it was with feelings of profound relief that he found he was enabled to make good salvage thereof.

The pitch, in conjunction with oakum (for the making of which he had a quantity of old junk), would be indispensable should he have occasion to caulk the seams of his boat at any time, or find it necessary to try shipbuilding or repairing in any shape.

The tar, too, would be wanted for many purposes, especially for making with pitch a tarpaulin material.

And, according to his present plans, that would be essential, for he had decided that, in order to get the treasure sunk in the wreck of the Thunder, it would be necessary to make diving operations of some kind.

Whether this should be of the nature of a diving bell or diver's suit would depend upon circumstances; but, in any event, a waterproof material to cover seams and cracks would be necessary.

Lastly, we would mention one other thing saved from the ruin with but trifling damage.

This was a large ship's signal lantern, only one square of the strong glass of which was broken.

Thus, it will be seen, that after taking things all in all, Crusoe Jack, after a week's steady work, found himself much better off than he had dared to hope.

He had saved at least half of all his stores, the whole of his tools, and many other things.

Moreover, he had rebuilt the hut, and made things tolerably comfortable.

La-loo-hee-ah, too, had again constructed a charming little bower.

There was but one utter and irremediable loss of any importance.

This was the powder!

That was gone, and could not be replaced.

CHAPTER LXII.

TUTOR AND PUPIL.

WARNED by past experience, Crusoe took ample precaution to prevent being surprised again. Although he quite believed that these savages, warlike and determined as they had proved themselves, had been frightened away for good by the explosion which caused death to so many of them, he made a point of taking a survey of the shores of the island and seaward at least twice a day, morning and evening.

Somewhat to his surprise, La-loo-hee-ah, who had expressed her firm opinion that they would return no more, seemed to grow restless and uneasy, and made frequent excursions alone to the high peak of land whence an uninterrupted view could be seen of the island.

She always accompanied him, too, when he went on these expeditions, at which he was very glad; for, as day by day his knowledge of the language increased, he experienced greater pleasure in her companionship.

Her vivacity, good temper, and spirits were unbounded.

Her intelligence and natural wit were something marvellous for an untutored savage, and one day the thought suddenly struck Crusoe.

"Why should he not teach her to read and speak the English tongue—educate her, in fact? Sure am I she would prove a most apt pupil."

He thought for a few moments, and then, as was his wont, made up his mind very quickly.

"By Jove! I'll do it," he cried, aloud.

La-loo-hee-ah heard him make some exclamation, and, though she did not understand his words, for he had thought it a better and more expeditious plan for him to learn her language

"NO, I AM ONLY A LITTLE SCORCHED," REPLIED THE INDIAN MAIDEN.

than to impose the task on her of acquiring English, which, before he became better acquainted with her marvellous quickness of apprehension, he naturally thought would prove a long and difficult task.

Now, however, he had excellent reason for altering his opinion, and fully determined to commence at once· remembering, as he did, that in the prosecution of his tremendous task of recovering the gold he might be be a very possibly be a couple of years on this island—perhaps more ; it was impossible to judge with any certainty.

When, however, he had succeeded in explaining to her that he wished her to learn his language, she readily acquiesced.

And when he proceeded to make her comprehend that he also wished her to learn to write as she had seen him in his diary and log-book, and to read, which, also, she had witnessed him do—looking on the while with an expression on her face of the greatest wonder and awe—she not only agreed to his proposal, but seemed half frantic with delight.

" Wota ! wota !" she cried, clapping her hands, and laughing gleefully. " La-loo-hee-ah mahina putah dela Falera !"

(Beautiful ! beautiful ! La-loo-hee-ah will speak like a white princess.)

She was in ecstasies at the idea, and would almost have insisted on Crusoe giving her the lesson on that very eve.

Having once made up his mind to it, he set to work with a will, and was perfectly astonished at the ease and quickness with which she picked up not only the pronunciation, but even the idiom—the spirit of the language.

By the dim light of a rude lamp—made out of a half cocoa-nut shell, filled with melted grease—this strange couple, tutor and pupil, sat till nearly midnight ; La-loo-hee-ah, even then being unwilling to finish the lesson, so eager was her craving for knowledge.

Fortunately, although the oil had been all lost, Crusoe had been able to collect a quantity of grease, or slush, as sailors call it, the captain of the American vessel having left him a half cask before sailing away.

Mention has just been made of our hero's log-book or diary, also books.

The diary and log-book had been fortunately saved ; in fact, he had by a fortunate accident placed them in the medicine chest, which, as has been described, escaped with its contents in a most wonderful manner.

For ink he used a dark, almost black fluid, which was peculiar to a sort of small cuttle fish, several specimens of which he had caught in the lagoon.

Herein appears the value of knowledge, which often proves useful, under the most unexpected circumstances.

Crusoe, as a boy at school, had always been fond of natural history.

Little did he dream, however, when he read of the cuttle fish discharging a quantity of black liquid when pursued by its enemies in order to escape their keen sight, that he himself would ever be glad to turn his knowledge to account, and use this fluid as ink.

When, at last, La-loo-hee-ah, in her melodious ce, wished him " good night !" in English—

for she had learned that—he walked down by the sea-shore.

It was a bright, moonlight night, and he felt more inclined for reverie and thought than sleep.

The time, the place, the view, and the surrounding circumstances all seemed favourable for quiet reflection.

A gentle breeze just rustled the leaves of the trees and the surface of the lagoon.

The murmuring of the little waves as they rippled on the sandy shore fell exceedingly pleasant on the ear, and in the distance could be heard the deeper, more solemn, but yet withal gentle boom of the breakers, as the long Pacific swell rolled on to the outer reef.

It was a scene of peaceful calmness only to be witnessed in tropical climes, the bright moon bathing the whole in a flood of her silver light.

Crusoe's thoughts wandered in fancy far away both in space and time.

But after a while, with a sigh, his truant thoughts came back to this, his kingdom—his island of the sea.

" How will it all end ? It seems like a dream, or a vision. Dangers surmounted, desperate conflicts, decisive victories, strange adventures. Shall I achieve final triumph ? Shall I recover the gold lost in the wreck of the Thunder ? What oracle can answer ?—

" None."

" Time alone can solve that momentous question."

He paused in his half-murmured words, his thoughts seeming to turn suddenly to some subject of absorbing interest.

In a few seconds they found utterance in speech ; for he broke forth aloud, in a manner almost passionate—

" And what of this island princess, Falera La-loo-hee-ah ? Day by day—hour by hour her destiny seems to link itself more closely with mine. Together we have endured, risked danger —together we have fought—conquered together —companions in adversity and good. And now she is rapidly learning the English tongue, and there will be a band of union between us.

" How will it all end ?"

He was silent ; and, after the lapse of a short time, spoke out.—

" Time alone—the unraveller of all mysteries —can tell. Che sara sara—what will be, will be. Time and fortune. We are but puppets, and can only in a measure shape our own destinies.

" Whatever will be, will be, and I will hope that it will be for the best whatever may yet be in store for me."

Slowly he walked up to the hut, but it was daylight ere sleep visited his eyes.

CHAPTER LXVIII.
CRUSOE'S DIARY.

WE have arrived at a time in the career of our hero when great and unexpected changes in his fortunes are about to occur.

And, moreover, experience, which teaches a but fools, had wrought considerable changes in himself, in his inner nature, in his thoughts as to the past—his hopes as to the future.

We before gave some extracts from his diary ; here is a good opportunity for a few more.

When speaking of himself, his wishes, hopes, and prospects in the first person, he may give the reader a better idea of the situation and chances.

EXTRACT FROM THE DIARY OF CRUSOE JACK, ONE TIME SECOND MATE OF THE THUNDER.

" 20th.—Days, weeks, months have passed since I landed on this island, and made the first entry in this diary of my fortunes and adventures.

" Although I have made but slow progress with the great work, events have marched apace.

" At the present time I have a strange, nervous feeling (I have experienced the like before) a sort of presentiment that some great change is about to occur—events of the utmost importance to my future.

" When I look back I am compelled to own that this in which I am engaged is a most rash and desperate enterprise—some might call it hopeless; but when I look forward I feel inspired with fresh confidence—nerved with fresh energy.

" But to get to actual facts, and drop vain speculations.

" I have put things straight again on Flagstaff Point, and already the rapid growth of the luxuriant tropical vegetation has almost effaced the traces of the explosion, the neighbourhood of the hut no longer exhibiting that scorched and blackened appearance it did after the terrible blow up.

" My labour at the wreck progresses slowly but steadily, and so far satisfactorily.

" This is my course of action—the routine of my life here at present—a routine which I feel, 1 know, cannot continue much longer. And, yet, strange to say, I do not dread a change, but look forward almost eagerly to some fresh excitement—fresh adventures.

" At early dawn I rise, have a hasty wash, and start off with La-loo-hee-ah to the Lion's Crown.

" She always accompanies me now; and, strange to say, appears more nervous and anxious than I am myself, looking out to the west, where lie the islands of which her father is king, with a strange, eager glance, which appears to increase in intensity day by day. She evidently expects to see something. What can it be? It would seem that she scarcely knows herself, or, perhaps, she is unwilling to alarm me.

" Be that as it may, her manner disquiets me a good deal.

" After satisfying ourselves that nothing in the shape of vessel, boat, or canoe dots the surface of the sea, we return to the hut. La-loo-hee-ah, agile and fleet-footed as an antelope, outstrips me, and when I arrive at our home, storeroom, and fortress—the hut—she has prepared our simple breakfast. This consists sometimes of fish baked amidst hot stones. This, with bread-fruit roasted, or biscuit and coffee—of which, and tobacco, thank heaven, I have a fair supply—we make a very excellent repast.

" After this, I go down to the boat and embark a load of rocks and stones; this I take out to the wreck, and throw overboard at a proper place, so as to build up the sea wall which, foot by foot, with monotonous and continual labour, I am building up around the wreck of the Thunder.

" I have now got so accustomed to the work, and so expert, that I can embark and deposit two boatloads before mid day, when the heat is too intense for me to labour exposed to the sun.

" At noon I bathe, and then go up to the hut; where, in the shade, I do not rest, but toil quietly at another work I have in hand—the construction of a diving apparatus and dress.

" La-loo-hee-ha, meanwhile, goes up to the high peak I call the Lion's Crown to reconnoitre; and, returning as soon as possible, proceeds to prepare our dinner, which she does with inimitable quickness and skill.

" This entry, though it only contains the history of half a day's work, is enough; I will write the other half to-morrow."

CHAPTER LXIV.

ANOTHER EXTRACT FROM CRUSOE JACK'S DIARY—LA-LOO-HEE-AH'S WATER-CLOCK.

" 21ST.—Another day has rolled on. It is now about half an hour past noon by La-loo-hee-ah's clock. Speaking of that, I will put in writing a description of this most ingenious contrivance, entirely her own manufacture.

" Then I will go on to narrate the course of our life day by day, one-half of which I wrote yesterday.

" About La-loo-hee-ah's clock.

" No complicated works, wheels, springs, pinions, fine screws, and so forth, did my island maiden require to construct this primitive and simple, but withal marvellously accurate, measurer of time.

" The device of King Alfred to measure the hours by means of marks on a candle burning in a lantern was but a clumsy contrivance to this of La-loo-hee-ah's.

" All that she required was one of my buckets and a cocoa-nut shell.

" Surely scanty material enough to make a clock which shall accurately measure the time. The polished shell of a cocoa-nut, carefully divided in the middle, so as to form two cups or bowls of exactly equal dimensions, was the first requisite, and the only one, save the bucket and water.

" In the bottom of one of these shells she proceeded, with great care, to drill four very small holes—so small as to be scarcely perceptible. This she accomplished by means of a sharp-pointed fish-bone, twisting it round and round until it had perforated the shell.

" She now placed this cocoa-nut bowl in the bucket of water, on which it floated. But through the small holes in the bottom of the shell there flowed little jets of water—so minute, indeed, as to be scarcely visible.

" As the water thus flowed into the shell, of course it sank lower and lower, until, when full, it gently disappeared beneath the surface and sank to the bottom.

" Now, by making the holes larger she could, of course, cause the shell to fill more rapidly and sink in a shorter time. At first she had made the holes very small, and gradually enlarged them until the shell would fill with water and sink in exactly an hour, measured by my watch.

"And once this result arrived at, the time never deviated a quarter of a minute; indeed, the accuracy of this water-clock was quite marvellous. The other shell was only perforated with one hole, and this being of the same size as the four, of course it took about four times as long to sink.

"This, then, numbered four hours. And so La-loo-hee-ah could, at any time, set her water-clock, and know exactly the time when each hour and period of four hours expired.

"On each of the shells, which floated side by side in the bucket of water, she had affixed to each edge very slender reeds about nine inches in length.

"At the top of these miniature flagstaffs she had fastened distinguishing pennons—a piece of white material for the one brown shell, and one of the bright golden-hued feathers of the wingless bird on the other.

"It is to me a most amusing sight, when sitting outside the hut at eventide, to watch the two little flags, which, of course, being about a half a foot over the edge of the bucket, are plainly visible.

"La-loo-hee-ah sets her clock say, for both, to sink, at six o'clock. About sundown, with my watch in hand, I look at the white and orange pennons, distant only some twenty yards. At the hour exactly I perceive a sort of tremulous motion—a gentle waving to and fro—and then slowly they sink, and are seen no more.

"Sometimes I amuse myself with making guesses with La-loo-hee-ah as to which will sink first. It may be imagined that she—the maker of the clock, and who has set the clock—generally wins.

"I have often thought what sport this simple mode of clock-making might afford to a number of schoolboys.

"There might be a grand prize competition, each competitor making a water-clock to run any specified time. Then the one that sank most exactly to time—as measured by a good watch—would be the winner.

"Nothing would be required beyond half a cocoa-nut shell and a vessel of any kind filled with water.

"A good-sized tub would hold half-a-dozen water-clocks.

"As for boring the holes, that might be done by means of bits of iron wire; some larger than the others, as it became necessary to increase the size of the holes.

"Of course, if the shell were found to sink very much too slowly, another small hole would be the simplest plan. But all this might be easily ascertained by experiments.

"If I had known how to make a water-clock when I was at school, I know I would have had some.

"Ah well! here am I writing in this gossiping way as though I were comfortably at home in dear old England, instead of thousands of miles away, denizen of an island hitherto unknown in the vast Pacific—bent on a difficult, tedious, and, withal, dangerous task, and with the knowledge that, even if I succeeded in my dive for half a million, and recover the treasure, I yet may

never have an opportunity of reaping the fruits of my labour—that I may be destined either to live and die on this island, or perish in the attempt to gain some port on the main land of South America.

"It is strange, but I am not down-hearted, and feel a certain assurance that, though I should be fated to leave my bones on this my kingdom of Lion Island, still this record of my adventures and experiences will yet fall into the hands of civilised men, and be read by many with, perhaps, profit and interest.

"This evening I can write no more. The light wanes, and La-loo-hee-ah is trimming our lamp, and is eager for me to commence my lesson in the English tongue, and in reading and writing."

CHAPTER LXV.

DIARY CONTINUED—THE DIVING DRESS AND THE HELMET.

"22ND.—An idle day, or nearly so far as work at the wreck of the Thunder is concerned.

"As I write, it is but an hour past noon.

"This morning early, in loading the boat with rocks, I slightly twisted my ancle, and decided to give the injured foot a rest; so came up to the hut, and shall spend the rest of the afternoon about my diving apparatus, and in writing up this diary.

"La-loo-hee-ah has been gone for more than three hours. She left me, saying she would bathe, and would then go up to the Lion's Crown after our mid-day meal.

"She set both her water-clocks before leaving.

"I watched the little flag of the hour one sink, and then began to expect her back. I cannot imagine what has detained her. Of late she has been more restless and uneasy than ever, making frequent excursions to the high peak.

"She seems constantly on the watch—constantly in expectation of something. She seeks every possible opportunity of scanning the sea, and, indeed, is always looking around her as though expecting to see something. I fancy, from some words she let drop, that she expects her own people will visit the island for the purpose of some solemn religious ceremony connected with the skeleton of the warrior, which lies at the top of the sarcophagus I discovered. But she is a strange girl, and appears very unwilling to discuss the subject, so I do not press her on the point. Of one thing I am sure—that she is thoroughly, heart, and soul, devoted to my interests.

"It is possible that she prolonged her bath—she is more like a fish than a woman in the water. And, then, she may have taken it into her head to ascend to the Lion's Crown. But, even if that were the case, what can have induced her to remain so long?

"I feel restless, and am half inclined to go in search of her. However, I conquer the inclination, and think it better to remain as I am and rest my foot.

"I am busily engaged in constructing a waterproof diver's dress. This is easy enough as regards the body, for I have sufficient pitch and grease to make a compound which, when spread over canvas, will keep out the water.

"Already I have completed the dress from the knee to the neck. It is of strong canvas three times doubled, and when it is covered with a solution of pitch and tar, it will be as strong and stiff as leather.

"I have most carefully double-stitched and middle-stitched the seams, and of course at these parts I shall put on an extra coat of the composition.

"It is fortunate that I am an excellent hand with the palm and needle. Indeed, at sea in fine weather, I was always fond of sailmaking and mending; now this comes in most usefully.

"At the knees, this dress, when completed, is to be attached to my heavy sea-boots, which I can easily render perfectly water-tight.

"The boots will of course be properly weighted; and I shall also distribute lead and iron in other parts to counteract the buoyancy of the sea. But my great difficulty will be the head-piece, and the making the joints water-tight. A helmet of some kind is, I know, absolutely necessary.

"Those I have seen have been very elaborately constructed with pipes, tubing, and valves, and with glass discs let in for eye-holes. How am I to accomplish this? I have asked myself the question scores and scores of times, and it was long ere I could find any sort of answer at all; but at last I did. I think some beneficent spirit must have whispered the suggestion in my ear.

"It was a strange idea; indeed, at first sight, there was something so comical in it that I could not refrain from laughing. It was nothing else than to make the ship's signal-lantern serve the purpose of a helmet. And yet, when I proceeded to particulars, I thought that, under the circumstances, it was an excellent idea.

"In the first place, it was amply large enough to contain my head. That fact I ascertained by knocking the bottom out, and "trying it on"— a very extraordinary kind of head gear; and as it struck me, what would any old friend or shipmate say who could see Crusoe Jack putting on the signal-lantern? I fairly roared with laughter at the idea.

"This fact will suffice, I hope, to convince any one into whose hands this record of my adventures may fall, that despite my lonely position—a solitary white man—on this island (longitude about 120 degrees west, latitude 9 degrees south) I was by no means cast down in spirits, or inclined to despond, despite the difficulties and dangers before me which may prove insurmountable, and under which I may finally perish.

"I have, to-day, a gossiping humour on me, and since there are none to whom I can unfold my thoughts, I relieve my mind by writing them down.

"But to resume about the old ship's lantern, which I shall transform into a diver's helmet; it is quite large enough; the framework is of iron and tin, and tolerably strong, also it is heavy. I shall now make it both heavier and stronger.

"Fortunately, I have, in addition to the lead and iron, a quantity of copper—old ship's copper. I wished to decline it when the captain of the American vessel offered it to me; but he would take no denial. It was partly because I thought it was trespassing on his liberality, and partly also because I thought this copper could be of no use to me. Iron was harder, and lead more ductile; and I had a supply of each.

"But herein was just its advantage over these two metals, another instance of the wonderful way in which Fortune favours me—or perhaps some higher influence than Fortune— who can tell?"

"I had almost made up my mind to refuse it definitely. when something, I know not what, put me in mind of the old saying—'Keep a stone for seven years, and you'll find a use for it.'

"Besides, it also struck me that it would be ungracious to refuse what was so freely offered. So I accepted it, and right glad am I now that I did; for without it, I should be sorely at a loss, and, indeed, I much doubt whether I could have any chance of carrying out my plans with regard to the diving dress and diving apparatus.

"This copper is in sheets—part of the sheathing of the American whaler, which had been taken off, and replaced with new. It is much more manageable than iron, not requiring heat, as that stubborn metal does, to deal with it, and it is infinitely stronger than that soft metal, lead.

"With the latter I could never succeed, I am sure, in making a case to the lantern which is to form my diving helmet. For lead, though easily moulded, would not have sufficient strength to resist the great pressure of the water at any considerable depth.

"It is with these copper plates, using strips of lead as bands, and soldering with the same easily melted metal, I am quite certain I can construct a strong and perfectly water-tight helmet, and complete my diving dress. I will now just proceed to give a few particulars as to how I propose to make it water-tight, particularly at the joint at the neck between the helmet and the body. Also how I will arrange the pipes for air, weights, and so forth, and other things which, though seemingly trifles, are really all-important.

"I hear the sound of a voice—the voice of La-loo-hee-ah—she is calling me. I hear her words plainly—'Omani putah! omani putah! ketango maika!' ('White warrior! white warrior! the enemy comes!')

*　*　*　*　*

"I resume the pen, to make what may, perhaps, prove the last entry in this record of my adventures.

"La-loo-hee-ah has arrived, breathless, panting, her eyes gleaming, her whole frame convulsed. I have never seen her so excited or terrified before—even when ill-used, tortured, and in danger of her life.

"'They are coming—they are coming! A thousand canoes!'

"This she said in English.

"A thousand canoes full of savages! A cheerful prospect before me, truly, even allowing for exaggeration on the part of La-loo-hee-ah. Thousands of warlike and furious savages about to land and attack me again in my island kingdom!

"Truly, I am in a fair way of destruction now. La-loo-hee-ah is standing by my side, as I write, wringing her hands, almost weeping, imploring me to put on one side my papers, and come with her to view the approaching fleet.

"But I shall finish this entry—put away my diary, log-book, and pen and papers, and then go forth to meet my fate like a man—be it death or victory.

"Victory! It seems like mockery to write the word; for there comes to me the bitter memory that I am but one against thousands, and that the source of my power is gone from me. I am like Samson shorn of his locks; a lion with his teeth drawn and claws pared.

"My guns, rifles, and muskets are to be mute —no longer death-dealing weapons, but useless lumber. No matter—I look calmly on the prospect. Death stares me in the face; but I can face it. I have but one regret, and that is, that I shall not recover the gold—not make a successful 'dive for half a million.'"

Here ends (in all likelihood) the last entry in the diary of Crusoe Jack.

CHAPTER LXVI.
PREPARING FOR THE FIGHT.

AFTER finishing the above entry, which he thought but too likely would prove his last, Crusoe rose, and proceeded carefully and deliberately to roll up the diary, log-book, and other papers, and tie them tightly together with twine; then he wrapped up this bundle of papers, and a few other articles he wished preserved, in canvas, and finally enclosed the whole in a piece of tarpaulin, which he bound tightly round with spun yarn.

Then he walked out to a palm tree standing about a hundred yards to the south side of the hut, and, taking his sheath knife, proceeded to carve an inscription thereon.

He had previously stripped the bark off, and had little trouble in cutting the letters on the somewhat soft wood.

"Stranger, traveller, mariner, or explorer, who reads this inscription, make search at the foot of a bread-fruit tree two hundred yards due west from here, and you will find, about a foot beneath the surface, the written record of the life of Crusoe Jack, one time second mate of the ship Thunder, wrecked on this island."

Though the wood was soft, and he worked pretty quickly, yet it took him fully an hour to complete this inscription.

This done, he proceeded to bury the papers he had so carefully wrapped up at the foot of the tree.

All the while La-loo-hee-ah was in a terrible state of agitation and excitement, urging him continually to come with her.

But Crusoe had determined to take things coolly, and acted up to his resolve.

Said he to himself—

"Probably this day will end my life and adventures together. I will, however, do two things; make the best possible fight, with a good heart, and leave behind me, where it will some day be found, a record of my life and doings on this island—for sure am I that one day or other this extraordinary episode in an adventurous life will yet be read by and excite the wonder and interest of thousands of my countrymen."

Having buried the tarpaulin packet, and concealed as carefully as possibly all traces, by smoothing the earth and scattering sticks and dry leaves over in a careless way, he turned his attention to other matters.

La-loo-hee-ah, who had been watching all his doings with the utmost impatience, ever and anon urging him to desist and come with her, seized his hand the moment he had finished, and endeavoured to lead him away in the direction of the high western peak of the island he had named the Lion's Crown.

But to this he objected.

"No, no, La-loo-hee-ah," he said; "I have work to do here."

"Yes, yes. Let us go to the Crown. They come —they come in their hundreds of thousands!"

This she said in English, in which she had become marvellously proficient, considering how short a time she had been learning.

Of course, it was a great exaggeration this hundreds of thousands; and Crusoe, despite the gravity of the situation, could not forbear from smiling.

"No, no, La-loo-hee-ah. If they come, they must come; I have no means of preventing them. It can do no good going up to the peak, only to look at them. It will be simply a waste of time. Since I am to have visitors, I must make the best possible preparations for their reception."

He said this with a sort of grim humour, which was lost upon her, and then proceeded to make use of the small quantity of powder he had left in the flask.

Using the greatest care and economy with the precious powder, he used it as follows:

First, he loaded all the barrels of his revolver.

These took but very small charges, which was the reason he began with the pistol.

Next he loaded the American doubled-barrelled carbine, using the smallest possible charges.

Then two rifles; which, from the smallness of their bore, also required but little powder.

After having done this, he found that only enough powder for about three more charges of a rifle, or the six barrels of the revolver remained.

He now proceeded to count the barrels he had loaded.

"Two rifles and double-barrelled carbine, that is four; six chambers of the pistol, that is ten. Ah! ten men's lives at all events, if I am careful. Then I shall use the rest of the powder for the revolver. That is six more dead men, for I shall reserve my fire to the very last. That makes sixteen shots I shall have, and I will do my very utmost not to waste any, but have a life for every one. Sixteen dead men; or, at all events, most of them dead, or all badly hurt; for I shall be careful—very careful how I shoot. Sixteen dead men out of thousands! What will be the use of that? Little, I fear. I may keep them at bay till my last charge is fired; but long ere that they will grow emboldened at my reluctance to fire. Ah well! it can't be helped—I must fight it out. 'Fortune favours the brave,' they say, and I'll bet I don't show the white feather' nor go down without some of them having a taste of my leaden pellets. Then, I may knock over a few of them with cutlass and the broad axe—if I hit with that they'll feel it, I wager," and he smiled grimly as he reached forth his hand and took up the tool in question. "Who knows?—

perhaps, after all, I may pull through. Fortune plays strange pranks sometimes. Who can tell what wonderful surprise the fickle jade may have for me? Nil desperandum! When I have recovered the treasure, made my own fortune, and been created a baronet, that shall be my family motto. Now to work again to prepare for the reception of messieurs the savages."

La-loo-hee-ah had now become so impatient and excited that she could no longer restrain herself.

She started off, and ran along the ridge forming the lion's back like a frightened deer, and was soon lost to the sight of our hero.

"Gone to have another look at the enemy's fleet approaching," said Crusoe. "Well, perhaps it's as well—she can't do any good here."

Then he proceeded to make the best preparations he could for defence—his brain at work all the time to devise some settled plan of action which might seem to offer a chance.

"It's tremendous odds," he muttered. "Success seems impossible; escape with life equally so. No matter! I will make a tough fight for it, and die like a hunted fox without a whimper."

CHAPTER LXVII.
THE RIVAL FLEETS.

CRUSOE JACK now set to work strengthening his position in the best way he could.

The new hut was not so solidly built as the one destroyed by gunpowder; but this was not a matter of any moment. Indeed, he had profited by experience; and in the construction of this second fortress had retrieved some errors he had made in the first.

Thus he had more carefully loopholed it and made provision, so that he could command a view on both sides, he himself being secured from spears and arrows.

The firearms he laid carefully on the rude table, as also the flask containing all that remained of the powder, so that they might be ready to hand.

A cutlass, a broad axe, and a tomahawk, he also ranged in readiness.

Having done the best he could in the way of fitting the hut for defence, he now went out, and with axe and cutlass set to work cutting down the undergrowth and small trees, so that the savages should have no cover to conceal them when they advanced.

He seriously took into consideration the wisdom of abandoning the hut, and removing with all speed stores, arms, tools, &c., to a higher spot more difficult to be approached.

Now the highest part of all, the Lion's Crown, was totally inaccessible, except from one direction, the east.

He might, he considered, move up there with the assistance of La-loo-hee-ah, a considerable portion of his goods before the savages could land and attack him.

And once perched up there, with numberless rugged rocks, and huge boulders lying about, he felt certain the savages could never ascend in the face of the opposition he could offer in the shape of rolling down these rocks on their heads.

There were some drawbacks to this plan, however, one of which was the absence of water on the peak.

Of course it was not practicable to carry a large barrel up such a steep ascent, and he would have to be contented with a few jars and bucketfuls should he resolve there to stand a siege.

And if the savages were obstinate, and maintained a strict blockade, the want of water, and in time, even of food, would place him at their mercy.

So, for the present, he resolved not thus to isolate himself, but defend the hut if need be, and be ever watchful to seize any favourable chance which might offer to confound and defeat the savage foe.

There was yet another reason why he was loth to take to the rocky fortress on the Lion's Crown—he would thus cut himself off from his boat; and last, not least, the Golden Reef and the wreck of the Thunder, amidst which lay gold to the value of half a million sterling.

So he worked on vigorously, and ere long had made a great clearance of the undergrowth—scrub and shrubs, and small trees.

While thus occupied, the voice of La-loo-hee-ah fell on his ears from a considerable distance.

Looking in the direction whence the sound came, he perceived her standing on a small hillock on the ridge or backbone of the hill.

She was pointing out to sea, in a southerly direction, with outstretched arm.

She was fully half a mile distant, her figure, however, clearly visible against the sky, for she stood on a small eminence.

Her words, too, he could distinguish, spoken as they were in a high-pitched tone—

"Ketango maika! ketango maiga; ho omani Huanita!"

(The enemy comes! the enemy comes, and the warriors of Huanita).

This last sentence caused Crusoe some surprise.

He quite understood that the enemy were coming; but the warriors of Huanita, the island of which her father was king!

What did she mean by that?

Presently the very obvious thought occurred to him.

"I had better go to her, and see what she means."

She still stood pointing to the southward, and calling out, though, from the breeze freshening just then, and rustling amongst the branches of the trees, he could not make out her words.

Placing the revolver in his belt, slinging the double-barrelled carbine over his shoulder, buckling on his cutlass, and not forgetting the tomahawk, he started up the ridge, and in a short time stood beside La-loo-hee-ah.

It was up hill, and, as he ran a great part of the way, he arrived quite out of breath.

La-loo-hee-ah, taking his arm, pointed with her other hand to the south-western extremity of the island.

And there a strange and bewildering sight met his eyes—a sight which to him was quite inexplicable.

A crowd of vessels—a fleet of some hundreds of canoes were seen rounding the south-west portion of the island.

Or rather, two fleets, one of which had already rounded the point, and was making slowly towards a wide gap in the reef as if to come to land on the south shore, where there were several good harbours and inlets.

The second fleet had not yet all rounded the point, as each moment fresh canoes came into view.

Those of the latter fleet, however, already in sight outnumbered the first.

It was some time before Crusoe Jack could take in all the facts of the case.

He saw a fleet of from a hundred and fifty to two hundred canoes filled with armed warriors closely followed by another and more numerous one.

Between the two were exchanged at intervals flights of arrows, and occasionally he observed a canoe, or perhaps two, of the first fleet lag behind; then there would dash out from the second fleet several canoes, and at great speed make for the lag-behinds—it seemed to him with the intention of cutting them off from the main body.

But Crusoe observed that such attempts were vigorously opposed and frustrated by the foremost fleet; for immediately several large canoes would put off from the rest, and hasten to the rescue.

Then would ensue a sharp conflict—spears, as well as arrows flying thick and fast.

Sometimes two canoes of the opposite sides would come together, when a hand-to-hand conflict of considerable severity would ensue. But always, on these occasions, the canoes of the foremost fleet would get the best of it to all appearance, as on each occasion the others would be beaten off.

Crusoe watched these singular manœuvres for fully quarter of an hour.

La-loo-hee-ah, standing by his side, was trembling with excitement, and kept up a running fire of remarks in her own tongue.

Presently Crusoe perceived that the whole of the second fleet had rounded the point and come into sight.

He reckoned, as near as he could count, that there were about two hundred and thirty of them, while the first fleet did not number more than a hundred and fifty; so that, as far as numbers were concerned, the pursuers had greatly the advantage of it.

The second fleet, as the first passed through the opening into the coral reef, ceased to follow. Sails were lowered, and the paddles ceased to work.

All the canoes now congregated round a very large war vessel flying a large flag with strange devices thereon.

Crusoe judged, with reason, that this was the canoe of the chief or admiral of the fleet, and that directions were being given for future proceedings.

This council, or whatever it might be called, seemed likely to occupy some time, and our hero guessed that warlike harangues and inspiriting speeches were being delivered, or about to be so.

As he could not hear them, there was nothing much to interest him.

So he took advantage of the opportunity, and asked La-loo-hee-ah for an explanation.

"What is the meaning of this? Who are these savages, evidently of hostile tribes?"

She answered shortly, and to the point.

Showing him the first fleet, slowly passing through the opening in the reef, she said, in her own tongue—

"The warriors of Huanita, commanded by Akah Malatieta, the king, my father."

Then, pointing to the others, said—

"The men of Talanaki; the deadly enemies of my people—your enemies also, O white king."

Crusoe, who was at first bewildered, now began to understand the true state of affairs.

CHAPTER LXVIII.

CRUSOE SURVEYS THE CAMP OF THE SAVAGE FOE—A TERRIBLE MEANS OF REVENGE SUGGESTS ITSELF TO HIM.

LA-LOO-HEE-AH, standing by his side, watched all that was going on with quite as much eagerness as himself, and presently began to explain to him what was now being done, and how it all came about.

She spoke partly in the English tongue, much of which she had learned with marvellous quickness, but at times habit would get the better of her, and she would launch out in her own language, speaking with great rapidity and vehemence.

"The enemy, the men of Talanaki, have surprised our warriors. They know that I am on the island. And they know that the bones of our great warrior, long since dead, who fights for us, rest here. Their wise men, their kadodos have long told them that if they destroy the tomb of our spirit king, and scatter his bones by the sea-shore, that then we shall fall into their power like children, that they will scatter our warriors like leaves before the wind.

"Yes, yes, it is so. But our warriors are great warriors, and Akah Malatieta, my father, is a great king. And my brother, Malatieta Nina is a great chief. And the spirit of the long dead king will fight for us, and you shall fight for us, great white chief. You shall make your thunder and lightning, death-dealing weapons to speak to them.

"Ah! yes. We will beat them off, we will conquer and slay, make them all prisoners, and you shall be prince of all the islands, next in power and glory to my father."

Her eyes sparkled as she spoke, and, giving way to her enthusiasm, she seized his hand and placed it on her forehead, after the fashion of her people.

Crusoe, who understood all she said, though spoken in a mixture of the languages smiled at the prospect she held forth, and remarked—

"See, they are moving! Ah! they are going back."

And sure enough the fleet of canoes of the savages of Talanaki was in motion, propelled by hundreds of paddles; not in the direction which the other fleet had taken.

They seemed now to be retracing their course, and soon the foremost vessels disappeared behind the south-western point of the island.

Meanwhile, the fleet of Huanita had passed on through the reef into the lagoon, and were now entering an inlet well-known to Crusoe, where they could safely and easily move their canoes alongside the shore.

The foremost canoes of Huanita were also disappearing from view, as they paddled up the inlet.

Crusoe hesitated what course to adopt.

In a minute or two all the canoes—those alike of Huanita and Talanaki, would be out of sight.

To remain where he was would be useless, and he now debated with himself what course he should adopt.

La-loo-hee-ah decided for him, for taking his hand, she pointed to the high peak—the Lion's Crown.

"Let us mount there," she said. "We shall then see the enemy. It matters not about the others—they are friends.

There was reason in this; so together they ascended to the high point. Crusoe as he walked questioned La-loo-hee-ah, so as to be able to form a just idea of the state of affairs.

From all appearances fortune had once more favoured him, and this time most bountifully.

For if La-loo-hee-ah was right in her opinion, and the first fleet of canoes carried her father and the people of her tribe, he would have a body of numerous and warlike allies to join him in defeating the savages of Talanaki, who had already proved such fierce and determined enemies.

For, of course, on La-loo-hee-ah relating how he had rescued her from her enemies, and how together they had again and again beaten off the Talanakis with great slaughter, they would hail him as a friend.

And, very probably, though he smiled at La-loo-hee-ah's words when she said he should be "prince of all the islands," next in power and glory to the king, he would be looked upon with great consideration.

And (his heart beat high at the thought) was it not reasonable to suppose that at his earnest desire they would help him with the work at the Thunder's wreck, and aid him to recover the gold sunk in the hull of the old ship?

That La-loo-hee-ah should be mistaken in saying that these were her people was most improbable. However, as they made their way along the shore, he proceeded to question her more closely.

She was certain that the canoes which had passed into the harbour on the south shore of the island were those of her people. But she had discovered something which gave her great concern.

The war canoes of Huanita were divided into two parts—there were, in fact, two fleets.

The last and most important was commanded by the king, her father, and it was this one they had seen.

The other fleet, numbering nearly a hundred canoes, was commanded by her brother, Mala-tieta Nina.

She had recognised the distinguishing flag of her father's war canoe, but could nowhere make out that of her brother.

Besides, the canoes were not enough in number to consist of the two fleets.

Therefore, she argued, her brother, with his war canoe, was not present.

Therefore, she went on, there was reason to fear that something had happened to him and his war canoes.

Or, otherwise, it was not likely that the fleet of Huanita would be so largely outnumbered by that of Talanaki.

La-loo-hee-ah feared that her brother's fleet had been surprised, perhaps, on some expedition, attacked unawares by a superior force, and captured or destroyed.

That would account for the Huanita fleet retreating before the enemy, in order to protect the sacred relics of the dead king from falling into the hands of King Junga and his men.

La-loo-hee-ah went on to say that the Talanakis had a very wholesome dread of the warriors of Huanita, having often, to their cost, experienced their prowess.

And she was sure they would be very cautious how they attacked such redoubtable warriors, even though they largely outnumbered them.

Especially on this, which all the men of Huanita regarded as a sacred island, where they would fight with the utmost desperation, protected and aided by the spirit of the dead king.

La-loo-hee-ah had just finished explaining this when they arrived on the Lion's Crown.

The face looking to the east was a perpendicular precipice.

Crusoe, gazing around on the sea, could see nothing of the fleet of canoes.

"Gone!" he exclaimed, in bewilderment.

La-loo-hee-ah shook her head.

"No, not gone," she replied, "they are there."

And she pointed downwards, over the precipice.

Crusoe, going on his hands and knees, crawled to the edge and looked over.

And there, sure enough, they were, all of them—savages and canoes. The latter they had hauled on shore, and the great mass of the men were assembled right under the precipitous rock.

Crusoe regarded them in silence for a few moments, and then, drawing back cautiously exclaimed—

"By Jove!" A couple of dozen men acting in concert could roll over many tons of huge rocks, and utterly crush hundreds of these savage wretches!"

CHAPTER LXIX.

EXCITEMENT IN THE CAMP OF THE HUANITANS.

THERE was one quality which Crusoe had in an eminent degree, and the possession of which had a great deal to do with his success in many most dangerous adventures.

He was not by any means quick in deciding on a plan of action under circumstances of doubt and difficulty. Indeed, he usually pondered deeply, and studied, and dismissed from his mind many schemes before hitting on one with which he could be satisfied.

But when once light began to dawn upon him, when he felt certain that he saw the outline of the plan to be pursued, then all the rest came to him like a flash, and without a moment's hesitation more than necessary he would proceed to action.

And, as this history shows, he was always prompt enough in that respect, striking quickly, and striking hard.

It was so in this case.

A few moments after he had discovered the hostile savages, totally unsuspicious of danger, quietly bivouacked under the precipitous face of the Lion's Crown, he hit upon a plan for destroying them wholesale.

In the first place it was necessary to get the friendship and assistance of the warriors of Huanita, La-loo-hee-ah's people.

This he had little doubt of being able to accomplish without trouble.

"Come," he said to La-loo-hee-ah, "let us leave this, and go down to the shore. I must be a friend of your father the king, and his warriors."

La-loo-hee-ah assented, somewhat wondering at the sudden decision of her companion, for of course she could not know of the plan which had struck him for discomfiting and destroying the enemy.

It was now approaching evening; the sun was sinking to the horizon in the west.

Striking off from the ridge about half-way between the Lion's Crown and Flagstaff Point, Crusoe led the way down the slope, following the same route as when he had accidentally discovered the defile or mountain pass leading to the valley and lake of fresh water where he first saw La-loo-hee-ah.

As they advanced along the margin of the placid lake (a favourite resort of La-loo-hee-ah's for bathing, preferring it often to the sea water of the lagoon), the distant hum of human voices fell upon their ears.

They passed from the valley down the rocky bed of the little rivulet, which fell into the creek where La-loo-hee-ah moored her canoe, and down which she fled in headlong terror from the white man only to fall into the clutches of her enemies.

The sound of voices became now plainer every moment, and Crusoe judged that they had selected for a landing-place the very creek as had previously the savages of Talanaki.

As they neared the edge of the undergrowth of shrubs which lined the sandy shore, Crusoe slackened his pace.

"Gently, La-loo-hee-ah," he said. "You are in a desperate hurry to join your people. I must be more cautious; for, appearing suddenly, they may regard me as an enemy, and welcome me with a shower of spears—a proceeding which would certainly not be pleasant, and might prove fatal."

"Ah, great white king!" cried La-loo-hee-ah, "fear not. They will not harm the friend of their princess, La-loo-hee-ah!"

"Probably not, if they knew the facts; but as they do not, and cannot until the whole matter is explained to them, I think I had better remain here under shelter, concealed by the brushwood, while you advance to the encampment, and relate the history of our adventures."

"You are the wisest. It shall be as you say," replied La-loo-hee-ah, and then, pushing the leaves and branches on one side, she passed out on the open strip of sand, which everywhere lined the bank.

The creek where the warriors of Huanita had landed and encamped was about two hundred yards distant in a westerly direction.

It was admirably selected for safety and convenience, as, though the canoes moored on either shore, to the number of six score or over, were concealed by the thick scrub and other tropical vegetation which lined the banks, the sentries posted on guard could obtain a clear view along the sands by peeping through the slight openings in the foliage, themselves remaining invisible.

As they could see for more than half a mile in either direction along the coast, surprise by the sea was impossible.

All they had to do was to guard against surprise by the land side.

This was comparatively an easy matter, as a little hill or knoll, about two hundred yards in the rear of the encampment by the sea-shore, commanded a good view.

So that, even if attacked from that direction, they would have ample time to get the canoes out into the open sea, and beyond danger of damage or capture.

This was a most important matter, as the canoes of Huanita were larger and better built than those of their enemies; and being also better mariners, they fought by sea at an advantage, although greatly outnumbered.

The Huanitans at this time, however, did not seek concealment and the shelter of the woods, but were mostly gathered on the open sands.

The smoke of a score of fires rose to the sky, and around these many of the savages were grouped, some cooking, some polishing up their weapons, whilst others appeared to take it easily, merely lounging about and keeping up an incessant chatter of talk.

Others were busy building fragile structures of bushes and leaves, rude huts, in fact, while some were taking a bath in the lagoon.

La-loo-hee-ah advanced, and, as she kept in the shade of the shrubs, bushes, and small trees, she was not perceived until within a hundred yards of the encampment.

Then one savage, casting his eye upon her, suddenly gave vent to a cry, and in a few seconds a great shout of astonishment arose on the evening air.

There was a rush for arms, and then the multitude, seeing only one person, stood as if spellbound, gazing in bewilderment at the girl.

For it must be remembered that she presented a very different appearance now to what she did when she left the friendly shores of Huanita on her pious mission to the tomb of their long since dead warrior saint.

Now her attire had something semi-civilised about it, she having yielded to Crusoe's wishes as regards more drapery for her figure.

La-loo-hee-ah perceiving that she was not recognised, stopped, and raising her right arm aloft, cried aloud—

"Nargo faudana La-loo-hee-ah? Sarang Faler-a La-loo-hee-ah, Omam Huanita!"

(Do you not know La-loo-hee-ah? Welcome to the Princess La-loo-hee-ah, O warriors of Huanita!)

Then, after a moment or two, there arose a tremendous shout of rejoicing, and the warriors of Huanita ran, with wild excitement, and surrounded the daughter of their king, so that their tall forms hid her from the view of Crusoe.

CHAPTER LXX.

THE SAFETY OF LA-LOO-HEE-AH IS MADE KNOWN TO THE KING.

CRUSOE, though he could not see, could hear, and was able to distinguish the clear, musical voice of La-loo-hee-ah speaking rapidly amidst a running fire of exclamations and cries of astonishment.

She soon finished her speech, which was brief and to the purpose, and then the crowd of people opened out, falling back right and left, and La-loo-hee-ah, carrying a tall spear, with a white pennon advanced towards him.

"Come forth, white chief," she cried aloud, "and receive the welcome of the warriors of Huanita!"

Right thankful at the thought of being in the presence of friends, Crusoe came out from the bush.

La-loo-hee-ah, advancing towards him, took him by the hand, and led him into the midst of the crowd, the men falling back respectfully a few paces from the pair.

La-loo-hee-ah, now that she was restored to her people, seemed suddenly to have acquired regal dignity; and now, in her behaviour and speech, she was every inch the princess.

In a commanding voice, she addressed them—

"All but the warriors of the first order, all but those who have slain a chief in battle, will make obeisance to the white king."

Then there ensued a strange scene.

There were now assembled around La-loo-hee-ah and Crusoe fully two hundred of these wild children of nature.

Almost without exception, tall and handsome men.

Some wore ornaments—shells, corals, fishbones, and ivory.

Some, evidently chiefs, had on their heads thin circlets of the glistening white metal, and round these were stuck plumes of waving feathers of various kinds.

Those thus adorned with head-dresses were tatooed in singular fashion.

A single bar coming across the face in an oblique direction, starting from the left temple, and ending on the right jaw-bone under the ear.

These warriors, evidently men of note, were also infinitely better off in the way of attire.

For, whereas the majority had nothing but a narrow waistcloth of tappa, or some such material, these had around their waists a belt of the silver-like metal, about two inches broad.

To this were attached feathers, small shells, strips of fine white material, pieces of coral, and other articles, forming a short skirt, both picturesque and fantastic in appearance.

Of those whom Crusoe knew to be warriors of the first order, each having slain at least one chief in battle, there were about twenty, and they alone, of the crowd which momentarily increased, remained standing.

All the rest, at the command of La-loo-hee-ah, knelt and touched the earth three times with their foreheads.

This done, they remained on their knees.

"They are your servants — your slaves," whispered La-loo-hee-ah, in English. "Bid them rise when it pleases you, they will not do so before."

Crusoe at once caught the spirit of the thing, and fortunately was able to speak to them in their own language.

"Rise, warriors of Huanita! I, the white king, am your friend, and have come to lead you to victory over the enemy of Talanaki."

As they arose to their feet, there went forth a great shout—harsh, loud, and discordant—the war-cry of Huanita.

Crusoe now found himself suddenly transformed from a solitary adventurer into a hero—a man of note—a powerful chief.

CHAPTER LXXI.
CRUSOE IN COMMAND.

THAT which La-loo-hee-ah said to them, when first she discovered herself, had obviously produced this effect, and there could be no doubt that the submission and devotion of these brave savages were perfect and sincere.

He was regarded by them with great curiosity, tempered by respect—almost awe. The fact of his having learned enough of their language during his companionship with La-loo-hee-ah was of great use to him, and enormously increased his prestige and the esteem in which he was held.

The loud shout which greeted his brief address to those around him had been heard afar off, and scores of others came running to learn the cause.

These were quickly informed, and in their turn made obeisance.

Then there came two fellows running, and each blowing a rude horn at the same time.

These were the couriers of the king.

His majesty had seen the commotion—had heard the shouting, and now sent to know what it meant.

He had heard a rumour that the Princess La-loo-hee-ah, who was supposed to have fallen into the hands of the enemy, had been discovered alive and well, and had sent these, the king's messengers, to ascertain the truth.

"Go back to the king," said La-loo-hee-ah, "with all speed, and inform him that I, his daughter, am safe and well, and will hasten and present myself before him. I will leave you now," said La-loo-hee-ah to Crusoe Jack. "In the absence of my father and myself your commands, be they what they may, will be instantly obeyed."

Then, with a few words to the same effect to the crowd of chiefs and warriors surrounding them, she bounded off, and, fleet-footed as a deer, soon came up with the couriers already on their way.

Our friend now found himself in a most extraordinary and unexpected position.

He had at his orders some hundreds of warriors and chiefs, and yet felt strange and doubtful what to do—how to act.

At present it seemed that there was nothing to be done but wait the course of events.

The shades of evening were now darkening the scene, the sun having already set behind the island.

His fortunes had now, it would seem, taken a sudden and decisive turn for the better; yet he was nervous and anxious lest bad management and carelessness might even yet prove disastrous.

For, with a white man's prudence and forethought, he had not forgotten the horde of hostile savages camped under the steep cliff at the western extremity of the island.

He learned that the royal tent, or hut, was pitched amidst a grove of palm and cocoa-nut trees, some half mile away, where, watched by his faithful body-guard, his majesty could be free from the noise and turmoil of the camp.

The king had, it appeared, been wounded in the head by an arrow two days previously, and, though able to take the command of his forces, craved rest and quiet as much as possible.

Crusoe passed the time whilst La-loo-hee-ah was absent in examining the camp and its surroundings.

He was far from satisfied with the precautions taken against a surprise, and proceeded to exercise the authority vested in him, by doubling the sentinels, and placing them where he thought advisable.

His orders in this respect, though met with surprise, were obeyed without dispute or question.

Having thus provided, to the best of his ability, for the safety of the camp, and gone the round of the sentinels to see that all were at their posts, he anxiously awaited the return of La-loo-hee-ah.

For, though he could give his orders, and make himself understood in their language, he yet wanted the advice and explanations of the island princess on many subjects.

When she returned, escorted by a portion of the king's body-guard, it was night, and the light of scores of fires, around which the savages were grouped, illumined the scene.

She announced that the king would remain in seclusion that night, and at the dawn of day proceed on a pious pilgrimage to the sarcophagus of the long since dead warrior king, the founder of their race.

A spacious hut and a special guard, consisting of two chiefs and twenty warriors, were appointed for Crusoe; but, notwithstanding the fatigues and troubles of the day, he was far too excited and eagerly anxious as to the future, to find repose in sleep until the night had well-nigh waned.

CHAPTER LXXII.

CRUSOE WITNESSES AN EXTRAORDINARY SCENE.

AT early dawn Crusoe was up and about; and La-loo-hee-ah was soon after him.

And before sunrise all the encampment was alive, presenting the appearance of an ant's nest suddenly disturbed.

A portion of high land to the westward hid the sea and horizon from view in that direction.

Crusoe noted that the faces of all the islanders were turned towards the tree-covered ridge, behind which was the orb of day. As his early rays gilded the tree tops, a musical sort of murmur ran through the assembled crowd, all eagerly gazing to the east.

The instant when a bright spot gleaming over the ridge announced the appearance of the sun, there arose a great shout from the whole assemblage.

And then, as this died away, a wailing sort of chant thrilled on the morning air.

Crusoe could not distinguish all the words of the refrain, but understood enough to know that it was a sort of invocation or prayer to the morning sun.

There could be no doubt as to the fact, and he was greatly surprised at this conclusive evidence of the existence of sun-worshippers amidst the islanders of the Pacific Ocean.

The chant lasted some five minutes, the whole of the savages taking part in it, all the while dancing, gesticulating, pointing towards the sun.

In a very short time after it was concluded the smoke from scores of fires arose in and around the encampment.

A sumptuous breakfast was prepared for Crusoe and La-loo-hee-ah, without any request or trouble on their part.

Roasted bread-fruit, the pulp of cocoa-nut stewed in its own milk, and seasoned with certain savoury leaves, were laid before them.

After they had partaken of these, calabashes containing turtles' eggs, and a sort of seaweed, which these people seemed to consider a great luxury, were submitted for their approval; and lastly, fishes of various kinds, baked in hot stones, and wrapped in palm leaves, with plenty of young cocoa-nut milk to wash down the whole, made up an excellent repast.

Meanwhile, beyond the extremity of the camp, towards where the king had taken up his abode, a sort of procession was formed.

Crusoe noticed the waving plumes of many chiefs, and that some of the warriors, whom he recognised as of the king's body-guard, carried banners or flags, composed of the strange white silk-like material.

All of them carried spears, from the tops of which fluttered little slips of the same stuff, like lancers' pennons.

And gradually there swelled on the air, a wild concert of strange sounds.

He could distinguish the shrill whistling of a sort of fife, the beating of a drum, and undefinable sort of sound, like the twanging of some stringed instrument, and the hoarse bellowing of a rude horn or trumpet.

Presently there appeared a litter, covered by a canopy or awning, and in this, in savage grandeur, reposed, on skins, the king of Huauita.

The litter was borne by eight warriors, who proceeded to take up a position at the head of the procession.

Then the strange music swelled up to its loudest pitch, and, amidst the bellowing of trumpets, beating of drums, shrill screeching of pipes, and wild shouts of the savages, the king, thus attended, started on his pilgrimage to the ancient pyramid which Crusoe had discovered, with a sarcophagus at the apex, the last resting place of the ancient chief.

It was a most strange and picturesque sight, and Crusoe stood watching them with curious admiration, until they disappeared out of the sunlight into the leafy shades of the forest groves.

Until the king and the party that had gone with him returned from the performance of this solemn ceremony, Crusoe could do little save plan schemes for the future.

The first thing, he decided to himself, was to attack, defeat, and drive away for ever the hostile savages, who had encamped under the Lion's Crown.

But of course, although he and La-loo-hee-ah were left nominally in command, it would be necessary to consult with the king her father,

CRUSOE JACK AWAITED THE SAVAGE INDIAN'S BLOW.

36

and the other chiefs and warriors before commencing a campaign.

He ascertained from La-loo-hee-ah that her father, and those who had gone with him, could not be expected back till long after noon, when the sun should be well down in the western horizon.

Always hating inaction, he proposed to La-loo-hee-ah that they should make an excursion to their old home, the hut on Flagstaff Point, and thence proceed to the Lion's Crown to reconnoitre.

La-loo-he-ah willingly agreed, and our hero, having given strict orders for vigilance, and himself seen that sentries were properly posted all around, started on his excursion.

The hut, untenanted for only one single day and night, seemed to him to have a desolate appearance.

No fire now burned or smouldered in front, and altogether the scene and its surroundings had a melancholy effect.

There were still visible the marks of combat, the burnt trees around, the ground torn up by the explosion, and the grove where had been La-loo-hee-ah's bower entirely uprooted and destroyed.

But still, notwithstanding all these evidences and reminders of war's alarms, and of the perils and disasters he had there passed through, he felt a sort of affection for the place which he had first fixed upon for his abode.

Without hindrance or adventure he and his companion reached the Lion's Crown, and cautiously looking over the edge of the almost perpendicular cliff facing to the west, he saw that the hostile savages were encamped as on the preceding day.

Their canoes were still by the shore, some moored, some dragged upon the sand, while great numbers of themselves were encamped at the foot of the precipice.

Having ascertained this fact, he and La-loo-hee-ah proceeded to retrace their steps, and, after a short delay at the hut, descended to the shore, and returned to the camp of the Huanitans, arriving there about three hours after noon.

Very shortly after this there came a sound from the direction in which he knew the sacred pyramid lay of loud and discordant shouting.

Moment by moment the noise grew louder and more discordant as the returning party approached. La-loo-hee-ah, who was at first indifferent, grew interested, presently started and listened intently, a look of surprise and uneasiness on her face.

"What is it which troubles you, my island princess?" asked Crusoe, carelessly, for he was now able to tell by the play of her features when anything excited her wonder or annoyance.

"Hush! I want to hear what they are shouting."

"Singing a song of joy and triumph, I suppose."

"No, no! it is a war song; they are shouting forth angry words threatening death to some one."

"To the enemy, doubtless," remarked Crusoe.

"No, no; it is not that," replied the girl quickly. "I cannot understand it."

"Come, then," said Crusoe, "let us go and meet them. See, they are emerging from the wood on to the open ground."

He now proceeded to walk towards the cortège, followed by La-loo-hee-ah, who from some cause seemed very ill at ease.

As Crusoe and La-loo-hee-ah approached the Akah Malatieta, the king gave the order for those around him to cease their noise.

The assemblage opened out to our friends, and Crusoe advanced, with La-loo-hee-ah by his side, to the gorgeous litter on which reclined his majesty of Huanita.

In front of this, however, was an extraordinary character, a grey-bearded old savage, at least six feet and a half in height, with a quantity of tangled, dry sea-weed hanging from a circlet or band which went round his head.

He also wore one solitary tall plume.

His body, arms, and legs were tattooed in a most extraordinary fashion.

His skin showed scores of scars, as if from knife wounds.

That this was the case his present proceedings would seem to prove most probable.

He was dancing about in a wild and most mad manner, gesticulating and shouting the while, and absolutely frothing at the mouth from excitement and exertion.

In one hand—the right—he held a sort of dagger, curved like a boar's tusk. With this he frequently gashed himself about the body, legs, and other arm.

Streams of blood were flowing from him in many places.

"A curious amusement," said Crusoe to La-loo-hee-ah. "Poor devil! He must be mad. Why don't they take the knife away from him, and not let him cut himself about in this fashion?"

"Ah," replied La-loo-hee-ah, "you do not understand. He is a holy man. He is sacrificing blood to the spirit of our great dead king, hoping to ward off some terrible disaster."

The King now said some words sharply, and the old savage ceased, and stood panting and bleeding, a piteous spectacle.

Crusoe now perceived that the old fellow held in his other hand a knife of European manufacture—a sheath knife.

No other than the very knife he had himself left by the side of the skeleton in the sarcophagus, when he first discovered it, and proceeded to examine it closely.

Urged by some unfortunate impulse, he stepped forward, and laid his hand on the knife.

"It is mine," he said, in the Huanitan tongue. "I left it at the tomb months ago. Give it to me."

Tremendous was the effect of these words.

In an instant all was confusion and consternation.

La-loo-hee-ah gave vent to a little shriek of dismay.

The king raised himself in his litter, and pointing to Crusoe said some words in a rapid, excited tone of voice.

The old greybeard with the strange locks of seaweed gave utterance to a terrific howl, and this was instantly taken up by the surrounding chiefs and warriors, till the din was something horrible.

Again the king, whose eyes glared fiercely,

and who seemed fully to participate in the general excitement, shouted forth some words.

When there was a sudden, surging rush, and in a moment Crusoe found himself surrounded, seized, overpowered.

He had not a chance for resistance.

His hands bound behind him, he was dragged to a tree, and made fast thereto by strong bonds of stringy bark.

Half a score of savage warriors danced before him, poising their spears and javelins, aiming them at him, drawing their bows, and some whirling their clubs, in close proximity to his head.

The shock was sudden and unexpected, and for a few moments Crusoe was utterly overcome by terror.

He grew deadly pale ; a cold sweat broke out on his face, and he all but fainted.

Presently, however he recovered himself a little, and looked around.

"It is all over. I am to die now—that seems certain!" he said to himself. "To think of perishing thus, like a rat in a corner! Farewell life—hope—dreams of ambition! Farewell bright and glorious world – the last hour of Crusoe Jack has arrived!"

CHAPTER LXXIII.

MOMENTS OF HORROR.

THIS wild and tumultuous scene, so terrible to Crusoe, who was all the while in peril of instant death, continued for some minutes.

La-loo-hee-ah's father now alighted from the royal litter, and in a stern voice bade the savages —who were howling, capering, and brandishing their weapons around Crusoe—cease their noise and be quiet.

Then, at a further command, all fell back and seated themselves in a semi-circle, in the centre of which were the litter, the king, and some of the principal chiefs and warriors.

A smaller semi-circle, was formed by these latter facing Crusoe bound to the tree.

All seated themselves save the king and the tall grey-bearded old man who had been howling, dancing, and cutting himself in such a frantic manner.

The latter, though he no longer shouted, yelled, and capered, was still obviously in a state of great excitement.

He was trembling and moving about in a nervous manner ; which, indeed, was not to be wondered at, for the many gashes he had cut in his skin were still raw and bleeding, and, though not deep, must have been exceedingly painful.

Also he kept muttering to himself, waving the knives he held—one in each hand—glaring now and again ferociously at Crusoe as though eager to plunge one into his heart.

The king now proceeded to address the assemblage, and Crusoe gathering the purport of his harangue, slowly began to understand why he had been thus unexpectedly attacked, overpowered, and bound.

Also he learned from the king's speech the terrible fate in store for him.

"Warriors of Huanita! the holy man, Lafum Tambaroora, declared the great spirit of our ancient king, who hitherto has always fought for us, was offended, and now, in his anger, suffered our enemies to kill and wound our people and destroy our villages and canoes.

"He said that nothing but blood would assuage the anger of the offended spirit, and with holy zeal has caused his own to flow freely. Behold him!"

A murmur of pity, determination, and respectful awe went through the assembly, as all eyes were turned on the old man, who indeed presented an appearance both grotesque and horrible enough.

"Warriors of Huanita! the holy man spoke the words of truth and wisdom when he said that the spirit of the great king had been grievously offended, and that blood only—the blood of the offender—could appease his wrath.

"The nature of the offence has been revealed by the criminal himself.

"The last sanctuary and the sacred solitude of the tomb, where lie the bones of our great chief, king, and guardian spirit, have been violated by one on the part of whom it was sacrilege even to cast eyes upon the funeral monument. For was it not laid down as irrevocable law—the last instructions of the great king, my ancestor—that no living man, save one, of our royal family, or the next heir to the throne, should ever presume to invade the sanctity of that last resting place?

"A man—a stranger to ourselves in race—a man of noble and godlike appearance, but none the less a man, has dared to penetrate to that sacred place. His unhallowed feet have climbed the monument ; his unhallowed eyes have gazed on the remains of the dead. More, he has even dared to profane the tomb itself ; and, in token of his having done so, left there this weapon of strange form and make.

"Behold the man—a prisoner—bound fast in our power. He must die. With his blood alone can he atone for his crime. Advance then, holy father, most reverend Lafum Tambaroora. Your blood has been shed by yourself. The glorious privilege rests with you—of driving a weapon to the heart of the criminal, and so appeasing the anger of the spirit.

"Warriors of Huanita! arise to your feet! Let your voices proclaim to the offended spirit that justice is about to be done, and vengeance inflicted."

Then the whole assemblage arose as one man, and an extraordinary scene commenced.

First, there went up to the sky a long-drawn wailing yell, like the howling of troops of wolves, jackals, and hyænas. At first this was inarticulate, but soon it assumed the shape of words ; and the unfortunate captive, who knew, from the King's speech, that he was to be murdered, listened to what was in reality his own death-song.

It was a sort of a war chant sung always by the Huanitans before they put to death criminals or prisoners, and was intended to inform the spirits of departed friends that they were about to sacrifice enemies to their memory.

This infernal song, accompanied by a wild and furious dancing, brandishing of spears, and so forth, was continued until sheer exhaustion caused the savages to relax in their efforts.

Gradually the shouting grew feebler, the dancing and leaping tamer, and presently King Akah Malatieta gave the signal for silence and quiet by holding up his hand.

Then, whilst the whole of the savages stood

around, panting with excitement, their eyes gleaming with cruel ferocity at the thought of the tragedy to be enacted, he pronounced the fatal words, which Crusoe knew but too well were his death warrant—

"Most holy and reverend kadodo, whom men call Lafum Tambaroora, behold the criminal—bound at your mercy. It is for you to let out his life-blood."

The old man trembling with excitement, eager for his murderous task, advanced.

Throwing down the knife which he had used to lacerate himself, he took the sheath-knife of Crusoe in his right hand, and brandished it before the unhappy victim.

Then his eyes, gleaming with horrible ferocity, with his left hand he felt the ribs of the captive in the region of the heart, as though feeling for a proper place into which to plunge the weapon.

Then he raised the cruel blade, and prepared to strike.

Crusoe now experienced all the bitterness of death.

The sweat broke out on his pallid face, and, spite of all his fortitude, a gasping cry broke from his livid lips.

"Oh, God ! to die thus—to be slaughtered like a sheep !"

After brandishing the knife several times, and performing various antics before the unhappy white man, he suddenly retreated a few paces. Then, in two bounds, he was again close to the victim.

With a yell of cruel joy, he raised the deadly sheath knife.

"Die, accursed one !" he screamed out.

And then the hand holding the executioner's knife descended.

A cry from Crusoe !

A yell from the savages !

And yet another cry !

CHAPTER LXXIV.
CRUSOE'S DELIVERANCE.

DEATH, in every form or shape, must always be to the human mind more or less terrible.

Even the pain-worn and weary invalid cannot regard the passage from this to another world without a sort of shuddering alarm.

Nor even can the man or woman, fortified by religion, though ever so firm a believer, look forward to the severing the bond between soul and body without fear and instinctive shrinking.

How much more terrible a sudden, violent, and agonising death !

Amidst the roar and excitement of battle the spirits are in such a whirl that the mind sometimes is unable to think of the prospect of death.

Brave men, by a supreme exercise of will and strength of mind, are able to despise death ; or, at all events, to act as though it had no terrors for them—sublime hypocrisy !

But nevertheless, in all human beings—rich or poor, brave or cowardly—there exists, as an essential part of man's nature, the fear of death.

Crusoe Jack was a brave man, and had proved his courage many times.

But in face of the prospect of a death—sudden enough to be terrible, yet sure enough to be accompanied by great agony—his heart sank within him.

As he saw the gleaming knife uplifted, preparatory to being plunged into his body, a shudder went through his frame. He felt a sudden faintness—a sickening feeling of helpless terror. His eyesight failed him—he saw as though through a mist, and his breath came in short gasps. Then, summoning all his resolution to meet the pain of the fatal wound and the last agonies of death as became a man, he clenched his teeth and hands, and awaited the stroke with closed eyes.

A sort of numbness came over his faculties ; and momentarily expecting to feel the deadly stab, he, in a measure, longed for it.

His hearing, like his eyesight, was rendered dull by the intense mental agony he had endured.

Even his thoughts—his powers of perception and reason seemed to have received a shock, which rendered their action slow and uncertain.

He was dimly conscious of a cry in a familiar voice—of the presence of a familiar form—of confusion, followed by other sounds, shouts, and exclamations.

And then, suddenly, he felt that the bonds which had bound him to the tree by the arms and body were loosed.

He staggered forward, opened his eyes, and was like to fall, but he felt himself suddenly seized around the waist in a soft though vigorous grasp, and heard close to his ear these words, spoken in a high-pitched but withal melodious voice—

"Saro, Omani Huanita ! Sumatabuka eixta puta kalila. Falera La-loo-hee-ah amalono ma purata—kaboom—Panabusa, Omani Huanita !"

He heard every word ; they rang in his ears and he was dimly conscious that the voice was familiar to him, but at the time they carried no impression to his mind, although he was by this time literally well acquainted with the language.

When his vision cleared, and his senses and faculties slowly resumed their functions, an extraordinary sight met his eyes.

The whole aspect of the scene had changed as though by enchantment.

A change came over the spirit of his dream.

*   *   *   *   *

La-loo-hee-ah was by his side, half supporting him with her left arm, while on her right she bore a small native shield.

Sticking in that shield, driven in deeply by a vigorous blow, was his own sheath knife—the knife, the discovery of which at the tomb, and its acknowledgment by him, had caused his being doomed to death.

It had been aimed at his breast, the blow given with all the strength of the fierce old grey beard —with such force indeed that he was unable to withdraw it, and left it sticking in the wood and shark skin, of which the shield was made.

It was to La-loo-hee-ah that he owed his life —it was her sudden and unexpected interference which had wrought such a sudden change in the aspect of affairs, and snatched him from the very jaws of death.

When first on his claiming the knife he had left at the tomb he was seized and bound, she, knowing the unpardonable enormity of the offence he had committed, was aghast and dismayed, and knew not what to do.

Trembling and agitated, she listened to the stern speech of the savage king her father, and hea:d Crusoe doomed to death. Too well she was aware of the relentless cruelty with which the sentence would be carried out, and her heart sank within her as she thought of the terrible scene about to be enacted.

Trembling and excited, her gaze wandered wildly between her father, the prisoner, and the fierce greybearded old madman who was to be executioner.

She thought of kneeling at the king's feet, and imploring pardon for the offender, on the ground of the services he had rendered her.

But she knew it would be useless, and would only serve further to inflame the anger of the king and chiefs.

It was not until the last moments approached, when the executioner, his cruel eyes gleaming with savage joy, advanced, knife in hand, to butcher the unfortunate prisoner, that a sudden thought flashed across her mind.

She remembered an ancient and inviolate law of her nation.

It was to this effect, and involved a most extraordinary law of succession to the throne.

The king reigning having sons and a daughter, the next heir, in the ordinary course, would be the first son.

But if, during the lifetime of the king, this daughter should resolve to take to herself a husband, by this strange law the succession would devolve upon this husband and the daughter, who, in due course, would reign jointly as king and queen.

Also, she was well aware that, according to Huanitan customs, all that was necessary to constitute a marriage—or rather, to render one inevitable—was for the woman publicly to acknowledge a man as her husband.

Strictly speaking, this was, perhaps, no more than a betrothal; but it was invariably followed by a more elaborate ceremony, and that immediately, if possible.

No sooner did the memory of this law occur to La-loo-hee-ah than she proceeded to make use of it for the benefit of the prisoner.

There was not a moment to spare.

She had barely time to seize a shield from one of her people and intercept the murderous blow of the old man.

The next instant the captive's bonds were severed—he was free ; and she, half supporting him, addressed the few short and commanding words to the assembled multitude which had such a powerful and astonishing effect—completely changing the whole aspect of affairs.

It has been said that Crusoe heard every word, but that they conveyed no impression to his mind, in such a state of mental prostration was he, having literally experienced all the bitterness of death.

This was, translated into English, the brief and impressive speech she made :—

"Hear, O warriors of Huanita. This great white chief and spirit, I, the Princess La-loo-hee-ah, take as my husband, now and for ever. Kneel and make obeisance, warriors of Huanita."

CHAPTER LXXV.

CRUSOE BECOMES A PRINCE.

IT is a well-known fact that savages of all descriptions, the most ferocious as well as the most gentle and inoffensive, are peculiarly liable suddenly—instantaneously sometimes—to reverse their whole course of action, looking on their hitherto foes as friends—their friends as enemies, and this with what would seem to white men a very insufficient reason.

It was so in the present case.

For a few moments after the sudden interference of La-loo-hee-ah, they looked amazed—inclined to be angry.

The greybearded old executioner did not disguise his indignation at being thus baulked of his prey. Once his cruel nature fully aroused, he was like a wild beast which had tasted blood.

"Stand back, woman! Though a king's daughter, you shall not stay the sacrifice and vengeance due to our great spirit. Am I not right, O Akah Malatieta ?" he added, turning to the king.

"You are right," replied La-loo-hee-ah's father, sternly. "Stand back, my daughter. Our laws are stern and not to be escaped. Our laws must be obeyed—he must die !"

But La-loo-hee-ah was now fully aroused ; and, as is often the case with women, combined quick intelligence with a brave heart and earnest determination in the moment of danger.

With quick perception and good judgment, she cried—

"Our laws shall be obeyed. Hearken while I speak ; and when I have spoken, he who wishes to injure him (laying her other hand on Crusoe's shoulder as she spoke) will be the offender and worthy of death !"

Then she said the words which had such a marvellous effect—

"Hear, warriors of Huanita. This great white chief and spirit, I, the Princess La-loo-hee-ah, take as my husband, now and for ever. Kneel and make obeisance, warriors of Huanita !"

*   *   *   *   *

In a very few moments after the delivery of this short and impassioned speech, the whole of the assembled crowd—chiefs, warriors, and young men, who had not yet earned for themselves the title of warriors—fell on their knees, and, seeming completely convinced by the words of La-loo-hee-ah, made the required obeisance of touching the earth with their forehead.

Akah Malatieta and the fierce old kadodo Tambaroora alone remained standing.

The latter was savage, and obviously disinclined to be baulked of his victim.

"Is the sacrifice to the offended spirit—the just vengeance on the criminal—to be stayed by a woman, O king ?"

"Holy kadodo," replied the king, "my daughter has spoken. Her words are the words of truth. The white stranger is now one of our royal family, heir to the kingdom of Huanita. So lays down our law. What is done cannot be undone. What is to be will be. Our law is not to be changed, and according to our law the white chief, now condemned to death, is safe from harm from any warrior of Huanita, and must be respected and obeyed by all warriors and chiefs of Huanita, next to myself, Akah Malatieta, your king."

This speech of the king, delivered solemnly and with deliberation, effectually silenced the old kadodo, who could not dispute its justice or accuracy in point of Huanitan law.

Yes, there was no doubt about it; the white man, Crusoe, a few minutes previously condemned to death, and about to be cruelly slaughtered in cold blood, was now the husband of the fair La-loo-hee-ah, heir to the throne of Huanita and the tributary islands.

A very extraordinary situation truly, and one for which our friend had never bargained.

However, even had he been so disposed, he was in no way in a position to decline the extraordinary honour thrust upon him. As he gradually recovered from the shock caused by the terrible ordeal through which he had passed, he slowly began to realise his position in all its bearings.

On all hands he was treated with the most extreme respect, amounting even to reverence.

La-loo-hee-ah, perceiving that he was in a manner dazed by the desperate peril he had gone through, and the sudden and extraordinary change in his fortunes, said to him—

"Arouse yourself, prince and husband. Do not let these people think that you are cast down, or in evil humour. Walk with me to the sea-shore—there you will recover yourself, and we can talk."

Crusoe Jack had sense enough to see the advantage of following this advice, and, summoning all his resolution and energy, was once again himself, and, save for a sort of numbed feeling of which he could not get rid, was none the worse for this terrible adventure.

It may be thought by some that, in the presence of what seemed immediate and inevitable death, he scarcely bore out the character for dauntless bravery he has earned in the course of this tale.

The author is aware that a certain school or class of authors would have represented their hero as gazing defiantly with bold eye, unblanched cheek, and in the face of his foes.

They would have represented that his heart never quailed, that death had no terrors for him.

All this, and much more, they would probably have narrated; but all this and the much more would have been simply bosh!

Death, more especially sudden death, always has and must have terrors for the bravest.

If death carried no terror to the soul, there would be no bravery in meeting it with becoming fortitude. Therefore, a brave man must suffer terror in the face of death, or in imminent danger of death.

Therefore, a brave man must be terrified, frightened, or he cannot be a brave man.

Leaving our readers to study this apparent paradox, we will conclude the chapter.

CHAPTER LXXVI.
THE CORONATION.

It has been said that Crusoe was able to recover himself by an effort from the effects of the ordeal he had undergone.

To tell the truth, however, he felt languid and weak, and very much inclined to seek some shady place, and there recruit his damaged energies by a rest—a sound sleep.

However, he was wise enough to know that it would be the height of folly to show any sign of weakness, bodily or mental, to the Huanitans, who now regarded him with respect, mingled with a certain amount of curiosity.

So, as the expressive colloquial saying has it, he pulled himself together, and walking firmly, with head erect, did his utmost to look and behave as became the husband elect of the Princess La-loo-hee-ah, and heir to the throne of Huanita.

If it is true that "there is but a step from the sublime to the ridiculous," the adage should also hold good of the "terrible," the "dreadful," as well as the "sublime."

Strange thoughts often come at most inopportune times.

So it was with Crusoe now.

When La-loo-hee-ah originally made her short and impressive speech—the speech which doubtless saved his life and changed his fortunes—he did not gather anything of the sense, though he heard all.

But the words remained, as it were, printed on his brain, and when he recovered his composure and power of reason and thought, the sense of the words came to him, and he knew all about it.

The reality of his position dawned on him slowly at first, in a misty, vague manner.

But presently all was clear as sunlight, and he was able to contemplate all the circumstances.

What a strange fate was his! With a savage princess for wife—himself one day to be king of Huanita, an island in an unknown archipelago.

Where now were his plans for the future—his hopes of adventure, discovery, and glory—his ambitious dreams?

What a termination to all!

But was it a termination?

Did it not seem like it?

Undoubtedly he actually was, or would be, married to this wild island beauty. It was certain that, but for her courage, presence of mind, and devotion, he would have been past marriage—or, indeed, any other of the joys or sorrows of human life.

As a matter of honour, he could not repudiate this hasty marriage, as thereby his life had been saved.

As a matter of inclination, he had no wish to do so at the moment.

Was not La-loo-hee-ah lovely and loving? Had she not given him ample proof of her courage and her devotion to him?

Was she not a princess?

And was it not a fact that her alliance would make all the warriors and chiefs of Huanita his willing servants?

Would he not be, in fact, from his superior knowledge and intelligence as a white man, as well as the consort of La-loo-hee-ah, really king at the present moment—king de facto, if not de jure?

Yes, king, it is true; but king of a tribe of nearly naked savages.

La-loo-hee-ah, too, was a princess; but none the less an uncivilised, savage girl.

But need she remain so?

Was it not possible to educate her—to cultivate her mind and guide her taste, so that she should be worthy to take her place in civilised society?

He had ample proof of her really wonderful intelligence, and capability of learning.

There was yet another reason, and, perhaps, the most powerful of all, why he could not refuse to complete the implied contract.

Nolens volens, he was and must be the the husband of La-loo-hee-ah, Princess of Huanita.

Honour, gratitude, and, lastly, self-interest —self-preservation even—bade him accept the situation.

Said he to himself, whatever is, is right, is the creed of some philosopher.

To quote the motto of the ducal house of Bedford, " Che sara sara."

" It is true," he went on, pursuing his soliloquy—" it is true that this somewhat tame and matrimonial end to my adventures is far from that which my ambition sketched out. No matter! it is the characteristic of a true philosopher to adapt himself to circumstances, and so bend fortune to his will.

" My hopes and dreams tended in quite a different direction. 'L'homme propose, mais Dieu dispose.'

" I accept my fate—not grumblingly, or with a downcast heart, but with all willingness and sincerity.

" Hail to myself, Crusoe Jack! Imperator, King of the Thousand Islands.

" Yes," he said to himself, smiling, " I like that. Not a bad title at all—it will look well in print."

As he thus communed with himself, they were walking slowly down towards the placid shore of the lagoon, La-loo-hee-ah gazing all the while in his countenance, gathering, by the expression of his features, the tenor of his thoughts.

She saw he was not ill-pleased, and presently said, in her soft, murmuring, melodious voice—

" My lord is a great chief; he will be the greatest king of Huanita since the beginning of time. The enemy shall be scattered from him like flying fish from the dolphin, and the whole world shall ring with the praises of the white king and his loving and lovely bride, Falera La-loo-hee-ah, Princess of Huanita."

With these words she dropped gracefully on one knee, and taking the hand of the white man, raised it to her lips.

Crusoe Jack was touched by the innocent devotion of his new-made island bride, and with a smile on his handsome, sunburnt features, said—

" Don't be absurd, La-loo-hee-ah, why kneel to me? It is I who should kneel at your feet in loving gratitude; for have you not saved me from a dreadful death?"

He raised her just as a savage, a courier from her father, Akah Malatieta, bounded up; first, he made obeisance, touching the earth with his forehead; then, with great reverence, he proceeded to place upon the head of Crusoe Jack a circlet or diadem of the glistening metal.

Around this, inserted in the edge, were feathers fully two feet high, standing upright, while there gracefully drooped from the back part and sides, the splendid golden orange plumes of the great bird of paradise.

Crusoe took it off, and gravely placed it upon the head of the savage to observe the effect. He looked at it, and pictured to himself his own appearance in the extravagant and gorgeous head-dress.

Less than half-an-hour previously, a certain and terrible death stared him in the face; nevertheless, so irresistibly droll did the thought of himself thus adorned appear, that he could not control his merriment, and, to the astonishment of La-loo-hee-ah and the savage messenger, burst into a fit of laughter, long, loud, and hearty.

Presently, having laughed to his heart's content, he donned the gorgeous head-dress, symbol of his new and exalted rank and with La-loo-hee-ah by his side, gazing at him in fond admiration, returned to the camp—all the savages, warrior and chief alike, regarding him with wondering awe, and making lowly obeisance.

CHAPTER LXXVII.
CRUSOE IS MARRIED.

No time was lost in the celebration of the nuptials of Crusoe and the king's daughter.

The white man would have preferred that the ceremony should, at all events, be postponed; for there was with him a vague feeling of dislike to having the marriage formally ratified, although he had previously acknowledged to himself that it was both necessary and prudent, and that, even if he felt so inclined, it was impossible now for him to escape from it.

He instructed La-loo-hee-ah to lay before the king the desirability of first defeating and driving away the hostile savages who they knew were encamped on the other side of the island.

But to this the answer was prompt and decisive, and La-loo-hee-ah confirmed the words of the king—

" From time immemorial amongst the Huanitans it had been the custom for the marriage ceremony to be performed on the same day as the announcement of the choice was made.

" As for the enemy of Talanaki, there was no fear of their attacking again for several days.

" Such a thing as a sudden attack which Crusoe feared had never been heard of. It was a custom which long observance had made almost sacred.

" Moreover," continued the king, " the white chief, his son-in-law, would now, in virtue of his rank, take the command of half the forces of Huanita. He could take any precautions he thought fit to guard against a sudden surprise."

Accordingly Crusoe submitted; and, after doubling the number of sentinels—posting some on elevated points, and two at the hut on Flagstaff Hill—signified himself ready to undergo the ordeal, the savage ceremony, by which he was to be formally united to La-loo-hee-ah.

It took place that very afternoon, and was conducted with great magnificence and uproar, beating of drums, and playing on wild instruments which gave forth unearthly music.

We have no space here to describe the furious dances—the mystic rites—which might have been solemn but for their grotesqueness—the loudly-yelled songs—the ravings, howlings, and universal madness.

Nor of the banquet which followed—whereat all gorged themselves to the top of their bent, and then proceeded to get drunk on poee, a native liquor distilled from the juice of a certain tree.

Nor can we speak of the wild doings which ensued when night closed on the scene and the faculties and reason of the Huanitans were entirely under the sway of the fiery poee.

There were songs and shoutings, and torch-light processions, and night dances till long after dusk; until, at last, the braves and warriors of Huanita, tired out and quite drunk, sought their huts, and proceeded to sleep off the effects of their debauch.

Crusoe could not help thinking all the while this wild scene was being enacted how terrible would be the consequences of a sudden attack by the enemy.

Totally unprepared—fatigued with their great exertions—dancing, singing, and shouting, and moreover very drunk, all of them, there could only follow on an attack panic and indiscriminate massacre.

As for the sentries the white man had posted, they were as nearly as possible useless.

It was only by severe threats and constant supervision they could be kept at their posts at all, and when this point was gained it was but of little advantage, for nothing could induce them to keep watch on the side whence the enemy must come, if at all.

Nothing could divert their attention from the fires and torches, the singing, shouting, dancing, and carousing going on at the camp.

However, the eventful day and night passed off without any alarm.

By order of King Malatieta, a large and handsome building—a sort of pavilion—had been constructed for the occupation of his daughter and new son-in-law.

Crusoe, however, preferred to take up his quarters at his own hut, on Flagstaff Point.

Some opposition was made to this; but he was determined to let all see that he had a will of his own, and would, moreover, act up to it.

So he held to his point, which was, after some discussion, granted.

A royal body-guard of twenty warriors and two chiefs were appointed him—the best and most trustworthy men in the tribe, he himself selecting them, prompted by La-loo-hee-ah.

And so ended the day of Crusoe's marriage to the island princess.

It was his wish and intention to commence hostilities immediately against the enemy, and drive them from the island.

Then he proposed at once to set to work at the wreck of the Thunder; and aided by at least a hundred strong savages, he hoped in a very short time to be able to get at and reclaim the treasure.

And this done, what next?

He could not answer the self-put question.

What should he do with it, supposing he succeeded in fetching it up from the bottom of the sea?

Now that he could count on the assistance of the friendly islanders of Huanita, who would be bound to work under his orders, it was almost a certainty that he would be able to construct a dam strong and compact enough to enable him to get at the hold of the ship with comparative ease.

His hope was to attack and drive off the enemy of Talanaki, and this done—which he doubted not would be an easy matter under his leadership—to set to work at once.

What, then, was his chagrin when he learned that another ancient custom of the Huanitans stood in his way?

No war, or, indeed, anything of importance, was ever undertaken within a week of either the birth, death, or marriage of a member of the royal family.

He soon found it was hopeless to seek to overcome this law, and forebore to try, as he had sense enough to know that he would only damage his own prestige and popularity thereby.

He had, then, a week in which to mature his plans, and make preparations both for the attack on the enemy and for working at the Golden Reef.

Somewhat to his surprise, he found that the Talanaki men, who had moored their canoes and pitched their camp right underneath the precipitous bluff, still remained inactive—only taking the precaution to have an advanced post of a dozen men or so, about a mile away on the shore, in the direction which the Huanitans must take should they advance against them.

Crusoe, however, observed that they had been largely reinforced, so that the Huanitans would soon have to fight against even greater odds.

This disadvantage would have been avoided if they could have been persuaded to attack the enemy at once, instead of waiting for a whole week; for it was not till three days had passed that the Talanakis received their reinforcements.

However, Crusoe had still perfect confidence in utterly routing them; relying on his own superior knowledge and genius for war, which would enable him to make the very best possible disposition of the warriors of Huanita.

His plan was, that the attack should be threefold—one party, commanded by the king himself, sailing round with a fleet of canoes, and attacking those of the enemy, which lay by the shore, or were hauled up.

The other to advance round the coast by land, and attack the enemy at the same time; while the third party would be commanded by himself, and consist of only about a dozen men.

And yet on this little band, on himself, and on the arrangements he had made, he chiefly depended for a great and decisive victory.

It has been mentioned before that the enemy had chosen to encamp right under the precipitous bluff at the top of which was the Lion's Crown.

They had chosen this spot because it was well sheltered from the morning and the noonday sun by the shadow of the great cliff.

He proposed, then, so to dig and undermine the whole top of this cliff that a very slight shock would detach it, and send it tumbling down on the heads of the unfortunate and astonished foe.

He planned so as to be able thus to **hurl down**

on them at one coup many hundreds of tons of rock and earth.

The ground sloped from the base of the mountains to the sea-shore, and he confidently anticipated that enormous fragments would go down to the sea itself, carrying havoc and destruction with them, and very likely smashing up many of the canoes.

At the end of the week all was in readiness, and the combined attack was fixed for the morning. at about two hours after sunrise.

The result we will leave to the next chapter.

CHAPTER LXXVIII.

ON THE "WAR PATH."

As the first grey light of dawn broke slowly over the island and surrounding sea on the day fixed for the grand attack, Crusoe was stirring betimes.

With his chosen body guard of twelve, and accompanied by La-loo-hee-ah (who declared that she would share all dangers her lord and master might be exposed to), he started up for the Lion's Crown, where he arrived almost a quarter of an hour before sunrise.

It had been arranged that all the forces—the part which would advance by land along the coast, and also the fleet of canoes, which was to make a simultaneous attack from the sea-side—should start together at earliest dawn.

When they reached the point—on rounding which they should be in full view of the enemy, and within half a mile—they were to stop, and remain concealed until the appointed signal was given for a general advance.

Then, with all possible speed, and shouting the war cry of Huanita, they were to rush on the astonished Talanakis, and totally annihilate them.

The signal was to be a loud report and a shout from the Lion's Crown, from which point Crusoe and his men were to commence the attack.

Crusoe, before starting himself, had received news by a running courier, from the king that the land force and canoe fleet were all ready, and on the point of setting out.

All necessary preparations had been made on the previous day, and there were only a few preliminary things to be now seen to.

We will briefly describe what had been already done, that the reader may the better understand what follows.

Along the edge of the Lion's Crown, about five feet from the brink, a very narrow ditch had been dug; not more than a foot wide at the bottom, but between eight and nine feet in depth.

At the top it was wider, of course, as otherwise it would have been impossible to dig the ditch.

At the bottom of this ditch, which thus ran parallel to the edge of the cliff, for a distance of twenty yards, gunpowder was placed, done up in canvas and tarpaulin, and then served with spunyarn which was tightly wound round the tightly bound-up packet, until it was nearly as strong as though made of solid metal.

These packets, duly charged with powder, and thus forming impromptu bomb shells, were laid along the ditch at a distance of about 6 feet.

To each of these there was attached a thin tube of canvas filled with gunpowder, which led up to the surface.

The earth was then thrown in again, mixed with big stones, and the whole tightly rammed down.

Now, obviously, by firing each of these tubes at the end above ground, the packets of powder alone must be exploded, for being connected with these improvised bombs they would act as fusees.

Of course, the ignition of all these together would cause a great explosion and shock, and Crusoe hoped and believed that this alone would be sufficient to tear asunder the whole top of the cliff from the ditch to the edge, and send it thundering down on the camp of the Talanakis at the foot of the cliff.

And not only would it be the top of the cliff, which, his plan succeeding, would be hurled down on their heads, but also a great number of huge rocks and stones, a wall of which had been piled all along the edge.

More than this. On the inside of the ditch was another great collection of big rocks, generally of such a shape that they could be rolled over the edge by the strength of one man.

In order further to make certain of the desired effect of the explosion, and to aid the gunpowder, Crusoe had planted upright in the ditch, the ends going right to the bottom, a number of tall saplings.

To the top of these, which reached some twenty feet above the ground, he had attached ropes, and, when all was in readiness, he placed men at the ends of these ropes, with orders to pull with all their strength when he should give the word.

These tall poles would act as powerful levers, and he thought would powerfully aid the gunpowder in blowing up the top of the cliff.

Having laid a train of powder, connecting all the fuses together, Crusoe was ready for action.

He had, he thought, provided for all emergencies.

Even if it should unfortunately happen that the explosive power of the gunpowder was not sufficient to blow off so large a piece from the top of the cliff, this would not prevent the attack from being made.

For, so soon as it was well ascertained that this portion of the plan had failed, he and his men would rush to the edge, and commence rolling over the huge rocks and boulders collected for that purpose, which alone must, Crusoe thought, cause great panic and destruction to the savages at the foot of the precipice.

All being in readiness, and having stationed his men, he was to give the preliminary signal by firing off the blunderbuss, which was heavily loaded.

The loud bang of this would certainly be heard by both the land and sea forces of the Huanitans; while it was possible that the explosion of the mine would produce a dull, rumbling, muffled sound.

Assuring himself that all was in readiness—that every man was at his post—Crusoe fired the blunderbuss, at the same time lighting the gunpowder train.

Then he ran back a few yards, and stood watching the effect.

Immediately following the report of the blunderbuss there was the flash of the gunpowder train, which ran along with a sputtering sort of noise.

But when each fuze was fired there came a violent fizzing and spurting of jets of flame from the ground. Then this ceased.

Crusoe stood in deep anxiety looking on, and when second after second passed without an explosion, he began to fear that his mine had missed fire.

Then there came an upheaval of the ground in several places, not exactly slow, but certainly not sudden or violent in appearance at first.

To this there quickly succeeded much greater commotion, the surface being for a second or so tossed about like a stormy sea.

Then all at once the earth appeared to split and open in several places, and jets of flame and gunpowder smoke burst out.

Then came a great flash, as the imprisoned blazing gases burst loose, followed by a dull, sullen roar.

"Now, men!" shouted Crusoe, in the Huanitan tongue, "all together and over it goes!"

With yells and shouts, the savages tugged at the ropes attached to the tops of the tall saplings.

Almost instantly they yielded—so suddenly, indeed, as to cause the white man, amongst others, to fall on his back.

Instantly scrambling to his feet, Crusoe advanced towards the edge of the cliff.

The whole scene was wrapped in a thick veil of gunpowder smoke, through which he could dimly see that a large chasm lay where had been the ditch and mine.

The effect was even greater than he had expected.

The whole top of the cliff had been riven off, not only to the depth of the ditch, but much deeper; for the shock had torn off a large slice of the mountain face lower down.

All this took place in a very short space of time.

Crusoe was slowly and cautiously groping his way though the smoke, when a loud, thundering crash told that the huge cliff, and the rocks thereon piled, had reached the bottom.

Almost instantly following thereon, and before the rumbling echoes had subsided, there arose on the morning air an awful din of human voices, shrieks, yells, and dreadful howls of fear and pain.

Then arose the war cry of the Huanitans, as the land force and fleet of canoes, rounding the point together, made straight for the enemy at utmost speed.

In the course of a minute or two there came a gust of wind, which dispelled the smoke, and allowed Crusoe to advance to the brink, and look down on the scene.

It was indeed an extraordinary one.

At the foot of the cliff there was a huge mound of rock and earth, caused by the masses which fell from the mountain.

Amidst this he could see struggling forms, some evidently too desperately hurt to rise, whilst others were half-buried in the earth.

Some could be seen slowly and painfully crawling away, while the groans and cries of the wounded and dying could plainly be heard at the top of the rock.

Crusoe, listening to these cries, gazing on the wounded and the half-buried savages, had a feeling of pity, almost of compunction, for the part he had played in the catastrophe.

Right well he knew that for every struggling form he saw at the surface of this mound of destruction, there were a dozen utterly buried, and the life crushed out of them beneath.

Beyond this great heap itself, right down to the shore, the ground was strewn with injured savages, and great rocks, which, becoming detached from the main body, had gone rolling down the slopes, crushing and maiming all who fell in the way.

Some of these huge boulders had gone thundering down right into the sea, smashing and damaging many of the canoes moored by the shore.

Those of the Talanaki savages who had escaped without injury were in a state of utter terror and panic.

The war cries of the Huanitans, now coming down rapidly to the attack by land and sea, completed their discomfiture.

The brave army of Talanaki now presented the spectacle of a mob of frightened fugitives, rushing in wild confusion to their canoes in hopes of escaping.

A very brief survey of the scene was sufficient to satisfy Crusoe.

The victory was won.

The defeat of the enemy utter and complete.

CHAPTER LXXIX.

VICTORY!

THE attack of the Huanitans on their detested foes completed the rout of the latter.

Although many of them turned and fought singly with considerable desperation, there was no general resistance. It was a complete rout, a great rush to the shore in order to escape by means of the canoes.

Only some, less than half of the whole army of Talanaki, succeeded in embarking and pushing out to sea.

The remainder were either killed, wounded, or made prisoners.

These latter would have been immediately tortured, and then put to death; but Crusoe had previously given strict orders (and the king sanctioned all his decrees) that their lives should be spared.

Under any circumstances, the Englishman would have insisted on this, for humanity's sake; but there were yet other reasons why the prisoners should be kept alive.

He intended to force the prisoners to toil as labourers at the great work, the prosecution of which he had for some time been compelled to relinquish.

And, moreover, to do the hardest and most disagreeable part of the work—a punishment he considered they had well earned by their wanton attack upon himself and the intended cruelty La-loo-hee-ah.

And so, as the they were bound to and marched off to escort.

Crusoe, from his high position on the top of the cliff, could see, and even hear, all that passed.

And by the aid of the speaking-trumpet he was able to bellow forth his orders, which were implicitly obeyed.

The fleeing warriors of Talanaki—no longer forming an army, only a horde of panic-stricken savages—gazed with wonder and fear on their old and terrible enemy, the all-victorious white man, who had inflicted on them before such defeats and dreadful slaughter.

He seemed to them, as he stood on his rocky eminence, like some terrible avenging spirit.

The loud bellowing of the speaking-trumpet, too (of course, an utter mystery to them), they not unnaturally thought to be the voice of the dreadful war-spirit of the Huanitans, who, under the guise of a man of strange appearance and pale face, had lured them on to their destruction.

And certain it is that, as the terrified fugitives plied their paddles with all their might and main to escape from the scene of their discomfiture, each of them firmly resolved that never again would he make one of a party to land on this, which had proved to them, an island of death.

No pursuit of the fleeing enemy was made by order of Crusoe, who considered that quite enough prisoners had been taken, and that the enemy after such a tremendous lesson would never again attempt to molest him on this his kingdom, Lion Island.

The explosion took place at sunrise, the attack taking place immediately after, as the reader already knows.

And before the sun had mounted half way to the meridian there was nothing to be seen of the fierce warrior army of Talanaki but a few dark spots on the western horizon, the remnant of the fleet of canoes—a hundred and five prisoners—some slightly hurt, and forty being desperately wounded.

As to the dead it was impossible to tell; for the mainbody of these lay buried beneath the dreadful mound, which had been hurled down on their heads by the explosion of Crusoe's gunpowder.

He had thus expended the whole of his ammunition, save enough for ten charges, which he retained.

Serious as this was, yet on consideration he was well satisfied with its expenditure and the results.

And so ended the final struggle for mastery between the Huanitans, aided by Crusoe, and the fierce warriors of Talanaki.

CHAPTER LXXX.

CRUSOE JACK KING OF HUANITA.

CRUSOE remained on the cliff overlooking the scene of the catastrophe, and the utter rout of the enemy, until he had seen the Huanitan force, both land and sea, start back for the encampment, on the south side of the island.

Then he and La-loo-hee-ah, with the warriors who had attended him, started back, down the lion's shoulder, along the ridge to Flagstaff Point, and so to the sea-shore, and along the sands to the Huanitan camp.

But Crusoe and La-loo-hee-ah were not permitted to walk back.

Whilst he was occupied in watching the proceedings from his commanding position, and shouting his orders to those below, through the speaking trumpet, the savages busied themselves in constructing a rustic litter of boughs and foliage, the gigantic leaves of the cocoa palm being used to form the roof and sides.

Wild flowers were collected, and in a very short time a picturesque and charming-looking palanquin was constructed.

They chanted a Huanitan song of triumph, not altogether unmelodious, in praise of the great warrior white king, who had led them to victory, and so utterly defeated the enemy by means of his power of " thunder-making."

This palanquin was borne to where Crusoe stood by four savages, the rest ranging themselves in front and behind as escort.

In this leafy, cool conveyance, our hero and La-loo-hee-ah entered, and were thus borne in triumph down from the mountains, as far as the Huanitan camp.

All the way, Crusoe's twelve picked men—chiefs, every one of them—kept up their song of praise, and so soon as the little party emerged from the dense foliage lining the sandy shore, on to the open ground, their voices swelled to the loudest pitch, so as to be heard at the camp.

Instantly there arose a great shout, and in a minute or so a large procession was formed, and advanced to meet them.

Soon Crusoe, looking out at the side of the palanquin, perceived the gorgeous litter of the king approaching, at the head of about two hundred of the principal warriors and chiefs.

The litter was borne by chiefs only, and none accompanied except those who had proved their right to be enrolled as warriors, by having slain, at least, one of the enemy in battle.

The royal litter was on this occasion a most gorgeous affair, and really would not have disgraced a courtly pageant of the middle ages of France or England.

The hangings and drapery were all of the glossy vegetable silk, before spoken of, which had been dyed various colours. There was wood of different sorts and tints, from pale yellow to ebony black.

Then there was abundance of the white ivory-like substance; and lastly, the glistening white metal, which Crusoe judged superior in every respect to the finest silver.

As the cortège advanced, the song of triumph, commenced on starting, swelled to a loud chorus of over two hundred voices, all singing or rather shouting, at top-voice.

When they arrived within a few feet, there went up to the skies one final, tremendous burst of harmony or discord—quite a matter of opinion, Crusoe said to himself—and then at a signal from the king, they were silent.

The magnificent litter was lowered to the ground, and in this position, formed a sort of confined throne.

The king, alighted, came towards the shady rustic palanquin of Crusoe.

The chiefs and warriors spread out, and arranged themselves on each side of the royal litter in a semi-circle.

Crusoe Jack also alighted; and leading La-loo-hee-ah by the hand, advanced, to pay his respects to his majesty, Akah Malatieta.

The king took him by the hand; and, in an excited manner, addressed the crowd, presenting Crusoe to the notice of his subjects.

Our hero supposed that his royal father-in-law was about to make a highly congratulatory and complimentary harangue, but had no idea of what was actually coming.

The king's speech was short and to the purpose; and Crusoe Jack, when he gathered its purport, scarcely knew whether to be pleased or dissatisfied; indeed, wonder was, for some time, the predominant feeling in his mind.

"Chiefs and warriors of Huanita, we have this day achieved a glorious victory over the ancient enemies of Huanita. Behold my son! to whose wise counsel and more than earthly skill and power our victory is owing. It is he who, henceforth, shall rule you; and lead you to victory in battle, and prosperity in peace."

"I am an old man, and would fain rest—leaving the welfare of my subjects in wiser and more powerful hands than mine.

"According to our laws, my son here—husband of my beloved daughter, Falera La-loo-hee-ah—is heir to the throne. He shall not wait for his inheritance. This very day, in accordance with our laws and customs, I yield in his favour, and now proclaim him King of Huanita—reigning jointly with my well-beloved daughter.

"Chiefs and warriors, acknowledge your new king."

Thus speaking, Akah Malatieta led Crusoe up to the throne-like litter, and insisted on his taking his seat there beneath the gorgeous canopy; whilst La-loo-hee-ah he placed in a position a little lower—as it were, on the top step of the throne.

"Chiefs and warriors!" cried the old king, in a loud voice, "behold your king! May he long reign and rule to the honour, glory, and prosperity of the kingdom of Huanita."

Then there arose a tremendous sound of shouting and wild cries of joy.

And Crusoe Jack knew that he was now absolute monarch of Huanita and all the surrounding islands.

CHAPTER LXXXI.

THE SAVAGES FORWARD CRUSOE'S WORK AT THE WRECK.

"KING of Huanita," said Crusoe to himself, a few days after he was installed on his new throne. "Monarch of all I survey, and a great deal more, for my kingdom extends to the east and the west, as far as I please, bar continents.

"And now to work! Now for the dive! Down I go, and up comes the half million!"

*   *   *   *   *

Crusoe now set to work systematically; and, as far as the labour was concerned, bearing in mind the old adage, "Never do to yourself what what you can make anyone else do for you," set thirteen hundred islanders at work to clear the wreck.

One thousand of those were prisoners, and had to do the disagreeable part of the work,

labouring up to their waists in water, and so forth, as they had to do in constructing the breakwater around the wreck of the Thunder.

Sharks were rather troublesome, but Crusoe made even these monsters of the deep serve his purpose, for, when more than two were seized and devoured by these hungry denizens of the deep, would explain to them that it was on account of his great White Spirit being displeased at their not working hard enough, and so, inch by inch, and foot by foot, down went the stone, and up grew the embankment.

A month's time witnessed a vast change in the whole aspect of Lion Island, and especially on the shores and bays of the eastern side, off which lay the wreck of the Thunder.

Crusoe, with his fair consort, had taken up his abode at the old hut on Flagstaff Point; but the rude building of slabs and logs was now scarcely recognisable, altered in appearance, and ornamented as it was by the fantastic taste of the islanders.

The hut was now not only a picturesque and comfortable dwelling, proof against sun and storm, but also a stout fortress.

Stout palisades of iron-bark wood now replaced the rough fence which Crusoe had originally put up, and in place of the shallow drain he had dug to carry off the water during the heavy tropical rains, there was a deep moat surrounding the whole of the enclosure, in which stood the hut.

Close to the flagstaff, which the crew of the American vessel had planted for him, there now stood another one, a tall, straight sapling of cocoa palm without bend or joint, and here, side by side of the British flag, there waved in the breeze the royal standard of Huanita.

Anxious to obtain and keep absolute supremacy over the minds of his savage subjects, Crusoe had made considerable concessions to their prejudices and opinions.

He stooped to conquer!

Notably in the way of attire.

Though he by no means gave up his European dress, shirt, trousers, and so forth, he yet allowed his person to be ornamented in native fashion, so far as plumes, feathers, skins, ivory and such like decorations were concerned. And but for the absence of tattooing (a process with which he would have nothing to do), he might have been mistaken for a native chief of the islands.

Strange to say, as he approximated, so to speak, to the savage style of attire, La-loo-hee-ah went nearer to the European type.

Let us endeavour to describe the ordinary dress of Her Majesty Queen of Huanita.

We will begin with the little feet.

These were encased in slippers made with the skins of flying-fish, ornamented with pearls and topazes.

Then came a skirt, pure white, of the finest vegetable silk, confined around the waist by a silver girdle ornamented with shark's teeth and dolphin's eyes, petrified after a manner known to the natives.

The ground work of white satin was absolutely blazing with ornaments for which land and sea had been ransacked.

There were three rows of the small, downlike feathers of the bird of paradise.

LA-LOO-HLE-AH COUNSELS THE INDIAN CHIEFS.

Between these, and contrasting admirably with the gorgeous golden hues of the plumes, there were stars and half-moons of small, delicately coloured pink shells, and amongst and between them innumerable spangles of silver.

On the upper part of the body she wore, loosely thrown over the left shoulder, scarfwise, a broad band of vegetable silk, died a rich purple colour.

This was ornamented in the most magnificent manner by large emeralds, the size of walnuts.

Beneath this gorgeous band La-loo-hee-ah—probably out of compliment to her lord and master—wore a plain body, or chemise, to speak plainly, of white calico.

Around her handsome throat she wore a necklet of pink coral, and on her head a plain silver tiara, with one enormous emerald in the centre.

Armlets of the same white, silvery metal above the elbow, bracelets on her wrists, and a wand, or sceptre, of vegetable ivory, completed the attire and belongings of La-loo-hee-ah, Queen of Huanita.

Crusoe Jack and his fair queen, whose attire we have just described, reigned supreme and with unquestioned authority, not only over Lion Island, but in Huanita itself, and all the group to the west.

Delegating his authority to a principal, or chief, he himself, with La-loo-hee-ah, was able to sail on a royal tour or progress to the great island of Huanita, and those others still further off, which formed his new dominions.

In the course of his expedition he sailed on, in command of a powerful fleet, far past the confines of the Huanitan Archipelago, and into the waters of Talanaki.

He thus discovered, to his great satisfaction, that these hostile savages, one time so fierce and implacable in their enmity, were now thoroughly cowed by the late terrible disaster sustained by them at the hands of himself and the warriors of Huanita.

Indeed he felt satisfied, from observations made in the course of this his royal voyage and progress, that he could, if he chose, subdue to his sway the whole of the Talanaki group.

But of this he was not ambitious, and having satisfied himself that there was no probability—scarcely a possibility even—of a renewal of hostilities by the savages of Talanaki, he directed the prows of his fleet to the eastward, and, after an absence of two weeks, set sail again for Lion Island, calling at Huanita and the surrounding islets on his way.

On his arrival at his own island kingdom he found that things had progressed most favourably during his absence.

The warrior chief to whom he had entrusted the prosecution of the great work during his absence had taken very strong measures.

Measures, indeed, which he himself would neither have sanctioned nor allowed, but which had a prodigious effect in hastening the work of the prisoner gang.

This chief, one evening, being dissatisfied with the progress made by the said prisoners during the day, favoured them with a short speech, expressing his displeasure, and then, by his orders, five of them were thrown to the sharks.

This summary proceeding had a very striking effect on the others, and the next day they did more work than they had in the previous week; and so, when Crusoe returned, he found, to his great satisfaction, that the breakwater had been built right up to the surface.

And now, looking down from Flagstaff Point, he beheld the top of a semi-circular wall, enclosing the wreck of the Thunder and the sunken treasure between itself and the reef.

This barrier, now so nearly completed, fully answered all his expectations.

Of course it was not watertight, as the sea permeated backwards and forwards through the interstices of the stones of which it was composed.

But nevertheless the space thus inclosed was always calm, for even in rough weather the power of the waves was broken against the stone barrier.

And beyond this—a very considerable advantage—there was yet another and indispensable one.

The entrance of sharks was entirely prevented, so that it was possible to carry on diving operations with perfect safety to life and limb.

A few more days' labour under his own supervision saw the completion of the breakwater, which was raised to an elevation of clear five feet above the surface.

He caused the top of it, and also the reef, to be levelled and covered with an admixture of sand and hard clods, so that on all sides of the wreck of the Thunder there was a smooth, level platform, from which to conduct operations.

This done, and all minor arrangements having been made, Crusoe Jack proceeded to the execution of his grand project, of which through all difficulties and danger, he had never lost sight—the dive for half-a-million.

CHAPTER LXXXII.
CRUSOE VISITS THE WRECK OF THE THUNDER.

AND now behold our hero, standing on the climax of this his enterprise, about to put to the test of stern experience the success or failure of this his grand project.

Shortly he would know, beyond all doubt, whether the perils and the toils of the last few months were labour lost, or destined to be crowned with success.

He had made many preliminary dives and explorations in and around the wreck; but his stay under water on these occasions was necessarily of short duration, being compelled to come to the surface for breath.

Now, however, his diving apparatus is all complete, and he stands on the edge of the Golden Reef, clad in a complete panoply of canvas and leather, with huge sea boots, heavily weighted with lead, and covering his head a helmet, made out of an old ship's lantern.

Pipes and tubings, valves and stopcocks, pumps, bladders and barrels, for supply of air—all these things he had provided, and with a short jump plunged into the sea, and disappeared from view.

The reef, the embankment, the sea, and the lagoon were crowded with the wondering and admiring Huanitans, assembled to witness this last and greatest achievement of their white king.

Their stoutest and most skilful divers had never succeeded in remaining beneath the surface, of the water more than a minute and a half.

But five—ten minutes passed, and still the all-conquering white man remained beneath the surface, an occasional shake of the rope telling that he was alive and at work.

Reader, let us descend and join him, and see what he is doing.

*   *   *   *   *

He was now about to prove, for the first time the prudence and wisdom of his arrangements.

It was, he knew, a most hazardous affair, for, as a chain is no stronger than its weakest link, so he knew that the failure of even one little matter of detail in his equipment might render the whole enterprise abortive.

To the edge of the Golden Reef, which at the point he selected went down perpendicularly to the bottom, there was attached a rope ladder, weighted at the end.

This was for the purpose of coming to the surface again, for the lead attached to his boots and other parts of his diving dress would be sufficient to sink him.

It was La-loo-hee-ah herself who put the finishing touch to his water toilet, by putting the helmet on his head, and securing the watertight fastenings round the neck.

CHAPTER LXXXIII.
CRUSOE AGAIN AT THE WRECK.

GREAT as was the surprise of the Huanitans at the prolonged submergence of their adored king, that of Crusoe himself was scarcely less, for he had never hoped to be able to remain so long a time with so little inconvenience.

His previous dives had been purely experimental, and before the whole of the tubing and air reservoirs attached thereto were completed.

This tubing arrangement, though simple in idea and theory, was, perforce, somewhat complicated in practice.

Previously to descending himself he had caused to be sunk two large barrels, empty in the ordinary sense, but of course, as our readers know, full of air.

At the bottom of each of these was an aperture—bung hole, in fact, you may call it.

This bung-hole, when the cask was sunk, was closed by a rudely constructed but effective valve, a string from which was attached to the outside of Crusoe's diving dress, within easy reach of his hand, so that he could easily pull it and open the valve.

But also at the top of this barrel again there was another opening or bung-hole, over which was securely fixed the mouth or end of a thin tube, not more than the thickness of a finger, and over thirty yards in length.

The other barrel was arranged in exactly the same manner, the two containing between them nearly a hundred cubic feet of air.

Both these thirty-yard tubes communicated, at the other end, with the helmet of the diving dress, one on each side.

They were closed by a valve, the opening and shutting of which was an ingenious contrivance on the part of Crusoe, obviating the use of his hands; attached to the valve, and running down each side of the helmet, was a canvas strap which went down one side of the head from above the ear, under the chin up to the opposite side.

This, as the reader will, I hope, understand, completely smothered up the chin, mummywise.

Now Crusoe calculated that if by any chance he should be suffocating for want of air, even though almost unconscious and incapable of voluntary motion, he would naturally open his mouth and gasp, and the very act of gasping would bring the muscles of the jaw into action, these would act upon the strap, open the valve, and a stream of pure air would immediately pour in.

On taking his first plunge, weighted as he was, he rapidly reached the bottom.

The stone barriers and the reef between them had insured almost perfectly calm water at that depth, and he found no difficulty in keeping his balance in an upright position.

It was some little time before the atmospheric air contained in the helmet and diving dress was expended or vitiated, but when this had taken place he had to depend upon his barrel tube and valve arrangements.

Accordingly he proceeded to pull the string, which would open the valve at the bottom of each barrel; the water then rushing in forced out a quantity of air at the top, and into the tubes connected with the helmet.

To his great satisfaction, he discovered that the arrangement for working the helmet valves acted perfectly.

There was a valve also in the top of the helmet, which was forced open by the air rushing in from the two barrels, so that the air which he had already breathed or vitiated was driven out, rising in big bubbles to the surface.

For fully five minutes our diver remained nearly still, accustoming his eyes to the dim, greenish light, and his system to the pressure of the sea without, and the air within the helmet.

At first he could scarcely see at all, and a feeling of great oppression and uneasiness, amounting almost to pain, caused him to fear that he would have to ascend to the surface without any practical result.

By degrees, however, this feeling wore off, and to his surprise and gratification he found that he was able to breathe more freely.

Slowly, too, as his eyes became accustomed to the light, he was enabled to discern objects— dimly, it is true, but still sufficiently to enable him to distinguish the inequalities of the ground at the bottom, and the huge black mass at a few yards' distance, which he knew to be the wreck of the Thunder.

Presently, using all due caution, and moving his heavily-laden feet slowly and with tottering steps, he approached the hull of the sunken ship.

It was more than half buried in the vast quantity of sand, the accumulation of many months, before the completion of the breakwater prevented further encroachment.

This was so far an advantage that it made a sort of a slope, up which he was able to climb to the bulwarks of the wreck.

Gaining confidence every minute, he struggled his way slowly on, taking care to let into the helmet a gust of air now and again from the tubes.

The longer he stayed below, the greater confidence he acquired in his powers of moving about, and of keeping an upright position.

And presently he stood on the deck of the old ship, with still slack tubing to spare.

It was at the port gangway where he found an entrance.

Thence he proceeded along the deck, by the side of the bulwarks, towards the after-hatch and cabin.

But arriving a yard or so abaft the former, he was brought to a sudden check.

He had now travelled as far as the length of the pipes would allow him, and at once saw that to work to any effect these must be lengthened.

Accordingly he made his way back from off the wreck, down the mound of sand, and gained the edge of the reef in safety.

Here without much difficulty he found the rope ladder, for now that he had got accustomed to the greenish gloom surrounding him, he was enabled to see objects at several yards' distance.

Great was the excitement and commotion of his assembled subjects, when, without warning or notice, he quietly came up from the sea, and clambered on to the reef.

Loud were the shouts of joy and exultation, for from his long submersion a terrible report had spread that he had gone below never to come up again, having met with some fatal mishap.

Crusoe himself, too, was a good deal surprised.

He knew he had made a considerable stay, but did not think the time amounted to a quarter of an hour.

La-loo-hee-ah, to whom he had entrusted his watch, now hastened to welcome her lord and master on his safe return from the depths of the sea.

Then, to his great surprise, he discovered that he had been submerged for thirty-five minutes.

Perfectly satisfied with the result of this his first serious dive, he instantly set to work to make a quantity of more tubing, intending before he again essayed the depths to have at least sixty or seventy yards' scope, more than double as much as at first.

The manufacture of this tube was a work requiring time and the greatest care, for it was of absolute importance that it should be strong and perfectly water-tight throughout its entire length.

In a few days, however, during which time he kept a number of his people at work, improveing and solidifying the embankment, he was prepared to make his second attempt, which he hoped and believed would be entirely successful.

CHAPTER LXXXIV.

CRUSOE'S PROSPECTS BRIGHTEN.

IT is not absolutely the fact that "practice makes perfect" (for, humanly speaking, there is no such thing as perfection), but it is undoubtedly true that, in all operations requiring nerve and skill, it is essential to success.

After this first attempt at a prolonged dive, in full costume, which had been more successful even than he hoped, Crusoe rapidly improved, gaining experience and confidence at every submersion.

Working steadily several hours a day from the time his new tubing was completed, in the course of a month he had effected a great alteration in the appearance of matters at the bottom of the sea all around, and on the wreck of the Thunder.

An enormous quantity of sand, which seemed likely to encumber his operations, had been removed, and an easy mode of access to the wreck made by still further cutting away the bulwarks.

All obstacles—such as spars, old rope, and so forth, which encumbered the deck, the approaches to the cabin, and the cabin itself—had been cleared away.

This was effected in a manner both simple and efficacious.

For example.: the remains of the bulkhead and barricade at the fore part of the cabin, from behind which such a desperate defence had been made against the mutineers of the Thunder, would be in the way, he thought.

Accordingly, working at the bottom of the sea — securely and comfortably enough in his diving suit, now greatly improved—he, in the course of an afternoon, affixed grapnels and chains to everything he thought should be removed.

Then, ascending to the surface, he caused to be strung on to the ropes attached to these grapnels a couple of hundred of his faithful subjects.

At the signal—a short blast on a shell trumpet—they bent their backs and strained their muscles to carry out his wishes. And lo! in the space of a minute, all the offending substances were dragged up from the bottom and hauled on to the reef.

While, however, these diving operations around the Golden Reef were vigorously carried on, there were other things to which Crusoe devoted a part of his time and energies.

One of these was the choice and felling of trees suitable for ship or boat timber. For he had long since decided that, so soon as he had recovered the sunken treasure, he would strengthen and alter his boat by building up her gunwale, half-decking her, and so make her seaworthy enough for a voyage to some port on the east coast of South America.

There he would purchase or charter a good-sized vessel, and then once more set sail for his island kingdom. And then—what then?

Ah! when his thoughts turned that way, it caused him many a pang and deep regret.

Of course he must embark the gold on board his vessel, and, bidding adieu to his kingdom and subjects, set sail for Old England with the crew he would have obtained at the South American port.

Well he knew what would be the grief and dismay of his subjects when he should announce to them that he was about to leave for ever.

And for ever he inwardly felt it would be, when the time came.

For, despite the glory, power, and state with which he was here invested—reigning in the hearts and affections of the faithful, simple-minded islanders—despite the glorious scenery and genial climate of these happy islands—despite the fertility of the valleys, and the proud thought that, standing on the high peak he called the Lion's Crown, he was absolutely monarch of all he surveyed—despite all these things, his heart yearned for the joys, troubles, and excitements of civilised life.

He felt that he could never content himself with imperial rank and power amidst these far away islands of the Pacific.

And what of La-loo-hee-ah, his queen and consort, to whom he owed so much—his present rank—life itself, even?

That was a subject which long sorely troubled him, and on which he found it a hard and painful task to come to a decision.

Finally, he made up his mind that under no circumstances could he desert her—even though he knew she would be in the midst of her own people, and sure of all the attentions and luxuries she was entitled to by her rank.

Of her deep affection for him there could be no doubt, and it would have been strange indeed had her constancy, her devotion, her intelligence, and great beauty produced no effect upon his heart.

"Come weal, come woe, whatever may betide, my fate is bound up with that of La-loo-hee-ah, though no priestly formula or ceremony of our religion has joined me to her in the bonds of matrimony! We were united solemnly, and with all the proper forms of her people in a manner befitting her rank. Had she not bestowed herself on me my life was forfeit. I should be an ingrate and coward indeed, did I, after reaping all the benefit, seek to repudiate the bargain."

This was the solemn conclusion Crusoe had come to in his own mind on the subject.

After long and painful self-discussion of her intelligence, fidelity, and dazzling beauty, there could be no two opinions.

In complexion, she was fairer than many an Italian or Spanish beauty, and, assuredly, she had greater claims on his love and gratitude than any other woman in the world.

And lastly, though of no mean importance in his mind, came this thought—amounting to sure conviction—

"Already she can speak and write the English tongue. She is apt and willing—ever anxious to learn.

"I will procure for her the best masters and means of instruction: and ere she has mingled for a year with civilised people, my island bride —Princess of Huanita—shall be fitted in every respect to take her place as a queen of beauty and fashion in English society."

Having once decided the course demanded of him by duty and honour, he ceased to discuss it with himself; but as his great project, the recovery of the gold, seemed every day more promising of complete success, he employed all his spare time in fitting La-loo-hee-ah for the great change which, he doubted not, would ere long take place in the current of her life.

Still the work went on until day by day our hero felt more certain of ultimate success.

He resolved not to attempt raising a single box of gold until he was pretty certain that the whole was fairly in his grasp, so that it should only be a question of time, a day or so, to place himself in posession of the half-million of gold sunk in the Thunder.

Meanwhile in the rear of the old hut on Flagstaff Point, which had stood him in such good stead as a fortress against the hostile savages, there arose rapidly a large building strongly built of logs.

This he intended as his warehouse, and while yet it was unfinished commenced storing therein quantities of the valuable productions of this and the islands to the west.

Already he had despatched two flotillas under the command of trusty chiefs, and each fleet had returned laden with valuable merchandise.

And as Crusoe beheld his store-house filled with the extraordinary and precious productions of the islands, he was able to say to himself—

"Even without any share of the gold I shall recover I must be a wealthy man, supposing I succeed in providing transport to a civilised country of the riches I am collecting."

CHAPTER LXXXV.
CRUSOE ESTIMATES THE VALUE OF HIS STOCK.

AN inspection of the great store-house which Crusoe had erected at the back of the "Old Hut," as he always called it, would have convinced any valuer as to the truth of the assertion of his being a wealthy man irrespective of the sunken treasure, could he only succeed in bringing his valuable wares to a market.

In good truth, such were the extraordinary nature and quantity of the contents of this said store-house, at one of his last ("and successful" he said to himself) dives for the half-million, that no valuer in the world could properly estimate it.

It was a large octagonal building, with only two floors.

The second floor had been put up with considerable difficulty, as every step and detail required Crusoe's personal attention; and this not from any fault on the part of his willing labourers, but from their utter ignorance of the construction of any building whatever above one storey—the ground one.

However, this second storey, though light enough—floored only with split palms, and with bamboos for rafters to support the roof—answered its purpose very well.

It was about half filled with great bundles, nearly the size of woolpacks, of the extraordinary vegetable substance, exceeding the finest silk in texture, which had quite early been brought under the notice of Crusoe—the same wondrous fabric which floated as a little flag from the shaft of La-loo-hee-ah's javelin.

As to the value of this, it was impossible to determine on the spot; but Crusoe felt certain that, weight for weight, it would fetch a better price in the market than the finest China silk.

Now it occurred to Crusoe one day that he would have a look around his store-room, and make a valuation of his own as to what the contents would be worth in an European country.

South Sea Island silk he determined to call the vegetable material.

And thus he appraised it—
South Sea Island silk, £70,000.

On this same second floor—being comparatively light, and so not likely to break down the bamboo flooring — there was stored, as he thought, ivory—or what was better than ivory (though no elephant died to find it), to the value of £10,000.

And this latter was much more easily attainable than the vegetable silk, so that its small ratio in proportion was nothing.

On this very day he had despatched two more flotillas to the islands to the west with orders to return laden with merchandise; but especially had he ordered as much as possible of the white silvery metal to be brought.

This he felt certain was the most valuable commodity of all ; and, believing that it was certainly much more valuable than silver, did not venture to price that which he already had, if wrought to an European market.

He had already safely stored of it more than five tons.

CHAPTER LXXXVI.

THE HUANITANS BECOME ALARMED.

ONCE more behold our hero under water—moving about carefully and slowly, but without difficulty, groping his way step by step in the dim greenish light which alone prevailed.

There was abundant tubing now, and as Crusoe intended this to be a grand and supreme effort, he had taken care before descending to see that nothing was neglected.

A complete labyrinth of ropes and chains came from the surface down to the hull, attached to different portions of the wreck.

He had now descended, in order to make quite sure that all was right, and that each rope, chain, and grapnel was properly affixed.

This done, he returned to the surface.

On the platform, on the barrier, and also on the reef, he had caused to be put up strong triangles, each consisting of three young trees, fixed in the ground at the bottom, and firmly bound together at the top, where were attached a number of blocks or roughly-made pulleys through which the ropes led.

All being in readiness, and some half dozen savages holding each rope, Crusoe gave the signal.

With loud shouts and yells, they evinced their zeal by tugging and struggling their best.

In a few seconds the fruits of these exertions were apparent.

The ropes yielded, at first slowly, then all together, and there was a great commotion in the water over and around the wreck.

Great pieces of timber shot up above the surface, as if some giant beneath had propelled them, and in a very short space of time the seat was covered with spars, planks, bulkheads, and chips and splinters of the wreck.

Crusoe's plan had been well laid, and he felt pretty confident that on descending he would find nearly all obstacles, preventing his getting at the after-hold, where the treasure was, removed.

For he had attached ropes and chains to almost every object and projection, believing that the rotting effect of the water would prove to have been so great that he could, had he wished it, have pulled the whole afterpart of the deck off the wreck.

Before he could descend again, it was necessary to clear away the débris, floating beams and timber, which covered the surface, as they might impede the working of his ropes, signal lines, &c.

This occupied some hours, and he resolved to postpone his descent—when he firmly believed he would bring up at least one box of gold—till the following day.

As for the state in which the gold would be found he felt pretty confident that the greater part of the boxes would be whole and sound.

True it was that one box, at least, must have been burst open in some manner, for La-loo-hee-ah had long previously brought up a handful of sand and gravel, mingled with gold.

Still he was firmly of opinion that nearly the whole of the treasure would be found in such a state that it would be an easy matter to raise it to the surface.

The rest of that day he employed in inspecting his other treasures, the valuable contents of the store-house.

The next morning, ere the sun was more than an hour above the horizon, Crusoe was again standing on the edge of the reef, clad cap-a-pie in his diving dress, ready to make one more plunge.

Before putting on the helmet he addressed the assembled people, telling them that he set great importance on this dive, and that they need not be alarmed should he not reappear for a considerable interval.

La-loo-lee-ah (who always attended to these matters herself) proceeded to fasten on the diving helmet, saying before she did so—

"A safe and speedy return to my lord and prince."

And then Crusoe disappeared beneath the surface.

As was always the case, the excitable savages gave a loud cheer, or rather a series of yells, as the waters closed over their king.

Then ensued a general hubbub and chattering, running to and fro on the reef, paddling of canoes about, a sort of thing which is inevitable with savages when under excitement.

After a bit they quieted down, and when they thought he had been beneath the surface long enough, they gathered to the edge of the barrier and reef, and anxiously looked for his coming.

Minute after minute passed, till even La-loo-hee-ah began to grow uneasy, although he had warned her that he should probably make a long stay.

All at once there came a violent pull at the signal rope.

Only one, and then it was still again.

La-loo-hee-ah, standing by the brink close to the rope-ladder, peered anxiously down into the sea, vainly striving to pierce it with her eyesight.

She could dimly see the dark shadow of the wreck of the Thunder; but that was all.

Suddenly a chief, standing on the barrier opposite to her, gave a cry, pointing with his finger.

Bubbles of air were to be seen bursting up to the surface.

Not one or two, but many—a stream, a succession.

La-loo-hee-ah gazed with eyes dilated with terror.

Partly by nature, partly by reason of the constant society and gentle teaching of Crusoe, she was infinitely more intelligent than any of their subjects, even the most trusted chief.

And so, while the crowd only gaped and wondered, without ascribing any importance to the stream of bubbles, she experienced a deadly fear; for well she knew that something must have happened for such a quantity of air to come bubbling up thus.

With clasped hands, leaning forward over the dark still waters, she seemed as though she would by the very force of intense will and desire pierce the depths.

Suddenly a scream broke from her—a scream wrung from her heart.

What was it she saw which could cause her face to wear such an expression of terrible agony?

The frothing waters where the bubbles had been coming up, and for some distance around, were now tinged red.

Blood!

Some terrible catastrophe had happened.

She stood for a moment or two the picture of grief and terror, and then, seeming to recover energy all at once, hastily tore off the encumbering garments, and plunged head-foremost into the sea.

The Huanitans knew now that there was something wrong, and a wailing shout went up to the sky.

Let us, too, good reader, plunge beneath the surface down to the wreck of the Thunder, and see for ourselves what is there being enacted.

CHAPTER LXXXVII.

A DISCOVERY.

On descending to the depths of the dark green sea on this momentous occasion Crusoe felt quite at his ease.

Long practice and familiarity had now caused him to be indifferent to the pressure of the water and the air in the helmet, and he was able to move about freely, and without any fear or even nervousness.

He found everything exactly as he could have wished.

The mound of sand just sloped enough to render the ascent to the deck of the sunken vessel easy.

She lay nearly on an even keel, so that when he gained the deck, he was able to walk, slowly and carefully towards the cabin.

All obstacles had been cleared away, and even a part of the poop deck, which formed the roof of the cabin, torn off by his last grand coup.

This greatly increased the light, and so he was able to advance steadily, and without check of any sort, right up to the little hatch of the lazarette abaft the mizzenmast.

Down here, only a few yards from him, lay the treasure, the half-million, to reclaim which he had toiled so long, suffered so much, and passed through such desperate peril.

He stood by the side of the square hole, and gazed down into what seemed the profound darkness below—seemed only, for he knew that once down, there would be some light, and his eyesight was now well accustomed to the gloomy depths, for his purpose.

There was ample tubing to keep up the supply of air, and all his ropes—his signal line and everything else—in perfect working order.

Still he hesitated, and for this reason: he had forgotten one thing.

How was he to get down to the lazarette or store-room where they had stored the gold?

When the Thunder sank it was full to within five or six feet of the hatchway with cases, boxes, and all sorts of stores.

But now, probably even the greater part of these had been washed away by the action of the water.

Would it be safe to hazard what would literally be a leap in the dark?

While he thus debated with himself, moving slightly, his foot kicked against something, and, stooping, he lifted a harpoon with a long handle.

The very thing—a perfect God-send!

With this, which was seven feet in length, he was able to probe down into the hold, and found, to his great satisfaction, that there was a footing at less than six feet.

He knew well that there was no time to be lost; for, of course, the supply of air would not last for ever. So, without a moment's hesitation, using the harpoon as a prod, he let himself drop gently down the hatchway.

It was a moment or two before his eyes were accustomed to the still deeper gloom, and then as he knew time was precious, he set to work.

*   *   *   *   *

Success! Triumph! Glory! Gold! gold! gold!

He soon discovered a pile of the well-remembered bullion boxes, and put the rope on to one of them.

He at first thought of giving the signal to haul up, as consideration led him to return to the surface himself to see all clear for the hoisting of the first box.

The first—the very first he had recovered.

The thought was enough to make him intoxicated with joy; and he felt, by the rush of blood to his head, that it was necessary for him to return to the surface sooner than he need have done had it not been for the excitement of finding this first box of gold, and the certainty that he should very shortly get many more.

He turned to ascend, blundering along in the gloom, dragging the gold-dust after him.

All at once he came face to face with a sight which made his heart stand still.

For a moment or two he thought he should faint.

He was incapable of motion—of anything beyond speechless terror.

There it was, right before him; a most hideous and terrible reality—no dream, or freak of the imagination.

CHAPTER LXXXVIII.

CRUSOE'S ENCOUNTER WITH A MONSTER OF THE DEEP.

YES, there it was, the terrible monster, floating with a quivering motion, and rolling slowly from side to side.

A huge shark, one of the largest size, of the most deadly and dangerous species—a ground shark.

Despite the gloom at that depth, the creature was plainly visible; its own body emitting a pale, phosphorescent light.

It seemed to be surrounded by a sort of halo, which flickered and trembled in a strange, weird manner.

Crusoe could see the brute quite plainly. It was not more than twelve feet distant, and he could observe even the rolling of the great goggle eyes in their sockets.

Slowly it approached him, rolling slowly on either side as it did so, like a ship in a gentle sea.

The phosphorescent greenish light grew brighter, and the diver could now make out the gleam of the horrid eyes, and the double row of glistening white teeth, as the monster half-opened its mouth.

Alone in the hold of a sunken ship, with that fearful great ground shark for a companion!

Well he knew that, when once the creature had fastened its grip, it could with perfect ease tear to ribands the stout diver's dress, and then with many a savage shake (as he had often seen a dog shake a rat) rend him limb from limb.

All this he well knew, and his heart now stood still—now pulsated furiously—under the influence of the great terror of that shining, slimy presence.

Oh, the horror of those few moments!

Never till then had Crusoe known what the agony of terror was.

The shark slowly crept up—a very slight play of the central fins, and the slow rolling to and fro of the huge body being the only motion perceptible.

Suddenly the shark made a lightning-like dart to the right hand.

Crusoe only saw a phosphorescent flash through the water, so rapid was the passage of the monster through its native element.

This sudden dart to a distance of about twenty feet seemed quite objectless—a sort of freak, a playful bit of a gambol on the part of the shark, for in half a minute afterwards it again came, slowly creeping up, with the same slow rolling motion.

Perhaps the shark had taken this sudden dart to the right just as exercise, to waken up its nerves and muscles.

Perhaps it had that effect on the shark.

It is certain, however, that it had a great effect upon Crusoe.

It caused him to start suddenly, and the shock revived him, and brought him to himself.

The shark soon made another sudden dart to the other side, and this over again, and commenced slowly creeping towards our hero.

But Crusoe had now thoroughly recovered his self-possession, and though fully awake to the desperate danger of his situation, was not altogether without hope of coming safely through this peril as he had so many previous ones.

What a happy accident his stumbling across the harpoon; at the time he regarded it only as a pole with which to sound the depth of the hold, and assist him in his descent.

As it turned out, this accident offered him his only chance of life.

He stood with the weapon in his hands, grasped firmly by the butt with the right hand, a little further up with the left, the barbed points raised slightly above the level of the shark's head.

Suddenly the monster, by one swift powerful swish of his great tail, propelled itself through the water towards Crusoe, at the same time turning half on its side.

Crusoe stood firm, and endeavoured to meet the brute full in the mouth with the barb of the harpoon.

But either his aim was too incorrect, or the shark swerved, for it only grazed the head.

This, however, was sufficient to turn it from its direct course, and it passed Crusoe with a rush, actually brushing him and making him stagger.

Again the shark returned to a similar position, and appeared about to repeat the manœuvre, this time, perhaps, with better success.

But Crusoe, now full of energy, and determined to make a hard fight for his life, was not disposed to allow this.

He himself advanced two or three paces with levelled harpoon.

At this moment the shark slowly rolled over on his side, half opening its mouth, and revealing its dreadful teeth—teeth which, ere long, might be tearing at his flesh and sinews.

Again a sudden swish with the tremendously-powerful tail ; again is the huge body of the fish propelled like a cannon ball through the water.

Not far without obstruction however.

For Crusoe, levelling the harpoon with steady nerve, and beautiful precision, met the monster full in the open jaws.

The impetuosity of the shark's rush was quite sufficient to seal its fate.

The creature impaled itself on the harpoon, the head of which was driven right through the stomach.

It was all over.

The sea became thick with blood.

It was this which had appeared at the surface, and so alarmed our hero's subjects and Queen La-loo-hee-ah.

CHAPTER LXXXIX.

A CRITICAL POSITION.

THE battle was over—at least so far as the shark was concerned, for that fierce and voracious monster of the deep after a few convulsive struggles and plunges, turned belly upwards, and, rising, became fixed across the small hatchway.

Crusoe, however, was still far from being in safety.

In the first place, he began to suffer dreadfully from want of air.

In the next, the hatchway was barred against him by the huge body of the shark.

Given plenty of time, and doubtless he would easily overcome this and all other difficulties.

But time was short because the supply of air was so.

Without his knowledge, the tube leading to one of his air barrels had sprung a leak, a slight hole having been torn in it. Through this hole the air of course rushed out, expelled from the cask by the pressure of the atmosphere.

Now Crusoe had been using the air from the other barrel, not having had occasion until after the encounter with the shark to apply to this one.

Great, then, was his dismay on opening the valve.

He expected a rush of fresh air, but instead thereof came a gush of sea water, which had filled the pipe through the hole.

He at once knew what had occurred, and realised the danger.

Breathing was now very oppressive and painful, and he was well aware that it was a matter of necessity to go to the surface at once.

Not without difficulty, he, by means of the harpoon, shoved the huge carcase a little backward.

So soon as the head got clear of the combings it shot up in such a natural manner as almost to seem alive.

This, however, was only the effect of the natural buoyancy of the sea, the dead fish being of less specific gravity than the water.

He now thought his task literally easy, and thought the worst he would have to suffer would be breathing foul air for a short time, and the consequent sickness and exhaustion—things which he had before experienced.

What, then, was his dismay, when he endeavoured to clamber up the hatch, to find that he was unable?

He strained every nerve.

In vain.

The heavily-loaded diving dress, especially the boots, kept him down.

Should he throw off all the weights?

If he did so, he knew that his feet would float upwards, his head down from the great weight of the helmet.

After a moment's thought he looked around, and presently dragged a wooden case from out of the sand, in which it was half buried, and placed it under the hatchway.

On this he mounted, which raised his arm-pits to a level with the cabin-deck, and enabled him to get his elbows over, and so endeavour to lift himself.

In vain.

His desperate efforts only made matters worse by increasing the difficulty of breathing, and causing a rush of blood to the head.

So he desisted, and went in search of another case or box, or anything to place on the top of the first.

He found one, but it was very heavy, and it was terrible work to drag it under the hatchway.

And when he got it there, he found himself utterly unable to lift it on top of the other one.

Then came black despair.

What more could he do?

Struggle again to climb to the deck above by his own unaided strength?

It would be the act of a fool, for he had before strained his very utmost, and failed.

And now he was, he knew, weaker, and much more oppressed for breath.

Panting, gasping, he made one more excursion around the hold, in hopes of finding something light and moveable.

But nothing could he find which could possibly be of any service.

Then he came back to the hatchway, placed his elbows over the combings, and rested on them the chin of the helmet.

The pain and oppression were now dreadful.

He thought his head would burst.

There was a loud humming noise in his ears, and the dim, greenish haze, caused by the light having to struggle through several fathoms of water, grew thicker, and more obscure.

Sparks, stars, comets—fireworks of all descriptions flashed about before his eyes, and he thought he heard the boom of a fierce cannonade.

Then he began to grow delirious, and saw strange shapes darting about—monsters of the deep, lovely mermaids, with long flowing hair, and eyes like electric sparks.

Hundreds of them!

Thousands of them!

They flocked all around him.

Some seemed to beckon to him, others laughed at him, pointing their dainty fingers; others merely looked at him, while some came up to him, and brandished sea shells for weapons in a threatening manner.

"So this is the end of all," thought Crusoe, as he felt the last stupor coming over him—"the end of all my labours and hopes! Farewell, this beautiful world! farewell, the old home in England! farewell all dreams of ambition! I perish thus, like a rat in a drain—drowned, drowned, within reach of a vast treasure! Ha! ha! (he laughed a short, delirious laugh, more like a

cough within the helmet). I can say I die a rich man, for I die worth half a million. I have made a successful dive for half a million. I have got it—I have got it! I will stick to it in death, as I did in life!"

Just then one of the mermaids came out from the crowd, and seized him by the throat.

He lost consciousness.

CHAPTER XC.
REJOICINGS ON LION ISLAND.

CRUSOE slightly recovering from the utter unconsciousness into which he fell when he fancied himself seized by a fierce mermaid or water-witch, felt himself dragged up through the lazarette hatch.

It seemed to him that some guiding power urged him to walk, or rather totter forward along the deck of the vessel, over the side, where the bulwarks were broken, and down the mound of sand.

Then he knew no more.

*   *   *   *   *

When he recovered consciousness he was lying prone on the Golden Reef, all encased in his diving armour. His head was reclining on the knee of La-loo-hee-ah, who was making all haste to unfasten and disencumber him of the diving helmet.

This done, he rapidly recovered, and was soon able to stand and look around him, and understand all which had occurred.

In a former chapter it has been related how his faithful queen and consort, La-loo-hee-ah, frantic with terror at his long submersion, and the appearance of blood at the surface, had thrown off her apparel and plunged beneath the sea.

Active and supple as a fish under water, so long as it was possible to hold breath, she had little difficulty in making her way to the interior of the cabin.

For some time she was unable to discover anything, by reason of the gloom which prevailed; but presently, as she swam rapidly to and fro, searching for Crusoe, she came across one of the air-tubes.

Following this down, she soon discovered our hero, leaning his elbows as we have described on the combings of the lazarette hatch.

At this time he was in a very bad way—almost at the last gasp, indeed. In his delirium he peopled the interior of the cuddy of the sunken Thunder with water-witches, mermaids, and monsters of the deep. And so it happened that when La-loo-hee-ah, instantly on discovering him, dragged him up (which she accomplished

BURNING OF THE MAN-OF-WAR.

without much difficulty, by reason of the buoy-ancy of her unweighted body) he fancied in his frenzy that he had been seized by some fierce and terrible mermaid denizen of the deep.

Fortunately, although all but entirely insen-sible as regarded thought and sensation, he had still power left in his limbs and muscles, and La-loo-he-ah was able to guide him safely to the foot of the ladder leading up along the steep side of the coral reef to the surface.

It was not so easy to accomplish the task of the ascent, heavily weighted as he was; but La-loo-hee-ah overcame all obstacles, and her-self, utterly exhausted by her exertions and long submersion, got him on the ladder, helped him to climb step by step, holding him on all the while.

The moment the top of the helmet appeared above the surface, there was a rush of the faith-ful Huanitans to the spot; and Crusoe and La-loo-hee-ah, again his preserver, were soon in safety on the Golden Reef.

On his recovery she told him, in a few words, how she had found him and brought him safe'y to the surface.

And then he proceeded to relate what had be-fallen himself—of his encounter with the shark, and afterwards the horror of his position when he found that he could not raise himself from the lazarette hold on to the deck.

To the Huanitans nothing was said, as it could do no good to inform them of the despé-rate peril he had safely passed through, while it might, and probably would, damage his prestige should they know that, but for La-loo-hee-ah, their own Island Princess, he, the great white king—the conqueror of all, from the hostile savages of Talanaki to the monster shark—would have perished miserably from suffocation.

So La-loo-hee-ah merely explained to some of the principal chiefs that the king had fought with and conquered an enormous shark, and had also succeeded in finding and attaching to a rope one of the boxes of yellow metal, which it was his will to have brought up from the wreck. As however he had suffered great fatigue in his con-test with the shark, and by so prolonged a dive, the work would be concluded on that day with the getting the body of the monster shark, and with raising the first box of gold.

The rest of the day would be devoted to a grand feast and festival, to be followed by a torchlight procession and night-dance in honour of the occasion—the hoisting to the surface of the first box of gold.

There was tumultuous joy amongst the Huani-tans at this announcement; and with loud shouts and songs they set to work to get up the box of gold and the shark's body, also to pre-pare for the promised festival.

A score of skilful divers plunged beneath tho surface; and soon the dead body of the shark was floated to the top, and dragged on to the Golden Reef, the Huanitans dancing and caper-ing around the corpse of the monster like maniacs.

Next came the raising of the gold box. There was some little difficulty about this, not because of its weight, but by reason of its having got jammed in the lazarette hold.

At last, however, it was hoisted above the surface, and deposited on the Golden Reef.

The feelings of Crusoe as he stood on the reef looking down on this box of gold—first fruits of the hardships, toils, and desperate dangers he had gone through—it is impossible to describe.

A species of intoxication took possession of him, and he shouted, and actually danced with joy, much to the delight of his faithful subjects, who saw nothing undignified therein.

Then he arranged a procession, with the box at the head thereof, carried in state in the royal litter.

Behind followed, in order of their rank, chiefs, warriors, and the others, all singing a war song of triumph.

And in the glorious afternoon sunshine the box of gold was carried up Flagstaff Hill to the hut on the top, and there safely deposited. Then the light-hearted natives gave way to their en-thusiastic, happy natures, and the sun went down on such a scene of feasting, rioting, uproarious noise, and wild, frantic dancing and screaming as Lion Island had never witnessed before.

And so ended the eventful day on which Crusoe approached the end of his task, and safely landed the first box of gold recovered from the Thunder on the Golden Reef.

The rest is yet to be accomplished—perchance with ease, perchance not without overcoming fresh obstacles, passing through fresh perils; perchance never to be accomplished at all.

We shall see in due course.

CHAPTER XCI.

THE LAST BOX OF GOLD.

BUT as things turned out, this first box of gold was but an instalment—all the remainder to be paid on demand—the demand requisite being simply labour skilfully applied.

Once the actual place where the gold boxes lay had been discovered and reached, it was not difficult to get at other boxes containing the same precious metal.

For it must not be forgotten that these

islanders were like fish—quite equal to fish, indeed—swimming at or near the surface, when respiration was possible, at short intervals.

It was only at depths and in power of living under water altogether, that fish got the upper hand of them.

Still, so long as breath held good, these children of the isles and the ocean were as nimble and as quick in every way under water as fishes, and, by reason of their human intelligence, superior in other respects.

Fifty of the most skilful divers were constantly employed in the work.

Crusoe found that his own presence in diving dress was not necessary at all. But though all the gold, to the very last box, might have been recovered without his again donning helmet, leather, and canvas, he had regard to other considerations.

They looked up to him as their chief—their KING—more than their king—as a deity—an invincible hero.

Beyond all things, his power of remaining beneath the water for a time—which appeared to them unlimited—was wonderful—awful, even, in their estimation.

Crusoe, in diving dress, was wont to go down once every day, remaining from half an hour to forty minutes, and then ascend to the surface, to see the gold boxes brought up and despatched to Flagstaff Point.

And so day by day the work went on.

After a while the toil became monotonous.

Crusoe began to tire of the simple easy way in which he fished up treasure from the hungry sea.

There was no excitement—no combating—no men to beat—no difficulties to surmount—no hardships to undergo—nothing to do but pull up lumps of gold—boxes of gold.

So long as he had danger and difficulty before him he was content; but now that all came to his hand he was discontented.

We have chronicled how our hero got the first box of gold from the wreck of the Thunder.

Now comes the last.

Not from any necessity, but merely from fancy—a desire himself to finish the work he had begun and so well carried through, Crusoe decided himself to descend and fasten a rope to the last box of gold.

Then he would ascend to the surface and himself haul it up, thus with his own hands landing the last box of the half-million on the Golden Reef.

The morning of the day which was to be the eventful one—that on which the long and arduously fought out enterprise was to be brought to a successful conclusion, broke.

There had been thunder, squalls, and rain in showers during the night, it being the time of the equinox, and when dawn broke there lay over the islands and surrounding sea a heavy canopy of mist, effectually bounding the view on all sides to a few hundred yards.

This, however, would in nowise interfere with the work to be done at the Golden Reef; and so soon as it was fairly light, Crusoe and his lovely consort, King and Queen of Huanita, went in grand procession to the Golden Reef.

The royal state-barge—no other than the old ship's boat altered, built upon, and gorgeously decorated—headed a fleet of three hundred canoes, all filled with armed warriors, ornamented and be-feathered in most magnificent style.

Crusoe was now so skilful and experienced a diver that it was a matter of the greatest ease—merely child's play to descend and remain under the water for half-an-hour at a spell.

Consequently he had little or no trouble in bending on the rope to the last box of gold.

However, to make perfectly certain that this was indeed the only remaining box, he remained below for some time, making a complete tour of the afterhold.

Having satisfied himself that he had really accomplished his task, and that there remained no more treasure in the hold of the Thunder, he made his way back to the foot of the rope-ladder, hanging from the Golden Reef.

Just as he placed his foot on the lowest step he suddenly felt a shock, so violent as to throw him backwards, and nearly cause him to fall.

Amazed and bewildered, he again made his way back to the ladder and began to mount.

Scarcely had he ascended half-way, however, when another tremendous shock almost caused him to lose his hold.

"In the name of all the gods," he said to himself, "what is the meaning of this?"

"Is it a torpedo, an electric eel? The sooner I get above water the better I shall be pleased. The shark was bad enough; but these shocks from an invisible source are quite beyond me."

Just as he reached the surface he felt another violent concussion, but prepared by the other two he held on like "grim death," as the saying is, and safely clambered on to the Golden Reef.

Eagerly and rapidly he stripped off his diving-dress and looked around him.

That something unusual had occurred was manifest by the excitement of the islanders.

They were talking, shouting, screaming, gesticulating, behaving, in fact, as all savages do when excited.

Presently the mystery of the great shocks he had received beneath the surface was partially revealed.

Boom!

His ear at once recognised the sound.

The report of a heavy gun.

Boom!

Again!

Quite close too!

The sound came from the south; and Crusoe judged that there must be a vessel within a very short distance.

Wildly his heart pulsated as he vainly strained his eyes in the endeavour to penetrate the mist.

But presently he felt a gentle aura on his cheek; a breeze arose which soon grew brisk, and then the veil of mist rolled away.

All the while the thundering boom of the cannon rang out at minute intervals—minute guns.

And when the canopy of vapour altogether lifted, a grand, a glorious sight fell on the eyes of our adventurer.

A vessel, with the glorious old British ensign flying at her peak, the old "red, red rag" as it has been called—red with the blood shed in a thousand victories—ragged from shot holes, but never yet torn down by an enemy!

Remember that, brave boys of England, and don't listen to Mr. John Bright and the Peace-at-any-price party, who would, if they had their way, place our "tight little island" on a level with thieving Greece or effete Turkey.

Yes, there she lay, a magnificent vessel, fast grounded on the Golden Reef, not a hundred yards away from the spot where lay the wreck of the Thunder.

The minute guns were fired, Crusoe concluded, as signals of distress.

"Man the stage barge!" shouted Crusoe, in the Huanitan tongue.

In two minutes he was seated in the stern, whilst a dozen skilful warriors wielded the paddles, and made the boat shoot through the water to the British vessel.

Was it not strange that on the very day he had accomplished his task this thing should happen—that he should be again within the reach of civilisation?

As to how it was, or what it all meant, he could form no idea.

And when he stepped on the deck of the vessel, and saw the jolly English faces of the sailors and officers, heard the dear old language spoken by English tongues—Crusoe, King of Huanita, Emperor of the Islands—what do you suppose he did, readers?

This strong, brave man, who had made such a good fight against dangers and difficulties, actually cried.

Big tears rolled down his cheeks.

Wasn't it babyish?

The sturdy sailors and the officers did not think so, for the latter led him into the cabin with all honour.

CHAPTER XCII.

THE KING OF HUANITA MEETS WITH A SURPRISE.

CRUSOE, as he made his way towards the cabin, conducted by the officers, was an object of intense interest to the crew.

And, indeed, his attire and appearance were sufficiently remarkable; for, although clothed in a manner after the European fashion, much of the material was of native manufacture. However, he wore rich ornaments and decorations of the white metal, vegetable ivory, coral, and other productions of the islands.

This he did out of deference to the prejudices of his subjects, well aware that by conforming to their customs he would have a firmer hold on their respect and loyalty.

In place of hat, he wore a strange native head-dress made of palm leaves, woven with silver thread, and ornamented with feathers. It was, in fact, a sort of crown or coronet.

Crusoe had become so accustomed to it that really, in the excitement of the moment, he had forgotten that it adorned his head, or assuredly he would have left it behind.

On his feet he wore, in place of shoes, sandals of shark skin, fastened by narrow thongs of the same.

His complexion was bronzed to the colour of the islanders whom he now ruled, and he let his hair grow long.

Altogether, he presented about as strange a figure for a white man it is possible to conceive.

As Crusoe entered the cabin he started back as if he had seen an apparition.

He had cause enough for surprise, for immediately confronting him stood the captain of the ship—his long-lamented friend, the companion of his boyish adventures, the man who had stood by him in many a death struggle, the gallant and invincible Starboard Tom!—who he had supposed was crushed amongst the icebergs thousands of miles from where they at present stood.

We drop the veil over the meeting of these well-tried and trusted friends.

After the excitement of the two fellow-adventurers had somewhat subsided, Crusoe's eyes fell on his reflection in a large mirror, and he absolutely started at the picture presented.

Starboard Tom laughed heartily on noticing this, and Crusoe joined in.

"You may well laugh, Tom," he said, "I had no idea I presented such an extraordinary appearance till I happened to cast my eyes in the mirror. But your vessel is aground, I think. I can place at your service some four hundred canoes, manned by two thousand of my people. They ought to be able to tow her off."

"Thanks, Jack. I will gladly avail myself of your offer at high water, of which it yet wants more than three hours. Your canoes ought to drag her off if she was high and dry. As it is, there is no harm done ; and if we get her off before a strong wind arises, she will be none the worse in any way. Meanwhile, Jack, suppose you give me a short history of your adventures since we were shipwrecked on the icebergs. Here, steward, bring the spirit-stand."

The spirit-stand was brought, and Crusoe, for the first time for many a long month, filled himself a glass of grog, his own small stock having been long since finished.

"I shall have much pleasure in doing as you wish, Tom," he replied ; "and really, without any vanity, I may say I have a very wonderful and startling series of adventures to tell you, and if we have time before high water you can tell me how you escaped what appeared to be certain death."

Crusoe Jack then recounted his wonderful exploits to Starboard Tom. He merely sketched the miseries he underwent after the wreck of the boat containing the two friends and the American crew, on the iceberg, when Crusoe thought all were lost except himself. But he gave Tom a vivid description of the meeting on board the Thunder—the wreck of that vessel and the consequent loss of half a million of money—the landing on the uninhabited island—the desperate encounter with the fierce natives of the island adjacent—the imminent peril in which he was placed when La-loo-hee-ah made the memorable declaration which caused him to become her husband, and eventually to be proclaimed King of Huanita, and finally he told him how he had resolved to recover the half-million sunk in the wreck of the Thunder, which he had finally achieved on that very morning.

Just as Jack had finished his remarkable tale a slight motion was felt in the vessel, and Tom jumped up saying, "I must reserve the account of my adventures till another time, Jack, or we shall have a hole through the bottom."

"What ballast have you?" asked Jack.

"Gravel and pig iron, about three hundred and fifty tons."

"Is the ballast to be got at?" pursued Jack.

"It can be, after a quarter of an hour's work."

"In less than half an hour I can have three hundred canoes alongside, and two thousand men to help to do the work. How she bumps, Tom! We'd best make haste; you set your crew to work, and I'll send off for a fleet of canoes instantly."

Meanwhile, the ship kept thumping and grinding in a most ominous manner. Tom Starboard urged the crew to work their utmost, and in less than a quarter of an hour the ballast was being got on deck and pitched. Very shortly, however, after this wasteful task began, a swarm of canoes were around the ship, stages were quickly rigged, and whilst a couple of hundred of the Huanitans aided the crew, the others, under the direction of Crusoe himself, carefully placed the iron pigs in the canoes.

And lo! in less than three quarters of an hour after the commencement of the work the big ship heeled over slightly to one side, and then feeling the buoyancy of the still rising tide, constantly being lightened as she was, glided gently and quietly off the reef and into deep water.

Starboard Tom, now the vessel was off the reef, wished to know in what state the ship's bottom was, as he feared that, although she did not leak at present, some serious damage might have been done.

Here, again, his friend Jack was able to do good service.

He pointed out a safe anchorage. The vessel was brought to, and moored bow and stern. Then he ordered a score of his most skilful and trustworthy divers to descend and report on the state of the ship's bottom.

Shortly afterwards he was able to inform Tom that the ship's bottom was quite uninjured beyond the fact of some sheets of copper having been torn off.

The effect of this would be to slightly retard her speed until such time as she could be taken into a suitable port and docked.

Before everything was put straight—"ship-shape and Bristol fashion," as the sailors phrase it—the day was well advanced, and Crusoe proposed to go on shore now, and send off at once a quantity of fresh vegetables, fruit, fish, and other productions of his fertile kingdom.

And so it was arranged.

He was conversing with Tom below, when suddenly a loud yelling and shouting was heard at some distance from the vessel.

Crusoe instantly knew that it was a native war-cry.

It increased; grew louder; seemed to approach nearer.

"What the deuce's up now, I wonder?" remarked Tom.

"I'm sure I don't know," replied Crusoe. "Suppose we go on deck and see.'"

Before they could reach the foot of the ladder it was plain something was the matter by the noise and apparent confusion on deck.

Directly he reached the deck Tom Starboard ordered every man to his post.

CHAPTER XCIII.

A SHARP ENGAGEMENT.

THE Golden Reef and its surroundings now presented an extraordinary and most exciting scene.

A fleet of several hundreds of canoes could be seen coming from the island, urged to the utmost speed by the strong and skilful natives, right down to the British vessel.

They were not more than a quarter of a mile distant at the most, and it was obvious that in a few minutes they would be alongside.

As to their intention, it seemed that it could scarcely be a matter of doubt. They were all thronged with armed warriors, who stood up, shouting cries of rage and defiance.

Crusoe Jack very soon comprehended the meaning of this extraordinary scene. He saw at once that the Huanitans, wild with excitement and fury, were about to attack the ship; their reason for doing so, he guessed, was an unfounded idea that he, their king, was detained prisoner in the great canoe.

It was to rescue him that all these warriors were urging on their war canoes towards the British vessel.

Well he knew the terrible slaughter which would come should the misguided natives persevere in their intention, and endeavour to board the ship. Grape shot would, he knew, soon mow down his unhappy subjects, and those who escaped death by lead and iron would infallibly be slain or driven overboard by cold steel.

He saw the necessity of prompt action, in order to arrest a terrible slaughter; and leaving Tom, who seemed lost in amazement at the scene, he ran forward to the forecastle, and standing on the heel of the bowsprit, so as to be in full view of the fleet of canoes, he waved his right arm aloft, and shouted out some words in the Huanitan tongue.

But as it happened, unfortunately, what with the distance and the noise, the advancing savages madly shouting and yelling, his word were inaudible to them; and to those on board the vessel what he said was unintelligible. Now, from the first, Crusoe, dressed and ornamented as he was in half savage style, was looked upon by the crew with curiosity and suspicion, they taking him to be, not a white man, but a native, or at most only a half-breed, which latter are notorious as the most hostile and bitter against white men. Crusoe then, his first hail not being heard by the Huanitans, proceeded to call out again.

Scarcely had he opened his mouth than he was set upon by the forecastle men, taken entirely unawares, was knocked down by a handspike, and secured before he could offer any resistance whatever.

The approaching Huanitans, though they could not hear his hail, saw him attacked, knocked down, and dragged away from the bowsprit by the men of the sloop.

Their fury at seeing their king thus treacherously made prisoner, as they imagined, exceeded all bounds, and redoubling their efforts, they urged their canoes through the water at a tremendous pace.

In a minute or two, and before the guns of the sloop could be loaded and run out, twenty or thirty of the canoes were around her bows, and the nearly naked savages began swarming on board.

They clambered up with such determination and agility and in such numbers as to gain a footing on the fore part of the deck before a shot could be fired.

The few sailors, who were on and about the forecastle, fell back before such odds, which was the more necessary because none of them had yet recovered their arms.

The seamen from the forecastle retreated, dragging our hero with them; who, out of breath, and overwhelmed by this sudden attack, was scarcely able to speak.

Of this episode Tom knew nothing, having been occupied in getting ready to resist what seemed a sudden unprovoked attack on the part of the savages.

Each moment the savages kept swarming up over the bows of the vessel in scores, and soon the crew were outnumbered more than three to one—odds which were constantly being increased.

But, notwithstanding this disproportion in numbers, and the fact of having been taken by surprise, the well-disciplined seamen were not in the least panic-stricken. Quietly, though quickly, preparations, the result of which must prove most disastrous and deadly to the intruders, were made.

Four carronades were run on to the quarter-deck, pointed forward, and doubly loaded with grape and cannister.

A few sharp-shooters ascended to the main and mizzentops, and there awaited the words to open fire.

The clang of the steel ramrods in the rifles was heard, and in a very brief space there was presented to the Huanitans a serried double rank on deck, Tom in the rear of the four carronades.

"Ready with the carronades?" shouted Tom.

"All ready, sir."

"Small arms men, ready?"

"All ready."

"Now, lads, look out—wait for the word, then let the vagabonds have it."

A terrible slaughter was on the eve of being enacted.

The arrows and spears of the Huanitans already had begun to whistle about the heads of the British, and an encounter seemed inevitable. Little effect, however, could the rude weapons of the savages have against the artillery and arms of precision of the Englishmen.

The seamen were all armed with Snider, Enfields (breech-loaders), and each man could fire from ten to fifteen bullets in a minute.

This, together with the carronades, loaded with grape, must cause awful carnage amidst the crowd of savages.

These latter, savage-like, were dancing and shouting, and working themselves up into a state of frenzy before attack, venting their rage on the rigging, the spars and even the solid deck, hacking and hewing in all directions.

Two mariners and a sailor were presently struck by spears, and had to be taken to the rear.

CHAPTER XCIV.

THE FIRST SHOT.

THE English blood was now pretty well up, and all waited eagerly for the word which should inaugurate such a scene of slaughter as few, if any, amongst those on board could ever have had an opportunity of witnessing.

"Ready in the tops?" cried Tom Starboard.

"All ready"

"Wait for the fire of the carronades; then blaze away."

"Ready with the carronades?"

"All ready."

It was his last chance, and in another quarter minute the decks of the ship would have been deluged with blood, the air hideous with the shrieks of wounded men.

Crusoe had vainly endeavoured to get a hearing from the excited and angry men by whom he was held captive; and up to this last moment had not been able to see or attract the attention of Tom, or any one to whom he could explain the true state of affairs; for, be it observed, it was all plain enough to him by this time—the double mistake through which a sanguinary encounter seemed inevitable between the warlike crew and the natives.

At that very moment there came a shower of spears, and the next instant Tom gave the order—

"Once more ready with the carronades—ready, marines—ready all—fire!"

Fortunately, in the interests of humanity, this order was never carried out.

Scarcely was the word out of the captain's mouth than Jack made a desperate effort, broke from his captors, and shouted out, "Hold on all; don't fire."

"It is quite a mistake, Tom," said Jack. "Let me speak to my people, let me show myself, and all will be well."

"What the devil's the meaning of all this?" cried Tom Starboard, looking with astonishment at our hero, who bore plain marks of the rough treatment to which he had been subjected.

"There is no time to explain now. Let me go and speak to them. I will stop my men, you hold yours in hand."

Another shower of spears, and a loud yell on the part of the savages, who were now advancing along the deck (encouraged at having hitherto met with so little resistance), showed the wisdom of Crusoe's words; and he was at once conducted through the compact body of seamen and the steady line in front.

It was fully time, for the Huanitans, headed by the bravest of the chiefs, were now within twenty yards, advancing after their fashion—not with the steady tramp of an impetuous charge by Europeans, but dancing, capering, leaping, and yelling at a great rate.

The moment Crusoe was perceived, there arose a yell louder than ordinary, and a shower of spears were thrown over his head.

"Hold! warriors of Huanita, hold!—death to the man who shoots an arrow or throws a spear!"

He spoke in the Huanitan tongue, and shouted his loudest, so that his words were plainly heard by the natives who were in front.

There was a momentary pause; but it would seem that those in the rear did not hear, or, at all events, understand, for there came some spears, which, falling amidst the seamen, inflicted several slight wounds, and exasperated the men, who were already impatient to attack the savages to such an extent that it seemed likely they would break out and fire and charge without orders.

"Hold!" again shouted Crusoe; but his voice was drowned in another series of yells, and the foremost of the Huanitans forced on by those behind pressed on. Spears were still flying from the rear, and it seemed that a conflict and terrible slaughter were inevitable, for the blood of the English was now thoroughly aroused.

"Confound you, you black skunk! Here's a bullet for you. 'Twas your spear hit my chum, Joe."

Then followed the report of a rifle.

This was the first shot, and the good aim of the speaker, a sharpshooter, in the mizzen-rigging, was dreadfully proved, for the savage chief, so addressed, fell, shot through the body.

Other scattering shots now followed, and the men cocked their rifles, and brought them to the present without orders.

The gunners at the carronades still stood steady, but it was certain that when their comrades fired a volley, the artillery fire would instantly follow, order or no order being given.

It seemed that Crusoe was too late in his interference, for the opposing ranks (if the loose, crowded array of the Huanitans deserves the name), were now close together, and our hero's voice was quite drowned in the uproar of yells from the savages and angry shouts from the English.

At last the infernal din was quelled, with only a few slight wounds on the side of the English; but the lovely La-loo-hee-ah, the consort of Crusoe, the Queen of Huanita, was shot dead by one of the sharpshooters in the rigging.

CHAPTER XCV.

EXPLANATORY.

CRUSOE was much grieved at the loss of his faithful and beautiful Indian wife, who had lost her life through her noble devotion to him.

He could not bear the idea of living on the island without her, so as soon as he had had the rescued treasure and the articles which the warehouse contained conveyed on board, he bid adieu to his faithful Huanitans, with the intention of returning to civilisation.

On the homeward passage, Tom Starboard recounted to Crusoe all the adventures he had undergone. Tom was thrown on to a cleft in the iceberg, and picked up the next morning by a passing ship and taken to England.

From thence he shipped in a vessel to Chili, to see the Merediths, and Mabel prevailed on her father to charter a vessel, and appoint Tom Starboard as captain to search for our hero.

Our readers know how successful he was in his search.

After an eventful voyage Crusoe Jack and gallant old Tom Starboard arrived safely at their destination, and the Merediths received Crusoe as one risen from the dead.

Crusoe and Mabel still loved each other, although separated for so long a time, and shortly after his return they were married, and Jack and his lovely bride, attended by Tom Starboard, then proceeded to England to claim the estates and title, which rightly belonged to Crusoe Jack, or, as he was afterwards called, when the estates were regained—Sir James Morland.

www.ingramcontent.com/pod-product-compliance
Lightning Source LLC
Chambersburg PA
CBHW080945020726
47505CB00009B/2146

* 9 7 8 1 5 3 5 8 0 2 9 9 4 *